THE
MALLOREON

VOLUME ONE

By David Eddings

THE BELGARIAD

Book One: *Pawn of Prophecy*
Book Two: *Queen of Sorcery*
Book Three: *Magician's Gambit*
Book Four: *Castle of Wizardry*
Book Five: *Enchanters' End Game*

THE MALLOREON

Book One: *Guardians of the West*
Book Two: *King of the Murgos*
Book Three: *Demon Lord of Karanda*
Book Four: *Sorceress of Darshiva*
Book Five: *The Seeress of Kell*

THE ELENIUM

Book One: *The Diamond Throne*
Book Two: *The Ruby Knight*
Book Three: *The Sapphire Rose*

THE TAMULI

Book One: *Domes of Fire*
Book Two: *The Shining Ones*
Book Three: *The Hidden City*

BELGARATH THE SORCERER

POLGARA THE SORCERESS

THE REDEMPTION OF ALTHALUS

THE RIVAN CODEX

REGINA'S SONG

THE
MALLOREON

VOLUME ONE

DAVID
EDDINGS

BALLANTINE BOOKS

NEW YORK

2005 Del Rey Trade Paperback Edition

Copyright © 1987, 1988 by David Eddings
Preface copyright © 2005 by David Eddings

Published in the United States by Del Rey Books, an imprint of The Random House
Publishing Group, a division of Random House, Inc., New York.

Del Rey is a registered trademark and the Del Rey colophon is a trademark
of Random House, Inc.

Originally published in three separate volumes in the United States by Del Rey Books,
an imprint of The Random House Publishing Group, a division of Random House, Inc.,
as *Guardians of the West* in 1987 and *King of the Murgos* and *Demon Lord of Karanda*
in 1988.

ISBN 0-345-48386-3

Printed in the United States of America

www.delreybooks.com

9 8 7 6 5 4 3 2

CONTENTS

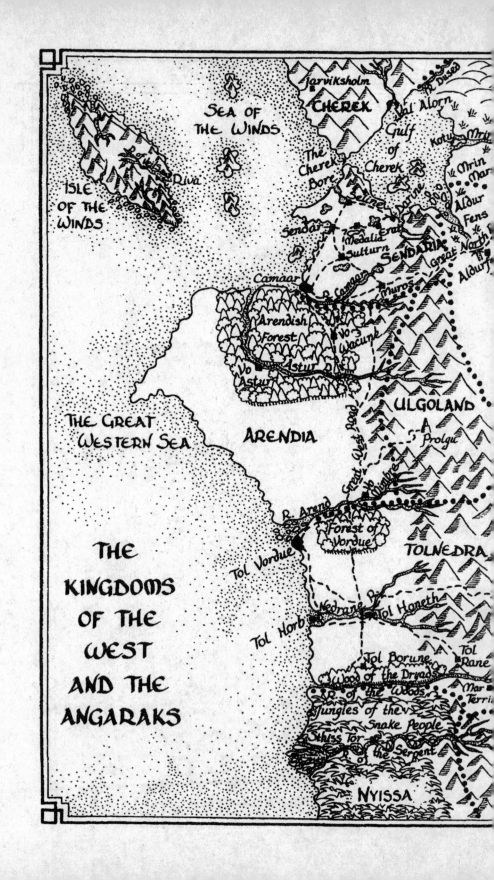

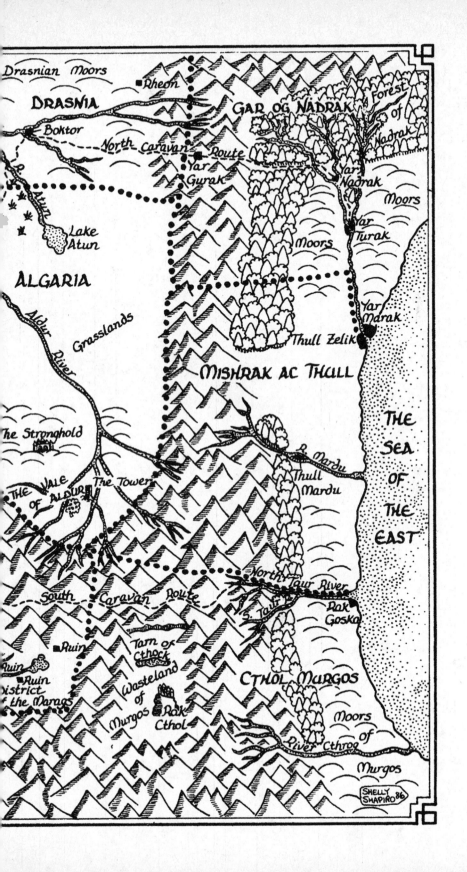

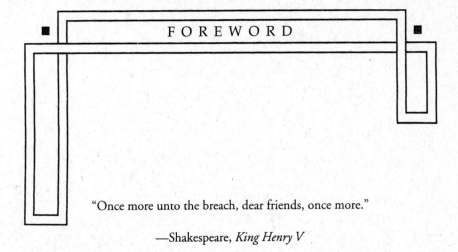

FOREWORD

"Once more unto the breach, dear friends, once more."

—Shakespeare, *King Henry V*

Now we have a two-volume Malloreon to accompany the earlier two-volume Belgariad. You will note that The Malloreon is significantly longer than The Belgariad. Certain restrictions were relaxed after the success of The Belgariad.

When we add the two prequels, *Belgarath the Sorcerer* and *Polgara the Sorceress,* we have the traditional twelve-book format established by Homer in *The Iliad* and *The Odyssey.* He was closely followed by Virgil in *The Aeneid,* and not quite so closely by Milton in *Paradise Lost.* (Take notes, I may give a test later.)

As we mentioned in *The Rivan Codex,* when we met Lester and Judy-Lynn Del Rey, I told him that I thought that there was more story left to tell after The Belgariad was completed. Lest agreed (and Judy-Lynn wanted to write a contract on the back of the menu in the restaurant where we were having dinner).

The Malloreon gave us the chance to get the smell of bubble gum out of my typewriter. Garion (and Ce'Nedra) grow up, so they're now adults and rule the Isle of the Winds. Then, as was fairly common in medieval Europe, we have a kidnapping, and that starts the ball rolling (through five more books). We got to introduce new villains, new heroes, and new allies.

There were many, many things that we didn't explain in these two pentologies, and that's what produced the two prequels, and that carried us into the standard twelve-book format. My unindicted coconspirator suggested several things that show up at the end of *Polgara the Sorceress* that links that book to *Pawn of Prophecy* (Book One of The Belgariad). In effect, the reader can go directly from the end of *Polgara* to the beginning of *Pawn.* The whole story, thus, becomes a circle that's approximately 4,600 pages long. I suppose that there might be readers out there who have been reading their way around that circle for the last twenty years or so, and thus we have the literary equivalent of peddling dope.

Ah well,
David Eddings

GUARDIANS
OF THE WEST

For Judy-Lynn:
A rose blooms and then fades,
    but the beauty and the fragrance
    are remembered always.

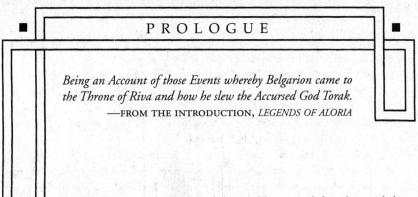

*Being an Account of those Events whereby Belgarion came to
the Throne of Riva and how he slew the Accursed God Torak.*
—FROM THE INTRODUCTION, *LEGENDS OF ALORIA*

After the seven Gods created the world, it is said that they and those
races of men they had chosen dwelt together in peace and harmony.
But UL, father of the Gods, remained aloof, until Gorim, leader of those who had
no God, went up on a high mountain and importuned him mightily. Then the
heart of UL melted, and he lifted up Gorim and swore to be his God and God of
his people, the Ulgos.

The God Aldur remained apart, teaching the power of the Will and the Word
to Belgarath and other disciples. And a time came when Aldur took up a globe-
shaped stone no larger than the heart of child. Men named the stone the Orb of
Aldur, and it was filled with enormous power, for it was the embodiment of a Necessity which had existed since the beginning of time.

Torak, God of the Angarak peoples, coveted lordship and dominion over all
things, for to him had come an opposing Necessity. When he learned of the Orb,
he was sorely troubled, fearing that it would counter his destiny. He went therefore
to Aldur to plead that the stone be set aside. When Aldur would not give up the
stone, Torak smote him and fled with the Orb.

Then Aldur summoned his other brothers, and they went with a mighty army
of their followers to confront Torak. But Torak, seeing that his Angaraks must be
defeated, raised the Orb and used its power to crack the world and bring in the Sea
of the East to divide him from his enemies.

But the Orb was angered that Torak should use it thus and it lashed him with
a fire whose agony could not be quenched. Torak's left hand was burned away, his
left cheek was seared and charred, and his left eye took flame and was ever after
filled with the fire of the Orb's wrath.

In agony, Torak led his people into the wastelands of Mallorea, and his people
built him a city in Cthol Mishrak, which was called the City of Night, for Torak hid
it under an endless cloud. There, in a tower of iron, Torak contended with the Orb,
trying in vain to quell its hatred for him.

Thus it endured for two thousand years. Then Cherek Bear-Shoulders, King of
the Alorns, went down to the Vale of Aldur to tell Belgarath the Sorcerer that the
northern way was clear. Together they left the Vale with Cherek's three mighty sons,
Dras Bull-neck, Algar Fleet-foot, and Riva Iron-grip. They stole through the
marches, with Belgarath taking the form of a wolf to guide them, and they crossed
over into Mallorea. By night, they stole into Torak's iron tower. And while the
maimed God tossed in pain-haunted slumber, they crept to the room where he kept

the Orb locked in an iron casket. Riva Iron-grip, whose heart was without ill intent, took up the Orb, and they left for the West.

Torak waked to find the Orb gone and he pursued them. But Riva lifted up the Orb, and its angry flame filled Torak with fear. Then the company passed from Mallorea and returned to their own lands.

Belgarath divided Aloria into four kingdoms. Over three he set Cherek Bear-Shoulders, Dras Bull-neck, and Algar Fleet-foot. To Riva Iron-grip and to his line he gave the Orb of Aldur and sent him to the Isle of the Winds.

Belar, God of the Alorns, sent down two stars, and from them Riva forged a mighty sword and placed the Orb on its pommel. And he hung the sword on the wall of the throne room of the Citadel, where it might ever guard the West from Torak.

When Belgarath returned to his home, he discovered that his wife, Poledra, had borne him twin daughters, but then had passed away. In heartsick sorrow, he named his daughters Polgara and Beldaran. And when they were of age, he sent Beldaran to Riva Iron-grip to be his wife and mother of the Rivan line. But Polgara he kept with him and instructed in the arts of sorcery.

In rage at the loss of the Orb, Torak destroyed the City of Night and divided the Angaraks. The Murgos, the Nadraks, and the Thulls he sent to dwell in the wastelands along the western shores of the Sea of the East. The Malloreans he kept to subdue all of the continent on which they dwelt. Over all, he set his Grolim priests to watch, to scourge any who faltered, and to offer human sacrifices to him.

Many centuries passed. Then Zedar the Apostate, who served Torak, conspired with Salmissra, Queen of the snake-people, to send emissaries to the Isle of the Winds to slay Gorek, Riva's descendant, and all his family. This was done, though some claimed that a lone child escaped; but none could say for certain.

Emboldened by the death of the guardian of the Orb, Torak gathered his host and invaded the West, planning to enslave the peoples and regain the Orb. At Vo Mimbre on the plains of Arendia, the hordes of Angaraks met the armies of the West in dreadful slaughter. And there Brand the Rivan Warder, bearing the Orb upon his shield, met Torak in single combat and struck down the maimed God. The Angaraks, seeing that, were disheartened and they were overthrown and destroyed. But at night, as the Kings of the West celebrated, Zedar the Apostate took the body of Torak and spirited it away. Then the High Priest of the Ulgos, named Gorim as all such High Priests had been, revealed that Torak had not been killed, but bound in slumber until a king of the line of Riva sat once more on the throne in the Hall of the Rivan King.

The Kings of the West believed that meant forever, for it was held that the line of Riva had perished utterly. But Belgarath and his daughter Polgara knew better. For a child *had* escaped the slaughter of Gorek's family, and they had concealed him and his descendants in obscurity for generations. But ancient prophecies revealed to them that the time for the return of the Rivan King was not yet come.

Many more centuries passed. Then, in a nameless city on the far side of the world, Zedar the Apostate came upon an innocent child and resolved to take the child and go secretly with him to the Isle of the Winds. There he hoped that the innocence of the child might enable that child to take the Orb of Aldur from the pommel of the sword of the Rivan King. It occurred as he wished, and Zedar fled with the child and the Orb toward the East.

Polgara the Sorceress had been living with a young boy, who called her Aunt Pol, in obscurity on a farm in Sendaria. This boy was Garion, the orphaned last descendant of the Rivan line, but he was unaware of his parentage.

When Belgarath learned of the theft of the Orb, he hastened to Sendaria to urge his daughter to join him in the search for Zedar and the Orb. Polgara insisted that the boy must accompany them on the quest, so Garion accompanied his Aunt Pol and Belgarath, whom he knew as a storyteller who sometimes visited the farm and whom he called Grandfather.

Durnik, the farm smith, insisted on going with them. Soon they were joined by Barak of Cherek and by Kheldar of Drasnia, whom men called Silk. In time, their quest for the Orb was joined by others: Hettar, horse-lord of Algaria; Mandorallen, the Mimbrate knight; and Relg, an Ulgo zealot. And seemingly by chance, the Princess Ce'Nedra, having quarreled with her father, Emperor Ran Borune XXIII of Tolnedra, fled his palace and became one of the companions, though she knew nothing of their quest. Thus was completed the company foretold by the prophecy of the Mrin Codex.

Their search led them to the Wood of the Dryads, where they were confronted by the Murgo Grolim Asharak, who had long spied secretly upon Garion. Then the voice of prophecy within Garion's mind spoke to Garion, and he struck Asharak with his hand and his Will. And Asharak was utterly consumed in fire. Thus Garion learned that he was possessed of the power of sorcery. Polgara rejoiced, telling him that henceforth he should be named Belgarion, as was proper for a sorcerer, for she knew then that the centuries of waiting were over and that Garion should be the one to reclaim the Rivan Throne, as foretold.

Zedar the Apostate fled from Belgarath in haste. Unwisely, he entered the realms of Ctuchik, High Priest of the western Grolims. Like Zedar, Ctuchik was a disciple of Torak, but the two had lived in enmity throughout the centuries. As Zedar crossed the barren mountains of Cthol Murgos, Ctuchik waited him in ambush and wrested from him the Orb of Aldur and the child whose innocence enabled him to touch the Orb and not die.

Belgarath went ahead to seek out the trail of Zedar, but Beltira, another disciple of Aldur, gave him the news that Ctuchik now held the child and the Orb. The other companions went on to Nyissa, where Salmissra, Queen of the snake-loving people, had Garion seized and brought to her palace. But Polgara freed him and turned Salmissra into a serpent, to rule over the snake-people in that form forever.

When Belgarath rejoined his companions, he led the company on a difficult journey to the dark city of Rak Cthol, which was built atop a mountain in the desert of Murgos. They accomplished the difficult climb to confront Ctuchik, who knew of their coming and awaited with the child and the Orb. Then Belgarath engaged Ctuchik in a duel of sorcery. But Ctuchik, hard-pressed, tried a forbidden spell, and it rebounded on him, destroying him so utterly that no trace of him remained.

The shock of his destruction tumbled Rak Cthol from its mountaintop. While the city of the Grolims shuddered into rubble, Garion snatched up the trusting child who bore the Orb and carried him to safety. They fled, with the hordes of Taur Urgas, King of the Murgos, pursuing them. But when they crossed into the lands of Algaria, the Algarians came against the Murgos and defeated them. Then at last, Belgarath could turn toward the Isle of the Winds to restore the Orb to its rightful place.

There in the Hall of the Rivan King at Erastide, the child whom they called Errand placed the Orb of Aldur into Garion's hand, and Garion stood on the throne to set it in its accustomed place on the pommel of the great Sword of the Rivan King. As he did so, the Orb leaped into flame, and the sword blazed with cold blue fire. By these signs, all knew that Garion was indeed the true heir to the throne of Riva and they acclaimed him King of Riva, Overlord of the West, and the Keeper of the Orb.

Soon, in keeping with the Accords signed after the Battle of Vo Mimbre, the boy who had come from a humble farm in Sendaria to become the Rivan King was betrothed to the Princess Ce'Nedra. But before the wedding could take place, the voice of prophecy that was within his head urged him to go to the room of documents and there take down the copy of the Mrin Codex.

In that ancient prophecy, he discovered that he was destined to take up Riva's sword and go with it to confront the maimed God Torak and to slay or be slain, thereby to decide the fate of the world. For Torak had begun to end his long slumber with the crowning of Garion, and in this meeting must be determined which of the two opposing Necessities or prophecies would prevail.

Garion knew that he could marshal an army to invade the East with him. But though his heart was filled with fear, he determined that he alone should accept the danger. Only Belgarath and Silk accompanied him. In the early morning, they crept out of the Citadel of Riva and set out on the long northern journey to the dark ruins of the City of Night where Torak lay.

But the Princess Ce'Nedra went to the Kings of the West and persuaded them to join her in an effort to distract the forces of the Angaraks, so that Garion might win through safely. With the help of Polgara, she marched through Sendaria, Arendia, and Tolnedra, raising a mighty army to follow her and to engage the hosts of the East. They met on the plain surrounding the city of Thull Mardu. Caught between the forces of Emperor 'Zakath of Mallorea and those of the mad King of the Murgos, Taur Urgas, Ce'Nedra's army faced annihilation. But Cho-Hag, Chief of the Clan-Chiefs of Algaria, slew Taur Urgas; and the Nadrak King Drosta lek Thun changed sides, giving her forces time to withdraw.

Ce'Nedra, Polgara, Durnik, and the child Errand, however, were captured and sent to 'Zakath, who sent them on to the ruined city of Cthol Mishrak for Zedar to judge. Zedar slew Durnik, and it was to see Polgara weeping over his body that Garion arrived.

In a duel of sorcery, Belgarath sealed Zedar into the rocks far below the surface. But by then Torak had awakened fully. The two destinies which had opposed each other since time began thus faced each other in the ruined City of Night. And there in the darkness, Garion, the Child of Light, slew Torak, the Child of Dark, with the flaming sword of the Rivan King, and the dark prophecy fled wailing into the void.

UL and the six living Gods came for the body of Torak. And Polgara importuned them to bring Durnik back to life. Reluctantly they consented. But since it would not be mete for her so far to exceed Durnik's abilities, they gave to him the gift of sorcery.

Then all returned to the city of Riva. Belgarion married Ce'Nedra, and Polgara took Durnik as her husband. The Orb was again in its rightful place to protect the West. And the war of Gods, kings, and men, which had endured for seven thousand years, was at an end.

Or so men thought.

PART ONE

THE VALE OF
ALDUR

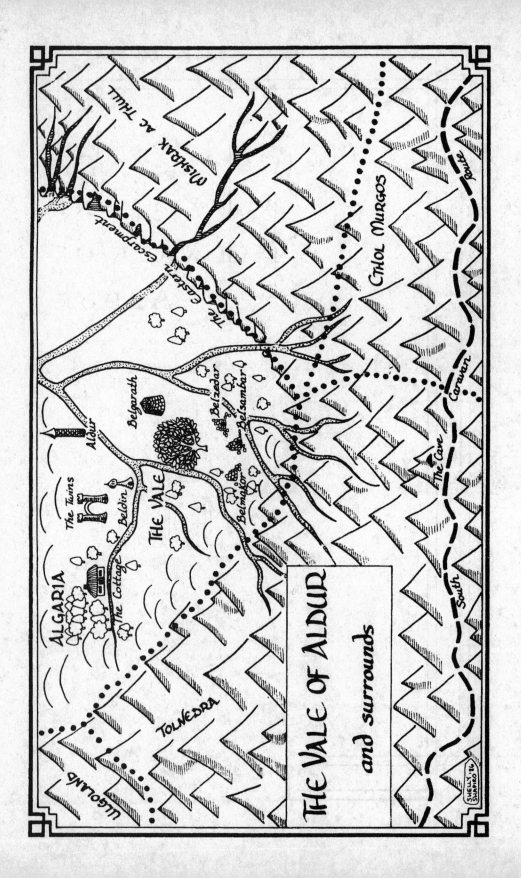

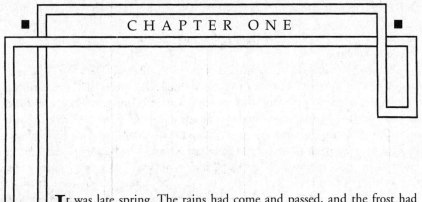

It was late spring. The rains had come and passed, and the frost had gone out of the ground. Warmed by the soft touch of the sun, damp brown fields lay open to the sky, covered only by a faint green blush as the first tender shoots emerged from their winter's sleep. Quite early one fine morning, when the air was still cool, but the sky gave promise of a golden day, the boy Errand, along with his family, left an inn lying in one of the quieter districts of the bustling port city of Camaar on the south coast of the kingdom of Sendaria. Errand had never had a family before, and the sense of belonging was new to him. Everything around him seemed colored, overshadowed almost, by the fact that he was now included in a small, tightly knit group of people bound together by love. The purpose of the journey upon which they set out that spring morning was at once simple and very profound. They were going home. Just as he had not had a family before, Errand had never had a home; and, though he had never seen the cottage in the Vale of Aldur which was their destination, he nonetheless yearned toward that place as if its every stone and tree and bush had been imprinted upon his memory and imagination since the day he was born.

A brief rain squall had swept in off the Sea of the Winds about midnight and then had passed as quickly as it had come, leaving the gray, cobbled streets and tall, tile-roofed buildings of Camaar washed clean to greet the morning sun. As they rolled slowly through the streets in the sturdy wagon which Durnik the smith, after much careful inspection, had bought two days earlier, Errand, riding burrowed amongst the bags of food and equipment which filled the wagon bed, could smell the faint, salt tang of the harbor and see the bluish morning cast in the shadows of the red-roofed buildings they passed. Durnik, of course, drove the wagon, his strong brown hands holding the reins in that competent way with which he did everything, transmitting somehow along those leather straps to the wagon team the comforting knowledge that he was completely in control and knew exactly what he was doing.

The stout, placid mare upon which Belgarath the Sorcerer rode, however, quite obviously did not share the comfortable security felt by the wagon horses. Belgarath, as he sometimes did, had stayed late in the taproom of the inn the previous night and he rode this morning slumped in the saddle, paying little or no heed to where he was going. The mare, also recently purchased, had not yet had the time to accustom herself to her new owner's peculiarities, and his almost aggressive inattention made her nervous. She rolled her eyes often, as if trying to determine if this immobile lump mounted on her back really intended for her to go along with the wagon or not.

Belgarath's daughter, known to the entire world as Polgara the Sorceress, viewed her father's semicomatose progress through the streets of Camaar with a steady gaze, reserving her comments for later. She sat beside Durnik, her husband of only a few weeks, wearing a hooded cape and a plain gray woolen dress. She had put aside the blue velvet gowns and jewels and rich, fur-trimmed capes which she had customarily worn while they had been at Riva and had assumed this simpler mode of dress as if almost with relief. Polgara was not averse to wearing finery when the occasion demanded it; and when so dressed, she appeared more regal than any queen in all the world. She had, however, an exquisite sense of the appropriate and she had dressed herself in these plain garments almost with delight, since they were appropriate to something she had wanted to do for uncounted centuries.

Unlike his daughter, Belgarath dressed entirely for comfort. The fact that his boots were mismatched was neither an indication of poverty nor of carelessness. It stemmed rather from conscious choice, since the left boot of one pair was comfortable upon his left foot and its mate pinched his toes, whereas his right boot—from another pair—was most satisfactory, while its companion chafed his heel. It was much the same with the rest of his clothing. He was indifferent to the patches on the knees of his hose, unconcerned by the fact that he was one of the few men in the world who used a length of soft rope for a belt, and quite content to wear a tunic so wrinkled and gravy-spotted that persons of only moderate fastidiousness would not even have considered using it for a scrub-rag.

The great oaken gates of Camaar stood open, for the war that had raged on the plains of Mishrak ac Thull, hundreds of leagues to the east, was over. The vast armies that had been raised by the Princess Ce'Nedra to fight that war had returned to their homes, and there was peace once more in the Kingdoms of the West. Belgarion, King of Riva and Overlord of the West, sat upon the throne in the Hall of the Rivan King with the Orb of Aldur once again in its proper place above his throne. The maimed God of Angarak was dead, and his eons-old threat to the West was gone forever.

The guards at the city gate paid scant attention to Errand's family as they passed, and so they left Camaar and set out upon the broad, straight imperial highway that stretched east toward Muros and the snow-topped mountains that separated Sendaria from the lands of the horse clans of Algaria.

Flights of birds wheeled and darted in the luminous air as the wagon team and the patient mare plodded up the long hill outside Camaar. The birds sang and trilled almost as if in greeting and hovered strangely on stuttering wings above the wagon. Polgara raised her flawless face in the clear, bright light to listen.

"What are they saying?" Durnik asked.

She smiled gently. "They're babbling," she replied in her rich voice. "Birds do that a great deal. In general they're happy that it's morning and that the sun is shining and that their nests have been built. Most of them want to talk about their eggs. Birds always want to talk about their eggs."

"And of course they're glad to see you, aren't they?"

"I suppose they are."

"Someday do you suppose you could teach me to understand what they're saying?"

She smiled at him. "If you wish. It's not a very practical thing to know, however."

"It probably doesn't hurt to know a *few* things that aren't practical," he replied with an absolutely straight face.

"Oh, my Durnik." She laughed, fondly putting her hand over his. "You're an absolute joy, do you know that?"

Errand, riding just behind them among the bags and boxes and the tools Durnik had so carefully selected in Camaar, smiled, feeling that he was included in the deep, warm affection they shared. Errand was not used to affection. He had been raised, if that is the proper term, by Zedar the Apostate, a man who had looked much like Belgarath. Zedar had simply come across the little boy in a narrow alleyway in some forgotten city and had taken him along for a specific purpose. The boy had been fed and clothed, nothing more, and the only words his bleak-faced guardian had ever spoken to him were, "I have an errand for you, boy." Because those were the only words he had heard, the only word the child spoke when he had been found by these others was "Errand." And since they did not know what else to call him, that had become his name.

When they reached the top of the long hill, they paused for a few moments to allow the wagon horses to catch their breath. From his comfortable perch in the wagon, Errand looked out over the broad expanse of neatly walled fields lying pale green in the long, slanting rays of the morning sun. Then he turned and looked back toward Camaar with its red roofs and its sparkling blue-green harbor filled with the ships of a half-dozen kingdoms.

"Are you warm enough?" Polgara asked him.

Errand nodded. "Yes," he said, "thank you." The words were coming more easily to him now, though he still spoke but rarely.

Belgarath lounged in his saddle, absently rubbing at his short white beard. His eyes were slightly bleary, and he squinted as if the morning sunlight was painful to him. "I sort of like to start out a journey in the sunshine," he said. "It always seems to bode well for the rest of the trip." Then he grimaced. "I don't know that it needs to be *this* bright, however."

"Are we feeling a bit delicate this morning, father?" Polgara asked him archly.

He turned to regard his daughter, his face set. "Why don't you go ahead and say it, Pol? I'm sure you won't be happy until you do."

"Why, father," she said, her glorious eyes wide with feigned innocence, "what makes you think I was going to say anything?"

He grunted.

"I'm sure you realize by now all by yourself that you drank a bit too much ale last night," she continued. "You don't need *me* to tell you that, do you?"

"I'm not really in the mood for any of this, Polgara," he told her shortly.

"Oh, poor old dear," she said in mock commiseration. "Would you like to have me stir something up to make you feel better?"

"Thank you, but no," he replied. "The aftertaste of your concoctions lingers for days. I think I prefer the headache."

"If a medicine doesn't taste bad, it isn't working," she told him. She pushed back the hood of the cape she wore. Her hair was long, very dark, and touched just over her left brow with a single lock of snowy white. "I *did* warn you, father," she said relentlessly.

"Polgara," he said, wincing, "do you suppose we could skip the 'I told you so'?"

"You heard me warn him, didn't you, Durnik?" Polgara asked her husband.

Durnik was obviously trying not to laugh.

The old man sighed, then reached inside his tunic and took out a small flagon. He uncorked it with his teeth and took a long drink.

"Oh, father," Polgara said disgustedly, "didn't you get enough last night?"

"Not if this conversation is going to linger on this particular subject, no." He held out the flagon to his daughter's husband. "Durnik?" he offered.

"Thanks all the same, Belgarath," Durnik replied, "but it's a bit early for me."

"Pol?" Belgarath said then, offering a drink to his daughter.

"Don't be absurd."

"As you wish." Belgarath shrugged, recorking the bottle and tucking it away again. "Shall we move along then?" he suggested. "It's a very long way to the Vale of Aldur." And he nudged his horse into a walk.

Just before the wagon rolled down on the far side of the hill, Errand looked back toward Camaar and saw a detachment of mounted men coming out through the gate. Glints and flashes of reflected sunlight said quite clearly that at least some of the garments the men wore were made of polished steel. Errand considered mentioning the fact, but decided not to. He settled back again and looked up at the deep blue sky dotted with puffy white clouds. Errand liked mornings. In the morning a day was always full of promise. The disappointments usually did not start until later.

The soldiers who had ridden out of Camaar caught up with them before they had gone another mile. The commander of the detachment was a sober-faced Sendarian officer with only one arm. As his troops fell in behind the wagon, he rode up alongside. "Your Grace," he greeted Polgara formally with a stiff little bow from his saddle.

"General Brendig," she replied with a brief nod of acknowledgement. "You're up early."

"Soldiers are almost always up early, your Grace."

"Brendig," Belgarath said rather irritably, "is this some kind of coincidence, or are you following us on purpose?"

"Sendaria is a very orderly kingdom, Ancient One," Brendig answered blandly. "We try to arrange things so that coincidences don't happen."

"I thought so," Belgarath said sourly. "What's Fulrach up to now?"

"His Majesty merely felt that an escort might be appropriate."

"I know the way, Brendig. I've made the trip a few times before, after all."

"I'm sure of it, Ancient Belgarath," Brendig agreed politely. "The escort has to do with friendship and respect."

"I take it then that you're going to insist?"

"Orders are orders, Ancient One."

"Could we skip the 'Ancient'?" Belgarath asked plaintively.

"My father's feeling his years this morning, General." Polgara smiled, "All seven thousand of them."

Brendig almost smiled. "Of course, your Grace."

"Just why are we being so formal this morning, my Lord Brendig?" she asked him. "I'm sure we know each other well enough to skip all that nonsense."

Brendig looked at her quizzically. "You remember when we first met?" he asked.

"As I recall, that was when you were arresting us, wasn't it?" Durnik asked with a slight grin.

"Well—" Brendig coughed uncomfortably. "—not exactly, Goodman Durnik. I was really just conveying his Majesty's invitation to you to visit him at the palace. At any rate, Lady Polgara—your esteemed wife—was posing as the Duchess of Erat, you may remember."

Durnik nodded. "I believe she was, yes."

"I had occasion recently to look into some old books of heraldry and I discovered something rather remarkable. Were you aware, Goodman Durnik, that your wife really *is* the Duchess of Erat?"

Durnik blinked. "Pol?" he said incredulously.

Polgara shrugged. "I'd almost forgotten," she said. "It was a very long time ago."

"Your title, nonetheless, is still valid, your Grace," Brendig assured her. "Every landholder in the District of Erat pays a small tithe each year into an account that's being held in Sendar for you."

"How tiresome," she said.

"Wait a minute, Pol," Belgarath said sharply, his eyes suddenly very alert. "Brendig, just how big is this account of my daughter's—in round figures?"

"Several million, as I understand it," Brendig replied.

"Well," Belgarath said, his eyes going wide. "Well, well, well."

Polgara gave him a level gaze. "What have you got in your mind, father?" she asked him pointedly.

"It's just that I'm pleased for you, Pol," he said expansively. "Any father would be happy to know that his child has done so well." He turned back to Brendig. "Tell me, General, just who's managing my daughter's fortune?"

"It's supervised by the crown, Belgarath," Brendig replied.

"That's an awful burden to lay on poor Fulrach," Belgarath said thoughtfully, "considering all his other responsibilities. Perhaps I ought to—"

"Never mind, Old Wolf," Polgara said firmly.

"I just thought—"

"Yes, father. I know what you thought. The money's fine right where it is."

Belgarath sighed. "I've never been rich before," he said wistfully.

"Then you won't really miss it, will you?"

"You're a hard woman, Polgara—to leave your poor old father sunk in deprivation like this."

"You've lived without money or possessions for thousands of years, father. Somehow I'm almost positive that you'll survive."

"How did you get to be the Duchess of Erat?" Durnik asked his wife.

"I did the Duke of Vo Wacune a favor," she replied. "It was something that no one else could do. He was very grateful."

Durnik looked stunned. "But Vo Wacune was destroyed thousands of years ago," he protested.

"Yes. I know."

"I think I'm going to have trouble getting used to all this."

"You knew that I wasn't like other women," she said.

"Yes, but—"

"Does it really matter to you how old I am? Does it change anything?"

"No," he said immediately, "not a thing."

"Then don't worry about it."

They moved in easy stages across southern Sendaria, stopping each night at the solid, comfortable hostels operated by the Tolnedran legionnaires who patrolled and maintained the imperial highway and arriving in Muros on the afternoon of the third day after their departure from Camaar. Vast cattle herds from Algaria were already filling the acre upon acre of pens lying to the east of the city, and the cloud of dust raised by their milling hooves blotted out the sky. Muros was not a comfortable town during the season of the cattle drives. It was hot, dirty, and noisy. Belgarath suggested that they pass it up and stop for the night in the mountains where the air would be less dust-clogged and the neighbors less rowdy.

"Are you planning to accompany us all the way to the Vale?" he asked General Brendig after they had passed the cattle pens and were moving along the Great North Road toward the mountains.

"Ah—no, actually, Belgarath," Brendig replied, peering ahead at a band of Algar horsemen approaching along the highway. "As a matter of fact, I'll be turning back about now."

The leader of the Algar riders was a tall, hawk-faced man in leather clothing, with a raven-black scalp lock flowing behind him. When he reached the wagon, he reined in his horse. "General Brendig," he said in a quiet voice, nodding to the Sendarian officer.

"My Lord Hettar," Brendig replied pleasantly.

"What are you doing here, Hettar?" Belgarath demanded.

Hettar's eyes went very wide. "I just brought a cattle herd across the mountains, Belgarath," he said innocently. "I'll be going back now and I thought you might like some company."

"How strange that you just happen to be here at this particular time."

"Isn't it, though?" Hettar looked at Brendig and winked.

"Are we playing games?" Belgarath asked the pair of them. "I don't need supervision and I definitely don't need a military escort every place I go. I'm perfectly capable of taking care of myself."

"We all know that, Belgarath," Hettar said placatingly. He looked at the wagon. "It's nice to see you again, Polgara," he said pleasantly. Then he gave Durnik a rather sly look. "Married life agrees with you, my friend," he added. "I think you've put on a few pounds."

"I'd say that *your* wife has been adding a few extra spoonfuls to your plate as well." Durnik grinned at his friend.

"Is it starting to show?" Hettar asked.

Durnik nodded gravely. "Just a bit," he said.

Hettar made a rueful face and then gave Errand a peculiar little wink. Errand and Hettar had always got on well together, probably because neither of them felt any pressing need to fill up the silence with random conversation.

"I'll be leaving you now," Brendig said. "It's been a pleasant journey." He bowed to Polgara and nodded to Hettar. And then, with his detachment of troops jingling along behind him, he rode back toward Muros.

"I'm going to have words with Fulrach about this," Belgarath said darkly to Hettar, "and with your father, too."

"It's one of the prices of immortality, Belgarath," Hettar said blandly. "People tend to respect you—even when you'd rather they didn't. Shall we go?"

The mountains of eastern Sendaria were not so high as to make travel across them unpleasant. With the fierce-looking Algar clansmen riding both to the front and to the rear of the wagon, they traveled at an easy pace along the Great North Road through the deep green forests and beside tumbling mountain streams. At one point, when they had stopped to rest their horses, Durnik stepped down from the wagon and walked to the edge of the road to gaze speculatively at a deep pool at the foot of a small, churning waterfall.

"Are we in any particular hurry?" he asked Belgarath.

"Not really. Why?"

"I just thought that this might be a pleasant place to stop for our noon meal," the smith said artlessly.

Belgarath looked around. "If you want, I suppose it's all right."

"Good." With that same slightly absent look on his face, Durnik went to the wagon and took a coil of thin, waxed cord from one of the bags. He carefully tied a hook decorated with some brightly colored yarn to one end of the cord and began looking about for a slender, springy sapling. Five minutes later he was standing on a boulder that jutted out into the pool, making long casts into the turbulent water just at the foot of the falls.

Errand drifted down to the edge of the stream to watch. Durnik was casting into the center of the main flow of the current so that the swiftly moving green water pulled his lure down deep into the pool.

After about a half an hour, Polgara called to them. "Errand, Durnik, your lunch is ready."

"Yes, dear," Durnik replied absently. "In a moment."

Errand obediently went back up to the wagon, though his eyes yearned back toward the rushing water. Polgara gave him one brief, understanding look, then laid the meat and cheese she had sliced for him on a piece of bread so that he could carry his lunch back to the stream bank.

"Thank you," he said simply.

Durnik continued his fishing, his face still intent. Polgara came down to the water's edge. "Durnik," she called. "Lunch."

"Yes," he replied, not taking his eyes off the water. "I'm coming." He made another cast.

Polgara sighed. "Oh, well," she said. "I suppose every man needs at least one vice."

After about another half-hour, Durnik looked baffled. He jumped from his boulder to the stream bank and stood scratching his head and staring in perplexity at the swirling water. "I *know* they're in there," he said to Errand. "I can almost feel them."

"Here," Errand said, pointing down at the deep, slow-moving eddy near the bank.

"I think they'd be farther out, Errand," Durnik replied doubtfully.

"Here," Errand repeated, pointing again.

Durnik shrugged. "If you say so," he said dubiously, flipping his lure out into the eddy. "I still think they'd be out in the main current, though."

And then his pole bent sharply into a tense, quivering bow. He caught four trout in rapid succession, thick, heavy-bodied trout with silvery, speckled sides and curved jaws filled with needlelike teeth.

"Why did it take you so long to find the right spot?" Belgarath asked later that afternoon when they were back on the highway.

"You have to work that kind of pool methodically, Belgarath," Durnik explained. "You start at one side and work your way across, cast by cast."

"I see."

"It's the only way to be really sure you've covered it all."

"Of course."

"I was fairly sure where they were lying, though."

"Naturally."

"It was just that I wanted to do it the right way. I'm sure you understand."

"Perfectly," Belgarath said gravely.

After they had passed through the mountains, they turned south, riding through the vast grasslands of the Algarian plain where herds of cattle and horses grazed in that huge green sea of grass that rippled and swayed under the steady easterly breeze. Although Hettar strongly urged them to stop by the Stronghold of the Algar clans, Polgara declined. "Tell Cho-Hag and Silar that we may visit later," she said, "but we really should get to the Vale. It's probably going to take most of the summer to make my mother's house habitable again."

Hettar nodded gravely and then waved a brief salute as he and his clansmen turned eastward and rode off across the rolling grasslands toward the mountainlike Stronghold of his father, Cho-Hag, Chief of the Clan-Chiefs of Algaria.

The cottage that had belonged to Polgara's mother lay in a valley among the rolling hills marking the northern edge of the Vale of Aldur. A sparkling stream flowed through the sheltered hollow, and there were woods, birch intermixed with cedar, stretching along the valley floor. The cottage was constructed of fieldstone, gray, russet, and earthy-brown, all neatly fitted together. It was a broad, low building, considerably larger than the word "cottage" suggested. It had not been occupied for well over three thousand years, and the thatching and the doors and windowframes had long since surrendered to the elements, leaving the shell of the house standing, bramble-filled and unroofed to the sky. There was, nonetheless, a peculiar sense of waiting about it, as if Poledra, the woman who had lived here, had instilled in the very stones the knowledge that one day her daughter would return.

They arrived in the middle of a golden afternoon, and Errand, lulled by a creaking wheel, had drifted into a doze. When the wagon stopped, Polgara shook him gently awake. "Errand," she said, "we're here." He opened his eyes and looked for the first time at the place he would forever call home. He saw the weathered shell of the cottage nestled in the tall green grass. He saw the woods beyond, with the white trunks of the birch trees standing out among the dark green cedars, and he saw the stream. The place had enormous possibilities. He realized that at once. The stream, of course, was perfect for sailing toy boats, for skipping stones, and, in the event of failing inspiration, for falling into. Several of the trees appeared to have been specifically designed for climbing, and one huge, white old birch overhanging the stream promised the exhilarating combination of climbing a tree and falling into the water, all at one time.

The land upon which their wagon had stopped was a long hill sloping gently down toward the cottage. It was the kind of a hill down which a boy could run on a day when the sky was a deep blue dotted with dandelion-puff clouds racing in the breeze. The knee-high grass would be lush in the sun, and the turf damply firm underfoot; the rush of sweet-smelling air as one ran down that long slope would be intoxicating.

And then he felt quite keenly a sense of deep sorrow, a sorrow which had endured unchanged for century upon century, and he turned to look at Belgarath's weathered face and the single tear coursing down the old man's furrowed cheek, to disappear in his close-cropped white beard.

In spite of Belgarath's sorrow for his lost wife, Errand looked out at this small, green valley with its trees and its stream and its lush meadow with a deep and abiding contentment. He smiled and said, "Home," trying the word and liking the sound of it.

Polgara looked gravely into his face. Her eyes were very large and luminous, and their color changed with her mood, ranging from a light blue so pale as to be virtually gray to a deep lavender. "Yes, Errand," she replied in her vibrant voice. "Home." Then she put her arms about him to hold him softly, and there was in that gentle embrace all the yearning toward this place which had filled her down through the weary centuries that she and her father had labored at their endless task.

Durnik the smith looked thoughtfully at the hollow spread out below in the warm sunshine, considering, planning, arranging, and rearranging things in his mind. "It's going to take a while to get everything the way we want it, Pol," he said to his bride.

"We have all the time in the world, Durnik," Polgara replied with a gentle smile.

"I'll help you unload the wagon and set up your tents," Belgarath said, scratching absently at his beard. "Then tomorrow I suppose I ought to go on down into the Vale—have a talk with Beldin and the twins, look in on my tower—that sort of thing."

Polgara gave him a long, steady look. "Don't be in such a hurry to leave, father," she told him. "You talked with Beldin just last month at Riva and on any number of occasions you've gone for decades without visiting your tower. I've noticed that every time there's work to be done, you suddenly have pressing business someplace else."

Belgarath's face assumed an expression of injured innocence. "Why, Polgara—" he started to protest.

"That won't work either, father," she told him crisply. "A few weeks—or a month or two—of helping Durnik isn't going to injure you permanently. Or did you plan to leave us abandoned to the winter snows?"

Belgarath looked with some distaste at the shell of the house standing at the foot of the hill, with the hours of toil it was going to take to make it livable stamped all over it. "Why, of course, Pol," he said somewhat too quickly. "I'd be happy to stay and lend a hand."

"I knew we could depend on you, father," she said sweetly.

Belgarath looked critically at Durnik, trying to assess the strength of the smith's convictions. "I hope you weren't intending to do everything by hand," he said tentatively. "What I mean is—well, we *do* have certain alternatives available to us, you know."

Durnik looked a little uncomfortable, his plain, honest face touched with the faintest hint of a disapproving expression. "I—uh—I really don't know, Belgarath," he said dubiously. "I don't believe that I'd really feel right about that. If I do it by hand, then I'll know that it's been done properly. I'm not all that comfortable with this other way of doing things yet. Somehow it seems like cheating—if you get what I mean."

Belgarath sighed. "Somehow I was afraid you might look at it that way." He shook his head and squared his shoulders. "All right, let's go on down there and get started."

It took about a month to dig the accumulated debris of three eons out of the corners of the house, to reframe the doors and windows and to re-beam and thatch the roof. It would have taken twice as long had Belgarath not cheated outrageously each time Durnik's back was turned. All manner of tedious tasks somehow performed themselves whenever the smith was not around. Once, for example, Durnik took out the wagon to bring in more timbers; as soon as he was out of sight, Belgarath tossed aside the adze with which he had been laboriously squaring off a beam, looked gravely at Errand, and reached inside his jerkin for the earthenware jar of ale he had filched from Polgara's stores. He took a long drink and then he directed the force of his will at the stubborn beam and released it with a single muttered word. An absolute blizzard of white wood chips went flying in all directions. When the beam was neatly squared, the old man looked at Errand with a self-satisfied smirk and winked impishly. With a perfectly straight face, Errand winked back.

The boy had seen sorcery performed before. Zedar the Apostate had been a sorcerer, and so had Ctuchik. Indeed, throughout almost his entire life the boy had been in the care of people with that peculiar gift. Not one of the others, however, had that air of casual competence, that verve, with which Belgarath performed his art. The old man's offhand way of making the impossible seem so easy that it was hardly worth mentioning was the mark of the true virtuoso. Errand knew how it was done, of course. No one can possibly spend that much time with assorted sorcerers without picking up the theory, at least. The ease with which Belgarath made things happen almost tempted him to try it himself; but whenever he considered the idea, he realized that there wasn't really anything he wanted to do that badly.

The things the boy learned from Durnik, while more commonplace, were nonetheless very nearly as profound. Errand saw almost immediately that there was virtually nothing the smith could not do with his hands. He was familiar with almost every known tool. He could work in wood and stone as readily as in iron and brass. He could build a house or a chair or a bed with equal facility. As Errand watched closely, he picked up the hundreds of little tricks and knacks that separated the craftsman from the bumbling amateur.

Polgara dealt with all domestic matters. The tents in which they slept while the cottage was being readied were as neatly kept as any house. The bedding was aired daily, meals were prepared, and laundry was hung out to dry. On one occasion Belgarath, who had come to beg or steal more ale, looked critically at his daughter, who was humming contentedly to herself as she cut up some recently cooked-down soap. "Pol," he said acidly, "you're the most powerful woman in the world. You've got more titles than you can count, and there's not a king in the world who doesn't bow to you automatically. Can you tell me exactly *why* you find it necessary to make soap that way? It's hard work, hot work, and the smell is awful."

She looked calmly at her father. "I've spent thousands of years being the most powerful woman in the world, Old Wolf," she replied. "Kings have been bowing to me for centuries, and I've lost track of all the titles. This *is*, however, the very first time I've ever married. You and I were always too busy for that. I've *wanted* to be married, though, and I've spent my whole life practicing. I know everything a good wife needs to know and I can do everything a good wife needs to do. Please don't criticize me, father, and please don't interfere. I've never been so happy in my life."

"Making soap?"

"That's part of it, yes."

"It's such a waste of time," he said. He gestured negligently, and a cake of soap that had not been there before joined the ones she had already made.

"Father!" she said, stamping her foot. "You stop that this minute!"

He picked up two cakes of soap, one his and one hers. "Can you really tell me the difference between them, Pol?"

"Mine was made with love; yours is just a trick."

"It's still going to get clothes just as clean."

"Not mine, it won't," she said, taking the cake of soap out of his hand. She held it up, balanced neatly on her palm. Then she blew on it with a slight puff, and it instantly vanished.

"That's a little silly, Pol," he told her.

"Being silly at times runs in my family, I think," she replied calmly. "Just go back to your own work, father, and leave me to mine."

"You're almost as bad as Durnik is," he accused her.

She nodded with a contented smile. "I know. That's probably why I married him."

"Come along, Errand," Belgarath said to the boy as he turned to leave. "This sort of thing might be contagious, and I wouldn't want you to catch it."

"Oh," she said. "One other thing, father. Stay out of my stores. If you want a jar of ale, ask me."

Assuming a lofty expression, Belgarath strode away without answering. As soon as they were around the corner, however, Errand pulled a brown jar from inside his tunic and wordlessly gave it to the old man.

"Excellent, my boy." Belgarath grinned. "You see how easy it is, once you get the hang of it?"

Throughout that summer and well into the long, golden autumn which followed it, the four of them worked to make the cottage habitable and weathertight for the winter. Errand did what he could to help, though more often than not his help consisted primarily of providing company while keeping out from underfoot.

When the snows came, the entire world seemed somehow to change. More than ever before, the isolated cottage became a warm, safe haven. The central room, where they took their meals and where they all sat in the long evenings, faced a huge stone fireplace that provided both warmth and light. Errand, whose time was spent out of doors on all but the most bitterly cold days, was usually drowsy during those golden, firelit hours between supper and bedtime and he often lay on a fur rug before the fire and gazed into the dancing flames until his eyes slowly closed. And later he waked in the cool darkness of his own room with warm, down-filled coverlets tucked up under his chin and he knew that Polgara had quietly carried him in and put him to bed. And he sighed happily and went back to sleep.

Durnik made him a sled, of course, and the long hill which ran down into the valley was perfect for sledding. The snow was not deep enough to make the runners of the sled bog down, and Errand was able to coast amazing distances across the meadow at the bottom of the hill because of the terrific momentum built up as he slid down the slope.

The absolute cap of the entire sledding season came late one bitingly cold afternoon, just after the sun had dropped into a bank of purple clouds on the western horizon and the sky had turned to a pale, icy turquoise. Errand trudged up the hill through the frozen snow, puffing his sled behind him. When he reached the top, he stopped for a moment to catch his breath. The thatched cottage below nestled in the surrounding snowbanks with the light from its windows golden and the column of pale blue smoke rising from its chimney as straight as an arrow into the dead calm air.

Errand smiled, lay down on his sled, and pushed off. The combination of circumstances was perfect for sledding. There was not even a breeze to impede his rapid descent, and he gathered astounding speed on his way down the hill. He flew across the meadow and in among the trees. The white-barked birches and dark, shadowy cedars flashed by as he sped through the woods. He might have gone even farther had the stream not been in his way. And even that conclusion to the ride was fairly exciting, since the bank of the stream was several feet high and Errand and his sled sailed out over the dark water in a long, graceful arc which ended abruptly in a spectacular, icy splash.

Polgara spoke to him at some length when he arrived home, shivering and with ice beginning to form up on his clothing and in his hair. Polgara, he noticed, tended to overdramatize things—particularly when an opportunity presented itself for her to speak to someone about his shortcomings. She took one long look at him and immediately fetched a vile-tasting medicine, which she spooned into him liberally. Then she began to pull off his frozen clothing, commenting extensively as she did so. She had an excellent speaking voice and a fine command of language. Her intonations and inflections added whole volumes of meaning to her commentary. On the whole, however, Errand would have preferred a shorter, somewhat less exhaustive discussion of his most recent misadventure—particularly in view of the fact that Belgarath and Durnik were both trying without much success to conceal broad grins as Polgara spoke to him while simultaneously rubbing him down with a large, rough towel.

"Well," Durnik observed, "at least he won't need a bath this week."

Polgara stopped drying the boy and slowly turned to gaze at her husband. There was nothing really threatening in her expression, but her eyes were frosty. "You said something?" she asked him.

"Uh—no, dear," he hastily assured her. "Not really." He looked at Belgarath a bit uncomfortably, then he rose to his feet. "Perhaps I'd better bring in some firewood," he said.

One of Polgara's eyebrows went up, and her gaze moved on to her father. "Well?" she said.

He blinked, his face a study in total innocence.

Her expression did not change, but the silence became ominous, oppressive.

"Why don't I give you a hand, Durnik?" the old man suggested finally, also getting up. Then the two of them went outside, leaving Errand alone with Polgara.

She turned back to him. "You slid all the way down the hill," she asked quite calmly, "and clear across the meadow?"

He nodded.

"And then through the woods?"

He nodded again.

"And then off the bank and into the stream?"

"Yes, ma'am," he admitted.

"I don't suppose it occurred to you to roll off the sled *before* it went over the edge and into the water?"

Errand was not really a very talkative boy, but he felt that his position in this affair needed a bit of explanation. "Well," he began, "I didn't really think of rolling off—but I don't think I would have, even if I *had* thought of it."

"I'm sure there's an explanation for that."

He looked at her earnestly. "Everything had gone so splendidly up until then that—well, it just wouldn't have seemed right to get off just because a few things started to go wrong."

There was a long pause. "I see," she said at last, her expression grave. "Then it was in the nature of a moral decision—this riding the sled all the way into the stream?"

"I suppose you might say that, yes."

She looked at him steadily for a moment and then slowly sank her face into her hands. "I'm not entirely certain that I have the strength to go through all of this again," she said in a tragic voice.

"Through what?" he asked, slightly alarmed.

"Raising Garion was almost more than I could bear," she replied, "but not even *he* could have come up with a more illogical reason for doing something." Then she looked at him, laughed fondly, and put her arms about him. "Oh, Errand," she said, pulling him tightly to her, and everything was all right again.

CHAPTER TWO

Belgarath the Sorcerer was a man with many flaws in his character. He had never been fond of physical labor and he was perhaps a bit *too* fond of dark brown ale. He was occasionally careless about the truth and had a certain grand indifference to some of the finer points of property ownership. The company of ladies of questionable reputation did not particularly offend his sensibilities, and his choice of language very frequently left much to be desired.

Polgara the Sorceress was a woman of almost inhuman determination and she had spent several thousand years trying to reform her vagrant father, but without much notable success. She persevered, however, in the face of overwhelming odds. Down through the centuries she had fought a valiant rearguard action against his bad habits. She had regretfully surrendered on the points of indolence and shabbiness. She grudgingly gave ground on swearing and lying. She remained adamant, however, even despite repeated defeats, on the points of drunkenness, thievery, and wenching. She felt for some peculiar reason that it was her duty to fight on those issues to the very death.

Since Belgarath put off his return to his tower in the Vale of Aldur until the following spring, Errand was able to witness at close hand those endless and unbelievably involuted skirmishes between father and daughter with which they filled the periodic quiet spaces in their lives. Polgara's comments about the lazy old man's lounging about in her kitchen, soaking up the heat from her fireplace and the well-chilled ale from her stores with almost equal facility, were pointed, and Belgarath's smooth evasions revealed centuries of highly polished skill. Errand, however, saw past those waspish remarks and blandly flippant replies. The bonds between Belgarath and his daughter were so profound that they went far beyond what others might conceivably understand, and so, over the endless years, they found it necessary to conceal their boundless love for each other behind this endless façade of contention. This is not to say that Polgara might not have preferred a more upstanding father, but she was not *quite* as disappointed in him as her observations sometimes indicated.

They both knew why Belgarath sat out the winter in Poledra's cottage with his daughter and her husband. Though not one word of the matter had ever passed between them, they knew that the memories the old man had of this house needed to be changed—not erased certainly, for no power on earth could erase Belgarath's memories of his wife, but rather they needed to be altered slightly so that this thatched cottage might also remind the old man of happy hours spent here, as well as that bleak and terrible day when he had returned to find that his beloved Poledra had died.

After the snow had been cut away by a week of warm spring rains and the sky had turned blue once again, Belgarath at last decided that it was time to take up his interrupted journey. "I don't really have anything pressing," he admitted, "but I'd like to look in on Beldin and the twins, and it might be a good time to tidy up my tower. I've sort of let that slide over the past few hundred years."

"If you'd like, we could go along," Polgara offered. "After all, you *did* help with the cottage—not enthusiastically, perhaps, but you did help. It only seems right that we help you with cleaning your tower."

"Thanks all the same, Pol," he declined firmly, "but your idea of cleaning tends to be a bit too drastic for my taste. Things that might be important later on have a way of winding up on the dust heap when you clean. As long as there's a clear space somewhere in the center, a room is clean enough for me."

"Oh, father," she said, laughing, "you never change."

"Of course not," he replied. He looked thoughtfully over at Errand, who was quietly eating his breakfast. "If it's all right, though," he said, "I'll take the boy with me."

She gave him a quick look.

Belgarath shrugged. "He's company and he might enjoy a change of scenery. Besides, you and Durnik haven't really had a chance to be alone since your wedding day. Call it a belated present if you want."

She looked at him. "Thank you, father," she said simply, and her eyes were suddenly very warm and filled with affection.

Belgarath looked away, almost as if her look embarrassed him. "Did you want your things? From the tower, I mean. You've left quite a few trunks and boxes there at one time or another over the years."

"Why, that's very nice of you, father."

"I need the space they're taking up," he said. Then he grinned at her.

"You *will* watch the boy, won't you? I know your mind sometimes wanders when you start puttering around in your tower."

"He'll be fine with me, Pol," the old man assured her.

And so the following morning Belgarath mounted his horse, and Durnik boosted Errand up behind him. "I'll bring him home in a few weeks," Belgarath said. "Or at least by midsummer." He leaned down, shook Durnik's hand, and then turned his mount toward the south.

The air was still cool, although the early spring sunshine was very bright. The scents of stirring growth were in the air, and Errand, riding easily behind Belgarath, could feel Aldur's presence as they pressed deeper into the Vale. He felt it as a calm and gentle kind of awareness, and it was dominated by an overpowering desire to know. The presence of the God Aldur here in the Vale was not some vague spiritual permeation, but rather was quite sharp, on the very edge of being palpable.

They moved on down into the Vale, riding at an easy pace through the tall, winter-browned grass. Broad trees dotted the open expanse, lifting their crowns to the sky, holding the tips of their branches, swollen with the urgency of budding leaves, up to receive the gentle kiss of sun-warmed air.

"Well, boy?" Belgarath said after they had ridden a league or more.

"Where are the towers?" Errand asked politely.

"A bit farther. How did you know about the towers?"

"You and Polgara spoke of them."

"Eavesdropping is a very bad habit, Errand."

"Was it a private conversation?"

"No, I suppose not."

"Then it wasn't eavesdropping, was it?"

Belgarath turned sharply, looking over his shoulder at the boy riding behind him. "That's a pretty fine distinction for somebody as young as you are. How did you arrive at it?"

Errand shrugged. "It just came to me. Do they always graze here like that?" He pointed at a dozen or so reddish-brown deer feeding calmly nearby.

"They have done so ever since I can remember. There's something about Aldur's presence that keeps animals from molesting each other."

They passed a pair of graceful towers linked by a peculiar, almost airy bridge arching between them, and Belgarath told him that they belonged to Beltira and Belkira, the twin sorcerers whose minds were so closely linked that they inevitably completed each other's sentences. A short while later they rode by a tower so delicately constructed of rose quartz that it seemed almost to float like a pink jewel in the lambent air. This tower, Belgarath told him, belonged to the hunchbacked Beldin, who had surrounded his own ugliness with a beauty so exquisite that it snatched one's breath away.

At last they reached Belgarath's own squat, functional tower and dismounted. "Well," the old man said, "here we are. Let's go up."

The room at the top of the tower was large, round, and incredibly cluttered. As he looked around at it, Belgarath's eyes took on a defeated look. "This is going to take weeks," he muttered.

A great many things in the room attracted Errand's eye, but he knew that, in Belgarath's present mood, the old man would not be inclined to show him or explain to him much of anything. He located the fireplace, found a tarnished brass scoop and a short-handled broom, and knelt in front of the cavernous, soot-darkened opening.

"What are you doing?" Belgarath asked.

"Durnik says that the first thing you should do in a new place is get a spot ready for your fire."

"Oh, he does, does he?"

"It's not usually a very big chore, but it gets you started—and once you get started, the rest of the job doesn't look so big. Durnik's very wise about things like that. Do you have a pail or a dust bin of some kind?"

"You're going to insist on cleaning the fireplace?"

"Well—if you don't mind too much. It *is* pretty dirty, don't you think?"

Belgarath sighed. "Pol and Durnik have corrupted you already, boy," he said. "I tried to save you, but a bad influence like that always wins out in the end."

"I suppose you're right," Errand agreed. "Where did you say that pail was?"

By evening they had cleared a semicircular area around the fireplace, finding in the process a couple of couches, several chairs, and a sturdy table.

"I don't suppose you have anything to eat stored anyplace?" Errand said wistfully. His stomach told him that it was definitely moving on toward suppertime.

Belgarath looked up from a parchment scroll he had just fished out from under one of the couches. "What?" he asked. "Oh yes. I'd almost forgotten. We'll go visit the twins. They're bound to have something on the fire."

"Do they know we're coming?"

Belgarath shrugged. "That doesn't really matter, Errand. You must learn that that's what friends and family are for—to be imposed upon. One of the cardinal rules, if you want to get through life without overexerting yourself, is that, when all else fails, fall back on friends and relations."

The twin sorcerers, Beltira and Belkira, were overjoyed to see them, and the "something on the fire" turned out to be a savory stew that was at least as good as one that might have emerged from Polgara's kitchen. When Errand commented on that, Belgarath looked amused. "Who do you think taught her how to cook?" he asked.

It was not until several days later, when the cleaning of Belgarath's tower had progressed to the point where the floor was receiving its first scrubbing in a dozen or more centuries, that Beldin finally stopped by.

"What are you doing, Belgarath?" the filthy, misshapen hunchback demanded. Beldin was very short, dressed in battered rags, and he was gnarled like an old oak stump. His hair and beard were matted, and twigs and bits of straw clung to him in various places.

"Just a little cleaning," Belgarath replied, looking almost embarrassed.

"What for?" Beldin asked. "It's just going to get dirty again." He looked at a number of very old bones lying along the curved wall. "What you really ought to do is render down your floor for soup stock."

"Did you come by to visit or just to be disagreeable?"

"I saw the smoke from your chimney. I wanted to see if anybody was here or if all this litter had just taken fire spontaneously."

Errand knew that Belgarath and Beldin were genuinely fond of each other and that this banter between them was one of their favorite forms of entertainment. He continued with the work he was doing even as he listened.

"Would you like some ale?" Belgarath asked.

"Not if *you* brewed it," Beldin replied ungraciously. "You'd think that a man who drinks as much as you do would have learned how to make decent ale by now."

"That last batch wasn't so bad," Belgarath protested.

"I've run across stump water that tasted better."

"Quit worrying. I borrowed this keg from the twins."

"Did they know you were borrowing it?"

"What difference does that make? We all share everything anyway."

One of Beldin's shaggy eyebrows raised. "They share their food and drink, and you share your appetite and thirst. I suppose that works out."

"Of course it does." Belgarath turned with a slightly pained look. "Errand," he said, "do you *have* to do that?"

Errand looked up from the flagstones he was industriously scrubbing. "Does it bother you?" he asked.

"Of course it bothers me. Don't you know that it's terribly impolite to keep working like that when I'm resting?"

"I'll try to remember that. How long do you expect that you'll be resting?"

"Just put the brush down, Errand," Belgarath told him. "That patch of floor has been dirty for a dozen centuries at least. Another day or so isn't going to matter all that much."

"He's a great deal like Belgarion was, isn't he?" Beldin said, sprawling in one of the chairs near the fire.

"It probably has something to do with Polgara's influence," Belgarath agreed, drawing two tankards of ale from the keg. "She leaves marks on every boy she meets. I try to moderate the effects of her prejudices as much as possible, though." He looked gravely at Errand. "I think this one is smarter than Garion was, but he doesn't seem to have Garion's sense of adventure—and he's just a bit too well behaved."

"I'm sure you'll be able to work on that."

Belgarath settled himself into another chair and pushed his feet out toward the fire. "What have you been up to?" he asked the hunchback. "I haven't seen you since Garion's wedding."

"I thought that somebody ought to keep an eye on the Angaraks," Beldin replied, scratching vigorously at one armpit.

"And?"

"And what?"

"That's an irritating habit you've picked up somewhere. What are the Angaraks doing?"

"The Murgos are still all in little pieces about the death of Taur Urgas." Beldin laughed. "He was completely mad, but he kept them unified—until Cho-Hag ran his saber through him. His son Urgit isn't much of a king. He's barely able to get their attention. The western Grolims can't even function any more. Ctuchik's dead, and Torak's dead, and about all the Grolims can do now is stare at the walls and count their fingers. My guess is that Murgo society is right on the verge of collapsing entirely."

"Good. Getting rid of the Murgos has been one of my main goals in life."

"I wouldn't start gloating just yet," Beldin said sourly. "After word reached 'Zakath that Belgarion had killed Torak, he threw off all pretenses about the fiction of Angarak unity and marched his Malloreans on Rak Goska. He didn't leave much of it standing."

Belgarath shrugged. "It wasn't a very attractive city anyway."

"It's a lot less attractive now. 'Zakath seems to think that crucifixions and impalings are educational. He decorated what was left of the walls of Rak Goska with object lessons. Every time he goes any place in Cthol Murgos, he leaves a trail of occupied crosses and stakes behind him."

"I find that I can bear the misfortunes of the Murgos with great fortitude," Belgarath replied piously.

"I think you'd better take a more realistic look at things, Belgarath," the hunchback growled. "We could probably match Murgo numbers if we really had to, but people don't talk about 'the uncountable hordes of boundless Mallorea' for nothing. 'Zakath has a *very* big army, and he commands most of the seaports on the east coast, so he can ship in as many more troops as he wants. If he succeeds in obliterating the Murgos, he's going to be camped on our southern doorstep with a lot of bored soldiers on his hands. Certain ideas are bound to occur to him at about that time."

Belgarath grunted. "I'll worry about that when the time comes."

"Oh, by the way," Beldin said suddenly with an ironic grin, "I found out what that apostrophe is doing in his name."

"Whose name?"

" 'Zakath's. Would you believe that it indicates the word 'Kal'?"

"Kal Zakath?" Belgarath stared at him incredulously.

"Isn't that outrageous?" Beldin chortled. "I guess that the Mallorean emperors have been secretly yearning to take that title since just after the battle of Vo Mimbre, but they were always afraid that Torak might wake up and take offense at their presumption. Now that he's dead, a fair number of Malloreans have begun to call their ruler 'Kal Zakath'—the ones who want to keep their heads do, at any rate."

"What does 'Kal' mean?" Errand asked.

"It's an Angarak word that means King and God," Belgarath explained. "Five hundred years ago, Torak set aside the Mallorean emperor and personally led his hordes against the west. The Angaraks—all of them: Murgos, Nedraks, and Thulls, as well as the Malloreans—called him Kal Torak."

"What happened?" Errand asked curiously. "When Kal Torak invaded the West, I mean?"

Belgarath shrugged. "It's a very old story."

"Not until you've heard it," Errand told him.

Beldin gave Belgarath a sharp look. "He *is* quick, isn't he?"

Belgarath looked at Errand thoughtfully. "All right," he said. "Putting it very briefly, Kal Torak smashed Drasnia, laid siege to the Algarian Stronghold for eight years, and then crossed Ulgoland to the plains of Arendia. The Kingdoms of the West met him at Vo Mimbre, and he was struck down in a duel with the Rivan Warder."

"But not killed."

"No. Not killed. The Rivan Warder struck him straight through the head with his sword, but Torak wasn't killed. He was only bound in slumber until a king sat once again on the throne of Riva."

"Belgarion," Errand said.

"Right. You know what happened then. You were there, after all."

Errand sighed. "Yes," he said sadly.

Belgarath turned back to Beldin. "All right," he said, "what's going on in Mallorea?"

"Things are about the same as always," Beldin replied, taking a drink of ale and belching thunderously. "The bureaucracy is still the glue that holds everything together. There are still plots and intrigues in Melcene and Mal Zeth. Karanda and Darshiva and Gandahar are on the verge of open rebellion, and the Grolims are still afraid to go near Kell."

"The Mallorean Grolims are still a functioning church then?" Belgarath seemed a little surprised. "I thought that the citizenry might have taken steps—the way they did in Mishrak ac Thull. I understand that the Thulls started building bonfires with Grolims."

"Kal Zakath sent a few orders back to Mal Zeth," Beldin told him, "and the army stepped in to stop the slaughter. After all, if you plan to be King *and* God, you're going to need yourself a church. 'Zakath seems to think that it might be easier to use one that's already established."

"What does Urvon think of that idea?"

"He's not making much of an issue of it right now. Before the army moved in, the people of Mallorea were finding a great deal of entertainment in hanging Grolims up on iron hooks. Urvon is staying in Mal Yaska and keeping very quiet. I think he believes that the fact that he's still alive might just be an oversight on the part of his exalted Majesty, Kal Zakath. Urvon is a slimy snake, but he's no fool."

"I've never met him."

"You haven't missed a thing," Beldin said sourly. He held out his tankard. "You want to fill this?"

"You're drinking up all of my ale, Beldin."

"You can always steal more. The twins never lock their doors. Anyway, Urvon was a disciple of Torak, the same as Ctuchik and Zedar. He doesn't have any of their good qualities, however."

"They didn't *have* any good qualities," Belgarath said, handing him back the refilled tankard.

"Compared to Urvon, they did. He's a natural-born bootlicker, a fawning, contemptible sneak. Even Torak despised him. But, like all people with those charming traits, as soon as he got the least little bit of power, he went absolutely berserk with it. He's not satisfied with bows as a sign of respect; he wants people to grovel before him."

"You seem moderately unfond of him," Belgarath noted.

"I *loathe* that piebald back stabber."

"Piebald?"

"He's got patches of skin on his face and hands with no color at all, so he looks all splotchy—as if he had some gruesome disease. I'm viewed in some quarters as passing ugly, but Urvon could scare a troll into fits. Anyway, if Kal Zakath wants to turn the Grolim church into a state religion with *his* face on the altars instead of Torak's, he's going to have to deal with Urvon first, and Urvon always stays holed up in Mal Yaska, completely surrounded by Grolim sorcerers. 'Zakath won't be able to get near him. *I* can't even get near him. I give it a try every hundred years or so, hoping that somebody might get careless or that I might get lucky enough to get a large, sharp hook into his guts. What I'd really like to do, though, is drag him facedown over red-hot coals for a few weeks."

Belgarath looked a little surprised at the little man's vehemence. "That's all he's doing then? Staying under cover in Mal Yaska?"

"Not hardly! Urvon plots and schemes even in his sleep. In the last year and a half—ever since Belgarion ran his sword through Torak—Urvon's been scrambling around, trying to preserve what's left of his church. There are some old, moth-eaten prophecies—the Grolims call them Oracles—from a place called Ashaba in the Karandese Mountains. Urvon dusted them off and he's been twisting them around so that they seem to say that Torak will return—that he's not dead, or that he'll be resurrected or possibly reborn."

Belgarath snorted. "What nonsense!"

"Of course it is, but he had to do something. The Grolim church was convulsing like a headless snake, and 'Zakath was right on the verge of putting his fist around everybody's throat to make sure that every time any Angarak bowed, it would be to *him*. Urvon made sure that there were very few copies of these Ashabine Oracles left lying about and he's been inventing all sorts of things and claiming that he found them in the prophecies. That's about the only thing holding 'Zakath off right now and probably *that* wouldn't even work, if the Emperor weren't so busy trying to decorate every tree he comes across with a Murgo or two."

"Did you have any trouble moving around in Mallorea?"

Beldin snorted a crude obscenity. "Of course not. Nobody even notices the face of a deformed man. Most people couldn't tell you if I'm an Alorn or a Marag. They can't see past the hump on my back." He rose from his chair, went to the cask, and refilled his tankard again. "Belgarath," he said very seriously, "does the name Cthrag Sardius mean anything to you?"

"Sardius? Sardonyx, you mean?"

Beldin shrugged. "The Mallorean Grolims call it Cthrag Sardius. What's the difference?"

"Sardonyx is a gemstone—sort of orange colored with milky-white stripes. It's not really very rare—or very attractive."

"That doesn't quite match up with the way I heard the Malloreans talk about it." Beldin frowned. "From the way they use the name Cthrag Sardius, I gather that it's a single stone—and that it's got a certain kind of importance."

"What sort of importance?"

"I can't say for sure. About all I could gather was that just about every Grolim in Mallorea would trade his soul for the chance to get his hands on it."

"It could just be some kind of internal symbol—something to do with the power struggle that's going on over there."

"That's possible, I suppose, but why would its name be Cthrag Sardius then? They called the Orb of Aldur 'Cthrag Yaska,' remember? There'd almost have to be a connection between Cthrag Sardius and Cthrag Yaska, wouldn't there? And if there is, maybe we ought to have a look into it."

Belgarath gave him a long look and then sighed. "I thought that, once Torak was dead, we might get a chance to rest."

"You've had a year or so." Beldin shrugged. "Much more than that and you start to get flabby."

"You're a very disagreeable fellow, do you know that?"

Beldin gave him a tight, ugly grin. "Yes," he agreed. "I thought you might have noticed that."

The next morning Belgarath began meticulously sorting though a mountainous heap of crackling parchments, trying to impose some kind of order upon centuries of chaos. Errand watched the old man quietly for a time, then drifted over to the window to look out at the sun-warmed meadows of the Vale. Perhaps a mile away, there was another tower, a tall, slender structure that looked somehow very serene.

"Do you mind if I go outside?" he asked Belgarath.

"What? No, that's all right. Just don't wander too far away."

"I won't," Errand promised, going to the top of the stairway that spiraled down into the cool dimness below.

The early morning sunlight slanted across the dew-drenched meadow, and sky-larks sang and spun through the sweet-smelling air. A brown rabbit hopped out of the tall grass and regarded Errand quite calmly. Then it sat on its haunches and began vigorously to scratch its long ears with a busy hind foot.

Errand had not come out of the tower for random play, however, nor to watch rabbits. He had someplace to go and he set out across the dewy green meadow in the direction of the tower he had seen from Belgarath's window.

He hadn't really counted on the dew, and his feet were uncomfortably wet by the time he reached the solitary tower. He walked around the base of the stone structure several times, his feet squelching in their sodden boots.

"I wondered how long it would take before you came by," a very calm voice said to him.

"I was busy helping Belgarath," Errand apologized.

"Did he really need help?"

"He was having a little trouble getting started."

"Would you like to come up?"

"If it's all right."

"The door's on the far side."

Errand went around the tower and found a large stone that had been turned to reveal a doorway. He went into the tower and on up the stairs.

One tower room was much like another, but there were certain differences be-tween this one and Belgarath's. As in Belgarath's tower, there was a fireplace here with a fire burning in it, but there appeared to be nothing in the flames here for them to feed upon. The room itself was strangely uncluttered, for the owner of *this* tower stored his parchment scrolls, tools, and implements in some unimaginable place, to be summoned as he required them.

The owner of the tower sat beside the fire. His hair and beard were white, and he wore a blue, loose-fitting robe. "Come over to the fire and dry your feet, boy," he said in his gentle voice.

"Thank you," Errand replied.

"How is Polgara?"

"Very well," Errand said, "And happy. She likes being married, I think." He lifted one foot and held it close to the fire.

"Don't burn your shoes."

"I'll be careful."

"Would you like some breakfast?"

"That would be nice. Belgarath forgets things like that sometimes."

"On the table there."

Errand looked at the table and saw a steaming bowl of porridge that had not been there before.

"Thank you," he said politely, going to the table and pulling up a chair.

"Was there something special you wanted to talk about?"

"Not really," Errand replied, picking up a spoon and starting on the porridge. "I just thought I should come by. The Vale *is* yours, after all."

"Polgara's been teaching you manners, I see."

Errand smiled. "And other things, too."

"Are you happy with her, Errand?" the owner of the tower asked.

"Yes, Aldur, I really am," Errand replied and continued to eat his porridge.

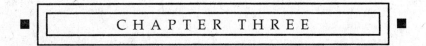

CHAPTER THREE

As the summer progressed, Errand found himself rather naturally more and more in the company of Durnik. The smith, he soon discovered, was an extraordinarily patient man who did things the old way, not so much because of some moral bias against what Belgarath called "the alternative we have available to us," but rather because he took a deep satisfaction in working with his hands. This was not to say that Durnik did not occasionally take short cuts. Errand noticed a certain pattern to the smith's evasions. Durnik absolutely would not cheat on any project involving making something for Polgara or for their home. No matter how laborious or tedious those projects might be, Durnik completed them with his hands and his muscles.

Certain outside activities, however, were not quite so closely tied up with Durnik's sense of ethics. Two hundred yards of rail fence, for example, appeared rather quickly one morning. The fence needed to be there; there was no question of that, since a nearby herd of Algar cattle had to be diverted from plodding with bovine stubbornness across Polgara's garden on their way to water. As a matter of fact, the fence actually began to appear instantly just in front of the startled cows. They regarded the first fifty feet or so in bafflement; then, after considering the problem for several minutes, they moved to go around the obstruction. Another fifty feet of fence appeared in their path. In time, the cows grew surly about the whole thing and even tried running, perhaps thinking in their sluggish way that they might be able to outrace this phantom fence builder. Durnik, however, sat planted on a stump, his eyes intent and his face determined, extending his fence section by section in front of the increasingly irritable cows.

One dark brown bull, finally goaded into a fury of frustration, lowered his head, pawed the earth a few times, and charged the fence with a great bellow. Durnik made a peculiar twisting gesture with one hand, and the bull was suddenly charging *away* from the fence, turned around somehow in midstride without even knowing it. He ran for several hundred yards before it occurred to him that his horns had not yet encountered anything substantial. He slowed and raised his head in astonishment. He looked dubiously back over his shoulder at the fence, then turned around and gave it another try. Once again Durnik turned him, and once again he charged ferociously off in the wrong direction. The third time he tried it, he charged over the top of the hill and disappeared on the other side. He did not come back.

Durnik looked gravely at Errand and then he winked. Polgara came out of the cottage, drying her hands on her apron, and noted the fence which had somehow constructed itself while she had been washing the breakfast dishes. She gave her husband a quizzical look, and Durnik seemed a bit abashed at having been caught using sorcery rather than an axe.

"Very nice fence, dear," she said encouragingly to him.

"We kind of needed one there," he said apologetically. "Those cows—well, I had to do it in a hurry."

"Durnik," she said gently, "there's nothing morally reprehensible about using your talent for this sort of thing—and you *should* practice every so often." She looked at the zig-zag pattern of the interlocking rail fence, and then her expression became concentrated. One after another, each of the junctures of the rails was suddenly bound tightly together with stout rosebushes in full bloom. "There," she said contentedly, patted her husband's shoulder, and went back inside.

"She's a remarkable woman, do you know that?" Durnik said to Errand.

"Yes," Errand agreed.

Polgara was not *always* pleased with her husband's ventures into this new field, however. On one occasion toward the hot, dusty end of summer when the vegetables in her garden were beginning to wilt, Polgara devoted the bulk of one morning to locating a small, black rain cloud over the mountains in Ulgoland and gently herding its sodden puffiness toward the Vale of Aldur and, more specifically, toward her thirsty garden.

Errand was playing along the fence when the cloud came in low over the hill to the west and then stopped directly over the cottage and the waiting garden. Durnik glanced up from the harness he was mending, saw the blond-haired boy at play and the ominous black cloud directly over his head, and rather negligently pulled in his will. He made a small flipping gesture with one hand. "Shoo," he said to the cloud.

The cloud gave a peculiar sort of twitch, almost like a hiccup, then slowly flowed on eastward. When it was several hundred yards beyond Polgara's parched garden, it began to rain—a nice, steady, soaking downpour that very satisfactorily watered several acres of empty grassland.

Durnik was not at all prepared for his wife's reaction. The door to the cottage banged open, and Polgara emerged with her eyes flashing. She gave the happily raining cloud a hard stare, and the soggy-looking thing gave another of those peculiar hiccups and actually managed to look guilty.

Then Polgara turned and looked directly at her husband, her eyes a bit wild. "Did you do that?" she demanded, pointing at the cloud.

"Why—yes," he replied. "I suppose I did, Pol."

"*Why* did you do that?"

"Errand was out there playing," Durnik said, still concentrating most of his attention on the harness. "I didn't think you'd want him to get wet."

Polgara looked at the cloud wasting all of its rain on grass so deeply rooted that it could have easily survived a ten-month drought. Then she looked at her garden and its drooping turnip tops and pathetic beans. She clenched her teeth tightly together to keep in certain words and phrases which she knew might shock her strait-laced and proper husband. She raised her face to the sky and lifted her arms in supplication. "Why me?" she demanded in a loud, tragic voice. "Why me?"

"Why, dear," Durnik said mildly, "whatever is wrong?"

Polgara told him what was wrong—at some length.

Durnik spent the next week putting in an irrigation system leading from the upper end of their valley to Polgara's garden, and she forgave him for his mistake almost as soon as he had finished it.

The winter came late that year, and autumn lingered in the Vale. The twins, Beltira and Belkira, came by just before the snows set in and told them that, after several weeks of discussion, both Belgarath and Beldin had left the Vale, and that each of them had gone away with that serious expression on his face that meant that there was trouble somewhere.

Errand missed Belgarath's company that winter. To be sure, the old sorcerer had, more often than not, managed to get him in trouble with Polgara, but Errand felt somehow that he shouldn't really be expected to devote *every* waking moment to staying out of trouble. When the snow came, he took up sledding again. After she had watched him come flying down the hill and across the meadow a few times, Polgara prudently asked Durnik to erect a barrier at the stream bank to prevent a recurrence of the previous winter's mishap. It was while the smith was erecting a woven wattle fence to keep Errand on dry land that he happened to glance down into the water. Because the often muddy little rills that emptied into their stream were all locked in ice now, the water was low and as clear as crystal. Durnik could very clearly see the long, narrow shapes hovering like shadows in the current above the beds of gravel that formed the bottom.

"What a curious thing," he murmured, his eyes taking on that peculiarly abstracted look. "I've never noticed them there before."

"I've seen them jumping," Errand said. "But most of the time, the water's too cloudy to see them when they're lying underwater."

"I imagine that's the reason for it, all right," Durnik agreed. He tied the end of the wattle fence to a tree and thoughtfully walked through the snow toward the shed he had built at the back of the cottage. A moment or so later he emerged with the skein of waxed cord in his hand; five minutes later he was fishing. Errand smiled and turned to trudge back up the long hill, towing his sled behind him. When he reached the top of the hill, a strange, hooded young woman awaited him.

"Can I help you?" he asked politely.

The young woman pushed back her hood to reveal the fact that a dark cloth was tightly bound across her eyes. "Thou art the one they call Errand?" she asked. Her voice was low and musical, and there was a peculiar lilt to her archaic speech.

"Yes," Errand replied, "I am. Did you hurt your eyes?"

"Nay, gentle child," she replied. "I must needs look upon the world by a light other than that of the mundane sun."

"Would you like to come down to our cottage?" Errand asked her. "You could warm yourself by our fire, and Polgara would welcome company."

"Though I revere the Lady Polgara, the time has not yet arrived for us to meet," the young woman said, "and it is not cold where I am." She paused and bent forward slightly as if she were in fact peering at him, though the cloth over her eyes was quite thick. "It *is* true, then," she murmured softly. "We could not be certain at such great distance, but now that I am face to face with thee, I know that there can be no mistake." She straightened then. "We will meet again," she told him.

"As you wish, ma'am," Errand replied, remembering his manners.

She smiled, and her smile was so radiant that it seemed almost to bring sunlight to the murky winter afternoon. "I am Cyradis," she said, "and I bear thee friendship, gentle Errand, even though the time may come when I must needs decide against thee." And then she vanished, disappearing so suddenly that she was there and then gone in the space of a single heartbeat.

Startled a bit, Errand glanced at the snow where she had stood and saw that there were no marks or footprints. He sat down on his sled to think about it. Nothing that the strange young woman had said really seemed to make much sense, but he was fairly sure that a time would come when it *would*. After a bit of thought, he concluded that this peculiar visit would upset Polgara if she heard about it. Since he was certain that this Cyradis posed no threat and meant him no harm, he decided that he would not mention the incident.

Then, because it was growing quite chilly atop the hill, he pushed his sled into motion and coasted down the long slope and across the meadow and to within a few dozen yards of where Durnik was fishing with such total concentration that he was oblivious of all that was going on around him.

Polgara was tolerant about Durnik's pastime. She was always suitably impressed at the length, weight, and silvery color of the prizes he brought home and she drew upon all her vast knowledge to find new and interesting ways to fry, bake, broil, roast, and even poach fish. She adamantly insisted, however, that *he* clean them.

When spring returned once again, Belgarath came by, mounted on a spirited roan stallion.

"What happened to your mare?" Durnik asked the old man as he dismounted in the dooryard of the cottage.

Belgarath made a sour face. "I was halfway to Drasnia when I discovered that she was pregnant. I traded her for *this* enthusiast." He gave the prancing roan a hard look.

"It looks as if you might have gotten the best of the bargain," Durnik mused, looking Belgarath's horse over.

"The mare was sedate and sensible," the old man disagreed. "This one doesn't have a brain in his head. All he wants to do is show off—running, jumping, rearing, and pawing the air with his hooves." He shook his head in disgust.

"Put him in the barn, father," Polgara suggested, "and wash up. You're just in time for supper. You can have a baked fish. As a matter of fact, you can have several baked fish if you'd like."

After they had eaten, Belgarath turned his chair around, leaned back, and pushed his feet out toward the fire. He looked around with a contented smile at the polished flagstone floor, the limed white walls with polished pots and kettles hanging on pegs, and at the dancing light and shadow coming from the arched fireplace. "It's good to relax a bit," he said. "I don't think I've stopped moving since I left here last autumn."

"What is it that's so pressing, father?" Polgara asked him as she cleared away the supper dishes.

"Beldin and I had quite a long talk," the old man replied. "There are some things going on in Mallorea that I don't quite like."

"What earthly difference can it make now, father? Our interest in Mallorea ended at Cthol Mishrak when Torak died. You were not appointed caretaker of the world, you know."

"I wish it were that easy, Pol," he said. "Does the name 'the Sardion' mean anything to you? Or 'Cthrag Sardius' perhaps?"

She was pouring hot water from a kettle into the large pan in which she customarily washed the dishes, but she stopped, frowning slightly. "I think I heard a Grolim say something about 'Cthrag Sardius' once. He was delirious and babbling in old Angarak."

"Can you remember what he was saying?" Belgarath asked intently.

"I'm sorry, father, but I don't *speak* old Angarak. You never got around to teaching me, remember?" She looked at Errand and crooked one finger at him.

Errand sighed disconsolately, got up, and fetched a dish towel.

"Don't make faces, Errand," she told him. "It doesn't hurt you to help clean up after supper." She looked back at Belgarath as she started to wash the dishes. "What's the significance of the 'Sardion' or whatever you call it?"

"I don't know," Belgarath replied, scratching at his beard in perplexity. "As Beldin pointed out, though, Torak called our Master's Orb 'Cthrag Yaska.' It's possible, I suppose, that 'Cthrag Sardius' might be connected in some way."

"I picked up a lot of 'possibles' and 'supposes' and 'mights' in there, father," she said. "I wonder if you aren't chasing after shadows out of habit—or just to keep busy."

"You know me well enough to know that I'm not all *that* enthusiastic about keeping busy, Pol," he said wryly.

"So I've noticed. Is anything else happening in the world?"

"Let's see." Belgarath leaned back and stared speculatively at the low-beamed ceiling. "The Grand Duke Noragon ate something that definitely didn't agree with him."

"Who is the Grand Duke Noragon? And why are we interested in his digestion?" Polgara asked.

"The Grand Duke Noragon *was* the candidate of the Honeth family to succeed Ran Borune on the Imperial Throne of Tolnedra." Belgarath smirked. "He was a complete and total jackass, and his ascension to the throne would have been an unmitigated disaster."

"You said *was*," Durnik noted.

"Right. Noragon's indigestion proved fatal. It is widely suspected that some splendid Horbite sympathizer used certain exotic condiments that come from the jungles of Nyissa to season the Grand Duke's last lunch. The symptoms, I understand, were quite spectacular. The Honeths are in total disarray, and the other families are gloating outrageously."

"Tolnedran politics are disgusting," Polgara declared.

"Our Prince Kheldar appears to be well on his way toward becoming the wealthiest man in the world," Belgarath continued.

"Silk?" Durnik looked a bit amazed. "Has he managed to steal *that* much already?"

"I gather that what he's doing is sort of legitimate this time," Belgarath said. "He and that rascal Yarblek have somehow managed to gain control of the entire Nadrak fur harvest. I wasn't able to get all the details, but the screams of anguish coming from the major commercial houses in Boktor would seem to indicate that our friends are doing rather well."

"I'm pleased to hear that," Durnik said.

"That's probably because you haven't been in the market for a fur cape lately." Belgarath chuckled. "The price has taken quite a jump, I understand." The old man rocked back in his chair. "In Cthol Murgos, your friend Kal Zakath is methodically butchering his way down the east coast. He's added Rak Cthan and Rak Hagga to the list of cities he's captured and depopulated. I'm not too fond of Murgos, but it's just possible that 'Zakath is going a little too far."

"Kal Zakath?" Polgara asked with one eyebrow slightly raised.

"An affectation." Belgarath shrugged.

"More likely a symptom," she observed. "Angarak rulers always seem to be unstable in one way or another." She turned to look at her father. "Well?"

"Well what?"

"Have you heard anything from Riva? How are Garion and Ce'Nedra doing?"

"I haven't heard a sound—oh, a few official things. 'The Rivan King is pleased to announce the appointment of Earl what's-his-name as Rivan ambassador to the Kingdom of Drasnia.' That sort of thing, but nothing in the least bit personal."

"We *are* sure he knows how to write, aren't we?" she demanded exasperatedly. "I'm sure that he's not so busy that he hasn't had the time to write at least *one* letter in the last two years."

"He did," Errand said quietly. He might not have mentioned the letter, but it seemed very important to Polgara.

She looked at him sharply. "What did you say?" she asked.

"Belgarion wrote to you last winter," Errand said. "The letter got lost, though, when the ship his messenger was aboard sank."

"If the ship sank, then how do you—"

"Pol," Belgarath said in a tone that seemed uncharacteristically firm, "why don't you let me handle this?" He turned to Errand. "You say that Garion wrote a letter to Polgara last winter?"

"Yes," Errand said.

"But that the letter was lost when the messenger's ship sank?"

Errand nodded.

"Why didn't he write another one then?"

"He doesn't know that the ship sank."

"But you do?"

Errand nodded again.

"Do you by any chance know what the letter said?"

"Yes."

"Do you suppose you could recite it for us?"

"I guess I could, if you want. Belgarion's going to write another one in a week or so, though."

Belgarath gave him a strange look. "Why don't you tell us what the first one said? That way we won't miss anything."

"All right," Errand agreed. He frowned, concentrating very hard. "He started out by saying, 'Dear Aunt Pol and Durnik.' I think that's sort of nice, don't you?"

"Just recite the letter, Errand," Belgarath said patiently. "Save the comments for later."

"All right." Errand stared thoughtfully into the fire. " 'I'm sorry I haven't written earlier,' " he recited, " 'but I've been terribly busy learning how to be a good king. It's easy enough to be King—all you need is to be born into the right family. To be a good king is harder, though. Brand helps me as much as he can, but I still have to make a lot of decisions about things that I don't really understand.

" 'Ce'Nedra is well—at least I think so. We're hardly talking to each other any more, so it's kind of hard to say for sure. Brand is a bit concerned that we haven't had any children yet, but I don't think he needs to worry. So far as I can tell, we're never going to have any children, and maybe it's just as well. I really think we should have gotten to know each other a little better before we got married. I'm sure that there's some way that we could have called it off. Now it's too late. We'll just have to make the best of it. If we don't see each other too much, we can usually manage to be civil to each other—at least civil enough to keep up appearances.

" 'Barak came by in that big war boat of his last summer, and we had a very good visit. He told me all about—' "

"Just a moment, Errand." Polgara stopped the recitation. "Does he say any more about the trouble he's having with Ce'Nedra?"

"No, ma'am," Errand replied after a moment during which he quickly ran through the rest of the letter in his mind. "He wrote about Barak's visit and some news he got from King Anheg and a letter from Mandorallen. That's about all. He said that he loves you and misses you very much. That's how he ended it."

Polgara and Belgarath exchanged a very long look. Errand could feel their perplexity, but he was not sure exactly how to set their minds at rest about the matter.

"You're sure that's the way the letter went?" Belgarath asked him.

Errand nodded. "That's what he wrote."

"And you knew what was in the letter as soon as he wrote it?"

Errand hesitated. "I don't know if it was like that, exactly. It doesn't really work that way, you know. You have to sort of think about it, and I didn't really think about it until the subject came up—when Polgara was talking about it just now."

"Does it matter how far away the other person is?" Belgarath asked curiously.

"No," Errand replied, "I don't think so. It just seems to be there when I want it to be."

"No one can do that, father," Polgara said to the old man. "No one has *ever* been able to do that."

"Apparently the rules have changed," Belgarath said thoughtfully. "I think we'll have to accept it as genuine, don't you?"

She nodded. "He doesn't have any reason to make it up."

"I think you and I are going to have to have some very long talks together, Errand," the old man said.

"Perhaps," Polgara said, "but not just yet." She turned back to the boy. "Could you repeat what Garion said about Ce'Nedra for me?"

Errand nodded. " 'Ce'Nedra is well—at least I think so. We're hardly talking to each other any more, so it's kind of hard to say for sure. Brand is a bit concerned that—' "

"That's fine, Errand," she said, raising one hand slightly. Then she looked into the boy's face. After a moment, one of her eyebrows shot up. "Tell me," she said, very carefully choosing her words, "do you know what's wrong between Garion and Ce'Nedra?"

"Yes," Errand replied.

"Would you tell me?"

"If you want. Ce'Nedra did something that made Garion *very* angry, and then he did something that embarrassed her in public, and that made *her* angry. She thinks that he doesn't pay enough attention to her and that he spends all his time on his work so that he won't have to spend any with her. He thinks that she's selfish and spoiled and doesn't think about anybody but herself. They're both wrong, but they've had a lot of arguments about it and they've hurt each other so much with some of the things they've said that they've both given up on being married to each other. They're terribly unhappy."

"Thank you, Errand," she said. Then she turned to Durnik. "We'll need to pack a few things," she said.

"Oh?" He looked a bit surprised.

"We're going to Riva," she said quite firmly.

CHAPTER FOUR

At Camaar, Belgarath ran across an old friend in a tavern near the harbor. When he brought the bearded, fur-clad Cherek to the inn where they were staying, Polgara gave the swaying sailor a penetrating look. "How long have you been drunk, Captain Greldik?" she asked bluntly.

"What day is it?" His reply was vague.

She told him.

"Astonishing." He belched. "Par'n me," he apologized. "I appear to have lost track of several days somewhere. Do you know by any chance what *week* it is?"

"Greldik," she said, "do you absolutely *have* to get drunk every time you're in port?"

Greldik looked thoughtfully at the ceiling, scratching at his beard. "Now that you mention it, Polgara, I believe I do. I hadn't really thought about it that way before, but now that you suggest it—"

She gave him a hard stare, but the look he returned was deliberately impudent. "Don't waste your time, Polgara," he suggested. "I'm not married; I've never *been* married; and I'm not ever going to *get* married. I'm not ruining any woman's life by the way I behave, and it's absolutely certain that no woman is ever going to ruin mine. Now, Belgarath says that you want to go to Riva. I'll round up my crew, and we'll leave on the morning tide."

"Will your crew be sober enough to find their way out of the harbor?"

He shrugged. "We might bump into a Tolnedran merchantman or two on the way out, but we'll find our way to the open sea eventually. Drunk or sober, my crew is the best afloat. We'll put you on the quay at Riva by midafternoon on the day after tomorrow—unless the sea freezes solid between now and then, in which case it might take a couple hours longer." He belched again. "Par'n me," he said, swaying back and forth and peering at her with his bleary eyes.

"Greldik," Belgarath said admiringly, "you're the bravest man alive."

"The sea doesn't frighten me," Greldik replied.

"I wasn't talking about the sea."

About noon of the following day, Greldik's ship was running before a freshening breeze through foaming whitecaps. A few of the less indisposed members of his crew lurched about the deck tending the lines and keeping a more or less alert eye on the stern where Greldik, puffy-eyed and obviously suffering, clung to the tiller.

"Aren't you going to shorten your sail?" Belgarath asked him.

"What for?"

"Because if you leave full sail up in this kind of wind, you'll uproot your mast."

"You stick to your sorcery, Belgarath," Greldik told him, "and leave the sailing to me. We're making good time, and the deck-planking starts to buckle up long before the mast is in any danger."

"How long before?"

Greldik shrugged. "Almost a minute or so—most of the time."

Belgarath stared at him. "I think I'll go below," he said at last.

"That's a good idea."

By evening the wind had abated, and Greldik's ship continued across a quieter sea as night fell. There were only occasional glimpses of the stars, but they were sufficient; when the sun rose the next morning, it was, as the wayward captain had predicted, dead astern. By midmorning, the dark, rocky crags and jagged peaks that formed the crest of the Isle of the Winds were poked above the western horizon, and their ship was once again plunging like a spirited horse through the whitecaps under a crisp blue sky. A broad grin split Greldik's bearded face as his ship swooped and lurched and shuddered her way through the hammering seas, throwing out great sheets of sparkling spray each time she knifed into a wave.

"That's a *very* unreliable man," Polgara said, giving the captain a disapproving stare.

"He really seems to be a good sailor, Pol," Durnik said mildly.

"That's not what I was talking about, Durnik."

"Oh."

The ship tacked smoothly between two rocky headlands and into the sheltered harbor of the city of Riva. The gray stone buildings mounted steeply upward toward the grim, menacing battlements of the Citadel which brooded over the city and the harbor below.

"This place always looks so bleak," Durnik noted. "Bleak and uninviting."

"That was sort of the idea when they built it, Durnik," Belgarath replied. "They didn't really want many visitors."

Then, at the end of a starboard tack, Greldik swung his tiller hard over, and his ship, her prow knifing through the dark water, ran directly at the stone quay jutting out from the foot of the city. At the last possible moment he swung his tiller again. To the flapping of her patched sails, the ship coasted the last few yards and bumped gently against the salt-crusted stones of the quay.

"Do you think anybody saw us coming and told Garion?" Durnik asked.

"Evidently so," Belgarath replied, pointing toward the arched gate that had just swung open to reveal the broad flight of stone stairs mounting upward within the thick, high walls protecting the seaward side of Riva. A number of official-looking men were coming through the gate; in the center of the group strode a tall young man with sandy-colored hair and a serious expression on his face.

"Let's step over to the other side of the ship," Belgarath suggested to Durnik and Errand. "I want to surprise him."

"Welcome to Riva, Captain Greldik." Errand recognized Garion's voice, even though it sounded older, more sure now.

Greldik squinted appraisingly over the rail. "You've grown, boy," he said to the King of Riva. A man as free as Greldik almost never felt the need for using customary terms of respect.

"It's been going around lately," Garion replied drily. "Almost everybody my age has come down with it."

"I've brought you some visitors," Greldik told him.

Grinning, Belgarath moved across the deck to the quayside railing with Durnik and Errand close behind him.

"Grandfather?" Garion's face was completely astonished. "What are you doing here? And Durnik—and Errand?"

"Actually it was your aunt's idea," Belgarath told him.

"Is Aunt Pol here, too?"

"Of course I am," Polgara replied calmly, emerging from the low-roofed cabin under the stern.

"Aunt Pol!" Garion exclaimed, looking dumfounded.

"Don't stare, Garion," she told him, adjusting the collar of her blue cloak. "It's impolite."

"But, why didn't you let me know you were coming? What are you all doing here?"

"Visiting, dear. People do that from time to time."

When they joined the young king on the quay, there were the usual embraces and handshakes and the long looks into each other's faces that go with reunions. Errand, however, was much more interested in something else. As they started the climb up through the gray city toward the Citadel brooding above it, he tugged once at Garion's sleeve. "Horse?" he asked.

Garion looked at him. "He's in the stables, Errand. He'll be happy to see you." Errand smiled and nodded.

"Does he still talk that way?" Garion asked Durnik. "Just one word at a time like that? I thought—well—"

"Most of the time he speaks normally—for his age," Durnik replied, "but he's been thinking about the colt ever since we left the Vale and sometimes, when he gets excited, he slips back to the old way."

"He listens, though," Polgara added, "which is more than I can say about another boy when he was that age."

Garion laughed. "Was I really that difficult, Aunt Pol?"

"Not difficult, dear. You just didn't listen."

When they arrived at the Citadel, the Rivan Queen greeted them under the high, thick-walled arch of the front gate. Ce'Nedra was as exquisite as Errand remembered her. Her coppery-colored hair was caught at the back of her head by a pair of golden combs, and the ringlets tumbled down her back in a flaming cascade. Her green eyes were large. She was tiny, not much taller than Errand, but she was every inch a queen. She greeted them all regally, embracing Belgarath and Durnik and lightly kissing Polgara's cheek.

Then she held out both hands to Errand, and he took them in his and looked into her eyes. There was a barrier there, the faintest hint of the defensive tightening with which she kept the hurt away. She drew him to her and kissed him; even in that gesture, he could feel the unhappy tenseness that she was probably no longer even aware of. As she removed her soft lips from his cheek, Errand once again looked deeply into her eyes, letting all the love and hope and compassion he felt for her flow into his gaze. Then, without even thinking, he reached out his hand and gently touched her cheek. Her eyes went very wide, and her lip began to tremble. That faint touch of agate-hard defensiveness about her face began to crumble. Two great tears welled up in her eyes; then, with a brokenhearted wail, she turned and stumbled blindly, her arms outstretched. "Oh, Lady Polgara!" she cried.

Polgara calmly took the sobbing little queen in her arms and held her. She looked directly into Errand's face, however, and one of her eyebrows was raised questioningly. Errand returned her look and gave her a calm, answering nod.

"Well," Belgarath said, slightly embarrassed by Ce'Nedra's sudden weeping. He scratched at his beard and looked around the inner courtyard of the Citadel and the broad granite steps leading up to the massive door. "Have you got anything to drink handy?" he asked Garion.

Polgara, her arms still about the weeping Ce'Nedra, gave him a level look. "Isn't it a bit early, father?" she asked.

"Oh, I don't think so," he replied blandly. "A bit of ale helps to settle the stomach after a sea voyage."

"There's always some excuse, isn't there?"

"I can usually manage to think of something."

Errand spent the afternoon in the exercise yard at the rear of the royal stables. The chestnut-colored colt was not really a colt any more, but rather a full-grown young stallion. His dark coat was glossy, and his muscles rippled under that coat as he ran in a wide circle about the yard. The single white patch on his shoulder seemed almost incandescent in the bright sunlight.

The horse had known somehow that Errand was coming and had been restive and high-strung all morning. The stableman cautioned Errand about that. "Be careful of him," he said. "He's a bit flighty today for some reason."

"He'll be fine now," Errand said, calmly unlatching the door to the young horse's stall.

"I wouldn't go—" the stableman started sharply, half-reaching out as if to pull the boy back, but Errand had already entered the stall with the wide-eyed animal. The horse snorted once and pranced nervously, his hooves thudding on the straw-covered floor. He stopped and stood quivering until Errand put out his hand and touched that bowed neck. Then everything was all right between them. Errand pushed the door of the stall open wider and, with the horse contentedly nuzzling at his shoulder, led the way out of the stable past the astonished groom.

For the time being, it was enough for the two of them just to be together—to share the bond which was between them and had somehow existed even before they had met and, in a peculiar way, even before either of them was born. There would be more later, but for now this was enough.

When the purple hue of evening began to creep up the eastern sky, Errand fed the horse, promised that he would come again the following day, and went back into the Citadel in search of his friends. He found them seated in a low-ceilinged dining hall. This room was smaller than the great main banquet hall and it was less formal. It was perhaps as close to being homey as any room in this bleak fortress could be.

"Did you have a pleasant afternoon?" Polgara asked him.

Errand nodded.

"And was the horse glad to see you?"

"Yes."

"And now you're hungry, I suppose?"

"Well—a little." He looked around the room, noting that the Rivan Queen was not present. "Where's Ce'Nedra?" he asked.

"She's a little tired," Polgara replied. "She and I had a long talk this afternoon."

Errand looked at her and understood. Then he looked around again. "I really *am* sort of hungry," he told her.

She laughed a warm, fond laugh. "All boys are the same," she said.

"Would you really want us to be different?" Garion asked her.

"No," she said, "I don't suppose I would."

The next morning, quite early, Polgara and Errand were in front of the fire in the apartment that had always been hers. Polgara sat in a high-backed chair with a fragrant cup of tea on the small table beside her. She wore a deep blue velvet dressing gown and held a large ivory comb. Errand sat on a carpet-covered footstool directly in front of her, enduring a part of the morning ritual. The washing of the face, ears, and neck did not take all that much time, but for some reason the combing of his hair always seemed to fill up the better part of a quarter hour. Errand's personal tastes in the arrangement of his hair were fairly elemental. As long as it was out of his eyes, it was satisfactory. Polgara, however, seemed to find a great deal of entertainment in pulling a comb through his soft, pale-blond curls. Now and then at odd times of the day, he would see that peculiar softness come into her eyes and see her fingers twitching almost of their own will toward a comb and he would know that, if he did not immediately become very busy with something, he would be wordlessly seated in a chair to have his hair attended to.

There was a respectful tap on the door.

"Yes, Garion?" she replied.

"I hope I'm not too early, Aunt Pol. May I come in?"

"Of course, dear."

Garion wore a blue doublet and hose and soft leather shoes. Errand had noticed that if he had any choice in the matter, the young King of Riva almost always wore blue.

"Good morning, dear," Polgara said, her fingers still busy with the comb.

"Good morning, Aunt Pol," Garion said. And then he looked at the boy who sat fidgeting slightly on the stool in front of Polgara's chair. "Good morning, Errand," he said gravely.

"Belgarion," Errand said, nodding.

"Hold your head still, Errand," Polgara said calmly. "Would you like some tea?" she asked Garion.

"No, thank you." He drew up another chair and sat down across from her. "Where's Durnik?" he asked.

"He's taking a walk around the parapet," Polgara told him. "Durnik likes to be outside when the sun comes up."

"Yes," Garion smiled. "I seem to remember that from Faldor's farm. Is everything all right? With the rooms, I mean?"

"I'm always very comfortable here," she said. "In some ways it was always was the closest thing I had to a permanent home—at least until now." She looked around with satisfaction at the deep crimson velvet drapes and the dark leather upholstery of her chairs and sighed contentedly.

"These have been your rooms for a long time, haven't they?"

"Yes. Beldaran set them aside for me after she and Iron-grip were married."

"What was he like?"

"Iron-grip? Very tall—almost as tall as his father—and immensely strong." She turned her attention back to Errand's hair.

"Was he as tall as Barak?"

"Taller, but not quite so thick-bodied. King Cherek himself was seven feet tall, and all of his sons were very big men. Dras Bull-neck was like a tree trunk. He blotted out the sky. Iron-grip was leaner and he had a fierce black beard and piercing blue eyes. By the time he and Beldaran were married, there were touches of gray in his hair and beard; but even so, there was a kind of innocence about him that we could all sense. It was very much like the innocence we all feel in Errand here."

"You seem to remember him very well. For me, he's always been just somebody in a legend. Everybody knows about the things he did, but we don't know anything about him as a real man."

"I'd remember him a bit more acutely, Garion. After all, there *had* been the possibility that I might have married him."

"Iron-grip?"

"Aldur told father to send one of his daughters to the Rivan King to be his wife. Father had to choose between Beldaran and me. I think the old wolf made the right choice, but I still looked at Iron-grip in a rather special way." She sighed and then smiled a bit ruefully. "I don't think I'd have made him a good wife," she said. "My sister Beldaran was sweet and gentle and very beautiful. I was neither gentle nor very attractive."

"But you're the most beautiful woman in the world, Aunt Pol," Garion objected quickly.

"It's nice of you to say that, Garion, but when I was sixteen, I wasn't what most people would call pretty. I was tall and gangly. My knees were always skinned, and my face was usually dirty. Your grandfather was never very conscientious about looking after the appearance of his daughters. Sometimes whole weeks would go by without a comb ever touching my hair. I didn't like my hair very much, anyway. Beldaran's was soft and golden, but mine was like a horse's mane, and there was this ugly white streak." She absently touched the white lock at her left brow with the comb.

"What caused that?" he asked curiously.

"Your grandfather touched me there with his hand the first time he saw me— when I was just a baby. The lock turned white instantly. We're all marked in one way or another, you know. You have the mark on your palm; I have this white lock; your grandfather has a mark just over his heart. It's in different places on each of us, but it means the same thing."

"What does it mean?"

"It has to do with what we are, dear." She turned Errand around and looked at him, her lips pursed. Then she gently touched the curls just over his ears. "Anyway, as I was saying, I was wild and willful and not at all pretty when I was young. The Vale of Aldur isn't really a very good place for a girl to grow up, and a group of crotchety old sorcerers is not really a very good substitute for a mother. They tend to forget that you're around. You remember that huge, ancient tree in the middle of the Vale?"

He nodded.

"I climbed up into that tree once and stayed there for two weeks before anyone noticed that I hadn't been underfoot lately. That sort of thing can make a girl feel neglected and unloved."

"How did you finally find out—that you're really beautiful, I mean?"

She smiled. "That's another story, dear." She looked at him rather directly. "Do you suppose we can stop tiptoeing around the subject now?"

"What?"

"That business in your letter about you and Ce'Nedra."

"Oh, that. I probably shouldn't have bothered you with it, Aunt Pol. It's my problem, after all." He looked away uncomfortably.

"Garion," she said firmly, "in our particular family there's no such thing as a private problem. I thought you knew that by now. Exactly what *is* the difficulty with Ce'Nedra?"

"It's just not working, Aunt Pol," he said disconsolately. "There are things that I absolutely *have* to see to by myself, and she wants me to spend every waking minute with her—well, at least she *used* to. Now we go for days without seeing each other at all. We don't sleep in the same bed any more, and—" He looked suddenly at Errand and coughed uncomfortably.

"There," Polgara said to Errand as if nothing had happened. "I guess you're presentable now. Why don't you put on that brown wool cape and go find Durnik? Then the two of you can go down to the stables and visit the horse."

"All right, Polgara," Errand agreed, slipping down off the stool and going to fetch the cape.

"He's a very good little boy, isn't he?" Garion said to Polgara.

"Most of the time," she replied. "If we can keep him out of the river behind my mother's house. For some reason, he seems to feel incomplete if he can't fall into the water once or twice a month."

Errand kissed Polgara and started toward the door.

"Tell Durnik that I said the two of you can enjoy yourselves this morning," she told him. She gave Garion a direct look. "I think I'm going to be busy here for a few hours."

"All right," Errand said, and went out into the corridor. He gave only the briefest of thoughts to the problem which had made Garion and Ce'Nedra so unhappy. Polgara had already taken the matter in hand, and Errand knew that she would fix things. The problem itself was not a large one, but it had somehow been exploded into something of monstrous proportions by the arguments it had caused. The smallest misunderstanding, Errand realized, could sometimes fester like a hidden wound, if words spoken in haste and in heat were allowed to stand without apology or forgiveness. He also realized that Garion and Ce'Nedra loved each other so much that they were both extremely vulnerable to those hasty and heated words. Each had an enormous power to hurt the other. Once they were both made fully aware of that, the whole business could be allowed to blow over.

The corridors of the Citadel of Riva were lighted by torches held in iron rings protruding from the stone walls. Errand walked down a broad hallway leading to the east side of the fortress and the steps leading to the parapet and the battlements above. When he reached the thick east wall, he paused to look out one of the narrow windows that admitted a slender band of steel-gray light from the dawn sky. The Citadel was high above the city, and the gray stone buildings and narrow, cobblestone streets below were still lost in shadows and morning mist. Here and there, lighted windows gleamed in the houses of early risers. The clean salt smell of the sea, carried by an onshore breeze, wafted over the island kingdom. Contained within the ancient stones of the Citadel itself was the sense of desolation the people of Riva Iron-grip had felt when they had first glimpsed this rocky isle rising grim and storm-lashed out of a laden sea. Also within those stones was that stern sense of duty that had made the Rivans wrest their fortress and their city directly from the rock itself, to stand forever in defense of the Orb of Aldur.

Errand climbed the flight of stone stairs and found Durnik standing at the battlements, looking out over the Sea of the Winds that was rolling endlessly in to crash in long, muted combers against the rocky shore.

"She finished with your hair, I see," Durnik noted.

Errand nodded. "Finally," he said wryly.

Durnik laughed. "We can both put up with a few things if they please her, can't we?" he said.

"Yes," Errand agreed. "She's talking with Belgarion right now. I think she wants us to stay away until they've talked it all out."

Durnik nodded. "That's the best way, really. Pol and Garion are very close. He'll tell her things when they're alone that he wouldn't say if we were around. I hope she can get things straightened out between him and Ce'Nedra."

"Polgara will fix it," Errand assured him.

From somewhere in a meadow high above them where the morning sun had already touched the emerald grass, a shepherdess lifted her voice to sing to her flock. She sang of love in a pure, unschooled voice that rose like bird song.

"That's the way love should be," Durnik said. "Simple and uncomplicated and clear—just like that girl's voice."

"I know," Errand said. "Polgara said we could go visit the horse—whenever you're finished up here."

"Of course," Durnik said, "and we could probably stop by the kitchen and pick up some breakfast along the way."

"That's an awfully good idea, too," Errand said.

The day went very well. The sun was warm and bright, and the horse frolicked in the exercise yard almost like a puppy.

"The king won't let us break him," one of the grooms told Durnik. "He hasn't even been trained to a halter yet. His Majesty said something about this being a very special horse—which I don't understand at all. A horse is a horse, isn't it?"

"It has to do with something that happened when he was born," Durnik explained.

"They're all born the same," the groom said.

"You had to have been there," Durnik told him.

At supper that evening, Garion and Ce'Nedra were looking rather tentatively across the table at each other, and Polgara had a mysterious little smile playing across her lips.

When they had all finished eating, Garion stretched and yawned somewhat theatrically. "For some reason I'm feeling very tired tonight," he said. "The rest of you can sit up and talk if you'd like, but I think I'll go to bed."

"That might not be a bad idea, Garion," Polgara told him.

He got to his feet, and Errand could feel his trembling nervousness. With an almost agonizing casualness he turned to Ce'Nedra. "Coming, dear?" he asked, putting an entire peace proposal into those two words.

Ce'Nedra looked at him, and her heart was in her eyes. "Why—uh—yes, Garion," she said with a rosy little blush, "I believe I will. I seem to be very tired, too."

"Good night, children," Polgara said to them in tones of warm affection. "Sleep well."

"What did you say to them?" Belgarath asked his daughter when the royal couple had left the room hand in hand.

"A great many things, father," she replied smugly.

"One of them must have done the trick," he said. "Durnik, be a good fellow and top this off for me." He passed his empty tankard to Durnik, who sat beside the ale barrel.

Polgara was so pleased with her success that she did not even comment on that.

It was well after midnight when Errand awoke with a slight start.

"You're a very sound sleeper," a voice that seemed to be inside his mind said to him.

"I was dreaming," Errand replied.

"I noticed that," the voice said drily. *"Pull on some clothes. I need you in the throne room."*

Errand obediently got out of bed and pulled on his tunic and his short, soft Sendarian boots.

"Be quiet," the voice told him. *"Let's not wake up Polgara and Durnik."*

Quietly they left the apartment and went down the long, deserted corridors to the Hall of the Rivan King, the vast throne room where, three years before, Errand had placed the Orb of Aldur in Garion's hand and had forever changed the young man's life.

The huge door creaked slightly as Errand pulled it open, and he heard a voice inside call out, "Who's there?"

"It's only me, Belgarion," Errand told him.

The great Hall was illuminated by the soft blue radiance of the Orb of Aldur, standing on the pommel of the huge sword of Riva, hanging point downward above the throne.

"What are you doing wandering around so late, Errand?" Garion asked him. The Rivan King was sprawled on his throne with his leg cocked up over one of the arms.

"I was told to come here," Errand replied.

Garion looked at him strangely. "Told? *Who* told you?"

"You know," Errand said, stepping inside the Hall and closing the door. "Him."

Garion blinked. "Does he talk to *you,* too?"

"This is the first time. I've known about him, though."

"If he's never—" Garion broke off and looked sharply up at the Orb, his eyes startled. The soft blue light of the stone had suddenly changed to a deep, angry red. Errand could very clearly hear a strange sound. For all of the time he had carried the Orb, his ears had been filled with the crystalline shimmer of its song, but now that shimmer seemed to have taken on an ugly iron overtone, as if the stone had encountered something or someone that filled it with a raging anger.

"Beware!" that voice which they both heard quite clearly said to them in tones which could not be ignored. *"Beware Zandramas!"*

CHAPTER FIVE

As soon as it was daylight, the two of them went in search of Belgarath. Errand could sense that Garion was troubled and he himself felt that the warning they had received concerned a matter of such importance that everything else must be set aside in the face of it. They had not really spoken much about it during those dark, silent hours while they sat together in the Hall of the Rivan King, waiting for the first light to touch the eastern horizon. Instead, they had both watched the Orb of Aldur closely, but the stone, after that one strange moment of crimson anger, had returned to its customary azure glow.

They found Belgarath seated before a recently rekindled fire in a low-beamed hall close to the royal kitchens. On the table not far from where he sat lay a large chunk of bread and a generous slab of cheese. Errand looked at the bread and cheese, realizing suddenly that he was hungry and wondering if Belgarath might be willing to share some of his breakfast. The old sorcerer seemed lost in thought as he gazed into the dancing flames, and his stout gray cloak was drawn about his shoulders, though the hall was not cold. "You two are up early," he noted as Garion and Errand entered and came to join him by the fireside.

"So are you, Grandfather," Garion said.

"I had a peculiar dream," the old man replied. "I've been trying to shake it off for several hours now. For some reason I dreamed that the Orb had turned red."

"It did," Errand told him quietly.

Belgarath looked at him sharply.

"Yes. We both saw it, Grandfather," Garion said. "We were in the throne room a few hours ago, and the Orb suddenly turned red. Then that voice that I've got in here—" He tapped his forehead. "—said to beware of Zandramas."

"Zandramas?" Belgarath said with a puzzled look. "Is that a name or a thing or what?"

"I don't really know, Grandfather," Garion replied, "but both Errand and I heard it, didn't we, Errand?"

Errand nodded, his eyes still on the bread and cheese.

"What were the two of you doing in the throne room at that hour?" Belgarath asked, his eyes very intent.

"I was asleep," Garion answered. Then his face flushed slightly. "Well, sort of asleep. Ce'Nedra and I talked until quite late. We haven't talked very much lately, and so we had a lot of things to say to each other. Anyway, *he* told me to get up and go to the throne room."

Belgarath looked at Errand. "And you?"

"He woke me up," Errand replied, "and he—"

"Hold it," Belgarath said sharply. "*Who* woke you up?"

"The same one who woke Garion."

"You know who he is?"

"Yes."

"And you know *what* he is?"

Errand nodded.

"Has he ever spoken to you before?"

"No."

"But you knew immediately who and what he is?"

"Yes. He told me that he needed me in the throne room, so I got dressed and went. When I got there, the Orb turned red, and the voice said to beware of Zandramas."

Belgarath was frowning. "You're both absolutely positive that the Orb changed color?"

"Yes, Grandfather," Garion assured him, "and it sounded different, too. It usually makes this kind of ringing noise—like the sound a bell makes after you strike it. This was altogether different."

"And you're sure that it turned red? I mean it wasn't just a darker shade of blue or something?"

"No, Grandfather. It was definitely red."

Belgarath got up out of his chair, his face suddenly grim. "Come with me," he said shortly and started toward the door.

"Where are we going?" Garion asked.

"To the library. I need to check on something."

"On what?"

"Let's wait until I read it. This is important, and I want to be sure that I've got it right."

As he passed the table, Errand picked up the piece of cheese and broke off part of it. He took a large bite as he followed Belgarath and Garion from the room. They went quickly through the dim, torchlit corridors and up a steep, echoing flight of narrow stone steps. In the past few years Belgarath's expression had become rather whimsical and touched with a sort of lazy self-indulgence. All trace of that was gone now, and his eyes were intent and very alert. When they reached the library, the old man took a pair of candles from a dusty table and lighted them from the torch hanging in an iron ring just outside the door. Then he came back inside and set one of the candles down. "Close the door, Garion," he said, still holding the other candle. "We don't want to be disturbed."

Wordlessly, Garion shut the solid oak door. Belgarath went over to the wall, lifted his candle and began to run his eyes over the row upon row of dusty, leather-bound books and the neatly stacked, silk-wrapped scrolls. "There," he said, pointing to the top shelf. "Reach that scroll down for me, Garion—the one wrapped in blue silk."

Garion stretched up on his tiptoes and took down the scroll. He looked at it curiously before handing it to his grandfather. "Are you sure?" he asked. "This isn't the Mrin Codex, you know."

"No," Belgarath told him. "It isn't. Don't get your attention so locked onto the Mrin Codex that you ignore all the others." He set down his candle and carefully untied the silver tassled cord binding the scroll. He stripped off the blue silk cover and began to unroll the crackling parchment, his eyes running quickly over the ancient script. "Here it is," he said at last. " 'Behold,' " he read, " 'in the day that

Aldur's Orb burns hot with crimson fire shall the name of the Child of Dark be revealed.' "

"But Torak was the Child of Dark," Garion protested. "What is that scroll?"

"The Darine Codex," Belgarath told him. "It's not always as reliable as the Mrin, but it's the only one that mentions this particular event."

"What does it mean?" Garion asked him, looking perplexed.

"It's a bit complicated," Belgarath replied, his lips pursed and his eyes still fixed on the passage in question. "Rather simply put, there are two prophecies."

"Yes, I knew that, but I thought that when Torak died, the other one just—well—"

"Not exactly. I don't think it's that simple. The two have been meeting in these confrontations since before the beginning of this world. Each time, there's a Child of Light and a Child of Dark. When you and Torak met at Cthol Mishrak, you were the Child of Light and Torak was the Child of Dark. It wasn't the first time the two had met. Apparently it was not to be the last, either."

"You mean that it's not over yet?" Garion demanded incredulously.

"Not according to this," Belgarath said, tapping the parchment.

"All right, if this Zandramas is the Child of Dark, who's the Child of Light?"

"As far as I know, you are."

"Me? Still?"

"Until we hear something to the contrary."

"Why me?"

"Haven't we had this conversation before?" Belgarath asked drily.

Garion's shoulders slumped. "Now I've got *this* to worry about again—on top of everything else."

"Oh, stop feeling sorry for yourself, Garion," Belgarath told him bluntly. "We're all doing what we have to do, and sniveling about it won't change a thing."

"I wasn't sniveling."

"Whatever you call it, stop it and get to work."

"What am I supposed to do?" Garion's tone was just a trifle sullen.

"You can start here," the old man said, waving one hand to indicate all the dusty books and silk-wrapped scrolls. "This is perhaps one of the world's best collections of prophecy—western prophecy at least. It doesn't include the Oracles of the Mallorean Grolims, of course, or the collection that Ctuchik had at Rak Cthol or the secret books of those people at Kell, but it's a place to start. I want you to read your way through this—all of it—and see if you can find out anything at all about this Zandramas. Make a note of every reference to 'the Child of Dark.' Most of them will probably have to do with Torak, but there might be some that mean Zandramas instead." He frowned slightly. "While you're at it, keep an eye out for anything that has to do with something called 'the Sardion' or 'Cthrag Sardius.' "

"What's that?"

"I don't know. Beldin ran across the term in Mallorea. It might be important—or it might not."

Garion looked around the library, his face blanching slightly. "Are you telling me that this is *all* prophecy?"

"Of course not. A lot of it—most of it probably—is the collected ravings of assorted madmen, all faithfully written down."

"Why would anybody want to write down what crazy people say?"

"Because the Mrin Codex is precisely that, the ravings of a lunatic. The Mrin prophet was so crazy that he had to be chained up. A lot of very conscientious people went out after he died and wrote down the gibberish of every madman they could find on the off chance that there might be prophecy hidden in it somewhere."

"How do I tell the difference?"

"I'm not really sure. Maybe after you've read them all, you'll be able to come up with a way to separate them. If you do, let us know. It could save us all a lot of time."

Garion looked around the library in dismay. "But, Grandfather," he protested, "this could take *years*!"

"You'd probably better get started then, hadn't you? Try to concentrate on things that are supposed to happen *after* the death of Torak. We're all fairly familiar with the things that led up to that."

"Grandfather, I'm not really a scholar. What if I miss something?"

"Don't," Belgarath told him firmly. "Like it or not, Garion, you're one of us. You have the same responsibilities that the rest of us do. You might as well get used to the idea that the whole world depends on you—and you *also* might just as well forget that you ever heard the words, 'why me?' That's the objection of a child, and you're a man now." Then the old man turned and looked very hard at Errand. "And what are *you* doing mixed up in all of this?" he asked.

"I'm not sure," Errand replied calmly. "We'll probably have to wait and see, won't we?"

That afternoon Errand was alone with Polgara in the warm comfort of her sitting room. She sat by the fire with her favorite blue robe about her and her feet on a carpeted footstool. She held an embroidery hoop in her hands and she was humming softly as her needle flashed in the golden firelight. Errand sat in the leather-covered armchair opposite hers, nibbling on an apple and watching her as she sewed. One of the things he loved about her was her ability to radiate a kind of calm contentment when she was engaged in simple domestic tasks. At such quiet times her very presence was soothing.

The pretty Rivan girl who served as Polgara's maid tapped softly and entered the room. "Lady Polgara," she said with a little curtsy, "My Lord Brand asks if he might have a word with you."

"Of course, dear," Polgara replied, laying aside her embroidery. "Show him in, please." Errand had noticed that Polgara tended to call all young people "dear," most of the time without even being aware that she was doing it.

The maid escorted the tall, gray-haired Rivan Warder into the room, curtsied again, and then quietly withdrew.

"Polgara," Brand greeted her in his deep voice. He was a large, bulky man with a deeply lined face and tired, sad eyes and he was the last Rivan Warder. During the centuries-long interregnum following the death of King Gorek at the hands of Queen Salmissra's assassins, the Isle of the Winds and the Rivan people had been ruled by a line of men chosen for their ability and their absolute devotion to duty. So selfless had been that devotion that each Rivan Warder had submerged his own personality and had taken the name Brand. Now that Garion had come at last to claim his throne, there was no further need for that centuries-old stewardship. So long as he lived, however, this big, sad-eyed man would be absolutely committed to the royal line—not perhaps so much to Garion himself, but rather to the concept of the line and to its perpetuation. It was with that thought uppermost in his mind that he came that quiet afternoon to thank Polgara for taking the estrangement of Garion and his queen in hand.

"How did they manage to grow so far apart?" she asked him. "When they married, they were so close that you couldn't pry them away from each other."

"It all started about a year ago," Brand replied in his rumbling voice. "There are two powerful families on the northern end of the island. They had always been friendly, but a dispute arose over a property arrangement that was involved in a wedding between a young man from one family and a girl from the other. People from one family came to the Citadel and presented their cause to Ce'Nedra, and she issued a royal decree supporting them."

"But she neglected to consult Garion about it?" Polgara surmised.

Brand nodded. "When he found out, he was furious. There's no question that Ce'Nedra had overstepped her authority, but Garion revoked her decree in public."

"Oh, dear," Polgara said. "So *that's* what all the bitterness was about. I couldn't really get a straight answer out of either of them."

"They were probably a little too ashamed to admit it," Brand said. "Each one had humiliated the other in public, and neither one was mature enough just to forgive and let it slide. They kept wrangling at each other until the whole affair got completely out of hand. There were times when I wanted to shake them both—or maybe spank them."

"That's an interesting idea." She laughed. "Why didn't you write and tell me they were having problems?"

"Belgarion told me not to," he replied helplessly.

"Sometimes we have to disobey that kind of order."

"I'm sorry, Polgara, but *I* can't do that."

"No, I suppose you couldn't." She turned to look at Errand, who was closely examining an exquisite piece of blown glass, a crystal wren perched on a budding twig. "Please don't touch it, Errand," she cautioned. "It's fragile and very precious."

"Yes," he agreed, "I know." And to reassure her, he clasped his hands firmly behind his back.

"Well." She turned back to Brand. "I hope the foolishness is all past now. I think we've restored peace to the royal house of Riva."

"I certainly hope so," Brand said with a tired smile. "I would definitely like to see an occupant in the royal nursery."

"That might take a bit longer."

"It's getting sort of important, Polgara," he said seriously. "We're all a bit nervous about the lack of an heir to the throne. It's not only me. Anheg and Rhodar and Cho-Hag have all written to me about it. All of Aloria is holding its breath waiting for Ce'Nedra to start having children."

"She's only nineteen, Brand."

"Most Alorn girls have had at least two babies by the time they're nineteen."

"Ce'Nedra isn't an Alorn. She's not even entirely Tolnedran. Her heritage is Dryad, and there are some peculiarities about Dryads and the way they mature."

"That's going to be a little hard to explain to other Alorns," Brand replied. "There *has* to be an heir to the Rivan throne. The line *must* continue."

"Give them a little time, Brand," Polgara said placidly. "They'll get around to it. The important thing was to get them back into the same bedroom."

Perhaps a day or so later, when the sun was sparkling on the waters of the Sea of the Winds and a stiff onshore breeze was flecking the tops of the green waves with frothy whitecaps, a huge Cherek war boat maneuvered its way ponderously between the two rocky headlands embracing the harbor at Riva. The ship's captain was also more than life-sized. With his red beard streaming in the wind, Barak, Earl of Trellheim, stood at his tiller, a look of studied concentration on his face as he worked his way through a tricky eddy just inside one of the protective headlands and then across the harbor to the stone quay. Almost before his sailors had made the ship fast, Barak was coming up the long flight of granite steps to the Citadel.

Belgarath and Errand had been on the parapet atop the walls of the fortress and had witnessed the arrival of Barak's ship. And so, when the big man reached the heavy gates, they were waiting for him.

"What are *you* doing here, Belgarath?" the burly Cherek asked. "I thought you were at the Vale."

Belgarath shrugged. "We came by for a visit."

Barak looked at Errand. "Hello, boy," he said. "Are Polgara and Durnik here, too?"

"Yes," Errand replied. "They're all in the throne room watching Belgarion."

"What's he doing?"

"Being king," Belgarath said shortly. "We saw you come into the harbor."

"Really impressive, wasn't it?" Barak said proudly.

"Your ship steers like a pregnant whale, Barak," Belgarath told him bluntly. "You don't seem to have grasped the idea that bigger is not necessarily better."

Barak's face took on an injured expression. "I don't make jokes about *your* possessions, Belgarath."

"I don't *have* any possessions, Barak. What brought you to Riva?"

"Anheg sent me. Is Garion going to be much longer at whatever he's doing?"

"We can go find out, I suppose."

The Rivan King, however, had concluded the formal audience for that morning and, in the company of Ce'Nedra, Polgara, and Durnik, had gone through a dim, private passageway which led from the great Hall of the Rivan King to the royal apartments.

"Barak!" Garion exclaimed, hurrying forward to greet his old friend in the corridor outside the door to the apartment.

Barak gave him a peculiar look and bowed respectfully.

"What's that all about?" Garion asked him with a puzzled look.

"You're still wearing your crown, Garion," Polgara reminded him, "and your state robes. All of that makes you look rather official."

"Oh," Garion said, looking a bit abashed, "I forgot. Let's go inside." He pulled open the door and led them all into the room beyond.

With a broad grin, Barak enfolded Polgara in a vast bear hug.

"Barak," she said a trifle breathlessly, "you'd be much nicer at close quarters if you'd remember to wash your beard after you've been eating smoked fish."

"I only had one," he told her.

"That's usually enough."

He turned then and put his bulky arms around Ce'Nedra's tiny shoulders and kissed her soundly.

The little queen laughed and caught her crown in time to keep it from sliding off her head. "You're right, Lady Polgara," she said, "he definitely has a certain fragrance about him."

"Garion," Barak said plaintively, "I'm absolutely dying for a drink."

"Did all the ale barrels on your ship run dry?" Polgara asked him.

"There's no drinking aboard the *Seabird*," Barak replied.

"Oh?"

"I want my sailors sober."

"Astonishing," she murmured.

"It's a matter of principle," Barak said piously.

"They *do* need their wits about them," Belgarath agreed. "That big ship of his is not exactly what you'd call responsive."

Barak gave him a hurt look.

Garion sent for ale, removed his crown and state robes with obvious relief, and invited them all to sit down.

Once Barak had quenched his most immediate thirst, his expression became serious. He looked at Garion. "Anheg sent me to warn you that we're starting to get reports about the Bear-cult again."

"I thought they were all killed at Thull Mardu," Durnik said.

"Grodeg's underlings were," Barak told him. "Unfortunately, Grodeg wasn't the whole cult."

"I don't exactly follow you," Durnik said.

"It gets a little complicated. You see, the Bear-cult has always been there, really. It's a fundamental part of the religious life of the more remote parts of Cherek, Drasnia, and Algaria. Every so often, though, somebody with more ambition than good sense—like Grodeg—gains control and tries to establish the cult in the cities. The cities are where the power is, and somebody like Grodeg automatically tries to use the cult to take them over. The problem is that the Bear-cult doesn't work in the cities."

Durnik's frown became even more confused.

"People who live in cities are always coming in contact with new people and new ideas," Barak explained. "Out in the countryside, though, they can go for generations without ever encountering a single new thought. The Bear-cult doesn't believe in new thoughts, so it's the natural sort of thing to attract country people."

"New ideas aren't *always* good ones," Durnik said stiffly, his own rural background painfully obvious.

"Granted," Barak agreed, "but old ones aren't necessarily good either, and the

Bear-cult's been working on the same idea for several thousand years now. About the last thing Belar said to the Alorns before the Gods departed was that they should lead the Kingdoms of the West against the people of Torak. It's that word 'lead' that's caused all the problems. It can mean many things, unfortunately. Bear-cultists have always taken it to mean that their very first step in obeying Belar's instructions should be a campaign to force the other Western Kingdoms to submit to Alorn domination. A good Bear-cultist isn't thinking about fighting Angaraks, because all of his attention is fixed on subduing Sendaria, Arendia, Tolnedra, Nyissa, and Maragor."

"Maragor doesn't even exist any more," Durnik objected.

"That news hasn't reached the cult yet," Barak said drily. "After all, it's only been about three thousand years now. Anyway, that's the rather tired idea behind the Bear-cult. Their first goal is to reunite Aloria; their next is to overrun and sub-jugate all of the Western Kingdoms; and only *then* will they start to give some thought to attacking Murgos and Malloreans."

"They *are* just a bit backward, aren't they?" Durnik observed.

"Some of them haven't even discovered fire yet." Barak snorted.

"I don't really see why Anheg is so concerned, Barak," Belgarath said. "The Bear-cult doesn't really cause any problems out there in the countryside. They jump around bonfires on midsummer's eve and put on bearskins and shuffle around in single file in the dead of winter and recite long prayers in smoky caves, until they get so dizzy that they can't stand up. Where's the danger in that?"

"I'm getting to that," Barak said, pulling at his beard. "Always before, the rural Bear-cult was just a reservoir of undirected stupidity and superstition. But in the last year or so, something new has been going on."

"Oh?" Belgarath looked at him curiously.

"There's a new leader of the cult—we don't even know who he is. In the past, Bear-cultists from one village didn't even trust the ones from another, so they were never organized enough to be any problem. This new leader of theirs has changed all of that. For the first time in history, rural Bear-cultists are all taking orders from one man."

Belgarath frowned. "That *is* serious," he admitted.

"This is very interesting, Barak," Garion said, looking a bit perplexed, "but why did King Anheg send you all the way here to warn *me*? From what I've been told, the Bear-cult has never been able to get a foothold here on the Isle of the Winds."

"Anheg wanted me to warn you to take a few precautions, since this new cult's antagonism is directed primarily at *you*."

"Me? What for?"

"You married a Tolnedran," Barak told him. "To a Bear-cultist, a Tolnedran is worse than a Murgo."

"That's a novel position," Ce'Nedra said with a toss of her curls.

"That's the way those people think," Barak told her. "Most of those blockheads don't even know what an Angarak *is*. They've all seen Tolnedrans though—usually merchants who deal quite sharply. For a thousand years, they've been waiting for a king to come and pick up Riva's sword and lead them on a holy war to crush all the

Kingdoms of the West into subjugation, and when he *does* finally show up, the very first thing he does is marry an Imperial Tolnedran Princess. The way they look at it, the next Rivan King is going to be a mongrel. They hate you like poison, my little sweetheart."

"What an absolute absurdity!" she exclaimed.

"Of course it is," the big Cherek agreed. "But absurdity has always been a characteristic of the mind dominated by religion. We'd all be a lot better off if Belar had just kept his mouth shut."

Belgarath laughed suddenly.

"What's so funny?" Barak asked.

"Asking Belar to keep his mouth shut would probably have been the most futile thing any human being could even contemplate," the old sorcerer said, still laughing. "I remember one time when he talked for a week and a half straight without stopping."

"What was he saying?" Garion asked curiously.

"He was explaining to the early Alorns why it wasn't a good idea to start a trek into the far north at the beginning of winter. Sometimes in those days you really had to talk to an Alorn to get an idea through to him."

"That hasn't really changed all that much," Ce'Nedra said with an arch look at her husband. Then she laughed and fondly touched his hand.

The next morning dawned clear and sunny, and Errand, as he usually did, went to the window as soon as he awoke to see what the day promised. He looked out over the city of Riva and saw the bright morning sun standing over the Sea of the Winds and smiled. There was not a hint of cloud. Today would be fine. He dressed himself in the tunic and hose which Polgara had laid out for him and then went to join his family. Durnik and Polgara sat in two comfortable, leather-upholstered chairs, one on each side of the fire, talking together quietly and sipping tea. As he always did, Errand went to Polgara, put his arms about her neck and kissed her.

"You slept late," she said, brushing his tousled hair back from his eyes.

"I was a little tired," he replied. "I didn't get much sleep the night before last."

"So I heard." Almost absently, she pulled him up into her lap and held him nestled against the soft velvet of her blue robe.

"He's growing a bit big for your lap," Durnik noted, smiling fondly at the two of them.

"I know," Polgara answered. "That's why I hold him as often as I can. Very soon he'll outgrow laps and cuddling, so I need to store up as much as I can now. It's all very well for them to grow up, but I miss the charm of having a small one about."

There was a brief tap on the door, and Belgarath entered.

"Well, good morning, father," Polgara greeted him.

"Pol." He nodded briefly. "Durnik."

"Did you manage to get Barak put to bed last night?" Durnik asked with a grin.

"We poured him in about midnight. Brand's sons helped us with him. He seems to be getting heavier as he puts on the years."

"You're looking surprisingly well," Polgara observed, "considering the fact that you spent the evening at Garion's ale barrel."

"I didn't drink all that much," he told her, coming to the fire to warm his hands. She looked at him with one raised eyebrow.

"I've got a lot on my mind," he said. Then he looked directly at her. "Is everything straightened out between Garion and Ce'Nedra?"

"I think so, yes."

"Let's be sure. I don't want things here to fly apart again. I'm going to have to get back to the Vale, but if you think you ought to stay and keep an eye on those two, I can go on ahead." His voice was serious, even decisive.

Errand looked at the old man, noting once again that Belgarath seemed sometimes to be two different people. When there was nothing of any urgency going on, he reveled in his leisure, amusing himself with drink, deception, and petty theft. When a serious problem arose, however, he could set all that aside and devote almost unlimited concentration and energy to solving it.

Polgara quietly put Errand down and looked at her father. "It's serious, then?"

"I don't know, Pol," he said, "and I don't like it when things are going on that I don't know about. If you've finished with what you came here to do, I think we'd better get back. As soon as we can get Barak on his feet, we'll have him take us to Camaar. We can pick up horses there. I need to talk with Beldin—see if *he* knows anything about this Zandramas thing."

"We'll be ready whenever you want to leave, father," she assured him.

Later that same morning Errand went to the stables to say good-bye to the frolicsome young horse. He was a bit sad to be leaving so soon. He was genuinely fond of Garion and Ce'Nedra. The young King of Riva was in many ways like a brother to Errand, and Ce'Nedra was delightful—when she was not going out of her way to be difficult. Most of all, however, he was going to miss the horse. Errand did not think of the horse as a beast of burden. They were both young and shared a wholehearted enthusiasm for each other's company.

The boy stood in the center of the exercise yard with the long-legged animal frisking about him in the bright morning sunlight. Then he caught a movement out of the corner of his eye, turned, and saw Durnik and Garion approaching.

"Good morning, Errand," the Rivan King said.

"Belgarion."

"You and the horse seem to be enjoying yourselves."

"We're friends," Errand said. "We like to be together."

Garion looked almost sadly at the chestnut-hued animal. The horse came to him and curiously nuzzled at his clothing. Garion rubbed the pointed ears and ran his hand down the smooth, glossy forehead. Then he sighed. "Would you like to have him for your very own?" he asked Errand.

"You don't own friends, Belgarion."

"You're right," Garion agreed, "but would you like it if he went back to the Vale with you?"

"But he likes you, too."

"I can always come and visit," the Rivan King said. "There isn't really much room for him to run here, and I'm always so busy that I don't have the time to spend with him the way I should. I think it would be best for him if he went with you. What do you think?"

Errand considered that, trying to think only of the well-being of the young animal and not of his own personal preferences. He looked at Garion and saw how much this generous offer had cost his friend. When he finally answered, his voice was quiet and very serious. "I think you're right, Belgarion. The Vale *would* be better for him. He wouldn't have to be penned up there."

"You'll have to train him," Garion said. "He's never been ridden."

"He and I can work on that," Errand assured him.

"He'll go with you, then," Garion decided.

"Thank you," Errand said simply.

"You're welcome, Errand."

"And done!" Errand could hear the voice as clearly as if it had spoken in his own mind.

"What?" Garion's silent reply was startled.

"Excellently done, Garion. I want these two to be together. They have things to do that need the both of them." Then the voice was gone.

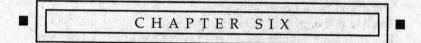

CHAPTER SIX

"The best way to begin is to lay a tunic or a coat across his back," Hettar said in his quiet voice. The tall Algar wore his usual black leather and he stood with Errand in the pasture lying to the west of Poledra's cottage. "Be sure that it's something that has your scent on it. You want him to get used to your smell and the idea that it's all right if something that smells like you is on his back."

"He already knows what I smell like, doesn't he?" Errand asked.

"This is just a little different," Hettar told him. "You have to go at these things slowly. You don't want to frighten him. If he's frightened, he'll try to throw you off his back."

"We're friends," Errand tried to explain. "He knows I won't do anything to hurt him, so why should he try to do something to hurt me?"

Hettar shook his head and looked out over the rolling grassland. "Just do it the way I explained, Errand," he said patiently. "Believe me, I know what I'm talking about."

"If you really want me to," Errand replied, "but I think it's an awful waste of time."

"Trust me."

Errand obediently laid one of his old tunics across the horse's back several times while the horse looked at him curiously, quite obviously wondering what he was doing. Errand wished that he could make Hettar understand. They had already wasted a good part of the morning on the hawk-faced Algar warrior's cautious approach to horse training. If they had just got right on with it, Errand knew that he and the horse could be galloping together across the free open expanse of hills and valleys stretched out before them.

"Is that enough?" Errand asked after he had put the tunic on the horse's back several times. "Can I get on him now?"

Hettar sighed. "It looks as if you're going to have to learn the hard way," he said. "Go ahead and climb on, if you want. Try to find a soft place to land when he throws you off, though."

"He wouldn't do that," Errand replied confidently. He put his hand on the chestnut's neck and gently led him over to where a white boulder stuck up out of the turf.

"Don't you think you ought to bridle him first?" Hettar asked him. "At least that gives you something to hang on to."

"I don't think so," Errand replied. "I don't believe he'd like that bridle."

"It's up to you," Hettar said. "Do it any way you like. Just try not to break anything when you fall."

"Oh, I don't think I'll fall."

"Tell me, do you know what the word 'wager' means?"

Errand laughed and climbed up on the boulder. "Well," he said, "here we go." He threw his leg over the horse's back.

The colt flinched slightly and stood trembling.

"It's all right," Errand assured him in a calm voice.

The horse turned and looked at him with soft astonishment in his large, liquid eyes.

"You'd better hang on," Hettar warned, but his eyes had an oddly puzzled look, and his voice was not quite as certain as the words.

"He's fine." Errand flexed his legs, not actually even bringing his heels in contact with the chestnut's flanks. The horse took a tentative step forward and then looked back inquiringly.

"That's the idea," Errand encouraged him.

The horse took several more steps, then stopped to look back over his shoulder again.

"Good," Errand said, patting his neck. "Very, very good."

The horse pranced about enthusiastically.

"Watch out!" Hetter said sharply.

Errand leaned forward and pointed toward a grassy knoll several hundred yards off to the southwest. "Let's go up there," he said into the sharply upstanding ear.

The horse gave a sort of delighted shudder, bunched himself, and ran for the hilltop as hard as he could. When, moments later, they crested the knoll, he slowed and pranced about proudly.

"All right," Errand said, laughing with sheer delight. "Now, why don't we go to that tree way over there on that other hillside?"

"It was unnatural," Hettar said moodily that evening as they all sat at the table in Poledra's cottage, bathed in the golden firelight.

"They seem to be doing all right," Durnik said mildly.

"But he's doing everything wrong," Hettar protested. "That horse should have gone absolutely wild when Errand just got on him like that without any warning. And you don't *tell* a horse where you want him to go. You have to steer him. That's what the reins are for."

"Errand's an unusual boy," Belgarath told him, "and the horse is an unusual horse. As long as they get along and understand each other, what difference does it make?"

"It's unnatural," Hettar said again with a baffled look. "I kept waiting for the horse to panic, but his mind stayed absolutely calm. I know what a horse is thinking, and about the only thing that colt was feeling when Errand got on his back was curiosity. *Curiosity!* He didn't do or think anything the way he should." He shook his head darkly, and his long black scalplock swung back and forth as if in emphasis. "It's unnatural," he growled as if that were the only word he could think of to sum up the situation.

"I think you've already said that several times, Hettar," Polgara told him. "Why don't we just drop the subject—since it seems to bother you so much—and you can tell me about Adara's baby instead."

An expression of fatuous pleasure came over Hettar's fierce, hawklike face. "He's a boy," he said with the overwhelming pride of a new father.

"We gathered that," Polgara said calmly. "How big was he when he was born?"

"Oh—" Hettar looked perplexed. "About so big, I'd say." He held his hands half a yard apart.

"No one took the trouble to measure him?"

"They might have done that, I suppose. My mother and the other ladies were doing all sorts of things right after he came."

"And would you care to estimate his weight?"

"Probably about as much as a full-grown hare, I suppose—a fairly good-sized one—or perhaps the weight of one of those red Sendarian cheeses."

"I see, perhaps a foot and a half long and eight or nine pounds—is that what you're trying to say?" Her look was steady.

"About that, I suppose."

"Why didn't you say so, then?" she demanded in exasperation.

He looked at her, startled. "Is it really *that* important?"

"Yes, Hettar, it really *is* that important. Women like to know these things."

"I'll have to remember that. About all I was really interested in was whether he had the usual number of arms, legs, ears, noses—things like that—that and making sure that his very first food was mare's milk, of course."

"Of course," she said acidly.

"It's very important, Polgara," he assured her. "Every Algar's first drink is mare's milk."

"That makes him part horse, I suppose."

He blinked. "No, of course not, but it establishes a sort of bond."

"Did you milk the mare for him? Or did you make him crawl out and find one for himself?"

"You're taking all this very oddly, Polgara."

"Blame it on my age," she said in a dangerous voice. He caught that tone almost immediately. "No, I don't think I'd want to do that."

"Wise decision," Durnik murmured. "You said that you were going up into the mountains of Ulgoland."

Hettar nodded. "You remember the Hrulgin?"

"The flesh-eating horses?"

"I have sort of an idea I want to try out. A full-grown Hrulga can't be tamed, of course, but maybe if I can capture some of their colts—"

"That's very dangerous, Hettar," Belgarath warned. "The whole herd will defend the young."

"There are some ways to separate the colts from the rest of the herd."

Polgara looked at him disapprovingly. "Even if you succeed, what do you plan to do with the beasts?"

"Tame them," Hettar replied simply.

"They can't be tamed."

"Nobody's ever tried it. And even if I can't tame them, perhaps I can breed them with ordinary horses."

Durnik looked puzzled. "Why would you want horses with fangs and claws?"

Hettar looked thoughtfully into the fire. "They're faster and stronger than ordinary horses," he replied. "They can jump much farther, and—" His voice drifted off into silence.

"And because you can't stand the idea of anything that looks like a horse that you can't ride," Belgarath finished for him.

"That might be a part of it," Hettar admitted. "They'd give a man a tremendous advantage in a battle, though."

"Hettar," Durnik said, "the most important thing in Algaria is the cattle, right?"

"Yes."

"Do you really want to start raising a breed of horses that would probably look at a cow as something to eat?"

Hettar frowned and scratched at his chin. "I hadn't thought about that," he admitted.

Now that he had the horse, Errand's range increased enormously. The young stallion's stamina was virtually inexhaustible, and he could run for most of the day without tiring. Because Errand was still only a boy, his weight was not enough to burden the enthusiastic animal, and they ran freely over the rolling, grass-covered hills of southern Algaria and down into the tree-dotted expanse of the Vale of Aldur.

The boy rose early each morning and ate his breakfast impatiently, knowing that the chestnut stallion was waiting just outside the cottage and that, as soon as breakfast was over, the two of them could gallop out through the dew-drenched grass glistening green and lush in the slanting, golden rays of the morning sun and pound up the long slopes of the hills lying before them with the cool, sweet morning air rushing past them. Polgara, who seemed to know instinctively why they both had this need to run, said nothing as Errand wolfed down his food, sitting on the very edge of his chair so that at the very instant his plate was clean he could bolt for the door and the day which lay before him. Her eyes were gentle as she watched him, and the smile she gave him when he asked to be excused was understanding.

On a dewy, sun-filled morning in late summer when the tall grass was golden and heavy with ripe seeds, Errand came out of the door of the cottage and touched the bowed neck of his waiting friend with a gentle, caressing hand. The horse quivered with pleasure and took a few prancing steps, eager to be off. Errand laughed, took a handful of the stallion's mane, swung his leg and flowed up onto the strong, glossy back in a single, fluid move. The horse was running almost before the boy was in place. They galloped up the long hill, paused to look out over the sun-touched grassland lying open before them, and then circled the small valley where the thatched stone cottage lay and headed south, down into the Vale.

This day's ride was not, as so many of the others had been, a random excursion with no particular goal or purpose. For several days now, Errand had felt the presence of a strange, subtle awareness emanating from the Vale that seemed to be calling to him and, as he had emerged from the cottage door, he had suddenly resolved to find out exactly what it was that seemed to summon him so quietly.

As they moved down into the quiet Vale, past placidly grazing deer and curious rabbits, Errand could feel that awareness growing stronger. It was a peculiar kind of consciousness, dominated more than anything by an incredible patience—an ability, it seemed, to wait for eons for a response to these occasional quiet calls.

As they crested a tall, rounded hill a few leagues to the west of Belgarath's tower, a brief shadow flickered across the bending grass. Errand glanced up and saw a blue-banded hawk circling on motionless wings on a rising column of sun-warmed air. Even as the boy watched, the hawk tilted, side-slipped, and then spiraled down in long, graceful circles. When it was no more than inches above the golden tassels of the ripe grass, it flared its wings, thrust down with its taloned feet and seemed somehow to shimmer in the morning air. When the momentary shimmer faded, the hawk was gone and the hunchbacked Beldin stood waist-deep in the tall grass, with one eyebrow cocked curiously. "What are you doing all the way down here, boy?" he asked without any kind of preamble.

"Good morning, Beldin," Errand said calmly, leaning back to let the horse know that he wanted to stop for a few minutes.

"Does Pol know how far from home you've been going?" the ugly man demanded, ignoring Errand's gesture toward politeness.

"Probably not entirely," Errand admitted. "She knows that I'm out riding, but she might not know how much ground we can cover."

"I've got better things to do than spend every day watching over you, you know," the irascible old man growled.

"You don't have to do that."

"Yes, as a matter of fact, I do. It's my month for it."

Errand looked at him, puzzled.

"Didn't you know that one of us watches you every time you leave the cottage?"

"Why would you want to do that?"

"You *do* remember Zedar, don't you?"

Errand sighed sadly. "Yes," he said.

"Don't waste your sympathy on him," Beldin said. "He got exactly what he deserved."

"Nobody deserves that."

Beldin gave a snort of ugly laughter. "He's lucky that it was Belgarath who caught up with him. If it had been me, I'd have done a lot more than just seal him up inside solid rock. But that's beside the point. You remember *why* Zedar found you and took you with him?"

"To steal the Orb of Aldur."

"Right. So far as we know, you're the only person beside Belgarion who can touch the Orb and keep on living. Other people know that, too, so you might as well get used to the idea of being watched. We are *not* going to let you wander around alone where somebody might get his hands on you. Now, you didn't answer my question."

"Which question?"

"What are you doing all the way down in this part of the Vale?"

"There's something I need to see."

"What's that?"

"I don't know. It's up ahead somewhere. What is it that's off in that direction?"

"There's nothing out there but the tree."

"That must be it, then. It wants to see me."

"See?"

"Maybe that's the wrong word."

Beldin scowled at him. "Are you sure it's the tree?"

"No. Not really. All I know is that something in that direction has been—" Errand hesitated. "I want to say *inviting* me to come by. Would that be the proper word?"

"It's talking to you, not me. Pick any word you like. All right, let's go then."

"Would you like to ride?" Errand offered. "Horse can carry us both."

"Haven't you given him a name yet?"

"Horse is good enough. He doesn't seem to feel that he needs one. Would you like to ride?"

"Why would I want to ride when I can fly?"

Errand felt a sudden curiosity. "What's it like?" he asked. "Flying, I mean?"

Beldin's eyes suddenly changed, to become distant and almost soft. "You couldn't even begin to imagine," he said. "Just keep your eyes on me. When I get over the tree, I'll circle to show you where it is." He stooped in the tall grass, curved out his arms, and gave a strong leap. As he rose into the air, he shimmered into feathers and swooped away.

The tree stood in solitary immensity in the middle of a broad meadow, its trunk larger than a house, its wide-spread branches shading entire acres, and its crown rising hundreds of feet into the air. It was incredibly ancient. Its roots reached down almost into the very heart of the world, and its branches touched the sky. It stood alone and silent, as if forming a link between earth and sky, a link whose purpose was beyond the understanding of man.

As Errand rode up to the vast shaded area beneath the tree's shelter, Beldin swooped in, hovered, and dropped, almost seeming to stumble into his natural form. "All right," he growled, "there it is. Now what?"

"I'm not sure." Errand slid down off the horse's back and walked across the soft, springy turf toward the immense trunk. The sense of the tree's awareness was very strong now, and Errand approached it curiously, still unable to determine exactly what it wanted with him.

Then he put out his hand and touched the rough bark; in the instant that he touched it, he understood. He quite suddenly knew the whole of the tree's existence. He found that he could look back over a million mornings to the time when the world had just emerged out of the elemental chaos from which the Gods had formed it. All at once, he knew of the incredible length of time that the earth had rolled in silence, awaiting the coming of man. He saw the endless turning of the seasons and felt the footsteps of the Gods upon the earth. And even as the tree knew, Errand came to know the fallacy which lay behind man's conception of the nature of time. Man needed to compartmentalize time, to break it into manageable pieces— eons, centuries, years, and hours. This eternal tree, however, understood that time was all one piece—that it was not merely an endless repetition of the same events, but rather that it moved from its beginning toward a final goal. All of that convenient segmenting which men used to make time more manageable had no real meaning. It was to tell him this simple truth that the tree had summoned him here. As he grasped that fact, the tree acknowledged him in friendship and affection.

Slowly Errand let his fingertips slide from the bark, then turned, and walked back to where Beldin stood.

"That's it?" the hunchbacked sorcerer asked. "That's all it wanted?"

"Yes. That's all. We can go back now."

Beldin gave him a penetrating look. "What did it say?"

"It's not the kind of thing you can put into words."

"Try."

"Well—it was sort of saying that we pay too much attention to years."

"That's enormously helpful, Errand."

Errand struggled with it, trying to formulate words that would express what he had just learned. "Things happen in their own time," he said finally. "It doesn't make any difference how many—or few—of what we call years come between things."

"What things are we talking about?"

"The important ones. Do you really have to follow me all the way home?"

"I need to keep an eye on you. That's about all. Are you going back now?"

"Yes."

"I'll be up there." Beldin made a gesture toward the arching blue dome of the sky. He shuddered into the form of a hawk and drove himself into the air with strong thrusts of his wings.

Errand pulled himself up onto the chestnut stallion's back. His pensive mood was somehow communicated to the animal; instead of a gallop, the horse turned and walked north, back toward the cottage nestling in its valley.

The boy considered the message of the eternal tree as he rode slowly through the golden, sun-drenched grass and, all lost in thought, he paid but little attention to his surroundings. It was thus that he was not actually aware of the robed and hooded figure standing beneath a broad-spread pine until he was almost on top of it. It was the horse that warned him with a startled snort as the figure made a slight move.

"And so *thou* art the one," it snarled in a voice which seemed scarcely human.

Errand calmed the horse with a reassuring hand on its quivering neck and looked at the dark figure before him. He could feel the waves of hatred emanating from that shadowy shape and he knew that, of all the things he had ever encountered, *this* was the thing he should most fear. Yet, surprising even himself, he remained calm and unafraid.

The shape laughed, an ugly, dusty kind of sound. "Thou art a fool, boy," it said. "Fear me, for the day will come when I shall surely destroy thee."

"Not surely," Errand replied calmly. He peered closely at the shadow-shrouded form and saw at once that—like the figure of Cyradis he had met on the snowy hilltop—this seemingly substantial shape was not really *here,* but somewhere else, sending its malevolent hatred across the empty miles. "Besides," he added, "I'm old enough now not to be afraid of shadows."

"We will meet in the flesh, boy," the shadow snarled, "and in that meeting shalt thou die."

"That hasn't been decided yet, has it?" Errand said. "That's why we have to meet—to decide which of us will stay and which must go."

The dark-robed shape drew in its breath with a sharp hiss. "Enjoy thy youth, boy," it snarled, "for it is all the life thou wilt have. I *will* prevail." Then the dark shape vanished.

Errand drew in a deep breath and glanced skyward at the circling Beldin. He realized that not even the hawk's sharp eyes could have penetrated the spreading tree limbs to where that strange, cowled figure had stood. Beldin could not know of the meeting. Errand nudged the stallion's flanks, and they moved away from the solitary tree at a flowing canter, riding in the golden sunlight toward home.

CHAPTER SEVEN

The years that followed were quiet years at the cottage. Belgarath and Beldin were often away for long periods of time, and when they returned, travel-stained and weary, their faces usually wore the frustrated look of men who have not found what they were looking for. Although Durnik was often on the stream bank, bending all of his attention to the problem of convincing some wary trout that a thumbnail-sized bit of polished metal with a few strands of red yarn trailing behind it in the current was not merely edible but irresistibly delicious, he nonetheless maintained the cottage and its immediate surroundings in that scrupu-

lously tidy condition which announced louder than words that the proprietor of
any given farmstead was a Sendar. Although rail fences, by their very nature,
zigzagged and tended to meander with the lay of the ground, Durnik firmly insisted
that *his* fence lines be absolutely straight. He was quite obviously constitutionally
incapable of going *around* any obstacle. Thus, if a large rock happened to intrude itself in the path of one of his fences, he immediately stopped being a fence builder
and became an excavator.

Polgara immersed herself in domesticity. The interior of her cottage was im-
maculate. Her doorstep was not merely swept but frequently scrubbed. The rows of
beans, turnips, and cabbages in her garden were as straight as any of Durnik's fences,
and weeds were absolutely forbidden. Her expression as she toiled at these seemingly endless tasks was one of dreamy contentment, and she hummed or sang very
old songs as she worked.

The boy, Errand, however, tended on occasion toward vagrancy. This was not
to say that he was indolent, but many of the chores around a rural farmstead were
tedious, involving repeating the same series of actions over and over again. Stacking
firewood was not one of Errand's favorite pastimes. Weeding the garden seemed
somehow futile, since the weeds grew back overnight. Drying the dishes seemed an
act of utter folly, since, left alone, the dishes would dry themselves without any assistance whatsoever. He made some effort to sway Polgara to his point of view in
this particular matter. She listened gravely to his impeccable logic, nodding her
agreement as he demonstrated with all the eloquence at his command that the
dishes did not really *need* to be dried. And when he had finished, summing up all
his arguments with a dazzling display of sheer brilliance, she smiled and said, "Yes,
dear," and implacably handed him the dishtowel.

Errand was hardly overburdened with unremitting toil, however. In point of
fact, not a day went by when he did not spend several hours on the back of the
chestnut stallion, roaming the grasslands surrounding the cottage as freely as the
wind.

Beyond the timeless, golden doze of the Vale, the world moved on. Although
the cottage was remote, visitors were not uncommon. Hettar, of course, rode by
often and sometimes he was accompanied by Adara, his tall, lovely wife, and their
infant son. Like her husband, Adara was an Algar to her fingertips, as much at home
in the saddle as she was on her feet. Errand was very fond of her. Though her face
always seemed serious, even grave, there lurked just beneath that calm exterior an
ironic, penetrating wit that absolutely delighted him. It was more than that, however. The tall, dark-haired girl, with her flawless features and alabaster skin, carried
about her a light, delicate fragrance that always seemed to tug at the outer edges of
his consciousness. There was something elusive yet strangely compelling about that
scent. Once, when Polgara was playing with the baby, Adara rode with Errand to
the top of a nearby hill and there she told him about how the perfume she wore
originated.

"You did know that Garion is my cousin?" she asked him.

"Yes."

"We had ridden out from the Stronghold once—it was in the winter when
everything was locked in frost. The grass was brown and lifeless, and all the leaves

had fallen from the bushes. I asked him about sorcery—what it was and what he could do with it. I didn't really believe in sorcery—I wanted to, but I just couldn't bring myself to believe. He took up a twig and wrapped some dry grass around it; then he turned it into a flower right in front of my eyes."

Errand nodded. "Yes, that's the kind of thing Garion would do. Did it help you to believe?"

She smiled. "Not right away—at least not altogether. There was something else I wanted him to do, but he said that he couldn't."

"What was that?"

She blushed rosily and then laughed. "It still embarrasses me," she said. "I wanted him to use his power to make Hettar love me."

"But he didn't have to do that," Errand said, "Hettar loved you already, didn't he?"

"Well—he needed a little help to make him realize it. But I was feeling very sorry for myself that day. When we rode back to the Stronghold, I forgot the flower and left it behind on the sheltered side of a hill. A year or so later, the whole hillside was covered with low bushes and these beautiful little lavender flowers. Ce'Nedra calls the flower 'Adara's rose,' and Ariana thought it might have some medicinal value, even though we've never been able to find anything it cures. I like the fragrance of the flower, and it *is* mine in a sort of special way, so I sprinkle petals in the chests where I keep my clothes." She laughed a wicked sort of little laugh. "It makes Hettar *very* affectionate," she added.

"I don't think that's entirely caused by the flower," Errand said.

"Perhaps, but I'm not going to take any chances with that. If the scent gives me an advantage, I'm certainly going to use it."

"That makes sense, I suppose."

"Oh, Errand," she laughed, "you're an absolutely delightful boy."

The visits of Hettar and Adara were not entirely social in nature. Hettar's father was King Cho-Hag, Chief of the Clan-Chiefs of Algaria, and Cho-Hag, the nearest of the Alorn monarchs, felt that it was his responsibility to keep Polgara advised of the events which were taking place in the world beyond the boundaries of the Vale. From time to time he sent reports of the progress of the bloody, endless war in southern Cthol Murgos, where Kal Zakath, Emperor of Mallorea, continued his implacable march across the plains of Hagga and into the great southern forest in Gorut. The Kings of the West were at a loss to explain 'Zakath's seemingly unreasoning hatred of his Murgo cousins. There were rumors of a personal affront at some time in the past, but that had involved Taur Urgas, and Taur Urgas had died at the Battle of Thall Mardu. 'Zakath's enmity for the Murgos, however, had not died with the madman who ruled them, and he now led his Malloreans in a savage campaign evidently designed to exterminate all of Murgodom and to erase from human memory all traces of the fact that the Murgos had ever even existed.

In Tolnedra, Emperor Ran Borune XXIII, the father of Queen Ce'Nedra of Riva, was in failing health; and because he had no son to succeed him on the Imperial Throne at Tol Honeth, the great families of the Empire were engaged in a vicious struggle over the succession. Enormous bribes changed hands, and assassins crept through the streets of Tol Honeth by night with sharpened daggers and vials of those deadly poisons purchased in secret from the snake-people of Nyissa. The wily Ran Borune, however, much to the chagrin and outrage of the Honeths, the Vordues, and the Horbites, had appointed General Varana, the Duke of Anadile, as his regent; and Varana, whose control of the legions was very nearly absolute, took firm steps to curb the excesses of the great houses in their scramble for the throne.

The internecine wars of the Angaraks and the only slightly less savage struggles of the Grand Dukes of the Tolnedran Empire, however, were of only passing interest to the Alorn Kings. The monarchs of the north were far more concerned with the troublesome resurgence of the Bear-cult and with the sad but undeniable fact that King Rhodar of Drasnia was quite obviously declining rapidly. Rhodar, despite his vast bulk, had demonstrated an astonishing military genius during the campaign which had culminated in the Battle of Thull Mardu, but Cho-Hag sadly reported that the corpulent Drasnian monarch had grown forgetful and in some ways even childish in the past few years. Because of his huge weight, he could no longer stand unaided and he frequently fell asleep, even during the most important state functions. His lovely young queen, Porenn, did as much as she possibly could to relieve the burdens imposed upon him by his crown, but it was quite obvious to all who knew him that King Rhodar would be unable to reign much longer.

At last, toward the end of a severe winter that had locked the north in snow and ice deeper than anyone could remember, Queen Porenn sent a messenger to the Vale to entreat Polgara to come to Boktor to try her healing arts on the Drasnian king. The messenger arrived late one bitter afternoon as the wan sun sank almost wearily into a bed of purple cloud lying heavy over the mountains of Ulgo. He was thickly wrapped in rich sable fur, but his long, pointed nose protruded from the warm interior of his deep cowl and immediately identified him.

"Silk!" Durnik exclaimed as the little Drasnian dismounted in the snowy dooryard. "What are you doing all the way down here?"

"Freezing, actually," Silk replied. "I hope you've got a good fire going."

"Pol, look who's here," Durnik called, and Polgara opened the door to look out at their visitor.

"Well, Prince Kheldar," she said, smiling at the rat-faced little man, "have you so completely plundered Gar og Nadrak that you've come in search of a new theater for your depredations?"

"No," Silk told her, stamping his half-frozen feet on the ground. "I made the mistake of passing through Boktor on my way to Val Alorn. Porenn dragooned me into making a side trip."

"Go inside," Durnik told him. "I'll tend to your horse."

After Silk had removed his sable cloak, he stood shivering in front of the arched fireplace with his hands extended toward the flames. "I've been cold for the last week," he grumbled. "Where's Belgarath?"

"He and Beldin are off in the East somewhere," Polgara replied, mixing the half-frozen man a cup of spiced wine to help warm him.

"No matter, I suppose. Actually I came to see you. You've heard that my uncle isn't well?"

She nodded, picking up a glowing-hot poker and plunging it into the wine with a bubbling hiss. "Hettar brought us some news about that last fall. Have his physicians put a name to his illness yet?"

"Old age." Silk shrugged, gratefully taking the cup from her.

"Rhodar isn't really that old."

"He's carrying a lot of extra weight. That tires a man out after a while. Porenn is desperate. She sent me to ask you—no, to *beg* you—to come to Boktor and see what *you* can do. She says to tell you that Rhodar won't see the geese come north if you don't come."

"Is it really that bad?"

"I'm not a physician," Silk replied, "but he doesn't look very good, and his mind seems to be slipping. He's even starting to lose his appetite, and that's a bad sign in a man who always ate seven big meals a day."

"Of course we'll come," Polgara said quickly.

"Just let me get warm first," Silk said in a plaintive tone.

They were delayed for several days just south of Aldurford by a savage blizzard that swept out of the mountains of Sendaria to howl across the open plains of northern Algaria. As luck had it, they reached the encampment of a nomadic band of roving herdsmen just as the storm broke and sat out the days of shrieking wind and driving snow in the comfortable wagons of the hospitable Algars. When the weather cleared at last, they pressed on to Aldurford, crossed the river, and reached the broad causeway that stretched across the snow-choked fens to Boktor.

Queen Porenn, still lovely despite the dark circles under her eyes that spoke so eloquently of her sleepless concern, greeted them at the gates of King Rhodar's palace. "Oh, Polgara," she said, overwhelmed with gratitude and relief as she embraced the sorceress.

"Dear Porenn," Polgara said, enfolding the careworn little Drasnian queen in her arms. "We'd have been here sooner, but we encountered bad weather. How's Rhodar?"

"A little weaker every day," Porenn replied with a kind of hopelessness in her voice. "Even Kheva tires him now."

"Your son?"

Porenn nodded. "The next king of Drasnia. He's only six—much too young to ascend the throne."

"Well, let's see what we can do to delay that."

King Rhodar, however, looked even worse than Silk's assessment of his condition had led them to believe. Errand remembered the King of Drasnia as a fat, jolly man with a quick wit and seemingly inexhaustible energy. Now he was listless, and his gray-hued skin hung on him in folds. He could not rise; perhaps even more serious was the fact that he could not lie down without his breath coming in painful, choking gasps. His voice, which had once been powerful enough to wake a sleeping army, had become a puny, querulous wheeze. He smiled a tired little smile of greeting when they entered, but after only a few minutes of conversation, he dozed off again.

"I think I need to be alone with him," Polgara told the rest of them in a crisp, efficient voice, but the quick look she exchanged with Silk carried little hope for the ailing monarch's recovery.

When she emerged from Rhodar's room, her expression was grave.

"Well?" Porenn asked, her eyes fearful.

"I'll speak frankly," Polgara said. "We've known each other too long for me to hide the truth from you. I can make his breathing a bit easier and relieve some of his discomfort. There are some things that will make him more alert—for short periods of time—but we have to use those sparingly, probably only when there are some major decisions to be made."

"But you cannot cure him." Porenn's quiet voice hovered on the very edge of tears.

"It's not a condition that's subject to cure, Porenn. His body is just worn out. I've told him for years that he was eating himself to death. He's as heavy as three normal men. A man's heart was simply not designed to carry that kind of weight. He hasn't had any real exercise in the past several years, and his diet is absolutely the worst he could possibly have come up with."

"Could you use sorcery?" the Drasnian queen asked desperately.

"Porenn, I'd have to rebuild him from the ground up. Nothing he has really functions right any more. Sorcery simply wouldn't work. I'm sorry."

Two great tears welled up in Queen Porenn's eyes. "How long?" she asked in a voice scarcely more than a whisper.

"A few months—six at the most."

Porenn nodded, and then, despite her tear-filled eyes, she lifted her chin bravely. "When you think he's strong enough, I'd like to have you give him those potions that will clear his mind. He and I will have to talk. There are arrangements that are going to have to be made—for the sake of our son, and for Drasnia."

"Of course, Porenn."

The bitter cold of that long, cruel winter broke quite suddenly a couple of days later. A warm wind blew in off the Gulf of Cherek during the night, bringing with it a gusty rainstorm that turned the drifts clogging the broad avenues of Boktor into sodden brown slush. Errand and Prince Kheva, the heir to the Drasnian throne, found themselves confined to the palace by the sudden change in the weather. Crown Prince Kheva was a sturdy little boy with dark hair and a serious expression. Like his father, the ailing King Rhodar, Kheva had a marked preference for the color red and he customarily wore a velvet doublet and hose in that hue. Though Errand was perhaps five years or so older than the prince, the two of them became friends almost immediately. Together they discovered the enormous entertainment to be found in rolling a brightly colored wooden ball down a long flight of stone stairs. After the bouncing ball knocked a silver tray from the hands of the chief butler, however, they were asked quite firmly to find other amusements.

They wandered for a time through the echoing marble halls of the palace, Kheva in his bright red velvet and Errand in sturdy peasant brown, until they came at last to the grand ballroom. At one end of the enormous hall, a broad marble staircase with a crimson carpet down the center descended from the upper floors of the palace, and along each side of that imposing stair was a smooth marble balustrade. The two boys looked speculatively at those twin banisters, both of them immediately recognizing the tremendous potential of all that slippery marble. There were polished chairs along each side of the ballroom, and each chair was padded with a red velvet cushion. The boys looked at the balustrades. Then they looked at the cushions. Then they both turned to be sure that no guard or palace functionary was in the vicinity of the large, double doors at the back of the ballroom.

Errand prudently closed the doors; then he and Prince Kheva went to work. There were many chairs and many red velvet cushions. When those cushions were all piled in two heaps at the bottom of the marble stair railings, they made a pair of quite imposing mountains.

"Well?" Kheva said when all was in readiness.

"I guess we might as well," Errand replied.

Together they climbed the stairs and then each of them mounted one of the smooth, cool banisters descending grandly toward the white marble floor of the ballroom far below.

"Go!" Kheva shouted, and the two of them slid down, gaining tremendous speed as they went and landing with soft thumps in the heaps of cushions awaiting them.

Laughing with delight, the two boys ran back up the stairs again and once again they slid down. All in all, the afternoon went very well, until at last one of the cushions burst its seams and filled the quiet air of the grand ballroom with softly drifting goose down. It was, quite naturally, at that precise moment that Polgara came looking for them. Somehow it always happened that way. The moment anything was broken, spilled, or tipped over, someone in authority would appear. There was never an opportunity to tidy up, and so such situations always presented themselves in the worst possible light.

The double doors at the far end of the ballroom opened, and Polgara, regally beautiful in blue velvet, stepped inside. Her face was grave as she regarded the guilty-looking pair lying at the foot of the stairs in their piles of cushions, with a positive blizzard of goose down swirling around them.

Errand winced and held his breath.

Very softly, she closed the doors behind her and walked slowly toward them, her heels sounding ominously loud on the marble floor. She looked at the denuded chairs lining each side of the ballroom. She looked at the marble balustrades. She looked at the boys with feathers settling on them. And then, without warning whatsoever, she began to laugh, a rich, warm, vibrant laugh that absolutely filled the empty hall.

Errand felt somehow betrayed by her reaction. He and Kheva had gone out of their way to get themselves into trouble, and all she did was laugh about it. There was no scolding, no acid commentary, nothing but laughter. He definitely felt that this levity was out of place, an indication that she was not taking this thing as seriously as she ought. He felt a trifle bitter about the whole thing. He had *earned* the scolding she was denying him.

"You boys *will* clean it up, won't you?" she asked them.

"Of course, Lady Polgara," Kheva assured her quickly. "We were just about to do that."

"Splendid, your Highness," she said, the corners of her mouth still twitching. "Do try to gather up *all* the feathers." And she turned and walked out of the ballroom, leaving the faint echo of her laughter hovering in the air behind her.

After that, the boys were watched rather closely. There was nothing really obvious about it; it was just that there always seemed to be someone around to call a halt before things got completely out of hand.

About a week later, when the rains had passed and the slush had mostly melted off the streets, Errand and Kheva were sitting on the floor of a carpeted room, building a fortress out of wooden blocks. At a table near the window Silk, splendidly dressed in rich black velvet, was carefully reading a dispatch he had received that morning from his partner, Yarblek, who had remained in Gar og Nadrak to tend the business. About midmorning, a servant came into the room and spoke briefly with the rat-faced little man. Silk nodded, rose, and came over to where the boys were playing. "What would you gentlemen say to a breath of fresh air?" he asked them.

"Of course," Errand replied, getting to his feet.

"And you, cousin?" Silk asked Kheva.

"Certainly, your Highness," Kheva said.

Silk laughed. "Must we be so formal, Kheva?"

"Mother says I should always use the proper forms of address," Kheva told him seriously. "I guess it's to help me keep in practice or something."

"Your mother isn't here," Silk told him slyly, "so it's all right to cheat a little."

Kheva looked around nervously. "Do you really think we should?" he whispered.

"I'm sure of it," Silk replied. "Cheating is good for you. It helps you to keep your perspective."

"Do *you* cheat often?"

"Me?" Silk was still laughing. "All the time, cousin. All the time. Let's fetch cloaks and take a turn about the city. I have to go by the headquarters of the intelligence service; and since I've been appointed your keeper for the day, the two of you had better come along."

The air outside was cool and damp, and the wind was brisk enough to whip their cloaks about their legs as they passed along the cobbled streets of Boktor. The Drasnian capital was one of the major commercial centers of the world, and the streets teemed with men of all races. Richly mantled Tolnedrans spoke on street corners with sober-faced Sendars in sensible brown. Flamboyantly garbed and richly jeweled Drasnians haggled with leather-garbed Nadraks, and there were even a few black-robed Murgos striding along the blustery streets, with their broad-backed Thullish porters trailing behind them, carrying heavy packs filled with merchandise. The porters, of course, were followed at a discreet distance by the ever-present spies.

"Dear, sneaky old Boktor," Silk declaimed extravagantly, "where at least every other man you meet is a spy."

"Are those men spies?" Kheva asked, looking at them with a surprised expression.

"Of course they are, your Highness." Silk laughed again. "Everybody in Drasnia is a spy—or wants to be. It's our national industry. Didn't you know that?"

"Well—I knew that there are quite a few spies in the palace, but I didn't think they'd be out in the streets."

"Why should there be spies in the palace?" Errand asked him curiously.

Kheva shrugged. "Everybody wants to know what everybody else is doing. The more important you are, the more spies you have watching you."

"Are any of them watching you?"

"Six that I know of. There are probably a few more besides—and of course, all the spies are being spied on by other spies."

"What a peculiar place," Errand murmured.

Kheva laughed. "Once, when I was about three or so, I found a hiding place under a stair and fell asleep. Eventually, all the spies in the palace joined in the search for me. You'd be amazed at how many there really are."

This time, Silk laughed uproariously. "That's really very bad form, cousin," he said. "Members of the royal family aren't supposed to hide from the spies. It upsets them terribly. That's the building over there." He pointed at a large stone warehouse standing on a quiet side street.

"I always thought that the headquarters was in the same building with the academy," Kheva said.

"Those are the *official* offices, cousin. *This* is the place where the work gets done."

They entered the warehouse and went through a cavernous room piled high with boxes and bales to a small, unobtrusive door with a bulky-looking man in a workman's smock lounging against it. The man gave Silk a quick look, bowed, and opened the door for them. Beyond that somewhat shabby-looking door lay a large, well-lighted room with a dozen or more parchment-littered tables standing along the walls. At each table sat four or five people, all poring over the documents before them.

"What are they doing?" Errand asked curiously.

"Sorting information," Silk replied. "There probably isn't much that happens in the world that doesn't reach this room eventually. If we really wanted to know, we could probably ask around and find out what the King of Arendia had for breakfast this morning. We want to go into that room over there." He pointed toward a solid-looking door on the far side of the room.

The chamber beyond the door was plain, even bare. It contained a table and four chairs—nothing more. The man seated at the table in one of the chairs wore black hose and a pearl-gray doublet. He was as thin as an old bone, and even here, in the very midst of his own people, there was about him the sense of a tightly coiled spring. "Silk," he said with a terse nod.

"Javelin," Silk replied. "You wanted to see me?"

The man at the table looked at the two boys. He inclined his head briefly to Kheva. "Your Highness," he said.

"Margrave Khendon," the prince responded with a polite bow.

The seated man looked at Silk, his idle-appearing fingers twitching slightly.

"Margrave," Kheva said almost apologetically, "my mother's been teaching me the secret language. I know what you're saying."

The man Silk called Javelin stopped moving his fingers with a rueful expression. "Caught by my own cleverness, I see," he said. He looked speculatively at Errand.

"This is Errand, the boy Polgara and Durnik are raising," Silk told him.

"Ah," Javelin said, "the bearer of the Orb."

"Kheva and I can wait outside if you want to speak privately," Errand offered.

Javelin thought about that. "That probably won't be necessary," he decided. "I think we can trust you both to be discreet. Sit down, gentlemen." He pointed at the other three chairs.

"I'm sort of retired, Javelin," Silk told him. "I've got enough other things to keep me busy just now."

"I wasn't really going to ask you to get personally involved," Javelin replied. "All I really want is for you to find room for a couple of new employees in one of your enterprises."

Silk gave him a curious look.

"You're shipping goods out of Gar og Nadrak along the Northern Caravan Route," Javelin continued. "There are several villages near the border where the citizens are highly suspicious of strangers with no valid reason for passing through."

"And you want to use *my* caravans to give your men an excuse for being in those villages," Silk concluded.

Javelin shrugged. "It's not an uncommon practice."

"What's going on in eastern Drasnia that you're so interested in?"

"The same thing that's always going on in the outlying districts."

"The Bear-cult?" Silk asked incredulously. "You're going to waste time on *them*?"

"They've been behaving peculiarly lately. I want to find out why."

Silk looked at him with one eyebrow raised.

"Just call it idle curiosity if you like."

The look Silk gave him then was very hard. "Oh, no. You're not going to catch me *that* easily, my friend."

"Aren't *you* the least bit curious?"

"No. As a matter of fact, I'm not. No amount of clever trickery is going to lure me into neglecting my own affairs to go off on another one of your fishing expeditions. I'm too busy, Javelin." His eyes narrowed ever so slightly. "Why don't you send Hunter?"

"Hunter's busy someplace else, Silk, and stop trying to find out who Hunter is."

"It was worth a try. Actually I'm not interested at all, not in the least." He sat back in his chair with his arms adamantly crossed. His long pointed nose, however, was twitching. "What do you mean by 'behaving peculiarly'?" he asked after a moment.

"I thought you weren't interested."

"I'm not," Silk repeated hastily. "I most definitely am *not*." His nose, however, was twitching even more violently. Angrily he got to his feet. "Give me the names of the men you want me to hire," he said abruptly. "I'll see what I can do."

"Of course, Prince Kheldar," Javelin said blandly. "I appreciate your sense of loyalty to your old service."

Errand remembered something that Silk had said in the large outer room. "Silk says that information about almost everything is brought to this building," he said to Javelin.

"That might be an exaggeration, but we try."

"Then perhaps you might have heard something about Zandramas."

Javelin looked at him blankly.

"It's something that Belgarion and I heard about," Errand explained. "And Belgarath is curious about it, too. I thought you might have heard about it."

"I can't say that I have," Javelin admitted. "Of course we're a long way from Darshiva."

"What's Darshiva?" Errand asked.

"It's one of the principalities of the old Melcene Empire in eastern Mallorea. Zandrama is a Darshivan name. Didn't you know that?"

"No. We didn't."

There was a light tap on the door.

"Yes?" Javelin answered.

The door opened, and a young lady of perhaps nineteen or twenty came in. Her hair was the color of honey, her eyes were a warm, golden brown, and she wore a plain-looking gray dress. Her expression was serious, but there was just the hint of a dimple in each of her cheeks. "Uncle," she said, and her voice had a kind of vibrancy about it that made it almost irresistibly compelling.

Javelin's hard, angular face softened noticeably. "Yes, Liselle?" he said.

"Is this little Liselle?" Silk exclaimed.

"Not quite so little any more," Javelin said.

"The last time I saw her she was still in braids."

"She combed out the braids a few years ago," Javelin said drily, "and look what was hiding under them."

"I am looking," Silk said admiringly.

"The reports you wanted, uncle," the girl said, laying a sheaf of parchment on the table. Then she turned to Kheva and curtsied to him with incredible grace. "Your Highness," she greeted him.

"Margravine Liselle," the little prince replied with a polite bow.

"And Prince Kheldar," the girl said then.

"We weren't at all so formal when you were a child," Silk protested.

"But then, I'm not a child any more, your Highness." Silk looked over at Javelin. "When she was a little girl, she used to pull my nose."

"But it's such a long, interesting nose," Liselle said. And then she smiled, and the dimples suddenly sprang to life.

"Liselle is helping out here," Javelin said. "She'll be entering the academy in a few months."

"You're going to be a spy?" Silk asked her incredulously.

"It's the family business, Prince Kheldar. My father and mother were both spies. My uncle here is a spy. All of my friends are spies. How could I possibly be anything else?"

Silk looked a trifle off balance. "It just doesn't seem appropriate, for some reason."

"That probably means that I'll be quite successful, doesn't it? You *look* like a spy, Prince Kheldar. I don't, so I won't have nearly as many problems as you've had."

Though the girl's answers were clever, even pert, Errand could see something in her warm, brown eyes that Silk probably could not. Despite the fact that the Margravine Liselle was obviously a grown woman, Silk just as obviously still thought of her as a little girl—one who had pulled his nose. The look she gave *him,* however, was not the look of a little girl, and Errand realized that she had been waiting for a number of years for the opportunity to meet Silk on adult terms. Errand covered his mouth with his hand to hide a smile. The wily Prince Kheldar had some *very* interesting times ahead of him.

The door opened again, and a nondescript man came in, quickly crossed to the table, and whispered something to Javelin. The man's face, Errand noticed, was pale, and his hands were trembling.

Javelin's face grew set, and he sighed. He gave no other outward sign of emotion, however. He rose to his feet and came around the table. "Your Majesty," he said formally to Prince Kheva, "I believe that you should return to the palace immediately."

Silk and Liselle both caught the changed form of address and looked sharply at the Chief of Drasnian Intelligence.

"I believe that we should all accompany the King back to the palace," Javelin said sadly. "We must offer our condolences to his mother and aid her in any way we can in her hour of grief."

The King of Drasnia looked at his intelligence chief, his eyes very wide and his lip trembling.

Errand gently took the little boy's hand in his. "We'd better go, Kheva," he said. "Your mother will need you very much right now."

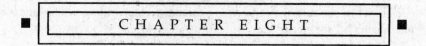

CHAPTER EIGHT

T he Kings of Aloria gathered in Boktor for the funeral of King Rhodar and the subsequent coronation of his son, Kheva. Such a gathering, of course, was traditional. Though the nations of the north had diverged somewhat over the centuries, the Alorns nonetheless had never forgotten their origins in the single kingdom of King Cherek Bear-shoulders five thousand years in the dim past, and they came together at such times in sadness to bury a brother. Because King Rhodar had been beloved and respected by other nations as well, Anheg of Cherek, Cho-Hag of Algaria, and Belgarion of Riva were joined by Fulrach of Sendaria, Korodullin of Arendia, and even by the erratic Drosta lek Thun of Gar og Nadrak. In addition, General Varana was present as the representative of Emperor Ran Borune XXIII of Tolnedra, and Sadi, Chief Eunuch of the palace of Queen Salmissra of Nyissa, was also in attendance.

The burial of an Alorn King was a serious matter, and it involved certain ceremonies at which only the other Alorn monarchs were present. No gathering of so
many kings and high-ranking functionaries, however, could ever be entirely ceremonial. Inevitably, politics were of major concern in the quiet discussions which
took place in the somberly draped corridors of the palace.

Errand, soberly dressed and quiet, drifted from one small gathering to another
in those days preceding the funeral. The Kings all knew him, but they seemed for
some reason to take little note of his presence, and so he heard many conversations
which he might perhaps not have heard had they stopped to consider the fact that
he was no longer the little boy they had known during the campaign in Mishrak ac
Thull.

The Alorn Kings—Belgarion in his usual blue doublet and hose, and the
brutish-looking Anheg in his rumpled blue robe and dented crown, and quiet-
voiced Cho-Hag in silver and black—stood together in a sable-draped embrasure in
one of the broad hallways of the palace.

"Porenn is going to have to serve as regent," Garion said. "Kheva is only six, and
somebody's going to have to run things until he's old enough to take charge himself."

"A *woman*?" Anheg said, aghast.

"Anheg, are we going to have *that* argument again?" Cho-Hag asked mildly.

"I don't see any alternative, Anheg," Garion said in his most persuasive manner. "King Drosta is almost drooling at the prospect of a boy king on the throne of
Drasnia. His troops will be biting off chunks of the borderlands before the rest of us
get home unless we put someone in charge here."

"But Porenn is so tiny," Anheg objected irrationally, "and so pretty. How can
she possibly run a kingdom?"

"Probably very well," Cho-Hag replied, shifting his weight carefully on his
crippled legs. "Rhodar confided in her completely, and she *was* behind the scheme
that eliminated Grodeg, after all."

"About the only other person in Drasnia competent enough to take charge here
is the Margrave Khendon," Garion told the King of Cherek. "The one they call
Javelin. Do you want the Chief of Drasnian Intelligence sitting behind the throne
giving orders?"

Anheg shuddered. "That's a ghastly thought. What about Prince Kheldar?"

Garion stared at him. "You're not serious, Anheg," he said incredulously. "Silk?
As regent?"

"You might be right," Anheg conceded after a moment's thought. "He *is* just a
little unreliable, isn't he?"

"A *little*?" Garion laughed.

"Are we agreed, then?" Cho-Hag asked. "It has to be Porenn, right?"

Anheg grumbled, but finally agreed.

The Algar King turned to Garion. "You'll probably have to issue a proclamation."

"Me? I don't have any authority in Drasnia."

"You're the Overlord of the West," Cho-Hag reminded him. "Just announce
that you recognize Porenn's regency and declare that anyone who argues about it or
violates her borders will have to answer to *you*."

"*That* should back Drosta off." Anheg chuckled grossly. "He's almost more frightened of you than he is of 'Zakath. He probably has nightmares about your flaming sword sliding between his ribs."

In another corridor, Errand came upon General Varana and Sadi the Eunuch. Sadi wore the mottled, iridescent silk robe of the Nyissans, and the general was draped in a silver Tolnedran mantle with broad bands of gold-colored trim across his shoulders.

"So, it's official, then?" Sadi said in his oddly contralto voice, eyeing the general's mantle.

"What's that?" Varana asked him. The general was a blocky-looking man with iron-gray hair and a slightly amused expression.

"We had heard rumors in Sthiss Tor that Ran Borune had adopted you as his son."

"Expediency." Varana shrugged. "The major families of the Empire were dismantling Tolnedra in their scramble for the throne. Ran Borune had to take steps to quiet things down."

"You *will* take the throne when he dies, though, won't you?"

"We'll see," Varana replied evasively. "Let's pray that his Majesty will live for many years yet."

"Of course," Sadi murmured. "The silver mantle of the crown prince *does* become you, however, my dear General." He rubbed one long-fingered hand over his shaved scalp.

"Thank you," Varana said with a slight bow. "And how are affairs in Salmissra's palace?"

Sadi laughed sardonically. "The same as they always are. We connive and plot and scheme against each other, and every scrap of food prepared in our kitchens is tainted with poison."

"I'd heard that was the custom," Vanara remarked. "How does one survive in such a lethal atmosphere?"

"Nervously," Sadi replied, making a sour face. "We are all on a strict regimen. We routinely dose ourselves with every known antidote to every known poison. Some of the poisons are actually quite flavorful. The antidotes all taste foul, however."

"The price of power, I suppose."

"Truly. What was the reaction of the Grand Dukes of Tolnedra when the Emperor designated you his heir?"

Varana laughed. "You could hear the screams echoing from the wood of the Dryads to the Arendish border."

"When the time comes, you may have to step on a few necks."

"It's possible."

"Of course the legions are all loyal to you."

"The legions are a great comfort to me."

"I think I like you, General Varana," the shaved-headed Nyissan said. "I'm certain that you and I will be able to come to some mutually profitable accommodations."

"I always like to be on good terms with my neighbors, Sadi," Varana agreed with aplomb.

In another corridor, Errand found a strangely assorted group. King Fulrach of Sendaria, dressed in sober, businesslike brown, was speaking quietly with the purple-garbed King Korodullin of Arendia and with the scabrous-looking Drosta lek Thun, who wore a richly jeweled doublet of an unwholesome-looking yellow.

"Have either of you heard anything about any decisions concerning a regency?" the emaciated Nadrak king asked in his shrill voice. Drosta's eyes bulged, seeming almost to start out of his pock-marked face, and he fidgeted continuously.

"I would imagine that Queen Porenn will guide the young king," Fulrach surmised.

"They surely wouldn't put a woman in charge," Drosta scoffed. "I know Alorns, and they all look at women as subhuman."

"Porenn is not exactly like other women," the King of Sendaria noted. "She's extraordinarily gifted."

"How could a woman possibly defend the borders of so large a kingdom as Drasnia?"

"Thy perception is awry, your Majesty," Korodullin told the Nadrak with uncharacteristic bluntness. "Inevitably, the other Alorn Kings will support her, and most particularly Belgarion of Riva will defend her. Methinks no monarch alive would be so foolhardy as to counter the wishes of the Overlord of the West."

"Riva's a long way away," Drosta suggested, his eyes narrowing.

"Not so far, Drosta," Fulrach told him. "Belgarion has a very long arm."

"What news hast thou heard from the south, your Majesty?" Korodullin asked the King of the Nadraks.

Drosta made an indelicate sound. "Kal Zakath is wading in Murgo blood," he said disgustedly. "He's pushed Urgit into the western mountains and he's butchering every Murgo he can lay his hands on. I keep hoping that someone will stick an arrow into him, but you can't depend on a Murgo to do anything right."

"Have you considered an alliance with King Gethell?" Fulrach asked.

"With the Thulls? You're not serious, Fulrach. I wouldn't saddle myself with the Thulls, even if it meant that I had to face the Malloreans alone. Gethell's so afraid of 'Zakath that he wets himself at the mention of his name. After the Battle of Thull Mardu, 'Zakath told my Thullish cousin that the very next time Gethell displeased him, he was going to have Gethell crucified. If Kal Zakath decides to come north, Gethell will probably hide himself under the nearest manure pile."

" 'Zakath is not overfond of thee either, I am told," Korodullin said.

Drosta laughed a shrill, somehow hysterical-sounding laugh. "He wants to grill me over a slow fire," he replied. "And possibly use my skin to make a pair of shoes."

"I'm amazed that you Angaraks didn't destroy each other eons ago." Fulrach smiled.

"Torak told us not to." Drosta shrugged. "And he told his Grolims to gut anybody who disobeyed. We may not always have *liked* Torak, but we always did what he told us to do. Only an idiot did otherwise—a dead idiot, usually."

On the following day, Belgarath the Sorcerer arrived from the East, and King

Rhodar of Drasnia was laid to rest. The small blonde Queen Porenn, dressed in deepest black, stood beside young King Kheva during the ceremony. Prince Kheldar stood directly behind the young king and his mother, and there was a strange, almost haunted look in his eyes. As Errand looked at him, he could see very plainly that the little spy had loved his uncle's tiny wife for years, but also that Porenn, though she was fond of him, did not return that love. State funerals, like all state functions, are long. Both Queen Porenn and her young son were very pale during the interminable proceedings, but at no time did either of them show any outward signs of grief.

Immediately following the funeral, Kheva's coronation took place, and the newly crowned Drasnian king announced in a piping but firm voice that his mother would guide him through the difficult years ahead.

At the conclusion of the ceremony, Belgarion, King of Riva and Overlord of the West, arose and briefly addressed the assembled notables. He welcomed Kheva to the rather exclusive fraternity of reigning monarchs, complimented him on the wisdom of the choice of the Queen Mother as regent, and then advised one and all that he fully supported Queen Porenn and that anyone offering her the slightest impertinence would most surely regret it. Since he was leaning on the massive sword of Riva Iron-grip as he made that declaration, everyone in the Drasnian throne room took him very seriously.

A few days later, the visitors all departed.

Spring had come to the plains of Algaria as Polgara, Durnik, Errand, and Belgarath rode southward in the company of King Cho-Hag and Queen Silar.

"A sad journey," Cho-Hag said to Belgarath as they rode. "I'm going to miss Rhodar."

"I think we all will," Belgarath replied. He looked ahead where a vast herd of cattle under the watchful eyes of a band of Algar clansmen was plodding slowly west toward the mountains of Sendaria and the great cattle fair at Muros. "I'm a little surprised that Hettar agreed to go back to Riva with Garion at this time of year. He's usually at the head of the cattle herds."

"Adara persuaded him," Queen Silar told the old man. "She and Ce'Nedra wanted to spend some time together, and there's almost nothing that Hettar won't do for his wife."

Polgara smiled. "Poor Hettar," she said. "With both Adara and Ce'Nedra working on him, he didn't stand a chance. That's a pair of very determined young ladies."

"The change of scenery will do him good," Cho-Hag noted. "He always gets restless in the summertime and, now that all the Murgos have retreated to the south, he can't even amuse himself by hunting down their raiding parties."

When they reached southern Algaria, Cho-Hag and Silar bade them farewell and turned eastward toward the Stronghold. The rest of the ride south to the Vale was uneventful. Belgarath stayed at the cottage for a few days and then prepared to return to his tower. Almost as an afterthought, he invited Errand to accompany him.

"We *are* a bit behind here, father," Polgara told him. "I need to get my garden in, and Durnik has a great deal of work ahead of him after this past winter."

"Then it's probably best if the boy is out from underfoot, isn't it?"

She gave him a long steady look and then finally gave up. "Oh, very well, father," she said.

"I knew you'd see it my way, Pol," he said.

"Just don't keep him all summer."

"Of course not. I want to talk with the twins for a while and see if Beldin has come back. I'll be off again in a month or so. I'll bring him home then."

And so Errand and Belgarath went on down into the heart of the Vale again and once more took up residence in the old man's tower. Beldin had not yet returned from Mallorea, but Belgarath had much to discuss with Beltira and Belkira, and so Errand and his chestnut stallion were left largely to find their own amusements.

It was on a bright summer morning that they turned toward the western edge of the Vale to explore the foothills that marked the boundary of Ulgoland. They had ridden for several miles through those rolling, tree-clad hills and stopped in a broad, shallow ravine where a tumbling brook babbled over mossy green stones. The morning sun was very warm, and the shade of the tall, fragrant pines was pleasant.

As they sat, a she-wolf padded quietly from out of the bushes at the edge of the brook, stopped, and sat on her haunches to look at them. There was about the she-wolf a peculiar blue nimbus, a soft glow that seemed to emanate from her thick fur.

The normal reaction of a horse to the presence or even the scent of a wolf would have been blind panic, but the stallion returned the blue wolf's gaze calmly, with not even so much as a hint of a tremor.

The boy knew who the wolf was, but he was surprised to meet her here. "Good morning," he said politely to her. "It's a pleasant day, isn't it?"

The wolf seemed to shimmer in the same way that Beldin shimmered as he assumed the shape of the hawk. When the air around her cleared, there stood in the animal's place a tawny-haired woman with golden eyes and a faintly amused smile on her lips. Though her gown was a plain brown such as one might see on any peasant woman, she wore it in a regal manner which any queen in jeweled brocade might envy. "Do you always greet wolves with such courtesy?" she asked him.

"I haven't met many wolves," he replied, "but I was fairly certain who you were."

"Yes, I suppose you would have been, at that."

Errand slid down off the horse's back.

"Does *he* know where you are this morning?"

"Belgarath? Probably not. He's talking with Beltira and Belkira, so the horse and I just came out to look at someplace new."

"It would be best perhaps if you didn't go too much farther into the Ulgo mountains," she advised. "There are creatures in these hills that are quite savage."

He nodded. "I'll keep that in mind."

"Will you do something for me?" she asked quite directly.

"If I can."

"Speak to my daughter."

"Of course."

"Tell Polgara that there is a great evil in the world and a great danger."

"Zandramas?" Errand asked.

"Zandramas is a part of it, but the Sardion is at the center of the evil. It must be destroyed. Tell my husband and my daughter to warn Belgarion. His task is not yet finished."

"I'll tell them," Errand promised, "but couldn't you just as easily tell Polgara yourself?"

The tawny-haired woman looked off down the shady ravine. "No," she replied sadly. "It causes her too much pain when I appear to her."

"Why is that?"

"It reminds her of all the lost years and brings back all the anguish of a young girl who had to grow up without her mother to guide her. All of that comes back to her each time she sees me."

"You've never told her then? Of the sacrifice you were asked to make?"

She looked at him penetratingly. "How is it that you know what even my husband and Polgara do not?"

"I'm not sure," he replied. "I *do,* though—just as I know that you did *not* die."

"And will you tell Polgara that?"

"Not if you'd rather I didn't."

She sighed. "Someday, perhaps, but not yet. I think it's best if she and her father aren't aware of it. My task still lies ahead of me and it's a thing I can face best without any distractions."

"Whatever you wish," Errand said politely.

"We'll meet again," she told him. "Warn them about the Sardion. Tell them not to become so caught up in the search for Zandramas that they lose sight of that. It is from the Sardion that the evil stems. And be a trifle wary of Cyradis when next you meet her. She means you no ill, but she has her own task as well and she will do what she must to complete it."

"I will, Poledra," he promised.

"Oh," she said, almost as an afterthought, "there's someone waiting for you just up ahead there." She gestured toward the long tongue of a rock-strewn ridge thrusting out into the grassy Vale. "He can't see you yet, but he's waiting." Then she smiled, shimmered back into the form of the blue-tinged wolf, and loped away without a backward glance.

Curiously, Errand remounted and rode up out of the ravine and continued on southward, skirting the higher hills that rose toward the glistening white peaks of the land of the Ulgos as he rode toward the ridge. Then, as his eyes searched the rocky slope, he caught a momentary flicker of sunlight reflected from something shiny in the middle of a brushy outcrop halfway up the slope. Without hesitation, he rode in that direction.

The man who sat among the thick bushes wore a peculiar shirt of mail, constructed of overlapping metal scales. He was short but had powerful shoulders, and his eyes were veiled with a gauzy strip of cloth that was not so much a blindfold as it was a shield against the bright sunlight.

"Is that you, Errand?" the veiled man asked in a harsh-sounding voice.

"Yes," Errand replied. "I haven't seen you in a long time, Relg."

"I need to talk with you," the harsh-voiced zealot said. "Can we get back out of the light?"

"Of course." Errand slid down off his horse and followed the Ulgo through the rustling bushes to a cave mouth running back into the hillside. Relg stooped slightly under the overhanging rock and went inside. "I thought I recognized you," he said as Errand joined him in the cool dimness within the cave, "but I couldn't be sure out there in all that light." He untied the cloth from across his eyes and peered at the boy. "You've grown."

Errand smiled. "It's been a few years. How is Taiba?"

"She has given me a son," Relg said, almost in a kind of wonder. "A very special son."

"I'm glad to hear that."

"When I was younger and filled with the notion of my own sanctity, UL spoke to me in my soul. He told me that the child who will be the new Gorim would come to Ulgo through me. In my pride I thought that he meant that I was to seek out the child and reveal him. How could I know that what he meant was a much simpler thing? It is my son that he spoke of. The mark is on my son—*my* son!" There was an awed pride in the zealot's voice.

"UL's ways are not the ways of men."

"How truly you speak."

"And are you happy?"

"My life is filled," Relg said simply. "But now I have another task. Our aged Gorim has sent me to seek out Belgarath. It is urgent that he come with me to Prolgu."

"He's not very far away," Errand said. He looked at Relg and saw how, even in this dim cave, the zealot kept his eyes squinted almost shut to protect them from the light. "I have a horse," he said. "I can go and bring him back here in a few hours, if you want. That way you won't have to go out into the sunlight."

Relg gave him a quick, grateful look and then nodded. "Tell him that he *must* come. The Gorim must speak with him."

"I will," Errand promised. Then he turned and left the cave.

"What does *he* want?" Belgarath demanded irritably when Errand told him that Relg wanted to see him.

"He wants you to go with him to Prolgu," Errand replied. "The Gorim wants to see you—the old one."

"The *old* one? Is there a new one?"

Errand nodded. "Relg's son," he said.

Belgarath stared at Errand for a moment and then he suddenly began to laugh. "What's so funny?"

"It appears that UL has a sense of humor," the old man chortled. "I wouldn't have suspected that of him."

"I don't quite follow."

"It's a very long story," Belgarath said, still laughing. "I guess that, if the Gorim wants to see me, we'd better go."

"You want me to go along?"

"Polgara would skin me alive if I left you here alone. Let's get started."

Errand led the old man back across the Vale to the ridge line in the foothills and the cave where Relg waited. It took a few minutes to explain to the young horse that he was supposed to go back to Belgarath's tower alone. Errand spoke with him at some length, and it finally appeared that the animal had grasped the edges, at least, of the idea.

The trip through the dark galleries to Prolgu took several days. For most of the way, Errand felt that they were groping along blindly; but for Relg, whose eyes were virtually useless in open daylight, these lightless passageways were home, and his sense of direction was unerring. And so it was that they came at last to the faintly lighted cavern with its shallow, glass-clear lake and the island rising in the center where the aged Gorim awaited them.

"*Yad ho*, Belgarath," the saintly old man in his white robe called when they reached the shore of the subterranean lake, "*Groja UL*."

"Gorim," Belgarath replied with a respectful bow, "*Yad ho, Groja UL*." Then they crossed the marble causeway to join the Gorim. Belgarath and the old man clasped each other's arms warmly. "It's been a few years, hasn't it?" the sorcerer said. "How are you bearing up?"

"I feel almost young." The Gorim smiled. "Now that Relg has found my successor. I can at last see the end of my task."

"Found?" Belgarath asked quizzically.

"It amounts to the same thing." The Gorim looked fondly at Relg. "We had our disagreements, didn't we, my son?" he said, "But as it turned out, we were all working toward the same end."

"It took me a little longer to realize it, Holy Gorim," Relg replied wryly. "I'm a bit more stubborn than most men. Sometimes I'm amazed that UL didn't lose patience with me. Please excuse me, but I must go to my wife and son. I've been many days away from them." He turned and went quickly back across the causeway.

Belgarath grinned. "A remarkably changed man."

"His wife is a marvel," the Gorim agreed.

"Are you sure that their child is the chosen one?"

The Gorim nodded. "UL has confirmed it. There were those who objected, since Taiba is a Marag rather than a daughter of Ulgo, but UL's voice silenced them."

"I'm sure it did. UL's voice is very penetrating, I've noticed. You wanted to see me?"

The Gorim's expression became grave. He gestured toward his pyramid-shaped house. "Let's go inside. There's a matter of urgency we need to discuss."

Errand followed along behind the two old men as they entered the house. The room inside was dimly lighted by a glowing crystal globe hanging on a chain from the ceiling, and there was a table with low stone benches. They sat at the table, and the old Gorim looked solemnly at Belgarath. "We are not like the people who live above in the light of the sun, my friend," he said. "For them, there is the sound of the wind in the trees, of rushing streams, and of birds filling the air with song. Here in our caves, however, we hear only the sounds of the earth herself."

Belgarath nodded.

"The earth and the rocks speak to the people of Ulgo in peculiar ways," the Gorim continued. "A sound can come to us from half around the world. Such a sound has been muttering in the rocks for some years now, growing louder and more distinct with each passing month."

"A fault perhaps?" Belgarath suggested. "Some place where the stone bed of a continent is shifting?"

"I don't believe so, my friend," the Gorim disagreed. "The sound we hear is not the shifting of the restless earth. It is a sound caused by the awakening of a single stone."

"I'm not sure I follow you," Belgarath said, frowning.

"The stone we hear is alive, Belgarath."

The old sorcerer looked at his friend. "There's only one living stone, Gorim."

"I had always believed so myself. I have heard the sound of Aldur's Orb as it moves about the world, and this new sound is also the sound of a living stone. It awakens, Belgarath, and it feels its power. It is evil, my friend—so evil that earth herself groans under its weight."

"How long has this sound been coming to you?"

"It began not long after the death of accursed Torak."

Belgarath pursed his lips. "We've known that something has been moving around over in Mallorea," he said. "We didn't know it was quite this serious, however. Can you tell me anything more about this stone?"

"Only its name," the Gorim replied. "We hear it whispered through the caves and galleries and the fissures of earth. It is called 'Sardius.' "

Belgarath's head came up. "*Cthrag Sardius?* The Sardion?"

"You have heard of it?"

"Beldin ran across it in Mallorea. It was connected with something called Zandramas."

The Gorim gasped, and his face went deathly pale. "Belgarath!" he exclaimed in a shocked voice.

"What's the matter?"

"That's the most dreadful curse in our language."

Belgarath stared at him. "I thought I knew most of the words in the Ulgo tongue. How is it that I've never heard that one before?"

"No one would have repeated it to you."

"I didn't think Ulgos even knew *how* to curse. What does it mean—in general terms?"

"It means confusion—chaos—absolute negation. It's a horrible word."

Belgarath frowned. "Why would an Ulgo curse word show up in Darshiva as the name of someone or something? And why in connection with the Sardion?"

"Is it possible that they are using the two words to mean the same thing?"

"I hadn't thought of that," Belgarath admitted. "I suppose they could be. The sense seems to be similar."

Polgara had rather carefully instructed Errand that he must not interrupt when his elders were talking, but this seemed so important that he felt that the rule needed to be broken. "They aren't the same," he told the two old men.

Belgarath gave him a strange look.

"The Sardion is a stone, isn't it?"

"Yes," the Gorim replied.

"Zandramas isn't a stone. It's a person."

"How could you know that, my boy?"

"We've met," Errand told him quietly. "Not exactly face to face, but—well—" It was a difficult thing to explain. "It was kind of like a shadow—except that the person who was casting the shadow was someplace else."

"A projection," Belgarath explained to the Gorim. "It's a fairly simple trick that the Grolims are fond of." He turned back to the boy. "Did this shadow say anything to you?"

Errand nodded. "It said that it was going to kill me."

Belgarath drew in his breath sharply. "Did you tell Polgara?" he demanded.

"No. Should I?"

"Didn't you think it was fairly significant?"

"I thought it was just a threat—meant to frighten me."

"Did it?"

"Frighten me? No, not really."

"Aren't you being just a little blasé, Errand?" Belgarath asked. "Do people go around threatening to kill you so often that it bores you or something?"

"No. That was the only time. It was only a shadow, though, and a shadow can't really hurt you, can it?"

"Have you run across many more of these shadows?"

"Just Cyradis."

"And who is Cyradis?"

"I'm not really sure. She talks the way Mandorallen does—thee's and thou's and all that—and she wears a blindfold over her eyes."

"A seeress." Belgarath grunted. "And what did *she* tell you?"

"She said that we were going to meet again and that she sort of liked me."

"I'm sure that was comforting," Belgarath said drily. "Don't keep secrets like this, Errand. When something unusual happens, *tell* somebody."

"I'm sorry," Errand apologized. "I just thought that—well—you and Polgara and Durnik had other things on your minds, that's all."

"We don't really mind being interrupted all *that* much, boy. *Share* these little adventures with us."

"If you want me to."

Belgarath turned back to the Gorim. "I think we're starting to get somewhere," he said, "thanks to our reticent young friend here. We know that Zandramas, if you'll pardon the word, is a person—a person that's somehow connected to this living stone that the Angaraks call Cthrag Sardius. We've had warnings about Zandramas before, so I think we'll have to assume that the Sardion is *also* a direct threat."

"What must we do now, then?" the Gorim asked him.

"I think we're all going to have to concentrate on finding out just exactly what's going on over there in Mallorea—even if we have to take the place apart stone by stone. Up until now, I was only curious. Now it looks as if I'd better start taking this whole thing seriously. If the Sardion is a living stone, then it's like the Orb, and I don't want something with that kind of power in the hands of the wrong person—and from everything I've been able to gather, this Zandramas is most *definitely* the wrong person." He turned then to look at Errand, his expression puzzled. "What's *your* connection with all of this, boy?" he asked. "Why is it that everyone and everything involved in this whole thing stops by to pay you a visit?"

"I don't know, Belgarath," Errand replied truthfully.

"Maybe that's the place we should start. I've been promising myself that I was going to have a long talk with you one of these days. Maybe it's time we did just that."

"If you wish," Errand said. "I don't know how much help I'll be, though."

"That's what we're going to find out, Errand. That's what we're going to find out."

PART TWO

RIVA

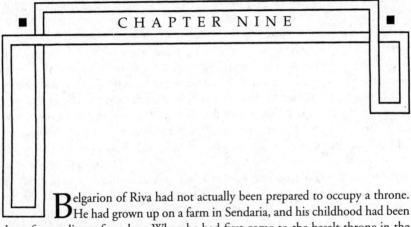
Belgarion of Riva had not actually been prepared to occupy a throne. He had grown up on a farm in Sendaria, and his childhood had been that of an ordinary farm boy. When he had first come to the basalt throne in the Hall of the Rivan King, he had known much more about farm kitchens and stables than he had about throne rooms and council chambers. Statecraft had been a mystery to him, and he had known no more of diplomacy than he had of algebra.

Fortunately, the Isle of the Winds was not a difficult kingdom to rule. The Rivan people were orderly, sober, and had a strong regard for duty and civic responsibility. This had made things much easier for their tall, sandy-haired monarch during the trying early years of his reign while he was learning the difficult art of ruling well. He made mistakes, naturally, but the consequences of those early slips and miscalculations were never dire, and his subjects were pleased to note that this earnest, sincere young man who had come so startlingly to the throne never made the same mistake twice. Once he had settled in and had become accustomed to his job, it was probably safe to say that Belgarion—or Garion, as he preferred to be called—almost never encountered major problems in his capacity as King of Riva.

He had other titles, however. Some were purely honorary, others not so much so. "Godslayer," for example, involved certain duties which were not likely to come up very often. "Lord of the Western Sea" caused him almost no concern whatsoever, since he had concluded quite early that the waves and tides need little supervision and that fish, for the most part, were entirely capable of managing their own government. Most of Garion's headaches stemmed directly from the grand-sounding title, "Overlord of the West." He had assumed at first—since the war with the Angaraks was over—that this title, like the others, was merely something in the nature of a formality, something impressive, but largely empty, which had been tacked on to all the rest, sort of to round them out. It earned him, after all, no tax revenue; it had no special crown or throne; and there was no administrative staff to deal with day-to-day problems.

But to his chagrin, he soon discovered that one of the peculiarities of human nature was the tendency to want to take problems to the person in charge. Had there *not* been an Overlord of the West, he was quite sure that his fellow monarchs would have found ways to deal with all those perplexing difficulties by themselves. But as long as he occupied that exalted position, they all seemed to take an almost childlike delight in bringing him the most difficult, the most agonizing, and the most utterly insoluble problems and then happily sitting back with trusting smiles on their faces while he struggled and floundered with them.

As a case in point, there was the situation which arose in Arendia during the summer of Garion's twenty-third year. The year had gone fairly well up until that point. The misunderstanding which had marred his relationship with Ce'Nedra had been smoothed over, and Garion and his complicated little wife were living together in what might best be described as domestic felicity. The campaign of Emperor Kal Zakath of Mallorea, whose presence on this continent had been a great cause for concern, had bogged down in the mountains of western Cthol Murgos and showed some promise of grinding on for decades far from the borders of any of the Kingdoms of the West. General Varana, the Duke of Anadile, functioning as regent for the ailing Emperor Ran Borune XXIII, had clamped down quite firmly on the excesses of the great families of Tolnedra in their unseemly scramble for the Imperial Throne. All in all, Garion had been looking forward to a period of peace and tranquility until that warm, early summer day when the letter arrived from King Korodullin of Arendia.

Garion and Ce'Nedra had been spending a quiet afternoon together in the comfortable royal apartment, talking idly of little, unimportant things—more for the pleasure of each other's company than out of any real concern for the subjects at hand. Garion lounged in a large, blue velvet armchair by the window, and Ce'Nedra sat before a gilt-edged mirror, brushing her long, copper-colored hair. Garion was very fond of Ce'Nedra's hair. Its color was exciting. It smelled good, and there was one delightfully vagrant curl that always seemed to want to tumble appealingly down the side of her smooth, white neck. When the servant brought the letter from the King of Arendia, tastefully carried on a silver tray, Garion took his eyes off his lovely wife almost regretfully. He broke the ornately stamped wax seal and opened the crackling parchment.

"Who is it from, Garion?" Ce'Nedra asked, still puffing the brush through her hair and regarding her reflection in the mirror with a kind of dreamy contentment.

"Korodullin," he replied and then began to read.

"To his Majesty, King Belgarion of Riva, Overlord of the West, greetings:" the letter began.

"It is our fervent hope that this finds thee and thy queen in good health and tranquil spirits. Gladly would I permit my pen the leisure to dwell fulsomely upon the regard and affection my queen and I bear thee and her Majesty, but a crisis hath arisen here in Arendia; and because it doth derive directly from the actions of certain friends of thine, I have resolved to seek thy aid in meeting it.

"To our great sorrow, our dear friend the Baron of Vo Ebor succumbed at last to those grievous wounds which he received upon the battlefield at Thull Mardu. His passing this spring hath grieved us more than I can tell thee. He was a good and faithful knight. His heir, since he and the Baroness Nerina were childless, is a distant nephew, one Sir Embrig, a somewhat rash knight more interested, I fear, in the title and lands of his inheritance than in the fact that he doth intrude himself upon the tragic baroness. With airs most unbecoming to one of gentle birth, he journeyed straightway to Vo Ebor to take possession of his new estates and with him he brought diverse other knights of his acquaintance, his cronies and drinking companions. When they reached Vo Ebor, Sir Embrig and his cohorts gave themselves over to unseemly carouse, and when they were all deep in their cups, one of these

rude knights expressed admiration for the person of the but recently widowed Nerina. Without pausing to think or to consider the lady's bereavement, Sir Embrig
promptly promised her hand to his drunken companion. Now in Arendia, by reason of certain of our laws, Sir Embrig hath indeed this right, though no true knight
would so incivilly insist on imposing his will upon a kinswoman in her time of grief.

"The news of this outrage was carried at once to Sir Mandorallen, the mighty
Baron of Vo Mandor, and that great knight went immediately to horse. What tran-
spired upon his arrival at Vo Ebor thou canst well imagine, given Sir Mandorallen's
prowess and the depth of his regard for the Baroness Nerina. Sir Embrig and his cohorts rashly attempted to stand in his path, and there were, as I understand, some
fatalities and a great number of grievous injuries as a result. Thy friend removed the
baroness to his own keep at Vo Mandor, where he holds her in protective custody.
Sir Embrig, who—regrettably perhaps—will recover from his wounds, hath declared that a state of war doth exist between Ebor and Mandor and he hath summoned to his cause diverse noblemen. Other noblemen flock to the banner of Sir
Mandorallen, and southwestern Arendia doth stand on the brink of general war. I
have even been informed that Lelldorin of Wildantor, ever a rash youth, hath raised
an army of Asturian bowmen and at this moment doth march southward with
them, intending to aid his old comrade in arms.

"Thus it doth stand. Know that I am reluctant to bring the power of the
Arendish crown to bear in this matter, since, should I be compelled to make a judgment, I would be forced by our laws to decide in favor of Sir Embrig.

"I appeal to thee, King Belgarion, to come to Arendia and to use thy influence
with thy former companions and dear friends to bring them back from the precipice
upon which they now stand. Only thy intercession, I fear, can avert this impending
disaster.

In hope and friendship,
Korodullin."

Garion stared helplessly at the letter. "Why me?" he demanded without even
thinking.

"What does he say, dear?" Ce'Nedra asked, laying aside her brush and picking
up an ivory comb.

"He says that—" Garion broke off. "Mandorallen and Lelldorin—" He got up
and began to swear. "Here," he said, thrusting the letter at her. "Read it." He began
to pace up and down with his fists clenched behind his back, still muttering curse
words.

Ce'Nedra read the letter as he continued pacing. "Oh dear," she said finally in
dismay. "Oh dear."

"That sums it up pretty well, I'd say." He started swearing again.

"Garion, please don't use that kind of language. It makes you sound like a pi-
rate. What are you going to do about this?"

"I haven't got the faintest idea."

"Well, you're going to have to do *something*."

"Why me?" he burst out. "Why do they always bring these things to me?"

"Because they all know that you can take care of these little problems better
than anybody else."

"Thanks," he said drily.

"Be nice," she told him. Then she pursed her lips thoughtfully, tapping her cheek with the ivory comb. "You'll need your crown, of course—and I think the blue and silver doublet would be nice."

"What are you talking about?"

"You're going to have to go to Arendia to get this all straightened out, and I think you should look your very best—Arends are so conscious of appearances. Why don't you go see about a ship? I'll pack a few things for you." She looked out the window at the golden afternoon sunlight. "Do you think it might be too warm for you to wear your ermine?"

"I won't be wearing ermine, Ce'Nedra. I'll be wearing armor and my sword."

"Oh, don't be so dramatic, Garion. All you have to do is go there and tell them to stop."

"Maybe, but I have to get their attention first. This is Mandorallen we're talk-ing about—and Lelldorin. We're not dealing with sensible people, remember?"

A little frown creased her forehead. "That *is* true," she admitted. But then she gave him an encouraging little smile. "I'm sure you can fix it, though. I have every confidence in you."

"You're as bad as all the rest," he said a bit sullenly.

"But you *can,* Garion. Everybody says so."

"I guess I'd better go talk to Brand," he said glumly.

"There are some things that need to be attended to, and this is likely to take me a few weeks."

"I'll take care of them for you, dear," she said reassuringly, reaching up and pat-ting his cheek. "You just run along now. I can manage things here very well while you're gone."

He stared at her with a sinking feeling in the pit of his stomach.

When he arrived at Vo Mandor on a cloudy morning several days later, the sit-uation had deteriorated even further. The forces of Sir Embrig were in the field, en-camped not three leagues from Mandorallen's castle, and Mandorallen and Lelldorin had marched from the city to meet them. Garion thundered up to the gates of his friend's stout fortress on the war horse he had borrowed from an accommodating baron upon his arrival in Arendia. He wore the full suit of steel armor that had been a gift from King Korodullin, and Iron-grip's enormous sword rode in its scab-bard across his back. The gates swung wide for him, and he entered the courtyard, swung awkwardly down from his saddle, and demanded to be taken immediately to the Baroness Nerina.

He found her pale-faced and dressed all in black, standing somberly on the bat-tlements, searching the cloudy sky to the east for the telltale columns of smoke which would announce that the battle had begun. "It doth lie upon me, King Bel-garion," she declared almost morbidly. "Strife and discord and anguish hath derived from me since the day I first wed my dear departed lord."

"There's no need to blame yourself," Garion told her. "Mandorallen can usually get himself into trouble without help from anyone. When did he and Lelldorin leave?"

"Somewhat past noon yesterday," she replied. "Methinks the battle will be joined 'ere long." She looked mournfully down at the flagstones of a courtyard lying far below and sighed.

"I guess I'd better go then," he said grimly. "Maybe if I can get there before they start, I can head this off."

"I have just had a most excellent thought, your Majesty," she declared, a bright little smile lighting up her pale face. "I can make thy task much easier."

"I hope *somebody* can," he said. "The way things look right now, I'm going to be in for a very bad morning."

"Make haste then, your Majesty, to the field where rude war even now doth hover above our dear friends, and advise them that the cause of their impending battle hath departed from this sad world."

"I'm not sure I follow that."

"It is most simple, your Majesty. Since *I* am the cause of all this strife, it doth lie upon me to end it."

He looked at her suspiciously. "Just what are we talking about here, Nerina? How do you propose to bring all those idiots to their senses?"

Her smile became actually radiant. "I have but to hurl myself from this lofty battlement, my Lord, and join my husband in the silence of the grave to end this dreadful bloodshed before it hath begun. Go quickly, my Lord. Descend to that courtyard far below and take to horse. I will descend by this shorter, happier route and await thee upon those rude stones below. Then mayest thou carry the news of my death to the battlefield. Once I am dead, no man's blood need be spilt over me." She put one hand on the rough stone of the parapet.

"Oh, stop that," he said in disgust, "and get away from there."

"Ah, nay, your Majesty," she said quite firmly. "This is the best of all possible answers. At one stroke I can avert this impending battle and rid myself of this burdensome life."

"Nerina," he said in a flat voice, "I'm not going to let you jump, and that's all there is to that."

"Surely thou wouldst not be so rude as to lay hands upon my person to prevent me," she said in a shocked tone of voice.

"I won't have to," he said. He looked at her pale, uncomprehending face and realized that she did not have the faintest idea of what he was talking about. "On second thought, maybe it's not such a bad idea after all. The trip down to that courtyard is likely to take you about a day and a half, so it should give you time to think this all the way through—besides, it might just possibly keep you out of mischief while I'm gone."

Her eyes went suddenly wide as what he was saying to her seeped ever so slowly into her mind. "Thou wouldst not use *sorcery* to foil my most excellent solution," she gasped.

"Try me."

She looked at him helplessly, tears coming to her eyes.

"This is most unchivalrous of thee, my Lord," she accused him.

"I was raised on a farm in Sendaria, my Lady," he reminded her. "I didn't have the advantages of a noble upbringing, so I have these little lapses from time to time. I'm sure you'll forgive me for not letting you kill yourself. Now, if you'll excuse me, I have to go stop that nonsense out there." He turned and clanked toward the stairs. "Oh," he said, looking over his shoulder at her, "don't get any ideas about jumping as soon as my back's turned either. I have a long arm, Nerina—a very long arm."

She stared at him, her lip trembling.

"That's better," he said and went on down the stairs.

The servants in Mandorallen's castle took one look at Garion's stormy face as he strode into the courtyard below and prudently melted out of his path. Laboriously, he hauled himself into the saddle of the huge roan war horse upon which he had arrived, adjusted the great sword of the Rivan King in its scabbard across his back, and looked around. "Somebody bring me a lance," he commanded.

They brought him several, stumbling over each other in their haste to comply. He selected one and then set off at a thundering gallop.

The citizens of the town of Vo Mandor, which lay just beyond the walls of Mandorallen's keep, were as prudent as the servants within the walls had been. A wide path was opened along the cobblestone streets as the angry King of Riva passed through, and the town gates stood wide open for him.

Garion knew that he was going to have to get their attention, and Arends on the verge of battle are notoriously difficult to reach. He would need to startle them with something. As he thundered through the green Arendish countryside, past neat, thatch-roofed villages and groves of beech and maple, he cast an appraising eye toward the gray, scudding clouds overhead, and the first faint hints of a plan began to form in his mind.

When he arrived, he found the two armies drawn up on opposite sides of a broad, open meadow. As was the age-old Arendish custom, a number of personal challenges had been issued, and those matters were in the process of being settled as a sort of prelude to the grand general mêlée which would follow. Several armored knights from either side were tilting in the center of the field as the two armies looked on approvingly. Enthusiastically, the brainless, steel-clad young nobles crashed into each other, littering the turf with splinters from the shattered remains of their lances.

Garion took in the situation at a single glance, scarcely pausing before riding directly into the middle of the fray. It must be admitted that he cheated just a little during the encounter. The lance he carried *looked* the same as those with which the Mimbrate knights were attempting to kill or maim each other. About the only real difference lay in the fact that *his* lance, unlike theirs, would not break, no matter what it encountered and was, moreover, enveloped in a kind of nimbus of sheer force. Garion had no real desire to run the sharp steel tip of that lance through anybody. He merely wanted them off their horses. On his first course through the center of the startled, milling knights, he hurled three of them from their saddles in rapid succession. Then he wheeled his charger and unhorsed two more so quickly that the vast clatter they made as they fell merged into a single sound.

It needed a bit more, however, something suitably spectacular to penetrate the solid bone Arends used for heads. Almost negligently, Garion discarded his invincible lance, reached back over his shoulder and drew the mighty sword of the Rivan King. The Orb of Aldur blazed forth its dazzling blue light, and the sword itself immediately burst into flame. As always, despite its vast size, the sword in his hand had no apparent weight, and he wielded it with blinding speed. He drove directly at one startled knight, chopping the amazed man's lance into foot-long chunks as he worked his way up the weapon's shaft. When only the butt remained, Garion smashed the knight from his saddle with the flat of the burning sword. He wheeled then, chopped an upraised mace neatly in two and rode the bearer of the mace into the ground, horse and all.

Stunned by the ferocity of his attack, the wide-eyed Mimbrate knights drew back. It was not merely his overwhelming prowess in battle, however, that made them retreat. From between clenched teeth, the King of Riva was swearing sulfurously, and his choice of oaths made strong men go pale. He looked around, his eyes ablaze, then gathered in his will. He raised his flaming sword and pointed it at the roiling sky overhead. *"NOW!"* he barked in a voice like the cracking of a whip.

The clouds shuddered, almost seeming to flinch as the full force of Belgarion's will smote them. A sizzling bolt of lightning as thick as the trunk of a mighty tree crashed to earth with a deafening thunderclap that shook the ground for miles in every direction. A great, smoking hole appeared in the turf where the bolt had struck. Again and again Garion called down the lightning. The noise of thunder ripped and rolled through the air, and the reek of burning sod and singed earth hung like a cloud over the suddenly terrified armies.

Then a great, howling gale struck; at the same time, the clouds ripped open to inundate the opposing forces in a deluge so intense that many knights were actually hurled from their saddles by the impact. Even as the gale shrieked and the driving downpour struck them, flickering bolts of lightning continued to stagger across the field which separated them, sizzling dreadfully and filling the air with steam and smoke. To cross that field was unthinkable.

Grimly, Garion sat his terrified charger in the very midst of that awful display, with the lightning dancing around him. He let it rain on the two armies for several minutes until he was certain that he had their full attention; then, with a negligent flick of his flaming sword, he turned off the downpour.

"I have had enough of this stupidity!" he announced in a voice as loud as the thunder had been. "Lay down your weapons at once!"

They stared at him and then distrustfully at each other.

"AT ONCE!" Garion roared, emphasizing his command with yet another lightning bolt and a shattering thunderclap.

The clatter of suddenly discarded weapons was enormous.

"I want to see Sir Embrig and Sir Mandorallen right *here,*" Garion said then, pointing with his sword at a spot directly in front of his horse. "Immediately!"

Slowly, almost like reluctant schoolboys, the two steel-clad knights warily approached him.

"Just exactly what do the two of you think you're doing?" Garion demanded of them.

"Mine honor compelled me, your Majesty," Sir Embrig declared in a faltering voice. He was a stout, florid-faced man of about forty with the purple-veined nose of one who drinks heavily. "Sir Mandorallen hath abducted my kinswoman."

"Thy concern for the lady extendeth only to thy authority over her person," Mandorallen retorted hotly. "Thou hast usurped her lands and chattels with churlish disregard for her feelings, and—"

"All right," Garion snapped, "that's enough. Your personal squabble has brought half of Arendia to the brink of war. Is that what you wanted? Are you such a pair of children that you're willing to destroy your homeland just to get your own way?"

"But—" Mandorallen tried to say.

"But nothing." Garion then proceeded—at some length—to tell them exactly what he thought of them. His tone was scornful, and his choice of language wide-ranging. The two frequently went pale as he spoke. Then he saw Lelldorin drawing cautiously near to listen.

"And you!" Garion turned his attention to the young Asturian. "What are *you* doing down here in Mimbre?"

"Me? Well—Mandorallen *is* my friend, Garion."

"Did he ask for your help?"

"Well—"

"I didn't think so. You just took it on yourself." He then included Lelldorin in his commentary, gesturing often with the burning sword in his right hand. The three watched that sword with a certain wide-eyed anxiety as he waved it in their faces.

"Very well, then," Garion said after he had cleared the air, "this is what we're going to do." He looked belligerently at Sir Embrig. "Do you want to fight me?" he challenged, thrusting out his jaw pugnaciously.

Sir Embrig's face went a pasty white, and his eyes started from his head. "*Me*, your Majesty?" he gasped. "Thou wouldst have *me* take the field against the God-slayer?" He began to tremble violently.

"I didn't think so." Garion grunted. "Since that's the case, you'll immediately relinquish all claim of authority over the Baroness Nerina to *me*."

"Most gladly, your Majesty." Embrig's words tumbled over themselves as they came out.

"Mandorallen," Garion said, "do *you* want to fight me?"

"Thou art my friend, Garion," Mandorallen protested. "I would die before I raised my hand against thee."

"Good. Then *you* will turn all territorial claims on behalf of the baroness over to me—at once. *I* am her protector now."

"I agree to this," Mandorallen replied gravely.

"Sir Embrig," Garion said then, "I bestow upon you the entirety of the Barony of Vo Ebor—including those lands which would normally go to Nerina. Will you accept them?"

"I will, your Majesty."

"Sir Mandorallen, I offer you the hand in marriage of my ward, Nerina of Vo Ebor. Will you accept her?"

"With all my heart, my Lord," Mandorallen choked, with tears coming to his eyes.

"Splendid," Lelldorin said admiringly.

"Shut up, Lelldorin," Garion told him. "That's it, then, gentlemen. Your war is over. Pack up your armies and go home—and if this breaks out again, I'll come back. The next time I have to come down here, I'm going to be *very* angry. Do we all understand each other?"

Mutely they nodded.

That ended the war.

The Baroness Nerina, however, raised certain strenuous objections when she was informed of Garion's decisions upon the return of Mandorallen's army to Vo Mandor. "Am I some common serf girl to be bestowed upon any man who pleases my lord?" she demanded with a fine air of high drama.

"Are you questioning my authority as your guardian?" Garion asked her directly.

"Nay, my Lord. Sir Embrig hath consented to this. Thou art my guardian now. I must do as thou commandest me."

"Do you love Mandorallen?"

She looked quickly at the great knight and then blushed.

"Answer me!"

"I do, my Lord," she confessed in a small voice.

"What's the problem then? You've loved him for years, but when I order you to marry him, you object."

"My Lord," she replied stiffly, "there are certain proprieties to be observed. A lady may not be so churlishly disposed of." And with that she turned her back and stormed away.

Mandorallen groaned, and a sob escaped him.

"What is it now?" Garion demanded.

"My Nerina and I will never be wed, I fear," Mandorallen declared brokenly.

"Nonsense. Lelldorin, do *you* understand what this is all about?"

Lelldorin frowned. "I think so, Garion. There are a whole series of rather delicate negotiations and formalities that you're leaping over here. There's the question of the dowry, the formal, written consent of the guardian—that's you, of course—and probably most important, there has to be a formal proposal—with witnesses."

"She's refusing over technicalities?" Garion asked incredulously.

"Technicalities are very important to a woman, Garion."

Garion sighed with resignation. This was going to take longer than he had thought. "Come with me," he told them.

Nerina had locked her door and refused to answer Garion's polite knock. Finally he looked at the stout oak planks barring his way. "Burst!" he said, and the door blew inward, showering the startled lady seated on the bed with splinters. "Now," Garion said, stepping over the wreckage, "let's get down to business. How big a dowry do we think would be appropriate?"

Mandorallen was willing—more than willing—to accept some mere token, but Nerina stubbornly insisted upon something significant. Wincing slightly, Garion made an offer acceptable to the lady. He then called for pen and ink and scribbled—with Lelldorin's aid—a suitable document of consent. "Very well," he said then to Mandorallen, "ask her."

"Such proposal doth not customarily come with such unseemly haste, your Majesty," Nerina protested. "It is considered proper for the couple to have some time to acquaint themselves with each other."

"You're already acquainted, Nerina," he reminded her. "Get on with it."

Mandorallen sank to his knees before his lady, his armor clinking on the floor. "Wilt thou have me as thy husband, Nerina?" he implored her.

She stared at him helplessly. "I have not, my Lord, had time to frame a suitable reply."

"Try 'yes,' Nerina," Garion suggested.

"Is such thy command, my Lord?"

"If you want to put it that way."

"I must obey, then. I will have thee, Sir Mandorallen—with all my heart."

"Splendid," Garion said briskly, rubbing his hands together. "Get up, Mandorallen, and let's go down to your chapel. We'll find a priest and get this all formalized by suppertime."

"Surely thou art not proposing such haste, my Lord," Nerina gasped.

"As a matter of fact, I am. I have to get back to Riva and I'm not going to leave here until the two of you are safely married. Things have a way of going wrong in Arendia if somebody isn't around to watch them."

"I am not suitably attired, your Majesty," Nerina protested, looking down at her black dress. "Thou wouldst not have me married in a gown of sable hue?"

"And I," Mandorallen also objected, "I am still under arms. A man should not approach his wedding clad in steel."

"I don't have the slightest concern about what either of you is wearing," Garion informed them. "It's what's in your hearts that's important, not what's on your backs."

"But—" Nerina faltered. "I do not even have a veil."

Garion gave her a long, steady look. Then he cast a quick look around the room, picked up a lace doily from a nearby table and set it neatly atop the lady's head. "Charming," he murmured. "Can anyone think of anything else?"

"A ring?" Lelldorin suggested hesitantly.

Garion turned to stare at him. "You, too?" he said.

"They really ought to have a ring, Garion," Lelldorin said defensively.

Garion considered that for a moment, concentrated, and then forged a plain gold ring out of insubstantial air. "Will this do?" he asked, holding it out to them.

"Might I not be attended?" Nerina asked in a small, trembling voice. "It is unseemly for a noblewoman to be wed without the presence of some lady of suitable rank to support and encourage her."

"Go fetch somebody," Garion said to Lelldorin.

"Whom should I select?" Lelldorin asked helplessly.

"I don't care. Just bring a lady of noble birth to the chapel—even if you have to drag her by the hair."

Lelldorin scurried out.

"Is there anything else?" Garion asked Mandorallen and Nerina in the slightly dangerous tone that indicated that his patience was wearing very thin.

"It is customary for a bridegroom to be accompanied by a close friend, Garion," Mandorallen reminded him.

"Lelldorin will be there," Garion said, "and so will I. We won't let you fall down or faint or run away."

"Might I not have a few small flowers?" Nerina asked in a plaintive voice.

Garion looked at her. "Certainly," he replied in a deceptively mild tone. "Hold out your hand." He then began to create lilies—rapidly—popping them out of empty air and depositing them one after another in the startled lady's hand. "Are they the right color, Nerina?" he asked her. "I can change them if you like—purple, perhaps, or chartreuse, or maybe bright blue would suit you."

And then he finally decided that he was not really getting anywhere. They were going to continue to raise objections for as long as they possibly could. They were both so accustomed to living in the very heart of their colossal tragedy that they were unwilling—unable even—to give up their mournful entertainment. The solution, of necessity, was going to be entirely up to him. Knowing that it was a trifle overdramatic, but considering the mental capabilities of the two involved, he drew his sword. "We are all now going directly to the chapel," he announced, "and the two of you are going to get married." He pointed at the splintered door with the sword. "Now march!" he commanded.

And so it was that one of the great tragic love stories of all time came at last to a happy ending. Mandorallen and his Nerina were married that very afternoon, with Garion quite literally standing over them with flaming sword to insure that no last-minute hitches could interrupt.

On the whole, Garion was rather pleased with himself and with the way he had handled things. His mood was self-congratulatory as he departed the following morning to return to Riva.

CHAPTER TEN

"Anyway," Garion was saying as he and Ce'Nedra relaxed in their blue-carpeted sitting room on the evening of his return to Riva, "when we got back to Mandorallen's castle and told Nerina that it was all right for them to get married, she raised all kinds of objections."

"I always thought she loved him," Ce'Nedra said.

"She does, but she's been in the very center of this great tragic situation for all these years, and she didn't really want to give that up. She hadn't got all that noble suffering out of her system yet."

"Don't be snide, Garion."

"Arends make my teeth ache. First she held out for a dowry—a very big one."

"That seems reasonable."

"Not when you consider the fact that *I* had to pay it."

"You? Why should you have to pay it?"

"I'm her guardian, remember? For all of her thee's and thou's and vaporish airs, she haggles like a Drasnian horse trader. By the time she was done, my purse was very lean. And she had to have a formal letter of consent—and a veil, a lady to attend her, a ring, and flowers. And I was getting more irritated by the minute."

"Aren't you forgetting something?"

"I don't think so."

"Didn't Mandorallen propose to her?" Ce'Nedra leaned forward, her little face very intent. "I'm certain that she would have insisted on that."

"You're right, I almost forgot that part."

She shook her head almost sadly. "Oh, Garion," she said in a disapproving tone.

"That came earlier—right after the business with the dowry. Anyway, he proposed, and I made her say yes, and then—"

"Wait a minute," Ce'Nedra said firmly, holding up one little hand. "Don't rush through that part. Exactly what did he say when he asked her?"

Garion scratched his ear. "I'm not sure I remember," he confessed.

"Try," she urged him. "Please."

"Let's see," he pondered, looking up at the ornately carved wooden beams of the ceiling. "First she objected to having the proposal come before they had gone through all the business of 'getting acquainted,' as she put it. I guess she meant all the sneaking around so that they could be alone together in secluded places—and the love poems and the flowers and all those calf-eyed looks."

Ce'Nedra gave him a hard little stare. "You know, sometimes you can be absolutely infuriating. You've got about as much sensitivity as a block of wood."

"What's that supposed to mean?"

"Never mind. Just tell me what happened next."

"Well, I told her straight off that I wasn't having any of *that* nonsense. I said that they were already acquainted and to get on with it."

"You're just full of charm, aren't you?" she said sarcastically.

"Ce'Nedra, what *is* the problem here?"

"Never mind. Just get on with the story. You always dawdle so when you're telling me about something like this."

"Me? You're the one who keeps interrupting."

"Just move along with it, Garion."

He shrugged. "There isn't much more. He asked her; she said yes; and then I marched them down to the chapel."

"The words, Garion," she insisted. "The words. Exactly what did he say?"

"Nothing very earth-shaking. It went sort of like 'Wilt thou have me as thy husband, Nerina?' "

"Oh," Ce'Nedra said with a catch in her voice. He was astonished to see tears in her eyes.

"What's the matter?" he demanded.

"Never mind," she replied, dabbing at her eyes with a wispy scrap of a handkerchief. "What did she say then?"

"She said that she hadn't had time to work up a suitable answer, so I told her just to say 'yes'."

"And?"

"She said, 'I will have thee, Sir Mandorallen—with all my heart.' "

"Oh," Ce'Nedra said again, her handkerchief going once more to her brimming eyes. "That's just lovely."

"If you say so," he said. "It seemed a little drawn-out to me."

"Sometimes you're hopeless," she told him. Then she sighed a little forlornly. "I never got a formal proposal," she said.

"You most certainly did," he said indignantly. "Don't you remember all that ceremony when you and the Tolnedran Ambassador came into the throne room?"

"*I* did the proposing, Garion," she reminded him with a toss of her flaming curls. "I presented myself before your throne and asked you if you would consent to take me to wife. You agreed, and that's all there was to it. You never once asked *me*."

He frowned and thought back. "I *must* have."

"Not once."

"Well, as long as we got married, anyway, it doesn't really matter all that much, does it?"

Her expression turned to ice.

He caught that look. "Is it really that important, Ce'Nedra?" he asked her.

"Yes, Garion. It is."

He sighed. "All right then. I guess I'd better do it."

"Do what?"

"Propose. Will you marry me, Ce'Nedra?"

"Is that the best you can do?"

He gave her a long, steady look. She was, he had to admit, very appealing. She was wearing a pale green dress, all frilly and touched here and there with lace, and she sat rather primly in her chair, looking pouty and discontented. He arose from his chair, crossed to where she sat, and sank extravagantly to his knees. He took her small hand in both of his and looked imploringly into her face, trying to match the look of fatuous adoration that Mandorallen had worn. "Will her Imperial Highness consent to have me as her husband?" he asked her. "I can offer little besides an honest, loving heart and boundless devotion."

"Are you making fun of me?" she asked suspiciously.

"No." he said. "You wanted a formal proposal, so I just gave you one. Well?"

"Well what?"

"Will you consent to marry me?"

She gave him an arch look, her eyes twinkling. Then she reached out fondly and tousled his hair. "I'll think about it," she replied.

"What do you mean, you'll think about it?"

"Who knows?" she said with a smirk. "I might get a better offer. Do get up, Garion. You'll make the knees of your hose all baggy if you stay down on the floor like that."

He got to his feet. "Women!" he said exasperatedly, throwing his arms in the air.

She gave him that tiny, wide-eyed look that at one time, before he had come to recognize it as pure deception, had always made his knees go weak. "Don't you love me any more?" she asked in that trembling, dishonest, little-girl voice.

"Didn't we decide that we weren't going to do that to each other any more?"

"This is a special occasion, dear," she replied. And then she laughed, sprang up from her chair, and threw her arms about his neck. "Oh, Garion," she said, still laughing. "I *do* love you."

"I certainly hope so," he said, wrapping his arms around her shoulders and kissing her upturned lips.

The following morning Garion dressed rather informally and then tapped on the door to Ce'Nedra's private sitting room.

"Yes?" she answered.

"It's Garion," he said. "May I come in?" His Sendarian good manners had been so deeply ingrained in him that even though he was the King here, he always asked permission before opening the door to someone else's room.

"Of course," she said.

He turned the latch and entered her frilly private domain, a room all pink and pale green flounces and with yards of rustling satin and brocade drapery. Ce'Nedra's favorite lady-in-waiting, Arell, rose in some confusion to perform the customary curtsy. Arell was Brand's niece, the daughter of his youngest sister, and she was one of several highborn Rivan ladies who attended the queen. She was very nearly the archetypical Alorn woman, tall, blond, and buxom, with golden braids coiled about her head, deep blue eyes and a complexion like new milk. She and Ce'Nedra were virtually inseparable, and the two spent much of their time with their heads together, whispering and giggling. For some reason, Arell always blushed rosily whenever Garion entered the room. He did not understand that at all, but privately suspected that Ce'Nedra had told her lady-in-waiting certain things that really *should* have remained private—things that brought a blush to the Rivan girl's cheeks whenever she looked at him.

"I'm going down into the city," Garion told his wife. "Did you want anything?"

"I prefer to do my own shopping, Garion," Ce'Nedra replied, smoothing the front of her satin dressing gown. "You never get things right anyway."

He was about to reply to that, but decided against it. "Whatever you want. I'll see you at luncheon then."

"As my Lord commands," Ce'Nedra said with a mocking little genuflection.

"Stop that."

She made a face at him and then came over and kissed him.

Garion turned to Arell. "My Lady," he said, bowing politely.

Arell's blue eyes were filled with suppressed mirth, and there was a slightly speculative look in them as well. She blushed and curtsied again. "Your Majesty," she said respectfully.

As Garion left the royal apartment, he wondered idly what Ce'Nedra had told Arell to cause all those blushes and peculiar looks. He was grateful to the blond girl, however. Her presence provided Ce'Nedra with company, which left him free to attend to other matters. Since Aunt Pol had intervened and healed the estrangement that had caused them both so much anguish, Ce'Nedra had become very possessive about Garion's spare time. On the whole he felt that being married was rather nice, but sometimes Ce'Nedra tended to overdo things a bit.

In the corridor outside, Brand's second son, Kail, was waiting, holding a parchment sheet in his hand. "I think this needs your immediate attention, Sire," he said formally.

Although Kail was a warrior, tall and broad-shouldered like his father and his brothers, he was nonetheless a studious man, intelligent and discreet, and he knew enough about Riva and its people to be able to sort through the voluminous petitions, appeals, and proposals directed to the throne and to separate the important from the trivial. When Garion had first come to the throne, the need for someone to manage the administrative staff had been painfully clear, and Kail had been the obvious choice for that post. He was about twenty-four years old and wore a neatly trimmed brown beard. The hours he had spent in study had given him a slight squint and a permanent furrow between his eyebrows. Since he and Garion spent several hours a day together, they had soon become friends, and Garion greatly respected Kail's judgment and advice. "Is it serious?" he asked, taking the parchment and glancing at it.

"It could be, Sire," Kail replied. "There's a dispute over the ownership of a certain valley. The families involved are both quite powerful, and I think we'll want to settle the matter before things go any further."

"Is there any clear-cut evidence of ownership on either side?"

Kail shook his head. "The two families have used the land in common for centuries. There's been some friction between them lately, however."

"I see," Garion said. He thought about it. "No matter what I decide, one side or the other is going to be unhappy with me, right?"

"Very probably, your Majesty."

"All right, then. We'll let them both be unhappy. Write up something that sounds sort of official declaring that this valley of theirs now belongs to me. We'll let them stew about that for a week or so, and then I'll divide the land right down the middle and give half to each of them. They'll be so angry with me that they'll forget that they don't like each other. I don't want this island turning into another Arendia."

Kail laughed. "Very practical, Belgarion," he said.

Garion grinned at him. "I grew up in Sendaria, remember? Oh, keep a strip of the valley—about a hundred yards wide right through the center. Call it crown land or something and forbid them to trespass on it. That should keep them from butting heads along the fence line." He handed the parchment back to Kail and went on down the corridor, rather pleased with himself.

His mission in the city that morning took him to the shop of a young glass blower of his acquaintance, a skilled artisan named Joran. Ostensibly the visit was for the purpose of inspecting a set of crystal goblets he had commissioned as a present for Ce'Nedra. Its real purpose, however, was somewhat more serious. Because his upbringing had been humble, Garion was more aware than most monarchs that the opinions and problems of the common people seldom came to the attention of the throne. He strongly felt that he needed a pair of ears in the city—not to spy out unfavorable opinion, but rather to give him a clear, unprejudiced awareness of the real problems of his people. Joran had been his choice for that task.

After they had gone through the motions of looking at the goblets, the two of them went into a small, private room at the back of Joran's shop.

"I got your note as soon as I got back from Arendia," Garion said. "Is the matter really that serious?"

"I believe so, your Majesty," Joran replied. "The tax was poorly thought out, I think, and it's causing a great deal of unfavorable comment."

"All directed at me, I suppose?"

"You *are* the king, after all."

"Thanks," Garion said drily. "What's the main dissatisfaction with it?"

"All taxes are odious," Joran observed, "but they're bearable as long as everybody has to pay the same. It's the exclusion that irritates people."

"Exclusion? What's that?"

"The nobility doesn't have to pay commercial taxes. Didn't you know that?"

"No," Garion said. "I didn't."

"The theory was that nobles have other obligations—raising and supporting troops and so on. That simply doesn't hold true any more. The crown raises its own army now. If a nobleman goes into trade, though, he doesn't have to pay any commercial taxes. The only real difference between him and any other tradesman is that he happens to have a title. His shop is the same as mine, and he spends his time the same way that I do—but I have to pay the tax, and he doesn't."

"That doesn't seem very fair," Garion agreed.

"What makes it worse is that I have to charge higher prices in order to pay the tax, but the nobleman can cut his rates and steal my customers away from me."

"That's going to have to be fixed," Garion said. "We'll eliminate that exclusion."

"The nobles won't like it," Joran warned.

"They don't have to like it," Garion said flatly.

"You're a very fair king, your Majesty."

"Fairness doesn't really have all that much to do with it," Garion disagreed. "How many nobles are in business here in the city?"

Joran shrugged. "A couple dozen, I suppose."

"And how many other businessmen are there?"

"Hundreds."

"I'd rather have two dozen people hate me than several hundred."

"I hadn't thought of it that way," Joran admitted.

"I sort of have to," Garion said wryly.

The following week a series of squalls swept in off the Sea of the Winds, raking the rocky isle with chill gales and tattered sheets of slanting rain. The weather at Riva was never really what one would call pleasant for very long, and these summer storms were so common that the Rivans accepted them as part of the natural order

of things. Ce'Nedra, however, had been raised far to the south in the endless sunshine at Tol Honeth, and the damp chill which invaded the Citadel each time the
sky turned gray and soggy depressed her spirits and made her irritable and out of
sorts. She customarily endured these spells of bad weather by ensconcing herself in
a large green velvet armchair by the fire with a warm blanket, a cup of tea, and an
oversized book—usually an Arendish romance which dwelt fulsomely on impossibly splendid knights and sighing ladies perpetually on the verge of disaster. Pro-
longed confinement, however, almost always drove her at last from her book in
search of other diversions.

One midmorning when the wind was moaning in the chimneys and the rain
was slashing at the windows, she entered the study where Garion was carefully
going over an exhaustive report on wool production on crown lands in the north.
The little queen wore an ermine-trimmed gown of green velvet and a discontented
expression. "What are you doing?" she asked.

"Reading about wool," he replied.

"Why?"

"I think I'm supposed to know about it. Everybody stands around talking
about wool with these sober expressions on their faces. It seems to be terribly important to them."

"Do you really care that much about it?"

He shrugged. "It helps to pay the bills."

She drifted over to the window and stared out at the rain. "Will it *never* stop?"
she demanded at last.

"Eventually, I suppose."

"I think I'll send for Arell. Maybe we can go down into the city and look
around the shops."

"It's pretty wet out there, Ce'Nedra."

"I can wear a cloak, and a little rain won't make me melt. Would you give me
some money?"

"I thought I gave you some just last week."

"I spent it. Now I need some more."

Garion put aside the report and went to a heavy cabinet standing against the
wall. He took a key from a pocket in his doublet, unlocked the cabinet, and pulled
out the top drawer. Ce'Nedra came over and looked curiously into the drawer. It
was about half-filled with coins, gold, silver, and copper, all jumbled together.

"Where did you get all of that?" she exclaimed.

"They give it to me from time to time," he answered. "I throw it in there because I don't want to carry it around. I thought you knew about it."

"How would I know about it? You never tell me anything. How much have
you got in there?"

He shrugged. "I don't know."

"Garion!" Her voice was shocked. "Don't you even count it?"

"No. Should I?"

"You're obviously not a Tolnedran. This isn't the whole royal treasury, is it?"

"No. They keep that someplace else. This is just for personal expenses, I think."

"It *has* to be counted, Garion."

"I don't really have the time, Ce'Nedra."

"Well, I do. Pull that drawer out and bring it over to the table."

He did that, grunting slightly at the weight, and then stood smiling fondly as she sat down and happily started counting money. He had not realized just how much sheer pleasure she could take in handling and stacking coins. She actually glowed as the merry tinkle of money filled her ears. A few of the coins had become tarnished. She looked at those disapprovingly and stopped her count to polish them carefully on the hem of her gown.

"Were you going to go down into the city?" he asked, resuming his seat at the other end of the table.

"Not today, I guess." She kept on counting. A single lock of her hair strayed down across her face, and she absently blew at it from time to time as she concentrated on the task at hand. She dug another handful of jingling coins out of the drawer and began to stack them carefully on the table in front of her. She looked so serious about it that Garion started to laugh.

She looked up sharply. "What's so funny?" she demanded.

"Nothing, dear," he said and went back to work to the clinking accompaniment of Ce'Nedra's counting.

As the summer wore on, the news from the southern latitudes continued to be good. King Urgit of Cthol Murgos had retreated deeper into the mountains, and the advance of the Emperor Kal Zakath of Mallorea slowed even more. The Mallorean army had suffered dreadful losses in its first efforts to pursue the Murgos in that craggy wasteland and it now moved with extreme caution. Garion received the news of the near-stalemate in the south with great satisfaction.

Toward the end of summer, word arrived from Algaria that Garion's cousin Adara had just presented Hettar with their second son. Ce'Nedra went wild with delight and dipped deeply into the drawer in Garion's study to buy suitable gifts for both mother and child.

The news which arrived in early autumn, however, was not so joyous. In a sadly worded letter, General Varana advised them that Ce'Nedra's father, Emperor Ran Borune XXIII, was sinking fast and that they should make haste to Tol Honeth. Fortunately, the autumn sky remained clear as the ship which carried the Rivan King and his desperately worried little wife ran south before a good following breeze. They reached Tol Horb at the broad mouth of the Nedrane within a week and then began rowing upriver to the Imperial Capital at Tol Honeth.

They had gone no more than a few leagues when their ship was met by a flotilla of white and gold barges, which formed up around them to escort them to Tol Honeth. Aboard those barges was a chorus of young Tolnedran women who strewed flower petals on the broad surface of the Nedrane and caroled a formal greeting to the Imperial Princess.

Garion stood beside Ce'Nedra on the deck of their ship, frowning slightly at this choral welcome. "Is that altogether appropriate?" he asked.

"It's the custom," she said. "Members of the Imperial Family are always escorted to the city."

Garion listened to the words of the song. "Haven't they heard about your wedding yet?" he asked. "They're greeting the Imperial Princess, not the Rivan Queen."

"We're a provincial people, Garion," Ce'Nedra said. "In a Tolnedran's eyes, an Imperial Princess is much more important than the queen of some remote island."

The singing continued as they moved on upriver. As the gleaming white city of Tol Honeth came into view, a huge brazen fanfare greeted them from the walls. A detachment of burnished legionnaires, their scarlet pennons snapping in the breeze and the plumes on their helmets tossing, awaited them on the marble quay to escort them through the broad avenues to the grounds of the Imperial Palace.

General Varana, a blocky-looking professional soldier with short-cropped, curly hair and a noticeable limp, met them at the palace gate. His expression was somber.

"Are we in time, uncle?" Ce'Nedra asked with an almost frightened note in her voice.

The general nodded, then took the little queen in his arms. "You're going to have to be brave, Ce'Nedra," he told her. "Your father is very, very ill."

"Is there any hope at all?" she asked in a small voice.

"We can always hope," Varana replied, but his tone said otherwise.

"Can I see him now?"

"Of course." The general looked gravely at Garion. "Your Majesty," he said, nodding.

"Your Highness," Garion replied, remembering that Ce'Nedra's wily father had "adopted" Varana several years back, and that the general was heir apparent to the Imperial Throne.

Varana led them with his limping gait through the marble corridors of the vast palace to a quiet wing and a door flanked by a towering pair of legionnaires in burnished breastplates. As they approached, the heavy door opened quietly, and Lord Morin, the brown-mantled Imperial Chamberlain emerged. Morin had aged since Garion had last seen him, and his concern for his failing Emperor was written clearly on his face.

"Dear Morin," Ce'Nedra said, impulsively embracing her father's closest friend.

"Little Ce'Nedra," he replied fondly. "I'm so glad you're in time. He's been asking for you. I think perhaps the fact you were coming is all he's been hanging on to."

"Is he awake?"

Morin nodded. "He dozes a great deal, but he's still alert most of the time."

Ce'Nedra drew herself up, squared her shoulders, and carefully assumed a bright, optimistic smile. "All right," she said. "Let's go in."

Ran Borune lay in a vast canopied bed beneath a gold-colored coverlet. He had never been a large man, and his illness had wasted him down to a near-skeleton. His complexion was not so much pale as it was gray, and his beaklike nose was pinched and rose from his drawn face like the prow of a ship. His eyes were closed, and his thin chest seemed almost to flutter as he struggled to breathe.

"Father?" Ce'Nedra said so softly that her voice was hardly more than a whisper.

The Emperor opened one eye. "Well," he said testily, "I see that you finally got here."

"Nothing could have kept me away," she told him, bending over the bed to kiss his withered cheek.

"That's hardly encouraging," he grunted.

"Now that I'm here, we'll have to see about getting you well again."

"Don't patronize me, Ce'Nedra. My physicians have given up entirely."

"What do they know? We Borunes are indestructible."

"Did someone pass that law while I wasn't looking?" The Emperor looked past his daughter's shoulder at his son-in-law. "You're looking well, Garion," he said. "And please don't waste your time on platitudes by telling me how well *I* look. I look awful, don't I?"

"Moderately awful, yes," Garion replied.

Ran Borune flashed him a quick little grin. Then he turned back to his daughter. "Well, Ce'Nedra," he said pleasantly, "what shall we fight about today?"

"Fight? Who said we were going to fight?"

"We always fight. I've been looking forward to it. I haven't had a really good fight since you stole my legions that day."

"Borrowed, father," she corrected primly, almost in spite of herself.

"Is that what you call it?" He winked broadly at Garion. "You should have been there," he chuckled. "She goaded me into a fit and then pinched my whole army while I was frothing at the mouth."

"Pinched!" Ce'Nedra exclaimed.

Ran Borune began to chuckle, but his laughter turned into a tearing cough that left him gasping and so weak that he could not even raise his head. He closed his eyes then and dozed for a while as Ce'Nedra hovered anxiously over him.

After a quarter of an hour or so, Lord Morin quietly entered with a small flask and a silver spoon. "It's time for his medicine," he said softly to Ce'Nedra. "I don't think it really helps very much, but we go through the motions anyway."

"Is that you, Morin?" the Emperor asked without opening his eyes.

"Yes, Ran Borune."

"Is there any word from Tol Rane yet?"

"Yes, your Majesty."

"What did they say?"

"I'm afraid the season's over there, too."

"There has to be *one* tree somewhere in the world that's still bearing fruit," the emaciated little man in the imperial bed said exasperatedly.

"His Majesty has expressed a desire for some fresh fruit," Morin told Ce'Nedra and Garion.

"Not just *any* fruit, Morin," Ran Borune wheezed. "Cherries. I want cherries. Right now I'd bestow a Grand Duchy on any man who could bring me ripe cherries."

"Don't be so difficult, father," Ce'Nedra chided him. "The season for cherries was over months ago. How about a nice ripe peach?"

"I don't *want* peaches. I want cherries!"

"Well, you can't have them."

"You're an undutiful daughter, Ce'Nedra," he accused her.

Garion leaned forward and spoke quietly to Ce'Nedra.

"I'll be right back," he told her and went out of the room with Morin. In the corridor outside they met General Varana.

"How is he?" the general asked.

"Peevish," Garion replied. "He wants some cherries."

"I know," Varana said sourly. "He's been asking for them for weeks. Trust a Borune to demand the impossible."

"Are there any cherry trees here on the palace grounds?"

"There are a couple in his private garden. Why?"

"I thought I might have a word with them," Garion said innocently, "explain a few things, and give them a bit of encouragement."

Varana gave him a look of profound disapproval.

"It's not really immoral," Garion assured him.

Varana raised one hand and turned his face away. "Please, Belgarion," he said in a pained voice, "don't try to explain it to me. I don't even want to hear about it. If you're going to do it, just do it and get it over with, but please don't try to convince me that it's in any way natural or wholesome."

"All right," Garion agreed. "Which way did you say that garden was?"

It wasn't really difficult, of course. Garion had seen Belgarath the Sorcerer do it on many occasions. It was no more than ten minutes later that he returned to the corridor outside the sickroom with a small basket of dark purple cherries.

Varana looked steadily at the basket, but said nothing. Garion quietly opened the door and went inside.

Ran Borune lay propped on his pillows, his drawn face sagging with exhaustion. "I don't see why not," he was saying to Ce'Nedra. "A respectful daughter would have presented her father with a half-dozen grandchildren by now."

"We'll get to it, father," she replied. "Why is everyone so worried about it?"

"Because it's important, Ce'Nedra. Not even *you* could be so silly as to—" He broke off, staring incredulously at the basket in Garion's hand. "Where did you get those?" he demanded.

"I don't think you really want to know, Ran Borune. It's the kind of thing that seems to upset Tolnedrans for some reason."

"You didn't just make them, did you?" the Emperor asked suspiciously.

"No. It's much harder that way. I just gave the trees in your garden a little encouragement, that's all. They were very cooperative."

"What an absolutely splendid fellow you married, Ce'Nedra," Ran Borune exclaimed, eying the cherries greedily. "Put those right here, my boy." He patted the bed at his side.

Ce'Nedra flashed her husband a grateful little smile, took the basket from him, and deposited it by her father's side. Almost absently she took one of the cherries and popped it into her mouth.

"Ce'Nedra! You stop eating my cherries!"

"Just checking to see if they're ripe, father."

"Any idiot can see that they're ripe," he said, clutching the basket possessively to his side. "If you want any, go get your own." He carefully selected one of the plump, glowing cherries and put it in his mouth. "Marvelous," he said, chewing happily.

"Don't spit the seeds on the floor like that, father," Ce'Nedra reproved him.

"It's my floor," he told her. "Mind your own business. Spitting the seeds is part of the fun." He ate several more cherries. "We won't discuss how you came by these, Garion," he said magnanimously. "Technically, it's a violation of Tolnedran law to practice sorcery anywhere in the Empire, but we'll let it pass—just this once."

"Thank you, Ran Borune," Garion said. "I appreciate that."

After he had eaten about half of the cherries, the Emperor smiled and sighed contentedly. "I feel better already," he said. "Ce'Vanne used to bring me fresh cherries in that same kind of basket."

"My mother," Ce'Nedra said to Garion.

Ran Borune's eyes clouded over. "I miss her," he said very quietly. "She was impossible to live with, but I miss her more every day."

"I scarcely remember her," Ce'Nedra said wistfully.

"I remember her very well," her father said. "I'd give my whole Empire if I could see her face just one more time."

Ce'Nedra took his wasted hand in hers and looked imploringly at Garion. "Could you?" she asked, two great tears standing in her eyes.

"I'm not entirely sure," he replied in some perplexity. "I think I know how it's done, but I never met your mother, so I'd have to—" He broke off, still trying to work it out in his mind. "I'm sure Aunt Pol could do it, but—" He came to the bedside. "We can try," he said. He took Ce'Nedra's other hand and then Ran Borune's, linking the three of them together.

It was extremely difficult. Ran Borune's memory was clouded by age and his long illness, and Ce'Nedra's remembrance of her mother was so sketchy that it could hardly be said to exist at all. Garion concentrated, bending all his will upon it. Beads of perspiration stood out on his forehead as he struggled to gather all those fleeting memories into one single image.

The light coming in through the flimsy curtains at the window seemed to darken as if a cloud had passed over the sun, and there was a faint, far-off tinkling sound, as if of small, golden bells. The room was suddenly filled with a kind of woodland fragrance—a subtle smell of moss and leaves and green trees. The light faded a bit more, and the tinkling and the odor grew stronger.

And then there was a hazy, nebulous luminosity in the air at the foot of the dying Emperor's bed. The glow grew brighter, and she was there. Ce'Vanne had been a bit taller than her daughter, but Garion saw instantly why Ran Borune had always so doted on his only child. The hair was precisely the same deep auburn; the complexion was that same golden-tinged olive; and the eyes were of that exact same green. The face was willful, certainly, but the eyes were filled with love.

The figure came silently around the bed, reaching out briefly in passing to touch Ce'Nedra's face with lingering, phantom fingertips. Garion could suddenly see the source of that small bell sound. Ce'Nedra's mother wore the two golden acorn earrings of which her daughter was so fond, and the two tiny clappers inside them gave off that faint, musical tinkle whenever she moved her head. For no particular reason, Garion remembered that those same earrings lay on his wife's dressing table back at Riva.

Ce'Vanne reached out her hand to her husband. Ran Borune's face was filled with wonder, and his eyes with tears. "Ce'Vanne," he said in a trembling whisper, struggling to raise himself from his pillow. He pulled his shaking hand free from Garion's grasp and reached out toward her. For a moment their hands seemed to touch, and then Ran Borune gave a long, quavering sigh, sank back on his pillows, and died.

Ce'Nedra sat for a long time holding her father's hand as the faint, woodland smell and the echo of the little golden bells slowly subsided from the room and the light from the window returned. Finally she placed the wasted hand gently back on the coverlet, rose, and looked around the room with an almost casual air. "It's going to have to be aired out, of course," she said absently. "Maybe some cut flowers to sweeten the air." She smoothed the coverlet at the side of the bed and gravely looked at her father's body. Then she turned. "Oh, Garion," she wailed, suddenly throwing herself into his arms.

Garion held her, smoothing her hair and feeling the shaking of her tiny body against him and looking all the while at the still, peaceful face of the Emperor of Tolnedra. It may have been some trick of the light, but it almost seemed that there was a smile on Ran Borune's lips.

CHAPTER ELEVEN

The state funeral for Emperor Ran Borune XXIII of the Third Borune Dynasty took place a few days later in the Temple of Nedra, Lion God of the Empire. The temple was a huge marble building not far from the Imperial Palace. The altar was backed by a vast fan of pure, beaten gold, with the head of a lion in its center. Directly in front of the altar stood the simple marble bier of Ce'Nedra's father. The late Emperor lay in calm repose, covered from the neck down by a cloth of gold. The column-lined inner hall of the temple was filled to overflowing as the members of the great families vied with one another, not so much to pay their respects to Ran Borune, but rather to display the opulence of their clothing and the sheer weight of their personal adornment.

Garion and Ce'Nedra, both dressed in deepest mourning, sat beside General Varana at the front of the vast hall as the eulogies were delivered. Tolnedran politics dictated that a representative of each of the major houses should speak upon this sad occasion. The speeches, Garion suspected, had been prepared long in advance. They were all quite flowery and tiresome, and each one seemed to be directed at the point that, although Ran Borune was gone, the Empire lived on. Many of the speakers seemed quite smug about that.

When the eulogies had at last been completed, the white-robed High Priest of Nedra, a pudgy, sweating man with a grossly sensual mouth, arose and stepped to the front of the altar to add his own contribution. Drawing upon events in the life of Ran Borune, he delivered a lengthy homily on the advantages of having wealth and using it wisely. At first Garion was shocked by the High Priest's choice of subject matter, but the rapt faces of the throng in the temple told him that a sermon about money was very moving to a Tolnedran congregation and that the High Priest, by selecting such a topic, was able thereby to slip in any number of laudatory comments about Ce'Nedra's father.

Once all the tedious speeches were completed, the little Emperor was laid to rest beside his wife under a marble slab in the Borune section of the catacombs beneath the temple. The so-called mourners then returned to the main temple hall to express their condolences to the bereaved family. Ce'Nedra bore up well, though she was very pale. On one occasion she swayed slightly, and Garion, without thinking, reached out to support her.

"Don't touch me!" she whispered sharply under her breath, raising her chin sharply.

"What?" Garion was startled.

"We can *not* show any sign of weakness in the presence of our enemies. I will *not* break down for the entertainment of the Honeths or the Horbites or the Vordues. My father would rise from his grave in disgust if I did."

The nobles of all the great houses continued to file past to offer their extensive and obviously counterfeit sympathy to the sable-gowned little Rivan Queen. Garion found their half-concealed smirks contemptible and their barbed jibes disgusting. His face grew more stern and disapproving as the moments passed. His threatening presence soon dampened the enjoyment of the Grand Dukes and their ladies and sycophants. The Tolnedrans were genuinely afraid of this tall, mysterious Alorn monarch who had come out of nowhere to assume Riva's throne and to shake the very earth with his footsteps. Even as they approached Ce'Nedra to deliver their poisonous observations, his cold, grim face made them falter, and many carefully prepared impertinences went unsaid.

At last, disgusted so much that even his Sendarian good manners deserted him, he placed his hand firmly on his wife's elbow. "We will leave now," he said to her in a voice which could be clearly heard by everyone in the vast temple. "The air in this place has turned a trifle rancid."

Ce'Nedra cast him one startled glance, then lifted her chin in her most regal and imperious manner, laid her hand lightly on his arm, and walked with him toward the huge bronze doors. The silence was vast as they moved with stately pace through the throng, and a wide path opened for them.

"That was very nicely done, dear," Ce'Nedra complimented him warmly as they rode in the gold-inlaid imperial carriage back toward the palace.

"It seemed appropriate," he replied. "I'd reached the point where I either had to say something rather pointed or turn the whole lot of them into toads."

"My, what an enchanting thought," she exclaimed. "We could go back, if you want."

When Varana arrived back at the palace an hour or so later, he was positively gloating. "Belgarion," he said with a broad grin, "you're a splendid young fellow, do you know that? With that one word you mortally offended virtually the entire nobility of northern Tolnedra."

"Which word was that?"

"Rancid."

"I'm sorry about that one."

"Don't be. It perfectly describes them."

"It is a bit coarse, though."

"Not under the circumstances. It *did* manage to make you any number of life-long enemies, however."

"That's all I need," Garion replied sourly. "Give me just a few more years, and I'll have enemies in all parts of the world."

"A king isn't really doing his job if he doesn't make enemies, Belgarion. Any jackass can go through life without offending people."

"Thanks."

There had been some uncertainty about which course Varana would follow once Ran Borune was gone. His "adoption" by the late Emperor had clearly been a ruse with very little in the way of legality to back it up. The candidates for the throne, blinded by their own lust for the Imperial Crown, had convinced themselves that he would merely serve as a kind of caretaker until the question of the succession had been settled in the usual fashion.

The issue remained in doubt until his official coronation, which took place two days after Ran Borune's funeral. The gloating exultation among the contenders for the throne was almost audible when the general limped into the Temple of Nedra dressed in his uniform, rather than the traditional gold mantle which only the Emperor was allowed to wear. Obviously this man did not intend to take his elevation seriously. It might cost a bit to bribe him, but the way to the Imperial Palace was still open. The grins were broad as Varana, gleaming in his gold-inlaid breastplate, approached the altar.

The pudgy High Priest bent forward for a moment of whispered consultation. Varana replied, and the ecclesiast's face suddenly went deathly pale. Trembling violently, he opened the gold and crystal cask on the altar and removed the jewel-encrusted Imperial Crown. Varana's short-cropped hair was annointed with the traditional ungent, and the High Priest raised the crown with shaking hands. "I crown thee," he declared in a voice almost squeaky with fright. "—I crown thee Emperor Ran Borune XXIV, Lord of all Tolnedra."

It took a moment for that to sink in. Then the temple was filled with howls of anguished protest as the Tolnedran nobility grasped the fact that by the choice of his imperial name, Varana was clearly announcing that he intended to keep the crown for himself. Those howls were cut off sharply as the Tolnedran legionnaires, who had quietly filed into place along the colonnade surrounding the main temple floor, drew their swords with a huge, steely rasp. The gleaming swords raised in salute.

"Hail Ran Borune!" the legions thundered. "Hail Emperor of Tolnedra!"

And that was that.

That evening as Garion, Ce'Nedra, and the newly crowned Emperor sat together in a crimson-draped private chamber filled with the golden glow of dozens of candles, Varana exclaimed, "Surprise is as important in politics as it is in military tactics, Belgarion. If your opponent doesn't know what you're going to do, there's no way he can prepare countermeasures." The general now openly wore the gold mantle of the Emperor.

"That makes sense," Garion replied, sipping at a goblet of Tolnedran wine. "Wearing your breastplate instead of the Imperial Mantle kept them guessing right up until the last minute."

"That was for a much more practical reason." Varana laughed. "Many of those young nobles have had military training, and we teach our legionnaires how to throw daggers. Since my back was going to be toward them, I wanted a good, solid layer of steel covering the area between my shoulder blades."

"Tolnedran politics are very nervous, aren't they?"

Varana nodded his agreement. "Fun, though," he added.

"You have a peculiar notion of fun. I've had a few daggers thrown at me and I didn't find it all that amusing."

"We Anadiles have always had a peculiar sense of humor."

"Borune, uncle," Ce'Nedra corrected primly.

"What was that, dear?"

"You're a Borune now, not an Anadile—and you should start acting like one."

"Bad-tempered, you mean? That's not really in my nature."

"Ce'Nedra could give you lessons, if you like," Garion offered, grinning fondly at his wife.

"*What?*" Ce'Nedra exclaimed indignantly, her voice going up an octave or so.

"I suppose she could at that," Varana agreed blandly. "She's always been very good at it."

Ce'Nedra sighed mournfully, eyeing the pair of grinning monarchs. Then her expression became artfully tragic. "What's a poor little girl to do?" she asked in a trembling voice. "Here I am, maltreated and abused by both my husband and my brother."

Varana blinked. "You know, I hadn't even thought of that. You *are* my sister now, aren't you?"

"Perhaps you aren't quite as clever as I thought, brother dear," she purred at him. "I *know* that Garion's not quite bright, but I thought better of you."

Garion and Varana exchanged rueful glances.

"Would you gentlemen like to play some more?" Ce'Nedra asked them, her eyes twinkling and a smug smile hovering about her lips.

There was a light tap on the door.

"Yes?" Varana said.

"Lord Morin to see you, your Majesty," the guard outside the door announced.

"Send him in, please."

The Imperial Chamberlain entered quietly. His face was marked by the sorrow he felt at the passing of the man he had served so long and faithfully, but he still performed his duties with the quiet efficiency that had always been his outstanding characteristic.

"Yes, Morin?" Varana said.

"There's someone waiting outside, your Majesty. She's rather notorious, so I thought I should speak to you privately before I presented her to you."

"Notorious?"

"It's the courtesan Bethra, your Majesty," Morin said with a faintly embarrassed look at Ce'Nedra. "She's been—ah—shall we say, useful to the crown in the past. She has access to a great deal of information as a result of her professional activities and she was a longtime friend of Ran Borune's. From time to time she kept him advised of the activities of certain unfriendly nobles. He made arrangements for there to be a way by which she could enter the palace unnoticed so that they could—ah—talk, among other things."

"Why, that sly old fox."

"I have never known her information to be inaccurate, your Majesty," Morin continued. "She says she has something very important to tell you."

"You'd better bring her in, then, Morin," Varana said. "With your permission, of course, dear sister," he added to Ce'Nedra.

"Certainly," Ce'Nedra agreed, her eyes afire with curiosity.

When Morin brought the woman in, she was wearing a light, hooded cloak, but when, with one smooth, round arm, she reached up and pushed the hood back, Garion started slightly. He knew her. He recalled that when he and Aunt Pol and the others had been passing through Tol Honeth during their pursuit of Zedar the Apostate and the stolen Orb, this same woman had accosted Silk for a bantering exchange. As she unfastened the neck of her cloak and let it slide almost sensuously from her creamy shoulders, he saw that she had not changed in the nearly ten years since he had last seen her. Her lustrous, blue-black hair was untouched by any hint of gray. Her startlingly beautiful face was still as smooth as a girl's, and her heavy-lidded eyes were still filled with a sultry wickedness. Her gown was of palest lavender and cut in such a way as to enhance rather than conceal the lush, almost overripe body it enclosed. It was the kind of body that was a direct challenge to every man she met. Garion stared openly at her until he caught Ce'Nedra's green eyes, agate-hard, boring into him, and he quickly looked away.

"Your Majesty," Bethra said in a throaty contralto as she curtsied gracefully to the new Emperor, "I would have waited a time before introducing myself, but I've heard a few things I thought you should know immediately."

"I appreciate your friendship, Lady Bethra," Varana replied with exquisite courtesy.

She laughed a warm, wicked laugh. "I'm not a lady, your Majesty," she corrected him. "Most definitely *not* a lady." She made a small curtsy to Ce'Nedra. "Princess," she murmured.

"Madame," Ce'Nedra responded with a faint chill in her voice and a very slight inclination of her head.

"Ah," Bethra said almost sadly. Then she turned back to Varana. "Late this afternoon I was entertaining Count Ergon and the Baron Kelbor at my establishment."

"A pair of powerful Honethite nobles," Varana explained to Garion.

"The gentlemen from the house of Honeth are less than pleased with your Majesty's choice of an official name," Bethra continued. "They spoke hastily and in some heat, but I think that you might want to take what they said seriously. Ergon is an unmitigated ass, all bluster and pomposity, but Baron Kelbor is not the sort to be taken lightly. At any rate, they concluded that, with the legions all around the palace, it would be unlikely that an assassin could reach you; but then Kelbor said, 'If you want to kill a snake, you cut off its tail—just behind the head. We can't reach Varana, but we *can* reach his son. Without an heir, Varana's line dies with him.' "

"My son?" Varana said sharply.

"His life is in danger, your Majesty. I thought you should know."

"Thank you, Bethra," Varana replied gravely. Then he turned to Morin. "Send a detachment of the third legion to my son's house," he said. "No one is to go in or out until I've had time to make other arrangements."

"At once, your Majesty."

"I would also like to speak with the two gentlemen from the House of Honeth. Send some troops to invite them to the palace. Have them wait in that little room adjoining the torture chamber down in the dungeons until I have the time to discuss this with them."

"You wouldn't," Ce'Nedra gasped.

"Probably not," Varana admitted, "but they don't have to know that, do they? Let's give them a nervous hour or two."

"I'll see to it immediately, your Majesty," Morin said. He bowed and quietly left the room.

"I'm told that you knew my father," Ce'Nedra said to the lushly curved woman standing in the center of the room.

"Yes, Princess," Bethra responded. "Quite well, actually. We were friends for years."

Ce'Nedra's eyes narrowed.

"Your father was a vigorous man, Princess," Bethra told her calmly. "I'm told that many people prefer not to believe that kind of thing about their parents, but it does happen now and again. I was quite fond of him and I'll miss him very much, I think."

"I don't believe you," Ce'Nedra said bluntly.

"That's up to you, of course."

"My father would not have done that."

"Whatever you say, Princess," Bethra said with a faint smile.

"You're lying!" Ce'Nedra snapped.

A momentary glint came into Bethra's eyes. "No, Princess. I don't lie. I might conceal the truth at times, but I never lie. Lies are too easily found out. Ran Borune and I were intimate friends and we enjoyed each other's company in many ways." Her look became faintly amused. "Your upbringing has sheltered you from certain facts, Princess Ce'Nedra. Tol Honeth is an extremely corrupt city, and I am fully at home here. Let's face a certain blunt truth. I'm a harlot and I make no apology for that fact. The work is easy—even pleasant at times—and the pay is very good. I'm on the best of terms with some of the richest and most powerful men in the world. We talk, and they value my conversation, but when they come to my house, it's not the talk they're interested in. The talk comes later. It was much the same when I visited your father. We *did* talk, Princess, but it was usually later."

Ce'Nedra's face was flaming, and her eyes were wide with shock. "No one has *ever* talked to me that way before," she gasped.

"Then it was probably overdue," Bethra said calmly. "You're much wiser now—not happier, perhaps, but wiser. Now, if you'll excuse me, I should probably leave. The Honeths have spies everywhere, and I think it might not be a good idea for them to find out about this visit."

"I want to thank you for the information you've just brought me, Bethra," Varana said to her. "Let me give you something for your trouble."

"That has never been necessary, your Majesty," she replied with an arch little smile. "Information is *not* what I sell. I'll go now—unless you want to talk business, of course." She paused in the act of putting her cloak back on and gave him a very direct look.

"Ah—this might not be the best time, Bethra," Varana said with a faintly regretful note in his voice and a quick sidelong glance at Ce'Nedra.

"Some other time then, perhaps." She curtsied again and quietly left the room, the musky fragrance of the scent she wore lingering in the air behind her.

Ce'Nedra was still blushing furiously, and her eyes were outraged. She spun to face Garion and Varana. "Don't either of you *dare* say anything," she commanded. "Not one single word."

The sad visit to Tol Honeth ended a few days later, and Garion and Ce'Nedra took ship again for the voyage back to the Isle of the Winds. Though Ce'Nedra seldom gave any outward hints of her grief, Garion knew her well enough to understand that her father's death had hurt her deeply. Because he loved her and was sensitive to her emotions, he treated her with a certain extra tenderness and consideration for the next several months.

In midautumn that year, the Alorn Kings and Queen Porenn, Regent of Drasnia, arrived at Riva for the traditional meeting of the Alorn Council. The meeting had none of the urgency which had marked those meetings previously. Torak was dead, the Angaraks were convulsed by war, and a king sat upon the Rivan throne. The entire affair was almost purely social, though the kings did make some pretense at holding business sessions in the blue-draped council chamber high in the south tower of the Citadel. They gravely talked about the stalemated war in southern Cthol Murgos and about the troubles Varana was having with the Vordue family of northern Tolnedra.

Warned perhaps by the failure of the Honeths in their attempts at assassination, the Vordues decided to try secession. Shortly after Varana's coronation as Ran Borune XXIV, the Vordue family declared that their Grand Duchy was no longer a part of Tolnedra but rather was a separate, independent kingdom—although they had not yet decided which of their number was to ascend the throne.

"Varana's going to have to move the legions against them," King Anheg declared, wiping the ale foam from his mouth with his sleeve. "Otherwise, the other families will secede too, and Tolnedra will fly apart like a broken spring."

"It's not really that simple, Anheg," Queen Porenn told him smoothly, turning back from the window out of which she had been watching the activity in the harbor far below. The Queen of Drasnia still wore deep mourning, and her black gown seemed to enhance her blonde loveliness. "The legions will gladly fight any foreign enemy, but Varana can't ask them to attack their own people."

Anheg shrugged. "He could bring up legions from the south. They're all Borunes or Anadiles or Ranites. They wouldn't mind trampling over the Vordues."

"But then the northern legions would step in to stop them. Once the legions start fighting each other, the Empire will *really* disintegrate."

"I guess I really hadn't thought of it that way," Anheg admitted. "You know, Porenn, you're extremely intelligent—for a woman."

"And you're extremely perceptive—for a man," she replied with a sweet smile.

"That's one for her side," King Cho-Hag said quietly.

"Were we keeping score?" Garion asked mildly.

"It helps us to keep track, sort of," the Chief of the Clan-Chiefs of Algaria answered with a straight face.

It was not until several days later that word reached Riva concerning Varana's rather novel approach to his problem with the Vordues. A Drasnian ship sailed into the harbor one morning, and an agent of the Drasnian Intelligence Service brought a sheaf of dispatches to Queen Porenn. After she read them, she entered the council chamber with a smug little smile. "I believe we can set our minds at rest about Varana's abilities, gentlemen," she told the Alorn Kings. "He appears to have found a solution to the Vordue question."

"Oh?" Brand rumbled. "What is it?"

"My informants advise me that he has made a secret arrangement with King Korodullin of Arendia. This so-called Kingdom of Vordue has suddenly become absolutely infested with Arendish bandits—most of them in full armor, oddly enough."

"Wait a minute, Porenn," Anheg interrupted. "If it's a secret arrangement, how is it that you know about it?"

The little blonde Queen of Drasnia lowered her eyelids demurely. "Why, Anheg, dear, weren't you aware of the fact that I know everything?"

"Another one for her side," King Cho-Hag said to Garion.

"I'd say so, yes," Garion agreed.

"At any rate," the Drasnian Queen continued, "there are now whole battalions of brainless young Mimbrate knights in Vordue, all posing as bandits and plundering and burning at will. The Vordues don't have what you could call an army, so they've been screaming for aid from the legions. My people managed to get their hands on a copy of Varana's reply." She unfolded a document. " 'To the government of the Kingdom of Vordue,' " she read, " 'Greetings: Your recent appeal for help came as a great surprise to me. Surely the esteemed gentlemen in Tol Vordue would not want me to violate the sovereignty of their newly established kingdom by sending Tolnedran legions across their borders to deal with a few Arendish brigands. The maintenance of public order is the paramount responsibility of any government, and I would not dream of intruding my forces into so fundamental an area. To do so would raise grave doubts in the minds of reasonable men the world over as to the viability of your new state. I do, however, send you my best wishes in your efforts to deal with what is, after all, a strictly internal matter.' "

Anheg began to laugh, pounding his heavy fist on the table in his glee. "I think that calls for a drink," he chortled.

"I think it might call for several," Garion agreed. "We can toast the efforts of the Vordues to maintain order."

"I trust you gentlemen will excuse me then," Queen Porenn said. "No mere woman could ever hope to compete with the Kings of Aloria when it comes to really serious drinking."

"Of course, Porenn," Anheg agreed magnanimously. "We'll even drink your share for you."

"You're too kind," she murmured and withdrew.

Much of the evening that followed was lost in a hazy fog of ale fumes for Garion. He seemed to remember weaving down a corridor with Anheg on one side and Brand on the other. The three of them had their arms about one another's shoulders, and they staggered in a peculiar kind of unison. He also seemed to remember that they were singing. When he was sober, Garion never sang. That night, however, it seemed like the most natural and enjoyable thing in the world.

He had not been drunk before. Aunt Pol had always disapproved of drinking, and, as he did in most things, he had deferred to her opinions about the matter. Thus, he was totally unprepared for the way he felt the next morning.

Ce'Nedra was unsympathetic, to say the least. Like every woman who had ever lived since the beginning of time, she smugly enjoyed her husband's suffering. "I told you that you were drinking too much," she reminded him.

"Please don't," he said, holding his head between his hands.

"It's your own fault," she smirked.

"Just leave me alone," he begged. "I'm trying to die."

"Oh, I don't think you'll die, Garion. You might wish you could, but you won't."

"Do you have to talk so loud?"

"We all just *loved* your singing," she congratulated him brightly. "I actually think you invented notes that didn't even exist before."

Garion groaned and once more buried his face between his trembling hands.

The Alorn Council lasted for perhaps another week. It might have continued longer had not a savage autumn storm announced with a howling gale that it was time for the assembled guests to return to the mainland while the Sea of the Winds was still navigable.

Not too many days later, Brand, the tall, aging Rivan Warder, requested a private audience with Garion. It was raining gustily outside, and sheets of water intermittently clawed at the windows of Garion's study as the two men sat down in comfortable chairs across the table from each other. "May I speak frankly, Belgarion?" the big, sad-eyed man asked.

"You know you don't have to ask that."

"The matter at hand is a personal one. I don't want you to be offended."

"Say what you think needs to be said. I promise not to be offended."

Brand glanced out the window at the gray sky and the wind-driven rain. "Belgarion, it's been almost eight years now since you married Princess Ce'Nedra."

Garion nodded.

"I'm not trying to intrude on your privacy, but the fact that your wife has not yet produced an heir to the throne is, after all, a state matter."

Garion pursed his lips. "I know that you and Anheg and the others are very concerned. I think your concern is premature, though."

"Eight years is a long time, Belgarion. We all know how much you love your wife. We're all fond of her." Brand smiled briefly. "Even though she's a little difficult at times."

"You've noticed."

"We followed her willingly to the battlefield at Thull Mardu—and probably would again if she asked us to—but I think we'd better face the possibility that she may be barren."

"I'm positive that she's not," Garion said firmly.

"Then why isn't she having children?"

Garion couldn't answer that.

"Belgarion, the fate of this kingdom—and of all Aloria—hangs on your weakest breath. There's virtually no other topic of conversation in all the northern kingdoms."

"I didn't know that," Garion admitted.

"Grodeg and his henchmen were virtually wiped out at Thull Mardu, but there's been a resurgence of the Bear-cult in remote parts of Cherek, Drasnia, and Algaria. You knew that, didn't you?"

Garion nodded.

"And even in the cities there are those elements that sympathize with the cult's aims and beliefs. Those people were not happy that you chose a Tolnedran princess for your wife. Rumors are already abroad that Ce'Nedra's inability to have children is a sign of Belar's disapproval of your marriage to her."

"That's superstitious nonsense," Garion scoffed.

"Of course it is, but if that kind of thinking begins to take hold, it's ultimately going to have some unpleasant effects. Other elements in Alorn society—friendly to you—are very concerned about it. To put it bluntly, there's a rather widely held opinion that the time has come for you to divorce Ce'Nedra."

"*What?*"

"You *do* have that power, you know. The way they all see it, the best solution might be for you to put aside your barren Tolnedran queen and take some nice, fertile Alorn girl, who'll present you with babies by the dozen."

"That's absolutely out of the question," Garion said hotly. "I won't do it. Didn't those idiots ever hear about the Accords of Vo Mimbre? Even if I wanted to divorce Ce'Nedra, I couldn't. Our marriage was agreed upon five hundred years ago."

"The Bear-cult feels that the arrangement was forced on the Alorns by Belgarath and Polgara," Brand replied. "Since those two are loyal to Aldur, the cult feels that it might have been done without Belar's approval."

"Nonsense," Garion snapped.

"There's a lot of nonsense in any religion, Belgarion. The point remains, however, that Ce'Nedra has few friends in any part of Alorn society. Even those who are friendly to you aren't very fond of her. Both your enemies *and* your friends would like to see you divorce her. They all know how fond of her you are, so they'll probably never approach you with the idea. They're likely to take more direct action instead."

"Such as?"

"Since they know that you can't be persuaded to divorce her, someone may try to remove her permanently."

"They wouldn't dare!"

"Alorns are almost as emotional as Arends are, Belgarion—and sometimes almost as thick-headed. We're all aware of it. Anheg and Cho-Hag both urged me to warn you about this possibility, and Porenn has put whole platoons of her spies to work on it so that we'll at least have some advance warning if someone starts plotting against the queen."

"And just where do you stand in this, Brand?" Garion asked quietly.

"Belgarion," the big man said firmly, "I love you as if you were my own son, and Ce'Nedra is as dear to me as the daughter I never had. Nothing in this world would make me happier than to see the floor of that nursery next to your bedroom absolutely littered with children. But it's been eight years. Things have reached the point where we must do something—if for no other reason, then to protect that tiny, brave girl we both love."

"What can we do?" Garion asked helplessly.

"You and I are only men, Garion. How can we know why a woman does or does not have children? And that's the crux of the whole situation. I implore you, Garion—I beg you—send for Polgara. We need her advice and help—and we need it now."

After the Warder had quietly left, Garion sat for a long while staring out at the rain. All in all, he decided that it might be wiser not to tell Ce'Nedra about the conversation. He did not want to frighten her with talk of assassins lurking in the dim corridors, and any hint that political expediency might compel consideration of divorce would *not* be well received. After careful thought, he concluded that the best course would be just to keep his mouth shut and send for Aunt Pol. Unfortunately, he had forgotten something rather important. When he entered the cheery, candle-lit royal apartment that evening, he wore a carefully assumed smile designed to indicate that nothing untoward had happened during the day.

The frosty silence which greeted him should have warned him; even had he missed that danger sign, he certainly should have noticed the scars on the door casing and the broken shards of several vases and assorted porcelain figurines that lay in the corners where they had been missed in the hasty cleanup following an explosion of some sort. The Rivan King, however, sometimes tended to be slightly unobservant. "Good evening, dear," he greeted his icy little wife in a cheerful voice.

"Really?"

"How did your day go?"

She turned to regard him with a look filled with daggers. "How can you possibly have the nerve to ask that?"

Garion blinked.

"Tell me," she said, "just when is it that I am to be put aside so that my Lord can marry the blonde-headed brood sow who's going to replace me in my Lord's bed and fill the entire Citadel with litters of runny-nosed Alorn brats?"

"How—?"

"My Lord appears to have forgotten the gift he chained about my neck when we were betrothed," she said. "My Lord also appears to have forgotten just exactly what Beldaran's amulet can do."

"Oh," Garion said, suddenly remembering. "Oh, my."

"Unfortunately, the amulet won't come off," Ce'Nedra told him bitingly. "You won't be able to give it to your next wife—unless you plan to have my head cut off so that you can reclaim it."

"*Will* you stop that?"

"As my Lord commands me. Did you plan to ship me back to Tolnedra—or am I just to be shoved out the front gate into the rain and left to fend for myself?"

"You heard the discussion I had with Brand, then, I take it."

"Obviously."

"If you heard part of it, then I'm sure you heard it all. Brand was only reporting a danger to you caused by the absurd notions of a group of frothing fanatics."

"You should not have even listened to him."

"When he's trying to warn me that somebody might attempt to kill you? Ce'Nedra, be serious."

"The thought is there now, Garion," she said accusingly. "Now you know that you can get rid of me any time you want. I've seen you ogling those empty-headed Alorn girls with their long blonde braids and their overdeveloped bosoms. Now's your chance, Garion. Which one will you choose?"

"Are you about finished with all of this?"

Her eyes narrowed. "I see," she said. "Now I'm not merely barren, I'm also hysterical."

"No, you're just a little silly now and then, that's all."

"*Silly?*"

"Everybody's silly once in a while," he added quite calmly. "It's part of being human. I'm actually a little surprised that you aren't throwing things."

She threw a quick, guilty glance in the direction of some of the broken fragments in the corner.

"Oh," he said, catching the glance. "You did that earlier, I see. I'm glad I missed that part. It's hard to try to reason with somebody when you're dodging flying crockery and the other person is shrieking curses."

Ce'Nedra blushed slightly.

"You did *that* too?" he asked mildly. "Sometimes I wonder where you managed to pick up all those words. How did you ever find out what they mean?"

"*You* swear all the time," she accused.

"I know," he admitted. "It's terribly unfair. I'm allowed to, but you're not."

"I'd like to know who made up that rule," she started, and then her eyes narrowed. "You're trying to change the subject," she accused him.

"No, Ce'Nedra, I already did. We weren't getting anywhere with the other topic. You are *not* barren, and I am *not* going to divorce you, no matter how long somebody else's braids are, or how—well, never mind."

She looked at him. "Oh, Garion, what if I am?" she said in a small voice. "Barren, I mean?"

"That's absurd, Ce'Nedra. We won't even discuss that."

The lingering doubt in the eyes of the Rivan Queen, however, said quite clearly that, even if they did not discuss it, she would continue to worry about it.

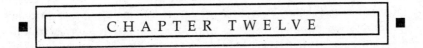

CHAPTER TWELVE

The season made the Sea of the Winds extremely hazardous, and Garion was forced to wait for a full month before he could dispatch a messenger to the Vale of Aldur. By then the late autumn snowstorms had clogged the passes in the mountains of eastern Sendaria, and the royal messenger was obliged literally to wade his way across the plains of Algaria. With all these delays, it was very nearly Erastide by the time Aunt Pol, Durnik, and Errand arrived at the snowy quay in the harbor at Riva. Durnik admitted to Garion that it had only been a chance meeting with the wayward Captain Greldik, who feared no storm that any sea could hurl at him, that had made the trip possible at all. Polgara spoke briefly with the vagabond seaman before they began the long climb up to the Citadel, and Garion noted with some surprise that Greldik slipped his hawsers immediately and sailed back out to sea.

Polgara seemed quite unconcerned about the gravity of the problem that had impelled Garion to send for her. She spoke with him only a couple of times about it, asking a few rather direct questions that set his ears to flaming. Her discussions with Ce'Nedra were a bit more lengthy, but only slightly so. Garion received the distinct impression that she was waiting for someone or something before proceeding.

The Erastide celebration at Riva that year was somewhat subdued. Although it was very pleasant to have Polgara, Durnik, and Errand with them to join in the festivities, Garion's concern over the problem Brand had raised dampened his enjoyment of the holiday.

Several weeks afterward, Garion entered the royal apartment one snowy midafternoon to find Polgara and Ce'Nedra seated by a cozy fire sipping tea and chatting together quietly. The curiosity which had been growing in him since the arrival of his visitors finally boiled to a head.

"Aunt Pol," he began.

"Yes dear?"

"You've been here for almost a month now."

"Has it been that long? The time certainly passes quickly when you're with people you love."

"There's still this little problem, you know," he reminded her.

"Yes, Garion," she replied patiently. "I'm aware of that."

"Are we doing anything about it?"

"No," she said placidly, "not yet, anyhow."

"It's sort of important, Aunt Pol. I don't want to seem to be trying to rush you or anything, but—" He broke off helplessly.

Polgara rose from her chair, went to the window, and looked out at the small private garden just outside. The garden was clogged with snow, and the pair of intertwined oak trees Ce'Nedra had planted there at the time of her betrothal to Garion were bowed slightly beneath the weight on their limbs. "One of the things you'll learn as you grow older, Garion," she said to him, gravely looking out at the snowy garden, "is patience. Everything has its proper season. The solution to your problem isn't all that complicated, but it's just not the proper time to come to grips with it yet."

"I don't understand at all, Aunt Pol."

"Then you'll just have to trust me, won't you?"

"Of course I trust you, Aunt Pol. It's just—"

"Just what, dear?"

"Nothing."

It was late winter before Captain Greldik returned from the south. A storm had sprung one of the seams of his ship, and she was taking water as she wallowed heavily around the headland and made for the quay.

"I thought for a while there that I might have to swim," the bearded Cherek growled as he jumped across to the quay. "Where's the best place to beach this poor old cow of mine? I'm going to have to calk her bottom."

"Most sailors use that inlet there," Garion replied, pointing.

"I *hate* to beach a ship in the winter," Greldik said bitterly. "Is there someplace where I can get a drink?"

"Up at the Citadel," Garion offered.

"Thanks. Oh, I brought that visitor Polgara wanted."

"Visitor?"

Greldik stepped back, squinted at his ship to determine the location of the aft cabin, then went over and kicked the planking several times. "We're here!" he bellowed. He turned back to Garion. "I really hate to sail with women on board. I'm not superstitious, but sometimes I really think they *do* bring bad luck—and you've always got to watch your manners."

"You have a woman aboard?" Garion asked curiously.

Greldik grunted sourly. "Pretty little thing, but she seems to expect deferential treatment; and when your whole crew is busy bailing seawater out of your bilges, you don't have much time for that."

"Hello, Garion," a light voice said from up on deck.

"Xera?" Garion stared up into the small face of his wife's cousin. "Is that really you?"

"Yes, Garion," the red-haired Dryad replied calmly. She was bundled up to the ears in thick, warm furs, and her breath steamed in the frosty air. "I got here as quickly as I could when I received Lady Polgara's summons." She smiled sweetly down at the sour-faced Greldik. "Captain," she said, "could you have some of your men bring those bales along for me?"

"Dirt," Greldik snorted. "I sail two thousand leagues in the dead of winter to carry one small girl, two casks of water, and four bales of dirt."

"Loam, Captain," Xera corrected meticulously, "loam. There's a difference, you know."

"I'm a sailor," Greldik said. "To me, dirt is dirt."

"Whatever you wish, Captain," Xera said winsomely. "Now do be a dear and have the bales carried up to the Citadel for me—and I'll need the casks as well."

Grumbling, Captain Greldik gave the orders.

Ce'Nedra was ecstatic when she learned that her cousin had arrived in Riva. The two of them flew into each other's arms and dashed off immediately to find Polgara.

"They're very fond of each other, aren't they?" Durnik observed. The smith was dressed in furs and wore a pair of well-tarred boots. Shortly after his arrival, despite the fact that it was in the dead of winter, Durnik had discovered a large, swirling pool in the river that dropped out of the mountains and ran just to the north of the city. With astounding self-restraint, he had actually stared at that ice-rimmed pool for a full ten minutes before going in search of a fishing pole. Now he happily spent most of each day probing those dark, churning waters with a waxed line and a bright lure in search of the silvery-sided salmon that lurked beneath the turbulent surface. The closest Garion had ever seen his Aunt Pol actually come to scolding her husband had been on the day when she had intercepted him on his way out of the Citadel into the very teeth of a screaming blizzard, whistling, and with his fishing pole over his shoulder.

"What am I supposed to do with all of this?" Greldik demanded, pointing at the six burly sailors who had carried Xera's bales and casks up the long stairway to the grim fortress brooding over the city.

"Oh," Garion said, "just have your men put them over there." He pointed toward a corner of the antechamber they had just entered. "I'll find out what the ladies want done with them later."

Greldik grunted. "Good." Then he rubbed his hands together. "Now, about that drink—"

Garion did not have the faintest idea what his wife and her cousin and Polgara were up to. Most of the time, their conversations broke off as soon as he entered the room. To his astonishment, the four bales of loam and the two casks of what seemed to be water were stacked rather untidily in one corner of the royal bedroom. Ce'Nedra adamantly refused to explain, but the look she gave him when he asked why they needed to be so close to the royal bed was not only mysterious, but actually faintly naughty.

It was perhaps a week or two after Xera's arrival that a sudden break in the weather brought the sun out, and the temperature soared up to almost freezing. Shortly before noon, Garion was in conference with the Drasnian ambassador when a wide-eyed servant hesitantly entered the royal study. "Please, your Majesty," the poor man stammered. "Please forgive me for interrupting, but Lady Polgara told me to bring you to her at once. I tried to tell her that we don't bother you when you're busy, but she—well, she sort of insisted."

"You'd better go see what she wants, your Majesty," the Drasnian ambassador suggested. "If the Lady Polgara had just summoned *me,* I'd be running toward her door already."

"You don't really have to be afraid of her, Margrave," Garion told him. "She wouldn't actually hurt you."

"That's a chance I'd prefer not to take, your Majesty. We can talk about the matter we were discussing some other time."

Frowning slightly, Garion went down the hall to the door of Aunt Pol's apartment. He tapped gently and then went in.

"Ah, there you are," she said crisply. "I was about to send another servant after you." She wore a fur-lined cloak with a deep hood pulled up until it framed her face. Ce'Nedra and Xera, similarly garbed, were standing just behind her. "I want you to go find Durnik," she said. "He's probably fishing. Find him and bring him back to the Citadel. Get a shovel and a pick from someplace and then bring Durnik and the tools to that little garden just outside your apartment window."

He stared at her.

She made a kind of flipping motion with one hand. "Quickly, quickly, Garion," she said. "The day is wearing on."

"Yes, Aunt Pol," he said without even thinking. He turned and went back out, half-running. He was nearly to the end of the hallway before he remembered that he was the king here, and that people *probably* shouldn't order him around like that.

Durnik, of course, responded immediately to his wife's summons—well, *almost* immediately. He *did* make one last cast before carefully coiling up his fishing line and following Garion back to the Citadel. When the two of them entered the small private garden adjoining the royal apartment, Aunt Pol, Ce'Nedra, and Xera were already there, standing beneath the intertwined oak trees.

"Here's what we're going to do," Aunt Pol said in a businesslike fashion. "I'd like to have the area around these tree trunks opened up to a depth of about two feet."

"Uh—Aunt Pol," Garion interposed, "the ground is sort of frozen. Digging is going to be a little difficult."

"That's what the pick is for, dear," she said patiently.

"Wouldn't it be easier to wait until the ground thaws?"

"Probably, but it needs to be done now. Dig, Garion."

"I've got gardeners, Aunt Pol. We could send for a couple of them." He eyed the pick and shovel uncomfortably.

"It's probably better if we keep it in the family, dear. You can start digging right here." She pointed.

Garion sighed and took up the pick.

What followed made no sense at all. Garion and Durnik picked and spaded at the frozen ground until late afternoon, opening up the area Aunt Pol had indicated. Then they dumped the four bales of loam into the hole they had prepared, tamped down the loose earth, and watered the dark soil liberally with the water from the two casks. After that, Aunt Pol instructed them to cover everything back up again with snow.

"Did you understand any of that?" Garion asked Durnik as the two of them returned their tools to the gardeners' shed in the courtyard near the stables.

"No," Durnik admitted, "but I'm sure she knows what she's doing." He glanced at the evening sky and then sighed. "It's probably a little late to go back to that pool," he said regretfully.

Aunt Pol and the two girls visited the garden daily, but Garion could never discover exactly what they were doing, and the following week his attention was diverted by the sudden appearance of his grandfather, Belgarath the Sorcerer. The young king was sitting in his study with Errand as the boy described in some detail the training of the horse Garion had given him a few years back when the door banged unceremoniously open and Belgarath, travel-stained and with a face like a thundercloud, strode in.

"Grandfather!" Garion exclaimed, starting to his feet. "What are—"

"Shut up and sit down!" Belgarath shouted at him.

"What?"

"Do as I tell you. We are going to have a talk, Garion—that is, *I'm* going to talk, and *you're* going to listen." He paused as if to get control of what appeared to be a towering anger. "Do you have any idea of what you've done?" he demanded at last.

"Me? What are we talking about, Grandfather?" Garion asked.

"We're talking about your little display of pyrotechnics on the plains of Mimbre," Belgarath replied icily. "That impromptu thunderstorm of yours."

"Grandfather," Garion explained as mildly as possible, "they were right on the brink of war. All Arendia would probably have gotten involved. You've said yourself that we didn't want that to happen. I had to stop them."

"We aren't talking about your motives, Garion. We're talking about your methods. What possessed you to use a thunderstorm?"

"It seemed like the best way to get their attention."

"You couldn't think of anything else?"

"They were already charging, Grandfather. I didn't have a lot of time to consider alternatives."

"Haven't I told you again and again that we don't tamper with the weather?"

"Well—it was sort of an emergency."

"If you thought *that* was an emergency, you should have seen the blizzard you touched off in the Vale with your foolishness—and the hurricanes it spawned in the Sea of the East—not to mention the droughts and tornados you kicked up all over the world. Don't you have any sense of responsibility at all?"

"I didn't know it was going to do that." Garion was aghast.

"Boy, it's your business to know!" Belgarath suddenly roared at him, his face mottled with rage. "It's taken Beldin and me six months of constant travel and the Gods only know how much effort to quiet things down. Do you realize that with that one thoughtless storm of yours you came very close to changing the weather patterns of the entire globe? And that change would have been a universal disaster?"

"One tiny little storm?"

"Yes, one tiny little storm," Belgarath said scathingly. "Your one tiny little storm in the right place at the right time came very close to altering the weather for the next several eons—all over the world—you blockhead!"

"Grandfather," Garion protested.

"Do you know what the term ice age means?"

Garion shook his head, his face blank.

"It's a time when the average temperature drops—just a bit. In the extreme north, that means that the snow doesn't melt in the summer. It keeps piling up, year after year. It forms glaciers, and the glaciers start to move farther and farther south. In just a few centuries, that little display of yours could have had a wall of ice two hundred feet high moving down across the moors of Drasnia. You'd have buried Boktor and Val Alorn under solid ice, you idiot. Is that what you wanted?"

"Of course not. Grandfather, I honestly didn't know. I wouldn't have started it if I'd known."

"That would have been a great comfort to the millions of people you very nearly entombed in ice," Belgarath retorted with a vast sarcasm. "Don't *ever* do that again! Don't even *think* about putting your hands on something until you're absolutely certain you know everything there is to know about it. Even then, it's best not to gamble."

"But—but—you and Aunt Pol called down the rainstorm in the Wood of the Dryads," Garion pointed out defensively.

"We knew what we were doing," Belgarath almost screamed. "There was no danger there." With an enormous effort, the old man got control of himself. "Don't *ever* touch the weather again, Garion—not until you've had at least a thousand years of study."

"A thousand years!"

"At least. In your case, maybe two thousand. You seem to have this extraordinary luck. You always manage to be in the wrong place at the wrong time."

"I won't do it again, Grandfather," Garion promised fervently, shuddering at the thought of towering ice walls creeping inexorably across the world.

Belgarath gave him a long, hard look and then let the matter drop. Later, when he had regained his composure, he lounged in a chair by the fire with a tankard of ale in one hand. Garion knew his grandfather well enough to be aware of the fact that ale mellowed the old man's disposition and he had prudently sent for some as soon as the initial explosion had subsided. "How are your studies going, boy?" the old sorcerer asked.

"I've been a little pressed for time lately, Grandfather," Garion replied guiltily.

Belgarath gave him a long, cold stare, and Garion could clearly see the mottling on his neck that indicated that the old man's interior temperature was rising again.

"I'm sorry Grandfather," he apologized quickly. "From now on, I'll *make* the time to study."

Belgarath's eyes widened slightly. "Don't do that," he said quickly. "You got into enough trouble fooling around with the weather. If you start in on time, not even the Gods could predict the outcome."

"I didn't exactly mean it that way, Grandfather."

"Say what you mean, then. This isn't a good area for misunderstandings, you know." He turned his attention then to Errand. "What are you doing here, boy?" he asked.

"Durnik and Polgara are here," Errand replied. "They thought I ought to come along."

"Polgara's here?" Belgarath seemed surprised.

"I asked her to come," Garion told him. "There's a little bit of a problem she's fixing for me—at least I *think* she's fixing it. She's been acting sort of mysterious."

"She overdramatizes things sometimes. Exactly what is this problem she's working on?"

"Uh—" Garion glanced at Errand, who sat watching the two of them with polite interest. Garion flushed slightly. "It—uh—has to do with the—uh—heir to the Rivan Throne," he explained delicately.

"What's the problem there?" Belgarath demanded obtusely. "*You're* the heir to the Rivan Throne."

"No, I mean the next one."

"I still don't see any problem."

"Grandfather, there *isn't* one—not yet, at least."

"There *isn't*? What have you been doing, boy?"

"Never mind," Garion said, giving up.

When spring arrived at last, Polgara's attention to the two embracing oak trees became all-consuming. She went to the garden at least a dozen times a day to examine every twig meticulously for signs of budding. When at last the twig ends began to swell, a look of strange satisfaction became apparent on her face. Once again she and the two young women, Ce'Nedra and Xera, began puttering in the garden. Garion found all these botanical pastimes baffling—even a little irritating. He had, after all, asked Aunt Pol to come to Riva to deal with a much more serious problem.

Xera returned home to the Wood of the Dryads at the first break in the weather. Not long afterward, Aunt Pol calmly announced that she and Durnik and Errand would also be leaving soon. "We'll take father with us," she declared, looking disapprovingly over at the old sorcerer, who was drinking ale and bantering outrageously with Brand's niece, the blushing Lady Arell.

"Aunt Pol," Garion protested, "what about that little—uh—difficulty Ce'Nedra and I were having?"

"What about it, dear?"

"Aren't you going to do something about it?"

"I did, Garion," she replied blandly.

"Aunt Pol, you spent all your time in that garden."

"Yes, dear. I know."

Garion brooded about the whole matter for several weeks after they had all left. He even began to wonder if he had somehow failed to explain fully the problem or if Aunt Pol had somehow misunderstood.

When spring was in full flower and the meadows rising steeply behind the city had turned bright green, touched here and there with vibrantly colored patches of wildflowers, Ce'Nedra began behaving peculiarly. He frequently found her seated in their garden, looking with an odd, tender expression at her oak trees, and quite often she was gone from the Citadel entirely, to return at the end of the day in the company of Lady Arell all bedecked with wildflowers. Before each meal, she took a sip from a small, silver flagon and made a dreadful face.

"What's that you're drinking?" he asked her curiously one morning.

"It's a sort of a tonic," she replied, shuddering. "It has oak buds in it and it tastes absolutely vile."

"Aunt Pol made it for you."

"How did you know that?"

"Her medicines always taste awful."

"Mmm," she said absently. Then she gave him a long look. "Are you going to be very busy today?"

"Not really. Why?"

"I thought that we might stop by the kitchen, pick up some meat, bread, and cheese, and then go spend a day out in the forest."

"In the forest? What for?"

"Garion," she said almost crossly, "I've been cooped up in this dreary old castle all winter. I'd like some fresh air and sunshine—and the smell of trees and wildflowers around me instead of damp stone."

"Why don't you ask Arell to go with you? I probably shouldn't really be gone all day."

She gave him an exasperated look. "You just said you didn't have anything important to do."

"You never know. Something might come up."

"It can wait," she said from between clenched teeth.

Garion shot her a quick glance, recognized the danger signals, and then replied as mildly as he could, "I suppose you're right, dear. I don't see any reason why we shouldn't have a little outing together. We could ask Arell—and maybe Kail—if they'd like to join us."

"No, Garion," she said quite firmly.

"No?"

"Definitely not."

And so it was that, shortly after breakfast, the Rivan King, hand in hand with his little queen, left the Citadel with a well-stocked basket, crossed the broad meadow behind the city, and strolled into the sunlight-dappled shade beneath the evergreens that mounted steeply toward the glistening, snow-capped peaks that formed the spine of the island.

Once they entered the woods, all traces of discontent dropped away from Ce'Nedra's face. She picked wildflowers as they wandered among the tall pines and firs and wove them into a garland for herself. The morning sun slanted down through the limbs high overhead, dappling the mossy forest floor with golden light and blue shadows. The resinous smell of the tall evergreens was a heady perfume, and birds swooped and spiraled among the tall, columnlike trunks, caroling to greet the sun.

After a time, they found a glade, a mossy, open clearing embraced by trees, where a brook gurgled and murmured over shining stones to drop into a gleaming forest pool and where a single, soft-eyed deer stood to drink. The deer raised her head from the water swirling about her delicate brown legs, looked at them quite unafraid, and then picked her way back into the forest, her hooves clicking on the stones and her tail flicking.

"Oh, this is just perfect," Ce'Nedra declared with a soft little smile on her face. She sat on a round boulder and began to unlace her shoes.

Garion put down the basket and stretched, feeling the cares of the past several weeks slowly draining out of him. "I'm glad you thought of this," he said, sprawling comfortably on the sun-warmed moss. "It's really a very good idea."

"Naturally," she said. "All my ideas are good ones."

"I don't know if I'd go *that* far." Then a thought occurred to him. "Ce'Nedra," he said.

"What?"

"I've been meaning to ask you something. All the Dryads have names that begin with an *X*, don't they? Xera, Xantha—like that."

"It's our custom," she replied, continuing to work on her shoelaces.

"Why doesn't yours, then? Begin with an *X*, I mean?"

"It does." She pulled off one of her shoes. "Tolnedrans just pronounce it a little differently, that's all. So they spell it that way. Dryads don't read or write very much, so they don't worry too much about spelling."

"X'Nedra?"

"That's fairly close. Make the *X* a little softer, though."

"You know, I've been wondering about that for the longest time."

"Why didn't you ask, then?"

"I don't know. I just never got around to it."

"There's a reason for everything, Garion," she told him, "but you'll never find it out if you don't ask."

"Now you sound just like Aunt Pol."

"Yes, dear. I know." She smiled, pulled off her other shoe and wriggled her toes contentedly.

"Why barefoot?" he asked idly.

"I like the feel of the moss on my feet—and I think that in a little bit I might go swimming."

"It's too cold. That brook comes right out of a glacier."

"A little cold water won't hurt me." She shrugged. Then, almost as if responding to a dare, she stood up and began to take off her clothes.

"Ce'Nedra! What if someone comes along?"

She laughed a silvery laugh. "What if they do? I'm not going to soak my clothes just for the sake of propriety. Don't be such a prude, Garion."

"It's not that. It's—"

"It's what?"

"Never mind."

She ran on light feet into the pool, squealing delightedly as the icy water splashed up around her. With a long clean dive, she disappeared beneath the surface of the pool, swam to the far side, where a large, mossy log angled down into the crystal-clear water, and surfaced with streaming hair and an impish grin. "Well?" she said to him.

"Well what?"

"Aren't you coming in?"

"Of course I'm not."

"Is the mighty Overlord of the West afraid of cold water?"

"The mighty Overlord of the West has better sense than to catch cold for the sake of a little splashing around."

"Garion, you're getting positively stodgy. Take off your crown and relax."

"I'm not wearing my crown."

"Take off something else, then."

"Ce'Nedra!"

She laughed another silvery peal of laughter and began kicking her bare feet, sending up showers of sparkling water drops that gleamed like jewels in the mid-morning sunlight. Then she lay back and her hair spread like a deep copper fan upon the surface of the pool. The garland of flowers she had woven for herself earlier had come apart as a result of her swimming, and the individual blossoms floated on the water, bobbing in the ripples.

Garion sat on a mossy hummock with his back resting comfortably against a tree trunk. The sun was warm, and the smell of trees and grass and wildflowers filled his nostrils. A breeze carrying the salt tang of the sea sighed among the green limbs of the tall fir trees surrounding the little glade, and golden sunlight fell in patches on the floor of the forest.

An errant butterfly, its patterned wings a blaze of iridescent blue and gold, flitted out from among the tall tree trunks into the sunlight. Drawn by color or scent or some other, more mysterious urge, it wavered through the lucid air to the pool and the flowers bobbing there. Curiously it moved from flower to floating flower, touching each of them lightly with its wings. With a breathless expression Ce'Nedra slowly sank her head into the water until only her upturned face was above the surface. The butterfly continued its curious investigation, coming closer and closer to the waiting queen. And then it hovered over her face, its soft wings brushing her lips ecstatically.

"Oh, fine." Garion laughed. "Now my wife is consorting with butterflies."

"I'll do whatever it takes in order to get a kiss," she replied, giving him an arch look.

"If it's kisses you want, I'll take care of that for you," he said.

"That's an interesting thought. I think I'd like one right now. My other lover seems to have lost interest." She pointed at the butterfly, which had settled with quivering wings on a bush near the foot of the pool. "Come and kiss me, Garion."

"You're right in the middle of the deepest part of the pool," he pointed out.

"So?"

"I don't suppose you'd consider coming out."

"You offered kisses, Garion. You didn't make any conditions."

Garion sighed, stood up, and began to remove his clothing. "We're both going to regret this," he predicted. "A cold in the summertime lasts for months."

"You're not going to catch cold, Garion. Come along now."

He groaned and then waded manfully into the icy water. "You're a cruel woman, Ce'Nedra," he accused, wincing at the shocking chill.

"Don't be such a baby. Come over here."

Gritting his teeth, he plowed through the water toward her, stubbing his toe on a large rock in the process. When he reached her, she slid her cold, wet little arms around his neck and glued her lips to his. Her kiss was lingering and it pulled him slightly off balance. He felt her lips tighten slightly as she grinned impishly, even in the midst of the kiss, and then without any warning, she lifted her legs, and her weight pulled him under.

He came up sputtering and swearing.

"Wasn't that fun?" she giggled.

"Not really," he grumbled. "Drowning isn't one of my favorite sports."

She ignored that. "Now that you're all wet, you might as well swim with me."

They swam together for about a quarter of an hour and then emerged from the pool, shivering and with their lips turning blue.

"Make a fire, Garion," Ce'Nedra said through chattering teeth.

"I didn't bring any tinder," he said "or a flint."

"Do it the other way, then."

"What other way?" he asked blankly.

"You know—" She made a sort of mysterious gesture.

"Oh. I forgot about that."

"Hurry, Garion. I'm freezing."

He gathered some twigs and fallen branches, cleared a space in the moss, and concentrated his will on the pile of wood. At first, a small tendril of smoke arose, then a tongue of bright orange flame. Within a few minutes, a goodly little fire was crackling just beside the moss-covered hummock upon which the shivering Ce'Nedra was huddled.

"Oh, that's much better," she said, stretching her hands out to the fire. "You're a useful person to have around, my Lord."

"Thank you, my Lady. Would my Lady like to consider putting on some clothes?"

"Not until she's dry, she wouldn't. I *hate* pulling on dry clothes over wet skin."

"Let's hope nobody comes along, then. We're not really dressed for company, you know."

"You're *so* conventional, Garion."

"I suppose so," he admitted.

"Why don't you come over here beside me?" she invited. "It's much warmer here."

He couldn't really think of any reason why he shouldn't, so he joined her on the warm moss.

"See," she said, putting her arms about his neck. "Isn't this much nicer?" She kissed him—a serious kind of kiss that made his breath catch in his throat and his heart pound.

When she finally released her grip about his neck, he looked around the glade nervously. A fluttering movement near the foot of the pool caught his eye. He coughed, looking slightly embarrassed.

"What's the matter?" she asked him.

"I think that butterfly is watching," he said with a slight flush.

"That's all right." she smiled, sliding her arms about his neck and kissing him again.

· · ·

The world seemed unusually quiet as spring gently slipped into summer that year. The secession of the Vordues crumbled under the onslaughts of the armored Mimbrate "brigands," and the Vordue family finally capitulated, pleading with an almost genuine humility to be readmitted to the Empire. While they were not fond of Varana's tax collectors, they all ran out into the streets to greet his legions as they returned.

The news from Cthol Murgos was sketchy at best, but it appeared that things in the far south remained at an impasse, with Kal Zakath's Malloreans holding the plains and Urgit's Murgos firmly entrenched in the mountains.

Periodic reports forwarded to Garion by Drasnian Intelligence seemed to indicate that the re-emergent Bear-cult was doing little more than milling around out in the countryside.

Garion enjoyed this respite from crisis and, since there was no really pressing business, he took to sleeping late, sometimes lying in bed in a kind of luxurious doze until two or three hours past sunrise.

On one such morning about midsummer, he was having an absolutely splendid dream. He and Ce'Nedra were leaping from the loft in the barn at Faldor's farm into the soft hay piled below. He was awakened rather rudely as his wife bolted from the bed and ran into an adjoining chamber where she was violently and noisily sick.

"Ce'Nedra!" he exclaimed, jumping out of bed to follow her. "What are you doing?"

"I'm throwing up," she replied, raising her pale face from the basin she was holding on her knees.

"Are you sick?"

"No," she drawled sarcastically. "I'm doing it for fun."

"I'll get one of the physicians," he said, grabbing, up a robe.

"Never mind."

"But you're sick."

"Of course I am, but I don't need a physician."

"That doesn't make any sense, Ce'Nedra. If you're sick, you need a doctor."

"I'm supposed to be sick," she told him.

"*What?*"

"Don't you know anything, Garion? I'll probably get sick every morning for the next several months."

"I don't understand you at all, Ce'Nedra."

"You're impossibly dense. People in my condition *always* get sick in the morning."

"Condition? What condition?"

She rolled her eyes upward almost in despair. "Garion," she said with exaggerated patience, "do you remember that little problem we had last fall? The problem that made us send for Lady Polgara?"

"Well—yes."

"I'm *so* glad. Well, we don't have that problem any more."

He stared at her, slowly comprehending. "You mean—?"

"Yes, dear," she said with a pale smile. "You're going to be a father. Now, if you'll excuse me, I think I'll throw up again."

CHAPTER THIRTEEN

They did not match. Now matter how hard Garion twisted and turned the sense of the two passages, there was no apparent way to make them match. Despite the fact that they both seemed to describe the same period of time, they simply went off in opposite directions. It was a bright, golden autumn morning outside, but the dusty library seemed somehow dim, chill, and uninviting.

Garion did not think of himself as a scholar and he had approached the task that Belgarath had laid upon him with some reluctance. The sheer volume of the documents he was obliged to read was intimidating, for one thing, and this gloomy little room with its smell of ancient parchment and mildewed leather bindings always depressed him. He had done unpleasant things before, however, and, although he was a bit grim about it, he nonetheless dutifully spent at least two hours a day confined in this prisonlike cell, struggling with ancient books and scrolls written in oftentimes difficult script. At least, he told himself, it was better than scrubbing pots in a scullery.

He set his teeth together and laid the two scrolls side by side on the table to compare them again. He read slowly and aloud, hoping perhaps to catch with his ears what his eyes might miss. The Darine Codex seemed relatively clear and straightforward. "Behold," it said, "in the day that Aldur's Orb burns hot with crimson fire shall the name of the Child of Dark be revealed. Guard well the son of the Child of Light for he shall have no brother. And it shall come to pass that those which once were one and now are two shall be rejoined, and in that rejoining shall one of them be no more."

The Orb *had* turned crimson, and the name of the Child of Dark—Zandramas—had been revealed. That matched what had taken place. The information that the son of the Child of Light—his son—would have no brother had concerned Garion a bit. At first he had taken it to mean that he and Ce'Nedra would only have one child, but the more he thought about that, the more he realized that his reasoning there was flawed. All it really said was that they would only have one son. It said nothing about daughters. The more he thought about it, the more the notion of a whole cluster of chattering little girls gathered about his knee appealed to him.

The last passage, however—the one about the two which once were one—didn't really make any sense yet, but he was quite certain that it would, eventually.

He moved his hand over to trace the lines of the Mrin Codex, peering hard at them in the flickering yellow candlelight. He read slowly and carefully once more. "And the Child of Light shall meet with the Child of Dark and shall overcome him—" That obviously referred to the meeting with Torak. "—and the Darkness shall flee." The Dark Prophecy *had* fled when Torak had died. "But behold, the stone which lies at the center of the light—" The Orb, obviously. "—shall—" One word seemed to be blotted at that point. Garion frowned, trying to make out what word might lie beneath that irregular splotch of ink. Even as he stared at it, a strange kind of weariness came over him, as if the effort to push aside that blot to see what lay beneath were as difficult as moving a mountain. He shrugged and went on, "—and this meeting will come to pass in a place which is no more, and there will the choice be made."

That last fragment made him want to howl in frustration. How could a meeting—or anything else—happen in a place which is no more? And what was the meaning of the word "choice"? What choice? Whose choice? Choice between what and what?

He swore and read it again. Once again he felt that peculiar lassitude when his eyes reached the blot on the page. He shrugged it off and went on. No matter what the word under the blot might be, it was still only one word, and one single word could not be *that* important. Irritably he put the scroll aside and considered the discrepancy. The most immediate explanation was that this spot, like so many others, was a place where the Mrin Prophet's well-known insanity had simply got the best of him. Another possibility was that this particular copy was not precisely accurate. The scribe who had copied it off had perhaps inadvertently skipped a line or two at the time when he had blotted the page. Garion recalled an occasion when he had done that himself, turning a perfectly bland proclamation into a horrendous declaration that he was on the verge of naming himself military dictator of all the kingdoms lying on this side of the Eastern Escarpment. When he had caught the blunder, he had not just erased the offending lines, he had shudderingly burned the whole sheet to make sure that no one ever saw it.

He stood up, stretching to relieve his cramped muscles and going to the small, barred window of the library. The autumn sky was a crisp blue. The nights had turned chilly in the past few weeks, and the higher meadows lying above the city were touched with frost when the sun arose. The days, however, were warm and golden. He checked the position of the sun to gauge the time. He had promised to meet with Count Valgon, the Tolnedran ambassador, at midday and he did not want to be late. Aunt Pol had stressed the importance of punctuality, and Garion always did his best to be on time.

He turned back to the table and absently rerolled the two scrolls, his mind still wrestling with the problem of the conflicting passages. Then he blew out the candles and left the library, carefully closing the door behind him.

Valgon, as always, was tedious. Garion felt that there was an innate pomposity in the Tolnedran character that made it impossible for them to say what they meant without extensive embellishment. The discussion that day had to do with "prioritizing" the unloading of merchant vessels in the harbor at Riva. Valgon seemed terribly fond of the word "prioritizing," finding a way to insert it into the discussion at least once in every other sentence. The essence of Valgon's presentation seemed to be a request—or a demand—that Tolnedran merchantmen should always have first access to the somewhat limited wharves at the foot of the city.

"My dear Valgon," Garion began, seeking some diplomatic way to refuse, "I actually believe that this matter needs—" He broke off, looking up as the great carved doors to the throne room swung inward.

One of the towering, gray-cloaked sentries who always stood guard outside when Garion was in the throne room stepped in, cleared his throat, and announced in a voice that probably could have been heard on the other side of the island, "Her Royal Majesty, Queen Ce'Nedra of Riva, Imperial Princess of the Tolnedran Empire, Commander of the Armies of the West, and beloved wife of his Majesty, Belgarion of Riva, Godslayer, Lord of the Western Sea, and Overlord of the West!"

Ce'Nedra, demure and tiny, entered on the sentry's heels, her shoulders unbowed by the weight of all those vast titles. She wore a teal-green velvet gown, gathered beneath the bodice to conceal her expanding waistline, and her eyes were sparkling mischievously.

Valgon turned and bowed smoothly.

Ce'Nedra touched the sentry's arm, strained up on tiptoe, and whispered to him. The sentry nodded, turned back toward the throne at the front of the hall, and cleared his throat again. "His Highness, Prince Kheldar of Drasnia, nephew of the beloved late King Rhodar, and cousin to King Kheva, Lord of the Marches of the North!"

Garion started up from the throne in astonishment.

Silk entered grandly. His doublet was a rich pearl gray, his fingers glittered with rings, and a heavy gold chain with a large pendant sapphire hung about his neck. "That's all right, gentlemen," he said to Garion and Count Valgon with an airy wave of his hand, "you needn't rise." He extended his arm grandly to Ce'Nedra, and the two of them came down the broad, carpeted aisle past the three glowing firepits in the floor.

"Silk!" Garion exclaimed.

"The very same," Silk replied with a mocking little bow. "Your Majesty is looking well—considering."

"Considering what?"

Silk winked at him.

"I am quite overwhelmed to meet so famous a merchant prince again," Valgon murmured politely. "Your Highness has become a legend in recent years. Your exploits in the East are the absolute despair of the great commercial houses in Tol Honeth."

"One *has* had certain modest success," Silk responded, breathing on a large ruby ring on his left hand and then polishing it on the front of his doublet. "In your next report, please convey my regards to your new Emperor. His handling of the Vordue situation was masterly."

Valgon permitted himself a faint smile. "I'm sure his Imperial Majesty will appreciate your good opinion, Prince Kheldar." He turned to Garion. "I know that your Majesty and his old friend will have many things to discuss," he said. "We can take up this other matter at a later date, perhaps." He bowed. "With your Majesty's permission, I will withdraw."

"Of course, Valgon," Garion replied. "And thank you."

The Tolnedran bowed again and quietly left the throne room.

Ce'Nedra came down to the foot of the throne and linked her arm affectionately with Silk's. "I hope you didn't mind being interrupted, Garion," she said. "I know that you and Valgon were having an absolutely *fascinating* talk."

Garion made a face. "What was the idea behind all that formality?" he asked curiously. "The business with all those titles, I mean?"

Silk grinned. "Ce'Nedra's idea. She felt that if we overwhelmed Valgon with enough titles, we could persuade him to go away. Did we interrupt anything important?"

Garion gave him a sour look. "He was talking about the problem of getting Tolnedran merchant vessels unloaded. I think that, if he'd thrown the word 'prioritizing' at me about one more time, I'd have jumped up and strangled him."

"Oh?" Ce'Nedra said, all wide-eyed and girlish. "Let's call him back, then."

"I take it that you're unfond of him," Silk suggested.

"He's a Honethite," Ce'Nedra replied, making an indelicate little sound. "I despise the Honeths."

"Let's go someplace where we can talk," Garion said, looking around at the formal throne room.

"Whatever your Majesty wishes," Silk said with a grand bow.

"Oh, stop that!" Garion said, coming down from the dais and leading the way to the side door.

When they reached the quiet, sunlit sanctuary of the royal apartment, Garion sighed with relief as he took off his crown and shrugged out of his formal state robes. "You have no idea how hot that thing gets," he said, tossing the robe in a heap on a chair in the corner.

"It also wrinkles, dear," Ce'Nedra reminded him, picking up the robe, folding it carefully, and hanging it over the chair back.

"Perhaps I could find one for you in Mallorean satin—suitable color and interwoven with silver thread," Silk suggested. "It would look very rich—tastefully understated—and not nearly so heavy."

"That's a thought," Garion said.

"And I'm sure I could offer it to you at a *very* attractive price."

Garion gave him a startled look, and Silk laughed.

"You never change, do you, Silk?" Ce'Nedra said.

"Of course not," the little thief replied, sprawling unasked in a chair.

"What brings you to Riva?" Garion asked him, taking a chair across the table from his friend.

"Affection—at least mostly. I haven't seen you two for several years now." He looked around. "I don't suppose you've got anything to drink handy?"

"We could probably find something." Garion grinned at him.

"We have a rather pleasant little wine," Ce'Nedra offered, going to a dark, polished sideboard. "We've been trying to keep Garion here away from ale."

One of Silk's eyebrows went up.

"He has an unfortunate tendency to want to sing when he drinks ale," the Queen explained. "I wouldn't really want to put you through that."

"All right," Garion said to her.

"It's not so much his voice," Ce'Nedra went on relentlessly. "It's the way he goes looking for the right notes—and doesn't find them."

"Do you *mind*?" Garion asked her.

She laughed a shimmering laugh and filled two silver goblets with a blood-red Tolnedran wine.

"Aren't you joining us?" Silk asked.

She made a face. "The heir to the Rivan Throne doesn't care much for wine," she replied, delicately placing one hand on her swelling abdomen. "Or perhaps he enjoys it too much. It makes him start kicking, and I'd rather that he didn't break too many of my ribs."

"Ah," Silk said delicately.

She brought the goblets to the table and set them down. "Now, if you two gentlemen will excuse me, it's time for my visit to the baths."

"Her hobby," Garion said. "She spends at least two hours of every afternoon down in the women's baths—even when she isn't dirty."

She shrugged. "It relaxes my back. I've been carrying this burden lately." Once again she touched her abdomen. "And it seems to get heavier every day."

"I'm glad that it's the women who have the babies," Silk said. "I'm sure I wouldn't really have the strength for it."

"You're a nasty little man, Kheldar," she retorted tartly.

"Of course I am." He smirked.

She gave him a withering look and went in search of Lady Arell, her usual companion in the baths.

"She looks absolutely blooming," Silk observed, "and she's not nearly as bad-tempered as I'd expected."

"You should have been around a few months ago."

"Bad?"

"You can't imagine."

"It happens, I suppose—or so I've been told."

"What have you been up to lately?" Garion asked, leaning back in his chair. "We haven't heard much about you."

"I've been in Mallorea," Silk replied, sipping at his wine. "The fur trade isn't very challenging any more, and Yarblek's been handling that end of the business. We felt that there was a great deal of money to be made in Mallorean silks, carpets, and uncut gemstones, so I went over to investigate."

"Isn't it a little dangerous for a Western merchant in Mallorea?"

Silk shrugged. "No worse than Rak Goska—or Tol Honeth, for that matter. I've spent my whole life in dangerous places, Garion."

"Couldn't you just buy your goods at Yar Marak or Thull Zelik when they come off the Mallorean ships?"

"The prices are better at the source. Every time an article goes through another pair of hands, the price doubles."

"That makes sense, I suppose." Garion looked at his friend, envying the freedom that made it possible for Silk to go anywhere in the world he wanted to go.

"What's Mallorea really like?" he asked. "We hear stories, but I think that's all they are most of the time."

"It's in turmoil just now," Silk replied gravely. "Kal Zakath's off fighting his war with the Murgos, and the Grolims went all to pieces when they heard about the death of Torak. Mallorean society has always been directed from either Mal Zeth or Mal Yaska—the emperor or the church—but now nobody seems to be in charge. The government bureaucracy tries to hold things together, but Malloreans need strong leadership and right now they don't have it. All sorts of strange things are beginning to surface—rebellions, new religions, that kind of thing."

A thought occurred to Garion. "Have you run across the name Zandramas?" he asked curiously.

Silk looked at him sharply. "It's odd you should ask that," he said. "When I was in Boktor, just before Rhodar died, I was talking with Javelin. Errand happened to be there and he asked Javelin the same question. Javelin told him that it's a Darshivan name and that was about all he knew. When I went back to Mallorea, I asked in a few places, but people got very tight-lipped and white-knuckled every time I mentioned it, so I let it drop. I gathered that it has something to do with one of those new religions I mentioned before."

"Did you happen to hear anything about something called the Sardion—or Cthrag Sardius, maybe?"

Silk frowned, tapping the rim of his goblet thoughtfully against his lower lip. "It's got a familiar ring to it, but I can't quite put my finger on where I heard it."

"If you happen to remember, I'd appreciate your telling me anything you can find out about it."

"Is it important?"

"I think it might be. Grandfather and Beldin have been trying to track it down."

"I've got some contacts in Mal Zeth and Melcene," Silk noted. "When I get back, I'll see what I can find out."

"You're going back soon, then?"

Silk nodded. "I'd have stayed there, but a little crisis came up in Yar Nadrak. King Drosta started to get greedy. We've been paying him some very healthy bribes to persuade him to look the other way about some of our activities in his kingdom. He got the notion that we were making a great deal of money and he was toying with the idea of expropriating our holdings in Gar og Nadrak. I had to come back and talk him out of the notion."

"How did you manage that? I've always had the impression that Drosta does pretty much what he wants in Gar og Nadrak."

"I threatened him," Silk said. "I pointed out that I'm closely related to the King of Drasnia and hinted that I was on very good terms with Kal Zakath. The prospect of an invasion from either the East or the West didn't appeal to him, so he dropped the idea."

"*Are* you on good terms with 'Zakath?"

"I've never met him—but Drosta doesn't know that."

"You lied? Isn't that dangerous?"

Silk laughed. "Lots of things are dangerous, Garion. We've both been in tight spots before. Rak Cthol wasn't the safest place in the world, if you'll recall, and Cthol Mishrak made me definitely edgy."

Garion toyed with his goblet. "You know something, Silk?" he said. "I sort of miss all that."

"All what?"

"I don't know—the danger, the excitement. Things have settled down pretty much for me. About the only excitement I get these days is in trying to maneuver my way around the Tolnedran ambassador. Sometimes I wish—" He left it hanging there.

"You can come to Mallorea with me, if you'd like," Silk offered. "I could find interesting work for a man of your talents."

"I don't think Ce'Nedra would be too pleased if I left just now."

"That's one of the reasons I never married," Silk told him. "I don't have to worry about things like that."

"Are you going to stop in Boktor on your way back?"

"Briefly, maybe. I visited the people I needed to see on my way here from Yar Nadrak. Porenn's doing very well with Kheva. He's probably going to be a good king when he grows up. And I stopped by to see Javelin, of course. It's more or less expected. He likes to get our impressions of foreign countries—even when we're not acting in any official capacity."

"Javelin's very good, isn't he?"

"He's the best."

"I always thought you were."

"Not by a long way, Garion." Silk smiled. "I'm too erratic—brilliant, maybe, but erratic. I get sidetracked too easily. When Javelin goes after something, he doesn't let anything distract him until he gets it. Right now, he's trying to get to the bottom of this Bear-cult thing."

"Is he having any luck?"

"Not yet. He's been trying for several years to get somebody into the inner councils of the cult, but he hasn't been able to manage it. I told him that he ought to send in Hunter, but he told me that Hunter's busy with something else and to mind my own business."

"Hunter? Who's Hunter?"

"I have no idea," Silk admitted. "It's not really a who, you see. It's a name that's applied to the most secret of our spies, and it changes from time to time. Only Javelin knows who Hunter is and he won't tell anybody—not even Porenn. Javelin himself was Hunter for a time—about fifteen years ago. It's not always necessarily a Drasnian, though—or even a man. It can be anybody in the world. It might even be somebody we know—Barak, maybe, or Relg—or maybe somebody in Nyissa."

"Mandorallen, perhaps?" Garion suggested, smiling.

Silk considered that. "No, Garion," he concluded. "I don't think Mandorallen has the right equipment. It can surprise you though. On several occasions, Hunter has even been a Murgo."

"A Murgo? How could you possibly trust a Murgo?"

"I didn't say we always have to *trust* Hunter."

Garion shook his head helplessly. "I'll never understand spies and spying."

"It's a game," Silk told him. "After you've played for a while, the game itself gets to be more important than which side you're on. Our reasons for doing things sometimes get pretty obscure."

"I've noticed that," Garion said. "And as long as the subject has come up, what's your *real* reason for coming to Riva?"

"It's nothing all that secret, Garion," Silk replied urbanely, adjusting the cuffs of his gray doublet. "I realized a few years ago that a traveling merchant tends to lose track of things. If you want to stay on top of a local situation, you need to have an agent on the scene—somebody who can take advantage of opportunities when they arise. I've located some markets for certain Rivan products—glass, good boots, those wool capes, that sort of thing—and I decided that it might not be a bad idea to have a representative here."

"That's really a very good idea, Silk. Things are a little static down in the city. We could use some new businesses to liven things up."

Silk beamed at him.

"And I can always use the additional revenue," Garion added.

"What?"

"There *are* a few taxes, Silk—nothing too burdensome, but I'm sure you understand. A kingdom is very expensive to run."

"Garion!" Silk's voice was anguished.

"It's one of the first things I learned. People don't mind taxes so much if they're sure that everybody's paying the same. I can't really make exceptions at all—not even for an old friend. I'll introduce you to Kail. He's my chief administrator. He'll set things up for you."

"I'm terribly disappointed in you, Garion," Silk said with a crestfallen look.

"As you've said so many times, business is business, after all."

There was a light tap on the door.

"Yes?" Garion answered.

"The Rivan Warder, your Majesty," the sentry outside announced.

"Send him in."

The tall, graying Rivan Warder entered quietly. "Prince Kheldar," he greeted Silk with a brief nod, then turned to Garion. "I wouldn't bother you, your Majesty," he apologized, "but a matter of some urgency has come up."

"Of course, Brand," Garion replied politely. "Sit down."

"Thank you, Belgarion," Brand said gratefully, sinking into a chair. "My legs aren't what they used to be."

"Isn't it a joy to grow older?" Silk said. "The mind gets better, but everything else starts to fall apart."

Brand smiled briefly. "There's been a bit of a squabble in the garrison here in the Citadel, Belgarion," he said, getting directly to the point. "I'll discipline the two young men involved myself, but I thought that perhaps if *you* spoke to them, it might head off bloodshed."

"Bloodshed?"

"They were bickering over something quite unimportant, and one thing led to another. They scuffled a bit and knocked a few of each other's teeth loose. That should have been the end of it, but they started issuing each other formal challenges. I was fairly sure that you would want to keep the swords out of it."

"Definitely."

"I can order them to withdraw the challenges, but there's always the possibility that they'll sneak out some night and find a private place to do war on each other. I think that if the king spoke with them, we might be able to head off that sort of foolishness. They're a couple of fairly good young men, and I don't think we want to have them chop each other into dog meat."

Garion nodded his agreement. "Send the pair of them to me first thing in the—"

The medallion he always wore gave a peculiar little twitch, and he broke off what he was saying, startled by the flutter against his chest. The amulet suddenly seemed to grow very hot, and there was a strange humming sound in his ears.

"What is it, Garion?" Silk asked him curiously.

Garion started to hold up one hand as he tried to pinpoint the source of the humming sound. Then his amulet gave a violent lurch that was almost like a blow to his chest. The humming shattered, and he heard Ce'Nedra's voice crying to him. *"Garion! Help me!"*

He sprang to his feet as Brand and Silk stared at him in amazement. "Ce'Nedra?" he shouted. "Where are you?"

"Help me, Garion! The baths!"

"Quick!" Garion exclaimed to the others. "Ce'Nedra needs us—in the baths!" and he ran from the room, grabbing up a plain sword standing sheathed in the corner as he passed.

"What is it?" Silk demanded, running along behind as they burst into the outer corridor.

"I don't know," Garion shouted. "She called me for help." He shook his sword as he ran, trying to free it of its sheath. "Something's happening down in the baths."

It was a long way down seemingly endless flights of torchlit stairs to the baths in the cellars of the Citadel. Garion went down those stairs three and four at a time with Silk and Brand hot on his heels. Startled servants and officials jumped out of their way as they rushed down, faces grim and with drawn weapons in their hands.

At the bottom of the last flight of stairs they found the heavy door to the women's baths bolted from the inside. Instantly summoning his will, Garion focused it and commanded, "Burst!" The iron-bound door blasted inward off its hinges.

The scene inside was one of horror. The Lady Arell lay in a crumpled heap on the tile floor with the hilt of a dagger protruding from between her shoulders. In the center of the steaming pool, a tall, raw-boned woman in a dark cloak was grimly holding something under the water—something that struggled weakly—and floating on the surface above that struggling form was a great fan of coppery red hair.

"Ce'Nedra!" Garion shouted, leaping feetfirst into the pool with his sword aloft.

The cloaked woman gave him one startled glance and fled, splashing frantically away from the enraged king.

Ce'Nedra's tiny body rose limply to the surface of the pool, and she floated facedown and bobbing slightly in the water. With a cry of anguish, Garion dropped his sword and struggled through the warm, waist-deep water, his desperate arms reaching out toward the limp body floating just beyond his grasp.

Roaring with rage, Brand ran around the tiled walkway surrounding the pool with his sword aloft to pursue the tall woman, who was fleeing through a narrow doorway on the far side of the bath, but Silk was already ahead of him, running swiftly after the woman with a long-bladed dagger held low.

Garion caught up the body of his wife in his arms and struggled toward the edge of the pool. With horror he realized that she was not breathing.

"What can I do?" he cried desperately. "Aunt Pol, what can I do?" But Aunt Pol was not there. He laid Ce'Nedra on the tiles on the edge of the pool. There was no sign of movement, no flutter of breath, and her face was a ghastly blue-gray color.

"Somebody help me!" Garion cried out, catching the tiny, lifeless form in his arms and holding it very close to him.

Something throbbed sharply against his chest, and he looked into his wife's still face, desperately searching for some sign of life. But Ce'Nedra did not move, and her little body was limp. Again he caught her to him.

Once again he felt that sharp throb—almost like a blow against his heart. He held Ce'Nedra away from him again, searching with tear-filled eyes for the source of that strange, jolting throb. The flickering light of one of the torches stuck in iron rings around the marble walls of the pool seemed to dance on the polished surface of the silver amulet at her throat. Could it have been—? With a trembling hand he put his fingertips to the amulet. He felt a tingling shock in his fingers. Startled, he jerked his hand away. Then he closed his fist about the amulet. He could feel it in his palm, throbbing like a silver heart, beating with a faltering rhythm.

"Ce'Nedra!" he said sharply. "You've got to wake up. Please don't die, Ce'Nedra!" But there was no sign, no movement from his wife. Still holding the amulet, Garion began to weep. "Aunt Pol," he cried brokenly, "what can I do?"

"Garion?" It was Aunt Pol's startled voice, coming to him across the empty miles.

"Aunt Pol," he sobbed, "help me!"

"What is it? What's wrong?"

"It's Ce'Nedra. She—she's been drowned!" And the full horror of it struck him like some great, overwhelming blow, and he began to sob again, great, tearing sobs.

"Stop that!" Aunt Pol's voice cracked like a whip. "Where?" she demanded. "When did this happen?"

"Here in the baths. She's not breathing, Aunt Pol. I think she's dead."

"Stop babbling, Garion!" Her voice was like a slap in the face. "How long has it been since her breathing stopped?"

"A few minutes—I don't know."

"You don't have any time to lose. Have you got her out of the water?"

"Yes—but she's not breathing, and her face is like ashes."

"Listen carefully. You've got to force the water out of her lungs. Put her down on her face and push on her back. Try to do it in the same rhythm as normal breathing, and be careful not to push too hard. You don't want to hurt the baby."

"But—"

"Do as I say, Garion!"

He turned his silent wife over and began to carefully push down on her ribs. An astonishing amount of water came out of the tiny girl's mouth, but she remained still and unmoving.

Garion stopped and took hold of the amulet again. "Nothing's happening, Aunt Pol."

"Don't stop."

He began pushing on Ce'Nedra's ribs again. He was about ready to despair, but then she coughed, and he almost wept with relief. He continued to push at her back. She coughed again, and then she began to cry weakly. Garion put his hand on the amulet. "She's crying, Aunt Pol! She's alive!"

"Good. You can stop now. What happened?"

"Some woman tried to kill her here in the baths. Silk and Brand are chasing the woman now."

There was a long silence. "I see," Aunt Pol said finally. "Now listen, Garion—carefully. Ce'Nedra's lungs will be very weak after this. The main danger right now is congestion and fever. You've got to keep her warm and quiet. Her life—and the baby's—depend on that. As soon as her breathing is stronger, get her into bed. I'll be there as soon as I can."

Garion moved quickly, gathering up every towel and robe he could find to make a bed for his weakly crying wife. As he covered her with a cloak, Silk returned, his face grim, and Brand, puffing noticeably, was right behind him.

"Is she all right?" the big Warder asked, his face desperately concerned.

"I think so," Garion said. "I got her breathing started again. Did the woman get away?"

"Not exactly," Silk replied. "She ran upstairs until she reached the battlements. When she got up there, I was right behind her. She saw that there was no way to escape, so she threw herself off."

Garion felt a surge of satisfaction at that. "Good," he said without thinking.

"No. Not really. We needed to question her. Now we'll never find out who sent her here to do this."

"I hadn't thought of that."

Brand had gone sadly to the silent body of his niece. "My poor Arell," he said, his voice full of tears. He knelt beside her and took hold of the dagger protruding from her back. "Even in death, she served her queen," he said almost proudly.

Garion looked at him.

"The dagger's stuck," Brand explained, tugging at it. "The woman who killed her couldn't get it out. That's why she was trying to drown Ce'Nedra. If she'd been able to use this knife, we'd have been too late."

"I'm going to find out who's responsible for this," Garion declared from between clenched teeth. "I think I'll have him flayed."

"Flaying is good," Silk agreed. "Or boiling. Boiling has always been my favorite."

"Garion," Ce'Nedra said weakly, and all thoughts of vengeance fled from Garion's mind as he turned to her. While he held his wife close to him, he dimly heard Silk speaking quietly to Brand.

"After somebody picks up what's left of our would-be assassin," the little man was saying in a terse voice, "I'd like to have all of her clothing brought to me."

"Her clothing?"

"Right. The woman isn't able to talk anymore, but her clothing might. You'd be surprised at how much you can learn about someone by looking at his undergarments. We want to find out who was behind this, and that dead woman out there is our only clue. I want to find out who she was and where she came from. The quicker I can do that, the quicker we can start heating up the oil."

"Oil?"

"I'm going to simmer the man who was behind this—slowly and with a great deal of attention to every exquisite detail."

CHAPTER FOURTEEN

Polgara arrived late that same afternoon. No one saw fit to raise the question of how she had crossed the hundreds of intervening leagues in the space of hours instead of weeks. The sentry who had been standing watch atop the battlements and who escorted her to the sickroom, however, had a slightly wild look in his eyes, as if he had just seen something about which he would prefer not to speak.

Garion, at the moment she arrived, was in the midst of a discussion with one of the court physicians about the therapeutic value of bleeding, and the conversation had reached the point where he had just picked up a sword to confront the startled medical man who was approaching the bed with lancet in hand. "If you try to open my wife's veins with that," the young king declared firmly, "I'm going to open yours with this."

"All right," Polgara said crisply, "that will do, Garion." She removed her cloak and laid it across the back of a chair.

"Aunt Pol," he gasped with relief.

She had already turned to face the four physicians who had been tending the little queen. "Thank you for your efforts, gentlemen," she told them. "I'll send for you if I need you." The note of dismissal in her voice was final, and the four quietly filed out.

"Lady Polgara," Ce'Nedra said weakly from the bed.

Polgara turned to her immediately. "Yes, dear," she said, taking Ce'Nedra's tiny hand in hers. "How do you feel?"

"My chest hurts, and I can't seem to stay awake."

"We'll have you up and about in no time at all, dear," Polgara assured her. She looked critically at the bed. "I think I'm going to need more pillows, Garion," she said. "I want to prop her up into a sitting position."

Garion quickly went through the sitting room to the door leading to the corridor outside.

"Yes, your Majesty?" the sentry said as Garion opened the door.

"Do you want to get me about a dozen or so pillows?"

"Of course, your Majesty." The sentry started down the corridor.

"On second thought, make that two dozen," Garion called after him. Then he went back to the bedroom.

"I mean it, Lady Polgara," Ce'Nedra was saying in a weak little voice. "If it ever gets to the point where you have to make a choice, save my baby. Don't even think about me."

"I see," Polgara replied gravely. "I hope you've purged yourself of that particular nonsense now."

Ce'Nedra stared at her.

"Melodrama has always made me just ever so faintly nauseous."

A slow flush crept up Ce'Nedra's cheeks.

"That's a very good sign," Aunt Pol encouraged her. "If you can blush, it means that you're well enough to take final note of trivial things."

"Trivial?"

"Such as being embarrassed about how truly stupid that last statement of yours really was. Your baby's fine, Ce'Nedra. In fact, he's better off right now than you are. He's sleeping at the moment."

Ce'Nedra's eyes had gone wide, and her hands were placed protectively over her abdomen. "You can see him?" she asked incredulously.

"See isn't exactly the right word, dear," Polgara said as she mixed two powders together in a glass. "I know what he's doing and what he's thinking about." She added water to the mixture in the glass and watched critically as the contents bubbled and fumed. "Here," she instructed, handing the glass to her patient, "Drink this." Then she turned to Garion. "Build up the fire, dear. It's autumn, after all, and we don't want her getting chilled."

Brand and Silk had rather carefully examined the broken body of the would-be assassin and had shifted their attention to her clothing by the time Garion joined them late that evening. "Have you found out anything yet?" he asked as he entered the room.

"We know that she was an Alorn," Brand replied in his rumbling voice. "About thirty-five years old, and she didn't work for a living. At least she didn't do anything strenuous enough to put calluses on her hands."

"That's not very much to go on," Garion said.

"It's a start," Silk told him, carefully examining the hem of a bloodstained dress.

"It sort of points at the Bear-cult then, doesn't it?"

"Not necessarily," Silk replied, laying aside the dress and picking up a linen shift. "When you're trying to hide your identity, you pick an assassin from another country. Of course, that kind of thinking might be a little too subtle for the Bear-cult." He frowned. "Now, where have I seen this stitch before?" he muttered, still looking at the dead woman's undergarment.

"I'm so very sorry about Arell," Garion said to Brand. "We were all very fond of her." It seemed like such an inadequate thing to say.

"She would have appreciated that, Belgarion," Brand said quietly. "She loved Ce'Nedra very much."

Garion turned back to Silk with a feeling of frustration boiling up in him. "What are we going to do?" he demanded. "If we can't find out who was behind this, he'll probably just try again."

"I certainly *hope* so," Silk said.

"You *what*?"

"We can save a lot of time if we can catch somebody who's still alive. You can only get so much out of dead people."

"I wish we'd been a little more thorough when we wiped out the Bear-cult at Thull Mardu," Brand said.

"I wouldn't get my mind *too* set on the notion that the Bear-cult was responsible for this," Silk told him. "There are some other possibilities."

"Who else would want to hurt Ce'Nedra?" Garion asked.

Silk sprawled in a chair, scratching absently at his cheek and with his forehead furrowed with thought. "Maybe it wasn't Ce'Nedra," he mused.

"What?"

"It's altogether possible, you know, that the attempt was directed at the baby she's carrying. There could be people out there in the world who do not want there to be an heir to Iron-grip's throne."

"Who?"

"The Grolims come to mind rather quickly," Silk replied. "Or the Nyissans— or even a few Tolnedrans. I want to keep an open mind on the matter—until I find out a few more things." He held up the stained undergarment. "I'm going to start with this. Tomorrow morning, I'm going to take it down to the city and show it to every tailor and seamstress I can find. I might be able to get something out of the weave, and there's a peculiar kind of stitching along the hem. If I can find somebody to identify it for me, it might give us something to work on."

Brand looked thoughtfully over at the still, blanket-draped form of the woman who had tried to kill Ce'Nedra. "She would have had to have entered the Citadel by way of one of the gates," he mused. "That means that she passed a sentry and that she had to have given him some kind of excuse for coming in. I'll round up every man who's been on sentry duty for the past week and bring them all down here to have a look at her. Once we know exactly when she got in, maybe we can start to backtrack her. I'd like to find the ship she arrived on and have a talk with the captain."

"What can I do?" Garion asked quickly.

"Probably you should stay close to Ce'Nedra's room," Silk suggested. "Any time Polgara leaves for any reason at all, you ought to go in and take her place. There could be other attempts, you know, and I think we'll all feel better if Ce'Nedra's guarded rather closely."

Under Polgara's watchful eyes, Ce'Nedra spent a quiet night, and her breathing was much stronger the next day. She complained bitterly about the taste of the medicines she was required to drink, and Polgara listened with a great show of interest to the queen's extensive tirade. "Yes, dear," she agreed pleasantly. "Now drink it all down."

"Does it have to taste so awful?" Ce'Nedra said with a shudder.

"Of course it does. If medicine tasted good, sick people might be tempted to stay sick so that they could enjoy the medicine. The worse it tastes, the quicker you get well."

Late that afternoon, Silk returned with a disgusted look on his face. "I hadn't realized how many ways it's possible to attach two pieces of cloth together," he grumbled.

"No luck, I take it," Garion said.

"Not really," Silk replied, throwing himself into a chair. "I managed to pick up all sorts of educated guesses, though."

"Oh?"

"One tailor was willing to stake his reputation on the fact that this particular stitch is used exclusively in Nyissa. A seamstress told me very confidently that this was an Ulgo garment. And one half-wit went so far as to say that the owner of the garment was a sailor, since this stitch is *always* used to repair torn sails."

"What are you talking about, Silk?" Polgara asked curiously as she passed through the sitting room on her way back to Ce'Nedra's bedside.

"I've been trying to get someone to identify the stitching on the hem of this thing," he said in a disgusted tone, waving the bloodstained shift.

"Here. Let me see it."

Silk wordlessly handed her the garment.

She glanced at it almost casually. "Northeastern Drasnia," she told him, "from somewhere near the town of Rheon."

"Are you sure?" Silk came to his feet quickly.

She nodded. "That kind of stitching was developed centuries ago—back in the days when all the garments up there were made from reindeer skin."

"That's disgusting," Silk said.

"What is?"

"I ran around with this thing all day long—up and down all those stairs and in and out of every tailor shop in Riva—and all I had to do to find out what I wanted to know was show it to you."

"That's not my fault, Prince Kheldar," she told him, handing back the shift. "If you don't know enough to bring these little problems to me by now, then there probably isn't much hope for you."

"Thanks, Polgara," he said drily.

"Then the assassin was a Drasnian," Garion said.

"A *northeastern* Drasnian," Silk corrected. "Those people up there are a strange sort—almost worse than the ones who live in the fens."

"Strange?"

"Standoffish, closemouthed, unfriendly, clannish, secretive. Everybody in northeast Drasnia behaves as if he had all the state secrets in the kingdom tucked up his sleeve."

"Why would they hate Ce'Nedra so much?" Garion asked with a puzzled frown.

"I wouldn't make too much of the fact that this assassin was a Drasnian, Garion," Silk told him. "People who hire other people to do their killing for them don't always go looking for their hirelings close to home—and, although there are a lot of assassins in the world, very few of them are women." He pursed his lips thoughtfully. "I *do* think that I'll take a trip up to Rheon and have a look around, however."

As the chill of winter set in, Polgara finally declared that Ce'Nedra was out of all danger. "I think I'll stay, though," she added. "Durnik and Errand can manage at home for a few months, and I'd probably no sooner get home than I'd have to turn around and come back."

Garion looked at her blankly.

"You didn't actually think that I was going to let anybody else deliver Ce'Nedra's first baby, did you?"

It snowed heavily just before Erastide, and the steep streets of the city of Riva became virtually impassable. Ce'Nedra's disposition soured noticeably. Her increasing girth made her awkward, and the depth of the snow in the city streets had rather effectively confined her to the Citadel. Polgara took the little queen's outbursts and crying fits calmly, scarcely changing expression, even at the height of the eruptions. "You *do* want to have this baby, don't you?" she asked pointedly on one such occasion.

"Of course I do," Ce'Nedra replied indignantly.

"Well then, you have to go through this. It's the only way I know of to fill the nursery."

"Don't try to be reasonable with me, Lady Polgara," Ce'Nedra flared. "I'm not in the mood for reasonableness right now."

Polgara gave her a faintly amused look, and Ce'Nedra, in spite of herself, began to laugh. "I'm being silly, aren't I?"

"A bit, yes."

"It's just that I feel so huge and ugly."

"That will pass, Ce'Nedra."

"Sometimes I wish I could just lay eggs—the way birds do."

"I'd stick to doing it the old way, dear. I don't think you have the disposition for sitting on a nest."

Erastide came and passed quietly. The celebration on the island was warm, but somewhat restrained. It seemed as if the whole population was holding its breath, waiting for a much larger reason for celebration. Winter ground on with each week adding more snow to the already high-piled drifts. A month or so after Erastide there was a brief thaw, lasting for perhaps two days, and then the frigid chill locked in again, turning the sodden snowbanks into blocks of ice. The weeks plodded by tediously, and everybody waited.

"Would you just look at that?" Ce'Nedra said angrily to Garion one morning shortly after they had arisen.

"At what, dear?" he replied mildly.

"At that!" She pointed disgustedly at the window. "It's snowing again." There was a note of accusation in her voice.

"It's not my fault," he said defensively.

"Did I say that it was?" She turned awkwardly to glare at him. Her tininess made her swollen belly appear all the larger, and she sometimes seemed to thrust it out at him as if it were entirely his doing.

"This is just absolutely insupportable," she declared. "Why have you brought me to this frozen—" She stopped in mid-tirade, a strange look crossing her face.

"Are you all right, dear?" Garion asked.

"Don't 'dear' me, Garion. I—" She stopped again. "Oh, my," she said breathlessly.

"What is it?" He got to his feet.

"Oh, dear," Ce'Nedra said, putting her hands to the small of her back. "Oh dear, oh dear, oh dear."

"Ce'Nedra, that's not very helpful. What's the matter?"

"I think perhaps I'd better go lie down," she said almost absently. She started across the room, moving at a stately waddle. She stopped. "Oh, dear," she said with much more vehemence. Her face was pale, and she put one hand on a chairback to support herself. "I think that it might be a good idea if you sent for Lady Polgara, Garion."

"Is it—? I mean, are you—?"

"Don't babble, Garion," she said tensely. "Just open the door and scream for your Aunt Pol."

"Are you trying to say that—?"

"I'm not trying, Garion. I'm saying it. Get her in here right now." She waddled to the bedroom door and stopped again with a little gasp. "Oh, my goodness," she said.

Garion stumbled to the door and jerked it open. "Get Lady Polgara!" he said to the startled sentry. "Immediately! Run!"

"Yes, your Majesty!" the man replied, dropping his spear and sprinting down the hall.

Garion slammed the door and dashed to Ce'Nedra's side. "Can I do anything?" he asked, wringing his hands.

"Help me to bed," she told him.

"Bed!" he said. "Right!" He grabbed her arm and began to tug at her.

"What are you doing?"

"Bed," he blurted, pointing at the royal four-poster.

"I know what it is, Garion. Help me. Don't yank on me."

"Oh." He took her hand, slipped his other arm about her, and lifted her off her feet. He stumbled toward the bed, his eyes wide and his mind completely blank.

"Put me down, you great oaf!"

"Bed," he urged her, trying with all the eloquence at his command to explain. He carefully set her back down on her feet and rushed on ahead. "Nice bed," he said, patting the coverlets encouragingly.

Ce'Nedra closed her eyes and sighed. "Just step out of my way, Garion," she said with resignation.

"But—"

"Why don't you build up the fire?" she suggested.

"What?" He stared around blankly.

"The fireplace—that opening in the wall with the burning logs in it. Put some more wood in there. We want it nice and warm for the baby, don't we?" She reached the bed and leaned against it.

Garion dashed to the fireplace and stood staring at it stupidly.

"What's the matter now?"

"Wood," he replied. "No wood."

"Bring some in from the other room."

What an absolutely brilliant suggestion she had just made! He stared at her gratefully.

"Go into the other room, Garion," she said, speaking very slowly and distinctly. "Pick up some wood. Carry it back in here. Put it on the fire. Have you got all that so far?"

"Right!" he said excitedly. He dashed into the other room, picked up a stick of firewood, and dashed back in with it. "Wood," he said, holding the stick up proudly.

"Very nice, Garion," she said, climbing laboriously into the bed. "Now put it on the fire and go back out and bring in some more."

"More," he agreed, flinging the stick into the fireplace and dashing out the door again.

After he had emptied the woodbin in the sitting room—one stick at a time—he stared around wildly, trying to decide what to do next. He picked up a chair. If he were to swing it against the wall, he reasoned, it ought to break up into manageable pieces.

The door to the apartment opened, and Polgara came in. She stopped to stare at the wild-eyed Garion. "What on earth are you doing with that chair?" she demanded.

"Wood," he explained, brandishing the heavy piece of furniture. "Need wood—for the fire."

She gave him a long look, smoothing down the front of her white apron. "I see," she said. "It's going to be one of those. Put the chair down, Garion. Where's Ce'Nedra?"

"Bed," he replied, regretfully setting down the polished chair. Then he looked at her brightly. "Baby," he informed her.

She rolled her eyes toward the ceiling. "Garion," she said, speaking carefully as if to a child, "it's much too early for Ce'Nedra to be taking to her bed. She needs to walk around—keep moving."

He shook his head stubbornly. "Bed," he repeated. "Baby." He looked around and picked up the chair again.

Polgara sighed, opened the door, and beckoned to the sentry. "Young man," she said, "why don't you take his Majesty here down to that courtyard just outside the kitchen? There's a large pile of logs there. Get him an axe so that he can cut up some firewood."

Everybody was being absolutely brilliant today. Garion marveled at the suggestion Aunt Pol had just made. He set down the chair again and dashed out with the baffled sentry in tow.

He chopped up what seemed like a cord of wood in the first hour, sending out a positive blizzard of chips as he swung the axe so fast that it seemed almost to blur in the air. Then he paused, pulled off his doublet, and really got down to work. About noon, a respectful cook brought him a slab of freshly roasted beef, a large chunk of bread, and some ale. Garion wolfed down three or four bites, took a couple of gulps of the ale, and then picked up his axe to attack another log. It was altogether possible that he might have finished up with the woodpile outside the kitchen and then gone in search of more trees had not Brand interrupted him shortly before the sun went down.

The big, gray-haired Warder had a broad grin on his face. "Congratulations, Belgarion," he said. "You have a son."

Garion paused, looking almost regretfully at the remaining logs. Then what Brand had just said finally seeped into his awareness. The axe slid from his fingers. "A son?" he said. "What an amazing thing. And so quickly, too." He looked at the woodpile. "I only just now got here. I always thought that it took much longer."

Brand looked at him carefully, then gently took him by the arm. "Come along now, Belgarion," he said. "Let's go up and meet your son."

Garion bent and carefully picked up an armload of wood. "For the fire," he explained. "Ce'Nedra wants a nice big fire."

"She'll be very proud of you, Belgarion," Brand assured him.

When they reached the royal bedchamber, Garion carefully put his armload of wood on the polished table by the window and approached the bed on tiptoe.

Ce'Nedra looked very tired and wan, but there was, nonetheless, a contented little smile on her face. Nestled beside her in a soft blanket was a very small person. The newcomer had a red face and almost no hair. He seemed to be asleep, but as Garion approached, his eyes opened. Gravely, the crown prince looked at his father, then sighed, burped, and went back to sleep.

"Oh, isn't he just beautiful, Garion?" Ce'Nedra said in a wondering little voice.

"Yes," Garion replied with a great lump coming up into his throat. "And so are you." He knelt beside the bed and put his arms about them both.

"Very nice, children," Polgara said from the other side of the bed. "You both did just fine."

The following day Garion and his newborn son went through a very ancient ceremony. With Polgara at his side in a splendid blue and silver gown, he carried the baby to the Hall of the Rivan King, where the nobles of the island kingdom awaited them. As the three of them entered the Hall, the Orb of Aldur, standing on the pommel of Iron-grip's sword, blazed forth with a great shimmer of blue light. Almost bemused, Garion approached his throne. "This is my son, Geran," he announced— in part to the gathered throng, but also, in a peculiar way, to the Orb itself. The choice of his son's name had not been difficult. Though he could not remember his father, Garion had wanted to honor him, and no way seemed more appropriate than to give *his* son his father's name.

He carefully handed the baby to Polgara, reached up, and took down the great sword. Holding it by the blade, he extended it toward the blanket-wrapped infant in Polgara's arms. The shimmering glow of the Orb grew brighter. And then, as if attracted by that light, Geran stretched forth his tiny pink hand and put it on the glowing jewel. A great aura of many-colored light burst from the Orb at the infant's touch, surrounding the three of them with a pulsating rainbow that illuminated the entire Hall. A vast chorus filled Garion's ears, rising to an enormous chord that seemed to shake the whole world.

"Hail Geran!" Brand boomed in a great voice, "heir to the throne of Iron-grip and keeper of the Orb of Aldur!"

"Hail Geran!" the throng echoed in a thunderous shout.

"Hail Geran," the dry voice in Garion's mind added quietly.

Polgara said nothing. She did not need to speak, since the look in her eyes said everything that needed saying.

Although it was winter and the Sea of the Winds was lashed by storms, the Alorn Kings all journeyed to Riva to celebrate the birth of Geran. Many others, friends and old acquaintances, joined with Anheg, Cho-Hag, and Queen Porenn on the journey to Riva. Barak was there, of course, accompanied by his wife Merel. Hettar and Adara arrived. Lelldorin and Mandorallen came up from Arendia with Ariana and Nerina.

Garion, now somewhat more sensitive to such things, was amazed at how many children his friends had produced. No matter which way he turned, there seemed to be babies, and the sound of little boys and girls running and laughing filled the sober halls of the Citadel. The boy-king Kheva of Drasnia and Barak's son Unrak soon became the closest of friends. Nerina's daughters romped with Adara's sons in endless games involving much giggling. Barak's eldest daughter, Gundred, now a ravishing young lady, cut a broad track through the hearts of whole platoons of young Rivan nobles, all the while under the watchful eye of her huge, red-bearded father, who never actually threatened any of his daughter's suitors, but whose looks said quite plainly that he would tolerate no foolishness. Little Terzie, Gundred's younger sister, hovered on the very brink of womanhood—romping one moment with the younger children and looking the next with devastating eyes at the group of adolescent Rivan boys who always seemed to be around.

King Fulrach and General Brendig sailed over from Sendaria about midway through the celebration. Queen Layla sent her fondest congratulations, but she did not make the trip with her husband. "She almost got on board the ship," Fulrach reported, "but then a gust of wind made a wave break over the stones of the quay, and she fainted. We decided not to subject her to the voyage at that point."

"It's probably best," Garion agreed.

Durnik and Errand came up from the Vale, naturally, and with them came Belgarath.

The celebration went on for weeks. There were banquets and formal presentations of gifts, both by the visitors and by the ambassadors of various friendly kingdoms. And, of course, there were hours of reminiscences and a fair amount of serious drinking. Ce'Nedra was in her glory, since she and her infant son were the absolute center of attention.

Garion found that the festivities, coupled with his normal duties, left him almost no free time at all. He wished that he could find an hour or two to talk with Barak, Hettar, Mandorallen, and Lelldorin; but no matter how he tried to rearrange his days, the time simply was not there.

Very late one evening, however, Belgarath came looking for him. Garion looked up from a report he had been reading as the old sorcerer entered his study. "I thought we might want to talk for a bit," the old man said.

Garion tossed aside the report. "I haven't meant to neglect you, Grandfather," he apologized, "but they're keeping my days pretty well filled up."

Belgarath shrugged. "Things are bound to settle down in a while. Did I ever get around to congratulating you?"

"I think so."

"Good. That's taken care of, then. People always make such a fuss about babies. I don't really care that much for them myself. They're all squally and wet, most of the time, and it's almost impossible to talk to them. You don't mind if I help myself, do you?" He pointed at a crystal decanter of pale wine standing on a table.

"No. Go ahead."

"You want some?"

"No thanks, Grandfather."

Belgarath poured himself a goblet of wine and then settled down in a chair across from Garion's. "How's the king business?" he asked.

"Tedious," Garion replied ruefully.

"Actually, that's not a bad thing, you know. When it gets exciting, that usually means that something pretty awful is happening."

"I suppose you're right."

"Have you been studying?"

Garion sat up quickly. "I'm glad you brought that up. Things have been so hectic that something sort of important had almost slipped my mind."

"Oh?"

"How careful were people when they made copies of those prophecies?"

Belgarath shrugged. "Fairly careful, I suppose. Why do you ask?"

"I think that something got left out of my copy of the Mrin Codex."

"What makes you think so?"

"There's a passage in there that just doesn't make sense."

"Maybe not to *you*, but you haven't been studying all that long."

"That's not what I mean, Grandfather. I'm not talking about an obscure meaning. When I'm getting at is a sentence that starts out and then just stops without going anywhere. I mean, it doesn't have any ending the way it should."

"You're concerned about grammar?"

Garion scratched at his head. "It's the only passage I found in there that breaks off that way. It goes, 'But behold, the stone which lies at the center of the light shall—' And then there's a blot, and it takes up again with '—and this meeting will come to pass in a place which is no more, and there will the choice be made.' "

Belgarath frowned. "I think I know the passage," he said.

"The two just don't fit together, Grandfather. The first part is talking about the Orb—at least that's the way I read it—and the second part is talking about a meeting. I don't know what word is under that blot, but I can't for the life of me figure out how the two parts could be hooked together. I think there's something missing. That's why I was asking about how they went about copying these things. Could the scribe who was doing it have skipped a couple of lines?"

"I don't think so, Garion," Belgarath said. "The new copy is always compared with the old one by somebody other than the scribe. We *are* fairly careful about things like that."

"Then what's under the blot?"

Belgarath scratched his beard thoughtfully. "I can't quite recall," he admitted. "Anheg's here. Maybe he remembers—or you can ask him to transcribe that part from his copy and send it to you when he gets back to Val Alorn."

"That's a good idea."

"I wouldn't worry too much about it, Garion. It's only part of one passage, after all."

"There are a lot of things in there that are only one passage, Grandfather, and they turned out to be sort of important."

"If it bothers you so much, chase it down. That's a good way to learn."

"Aren't you the least bit curious about it?"

"I have other things on my mind. You're the one who found this discrepancy, so I'll give you all the glory of exposing it to the world and working out the solution."

"You're not being very much help, Grandfather."

Belgarath grinned at him. "I'm not really trying to be, Garion. You're grown up enough now to solve your own problems." He looked over at the decanter. "I believe I'll have just another little touch of that," he said.

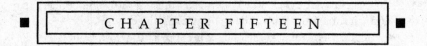

CHAPTER FIFTEEN

" And they shall number twelve, for twelve is a number which is pleas-
... ing to the Gods. I know this to be true, for a raven once came to me in a dream and told me so. I have always loved the number twelve, and it is for this reason that the Gods have chosen me to reveal this truth to all the nations. . . ."

Garion scowled at the musty-smelling book. There had been some hope in the earlier pages—some obscure references to Light and Dark and a tantalizing fragment which had stated quite clearly that, "The holiest of things will always be the color of the sky, save only when it perceives great evil, and then will it burn hot with scarlet flame." When he had found that passage, he had read on avidly, convinced that he had stumbled across a genuine and hitherto undiscovered prophecy. The rest of the book, unfortunately, proved to be absolute gibberish. The brief biographical note at the beginning of the book indicated that its author had been a Drasnian merchant of some substance during the third millennium and that these secret jottings had been found only after his death. Garion wondered how a man with so disturbed a mind could have even functioned in a normal society.

He closed the book in disgust and added it to the growing pile of ravings that was accumulating on the table in front of him. Next he picked up a slender volume that had been found in a deserted house in Arendia. The first few pages were devoted to the household accounts of a very minor Arendish nobleman. Then, on the fourth page, the mundane broke off quite suddenly. "The Child of Light shall take up the sword and go in search of that which is hidden," Garion read. This was immediately followed by a tediously detailed account of the purchase of a dozen or so pigs from a neighbor. Then once again the unknown writer jumped into prophecy. "The quest of the Child of Light shall be for one whose soul has been reft away, for a stone that is empty at its center and for the babe who will hold the Light in one hand and the Dark in the other." That definitely seemed to be getting somewhere. Garion pulled one of his guttering candles closer and hunched over the book, reading each page carefully. Those two passages, however, proved to be the only ones in the entire volume that did not speak of the day-to-day business of that forgotten farm somewhere in Arendia.

Garion sighed, leaned back, and looked around at the dimly lighted library. The bound books stood in their dusty rows on the dark shelves, and the linen-covered scrolls lay along the top of each bookcase. The light of his two candles flickered, making the room seem almost to dance.

"There has to be a faster way to do this," he muttered.

"Actually there is," the dry voice in his mind said to him.

"What?"

"You said that there had to be a faster way. I said that there is."

"Where have you been?"

"Here and there."

Garion knew this other awareness well enough by now to be certain that it would tell him only what it wanted him to know. "All right," he said, "what is this faster way?"

"You don't have to read every single word the way you have been doing. Open your mind and just leaf through the pages. The things I put in each book will sort of leap out at you."

"Are the prophecies always mixed right in with all this other nonsense?"

"Usually, yes."

"Why did you do it that way?"

"Several reasons. Most of the time I didn't want the man who was doing the actual writing even to know what I was hiding in his book. Then, of course, it's a good way to keep things from falling into unfriendly hands."

"And friendly ones too, for that matter."

"Did you want me to explain, or were you just looking for an excuse to make clever remarks?"

"All right." Garion sighed, giving up.

"I think I've told you before that the word gives meaning to the event. The word has to be there, but it doesn't have to be right out in the open where just anybody can find it."

Garion frowned. "Do you mean that you put all these things in all these books for just a few people to read?"

"The term 'a few' isn't really accurate. Try 'one' instead."

"One? Who?"

"You, obviously."

"Me? Why me?"

"Are we going to go through that again?"

"Are you trying to say that all of this was sort of like a personal letter—just to me?"

"In a manner of speaking, yes."

"What if I hadn't gotten around to reading it?"

"Why are you reading it now?"

"Because Belgarath told me to."

"Why do you think Belgarath told you that?"

"Because—" Garion broke off. "*You* told him to say it to me?"

"Naturally. He didn't know about it, of course, but I nudged him. All sorts of people have access to the Mrin Codex. That's why I made it so cryptic. These personal instructions to you, however, should be fairly clear—if you pay attention."

"Why don't you just *tell* me what I'm supposed to do?"

"I'm not permitted to do that."

"Permitted?"

"We have our rules, my opposite and I. We're very carefully balanced and we have to stay that way. We agreed only to act through our instruments, and if I intervene in person—with such things as telling you directly what you must do—then my opposite will also be free to step over the line. That's why we both work through what are called prophecies."

"Isn't that a little complicated?"

"The alternative would be absolute chaos. My opposite and I are limitless. If we confront each other directly, whole suns will be destroyed."

Garion shuddered and swallowed hard. "I didn't realize that," he admitted. Then an idea occurred to him. "Would you be permitted to tell me about that line in the Mrin Codex—the one that's got the blotted word in the middle of it?"

"That depends on how much you want to know about it."

"What's the word under the blot?"

"There are several words there. If you look at it in the right kind of light, you should be able to see them. As for these other books, try reading them the way I told you to. I think you'll find that it saves a lot of time—and you really don't have all that much time to spare."

"What's that supposed to mean?"

But the voice was gone.

The door to the library opened, and Ce'Nedra came in, wearing her nightdress and a warm robe. "Garion," she said, "aren't you *ever* coming to bed?"

"What?" He looked up. "Oh—yes. Right away."

"Who was in here with you?"

"Nobody. Why?"

"I heard you talking to someone."

"I was just reading, that's all."

"Come to bed, Garion," she said firmly. "You can't read the whole library in one evening."

"Yes, dear," he agreed.

· · ·

Not long after that, when spring had begun to touch the lower meadows on the slopes behind the Citadel, the promised letter from King Anheg arrived. Garion immediately took the copy of that baffling passage in the Mrin Codex to the library to compare it with *his* copy. When he put the two side by side, he began to swear. Anheg's copy was blotted in exactly the same place. "I told him!" Garion fumed. "I told him specifically that I needed to see that particular spot! I even showed him!" Swearing angrily, he began to pace up and down, waving both arms in the air.

Rather surprisingly, Ce'Nedra took her husband's near-obsession with the Mrin Codex in stride. Of course, the little queen's attention was almost totally riveted on her new son, and Garion was fairly certain that anything he said or did was only on the very edge of her awareness. Young Prince Geran was grossly overmothered. Ce'Nedra held him in her arms almost every minute that he was awake and frequently even when he was asleep. He was a good-natured baby and seldom cried or fussed. He took his mother's constant attention quite calmly and accepted all the cuddling and cooing and impulsive kisses with equanimity. Garion, however, felt that Ce'Nedra really overdid things just a bit. Since she insisted on holding Geran constantly, it definitely cut into the time when *he* might be able to hold his son. Once he almost asked her when his turn was going to come, but decided at the last minute not to. The thing that he really felt was unfair was Ce'Nedra's sense of timing. Whenever she *did* put Geran in his cradle for a few moments and Garion finally got the chance to pick him up, the little queen's hands seemed almost automatically to go to the buttons on the front of her dress, and she would placidly announce that it was time for Geran to nurse. Garion certainly did not begrudge his son his lunch, but the baby really didn't look all that hungry most of the time.

After a time, however, when he finally became adjusted to Geran's undeniable presence in their lives, the call of the dim, musty library began to reassert itself. The procedure that had been suggested to him by the dry voice worked surprisingly well. After a little practice, he found that he could skim rapidly over page after page of mundane material and that his eye would stop automatically at the prophetic passages buried in the midst of ordinary text. He was surprised to find so many of these passages hidden away in the most unlikely places. In most cases it was obvious that the writers had not even been aware of what they had inserted. A sentence would frequently break off, leap into prophecy, and then take up again exactly where it had stopped. Garion was positive that upon rereading the text, the unconscious prophet who had inserted the material would not even see what he had just written.

The Mrin Codex, however, and to a lesser degree the Darine, remained the core of the whole thing. Passages from other works clarified or expanded, but the two major prophecies put it all down in uncontaminated form. Garion began to cross index as he went along, identifying each new passage with a number and then linking those numbers to the series of letter codes he had assigned to the paragraphs of the Mrin scroll. Each paragraph of the Mrin, he discovered, usually had three or four corroborating or explanatory lines gleaned from other works—all except that crucial blotted passage.

"And how did the search go today, dear?" Ce'Nedra asked brightly one evening when he returned, grouchy and out of sorts, to the royal apartment. She was nursing Geran at the time, and her face was aglow with tenderness as she held her baby to her breast.

"I'm just about to give it all up," he declared, flinging himself into a chair. "I think it might be better just to lock up that library and throw away the key."

She looked at him fondly and smiled. "Now you know that wouldn't do any good, Garion. You know that after a day or so you wouldn't be able to stand it, and no door is so stout that you can't break it down."

"Maybe I should just burn all those books and scrolls," he said morosely. "I can't concentrate on anything else any more. I *know* there's something hidden under that blot, but I can't find a single clue anywhere to what it might be."

"If you burn that library, Belgarath will probably turn you into a radish," she warned with a smile. "He's very fond of books, you know."

"It might be nice to be a radish for a while," he replied.

"It's really very simple, Garion," she said with that infuriating placidity. "Since all the copies are blotted, why don't you go look at the original?"

He stared at her.

"It has to be *somewhere,* doesn't it?"

"Well—I suppose so, yes."

"Find out where it is, then, and go look—or send for it."

"I never thought of that."

"Obviously. It's much more fun to rant and rave and be unpleasant about it."

"You know, that's really a very good idea, Ce'Nedra."

"Naturally. You men always want to complicate things so much. Next time you have a problem, dear, just bring it to me. I'll tell you how to solve it."

He let that pass.

The first thing the following morning, Garion went down into the city and called on the Rivan Deacon in the Temple of Belar. The Rivan Deacon was a sober-faced, gentle man. Unlike the priests of Belar in the major temples on the continent, who were frequently more involved in politics than in the care of their flocks, the leader of the Rivan Church concerned himself almost exclusively with the well-being—physical as well as spiritual—of the common people. Garion had always rather liked him.

"I've never actually seen it myself, your Majesty," the Deacon replied in response to Garion's question, "but I've always been told that it's kept in that shrine on the banks of the Mrin River—between the edge of the fens and Boktor."

"Shrine?"

"The ancient Drasnians erected it on the site where the Mrin Prophet was kept chained," the Deacon explained. "After the poor man died, King Bull-neck directed that a memorial of some sort be put up there. They built the shrine directly over his grave. The original scroll is kept there in a large crystal case. A group of priests is there to protect it. Most people wouldn't be allowed to touch it; but considering the fact that you're the Rivan King, I'm sure that they'll make an exception."

"Then it's always been there?"

"Except during the time of the Angarak invasion during the fourth millennium. It was taken by ship to Val Alorn for safekeeping just before Boktor was burned. Torak wanted to get his hands on it, so it was felt wiser to get it out of the country."

"That makes sense," Garion said. "Thank you for the information, your Reverence."

"Glad to be of help, your Majesty."

It was going to be hard to get away. This week was completely out of the question, since there was that meeting with the port authorities the day after tomorrow. And next week would be even worse. There were always so many official meetings and state functions. Garion sighed as he climbed back up the long stairs to the Citadel with his inevitable guard at his side. It somehow seemed that he was almost a prisoner here on this island. There were always so many demands on his time. He could remember a time, not really that long ago, when he started each day on horseback and seldom slept in the same bed two nights in a row. Upon consideration, however, he was forced to admit that even then he had not been free to do as he wished. Though he had not known it, this burden of responsibility had descended upon him on that windy autumn night so many years ago when he, Aunt Pol, Belgarath, and Durnik had crept through the gate at Faldor's farm and out into the wide world that lay before them.

"Well," he muttered under his breath, "this is important too. Brand can manage here. They'll just have to get along without me for a while."

"What was that, your Majesty?" the guard asked politely.

"Just thinking out loud," Garion replied, a little embarrassed.

Ce'Nedra seemed moody and out of sorts that evening. She held Geran almost abstractedly, paying scant attention to him as he played with the amulet at her throat with a look of serious concentration on his face.

"What's the matter, dear?" Garion asked her.

"Just a headache, that's all," she replied shortly. "And a strange sort of ringing in my ears."

"You're tired."

"Maybe that's it." She arose. "I think I'll put Geran in his cradle and go to bed," she declared. "Maybe a good night's sleep will make me feel better."

"I can put him to bed," Garion offered.

"No," she said with a strange look. "I want to be sure that he's safely in his cradle."

"Safe?" Garion laughed. "Ce'Nedra, this is Riva. It's the safest place in the world."

"Go tell that to Arell," she told him and went into the small room adjoining their bedchamber where Geran's cradle stood.

Garion sat up and read until rather late that evening. Ce'Nedra's restless moodiness had somehow communicated itself to him, and he did not feel ready for bed. Finally, he put aside his book and went to the window to look out across the moon-touched waters of the Sea of the Winds lying far below. The long, slow waves seemed almost like molten silver in the pale light, and their stately pace was oddly hypnotic. Finally he blew out the candles and went quietly into the bedroom.

Ce'Nedra was tossing restlessly in her sleep and muttering half-formed phrases—

meaningless snatches of fragmentary conversation. Garion undressed and slipped into bed, trying not to disturb her.

"No," she said in a peremptory tone of voice. "I won't let you do that." Then she moaned and tossed her head on the pillow.

Garion lay in the soft darkness, listening to his wife talking in her sleep.

"Garion!" she gasped, coming suddenly awake. "Your feet are cold!"

"Oh," he said, "Sorry."

She drifted almost immediately back into sleep, and the muttering resumed.

It was the sound of a different voice that awoke him several hours later. The voice was oddly familiar, and Garion lay, still almost asleep, trying to remember exactly where he had heard it before. It was a woman's voice, low and musical and speaking in a peculiarly soothing tone.

Then he suddenly realized that Ce'Nedra was not in the bed beside him and he came fully awake instantly.

"But I have to hide him so that they can't find him," he heard Ce'Nedra say in a strangely numb voice. He tossed back the covers and slid out of bed.

A faint light gleamed through the open door to the nursery, and the voices seemed to be coming from there. Garion moved quickly to that door, his bare feet making no sound on the carpet.

"Uncover your baby, Ce'Nedra," the other woman was saying in a calm, persuasive voice. "You'll hurt him."

Garion looked through the doorway. Ce'Nedra was standing by the cradle in her white nightdress, her eyes vacant and staring, with another figure beside her. On the chair at the foot of the cradle was a great heap of blankets and pillows. Dreamily, the Rivan Queen was methodically piling the bedclothes on top of her baby.

"Ce'Nedra," the woman said to her. "Stop. Listen to me."

"I have to hide him," Ce'Nedra replied stubbornly. "They want to kill him."

"Ce'Nedra. You'll smother him. Now take all the blankets and pillows out again."

"But—"

"Do as I said, Ce'Nedra," the woman said firmly. "Now."

Ce'Nedra made a little whimpering sound and began to remove the bedding from the cradle.

"That's better. Now listen to me. You must ignore him when he tells you things like this. He is not your friend."

Ce'Nedra's face grew puzzled. "He isn't?"

"He's your enemy. *He* is the one who wants to hurt Geran."

"My baby?"

"Your baby's all right, Ce'Nedra, but you have to fight this voice that comes to you in the night."

"Who—" Garion started, but then the woman turned to look at him, and he broke off, his mouth agape with astonishment. The woman had tawny-colored hair and warm, golden eyes. Her dress was plain and brown, almost earth-colored. Garion knew her. He had met her once before on the moors of eastern Drasnia when he and Belgarath and Silk had been on their way to that dreadful meeting in the haunted ruins of Cthol Mishrak.

Aunt Pol's mother closely resembled her daughter. Her face had that same calm, flawless beauty, and her head that same proud, erect carriage. There was about this timeless face, however, a strange, almost eternal kind of regret that caught at Garion's throat. "Poledra!" he gasped. "What—"

Aunt Pol's mother put one finger to her lips. "Don't wake her, Belgarion," she cautioned. "Let's get her back to bed."

"Geran—?"

"He's all right. I arrived in time. Just lead her gently back to bed. She'll sleep now without any more of these adventures."

Garion went to his wife's side and put his arm about her shoulders. "Come along now, Ce'Nedra," he said gently to her.

She nodded, her eyes still vacant, and obediently went with him back into the royal bedroom.

"Could you pull back that bolster for me?" he quietly asked Poledra.

She laughed. "As a matter of fact, I can't," she said. "You forget that I'm not really here, Belgarion."

"Oh," he said. "I'm sorry. It just seemed—" He pushed the bolster out of the way, carefully laid Ce'Nedra in bed, and pulled the coverlets up around her chin. She sighed and snuggled down to sleep.

"Let's go into the other room," Poledra suggested.

He nodded and quietly followed her into the adjoining room which was still dimly lighted by the glowing embers of the dying fire. "What was that all about?" he asked, softly closing the door.

"There's someone who hates and fears your son, Belgarion," she told him gravely.

"He's only a baby," Garion protested.

"His enemy fears him for what he may become—not for what he is now. It's happened that way before, you'll recall."

"You mean when Asharak killed my parents?"

She nodded. "He was actually trying to get at you."

"But how can I protect Geran from his own mother? I mean—if this man can come to Ce'Nedra in her sleep like that and make her do things, how can I possibly—?"

"It won't happen again, Belgarion. I took care of that."

"But how could you? I mean, you're—well—"

"Dead? That's not altogether accurate, but no matter. Geran is safe for the moment, and Ce'Nedra won't do this again. There's something else we need to discuss."

"All right."

"You're getting very close to something important. I can't tell you everything, but you *do* need to look at the Mrin Codex—the real one, not one of the copies. You must see what's hidden there."

"I can't leave Ce'Nedra—not now."

"She's going to be all right, and this is something that only you can do. Go to that shrine on the River Mrin and look at the Codex. It's desperately important."

Garion squared his shoulders. "All right," he said. "I'll leave in the morning."

"One other thing."

"What?"

"You must take the Orb with you."

"The Orb?"

"You won't be able to see what you have to see without it."

"I don't quite understand."

"You will when you get there."

"All right, Poledra," he said. Then he made a rueful face. "I don't know why I'm objecting. I've been doing things I didn't understand all my life now."

"Everything will become clear in time," she assured him. Then she looked at him rather critically. "Garion," she said in a tone so like Aunt Pol's that he answered automatically.

"Yes?"

"You really shouldn't run around at night without a robe, you know. You'll catch cold."

The ship he hired at Kotu was small, but well designed for river travel. It was a shallow-draft, broad-beamed little ship that sometimes bobbed like a chip of wood. The oarsmen were sturdy fellows and they made good time rowing against the sluggish current of the Mrin River as it meandered its slow way through the fens.

By nightfall they were ten leagues upriver from Kotu, and the captain prudently moored his ship to a dead snag with one of the tar-smeared hawsers. "It's not a good idea to try to find the channel in the dark," he told Garion. "One wrong turn and we could spend the next month wandering around in the fens."

"You know what you're doing, Captain," Garion told him. "I'm not going to interfere."

"Would you like a tankard of ale, your Majesty?" the captain offered.

"That might not be a bad idea," Garion agreed.

Later, he leaned against the railing with his tankard in hand, watching the darting lights of the fireflies and listening to the endless chorus of the frogs. It was a warm spring night, and the damp, rich odor of the fens filled his nostrils.

He heard a faint splash, a fish maybe, or perhaps a diving otter.

"Belgarion?" It was a strange, piping kind of voice, but it was quite distinct. It was also coming from the other side of the railing.

Garion peered out into the velvet darkness.

"Belgarion?" The voice came again. It was somewhere below him.

"Yes?" Garion answered cautiously.

"I need to tell you something." There was another small splash, and the ship rocked slightly. The hawser that moored her to the snag dipped, and a scampering shadow ran quickly up it and slid over the railing in a curiously fluid way. The shadow stood up, and Garion could clearly hear the water dripping from it. The figure was short, scarcely more than four feet tall, and it moved toward Garion with a peculiarly shuffling gait.

"You are older," it said.

"That happens," Garion replied, peering at the form as he tried to make out its

face. Then the moon slid out from behind a cloud, and Garion found himself staring directly into the furry, wide-eyed face of a fenling. "Tupik?" he asked incredulously. "Is that you?"

"You remember." The small, furry creature seemed pleased.

"Of course I remember."

The ship rocked again, and another furry shadow ran up the hawser. Tupik
turned with irritation. "Poppi!" he chittered angrily. "Go home!"

"No," she answered quite calmly.

"You must do as I say!" he told her, stamping his feet on the deck.

"Why?"

Tupik stared at her in obvious frustration. "Are they all like that?" he demanded
of Garion.

"All what?"

"Females." Tupik said the word with a certain disgust.

"Most of them, yes."

Tupik sighed.

"How is Vordai?" Garion asked them.

Poppi made a peculiarly disconsolate whimpering sound. "Our mother is
gone," she said sadly.

"I'm sorry."

"She was very tired," Tupik said.

"We covered her with flowers," Poppi said. "And then we closed up her house."

"She would have liked that."

"She said that one day you would come back," Tupik told him. "She was very
wise."

"Yes."

"She said that we should wait until you came and then we were to give you a
message."

"Oh?"

"There is an evil that moves against you."

"I was beginning to suspect that."

"Mother said to tell you that the evil has many faces and that the faces do not
always agree, but that which is behind it all has no face and that it comes from much
farther than you think."

"I don't quite follow."

"It is from beyond the stars."

Garion stared at him.

"That is what we were told to say," Poppi assured him. "Tupik said it exactly as
mother told it to him."

"Tell Belgarath about mother," Tupik said then. "And tell him that she sent
him her thanks."

"I will."

"Good-bye, Belgarion," the fenling said. Poppi made a small, affectionate
sound in her throat, pattered over, and nuzzled briefly at Garion's hand.

And then the two of them slipped over the side and vanished in the dark waters of the fens.

CHAPTER SIXTEEN

It was a dreary-looking place. The village huddled on the river bank at the edge of a flat, featureless plain covered with coarse, dark-green grass. The underlying soil was alluvial clay, slick, gray, and unwholesome-looking, and just beyond the wide bend in the Mrin River lay the endless green and brown expanse of the fens. The village itself consisted of perhaps two dozen dun-colored houses, huddled all together about the square stone structure of the shrine. Rickety docks, constructed of bone-white driftwood, stuck out into the river like skeletal fingers, and fishing nets hung on poles, drying and smelling in the humid, mosquito-infested air.

Garion's ship arrived about noon, and he went immediately up from the creaking dock along the muddy, rutted street to the shrine itself, walking carefully to avoid slipping, and feeling the curious stares of the dull-eyed villagers directed at him and at the great sword of the Rivan King strapped to his back.

The priests of Belar who guarded the shrine were obsequious, almost fawning, when he arrived at the tarnished bronze gates and requested entry. They led him through a flagstone-covered courtyard, pointing proudly at the rotting kennel and the stout, tar-smeared post with its fragment of heavy, rusting chain where the mad prophet of Mrin had spent his last days.

Within the shrine itself stood the customary altar with its great carved-stone bearhead. Garion noted that the interior of the shrine stood in need of a good cleaning and that the priest-guardians themselves were rumpled and unwashed. One of the first manifestations of religious enthusiasm, he had noted, was a powerful aversion to soap and water. Holy places—and those who attended them—always seemed to smell bad.

There was some small problem when they reached the vaulted sanctorum where the yellowed parchment scroll of the original Mrin Codex lay in its crystal case with two man-high candles flanking it. One of the priests, a wild-eyed fanatic whose hair and beard resembled a wind-ravaged strawstack, objected shrilly— almost hysterically—when Garion politely requested that the case be opened. The ranking priest, however, was enough of a politician to recognize the preeminent claim of the Rivan King—particularly since he bore Aldur's Orb—to examine any holy object he pleased. Garion realized once again that, in a peculiar way, he himself was a holy object in the minds of many Alorns.

The fanatic at last retreated, muttering the word "blasphemy" over and over again. The crystal case was opened with a rusty iron key, and a small table and chair were brought into the circle of candlelight so that Garion might examine the Codex.

"I think I can manage now, your Reverences," he told them rather pointedly. He did not like having people read over his shoulder and he felt no particular need of company. He sat at the table, put his hand on the scroll, and looked directly at the little clot of priests. "I'll call if I need anything," he added.

Their expressions were disapproving, but the overpowering presence of the Rivan King made them too timid to protest his peremptory dismissal; they quietly filed out, leaving him alone with the scroll.

Garion was excited. The solution to the problem that had plagued him for all these months lay at last in his hands. With nervous fingers, he untied the silken cord and began to unroll the crackling parchment. The script was archaic, but gorgeously done. The individual letters had not so much been written as they had been meticulously drawn. He perceived almost at once that an entire lifetime had been devoted to the production of this single manuscript. His hands actually trembling with his eagerness, Garion carefully unrolled the scroll, his eyes running over the now-familiar words and phrases, searching for the line that would once and for all clear up the mystery.

And there it was! Garion stared at it incredulously, not believing what he saw. The blot was exactly the same as it was on all the copies. He almost screamed with frustration.

With a sick feeling of defeat, he read once again that fatal line: "And the Child of Light shall meet with the Child of Dark and shall overcome him, and the Darkness shall flee. But behold, the Stone which lies at the center of the Light shall—" And there was that accursed blot again.

A peculiar thing happened as he read it again. An odd sort of indifference seemed to come over him. Why was he making such a fuss about a single blotted word? What difference could one word make? He almost rose from his chair with the intention of putting the scroll back in its case and leaving this foul-smelling place for home. Then he stopped quite suddenly, remembering all the hours he had spent trying to puzzle out the meaning of that blot on the page. Perhaps it wouldn't hurt to read it one more time. He had, after all, come a very long way.

He started over again, but his distaste became so acute that he could hardly stand it. Why was he wasting his time with this nonsense? He had traveled all this way to wear out his eyes on this moldering scrap of insane gibberish—this stinking, half-rotten sheet of poorly tanned sheepskin. He shoved the Codex away in disgust. This was sheer idiocy. He pushed back the chair and stood up, shifting Iron-grip's great sword on his back. His ship would still be there, moored to that rickety dock. He could be halfway to Kotu by nightfall and back at Riva within the week. He would lock the library once and for all and tend to his business. A king, after all, did not have time for all this idle, brainsickly speculation. Decisively, he turned his back on the scroll and started toward the door.

As soon as he was no longer looking at the scroll, however, he stopped. What was he doing? The puzzle was still there. He had made no effort to solve it. He *had* to find out. But as he turned back and looked at the scroll again, that same wave of insupportable disgust almost overwhelmed him. It was so strong that it made him feel faint. Once again he turned his back, and once again the feeling vanished. There was something about the scroll itself that was trying to drive him away.

He began to pace up and down, carefully keeping his eyes away from the scroll. What had the dry voice in his mind told him? "There are several words there. If you look at them in the right kind of light, you should be able to see them." *What* kind of light? The candles in this vaulted room obviously weren't what the voice had meant. Sunlight? That hardly seemed likely. Poledra had said that he *must* read the hidden words, but how could he, when the Codex literally drove him away each time he looked at it?

Then he stopped. What else had she said? Something about not being able to see without . . .

The wave of disgust which struck him was so strong that he felt his stomach constrict. He spun quickly so that his back was toward that hateful document; as he did so, the hilt of Iron-grip's sword jabbed him painfully in the side of the head. Angrily he reached over his shoulder to grasp the handle and push it back, but instead, his hand touched the Orb. The feeling of revulsion evaporated instantly, and his mind became clear, and his thoughts lucid. The light! Of course! He had to read the Codex by the light of the Orb! That is what both Poledra and the dry voice had been trying to tell him. Awkwardly, he reached up and back, seizing the Orb. "Come off," he muttered to it. With a faint click, the Orb came free in his hand. The sudden weight of the huge sword strapped across his back very nearly drove him to his knees. In astonishment, he realized that the seeming weightlessness of the great weapon had been the work of the Orb itself. Struggling under that gross weight, he fumbled with the buckle at his chest, unfastened it, and felt the enormous bulk slide free. Iron-grip's sword fell to the floor with a loud clatter.

Holding the Orb in front of him, Garion turned and looked directly at the scroll. He could almost hear an angry snarl hovering in the air, but his mind remained clear. He stepped to the table and pulled the scroll open with one hand, holding the glowing Orb above it with the other.

At last he saw the meaning of the blot that had frustrated him for so long. It was not some random splotch of spilled ink. The message was there—all of it, but the words had all been written down on top of one another! The entire prophecy lay in that one single spot! By the blue, unwavering light of Aldur's Orb, his eyes seemed actually to plunge down and down beneath the surface of the parchment, and the words, hidden for eons, rose like bubbles out of the substance of the scroll.

"But Behold," the crucial passage read, "the Stone which lies at the center of the Light shall burn red, and my voice shall speak unto the Child of Light and reveal the name of the Child of Dark. And the Child of Light will take up the Guardian's sword and go forth to seek out that which is hidden. Long will be his quest, and it shall be threefold. And ye shall know that the quest hath begun when the Keeper's Line is renewed. Guard well the seed of the Keeper, for there shall be no other. Guard it well, for should that seed fall into the hands of the Child of Dark and be taken to the place where the evil dwells, then blind choice alone can decide the outcome. Should the Keeper's seed be reft away, then must the Beloved and Eternal lead the way. And he shall find the path to the place where the evil dwells in the Mysteries. And in each Mystery shall lie but a part of the path, and he must find them all—all—or the path will lead awry, and the Dark shall triumph. Hasten therefore to the meeting where the threefold quest will end. And this meeting will come to pass in a place which is no more, and there will the choice be made."

Garion read it again, and then a third time, feeling an ominous chill as the words echoed and thundered through his consciousness. Finally he rose and went to the door of the candlelit, vaulted chamber. "I'll need something to write with," he told the priest standing just outside. "And send someone down to the river. Have him tell the captain of my ship to get things ready. Just as soon as I finish here, I have to leave for Kotu."

The priest was staring wide-eyed at the incandescently glowing Orb in Garion's hand. "Don't just stand there, man, move!" Garion told him. "The whole world's hanging on this!"

The priest blinked and then scurried away.

The following day, Garion was in Kotu, and about a day and a half later, he reached Aldurford in northern Algaria. As luck had it, a herd of half-wild Algarian cattle was being driven across that wide, shallow place in the mighty river on their way to Muros, and Garion went immediately in search of the herd master.

"I'm going to need two horses," he said, skipping the customary courtesies. "The best you have. I have to be in the Vale of Aldur before the week is out."

The herd master, a fierce-looking Algar warrior in black leather, looked at him speculatively. "Good horses are expensive, your Majesty," he ventured, his eyes coming alight.

"That's beside the point. Please have them ready in a quarter of an hour—and throw some food in a saddlebag for me."

"Doesn't your Majesty even want to discuss the price?" The herd master's voice betrayed his profound disappointment.

"Not particularly," Garion told him. "Just add it all up, and I'll pay it."

The herd master sighed. "Take them as a gift, your Majesty," he said. Then he looked mournfully at the Rivan King. "You *do* realize, of course, that you've absolutely ruined my whole afternoon."

Garion gave him a tight, knowing grin. "If I had the time, good herd master, I'd haggle with you for the whole day—right down to the last penny—but I have urgent business in the south."

The herd master shook his head sadly.

"Don't take it so hard, my friend," Garion told him. "If you like, I'll curse your name to everyone I meet and tell them all how badly you cheated me."

The herd master's eyes brightened. "That would be extremely kind of your Majesty," he said. He caught Garion's amused look. "One *does* have a certain reputation to maintain, after all. The horses will be ready whenever you are. I'll select them for you myself."

Garion made good time as he galloped south. He kept his horses fresh and strong by changing mounts every two or three leagues. The long journey in quest of the Orb had taught him many ways to conserve the strength of a good horse, and he utilized them all. When a steep hill stood in his path, he slowed to a walk and made up the lost time on the long downhill slope on the other side. When he could, he went around rough terrain. He stopped for the night late and was on the move again at first light in the morning.

Steadily he moved south through the knee-high sea of waving prairie grass lying lush and green under the warm spring sun. He avoided the man-made mountain of the Algarian Stronghold, knowing that King Cho-Hag and Queen Silar, and certainly Hettar and Adara, would insist that he stop over for a day or so. Regretfully, he also passed a league or so to the west of Poledra's cottage. He hoped that there would be time later to visit Aunt Pol, Durnik, and Errand. Right now he had to get to Belgarath with the passage of the Codex he had so carefully copied and which now rode in the inside pocket of his doublet.

When at last he arrived at Belgarath's squat, round tower, his legs were so tired that they trembled under him as he swung down from his lathered horse. He went immediately to the large, flat-faced rock that was the door to the tower. "Grandfather!" he shouted at the windows above, "Grandfather, it's me!"

There was no answer. The squat tower loomed silently up out of the tall grass, etched sharply against the sky. Garion had not even considered the possibility that the old man might not be here. "Grandfather!" he called again. There was still no answer. A red-winged blackbird swooped in, landed atop the tower, and peered curiously down at Garion. Then it began to preen its feathers.

Almost sick with disappointment, Garion stared at the silent rock that always swung aside for Belgarath. Although he knew that it was a serious breach of etiquette, he pulled in his concentration, looked at the rock, and said, "Open."

The stone gave a startled little lurch and swung obediently aside. Garion went in and quickly mounted the stairs, remembering at the last instant to step up over the one where the loose stone still lay unrepaired. "Grandfather!" he called up the stairway.

"Garion?" the old man's voice coming from above sounded startled. "Is that you?"

"I called," Garion said, coming up the cluttered, round room at the top of the stairs. "Didn't you hear me?"

"I was concentrating on something," the old man replied. "What's the matter? What are you doing here?"

"I finally found that passage," Garion told him.

"What passage?"

"The one in the Mrin Codex—the one that was missing."

Belgarath's expression grew suddenly tense, even wary. "What are you talking about, boy? There's no missing passage in the Mrin Codex."

"We talked about it at Riva. Don't you remember? It's the place where there's a blot on that page. I pointed it out to you."

Belgarath's look grew disgusted. "You came here and interrupted me over *that*?" His tone was scathing.

Garion stared at him. This was not the Belgarath he knew. The old man had never treated him so coldly before. "Grandfather," he said, "what's wrong with you? This is very important. Somebody has somehow obscured a part of the Codex. When you read it, there's a part you don't see."

"But *you* can see it?" Belgarath said in a voice filled almost with contempt. "*You?* A boy who couldn't even read until he was almost grown? The rest of us have been studying that Codex for thousands of years, and now you come along and tell us that we've been missing something?"

"Listen to me, Grandfather. I'm trying to explain. When you come to that place, something happens to your mind. You don't pay any attention to it because, for some reason, you don't want to."

"Nonsense!" Belgarath snorted. "I don't need some rank beginner trying to tell *me* how to study."

"Won't you at least look at what I found?" Garion begged, taking the parchment out of his inside pocket and holding it out.

"No!" Belgarath shouted, slapping the parchment away. "Take that nonsense away from me. Get out of my tower, Garion!"

"Grandfather!"

"Get out of here!" The old man's face was pale with anger, and his eyes flashed.

Garion was so hurt by his grandfather's words that tears actually welled up in his eyes. How could Belgarath talk to him this way?

The old man became even more agitated. He began to pace up and down, muttering angrily to himself. "I have work to do—important work—and you come bursting in here with this wild tale about something being missing. How dare you? How dare you interrupt me with this idiocy? Don't you know who I am?" He gestured at the parchment Garion had picked up and was holding again. "Get that disgusting thing out of my sight!"

And then Garion suddenly understood. Whatever or whoever it was that was trying to conceal the words hidden in that strange blot of ink was growing desperate, driving Belgarath into this uncharacteristic rage to keep him from reading the passage. There was only one way to break that strange compulsion not to see. Garion laid the parchment on a table, then coldly and deliberately unbuckled the heavy belt running across his chest, removed Iron-grip's sword from his back, and stood it against the wall. He put his hand to the Orb on the pommel of the sword and said, "Come off." The Orb came free in his hand, glowing at his touch.

"What are you doing?" Belgarath demanded of him.

"I'm going to have to *make* you see what I'm talking about, Grandfather," Garion said unhappily. "I don't want to hurt you, but you have to look." He walked slowly and deliberately toward Belgarath, the Orb extended before him.

"Garion," Belgarath said, backing away apprehensively, "Be careful with that."

"Go to the table, Grandfather," Garion told him grimly. "Go to the table and read what I found."

"Are you threatening me?" Belgarath demanded incredulously.

"Just do it, Grandfather."

"We don't behave this way toward each other, Garion," the old man said, still backing away from the glowing Orb.

"The table," Garion repeated. "Go over there and read."

Sweat was standing out on Belgarath's forehead. Reluctantly, almost as if it were causing him some obscure kind of pain, he went to the table and bent over the parchment sheet. Then he shook his head. "I can't see it," he declared, though a burning candle stood right beside the sheet. "It's too dark in here."

"Here," Garion said, reaching forth with the glowing Orb, "I'll light it for you." The Orb flared, and its blue light fell across the sheet and filled the room. "Read it, Grandfather," Garion said implacably.

Belgarath stared at him with an almost pleading expression. "Garion—"

"Read it."

Belgarath dropped his eyes to the page lying before him, and suddenly he gasped. "Where—? How did you get this?"

"It was under that blot. Can you see it now?"

"Of course I can see it." Excitedly Belgarath picked up the sheet and read it again. His hands were actually trembling. "Are you sure this is exactly what it said?"

"I copied it word for word, Grandfather—right off the original scroll."

"How were you able to see it?"

"The same way you are—by the light of the Orb. Somehow that makes it clear."

"Astonishing," the old man said. "I wonder—" He went quickly to a cabinet standing by the wall, rummaged around for a moment, and then came back to the table with a scroll in his hands. He quickly unrolled it. "Hold the Orb closer, boy," he said.

Garion held out the Orb and watched with his grandfather as the buried words slowly rose to the surface just as they had in the shrine.

"Absolutely amazing," Belgarath marveled. "It's blurred, and some of the words aren't clear, but it's there. It's all there. How is it possible that none of us noticed this before—and how did *you* discover it?"

"I had help, Grandfather. The voice told me that I had to read it in a certain kind of light." He hesitated, knowing how much pain what he had to say would cause the old man. "And then, Poledra came to visit us."

"Poledra?" Belgarath spoke his wife's name with a little catch in his voice.

"Someone was making Ce'Nedra do something in her sleep—something very dangerous—and Poledra came and stopped her. Then she told me that I had to go to the shrine in Drasnia and read the Codex and she specifically told me to take the Orb along. When I got there and started reading, I almost left. It all seemed so stupid somehow. Then I remembered what they had told me and I put it together. As soon as I started reading by the light of the Orb, that feeling that I was wasting my time disappeared. Grandfather, what causes that? I thought it was only me, but it affected you, too."

Belgarath thought a moment, frowning. "It was an interdiction," he explained finally. "Someone at some time put his will to that one spot and made it so repulsive that no one could even see it."

"But it's right there—even on your copy. How is it that the scribe who copied it could see it well enough to write it down, but we couldn't?"

"Many of the scribes in the old days were illiterate," Belgarath explained. "You don't have to be able to read in order to copy something. All those scribes were doing was drawing exact duplicates of the letters on the page."

"But this—what was it you called it?"

"Interdiction. It's a fancy word for what happens. I think Beldin invented it. He's terribly impressed by his own cleverness sometimes."

"The interdiction made the scribes pile all the words on top of each other—even though they didn't know what the words meant?"

Belgarath grunted, his eyes lost in thought. "Whoever did this is very strong—and very subtle. I didn't even suspect that someone was tampering with my mind."

"When did it happen?"

"Probably at the same time the Mrin Prophet was speaking the words originally."

"Would the interdiction keep working after the person who caused it was dead?"

"No."

"Then—"

"Right. He's still around somewhere."

"Could it be this Zandramas we keep hearing about?"

"That's possible, I suppose." Belgarath picked up the sheet Garion had copied. "I can see it by ordinary light now," he said. "Apparently once you break the interdiction for somebody, it stays broken." He carefully read the sheet again. "This is really important, Garion."

"I was fairly sure it was," Garion replied. "I don't understand it all, though. The first part is fairly simple—the part about the Orb turning red and the name of the Child of Dark being revealed. It sort of looks as if I'm going to have to make another one of those trips."

"A long one, if this is right."

"What's this next part mean?"

"Well, as nearly as I can make it out, this quest of yours—whatever it is—has already started. It began when Geran was born." The old man frowned. "I don't like this part that says that blind choice might make the decision, though. That's the sort of thing that makes me very nervous."

"Who is the Beloved and Eternal?"

"Probably me."

Garion looked at him.

Belgarath shrugged. "It's a little ostentatious," he admitted, "but some people do call me 'the Eternal Man'—and when my master changed my name, he added the syllable 'Bel' to my old one. In the old language 'Bel' meant 'beloved.'" He smiled a bit sadly. "My master had a way with words sometimes."

"What are these mysteries it talks about?"

"It's an archaic term. In the old days they used the word 'mystery' instead of 'prophecy.' As cryptic as some of them are, it sort of makes sense, I guess."

"Ho! Garion! Belgarath!" The voice came to them from outside the tower.

"Who's that?" Belgarath asked. "Did you tell anybody you were coming here?"

"No," Garion frowned, "not really." He went to the window and looked down. A tall, hawk-faced Algar with a flowing back scalp lock sat astride a lathered and exhausted-looking horse. "Hettar!" Garion called down to him.

"What's the matter?"

"Let me in, Garion," Hettar replied. "I have to talk with you."

Belgarath joined Garion at the window. "The door's around on the other side," he called down. "I'll open it for you. Be careful of the stone on that fifth step," he cautioned, as the tall man started around the tower. "It's loose."

"When are you going to fix that, Grandfather?" Garion asked. He felt the faint, familiar surge as the old man opened the door.

"Oh, I'll get to it one of these days."

Hettar's hawklike face was bleak as he came up into the round room at the top of the tower.

"What's all the urgency, Hettar?" Garion asked. "I've never seen you ride a horse into the ground like that."

Hettar took a deep breath. "You've got to go back to Riva immediately, Garion," he said.

"Is something wrong there?" Garion asked, a sudden chill coming over him.

Hettar sighed. "I hate to be the one to have to tell you this, Garion, but Ce'Nedra sent word for me to get you as fast as I possibly could. You've got to go back to Riva at once."

Garion steeled himself, a dozen dreadful possibilities arising in his imagination. "Why?" he asked quietly.

"I'm sorry, Garion—more sorry than I can possibly say—but Brand has been murdered."

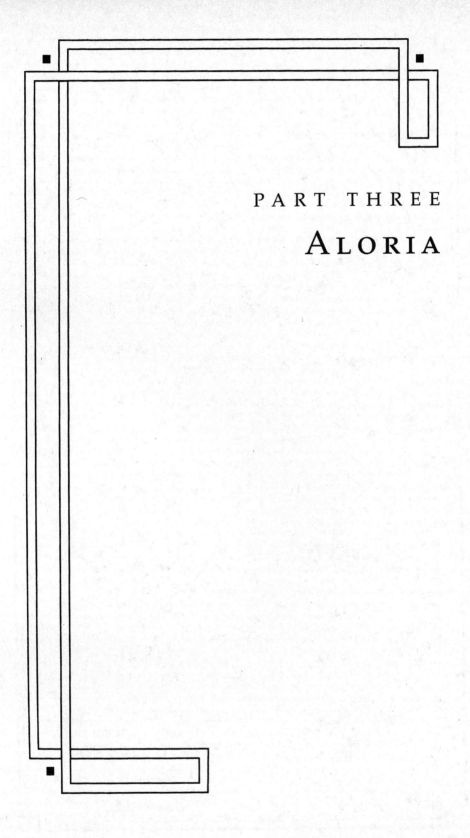

PART THREE

ALORIA

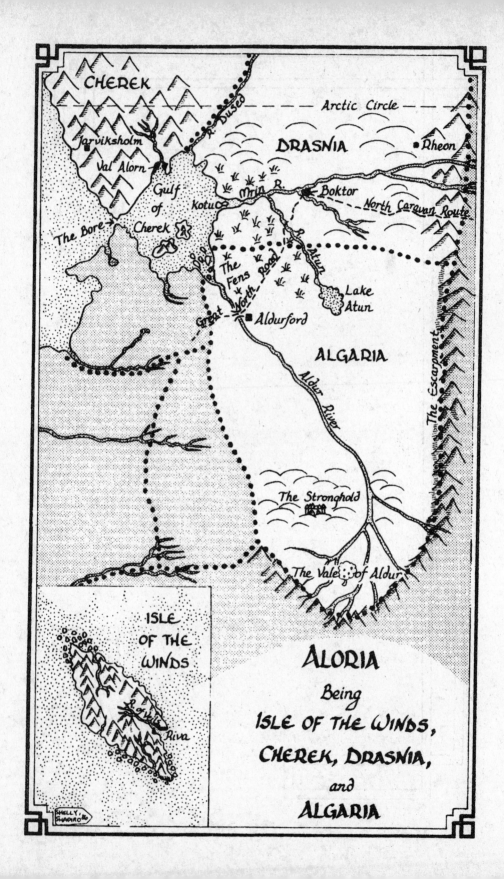

CHEREK

Arctic Circle

R. Dused

DRASNIA

Rheon

Jarviksholm

Val Alorn

Mrin R.

Boktor

North Caravan Route

Gulf of Cherek

kotu

The Bore

The Fens

Atun

Lake Atun

Great North Road

Aldurford

ALGARIA

The Escarpment

Aldur River

The Stronghold

The Vale of Aldur

ISLE OF THE WINDS

Riva

ALORIA

Being

ISLE OF THE WINDS,

CHEREK, DRASNIA,

and

ALGARIA

SHELLY SHAPIRO

Lieutenant Bledik was one of those sober-minded young Sendarian officers who took everything very seriously. He arrived at the Lion Inn in the port city of Camaar promptly on time and was escorted upstairs by the aproned innkeeper. The rooms in which Garion and the others were staying were airy and well-furnished and looked out over the harbor. Garion stood at the window holding aside one of the green drapes and looking out as if it might be possible to penetrate all those leagues of open water and see what was happening at Riva.

"You sent for me, your Majesty?" Bledik asked with a respectful bow.

"Ah, Lieutenant, come in," Garion said, turning from the window. "I have an urgent message for King Fulrach. How fast do you think you can get to Sendar?"

The lieutenant considered it. One look at his sober face told Garion that the young man always considered everything. Bledik pursed his lips, absently adjusting the collar of his scarlet uniform. "If I ride straight through and change horses at every hostel along the way, I can be at the palace by late tomorrow afternoon."

"Good," Garion said. He handed the young officer the folded and sealed letter to the Sendarian king. "When you see King Fulrach, tell him that I've sent Lord Hettar of Algaria to all of the Alorn Kings to tell them that I'm calling a meeting of the Alorn Council at Riva and that I'd like to have him there as well."

"Yes, your Majesty."

"And tell him that the Rivan Warder has been murdered."

Bledik's eyes widened, and his face went pale. "No!" he gasped. "Who was responsible?"

"I don't know any of the details yet, but, as soon as we can hire a ship, we're going across to the island."

"Garion, dear," Polgara said from her chair by the window, "you explained everything in the letter. The lieutenant has a long way to go, and you're delaying him."

"You're probably right, Aunt Pol," he admitted. He turned back to Bledik. "Will you need any money or anything?" he asked.

"No, your Majesty."

"You'd better get started then."

"At once, your Majesty." The lieutenant saluted and went out.

Garion began to pace up and down on the costly Mallorean carpet while Polgara, dressed in a plain blue traveling gown, continued to mend one of Errand's tunics, her needle flashing in the sunlight streaming through the window. "How can you be so calm?" he demanded of her.

"I'm not, dear," she replied. "That's why I'm sewing."

"What's taking them so long?" he fretted.

"Hiring a ship takes time, Garion. It's not exactly like buying a loaf of bread."

"Who could possibly have wanted to hurt Brand?" he burst out. He had asked that same question over and over in the week or more since they had left the Vale. The big, sad-faced Warder had been so totally devoted to Garion and the Rivan Throne that he had possessed virtually no separate identity. So far as Garion knew, Brand had not had an enemy in the world.

"That's one of the first things we'll want to find out when we get to Riva," she said. "Now please try to calm yourself. Pacing about doesn't accomplish anything and it's very distracting."

It was almost evening when Belgarath, Durnik, and Errand returned, bringing with them a tall, gray-haired Rivan whose clothing carried those distinctive smells of salt water and tar that identified him as a sailor.

"This is Captain Jandra," Belgarath introduced him. "He's agreed to ferry us across to the Isle."

"Thank you, Captain," Garion said simply.

"My pleasure, your Majesty," Jandra replied with a stiff bow.

"Have you just come in from Riva?" Polgara asked him.

"Yesterday afternoon, my Lady."

"Have you any idea at all about what happened there?"

"We didn't get too many details down at the harbor, my Lady. Sometimes the people up at the Citadel are sort of secretive—no offense, your Majesty. There are all kinds of rumors going about the city, though—most of them pretty farfetched. About all I can say for certain is that the Warder was attacked and killed by a group of Chereks."

"*Chereks!*" Garion exclaimed.

"Everyone agrees on that point, your Majesty. Some people say that all the assassins were killed. Others say that there were some survivors. I couldn't really say for sure, but I know that they *did* bury six of them."

"Good," Belgarath grunted.

"Not if there were only six to begin with, father," Polgara told him. "We need answers, not bodies."

"Uh—pardon me, your Majesty," Jandra said a little uncomfortably. "It might not be my place to say this, but some of the rumors in the city say that the Chereks were officials of some kind from Val Alorn and that they were sent by King Anheg."

"Anheg? That's absurd."

"That's what some people are saying, your Majesty. I don't put much stock in it myself, but it might just be the kind of talk you wouldn't want going much further. The Warder was well-liked in Riva, and a lot of people have taken to polishing their swords—if you take my meaning."

"I think I'd better get home as soon as possible," Garion said. "How long will it take us to get to Riva?"

The captain thought it over. "My ship isn't as fast as a Cherek warship," he apologized. "Let's say three days—if the weather holds. We can leave on the morning tide, if you can be ready."

"We'll do that, then," Garion said.

. . .

It was late summer on the Sea of the Winds, and the weather held clear and sunny. Jandra's ship plowed steadily through the sparkling, sun-touched waves, heeling to one side under a quartering wind. Garion spent most of the voyage pacing moodily up and down the deck. When, on the third day out from Camaar, the jagged shape of the Isle of the Winds appeared low on the horizon ahead, a kind of desperate impatience came over him. There were so many questions that had to be answered and so many things that had to be done that even the hour or so that it would take to reach the harbor seemed an intolerable delay.

It was midafternoon when Jandra's ship rounded the headland at the harbor mouth and made for the stone quays at the foot of the city. "I'm going on ahead," Garion told the others. "Follow me as soon as you can." And even as the sailors were making fast the hawsers, he leaped across to the salt-crusted stones of the quay and started up toward the Citadel, taking the steps two at a time.

Ce'Nedra was waiting for him at the massive main doors of the Citadel, garbed in a black mourning dress. Her face was pale, and her eyes full of tears. "Oh, Garion," she cried as he reached her. She threw her arms about his neck and began to sob against his chest.

"How long ago did it happen, Ce'Nedra?" he asked, holding her in his arms. "Hettar didn't have too many details."

"It was about three weeks ago," she sobbed. "Poor Brand. That poor, dear man."

"Do you know where I can find Kail?"

"He's been working at Brand's desk," she replied. "I don't think he's slept for more than a few hours any night since it happened."

"Aunt Pol and the others should be along shortly. I'm going to talk with Kail. Would you bring them as soon as they get here?"

"Of course, dear," she replied, wiping her eyes with the back of her hand.

"We'll talk later," he said. "Right now I've got to find out what happened."

"Garion," she said gravely, "they were Chereks."

"That's what I'd heard," he said, "and that's why I've got to get to the bottom of this as quickly as possible."

The corridors of the Citadel were muted and oddly silent. As Garion strode toward that group of rooms in the west wing from which Brand had always conducted the day-to-day business of the kingdom, the servants and functionaries he encountered bowed soberly and stood aside for him.

Kail was dressed in deepest black, and his face was gray with fatigue and deep sorrow. The orderly stacks of documents on the top of Brand's heavy desk, however, gave evidence that despite his grief he had been working not only at his own duties but at his father's as well. He looked up as Garion entered the room and started to rise.

"Don't," Garion said. "We have too much to do for formalities." He looked at his weary friend. "I'm sorry, Kail," he said sadly. "I'm more sorry than I can possibly tell you."

"Thank you, your Majesty."

Garion sank into the chair across the desk from him, his own weariness coming over him in a wave. "I haven't been able to get any details," he said. "Could you tell me exactly what happened?"

Kail nodded and leaned back in his chair. "It was about a month ago," he began, "not long after you left for Drasnia. A trade deputation from King Anheg arrived. All their credentials seemed to be in order, but they were a bit vague about exactly what the purpose of their visit was. We extended them the customary courtesies, and most of the time they stayed in the rooms we assigned them. Then, late one night, my father had been discussing some matters with Queen Ce'Nedra and was on his way back to his own quarters when he encountered them in the corridor leading to the royal apartments. He asked if he could help them, and they attacked him without any warning whatsoever." Kail stopped, and Garion could see his jaws tightly clenched. He drew in a deep breath and passed one weary hand across his eyes. "Your Majesty, my father wasn't even armed. He did his best to defend himself, and he was able to call for help before they cut him down. My brothers and I ran to his aid—along with several of the Citadel guards—and we all did our best to capture the assassins, but they absolutely refused to surrender." He frowned. "It was almost as if they were deliberately throwing their lives away. We had no choice but to kill them."

"All of them?" Garion asked with a sinking feeling in the pit of his stomach.

"All but one," Kail replied. "My brother, Brin, hit him across the back of the head with the butt of an axe. He's been unconscious ever since."

"Aunt Pol's with me," Garion said. "She'll wake him—if anybody can." His face went bleak. "And when he *does* wake up, he and I are going to have a little talk."

"I want some answers, too," Kail agreed. He paused, his face troubled. "Belgarion, they carried a letter from King Anheg. That's why we let them into the Citadel."

"I'm sure there's a logical explanation."

"I have the letter. It's over his seal and his signature."

"I've called a meeting of the Alorn Council," Garion told him. "As soon as Anheg gets here, we'll be able to clear this up."

"If he comes," Kail added somberly.

The door opened quietly, and Ce'Nedra led the others into the room.

"All right," Belgarath said crisply, "let's see if we can sort this out. Did any of them survive?"

"One, Ancient One," Kail replied, "but he's unconscious."

"Where is he?" Polgara asked.

"We put him in a room in the north tower, my Lady. The physicians have been tending his injuries, but they haven't been able to revive him yet."

"I'll go at once," she said.

Errand crossed the room to where Kail sat and wordlessly laid a sympathetic hand on the young Rivan's shoulder. Kail's jaws clenched again, and tears suddenly welled up in his eyes.

"They had a letter from Anheg, Grandfather," Garion told the old man. "That's how they got inside the Citadel."

"Do you have the letter anywhere?" Belgarath asked Kail.

"Yes, Ancient One. It's right here." Kail began to leaf through a stack of documents.

"That seems to be the best place to start," the old man said. "The entire Alorn alliance is hanging on this, so we'd better get it straightened out fast."

It was late evening by the time Polgara completed her examination of the lone surviving assassin. When she came into the royal apartment where the discussions had been continuing, her face was bleak. "I'm sorry, but there's absolutely nothing I can do with him," she reported. "The entire back of his skull has been crushed. He's only barely alive; if I try to wake him, he'll die immediately."

"I need some answers, Aunt Pol," Garion said. "How long do you think it's going to be until he wakes up?"

She shook her head. "I doubt that he ever will—and even if he does, it's unlikely that he's going to be able to say anything coherent. About all that's holding his brains together right now is his scalp."

He looked at her helplessly. "Couldn't you—"

"No, Garion. There's nothing left of his mind to work with."

Two days later, King Cho-Hag, Chief of the Clan-Chiefs of the Algar horsemen, arrived, accompanied by Queen Silar and Adara, Garion's tall, dark-haired cousin. "A very sad occasion," Cho-Hag said to Garion in his quiet voice as they clasped hands on the quay.

"It seems lately that about the only time we all get together is to attend funerals," Garion agreed. "Where's Hettar?"

"I think he's at Val Alorn," Cho-Hag replied. "He'll probably come here with Anheg."

"That's something we're going to have to talk about," Garion said.

Cho-Hag lifted one eyebrow.

"The people who killed Brand were Chereks," Garion explained quietly. "They had a letter from Anheg."

"Anheg could not have had anything to do with it," Cho-Hag declared. "He loved Brand like a brother. There had to be somebody else behind it."

"I'm sure you're right, but there's a great deal of suspicion here in Riva right now. There are some people who are even talking war."

Cho-Hag's face went grim.

"That's why we have to get to the truth in a hurry," Garion told him. "We've got to head that kind of thinking off before it gets completely out of hand."

The next day King Fulrach of Sendaria arrived in the harbor; with him on their stout, broad-beamed ship was the one-armed General Brendig, the ancient but still-vigorous Earl of Seline, and, surprisingly, Queen Layla herself, the lady whose fear of sea travel had become almost legendary. That same afternoon, Queen Porenn, still in deepest mourning for her husband, disembarked from the black-painted Drasnian vessel that had carried her from Boktor, along with her son, the boy-king Kheva and the bone-thin Margrave Khendon, the man known as Javelin.

"Oh, my dear Garion," Porenn said, embracing him at the foot of the gangway. "I cannot tell you how sorry I am."

"We've all lost one of our dearest friends," he replied. He turned to Kheva. "Your Majesty," he said with a formal bow.

"Your Majesty," Kheva replied, also bowing.

"We heard that there's some mystery surrounding the assassination," Porenn said. "Khendon here is very good at clearing up mysteries."

"Margrave," Garion greeted the Drasnian Chief of Intelligence.

"Your Majesty," Javelin responded. He turned and extended one hand to a young woman with honey-blond hair and soft brown eyes who was coming down the gangway. "You do remember my niece, don't you?"

"Margravine Liselle," Garion greeted her.

"Your Majesty," she replied with a formal curtsy. Although she was probably not even aware of it, the hint of a dimple in each of her cheeks gave her expression a slightly impish cast. "My uncle has pressed me into service as his secretary. He pretends failing eyesight, but I think perhaps it's just an excuse to avoid giving me a genuine assignment. Older relatives tend to be overprotective sometimes, don't you think?"

Garion smiled briefly. "Has anyone heard from Silk?" he asked.

"He's at Rheon," Javelin replied, "trying to gather information about the activities of the Bear-cult. We've sent messengers, but sometimes he can be hard to find. I expect he'll be along soon, though."

"Has Anheg arrived yet?" Queen Porenn asked.

Garion shook his head. "Cho-Hag and Fulrach are here, but there's no word from Anheg yet."

"We've heard that some people suspect him," the little blond queen said. "It simply cannot be true, Garion."

"I'm sure he'll be able to explain everything as soon as he arrives."

"Did any of the assassins survive?" Javelin asked.

"One," Garion told him, "but I'm afraid that he won't be much help to us. One of Brand's sons bashed in his head. It doesn't appear that he's ever going to wake up."

"Pity," Javelin murmured briefly, "but a man doesn't always have to be able to talk in order to provide information."

"I hope you're right," Garion said fervently.

The discussions at supper and later that evening were subdued. Though no one stated it openly, they were all reluctant to speak of the bleak possibility which faced them. To raise that question without Anheg's being present might have solidified the doubts and suspicions and given the entire meeting a tone none of them were willing to assume.

"When is Brand's funeral to be held?" Porenn asked quietly.

"As soon as Anheg arrives, I guess," Garion replied.

"Have you made any decisions concerning his office?" Fulrach asked.

"I don't quite follow you."

"The position of Warder originated a long time ago in order to fill the vacuum that existed after the Nyissans murdered King Gorek and his family. Now that you occupy the throne, do you really *need* a Warder?"

"To be honest with you, I hadn't really thought about it. Brand's always been here. He seemed as permanent as the stones of the Citadel itself."

"Who's been doing his work since he was killed, your Majesty?" the silvery-haired old Earl of Seline asked.

"His second son, Kail."

"You have many other responsibilities, Belgarion," the Earl pointed out. "You really do need someone here to manage the day-to-day details—at least until the present crisis has passed. I don't think, however, that any final decision about the post of Warder needs to be made just now. I'm sure that if you asked him, Kail would continue to perform his father's duties without a formal appointment."

"He's right, Garion," Ce'Nedra said. "Kail's absolutely devoted to you. He'll do anything you ask him to do."

"If this young man is doing an adequate job, it's probably best to let him continue," Seline suggested. Then he smiled briefly. "There's an old Sendarian adage that says, 'If it isn't broken, don't try to fix it.'"

The following morning an ungainly-looking ship with elaborate structures fore and aft wallowed into the harbor under an obviously top-heavy spread of sail. Garion, who stood atop the battlements of the Citadel talking quietly with Javelin, frowned as he looked down at it. "What kind of ship is that?" he asked. "I don't recognize the construction."

"It's Arendish, your Majesty. They feel the need to make everything look like a castle."

"I didn't know that the Arends even *had* any ships."

"They don't have very many," Javelin replied. "Their vessels have a tendency to capsize whenever they encounter a stiff breeze."

"I guess we'd better go down and see who it is."

"Right," Javelin agreed.

The passengers aboard the clumsy Arendish vessel proved to be old friends. Mandorallen, the mighty Baron of Vo Mandor, stood at the rail, gleaming in full armor. At his side stood Lelldorin of Wildantor, and with them were their wives, Nerina and Ariana, both ornately gowned in dark, rich brocades.

"We came instantly upon our receipt of the news of thy tragedy, Garion," Mandorallen shouted across the intervening water as the Arendish crew laboriously maneuvered their awkward ship toward the quay upon which Garion and Javelin waited. "Duty and affection, both for thee and thy foully murdered Warder, impell us to aid thee in thy rightful search for vengeance. Korodullin himself would have joined us but for an illness which hath laid him low."

"I suppose I should have expected this," Garion murmured.

"Are they likely to complicate matters?" Javelin asked quietly.

Garion shuddered. "You have no idea."

It was not until two days later that the *Seabird*, with Barak at the tiller, rounded the headland and sailed into the harbor. The rails were lined with burly Cherek warriors in chain-mail shirts. Their faces were alert, and their eyes were wary as Barak steered his ship up to the quay.

When Garion reached the foot of the long flight of stone steps leading down from the Citadel, a sizeable crowd had gathered. The mood of that crowd was ugly, and most of the men who stood there with grim faces had weapons at their sides.

"It looks as if we've got a situation on our hands here," Garion said quietly to Kail, who had accompanied him. "I think we'd better try to put the best face on this meeting."

Kail looked at the angry faces of the townspeople pressing toward the wharves. "Perhaps you're right, Belgarion," he agreed.

"We're going to have to put on a show of cordiality when we greet Anheg."

"You ask a great deal, Belgarion."

"I hate to put it this way, Kail, but I'm not *asking*. Those Chereks along the rail are Anheg's personal bodyguard. If anything starts here, there's going to be a lot of bloodshed—and probably the beginning of a war that none of us wants. Now smile, and let's go welcome the King of Cherek."

To give it the best possible appearance, Garion led Kail up the gangway to the deck of Barak's ship so that his meeting with King Anheg could take place in full view of the angry crowd. Barak, clad in a formal green doublet and looking even larger than he had the last time Garion had seen him, strode down the deck to meet them. "This is a very bleak time for us all," he declared as he shook hands first with Garion and then with Kail. "Anheg and Hettar are below with the ladies."

"Ladies?" Garion asked.

"Islena and Merel."

"You've heard the rumors?" Garion asked him.

Barak nodded. "That's one of the reasons we brought our wives."

"Good idea," Garion said approvingly. "A man who's coming someplace to pick a fight doesn't usually bring his wife along, and we all want to give this the best possible appearance."

"I'll go down and get Anheg," Barak said, casting a quick glance at the ugly crowd gathered at the foot of his gangway.

King Anheg's brutish, black-bearded face was haggard and drawn when he emerged from belowdecks in his usual blue robe.

"Anheg, my friend," Garion said in a voice intended to carry to the crowd. He hurried forward and caught the Cherek king in a rough embrace. "I think we should smile," he whispered. "We want to let those people know we're still the best of friends."

"Are we, Garion?" Anheg asked in a subdued voice.

"Nothing has changed at all, Anheg," Garion said firmly.

"Let's get on with this, then." Anheg raised his voice. "The royal house of Cherek extends its condolences to the Rivan Throne in this hour of grief," he declared formally.

"Hypocrite!" a voice from the crowd bellowed.

Anheg's face went bleak, but Garion moved quickly to the rail, his eyes angry. "Any man who insults my friend insults me," he said in a dreadfully quiet voice. "Does anyone here want to say anything to *me*?"

The crowd drew back nervously.

Garion turned back to Anheg. "You look tired," he said.

"I've been tearing the palace apart—and most of Val Alorn as well—ever since I heard about what happened, but I haven't been able to find a single clue." The black-bearded Cherek king stopped and looked straight into Garion's face. His eyes had a pleading look in them. "I swear to you, Garion, upon my life, that I had nothing whatsoever to do with the death of Brand."

"I know that, Anheg," Garion said simply. He glanced at the still-angry crowd.

"Maybe we'd better get Hettar and the ladies and go on up to the Citadel. The others are all there, and we want to get started." He turned to Kail. "As soon as we get there, I want you to send down some men to disperse these people. Have them seal off the foot of this quay. I don't want any trouble here."

"Is it that bad?" Anheg asked very quietly.

"Just a precaution," Garion said. "I want to keep things under control until we get to the bottom of this."

■ CHAPTER EIGHTEEN ■

The funeral of Brand, the Rivan Warder, took place the following day in the Hall of the Rivan King. Garion, dressed all in black, sat on the basalt throne with Ce'Nedra at his side as the Rivan Deacon delivered the eulogy to the crowded Hall.

The presence of King Anheg of Cherek at that sorrowful ceremony caused an angry undertone among the members of the Rivan nobility, and it was only their profound respect for Brand and Garion's flinty gaze that prevented the whispers at the back of the Hall from becoming open accusations. Anheg, seated between Porenn and Cho-Hag, remained stony-faced throughout the services and he left the Hall immediately upon their conclusion.

"I've never seen him like this," Barak said quietly to Garion after the ceremony. "No one has ever accused him of murder before, and he doesn't know how to deal with it."

"No one's accusing him now," Garion replied quickly.

"Turn around and look at the faces of your subjects, Garion," Barak said sadly. "There's an accusation in every single eye."

Garion sighed. "I don't have to look. I know exactly what they're thinking."

"When do you want to start the meetings?"

"Let's wait a bit," Garion decided. "I don't particularly want Anheg going through the corridors of the Citadel while all these mourners are drifting about with daggers in their belts."

"Sound thinking," Barak agreed.

They gathered about midafternoon in the blue-draped council chamber in the south tower. As soon as Kail had closed the door, Anheg rose and faced them. "I want to state right at the outset that I had absolutely nothing to do with what happened here," he declared. "Brand was always one of my closest friends, and I'd have cut off my arm before I'd have hurt him. You have my word for that—both as a king and as an Alorn."

"No one's accusing you of anything, Anheg," Cho-Hag said quietly.

"Ha! I'm not nearly as stupid as I look, Cho-Hag—and even if I were, I still have ears. The people here in Riva have done everything short of spitting in my face."

The silvery-haired Earl of Seline leaned back in his chair. "I think perhaps that all of these suspicions—totally unfounded, of course—stem from that letter the assassins presented when they came here. Might it not be the quickest way to proceed to begin by examining that document?"

"Not a bad idea," Garion said. He turned to Kail. "Could we see the letter?"

"Ah—Ancient Belgarath has it, Sire," Kail said.

"Oh—that's right," Belgarath said. "I'd almost forgotten." He reached inside his gray tunic, drew out a folded parchment, and handed it to the old Sendarian nobleman.

"It looks more or less in order," the Earl mused after he had read it.

"Let me see that," Anheg demanded. He held the document distastefully, scowling as he read. "That's my signature, all right," he admitted, "and my seal, but I certainly didn't write this."

Garion had a thought. "Do you always read everything they bring you to sign?" he asked. "I know that there are times when they bring me whole stacks of things to sign, and I just write my name at the bottom of each one. What I'm getting at is—could someone have slipped this into a pile of other documents so that you signed it without knowing what it said?"

Anheg shook his head. "That happened to me once," he said. "Now I read everything before I sign it. Not only that, I dictate every document I put my name to. That way I know it says exactly what I want it to say." He thrust the letter toward Garion. "Look at this," he said, pointing at the second paragraph. " 'Foreasmuch as trade is the lifeblood of both our kingdoms—' and so on. Blast it, Garion! I've never used the word 'foreasmuch' in my entire life."

"How do we reconcile this, then?" the Earl of Seline asked. "We have authenticated the signature and seal. King Anheg declares that he not only reads everything he signs but that he also dictates every letter and proclamation personally. And yet we find textual inconsistencies in the document."

"Seline," Anheg said acidly, "did you ever dabble in law? You sound a great deal like a lawyer."

The Earl laughed. "Merely trying to be concise, your Majesty," he said.

"I *hate* lawyers."

The damning letter was central to the discussions for the remainder of the day, but nothing was resolved. Garion went wearily to bed that night as confused and filled with doubts as he had been when they started.

He slept badly and woke late. As he lay in the canopied royal bed, still trying to sort out his thoughts, he could hear voices coming from the adjoining room. Almost idly he began to identify those voices. Ce'Nedra was there, of course, and Aunt Pol. Queen Layla's giddy laugh made her easily identifiable. Nerina and Ariana, because of their Mimbrate dialect, were as easy. There were others as well, but the individuality of their voices was lost in the general chatter.

Garion slowly sat up, feeling almost as if he had not slept at all. He pushed the down-filled comforter aside and swung his feet to the floor. He did not really want to face this day. He sighed and stood up. Briefly he looked at the solid black doublet and hose he had worn the day before, then shook his head. To continue to dress in mourning might in some obscure way be taken as a silent accusation. That must be avoided at all costs. The situation involving King Anheg was so delicate at the moment that the slightest hint could push it into crisis. He crossed to the heavy wardrobe where he kept his clothes, selected one of his customary blue doublets, and began to dress.

The conversation in the adjoining room broke off suddenly at the sound of a knock on the door.

"Am I welcome here?" he heard Queen Islena ask in a subdued voice.

"Of course you are," Aunt Pol replied.

"I had thought that—" Islena faltered, then began again. "Considering everything, I had thought that perhaps it might be better if I stayed away."

"Nonsense," Queen Layla declared. "Do come in, Islena."

There was a general murmur of agreement.

"I swear to you all that my husband is innocent of this atrocity," Islena said in a clear voice.

"No one is saying that he was not, Islena," Aunt Pol replied quietly.

"Not openly perhaps, but there are ugly suspicions everywhere."

"I'm certain that Garion and the others will get to the bottom of it," Ce'Nedra said firmly. "Then everything will be cleared up."

"My poor Anheg did not sleep at all last night," Islena told them sadly. "I know that he looks brutish, but inside he's really very sensitive. This has hurt him deeply. Once he even cried."

"Our lords will requite the tears thy husband hath shed upon the body of the foul villain who lurks behind this monstrous act," the Baroness Nerina declared. "And the foolish men who doubt his true fidelity shall be covered with shame for their lack of trust, once the truth is out."

"I can only hope that you're right," Islena said.

"This is a mournful topic, ladies," Garion's cousin Adara told the rest of them, "and it has nothing to do with the real reason we're all here."

"And what reason is that, gentle Adara?" Ariana asked.

"The baby, Ariana," Adara replied. "We've come to see your baby again, Ce'Nedra. I'm sure he's not still sleeping, so why don't you bring him in here so that we can all fuss over him?"

Ce'Nedra laughed. "I thought you'd never ask."

The council meeting began about midmorning. The kings and their advisors gathered once more in a blue-draped council chamber. The golden sunlight of a late summer morning streamed in through the windows and a gentle sea breeze stirred the draperies. There was no particular formality in these sessions, and the monarchs and the others lounged comfortably in the velvet-upholstered chairs scattered about the room.

"I really don't think we'll accomplish too much by chewing on that letter for another day," Belgarath began. "Let's agree that it's obviously a forgery of some kind and move on." He looked at Kail. "Did your father have any enemies here on the island?" he asked, "Someone wealthy enough and powerful enough to hire Cherek assassins?"

Kail frowned. "No one can go through life without stepping on a few toes, Ancient One," he replied, "but I don't think anybody was holding that kind of grudge."

"In truth, my friend," Mandorallen told him, "some men, when they feel that they have been offended, will nurture their rancor in silence and with dissembling guise conceal their enmity until opportunity doth present itself to revenge themselves. The history of Arendia is replete with stories of such acts."

"It's a possibility," King Fulrach agreed. "And it might be better if we start close to home before we begin to go further afield."

"A list might be useful," Javelin suggested. "If we write down the name of every man on the Isle of the Winds whom Brand might possibly have offended, we can start eliminating them. Once we have the list narrowed down, we can start investigating. If the man behind this is a Rivan, he'd either have had to visit Cherek or had some contact with Chereks sometime in the recent past."

It took the remainder of the morning to compile the list. Kail sent for certain documents, and they all considered each of the decisions Brand had made during the past five years. Since the Warder had functioned as the kingdom's chief magistrate, there had been many decisions and usually a winner and a loser in each case.

After lunch, they began the winnowing process, discarding the names of those men without sufficient wealth or power to be able to obtain the services of paid assassins.

"It's narrowing down a bit," Javelin said as he struck off another name. He held up the list. "We've got this down to almost manageable proportions."

There was a respectful knock on the door. One of the guards posted there spoke briefly with someone outside, then came over to Barak and murmured something to him. The big red-bearded man nodded, rose, and followed him from the room.

"How about this one?" Javelin asked Kail, pointing at another name.

Kail scratched at one cheek. "I don't think so," he replied.

"It was a dispute over land," Javelin pointed out, "and some people get very intense where land is concerned."

"It was only a pasture," Kail recalled, "and not a very big one. The man has more land than he can keep track of anyway."

"Why did he go to the law, then?"

"It was the other man who brought the matter to my father."

Barak came back into the room. "Anheg," he said to his cousin, "Greldik's here. He's got something fairly important to tell you."

Anheg started to rise, then looked around. "Have him come in here," he said shortly. "I don't want anybody thinking that I've got any secrets."

"We've all got secrets, Anheg," Queen Porenn murmured.

"My situation is somewhat peculiar, Porenn." He pushed his dented crown back into place from where it had slipped down over one ear.

The bearded and fur-clad Greldik pushed past the guards and came into the chamber at that point. "You've got trouble at home, Anheg," he growled bluntly.

"What kind of trouble?"

"I just came back from Jarviksholm," Gredlik replied. "They're very unfriendly there."

"There's nothing new about that."

"They tried to sink me," Greldik said. "They've lined the tops of the cliffs on both sides of the inlet leading up to the city with catapults. The boulders were coming down like hailstones for a while."

Anheg scowled. "Why would they do that?"

"Probably because they didn't want me to see what they're doing."

"What could they be doing that they'd want to keep *that* secret?"

"They're building a fleet."

Anheg shrugged. "Lots of people build ships in Cherek."

"A hundred at a time?"

"How many?"

"I was busy dodging boulders, so I couldn't get an exact count, but the entire upper end of the inlet is lined with yards. The keels have all been laid, and they're starting on the ribs. Oh, they're working on the city walls, too."

"The walls? They're already higher than the walls of Val Alorn."

"They're even higher now."

Anheg scowled. "What are they up to?"

"Anheg, when you build a fleet and start strengthening your fortifications, it usually means that you're getting ready for a war. And when you try to sink the ship of a man known to be friendly to the crown, that usually means that the war is going to be with your king."

"He does have a point, Anheg," Barak said.

"Who's in control at Jarviksholm right now?" Garion asked curiously.

"The Bear-cult," Anheg said in disgust. "They've been filtering into the town from all over Cherek for the past ten years."

"This is very serious, Anheg," Barak said.

"It's also totally out of character," Javelin pointed out. "The cult has never been interested in confrontational politics before."

"*What* kind of politics?" Anheg asked.

"Another way of saying open war with the crown," the Drasnian Chief of Intelligence explained.

"Say what you mean, man."

"An occupational peculiarity," Javelin shrugged. "Always before, the cult has tried to work from within—trying to gather enough support to be able to coerce the kings of the Alorn nations to follow *their* policies. I don't think they've ever even considered open rebellion before."

"There's a first time for everything, I guess," Hettar suggested.

Javelin was frowning. "It's not at all like them," he mused, "and it's a direct reversal of a policy they've followed for the past three thousand years."

"People change sometimes," General Brendig said.

"Not the Bear-cult," Barak told him. "There isn't room enough in a cultist's mind for more than one idea."

"I think you'd better get off your behind and get back to Val Alorn, Anheg," Greldik suggested. "If they get those ships in the water, they'll control the whole west coast of Cherek."

Anheg shook his head. "I have to stay here," he declared. "I've got another matter that's more important right now."

Greldik shrugged. "It's your kingdom," he said, "at least for the time being."

"Thanks, Greldik," Anheg said drily. "You have no idea how that notion comforts me. How long will it take you to get to Val Alorn?"

"Three—maybe four days. It depends on how I catch the tides at the Bore."

"Go there," Anheg told him. "Tell the fleet admirals that I want them to move out of Val Alorn and take up stations off the Halberg straits. I think that when this council is over, I'll want to take a little journey up to Jarviksholm. It shouldn't take much to burn out those shipyards."

Greldik's answering grin was positively vicious.

After the council adjourned for the evening, Kail caught up with Garion in the torchlit corridor. "I think there's something you should consider, Belgarion," he said quietly.

"Oh?"

"This moving of the Cherek fleet concerns me."

"It's Anheg's fleet," Garion replied, "and his kingdom."

"There is only this Greldik's unsupported word about the shipyards at Jarviksholm," Kail pointed out. "And the Halberg straits are only three days from Riva."

"Aren't we being overly suspicious, Kail?"

"Your Majesty, I agree completely that King Anheg deserves every benefit of doubt concerning the assassination of my father, but this coincidence that puts the Cherek fleet within striking distance of Riva is an altogether different matter. I think we should quietly look to our defenses—just to be on the safe side."

"I'll think about it," Garion said shortly and moved on down the corridor.

About noon on the following day, Silk arrived. The little man was richly dressed in a gray velvet doublet; as had become his custom of late, his fingers glittered with costly jewels. After only the briefest of greetings to his friends, he went into private discussions with Javelin.

When Belgarath entered the council chamber that afternoon, he had a self-satisfied smirk on his face and the letter from King Anheg in his hand.

"What is it, father?" Polgara asked curiously. "You look like the ship's cat on a fishing boat."

"I'm always pleased when I solve a riddle, Pol." He turned to the rest of them. "As it turns out, Anheg *did* write this letter."

King Anheg jumped to his feet, his face livid.

Belgarath held up one hand. *"But,"* he continued, "what Anheg wrote is *not* what the letter seems to say." He laid the sheet of parchment on the table. "Have a look," he invited them.

When Garion looked at the letter, he could clearly see red-colored letters lying behind the ones which spelled out the message that seemed to place responsibility for Brand's death at Anheg's door.

"What is this, Belgarath?" King Fulrach asked.

"Actually, it's a letter to the Earl of Maelorg," the old man replied. "It has to do with Anheg's decision to raise the taxes on the herring fishery."

"I wrote *that* letter four years ago," Anheg declared, a baffled look crossing his face.

"Exactly," Belgarath said. "And if memory serves me, didn't the Earl of Maelorg die last spring?"

"Yes," Anheg said. "I attended the funeral."

"It appears that, after his death, someone got into his papers and filched this letter. Then they went to a great deal of trouble to bleach out the original message—all but the signature, of course—and to write one that introduced this so-called trade deputation."

"Why couldn't we see it before?" Barak asked.

"I had to tamper with it a bit," the old man admitted.

"Sorcery?"

"No. Actually I used a solution of certain salts. Sorcery might have raised the old message, but it probably would have erased the new one, and we might need that later on for evidence."

Barak's expression was slightly disappointed.

"Sorcery is not the *only* way do things, Barak."

"How did you find out?" Garion asked the old man, "That there was another message, I mean?"

"The bleach the fellow used leaves a very faint odor on the page." The sorcerer made a wry face. "It wasn't until this morning that I finally realized what I was smelling." He turned to Anheg. "I'm sorry it took me so long to exonerate you," he said.

"That's quite all right, Belgarath," Anheg said expansively. "It gave me the chance to find out who my *real* friends are."

Kail rose to his feet, his face a study in conflicting emotions. He went to Anheg's chair and dropped to one knee. "Forgive me, your Majesty," he said simply. "I must confess that I suspected you."

"Of course I forgive you." Anheg laughed suddenly. "Belar's teeth," he said. "After I read that letter, I even suspected myself. Get up, young man. Always stand on your feet—even when you've made a mistake."

"Kail," Garion said, "would you see to it that word of this discovery gets the widest possible circulation? Tell the people down in the city to stop sharpening their swords."

"I'll see to it at once, your Majesty."

"That still leaves us with an unsolved riddle," the Earl of Seline noted. "We know that King Anheg wasn't behind this, but who was?"

"We already have a good start on that," Lelldorin declared. "We've got that list of men who might have had reason to hate Brand."

"I think we're following the wrong track there," Queen Porenn disagreed. "The murder of the Rivan Warder was one thing, but trying to make it look as if Anheg had been responsible is something else entirely."

"I don't quite follow you, Porenn," Anheg admitted.

"If you had a very close friend—you *do* have a few friends, don't you, Anheg, dear?—and if this friend of yours was also a high-ranking official in your government, and the king of another country had him murdered, what would you do?"

"My warships would sail on the next tide," he replied.

"Exactly. The murder of Brand may not have been the result of a personal grudge. It might have been an attempt to start a war between Riva and Cherek."

Anheg blinked. "Porenn, you are an extraordinary woman."

"Why, thank you, Anheg."

The door opened, and Silk and Javelin entered. "Our most excellent Prince Kheldar here has a very interesting report for us," Javelin announced.

Silk stepped forward and bowed grandiosely. "Your Majesties," he said, "and dear friends. I can't say for certain just how relevant this is to your current discussions, but it's a matter that should be brought to your attention, I think."

"Have you ever noticed how a little prosperity makes certain people very pompous?" Barak asked Hettar.

"I noticed that," Hettar agreed mildly.

"I thought you might have."

Silk flashed his two friends a quick grin. "Anyway," he continued in a more conversational tone, "I've spent the past several months in the town of Rheon on the eastern frontier of dear old dreary Drasnia. Interesting town, Rheon. Very picturesque—particularly now that they've doubled the height of the walls."

"Kheldar," Queen Porenn said, tapping her fingers impatiently on the arm of her chair, "you *do* plan to get to the point eventually, don't you?"

"Why, of course, Auntie dear," he replied mockingly. "Rheon has always been a fortified town, largely because of its proximity to the Nadrak border. It is also filled with a citizenry so archconservative that most of them disapprove of the use of fire. It's a natural breeding ground for the Bear-cult. After the attempt on Ce'Nedra's life last summer, I sort of drifted into town to do a bit of snooping."

"That's an honest way to put it," Barak said.

"I'm going through an honest phase," Silk shrugged. "Enjoy it while you can, because it's starting to bore me. Now, it seems that the Bear-cult has a new leader— a man named Ulfgar. After Grodeg got that Murgo axe stuck in his back at Thull Mardu, the cult was pretty well demoralized. Then this Ulfgar comes out of nowhere and begins to pull them all together. This man can quite literally talk the birds out of the trees. Always before the leadership of the cult was in the hands of the priesthood, and always before it was centered in Cherek."

"Tell me something new," Anheg growled sourly.

"Ulfgar does not appear to be a priest of Belar," Silk continued, "and his center of power is at Rheon in eastern Drasnia."

"Kheldar, *please* come to the point," Porenn said.

"I'm getting there, your Majesty," he assured her. "In the last few months, very quietly, our friend Ulfgar has been calling in his cohorts. Cultists have been drifting up from Algaria and filtering into Rheon from all over Drasnia. The town is literally bulging with armed men. I'd guess that Ulfgar currently has a force at Rheon at least equal to the entire Drasnian army." He looked at young King Kheva. "Sorry, cousin," he said, "but it rather looks as if you now have only the second biggest army in Drasnia."

"I can correct that if I have to, cousin," Kheva replied firmly.

"You're doing a wonderful job with this boy, Auntie," Silk congratulated Porenn.

"Kheldar," she said acidly, "am I going to have to put you on the rack to pull this story out of you?"

"Why, Auntie dearest, what a shocking thing to suggest. This mysterious Ulfgar has resurrected a number of very ancient rituals and ceremonies—among them a permanent means of identifying kindred spirits—so to speak. At his orders, every cultist in Aloria has had a distinctive mark branded on the sole of his right foot. The chances are rather good that anyone you see limping is a new convert to the Bear-cult."

Barak winced. "That would *really* hurt," he said.

"They wear it rather proudly," Silk told him, "Once it heals, anyway."

"What does this mark look like?" King Cho-Hag asked.

"It's a symbolic representation of a bear paw," Silk explained. "It's shaped sort of like the letter U with a couple of marks at its open end to represent claws."

"After Kheldar told me this," Javelin took up the story, "we paid a short visit to that surviving assassin. His right foot has been branded with that particular mark."

"So now we know," Hettar said.

"We do indeed," Belgarath replied.

"Prithee," Mandorallen said, frowning in perplexity, "I have always been advised that the aim of this obscure religious denomination hath been the reunification of Aloria, that titanic empire of the north which existed under the reign of King Cherek Bear-shoulders, the mightiest ruler of antiquity."

"It may very well still be," Belgarath told him, "but if this Ulfgar had succeeded in putting Riva and Cherek at each other's throats, he might have been able to topple Drasnia and possibly Algaria as well. With Anheg and Garion concentrating on destroying each other, it probably wouldn't have been all that difficult for him to have taken their two kingdoms as well."

"Particularly with that fleet his people are building at Jarviksholm," Anheg added.

"His strategy seems at once very simple and yet very complex," General Brendig mused, "and I think it came very close to working."

"Too close," Polgara said. "What are we going to do about this, father?"

"I think we'll have to take steps," Belgarath replied. "This fellow Ulfgar still wants to reunite Aloria—but with himself as the successor to Bear-shoulders. The cult has tried subversion for three millennia. Now apparently they're going to try open war."

Garion's face grew bleak. "Well," he said, "if it's a war they want, they've come to the right place."

"I might drink to that," Anheg agreed. He thought for a moment. "If you're open to any suggestions, I think it might be a good idea if we destroy Jarviksholm before we move on Rheon. We don't want those Cherek cultists coming up behind us on the moors of eastern Drasnia and we *definitely* don't want a cult fleet in the Sea of the Winds. If even half of what Greldik says is true, we're going to have to burn out those shipyards before they get their warships into the water. You could mount a very successful attack on Rheon, Garion, and then come home to find a hostile force occupying Riva itself."

Garion considered that. "All right, then," he agreed. "We'll go to Jarviksholm first. Then we'll go to Rheon and have a little chat with this Ulfgar. I really want to look at a man who thinks he's big enough to fill Bear-shoulders' shoes."

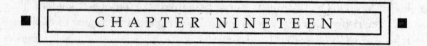

CHAPTER NINETEEN

"I'm sorry, Kail," Garion told his friend as they sat together in Garion's study with the morning sun streaming golden through the window, "but I have to have you and your brothers here at Riva. I'm taking most of our forces with me, and someone has to stay here to defend the city in case some of the cultists' ships slip around behind us."

Kail's face was angry. "That's not the real reason, is it?" he accused.

"Not entirely, no," Garion admitted. "I know how much you all loved your father and I know how much you want revenge on the people responsible for his murder."

"Isn't that only natural?"

"Of course it is, but people caught up in those feelings don't think clearly. They get rash and do things that put them in danger. Your family has shed enough blood already—first your brother Olban, then Arell, and now your father—so I'm not taking any chances with the rest of you."

Kail stood up, his face red with suppressed anger. "Does your Majesty have any further instructions for me?" he asked stiffly.

Garion sighed. "No, Kail," he said, "not at the moment. You know what to do here."

"Yes, your Majesty." Kail bowed curtly, turned and left the room.

Belgarath came into Garion's study through the other door.

"He didn't like it," Garion said.

"I didn't think he would." The old man shrugged, scratching at one bearded cheek. "But he's too important here in the Citadel for us to be risking his life. He'll be angry for a while, but he'll get over it."

"Is Aunt Pol staying behind, too?"

Belgarath made a face. "No. She insists on going. At least the other ladies have sense enough to realize that a battlefield is no place for a woman. I think we ought to leave Errand here, too. He has no sense of personal danger, and that's not a good trait when the fighting starts. You'd better finish here. The morning tide's turning, and we're almost ready to start."

As the *Seabird* moved out of the harbor that sunny morning with a flotilla of stout Rivan ships following her, Garion and the others gathered in the spacious, low-beamed aft cabin, poring over maps and discussing strategy.

"The inlet that runs up to Jarviksholm is very narrow," Anheg advised them, "and it's got more twists and turns to it than a Tolnedran trade agreement. It's going to slow us to a crawl."

"And then those catapults on top of the cliffs will sink half the fleet," Barak added gloomily.

"Is there any way we can come to the city from behind?" Hettar asked.

"There's a road coming up from Halberg," Barak replied, "but it goes through several passes fifteen leagues or so to the south of the city. Those passes are ideal for ambushes."

General Brendig had been studying the map. "What's this terrain like?" he asked, pointing at a spot on the south side of the mouth of the inlet.

"Rough," Barak said, "and steep."

"That's a description of most of Cherek," Silk observed.

"Is it passable?" Brendig persisted.

"Oh, you could climb it," Barak said, "but you'd be in plain view of the cata-pultists up on the cliffs. There's be a whole army waiting for you by the time you got to the top."

"Not if you did it at night," Brendig said.

"At night?" the big man scoffed. "Brendig, do you really want to take up night-time mountain climbing at your age?"

Brendig shrugged. "If it's the only way to get there."

Mandorallen had also been studying the map. "Prithee, my Lord," he said to Barak, "is this slope to the north also gentle enough to afford access to the clifftop?"

Barak shook his head. "It's a sheer face."

"Then we must needs seek other means to neutralize the catapults on that side." The knight thought a moment, then he smiled. "We have the means at our immediate disposal," he declared.

"I'd be interested to know what they are," King Fulrach said to him.

"It is the simplest possible solution, your Majesty," Mandorallen beamed. "To convey siege engines up the south slope would be tiresome—particularly during the hours of darkness. It would, moreover, be totally unnecessary, since the means of destroying the engines on the north side are already in place."

"I don't quite follow what you're suggesting," Garion admitted.

"I do," Hettar said. "All we have to do is climb the south slope at night, cap-ture the catapults on top, and then start lobbing boulders at the engines across the inlet."

"And once you distract *those* people, I can sweep up the inlet with fireboats and burn out the shipyards," Anheg added.

"But doesn't that still leave the city intact?" King Fulrach asked dubiously.

Garion stood up and began to pace up and down, thinking hard. "Once we start throwing rocks back and forth across the inlet and the fireboats start moving up toward the yards, it's going to attract quite a bit of attention from the city, wouldn't you say?"

"I could almost guarantee that," Brendig replied.

"Then wouldn't that be a perfect time to mount an attack on the landward side of the town? Everybody's going to be lining the front wall. The back side will be only lightly defended. If we strike fast enough, we could be inside before most of the defenders knew we were coming."

"Very good, Belgarion," King Cho-Hag murmured.

"It's all going to have to be carefully timed, though," Barak said thoughtfully. "We'll have to work out a way to pass signals back and forth."

"That's not really a problem, Barak," Aunt Pol told the big man. "We can take care of that."

"You know," Anheg said, "I think it might work. If we get lucky, we could take Jarviksholm in a single day."

"I never cared much for long sieges anyway," Silk noted, carefully polishing one of his rings.

Two days later they found the Cherek fleet standing at anchor off the Halberg straits, a narrow passage leading through a cluster of small, rocky islets jutting up out of the coastal waters of the west coast of the Cherek peninsula. The islets were topped with scrubby trees and they stood out, green against the snowfields covering the higher mountains lying inland. Garion stood at the rail of the *Seabird*, drinking in the beauty of that wild coast. A light step behind him and a familiar fragrance announced his Aunt Pol's approach.

"It's lovely, isn't it, Garion?" she said.

"Breathtaking," he agreed.

"It always seems this way," she mused. "Somehow it's when you're on your way to something very ugly that you come across these glimpses of beauty." She looked at him gravely. "You *will* be careful at Jarviksholm, won't you?"

"I'm always careful, Aunt Pol."

"Really? I seem to remember a number of incidents not too many years ago."

"I was a child then."

"Some things never change, I'm afraid." She suddenly put her arms about his neck and sighed. "Oh, my Garion," she said, "I've missed you in the past few years, do you know that?"

"I've missed you, too, Aunt Pol. Sometimes I wish—" He left it hanging.

"That we could have just stayed at Faldor's farm?"

"It really wasn't such a bad place, was it?"

"No. It was a very good place—for a child. But you're grown now. Would you really have been content there? Life was quite placid at Faldor's."

"If we hadn't left, I'd never have known what it was like to live any other way."

"But if we hadn't left, you never would have met Ce'Nedra, would you?"

"I suppose I hadn't thought about that."

"Let's go below, shall we?" she suggested. "That breeze is really rather brisk."

They encountered King Anheg and Barak in a narrow companionway just outside the main cabin belowdecks. "Barak," Anheg was saying acidly, "you're getting to be worse than an old woman."

"I don't care what you say, Anheg," the red-bearded Barak growled. "You're not going to take the *Seabird* up that inlet until all those catapults have been cleared. I didn't spend that much money on her to have somebody drop boulders on her decks from those cliffs. My boat, my rules."

The lean-faced Javelin approached from down the companionway. "Is there some problem, my Lords?" he asked.

"I was just laying down a few rules for Anheg here," Barak replied. "He's going to be in charge of my ship while I'm gone."

"Were you going somewhere, my Lord of Trellheim?"

"I'll be going with Garion when he mounts his attack on the city."

"As you think best, my Lord. How long do you think it's going to take to reach the mouth of the inlet?"

Barak tugged at his luxuriant red beard. "Those Rivan ships carrying Garion's troops aren't quite as fast as our warships," he mused. "I make it about a day and a half. Wouldn't you agree, Anheg?"

"About that, yes."

"That should put us there tomorrow evening, then?" Javelin asked.

"Right," Barak said, "and that's when the fun starts."

Aunt Pol sighed. "Alorns!"

After a few shouted conferences from ship to ship, the combined fleet heeled over sharply in the quickening breeze and beat northward along the rugged west coast of the Cherek peninsula toward Jarviksholm.

The following morning, Garion went up on deck with Barak and Hettar to watch the sun come up above the forested and snow-capped peaks of Cherek. The shadows back in the wooded valleys were a kind of misty blue, and the sun sparkled on the waves.

A mail-shirted Cherek sailor, who had been ostensibly coiling a rope, turned from his task, then suddenly plunged a dagger directly at Garion's unprotected back as the King stood at the rail.

The attack might well have proved fatal had Durnik not shouted a quick warning. Garion half-turned in time to see the dagger go skittering across the deck. At the same time, he heard a startled exclamation and a splash. He wheeled about to see a desperately clutching hand sink beneath the waves about thirty yards to port. He looked questioningly at Polgara, but she shook her head.

"I forgot about the mail shirt," Durnik said apologetically. "It's sort of hard to swim with one of those on, isn't it?"

"More than sort of," Barak assured him.

"You'll want to question him, I suppose," Durnik said. "I can fish him out, if you like."

"What do you think, Hettar?" Barak asked.

Hettar considered the notion for several moments, looking out at the bubbles coming up from somewhere far beneath the surface. "These are Cherek waters, aren't they?"

Barak nodded.

"Then I think we should consult King Anheg and get his opinion."

"Anheg's sleeping late this morning," Barak told him, also looking out at the bubbles.

"I'd hate to wake him," Hettar said. "He's had a lot on his mind lately, and I'm sure he needs his rest." The tall Algar turned to Durnik with an absolutely straight face. "I'll tell you what, Durnik. The very moment King Anheg wakes up, we'll bring the matter immediately to his attention."

"Have you ever translocated anything before, Durnik?" Polgara asked her husband.

"No, not really. I knew how it was done, of course, but I've never had the occasion to try it myself. I threw him just a little farther than I'd intended, I'm afraid."

"You'll get better with practice, dear," she assured him. Then she turned to Garion. "Are you all right?" she asked.

"I'm fine, Aunt Pol. He didn't even get close to me—thanks to Durnik."

"He's always been very useful to have around," she replied, giving Durnik a warm smile.

"Where did the fellow come from, Barak?" Hettar asked.

"Val Alorn, of all places. He always seemed like a good man, too. He did his work and kept his mouth shut. I'd never have suspected that he might have had religious convictions."

"Maybe it's time for us to examine everybody's feet," Hettar suggested.

Barak looked at him quizzically.

"If Silk's right, then all the Bear-cultists have that brand on the soles of their right feet. It's probably easier in the long run to examine feet rather than have Garion offer his back to every dagger aboard your ship."

"You might be right," Barak agreed.

They sailed into the wide mouth of the inlet that wound its way up to Jarviksholm just as the sun was setting. "Shouldn't we have waited until after dark to come this close?" Garion asked as he and the other kings stood on the foredeck of the *Seabird*.

Anheg shrugged. "They knew we were coming. They've been watching us ever since we left the Halberg straits. Besides, now that they know that we're here, those catapultists up there will concentrate on watching the ships. That ought to make it easier for you and Brendig to slip up behind them when the time comes."

"That makes sense, I guess."

Barak came forward with the one-armed General Brendig. "As close as we can figure it, we ought to start about midnight," he said. "Garion and the rest of us will climb up first and circle around until we're behind the city. Brendig and his men can follow us up and start taking over the catapults. As soon as it gets light enough to see, he's going to start throwing boulders across the inlet."

"Will that give Garion time enough to get into position?" King Fulrach asked.

"It should be plenty of time, your Majesty," Brendig assured him. "Lord Barak says that once we get to the top, the terrain is fairly flat."

"There are trees, too," Barak told them. "That should give us plenty of concealment."

"How much open space are we going to have to charge across when we attack the city?" Garion asked.

"Oh, maybe five hundred yards," Barak replied.

"That's quite a ways."

"It's about as far as *I* want to run."

Evening settled slowly over the calm waters of the inlet, purpling the sheer cliffs rising on either side. Garion used the last bit of light carefully to examine every inch of the steep slope which he and his men would be climbing in just a few hours. A flicker of movement just overhead caught his eye, and he looked up in time to see a ghostly white shape sliding silently through the calm, purple air. A single soft white feather slowly sifted down to settle on the deck not far away. Gravely, Hettar went over and picked it up.

A moment or two later, Aunt Pol, wrapped in her blue cloak, came down the deck and joined them. "You're going to have to be very careful when you approach the shipyards," she told Anheg, who stood nearby with Brendig. "They've moved catapults down to the beaches to try to hold you off."

"I expected that," he replied with an indifferent shrug.

"You'd better pay attention to her, Anheg," Barak said in a threatening tone, "because if you get my ship sunk, I'll pull out your beard one whisker at a time."

"What a novel way to address one's king," Silk murmured to Javelin.

"How heavily is the rear of the city defended?" Garion asked Polgara.

"The walls are high," she answered, "and the gate looks impressive. There aren't very many men there, though."

"Good."

Hettar silently handed her the feather.

"Why, thank you," she said to him. "I would have missed that."

The slope of the hill leading to the rolling plateau high above was even steeper than Garion's examination from the deck of the *Seabird* had led him to believe. Clumps of broken rock, almost invisible in the midnight darkness, rolled treacherously underfoot, and the stiff limbs of the scrubby bushes that choked the hillside seemed almost to push deliberately at his face and chest as he struggled upward. His mail shirt was heavy, and he was soon dripping with sweat.

"Rough going," Hettar observed laconically.

A pale sliver of a moon had risen when they finally crested that brutal slope. As they reached the top, they found that the plateau above was covered with a dense forest of fir and spruce trees.

"This might take us a little longer than I'd thought," Barak muttered, eyeing the thick undergrowth.

Garion paused to get his breath. "Let's stop for a moment," he told his friends. He stared glumly at the forest barring their way. "If all of us start crashing through that, we're going to alert the catapultists along the top of the cliff," he said. "I think we'd better send out some scouts to see if we can find a path or a track of some kind."

"Give me a while," Silk told him.

"You'd better take some men with you."

"They'd just slow me down. I'll be back before long." The little man vanished into the trees.

"He never changes, does he?" Hettar murmured.

Barak laughed shortly. "Did you really think he would?"

"How long thinkest thou it will be until dawn, my Lord?" Mandorallen asked the big Cherek.

"Two—maybe three hours," Barak replied. "That hill took a long time."

Lelldorin, his bow slung across his back, joined them at the edge of the dark wood. "General Brendig's started up," he told them.

"I wonder how he's going to manage that climb with only one arm," Barak said.

"I don't think you need to worry too much about Brendig," Hettar replied. "He usually does what he sets out to do."

"He's a good man," Barak agreed.

They waited in the warm summer darkness as the moon slowly climbed the eastern sky. From far below Garion could hear the calls of Anheg's men and the rasp of windlasses as the sailors strove to make enough noise to cover any inadvertant sounds Brendig's men might make as they struggled up the brushy slope. Finally Silk returned, appearing soundlessly out of the bushes. "There's a road about a quarter of a mile south of here," he reported quietly. "It seems to go toward Jarviksholm."

"Excellent," Mandorallen said gaily. "Let us proceed, my Lords. The city doth await our coming."

"I hope not," Garion said. "The whole idea is to surprise them."

The narrow road Silk had found proved to be a woodcutter's track and it meandered in a more or less easterly direction, leading them inland. Behind him Garion could hear the jingle of mail shirts and the steady, shuffling tread of his soldiers as they moved through the tag end of night in the deep shadows of the surrounding forest. There was a sense of inexorable purpose involved in this leading a mass of faceless men through the darkness. A tense excitement had been building in him since they had left the ships. His impatience to begin the attack was so strong now that it was all he could do to keep himself from breaking into a run.

They reached a large cleared area. At the far side of that open field, the white ribbon of a well-traveled highway cut due north across the moonlit pastureland. "That's the Halberg road," Barak told them. "We're almost there."

"I'd better see how Brendig's doing," Garion said. He carefully reached out, skirting the thoughts of the troops massed at his back and seeking the familiar touch of Durnik's mind. *"Durnik,"* he said silently, *"can you hear me?"*

"Garion?" the smith's thought came back.

"Right," Garion replied. *"Have you captured the catapults yet?"*

"We've still got a dozen or so to take. Brendig's moving slowly to keep down unnecessary noise."

"Will you have them all by the time it starts getting light?"

"I'm sure we will."

"Good. Let me know when you capture the last one."

"I will."

"How are they doing?" Lelldorin asked. The young bowman's voice was tight with excitement.

"They'll be ready when it's time," Garion replied.

"What thinkest thou, my Lord?" Mandorallen asked Barak. "Might it not be the proper moment to select some few stout trees to serve as rams to reduce the city gates?"

"I'll deal with the gate," Garion told them firmly.

Barak stared at him. "You mean that you're going to——?" He made a gesture with one thick-fingered hand.

Garion nodded.

"That hardly seems proper, Garion," Barak objected disapprovingly.

"Proper?"

"There are certain ways that things are done. City gates are supposed to be knocked in with battering rams."

"While the people inside pour boiling pitch down on the men trying to break in?"

"That's part of the risk," Barak explained. "Without a little risk, a battle isn't very much fun."

Hettar laughed quietly.

"I hate to fly in the face of tradition," Garion said, "but I'm not going to let a lot of people get killed unnecessarily just for the sake of an old custom."

A hazy ground fog, glowing in the moonlight, lay low on the broad, open expanse between the edge of the forest and the towering walls of Jarviksholm. Off to the east, the first pale glimmer of the approaching dawn stained the velvet sky. There were ruddy torches along the top of the heavy battlements of the city; by their light Garion could see a number of armed men.

"How close do you need to get to break in the gate?" Silk whispered to Garion.

"The closer the better," Garion replied.

"All right. We'll have to move up a bit, then. The fog and the tall grass should help."

"I'll go along with you," Barak said. "Is it likely to make much noise?"

"Probably," Garion said.

The big man turned to Hettar and Mandorallen. "Use that as your signal. When Garion knocks the gate down, you start the charge."

Hettar nodded.

Garion drew in a deep breath. "All right," he said, "let's go." Crouched low, the three of them started across the open field toward the city. When they were no more than a hundred yards from the gate, they sank down in the tall grass.

"Garion," Durnik's thought came from out of the growing light, *"we've captured all the catapults."*

"Can you see the ones on the north cliffs yet?"

"It's probably going to be just a few more minutes."

"Tell Brendig to start just as soon as he can make them out."

They waited as the eastern sky grew steadily lighter. Then a series of solid thuds came from beyond the city, followed after an interval by the sound of heavy rocks crashing through timbers and by startled shouts and cries of pain.

"We've started," Durnik reported.

"Garion," Polgara's thought came to him, *"are you in position?"*

"Yes, Aunt Pol."

"We're going to start up the inlet now."

"Let me know when you're in sight of the city."

"Be careful, Garion."

"I will."

"What's happening?" Barak whispered, eyeing the men atop the city walls.

"They've started dropping rocks on the north cliff," Garion replied softly, "and Anheg's got the fleet moving."

Barak ground his teeth together. "I told him to wait until all the catapults were out of action."

"Don't worry so much about that ship of yours," Silk murmured. "It's very hard to aim a catapult when you're dodging boulders."

"Somebody might get lucky."

They waited tensely as the light slowly grew stronger. Garion could smell the salt tang of the sea and the heavy odor of evergreens as he surveyed the stout gate.

"We can see the city now, Garion," Aunt Pol reported.

Shouts of alarm came from inside the city, and Garion saw the armed men atop the walls running along the parapet, making for the seaward side of Jarviksholm. "Are we ready?" he whispered to his two friends.

"Let's do it," Silk said tensely.

Garion rose to his feet and concentrated. He felt something that was almost like an inrushing of air as he drew in and concentrated his will. He seemed to be tingling all over as the enormous force built up in him. Grimly he drew Iron-grip's sword, which he had left sheathed until now in order to conceal that telltale blue fire. The Orb leaped joyously into flame. "Here we go," he said from between clenched teeth. He pointed the sword at the gate, standing solid and impenetrable-looking a hundred yards in front of him. "Burst!" he commanded, and all his clenched-in will surged into the sword and out through its flaming tip.

The one thing that he had overlooked, of course, was the Orb's desire to be helpful. The force which struck the gates of Jarviksholm was, to put it very mildly, excessive. The logs disappeared entirely, and chunks and splinters of that tar-smeared gate were later found as much as five miles distant. The solid stone wall in which the gate had been mounted also blew apart, and many of the huge, rough-hewn blocks sailed like pebbles to splash into the harbor and the inlet far from the city. Most of the back wall of Jarviksholm crumbled and fell in on itself. The noise was awful.

"Belar!" Barak swore in amazement as he watched the nearly absolute destruction.

There was a stunned silence for a moment, and then a great shout came from the edge of the woods as Hettar and Mandorallen led the charge of the massed Rivans and Chereks into the stunned city.

It was not what warriors call a good fight. The Bear-cult was not composed entirely of able-bodied men. It had also attracted into its ranks old men, women, and children. Because of the raging fanaticism of the cult, the warriors entering the city frequently found it necessary to kill those who might otherwise have been spared. By late afternoon, there were only a few small pockets of resistance remaining in the northwest quarter of Jarviksholm, and much of the rest of the city was on fire.

Garion, half-sickened by the smoke and the slaughter, stumbled back through the burning city, over that shattered wall, and out into the open fields beyond. He wandered, tired and sick, for a time until he came across Silk, seated comfortably on a large rock, casually watching the destruction of the city. "Is it just about finished?" the little man asked.

"Nearly," Garion replied. "They only have a few buildings left in their control."

"How was it?"

"Unpleasant. A lot of old people and women and children got killed."

"That happens sometimes."

"Did Anheg say what he was going to do with the survivors? I think there's been enough killing already."

"It's hard to say," Silk replied. "Our Cherek cousins tend sometimes to be a bit savage, though. Some things are likely to happen in the next day or so that you probably won't want to watch—like that." He pointed toward the edge of the wood where a crowd of Chereks were working on something. A long pole was raised and set into the ground. A crosspiece was attached to the top of the pole, and a man was tied by his outspread arms to that crosspiece.

"No!" Garion exclaimed.

"I wouldn't interfere, Garion," Silk advised. "It is Anheg's kingdom, after all, and he can deal with traitors and criminals in any way he sees fit."

"That's barbaric!"

"Moderately so, yes. As I said, though, Chereks have a certain casual brutality in their nature."

"But shouldn't we at least question the prisoners first?"

"Javelin's attending to that."

Garion stared at the crowd of soldiers working in the last ruddy light of the setting sun. "I'm sorry," he said, choking in revulsion, "but that's going entirely too far. I'm going to put a stop to it right now."

"I'd stay out of it, Garion."

"Oh, no—not when he starts crucifying women!"

"He's what?" Silk turned to stare at the soldiers. Suddenly the blood drained from the little man's face, and he sprang to his feet. With Garion close on his heels, he ran across the intervening turf. "Have you lost your mind entirely?" he demanded hotly of the bony Chief of Drasnian Intelligence, who sat calmly at a rough table in the center of a group of soldiers.

"What seems to be your problem, Kheldar?"

"Do you know who that is that you just crucified?"

"Naturally. I questioned her myself." His fingers moved almost idly, but Silk stood directly in front of the table, cutting off Garion's view of the thin man's hands.

"Get her down from there!" Silk said, though his voice seemed for some reason to have lost the edge of its outrage.

"Why don't you attend to your own business, Kheldar?" Javelin suggested. "Leave me to mine." He turned to a burly Cherek standing nearby. "Prince Kheldar and the Rivan King will be leaving now," he said coldly. "Would you escort them, please. I think that they should be somewhere at least a quarter of a mile from here."

"I'll kill him," Silk fumed as he and Garion were herded away. "I'll kill him with my own two bare hands."

As soon as the soldiers had led them to a spot some distance from Javelin and had turned to go back to their grisly work, however, the little man regained his composure with astonishing speed.

"What was that all about?" Garion asked.

"The girl he just crucified is his own niece, Liselle," Silk replied quite calmly.

"You can't be serious!"

"I've known her since she was a child. He promised to explain later. His explanation had better be very good, though, or I'm going to carve out his tripes." He removed a long dagger from under his pearl-gray doublet and tested the edge with his thumb.

It was after dark when Javelin came looking for them. "Oh, put that away, Kheldar," he said disgustedly, looking at Silk's dagger.

"I may need it in a minute," Silk replied. "Start talking, Javelin, and you'd better make it very convincing, or I'll have your guts in a pile right between your feet."

"You seem upset."

"You noticed. How clever of you."

"I did what I did for a very specific reason."

"Wonderful. I thought you were just amusing yourself."

"I can do without the sarcasm, Silk. You should know by now that I never do anything without a reason. You can put your mind at rest about Liselle. She's probably already been released."

"Released?"

"Escaped, actually. There were dozens of cultists hiding in those woods. Your eyes must be going bad on you if you didn't see them. Anyway, by now, every prisoner we crucified has been released and is on the way to safety back in the mountains."

"Exactly what is this all about, Javelin?"

"It's really very simple. We've been trying for years to get someone into the upper echelons of the Bear-cult. They have just rescued a genuine heroine—a martyr to the cause. Liselle's clever enough to use that to work her way into their higher councils."

"How did she get here in the first place?"

Javelin shrugged. "She put on a mail shirt, and I slipped her on board Trellheim's ship. After the fighting was nearly over, I just slipped her in with the other prisoners."

"Won't the others who were just rescued say that she was never in the city?" Garion asked.

"No, your Majesty, I don't think so," Javelin replied. "She's going to say that she lived in the northeast quarter of Jarviksholm. The others we crucified all came from the southwest quarter. Jarviksholm is a fairly good-sized town. Nobody could really say for sure that she wasn't there all along."

"I still can't believe that you would actually do that to her," Silk said.

"It took a fair amount of convincing and a great deal of fast talking on her part to persuade me," Javelin admitted.

Silk stared at him.

"Oh, yes," Javelin said. "Hadn't you guessed? The whole thing was her idea in the first place."

Suddenly Garion heard a hollow rushing sound, and a moment later Ce'Nedra's voice came to him quite clearly.

"Garion!" she cried out in anguish. *"Garion, come home immediately! Someone has stolen our baby!"*

CHAPTER TWENTY

Polgara looked at Garion critically as they stood together in a high, open meadow above the still-burning city of Jarviksholm while the pale light of dawn washed the stars out of the sky. "Your wing feathers are too short," she told him.

Garion made the feathers longer.

"Much better," she said. Then her look became intense, and she also shimmered into the shape of a speckled falcon. "I've never liked these hard feathers," she murmured, clicking her hooked beak. Then she looked at Garion, her golden eyes fierce. "Try to remember everything I told you, dear. We won't go too high on your first flight." She spread her wings, took a few short steps with her taloned feet, and lifted herself effortlessly into the air.

Garion tried to imitate what she had just done and drove himself beak-first into the turf.

She swooped back in. "You have to use your tail, too, Garion," she said. "The wings give the power, but the tail gives direction. Try it again."

The second attempt was a bit smoother. He actually flew for about fifty yards before he crashed into a tree.

"That was very nice, dear. Just try to watch where you're going."

Garion shook his head, trying to clear the ringing from his ears and the speckles of light from in front of his eyes.

"Straighten your feathers, dear, and let's try it again."

"It's going to take months for me to learn this, Aunt Pol. Wouldn't it just be faster to sail to Riva on the *Seabird*?"

"No, dear," she said firmly. "You just need a bit of practice, that's all."

His third attempt was somewhat more successful. He was beginning to get the knack of coordinating his wings and tail, but he still felt clumsy and he seemed to do a great deal of clawing ineffectually at the air.

"Garion, don't fight with it. Let it lift you."

They circled the meadow several times in the shadowless luminosity of dawn. Garion could see the smoke rising black from the city and the burned-out shipyards in the harbor as he followed Polgara in a steady upward spiral. As his confidence increased, he began to feel a fierce exhilaration. The rush of cool morning air through his feathers was intoxicating, and he found that he could lift himself higher and higher almost effortlessly. By the time the sun was fully up, the air was no longer an enemy, and he had begun to master the hundreds of minute muscular adjustments necessary to get the greatest possible efficiency out of his feathers.

Belgarath swooped in to join them with Durnik not far behind. "How's he doing?" the fierce-looking falcon asked Polgara.

"He's almost ready, father."

"Good. Let him practice for another fifteen minutes or so, and then we'll get started. There's a column of warm air rising off that lake over there. That always makes it easier." He tilted on one wing and veered away in a long, smooth arc.

"This is really very fine, Pol," Durnik said. "I should have learned how to do this years ago."

When they moved into the column of air rising from the surface of the warm waters of the lake, Garion learned the secret of effortless flight. With his wings spread and unmoving, he let the air lift him up and up. Objects on the ground far below shrank as he rose higher and higher. Jarviksholm now looked like a toy village, and its harbor was thick with miniature ships. The hills and forests were bright green in the morning sunshine. The sea was azure, and the snowfields on the higher peaks were so intensely white that they almost hurt his eyes.

"How high would you say we are?" he heard Durnik ask Belgarath.

"Several thousand feet."

"It's sort of like swimming, isn't it? It doesn't really matter how deep the water is, because you're only using the top of it anyway."

"I never really thought of it that way." Belgarath looked over at Aunt Pol. "This should be high enough," he said in the shrill, falcon's whistle. "Let's go to Riva."

The four of them beat steadily southwest, leaving the Cherek coast behind and flying out over the Sea of the Winds. For a time, a following breeze aided them, but at midday the breeze dropped, and they had to work for every mile. Garion's shoulders ached, and the unaccustomed effort of flying made the muscles in his chest burn. Grimly, he flew on. Far below him he could see the miles-long waves on the Sea of the Winds, looking from this height almost like ripples roughening the surface in the afternoon sunlight.

The sun was low over the western horizon when the rocky coast of the Isle of the Winds came into view. They flew southward along the east coast and spiraled down at last toward the uplifted towers and battlements of the Citadel, standing grim and gray over the city of Riva.

A sentry, leaning idly on his spear atop the highest parapet, looked startled as the four speckled falcons swooped in to land around him, and his eyes bulged with astonishment as they shimmered into human form. "Y-your Majesty," he stammered to Garion, awkwardly trying to bow and hold on to his spear at the same time.

"What happened here?" Garion demanded.

"Someone has abducted your son, Sire," the sentry reported. "We've sealed off the island, but we haven't caught him yet."

"Let's go down," Garion said to the others. "I want to talk to Ce'Nedra."

But that, of course, was nearly impossible. As soon as Garion entered the blue-carpeted royal apartment, she flew into his arms and collapsed in a storm of hysterical weeping. He could feel her tiny body trembling violently against him, and her fingers dug into his arms as she clung to him. "Ce'Nedra," he pleaded with her, "you've got to stop. You have to tell us what happened."

"He's gone, Garion," she wailed. "S-somebody came into the n-nursery and t-took him!" She began to cry again.

Ariana, Lelldorin's blond Mimbrate wife, stood not far away, and the dark-haired Adara stood at the window, looking on with a grieved expression.

"Why don't you see what you can do, Pol," Belgarath said quietly. "Try to get her calmed down. I'll need to talk to her—but probably later. Right now, I think the rest of us should go talk to Kail."

Polgara had gravely removed her cloak, folded it carefully, and laid it across the back of a chair. "All right, father," she replied. She came over and gently took the sobbing little queen out of Garion's arms. "It's all right, Ce'Nedra," she said soothingly. "We're here now. We'll take care of everything."

Ce'Nedra clung to her. "Oh, Lady Polgara," she cried.

"Have you given her anything?" Aunt Pol asked Ariana.

"Nay, my Lady Polgara," the blond girl replied. "I feared that in her distraught condition those potions which most usually have a calming effect might do her injury."

"Let me have a look at your medicine kit."

"At once, Lady Polgara."

"Come along," Belgarath said to Garion and Durnik, a steely glint coming into his eyes. "Let's go find Kail and see if we can get to the bottom of this."

They found Kail sitting wearily at a table in his father's office. Spread before him was a large map of the island, and he was poring over it intently.

"It happened sometime yesterday morning, Belgarion," he said gravely after they had exchanged the briefest of greetings. "It was before daybreak. Queen Ce'Nedra looked in on the prince a few hours past midnight, and everything was fine. A couple of hours later, he was gone."

"What have you done so far?" Belgarath asked him.

"I ordered the island sealed," Kail replied, "and then we searched the Citadel from one end to the other. Whoever took the prince was nowhere in the fortress, but no ship has arrived or departed since I gave that order, and the harbor master reports that nobody sailed after midnight yesterday. So far as I know, the abductor has not left the Isle of the Winds."

"Good," Garion said, a sudden hope welling up in him.

"At the moment, I have troops searching house by house in the city, and ships are patrolling every inch of the coastline. The island is completely sealed off."

"Have you searched the forests and mountains?" the old man asked.

"We want to finish the search of the city first," Kail said. "Then we'll seal the city and move the troops out into the surrounding countryside."

Belgarath nodded, staring at the map. "We want to move carefully," he said. "Let's not back this child stealer into a corner—at least not until we have my great-grandson safely back where he belongs."

Kail nodded his agreement. "The safety of the prince is our primary concern," he said.

Polgara quietly entered the room. "I gave her something that will make her sleep," she said, "and Ariana's watching her. I don't think it would do any good to try to question her just yet, and sleep is what she needs right now."

"You're probably right, Aunt Pol," Garion said, "but I'm not going to sleep—not until I find what happened to my son."

Early the following morning, they gathered again in Kail's orderly study to pore once again over the map. Garion was about to ask Kail about the search of the city, but he stopped as he felt a sudden tug of the great sword strapped across his back. Absently, still staring at the yellowed parchment map on Kail's desk, he adjusted the strap. It tugged at him again, more insistently this time.

"Garion," Durnik said curiously, "does the Orb sometimes glow like that when you aren't actually holding the sword?"

Garion looked over his shoulder at the flaring Orb. "What's it doing that for?" he asked, baffled.

The next tug nearly jerked him off his feet. "Grandfather," he said, a bit alarmed.

Belgarath's expression grew careful. "Garion," he said in a level voice, "I want you to take the sword out of its scabbard. I think the Orb is trying to tell you something."

Garion reached back over his shoulder and drew Iron-grip's great sword from its sheath with a steely slither. Without even stopping to think how irrational it might sound, he spoke directly to the glowing stone on the pommel. "I'm awfully busy right now. Can't this wait?"

The answer was a steady pull toward the door.

"What is it *doing*?" Garion demanded irritably.

"Let's just follow it," Belgarath told him.

Helplessly, Garion followed the powerful urging through the door and out into the torchlit corridor, with the others trailing curiously along behind him. He could sense the peculiarly crystalline awareness of the Orb and feel its overwhelming anger. Not since the dreadful night in Cthol Mishrak when he had faced the maimed God of Angarak had he felt so much outrage emanating from that living stone. The sword continued to pull him down the corridor, moving faster and faster until he was half running to keep up.

"What's it trying to do, father?" Polgara asked in a puzzled tone. "It's never done anything like this before."

"I'm not sure," the old man replied. "We'll just have to follow it and find out. I think it might be important, though."

Kail stopped briefly in front of a sentry posted in the corridor. "Would you go get my brothers?" he asked the man. "Have them come to the royal apartment."

"Yes sir," the sentry replied, with a quick salute.

Garion stopped at the dark, polished door to the apartment, opened it, and went inside with the sword still pulling at him.

Queen Layla was just in the act of drawing a blanket over the exhausted Adara, who lay asleep on the couch, and she looked up with astonishment. "What on earth—?" she began.

"Hush, Layla," Polgara told her. "Something's happening that we don't quite understand."

Garion steeled himself and went on into the bedroom. Ce'Nedra lay in the bed, tossing and whimpering in her sleep. At her bedside sat Queen Islena and Barak's wife Merel. Ariana dozed in a deep chair near the window. He was only able to give the ladies attending his wife the briefest of glances, however, before the sword pulled him on into the nursery, where the sight of the empty cradle wrenched at his heart. The great sword dipped over the cradle, and the Orb glowed. Then the stone flickered with a pulsating light for a moment.

"I think I'm starting to understand," Belgarath said. "I won't absolutely swear to this, but I think it wants to follow Geran's trail."

"Can it do that?" Durnik asked.

"It can do almost anything, and it's totally committed to the Rivan line. Let it go, Garion. Let's see where it leads you."

In the corridor outside, Kail's two brothers, Verdan and Brin, met them. Verdan, the eldest of the three, was as burly as an ox, and Brin, the youngest, only slightly less so. Both men wore mail shirts and helmets and had heavy broadswords belted to their sides.

"We think that the Orb may be trying to lead us to the prince," Kail explained tersely to them. "We might need you two when we find him."

Brin flashed a broad, almost boyish grin. "We'll have the abductor's head on a pole before nightfall, then," he said.

"Let's not be too hasty about removing heads," Belgarath told him. "I want the answers to some questions first."

"One of you stay with Ce'Nedra at all times," Aunt Pol told Queen Layla, who had curiously trailed along behind them. "She'll probably wake up sometime this afternoon. Let Ariana sleep for now. Ce'Nedra might need her when she awakens."

"Of course, Polgara," the plump queen of Sendaria replied.

"And you," Aunt Pol said firmly to Errand, who was just coming down the hall. "I want you to stay in the royal apartment and do exactly what Layla tells you to do."

"But—" he started to protest.

"No buts, Errand. What we have to do might be dangerous, and that's something you haven't quite learned to understand yet."

He sighed. "All right, Polgara," he said disconsolately.

With the Orb on the pommel of the massive sword pulling him along, Garion followed the unseen track of his son's abductor out through one of the side gates with the rest of them close on his heels.

"It seems to want to go toward the mountains," Garion said. "I thought the trail would lead down into the city."

"Don't think, Garion," Polgara told him. "Just go where the Orb leads you."

The trail led across the meadow rising steeply behind the Citadel and then into the forest of dark fir and spruce where Garion and Ce'Nedra had often strolled on their summer outings.

"Are you sure it knows what it's doing?" Garion asked as he pushed his way through a tangled patch of undergrowth. "There's no path here at all. I don't think anyone would have come this way."

"It's following some kind of trail, Garion," Belgarath assured him. "Just keep up with it."

They struggled through the thick underbrush for an hour or so. Once a covey of grouse exploded from under Garion's feet with a heart-stopping thunder of wings.

"I'll have to remember this place," Brin said to Kail. "The hunting here might be very good."

"We're hunting other game at the moment. Keep your mind on your work."

When they reached the upper edge of the forest, Garion stared up at the steep, rock-strewn meadow rising above the timberline. "Is there a pass of any kind through these mountains?" he asked.

"Off to the left of that big peak," Brin replied, pointing. "I use it when I go out to hunt wild stags, and the shepherds take their flocks through it to the pastures in the interior valleys."

"Also the shepherdesses," Verdan added drily. "Sometimes the game my brother chases doesn't have horns."

Brin threw a quick, nervous glance at Polgara, and a slow blush mounted his cheeks.

"I've always been rather fond of shepherdesses," Belgarath noted blandly. "For the most part, they're gentle, understanding girls—and frequently lonely, aren't they, Brin?"

"That will do, father," Aunt Pol said primly.

It took the better part of the day to go over the pass and through the green meadows lying in the hidden valleys among the mountains beyond. The sun hovered just above the gleaming, almost molten-looking sea on the western side of the Isle when they crested a boulder-covered ridge and started down the long, rocky slope toward the cliffs and the frothy surf pounding endlessly against the western coast.

"Could a ship have landed on this side?" Garion asked Kail as they went downhill.

Kail was puffing noticeably from the strenuous trek across the island and he mopped his streaming face with his sleeve. "There are a few places where it's possible, Belgarion—if you know what you're doing. It's difficult and dangerous, but it *is* possible."

Garion's heart sank. "Then he could very well have gotten away," he said.

"I had ships out there, Belgarion," Kail said to him, pointing at the sea. "I sent them out as soon as we found out that the prince had been taken. About the only way someone could have gotten all the way across the island to this side in time to sail away before those ships got around here would be if he could fly."

"We've got him, then," the irrepressible Brin exclaimed, loosening his sword in its scabbard and searching the boulder-strewn slope and the brink of the cliffs with a hunter's trained eye.

"Hold it a second," Durnik said sharply. He lifted his head and sniffed at the onshore breeze. "There's somebody up ahead."

"What?" Garion said, a sudden excitement building up in him.

"I just caught a distinct whiff of somebody who doesn't bathe regularly."

Belgarath's face took on an intense expression. "Pol," he said, "why don't you take a quick look down there?"

She nodded tersely, and her forehead furrowed with concentration. Garion felt and heard the whispered surge as she probed the empty-looking terrain ahead. "Chereks," she said after a moment. "About a dozen of them. They're hiding behind those boulders at the edge of the cliffs. They're watching us and planning an ambush."

"Chereks?" Brin exclaimed. "Why would Chereks want to attack us?"

"They're Bear-cultists," she told him, "and nobody knows why those madmen do anything."

"What do we do?" Brin asked in a half whisper.

"An ambusher always has the advantage," Verdan replied, "unless the person about to be ambushed knows that he's there. Then it's the other way around." He looked down the slope grimly, his big hand on his sword hilt.

"Then we just go down there and spring their trap?" Brin asked eagerly.

Kail looked at Belgarath. "What do you think, Ancient One? We have the advantage now. They're going to expect us to be startled when they jump out at us, but we'll be ready for them. We could have half of them down before they realize their mistake."

Belgarath squinted at the setting sun. "Normally, I'd say no," he said. "These little incidental fights aren't usually very productive, but we're losing the light." He turned to Aunt Pol. "Is Geran anywhere in the vicinity?"

"No," she replied. "There's no sign of him."

Belgarath scratched at his beard. "If we leave the Chereks there, they're going to follow us, and I don't think I want them creeping along behind—particularly once it gets dark." His lined old face tightened into a wolfish grin. "All right, let's indulge ourselves."

"Save a few of them, though, father," Polgara said. "I have some questions I'd like answered. And try not to get yourselves hurt, gentlemen. I'm a little tired for surgery today."

"No surgery today, Lady Polgara," Brin promised blithely. "A few funerals, perhaps, but no surgery."

She raised her eyes toward the sky. "Alorns," she sighed.

The ambush did not turn out at all as the hidden Bear-cultists had anticipated. The fur-clad Cherek who leaped howling at Garion was met in midair by the flaming sword of the Rivan King and was sheared nearly in two at the waist by the great blade. He fell to the suddenly blood-drenched grass, writhing and squealing. Kail coolly split a charging cultist's head while his brothers fell on the startled attackers and savagely but methodically began to hack them to pieces.

One cultist leaped atop a large rock, drawing a bow with his arrow pointed directly at Garion, but Belgarath made a short gesture with his left hand, and the bowman was suddenly hurled backward in a long, graceful arc that carried him out over the edge of the nearby cliff. His arrow went harmlessly into the air as he fell shrieking toward the foamy breakers five hundred feet below.

"Remember, I need a few of them alive!" Polgara sharply reminded them, as the carnage threatened to get completely out of hand.

Kail grunted, then neatly parried the thrust of a desperate Cherek. His big left fist swung in a broad arc and smashed solidly into the side of the Cherek's head, sending him spinning to the turf.

Durnik was using his favorite weapon, a stout cudgel perhaps three feet long. Expertly, he slapped a cultist's sword out of his hand and cracked him sharply alongside the head. The man's eyes glazed, and he tumbled limply to the ground. Belgarath surveyed the fight, selected a likely candidate, and then levitated him about fifty feet into the air. The suspended man was at first apparently unaware of his new location and kept slashing ineffectually at the surrounding emptiness.

The fight was soon over. The last crimson rays of the setting sun mingled with the scarlet blood staining the grass near the edge of the cliff, and the ground was littered with broken swords and scraps of bloody bearskin. "For some reason, that makes me feel better," Garion declared, wiping his sword on the fallen body of one of the cultists. The Orb, he noted, was also blazing with a kind of fiery satisfaction.

Polgara was coolly inspecting a couple of unconscious survivors. "These two will sleep for a while," she noted, rolling back an eyelid to examine the glazed eye underneath. "Bring that one down, father," she said, pointing at the man Belgarath had suspended in midair. "In one piece, if you can manage it. I'd like to question him."

"Of course, Pol." The old man's eyes were sparkling, and his grin very nearly split his face.

"Father," she said, "when *are* you ever going to grow up?"

"Why, Polgara," he said mockingly, "what a thing to say."

The floating cultist had finally realized his situation and had dropped his sword. He stood trembling on the insubstantial air, with his eyes bulging in terror and his limbs twitching violently. When Belgarath gently lowered him to the ground, he immediately collapsed in a quivering heap. The old man firmly grasped him by the front of his fur tunic and hauled him roughly into a half-standing position. "Do you know who I am?" he demanded, thrusting his face into that of the cringing captive.

"You—I—"

"Do you?" Belgarath's voice cracked like a whip.

"Yes," the man choked.

"Then you know that if you try to run away, I'll just hang you back up in the air again and leave you there. You know that I can do that, don't you?"

"Yes."

"That won't be necessary, father," Polgara said coolly. "This man is going to be very cooperative."

"I will say nothing, witch-woman," the captive declared, though his eyes were still a bit wild.

"Ah, no, my friend," she told him with a chilly little smile. "You will say everything. You'll talk for weeks if I need you to." She gave him a hard stare and made a small gesture in front of his face with her left hand. "Look closely, friend," she said. "Enjoy every single detail."

The bearded Bear-cultist stared at the empty air directly in front of his face, and the blood drained from his cheeks. His eyes started from his head in horror, and he shrieked, staggering back. Grimly, she made a sort of hooking gesture with her still-extended hand, and his retreat stopped instantly. "You can't run away from it," she said, "and unless you talk—right now—it will stand in front of your face until the day you die."

"Take it away!" he begged in an insane shriek. "Please, I'll do anything—anything!"

"I wonder where she learned to do that," Belgarath murmured to Garion. "I could never do it to anybody—and I've tried."

"He'll tell you whatever he knows now, Garion," Polgara said then. "He's aware of what will happen if he doesn't."

"What have you done with my son?" Garion demanded of the terrified man.

The prisoner swallowed hard, and then he straightened defiantly. "He's far beyond your reach now, King of Riva."

The rage welled up in Garion again, and, without thinking, he reached over his shoulder for his sword.

"Garion!" Polgara said sharply.

The cultist flinched back, his face going pale. "Your son is alive," he said hastily. Then a smug look crossed his face. "But the next time you meet him, he will kill you."

"What are you talking about?"

"Ulfgar has consulted the oracles. You are not the Rivan King we have awaited for all these centuries. It's the *next* King of Riva who will unite Aloria and lead us against the kingdoms of the south. It is your son, Belgarion, and he will lead us because he will be raised to share our beliefs."

"Where is my son?" Garion shouted at him.

"Where you will never find him," the prisoner taunted. "We will raise and nurture him in the true faith, as befits an Alorn monarch. And when he is grown, he will come and kill you and take his crown and his sword and his Orb from your usurping hand." The man's eyes were bulging, his limbs shook with religious ecstasy, and there was foam on his lips. "You will die by your own son's hand, Belgarion of Riva," he shrieked, "and King Geran will lead all Alorns against the unbelievers of the south, as Belar commanded."

"We're not getting too far with this line of questioning," Belgarath said. "Let me try for a while." He turned to the wild-eyed captive. "How much do you know about this Ulfgar?" he asked.

"Ulfgar is the Bear-lord, and he has even more power than you, old man."

"Interesting notion," Belgarath murmured. "Have you ever met this master sorcerer—or even seen him, for that matter?"

"Well—" the captive hedged.

"I didn't think so. How did you know he wanted you to come here and abduct Belgarion's son, then?"

The captive bit his lip.

"Answer me!"

"He sent a messenger," the man replied sullenly.

A sudden thought occurred to Garion. "Was this Ulfgar of yours behind the attempt to kill my wife?" he demanded.

"Wife!" The cultist sneered. "No Alorn takes a Tolnedran mongrel to wife. You—Iron-grip's heir—should know that better than any man. Naturally we tried to kill the Tolnedran wench. It was the only way to rid Aloria of the infection you brought here."

"You're starting to irritate me, friend," Garion said bleakly. "Don't do that."

"Let's get back to this messenger," Belgarath said. "You say that the baby is where we can't reach him, but you're still here, aren't you? Could it just possibly be that it was the messenger who was the actual abductor and that you and your friends are merely underlings?"

The cultist's eyes grew wild, and he looked this way and that like a trapped animal. His limbs began to tremble violently.

"I think we're approaching a question that you don't want to answer, friend," Belgarath suggested.

It came almost like a blow. There was a wrenching kind of feeling to it, almost as if someone were reaching inside a skull to twist and crush the brain within. The captive shrieked, gave Belgarath one wild look, then spun, took three quick steps, and hurled himself off the edge of the cliff behind him.

"Question me now!" he shrieked as he plummeted down into the twilight that was rising out of the dark, angry waters surging about the rocks at the foot of the cliff. Then, even as he fell, Garion heard peal upon peal of insane laughter fading horribly as the fanatic dropped away from them.

Aunt Pol started quickly toward the edge, but Belgarath reached out and took her arm. "Let him go, Pol," he said. "It wouldn't be a kindness to save him now. Someone put something in his mind that crushed out his sanity as soon as he was asked that certain question."

"Who could possibly do that?" she asked.

"I don't know, but I'm certainly going to find out."

The shrieking laughter, still fading, continued to echo up to where they stood. And then it ended abruptly far below.

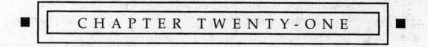

CHAPTER TWENTY-ONE

A sudden summer storm had come howling in off the Great Western Sea two days after the fight on the cliffs and it raked the island with shrieking winds and sheets of rain that rattled against the windows of the council chamber high in the south tower. The bone-thin Javelin, who had arrived with the others aboard the *Seabird* that morning, slouched in his chair, looking out at the raging storm and thoughtfully tapping his fingers together. "Where did the trail finally lead?" he asked.

"Right down to the water's edge in a secluded cove," Garion replied.

"Then I think we'll have to assume that this abductor made a clean escape with the prince. The timing might have been a little tight, but the men aboard the ships that were patrolling the coast would have been concentrating on the shore line, and a ship that had gotten well out to sea before they arrived could have escaped their notice."

Barak was piling an armload of logs in the cavernous fireplace. "Why were those others left behind, then?" he asked. "That doesn't make any sense at all."

"We're talking about Bear-cultists, Barak," Silk told him. "They're not *supposed* to make sense."

"There's a certain logic to it, though," the Earl of Seline pointed out. "If what the cultist said before he died is true, this Ulfgar has declared war on Belgarion. Isn't it entirely possible that those men were left behind specifically to waylay him? One way or another, he was certain to follow that trail."

"There's still something that doesn't quite ring true." Javelin frowned. "Let me think about it for a bit."

"We can sort out their motives later," Garion said. "The important thing right now is to find out where they've taken my son."

"Rheon, most likely," Anheg said. "We've destroyed Jarviksholm. Rheon's the only strong point they've got left."

"That's not entirely certain, Anheg," Queen Porenn disagreed. "This scheme to abduct Prince Geran was obviously planned quite some time ago, and you destroyed Jarviksholm only last week. It's unlikely that the abductors even knew about it. I don't think we can rule out the possibility that the prince was taken to Cherek."

Anheg rose and began pacing up and down, a dark scowl on his face. "She's got a point," he admitted finally. "These child stealers were Chereks, after all. It's quite possible that they tried to take him to Jarviksholm, but when they found the city destroyed, they had to go someplace else. We could very well find them holed up in a fishing village somewhere on the west coast."

"What do we do now, then?" Garion asked helplessly.

"We split up," King Cho-Hag said quietly. "Anheg turns out all his forces, and they search every village and farm in Cherek. The rest of us go to Rheon and deal with those people there."

"There's only one difficulty with that," Anheg said. "A baby is a baby. How do my men recognize Garion's son if they *do* run across him?"

"That's no real problem, Anheg," Polgara told him from her chair by the fire where she sat sipping a cup of tea. "Show them your palm, Garion."

Garion held up his right hand to show the King of Cherek the silvery mark there.

"I'd almost forgotten that," Anheg grunted. "Does Prince Geran have the same mark?"

"All heirs to the Rivan Throne have that mark on their palms," she replied. "It's been that way since the birth of Iron-grip's first son."

"All right," Anheg said. "My men will know what to look for, but will the rest of you have enough men to take Rheon? With the Algar and Drasnian cultists there, Ulfgar's got quite an army."

General Brendig rose and went over to a large map tacked up on one of the walls. "If I leave immediately for Sendar, I can put together a sizeable army in a few days. A forced march could put us in Darine within a week."

"I'll have ships waiting there to ferry you and your men to Boktor, then," Anheg promised.

"And I'll go south and raise the clans," Hettar said. "We'll ride straight north to Rheon."

Garion was also peering at the map. "If Anheg's ships take me and my troops to Boktor, we can join with the Drasnian pikemen there and march toward Rheon from the west," he said. "Then the ships can go back to Darine and pick up Brendig."

"That would save some time," Brendig agreed.

"With the Rivans and Drasnians, you're going to have enough troops to encircle Rheon," Silk said. "You might not have enough men to take the city, but you *will* have enough to keep anybody from going in or out. Then all you have to do is sit and wait for Brendig and Hettar. Once they join you, you'll have an overwhelming force."

"It's a sound plan, Garion," Barak said approvingly.

Mandorallen stood up. "And when we arrive at this fortified city on the moors of eastern Drasnia, I will undertake with siege engines and diverse other means to weaken the walls so that we may more easily gain access when we make our final assault," he noted. "Rheon will fall, and we will bring this miscreant Ulfgar to swift and terrible justice."

"Not *too* swift, I hope," Hettar murmured. "I was thinking along the lines of something more lingering."

"We'll have time to think about that after we catch him," Barak said.

The door opened, and Ce'Nedra, pale and wan-looking and accompanied by Queen Layla and the other ladies, entered. "Why are you all still here?" she demanded. "Why aren't you taking the world apart to find my baby?"

"That's hardly fair, Ce'Nedra," Garion chided her gently.

"I'm not trying to be fair. I want my baby."

"So do I, but we're not going to accomplish much by dashing around in circles, are we?"

"I'll raise an army myself, if I have to," she declared hotly. "I did it before and I can certainly do it again."

"And just where would you take them, dear?" Polgara asked her.

"Wherever it is that they've got my baby."

"And where is that? If you know something that we don't, shouldn't you share it with us?"

Ce'Nedra stared at her helplessly, her eyes filling with tears.

Belgarath had not contributed anything to the discussions, but rather had sat brooding out at the storm from a deep-cushioned chair by the window. "I've got the feeling that I'm missing something," he muttered as Adara and Nerina led the distraught Ce'Nedra to a chair near the council table.

"What did you say, Belgarath?" Anheg asked, removing his dented crown and tossing it on the table.

"I said that I think I'm missing something," the old man replied. "Anheg, just how extensive is your library?"

The Cherek King shrugged, scratching at his head. "I don't know that I could match the university library at Tol Honeth," he admitted, "but I've gathered *most* of the significant books in the world."

"How does your collection stack up in the area of the mysteries?"

"Of what?"

"Prophecies—not so much the Mrin Codex or the Darine—but the others: the Gospels of the Seers at Kell, the Grolim Prophecies of Rak Cthol, the Oracles of Ashaba."

"I've got that one," Anheg told him, "the Ashaba thing. I picked it up about a dozen years ago."

"I think I'd better go to Val Alorn and have a look at it."

"This is hardly the time for side trips, Grandfather," Garion objected.

"Garion, we know that something's happening that goes beyond an insurrection by a group of religious fanatics. That passage you found in the Mrin Codex was very specific. It instructed me to look into the mysteries, and I think that if I don't do exactly that, we're all likely to regret it." He turned to Anheg. "Where's your copy of the Ashabine Oracles?"

"In the library—up on the top shelf. I couldn't make any sense out of it, so I stuck it up there. I always meant to get back to it one day." Then a thought occurred to him. "Oh, by the way, there's a copy of the Mallorean Gospels in the monastery at Mar Terrin."

Belgarath blinked.

"That's one of the other books you wanted to see, wasn't it? The one by the Seers of Kell?"

"How could you possibly know what's in the library at Mar Terrin?"

"I heard about it a few years back. I have people who keep their eyes open for rare books. Anyway, I made the monks an offer for it—quite generous, I thought—but the negotiations fell through."

"You're a positive sink of information, Anheg. Can you think of anything else?"

"I can't help you with the Grolim Prophecies of Rak Cthol, I'm afraid. The only copy I know of was in Ctuchik's library, and that was probably buried when you blew Rak Cthol off its mountaintop. You could go dig for it, I suppose."

"Thanks, Anheg," Belgarath said drily. "You have no idea how much I appreciate your help."

"I can't believe that I'm hearing this," Ce'Nedra said accusingly to Belgarath. "Someone has stolen my baby—your great-grandson—and instead of trying to find him, you're planning to go off chasing obscure manuscripts."

"I'm not abandoning the child, Ce'Nedra. I'm just looking for him in a different place, that's all." He looked at her with a great sympathy in his eyes. "You're still very young," he said, "and all you can see is the one reality that your baby has been taken from you. There are two kinds of reality, however. Garion is going to follow your child in *this* reality. I'm going to follow him in the other. We're all after the same thing and this way we cover all the possibilities."

She stared at him for a moment, and then she suddenly covered her face with her hands and began to cry. Garion rose, went to her, and put her arms around her. "Ce'Nedra," he said soothingly, "Ce'Nedra, it's going to be all right."

"Nothing will be all right," she sobbed brokenly. "I'm so afraid for my baby, Garion. Nothing will ever be all right again."

Mandorallen rose to his feet, tears standing in his eyes. "As I am thy true knight and champion, dearest Ce'Nedra, I vow upon my life that the villain Ulfgar will never see another summer."

"That sort of gets to the point," Hettar murmured. "Why don't we all go to Rheon and nail Ulfgar to a post someplace—with very long nails?"

Anheg looked at Cho-Hag. "Your son has a remarkably firm grasp of the realities of this situation," he observed.

"He's the delight of my twilight years," Cho-Hag said proudly.

The argument with Ce'Nedra began immediately upon their return to the royal apartment. Garion tried reason first, then commands. Finally, he resorted to threats.

"I don't care what you say, Garion, I *am* going to Rheon."

"You are *not!*"

"I am *so!*"

"I'll have you locked in the bedroom."

"And as soon as you leave, I'll order someone to unlock the door—or I'll chop it down—and I'll be on the next boat out of the harbor."

"Ce'Nedra, it's too dangerous."

"So was Thull Mardu—and Cthol Mishrak—and I didn't flinch from either one. I'm going to Rheon, Garion—either with you or by myself. I'm going to get my baby back—even if I have to tear down the city walls with my bare hands."

"Ce'Nedra, please."

"No!" she exclaimed, stamping her foot. "I'm going, Garion, and nothing you can say or do is going to stop me!"

Garion threw his arms in the air. "Women!" he said in a despairing tone.

The fleet left at dawn the following morning, sailing out of the harbor into rough seas and the dirty scud and wrack of the tail end of the storm.

Garion stood on the aft deck of the *Seabird* beside Barak, whose thick hands firmly grasped the tiller. "I didn't think I was ever going to have to do this again," he said morosely.

"Oh, sailing in rough weather isn't all that bad." Barak shrugged as the wind tossed his red beard.

"That's not what I meant. I thought that after Torak died, I could live out my life in peace."

"You got lucky," Barak told him.

"Are you trying to be funny?"

"All anybody ever got out of peace was a fat behind and cobwebs in his head," the big man said sagely. "Give me a nice friendly little war any time."

When they were some leagues at sea, a detachment of ships separated from the fleet to sail due east toward Sendar, bearing with them King Fulrach, General Brendig, the Earl of Seline, and the heavily sedated Queen Layla.

"I hope Brendig gets to Darine on time," Anheg said, standing at the rail. "I'm really going to need those ships during the search."

"Where do you plan to start?" Queen Porenn asked him.

"The cult's largely concentrated on the west coast," he replied. "If Prince Geran's abductors went to Cherek, they'd most likely head for a cult stronghold. I'll start along the coast and work my way inland."

"That seems like sound strategy," she agreed. "Deploy your men and sweep the area."

"Porenn," he said with a pained look, "I love you like a sister, but please don't use military terms when you talk to me. It sets my teeth on edge to hear that sort of language in a woman's mouth."

The passage through the Cherek Bore delayed them for two days. Although Greldik and a few other hardy souls were willing—even eager—to attempt the Great Maelstrom in the heavy seas that were the aftermath of the storm, cooler and more prudent heads prevailed. "I'm sure the sea will quiet down in a bit," Barak shouted across to his friend, "and Rheon isn't going anyplace. Let's not lose any ships if we don't have to."

"Barak," Greldik shouted back, "you're turning into an old woman."

"Anheg said the same thing just before Jarviksholm," Barak noted.

"He's a wise king."

"It isn't his ship."

After they passed the Bore and entered the calmer waters of the Gulf of Cherek, King Anheg took a sizeable portion of the fleet and sailed northward toward Val Alorn. Before making the transfer to one of Anheg's ships, Belgarath stood on deck, talking quietly with Garion and Polgara. "As soon as I finish at Val Alorn, I'll go on down to Mar Terrin," he told them. "If I don't get back before you arrive at Rheon, be careful. The cult's pretty fanatic, and this war they've started is directed at you personally, Garion."

"I'll watch out for him, father," Polgara assured him.

"I can more or less take care of myself, Aunt Pol," Garion told her.

"I'm sure you can, dear," she replied, "but old habits die hard."

"How old am I going to have to be before you realize that I'm grown up?"

"Why don't you check back with me in a thousand years or so?" she said. "Maybe we can talk about it then."

He smiled, then sighed. "Aunt Pol," he said, "I love you."

"Yes, dear," she replied, patting his cheek, "I know, and I love you, too."

At Kotu, the ship carrying Hettar and his wife and parents turned south toward Aldurford. "I'll meet you at Rheon in about three weeks," the hawk-faced Algar called across to the *Seabird*. "Save a little bit of the fighting for me."

"Only if you hurry," Lelldorin shouted back blithely.

"I'm not sure which are worse," Polgara murmured to Ce'Nedra, "Arends or Alorns."

"Could they possibly be related?" Ce'Nedra asked.

Aunt Pol laughed, then wrinkled her nose as she looked at the wharves of Kotu. "Come, dear," she said, "let's go below. Harbors always have the most distressing odors about them."

The fleet passed Kotu and filed into the mouth of the Mrin River. The current was sluggish, and the fens lay green and soggy on either side. Garion stood near the bow of the *Seabird,* idly watching the gray-green reeds and scrubby bushes slide by as the oarsmen pulled steadily upstream.

"Ah, there you are, Garion," Queen Porenn said, coming up behind him. "I thought we might talk for a few minutes."

"Of course." He had a rather special feeling for this small, blonde woman, whose courage and devotion bespoke at once an enormous affection and an iron-clad resolve.

"When we reach Boktor, I want to leave Kheva at the palace. I don't think he's going to like it very much, but he's just a little young for battles. If he gets stubborn about it, could you order him to stay behind?"

"Me?"

"You're the Overlord of the West, Garion," she reminded him. "I'm only his mother."

"Overlord of the West is an overrated title, I'm afraid." He tugged absently at one ear. "I wonder if I could possibly persuade Ce'Nedra to stay in Boktor as well," he mused.

"I doubt it," she said. "Kheva might accept you as his superior, but Ce'Nedra looks upon you as her husband. There's a difference, you know."

He made a wry face. "You're probably right," he admitted. "It's worth a try, though. How far up the Mrin can we go by boat?"

"The north fork runs into a series of shallows about twenty leagues above Boktor," she replied. "I suppose we could portage around them, but it wouldn't accomplish very much. Ten leagues farther upstream you come to another stretch of shallows, and then there are the rapids. We could spend a great deal of time pulling the boats out of the water and then putting them back in again."

"Then it would be faster just to start marching when we get to the first shallows?"

She nodded. "It's likely to take several days for my generals to assemble their troops and get their supplies together," she added. "I'll instruct them to follow us as quickly as they can. Once they join us, we can go on to Rheon and lay siege until Brendig and Hettar arrive."

"You know, you're really very good at this, Porenn."

She smiled sadly. "Rhodar was a very good teacher."

"You loved him very much, didn't you?"

She sighed. "More than you can possibly imagine, Garion."

They reached Boktor the following afternoon, and Garion accompanied Queen Porenn and her slightly sullen son to the palace, with Silk tagging along behind. As soon as they arrived, Porenn sent a messenger to the headquarters of the Drasnian military forces.

"Shall we take some tea while we're waiting, gentlemen?" the little blonde queen offered as the three of them sat comfortably in a large, airy chamber with red velvet drapes at the windows.

"Only if you can't find anything stronger," Silk replied with an impudent grin.

"Isn't it a trifle early in the day for that, Prince Kheldar?" she asked him reprovingly.

"I'm an Alorn, Auntie dear. It's never too early in the day."

"Kheldar, please don't call me that. It makes me feel positively antique."

"But you *are*, Porenn—my aunt, I mean, not antique, of course."

"Are you ever serious about anything?"

"Not if I can help it."

She sighed and then laughed a warm tinkle of a laugh.

Perhaps a quarter of an hour later, a stocky man with a red face and a somewhat gaudy orange uniform was shown into the room. "Your Majesty sent for me?" he asked, bowing respectfully.

"Ah, General Haldar," she replied. "Are you acquainted with his Majesty, King Belgarion?"

"We met briefly, ma'am—at your late husband's funeral." He bowed floridly to Garion. "Your Majesty."

"General."

"And of course you've met Prince Kheldar."

"Of course," the general replied. "Your Highness."

"General." Silk looked at him closely. "Isn't that a new decoration, Haldar?" he asked.

The red-faced general touched the cluster of medals on his chest somewhat deprecatingly. "That's what generals do in peacetime, Prince Kheldar. We give each other medals."

"I'm afraid that the peacetime is at an end, General Haldar," Porenn said rather crisply. "You've heard what happened at Jarviksholm in Cherek, I presume."

"Yes, your Majesty," he replied. "It was a well-executed campaign."

"We are now going to proceed against Rheon. The Bear-cult has abducted King Belgarion's son."

"Abducted?" Haldar's expression was incredulous.

"I'm afraid so. I think the time has come to eliminate the cult entirely. That's why we're moving on Rheon. We have a fleet in the harbor loaded with Belgarion's Rivans. Tomorrow, we'll sail up to the shallows and disembark. We'll march overland toward Rheon. I want you to muster the army and follow us as quickly as you possibly can."

Haldar was frowning as if something he had heard had distracted him. "Are you sure that the Rivan Prince was abducted, your Majesty?" he asked. "He was not killed?"

"No," Garion answered firmly. "It was clearly an abduction."

Haldar began to pace up and down agitatedly. "That doesn't make any sense," he muttered, almost to himself.

"Do you understand your instructions, General?" Porenn asked him.

"What? Oh yes, your Majesty. I'm to gather the army and catch up with King Belgarion's Rivans before they reach Rheon."

"Precisely. We'll besiege the town until the rest of our forces arrive. We'll be joined at Rheon by Algars and elements of the Sendarian army."

"I'll start at once, your Majesty," he assured her. His expression was still slightly abstracted, and his frown was worried.

"Is there anything wrong, General?" she asked him.

"What? Oh, no, your Majesty. I'll go to headquarters and issue the necessary orders immediately."

"Thank you, General Haldar. That will be all."

"He certainly heard something he didn't like," Silk observed after the general had left.

"We've all heard things lately that we haven't liked," Garion said.

"It wasn't quite the same, though," Silk muttered. "Excuse me for a bit. I think I'm going to go ask a few questions." He rose from his chair and quietly left the room.

Early the next morning, the fleet weighed anchor and began to move slowly upstream from Boktor. Though the day had dawned clear and sunny, by noon a heavy cloud cover had swept in off the Gulf of Cherek to turn the Drasnian countryside gray and depressing.

"I hope it doesn't rain," Barak growled from his place at the tiller. "I hate slogging through mud on my way to a fight."

The shallows of the Mrin proved to be a very wide stretch of river where the water rippled over gravel bars.

"Have you ever considered dredging this?" Garion asked the Queen of Drasnia.

"No," she replied. "As a matter of policy I don't want the Mrin navigable beyond this point. I'd rather not have Tolnedran merchantmen bypassing Boktor." She smiled sweetly at Ce'Nedra. "I'm not trying to be offensive, dear," she said, "but your countrymen always seem to want to avoid customs. As things now stand, I control the North Caravan Route and I need that customs revenue."

"I understand, Porenn," Ce'Nedra assured her. "I'd do it that way myself."

They beached the fleet on the northern bank of the river, and Garion's forces began to disembark. "You'll lead the ships back downriver and across to Darine, then?" Barak said to the bearded Greldik.

"Right," Greldik said. "I'll have Brendig and his Sendars back here within a week."

"Good. Tell him to follow us to Rheon as quickly as he can. I've never been happy with the idea of long sieges."

"Are you going to send *Seabird* back with me?"

Barak scratched at his beard thoughtfully. "No," he said finally. "I think I'll leave her here."

"Believe me, I'm not going to get her sunk, Barak."

"I know, but I just feel better about the idea of having her here in case I need her. Will you come to Rheon with Brendig? There's bound to be some good fighting."

Greldik's face grew mournful. "No," he replied. "Anheg ordered me to come back to Val Alorn when I finish freighting the Sendars here."

"Oh. That's too bad."

Greldik grunted sourly. "Have fun at Rheon," he said, "and try not to get yourself killed."

"I'll make a special point of it."

By the time the troops and supplies had all been unloaded, it was late afternoon. The clouds continued to roll in, though there was as yet no rain. "I think we may as well set up a camp here," Garion said to the others as they all stood on the gently sloping river bank. "We wouldn't get too far before dark anyway, and if we get a good night's sleep, we can start early in the morning."

"That makes sense," Silk agreed.

"Did you find out anything about Haldar?" Queen Porenn asked the rat-faced little man. "I know there was something about him that was bothering you."

"Nothing really very specific." Silk shrugged. "He's been doing a lot of traveling lately, though."

"He's a general, Kheldar, and my Chief of Staff. Generals *do* have to make inspection tours from time to time, you know."

"But usually not alone," Silk replied. "When he makes these trips, he doesn't even take his aide along."

"I think you're just being overly suspicious."

"It's my nature to be suspicious, Auntie dear."

She stamped her foot. "*Will* you stop calling me that?"

He looked at her mildly. "Does it really bother you, Porenn?" he asked.

"I've told you that it bothers me."

"Maybe I ought to try to remember that, then."

"You're absolutely impossible, do you know that?"

"Of course I do, Auntie dear."

For the next two days the Rivan army marched steadily eastward across the desolate, gray-green moors, a wasteland of barren, sparsely vegetated hills interspersed with rank patches of thorn and bramble springing up around dark pools of stagnant water. The sky remained gray and threatening, but there was as yet no rain.

Garion rode at the head of the column with a bleakly determined look on his face, speaking infrequently except to issue commands. His scouts reported at intervals, announcing that there was no sign of cult forces ahead and with equal certainty that there was as yet no evidence that the Drasnian pikemen under General Haldar were coming up from the rear.

When they stopped for a hasty midday meal on that second day, Polgara approached him gravely. Her blue cloak seemed to whisper through the tall grass as she came, and her familiar fragrance came to him on the vagrant breeze. "Let's walk a bit, Garion," she said quietly. "There's something we need to discuss."

"All right." His reply was short, even curt.

She did something then that she had rarely done in the past several years. With a kind of solemn affection, she linked her arm in his, and together they walked away from the army and the rest of their friends, moving up a grassy knoll.

"You've grown very grim in the past few weeks, dear," she said as they stopped at the crest of the knoll.

"I think I've got reason enough, Aunt Pol."

"I know that you've been hurt deeply by all of this, Garion, and that you're filled with a great rage; but don't let it turn you into a savage."

"Aunt Pol, I didn't start this," he reminded her. "They tried to kill my wife. Then they murdered one of my closest friends and tried to start a war between me and Anheg. And now they've stolen my son. Don't you think that a little punishment might be in order?"

"Perhaps," she replied, looking directly into his face, "but you must not allow your sense of outrage to run away with you and make you decide to start wading in blood. You have tremendous power, Garion, and you could very easily use it to do unspeakable things to your enemies. If you do that, the power will turn you into something as vile as Torak was. You'll begin to take pleasure in the horrors you inflict. In time, that pleasure will come to own you."

He stared at her, startled by the intensity in her voice and by the way the single white lock at her brow seemed to blaze up suddenly.

"It's a very real danger, Garion. In a peculiar way, you're in more peril right now than you were when you faced Torak."

"I'm not going to let them get away with what they've done," he said stubbornly. "I'm not just going to let them go."

"I'm not suggesting that, dear. We'll be at Rheon soon, and there'll be fighting. You're an Alorn, and I'm sure that you'll be very enthusiastic about the fighting. I want you to promise me that you won't let that enthusiasm and your sense of outrage push you over the line into wanton slaughter."

"Not if they surrender," he replied stiffly.

"And what then? What will you do with your prisoners?"

He frowned. He hadn't really considered that.

"For the most part, the Bear-cult is composed of the ignorant and the misguided. They're so obsessed with a single idea that they can't even comprehend the enormity of what they've done. Will you butcher them for stupidity? Stupidity is unfortunate, but it hardly deserves *that* kind of punishment."

"What about Ulfgar?" he demanded.

She smiled a bleak little smile. "Now *that*," she said, "is another matter."

A large, blue-banded hawk spiraled down out of the murky sky. "Are we having a little family get-together?" Beldin asked harshly, even as he shimmered into his own form.

"Where have you been, uncle?" Aunt Pol asked him quite calmly. "I left word with the twins for you to catch up with us."

"I just got back from Mallorea," he grunted, scratching at his stomach. "Where's Belgarath?"

"At Val Alorn," she replied, "and then he's going on to Mar Terrin. He's trying to follow the trail that's supposed to be hidden in the mysteries. You've heard about what's happened?"

"Most of it, I think. The twins showed me the passage that was hidden in the Mrin Codex, and I heard about the Rivan Warder and Belgarion's son. You're moving against Rheon, right?"

"Naturally," she answered. "That's the source of the infection."

The hunchback looked speculatively at Garion. "I'm sure you're an expert tactician, Belgarion," he said, "but your reasoning escapes me this time."

Garion looked at him blankly.

"You're moving to attack a superior force in a fortified city, right?"

"I suppose you could put it that way."

"Then why is more than half your army camped at the shallows of the Mrin, two days behind you? Don't you think you might need them?"

"What are you talking about, uncle?" Aunt Pol asked sharply.

"I thought I was speaking quite plainly. The Drasnian army's camped at the shallows. They don't show signs of planning to move at any time in the near future. They're even fortifying their positions."

"That's impossible."

He shrugged. "Fly back and have a look for yourself."

"We'd better go tell the others, Garion," Aunt Pol said gravely. "Something has gone terribly wrong somewhere."

CHAPTER TWENTY-TWO

"What is that man thinking of?" Queen Porenn burst out in a sudden uncharacteristic fury. "I specifically ordered him to catch up with us."

Silk's face was bleak. "I think we should have checked the inestimable General Haldar's feet for that telltale brand," he said.

"You're not serious!" Porenn exclaimed.

"He's deliberately disobeying your orders, Porenn, and he's doing it in such a way as to endanger you and all the rest of us."

"Believe me, I'll get to the bottom of this as soon as I get back to Boktor."

"Unfortunately, we're not going in that direction just now."

"Then I'll go back to the shallows alone," she declared. "If necessary, I'll relieve him of his command."

"No," he said firmly, "you won't."

She stared at him incredulously. "Kheldar, do you realize to whom you're speaking?"

"Perfectly, Porenn, but it's too dangerous."

"It's my duty."

"No," he corrected. "Actually, your duty is to stay alive long enough to raise Kheva to be King of Drasnia."

She bit her lip. "That's unfair, Kheldar."

"Life is hard, Porenn."

"He's right, your Majesty," Javelin said. "General Haldar has already committed treason by disobeying you. I don't think he'd hesitate to add your murder to that crime."

"We're going to need some men," Barak rumbled, "A few anyway. Otherwise we're going to have to stop and wait for Brendig."

Silk shook his head. "Haldar's camped at the shallows. If what we suspect is true, he can keep Brendig from ever disembarking his troops."

"Well," Ce'Nedra demanded angrily, "what do we do now?"

"I don't think we've got much choice," Barak said. "We'll have to turn around and go back to the shallows and arrest Haldar for treason. Then we turn around and come back with the pikemen."

"That could take almost a week," she protested.

"What other alternatives do we have? We have to have those pikemen."

"I think you're overlooking something, Barak," Silk said. "Have you noticed a slight chill in the air the last two days?"

"A little—in the mornings."

"We're in northeastern Drasnia. Winter comes very early up here."

"Winter? But it's only early autumn."

"We're a long way north, my friend. We could get the first snowfall at any time now."

Barak started to swear.

Silk motioned Javelin aside, and the two of them spoke together briefly.

"It's all falling apart, isn't it, Garion?" Ce'Nedra said, her lower lip trembling.

"We'll fix it, Ce'Nedra," he said, taking her in his arms.

"But how?"

"I haven't quite worked that out yet."

"We're vulnerable, Garion," Barak said seriously. "We're marching directly into cult territory with a vastly inferior force. We're wide open to ambush."

"You'll need somebody to scout on ahead," Beldin said, looking up from the piece of cold meat he had been tearing with his teeth. He stuffed the rest of the chunk in his mouth and wiped his fingers on the front of his filthy tunic. "I can be fairly unobtrusive if I want to be."

"I'll take care of that, uncle," Polgara told him. "Hettar's coming north with the Algar clans. Could you go to him and tell him what's happened? We need him as quickly as he can get here."

He gave her an appraising look, still chewing on the chunk of meat. "Not a bad idea, Pol," he admitted. "I thought that married life might have made your wits soft, but it looks as if it's only your behind that's getting flabby."

"Do you mind, uncle?" she asked acidly.

"I'd better get started," he said. He crouched, spread his arms, and shimmered into the form of a hawk.

"I'll be away for a few days," Silk said, coming back to join them. "We might be able to salvage this yet." Then he turned on his heel and went directly to his horse.

"Where's he going?" Garion asked Javelin.

"We need men," Javelin replied. "He's going after some."

"Porenn," Polgara said, trying to look back down over her shoulder, "does it seem to you that I've been putting on a few extra pounds in the past months?"

Porenn smiled gently. "Of course not, Polgara," she said. "He was only teasing you."

Polgara, however, still had a slightly worried look on her face as she removed her blue cloak. "I'll go on ahead," she told Garion. "Keep your troops moving, but don't run. I don't want you to blunder into something before I have a chance to warn you." Then she blurred, and the great snowy owl drifted away on soft, noiseless wings.

Garion moved his forces carefully after that, deploying them into the best possible defensive posture as they marched. He doubled his scouts and rode personally to the top of every hill along the way to search the terrain ahead. The pace of their march slowed to be no more than five leagues a day; though the delay fretted him, he felt that he had no real choice in the matter.

Polgara returned each morning to report that no apparent dangers lay ahead and then she flew away again on noiseless wings.

"How does she manage that?" Ce'Nedra asked. "I don't think she's sleeping at all."

"Pol can go for weeks without sleep," Durnik told her. "She'll be all right—if it doesn't go on for *too* long."

"Belgarion," Errand said in his light voice, pulling his chestnut stallion in beside Garion's mount, "you did know that we're being watched, didn't you?"

"What?"

"There are men watching us."

"Where?"

"Several places. They're awfully well hidden. And there are other men galloping back and forth between that town we're going to and the army back at the river."

"I don't like that very much," Barak said. "It sounds as if they're trying to co-ordinate something."

Garion looked back over his shoulder at Queen Porenn, who rode beside Ce'Nedra. "Would the Drasnian army attack us if Haldar ordered them to?" he asked.

"No," she said quite firmly. "The troops are absolutely loyal to me. They'd refuse that kind of order."

"What if they thought they were rescuing you?" Errand asked.

"Rescuing?"

"That's what Ulfgar is suggesting," the young man replied. "The general's supposed to tell his troops that our army here is holding you prisoner."

"I think they *would* attack under those circumstances, your Majesty," Javelin said, "and if the cult and the army catch us between them, we could be in very deep trouble."

"What *else* can go wrong?" Garion fumed.

"At least it isn't snowing," Lelldorin said. "Not yet, anyway."

The army seemed almost to crawl across the barren landscape as the clouds continued to roll ponderously overhead. The world seemed locked in a chill, colorless gray, and each morning the scum of ice lying on the stagnant pools was thicker.

"We're never going to get there at this rate, Garion," Ce'Nedra said impatiently one gloomy midday as she rode beside him.

"If we get ambushed, we might not get there at all, Ce'Nedra," he replied. "I don't like this any more than you do, but I don't think we've really got much choice."

"I want my baby."

"So do I."

"Well, do something then."

"I'm open to suggestions."

"Can't you—?" She made a vague sort of gesture with one hand.

He shook his head. "You know that there are limits to that sort of thing, Ce'Nedra."

"What good is it then?" she demanded bitterly, pulling her gray Rivan cloak more tightly about her against the chill.

The great white owl awaited them just over the next rise. She sat on a broken limb of a dead-white snag, observing them with her unblinking golden eyes.

"Lady Polgara," Ce'Nedra greeted her with a formal inclination of her head.

Gravely the white owl returned her a stiff little bow. Garion suddenly laughed.

The owl blurred, and the air around it wavered briefly. Then Polgara was there, seated sedately on the limb with her ankles crossed. "What's so amusing, Garion?" she asked him.

"I've never seen a bird bow before," he replied. "It just struck me as funny, that's all."

"Try not to let it overwhelm you, dear," she said primly. "Come over here and help me down."

"Yes, Aunt Pol."

After he had helped her to the ground, she looked at him soberly. "There's a large cult force lying in wait two leagues ahead of you," she told him.

"How large?"

"Half again as large as yours."

"We'd better go tell the others," he said grimly, turning his horse.

"Is there any way we could slip around them?" Durnik asked after Polgara had told them all of the cultists lying in ambush ahead.

"I don't think so, Durnik," she replied. "They know we're here, and I'm sure we're being watched."

"We must needs attack them, then," Mandorallen asserted. "Our cause is just, and we must inevitably prevail."

"That's an interesting superstition, Mandorallen," Barak told him, "but I'd prefer to have the numbers on my side." The big man turned to Polgara. "How are they deployed? What I mean is—"

"I know what the word means, Barak." She scraped a patch of ground bare with her foot and picked up a stick. "This trail we're following runs through a ravine that cuts through that low range of hills just ahead. At about the deepest part of the ravine, there are several gullies running up the sides. There are four separate groups of cultists, each one hiding in a different gully." She sketched out the terrain ahead with her stick. "They obviously plan to let us march right into the middle of them and then attack us from all sides at once."

Durnik was frowning as he studied her sketch. "We could easily defeat any one of those groups," he suggested, rubbing thoughtfully at one cheek. "All we really need is some way to keep the other three groups out of the fight."

"That sort of sums it up," Barak said, "but I don't think they'll stay away just because they weren't invited."

"No," the smith agreed, "so we'll probably have to put up some kind of barrier to prevent their joining in."

"You've thought of something, haven't you, Durnik?" Queen Porenn observed.

"What manner of barrier could possibly keep the villains from rushing to the aid of their comrades?" Mandorallen asked.

Durnik shrugged. "Fire would probably work."

Javelin shook his head and pointed at the low gorse bushes in the field beside them. "Everything in this area is still green," he said. "I don't think it's going to burn very well."

Durnik smiled. "It doesn't have to be a *real* fire."

"Could you do that, Polgara?" Barak asked, his eyes coming alight.

She considered it a moment. "Not in three places at once," she replied.

"But there *are* three of us, Pol," the smith reminded her. "You could block one group with an illusion of fire; I could take the second; and Garion the third. We could pen all three groups in their separate gullies, and then, after we've finished with the first group, we could move on to the next." He frowned slightly. "The only problem with it is that I'm not sure exactly how to go about creating the illusion."

"It's not too difficult, dear," Aunt Pol assured him. "It shouldn't take long for you and Garion to get the knack of it."

"What do you think?" Queen Porenn asked Javelin.

"It's dangerous," he told her, "very dangerous."

"Do we have any choice?"

"Not that I can think of right offhand."

"That's it, then," Garion said. "If the rest of you will tell the troops what we're going to do, Durnik and I can start learning how to build imaginary bonfires."

It was perhaps an hour later when the Rivan troops moved out tensely, each man walking through the gray-green gorse with his hand close to his weapon. The low range of hills lay dark ahead of them, and the weedy track they followed led directly into the boulder-strewn ravine where the unseen Bear-cultists waited in ambush. Garion steeled himself as they entered that ravine, drawing in his will and carefully remembering everything Aunt Pol had taught him.

The plan worked surprisingly well. As the first group of cultists dashed from the concealment of their gully with their weapons aloft and shouts of triumph on their lips, Garion, Durnik, and Polgara instantly blocked the mouths of the other three gullies. The charging cult members faltered, their triumph changing to chagrin as they gaped at the sudden flames that prevented their comrades from joining the fray. Garion's Rivans moved immediately to take advantage of that momentary hesitation. Step by step the first group of cultists were pushed back into the narrow confines of the gully that had concealed them.

Garion could pay only scant attention to the progress of the fight. He sat astride his horse with Lelldorin at his side, concentrating entirely upon projecting the images of flame and the sense of heat and the crackle of fire across the mouth of the gully opposite the one where the fight was in progress. Dimly through the leaping flames, he could see the members of the cult trying to shield their faces from an intense heat that was not really there. And then the one thing that had not occurred to any of them happened. The trapped cult members in Garion's gully began to throw bucketsful of water hastily dipped from a stagnant pond on the imaginary flames. There was, of course, no hiss of steam nor any other visible effect of that attempt to quench the illusion. After several moments a cult member, cringing and wincing, stepped through the fire. "It isn't real!" he shouted back over his shoulder. "The fire isn't real!"

"*This* is, though," Lelldorin muttered grimly, sinking an arrow into the man's chest. The cultist threw up his arms and toppled over backward into the fire—which had no effect on his limp body. That, of course, gave the whole thing away. First a few and then a score or more cult members ran directly through Garion's illusion. Lelldorin's hands blurred as he shot arrow after arrow into the milling ranks at the mouth of the gully. "There're too many of them, Garion," he shouted. "I can't hold them. We'll have to fall back."

"Aunt Pol!" Garion yelled. "They're breaking through!"

"Push them back," she called to him. "Use your will."

He concentrated even more and pushed a solid barrier of his will at the men emerging from the gully. At first it seemed that it might even work, but the effort he was exerting was enormous, and he soon began to tire. The edges of his hastily erected barrier began to fray and tatter, and the men he was trying so desperately to hold back began to find those weak spots.

Dimly, even as he bent all of his concentration on maintaining the barrier, he heard a sullen rumble, almost like distant thunder.

"Garion!" Lelldorin cried. "Horsemen—hundreds of them!"

In dismay, Garion looked quickly up the ravine and saw a sudden horde of riders coming down the steep cut from the east. "Aunt Pol!" he shouted, even as he reached back over his shoulder to draw Iron-grip's great sword.

The wave of riders, however, veered sharply just as they reached him and crashed directly into the front ranks of the cultists who were on the verge of breaking through his barrier. This new force was composed of lean, leather-tough men in black, and their eyes had a peculiar angularity to them.

"Nadraks! By the Gods, they're Nadraks!" Garion heard Barak shout from somewhere across the ravine.

"What are *they* doing here?" Garion muttered, half to himself.

"Garion!" Lelldorin exclaimed. "That man in the middle of the riders—isn't that Prince Kheldar?"

The new troops charging into the furious mêlée quickly turned the tide of battle. They charged directly into the faces of the startled cultists who were emerging from the mouths of the gullies, inflicting dreadful casualties.

Once he had committed his horsemen, Silk dropped back to join Garion and Lelldorin in the center of the ravine. "Good day, gentlemen," he greeted them with aplomb. "I hope I didn't keep you waiting."

"Where did you get all the Nadraks?" Garion demanded, trembling with sudden relief.

"In Gar og Nadrak, of course."

"Why would they want to help us?"

"Because I paid them." Silk shrugged. "You owe me a great deal of money, Garion."

"How did you find so many so fast?" Lelldorin asked.

"Yarblek and I have a fur-trading station just across the border. The trappers who brought in their furs last spring were just lying around, drinking and gambling, so I hired them."

"You got here just in time," Garion said.

"I noticed that. Those fires of yours were a nice touch."

"Up until the point where they started throwing water on them. That's when things started to get tense."

A few hundred of the trapped cultists managed to escape the general destruction by scrambling up the steep sides of the gullies and fleeing out onto the barren moors; but for most of their fellows, there was no escape.

Barak rode out of the gully where the Rivan troops were mopping up the few survivors of the initial charge. "Do you want to give them the chance to surrender?" he asked Garion.

Garion remembered the conversation he and Polgara had had several days previously. "I suppose we should," he said after a moment's thought.

"You don't *have* to, you know," Barak told him. "Under the circumstances, no one would blame you if you wiped them out to the very last man."

"No," Garion said, "I don't think I really want to do that. Tell the ones that are left that we'll spare their lives if they throw down their weapons."

Barak shrugged. "It's up to you."

"Silk, you lying little thief!" a tall Nadrak in a felt coat and an outrageous fur hat exclaimed. He was roughly searching the body of a slain cultist. "You said that they all had money on them and that they were loaded down with gold chains and bracelets. All this one has on him is fleas."

"Perhaps I exaggerated just a trifle, Yarblek," Silk said urbanely to his partner.

"I ought to gut you, do you know that?"

"Why, Yarblek," Silk replied with feigned astonishment, "is that any way to talk to your brother?"

"Brother!" the Nadrak snorted, rising and planting a solid kick in the side of the body that had so sorely disappointed him.

"That's what we agreed when we went into partnership—that we were going to treat each other like brothers."

"Don't twist words on me, you little weasel. Besides, I stuck a knife in my brother twenty years ago—for lying to me."

As the last of the trapped and outnumbered cultists threw down their arms in surrender, Polgara, Ce'Nedra, and Errand came cautiously up the ravine, accompanied by the filthy, hunchbacked Beldin.

"Your Algar reinforcements are still several days away," the ugly little sorcerer told Garion. "I tried to hurry them along, but they're very tenderhearted with their horses. Where did you get all the Nadraks?"

"Silk hired them."

Beldin nodded approvingly. "Mercenaries always make the best soldiers," he said.

The coarse-faced Yarblek had been looking at Polgara, his eyes alight with recognition. "You're still as handsome as ever, girl," he said to her. "Have you changed your mind about letting me buy you?"

"No, Yarblek," she replied. "Not yet, anyway. You arrived at an excellent time."

"Only because some lying little thief told me there was loot to be had." He glared at Silk and then nudged the body he was standing over with his foot. "Frankly, I'd make more money plucking dead chickens."

Beldin looked at Garion. "If you intend to see your son again before he has a full beard, you'd better get moving," he said.

"I've got to make some arrangements about the prisoners," Garion replied.

"What's to arrange?" Yarblek shrugged. "Line them up and chop off their heads."

"Absolutely not!"

"What's the point of fighting if you can't butcher the prisoners when it's over?"

"Someday when we have some time, I'll explain it to you," Silk told him.

"Alorns!" Yarblek sighed, casting his eyes toward the murky sky.

"Yarblek, you mangy son of a dog!" It was a raven-haired woman in leather breeches and a tight-fitting leather vest. There was at once a vast anger and an overwhelming physical presence about her. "I thought you said we could make a profit by picking over the dead. These vermin don't have a thing on them."

"We were misled, Vella," he replied somberly, giving Silk a flinty look.

"I told you not to trust that rat-faced little sneak. You're not only ugly, Yarblek, you're stupid as well."

Garion had been looking curiously at the angry woman. "Isn't that the girl who danced in the tavern that time in Gar og Nadrak?" he asked Silk, remembering the girl's overwhelming sensuality that had stirred the blood of every man in that wayside drinking establishment.

The little man nodded. "She married that trapper—Tekk—but he came out second best in an argument with a bear a few years back, and his brother sold her to Yarblek."

"Worst mistake I ever made," Yarblek said mournfully. "She's almost as fast with her knives as she is with her tongue." He pulled back one sleeve and showed them an angry red scar. "And all I was trying to do was to be friendly."

She laughed. "Ha! You know the rules, Yarblek. If you want to keep your guts on the inside, you keep your hands to yourself."

Beldin's eyes had a peculiar expression in them as he looked at her. "Spirited wench, isn't she?" he murmured to Yarblek. "I admire a woman with a quick wit and a ready tongue."

A wild hope suddenly flared in Yarblek's eyes. "Do you like her?" he asked eagerly. "I'll sell her to you, if you want."

"Have you lost your mind entirely, Yarblek?" Vella demanded indignantly.

"Please, Vella, I'm talking business."

"This shabby old troll couldn't buy a tankard of cheap ale, much less me." She turned to Beldin. "Have you even got two coins to rub together, you jackass?" she demanded.

"Now you've gone and spoiled the whole negotiation," Yarblek accused her plaintively.

Beldin, however, gave the dark-haired woman a wicked, lopsided grin. "You interest me, girl," he told her, "and nobody's done that for longer than I can remember. Try to work on your threats and curses a bit, though. The rhythm isn't quite right." He turned to Polgara. "I think I'll go back and see what those Drasnian pikemen are up to. Somehow I don't believe that we want them creeping up behind us." Then he spread his arms, crouched, and became a hawk.

Vella stared incredulously after him as he soared away. "How did he do that?" she gasped.

"He's very talented," Silk replied.

"He is indeed." She turned on Yarblek with fire in her eyes. "Why did you let me talk to him like that?" she demanded. "You know how important first impressions are. Now he'll never make a decent offer for me."

"You can tell for yourself that he doesn't have any money."

"There are other things than money, Yarblek."

Yarblek shook his head and walked away muttering to himself.

Ce'Nedra's eyes were as hard as green agates. "Garion," she said in a deceptively quiet voice, "one day very soon we'll want to talk about these taverns you mentioned—and dancing girls—and a few other matters as well."

"It was a long time ago, dear," he said quickly.

"Not nearly long enough."

"Does anybody have anything to eat?" Vella demanded, looking around. "I'm as hungry as a bitch wolf with ten puppies."

"I can probably find something for you," Polgara replied. Vella looked at her, and her eyes slowly widened. "Are you who I think you are?" she asked in an awed voice.

"That depends on who you think I am, dear."

"I understand that you dance," Ce'Nedra said in a chilly voice.

Vella shrugged. "All women dance. I'm just the best, that's all."

"You seem very sure of yourself, Mistress Vella."

"I just recognize facts." Vella looked curiously at Ce'Nedra. "My, you're a tiny one, aren't you?" she asked. "Are you really full-grown?"

"I am the Queen of Riva," Ce'Nedra replied, drawing herself up to her full height.

"Good for you, girl," Vella said warmly, clapping her on the shoulder. "I always enjoy seeing a woman get ahead."

It was midmorning of a gray, cloudy day when Garion crested a hill and looked across a shallow valley at the imposing bulk of Rheon. The town stood atop a steep hill, and its walls reared up sharply out of the rank gorse covering the slopes.

"Well," Barak said quietly as he joined Garion, "there it is."

"I didn't realize the walls were quite so high," Garion admitted.

"They've been working on them," Barak said, pointing. "You can see that new stonework on the parapet."

Flying defiantly above the city, the scarlet banner of the Bear-cult, a blood-red flag with the black outline of a shambling bear in the center, snapped in the chill breeze. For some reason that flag raised an almost irrational rage in Garion. "I want that thing down," he said from between clenched teeth.

"That's why we came," Barak told him.

Mandorallen, burnished in his armor, joined them.

"This isn't going to be easy, is it?" Garion said to them.

"It won't be so bad," Barak replied, "once Hettar gets here."

Mandorallen had been assessing the town's fortifications with a professional eye. "I foresee no insurmountable difficulties," he declared confidently. "Immediately upon the return of the several hundred men I dispatched to procure timbers from the forest lying some leagues to the north, I shall begin the construction of siege engines."

"Can you actually throw a rock big enough to knock a hole in walls that thick?" Garion asked dubiously.

" 'Tis not the single stroke that reduces them, Garion," the knight replied. " 'Tis the repetition of blow after blow. I will ring the town with engines and rain stones upon their walls. I doubt not that there will be a breach or two 'ere my Lord Hettar arrives."

"Won't the people inside repair them as fast as you break them?" Garion asked.

"Not if you've got other catapults throwing burning pitch at them," Barak told him. "It's very hard to concentrate on anything when you're on fire."

Garion winced. "I hate using fire on people," he said, briefly remembering Asharak the Murgo.

"It's the only way, Garion," Barak said soberly. "Otherwise you're going to lose a lot of good men."

Garion sighed. "All right," he said. "Let's get started then."

Reinforced by Yarblek's trappers, the Rivans drew up in a wide circle around the fortified town. Though their combined numbers were not yet sufficient to mount a successful assault on those high, grim walls, they were nonetheless enough to seal the town effectively. The construction of Mandorallen's siege engines took but a few days; once they were completed and moved into position, the steady twang of tightly twisted ropes uncoiling with terrific force and the sharp crack of heavy rocks shattering against the walls of Rheon was almost continual.

Garion watched from a vantage point atop a nearby hill as rock after rock lofted high into the air to smash down on those seemingly impregnable walls.

"It's a sad thing to watch," Queen Porenn noted as she joined him. A stiff breeze tugged at her black gown and stirred her flaxen hair as she moodily watched Mandorallen's engines pound relentlessly at the walls. "Rheon has stood here for almost three thousand years. It's been like a rock guarding the frontier. It seems very strange to attack one of my own cities—particularly when you consider the fact that half of our forces are Nadraks, the very people Rheon was built to hold off in the first place."

"Wars are always a little absurd, Porenn," Garion agreed.

"More than just a little. Oh, Polgara asked me to tell you that Beldin has come back. He has something to tell you."

"All right. Shall we go back down, then?" He offered the Queen of Drasnia his arm.

Beldin was lounging on the grass near the tents, gnawing the shreds of meat off a soup bone and exchanging casual insults with Vella. "You've got a bit of a problem, Belgarion," he told Garion. "Those Drasnian pikemen have broken camp and they're marching this way."

Garion frowned. "How far away is Hettar?" he asked.

"Far enough to turn it into a race," the little hunchback replied. "I expect that the whole outcome is going to depend on which army gets here first."

"The Drasnians wouldn't really attack us, would they?" Ce'Nedra asked.

"It's hard to say," Porenn replied. "If Haldar has convinced them that Garion is holding me prisoner, they might. Javelin took a horse and rode back to see if he could find out exactly what's going on."

Garion began to pace up and down, gnawing worriedly on one fingernail.

"Don't bite your nails, dear," Polgara told him.

"Yes, ma'am," he replied automatically, still lost in thought. "Is Hettar coming as fast as he can?" he asked Beldin.

"He's pushing his horses about as hard as they can be pushed."

"If there was only some way to slow down the pikemen."

"I've got a couple of ideas," Beldin said. He looked at Polgara. "What do you say to a bit of flying, Pol?" he asked her. "I might need some help with this."

"I don't want you to hurt those men," Queen Porenn said firmly. "They're my people—even if they are being misled."

"If what I've got in mind works, nobody's going to get hurt," Beldin assured her. He rose to his feet and dusted off the back of his filthy tunic. "I've enjoyed chatting with you, girl," he said to Vella.

She unleashed a string of expletives at him that turned Ce'Nedra's face pale.

"You're getting better at that," he approved. "I think you're starting to get the hang of it. Coming, Pol?"

Vella's expression was indecipherable as she watched the blue-banded hawk and the snowy owl spiral upward.

CHAPTER TWENTY-THREE

Later that day, Garion rode out to continue his observations of the ongoing siege of the town of Rheon and he found Barak, Mandorallen, and Durnik in the midst of a discussion. "It has to do with the way walls are built, Mandorallen," Durnik was trying to explain. "A city wall is put together to withstand exactly what you're trying to do to that one."

Mandorallen shrugged. "It becomes a test then, Goodman, a test to discover which is the stronger—their walls or mine engines."

"That's the kind of test that could take months," Durnik pointed out. "*But,* if instead of throwing rocks at the *outside* of the wall, you lobbed them all the way over to hit the *inside* of the wall on the far side, you'd stand a pretty fair chance of toppling them outward."

Mandorallen frowned, mulling it over in his mind.

"He could be right, Mandorallen," Barak said. "City walls are usually buttressed from the inside. They're built to keep people out, not in. If you bang rocks against the inside of the walls, you won't have the strength of the buttresses to contend with. Not only that—if the walls fall outward, they'll provide us with natural ramps in the city. That way we won't need scaling ladders."

Yarblek sauntered over to join the discussion, his fur cap at a jaunty angle. After Durnik had explained his idea, the rangy-looking Nadrak's eyes narrowed thoughtfully. "He's got a point, Arend," he said to Mandorallen. "And after you've pounded the walls from the inside for a while, we can throw a few grappling hooks over the tops of them. If the walls have already been weakened, we should be able to pull them down."

"I must admit the feasibility of these most unorthodox approaches to the art of the siege," Mandorallen said. "Though they both do fly in the face of long-established tradition, they show promise of shortening the tedious procedure of reducing the walls." He looked curiously at Yarblek. "I had not previously considered this notion of using grappling hooks so," he admitted.

Yarblek laughed coarsely. "That's probably because you're not a Nadrak. We're an impatient people, so we don't build very good walls. I've pulled down some pretty stout-looking houses in my time—for one reason or another."

"I think, though, that we don't want to yank down the walls too soon," Barak cautioned. "The people inside outnumber us just now, and we don't want to give them any reason to come swarming out of that place—and if you pull a man's walls down, it usually makes him very grouchy."

The siege of Rheon continued for two more days before Javelin returned astride an exhausted horse. "Haldar's put his own people in most of the positions of authority in the army," he reported, once they had all gathered in the large, dun-colored tent that served as the headquarters of the besieging army. "They're all going around making speeches about Belgarion taking Queen Porenn prisoner. They've about halfway persuaded the troops that they're coming to her rescue."

"Was there any sign of Brendig and the Sendars yet?" Garion asked him.

"I didn't see them personally, but Haldar has his troops moving at a forced march, and he's got a lot of scouts out behind him. I think he believes that Brendig's right on his heels. On the way back, I ran into Lady Polgara and the sorcerer Beldin. They seem to be planning something, but I didn't have time to get any details." He slumped in his chair with a look of exhaustion on his face.

"You're tired, Khendon," Queen Porenn said. "Why don't you get a few hours' sleep, and we'll gather here again this evening."

"I'm all right, your Majesty," he said quickly.

"Go to bed, Javelin," she said firmly. "Your contributions to our discussions won't be very coherent if you keep falling asleep in your chair."

"You might as well do as she says, Javelin," Silk advised. "She's going to mother you whether you like it or not."

"That will do, Silk," Porenn said.

"But you *will*, Auntie. You're known far and wide as the little mother of Drasnia."

"I said, that will do."

"Yes, mother."

"I think you're walking on very thin ice, Silk," Yarblek said.

"I always walk on thin ice. It gives my life a certain zest."

The gloomy days were slowly settling into an even gloomier evening as Garion and his friends gathered once more in the large tent near the center of the encampment. Yarblek had brought a number of rolled-up rugs with him and several iron braziers, and these contributions to their headquarters added certain garish, even barbaric, touches to the interior of the tent.

"Where's Silk?" Garion asked, looking around as they all seated themselves around the glowing braziers.

"I think he's out snooping," Barak replied.

Garion made a face. "I wish that just once he'd be where he's supposed to be."

Javelin looked much more alert after his few hours' sleep. His expression, however, was grave. "We're starting to run out of time," he told them. "We've got three armies converging on this place. Lord Hettar is coming up from the south, and General Brendig is coming in from the west. Unfortunately, the Drasnian pikemen are very likely to get here first."

"Unless Pol and Beldin can slow them down," Durnik added.

"I have every confidence in Lady Polgara and Master Beldin," Javelin said, "but I think we should decide what we're going to do in the event that they aren't successful. It's always best to prepare for the worst."

"Wisely spoken, my Lord," Mandorallen murmured.

"Now," the Chief of Drasnian Intelligence continued, "we don't truly want to fight the pikemen. First of all, they aren't really our enemies; secondly, a battle with them is going to weaken our forces to the point that a sortie in force from the city could conceivably defeat us."

"What are you leading up to, Javelin?" Porenn asked him.

"I think we're going to have to get into the city."

"We haven't got enough men," Barak said flatly.

"And 'twill take several more days to reduce the walls," Mandorallen added.

Javelin held up one hand. "If we concentrate the siege engines on one section of wall, we should be able to bring it down within one day," he declared.

"But that just announces which quarter we'll attack from," Lelldorin protested. "The forces in the city will be concentrated there to repel us."

"Not if the rest of the city's on fire," Javelin replied.

"Absolutely out of the question," Garion said flatly. "My son could be in that town, and I'm not going to risk his life by setting the whole place on fire."

"I still say that we haven't got enough men to take the city," Barak maintained.

"We don't have to take the *whole* city, my Lord of Trellheim," Javelin said. "All we need to do is get our men inside. If we take one quarter of the town and fortify it, we can hold off the cult from the inside and Haldar from the outside. Then we simply sit tight and wait for Lord Hettar and General Brendig."

"It's got some possibilities," Yarblek said. "The way things stand right now, we're caught in a nutcracker. If those pikemen get here first, about all your friends are going to be able to do when they arrive is to pick up the pieces."

"No fire," Garion declared adamantly.

"I do fear me that however we proceed, we may not gain entry into the city 'ere the walls are breached," Mandorallen observed.

"The walls aren't really any problem," Durnik said quietly. "No wall is any better than its foundation."

"It is quite impossible, Goodman," Mandorallen told him. "A wall's foundation hath the entire weight resting upon it. No engine in the world can move such a mass."

"I wasn't talking about an engine," Durnik said.

"What have you got in mind, Durnik?" Garion asked him.

"It's not really going to be that hard, Garion," Durnik said. "I did a bit of looking around. The walls aren't resting on rock. They're resting on packed dirt. All we have to do is soften that dirt a bit. There's plenty of underground water in this region. If we put our heads together, you and I ought to be able to bring it up under one section of wall without anybody inside the city knowing what we've done. Once the ground is soft enough, a few dozen of Yarblek's grappling hooks ought to be enough to topple it."

"Can it be done, Garion?" Lelldorin asked doubtfully.

Garion thought it through. "It's possible," he conceded. "It's very possible."

"And if we did it at night, we could be in position to rush into the city just as soon as the wall falls," Barak said. "We could get inside without losing a single man."

"It's a novel solution," Silk observed from the doorway of the tent. "A little unethical, perhaps, but novel all the same."

"Where have you been, you little sneak?" Yarblek demanded.

"In Rheon, actually," Silk replied.

"You were inside the city?" Barak asked in surprise.

Silk shrugged. "Of course. I though it might be appropriate to get a friend of ours out of there before we took the place apart." He stepped aside with a mocking little bow to admit the honey-blonde Margravine Liselle.

"Now *that* is a splendid-looking young woman," Yarblek breathed in admiration.

Liselle smiled at him, the dimples dancing in her cheeks.

"How did you get inside?" Garion asked the rat-faced little man.

"You really wouldn't want to know, Garion," Silk told him. "There's always a way in or out of a city, if you're really serious about it."

"You two don't smell too good," Yarblek noted.

"It has to do with the route we took," Liselle replied, wrinkling her nose.

"You're looking well," Javelin said conversationally to his niece, "all things considered."

"Thank you, uncle," she replied. Then she turned to Garion. "Are the rumors going about the city true, your Majesty?" she asked. "Has your son been abducted?"

Garion nodded grimly. "It happened just after we took Jarviksholm. That's why we're here."

"But Prince Geran doesn't seem to be in Rheon," she told him.

"Are you sure?" Ce'Nedra demanded.

"I think so, your Majesty. The cultists inside the city are baffled. They seem to have no idea who took your son."

"Ulfgar may be keeping it secret," Javelin said. "Only a small group may know."

"Perhaps, but it doesn't look that way. I wasn't able to get close enough to him to make sure, but he has the look of a man whose plans have gone all awry. I don't think he expected this attack on Rheon. His fortifications are not nearly as complete as they might appear from the outside. The north wall in particular is rather flimsy. His reinforcement of the walls seems a desperation move. He was not expecting a siege. If he'd been behind the abduction, he would have been prepared for the attack—unless he thought you could never trace it to him."

"This is most excellent news, my Lady," Mandorallen praised her. "Since we know of the weakness of the north fortifications, we can concentrate our efforts there. If Goodman Durnik's plan proves workable, a weakening of the foundations of the north wall should bring it down most speedily."

"What can you tell us about Ulfgar?" Barak asked the girl.

"I only saw him briefly at a distance. He spends most of his time inside his house, and only his closest cohorts are allowed near him. He made a speech, though, just before he sent his forces to attack you. He speaks very passionately and he had the crowd absolutely under his control. I *can* tell you one thing about him, though. He's not an Alorn."

"He's not?" Barak looked dumfounded.

"His face doesn't give away his nationality, but his speech is not that of an Alorn."

"Why would the cult accept an outsider as their leader?" Garion demanded.

"They aren't aware of the fact that he is an outsider. He mispronounces a few words—just a couple, actually, and only a trained ear would catch them. If I'd been able to get closer to him, I might have been able to steer him toward those words that would have betrayed his origins. I'm sorry that I can't be of more help."

"How strong is his grip on the cult?" Javelin asked.

"It's absolute," she replied. "They'll do anything he tells them to do. They look upon him as something very akin to a God."

"We're going to have to take him alive," Garion said grimly. "I have to have some answers."

"That may be extremely difficult, your Majesty," she said gravely. "It's widely believed in Rheon that he's a sorcerer. I didn't actually see any evidence of it myself, but I talked with a number of people who have, or at least who claimed they have done so."

"You have performed a great service for us, Margravine," Queen Porenn said gratefully. "It shall not be forgotten."

"Thank you, your Majesty," Liselle replied simply, with a formal little curtsy. Then she turned back to Garion. "What information I was able to glean says quite strongly that the cult forces within the walls are not nearly so formidable as we were led to believe. Their numbers are impressive, but they include a great many young boys and old men. They appear to be counting rather desperately on a force that's marching toward the city under the command of a hidden cult member."

"Haldar," Barak said.

She nodded.

"And that brings us right back to the absolute necessity of getting inside those walls," Javelin told them. He looked at Durnik. "How long do you estimate that it's going to take for the ground under the north wall to soften enough to topple the structure?"

Durnik sat back, staring thoughtfully at the ceiling of the tent. "We want to take them by surprise," he said, "so I don't think we want the water to come gushing out—not at first, anyway. A gradual seepage would be far less noticeable. It's going to take a while to saturate the ground."

"And we're going to have to be very careful," Garion added. "If this Ulfgar really is a sorcerer, he'll hear us if we make too much noise."

"There'll be plenty of noise when the wall comes down," Barak said. "Why don't you just blow it apart the way you did the back wall of Jarviksholm?"

Garion shook his head. "There are a couple of moments after you unleash your will when you're absolutely vulnerable to attack by anybody who has the same kind of talent. I'd sort of like to be alive and sane when I find my son."

"How long will it take to soak the ground under the wall?" Javelin asked.

Durnik scratched at his cheek. "Tonight," he replied, "and all day tomorrow. By midnight tomorrow, the wall ought to be sufficiently undermined. Then, just before we attack, Garion and I can speed up the flow of water and wash out most of the dirt. It's going to be very wet and soft already, and a good stream of water ought to cut it right out from under the wall. If we lob stones at it from the far side and get a few dozen grappling hooks into it, we should be able to pull it down in short order."

"You might want to pick up the pace with your engines," Yarblek said to Mandorallen. "Give them time to get used to the idea of rocks coming out of the sky. That way they won't pay any attention when you start pounding on their walls tomorrow night."

"Midnight tomorrow, then?" Barak said.

"Right," Garion said firmly.

Javelin looked at his niece. "Do you have the layout of the north quarter of the city fairly well in mind?" he asked.

She nodded.

"Make a sketch for us. We'll need to know where to set up our defenses once we get inside."

"Right after I bathe, uncle."

"We need that sketch, Liselle."

"Not nearly as badly as I need a bath."

"You too, Kheldar," Queen Porenn said firmly.

Silk gave Liselle a speculative look.

"Never mind, Kheldar," she said. "I can wash my own back, thank you."

"Let's go find some water, Durnik," Garion said, getting to his feet. "Underground, I mean."

"Right," the smith replied.

There was no moon, of course. The clouds that had hovered over the area for the past week and more obscured the sky. The night air was chill as Garion and Durnik moved carefully across the shallow valley toward the besieged city.

"Cold night," Durnik murmured as they walked through the rank gorse.

"Umm," Garion agreed. "How deep do you think the water might be lying?"

"Not too deep," Durnik replied. "I asked Liselle how deep the wells are in Rheon. She said that they were all fairly shallow. I think we'll hit water at about twenty-five feet."

"What gave you this idea, anyway?"

Durnik chuckled softly in the darkness. "When I was much younger, I worked for a farmer who gave himself great airs. He thought it might impress his neighbors if he had a well right inside his house. We worked at it all one winter and finally tapped into an artesian flow. Three days later, his house collapsed. He was very upset about it."

"I can imagine."

Durnik looked up at the looming walls. "I don't know that we need to get any closer," he said. "It might be hard to concentrate if they see us and start shooting arrows at us. Let's work around to the north side."

"Right."

They moved even more carefully now, trying to avoid making any sound in the rustling gorse.

"This should do it," Durnik whispered. "Let's see what's down there."

Garion let his thoughts sink quietly down through the hard-packed earth under the north wall of the city. The first few feet were difficult, since he kept encountering moles and earthworms. An angry chittering told him that he had briefly disturbed a badger. Then he hit a layer of rock and probed his thought along its flat surface, looking for fissures.

"Just to your left," Durnik murmured. "Isn't that a crack?"

Garion found it and wormed his way downward. The fissure seemed to grow damper and damper the deeper he went. "It's wet down there," he whispered, "but the crack's so narrow that the water's barely seeping up."

"Let's widen the crack—but not too much. Just enough to let a trickle come up."

Garion bent his will and felt Durnik's will join with his. Together they shouldered the crack in the rock a bit wider. The water lying beneath the rock layer gushed upward. Together they pulled back and felt the water begin to erode the hard-packed dirt under the wall, seeping and spreading in the darkness beneath the surface.

"Let's move on," Durnik whispered. "We ought to open up six or eight places under the wall in order to soak the ground thoroughly. Then tomorrow night we can push the cracks wide open."

"Won't that wash out this whole hillside?" Garion asked, also whispering.

"Probably."

"That's going to make it a little hard for our troops when they rush this place."

"There's not much question about the fact that they're going to get their feet wet," Durnik said, "but that's better than trying to scale a wall with somebody pouring boiling oil on your head, wouldn't you say?"

"Much, much better," Garion agreed.

They moved on through the chill night. Then something brushed Garion's cheek. At first he ignored it, but it came again—soft and cold and damp. His heart sank. "Durnik," he whispered, "it's starting to snow."

"I thought that's what it was. I think this is going to turn very unpleasant on us."

The snow continued to fall through the remainder of the night and on into the next morning. Though there were occasional flurries that swirled around the bleak fortress, the snowfall for the most part was intermittent. It was a wet, sodden kind of snow that turned to slush almost as soon as it touched the ground.

Shortly before noon, Garion and Lelldorin donned heavy wool cloaks and stout boots and went out of the snow-clogged encampment toward the north wall of Rheon. When they were perhaps two hundred paces from the base of the hill upon which the city rested, they sauntered along with a great show of casualness, trying to look like nothing more dangerous than a pair of soldiers on patrol. As Garion looked at the fortress city, he saw the red and black bear-flag once more, and once again that banner raised an irrational rage in him. "Are you sure that you'll be able to recognize your arrows in the dark?" he asked his friend. "There are a lot of arrows sticking in the ground out there, you know."

Lelldorin drew his bow and shot an arrow in a long arc toward the city. The feathered shaft rose high in the air and then dropped to sink into the snow-covered turf about fifty paces from the beginning of the slope. "I made the arrows myself, Garion," he said, taking another shaft from the quiver at his back. "Believe me, I can recognize one of them as soon as my fingers touch it." He leaned back and bent his bow again. "Is the ground getting soft under the wall?"

Garion sent out his thought toward the slope of the hill and felt the chill, musty dampness of the soil lying under the snow. "Slowly," he replied, "it's still pretty firm, though."

"It's almost noon, Garion," Lelldorin said seriously, reaching for another arrow. "I know how thoroughly Goodman Durnik thinks things through, but is this really working?"

"It takes a while," Garion told him. "You have to soak the lower layers of earth first. Then the water starts to rise and saturate the dirt directly under the wall itself. It takes time; but if the water started gushing out of rabbit holes, the people on top of the wall would know that something's wrong."

"Think of how the rabbits would feel." Lelldorin grinned and shot another arrow.

They moved on as Lelldorin continued to mark the jumping-off line of the coming night's assault with deceptive casualness.

"All right," Garion said. "I know that *you* can recognize your own arrows, but how about the rest of us? One arrow feels just like another to me."

"It's simple," the young bowman replied. "I just creep up, find my arrows, and string them all together with twine. When you hit that string, you stop and wait for the wall to topple. Then you charge. We've been making night assaults on Mimbrate houses in Asturia for centuries this way."

Throughout the remainder of that snowy day, Garion and Durnik periodically checked the level of moisture in the soil of the north slope of the steep knoll upon which the city of Rheon stood. "It's getting very close to the saturation point, Garion," Durnik reported as dusk began to fall. "There are a few places on the lower slope where the water's starting to seep through the snow."

"It's a good thing it's getting dark," Garion said, shifting the weight of his mail shirt nervously. Armor of any kind always made him uncomfortable, and the prospect of the upcoming assault on the city filled him with a peculiar emotion, part anxiety, and part anticipation.

Durnik, his oldest friend, looked at him with an understanding that pierced any possible concealment. He grinned a bit wryly. "What are a pair of sensible Sendarian farm boys doing fighting a war in the snow in eastern Drasnia?" he asked.

"Winning—I hope."

"We'll win, Garion," Durnik assured him, laying an affectionate hand on the younger man's shoulder. "Sendars always win—eventually."

About an hour before midnight, Mandorallen began to move his siege engines, leaving only enough of them on the eastern and western sides to continue the intermittent barrage that was to mask their real purpose. As the hour wore on, Garion, Lelldorin, Durnik, and Silk crept forward at a half crouch toward the invisible line of arrows sticking up out of the snow.

"Here's one," Durnik whispered as his outstretched hands encountered the shaft of an arrow.

"Here," Lelldorin murmured, "let me feel it." He joined the smith, the both of them on their knees in the slush. "Yes, it's one of mine, Garion," he said very quietly. "They should be about ten paces apart."

Silk moved quickly to where the two of them crouched over the arrow. "Show me how you recognize them," he breathed.

"It's in the fletching," Lelldorin replied. "I always use twisted gut to attach the feathers."

Silk felt the feathered end of the arrow. "All right," he said. "I can pick them out now."

"Are you sure?" Lelldorin asked.

"If my fingertips can find the spots on a pair of dice, they can certainly tell the difference between gut and linen twine," Silk replied.

"All right. We'll start here." Lelldorin attached one end of a ball of twine to the arrow. "I'll go this way, and you go that."

"Right." Silk tied the end of his ball of string to the same shaft. He turned to Garion and Durnik. "Don't overdo it with the water, you two," he said. "I don't particularly want to get buried in a mudslide out here." Then he moved off, crouched low and groping for the next arrow. Lelldorin touched Garion's shoulder briefly, then disappeared in the opposite direction.

"The ground's completely soaked now," Durnik murmured. "If we open those fissures about a foot wide, it's going to flush most of the support out from under the wall."

"Good."

Again, they sent their probing thoughts out through the sodden earth of the hillside, located the layer of rock, and then swept back and forth along its irregular upper side until they located the first fissure. Garion felt a peculiar sensation as he began to worm his thought down that narrow crack where the water came welling up from far below, almost as if he were extending some incredibly long though invisible arm with slender, supple fingers at its end to reach down into the fissure. "Have you got it?" he whispered to Durnik.

"I think so."

"Let's pull it apart then," Garion said, bracing his will.

Slowly, with an effort that made the beads of sweat stand out on their foreheads, the two of them forced the fissure open. A sharp, muffled crack reverberated up from beneath the sodden slope of the hillside as the rock broke under the force of their combined wills.

"Who's there?" a voice demanded from atop the city wall.

"Is it open wide enough?" Garion whispered, ignoring that alarmed challenge.

"The water's coming up much faster," Durnik replied after a moment's probing. "There's a lot of pressure under that layer of rock. Let's move on to the next place."

A heavy twang came from somewhere behind them, and a peculiar slithering whistle passed overhead as the line from one of Yarblek's catapult-launched grappling hooks arched up and over the north wall. The hook made a steely clink as it slapped against the inside of the wall, and then there was a grating sound as the points dug in.

Crouched low, Garion and Durnik moved carefully on to their left, trying to minimize the soggy squelching sound their feet made in the slush and probing beneath the earth for the next fissure. When Lelldorin came back to rejoin them, they had already opened two more of those hidden cracks lying beneath the saturated slope; behind and above them, there was a gurgling sound as the soupy mud oozed out of the hillside to cascade in a brown flood down the snowy slope. "I got all the way to the end of the line of arrows," Lelldorin reported. "The string's in place on this side."

"Good," Garion said, panting slightly from his exertions. "Go back and tell Barak to start moving the troops into place."

"Right." Lelldorin turned and went off into the swirl of a sudden snow flurry.

"We'll have to be careful with this one," Durnik murmured, searching along under the soil. "There are a lot of fractures in the rock here. If we pull it too far apart, we'll break up the whole layer and turn loose a river."

Garion grunted his agreement as he sent the probing fingers of his will out toward the fissure.

When they reached the last of their subterranean well springs, Silk came out of the dark behind them, his nimble feet making no sound as he moved through the slush.

"What kept you?" Durnik whispered to the little man. "You only had about a hundred yards to go."

"I was checking the slope," Silk replied. "The whole thing is starting to ooze through the snow like cold gravy. Then I went up and pushed my foot against one of the foundation stones of the wall. It wobbled like a loose tooth."

"Well," Durnik said in a tone of self-satisfaction, "it worked after all."

There was a pause in the snowy darkness. "You mean you weren't actually sure?" Silk asked in a strangled voice.

"The theory was sound," the smith answered in an offhand sort of way. "But you can never be actually positive about a theory until you try it."

"Durnik, I'm getting too old for this."

Another grappling hook sailed overhead.

"We've got one more to open," Garion murmured. "Barak's moving the troops into place. Do you want to go back and tell Yarblek to send up the signal to Mandorallen?"

"My pleasure," Silk replied. "I want to get out of here before we're all hip-deep in mud anyway." He turned and went off into the dark.

Perhaps ten minutes later, when the last fissure had been opened and the entire north slope of the hill had turned into a slithering mass of oozing mud and freely running water, an orange ball of blazing pitch arched high in the air over the city. In response to that prearranged signal, Mandorallen's engines emplaced to the south began a continuous barrage, lofting their heavy stones high over the rooftops of Rheon to slam against the inside of the north wall. At the same time, the lines on Yarblek's grappling hooks tautened as the Nadrak mercenaries began to move their teams of horses away from the wall. There was an ominous creaking and grinding along the top of the hill as the weakened wall began to sway.

"How much longer do you think it's going to stand?" Barak asked as he came out of the darkness with Lelldorin at his side to join them.

"Not very," Durnik replied. "The ground's starting to give way under it."

The groaning creak above them grew louder, punctuated by the continual sharp crashes along the inside as Mandorallen's catapults stepped up the pace of their deadly rain. Then, with a sound like an avalanche, a section of the wall collapsed with a peculiarly sinuous motion as the upper portion toppled outward and the tower sank into the sodden earth. There was a great, splashing rumble as the heavy stones cascaded into the slush and mud of the hillside.

"A man should never try to put up stonework resting only on dirt," Durnik observed critically.

"Under the circumstances, I'm glad they did," Barak told him.

"Well, yes," Durnik admitted, "but there *are* right ways to do things."

The big Cherek chuckled. "Durnik, you're an absolute treasure, do you know that?"

Another section of the wall toppled outward to splash onto the slope. Shouts of alarm and the clanging of bells began to echo through the streets of the fortified town.

"You want me to move the men out?" Barak asked Garion, his voice tense with excitement.

"Let's wait until the whole wall comes down," Garion replied. "I don't want them charging up the hill with all those building stones falling on top of them."

"There it goes." Lelldorin laughed gleefully, pointing toward the last, toppling section of the wall.

"Start the men," Garion said tersely, reaching over his shoulder for the great sword strapped to his back.

Barak drew in a deep breath. "Charge!" he roared in a vast voice.

With a concerted shout, the Rivans and their Nadrak allies plunged up through the slush and mud and began clambering over the fallen ruins of the north wall and on into the city.

"Let's go!" Barak shouted. "We'll miss all the fighting if we don't hurry!"

■ | CHAPTER TWENTY-FOUR | ■

The fight was short and in many cases very ugly. Each element of Garion's army had been thoroughly briefed by Javelin and his niece, and they had all been given specific assignments. Unerringly, they moved through the snowy, fire-lit streets to occupy designated houses. Other elements, angling in from the edges of the breach in the north wall, circled the defensive perimeter Javelin had drawn on Liselle's map to pull down the houses and fill the streets with obstructing rubble.

The first counterattack came just before dawn. Howling Bear-cultists clad in shaggy furs swarmed out of the narrow streets beyond the perimeter to swarm up over the rubble of the collapsed houses, only to run directly into a withering rain of arrows from the rooftops and upper windows. After dreadful losses, they fell back.

As dawn broke pale and gray along the snowy eastern horizon, the last few pockets of resistance inside the perimeter crumbled, and the north quarter of Rheon was secure. Garion stood somberly at a broken upper window of a house overlooking the cleared area that marked the outer limits of that part of the town that was under his control. The bodies of the cultists who had mounted the counterattack lay sprawled in twisted, grotesque heaps, already lightly dusted with snow.

"Not a bad little fight," Barak declared, coming into the room with his blood-stained sword still in his hand. He dropped his dented shield in a corner and came over to the window.

"I didn't care much for it," Garion replied, pointing at the windrows of the dead lying below. "Killing people is a very poor way of changing their minds."

"They started this war, Garion. You didn't."

"No," Garion corrected. "Ulfgar started it. He's the one I actually want."

"Then we'll have to go get him for you," Barak said, carefully wiping his sword with a bit of tattered cloth.

During the course of the day, there were several more furious counterattacks from inside the city, but the results were much the same as had been the case with the first. Garion's positions were too secure and too well covered by archers to fall to these sporadic sorties.

"They don't actually fight well in groups, do they?" Durnik said from the vantage point of the upper story of that half-ruined house.

"They don't have that kind of discipline," Silk replied. The little man was sprawled on a broken couch in one corner of the room, carefully peeling an apple with a small, sharp knife. "Individually, they're as brave as lions, but the concept of unified action hasn't quite seeped into their heads yet."

"That was an awfully good shot," Barak congratulated Lelldorin, who had just loosed an arrow through the shattered window.

Lelldorin shrugged. "Child's play. Now, that fellow creeping along the roof-line of the house several streets back—that's a bit more challenging." He nocked another arrow, drew, and released all in one smooth motion.

"You got him," Barak said.

"Naturally."

As evening approached, Polgara and Beldin returned to the camp outside the city. "Well," the gnarled sorcerer said with a certain satisfaction, "you won't have to worry about the pikemen for a while." He held out his twisted hands to one of Yarblek's glowing braziers.

"You didn't hurt them, did you?" Porenn asked quickly.

"No." He grinned. "We just bogged them down. They were going through a marshy valley, and we diverted a river into it. The whole place is a quagmire now. They're perched on hummocks and in the branches of trees waiting for the water to subside."

"Won't that stall Brendig as well?" Garion asked.

"Brendig's marching around that valley," Polgara assured him, sitting near one of the braziers with a cup of tea. "He should be here in a few days." She looked at Vella. "This tea is really excellent," she said.

"Thank you, Lady Polgara," the dark-haired dancer replied. Her eyes were fixed on Ce'Nedra's copper curls, radiant in the golden candlelight. She sighed enviously. "If I had hair like that, Yarblek could sell me for double the price."

"I'd settle for half," Yarblek muttered, "just to avoid all those incidental knifings."

"Don't be such a baby, Yarblek," she told him. "I didn't really hurt you all that much."

"You weren't the one who was doing the bleeding."

"Have you been practicing your curses, Vella?" Beldin asked.

She demonstrated—at some length.

"You're getting better," he congratulated her.

For the next two days, Garion's forces worked to heap obstructions along the rubble-choked perimeter of the north quarter of Rheon to prevent a counterattack in force from crossing that intervening space. Garion and his friends observed the process from a large window high up in the house which they had converted into a headquarters.

"Whoever's in charge over there doesn't seem to have a very good grasp of basic strategy," Yarblek noted. "He's not making any effort to block off *his* side of that open space to keep us out of the rest of his city."

Barak frowned. "You know, Yarblek, you're right. That should have been his first move after we secured this part of town."

"Maybe he's too arrogant to believe that we can take more of his houses," Lelldorin suggested.

"Either that or he's laying traps for us back out of sight," Durnik added.

"That's possible, too," Barak agreed. "More than possible. Maybe we ought to do a little planning before we start any more attacks."

"Before we can plan anything, we have to know exactly what kind of traps Ulfgar has waiting for us," Javelin said.

Silk sighed and made a wry face. "All right. After dark I'll go have a look."

"I wasn't really suggesting that, Kheldar."

"Of course you weren't."

"It's a very good idea, though. I'm glad you thought of it."

It was some time after midnight when Silk returned to the large, firelit room in Garion's headquarters. "It's a very unpleasant night out there," the little man said, shivering and rubbing his hands together. He went over to stand in front of the fire.

"Well, are they planning any surprises for us?" Barak asked him, lifting a copper tankard.

"Oh, yes," Silk replied. "They're building walls across the streets several houses back from our perimeter and they're putting them just around corners so you won't see them until you're right on top of them."

"With archers and tubs of boiling pitch in all the houses nearby?" Barak asked glumly.

"Probably." Silk shrugged. "Do you have any more of that ale? I'm chilled to the bone."

"We'll have to work on this a bit," Javelin mused.

"Good luck," Barak said sourly, going to the ale keg. "I *hate* fighting in towns. Give me a nice open field any time."

"But the towns are where all the loot is," Yarblek said to him.

"Is that all you ever think about?"

"We're in this life to make a profit, my friend," the raw-boned Nadrak replied with a shrug.

"You sound just like Silk."

"I know. That's why we went into partnership."

It continued to snow lightly throughout the following day. The citizens of Rheon made a few more probing attacks on Garion's defensive perimeter, but for the most part they contented themselves with merely shooting arrows at anything that moved.

About midmorning the next day, Errand picked his way over the rubble of the fallen north wall and went directly to the house from which Garion was directing operations. When he entered, his young face was tight with exhilaration, and he was panting noticeably. "That's exciting," he said.

"What is?" Garion asked him.

"Dodging arrows."

"Does Aunt Pol know you're here?"

"I don't think so. I wanted to see the city, so I just came."

"You're going to get us both in trouble, do you know that?"

Errand shrugged. "A scolding doesn't hurt all that much. Oh, I thought you ought to know that Hettar's here—or he will be in an hour or so. He's just a few miles to the south."

"Finally!" Garion said with an explosive release of his breath. "How did you find out?"

"Horse and I went out for a ride. He gets restless when he's penned up. Anyway, we were up on that big hill to the south, and I saw the Algars coming."

"Well, let's go meet them."

"Why don't we?"

When Garion and his young friend reached the top of the hill south of Rheon, they saw wave upon wave of Algar clansmen flowing over the snowy moors at a brisk canter. A single horseman detached himself from the front rank of that sea of horses and men and pounded up the hill, his long black scalplock flowing behind him. "Good morning, Garion," Hettar said casually as he reined in. "You've been well, I trust?"

"Moderately." Garion grinned at him.

"You've got snow up here."

Garion looked around in feigned astonishment. "Why, I do believe you're right. I hadn't even noticed that."

Another rider came up the hill, a man in a shabby, hooded cloak. "Where's your aunt, Garion?" the man called when he was halfway up the hill.

"Grandfather?" Garion exclaimed with surprise. "I thought you were going to Mar Terrin."

Belgarath made an indelicate sound. "I did," he replied as he reined in his horse, "and it was an absolutely wasted trip. I'll tell you about it later. What's been going on here?"

Briefly Garion filled them in on the events of the past several weeks.

"You've been busy," Hettar noted.

"The time goes faster when you keep occupied."

"Is Pol inside the city, then?" Belgarath asked him.

"No. She and Ce'Nedra and the other ladies are staying in the camp we built when we first got here. The cultists have been counterattacking against our positions inside, so I didn't think it was entirely safe for them to be there."

"That makes sense. Why don't you round up everybody and bring them to the camp. I think we need to talk about a few things."

"All right, Grandfather."

It was shortly after noon when they gathered in the main tent in the Rivan encampment outside the city.

"Were you able to find anything useful, father?" Polgara asked Belgarath as the old man entered the tent.

Belgarath sprawled in a chair. "Some tantalizing hints was about all," he replied. "I get the feeling that Anheg's copy of the Ashabine Oracles has been rather carefully pruned somewhere along the way—or more likely at the very beginning. The modifications seem to be a part of the original text."

"Prophets don't usually tamper with their own prophecies," Polgara noted.

"*This* one would have—particularly if parts of the prophecy said things he didn't want to believe."

"Who was it?"

"Torak. I recognized his tone and his peculiar turn of phrase almost immediately."

"Torak?" Garion exclaimed, feeling a sudden chill.

Belgarath nodded. "There's an old Mallorean legend that says that after he destroyed Cthol Mishrak, Torak had a castle built at Ashaba in the Karandese Mountains. Once he moved in, an ecstasy came over him, and he composed the Ashabine Oracles. Anyway, the legend goes on to say that after the ecstasy had passed, Torak fell into a great rage. Apparently there were things in the prophecy that he didn't like. That could very well account for the tampering I detected. We've always been told that the word gives meaning to the event."

"Can you do that?"

"No. But Torak was so arrogant that he may have believed he could."

"But that puts us at a dead end, doesn't it?" Garion asked with a sinking feeling. "I mean—the Mrin Codex said that you had to look at all the mysteries, and if the Ashabine Oracles aren't correct—" He lifted his hands helplessly.

"There's a true copy somewhere," Belgarath replied confidently. "There has to be—otherwise the Codex would have given me different instructions."

"You're operating on pure faith, Belgarath," Ce'Nedra accused him.

"I know," he admitted. "I do that when I don't have anything else to fall back on."

"What did you find at Mar Terrin?" Polgara asked.

Belgarath made a vulgar sound. "The monks there may be very good at comforting the spirits of all those slaughtered Marags, but they're very bad at protecting manuscripts. The roof leaks in their library, and the copy of the Mallorean Gospels, naturally, was on a shelf right under the leak. It was so soggy that I could barely get the leaves apart, and the ink had run and smeared all over the pages. It was almost totally illegible. I spoke with the monks at some length about that." He scratched at one bearded cheek. "It looks as if I'm going to have to go a bit further afield to get what we need."

"You found nothing at all, then?" Beldin asked.

Belgarath grunted. "There was one passage in the Oracles that said that the Dark God will come again."

Garion felt a sudden chill grip his stomach. "Torak?" he said. "Is that possible?"

"I suppose you *could* take it to mean that, but if that's what it really means, then why would Torak have gone to the trouble of destroying so many of the other passages? If the entire purpose of the Oracles was to predict his own return, I expect that he'd have been overjoyed to keep them intact."

"You're assuming that old burnt-face was rational," Beldin growled. "I never noticed that quality in him very often."

"Oh, no," Belgarath disagreed. "Everything Torak did was perfectly rational—as long as you accepted his basic notion that he was the sole reason for creation. No, I think the passage means something else."

"Could you read any part of the Mallorean Gospels at all, father?" Aunt Pol asked him.

"Just one little fragment. It said something about a choice between the Light and the Dark."

Beldin snorted. "Now *that* would be something very unusual," he said. "The Seers at Kell haven't made a choice about anything since the world was made. They've been sitting on the fence for millennia."

Late the following afternoon, the Sendarian army came into view on the snowy hilltops to the west. Garion felt a peculiar twinge of pride as the solid, steady men he had always thought of as his countrymen marched purposefully through the snow toward the now-doomed city of Rheon.

"I might have gotten here sooner," General Brendig apologized as he rode up, "but we had to march around that quagmire where the Drasnian pikemen are bogged down."

"Are they all right?" Queen Porenn asked him quickly.

"Perfectly, your Majesty," the one-armed man replied. "They just can't go anywhere, that's all."

"How much rest will your troops need before they'll be ready to join the assault, Brendig?" Belgarath asked him.

Brendig shrugged. "A day ought to do it, Ancient One."

"That will give us time enough to make our plans," the old man said. "Let's get your men bivouacked and fed, and then Garion can brief you on the way things stand here."

In the strategy meeting in the garishly carpeted main tent that evening, they smoothed out the rough edges of their relatively simple plan of attack. Mandorallen's siege engines would continue to pound the city throughout the next day and on into the following night. On the next morning, a feigned assault would be mounted against the south gate to draw as many cultists as possible away from the hastily erected fortification inside the city. Another force would march out of the secure enclave in the north quarter of Rheon to begin the house-by-house occupation of the buildings facing the perimeter. Yet another force, acting on an inspired notion of General Brendig's, would use scaling ladders as bridges to go across the housetops and drop in behind the newly erected walls inside the city.

"The most important thing is to take Ulfgar alive," Garion cautioned. "We have to get some answers from him. I need to know just what part he played in the abduction of my son and where Geran is, if he knows."

"And I want to know just how many of the officers in my army he's subverted," Queen Porenn added.

"It looks as if he's going to be doing a lot of talking," Yarblek said with an evil grin. "In Gar og Nadrak we have a number of very entertaining ways of loosening people's tongues."

"Pol will handle that," Belgarath told him firmly. "She can get the answers we need without resorting to that sort of thing."

"Are you getting soft, Belgarath?" Barak asked.

"Not likely," the old man replied, "but if Yarblek here gets carried away, it might go a little too far, and you can't get answers out of a dead man."

"But afterward?" Yarblek asked eagerly.

"I don't really care what you do with him afterward."

The next day, Garion was in a small, curtained-off area in the main tent going over his maps and his carefully organized lists, trying to determine if there was anything he had overlooked. He had begun of late to feel as if the entire army were resting directly on his shoulders.

"Garion," Ce'Nedra said, entering his cubicle, "some friends have arrived."

He looked up.

"Brand's three sons," she told him, "and that glass blower Joran."

Garion frowned. "What are they doing here?" he asked. "I told them all to stay at Riva."

"They say that they've got something important to tell you."

He sighed. "You'd better have them come in, then."

Brand's three gray-cloaked sons and the serious-faced Joran entered and bowed. Their clothes were mud-spattered, and their faces weary.

"We are not deliberately disobeying your orders, Belgarion," Kail assured him quickly, "but we discovered something very important that you have to know."

"Oh? What's that?"

"After you left Riva with the army, your Majesty," Kail's older brother Verdan explained, "we decided to go over the west coast of the island inch by inch. We thought there might be some clues that we overlooked in our first search."

"Besides," Brin added, "we didn't have anything else to do."

"Anyway," Verdan continued, "we finally found the ship those Chereks had used to come to the island."

"Their ship?" Garion asked, suddenly sitting up. "I thought that whoever it was who abducted my son used it to get off the island."

Verdan shook his head. "The ship had been deliberately sunk, your Majesty. They filled it with rocks and then chopped holes in the bottom. We sailed right over it five times until a calm day when there wasn't any surf. It was lying on the bottom in about thirty feet of water."

"How did the abductor get off the island, then?"

"We had that same thought, Belgarion," Joran said. "It occurred to us that, in spite of everything, the abductor might still be on the Isle of the Winds. We started searching. That's when we found the shepherd."

"Shepherd?"

"He'd been alone with his flock up in the meadows on the western side of the Isle," Kail explained. "He was completely unaware of what had happened in the city. Anyway, we asked him if he had seen anything unusual at about the time Prince Geran was taken from the Citadel, and he said that he had seen a ship sail into a cove on the west coast at about that time and that somebody carrying something wrapped in a blanket got on board. Then the ship put out to sea, leaving the others behind. Belgarion, it was the same cove where the trail the Orb was following ended."

"Which way did the ship go?"

"South."

"There's one other thing, Belgarion," Joran added. "The shepherd was positive that the ship was Nyissan."

"Nyissan?"

"He was absolutely certain. He even described the snake banner she was flying."

Garion got quickly to his feet. "Wait here," he told them. Then he went to the flap in the partition. "Grandfather, Aunt Pol, could you step in here for a moment?"

"What is it, dear?" Polgara asked as she and the old sorcerer came into Garion's makeshift office, with Silk trailing curiously behind.

"Tell them," Garion said to Kail.

Quickly, Brand's second son repeated what they had just told Garion.

"Salmissra?" Polgara suggested to her father.

"Not necessarily, Pol. Nyissa is full of intrigue, and the Queen isn't behind it all—particularly after what you did to her." He frowned. "Why would a Cherek abandon one of his own boats to ride aboard a Nyissan scow? That doesn't make sense."

"That's another question we'll have to ask Ulfgar, once we get our hands on him," Silk said.

At dawn the next morning, a large body of troops comprised of elements from all the forces gathered for the siege began to march across the valley to the south of the city toward the steep hill and Rheon. They carried scaling ladders and battering rams in plain sight to make the defenders believe that this was a major assault.

In the quarter of the city occupied by Garion's troops, however, Silk led a sizeable detachment of men through the dawn murk across the rooftops to clear away the cult archers and the smeared men with their boiling pitch pots occupying those houses on either side of the hastily built walls erected to bar entrance into the rest of the city.

Garion, flanked by Barak and Mandorallen, waited in a snowy street near the perimeter of the occupied quarter. "This is the part I hate," he said tensely. "The waiting."

"I must confess to thee that I myself find this lull just before a battle unpleasant," Mandorallen replied.

"I thought Arends loved a battle." Barak grinned at his friend.

"It is our favorite pastime," the great knight admitted, checking one of the buckles under his armor. "This interim just 'ere we join with the enemy, however, is irksome. Sober, even melancholy, thoughts distract the mind from the main purpose at hand."

"Mandorallen," Barak laughed. "I've missed you."

The shadowy form of Yarblek came up the street to join them. He had put aside his felt overcoat and now wore a heavy steel breastplate and carried a wicked-looking axe. "Everything's ready," he told them quietly. "We can start just as soon as the little thief gives us the signal."

"Are you sure your men can pull down those walls?" Barak asked him.

Yarblek nodded. "Those people didn't have time enough to set the stones in mortar," he said. "Our grappling hooks can jerk down the walls in a few minutes."

"You seem very fond of that particular tool," Barak observed.

Yarblek shrugged. "I've always found that the best way to get through a wall is to yank it down."

"In Arendia, our preference is the battering ram," Mandorallen said.

"Those are good, too," Yarblek agreed, "but the trouble with a ram is that you're right under the wall when it falls. I've never particularly enjoyed having building stones bouncing off the top of my head."

They waited.

"Has anybody seen Lelldorin?" Garion asked.

"He went with Silk," Barak replied. "He seemed to think that he could find more targets from up on a roof."

"He was ever an enthusiast." Mandorallen smiled. "I must confess, however, that I have never seen his equal with the longbow."

"There it is," Barak said, pointing at a flaming arrow arching high above the rooftops. "That's the signal."

Garion drew in a deep breath and squared his shoulders. "All right. Sound your horn, Mandorallen, and let's get started."

The brazen note of Mandorallen's horn shattered the stillness. From every street and alleyway, Garion's army poured out to begin the final assault on Rheon. Rivans, Algars, Nadraks, and the solid men of Sendaria crunched through the snow toward the perimeter with their weapons in their hands. Three score of Yarblek's leather-clad mercenaries ran on ahead, their grappling hooks swinging from their hands.

With Barak at his side, Garion clambered over the treacherous, sliding rubble of the houses that had been pulled down to form the perimeter and over the half-frozen bodies of arrow-stitched cultists who had fallen earlier. A few—though not many—cultists had escaped the hasty floor-by-floor search of Silk's men in the houses facing the perimeter and they desperately showered the advancing troops with arrows. At Brendig's sharp command, detachments of Sendars veered and broke into each house to neutralize those remaining defenders efficiently.

The scene beyond the perimeter was one of enormous confusion. Advancing behind a wall of shields, Garion's army swept the streets clear of the now-desperate cultists. The air was thick with arrows and curses, and several houses were already shooting flames out through their roofs.

True to Yarblek's prediction, the loosely stacked walls blocking the streets some way into the city fell easily to the dozens of grappling hooks that sailed up over their troops to bite into the other sides.

The grim advance continued, and the air rang with the steely clang of sword against sword. Somehow, in all the confusion, Garion became separated from Barak and found himself fighting shoulder to shoulder beside Durnik in a narrow alley-way. The smith carried no sword or axe, but fought instead with a large, heavy club. "I just don't like chopping into people," he apologized, felling a burly opponent with one solid blow. "If you hit somebody with a club, there's a fair chance that he won't die, and there isn't all that blood."

They pushed deeper into the city, driving the demoralized inhabitants before them. The sounds of heavy fighting at the southern end of town gave notice that Silk and his men had reached the south wall and opened the gates to admit the massed troops whose feigned attack had fatally divided the cult forces.

And then Garion and Durnik burst out of the narrow alleyway into the broad, snowy central square of Rheon. Fighting raged all over the square; but on the east side, a thick knot of cultists was tightly packed about a high-wheeled cart. Atop the cart stood a black-bearded man in a rust-colored brocade doublet.

A lean Nadrak with a slender spear in his hand arched back, took aim, and hurled his weapon directly at the man on the cart. The black-bearded man raised one hand in a peculiar gesture, and the Nadrak spear suddenly sheered off to the right to clatter harmlessly on the snow-slick cobblestones. Garion clearly heard and felt the rushing surge that could only mean one thing. "Durnik!" he shouted. "The man on the cart. That's Ulfgar!"

Durnik's eyes narrowed. "Let's take him, Garion," he said.

Garion's anger at this stranger who was the cause of all this warfare and carnage and destruction suddenly swelled intolerably, and his rage communicated itself to the Orb on the pommel of his sword. The Orb flared, and Iron-grip's burning sword suddenly flamed out in searing blue fire.

"There! It's the Rivan King!" the black-bearded man on the cart screamed. "Kill him!"

Momentarily Garion's eyes locked on the eyes of the man on the cart. There was hate there and, at the same time, an awe and a desperate fear. But, blindly obedient to their leader's command, a dozen cultists ran through the slush toward Garion with their swords aloft. Suddenly they began to tumble into twitching heaps in the sodden snow in the square as arrow after arrow laced into their ranks.

"Ho, Garion!" Lelldorin shouted gleefully from a nearby housetop, his hands blurring as he loosed his arrows at the charging cultists.

"Ho, Lelldorin!" Garion called his reply, even as he ran in amongst the fur-clad men, flailing about him with his burning sword. The attention of the group around the cart was riveted entirely on the horrifying spectacle of the enraged King of Riva and his fabled sword. They did not, therefore, see Durnik the smith moving in a catlike crouch along the wall of a nearby house.

The man on the cart raised one hand aloft, seized a ball of pure fire, and hurled it desperately at Garion. Garion flicked the fireball aside with his flaming blade and continued his grim advance, swinging dreadful strokes at the desperate men garbed in bearskins in front of him without ever taking his eyes off of the pasty-faced man in the black beard. His expression growing panicky, Ulfgar raised his hand again, but suddenly seemed almost to lunge forward off the cart into the brown slush as Durnik's cudgel cracked sharply across the back of his head.

There was a great cry of chagrin as the cult leader fell. Several of his men tried desperately to lift his inert body, but Durnik's club, whistling and thudding solidly, felled them in their tracks. Others tried to form a wall with their bodies in an effort to keep Garion from reaching the body lying facedown in the snow, but Lelldorin's steady rain of arrows melted the center of that fur-clad wall. Garion, feeling strangely remote and unaffected by the slaughter, marched into the very midst of the disorganized survivors, swinging his huge sword in great, sweeping arcs. He barely felt the sickening shear as his sword cut through bone and flesh. After he had cut down a half a dozen or so, the rest broke and ran.

"Is he still alive?" Garion panted at the smith.

Durnik rolled the inert Ulfgar over and professionally peeled back one of his eyelids to have a look. "He's still with us," he said. "I hit him rather carefully."

"Good," Garion said. "Let's tie him up—and blindfold him."

"Why blindfold?"

"We both saw him use sorcery, so we've answered that particular question, but I think it might be a little hard to do that sort of thing if you can't see what you're aiming at."

Durnik though about it for a moment as he tied the unconscious man's hands. "You know, I believe you're right. It would be difficult, wouldn't it?"

CHAPTER TWENTY-FIVE

With the fall of Ulfgar, the cult's will to resist broke. Though a few of the more rabid continued to fight, most threw down their weapons in surrender. Grimly, Garion's army rounded them up and herded them through the snowy, bloodstained streets into the town's central square.

Silk and Javelin briefly questioned a sullen captive with a bloody bandage wrapped around his head, then joined Garion and Durnik, who stood watch over their still-unconscious prisoner. "Is that him?" Silk asked curiously, absently polishing one of his rings on the front of his gray doublet.

Garion nodded.

"He doesn't look all that impressive, does he?"

"The large stone house over there is his," Javelin said, pointing at a square building with red tiles on its roof.

"Not any more," Garion replied. "It's mine now."

Javelin smiled briefly. "We'll want to search it rather thoroughly," he said. "People sometimes forget to destroy important things."

"We might as well take Ulfgar in there, too," Garion said. "We need to question him, and that house is as good as any."

"I'll go get the others," Durnik offered, pulling off his pot-shaped helmet. "Do you think it's safe enough to bring Pol and the other ladies into the city yet?"

"It should be," Javelin replied. "What little resistance there is left is in the southeast quarter of the city."

Durnik nodded and went on across the square, his mail shirt jingling.

Garion, Silk, and Javelin picked up the limp form of the black-bearded man and carried him toward the stately house with the banner of a bear flying from a staff in front of it. As they started up the stairs, Garion glanced at a Rivan soldier standing guard over some demoralized prisoners huddled miserably in the slush. "Would you do me a favor?" he asked the gray-cloaked man.

"Of course, your Majesty," the soldier said, saluting.

"Chop that thing down." Garion indicated the flagstaff with a thrust of his jaw.

"At once, your Majesty." The soldier grinned. "I should have thought of it myself."

They carried Ulfgar into the house and through a polished door. The room beyond the door was luxuriously furnished, but the chairs were mostly overturned, and there were sheets of parchment everywhere. A crumpled heap of them had been stuffed into a large stone fireplace built into the back wall, but the fireplace was cold.

"Good," Javelin muttered. "He was interrupted before he could burn anything."

Silk looked around at the room. Rich, dark-colored tapestries hung on the walls, and the green carpeting was thick and soft. The chairs were all upholstered in scarlet velvet, and unlighted candles stood in silver sconces along the wall. "He managed to live fairly well, didn't he?" the little man murmured as they unceremoniously dumped the prisoner in the rust-colored doublet in one corner.

"Let's gather up these documents," Javelin said. "I want to go over them."

Garion unstrapped his sword, dropped his helmet on the floor, and shrugged himself out of his heavy mail shirt. Then he sank wearily onto a soft couch. "I'm absolutely exhausted," he said. "I feel as if I haven't slept for a week."

Silk shrugged. "One of the privileges of command."

The door opened, and Belgarath came into the room. "Durnik said I could find you here," he said, pushing back the hood of his shabby old cloak. He crossed the room and nudged the limp form in the corner. "He isn't dead, is he?"

"No," Garion replied. "Durnik put him to sleep with a club is all."

"Why the blindfold?" the old man asked, indicating the strip of blue cloth tied across the captive's face.

"He was using sorcery before we captured him. I thought it might not be a bad idea to cover his eyes."

"That depends on how good he is. Durnik sent soldiers out to round up the others and then he went over to the encampment to get Pol and the other ladies."

"Can you wake him up?" Silk asked.

"Let's have Pol do it. Her touch is a little lighter than mine, and I don't want to break anything accidentally."

It was perhaps three-quarters of an hour later when they all finally gathered in the green-carpeted room. Belgarath looked around, then straddled a straight-backed chair in front of the captive. "All right, Pol," he said bleakly. "Wake him up."

Polgara unfastened her blue cloak, knelt beside the prisoner, and put one hand on each side of his head. Garion heard a whispered rushing sound and felt a gentle surge. Ulfgar groaned.

"Give him a few minutes," she said, rising to her feet. "Then you can start questioning him."

"He's probably going to be stubborn about it," Brin predicted with a broad grin.

"I'll be terribly disappointed in him if he isn't," Silk said as he rifled through a drawer in a large, polished cabinet.

"Have you barbarians blinded me?" Ulfgar said in a weak voice as he struggled into a sitting position.

"No," Polgara told him. "Your eyes are covered to keep you out of mischief."

"Are my captors women, then?" There was contempt in the black-bearded man's voice.

"This one of them is," Ce'Nedra said, pushing her dark green cloak slightly to one side. It was the note in her voice that warned Garion and saved the prisoner's life. With blazing eyes, she snatched one of the daggers from Vella's belt and flew at the blindfolded man with the gleaming blade held aloft. At the last instant, Garion caught her upraised arm and wrested the knife from her grasp.

"Give me that!" she cried.

"No, Ce'Nedra."

"He stole my baby!" she screamed. "I'll kill him!"

"No, you won't. We can't get any answers out of him if you cut his throat." With one arm still about her, he handed the dagger back to Vella.

"We have a few questions for you, Ulfgar," Belgarath said to the captive.

"You're going to have to wait a long time for the answers."

"I'm *so* glad he said that," Hettar murmured. "Who wants to start cutting on him?"

"Do whatever you wish," Ulfgar sneered. "My body is of no concern to me."

"We'll do everything we can to change your mind about that," Vella said in a chillingly sweet voice as she tested the edge of her dagger with her thumb.

"Just what was it you wanted to know, Belgarath?" Errand asked, turning from his curious examination of a bronze statue standing in the corner. "I can give you the answers, if you want."

Belgarath looked at the blond boy sharply. "Do you know what's in his mind?" he asked, startled.

"More or less, yes."

"Where's my son?" Garion asked quickly.

"That's one thing he doesn't know," Errand replied. "He had nothing to do with the abduction."

"Who did it then?"

"He's not sure, but he thinks it was Zandramas."

"Zandramas?"

"That name keeps cropping up, doesn't it?" Silk said.

"Does he know who Zandramas is?"

"Not really. It's just a name he's heard from his Master."

"Who is his Master?"

"He's afraid to even think the name," Errand said. "It's a man with a splotchy face, though."

The prisoner was struggling desperately, trying to free himself from the ropes which bound him. "Lies!" he screamed. "All lies!"

"This man was sent here by his master to make sure that you and Ce'Nedra didn't have any children," Errand continued, ignoring the screaming captive, "or to see to it that, if you did, the children didn't live. He couldn't have been behind the abduction, Belgarion. If *he* had been the one who crept into the nursery at Riva, he would have killed your son, not taken him away."

"Where does he come from?" Liselle asked curiously as she removed her scarlet cloak. "I can't quite place his accent."

"That's probably because he's not really a man," Errand told her. "At least not entirely. He remembers being an animal of some sort."

They all stared at the boy and then at Ulfgar.

At that point the door opened again, and the hunchbacked Beldin came into the room. He was about to say something, but stopped, staring at the bound and blindfolded prisoner. He stumped across the floor, bent, and ripped the blue cloth away from the man's eyes to stare into his face. "Well, dog," he said. "What brings you out of your kennel?"

"You!" Ulfgar gasped, his face growing suddenly pale.

"Urvon will have your heart for breakfast when he finds out how badly you've botched things," Beldin said pleasantly.

"Do you know this man?" Garion asked sharply.

"He and I have known each other for a long, long time, haven't we, Harakan?" The prisoner spat at him.

"I see you will need a little bit of housebreaking." Beldin grinned.

"Who is he?" Garion demanded.

"His name is Harakan. He's a Mallorean Grolim—one of Urvon's dogs. The last time I saw him, he was whining and fawning all over Urvon's feet."

Then, quite suddenly, the captive vanished.

Beldin unleased a string of foul curses. Then he, too, flickered out of sight.

"What happened?" Ce'Nedra gasped. "Where did they go?"

"Maybe Beldin isn't as smart as I thought," Belgarath said. "He should have left that blindfold alone. Our prisoner translocated himself outside the building."

"Can you do that?" Garion asked incredulosly. "Without being able to see what you're doing, I mean?"

"It's very, very dangerous, but Harakan seems to have been desperate. Beldin's following him."

"He'll catch him, won't he?"

"It's hard to say."

"I still have questions that have to be answered."

"I can answer them for you, Belgarion," Errand told him quite calmly.

"You mean that you still know what's in his mind—even though he's not here any more?"

Errand nodded.

"Why don't you start at the beginning, Errand?" Polgara suggested.

"All right. This Harakan, I guess his real name is, came here because his Master, the one Beldin called Urvon, sent him here to make sure that Belgarion and Ce'Nedra never had any children. Harakan came here and gained control of the Bear-cult. At first he stirred up all kinds of talk against Ce'Nedra, hoping that he could force Belgarion to set her aside and marry someone else. Then, when he heard that she was going to have a baby, he sent someone to try to kill her. That didn't work, of course, and he started to get desperate. He was terribly afraid of what Urvon would do to him if he failed. He tried to gain control of Ce'Nedra when she was asleep once, to make her smother the baby, but someone—he doesn't know who—stepped in and stopped him."

"It was Poledra," Garion murmured. "I was there that night."

"Is that when he came up with the idea of murdering Brand and laying the blame at King Anheg's door?" General Brendig asked.

Errand frowned slightly. "Killing Brand was an accident," he replied. "As closely as Harakan could work it out, Brand just happened along and caught the cultists in that hallway when they were about to do what he really sent them to Riva to do."

"And what was that?" Ce'Nedra asked him.

"They were on their way to the royal apartments to kill you and your baby." Her face paled.

"And then they were supposed to kill themselves. *That* was what was supposed to start the war between Belgarion and King Anheg. Anyway, something went wrong. Brand got killed instead of you and your baby, and we found out that the cult was responsible instead of Anheg. He didn't dare go back to Urvon and admit that he had failed. Then Zandramas took your baby and got away from the Isle of the Winds with him. Harakan couldn't follow because Belgarion was already marching on Rheon by the time he found out about it. He was trapped here, and Zandramas was getting away with your baby."

"That Nyissan ship!" Kail exclaimed. "Zandramas stole your son, Belgarion, and then sailed off to the south and left us all floundering around here in Drasnia."

"What about the story we got from that Cherek cultist right after the abduction?" Brin asked.

"A Bear-cultist isn't usually very bright," Kail replied. "I don't think this Zandramas would have had too much difficulty in persuading those Chereks that the abduction was on Harakan's orders, and all that gibberish about the prince being raised in the cult so that one day he could claim the Rivan throne is just kind of brainsick nonsense men like that would believe."

"That's why they were left behind, then," Garion said. "We were *supposed* to capture at least one of them and get the carefully prepared story that sent us off here to Rheon, while Zandramas sailed away to the south with my son."

"It looks as if we've all been very carefully manipulated," Javelin said, sorting through some parchment sheets he had stacked on a polished table. "Harakan as well as the rest of us."

"We can be clever, too," Belgarath said. "I don't think Zandramas realizes that the Orb will follow Geran's trail. If we move fast enough, we can sneak up from behind and take this clever manipulator by surprise."

"It won't work across water," the dry voice in Garion's mind said laconically.

"What?"

"The Orb can't follow your son's trail over water. The ground stays in one place. Water keeps moving around—wind, tides, that sort of thing."

"Are you sure?"

But the voice was gone.

"There's a problem, Grandfather," Garion said. "The Orb can't find a trail on water."

"How do you know that?"

Garion tapped his forehead. "*He* just told me."

"That complicates things a bit."

"Not too much," Silk disagreed. "There are very few places where a Nyissan ship can land without being searched from keel to topmast. Most monarchs don't care much for the idea of having drugs and poisons slipped into their kingdoms.

Zandramas would definitely not want to sail into some port and get caught with the heir to the Rivan Throne aboard ship."

"There are many hidden coves along the coast of Arendia," Lelldorin suggested.

Silk shook his head. "I don't think so," he said. "I think the ship would have just stayed out to sea. I'm sure Zandramas wanted to get as far away from the Alorn kingdoms as possible—and as quickly as possible. If this ruse that sent us here to Rheon hadn't worked, Garion would have had every man and every ship in the West out looking for his son."

"How about southern Cthol Murgos?" General Brendig suggested.

Javelin frowned. "No," he said. "There's a war going on down there and the whole west coast is being patrolled by Murgo ships. The only safe place for a Nyissan ship to land is in Nyissa itself."

"And that brings us back to Salmissra, doesn't it?" Polgara said.

"I think that if there had been any kind of official involvement in this, my people would have found out about it, Lady Polgara," Javelin said. "I've got Salmissra's palace thoroughly covered. The actual orders would have had to come from Sadi, Salmissra's Chief Eunuch, and we watch him all the time. I don't think this came out of the palace."

The door opened and Beldin, his face as dark as a thundercloud, entered. "By the Gods!" he swore. "I lost him!"

"Lost him?" Belgarath asked. "How?"

"When he got to the street, he turned himself into a hawk. I was right on his tail, but he went into the clouds and changed form on me again. When he came out, he was mixed up in the middle of a flock of geese flying south. Naturally, when the geese saw me, they flew off squawking in all directions. I couldn't tell which one of them he was."

"You must be getting old."

"Why don't you shut up, Belgarath?"

"He's not important anymore, anyway." Belgarath shrugged. "We got what we needed out of him."

"I think I'd prefer it if he were safely dead. If nothing else, the loss of one of his favorite dogs would irritate Urvon, and I'll go out of my way to do that any day in the week."

"Why do you keep calling him a dog?" Hettar asked curiously.

"Because he's one of the Chandim—and that's what they are—the Hounds of Torak."

"Would you like to explain that?" Queen Porenn asked him.

Beldin took a deep breath to get his irritation under control. "It's not too complicated," he said. "When they built Cthol Mishrak in Mallorea, Torak set certain Grolims the task of guarding the city. In order to do that, they became hounds."

Garion shuddered, the memory of the huge dog-shapes they had encountered in the City of Night coming back to him with painful clarity.

"Anyway," Beldin continued, "after the Battle of Vo Mimbre when Torak was put to sleep for all those centuries, Urvon went into the forbidden area around the ruins and managed to persuade a part of the pack of hounds that he was acting on behalf of old burnt-face. He took them back to Mal Yaska with him and gradually changed them back into Grolims, even though he had to kill about half of them in the process. Anyhow, they call themselves the Chandim—a sort of secret order within the Grolim church. They're absolutely loyal to Urvon. They're pretty fair sorcerers and they dabble a bit in magic as well. Underneath it all, though, they're still dogs—very obedient and much more dangerous in packs than they are as individuals."

"What a fascinating little sidelight," Silk observed, looking up from a parchment scroll he had found in one of the cabinets.

"You have a very clever mouth, Kheldar," Beldin said testily. "How would you like to have me brick it up for you?"

"No, that's quite all right, Beldin."

"Well, what now, Belgarath?" Queen Porenn asked.

"Now? Now we go after Zandramas, of course. This hoax with the cult has put us a long way behind, but we'll catch up."

"You can count on that," Garion said. "I dealt with the Child of Dark once before and I can do it again if I have to." He turned back to Errand. "Do you have any idea of why Urvon wants my son killed?"

"It's something he found in a book of some kind. The book says that if your son ever falls into the hands of Zandramas, then Zandramas will be able to use him to do something. Whatever it is, Urvon would be willing to destroy the world to prevent it."

"What is it that Zandramas would be able to do?" Belgarath asked, his eyes intent.

"Harakan doesn't know. All he knows is that he's failed in the task Urvon set him."

Belgarath smiled slowly, a cold, wintery kind of smile. "I don't think we need to waste any time chasing down Harakan," he said.

"Not chase him?" Ce'Nedra exclaimed, "After all he's done to us?"

"Urvon will take care of him for us and Urvon will do things to him that we couldn't even begin to think of."

"Who is this Urvon?" General Brendig asked.

"Torak's third disciple," Belgarath replied. "There used to be three of them—Ctuchik, Zedar, and Urvon. But he's the only one left."

"We still don't know anything about Zandramas," Silk said.

"We know a few things. We know that Zandramas is now the Child of Dark, for example."

"That doesn't fit together, Belgarath," Barak rumbled. "Why would Urvon want to interfere with the Child of Dark? They're on the same side, aren't they?"

"Apparently not. It begins to look as if there's a little dissension in the ranks on the other side."

"That's always helpful."

"I'd like to know a bit more before I start gloating, though."

It was midafternoon before the last fanatic resistance collapsed in the southeastern quarter of Rheon and the demoralized prisoners were herded through the streets of the burning town to join the others in the town square.

Garion and General Brendig stood on the second floor balcony of the house where they had taken Harakan, talking quietly with the small, black-gowned Queen of Drasnia. "What will you do with them now, your Majesty?" General Brendig asked her, looking down at the frightened prisoners in the square.

"I'm going to tell them the truth and let them go, Brendig."

"Let them go?"

"Of course."

"I'm afraid I don't quite follow you."

"They're going to be just a little upset when I tell them that they've been duped into betraying Aloria by a Mallorean Grolim."

"I don't think they'll believe you."

"Enough of them will," she replied placidly, adjusting the collar of her black dress. "I'll manage to convince at least some of them of the truth, and they'll spread the word. Once it becomes general knowledge that the cult fell under the domination of this Grolim Harakan, it's going to be more difficult for them to gain new converts, don't you think?"

Brendig considered that. "I suppose you're right," he admitted. "But will you punish the ones who won't listen?"

"That would be tyranny, General, and one should always try to avoid the appearance of tyranny—particularly when it's unnecessary. Once word of this gets around, I think that anyone who starts babbling about the divine mission of Aloria to subjugate the southern kingdoms is going to be greeted with a barrage of stones."

"All right, then, what are you going to do about General Haldar?" he asked seriously. "You're not just going to let *him* go, too, are you?"

"Haldar's quite another matter," she replied. "He's a traitor, and that sort of thing ought to be discouraged."

"When he finds out what happened here, he'll probably try to run."

"Appearances can be deceiving, General Brendig," she told him with a chill smile. "I may look like a helpless woman, but I have a very long arm. Haldar can't run far enough or fast enough to escape me. And when my people catch him, he'll be brought back to Boktor in chains to stand trial. I think the outcome of that trial will be fairly predictable."

"Would you excuse me?" Garion asked politely. "I need to go talk with my grandfather."

"Of course, Garion," Queen Porenn said with a warm little smile.

He went back downstairs and found Silk and Javelin still ransacking the chests and cabinets in the green-carpeted room. "Are you finding anything useful?" he asked.

"Well, quite a bit, actually," Javelin replied. "I expect that by the time we're finished, we'll have the name of every cult member in Aloria."

"It just proves something I've always said," Silk noted as he continued to read. "A man should never put anything down in writing."

"Have either of you any idea where I can find Belgarath?"

"You might try the kitchens at the back of the house," Silk replied. "He said something about being hungry. I think Beldin went with him."

The kitchen in Harakan's house had escaped the general ransacking by Yarblek's men, who appeared to be more interested in loot than food, and the two old sorcerers sat comfortably at a table near a low, arched window picking at the remains of a roasted chicken. "Ah, Garion, my boy," Belgarath said expansively. "Come in and join us."

"Do you suppose there's anything to drink around here?" Beldin asked, wiping his fingers on the front of his tunic.

"There should be," Belgarath replied. "It's a kitchen, after all. Why don't you look in that pantry?"

Beldin rose and crossed the kitchen floor toward the pantry.

Garion bent slightly to look out the low window at the houses burning one street over. "It's starting to snow again," he observed.

Belgarath grunted. "I think we'll want to get out of here as quickly as we can," he said. "I don't really want to spend the winter here."

"Ah, ha!" Beldin said from the pantry. He emerged with a triumphant grin carrying a small wooden cask.

"You'd better taste it first," Belgarath told him. "It might be vinegar."

Beldin set the cask on the floor and bashed in its top with his fist. Then he licked his fingers and smacked his lips. "No," he said, "it's definitely not vinegar." He rummaged through a nearby cupboard and produced three earthenware cups.

"Well, brother," Belgarath said, "what are your plans?"

Beldin dipped into the cask with one of the cups. "I think I'll see if I can track down Harakan. I'd like to finish him off before I go back to Mallorea. He's not the kind you want lurking in alleys behind you as you go by."

"You're going to Mallorea, then?" Belgarath tore a wing off the chicken lying on the table.

"That's possibly the only place where we can get any solid information about this Zandramas." Beldin belched.

"Javelin says that he thinks it's a Darshivan name," Garion told him.

Beldin grunted. "That could help a little. This time I'll start there. I couldn't get anything at all at Mal Zeth, and those half-wits in Karanda fell over in a dead faint every time I mentioned the name."

"Did you try Mal Yaska?" Belgarath asked him.

"Hardly. Urvon's got my description posted on every wall in that place. For some reason, he's afraid that someday I might show up and yank out several yards of his guts."

"I wonder why."

"I told him so, that's why."

"You'll be in Darshiva, then?"

"For the time being—at least, I will after I've got Harakan safely under the ground. If I find out anything about Zandramas, I'll get word to you."

"Keep your eyes open for clear copies of the Mallorean Gospels and the Ashabine Oracles, too," Belgarath told him. "According to the Codex, I'm supposed to find clues in them."

"And what are you going to do?"

"I think we'll go on down to Nyissa and see if the Orb can pick up the trail of my great-grandson."

"The fact that some Rivan shepherd saw a Nyissan ship is a pretty slender lead, Belgarath."

"I know, but at the moment it's the only one we've got."

Garion absently pulled a few fragments off the picked-over chicken and put them in his mouth. He suddenly realized that he was ravenously hungry.

"Are you going to take Polgara with you?" Beldin asked.

"I don't think so. Garion and I are likely to be out of touch, and we'll need somebody here in the north to keep an eye on things. The Alorns are feeling muscular at the moment and they're going to need a firm hand to keep them out of mischief."

"That's a normal condition for Alorns. You realize that Polgara's not going to be happy when you tell her she has to stay behind, don't you?"

"I know," Belgarath replied with a gloomy look. "Maybe I'll just leave her a note. That worked pretty well last time."

"Just try to make sure she's not in the vicinity of anything breakable when she gets the note." Beldin laughed. "Like large cities and mountain ranges. I heard what happened when she got the last note you left."

The door opened, and Barak stuck his head into the kitchen. "Oh," he said. "There you are. There are a couple of people out here who want to see you. Mandorallen found them on the outskirts of town—a very strange pair."

"How do you mean strange?" Garion asked.

"The man's as big as a house. He's got arms like tree trunks, but he can't talk. The girl's pretty enough, but she's blind."

Belgarath and Beldin exchanged a quick look. "How do you know she's blind?" Belgarath asked.

"She's got a cloth tied across her eyes." Barak shrugged. "I just assumed that was what it meant."

"I guess we'd better go talk to her," Beldin said, rising from his seat. "A seeress wouldn't be in this part of the world unless it was pretty important."

"A seeress?" Garion asked.

"One of those people from Kell," Belgarath explained. "They're always blindfolded, and their guides are always mutes. Let's go see what she has to say."

When they entered the large main room, they found the others curiously eyeing the two strangers. The blindfolded seeress was a slight girl in a white robe. She had dark blond hair, and a serene smile touched her lips. She stood quietly in the center of the room, patiently waiting. Beside her stood one of the largest men Garion had ever seen. He wore a kind of sleeveless kirtle of coarse, undyed cloth belted at the waist, and he carried no weapon except for a stout, polished staff. He towered above even Hettar, and his bare arms were awesomely muscled. In a curious way, he seemed almost to hover over his slender mistress, his eyes watchful and protective.

"Has she said who she is?" Belgarath quietly asked Polgara as they joined the others.

"No," she replied. "All that she says is that she has to speak with you and Garion."

"Her name is Cyradis," Errand said from nearby.

"Do you know her?" Garion asked him.

"We met once—in the Vale. She wanted to find out something about me, so she came there, and we talked."

"What did she want to find out?"

"She didn't say."

"Didn't you ask her?"

"I think that if she'd wanted me to know, she'd have told me."

"I would speak with thee, Ancient Belgarath," the seeress said then in a light, clear voice, "and with thee, also, Belgarion."

They drew closer.

"I am permitted a short time here to tell thee certain truths. First, know that your tasks are not yet completed. Necessity doth command yet one more meeting between the Child of Light and the Child of Dark; and mark me well—this meeting shall be the last, for it is during this meeting that the final choice between the Light and the Dark shall be made."

"And where will this meeting take place, Cyradis?" Belgarath asked her, his face intent.

"In the presence of the Sardion—in the place which is no more."

"And where is that?"

"The path to that dread place lies in the mysteries, Ancient One. Thou must seek it there." She turned her face toward Garion, half-reaching out to him with one slender hand. "Thy heart is sore, Belgarion," she said with a great sympathy in her voice, "for Zandramas, the Child of Dark, hath reft away thy son and even now doth flee with him toward the Sardion. It lies upon thee to bar the path of Zandramas to that stone—for the stars and the voices of the earth proclaim that the power of the Dark doth reside in the Sardion, even as the power of the Light doth reside in the Orb of Aldur. Should Zandramas reach the Dark Stone with the babe, the Dark shall triumph, and its triumph shall be eternal."

"Is my baby all right?" Ce'Nedra demanded, her face pale and a dreadful fear in her eyes.

"Thy child is safe and well, Ce'Nedra," Cyradis told her. "Zandramas will protect him from all harm—not out of love, but out of Necessity." The seeress' face grew still. "Thou must steel thy heart, however," she continued, "for should there be no other way to prevent Zandramas from reaching the Sardion with thine infant son, it falls to thee—or to thy husband—to slay the child."

"Slay?" Ce'Nedra exclaimed, "Never!"

"Then the Dark shall prevail," Cyradis said simply. She turned back to Garion. "My time grows short," she said to him. "Heed what I say. Thy choice of companions to aid thee in this task of thine must be guided by Necessity and not thine own preference. Shouldst thou choose awry, then shalt thou fail thy task, and Zandramas will defeat thee. Thy son shall be lost to thee forever, and the world as thou knowest it shall be no more."

Garion's face was bleak. "Go ahead," he told her shortly. "Say the rest of what you have to say." Her suggestion that either he or Ce'Nedra could ever under any circumstances kill their own child had filled him with a sudden anger.

"Thou wilt leave this place in the company of Ancient Belgarath and his most revered daughter. Thou must also take with thee the Bearer of the Orb and thy wife."

"Absurd!" he burst out. "I'm not going to expose Ce'Nedra—or Errand—to that kind of danger."

"Then thou wilt surely fail."

He looked at her helplessly.

"Thou must have with thee as well the Guide and the Man with Two Lives—and one other whom I will reveal to thee. Thou wilt be joined at some later times by others—the Huntress, the Man Who Is No Man, the Empty One, and by the Woman Who Watches."

"That's fairly typical seer gibberish," Beldin muttered sourly.

"The words are not mine, gentle Beldin," she told him. "These are the names as they are written in the stars—and in the prophecies. The incidental and worldly names which were given them at the time of their births are of no moment in the timeless realm of the two Necessities which contend with each other at the center of all that is or ever will be. Each of these companions hath a certain task, and all tasks must be completed 'ere the meeting which is to come, else the Prophecy which hath guided thy steps since time began will fail."

"And what is my task, Cyradis?" Polgara asked her coolly.

"It is as it hath ever been, Holy Polgara. Thou must guide, and nurture, and protect, for thou art the mother—even as Ancient Belgarath is the father." The faintest of smiles touched the blindfolded girl's lips. "Others will aid thee in thy quest from time to time, Belgarion," she continued, "but those I have named must be with thee at that final meeting."

"What about us?" Barak demanded, "Hettar and Mandorallen and Lelldorin and me?"

"The tasks of each of you are complete, most Dreadful Bear, and the responsibility for them hath descended to your sons. Shouldst thou or the Bowman or the Horse Lord or the Knight Protector seek to join with Belgarion in this quest, thy presence will cause him to fail."

"Ridiculous!" the big man sputtered. "I'm certainly not staying behind."

"That choice is not thine to make." She turned back to Garion, laying her hand on the massive arm of her mute protector. "This is Toth," she said, slumping as if a great weariness were about to overcome her. "He hath guided my faltering steps since the day that other sight came upon me and I bound up mine eyes that I might better see. Though it doth rend my soul, he and I must now part for a little while. I have instructed him to aid thee in thy search. In the stars, he is called the Silent Man, and it is his destiny to be one of thy companions." She began to tremble as if in exhaustion. "One last word for thee, Belgarion," she said in a quavering voice. "Thy quest will be fraught with great peril, and one of thy companions shall lose his life in the course of it. Prepare thine heart therefore, for when this mischance occurs, thou must not falter, but must press on to the completion of the task which hath been laid upon thee."

"Who?" he said quickly. "Which one of them is going to die?"

"That hath not been revealed to me," she said. And then with an obvious effort, she straightened. "Remember me," she said, "for we shall meet anon." With that she vanished.

"Where did she go?" General Brendig exclaimed.

"She was never really here," Errand replied.

"It was a projection, Brendig," Belgarath said. "But the man—Toth—is solid. Now how did they work that? Do you know, Errand?"

Errand shrugged. "I can't tell, Belgarath. But it took the combined power of all the Seers at Kell."

"What absolute nonsense!" Barak burst out angrily, pounding one huge fist on the table. "Nothing in this world could make me stay behind!" Mandorallen, Hettar, and Lelldorin vehemently nodded their agreement.

Garion looked at Polgara. "Could she possibly have been lying?" he asked.

"Cyradis? No. A seeress isn't capable of lying. She may have concealed a few things, but she could never have lied. What she told us was what she saw in the stars."

"How can she see the stars with that blindfold over her eyes?" Lelldorin objected.

Polgara spread her hands. "I don't know. The seers perceive things in ways we don't entirely understand."

"Maybe she read them wrong," Hettar suggested.

"The Seers at Kell are usually right," Beldin growled, "so I wouldn't necessarily want to bet my life on that."

"That brings us right to the point," Garion said. "I'm going to have to go alone."

"*Alone?*" Ce'Nedra gasped.

"You heard what she said. Somebody who goes with me is going to get killed."

"That hath ever been a possibility, Garion," Mandorallen said soberly.

"But never a certainty."

"I won't let you go by yourself," Barak declared.

Garion felt a peculiar wrench, almost as if he had been rudely pushed aside. He was powerless as a voice which was not his came from his lips. "Will you people stop all this babbling?" it demanded. "You've been given your instructions. Now follow them."

They all stared at Garion in amazement. He spread his hands helplessly, trying to let them know that he had no control over the words coming from his mouth.

Belgarath blinked. "This must be important, if it can make *you* take a hand directly," he said to the awareness that had suddenly usurped Garion's voice.

"You don't have time to sit around debating the issue, Belgarath. You have a very long way to go and only so much time."

"Then what Cyradis said was true?" Polgara asked.

"As far as it went. She's still not taking sides, though."

"Then why did she come at all?" Beldin asked.

"She has her own task, and this was part of that. She must also give instructions to Zandramas."

"I don't suppose you could give us a hint or two about this place we're supposed to find?" Belgarath asked hopefully.

"Belgarath, don't do that. You know better. You have to stop at Prolgu on your way south."

"Prolgu?"

"Something that has to occur is going to happen there. Time is running out on you, Belgarath, so stop wasting it."

"You keep talking about time. Could you be a bit more specific?"

"He's gone, Grandfather," Garion said, regaining control of his voice.

"He always does that," Belgarath complained. "Just when the conversation gets interesting, he leaves."

"You know why he does it, Belgarath," Beldin said.

Belgarath sighed. "Yes, I suppose I do." He turned to the others. "That's it, then," he said. "I guess we do exactly what Cyradis told us to do."

"You're surely not going to take Ce'Nedra with you," Porenn objected.

"Of course I'm going, Porenn," Ce'Nedra declared with a little toss of her head. "I'd have gone anyway—no matter what that blind girl said."

"But she said that one of Garion's companions would die."

"I'm not his companion, Porenn. I'm his wife."

There were actual tears in Barak's eyes. "Isn't there anything I can say to persuade you to change your mind?" he pleaded.

Garion felt the tears also welling up in his own eyes. Barak had always been one of the solid rocks in his life, and the thought of beginning this search without the big red-bearded man at his side left a great emptiness inside him. "I'm afraid we don't have any choice, Barak," he said very sadly. "If it were up to me—" He left it hanging, unable to go on.

"This hath rent mine heart, dearest Ce'Nedra," Mandorallen said, kneeling before the queen. "I am thy true knight, thy champion and protector, and yet I am forbidden to accompany thee on thy perilous quest."

Great, glistening tears suddenly streamed down Ce'Nedra's cheeks. She put her arms about the great knight's neck. "Dear, dear Mandorallen," she said brokenly, kissing his cheek.

"I've got some people working on a few things in Mallorea," Silk said to Yarblek. "I'll give you a letter to them so that they can keep you advised. Don't make any hasty decisions, but don't pass up any opportunities, either."

"I know how to run the business, Silk," Yarblek retorted. "At least as well as you do."

"Of course you do, but you get excited. All I'm saying is that you should try to keep your head." The little man looked down rather sadly at his velvet doublet and all the jewels he was wearing. He sighed. "Oh, well, I've lived without all this before, I suppose." He turned to Durnik. "I guess we should start packing," he said.

Garion looked at him in perplexity.

"Weren't you listening, Garion?" the little man asked him. "Cyradis told you whom you were supposed to take along. Durnik's the Man with Two Lives, Errand is the Bearer of the Orb, and in case you've forgotten, I'm the Guide."

Garion's eyes widened.

"Naturally I'm going with you," Silk said with an impudent grin. "You'd probably get lost if I weren't along to show you the way."

KING OF
THE MURGOS

For Den, for reasons he will understand—
—and for our dear Janie,
just for being the way she is.

At this time I would like to express my indebtedness to my wife, Leigh Eddings, for her support, her contributions, and her wholehearted collaboration in this ongoing story. Without her help, none of this would have been possible.

I would also like to take this opportunity to thank my editor, Lester del Rey, for his patience and forbearance, as well as for contributions too numerous to mention.

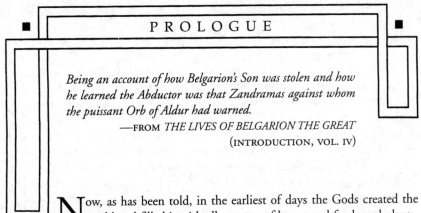

PROLOGUE

Being an account of how Belgarion's Son was stolen and how he learned the Abductor was that Zandramas against whom the puissant Orb of Aldur had warned.
—FROM *THE LIVES OF BELGARION THE GREAT*
(INTRODUCTION, VOL. IV)

Now, as has been told, in the earliest of days the Gods created the world and filled it with all manner of beasts and fowls and plants. Men also they created, and each God chose from among the races of men those whom they would guide and over whom they would rule. The God Aldur, however, took none, choosing to live apart in his tower and study the creation which they had made.

But a time came when a hungry child arrived at Aldur's tower, and Aldur took the child in and taught him the Will and the Word, by which all power may be used, in the manner that men call sorcery. And when the boy showed promise, Aldur named him Belgarath and made him a disciple. Then in time others came, and Aldur taught them and made them also his disciples. Among these was a malformed child whom Aldur named Beldin.

There came a day when Aldur took up a stone and shaped it and he called it his Orb, for the stone had fallen from beyond the stars and was a seat of great power, a center for one of the two Destinies which had been in conflict for control of all creation since the beginning of days.

But the God Torak coveted the stone and stole it, for the Dark Destiny had claimed his soul for its agent. Then the men of Aloria, known as Alorns, met with Belgarath, who led Cherek Bear-shoulders and his three sons into the far East where Torak had built Cthol Mishrak, the City of Eternal Night. By stealth, they stole back the Orb and returned with it.

With the counsel of the Gods, Belgarath divided Aloria into the kingdoms of Cherek, Drasnia, Algaria, and Riva, naming each for one who had accompanied him. And to Riva Iron-grip, who was to rule over the Isle of the Winds, he gave the keeping of the Orb, which Riva placed on the pommel of the great sword that he hung upon the wall of the Hall of the Rivan King, behind his throne.

Then Belgarath sought his home, but found tragedy awaiting him. His beloved wife Poledra had passed from the world of the living in giving birth to twin girls. In time, he sent Beldaran, the fairer of these, to be a wife to Riva Iron-grip to found the line of Rivan kings. His other daughter, Polgara, he kept with him, since her dark hair bore a single lock of white, the mark of a sorceress.

Guarded by the power of the Orb, all went well with the West for thousands of years. Then, on an evil day, King Gorek of Riva and his sons and sons' sons were slain by foul treachery. One child escaped, however, to be henceforth guarded in secret by Belgarath and Polgara. On the Isle, the Rivan Warder, Brand, sorrowfully took over the authority of his slain lord, and his sons continued to guard Aldur's Orb and all were known as Brand.

But there came a time when Zedar the Apostate found a child of such innocence that he could touch the Orb without being destroyed by its fire. Thus Zedar stole the Orb and fled with it toward the place where his dread Master, Torak, lay hidden.

When Belgarath learned of this, he went up to the quiet farm in Sendaria where Polgara was rearing a boy named Garion, who was the last descendant of the Rivan line. Taking the boy with them, they set out after the Orb. After many perilous adventures, they found the child, whom they named Errand. And, with Errand bearing the Orb, they returned to set the Orb back upon the sword.

Then Garion, now named Belgarion for the powers of sorcery he had shown, learned of the Prophecy, which revealed that the time was at hand when he, as the Child of Light, must confront the evil God Torak, to kill or to be killed. Fearfully, he departed eastward for the City of Endless Night to meet his fate. But with the aid of the great sword that bore the Orb of Aldur, he prevailed and slew the God.

Thus Belgarion, descendant of Riva Iron-grip, was crowned King of Riva and Overlord of the West. He took to wife the Tolnedran Princess Ce'Nedra, while Polgara took the faithful smith Durnik as her husband, since the Gods had raised him from the dead and had given him the power of sorcery to be her equal. With Belgarath, she and Durnik left for the Vale of Aldur in Algaria, where they planned to rear the strange, gentle child Errand.

The years passed as Belgarion learned to be a husband to his young bride and began mastering his powers of sorcery and the power of his throne. There was peace in the West, but trouble stirred in the South, where Kal Zakath, Emperor of Mallorea, waged war upon the King of the Murgos. And Belgarath, returning from a trip to Mallorea, reported dark rumors of a stone known as the Sardion. But what it might be, other than an object of fear, he could not say.

Then on a night when young Errand was visiting in the Citadel at Riva, he and Belgarion were awakened by the voice of the Prophecy within their minds and directed to the throne room. And there the blue Orb on the pommel of the sword turned angry red of a sudden and it spoke, saying, *"Beware Zandramas!"* But none could learn who or what Zandramas was.

Now, after years of waiting, Ce'Nedra found herself with child. But the fanatic followers of the Bear-cult were active again, crying that no Tolnedran should be Queen and that she must be set aside for one of the true blood of the Alorns.

When the Queen was great with child, she was set upon by an assassin in her bath and almost drowned. The assassin fled to the tower of the Citadel and from there threw herself to her death. But Prince Kheldar, the Drasnian adventurer who was also known as Silk, saw from her garments that she might be a follower of the cult. Belgarion was wroth, but he did not yet move to war.

Time passed, and Queen Ce'Nedra was delivered of a healthy male heir to the Throne of Riva. And great was the rejoicing from all the lands of the Alorns and beyond, and notables assembled at Riva to rejoice and celebrate this happy birth.

When all had departed and peace again descended upon the Citadel, Belgarion resumed his studies of the ancient Prophecy which men called the Mrin Codex. A strange blot had long troubled him, but now he found that he could read it in the light cast by the Orb. Thus he learned that the Dark Prophecy and his obligations as the Child of Light had not ended with the slaying of Torak. The Child of Dark was now Zandramas, whom he must meet in time to come "in the place which is no more."

His soul was heavy within him as he journeyed hastily to confer with his grandfather Belgarath in the Vale of Aldur. But even as he was speaking with the old man, new words of ill were brought him by messenger. Assassins had penetrated the Citadel at night, and the faithful Rivan Warder, Brand, had been killed.

With Belgarath and his Aunt Polgara, Belgarion sped to Riva, where one assassin weakly clung to life. Prince Kheldar arrived and was able to identify the comatose assassin as a member of the Bear-cult. New evidence revealed that the cult was massing an army at Rheon in Drasnia and was building a fleet at Jarviksholm on the coast of Cherek.

Now King Belgarion declared war upon the Bear-cult. Upon the advice of the other Alorn monarchs, he moved first against the shipyards at Jarviksholm to prevent the threat of a hostile fleet in the Sea of the Winds. His attack was quick and savage. Jarviksholm was razed to the ground, and the half-built fleet was burned before a single keel touched water.

But victory turned to ashes when a message from Riva reached him. His infant son had been abducted.

Belgarion, Belgarath, and Polgara turned themselves into birds by sorcery and flew back to Riva in a single day. The city of Riva had already been searched house by house. But with the aid of the Orb, Belgarion was able to follow the trail of the abductors to the west coast of the Isle. There they came upon a band of Cherek cultists and fell upon them. One survived, and Polgara forced him to speak. He declared that the child had been stolen on the orders of Ulfgar, leader of the Bear-cult, whose headquarters were at Rheon in eastern Drasnia. Before Polgara could wrest further information from him, however, the cultist leaped from the top of the cliff upon which they stood and dashed himself to death on the rocks below.

Now the war turned to Rheon. Belgarion found his troops badly outnumbered and an ambush awaiting his advance toward the city. He was facing defeat when Prince Kheldar arrived with a force of Nadrak mercenaries to turn the tide of battle. Reinforced by the Nadraks, the Rivans besieged the city of Rheon.

Belgarion and Durnik combined their wills to weaken the walls of the city until the siege engines of Baron Mandorallen could bring them down. The Rivans and Nadraks poured into the city, led by Belgarion. The battle inside was savage, but the cultists were driven back and most of them were slaughtered. Then Belgarion and Durnik captured the cult leader, Ulfgar.

Though Belgarion had already learned that his son was not within the city, he hoped that close questioning might drag the child's whereabouts from Ulfgar. The cult leader stubbornly refused to answer; then, surprisingly, Errand drew the information directly from Ulfgar's mind.

While it became clear that Ulfgar had been responsible for the attempt on

Ce'Nedra's life, he had played no part in the theft of the child. Indeed, his chief goal had been the death of Belgarion's son, preferably before its birth. He obviously knew nothing of the abduction, which did not at all suit his purpose.

Then the sorcerer Beldin joined them. He quickly recognized Ulfgar as Harakan, an underling of Torak's last living disciple Urvon. Harakan suddenly vanished, and Beldin sped in pursuit.

Messengers now arrived from Riva. Investigations following Belgarion's departure had discovered a shepherd in the hills who had seen a figure carrying what might have been a baby embark upon a ship of Nyissan design and sail southward.

Then Cyradis, a Seeress of Kell, sent a projection of herself to tell them more. The child, she claimed, had been taken by Zandramas, who had spun such a web of deceit to throw the blame upon Harakan that even the cult members who had been left behind to be discovered had believed what Polgara had extracted from the captive on the cliff of the Isle of the Winds.

Clearly, she said, the Child of Dark had stolen the baby for a purpose. That purpose was connected with the Sardion. Now they must pursue Zandramas. Beyond that she would not speak, except to identify those who must go with Belgarion. Then, leaving her huge, mute guide Toth behind to accompany them, she vanished.

Belgarion's heart sank within him as he realized that his son's abductor was now months ahead and that the trail had grown extremely dim. But he grimly gathered his companions to pursue Zandramas, even to the edge of the world or beyond, if need be.

PART ONE

THE SERPENT
QUEEN

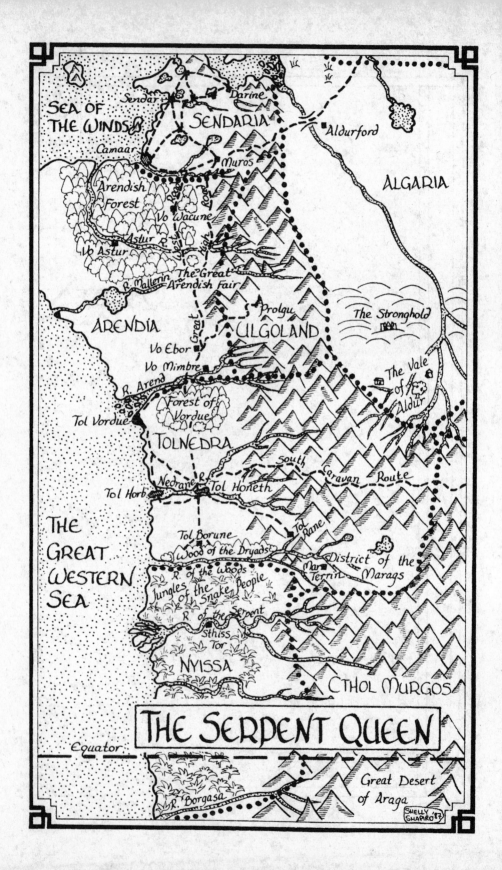

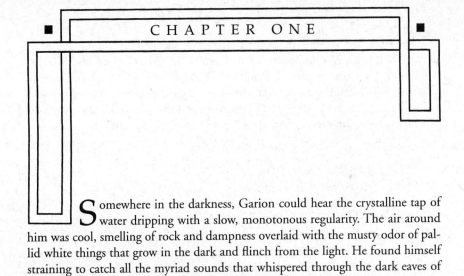

S omewhere in the darkness, Garion could hear the crystalline tap of water dripping with a slow, monotonous regularity. The air around him was cool, smelling of rock and dampness overlaid with the musty odor of pallid white things that grow in the dark and flinch from the light. He found himself straining to catch all the myriad sounds that whispered through the dark eaves of Ulgo—the moist trickle of water, the dusty slither of dislodged pebbles slowly running down a shallow incline, and the mournful sighing of air coming down from the surface through minute fissures in the rock.

Belgarath stopped and lifted the smoky torch that filled the passageway with flickering orange light and leaping shadows. "Wait here a moment," he said, and then he moved off down the murky gallery with his scuffed, mismatched boots shuffling along the uneven floor. The rest of them waited with the darkness pressing in all around them.

"I hate this," Silk muttered, half to himself. "I absolutely hate it."

They waited.

The ruddy flicker of Belgarath's torch reappeared at the far end of the gallery. "All right," he called. "It's this way."

Garion put his arm about Ce'Nedra's slender shoulders. A kind of deep silence had fallen over her during their ride south from Rheon as it had grown increasingly evident that their entire campaign against the Bear-cult in eastern Drasnia had done little more than give Zandramas a nearly insurmountable lead with the abducted Geran. The frustration that made Garion want to beat his fists against the rocks around him and howl in impotent fury had plunged Ce'Nedra into a profound depression instead, and now she stumbled through the dark caves of Ulgo, sunk in a kind of numb misery, neither knowing nor caring where the others led her. He turned his head to look back at Polgara, his face mirroring all his deep concern. The look she returned him was grave, but seemingly unperturbed. She parted the front of her blue cloak and moved her hands in the minute gestures of the Drasnian secret language. —*Be sure she stays warm*—she said. —*She's very susceptible to chills just now.*—

A half-dozen desperate questions sprang into Garion's mind; but with Ce'Nedra at his side with his arm about her shoulders, there was no way he could voice them.

—*It's important for you to stay calm, Garion*—Polgara's fingers told him. —*Don't let her know how concerned you are. I'm watching her, and I'll know what to do when the time comes.*—

Belgarath stopped again and stood tugging at one earlobe, looking dubiously down a dark passageway and then down another which branched off to the left.

"You're lost again, aren't you?" Silk accused him. The rat-faced little Drasnian had put aside his pearl-gray doublet and his jewels and gold chains and now wore an old brown tunic, shiny with age, a moth-eaten fur cloak, and a shapeless, battered hat, once again submerging himself in one of his innumerable disguises.

"Of course I'm not lost," Belgarath retorted. "I just haven't pinpointed exactly where we are at the moment."

"Belgarath, that's what the word *lost* means."

"Nonsense. I think we go this way." He pointed down the left-hand passageway.

"You *think*?"

"Uh—Silk," Durnik the smith cautioned quietly, "you really ought to keep your voice down. That ceiling up there doesn't look all that stable to me, and sometimes a loud noise is all it takes to bring one of them down."

Silk froze, his eyes rolling apprehensively upward and sweat visibly standing out on his forehead. "Polgara," he whispered in a strangled tone, "make him stop that."

"Leave him alone, Durnik," she said calmly. "You know how he feels about caves."

"I just thought he ought to know, Pol," the smith explained. "Things *do* happen in caves."

"Polgara!" Silk's voice was agonized. *"Please!"*

"I'll go back and see how Errand and Toth are doing with the horses," Durnik said. He looked at the sweating little Drasnian. "Just try not to shout," he advised.

As they rounded a corner in the twisting gallery, the passageway opened out into a large cavern with a broad vein of quartz running across its ceiling. At some point, perhaps even miles away, the vein reached the surface, and refracted sunlight, shattered into its component elements by the facets of the quartz, spilled down into the cavern in dancing rainbows that flared and faded as they shifted across the sparkling surface of the small, shallow lake in the center of the cave. At the far end of the lake, a tiny waterfall tinkled endlessly from rock to rock to fill the cavern with its music.

"Ce'Nedra, look!" Garion urged.

"What?" She raised her head. "Oh, yes," she said indifferently, "very pretty." And she went back to her abstracted silence.

Garion gave Aunt Pol a helpless look.

"Father," Polgara said then, "I think it's just about lunch time. This seems like a good place to rest a bit and have a bite to eat."

"Pol, we're never going to get there if we stop every mile or two."

"Why do you always argue with me, father? Is it out of some obscure principle?"

He glowered at her for a moment, then turned away, muttering to himself.

Errand and Toth led the horses down to the shore of the crystal lake to water them. They were a strangely mismatched pair. Errand was a slight young man with blond, curly hair and he wore a simple brown peasant smock. Toth towered above him like a giant tree looming over a sapling. Although winter was coming on in the Kingdoms of the West, the huge mute still wore only sandals, a short kirtle belted at the waist, and an unbleached wool blanket drawn over one shoulder. His bare arms and legs were like tree trunks, and his muscles knotted and rippled whenever he moved. His nondescript brown hair was drawn straight back and tied at the nape of his neck with a short length of leather thong. Blind Cyradis had told them that this silent giant was to aid them in the search for Zandramas and Garion's stolen son, but so far Toth seemed content merely to follow them impassively, giving no hint that he even cared where they were going.

"Would you like to help me, Ce'Nedra?" Polgara asked pleasantly, unbuckling the straps on one of the packs.

Ce'Nedra, numb-faced and inattentive, walked slowly across the smooth stone floor of the cavern to stand mutely beside the pack horse.

"We'll need bread," Polgara said, rummaging through the pack as if unaware of the young woman's obvious abstraction. She took out several long, dark brown loaves of peasant bread and piled them like sticks of firewood in the little queen's arms. "And cheese, of course," she added, lifting out a wax-covered ball of Sendarian cheddar. She pursed her lips. "And perhaps a bit of the ham as well, wouldn't you say?"

"I suppose so," Ce'Nedra replied in an expressionless tone.

"Garion," Polgara went on, "would you lay this cloth on that flat rock over there?" She looked back at Ce'Nedra. "I hate to eat off an uncovered table, don't you?"

"Umm," Ce'Nedra replied.

The two of them carried the loaves of bread, the wax-coated cheese, and the ham to the improvised table. Polgara snapped her fingers and shook her head. "I forgot the knife. Would you get it for me?"

Ce'Nedra nodded and started back toward the pack horse.

"What's wrong with her, Aunt Pol?" Garion asked in a tense whisper.

"It's a form of melancholia, dear."

"Is it dangerous?"

"It is if it goes on for too long."

"Can you do anything? I mean, could you give her some kind of medicine or something?"

"I'd rather not do that unless I have to, Garion. Sometimes the medicines just mask the symptoms, and other problems start to crop up. Most of the time, it's best to let these things run their natural course."

"Aunt Pol, I can't stand to see her like this."

"You're going to have to endure it for a while, Garion. Just behave as if you weren't aware of the way she's acting. She's not quite ready to come out of it yet." She turned with a warm smile. "Ah, there it is," she said, taking the knife from Ce'Nedra. "Thank you, dear."

They all gathered around Polgara's makeshift table for their simple lunch. As he ate, Durnik the smith gazed thoughtfully at the small crystal lake. "I wonder if there could be any fish in there," he mused.

"No, dear," Polgara said.

"It *is* possible, Pol. If the lake's fed by streams from the surface, the fish could have been washed down here when they were minnows, and—"

"No, Durnik."

He sighed.

After lunch, they re-entered the endless, twisting galleries, once again following Belgarath's flickering torch. The hours limped by as they trudged mile after mile with the darkness pressing palpably in around them.

"How much farther do we have to go, Grandfather?" Garion asked, falling in beside the old man.

"It's hard to say exactly. Distances can be deceptive here in the caves."

"Have you got any idea at all about why we had to come here? I mean, is there anything in the Mrin Codex—or maybe the Darine—that talks about something that's supposed to happen here in Ulgo?"

"Not that I remember, no."

"You don't suppose we might have misunderstood, do you?"

"Our friend was pretty specific, Garion. He said that we have to stop at Prolgu on our way south, because something that has to happen is going to happen here."

"Can't it happen without us?" Garion demanded. "We're just floundering around here in these caves, and all the while Zandramas is getting farther and farther ahead of us with my son."

"What's that?" Errand asked suddenly from somewhere behind them. "I thought I heard something."

They stopped to listen. The guttering sound of Belgarath's torch suddenly sounded very loud as Garion strained his ears, trying to reach out into the darkness to capture any wayward sound. The slow drip of water echoed its soft tapping from somewhere in the dark, and the faint sigh of air coming down through the cracks and crevices in the rock provided a mournful accompaniment. Then, very faintly, Garion heard the sound of singing, of choral voices raised in the peculiarly discordant but deeply reverent hymn to UL that had echoed and re-echoed through these dim caverns for over five millennia.

"Ah, the Ulgos," Belgarath said with satisfaction. "We're almost to Prolgu. Now maybe we'll find out what it is that's supposed to happen here."

They went perhaps another mile along the passageway which rather suddenly became steeper, taking them deeper and deeper into the earth.

"*Yakk!*" a voice from somewhere ahead barked sharply. "*Tacha velk?*"

"*Belgarath, Iyun hak,*" the old sorcerer replied calmly in response to the challenge.

"*Belgarath?*" The voice sounded startled. "*Zajek kallig, Belgarath?*"

"*Marekeg Gorim, Iyun zajek.*"

"*Veed mo. Mar ishum Ulgo.*"

Belgarath extinguished his torch as the Ulgo sentry approached with a phosphorescently glowing wooden bowl held aloft.

"*Yad ho, Belgarath. Groja UL.*"

"*Yad ho,*" the old man answered the ritual greeting. "*Groja UL.*"

The short, broad-shouldered Ulgo bowed briefly, then turned and led them on down the gloomy passageway. The greenish, unwavering glow from the wooden bowl he carried spread its eerie light in the dim gallery, painting all their faces with a ghostly pallor. After another mile or so, the gallery opened out into one of those vast caverns where the pale glow of that strange, cold light the Ulgos contrived winked at them from a hundred openings high up in the stone wall. They carefully moved along a narrow ledge to the foot of a stone stairway that had been chipped from the rock wall of the cave. Their guide spoke briefly to Belgarath.

"We'll have to leave the horses here," the old man said.

"I can stay with them," Durnik offered.

"No. The Ulgos will tend to them. Let's go up." And he started up the steep flight of stairs.

They climbed in silence, the sound of their footsteps echoing back hollowly from the far side of the cavern.

"Please don't lean out over the edge like that, Errand," Polgara said when they were about halfway up.

"I just wanted to see how far down it goes," he replied. "Did you know that there's water down there?"

"That's one of the reasons I'd rather you stayed away from the edge."

He flashed her a sudden smile and went on up.

At the top of the stairs, they skirted the edge of the dim subterranean abyss for several hundred yards, then entered one of the galleries where the Ulgos lived and worked in small cubicles carved from the rock. Beyond that gallery lay the Gorim's half-lit cavern with its lake and its island and the peculiarly pyramid-shaped house surrounded by solemn white pillars. At the far end of the marble causeway which crossed the lake, the Gorim of Ulgo, dressed as always in his white robe, stood peering across the water. "Belgarath?" he called in a quavering voice, "is that you?"

"Yes, it's me, Holy One," the old man replied. "You might have guessed that I'd turn up again."

"Welcome, old friend."

Belgarath started toward the causeway, but Ce'Nedra darted past him with her coppery curls flying and ran toward the Gorim with her arms outstretched.

"Ce'Nedra?" he said, blinking as she threw her arms about his neck.

"Oh, Holy Gorim," she sobbed, burying her face in his shoulder, "someone's taken my baby."

"They've done what?" he exclaimed.

Garion had started almost involuntarily to cross the causeway to Ce'Nedra's side, but Polgara put her hand on his arm to stop him. "Not just yet, dear," she murmured.

"But—"

"This may be what she needs, Garion."

"But, Aunt Pol, she's crying."

"Yes, dear. That's what I've been waiting for. We have to let her grief run its course before she can begin to come out of it."

The Gorim held the sobbing little queen in his arms, murmuring to her in a soft, comforting tone. After the first storm of her weeping had subsided, he raised his lined old face. "When did all this happen?" he asked.

"Late last summer," Belgarath told him. "It's a fairly involved story."

"Come inside then, all of you," the Gorim said. "My servants will prepare food and drink for you, and we can talk while you eat."

They filed into the pyramid-shaped house standing on the Gorim's island and entered the large central room with its stone benches and table, its glowing crystal lamps hanging on chains from the ceiling, and its peculiar, inward-sloping walls. The Gorim spoke briefly with one of his silent servants, then turned with his arm still about Ce'Nedra's shoulders. "Sit, my friends," he said to them.

As they sat at the stone table, one of the Gorim's servants entered, carrying a tray of polished crystal goblets and a couple of flagons of the fiery Ulgo drink.

"Now," the saintly old man said, "what has happened?"

Belgarath filled himself one of the goblets and then quickly sketched in the events of the past several months, telling the Gorim of the murder of Brand, of the attempt to sow dissention in the Alorn ranks, and of the campaign against the cult stronghold at Jarviksholm.

"And then," he went on as the Gorim's servants brought in trays of raw fruits and vegetables and a smoking roast hot from the spit, "right about at the same time we captured Jarviksholm, someone crept into the nursery in the Citadel at Riva and took Prince Geran out of his cradle. When we got back to the Isle, we discovered that the Orb will follow the baby's trail—as long as it stays on dry land, anyway. It led us to the west side of the island, and we encountered some Cherek Bear-cultists the abductor had left behind. When we questioned them, they told us that the new cult leader, Ulfgar, had ordered the abduction."

"But what they told you was not true?" the Gorim asked shrewdly.

"Not by half," Silk replied.

"Of course the problem there was that they didn't *know* they were lying," Belgarath continued. "They'd been very carefully prepared, and the story we got from them sounded quite plausible—particularly in view of the fact that we were already at war with the cult. Anyway, we mounted a campaign against the last cult stronghold at Rheon in northeastern Drasnia. After we took the town and captured Ulfgar, the truth started to come out. Ulfgar turned out to be a Mallorean Grolim named Harakan and he had absolutely nothing to do with the abduction. The real culprit was this mysterious Zandramas I told you about several years ago. I'm not sure exactly what part the Sardion plays in all this; but for some reason, Zandramas wants to take the baby to the place mentioned in the Mrin Codex—the place which is no more. Urvon desperately wants to prevent that, so he sent his henchman here to the west to kill the baby to keep it from happening."

"Have you any idea at all about where to begin the search?" the Gorim asked.

Belgarath shrugged. "A couple of clues is all. We're fairly sure that Zandramas left the Isle of the Winds aboard a Nyissan ship, so that's where we're going to start. The Codex says that I'm supposed to find the path to the Sardion in the mysteries, and I'm fairly certain that when we find the Sardion, Zandramas and the baby won't be far away. Maybe I can get some hints in those prophecies—if I can ever find any uncorrupted copies."

"It also appears that the Seers of Kell are directly involving themselves," Polgara added.

"The seers?" The Gorim's voice was startled. "They've never done that before."

"I know," she replied. "One of them—a girl named Cyradis—appeared at Rheon and gave us some additional information, and certain instructions."

"That is very unlike them."

"I think that things are moving toward the ultimate climax, Holy One," Belgarath said. "We were all concentrating so much on the meeting between Garion and Torak that we lost sight of the fact that the *real* meetings are the ones between the Child of Light and the Child of Dark. Cyradis told us that this is going to be the last meeting, and that *this* time, everything's going to be decided once and for all. I rather suspect that's the reason that the seers are finally coming out into the open."

The Gorim frowned. "I would not have ever thought to see them concern themselves with the affairs of other men," he said gravely.

"Just who *are* these seers, Holy Gorim?" Ce'Nedra asked in a subdued voice.

"They are our cousins, child," he replied simply.

Her look betrayed her bafflement.

"After the Gods made the races of man, there came the time of the choosing," he explained. "There were seven races of man—even as there are seven Gods. Aldur chose to go his way alone, however, and that meant that one of the races of man remained unchosen and Godless."

"Yes," she nodded, "I've heard that part of the story."

"We were all of the same people," the Gorim continued. "Us, the Morindim, the Karands in the north of Mallorea, the Melcenes far to the east, and the Dals. We were closest to the Dals, but when we went forth in search of the God UL, they had already turned their eyes to the skies in their attempt to read the stars. We urged them to come with us, but they would not."

"And you've lost all contact with them, then?" she asked.

"On occasion, some few of their seers have come to us, usually on some quest of which they would not speak. The seers are very wise, for the Vision which comes to them gives them knowledge of the past, the present, and the future—and more importantly, the meaning of it."

"Are they all women, then?"

"No. There are men as well. When the sight comes to them, they always bind their eyes to exclude all common light so that this other light can be seen more clearly. Inevitably, when a seer appears, there also appears a mute to be guide and protector. They are always paired—forever."

"Why are the Grolims so afraid of them?" Silk asked suddenly. "I've been in Mallorea a few times and I've seen Mallorean Grolims go all to pieces at just the mention of Kell."

"I suspect that the Dals have taken steps to keep the Grolims away from Kell. It's the very center of their learning, and Grolims are intolerant of non-Angarak things."

"What is the purpose of these seers, Holy One?" Garion asked.

"It's not only the seers, Belgarion," the Gorim replied. "The Dals are involved in all branches of arcane knowledge—necromancy, wizardry, magic, witchcraft—all of these and more. No one—except the Dals themselves—seems to know exactly what their purpose might be. Whatever it is, though, they are entirely committed to it—both the ones in Mallorea and those here in the west."

"In the west?" Silk blinked. "I didn't know that there were any Dals here."

The Gorim nodded. "They were divided by the Sea of the East when Torak used the Orb to crack the world. The western Dals were enslaved by the Murgos during the third millennium. But wherever they live—east or west—they have labored for eons at some task. Whatever that task may be, they are convinced that the fate of all creation depends on it."

"Does it?" Garion asked.

"We don't know, Belgarion. We don't know what the task is, so we can't even guess at its significance. We *do* know that they follow neither of the Prophecies which dominate the universe. They believe that their task was laid upon them by some higher destiny."

"And *that's* the thing that concerns me," Belgarath said. "Cyradis is manipulating us with these cryptic little announcements of hers; and for all I know, she's manipulating Zandramas as well. I don't like being led around by the nose—particularly by someone whose motives I don't understand. She complicates this whole business, and I don't like complications. I like nice, simple situations and nice, easy solutions."

"Good and Evil?" Durnik suggested.

"That's a difficult one, Durnik. I prefer 'them and us.' That clears away all the excess baggage and allows you to get right down to cases."

Garion slept restlessly that night and he rose early with his head feeling as if it were stuffed with sand. He sat for a time on one of the stone benches in the central room of the Gorim's house; then, caught in a kind of moody restlessness, he went outside to look across the quiet lake surrounding the island. The faint light from the globes hanging on their chains from the ceiling of the cavern cast a dim glow on the surface of the lake, and that glow filled the cave with a pale luminosity that seemed more like a light seen in a dream than any kind of illumination to be found in the real world. As he stood lost in thought at the water's edge, a movement on the far shore caught his eye.

They came singly and in groups of two and three, pale young women with the large, dark eyes and colorless hair of the Ulgos. They all wore modest white gowns, and they gathered shyly on the shore on the far side of the marble causeway, waiting in the dim light. Garion looked across the lake at them, then raised his voice to call, "Was there something you wanted?"

They whispered together for a moment, then pushed one of their number forward to speak for them. "We—we wanted to see the Princess Ce'Nedra," she blurted bashfully, her face dyed with a rosy blush. "If she's not too busy, that is." Her speech was halting, as if she were talking in a language not wholly familiar to her.

"I'll go see if she's awake," Garion offered.

"Thank you, sir," she replied, shrinking back into the protection of her group of friends.

Garion went back inside and found Ce'Nedra sitting up in bed. Her face had none of that numb indifference that had marked it for the past several weeks, and her eyes seemed alert. "You're up early," she noted.

"I had a little trouble sleeping. Are you all right?"

"I'm fine, Garion. Why do you ask?"

"I was just—" He broke off with a shrug. "There are some young Ulgo women outside. They want to see you."

She frowned. "Who could they possibly be?"

"They seemed to know you. They said that they wanted to see the Princess Ce'Nedra."

"Of course!" she exclaimed, springing from her bed. "I'd almost forgotten them." She quickly pulled on a teal-green dressing gown and dashed from the room.

Curiously, Garion started to follow her, but stopped in the central hall of the house when he saw Polgara, Durnik, and the Gorim sitting quietly at the stone table.

"What was that all about?" Polgara asked, looking after the scurrying little queen.

"There are some Ulgo women outside," Garion replied. "They seem to be friends of hers."

"She was very popular during her visit here," the Gorim said. "Ulgo girls are very shy, but Ce'Nedra befriended them all. They adored her."

"Excuse me, your Worship," Durnik said, "but is Relg anywhere about? I thought I might look in on him, as long as we're here."

"Relg and Taiba have taken their children and moved to Maragor," the Gorim replied.

"Maragor?" Garion blinked. "What about the ghosts there?"

"They are under the protection of the God Mara," the Gorim told him. "There seems to be some kind of understanding between Mara and UL. I'm not sure I entirely understand it, but Mara insists that Taiba's children are Marags and he has vowed to watch over them in Maragor."

Garion frowned. "But isn't their first-born son going to be Gorim someday?"

The old man nodded. "Yes. His eyes are still as blue as sapphires. I was concerned myself at first, Belgarion, but I'm certain that UL will return Relg's son to the caves of Ulgo at the proper time."

"How is Ce'Nedra this morning, Garion?" Polgara asked seriously.

"She seems to be almost back to normal. Does that mean that she's all right?"

"It's a good sign, dear, but it might be a little early to be sure. Why don't you go keep an eye on her?"

"All right."

"Just try not to be obvious. This is a rather critical time, and we don't want her getting the idea that we're spying on her."

"I'll be careful, Aunt Pol." He went outside and began walking around the small island as if he were only stretching his legs. He cast frequent glances at the group on the far shore. The pale, white-gowned Ulgo women were clustered about Ce'Nedra. Her green robe and her flaming red hair stood out in sharp contrast in the midst of the group. A sudden image came into Garion's mind. With her vibrant coloring, Ce'Nedra looked very much like a single crimson rose growing in the midst of a bed of white lilies.

After about a half an hour, Polgara came out of the house. "Garion," she said, "have you seen Errand this morning?"

"No, Aunt Pol."

"He's not in his room." She frowned slightly. "What *is* that boy thinking of? Go see if you can find him."

"Yes, ma'am," he replied automatically. As he started across the causeway, he smiled to himself. In spite of all that had happened, he and Aunt Pol always returned to the same relationship they had shared when he was a boy. He was fairly certain that most of the time she did not even remember that he was a king, and so she often sent him on menial errands with no real awareness that they might be beneath his dignity. Moreover, he found that he did not really mind. To fall back into the pattern of immediately obeying her peremptory commands relieved him of the necessity of making difficult decisions and took him back to those days when he was just a simple farm boy with none of the cares and responsibilities that had come to him with the crown of Riva.

Ce'Nedra and her friends were seated on rocks not far from the dim lake shore. Their conversation was subdued, and Ce'Nedra's face was somber again.

"Are you all right?" he asked her as he approached them.

"Yes," she replied. "We were just talking, that's all."

He looked at her, but decided not to say anything more. "Have you seen Errand?" he asked instead.

"No. Isn't he in the house?"

He shook his head. "I think he's gone exploring. Aunt Pol asked me to find him."

One of the young Ulgo women whispered something to Ce'Nedra.

"Saba says that she saw him in the main gallery when she was coming here," Ce'Nedra told him. "It was about an hour ago."

"Which way is that?" he asked.

"Over there." She pointed toward an opening leading back into the rock.

He nodded. "Are you warm enough?" he asked her.

"I'm fine, Garion."

"I'll be back in a bit," he said and walked toward the gallery she had pointed out. It made him uncomfortable to be forced to step around her this way, but the possibility that a chance remark might push her back into that bleak depression made him wary and half-afraid to speak at all. A purely physical ailment was one thing, but an illness of the mind was something horrifying.

The gallery he entered, like all the caves and passageways in which the Ulgos lived out their lives, was faintly illuminated by the dim glow of phosphorescent rocks. The cubicles on either side of the gallery were scrupulously neat, and he saw entire families gathered about stone tables for their morning meal, apparently oblivious to the fact that the fronts of their quarters were open to scrutiny by anyone who chanced to pass this way.

Since few of the Ulgos could speak his language, it was impossible for Garion to ask anyone if Errand had passed, and he soon found that he was wandering more or less aimlessly, hoping that he might chance across his friend. At the far end of the gallery, he emerged into the vast cavern where that flight of chiseled stairs led downward toward the dim reaches below.

He considered the possibility that Errand might have gone down to visit his horse, but something seemed to tell him that he should turn instead to follow the broad ledge circling the edge of the chasm. He had gone no more than a few hundred yards when he heard the sound of voices issuing from the mouth of a dark passageway angling back into the rock face. The shifting echoes made it impossible to distinguish individual words, but it seemed to Garion that one of the voices was Errand's. He entered the passageway, following the sound alone.

At first there was no light in the unused gallery, and he put his hand to the rough rock wall to grope his way along; but as he rounded a corner, he saw a light coming from somewhere ahead—a peculiar kind of steady white radiance quite unlike the faint greenish glow of phosphorescence that normally illuminated this dark world of the caves. And then the corridor he was following bent sharply to the left, and he rounded that corner to see Errand talking with a tall, white-robed figure. Garion's eyes widened. The light he had seen was emanating from that figure, and he felt the awesome presence of a transcendent being.

The glowing figure did not turn, but spoke in a calm, quiet voice. "Join us, Belgarion, and welcome."

Garion found that he was actually trembling as he wordlessly obeyed. Then the figure in white turned, and he found himself looking directly into the timeless face of UL himself.

"I have been instructing young Eriond here in the task which lies before him," the Father of the Gods said.

"Eriond?"

"It is his true name, Belgarion. It is time for him to put aside the childish name of his boyhood and to assume his true one. Even as thou wert concealed beneath thy simple 'Garion,' so hath he lain hidden under that 'Errand.' There is wisdom in this, for the true name of a man with a great task lying before him can ofttimes bring danger when its owner hath not yet come into his inheritance."

"It's a good name, don't you think, Belgarion?" Eriond said proudly.

"It's an excellent name, Eriond," Garion agreed.

The Orb, standing on the pommel of the great sword sheathed across Garion's back, glowed its blue response to the incandescently white radiance of UL, and the God nodded his acknowledgement of the stone.

"Tasks have been set for each of you," UL continued, "and for the companions who accompany you. All these tasks must be completed ere the meeting between the Child of Light and the Child of Dark may come again."

"Please, Holy UL," Garion said, "can you tell me—is my son all right?"

"He is well, Belgarion. The one who holds him will see to his needs. For the moment he is in no danger."

"Thank you," Garion said gratefully. Then he squared his shoulders. "And what is my task?" he asked.

"Thy task hath already been revealed to thee by the Seeress of Kell, Belgarion. Thou must bar the path of Zandramas to the Sardion; for should the Child of Dark reach that dread stone with thy son, the Dark shall prevail in this final meeting."

Garion steeled himself and then blurted his next question, afraid of what the answer might be. "In the Oracles of Ashaba it says that the Dark God will come again," he said. "Does that mean that Torak will be reborn and that I'm going to have to fight him again?"

"Nay, Belgarion. My son himself will not return. Thy flaming sword reft him of his life, and he is no more. The enemy in *this* meeting will be more perilous. The spirit which infused Torak hath found another vessel. Torak was maimed and imperfect by reason of his pride. The one who shall rise in his stead—shouldst thou fail in thy task—will be invincible; and not thy sword nor all the swords in all this world will be enough to withstand him."

"Then it's Zandramas that I have to fight," Garion said grimly. "I've got reason enough, that's certain."

"The meeting between the Child of Light and the Child of Dark shall not be a meeting between thee and Zandramas," UL told him.

"But the Codex says that Zandramas is the Child of Dark," Garion protested.

"At this present time, yes—even as at this present time thou art the Child of Light. That burden, however, shall pass from each of you ere the final meeting can take place. Know this, moreover. The event which began with the birth of thy son must be completed in a certain time. The tasks which lie before thee and thy companions are many, and all must be completed ere the time appointed for this meeting. Shouldst thou or any of thy companions fail in the completion of any task, then shall all our striving for uncounted ages come to naught. This final meeting between the Child of Light and the Child of Dark must be complete, and all of the necessary conditions must be met, for it is in *this* meeting that all that was divided shall be made one again. The fate of this world—and of all other worlds—lies in *thy* hands, Belgarion, and the outcome will not depend upon thy sword but upon a choice which thou must make."

The Father of the Gods looked at the two of them fondly. "Be not afraid, my sons," he told them, "for though you are different in many ways, you share the same spirit. Aid and sustain each other and be comforted in the knowledge that I am with you." Then the glowing figure shimmered and was gone, and the caves of Ulgo resounded with an echo like the aftersound of some unimaginably huge bell.

CHAPTER TWO

A kind of unthinking serenity had come over Garion, a calm resolve much akin to that which he had felt when he had faced Torak in the decaying ruins of the City of Endless Night half a world away. As he thought back on that dreadful night, he began to grope his way toward a startling truth. The maimed God had not been striving for a purely physical victory. He had been trying with all the dreadful force of his will to force them to submit to him, and it had been their steadfast refusal to yield, more than Garion's flaming sword, which had defeated him in the end. Slowly, almost like the onset of dawn, the truth came to Garion. Although evil might seem invincible as it stalked the world in darkness, it nonetheless yearned toward the light, and only in the surrender of the light could the darkness prevail. So long as the Child of Light remained firm and unyielding, he was still invincible. As he stood in the dark cave listening to the shimmering aftersound of UL's departure, Garion seemed to see directly into the mind of his enemy. Beneath it all, Torak had been afraid, and even now that same fear gnawed at the heart of Zandramas.

And then Garion perceived yet another truth, a truth at once enormously simple and at the same time so profound that the scope of it shook every fiber of his being. There was no such thing as darkness! What seemed so vast and overwhelming was nothing more than the absence of light. So long as the Child of Light kept that firmly in mind, the Child of Dark could never win. Torak had known this; Zandramas knew it; and now at last Garion himself understood it, and the knowledge brought with it a surging exultation.

"It gets easier once you understand, doesn't it?" the young man they had always called Errand asked quietly.

"You knew what I was thinking, didn't you?"

"Yes. Does that bother you?"

"No. I suppose not." Garion looked around. The gallery in which they stood suddenly seemed very dark now that UL was gone. Garion knew the way back, but the idea which he had just grasped seemed to require some kind of affirmation. He turned his head and spoke directly to the Orb riding on the pommel of his great sword. "Could you give us a bit of light?" he asked it.

The Orb responded by igniting into blue fire and at the same time filling Garion's mind with its crystal song. Garion looked at Eriond. "Shall we go back now? Aunt Pol was sort of worried when she couldn't find you."

As they turned and followed the deserted gallery back along the way they had come, Garion laid his arm affectionately across his young friend's shoulders. For some reason they seemed very close just now.

They emerged from the gallery at the brink of the dim abyss where pale lights dotted the sheer walls and the murmur of a waterfall far below came whispering up to them.

Garion suddenly remembered something that had happened the day before. "What is it about you and water that concerns Aunt Pol so much?" he asked curiously.

Eriond laughed. "Oh, that. When I was little—just after we moved into Poledra's cottage in the Vale—I used to fall into the river fairly often."

Garion grinned. "That seems like a perfectly natural thing to me."

"It hasn't happened for a long time now, but I think that Polgara feels that maybe I'm saving it up for a special occasion of some sort."

Garion laughed, and they entered the cubicle-lined corridor that led toward the Gorim's cavern. The Ulgos who lived and worked there threw startled glances in their direction as they passed.

"Uh—Belgarion," Eriond said, "the Orb is still glowing."

"Oh," Garion replied, "I'd forgotten about that." He looked back over his shoulder at the cheerfully burning stone. "It's all right now," he told it. "You can stop."

The Orb's final flicker seemed faintly disappointed.

The others were gathered at breakfast in the central room of the Gorim's house. Polgara looked up as the two of them entered. "Where have you—" she began, then stopped as she looked into Eriond's eyes more closely. "Something's happened, hasn't it?" she asked instead.

Eriond nodded. "Yes," he replied. "UL wanted to talk with us. There were some things we needed to know."

Belgarath pushed aside his plate, his face becoming intent.

"I think you'd better tell us about this," he said to them. "Take your time and don't skip over anything."

Garion crossed to the table and sat down beside Ce'Nedra. He described the meeting with the Father of the Gods carefully, trying as best he could to repeat UL's exact words.

"And then he said that Eriond and I shared the same spirit and that we were supposed to aid and sustain each other," he concluded.

"Was that all he said?" Belgarath asked.

"Pretty much, yes."

"Except that he told us he was with us," Eriond added.

"He didn't say anything more specific about this certain time when everything has to be completed?" the old man demanded with a slightly worried expression.

Garion shook his head. "No. I'm sorry, Grandfather. I'm afraid not."

Belgarath's expression suddenly became exasperated. "I *hate* working to a schedule I haven't seen," he muttered. "I can't tell if I'm ahead or behind."

Ce'Nedra had been clinging to Garion, her face filled with both concern and relief. "Are you really sure he said that our baby is all right?" she demanded.

"He said that he is well," Eriond assured her. "He told us that the one who holds him will see to his needs and that for the moment he's in no danger."

"For the moment?" Ce'Nedra exclaimed. "What's that supposed to mean?"

"He didn't get any more specific, Ce'Nedra," Garion said.

"Why didn't you ask UL where he is?"

"Because I'm sure he wouldn't have told me. Finding Geran and Zandramas is my job, and I don't think they're going to let me evade it by getting somebody else to do it for me."

"They? Who are they?"

"The Prophecies—both of them. They're playing a game, and we all have to follow the rules—even if we don't know what they are."

"That's nonsense."

"Go tell them. It wasn't my idea."

Aunt Pol was looking oddly at Eriond. "Have you known?" she asked him. "About your name, I mean?"

"I knew I had another name. When you called me Errand, it didn't seem quite right, for some reason. Do you mind very much, Polgara?"

She rose with a smile, came around the table, and embraced him warmly. "No, Eriond," she told him, "I don't mind at all."

"Just exactly what is the task UL set for you?" Belgarath asked.

"He said that I'd recognize it when I came to it."

"Is that all he said about it?"

"He said that it was very important and that it was going to change me."

Belgarath shook his head. "Why does everything always have to be in riddles?" he complained.

"It's another one of those rules Garion mentioned," Silk told him, refilling his goblet from one of the flagons. "Well, what next, old man?"

Belgarath thought about it, tugging at an earlobe and looking up at one of the faintly glowing lamps. "I think it's fairly safe to say that this meeting was the thing that was supposed to happen here at Prolgu," he said, "so I expect that it's time for us to move along. It might not hurt for us to get where we're going a little early, but I'm positive that it's going to be a disaster if we get there late." He rose from his seat and put his hand on the Gorim's frail shoulder. "I'll try to get word to you from time to time," he promised. "Could you ask some of your people to lead us through the caves to Arendia? I want to get out into the open as soon as possible."

"Of course, my old friend," the Gorim replied, "and may UL guide your steps."

"I hope *somebody* does," Silk murmured.

Belgarath gave him a hard look.

"It's all right, Belgarath," Silk said expansively. "The fact that you get lost all the time doesn't diminish our respect for you in the slightest. I'm sure it's just a bad habit you picked up somewhere—probably because your mind was on weightier matters."

Belgarath looked at Garion. "Did we really *have* to bring him along?"

"Yes, Grandfather, we really did."

It was shortly after sunrise two days later when they reached the irregularly shaped cave mouth that opened out into a birch forest. The white trees lifted their bare limbs toward an intensely blue sky, and fallen leaves covered the ground with a carpet of gold. The Ulgos who had guided them through the caves winced visibly and drew back from the sunlight. They murmured a few words to Belgarath, he thanked them, and then they retreated back into the protective darkness.

"You have absolutely no idea how much better I feel now," Silk said with relief as he emerged from the cave and looked around at the frosty morning sunlight. Here and there back among the trees were patches of frozen snow, crusty and sparkling in the slanting rays of the morning sun; somewhere off to the left, they could hear the rush and babble of a mountain brook tumbling over stones.

"Have you any notion of exactly where we are?" Durnik asked Belgarath as they rode out into the birch trees.

The old man squinted back over his shoulder, gauging the angle of the new-risen sun. "My guess is that we're in the foothills above central Arendia," he replied.

"South of the lower end of the Arendish forest?" Silk asked.

"That's hard to say for sure."

The little Drasnian looked around. "I'd better take a look," he said. He pointed at a hill rising out of the forest. "I might be able to see something from up there."

"And I think some breakfast might be in order," Polgara said. "Let's find a clear spot and build a fire."

"I won't be too long," Silk said, turning his horse and riding off through the white trunks of the birches.

The rest of them rode on down the slope, the hooves of their horses rustling the deep-piled carpet of golden leaves. Several hundred yards into the forest, they reached a clearing on the banks of the brook they had heard when they had emerged from the cave. Polgara drew in her horse. "This should do," she decided. "Garion, why don't you and Eriond gather some firewood? I think some bacon and toasted bread might be nice."

"Yes, Aunt Pol," he said automatically, swinging down from his saddle. Eriond joined him, and the two of them went back in among the white trees in search of fallen limbs.

"It's pleasant being back out in the sunlight again," Eriond said as he pulled a large branch out from under a fallen tree. "The caves are nice enough, I suppose, but I like to be able to look at the sky."

Garion felt very close to this open-faced young man. The experience they had shared in the cave had brought them even closer together and had focused an idea that had hovered on the edge of Garion's awareness for several years now. The fact that both he and Eriond had been raised by Aunt Pol and Durnik had made them in many respects very much like brothers. He considered that as he bundled several large limbs together with a length of rope. He realized at the same time that he knew very little about Eriond and what might have happened to him before they had found him at Rak Cthol. "Eriond," he said curiously, "can you remember anything at all about where you lived before Zedar found you?"

The young man looked up toward the sky, his eyes lost in thought. "It was in a city of some kind, I think," he replied. "I seem to remember streets—and shops."

"Do you remember your mother at all?"

"I don't think so. I don't remember living in any place for very long—or staying with the same people. It seems that I just used to go to a door, and people would take me inside and give me something to eat and a place to sleep."

Garion felt a sudden sharp pang of sympathy. Eriond was as much—or even more—an orphan as he was himself. "Do you remember the day when Zedar found you?" he asked.

Eriond nodded. "Yes," he replied, "quite clearly. It was cloudy, and there weren't any shadows, so I couldn't tell exactly what time of day it was. I met him in a very narrow street—an alley of some kind, I think. I remember that his eyes had a sort of injured look in them—as if something terrible had happened to him." He sighed. "Poor Zedar."

"Did he ever talk to you?"

"Not very often. About all he ever said was that he had an errand for me. He used to talk in his sleep once in a while, though. I remember that he used to say 'Master.' Sometimes when he said it, his voice would be full of love. Other times it was full of fear. It was almost as if he had two entirely different Masters."

"He did. At first he was one of the disciples of Aldur. Then later, his master was Torak."

"Why do you suppose he did that, Belgarion? Changed Masters, I mean?"

"I don't know, Eriond. I really don't know."

Durnik had built a small fire in the center of the clearing, and Polgara, humming softly to herself, was setting out her pots and pans beside it. As Garion and Eriond began breaking the branches they had gathered into manageable lengths, Silk rode back down the hill to rejoin them. "You can see quite a way from up there," he reported as he swung down from his saddle. "We're about ten leagues above the high road from Muros."

"Could you see the River Malerin?" Belgarath asked him.

Silk shook his head. "Not the river itself," he replied, "but there's a fairly good-sized valley off to the south. I'd imagine that it runs through there."

"I was fairly close then. How's the terrain look between here and the high road?"

"We've got some rough going ahead of us," Silk told him. "It's steep, and the woods look pretty dense."

"We'll have to make the best time we can. Once we get to the high road, we'll be all right."

Silk made a sour face. "There's another problem, though," he said. "There's a storm coming in from the west."

Durnik lifted his face to sniff at the frosty air and nodded. "Snow," he confirmed. "You can smell it coming."

Silk gave him a disgusted look. "You had to say it, didn't you, Durnik?" he said almost accusingly.

Durnik's look was slightly puzzled.

"Didn't you know that talking about unpleasant things makes them happen?"

"Silk, that's pure nonsense."

The little man sniffed. "I know—but it's true all the same."

The breakfast of bread, dried fruit, and bacon Aunt Pol prepared for them was simple, but there was more than enough to satisfy them all. When they had finished, they repacked, quenched their fire with water from the icy brook, and rode on down the steep slope, following the course of the tumbling stream through the white-trunked birch forest.

Durnik fell in beside the mute Toth as they rode. "Tell me, Toth," he said tentatively, eyeing the frothy white water pitching down over mossy green boulders, "have you ever done any fishing?"

The huge man smiled shyly.

"Well, I've got lines and hooks in one of the packs. Maybe if we get the chance . . ." Durnik left it hanging.

Toth's smile broadened into a grin.

Silk stood up in his stirrups and peered on ahead. "That storm isn't much more than a half-hour away," he told them.

Belgarath grunted. "I doubt that we'll make very good time once it hits," he replied.

"I *hate* snow." Silk shivered glumly.

"That's a peculiar trait in a Drasnian."

"Why do you think I left Drasnia in the first place?"

The heavy bank of cloud loomed in front of them as they continued on down the hill. The morning sunlight paled and then disappeared as the leading edge of the storm raced high overhead to blot out the crisp blue of the autumn sky. "Here it comes," Eriond said cheerfully as the first few flakes began to dance and swirl in the stiff breeze moving up the ridge toward them.

Silk gave the young man a sour look, crammed his battered hat down lower over his ears and pulled his shabby cloak tighter about him. He looked at Belgarath. "I don't suppose you'd consider doing something about this?" he asked pointedly.

"It wouldn't be a good idea."

"Sometimes you're a terrible disappointment to me, Belgarath," Silk said, drawing himself even more deeply into his cloak.

It began to snow harder, and the trees about them became hazy and indistinct in the shifting curtain of white that came seething up through the forest.

A mile or so farther down the hill they left the birch trees and entered a dark green forest of towering firs. The thick evergreens broke the force of the wind, and the snow sifted lazily down through the boughs, lightly dusting the needle-strewn floor of the forest. Belgarath shook the snow out of the folds of his cloak and looked around, choosing a route.

"Lost again?" Silk asked.

"No, not really." The old man looked back at Durnik. "How far down this hill do you think we're going to have to go to get below this?" he asked.

Durnik scratched at his chin. "It's sort of hard to say," he replied. He turned to the mute at his side. "What do you think, Toth?" he asked.

The giant lifted his head and sniffed at the air, then made a series of obscure gestures with one hand.

"You're probably right," Durnik agreed. He turned back to Belgarath. "If the slope stays this steep, we ought to be able to get below the snowline sometime this afternoon—if we keep moving."

"Well, I guess we'd better move along then," Belgarath said and led the way on down the hill at a jolting trot.

It continued to snow. The light dusting on the ground beneath the firs became a covering, and the dimness that had hovered among the dark tree trunks faded as the white snow brought its peculiar, sourceless light.

They stopped about noon and took a quick lunch of bread and cheese, then continued to descend through the forest toward Arendia. By midafternoon, as Durnik and Toth had predicted, the snow was mixed with a chill rain. Soon the few large, wet flakes were gone, and they rode through a steady drizzle that wreathed down among the trees.

Late in the afternoon the wind picked up, and the rain driven before it was cold and unpleasant. Durnik looked around. "I think that it's about time for us to find a place to stop for the night," he said. "We'll need shelter from this wind, and finding dry firewood might be a bit of a problem."

The huge Toth, whose feet very nearly dragged on the ground on either side of his horse, looked around and then pointed toward a dense thicket of sapling evergreens standing at the far edge of the broad clearing they had just entered. Once again he began to move his hands in those peculiar gestures. Durnik watched him intently for a few moments, then nodded, and the two of them rode on across to the thicket, dismounted, and went to work.

The campsite they constructed was well back among the slender tree trunks of the thicket where the force of the wind was broken and the dense branches shed the rain like a thatched roof. The two of them bent a half circle of the tall saplings over and tied their tips to the trunks of other trees to form a domelike framework of considerable size. Then they covered the frame with tent canvas and tied it in place securely. The resulting structure was a round-topped, open-fronted pavilion perhaps as big as a fair-sized room. At the front, they dug in a firepit and lined it with rocks.

The rain had soaked down the forest, and collecting dry firewood was difficult, but Garion drew upon the experience he had gained during the quest for the Orb to seek out those sheltered hollows under fallen trees, the spots on the leeward sides of large tree trunks and the brush-choked areas under overhanging rocks where dry twigs and branches could be found. By evening he and Eriond had piled up a considerable supply of wood not far from the fire pit where Polgara and Ce'Nedra were preparing supper.

There was a small spring several hundred yards on down the slope, and Garion slipped and slid downhill with two leather waterbags slung over his shoulders. The light was fading rapidly under the dark, windswept evergreens, and the ruddy glow of their campfire beckoned cheerfully as he started back up through the trees with the full waterbags hanging pendulously down against his thighs.

Polgara had hung her damp cloak on a tree limb and was humming softly to herself as she and Ce'Nedra worked over the fire.

"Why, thank you, your Majesty," Ce'Nedra said as Garion handed her the waterbags. Her little smile was somehow wistful, as if she were making a conscious effort to be lighthearted.

"It's my pleasure, your Majesty," he replied with a florid bow. "A good scullion can always find water when the cook's helper needs it."

She smiled briefly, kissed his cheek, and then sighed and went back to dicing vegetables for the stew Polgara was stirring.

After they had eaten, they all sat drowsily before the fire, listening to the sound of the wind in the treetops and the seething hiss of the rain in the forest about them.

"How far did we come today?" Ce'Nedra asked in a voice near sleep as she leaned wearily against Garion's shoulder.

"Seven or eight leagues, I'd guess," Durnik replied. "It's slow going when you don't have a road to follow."

"We'll make better time, once we hit the high road from Muros to the Great Fair," Silk added. His eyes brightened at that thought, and his long, pointed nose started to twitch.

"Never mind," Belgarath told him.

"We *will* need supplies, Belgarath," Silk said, his eyes still bright.

"I think we'll let Durnik take care of that. People who do business with you always seem to develop this sense of outrage once they've had time to think things through."

"But, Belgarath, I thought you said that you were in a hurry."

"I don't quite get the connection."

"People always travel faster when somebody's chasing them—or hadn't you noticed that?"

Belgarath gave him a long, hard look. "Just let it drop, Silk," he said. "Why don't we all get some sleep?" he suggested to the rest of them. "We've got a long day tomorrow."

It was well after midnight when Garion suddenly started into wakefulness. He lay rolled up in his blankets beside Ce'Nedra, listening to her regular breathing and the soft patter of the rain on the tree limbs. The wind had died, and the fire at the front of their snug shelter had burned down to a few ruddy coals. He shook the last remnants of sleep from his mind, trying to remember what it was that had awakened him.

"Don't make any noise," Belgarath said softly from the far side of the shelter.

"Did something wake you, too, Grandfather?"

"I want you to get out of your blankets very slowly," the old man said in a voice so quiet that it scarcely reached Garion's ears, "and get your hands on your sword."

"What is it, Grandfather?"

"Listen!" Belgarath said.

From high overhead in the rainy darkness there came the ponderous flap of vast wings and a sudden flare of sooty red light. The wings flapped again, and then the sound was gone.

"Move, Garion," Belgarath said urgently. "Get your sword—and put something over the Orb so that she can't see the glow from it."

Garion untangled his legs from his blankets and groped in the darkness for Iron-grip's sword.

Again there was the vast flapping sound overhead, and then a strange, hissing cry, accompanied by another flare of that sooty red light.

"What's that?" Ce'Nedra cried out.

"Be still, girl!" Belgarath snapped.

They lay tensely in the darkness as the flapping sound faded off into the rain-swept night.

"What's out there, Belgarath?" Silk asked tensely.

"She's a very large beast," the old man replied quietly. "Her eyes aren't very good, and she's as stupid as a stump, but she's very dangerous. She's hunting. Possibly she smells the horses—or us."

"How do you know it's a she?" Durnik asked.

"Because there's only one of them left in the world. She doesn't come out of her cave very often, but over the centuries enough people have caught glimpses of her to give rise to all those legends."

"I'm starting to get a very uneasy feeling about this," Silk murmured.

"She doesn't really look that much like the dragons in all those drawings," Belgarath continued, "but she *is* big, and she *does* fly."

"Oh, come now, Belgarath," Durnik scoffed. "There's no such thing as a dragon."

"I'm glad to hear it. Now, why don't you go out and explain that to her?"

"Is she the same creature we heard that night in the mountains above Maragor?" Garion asked.

"Yes. Have you got your sword?"

"Right here, Grandfather."

"Good. Now, very slowly, creep out and smother the last of those coals with dirt. Fire attracts her, so let's not take any chances on a sudden flare-up."

Garion inched his way out through the open front of the shelter and hurriedly scooped dirt over the fire pit with his hands.

"Is it really a flying lizard?" Silk whispered hoarsely.

"No," Belgarath replied, "actually she's a species of bird. She has a long, snake-like tail, and what she's covered with looks more like scales than feathers. She also has teeth—lots of very long, sharp teeth."

"Just exactly how big is she?" Durnik asked.

"You remember Faldor's barn?"

"Yes."

"About that big."

From quite some distance off there came another screeching bellow and the murky red flare.

"Her fire isn't really all that serious," Belgarath continued in the same low voice, "particularly since these woods are so wet. It's when she catches you in dry grass that it starts to be a problem. She's big, but she's not very brave—and on the ground she's as clumsy as a pig on a frozen pond. If it gets down to a fight, we probably won't be able to hurt her very much. About the best we can hope for is to frighten her off."

"Fight?" Silk choked. "You're not serious."

"We may not have any choice. If she's hungry and picks up our scent or the scent of the horses, she'll tear these woods apart looking for us. She has a few sensitive spots. Her tail is probably the best. Her wings get in the way, so she can't see behind her too well, and when she's on the ground, she can't turn very fast."

"Let's see if I've got this straight," Silk said. "You want us to sneak up behind this dragon and hit it on the tail, is that it?"

"Approximately, yes."

"Belgarath, have you lost your mind? Why not just use sorcery to drive it away?"

"Because she's immune to sorcery," Polgara explained calmly. "It was one of the little refinements Torak added when he and the other Gods created her species. He was so impressed with the concept of a dragon that he chose it as his totem creature. He tried in every way he could to make it invincible."

"It was one of his character defects," Belgarath added sourly. "All right, the dragon is clumsy and stupid and she's not used to pain. If we're careful, we can probably frighten her away without anyone getting hurt."

"She's coming back," Eriond said.

They listened as the flapping of those huge wings reverberated again through the sodden forest.

"Let's get out into the open," Belgarath said tensely.

"That's a good idea," Silk agreed. "If I have to do this, I want lots of level running room around me."

"Ce'Nedra," Polgara said, "I want you to get as far back into this thicket as you can. Find a place to hide."

"Yes, Lady Polgara," Ce'Nedra replied in a frightened little voice.

They crept out of the shelter into the darkness. The rain had slackened to a kind of misty drizzle wreathing down among the trees. Their horses, picketed not far away, snorted nervously, and Garion could smell the sharp odor of their fear over the resinous scent of wet evergreens.

"All right," Belgarath whispered. "Spread out—and be careful. Don't try to attack her unless you're sure that her attention is someplace else."

They crept out of the thicket into the broad clearing and started across. Garion, sword in hand, moved carefully, feeling for obstructions with his feet. When he reached the far side, he located a large tree trunk and went around behind it.

They waited tensely, straining their eyes toward the rain-swept night sky.

The heavy flapping of great wings reverberated down among the trees, and once again they heard that vast bellow. Even as the sound crashed down on them, Garion saw the huge billow of smoky flame in the sky overhead and, outlined by that flame, the shape of the dragon herself. She was even bigger than he had imagined. Her wings might easily have shaded an acre. Her cruel beak was agape, and he could clearly see her pointed teeth with the flames writhing about them. She had a very long, snakelike neck, huge talons, and a long, reptilian tail that lashed at the air behind her as she plunged down toward the clearing.

Then Eriond stepped out from behind a tree trunk and walked out into the center of the clearing as calmly as if he were merely taking a midmorning stroll.

"Eriond!" Polgara cried as, with a triumphant shriek, the dragon swooped down into the clearing. Talons extended, she struck at the unprotected young man. Her beak gaped, and vast billows of sooty orange flame poured forth to engulf him. With fear for the boy clutching at his heart, Garion ran forward with his sword aloft; but even as he ran at the huge beast, he felt the sudden familiar surge of Aunt Pol's will, and Eriond vanished as she translocated him to safety.

The earth shook as the dragon struck the ground, and her vast roar of frustration filled the clearing with the ruddy light of her fire. She was enormous. Her half-folded, scaly-looking wings reared above her higher than any house. Her lashing tail was thicker than the body of a horse, and her curved, tooth-studded beak was dreadful. A sickening stench filled the clearing each time she belched forth her billows of flame. By the light of her fire, Garion could clearly see her slitted yellow eyes. From what Belgarath had said, he expected a look of dull stupidity, but the burning eyes that searched the clearing were alert and filled with an intense, frightening eagerness.

Then Durnik and Toth were upon her. They dashed from the shelter of the trees, Durnik with his axe and Toth with the smith's sharp-bladed spade, and methodically they began to chop at the dragon's writhing tail. She shrieked, belching flame into the air, and began to claw at the sodden forest loam with her talons.

"Look out!" Silk shouted. "She's turning!"

The dragon whirled awkwardly, her wings beating at the air and her talons throwing up huge clots of earth, but Durnik and Toth had already run back into the shelter of the trees. As she swept the clearing with her burning eyes, Silk nimbly darted out behind her with his short, broad-bladed Drasnian sword in his hand. Again and again he drove it into the base of her huge tail. Then, as she floundered around to meet his attack, he danced clear to regain the safety of the surrounding forest.

And then Eriond stepped into the clearing again. Without any sign of fear but with a grave expression on his face, he walked out of the trees and moved directly toward the raging beast. "Why are you doing this?" he asked her calmly. "You know that this isn't the time or place."

The dragon almost seemed to flinch back at the sound of his voice, and her burning eyes grew wary.

"You can't avoid what's going to happen," he continued seriously. "None of us can—and you can't change it with this kind of foolishness. You'd better go. We really don't want to have to hurt you."

The dragon faltered, and Garion suddenly sensed that she was not only baffled, but that she was also afraid. Then she seemed to clench herself. With an enraged bellow, she sent out a vast sheet of flame from her gaping beak to engulf Eriond, who made no effort to escape.

Every nerve in Garion's body shrieked at him to run to his young friend's aid, but he found that he could not move so much as a muscle. He stood, sword in hand, locked in a kind of helpless stasis.

As the billow of flame subsided, Eriond emerged from it unscathed and with an expression of regretful firmness on his face. "I'd hoped that we wouldn't have to do this," he said to the dragon, "but you aren't giving us too much choice, you know." He sighed. "All right, Belgarion," he said, "make her go away—but please try not to hurt her too much."

With a kind of surging exultation, as if those words had somehow released him from all restraint, Garion ran directly up behind the dragon with his suddenly blazing sword and began to rain blows on her unprotected back and tail. The awful reek of burning flesh filled the clearing, and the dragon shrieked in pain. She flailed her huge tail in agony, and it was more to protect himself from that ponderous lashing than out of any conscious effort to injure the beast that Garion swung a massive blow with Iron-grip's sword. The sharp edge sheared effortlessly through scale and flesh and bone, smoothly lopping off about four feet of the writhing tip of the tail.

The shriek which thundered from the dragon's beak was shattering, and her fire boiled skyward in a huge cloud. A great jet of streaming blood spurted from the wound the sword had left, splashing into Garion's face and momentarily blinding him.

"Garion!" Polgara shouted. "Look out!"

He clawed at his eyes to clear away the hot blood. With terrifying agility, the dragon whirled, her talons tearing at the earth and her wings thundering. The Orb exploded into intense fire, and its blue flame ran anew up the sword, hissing and smoking as it burned away the thick blood which besmeared the blade. In the very act of striking at him with her beak, the dragon flinched back from the incandescence of the burning sword. Garion raised his blade, and once again the dragon flinched, retreating step by step across the wet clearing.

She was afraid! For some reason, the blue fire of the sword frightened her! Shrieking and trying desperately to defend herself with furnacelike gusts of fire, she backed away, her wounded tail still spraying the clearing with blood. There was clearly something about the fire of the Orb which she found unbearable. Once again filled with that wild surge of excitement, Garion raised his sword, and a searing pillar of fire erupted from its tip. He began to lash at the dragon with that whip of flame and heard the crackling sizzle as it seared her wings and shoulders. Fiercely he flogged her with the flame of his sword until, with a howl of agony, she turned and fled, tearing the earth with her talons and desperately flapping the huge sails of her wings.

Ponderously, she hurled herself into the air and clawed at the night with her wings, struggling to lift her vast bulk. She crashed through the upper branches of the firs at the edge of the clearing, fighting in panic to rise above the forest until she was clear. Shrieking, she flew off toward the southwest, filling the murky air with seething clouds of fire and streaming blood behind her as she went.

A stunned silence fell over them all as they looked up at the great beast fleeing through the rainy sky.

Polgara, her face dreadfully pale, came out from under the trees to confront Eriond. "Just exactly what were you thinking of?" she asked him in a terribly quiet voice.

"I don't quite follow you, Polgara," he replied, looking puzzled.

She controlled herself with an obvious effort. "Doesn't the word 'danger' have any meaning to you at all?"

"You mean the dragon? Oh, she wasn't really all that dangerous."

"She *did* sort of bury you up to the eyebrows in fire, Eriond," Silk pointed out.

"Oh, that," Eriond smiled. "But the fire wasn't real." He looked around at the rest of them. "Didn't you all know that?" he asked, looking slightly surprised. "It was only an illusion. That's all that evil ever really is—an illusion. I'm sorry if any of you were worried, but I didn't have time to explain."

Aunt Pol stared at the unperturbed young man for a moment, then turned her eyes on Garion, who stood still holding his burning sword. "And you—you—" Words somehow failed her. Slowly she sank her face into her trembling hands. "Two of them," she said in a terrible voice. "Two of them! I don't think I can stand this—not two of them."

Durnik looked at her gravely, then handed his axe to the giant Toth. He stepped over and put his arm about her shoulders. "There, there," he said. For a moment she seemed to resist, but then she suddenly buried her face in his shoulder. "Come along now, Pol," he said soothingly and gently turned her around to walk her back to their shelter. "Things won't seem nearly so bad in the morning."

CHAPTER THREE

Garion slept very little during the remainder of that rainy night. His pulse still raced with excitement, and he lay under his blankets beside Ce'Nedra, living and reliving his encounter with the dragon. It was only toward the tag end of the night that he became calm enough to consider an idea that had come

to him in the midst of the fight. He had *enjoyed* it. He had actually enjoyed a struggle that should have terrified him; the more he thought about it, the more he realized
that this was not the first time that this had happened. As far back as his early childhood, this same wild excitement had filled him each time he had been in danger.

The solid good sense of his Sendarian upbringing told him that this enthusiasm
for conflict and peril was probably an unhealthy outgrowth of his Alorn heritage and
that he should strive to keep it rigidly controlled, but deep inside he knew that he
would not. He had finally found the answer to the plaintive "Why me?" which he
had voiced so often in the past. He was inevitably chosen for these dreadful, frightening tasks because he was perfectly suited for them.

"It's what I do," he muttered to himself. "Any time there's something so ridicu-
lously dangerous that no rational human being would even consider trying it, they
send for me."

"What was that, Garion?" Ce'Nedra murmured drowsily.

"Nothing, dear," he replied. "I was just thinking out loud. Go back to sleep."

"Ummm," she murmured and snuggled closer to him, filling his nostrils with
the warm fragrance of her hair.

Dawn crept slowly under the overspreading limbs of the sodden forest with a
kind of growing paleness. The persistent drizzle joined with a morning mist rising
from the forest floor to form a kind of damp, gray cloud enveloping the dark trunks
of fir and spruce.

Garion awoke from a half doze and saw the shadowy forms of Durnik and Toth
standing quietly beside the cold fire pit at the front of the shelter. He slipped out
from under the blankets, moving carefully to avoid waking his sleeping wife, and
pulled on his clammy boots. Then he stood up, pulled on his cloak, and moved out
from under the tent canvas to join them.

He looked up toward the gloomy morning sky. "Still raining, I see," he noted
in that quiet tone people use when they rise before the sun.

Durnik nodded. "At this time of year it probably won't blow over for a week or
so." He opened the leather pouch at his hip and took out his wad of tinder. "I suppose we'd better get a fire going," he said.

Toth, huge and silent, went over to the side of their shelter, picked up two
leather water bags, and started down the steep slope toward the spring. Despite his
enormous size, he made almost no sound as he moved through the fog-shrouded
bushes.

Durnik knelt by the fire pit and carefully heaped dry twigs in the center. Then
he laid his ball of tinder beside the twigs and took out his flint and steel.

"Is Aunt Pol still asleep?" Garion asked him.

"Dozing. She says that it's very pleasant to lie in a warm bed while somebody
else builds up the fire." Durnik smiled gently.

Garion also smiled. "That's probably because for all those years she was usually
the first one up." He paused. "Is she still unhappy about last night?" he asked.

"Oh," Durnik said, bending over the pit and striking at his flint with his steel,
"I think she's regained her composure a bit." His flint and steel made a subdued
clicking sound; with each click a shower of bright, lingering sparks spilled down
into the pit. One of them fell glowing onto the tinder, and the smith gently blew on

it until a tiny tongue of orange flame rose from the center. Then he carefully moved the tinder under the twigs, and the flame grew and spread with a dry crackling. "There we are," he said, brushing the fire from the tinder and returning it to his pouch along with his flint and steel.

Garion knelt beside him and began snapping a dry branch into short lengths.

"You were very brave last night, Garion," Durnik said as the two of them fed the small fire.

"I think the word is insane," Garion replied wryly. "Would anybody in his right mind try to do something like that? I think the trouble is that I'm usually right in the middle of those things before I give any thought to how dangerous they are. Sometimes I wonder if Grandfather wasn't right. Maybe Aunt Pol *did* drop me on my head when I was a baby."

Durnik chuckled softly. "I sort of doubt it," he said. "She's very careful with children and other breakable things."

They added more branches to the fire until they had a cheerful blaze going, and then Garion stood up. The firelight reflected back from the fog with a soft, ruddy glow that had about it a kind of hazy unreality, as if, all unaware, they had inadvertently crossed the boundaries of the real world sometime during the night and entered the realms of magic and enchantment.

As Toth came back up from the spring with the two dripping waterbags, Polgara emerged from their shelter, brushing her long, dark hair. For some reason the single white lock above her left brow seemed almost incandescent this morning. "It's a very nice fire, dear," she said, kissing her husband. Then she looked at Garion. "Are you all right?" she asked him.

"What? Oh, yes. I'm fine."

"No cuts or bruises or singes you might have overlooked last night?"

"No. I seem to have gotten through it without a scratch." He hesitated. "Were you really upset last night, Aunt Pol—with Eriond and me, I mean?"

"Yes, Garion, I really was—but that was last night. What would you like for breakfast this morning?"

Some time later, as the pale dawn crept steadily under the trees, Silk stood shivering on one side of the fire pit with his hands stretched out to the flames and his eyes suspiciously fixed on the bubbling pot Aunt Pol had set on a flat rock at the very edge of the fire. "Gruel?" he asked. "Again?"

"Hot porridge," Aunt Pol corrected, stirring the contents of the pot with a long-handled wooden spoon.

"They're the same thing, Polgara."

"Not really. Gruel is thinner."

"Thick or thin, it's all the same."

She looked at him with one raised eyebrow. "Tell me, Prince Kheldar, why are you always so disagreeable in the morning?"

"Because I detest mornings. The only reason there's such a thing as morning in the first place is to keep night and afternoon from bumping into each other."

"Perhaps one of my tonics might sweeten your blood."

His eyes grew wary. "Ah—no. Thanks all the same, Polgara. Now that I'm all the way awake, I feel much better."

"I'm so glad for you. Now, do you suppose you could move away a bit? I'm going to need that side of the fire for the bacon."

"Anything you say." And he turned and went quickly back into the shelter.

Belgarath, who was lounging on top of his blankets, looked at the little man with an amused expression. "For a supposedly intelligent man, you *do* have a tendency to blunder from time to time, don't you?" he asked. "You should have learned by now not to bother Pol when she's cooking."

Silk grunted and picked up his moth-eaten fur cape. "I think I'll go check the horses," he said. "Do you want to come along?"

Belgarath cast an appraising eye at Polgara's dwindling supply of firewood. "That might not be a bad idea," he agreed, rising to his feet.

"I'll go with you," Garion said. "I've got a few kinks I'd like to work out. I think I slept on a stump last night." He slung the loop of his sword belt across one shoulder and followed the other two out of the shelter.

"It's sort of hard to believe that it really happened, isn't it?" Silk murmured when they reached the clearing. "The dragon, I mean. Now that it's daylight, everything looks so prosaic."

"Not quite," Garion said, pointing at the scaly chunk of the dragon's tail lying on the far edge of the clearing. The tip end of it was still twitching slightly.

Silk nodded. "That *is* the sort of thing you wouldn't ordinarily run across on a casual morning stroll." He looked at Belgarath. "Is she likely to bother us again?" he asked. "This is going to be a very nervous journey if we have to keep looking back over our shoulders every step of the way. Is she at all vindictive?"

"How do you mean?" the old man asked him.

"Well, Garion *did* kind of cut her tail off, after all. Do you think she might take it personally?"

"Not usually," Belgarath replied. "She doesn't really have that much in the way of a brain." He frowned thoughtfully. "What bothers me is that there was something about the whole encounter that was all wrong."

"Even the idea of it was wrong," Silk shuddered.

Belgarath shook his head. "That's not what I mean. I can't be sure if I imagined it or not, but she seemed to be looking specifically for one of us."

"Eriond?" Garion suggested.

"It sort of seemed that way, didn't it? But when she found him, she looked almost as if he frightened her. And what did he mean by those peculiar things he said to her?"

"Who knows?" Silk shrugged. "He's always been a strange boy. I don't think he lives in the same world with the rest of us."

"But why was the dragon so afraid of Garion's sword?"

"That sword frightens whole armies, Belgarath. The fire alone is pretty terrifying."

"She *likes* fire, Silk. I've seen her try to be coy and seductive for the benefit of a burning barn, and one time she flew around for a week making calves' eyes at a forest fire. There's something about last night that keeps nagging at me."

Eriond came out of the thicket where the horses were picketed, walking carefully around the dripping bushes.

"Are they all right?" Garion asked.

"The horses? They're fine, Belgarion. Is breakfast almost ready?"

"If that's what you want to call it," Silk replied sourly.

"Polgara's really a very good cook, Kheldar," Eriond assured him earnestly.

"Not even the best cook in the world can do very much with porridge."

Eriond's eyes brightened. "She's making porridge? I love porridge."

Silk gave him a long look, then turned sadly to Garion. "You see how easily the young are corrupted?" he observed. "Just give them the faintest hint of a wholesome upbringing, and they're lost forever." He squared his shoulders. "All right," he said grimly, "let's go get it over with."

After breakfast, they broke down their night's encampment and set out through the soft drizzle falling from the weeping sky. It was about noon when they reached a wide swath of cleared land, a stretch of bushy, stump-dotted ground perhaps a quarter of a mile wide, and in the center of that swath lay a wide, muddy road.

"The high road from Muros," Silk said with some satisfaction.

"Why did they cut down all the trees?" Eriond asked him.

"They used to have trouble with robbers lying in ambush right beside the road. The cleared space on each side gives travelers a sporting chance to get away."

They rode out from under the dripping trees and across the weed-grown clearing to the muddy road. "Now we should be able to make better time," Belgarath said, nudging his horse into a trot.

They followed the road south for several hours, moving at a steady canter. As they rode down out of the forested foothills, the trees gave way to rolling grasslands. They crested a hilltop and reined in to give their steaming mounts a brief rest. Somewhat to the northwest they saw the dark border of the great Arendish forest, hazy in the misty drizzle, and not far ahead the grim, gray-walled pile of Mimbrate castle brooding down on the grasslands lying below. Ce'Nedra sighed as she stared out over the sodden plain and at the fortress that seemed to hold in its very stones all the stiff-necked, wary suspicion that was at the core of Arendish society.

"Are you all right?" Garion asked her, fearful that her sigh might signify a return to that bleak melancholy which she had so recently shaken off.

"There's something so mournful about Arendia," she replied. "All those thousands of years of hatred and grief, and what did they prove? Even that castle seems to be weeping."

"That's just the rain, Ce'Nedra," he said carefully.

"No," she sighed again. "It's more than that."

The road from Muros was a muddy yellow scar, stretching between fields of browned, drooping grasses as it wound down to the Arendish plain, and for the next several days they rode past great, rearing Mimbrate castles and through dirty thatch-and-wattle villages where acrid wood smoke hung in the chill air like a miasma and the hopeless expressions on the faces of the ragged serfs bespoke lives lived out in misery and despair. They stopped each night in mean, shabby wayside inns reeking of spoiled food and unwashed bodies.

On the fourth day, they crested a hill and looked down at the garish sprawl of the Great Arendish Fair, standing at the junction of the high road from Muros and the Great West Road. The tents and pavilions spread for a league or more in every direction in a gaudy profusion of blue and red and yellow beneath a weeping gray sky, and pack-trains going to and from that great commercial center crawled across the plain like streams of ants.

Silk pushed his shabby hat back from his face. "Maybe I'd better go down and take a quick look around before we all ride in," he said. "We've been out of touch for a while, and it might not hurt to get the feel of things."

"All right," Belgarath agreed, "but no chicanery."

"Chicanery?"

"You know what I mean, Silk. Keep your instincts under control."

"Trust me, Belgarath."

"Not if I can help it."

Silk laughed and thumped his heels to his horse's flanks.

The rest of them rode at a walk down the long slope as Silk galloped on ahead toward that perpetually temporary tent-city standing in its sea of mud. As they approached the fair, Garion could hear a cacophonous tumult filling the air—a sort of bawling clamor of thousands of voices shouting all at once. There was also a myriad of scents—of spices and cooking food, of rare perfumes, and of horse corrals.

Belgarath drew in his mount. "Let's wait here for Silk," he said. "I don't want to blunder into anything."

They sat their horses to one side of the road in the chill rain, watching the slow crawl of pack trains slipping and sliding up the muddy road toward them.

About three-quarters of an hour later, Silk came pounding back up the hill. "I think we might want to approach carefully," he said, his pointed face serious.

"What's the matter?" Belgarath asked.

"I ran into Delvor," Silk replied, "and he told me that there's an Angarak merchant who's been asking questions about us."

"Maybe we should just bypass the fair, then," Durnik suggested.

Silk shook his head. "I think we ought to find out a little bit more about this curious Angarak. Delvor's offered to put us up in his tents for a day or so, but it might not be a bad idea if we circle the fair and come in from the south. We can join one of the caravans coming up from Tol Honeth. That way we won't be quite so obvious."

Belgarath considered it, squinting up at the rainy sky. "All right," he decided. "I don't want to waste too much time, but I don't like the idea of someone following us, either. Let's go see what Delvor can tell us."

They rode in a wide half circle through the rain-drenched grass and reached the muddy track of the Great West Road a mile or so south of the fair. A half-dozen Tolnedran merchants wrapped in rich fur cloaks rode at the head of a string of creaking wagons, and Garion and his friends unobtrusively fell in at the tail end of their column as the gradual darkening of the sky announced the approach of a dreary, rain-swept evening.

The narrow lanes lying between the tents and pavilions seethed with merchants from all parts of the world. The soupy mud was ankle-deep, churned by the hooves of hundreds of horses and the feet of brightly dressed men of trade, who bawled and shouted and haggled with each other, ignoring the mud and rain. Torches and lanterns hung at the sides of open-fronted booths made of canvas, where treasures of incalculable worth stood in curious proximity to brass pots and cheap tin plates.

"It's this way," Silk said, turning into a side lane. "Delvor's tents are a few hundred yards on up ahead."

"Who's Delvor?" Ce'Nedra asked Garion as they rode past a noisy tavern pavilion.

"A friend of Silk's. We met him the last time we were here. I think he's a member of Drasnian Intelligence."

She sniffed. "Aren't all Drasnians members of the intelligence service?"

He grinned. "Probably," he agreed.

Delvor was waiting for them in front of his blue and white striped pavilion. Silk's friend had changed very little in the years since Garion had last seen him. He was as bald as an egg, and his expression was still as shrewd and cynical as it had been before. He wore a fur-trimmed cloak pulled tightly about his shoulders, and his bald head gleamed wetly in the rain. "My servants will care for your horses," he told them as they dismounted. "Let's get in out of sight before too many people see you."

They followed him into his warm, well-lighted pavilion, and he carefully tied down the tent flap behind them. The pavilion was very nearly as comfortable-looking as a well-appointed house. There were chairs and divans and a large, polished table set with a splendid supper. The floors and walls were carpeted in blue, oil lamps hung on chains from the ceiling, and in each corner there was an iron brazier filled with glowing coals. Delvor's servants all wore sober livery and they wordlessly took the dripping cloaks from Garion and his friends and carried them through a canvas partition to an adjoining tent.

"Please," Delvor said politely, "seat yourselves. I took the liberty of having a bit of supper prepared."

Silk looked around as they all sat down at the table. "Opulent," he noted.

Delvor shrugged. "A little planning—and quite a bit of money. A tent doesn't *have* to be uncomfortable."

"And it's portable," Silk added. "If one has to leave someplace in a hurry, a tent can be folded up and taken along. That's hard to do with a house."

"There's that, too," Delvor admitted blandly. "Please eat, my friends. I know the kind of accommodations—and meals—that are offered in the inns here in Arendia."

The supper that had been set for them was as fine as one that might have come to the table of a nobleman. A heap of smoking chops lay on a silver platter, and there were boiled onions and peas and carrots swimming in a delicate cheese sauce. The bread was of the finest white, still steaming hot from the oven, and there was a wide selection of excellent wines.

"Your cook appears to be a man of some talent, Delvor," Polgara noted.

"Thank you, my Lady," he replied. "He costs me a few dozen extra crowns a year and he's got a foul temper, but I think he's worth the expense and aggravation."

"What's this about a curious Angarak merchant?" Belgarath asked, helping himself to a couple of the chops.

"He rode into the fair a few days ago with a half-dozen servants, but no pack horses or wagons. Their horses looked hard-ridden, as if he and his men had come here in a hurry. Since he arrived, he hasn't done any business at all. He and his people have spent all their time asking questions."

"Are they specifically asking for us?"

"Not by name, Ancient One, but the way they've been describing you didn't leave much doubt. He's been offering money for information—quite a bit of money."

"What kind of Angarak is he?"

"He claims to be a Nadrak, but if he's a Nadrak, I'm a Thull. I think he's a Mallorean. He's about medium height and build, clean-shaven and soberly dressed. About the only thing unusual about him is his eyes. They seem to be completely white—except for the pupils. There's no color to them at all."

Aunt Pol raised her head quickly. "Blind?" she asked.

"Blind? No, I don't think so. He seems to be able to see where he's going. Why do you ask, my Lady?"

"What you just described is the result of a very rare condition," she replied. "Most of the people who suffer from it are blind."

"If we're going to ride out of here without having him about ten minutes behind us, we're going to need some kind of distraction to delay him," Silk said, toying with a crystal goblet. He looked at his friend. "I don't suppose you still have any of those lead coins you hid in that Murgo tent the last time we were here, do you?"

"I'm afraid not, Silk. I had to go through customs at the Tolnedran border a few months ago. I didn't think it would be wise to have the customs people find that kind of thing in my packs, so I buried them under a tree."

"Lead coins?" Ce'Nedra said with a puzzled look. "What could you possibly buy with coins made of lead?"

"They're gilded, your Majesty," Delvor told her. "They look exactly like Tolnedran gold crowns."

Ce'Nedra's face suddenly went pale. "That's horrible!" she gasped.

Delvor's face mirrored his puzzlement at the vehemence of her reaction.

"Her Majesty is a Tolnedran, Delvor," Silk reminded him, "and counterfeit money strikes at the very core of a Tolnedran's being. I think it has something to do with their religion."

"I don't find that particularly amusing, Prince Kheldar," Ce'Nedra said tartly.

After supper they talked for a while longer, the comfortable talk of people who are warm and well fed, and then Delvor led them into an adjoining tent that had been partitioned off into sleeping chambers. Garion fell asleep almost as soon as his head touched the pillow and he awoke the following morning feeling more refreshed than he had in weeks. He dressed quietly to avoid waking Ce'Nedra and went out into the main pavilion.

Silk and Delvor sat at the table talking quietly. "There's a great deal of ferment going on here in Arendia," Delvor was saying. "The news of the campaign against the Bear-cult in the Alorn kingdoms has stirred the blood of all the young hotheads—both Mimbrate and Asturian. The thought of a fight someplace that they weren't invited to attend fills young Arends with anguish."

"There's nothing new about that," Silk said. "Good morning, Garion."

"Gentlemen," Garion said politely, pulling up a chair.

"Your Majesty," Delvor greeted him. Then he turned back to Silk. "The thing that concerns everybody more than the casual belligerence of the young nobles, though, is the unrest that's arisen among the serfs."

Garion remembered the miserable hovels in the villages they had passed in the last few days and the hopeless looks on the faces of their inhabitants. "They have reason enough for discontent, don't you think?" he said.

"I'd be the first to agree, your Majesty," Delvor said, "and it's not the first time it's happened. This time, though, it's a little more serious. The authorities have been finding caches of weapons—fairly sophisticated ones. A serf with a pitchfork isn't much of a match for an armored Mimbrate knight. A serf with a crossbow, however, is an altogether different matter. There have been several incidents—and some reprisals."

"How could serfs get those kinds of weapons?" Garion asked him. "Most of the time they don't even have enough to eat. How could they possibly afford to buy crossbows?"

"They're coming in from outside the country," Delvor told him. "We haven't been able to pinpoint the source yet, but it's fairly obvious that *somebody* wants to make sure that the Arendish nobility is too busy at home to get involved in anything anyplace else."

"Kal Zakath, perhaps?" Silk suggested.

"It's entirely possible," Delvor agreed. "There's no question that the Emperor of Mallorea has global ambitions, and turmoil in the Kingdoms of the West would be his best ally if he decides to turn his armies northward after he finally kills King Urgit."

Garion groaned. "That's all I need," he said, "one *more* thing to worry about."

When the others joined them in the main pavilion, Delvor's servants brought in a huge breakfast. There were whole platters of eggs, heaps of bacon and sausage, and plate after plate of fruit and rich pastries.

"Now *this* is what I call a breakfast," Silk said enthusiastically.

Polgara gave him a cool look. "Go ahead and say it, Prince Kheldar," she said. "I'm sure that you have all sorts of interesting observations to make."

"Would *I* say anything about that excellent gruel you offer us every morning, dear lady?" he asked with exaggerated innocence.

"Not if you're at all concerned about your health, you wouldn't," Ce'Nedra said sweetly.

One of the servants entered the tent with an offended expression on his face. "There's an obnoxious, filthy hunchback outside, Delvor," he reported. "He has the foulest mouth I've ever run across and he's demanding to be let in. Do you want us to chase him off?"

"Oh, that would be Uncle Beldin," Polgara said.

"You know him?" Delvor seemed surprised.

"I've known him since I was a baby," she replied. "He's not really as bad as he seems—once you get used to him." She frowned slightly. "You probably ought to let him come in," she advised. "He can be *terribly* unpleasant when people irritate him."

"Belgarath," Beldin growled, roughly pushing his way past the protesting servant, "is this all the farther you've come? I thought you'd be in Tol Honeth by now."

"We had to stop at Prolgu to see the Gorim," Belgarath replied mildly.

"This isn't a grand tour, you blockhead," Beldin snapped irritably. The little hunchback was as filthy as ever. The wet rags he wore for clothes were tied to his body here and there with lengths of rotten twine. His hair was matted and had twigs and bits of straw clinging to it. His hideous face was as black as a thundercloud as he stumped to the table on his short, gnarled legs and helped himself to a bit of sausage.

"Please try to be civil, uncle," Aunt Pol said.

"Why?" He pointed at a small pot standing on the table. "What's in that?"

"Jam," Delvor replied, looking slightly intimidated.

"Interesting," Beldin said. He dipped one dirty hand into the pot and began feeding gobs of jam into his mouth. "Not bad," he said, licking his fingers.

"There's bread right there, uncle," Aunt Pol said pointedly.

"I don't like bread," he grunted, wiping his hand on his clothes.

"Did you manage to catch up with Harakan?" Belgarath asked him.

Beldin retorted with a number of expletives that made Ce'Nedra's face blanch. "He gave me the slip again. I don't have the time to waste chasing him, so I'll have to forgo the pleasure of splitting him up the middle." He dipped his hand into the jam pot again.

"If we run across him, we'll take care of it for you," Silk offered.

"He's a sorcerer, Kheldar. If you get in his way, he'll hang your guts on a fence."

"I was going to let Garion do it."

Beldin set down the empty jam pot and belched.

"Can I offer you anything else?" Delvor asked him.

"No, thanks all the same, but I'm full now." He turned back to Belgarath. "Were you planning to get as far as Tol Honeth before summer?"

"We're not really *that* far behind, Beldin," Belgarath protested.

Beldin made an indelicate sound. "Keep your eyes open on the way south," he advised. "There's a Mallorean who's been asking questions about you and the others. He's been hiring people all up and down the Great West Road."

Belgarath looked at him sharply. "Could you get any kind of name?"

"He uses several. The one that crops up most often is Naradas."

"Have you got any idea of what he looks like?" Silk asked.

"About all I've been able to pick up is the fact that he's got funny eyes. From what I've been told, they're all white."

"Well," Delvor said, "well, well, well."

"What's that supposed to mean?" Beldin asked him.

"The man with white eyes is right here in the fair. He's been asking questions here, too."

"That makes it fairly easy, then. Have somebody go run a knife into his back."

Belgarath shook his head. "The legionnaires who police the fair get excited when unexplained bodies start showing up," he said.

Beldin shrugged. "Rap him on the head with something, then drag him a few miles out onto the plain. Cut his throat and dump him in a hole. He probably won't sprout until spring." He looked over at Polgara with a sly grin creasing his ugly face. "If you keep nibbling on that pastry, girl, you're going to spread. You're chubby enough already."

"*Chubby?*"

"That's all right, Pol. Some men like girls with fat bottoms."

"Why don't you wipe the jam out of your beard, uncle?"

"I'm saving it for lunch." He scratched one armpit.

"Lice again?" she asked coolly.

"It's always possible. I don't mind a few lice, though. They're better company than most people I know."

"Where are you going now?" Belgarath asked him.

"Back to Mallorea. I want to root around in Darshiva for a while and see what I can dig up about Zandramas."

Delvor had been looking at the grimy little man with a speculative squint. "Were you planning to leave immediately, Master Beldin?" he asked.

"Why?"

"I'd like a word with you in private, if you've got a few moments."

"Secrets, Delvor?" Silk asked.

"Not really, old boy. I've got a sort of an idea, but I'd like to get it a bit more developed before I tell you about it." He turned back to the hunchback. "Why don't we take a little stroll, Master Beldin? I have a notion that might appeal to you, and it really won't take very long."

Beldin's look was curious. "All right," he agreed, and the two of them went outside into the drizzling morning.

"What was that all about?" Garion asked Silk.

"It's an irritating habit Delvor picked up at the Academy. He likes to pull off clever ploys without any advance warning. That way he can sit around afterward and bask in everyone's stunned admiration." The little man looked at the table. "I believe I'll have just a bit more of that sausage," he said, "and maybe a few more eggs. It's a long way to Tol Honeth, and I'd like to put in a buffer against all that gruel."

Polgara looked at Ce'Nedra. "Have you ever noticed that when some people find a notion they think is funny, they tend to keep playing with it long past the point where it bores everyone else to tears?"

Ce'Nedra looked at Silk with a sly little twinkle in her eyes. "I've noticed that, Lady Polgara. Do you suppose it might be the result of a limited imagination?"

"I'm sure that has something to do with it, dear." Aunt Polgara looked at Silk with a serene smile. "Now, did you want to play some more, Kheldar?"

"Ah—no, Polgara. I don't really think so."

It was shortly before noon when Delvor and Beldin returned, each with a self-satisfied smirk on his face. "It was a truly masterful performance, Master Beldin," Delvor congratulated the little hunchback as they entered.

"Child's play." Beldin shrugged deprecatingly. "People inevitably believe that a deformed body houses a defective brain. I've used that to my advantage many times."

"I'm sure they'll tell us what this is all about eventually," Silk said.

"It wasn't too complicated, Silk," Delvor told him. "You'll be able to leave now without any worries about that curious Mallorean."

"Oh?"

"He was trying to buy information." Delvor shrugged. "So we sold him some, and he left—at a full gallop."

"What sort of information did you sell him?"

"It went sort of like this," Beldin said. He stooped a bit more, deliberately exaggerating his deformity, and his face took on an expression of vapid imbecility. "An' it please yer honor," he said in a squeaky voice dripping with servile stupidity, "I hears that you wants to find some people an' that you says you'll pay to know where they be. I seed the people yer lookin fer, an' I kin tell you where they was—if you gimme enough money. How much was you willin' to pay?"

Delvor laughed delightedly. "Naradas swallowed it whole. I took Master Beldin to him and told him that I'd found someone who knew about the people he was looking for. We agreed to a price, and then your friend here gulled him completely."

"Which way did you send him?" Belgarath asked.

"North." Beldin shrugged. "I told him that I'd seen you camped by the roadside up in the Arendish forest—that one of the members of your party had fallen sick and that you'd stopped to nurse him back to health."

"Wasn't he at all suspicious?" Silk asked.

Delvor shook his head. "The thing that makes people suspicious is help that comes for no particular reason. I gave Naradas every reason to believe that I was sincere. I cheated Master Beldin—outrageously. Naradas gave him a few silver coins for his information. *My* price, however, was much higher."

"Brilliant," Silk murmured admiringly.

"There's something you ought to know about White Eyes, though," Beldin told Belgarath. "He's a Mallorean Grolim. I didn't probe into him too hard, because I didn't want him to catch what I was doing, but I *was* able to get that much. He's got a great deal of power, so watch out for him."

"Did you find out whom he's working for?"

Beldin shook his head. "I pulled back as soon as I found out what he was." The hunchback's face grew bleak. "Be careful about this one, Belgarath. He's very dangerous."

Belgarath's face grew grim. "So am I, Beldin," he said.

I know, but there are some things you *won't* do. Naradas doesn't feel that kind of restraint."

CHAPTER FOUR

They rode south under clearing skies for the next six days. A cold wind bent the winter-browned grass at the sides of the road, and the rolling plain of southern Arendia lay dead and sere beneath a chill blue sky. They passed an occasional mud-and-wattle village where ragged serfs clenched themselves to endure yet another winter and more infrequently a rearing stone keep where a proud Mimbrate baron kept a watchful eye on his neighbors.

The Great West Road, like all roads that formed a part of the Tolnedran highway system, was patrolled by scarlet-cloaked Imperial Legionnaires. Garion and his friends also encountered an occasional merchant traveling northward with wary eyes and accompanied by burly hirelings whose hands never strayed far from their weapons.

They reached the River Arend on a frosty midmorning and looked across the sparkling ford at the Forest of Vordue in northern Tolnedra. "Did you want to stop at Vo Mimbre?" Silk asked Belgarath.

The old man shook his head. "Mandorallen and Lelldorin have probably already advised Korodullin about what happened in Drasnia, and I'm not really in the mood for three or four days of speeches filled with thee's and thou's and forasmuches. Besides, I want to get to Tol Honeth as soon as possible."

As they splashed through the shallow waters of the ford, Garion remembered something. "Will we have to stop at that customs station?" he asked.

"Naturally," Silk replied. "Everybody has to go through customs—except for licensed smugglers, of course." He looked over at Belgarath. "Do you want me to handle things when we get there?"

"Just don't get too creative."

"Nothing could have been further from my mind, Belgarath. All I want is a chance to try these out." He indicated the seedy clothing he wore.

"I've been sort of wondering what you had in mind when you picked out your wardrobe," Durnik said.

Silk gave him a sly wink.

They rode up out of the ford and on into the Forest of Vordue with its neatly spaced trees and groomed undergrowth. They had gone no more than a league when they came to the whitewashed building that housed the customs station. One corner of the long, shedlike structure showed signs of a recent fire, and the red-tile roof was badly soot-darkened at that end. A half-dozen slovenly soldiers of the customs service were huddled in the muddy yard about a small open fire, drinking cheap wine to ward off the chill. One of them, a stubble-faced man in a patched cloak and rusty breastplate, indolently rose, stepped into the middle of the road, and held up one beefy hand. "That's as far as you go," he declared. "Take your horses over there beside the building and open your packs for inspection."

Silk pushed forward. "Of course, Sergeant," he replied in an obsequious, fawning tone. "We have nothing to hide."

"We'll decide that," the unshaven soldier said, swaying slightly as he barred their path.

The customs agent emerged from the station with a blanket wrapped about his shoulders. It was the same stout man whom they had encountered years before when they had passed this way during their pursuit of Zedar and the stolen Orb. On their previous meeting, however, there had been a certain smug self-satisfaction about him. Now his florid face bore the discontented expression of a man who lives with the conviction that life has somehow cheated him. "What do you have to declare?" he demanded brusquely.

"Nothing on this trip, I'm afraid, your Excellency," Silk answered in a whining voice. "We're just poor travelers on our way to Tol Honeth."

The paunchy agent peered at the little man. "I think we've met before, haven't we? Aren't you Radek of Boktor?"

"The same, your Excellency. You have an extremely good memory."

"In my business, you have to. How did you do with your Sendarian woolens that time?"

Silk's face grew melancholy. "Not nearly as well as I'd hoped. The weather broke before I got to Tol Honeth, so the price was less than half of what it should have been."

"I'm sorry to hear that," the agent said perfunctorily. "Would you mind opening your packs?"

"All we have is food and spare clothing." The little Drasnian was actually sniveling.

"It's been my experience that people sometimes forget that they're carrying things of value. Open the packs, Radek."

"Anything you say, Excellency." Silk clambered down from his horse and began unbuckling the straps on the packs. "I wish I *did* have things of value in here," he sighed tragically, "but that unfortunate venture in the wool market started a long decline for me, I'm afraid. I'm virtually out of business."

The agent grunted and rummaged through their packs for several minutes, shivering all the while. Finally he turned back to Silk with a sour look. "It seems that you're telling the truth, Radek. I'm sorry I doubted you." He blew on his hands trying to warm them. "Times have been hard of late. Nothing's come through here in the last six months that was even worth a decent bribe."

"I've heard that there's been some trouble down here in Vordue," Silk whined as he buckled the packs shut again. "Something about a secession from the rest of Tolnedra."

"The most idiotic thing in the history of the Empire," the agent exploded. "All the brains went out of the Vordue family after the Grand Duke Kador died. They should have known that fellow was an agent for a foreign power."

"Which fellow was that?"

"The one who claimed that he was an eastern merchant. He wormed his way into the confidence of the Vordues and puffed them up with flattery. By the time he was done, they actually believed that they were competent enough to run their own kingdom, independent of the rest of Tolnedra. But that Varana's a sly one, let me tell you. He struck a bargain with King Korodullin, and before long all of Vordue was crawling with Mimbrate knights stealing everything in sight." He pointed at the scorched corner of his station. "You see that? A platoon or so of them came by here and sacked the building. Then they set fire to the place."

"Tragic," Silk commiserated with him. "Did anyone ever find out just who that so-called merchant was working for?"

"Those idiots in Tol Vordue didn't, that's for certain, but I knew who he was the minute I laid eyes on him."

"Oh?"

"The man was a Rivan, and that puts the whole thing right in the lap of King

Belgarion. He's always hated the Vordues anyway, so he came up with this scheme to break their power in northern Tolnedra." He smiled bleakly. "He's getting exactly what he's got coming to him, though. They forced him to marry the Princess Ce'Nedra, and she's making his life miserable."

"How were you able to tell that the agent was Rivan?" Silk asked curiously.

"That's easy, Radek. The Rivans have been isolated on that island of theirs for thousands of years. They're so inbred that all kinds of defects and deformities crop up in them."

"He was deformed?"

The agent shook his head. "It was his eyes," he said. "They didn't have any color to them at all—absolutely white." He shuddered. "It was a chilling thing to see." He pulled his blanket tighter about his shoulders. "I'm sorry, Radek, but I'm freezing out here. I'm going back inside where it's warm. You and your friends are free to go." And with that he hurried back into the station and the warmth of his fireside.

"Isn't *that* interesting?" Silk said as they rode away.

Belgarath was frowning. "The next question is who this busy man with the white eyes is working for," he said.

"Urvon?" Durnik suggested. "Maybe he put Harakan to work in the north and Naradas here in the south—both of them trying to stir up as much turmoil as possible."

"Maybe," Belgarath grunted, "but then again maybe not."

"My dear Prince Kheldar," Ce'Nedra said, pushing back the hood of her cloak with one mittened hand, "what exactly was the purpose of all that cringing and sniveling?"

"Characterization, Ce'Nedra," he replied airily. "Radek of Boktor was a pompous, arrogant ass—as long as he was rich. Now that he's poor, he's gone the other way entirely. It's the nature of the man."

"But, there *isn't* any such person as Radek of Boktor."

"Of course there is. You just saw him. Radek of Boktor exists in the memories of people all over this part of the world. In many ways he's even more real than that bloated time-server back there."

"But he's *you*. You just made him up."

"Certainly I did, and I'm really rather proud of him. His existence, his background, and his entire life history are a matter of public record. He's as real as you are."

"That doesn't make sense at all, Silk," she protested.

"That's because you aren't Drasnian, Ce'Nedra."

They reached Tol Honeth several days later. The white marble Imperial City gleamed in the frosty winter sunshine, and the legionnaires standing guard at the carved bronze gates were as crisp and burnished as always. As Garion and his friends clattered across the marble-paved bridge to the gate, the officer in charge of the guard detachment took one look at Ce'Nedra and banged his clenched fist on his polished breastplate in salute. "Your Imperial Highness," he greeted her. "If we had known you were approaching, we would have sent out an escort."

"That's all right, Captain," she replied in a tired little voice. "Do you suppose you could send one of your men on ahead of us to the palace to advise the Emperor that we're here?"

"At once, your Imperial Highness," he said, saluting again and standing aside to let them pass.

"I just wish that someday somebody in Tolnedra would remember that you're married," Garion muttered, feeling a bit surly about it.

"What was that, dear?" Ce'Nedra asked.

"Can't they get it through their heads that you're the Queen of Riva now? Every time one of them calls you 'Your Imperial Highness,' it makes me feel like some kind of hanger-on—or a servant of some sort."

"Aren't you being a little oversensitive, Garion?"

He grunted sourly, still feeling just a bit offended.

The avenues of Tol Honeth were broad and faced with the proud, lofty houses of the Tolnedran elite. Columns and statuary abounded on the fronts of those residences in vast, ostentatious display, and the richly garbed merchant princes in the streets were bedecked with jewels beyond price. Silk looked at them as he rode past and then ruefully down at his own shabby, threadbare garments. He sighed bitterly.

"More characterization, Radek?" Aunt Polgara asked him.

"Only in part," he replied. "Of course Radek *would* be envious, but I have to admit that I do sort of miss my own finery."

"How on earth do you keep all these fictitious people straight?"

"Concentration, Polgara," he said, "concentration. You can't succeed at any game if you don't concentrate."

The Imperial Compound was a cluster of sculptured marble buildings enclosed within a high wall and situated atop a hill in the western quarter of the city. Warned in advance of their approach, the legionnaires at the gate admitted the party immediately with crisp military salutes. Beyond the gate lay a paved courtyard, and standing at the foot of the marble stairs leading up to a column-fronted building stood the Emperor Varana. "Welcome to Tol Honeth," he said to them as they dismounted. Ce'Nedra hurried toward him, but stopped at the last moment and curtsied formally. "Your Imperial Majesty," she said.

"Why so ceremonial, Ce'Nedra?" he asked, holding out his arms to her.

"Please, uncle," she said, glancing at the palace functionaries lining the top of the stairs, "not here. If you kiss me here, I'll break down and cry, and a Borune never cries in public."

"Ah," he said with an understanding look. Then he turned to the rest of them. "Come inside, all of you. Let's get in out of the cold." He turned, offered Ce'Nedra his arm, and limped up the stairs.

Just inside the doors, there was a large circular rotunda, lined along its walls with marble busts of the last thousand years or so of Tolnedran Emperors. "Look like a gang of pickpockets, don't they?" Varana said to Garion with a wry smile.

"I don't see yours anywhere," Garion replied.

"The royal sculptor is having trouble with my nose. The Anadiles descended from peasant stock, and my nose isn't suitably imperial for his taste." He led them down a broad hallway to a large, candlelit room with a crimson carpet and drapes and deeply upholstered furniture of the same hue. In each corner stood a glowing iron brazier, and the room was pleasantly warm. "Please," the Emperor said, "make yourselves comfortable. I'll send for something hot to drink and have the kitchen prepare a dinner for us." He spoke briefly with the legionnaire at the door as Garion and his friends removed their cloaks and seated themselves.

"Now," Varana said, closing the door, "what brings you to Tol Honeth?"

"You've heard about our campaign against the Bear-cult?" Belgarath asked him, "and the reason for it?"

The Emperor nodded.

"As it turned out, the campaign was misdirected. The cult was not involved in the abduction of Prince Geran, although there was an effort to implicate them. The person we're looking for is named Zandramas. Does that name mean anything to you?"

Varana frowned. "No," he replied, "I can't say that it does."

Belgarath rapidly sketched in the situation, telling Varana what they had learned about Zandramas, Harakan, and the Sardion. When he had finished, the Emperor's expression was slightly dubious.

"I can accept most of what you say, Belgarath," he said, "but some of it—" He shrugged, holding up both hands.

"What's the problem?"

"Varana's a skeptic, father," Polgara said. "There are certain things he prefers not to think about."

"Even after everything that happened at Thull Mardu?" Belgarath looked surprised.

"It's a matter of principle, Belgarath." Varana laughed. "It has to do with being a Tolnedran—and a soldier."

Belgarath gave him an amused look. "All right, then, can you accept the fact that the abduction might have been *politically* motivated?"

"Of course. I understand politics."

"Good. There have always been two major centers of power in Mallorea—the throne and the church. Now it looks as if this Zandramas is raising a third. We can't tell if Kal Zakath is directly involved in any way, but there's some kind of power struggle going on between Urvon and Zandramas. For some reason Garion's son is central to that struggle."

"We've also picked up some hints along the way that for one reason or another the Malloreans don't want us to become involved," Silk added. "There are agents stirring up trouble in Arendia, and it may have been a Mallorean who was behind the Vordue secession."

Varana looked at him sharply.

"A man named Naradas."

"Now that's a name I *have* heard," the Emperor said. "Supposedly he's an Angarak merchant here to negotiate some very sweeping trade agreements. He travels a great deal and spends a lot of money. My commercial advisors think that he's an agent for King Urgit. Now that 'Zakath controls the mining regions in eastern Cthol Murgos, Urgit desperately needs money to finance the war he's got going on down there."

Silk shook his head. "I don't think so," he said. "Naradas is a Mallorean Grolim. It's not likely that he'd be working for the King of the Murgos."

There was a respectful tap at the door.

"Yes?" Varana said.

The door opened and Lord Morin, the Imperial Chamberlain, entered. He was an old man now and very thin. His hair had gone completely white and it stood out in wisps. His skin had that waxy transparency one sees in the very old, and he moved slowly. "The Drasnian Ambassador, your Majesty," he announced in a qua-vering voice. "He says that he has some information of great urgency for you—and for your guests."

"You'd better show him in then, Morin."

"There's a young lady with him, your Majesty," Morin added. "A Drasnian noblewoman, I believe."

"We'll see them both," Varana said.

"As you wish, your Majesty," Morin replied with a creaky bow.

When the aged Chamberlain escorted the ambassador and his companion into the room, Garion blinked in surprise.

"His Excellency, Prince Khaldon, Ambassador of the Royal Court of Drasnia," Morin announced, "and her Ladyship, the Margravine Liselle, a—uh—" He faltered.

"Spy, your Excellency," Liselle supplied with aplomb.

"Is that an official designation, your Ladyship?"

"It saves a great deal of time, Excellency."

"My," Morin sighed, "how the world changes. Should I introduce your Lady-ship to the Emperor as an official spy?"

"I think he's gathered that already, Lord Morin," she said, touching his thin hand affectionately.

Morin bowed and tottered slowly from the room. "What a dear old man," she murmured.

"Well, hello, cousin," Silk said to the ambassador.

"Cousin," Prince Khaldon replied coolly.

"Are you two somehow related?" Varana asked. "Distantly, your Majesty," Silk told him. "Our mothers were second cousins—or was it third?"

"Fourth, I think," Khaldon said. He eyed his rat-faced relative. "You're looking a bit seedy, old man," he noted. "The last time I saw you, you were dripping gold and jewels."

"I'm in disguise, cousin," Silk said blandly. "You're not supposed to be able to recognize me."

"Ah," Khaldon said. He turned to the Emperor. "Please excuse our banter, your Majesty. Kheldar here and I have loathed each other since childhood."

Silk grinned. "It was hate at first sight," he agreed. "We absolutely detest each other."

Khaldon smiled briefly. "When we were children, they used to hide all the knives every time our families visited each other."

Silk looked curiously at Liselle. "What are you doing in Tol Honeth?" he asked her.

"It's a secret."

"Velvet brought several dispatches from Boktor," Khaldon explained, "and certain instructions."

"Velvet?"

"Silly, isn't it?" Liselle laughed. "But then, I suppose they could have chosen a worse nickname for me."

"It's better than some that spring to mind," Silk agreed.

"Be nice, Kheldar."

"There was something you thought we ought to know, Prince Khaldon?" Varana asked.

Khaldon sighed. "It saddens me to report that the courtesan Bethra has been murdered, your Majesty."

"*What?*"

"She was set upon by assassins in a deserted street last night when she was returning from a business engagement. She was left for dead, but she managed to drag herself to our gate, and she was able to pass on some information before she died."

Silk's face had gone quite white. "Who was responsible for it?" he demanded.

"We're still working on that, Kheldar," his cousin replied. "We have some suspicions, of course, but nothing concrete enough to take before a magistrate."

The Emperor's face was bleak, and he rose from the chair in which he had been sitting. "There are some people who will need to know about this," he said grimly. "Would you come with me, Prince Khaldon?"

"Of course, your Majesty."

"Please excuse us," Varana said to the rest of them. "This is a matter that needs my immediate attention." He led the Drasnian Ambassador from the room.

"Did she suffer greatly?" Silk asked the girl known as Velvet in a voice filled with pain.

"They used knives, Kheldar," she replied simply. "That's never pleasant."

"I see." His ferretlike face hardened. "Could she give you any kind of idea what might have been behind it?"

"I gather that it had to do with several things. She mentioned the fact that she once informed Emperor Varana of a plot against the life of his son."

"The Honeths!" Ce'Nedra grated.

"What makes you say that?" Silk asked quickly.

"Garion and I were here when she told Varana. It was at the time of my father's funeral. Bethra came secretly to the palace and said that two Honethite nobles—Count Elgon and Baron Kelbor—were hatching a scheme to murder Varana's son."

Silk's face was stony. "Thank you, Ce'Nedra," he said grimly.

"There's something else you should know, Kheldar," Velvet said quietly. She looked at the rest of them. "We all *will* be discreet about this, won't we?"

"Of course," Belgarath assured her.

Velvet turned back to Silk. "Bethra was Hunter," she told him.

"Hunter? *Bethra?*"

"She has been for several years now. When the struggle over the succession started heating up here in Tolnedra, King Rhodar instructed Javelin to take steps to make sure that the man who followed Ran Borune to the throne would be someone the Alorns could live with. Javelin came to Tol Honeth and recruited Bethra to see to it."

"Excuse me," Belgarath interrupted, his eyes alight with curiosity, "but exactly what is this 'Hunter'?"

"Our most secret spy," Velvet replied. "Hunter's identity is known only to Javelin, and Hunter deals with only the most sensitive situations—things that the Drasnian crown simply cannot openly become involved in. Anyway, when it appeared that the Grand Duke Noragon of the House of Honeth was almost certain to be the next Emperor, King Rhodar made a certain suggestion to Javelin, and a few months later, Noragon accidentally ate some bad shellfish—some *very* bad shellfish."

"Bethra did that?" Silk's tone was amazed.

"She was extraordinarily resourceful."

"Margravine Liselle?" Ce'Nedra said, her eyes narrowed thoughtfully.

"Yes, your Majesty?"

"If the identity of Hunter is the deepest state secret in Drasnia, how is it that *you* were aware of it?"

"I was sent from Boktor with certain instructions for her. My uncle knows that I can be trusted."

"But you're revealing it now, aren't you?"

"It's after the fact, your Majesty. Bethra's dead. Someone else will be Hunter now. Anyway, before she died, Bethra told us that someone had found out about her involvement in the death of Grand Duke Noragon and had passed the information on. She believed that it was that information that triggered the attack on her."

"It's definitely narrowing down to the Honeths then, isn't it?" Silk said.

"It's not definite proof, Kheldar," Velvet warned him.

"It's definite enough to satisfy me."

"You're not going to do anything precipitous, are you?" she asked him. "Javelin wouldn't like that, you know."

"That's Javelin's problem."

"We don't have time to get involved in Tolnedran politics, Silk," Belgarath added firmly. "We're not going to be here that long."

"It's not going to *take* me all that long."

"I'll have to report what you're planning to Javelin," Velvet warned.

"Of course. But I'll be finished with it by the time your report reaches Boktor."

"It's important that you don't embarrass us, Kheldar."

"Trust me," he said and quietly left the room.

"It always makes me nervous when he says that," Durnik murmured.

Early the following morning, Belgarath and Garion left the Imperial Palace to visit the library at the university. It was chilly in the broad streets of Tol Honeth, and a raw wind was blowing in off the Nedrane River. The few merchants abroad at that hour walked briskly along the marble thoroughfares with fur cloaks pulled tightly about them, and gangs of roughly dressed laborers thronged up out of the poorer sections of the city with their heads bent into the wind and their chapped hands burrowed deep into their clothing.

Garion and his grandfather passed through the deserted central marketplace and soon reached a large cluster of buildings enclosed by a marble wall and entered through a gate stamped with the Imperial Seal. The grounds inside the compound were as neatly trimmed as those surrounding the palace, and there were broad marble walks stretching from building to building across the lawns. As they moved along one of those walks, they encountered a portly, black-robed scholar pacing along with his hands clasped behind his back and his face lost in thought.

"Excuse me," Belgarath said to him, "but could you direct us to the library?"

"What?" The man looked up, blinking.

"The library, good sir," Belgarath repeated. "Which way is it?"

"Oh," the scholar said. "It's over there someplace." He gestured vaguely.

"Do you suppose you could be a bit more precise?"

The scholar gave the shabbily dressed old man an offended look. "Ask one of the porters," he said brusquely. "I'm busy. I've been working on a problem for twenty years now and I've almost found the solution."

"Oh? Which problem is that?"

"I doubt that it would be of much interest to an uneducated mendicant," the scholar replied loftily, "but if you really must know, I've been trying to calculate the exact weight of the world."

"Is that all? And it's taken you twenty years?" Belgarath's face was astonished. "I solved *that* problem a long time ago—in about a week."

The scholar stared at him, his face going dead white. "That's impossible!" he exclaimed. "I'm the only man in the world who's looking into it. No one has ever asked the question before."

Belgarath laughed. "I'm sorry, learned scholar, but it's been asked several times already. The best solution I ever saw was by a man named Talgin—at the University of Melcena, I think. It was during the second millennium. There should be a copy of his calculations in your library."

The scholar began to tremble violently, and his eyes bulged. Without a word he spun on his heel and dashed across the lawn with the skirts of his robe flapping behind him.

"Keep an eye on him, Garion," Belgarath said calmly. "The building he runs to should be the library."

"Just how much *does* the world weigh?" Garion asked curiously.

"How should I know?" Belgarath replied. "No sane man would even be curious about it."

"But what about this Talgin you mentioned—the one who wrote the solution?"

"Talgin? Oh, there's no such person. I just made him up."

Garion stared at him. "That's a dreadful thing to do, Grandfather," he accused. "You've just destroyed a man's entire life work with a lie."

"But it *did* get him to lead us to the library," the old man said slyly. "Besides, maybe now he'll turn his attention to something a bit more meaningful. The library's in that building with the tower. He just ran up the steps. Shall we go?"

There was a marble rotunda just inside the main entrance to the library, and in the precise center of that rotunda stood a high, ornately carved desk. A bald, skinny man sat behind the desk laboriously copying from a huge book. For some reason the man looked familiar to Garion, and he frowned as they approached the desk, trying to remember where he had seen him before.

"May I help you?" the skinny man asked, looking up from his copying as Belgarath stopped in front of his desk.

"Possibly so. I'm looking for a copy of the Prophecies of the Western Grolims."

The skinny man frowned, scratching at one ear. "That would be in the comparative theology section," he mused. "Could you hazard a guess as to the date of composition?"

Belgarath also frowned, staring up into the vault of the rotunda as he considered it. "My guess would be early third millennium," he said finally.

"That would put it at the time of either the second Honethite Dynasty or the second Vorduvian," the scholar said. "We shouldn't have too much trouble finding it." He rose to his feet. "It's this way," he said, pointing toward one of the hallways fanning out from the rotunda. "If you'll follow me, please."

Garion still felt the nagging certainty that he knew this polite, helpful scholar. The man certainly had better manners than the pompous, self-important worldweighter they had met outside, and—Then it came to him. "Master Jeebers?" he said incredulously, "is that you?"

"Have we met before, sir?" Jeebers asked politely, looking at Garion with a puzzled squint.

Garion grinned broadly. "We have indeed, Master Jeebers. You introduced me to my wife."

"I don't seem to recall—"

"Oh, I think you do. You crept out of the palace with her one night and rode south toward Tol Borune. Along the way, you joined a party of merchants. You left rather suddenly when my wife told you that leaving Tol Honeth was *her* idea instead of Ran Borune's."

Jeebers blinked and then his eyes widened. "Your Majesty," he said with a bow. "Forgive me for not recognizing you at once. My eyes aren't what they once were."

Garion laughed, clapping him on the shoulder in delight. "That's quite all right, Jeebers," he said. "I'm not going about announcing who I am on this trip."

"And how is little Ce'Nedra—Uh, her Majesty, that is?"

Garion was about to tell his wife's former tutor about the abduction of their son, but Belgarath gave him a discreet nudge. "Uh—fine, just fine," he said instead.

"I'm so glad to hear it," Jeebers said with a fond smile. "She was an absolutely impossible student, but strangely I find that much of the fun went out of my life after she and I parted company. I was delighted to hear of her fortuitous marriage and not nearly as surprised as my colleagues here when we heard that she had raised an army and marched on Thull Mardu. She always was a fiery little thing—and brilliant." He gave Garion a rather apologetic look. "To be honest, though, I have to tell you that she was an erratic and undisciplined student."

"I've noticed those qualities in her from time to time."

Jeebers laughed. "I'm sure you have, your Majesty," he said. "Please convey my regards to her—" He hesitated. "And if you don't think it's presumptuous—my affection as well."

"I will, Jeebers," Garion promised. "I will."

"This is the comparative theology section of our library," the bald scholar said, pushing open a heavy door. "All the items are catalogued and stored by Dynasty. The antiquity sections are back this way." He led them along a narrow aisle between tall book racks filled with leather-bound volumes and tightly rolled scrolls. The skinny man paused once and rubbed his finger along one of the shelves. "Dust," he sniffed disapprovingly. "I expect I'd better speak sharply to the custodians about that."

"It's the nature of books to collect dust," Belgarath said.

"And it's the nature of custodians to avoid doing anything about it," Jeebers added with a wry smile. "Ah, here we are." He stopped in the center of a somewhat broader aisle where the books showed marked signs of extreme age. "Please be gentle with them," he said, touching the backs of the volumes with an odd kind of affection. "They're old and brittle. The works written during the Second Honethite Dynasty are on this side, and those dating back to the Second Vordue Dynasty are over here. They're further broken down into kingdom of origin, so it shouldn't be hard for you to locate the one you want. Now, if you'll excuse me, I shouldn't stay away from my desk for too long. Some of my colleagues get impatient and start rooting through the shelves on their own. It takes weeks sometimes to get things put right again."

"I'm sure we can manage from here, Master Jeebers," Belgarath assured him, "and thank you for your assistance."

"It's my pleasure," Jeebers replied with a slight bow. He looked back at Garion. "You *will* remember to give little Ce'Nedra my greetings, won't you?"

"You have my word on it, Master Jeebers."

"Thank you, your Majesty." And the skinny man turned and went on out of the book-lined room.

"An enormous change there," Belgarath noted. "Probably the little fright Ce'Nedra gave him at Tol Borune that time knocked all the pomposity out of him." The old man was peering intently at the shelves. "I'll have to admit that he's a very competent scholar."

"Isn't he just a librarian?" Garion asked, "somebody who looks after books?"

"That's where all the rest of scholarship starts, Garion. All the books in the world won't help you if they're just piled up in a heap." He bent slightly and pulled a black-wrapped scroll from a lower shelf. "Here we are," he said triumphantly. "Jeebers led us right to it." He moved to the end of the aisle where a table and bench sat before a tall, narrow window and where the pale winter sunlight fell golden on the stone floor. He sat and carefully undid the ties that held the scroll tightly rolled inside its black velvet cover. As he pulled the scroll out, he muttered a number of fairly sulfurous oaths.

"What's the matter?" Garion asked.

"Grolim stupidity," Belgarath growled. "Look at this." He held out the scroll. "Look at the parchment."

Garion peered at it. "It looks like other parchment to me."

"It's human skin," the old man snorted disgustedly.

Garion drew back in revulsion. "That's ghastly."

"That's not the point. Whoever provided the skin was finished with it anyway.

The problem is that human skin won't hold ink." He unrolled a foot or so of the scroll. "Look at that. It's so faded that you can't even make out the words."

"Could you use something to bring them out again—the way you did with Anheg's letter that time?"

"Garion, this scroll's about three thousand years old. The solution of salts I used on Anheg's letter would probably dissolve it entirely."

"Sorcery then?"

Belgarath shook his head. "It's just too fragile." He started to swear again even as he carefully unrolled the scroll inch by inch, moving it this way and that to catch the sunlight. "Here's something," he grunted with some surprise.

"What does it say?"

" '. . . seek the path of the Child of Dark in the land of the serpents . . .' " The old man looked up. "That's something, anyway."

"What does it mean?"

"Just what it says. Zandramas went to Nyissa. We'll pick up the trail there."

"Grandfather, we already knew that."

"We *suspected* it, Garion. There's a difference. Zandramas has tricked us into following false trails before. Now we know for certain that we're on the right track."

"It isn't very much, Grandfather."

"I know, but it's better than nothing."

CHAPTER FIVE

"Would you just look at that?" Ce'Nedra said indignantly the following morning. She had just arisen and stood at the window, wrapped in a warm robe.

"Hmmm?" Garion murmured drowsily. "Look at what, dear?" He was burrowed deeply under the warm quilts and was giving some serious thought to going back to sleep.

"You can't see it from there, Garion. Come over here."

He sighed, slipped out of bed, and padded barefoot over to the window.

"Isn't that disgusting?" she demanded.

The grounds of the Imperial Compound were blanketed in white, and large snowflakes were settling lazily through the dead-calm air.

"Isn't it sort of peculiar for it to snow in Tol Honeth?" he asked.

"Garion, it *never* snows in Tol Honeth. The last time I saw snow here was when I was five years old."

"It's been an unusual winter."

"Well, I'm going back to bed, and I'm not going to get up until every bit of it melts."

"You don't really have to go out in it, you know."

"I don't even want to *look* at it." She flounced back to their canopied bed, let her robe drop to the floor, and climbed back under the quilts. Garion shrugged and started back toward the bed. Another hour or two of sleep seemed definitely in order.

"Please pull the curtains on the bed shut," she told him, "and don't make too much noise when you leave."

He stared at her for a moment, then sighed. He closed the heavy curtains around the bed and sleepily began to dress.

"Do be a dear, Garion," she said sweetly. "Stop by the kitchen and tell them that I'll want my breakfast in here."

Now that, he felt, was *distinctly* unfair. He pulled on the rest of his clothes, feeling surly.

"Oh, Garion?"

"Yes, dear?" He kept it neutral with some effort.

"Don't forget to comb your hair. You always look like a straw stack in the morning." Her voice already sounded drowsy and on the edge of sleep.

He found Belgarath sitting moodily before the window in an unlighted dining room. Although it was quite early, the old man had a tankard on the table beside him. "Can you believe this?" he said disgustedly, looking out at the softly falling snow.

"I don't imagine that it's going to last very long, Grandfather."

"It *never* snows in Tol Honeth."

"That's what Ce'Nedra was just saying." Garion held out his hands to a glowing iron brazier.

"Where is she?"

"She went back to bed."

"That's probably not such a bad idea. Why didn't you join her?"

"She decided that it was time for me to get up."

"That hardly seems fair."

"The same thought occurred to me."

Belgarath scratched absently at his ear, still looking out at the snow. "We're too far south for this to last for more than a day or so. Besides, the day after tomorrow is Erastide. A lot of people will be traveling after the holiday, so we won't be quite so conspicuous."

"You think we should wait?"

"It's sort of logical. We wouldn't make very good time slogging through all that, anyway."

"What do you plan to do today, then?"

Belgarath picked up his tankard. "I think I'll finish this and then go back to bed."

Garion pulled up one of the red velvet upholstered chairs and sat down. Something had been bothering him for several days now, and he decided that this might be a good time to bring it out into the open. "Grandfather?"

"Yes?"

"Why is it that all of this seems to have happened before?"

"All of what?"

"Everything. There are Angaraks in Arendia trying to stir up trouble—just as they were when we were following Zedar. There are intrigues and assassinations in Tolnedra—the same as last time. We ran into a monster—a dragon this time instead of the Algroths—but it's still pretty close to the same sort of thing. It seems almost as if we were repeating everything that happened when we were trying to find the Orb. We've even been running into the same people—Delvor, that customs man, even Jeebers."

"You know, that's a very interesting question, Garion." Belgarath pondered for a moment, absently taking a drink from his tankard. "If you think about it in a certain way, though, it does sort of make sense."

"I don't quite follow you."

"We're on our way to another meeting between the Child of Light and the Child of Dark," Belgarath explained. "That meeting is going to be a repetition of an event that's been happening over and over again since the beginning of time. Since it's the same event, it stands to reason that the circumstances leading up to it should also be similar." He thought about it a moment longer. "Actually," he continued, "they'd almost have to be, wouldn't they?"

"That's a little deep for me, I'm afraid."

"There are two Prophecies—two sides of the same thing. Something happened an unimaginably long time ago to separate them."

"Yes. I understand that."

"When they got separated, things sort of stopped."

"What things?"

"It's kind of hard to put into words. Let's call it the course of things that were supposed to happen—the future, I suppose. As long as those two forces are separate—and equal—the future can't happen. We all just keep going through the same series of events over and over again.

"When will it end?"

"When one of the Prophecies finally overcomes the other. When the Child of Light finally defeats the Child of Dark—or the other way around."

"I thought I already did that."

"I don't think it was conclusive enough, Garion."

"I killed Torak, Grandfather. You can't get much more conclusive than that, can you?"

"You killed *Torak*, Garion. You didn't kill the Dark Prophecy. I think it's going to take something more significant than a sword fight in the City of Night to settle this."

"Such as what?"

Belgarath spread his hands. "I don't know. I really don't. This idea of yours could be very useful, though."

"Oh?"

"If we're going to go through a series of events that are similar to what happened last time, it could give us a notion of what to expect, couldn't it? You might want to think about that—maybe spend a little time this morning remembering exactly what happened last time."

"What are you going to do?"

Belgarath drained his tankard and stood up. "As I said—I'm going back to bed."

That afternoon, a polite official in a brown mantle tapped on the door of the room where Garion sat reading and advised him that the Emperor Varana wanted to see him. Garion set aside his book and followed the official through the echoing marble halls to Varana's study.

"Ah, Belgarion," Varana said as he entered. "A bit of news has just reached me that you might find interesting. Please, have a seat."

"Information?" Garion asked, sitting in the leather-upholstered chair beside the Emperor's desk.

"That man you mentioned the other day—Naradas—has been seen here in Tol Honeth."

"Naradas? How did he manage to get down here that fast? The last I heard, he was riding north from the Great Fair in Arendia."

"Has he been following you?"

"He's been asking a lot of questions and spreading money around."

"I can have him picked up, if you want. I have a few questions I'd like to ask him myself, and I could hold him for several months if need be."

Garion thought about it. Finally he shook his head rather regretfully. "He's a Mallorean Grolim, and he could be out of any kind of prison cell you could put him in within a matter of minutes."

"The Imperial Dungeon is quite secure, Belgarion," Varana said a bit stiffly.

"Not that secure, Varana." Then Garion smiled briefly, remembering the Emperor's stubborn convictions about such things. "Let's just say that Naradas has some out-of-the-ordinary resources available to him. It's one of those things that makes you uncomfortable to talk about."

"Oh," Varana said distastefully, "that."

Garion nodded. "It might be better in the long run just to have your people keep an eye on him. If he doesn't know that we're aware that he's here, he might lead us to others—or at least to certain information. Harakan's been seen here in Tolnedra, too, I understand, and I'd like to find out if there's some kind of connection between the two of them."

Varana smiled. "Your life is a great deal more complicated than mine, Belgarion," he said. "I only have one reality to deal with."

Garion gave a wry shrug. "It helps to fill up my spare time," he replied.

There was a light tap on the door, and Lord Morin slowly shuffled into the room. "I'm sorry to disturb your Majesties, but there's some unsettling news from the city."

"Oh?" Varana said. "What's been happening, Morin?"

"Someone's been killing members of the Honeth family—very quietly, but very efficiently. Quite a few have died in the last two nights."

"Poison?"

"No, your Majesty. This assassin is more direct. He smothered a few with their own pillows night before last, and there was one nasty fall. At first the deaths appeared to be of natural causes. Last night, though, he started using a knife." Morin shook his head disapprovingly. "Messy," he sniffed. "Very messy."

Varana frowned. "I thought that all the old feuds had settled down. Do you think it might be the Horbites? They hold grudges forever sometimes."

"No one seems to know, your Majesty. The Honeths are terrified. They're either fleeing the city or turning their houses into forts."

Varana smiled. "I think I can live with the discomfort of the Honeth family. Did this fellow leave any kind of trademark? Can we identify him as a known assassin?"

"We haven't a clue, your Majesty. Should I put guards around the houses of the Honeths—the ones who are left?"

"They have their own soldiers." Varana shrugged. "But put out some inquiries and let this fellow know that I'd like to have a little talk with him."

"Are you going to arrest him?" Garion asked.

"Oh, I don't know that I want to go *that* far. I just want to find out who he is and suggest to him that he ought to follow the rules a little more closely, that's all. I wonder who he could possibly be."

Garion, however, had a few private suspicions about the matter.

The Erastide festivities were in full swing in Tol Honeth, and the revelers, many far gone in drink, lurched and staggered from party to party as the great families vied with one another in a vulgar display of ostentatious wealth. The huge mansions of the rich and powerful were festooned with gaily hued buntings and hung with colored lanterns. Fortunes were spent on lavish banquets, and the entertainments provided often exceeded the bounds of good taste. Although the celebrations at the palace were more restrained, Emperor Varana nonetheless felt obliged to extend his hospitality to many people he privately loathed.

The event which had been long in the planning for that particular evening was a state banquet to be followed by a grand ball. "And you two will be my guests of honor," Varana firmly told Garion and Ce'Nedra. "If *I* have to endure this, then so do you."

"I'd really rather not, uncle," Ce'Nedra told him with a sad little smile. "I'm not much in the mood for festivities just now."

"You can't just turn off your life, Ce'Nedra," he said gently. "A party—even one of the stuffy ones here in the palace—might help to divert your mind from your tragic circumstances." He gave her a shrewd look. "Besides," he added, "if you don't attend, the Honeths, Horbites, and Vordues will all be smirking up their sleeves about your absence."

Ce'Nedra's head came up quickly, and her eyes took on a flinty look. "That's true, isn't it?" she replied. "Of course, I really don't have a thing to wear."

"There are whole closets filled with your gowns in the imperial apartments, Ce'Nedra," he reminded her.

"Oh, yes. I'd forgotten those. All right, uncle, I'll be happy to attend."

And so it was that Ce'Nedra, dressed in a creamy white velvet gown and with a jeweled coronet nestling among her flaming curls, entered the ballroom that evening on the arm of her husband, the King of Riva. Garion, dressed in a borrowed blue doublet that was noticeably tight across the shoulders, approached the entire affair with a great lack of enthusiasm. As a visiting head of state, he was obliged to stand for an hour or so in the reception line in the grand ballroom, murmuring empty responses to the pleasantries offered by assorted Horbites, Vordues, Ranites, and Borunes—and their often giddy wives. The Honeths, however, were conspicuous by their absence.

Toward the end of that interminable ceremony, Javelin's honey-blond niece, the Margravine Liselle, dressed in a spectacular gown of lavender brocade, came past on the arm of Prince Khaldon. "Courage, your Majesty," she murmured as she curtsied to Garion. "Not even this can last forever—though it might seem like it."

"Thanks, Liselle," he replied drily.

After the reception line had wound to its tedious conclusion, Garion circulated politely among the other guests, enduring the endlessly repeated comment: "It *never* snows in Tol Honeth."

At the far end of the candlelit ballroom, a group of Arendish musicians sawed and plucked and tootled their way through a repertoire of holiday songs that were common to all the Kingdoms of the West. Their lutes, violas, harps, flutes, and oboes provided a largely unheard background to the chattering of the Emperor's guests.

"I had engaged Madame Aldima to entertain us this evening," Varana was saying to a small cluster of Horbites. "Her singing was to have been the high point of the festivities. Unfortunately, the change in the weather has made her fearful of coming out of her house. She's most protective of her voice, I understand."

"And well she should be," a Ranite lady standing just behind Garion murmured to her companion. "It wasn't much of a voice to begin with, and time hasn't been kind to it—all those years Aldima spent singing in taverns, no doubt."

"It hardly seems like Erastide without singing," Varana continued. "Perhaps we might persuade one of these lovely ladies to grace us with a song or two."

A stout Borune lady of middle years quickly responded to the Emperor's suggestion, joining with the orchestra in a rendition of an old favorite delivered in a warbling soprano voice that struggled painfully to reach the higher registers. When she had finished and stood red-faced and gasping, the Emperor's guests responded to her screeching with polite applause which lasted for almost five seconds. Then they returned to their inane chatter.

And then the musicians struck up an Arendish air so old that its origins were lost in the mists of antiquity. Like most Arendish songs, it was of a melancholy turn, beginning in a minor key with an intricate waterfall of notes from the lute. As the deep-toned viola entered with the main theme, a rich contralto voice joined in. Gradually, the conversations died out as that voice poignantly touched the guests into silence. Garion was startled. Standing not far from the orchestra, the Margravine Liselle had lifted her head in song. Her voice was marvelous. It had a dark, thrilling timbre and was as smooth as honey. The other guests drew back from her in profound respect for that glorious voice, leaving her standing quite alone in a golden circle of candlelight. And then, to Garion's astonishment, Ce'Nedra stepped into that candlelight to join the lavender-gowned Drasnian girl. As the flute picked up the counterharmony, the tiny Rivan Queen raised her sad little face and joined her voice with that of the Margravine. Effortlessly, her clear voice rose with that of the flute, so perfectly matching its tone and color that one could not separate exactly the voice of the instrument from hers. And yet, there was a sadness bordering on heartbreak in her singing, a sorrow that brought a lump to Garion's throat and tears to his eyes. Despite the festivities around her, it was clearly evident that Ce'Nedra still nursed her abiding anguish deep in her heart, and no gaiety nor entertainment could lessen her suffering.

As the song drew to its conclusion, the applause was thunderous. "More!" they shouted. "More!"

Encouraged by the ovation, the musicians returned to the beginning of that same ancient air. Once again the lute spilled out its heart in that rippling cascade, but this time as the viola led Liselle into the main theme, yet a third voice joined in—a voice Garion knew so well that he did not even have to look to see who was singing.

Polgara, dressed in a deep blue velvet gown trimmed in silver, joined Liselle and Ce'Nedra in the candlelit circle. Her voice was as rich and smooth as the Margravine's, and yet there was in it a sorrow that went even beyond Ce'Nedra's—a sorrow for a place that had been lost and could never return again. Then, as the flute accompanied Ce'Nedra into the rising counterpoint, Polgara's rose to join hers as well. The harmony thus created was not the traditional one which was so familiar in all the Kingdoms of the West. The Arendish musicians, their eyes filled with tears, took up those strange antique chords to recreate a melody that had not been heard in thousands of years.

As the last notes of that glorious song faded, there was an awed silence. And then, many of them weeping openly, the guests burst into applause as Polgara silently led the two young women out of that golden circle of light.

Belgarath, looking somewhat unusually regal in a snowy Tolnedran mantle, but holding nonetheless a full silver goblet, stood in her path, his eyes a mystery.

"Well, father?" she asked.

Wordlessly he kissed her forehead and handed her the goblet. "Lovely, Pol, but why revive something that's been dead and gone for all these centuries?"

Her chin lifted proudly. "The memory of Vo Wacune will never die so long as I live, father. I carry it forever in my heart, and every so often I like to remind people that there was once a shining city filled with grace and courage and beauty and that this mundane world in which we now live allowed it to slip away."

"It's very painful for you, isn't it, Polgara?" he asked gravely.

"Yes, father, it is—more painful than I can say—but I've endured pain before, so . . ." She left it hanging with a slight shrug and moved with regal step from the hall.

After the banquet, Garion and Ce'Nedra took a few turns about the ballroom floor, more for the sake of appearances than out of any real desire for it.

"Why does Lady Polgara feel so strongly about the Wacite Arends?" Ce'Nedra asked as they danced.

"She lived in Vo Wacune for quite some time when she was young," Garion replied. "I think she loved the city—and the people—very much."

"I thought my heart would break when she sang that song."

"Mine nearly did," Garion said quietly. "She's suffered so very much, but I think that the destruction of Vo Wacune hurt her more than anything else that's ever happened. She's never forgiven Grandfather for not coming to the aid of the city when the Asturians destroyed it."

Ce'Nedra sighed. "There's so much sorrow in the world."

"There's hope, too," he reminded her.

"But only such a little." She sighed again. Then a sudden impish smile crossed her lips. "That song absolutely destroyed all the ladies who are here," she smirked. "Absolutely *destroyed* them."

"Try not to gloat in public, love," he gently chided her. "It's really not very becoming."

"Didn't Uncle Varana say that I was one of the guests of honor?"

"Well—yes."

"It's my party then," she said with a toss of her head, "so I'll gloat if I want to."

When they all returned to the set of rooms Varana had provided for their use, Silk was waiting for them, standing by the fire and warming his hands. The little man had a furtive, slightly worried look on his face, and he was covered from top to toe with reeking debris. "Where's Varana?" he asked tensely as they entered the candlelit sitting room.

"He's down in the ballroom entertaining his guests," Garion said.

"What *have* you been doing, Prince Kheldar?" Ce'Nedra asked, wrinkling her nose at the offensive odors emanating from his clothes.

"Hiding," he replied, "under a garbage heap. I think we might want to leave Tol Honeth—fairly soon."

Belgarath's eyes narrowed. "Exactly what have you been up to, Silk?" he demanded, "and where have you been for the past couple of days?"

"Here and there," Silk said evasively. "I really should go get cleaned up."

"I don't suppose you know anything about what's been happening to the Honeth family, do you?" Garion asked.

"What's this?" Belgarath said.

"I was with Varana this afternoon when Lord Morin brought the report. The Honeths have been dying at a surprising rate. Eight or ten at last count."

"Twelve, actually," Silk corrected meticulously.

Belgarath turned on the rat-faced man. "I think I'd like an explanation."

"People die," Silk shrugged. "It happens all the time."

"Did they have help?"

"A little, maybe."

"And were *you* the one who provided this assistance?"

"Would I do that?"

Belgarath's face grew bleak. "I want the truth, Prince Kheldar."

Silk spread his hands extravagantly. "What is truth, old friend? Can any man ever really know what the truth is?"

"This isn't a philosophical discussion, Silk. Have you been out butchering Honeths?"

"I don't know that I'd say 'butchering' exactly. That word smacks of a certain crudity. I pride myself on my refinement."

"Have you been killing people?"

"Well," Silk's face took on a slightly offended expression, "if you're going to put it *that* way—"

"Twelve people?" Durnik's tone was incredulous.

"And another that isn't very likely to survive," Silk noted. "I was interrupted before I had time to make sure of him, but I probably did enough to get the job done."

"I'm still waiting, Silk," Belgarath said darkly.

Silk sniffed at one rancid sleeve and made a face. "Bethra and I were very good friends." He shrugged as if that explained everything.

"But—" Durnik objected. "Didn't she try to have you killed once?"

"Oh, that. That wasn't anything important. It was business—nothing personal."

"Isn't trying to kill somebody about as personal as you can get?"

"Of course not. I was interfering with something she was working on. You see, she had this arrangement with the Thullish ambassador, and—"

"Quit trying to change the subject, Silk," Belgarath said.

Silk's eyes grew hard. "Bethra was a special woman," he replied. "Beautiful, gifted, and totally honest. I admired her very much. You could almost say that I loved her—in a rather special kind of way. The idea that someone saw fit to have her cut down in the street greatly offended me. I did what I thought was appropriate."

"Despite the importance of what we're doing?" Belgarath's face was like a thundercloud. "You just dropped everything and ran out to do a little private killing?"

"There are some things you just don't let slide, Belgarath. There's also a principle involved. We do *not* allow the killing of a member of Drasnian intelligence to go unpunished. It's bad for business if people get the idea that they can get away with that sort of thing. Anyway, the first night I went to some pains to make things look sort of natural."

"Natural?" Durnik asked. "How can you make a murder look natural?"

"Please, Durnik. Murder is such an ugly word."

"He smothered them in their beds with their own pillows," Garion explained.

"And one fellow sort of accidentally fell out of a window," Silk added. "Rather a high one as I recall. He came down on an iron fence."

Durnik shuddered.

"I managed to visit five of them night before last, but the methods were taking entirely too long, so last night I was a bit more direct. I *did* sort of linger for a time with the Baron Kelbor, though. He was the one who actually gave the order to have Bethra killed. We had a very nice chat before he left us."

"Kelbor's house is the most closely guarded in Tol Honeth," Ce'Nedra said. "How did you manage to get in?"

"People seldom look up at night—particularly when it's snowing. I went in over the rooftops. Anyway, Kelbor gave me some very useful information. It seems that the man who told the Honeths about Bethra's activities was a Mallorean."

"Naradas?" Garion asked quickly.

"No. This one had a black beard."

"Harakan, then?"

"Lots of people have beards, Garion. I'd like a little bit more confirmation—

not that I'd object to cutting Harakan up into little pieces, but I'd hate to let the real culprit get away because I was concentrating too much on our old friend." His face went bleak again. "That's particularly true in view of the fact that, from what Kelbor said, this helpful Mallorean arranged and participated in Bethra's murder—sort of as a favor to the Honeth family."

"I *do* wish that you'd go take a bath, Prince Kheldar," Ce'Nedra said. "What on earth possessed you to take up residence in a garbage heap?"

He shrugged. "I was interrupted during my last visit, and a number of people were chasing me. This snow complicated things a bit. My tracks were fairly easy for them to follow. I needed a place to hide, and the garbage heap was handy." His look became disgusted. "It *never* snows in Tol Honeth."

"You'd be amazed at how many people have told me the same thing today," Garion murmured.

"I really think we should leave almost immediately," Silk said.

"What for?" Durnik asked. "You got away, didn't you?"

"You forget the tracks, Durnik." Silk held up one foot. "Rivan boots—an affectation, perhaps. They're very comfortable, but they do leave distinctive tracks. I expect that it's only going to be a matter of time before somebody puts a few things together and I'm not really in the mood for dodging Honethite assassins. They're fairly inept, but they can be an inconvenience."

The door opened rather quietly, and Silk instantly went into a crouch, his hands diving inside his smeared doublet for his daggers.

"My goodness," the lavender-gowned Velvet said mildly, entering and closing the door behind her, "aren't we jumpy this evening?"

"What are you doing in here?" Silk demanded.

"I was attending the Imperial Ball. You have no idea how much gossip one can pick up at such affairs. The whole ballroom is buzzing with the accidents that have been befalling the Honeths in the past couple nights. Under the circumstances, I thought it might have occurred to you that it was time for us to leave."

"Us?"

"Oh, didn't I tell you? How forgetful of me. I'll be joining you."

"You most certainly will *not*!" Belgarath said.

"I hate to contradict you, Ancient One," she said regretfully, "but I'm acting on orders." She turned to Silk. "My uncle has been a little nervous about some of your activities during the past few years. He *trusts* you, my dear Kheldar—you must never think that he doesn't trust you—but he *does* sort of want somebody to keep an eye on you." She frowned. "I think that he's going to be quite cross when he hears about your midnight visits to the Honeth family."

"You know the rules, Liselle," Silk replied. "Bethra was one of our people. We don't let those things go."

"Naturally not. But Javelin prefers to order that sort of retaliation personally. Your somewhat hasty vengeance has robbed him of that opportunity. You're just too independent, Silk. He's right, you know. You *do* need to be watched." She pursed her lips slightly. "I must admit, though, that it *was* a very nice job."

"Now you listen to me, young lady," Belgarath said hotly. "I am *not* conducting a guided tour for the benefit of the Drasnian spy network."

She gave him a disarming little smile and fondly patted his bearded cheek. "Oh, come now, Belgarath," she said, her soft brown eyes appealing, "do be reasonable. Wouldn't it be more civilized—and convenient—to have me in your party rather than trailing along behind you? I *am* going to follow my orders, Revered One, whether you like it or not."

"Why is it that I have to be surrounded by women who won't do as they're told?"

Her eyes went very wide. "Because we love you, Immortal One," she explained outrageously. "You're the answer to every maiden's dreams, and we follow you out of blind devotion."

"That's about enough of that, Miss," he said ominously. "You're not going with us, and that's final."

"*You know,*" the dry voice in Garion's mind mused, "*I think I've finally isolated the difficulty I've always had with Belgarath. It's his pure, pigheaded contrariness. He doesn't really have any reason for these arbitrary decisions of his. He just does it to irritate me.*"

"Do you mean that she's *supposed* to go along?" Garion blurted, so startled that he said it aloud.

"*Of course she is. Why do you think I went to all the trouble to get her to Tol Honeth before you all left. Go ahead and tell him.*"

Belgarath's expression, however, clearly showed that Garion's inadvertent exclamation had already told him that he had just been overruled. "Another visitation, I take it?" he said in a slightly sick tone of voice.

"Yes, Grandfather," Garion said. "I'm afraid so."

"She goes along then?"

Garion nodded.

"*I love to watch his expression when he loses one of these arguments,*" the dry voice said smugly.

Polgara began to laugh.

"What's so funny, Pol?" Belgarath demanded.

"Nothing, father," she replied innocently.

He suddenly threw his hands into the air. "Go ahead," he said in exasperation. "Invite all of Tol Honeth to come along. I don't care."

"Oh, father," Polgara said to him, "stop trying to be such a curmudgeon."

"Curmudgeon? Pol, you watch your tongue."

"That's really very difficult, father, and it makes one look ridiculous. Now, I think we should make a few plans. While the rest of us are changing clothes and packing, why don't you and Garion go explain to Varana that we're going to have to leave. Think up some suitable excuse. I don't know that we necessarily want him to know about Silk's nocturnal activities." She looked at the ceiling thoughtfully. "Durnik and Eriond and Toth will see to the horses, of course," she mused, "and I have a rather special little job for you, Prince Kheldar."

"Oh?"

"Go wash—thoroughly."

"I suppose I should have my clothes laundered as well," he noted, looking down at his garbage-saturated doublet and hose.

"No, Silk. Not laundered—burned."

"We can't leave tonight, Lady Polgara," Ce'Nedra said. "All the gates of the city are locked, and the legionnaires won't open them for anybody—except on the Emperor's direct orders."

"I can get us out of the city," Velvet said confidently.

"How are you going to manage that?" Belgarath asked her.

"Trust me."

"I *wish* people wouldn't keep saying that to me."

"Oh, by the way," she continued, "I saw an old friend of ours today. A large group of Honeths were riding toward the south gate." She looked over at Silk. "You really must have frightened them, Kheldar. They had whole battalions of their soldiers drawn up around them to keep you at a distance. Anyway, riding right in the middle of them and looking every inch a Tolnedran gentleman was the Mallorean, Harakan."

"Well, well," Silk said. "Isn't *that* interesting?"

"Prince Kheldar," Velvet said pleasantly, "please *do* go visit the baths—or at the very least, don't stand quite so close."

CHAPTER SIX

A chill gray fog had risen from the river to shroud the broad avenues of Tol Honeth. The snow had turned to rain—a cold drizzle that sifted down through the fog, and, although the roofs and courtyards were still mantled in white, the thoroughfares and avenues were clogged with seeping brown slush, crossed and crisscrossed with the tracks of wagons and carriages. It was nearly midnight when Garion and the others quietly left the grounds of the Imperial Compound, and the few bands of holiday revelers they encountered in the streets were much the worse for drink.

Velvet, riding a chestnut mare and wrapped and cowled in a heavy gray cloak, led them down past the marble-fronted houses of the merchant barons of Tol Honeth, through the empty central marketplace and into the poorer quarters of the city lying to the south. As they turned the corner of a side street, an authoritative voice came out of the fog. "Halt!"

Velvet reined in her horse and sat waiting as a squad of helmeted and red-cloaked legionnaires armed with lances marched out of the rainy mist. "State your business, please," the sergeant in charge of the patrol said brusquely.

"It's not really business, dear fellow," Velvet replied brightly. "We're on our way to an amusement. Count Norain is giving a party at his house. You *do* know the count, don't you?"

Some of the suspicion faded from the sergeant's face. "No, your Ladyship," he answered. "I'm afraid not."

"You don't know Norry?" Velvet exclaimed. "What an extraordinary thing! I thought everyone in Tol Honeth knew him—at least he always says so. Poor Norry's going to be absolutely crushed. I'll tell you what. Why don't you and your men come along with us so that you can meet him? You'll adore it. His parties are always so amusing." She gave the sergeant a wide-eyed, vapid smile.

"I'm sorry, your Ladyship, but we're on duty. Are you certain that you're following the right street, though? You're entering one of the meaner sections of the city, and I don't recall any noblemen's houses hereabouts."

"It's a short cut," Velvet told him. "You see, we go down through here, and then we turn left." She hesitated, "Or was it right? I forget exactly, but I'm sure one of my friends knows the way."

"You must be careful in this part of town, your Ladyship. There are footpads and cutpurses about."

"My goodness!"

"You really ought to be carrying torches."

"Torches? Great Nedra, no! The smell of the smoke from a torch lingers in my hair for weeks. Are you sure you can't join us? Norry's parties are *so* delightful."

"Give the count our regrets, your Ladyship."

"Come along, then," Velvet said to the others. "We really must hurry. We're terribly late as it is. Good-bye, Captain."

"Sergeant, your Ladyship."

"Oh? Is there a difference?"

"Never mind, your Ladyship. Hurry along now. You wouldn't want to miss any of the fun."

Velvet laughed gaily and moved her horse out at a steady trot.

"Who is Count Norain?" Durnik asked her curiously when they were out of earshot of the patrol.

"A figment of my imagination, Goodman Durnik." Velvet laughed.

"She's a Drasnian, all right," Belgarath murmured.

"Did you have any doubts, Eternal One?"

"Exactly where are you taking us, Liselle?" Polgara asked as they rode on down the foggy street.

"There's a house I know, Lady Polgara. It's not a very nice house, but it's built up against the south wall of the city, and it has a very useful back door."

"How can it have a back door if it's up against the city wall?" Ce'Nedra asked, pulling the hood of her green cloak forward to shield her face from the rainy mist.

Velvet winked at her. "You'll see," she said.

The street down which they rode grew shabbier and shabbier. The buildings looming out of the fog were built of plain stone instead of marble, and many of them were windowless warehouses, presenting blank faces to the street.

They passed a rank-smelling tavern from which came shouts and laughter and snatches of bawdy songs. Several drunken men burst from the door of the tavern and began pummeling each other with fists and clubs. One burly, unshaven ruffian lurched into the street and stood swaying in their path.

"Stand aside," Velvet said coolly to him.

"Who says so?"

The impassive Toth moved his horse up beside Velvet's mount, reached out with one huge arm, set the tip of the staff he carried against the man's chest, and gave him a light push.

"Just watch out who you're shoving!" the drunken man said, knocking the staff aside.

Without changing expression, Toth flicked his wrist, and the tip of the staff cracked sharply against the side of the fellow's head, sending him reeling, vacant-eyed and twitching, into the gutter.

"Why, thank you," Velvet said pleasantly to the mute giant, and Toth inclined his head politely as they rode on down the shabby street.

"What in the world were they fighting about?" Ce'Nedra asked curiously.

"It's a way to keep warm," Silk replied. "Firewood's expensive in Tol Honeth, and a nice friendly fight stirs up the blood. I thought that everybody knew that."

"Are you making fun of me?"

"Would I do that?"

"He's always had a certain streak of flippancy in his nature, your Majesty," Velvet said.

"Liselle," Ce'Nedra told her quite firmly, "since we're going to be traveling together, let's drop the formalities. My name is Ce'Nedra."

"If your Majesty prefers it that way."

"My Majesty does."

"All right then, Ce'Nedra," the blond girl said with a warm smile.

They rode on through the unlighted streets of the Imperial City until they reached the looming mass of the south wall. "We go this way," Velvet told them, turning down a rainy street lying between the wall and a long string of warehouses. The house to which she led them was a stout, two-story building, its stones black and shiny from the rain and fog, and it was set about a central courtyard and had a heavy front gate. Its narrow windows were all tightly shuttered, and a single small lantern gleamed over its gate.

Velvet dismounted carefully, holding her skirt up to keep its hem out of the slush. She stepped to the gate and tugged at a rope. Inside the courtyard a small bell tinkled. A voice from inside answered, and she spoke quietly for a moment to the gatekeeper. Then there was the sound of a clanking chain, and the gate swung open. Velvet led her horse into the courtyard, and the rest followed her. Inside, Garion looked around curiously. The courtyard had been cleared of snow, and the cobble-stones gleamed wetly in the still-falling drizzle. Several saddled horses stood under an overhanging roof, and a couple of well-appointed carriages were drawn up to a solid-looking door.

"Are we going inside?" Ce'Nedra asked, looking about curiously.

Velvet gave her a speculative look, then turned to look at Eriond. "Perhaps that might not be such a good idea," she said.

The muffled sound of laughter came from somewhere inside, followed by a woman's shrill squeal.

One of Polgara's eyebrows went up. "I think Liselle is right," she said firmly. "We'll wait out here."

"I'm a grown woman, Lady Polgara," Ce'Nedra objected.

"Not *that* grown, dear."

"Will you accompany me, Prince Kheldar?" Velvet asked the little man. "The presence of an unescorted woman in this house is sometimes misunderstood."

"Of course," he replied.

"We won't be long," Velvet assured the rest of them. With Silk at her side, she went to the door, rapped on its panels, and was immediately admitted.

"I still don't see why we can't wait inside where it's warm and dry," Ce'Nedra complained, shivering and puffing her cloak more tightly about her.

"I'm sure you would if you went in there," Polgara told her. "A little rain won't hurt you."

"What could possibly be *that* bad about this house?" There was another squeal from inside followed by more raucous laughter.

"That, for one thing," Polgara replied.

Ce'Nedra's eyes grew wide. "You mean that it's one of *those* places?" Her face suddenly went bright red.

"It's got all the earmarks of it."

After about a quarter of an hour, a slanting cellar door at the rear of the rain-drenched courtyard creaked open, and Silk came up from below carrying a gleaming lantern. "We're going to have to lead the horses down," he told them.

"Where are we going?" Garion asked.

"Down to the cellars. This place is full of surprises."

In single file, leading their skittish horses, they followed down a slanting stone ramp. From somewhere below, Garion could hear the gurgle and wash of running water; when they reached the foot of the ramp, he saw that the narrow passageway opened out into a large, cavelike chamber, roofed over with massive stone arches and dimly lighted by smoky torches. The center of the chamber was filled with dark, oily-looking water, and a narrow walkway ran around three sides of the pool. Moored to the walkway was a fair-sized barge, painted black and with a dozen dark-cloaked oarsmen on each side.

Velvet stood on the walkway beside the barge. "We can only cross two at a time," she said to them, her voice echoing hollowly in the vaulted chamber, "because of the horses."

"Cross?" Ce'Nedra said. "Cross where?"

"To the south bank of the Nedrane," Velvet replied.

"But we're still inside the city walls."

"Actually, we're *under* the city wall, Ce'Nedra. The only thing between us and the river are two of the marble slabs that form the exterior facing."

There came then the clanking of a heavy windlass somewhere in the dimness, and the front wall of the subterranean harbor creaked slowly open, dividing in the middle and swinging ponderously on great, well-greased iron hinges. Through the opening between the two slowly moving stone slabs, Garion could see the rain-dimpled surface of the river moving slowly by with its far shore lost in the dripping fog.

"Very clever," Belgarath said. "How long has this house been here?"

"Centuries," Velvet replied. "It was built to provide just about anything anyone could desire. Occasionally, one of the customers wants to leave—or enter—the city unobserved. That's what this place is for."

"How did you find out about it?" Garion asked her.

She shrugged. "Bethra owned the house. She told Javelin about its secrets."

Silk sighed. "She even reaches out from the grave to help us."

They were ferried in pairs across the foggy, rain-swept expanse of the Nedrane to land on a narrow, mist-shrouded sand beach backed by a thicket of willows. When Velvet finally joined them, it was perhaps three hours past midnight. "The oarsmen will brush our tracks out of the sand," she told them. "It's part of the service."

"Did this cost very much?" Silk asked her.

"A great deal, actually, but it comes out of the budget of the Drasnian Embassy. Your cousin didn't like that too much, but I persuaded him to pay—finally."

Silk grinned viciously.

"We have a few hours left until daylight," Velvet continued. "There's a wagon road on the other side of these willows, and it joins the Imperial Highway about a mile or so downriver. We should probably travel at a walk until we're out of earshot of the city. The legionnaires at the south gate might become curious if they hear galloping."

They mounted their horses in the soggy darkness and rode through the willows, down onto the muddy wagon track. Garion pulled his horse in beside Silk's. "What was going on in that place?" he asked curiously.

"Almost anything you could imagine." Silk laughed. "And probably a number of things you couldn't. It's a very interesting house with all sorts of diversions for people with enough money to be able to afford them."

"Did you recognize anybody there?"

"Several, actually—some highly respected members of the noble houses of the Empire."

Ce'Nedra, who rode directly behind them, sniffed disdainfully. "I cannot understand why any man would choose to frequent that sort of place."

"The customers are not exclusively male, Ce'Nedra," Silk told her.

"You can't be serious."

"A fair number of the highborn ladies of Tol Honeth have found all kinds of interesting ways to relieve their boredom. They wear masks, of course—although very little else. I recognized one countess, however—one of the pillars of the Horbite family."

"If she was wearing a mask, how could you recognize her?"

"She has a distinctive birthmark—in a place where it's seldom seen. Some years back, she and I were quite friendly, and she showed it to me."

There was a long silence. "I don't know that I really want to discuss this any more," Ce'Nedra said primly and nudged her horse past them to join Polgara and Velvet.

"She *did* ask," Silk protested innocently to Garion. "You heard her, didn't you?"

They rode south for several days in clearing weather. Erastide had passed virtually unnoticed while they were on the road, and Garion felt a strange kind of regret about that. Since his earliest childhood, the midwinter holiday had been one of the high points of the year. To allow it to pass unobserved seemed somehow to violate something very sacred. He wished that there might have been time to buy something special for Ce'Nedra, but about the best he could manage in the way of a gift was a tender kiss.

Some leagues above Tol Borune, they met a richly dressed couple riding north toward the Imperial Capital, accompanied by a dozen or so liveried servants. "You there, fellow," the velvet-clad nobleman called condescendingly to Silk, who happened to be riding in the lead, "what news from Tol Honeth?"

"The usual, your Lordship," Silk replied obsequiously. "Assassinations, plots, and intrigues—the normal amusements of the highborn."

"I don't care much for your tone, fellow," the nobleman said.

"And I don't care much for being called 'fellow,' either."

"We've heard such amazing stories," the giddy-looking lady in a fur-lined red velvet cape said breathlessly. "Is it true that someone is actually trying to kill all the Honeths? We heard that whole families have been murdered in their beds."

"Balera," her husband said in disgust, "you're just repeating wild rumors. What could a seedy-looking commoner like this know about what's really happening in the capital? I'm sure that if there were any substance to those wild stories, Naradas would have told us."

"Naradas?" Silk's eyes suddenly filled with interest. "An Angarak merchant with colorless eyes?"

"You know him?" the nobleman asked with some surprise.

"I know *of* him, your Lordship," Silk replied carefully. "It's not wise to go around announcing that you're acquainted with that one. You *did* know that the Emperor has put a price on his head, didn't you?"

"Naradas? Impossible!"

"I'm sorry, your Honor, but it's common knowledge all over Tol Honeth. If you know where to put your hands on him, you can earn yourself a thousand gold crowns without much effort."

"A thousand crowns!"

Silk looked around conspiratorially. "I wouldn't really want this to go any further," he said in a half whisper, "but it's widely rumored in Tol Honeth that those gold coins he's so free with are false."

"False?" the noble exclaimed, his eyes suddenly bulging.

"Very clever imitations," Silk continued. "Just enough gold is mixed with baser metals to make the coins look authentic, but they aren't worth a tenth of their face value."

The noble's face turned pasty white, and he clutched involuntarily at the purse attached to his belt.

"It's all part of a plot to destroy the Tolnedran economy by debasing the coinage," Silk added. "The Honeths were involved in it in some way, and that's why they're all being murdered. Of course, anyone caught with any of those coins in his possession is immediately hanged."

"*What?*"

"Naturally." Silk shrugged. "The Emperor intends to root out this monstrous business immediately. Stern measures are absolutely essential."

"I'm ruined!" the nobleman groaned. "Quickly, Balera!" he said, wheeling his horse, "we must return to Tol Borune at once!" And he led his frightened wife back southward at a dead run.

"Don't you want to hear about which kingdom was behind it all?" Silk called after them. Then he doubled over in his saddle, convulsed with laughter.

"Brilliant, Prince Kheldar," Velvet murmured admiringly.

"This Naradas moves around quite a bit, doesn't he?" Durnik said.

"I think I just put a bit of an anchor on him," Silk smirked. "Once that rumor spreads, I expect that he's going to have a little trouble spending his money—not to mention the interest that reward I mentioned is going to generate in certain quarters."

"That was a dreadful thing you did to that poor nobleman, though," Velvet said disapprovingly. "He's on his way back to Tol Borune to empty out all his strongboxes and bury the money."

Silk shrugged. "That's what he gets for consorting with Angaraks. Shall we press on?"

They passed Tol Borune without stopping and rode on south toward the Wood of the Dryads. When the ancient forest came into view on the southern horizon, Polgara pulled her horse in beside the mount of the dozing Belgarath. "I think we should stop by and pay our respects to Xantha, father," she said.

The old man roused himself and squinted in the direction of the Wood. "Maybe," he grunted doubtfully.

"We owe her the courtesy, father, and it's not really out of our way."

"All right, Pol," he said, "but just a brief stop. We're months behind Zandramas already."

They crossed the last band of open fields and rode in under the ancient, mossy oaks. The leaves had fallen to the chill winds of winter, and the bare limbs of the huge trees were starkly etched against the sky.

A peculiar change came over Ce'Nedra as they entered the Wood. Although it was still not really warm, she pushed back the hood of her cloak and shook out her coppery curls, causing her tiny, acorn-shaped gold earrings to tinkle musically. Her face became strangely calm, no longer mirroring the sorrow that had marked it since the abduction of her son. Her eyes became soft, almost unfocused. "I have returned," she murmured into the quiet air beneath the spreading trees.

Garion felt, rather than heard, the soft, murmuring response. From all around him he seemed to hear a sibilant sighing, although there was no trace of a breeze. The sighing was almost like a chorus, joining just below the level of hearing into a quiet, mournful song, a song filled with a gentle regret and at the same time an abiding hope.

"Why are they sad?" Eriond quietly asked Ce'Nedra.

"Because it's winter," she replied. "They mourn the falling of their leaves and regret the fact that the birds have all flown south."

"But spring will come again," he said.

"They know, but winter always saddens them."

Velvet was looking curiously at the little queen.

"Ce'Nedra's background makes her peculiarly sensitive to trees," Polgara explained.

"I didn't know that Tolnedrans were that interested in the out-of-doors."

"She's only half Tolnedran, Liselle. Her love of trees comes from the other side of her heritage."

"I'm a Dryad," Ce'Nedra said simply, her eyes still dreamy.

"I didn't know that."

"We didn't exactly make an issue of it," Belgarath told her. "We were having trouble enough getting the Alorns to accept a Tolnedran as the Rivan Queen without complicating matters by telling them that she was a nonhuman as well."

They made a simple camp not far from the place where they had been set upon by the hideous mud-men Queen Salmissra had dispatched to attack them so many years before. Because they could not hew limbs from live trees in this sacred wood, they were obliged to make shelters as best they could with what they found lying on the leaf-strewn forest floor, and their fire was of necessity very small. As twilight settled slowly over the silent Wood, Silk looked dubiously at the tiny, flickering flame and then out at the vast darkness moving almost visibly out from among the trees. "I think we're in for a cold night," he predicted.

Garion slept badly. Although he had piled fallen leaves deeply in the makeshift bed he shared with Ce'Nedra, their damp cold seemed to seep through to chill his very bones. He awoke from a fitful doze just as the first pale, misty light seeped in among the trees. He sat up stiffly and was about to throw off his blanket, but stopped. Eriond was sitting on a fallen log on the other side of their long-dead campfire, and sitting beside him was a tawny-haired Dryad.

"The trees say that you are a friend," the Dryad was saying as she absently toyed with a sharp-tipped arrow.

"I'm fond of trees," Eriond replied.

"That's not exactly the way they meant it."

"I know."

Garion carefully pushed his blankets aside and stood up.

The Dryad's hand moved swiftly toward the bow lying at her side, then she stopped. "Oh," she said, "it's you." She looked at him critically. Her eyes were as gray as glass. "You've gotten older, haven't you?"

"It's been quite a few years," he said, trying to remember just exactly where he had seen her before.

A faint hint of a smile touched her lips. "You don't remember me, do you?"

"Well, sort of."

She laughed, then picked up her bow. She set the arrow she was holding to the string and pointed it at him. "Does this help your memory at all?"

He blinked. "Weren't you the one who wanted to kill me?"

"It was only fair, after all. I was the one who caught you, so I should have been the one who got to kill you."

"Do you kill every human you catch?" Eriond asked her.

She lowered her bow. "Well, not *every* one of them. Sometimes I find other uses for them."

Garion looked at her a bit more closely. "You haven't changed a bit. You still look the same as before."

"I know." Her eyes grew challenging. "And pretty?" she prompted.

"Very pretty."

"What a nice thing for you to say. Maybe I'm glad that I didn't kill you after all. Why don't you and I go someplace, and you can say some more nice things to me?"

"That's enough, Xbel," Ce'Nedra said tartly from her bed of leaves. "He's mine, so don't get any ideas."

"Hello, Ce'Nedra," the tawny-haired Dryad said as calmly as if they had talked together within the past week. "Wouldn't you be willing to share him with one of your own sisters?"

"You wouldn't lend me your comb, would you?"

"Certainly not—but that's entirely different."

"There's no way that I could ever make you understand," Ce'Nedra said, pushing back her blankets and rising to her feet.

"Humans." Xbel sighed. "You all have such funny ideas." She looked speculatively at Eriond, her slim little hand softly touching his cheek. "How about this one? Does it belong to you, too?"

Polgara came out of another one of their makeshift shelters. Her face was calm, although one of her eyebrows was raised. "Good morning, Xbel," she said. "You're up early."

"I was hunting," the Dryad replied. "Does this blond one belong to you, Polgara? Ce'Nedra won't share that one of hers with me, but maybe—" Her hand lingeringly touched Eriond's soft curls.

"No, Xbel," Polgara said firmly.

Xbel sighed again. "None of you are any fun at all," she pouted. Then she stood up. She was as tiny as Ce'Nedra and as slender as a willow. "Oh," she said, "I almost forgot. Xantha says that I'm supposed to take you to her."

"But you got sidetracked, didn't you?" Ce'Nedra added drily.

"The day hasn't even got started yet." The Dryad shrugged.

Then Belgarath and Silk came out into the open area around the cold fire pit; a moment later, Durnik and Toth joined them.

"You have such a *lot* of them," Xbel murmured warmly. "Surely you can spare me one for just a little while."

"What's this?" Silk asked curiously.

"Never mind, Silk," Polgara told him. "Xantha wants to see us. Right after breakfast, Xbel here will show us the way—won't you, Xbel?"

"I suppose so." Xbel sighed a bit petulantly.

After their simple breakfast, the tawny-haired Dryad led them through the ancient Wood. Belgarath, leading his horse, walked beside her, and the two of them seemed deep in a conversation of some kind. Garion noticed that his grandfather furtively reached into his pocket from time to time and offered something to the slim Dryad—something she greedily snatched and popped into her mouth.

"What's he giving her?" Velvet asked.

"Sweets," Polgara said, sounding disgusted. "They're not good for her, but he always brings sweets with him when he comes into this Wood."

"Oh," Velvet said. "I see." She pursed her lips. "Isn't she a bit young to be so—well—"

Ce'Nedra laughed. "Appearances can be deceiving, Liselle. Xbel is quite a bit older than she looks."

"How old would you say?"

"Two or three hundred years at least. She's the same age as her tree, and oak trees live for a very long time."

Back in the forest, Garion heard giggles, whispers, and the faint tinkle of little golden bells; once in a while he caught a glimpse of a flitting patch of color as a Dryad scampered through the trees, her earrings jingling.

Queen Xantha's tree was even more vast than Garion remembered it, its branches as broad as highways and the hollows in its bole opening like the mouths of caves. The Dryads in their brightly colored tunics bedecked the huge limbs like flowers, giggling and whispering and pointing at the visitors. Xbel led them into the broad, moss-covered clearing beneath the tree, put her fingers to her lips, and made a curiously birdlike whistle.

Queen Xantha, with her red-haired daughter Xera at her side, emerged from one of the hollows in the vast trunk and greeted them as they dismounted. Ce'Nedra and Xera flew into each other's arms even as the queen and Polgara warmly embraced. Xantha's golden hair was touched with gray at the temples, and her gray-green eyes were tired.

"Are you unwell, Xantha?" Polgara asked her.

The queen sighed. "The time is growing close, that's all." She looked up affectionately at her enormous oak. "He's growing very tired, and his weight presses down upon his roots. He finds it harder and harder each spring to revive himself and put forth leaves."

"Can I do anything?"

"No, dearest Polgara. There's no pain—just a great weariness. I won't mind sleeping. Now, what brings you into our Wood?"

"Someone has taken my baby," Ce'Nedra cried, flying into her aunt's arms.

"What are you saying, child?"

"It happened last summer, Xantha," Belgarath told her. "We're trying to find the trail of the one who stole him—a Mallorean named Zandramas. We think that the abductor sailed south aboard a Nyissan ship."

Xbel was standing not far from the giant Toth, eyeing his awesomely muscled arms speculatively. "I saw one of the boats of the snake-people late last summer," she mentioned, not taking her eyes off the huge mute, "down where our river empties out into the big lake."

"You never mentioned it, Xbel," Xantha said.

"I forgot. Is anybody really interested in what the snake-people do?"

"Big lake?" Durnik said with a puzzled frown. "I don't remember any big lakes here in this Wood."

"It's the one that tastes funny," Xbel told him. "And you can't see the other side."

"You must mean the Great Western Sea, then."

"Whatever you want to call it," she replied indifferently. She continued to look Toth up and down.

"Did this Nyissan ship just sail on by?" Belgarath asked her.

"No," she said. "It got burned up. But that was after somebody got off."

"Xbel," Polgara said, stepping between the tawny-haired little Dryad and the object of her scrutiny, "do you think you can remember exactly what you saw?"

"I suppose so. It wasn't really very much, though. I was hunting, and I saw a boat go up to the beach on the south side of the river. This human in a black cloak with the hood pulled up got off with something in its arms. Then the black boat went back out into the water, and the human on the beach waved one hand at it. That's when the ship caught on fire—all over. All at once."

"What happened to the crew?" Durnik asked her.

"You know those big fish with all the teeth?"

"Sharks?"

"I guess so. Anyway, the water around the boat was full of them. When the humans jumped off the boat to get away from the fire, the fish ate them all up." She sighed. "It was a terrible waste. I was hoping that maybe one or two might have gotten away—or maybe even three." She sighed again.

"What did the human on the beach do then?" Polgara asked.

Xbel shrugged. "It waited until the ship burned all up and then it went into the woods on the south side of the river." She stepped around Polgara, her eyes still fixed on the huge mute. "If you're not using this one, Polgara, do you suppose I could borrow it for a little while? I've never seen one quite as big."

Garion spun and ran toward his horse, but Eriond was already there. He held out the reins of his own chestnut stallion. "He's faster, Belgarion," he said. "Take him."

Garion nodded shortly and swung into the saddle.

"Garion!" Ce'Nedra cried, "where are you going?"

But he was already plunging into the forest at a gallop. He was not really thinking as the stallion thundered through the leafless Wood. The only semblance of a thought in his mind was the image the indifferent Xbel had implanted there—a dark figure on the beach with something in its arms. Slowly, however, something else intruded itself on his awareness. There was something strange about the stallion's gait. About every fourth or fifth stride, the horse gave a peculiar lurch, and the wood seemed to blur for an instant. Then the gallop would continue until the next lurch and blurring.

The distance from Xantha's tree to the beach where the River of the Woods emptied into the Great Western Sea was considerable, he knew. At even the fastest gallop, it would take the better part of a day and a half to cover it. But wasn't that the glint of winter sunlight on a huge body of water coming through the trees just ahead?

There was another lurch and that odd blurring; quite suddenly the stallion set his forelegs stiffly, sliding through the sand at the very edge of the rolling surf.

"How did you do that?"

The horse looked back over one shoulder inquiringly.

Then Garion looked around in dismay. "We're on the wrong side of the river," he cried. "We're supposed to be over there." He drew on his will, preparing to translocate himself to the south beach, but the horse wheeled, took two steps, and lurched again.

They were suddenly on the sandy south beach, and Garion was clinging to the saddle to keep from falling off. For an irrational moment, he wanted to scold the animal for not warning him, but there was something much more important to attend to. He slid down from his saddle and ran along the damp sand at the edge of the water, drawing Iron-grip's sword as he went. The Orb glowed eagerly as he held up the blade. "Geran!" he shouted to it. "Find my son."

Between two strides, the Orb tugged at him, almost jerking him off balance. He slid to a stop on the hard-packed sand, feeling the powerful pull of the sword in his hands. The tip lowered, touched the sand once, and then the Orb flared triumphantly as the blade pointed unerringly up the driftwood-littered beach toward the scrubby forest at its upper end.

It was true! Although he had secretly feared that the hints they had received might have been just another clever ruse, the trail of Zandramas and of his infant son was here after all. A sudden wave of exultation surged through him.

"Run, Zandramas!" he called out. "Run as fast as you can! I have your trail now, and the world isn't big enough for you to find any place to hide from me!"

CHAPTER SEVEN

A chill dampness hung in the air beneath the tangled limbs overhead, and the smell of stagnant water and decay filled their nostrils. The trees twisted upward from the dark floor of the jungle, seeking the light. Gray-green moss hung in streamers from the trees, and ropy vines crawled up their trunks like thick-bodied serpents. A pale, wispy fog hovered back among the trees, rising foul-smelling and dank from black ponds and sluggishly moving streams.

The road they followed was ancient, and it was overgrown with tangled brush. Garion rode now at the head of the party with his sword resting on the pommel of his saddle and the Orb eagerly tugging him on. It was late afternoon, and the day that had been gray and overcast to begin with settled slowly, almost sadly toward evening.

"I didn't know that the Nyissans had ever built roads," Ce'Nedra said, looking at the weed-choked track lying ahead of them.

"They were all abandoned after the Marag invasion at the end of the second millennium," Belgarath told her. "The Nyissans discovered that their highway system provided too easy a route for a hostile army, so Salmissra ordered that all the roads be allowed to go back to the jungle."

The sword in Garion's hands swung slightly, pointing toward the thick undergrowth at the side of the road. He frowned slightly, reining in. "Grandfather," he said, "the trail goes off into the woods."

The rest of them pulled up, peering into the obscuring bushes. "I'll go take a look," Silk said, sliding down from his horse and walking toward the side of the road.

"Watch out for snakes," Durnik called after him.

Silk stopped abruptly. "Thanks," he said in a voice dripping with sarcasm. Then he pushed into the brush, moving carefully and with his eyes fixed on the ground.

They waited, listening to the rustling crackle as Silk moved around back in the undergrowth. "There's a campsite back here," he called to them, "an old fire pit and several lean-tos."

"Let's have a look," Belgarath said, swinging down out of his saddle.

They left Toth with the horses and pushed back into the stiffly rustling brush. Some yards back from the road they came to a clearing and found Silk standing over a cold fire pit with a number of charred sticks lying at the bottom. "Was Zandramas here?" he asked Garion.

Garion moved forward, holding out his sword. It moved erratically in his hands, pointing first this way and then that. Then it tugged him toward one of the partially collapsed shelters. When he reached it, the sword dipped, touched the ground inside the rude lean-to, and the Orb flared.

"I guess that answers that question," Silk said with a certain satisfaction.

Durnik had knelt by the fire pit and was carefully turning over the charred sticks and peering into the ashes beneath. "It's been several months," he said.

Silk looked around. "From the number of shelters I'd say that at least four people made camp here."

Belgarath grunted. "Zandramas isn't alone any more, then."

Eriond had been curiously poking into the crude shelters and he reached down, picked something up from the ground inside one of them, and came back to join the rest. Wordlessly, he held out the object in his hand to Ce'Nedra.

"Oh," she cried, taking it quickly and clutching it tightly against her.

"What is it, Ce'Nedra?" Velvet asked.

The little queen, her eyes brimming, mutely held out the object Eriond had just given her. It was a small, wool-knit cap, lying damp and sad-looking in her hand. "It's my baby's," she said in a choked voice. "He was wearing it the night he was stolen."

Durnik cleared his throat uncomfortably. "It's getting late," he said quietly. "Did we want to set up for the night here?"

Garion looked at Ce'Nedra's agonized face. "I don't think so," he replied. "Let's go on just a little farther."

Durnik also looked at the grieving queen. "Right," he agreed.

About a half mile farther down the road, they reached the ruins of a long-abandoned city, half buried in the rank jungle growth. Trees buckled up the once-broad streets, and climbing vines wreathed their way upward about the empty towers.

"It seems like a good location," Durnik said, looking around the ruins. "Why did the people just go away and leave it empty?"

"There could be a half-dozen reasons, Durnik," Polgara said. "A pestilence, politics, war—even a whim."

"A whim?" He looked startled.

"This is Nyissa," she reminded him. "Salmissra rules here, and her authority over her people is the most absolute in all the world. If she came here at some time in the past and told the people to leave, they'd have left."

He shook his head disapprovingly. "That's wrong," he said.

"Yes, dear," she agreed. "I know."

They made camp in the abandoned ruins, and the next morning they continued to ride in a generally southeasterly direction. As they pushed deeper and deeper into the Nyissan jungle, there was a gradual change in the vegetation. The trees loomed higher, and their trunks grew thicker. The underbrush became more dense, and the all-pervading reek of stagnant water grew stronger. Then, shortly before noon, a slight, vagrant breeze suddenly brought another scent to Garion's nostrils. It was an odor of such overpowering sweetness that it almost made him giddy.

"What is that lovely fragrance?" Velvet asked, her brown eyes softening.

Just then they rounded a bend, and there, standing in glory at the side of the road, rose the most beautiful tree Garion had ever seen. Its leaves were a shimmering gold, and long crimson vines hung in profusion from its limbs. It was covered with enormous blossoms of red, blue, and vivid lavender, and among those blossoms hung rich-looking clusters of shiny purple fruit that seemed almost ready to burst. An overwhelming sense of longing seemed to come over him as the sight and smell of that glorious tree touched his very heart.

Velvet, however, had already pushed past him, her face fixed in a dreamy smile as she rode toward the tree.

"Liselle!" Polgara's voice cracked like a whip. "Stop!"

"But—" Velvet's voice was vibrant with longing.

"Don't move," Polgara commanded. "You're in dreadful danger."

"Danger?" Garion said. "It's only a tree, Aunt Pol."

"Come with me, all of you," she commanded. "Keep a tight rein on your horses, and don't go anywhere near that tree." She rode slowly forward at a walk, holding her horse's reins firmly in both hands.

"What's the matter, Pol?" Durnik asked.

"I thought that all of those had been destroyed," she muttered, looking at the gorgeous tree with an expression of flinty hatred.

"But—" Velvet objected, "why would anyone want to destroy something so lovely?"

"Of course it's lovely. That's how it hunts."

"Hunts?" Silk said in a startled voice. "Polgara, it's only a tree. Trees don't hunt."

"This one does. One taste of its fruit is instant death, and the touch of its blossoms paralyzes every muscle in the body. Look there." She pointed at something in the high grass beneath the tree. Garion peered into the grass and saw the skeleton of a large-sized animal. A half-dozen of the crimson tendrils hanging from one of the flower-decked branches had poked their way down into the animal's rib cage and interwoven themselves into the mossy bones.

"Do not look at the tree," Polgara told them all in a deadly tone. "Do not think about the fruit, and try not to inhale the fragrance of its flowers too deeply. The tree is trying to lure you to within range of its tendrils. Ride on and don't look back." She reined in her horse.

"Aren't you coming, too?" Durnik asked with a worried look.

"I'll catch up," she replied. "I have to attend to this monstrosity first."

"Do as she says," Belgarath told them. "Let's go."

As they rode on past that beautiful, deadly tree, Garion felt a wrench of bitter disappointment; as they moved farther down the road away from it, he seemed to hear a silent snarl of frustration. Startled, he glanced back once and was amazed to see the crimson tendrils hanging from the branches writhing and lashing at the air in a kind of vegetative fury. Then he turned back quickly as Ce'Nedra made a violent retching sound.

"What's the matter?" he cried.

"The tree!" she gasped. "It's horrible! It feeds on the agony of its victims as much as upon their flesh!"

As they rounded another bend in the road, Garion felt a violent surge, and there was a huge concussion behind them, followed by the sizzling crackle of a fire surging up through living wood. In his mind he heard an awful scream filled with pain, anger, and a malevolent hatred. A pall of greasy black smoke drifted low to the ground, bringing with it a dreadful stench.

It was perhaps a quarter of an hour later when Polgara rejoined them. "It will not feed again," she said with a note of satisfaction in her voice. She smiled almost wryly. "That's one of the few things Salmissra and I have ever agreed upon," she added. "There's no place in the world for that particular tree."

They rode on down into Nyissa, following the weed-choked track of the long-abandoned highway. About noon of the following day, Eriond's chestnut stallion grew restive, and the blond young man pulled up beside Garion, who still rode in the lead with his sword on the pommel of his saddle. "He wants to run." Eriond laughed gently. "He always wants to run."

Garion looked over at him. "Eriond," he said, "there's something I've been meaning to ask you."

"Yes, Belgarion?"

"When I was riding your horse to the beach back up there in the Wood of the Dryads, he did something that was sort of odd."

"Odd? How do you mean?"

"It should have taken nearly two days to reach the sea, but he did it in about a half an hour."

"Oh," Eriond said, "that."

"Can you explain how he does it?"

"It's something he does sometimes when he knows that I'm in a hurry to get someplace. He kind of goes to another place, and when he comes back, you're much farther along than you were when he started."

"Where is this other place?"

"Right here—all around us—but at the same time, it's not. Does that make any sense?"

"No. Not really."

Eriond frowned in concentration. "You told me one time that you could change yourself into a wolf—the same way Belgarath does."

"Yes."

"And you said that when you do that, your sword is still with you, but at the same time it's not."

"That's what Grandfather told me."

"I think that's where this other place is—the same place where your sword goes. Distance doesn't seem to mean the same thing there as it does here. Does that explain it at all?"

Garion laughed. "It doesn't even come close, Eriond, but I'll take your word for it."

About midafternoon the next day, they reached the marshy banks of the River of the Serpent where the highway turned toward the east, following the winding course of that sluggish stream. The sky had cleared, though the pale sunlight had little warmth to it.

"Maybe I'd better scout on ahead," Silk said. "The road looks a bit more well traveled along this stretch, and we didn't exactly make a lot of friends the last time we were here." He spurred his horse into a brisk canter; in a few minutes he was out of sight around a bend in the weed-choked road.

"We won't have to go through Sthiss Tor, will we?" Ce'Nedra asked.

"No," Belgarath replied. "It's on the other side of the river." He looked at the screen of trees and brush lying between the ancient highway and the mossy river bank. "We should be able to slip past it without too much trouble."

An hour or so later, they rounded a bend in the road and caught a glimpse of the strange, alien-looking towers of the capital of the snake-people rising into the air on the far side of the river. There seemed to be no coherent pattern to Nyissan architecture. Some of the towers rose in slender spires, and others were bulky, with bulblike tops. Some even twisted in spirals toward the sky. They were, moreover, painted every possible hue—green, red, yellow, and even some in a garish purple. Silk was waiting for them a few hundred yards farther along the road. "There won't be any trouble getting past here without being seen from the other side," he reported, "but there's someone on up ahead who wants to talk to us."

"Who?" Belgarath asked sharply.

"He didn't say, but he seemed to know we were coming."

"I don't like that very much. Did he say what he wants?"

"Only that he's got a message of some kind for us."

"Let's go find out about this." The old man looked at Garion. "You'd better cover the Orb," he suggested. "Let's keep it out of sight—just to be on the safe side."

Garion nodded, took out a soft, tight-fitting leather sleeve and pulled it down over the hilt of Iron-grip's sword.

The shaven-headed Nyissan who awaited them was dressed in shabby, stained clothing and he had a long scar running from forehead to chin across an empty eye socket. "We thought you'd get here earlier," he said laconically as they all reined in. "What kept you?"

Garion looked at the one-eyed man closely. "Don't I know you?" he asked. "Isn't your name Issus?"

Issus grunted. "I'm surprised you remember. Your head wasn't too clear the last time we met."

"It wasn't the sort of thing I'd be likely to forget."

"Somebody in the city wants to see you," Issus said.

"I'm sorry, friend," Belgarath told him, "but we're pressed for time. I don't think there's anybody in Sthiss Tor that we need to talk with."

Issus shrugged. "That's up to you. I was paid to meet you and give you the message." He turned and started back through the slanting, late-afternoon sunlight toward the rank growth along the river bank. Then he stopped. "Oh. I almost forgot. The man who sent me said to tell you that he has some information about somebody named Zandramas, if that means anything to you."

"Zandramas?" Ce'Nedra said sharply.

"Whoever that is," Issus replied. "If you're interested, I've got a boat. I can take some of you across to the city if you want."

"Give us a minute or two to talk it over," Belgarath said to him.

"Take as long as you want. We can't cross until after dark anyway. I'll wait in the boat while you decide." He went on down through the bushes toward the river bank.

"Who is he?" Silk asked Garion.

"His name is Issus. He's for hire. Last time I saw him, he was working for Sadi—the Chief Eunuch in Salmissra's palace—but I get the feeling that he'll work for anybody as long as he gets paid." He turned to Belgarath. "What do you think, Grandfather?"

The old man tugged at one earlobe. "It could be some kind of ruse," he said, "but somebody over there knows enough about what we're doing to realize that we're interested in Zandramas. I think I'd like to find out who this well-informed citizen is."

"You won't get anything out of Issus," Silk told him. "I've already tried."

Belgarath pondered a moment. "Go see how big this boat of his is."

Silk went over to the edge of the road and peered down through the bushes. "We can't all go," he reported. "Maybe four of us."

Belgarath scratched his chin. "You, me, Pol, and Garion," he decided. He turned to Durnik. "Take the others—and the horses—and go back into the jungle a ways. This might take us a while. Don't build up any fires that can be seen from the city."

"I'll take care of things, Belgarath."

The boat Issus had rowed across from the city was painted a dull black, and it was moored to a half-sunken log, and screened by overhanging tree limbs. The one-eyed man looked critically at Garion. "Do you have to take that big sword?" he asked.

"Yes," Garion replied.

Issus shrugged. "Suit yourself."

As twilight settled on the river, a mist of tiny gnats rose from the surrounding bushes and swarmed about them as they sat in the boat waiting for darkness. Silk absently slapped at his neck.

"Don't jiggle the boat," Issus warned. "The leeches are hungry this time of year, so it's not a good time for swimming."

They sat huddled in the small boat enduring the biting of the gnats as the light gradually faded. After about a half-hour of discomfort, Issus peered out through the concealing branches. "It's dark enough," he said shortly. He untied the boat and pushed it out from the bank with one oar. Then he settled himself and started to row toward the lights of Sthiss Tor on the far side. After about twenty minutes, he swung his boat into the deep shadows beneath the wharf jutting out into the water from the Drasnian enclave, that commercial zone on the river front where northern merchants were permitted to conduct business. A tar-smeared rope was slung under the wharf, and Issus pulled them hand over hand beneath the protecting structure until they reached a ladder. "We go up here," he said, tying his boat to a piling beside the ladder. "Try not to make too much noise."

"Exactly where are you taking us?" Polgara asked him.

"It's not far," he replied and quietly went up the ladder.

"Keep your eyes open," Belgarath muttered. "I don't altogether trust that fellow."

The streets of Sthiss Tor were dark, since all the ground-level windows were thickly shuttered. Issus moved on catlike feet, keeping to the shadows, although Garion could not be sure if his stealth was out of necessity or merely from habit. As they passed a narrow alleyway, Garion heard a skittering noise coming from somewhere in the darkness, and his hand flew to his sword hilt. "What's that?" he asked.

"Rats." Issus shrugged. "They come up from the river at night to feed on garbage—and then the snakes crawl in out of the jungle to eat the rats." He held up one hand. "Wait here a moment." He moved on ahead to peer cautiously up and down a broad street lying just ahead of them. "It's clear," he said. "Come ahead. The house we want is just across the street."

"That's Droblek's house, isn't it?" Polgara asked as they joined the furtive Nyissan, "the Drasnian Port Authority?"

"You've been here before, I see. Let's go. They're expecting us."

Droblek himself opened the door of his house in response to Issus' light tap. The Drasnian port official wore a loose-fitting brown robe and was, if anything, more grossly fat than he had been when Garion had last seen him. As he opened the door, he looked nervously out into the street, peering this way and then that in the gloom. "Quickly," he whispered, "Inside—all of you." Once he had closed the door behind them and secured it with a stout lock, he seemed to relax a bit. "My Lady," he wheezed to Polgara with a portly bow, "my house is honored."

"Thank you, Droblek. Are you the one who sent for us?"

"No, my Lady. I helped to make the arrangements, though."

"You seem a bit nervous, Droblek," Silk said to him.

"I'm concealing something in my house that I'd rather not have here, Prince Kheldar. I could get into a lot of trouble if anyone found out about it. The Tolnedran Ambassador always has people watching my house, and he'd delight in embarrassing me."

"Where's the man we're supposed to meet?" Belgarath asked brusquely.

Droblek's face was awed as he replied. "I have a hidden chamber at the back of the house, Ancient One. He's waiting there."

"Let's go see him, then."

"At once, Eternal Belgarath." Waddling and puffing noticeably, the Drasnian official led them down a dimly lighted hallway. At its far end, he ran his hand down the wall and touched one of its stones. With a loud click, an irregularly shaped section of the wall came unlatched to protrude slightly from the rest.

"Exotic," Silk murmured.

"Who's there?" a shrill voice came from the other side of that hidden door.

"It's me—Droblek," the fat man answered. "The people you wanted to see have arrived." He pulled the stone-slab-covered door open. "I'll go keep watch," he said to them.

Beyond the door was a small, dank, hidden chamber lighted by a single candle. Sadi the eunuch stood fearfully beside a battered wooden table. His shaven head was stubbled and his scarlet silk robe tattered. There was a hunted look about his eyes. "At last," he said with relief.

"What on earth are you doing here, Sadi?" Polgara asked him.

"Hiding," he said. "Come in, please, all of you, and close the door. I don't want anybody to find out accidentally where I am."

They stepped into the small room, and Droblek pushed the door shut behind them.

"Why is the Chief Eunuch of Salmissra's palace hiding in the house of the Drasnian Port Authority?" Silk asked curiously.

"There's been a slight misunderstanding at the palace, Prince Kheldar," Sadi replied, sinking into a chair by the wooden table. "I'm not Chief Eunuch any more. As a matter of fact, there's a price on my head—a fairly large one, I'm told. Droblek owed me a favor, so he let me hide here—not very willingly, but—" He shrugged.

"Since we're talking about prices, I'll take my money now," Issus said.

"I have one more little job for you, Issus," the eunuch said in his oddly contralto voice. "Do you think that you could get into the palace?"

"If I need to."

"There's a red leather case in my quarters—under the bed. It has brass hinges. I need it."

"Did you want to discuss the price?"

"I'll pay you whatever you think is fair."

"All right. Let's say double what you already owe me."

"Double?"

"The palace is very dangerous right now."

"You're taking advantage of the situation, Issus."

"Go fetch it yourself then."

Sadi looked at him helplessly. "All right," he surrendered, "double."

"It's always a pleasure doing business with you, Sadi," Issus said flatly. Then he went to the door and slipped out.

"What happened here?" Silk asked the nervous eunuch.

Sadi sighed. "Certain accusations were made against me," he said in a pained voice. "I wasn't entirely prepared to defend myself against them, so I thought it might be wiser to take an extended leave from my duties. I've been working too hard lately anyway."

"Were the accusations unfounded?"

Sadi ran one long-fingered hand over his stubbled scalp. "Well—not entirely," he admitted, "but the matter was blown all out of proportion."

"Who took your place at the palace?"

"Sariss." Sadi almost spat the name. "He's a third-rate schemer with no real sense of style at all. Someday I'm going to take a great deal of pleasure in cutting out several things he needs rather badly—with a dull knife."

"Issus told us that you had some information about someone called Zandramas," Belgarath said.

"I do indeed," Sadi replied. He rose from his chair and went to the narrow, unmade bed standing against one wall. He rummaged around under the dirty brown blanket, took out a small silver flask, and opened it. "Excuse me," he said, taking a small sip. He grimaced. "I wish it didn't taste so bad."

Polgara gave him a cool look. "Do you suppose you could tell us what you know about Zandramas—before you start seeing the butterflies?"

Sadi looked at her innocently. "Oh, no. This isn't one of those, Lady Polgara," he assured her, shaking the flask. "It just has a certain calming effect. My nerves have been absolutely destroyed by what's been happening in the past few months."

"Why don't we get down to business?" Belgarath suggested.

"Very well. I have something you want, and you have something I want. I think a trade is in order."

"Why don't we discuss that?" Silk said, his eyes suddenly brightening and his long nose twitching.

"I'm very much aware of your reputation, Prince Kheldar." Sadi smiled. "I'm not foolish enough to try to bargain with *you*."

"All right, just what *is* this thing you want from us, Sadi?" Belgarath asked the dead-eyed eunuch.

"You're on your way out of Nyissa. I want you to take me with you. In exchange, I'll tell you everything I've learned about Zandramas."

"Totally out of the question."

"I think you're speaking in haste, Ancient One. Hear me out first."

"I don't trust you, Sadi," Belgarath said bluntly.

"That's quite understandable. I'm not the sort of man who *should* be trusted."

"Then why should I saddle myself with you?"

"Because I know why you're following Zandramas—and more importantly, I know where Zandramas is going. It's a very dangerous place for *you*, but I can arrange a way for us to move around freely once we get there. Now, why don't we put aside all this childishness about trusting each other and get down to business?"

"We're just wasting time here," Belgarath said to the rest of them.

"I can be very useful to you, Ancient One," Sadi told him.

"Or to anyone who might want to know where we are," Silk added.

"That wouldn't be in my own best interests, Kheldar."

"Which brings up an interesting point," Silk said. "I have a splendid opportunity here to turn a quick profit. You mentioned the fact that there's a large price on your head. If you don't want to be cooperative, I might just decide to collect that price. How much did you say it was?"

"You won't do that, Kheldar," Sadi replied placidly. "You're in a hurry to catch up with Zandramas, and there are always a hundred administrative details involved in collecting a reward. It would probably be a month before you saw any of the money, and Zandramas would be that much farther ahead of you by then."

"That's probably true," Silk admitted. He reached for one of his daggers with a regretful expression. "There's this other alternative, however—messy, but usually fairly effective."

Sadi backed away from him. "Belgarath," he said in a faintly alarmed voice.

"That won't be necessary, Silk," the old man said. He turned to Polgara. "See what you can do, Pol," he suggested.

"All right, father." She turned to the eunuch. "Sit down, Sadi," she told him. "I want you to look at something."

"Of course, Lady Polgara," he agreed amiably, seating himself in a chair by the table.

"Look closely," she said, making a curious gesture in front of his eyes.

The eunuch continued to smile. "How charming," he murmured, looking at something which seemed to have appeared before his eyes. "Can you make it do any other tricks, too?"

She bent forward and looked closely into his eyes. "I see. You're more clever than I thought, Sadi." She turned back to the rest of them. "He's drugged," she said. "Probably what he drank out of that flask. Right now there's absolutely nothing I can do with him."

"That takes us back to the other alternative, doesn't it?" Silk said, reaching for his dagger again.

Polgara shook her head. "Right now, he wouldn't even feel it."

"Oh," Sadi said in a disappointed voice, "you made it go away—and I rather liked it."

"The drug won't last forever." Silk shrugged. "And by the time it wears off, we should be far enough from the city to be able to carve some answers out of him without the screams attracting any attention." His hand strayed again to the hilt of his dagger.

"*Alorns,*" the dry voice in Garion's mind said disgustedly. "*Why is it that your solution to every problem comes out of a scabbard?*"

"*What?*"

"*Tell the little thief to put away his knife.*"

"*But—*"

"*Don't argue with me, Garion. You have to have Sadi's information about Zandramas, and I can't give it to you.*"

"*You're not suggesting that we take him along?*" Garion was profoundly shocked at the idea.

"*I'm not suggesting anything, Garion. I'm telling you. Sadi goes along. You can't do what you have to do without him. Now tell your grandfather.*"

"*He's not going to like it.*"

"I can face that prospect with enormous fortitude." Then the voice was gone.

"Grandfather," Garion said in a sick tone.

"What?" The old man's tone was testy.

"This isn't my idea, Grandfather, but—" Garion looked at the dreamy-faced eunuch with distaste and then lifted his hands helplessly.

"You're not serious!" Belgarath exclaimed after a moment.

"I'm afraid so."

"Am I missing something?" Sadi asked curiously.

"Shut up!" Belgarath snapped. Then he turned back to Garion. "Are you absolutely sure?"

Garion nodded dejectedly.

"This is sheer idiocy!" The old man turned and glared at Sadi. Then he reached across the table and took the front of the eunuch's iridescent robe in his fist. "Listen to me very carefully, Sadi," he said from between clenched teeth. "You're going with us, but keep your nose out of that flask. Do you understand me?"

"Of course, Ancient One," the eunuch replied in that same dreamy voice.

"I don't think you fully grasp what I'm talking about," Belgarath continued in a dreadfully quiet voice. "If I catch you with your brains full of dandelion fluff just once, I'll make you wish that Kheldar had gotten to you with his knife first. Do you follow me?"

Sadi's eyes grew wide, and his face blanched. "Y—yes, Belgarath," he stammered fearfully.

"Good. Now start talking. Just exactly what do you know about Zandramas?"

CHAPTER EIGHT

"It all started last year," Sadi began, still eyeing Belgarath apprehensively. "A Mallorean posing as a jewel merchant came to Sthiss Tor and sought out my chief rival at the palace—a petty schemer named Sariss. It was rather general knowledge that Sariss had long coveted my position, but I hadn't gotten around to having him killed yet." He made a face. "A grave oversight, as it turned out. Anyway, Sariss and the Mallorean negotiated for a bit, and the bargain they struck had nothing to do with gem stones. This so-called jeweler needed something that only someone in a position of authority could provide, so he gave Sariss certain information that Sariss was able to use to discredit me and usurp my position."

"I just love politics, don't you?" Silk said to no one in particular.

Sadi grimaced again. "The details of my fall from the queen's favor are tedious," he continued, "and I really don't want to bore you with them. At any rate, Sariss supplanted me as Chief Eunuch, and I barely escaped from the palace with my life. Once Sariss had consolidated his position, he was able to keep his part of the bargain he had reached with his Mallorean friend."

"And what exactly did the Mallorean want?" Silk asked.

"This, Prince Kheldar," Sadi said, rising and going to his rumpled cot. He drew a carefully folded parchment from beneath the mattress and handed it to the little man.

Silk read it quickly and then whistled.

"Well?" Belgarath said.

"It's an official document," Silk replied. "At least, it's over the queen's seal. Early last spring, Salmissra dispatched a diplomatic mission to Sendaria."

"That's fairly routine, Silk."

"I know, but there are also some secret instructions to the diplomats. She tells them that they will be met at the mouth of the River of the Serpent by a foreigner, and that they are to render this stranger every possible aid. The gist of the whole thing is that these diplomats were to make arrangements to get the foreigner to the port of Halberg on the west coast of Cherek *and* to have a Nyissan ship standing off the Rivan coast on a certain date about the middle of last summer."

"Coincidence, perhaps?" Belgarath suggested.

Silk shook his head and held up the parchment. "It identifies the foreigner by name. The diplomats were supposed to identify their passenger by the name 'Zandramas.' "

"That explains a few things, doesn't it?" Garion said.

"May I see that?" Polgara asked.

Silk handed her the parchment.

She looked at it briefly and then held it out to Sadi. "Are you positive that this is Salmissra's seal?" she asked him.

"There's no question about it, Polgara," he replied, "and no one dares to touch that seal without her consent."

"I see."

"How did you come by the document, Sadi?" Silk asked curiously.

"Four copies of all official documents are routinely made, Prince Kheldar. It's one of the resources of those with access to the queen's favor. The purchase price of the extra copies has been established for centuries."

"All right," Garion said, "so Zandramas came to Nyissa posing as a merchant, arranged to have Sariss replace you as Chief Eunuch, and somehow managed to get Salmissra to issue that order. Is that it?"

"It's not quite that simple, Belgarion," Sadi told him. "The Mallorean merchant was *not* Zandramas. No one here in Sthiss Tor ever saw Zandramas. The 'stranger' the document talks about joined the diplomats on their way to Sendaria. So far as I've been able to determine, Zandramas never passed through Sthiss Tor. Not only that, but after the arrangements for the ship to Halberg had been made, all the diplomats conveniently died. They were stopping over at an inn in Camaar on their way to the capital, and there was a fire in the middle of the night. No one escaped the fire."

"That's got a familiar ring to it," Silk said.

"All right then," Garion said, "who *was* the Mallorean jeweler?"

Sadi spread his hands helplessly. "I was never able to find out," he confessed.

"Did you ever see him?"

"Once. He was a strange-looking fellow. His eyes were absolutely colorless."

There was a long pause, and then Silk said, "That clears up a few other things, doesn't it?"

"Maybe so," Garion said, "but it still doesn't answer my main question. We know who Naradas is working for now. We know how Zandramas got to Cherek and escaped from the Isle of the Winds with my son, but what I need to know is where the trail we're following is going to lead."

Sadi shrugged. "Rak Verkat."

"How did you arrive at that conclusion?" Silk asked him.

"Sariss hasn't been in power long enough to weed out the more untrustworthy of his underlings. I found one who was open to the notion of private enterprise. Zandramas has to be in Mallorea with Prince Geran by this coming spring, and the route must be by way of Rak Verkat."

"Wouldn't it be shorter to sail from Rak Cthan?" Silk asked.

Sadi looked at him with a faintly surprised expression. "I thought you knew," he said. "Kal Zakath has put a very handsome price on the head of Zandramas, and the Mallorean reserves are concentrated at Rak Hagga. If Zandramas tried to go through Hagga to reach Cthan, all those troops would drop whatever they were doing to go head-hunting. The only safe port for Zandramas to sail from is Rak Verkat."

"Was this underling you bribed reliable?" Silk demanded.

"Of course not. As soon as he had finished telling me all this, he had planned to turn me in for the reward—dead, naturally, so he didn't really have any reason to lie to me, and he was too stupid to make up a coherent lie anyway." The eunuch smiled bleakly. "I know of a certain plant, though. It's a *very* reliable plant. The man was telling me the absolute truth. As a matter of fact, he kept telling me the truth long after it had begun to bore me. Sariss provided Zandramas with an escort across Nyissa and detailed maps of the shortest route to the Isle of Verkat."

"Was that all the fellow said?" Garion asked.

"Oh, no," Sadi replied. "He was busy confessing to me that he had cheated on an examination in school when I finally had Issus cut his throat. I can only deal with so much truth in one day."

"All right," Garion said, ignoring that, "Zandramas is going to the Isle of Verkat. How does that help us?"

"The route Zandramas will have to follow will be roundabout—because of that reward I mentioned. We, on the other hand, can go straight across southern Cthol Murgos to the Isle. It will save us months."

"That route goes right through the war zone," Silk protested.

"That's no particular problem. I can take you directly through to Verkat without any hindrance from either the Murgos or the Malloreans."

"How do you propose to manage that?"

"When I was younger, I was engaged in the slave trade in Cthol Murgos. I know all the routes and I know whom to bribe and whom to avoid. Slavers are useful to both sides in the war between the Murgos and Malloreans, so they're allowed to move around freely. All we have to do is dress as slave traders, and no one will interfere with us."

"What's to keep you from selling us to the Grolims as soon as we cross the border?" Silk asked bluntly.

"Self-interest." Sadi shrugged. "Grolims are an ungrateful lot. If I sell you to them, it's quite likely that they'll turn around and sell me to Salmissra. I don't think I'd like that at all."

"Is she really that angry with you?" Garion asked.

"Irritated," Sadi said. "A snake doesn't really get angry. I've heard, however, that she wants to bite me personally. That's a great honor, of course, but one I'd prefer to forgo."

The door to the hidden room clicked open, and Droblek looked in. "Issus is back," he said.

"Good," Belgarath replied. "I want to get back across the river before morning."

The one-eyed man came in carrying the case Sadi had described. It was a flat, square box a couple of feet across and several inches thick. "What's in this, Sadi?" he asked. "It gurgles." He took the case.

"Be careful man!" Sadi exclaimed. "Some of those bottles are fragile."

"What's this?" Belgarath demanded.

"A bit of this, a bit of that," Sadi replied evasively.

"Drugs?"

"And poisons and antidotes—a few aphrodisiacs, an anesthetic or two, a fairly effective truth drug—and Zith."

"What is Zith?"

"Zith is a who, Ancient One, not a what. I never go anywhere without her." He opened the case and lovingly took out a small earthenware bottle, securely corked and with a series of small holes encircling its neck. "Would you hold this, please?" he said, handing the bottle to Silk. "I want to make sure Issus didn't break anything." He began to carefully examine the row after row of little vials nested in velvet-lined pockets inside the case.

Silk looked curiously at the bottle, then took hold of the cork.

"I really wouldn't do that, Prince Kheldar," Sadi advised. "You might get a nasty surprise."

"What's in here?" Silk asked, shaking the bottle.

"Please, Kheldar. Zith becomes vexed when people shake her." Sadi closed the case, set it aside, and took the bottle from Silk. "There, there," he said to it in a crooning voice. "It's nothing to be alarmed about, dear. I'm right here and I won't let him disturb you any more."

From inside the bottle came a peculiar purring sound.

"How did you get a cat in there?" Garion asked.

"Oh, Zith isn't a cat, Belgarion," Sadi assured him. "Here, I'll show you." Carefully he worked the cork out and laid the bottle on its side on the table. "You can come out now, dear," he crooned to it.

Nothing happened.

"Come along now, Zith. Don't be shy."

Then a small, bright-green snake slithered obediently from the mouth of the bottle. She had gleaming yellow eyes and a vibrant red stripe running down her back from nose to tail. Her forked tongue flickered out, touching Sadi's outstretched hand.

Silk recoiled with a sharp intake of breath.

"Isn't she beautiful?" Sadi said, gently stroking the little snake's head with one finger. The snake began to purr contentedly, then raised her head, fixed Silk with a cold, reptilian eye, and hissed spitefully at him.

"I do believe that you offended her, Prince Kheldar," Sadi said. "Maybe you should stay away from her for a while."

"Don't worry," Silk said fervently, backing away. "Is she venomous?"

"She's the deadliest little snake in the world, aren't you, dear?" Sadi stroked the snake's head again. "Also the rarest. Her species is highly prized in Nyissa because they're the most intelligent of all reptiles. They're friendly—even affectionate—and, of course, the purr is absolutely delightful."

"But she *does* bite," Silk added.

"Only people who irritate her—and never a friend. All you have to do is feed her and keep her warm and show her a little affection now and then, and she'll follow you around like a puppy."

"Not *me,* she won't."

"Sadi," Belgarath said, pointing at the case, "what's the idea of all this? I don't need a walking apothecary shop trailing along behind me."

Sadi held up one hand. "Murgos aren't really very interested in money, Ancient One, but there are people I'll have to bribe when we go across Cthol Murgos. Some of them have picked up certain habits. That case is going to be worth more to us than a pack horse loaded down with gold."

Belgarath grunted. "Just keep *your* face out of it. I don't want your head full of smoke at a crucial moment—and keep your snake under control."

"Of course, Belgarath."

The old sorcerer turned to Issus. "Can you get a bigger boat? We need to get back across the river, and that one of yours won't hold all of us."

Issus nodded.

"Not just yet, father," Polgara said. "I'm going to need him for a while."

"Pol, we need to get back on the other side of the river before dawn."

"I won't be too long, father, but I have to go to the palace."

"The palace?"

"Zandramas went to Cherek—where no Angarak has been allowed since the days of Bear-shoulders. Salmissra arranged that and she also engineered the escape from the Isle of the Winds after the abduction of Ce'Nedra's baby. I want to know why."

"We're a bit pressed for time, Polgara. Can't this wait?"

"I don't think so, father. I think we need to know if there were any *other* arrangements. I'd rather not be surprised by a battalion or so of Nyissan troops lurking in the jungle along the trail we're following."

He frowned. "You might be right."

"You're going to the palace?" Garion asked her.

"I must, dear."

"All right," he said, squaring his shoulders. "Then I'm going with you."

She gave him a long, steady look. "You're going to insist, I take it?"

He nodded. "Yes, Aunt Pol, I think I am." He said it quite decisively.

She sighed. "How quickly they grow up," she said. Then she turned to Issus. "Do you know a back way to the palace?" she asked him.

The one-eyed man nodded.

"Will you show us?"

"Of course," he replied. He paused. "We can discuss the price later."

"Price?"

"Nothing for nothing, Lady," he shrugged. "Shall we go?"

It was nearly midnight when Issus led Polgara and Garion out the rear door of Droblek's house into a narrow alleyway that smelled strongly of rotting garbage. They made their way furtively through a twisting series of similar alleys, sometimes passing through the lower corridors of houses to move from one alley to another.

"How do you know which houses have unlocked doors?" Garion whispered as they emerged from a tall, narrow house in a run-down quarter of the city.

"It's my business to know," Issus replied. He straightened and looked around. "We're getting close to the palace," he told them. "The streets and alleys in this part of the city are patrolled. Wait here a minute." He stealthily crossed the alley, opened a recessed door, and slipped inside. A couple of moments later he emerged, carrying two silk robes, a pair of lances, and a couple of brass helmets. "We'll wear these," he said to Garion, "and if you don't mind, Lady, pull your hood farther over your face. If anybody stops us, let me do the talking."

Garion pulled on the robe and helmet and took one of the lances from the assassin.

"Tuck your hair up under the helmet," Issus instructed. Then he stepped out boldly, trusting to their disguises rather than to stealth.

They had no sooner entered the next street than they were stopped by a half-dozen armed men.

"What's your business?" the man in charge of the patrol demanded.

"We're escorting a visitor to the palace," Issus replied.

"What kind of visitor?"

Issus gave him a disgusted look. "You don't really want to interfere, Corporal," he said. "The one she's visiting wouldn't like it."

"And who is that?"

"Now, that's a very stupid question, man. If this woman's friend finds out that I told you, we'll probably *both* wind up in the river."

"How do I know that you're telling me the truth?"

"You don't—but do you really want to take a chance on it?"

The corporal's expression grew faintly nervous as he thought about it. "You'd better move along," he said finally.

"I was sure you'd see it my way," Issus observed. He roughly took hold of Polgara's arm. "Move, you," he commanded.

When they reached the end of the street, Garion glanced back. The soldiers were still watching them, but made no move to follow.

"I hope you aren't offended, Lady," Issus apologized.

"No," Polgara replied. "You're a very resourceful fellow, Issus."

"That's what I get paid for. We go this way."

The wall of Salmissra's palace was very high, constructed of great roughhewn stone blocks that had stood for eons in this dank city by the river. Issus led them into the dense shadows under the wall and to a small, iron-barred gate. He fumbled with the lock for a moment, then carefully swung the gate open. "Let's go," he muttered.

The palace was a maze of dimly lighted corridors, but Issus led them confidently, moving along as if he were on an important mission. As they approached the broader, somewhat more brightly lighted hallways near the center of the palace, a grotesquely made-up eunuch lurched by, his legs stiff and his eyes unfocused. His mouth was fixed in a stupefied grin, and his body twitched spasmodically as he stumbled past them. They passed an open doorway and heard someone inside giggling uncontrollably. Garion could not be sure if that unseen person was a man or a woman.

The one-eyed man stopped and opened a door. "We have to go through here," he said, taking a smoky lamp from the niche beside the door. "Be careful. It's dark, and there are snakes on the floor."

The room was cool and had a musty smell. Garion could clearly hear the dry, dusty hiss of scales rubbing against each other in the corners. "It's fairly safe," Issus said. "They were fed today, and that always makes them sluggish." He stopped at the door, opened it a crack, and peered out. "Wait," he whispered.

Garion heard a couple of men talking and the sound of their footsteps in the corridor outside. Then a door opened and closed.

"It's clear," Issus said quietly. "Let's go." He led them out into the corridor and along its dimly lighted length to a polished door. He looked at Polgara. "Are you sure you want to see the queen?" he asked her.

She nodded.

"All right," he said. "Sariss is in here. He'll take us to the throne room."

"Are you sure?" Garion whispered.

Issus reached under the robe he had donned in the alley and drew out a long, saw-edged dagger. "I can practically guarantee it," he said. "Give me a moment. Then come in and close the door." He shoved the door open and jumped into the room like a great, soft-footed cat.

"What—" someone inside the room cried out in a high-pitched voice. Then there was a terrified silence.

Garion and Polgara entered quickly, closing the door behind them. A man sat at the table, his eyes bulging with fright and with the needlepoint of Issus' dagger pushed against his throat. He wore a crimson silk robe, and his shaven head was pasty white. Rolls of greasy, unhealthy-looking fat drooped from his jowls, and his frightened eyes were small and piglike.

Issus was talking to him in a dreadfully quiet voice, emphasizing what he was saying by pressing the point of his knife into the skin of the fat man's throat. "This is an Ulgo knife, Sariss. It causes almost no damage when it goes in, but when you pull it out, it jerks out all kinds of things along with it. Now, we aren't going to make any kind of outcry, are we?"

"N-no," Sariss stammered in a squeaky voice.

"I was sure you'd see it my way. This is what we're going to do. This lady and her young friend want to have a word with the queen, so you're going to take us to the throne room."

"The queen?" Sariss gasped. "No one goes into her presence without permission. I-I can't do it."

"This conversation has suddenly taken a definite turn for the worse." Issus looked over at Polgara. "Would you like to turn your head, Lady?" he asked politely. "The sight of a man with his brains oozing out of his ears makes some people queasy."

"Please," Sariss begged him. "I can't. The queen will kill me if I take you into the throne room without being summoned."

"And I'll kill you if you don't. Somehow, I've got the feeling that this isn't going to be one of your good days, Sariss. Now get on your feet." The assassin jerked the trembling fat man from his chair.

They stepped out into the corridor with the eunuch leading the way. Sweat was streaming down his face, and there was a wild look in his eyes.

"No blunders, Sariss," Issus warned. "Remember that I'm right behind you."

The two burly guards at the entrance to the throne room bowed respectfully to the Chief Eunuch and swung the heavy doors open for him.

Salmissra's throne room was unchanged. The enormous stone statue of Issa, the Serpent God, still loomed behind the dais at the far end of the room. The crystal lamps still glowed dimly on their silver chains, and the two dozen bald and crimson-robed eunuchs still knelt on the polished floor, ready to murmur in unison their phrases of adoration. Even the gold-framed mirror still stood on its pedestal at the side of the divanlike throne.

Salmissra herself, however, was dreadfully changed. She was no longer the beautiful, sensuous woman Garion had seen when, drugged and bemused, he had first been led into her presence. She lay on her throne with her mottled coils undulating restlessly. Her polished scales gleamed in the lamplight, and her flat reptile's head rose on its long, thin neck, with the golden crown of the serpent queen resting lightly above her dead, incurious eyes.

She glanced briefly at them as they entered, then turned back to regard her reflection in the mirror. "I do not recall having summoned you, Sariss," she said in a dry, dusty whisper.

"The queen questions the Chief Eunuch," the two dozen shaven-headed men kneeling near the dais intoned in unison.

"Forgive me, Eternal Salmissra," the eunuch pleaded, prostrating himself on the floor before the throne. "I was forced to bring these strangers into your presence. They threatened to kill me if I refused."

"Then you should have died, Sariss," the serpent whispered. "You know that I do not like to be disturbed."

"The queen is displeased," half of the kneeling eunuchs murmured.

"Ah," the other half responded with a certain spiteful satisfaction.

Salmissra swung her swaying head slightly to fix her eyes on Issus. "I seem to know you," she said.

The one-eyed man bowed. "Issus, your Majesty," he replied. "The assassin."

"I do not wish to be disturbed just now," the Serpent Queen told him in her emotionless whisper. "If that means that you're going to kill Sariss, please take him out into the corridor to do it."

"We will not disturb you for long, Salmissra," Polgara said, pushing back the hood of her cloak.

The snake's head turned slowly, her forked tongue tasting the air. "Ah, Polgara," she hissed without any evident surprise. "It has been some time since your last visit."

"Several years," Polgara agreed.

"I no longer take note of the years." Salmissra's dead gaze turned to Garion. "And Belgarion," she said. "I see that you're not a boy any more."

"No," he replied, fighting down an involuntary shudder.

"Come closer," she whispered. "Once you thought that I was beautiful and yearned for my kiss. Would you like to kiss me now?"

Garion felt a strange compulsion to obey and found that he could not take his eyes from those of the Serpent Queen. Not even aware that he did it, he took a hesitant step toward the dais.

"The fortunate one approaches the throne," the eunuchs murmured.

"Garion!" Polgara said sharply.

"I will not hurt him, Polgara. I never intended to hurt him."

"I have a few questions for you, Salmissra," Polgara said coldly. "Once you answer them, we'll leave you to your entertainments."

"What manner of questions, Polgara? What could I possibly know that your sorcery could not ferret out?"

"You recently met a Mallorean named Naradas," Polgara said. "A man with colorless eyes."

"Is that his name? Sariss never told me."

"You made an arrangement with him."

"Did I?"

"At his request, you sent diplomats to Sendaria. Among them was a foreigner named Zandramas. Your diplomats were instructed to give the foreigner every possible assistance in getting to Halberg on the west coast of Cherek. You also ordered a ship to the Isle of the Winds to bring Zandramas back to Nyissa."

"I gave no such orders, Polgara. I have no interest in the affairs of Zandramas."

"The name is familiar to you?"

"Of course. I told you once that the priests of Angarak and the sorcerers of Aloria are not the only ones who can find a truth that lies hidden. I know of your desperate pursuit of the one who took Belgarion's son from the Citadel at Riva."

"But you say that you were in no way involved in the arrangements?"

"The one you call Naradas came to me with gifts," Salmissra whispered, "but said nothing more than that he wished my permission to trade here in Nyissa."

"Then how do you explain this?" Aunt Pol took the parchment sheet Sadi had given her from under her cloak.

Salmissra flicked her tongue at one of the kneeling eunuchs. "Bring it to me," she ordered.

The eunuch leaped to his feet, took the parchment from Aunt Pol, and then knelt on the edge of the dais, holding the sheet open and extended toward his queen.

"This is not the order I gave," Salmissra said flatly after the briefest of glances. "I ordered the diplomats to Sendaria—nothing more. Your copy is not accurate, Polgara."

"Would the original be about anywhere?" Garion asked her.

"Sariss should have it."

Garion looked at the fat eunuch groveling on the floor. "Where is it?" he demanded.

Sariss stared at him, then his gaze went in terror to the enthroned serpent.

Garion considered several alternatives but discarded most of them in favor of simplicity. "Make him talk, Issus," he said shortly.

The one-eyed man stepped over, straddled the trembling eunuch, and grasped his chin firmly from behind. Then he pulled up sharply until Sariss was arched backward. The saw-edged dagger made a steely grating sound as it came out of its sheath.

"Wait!" Sariss begged in a choked voice. "It—it's in the drawer at the bottom of my wardrobe in my room."

"Your methods are direct, assassin," the queen observed.

"I'm a simple man, your Majesty," Issus replied. "I do not have the temperament for subtlety nor intricacy. I've found that directness saves time in the long run." He released the terrified Sariss and pushed his Ulgo dagger back into his sheath. He looked at Garion. "Do you want me to go get the parchment?" he asked.

"I think we're going to need it."

"All right." Issus turned and left the room.

"An interesting man," Salmissra noted. She bent and caressingly touched her mottled coils with her blunt nose. "My life is much changed since you were last here, Polgara," she whispered in her dusty voice. "I am no longer driven by those hungers I had before, but pass my days instead in restless doze. I lull myself into slumber with the sweet sound of my own scales caressing each other. As I sleep, I dream. I dream of mossy caves in deep, cool forests, and I dream of the days when I was still a woman. But sometimes in my dreams, I am a bodiless spirit, seeking out the truths that others would hide. I know of the fear which lies in your heart, Polgara, and the desperate need that drives Zandramas. I even know of the terrible task which lies upon Cyradis."

"But you still say that you are not involved in this matter?"

"I have no interest in it. You and Zandramas can pursue each other across all the kingdoms of the world, but I am incurious as to the outcome."

Aunt Pol's eyes narrowed as she looked at her.

"I have no reason to lie to you, Polgara," Salmissra said, sensing the suspicion in that look. "What could Zandramas possibly offer me that would buy my aid? All of my needs are satisfied, and I no longer have desires." Her blunt head came up and her tongue flickered. "I rejoice, however, that your quest has brought you again into my presence so that I may gaze once more upon the perfection of your face."

Polgara's chin lifted. "Look quickly then, Salmissra. I have little patience for the involuted amusements of a snake."

"The centuries have made you waspish, Polgara. Let us be civil to one another. Would you like to have me tell you what I know of Zandramas? She is no longer what she once was."

"*She!*" Garion exclaimed.

"You did not even know that?" the serpent hissed maliciously. "Your sorcery is a sham, then, Polgara. Could you not sense your enemy is a woman? And did you perhaps not even realize that you have already met her?"

"What are you talking about, Salmissra?"

"Poor, dear Polgara. The long, long centuries have filled your wits with cobwebs. Did you really think that you and Belgarath are the only ones in the world who can change their shapes? The dragon who visited you in the mountains above Arendia appears quite different when she resumes her natural form."

The door to the throne room opened and Issus came back in, holding a parchment sheet with a red wax seal on the bottom of it.

"Bring it to me," Salmissra commanded.

Issus looked at her, his single eye narrowing as he gauged the distance between the serpent's throne and his own unprotected skin. Then he went over to the prostrate eunuch who had presented Polgara's document to the queen. Without changing expression, he kicked the man solidly in the ribs. "Here," he said, thrusting out the parchment. "Take this to her Majesty."

"Are you afraid of me, Issus?" Salmissra asked, sounding faintly amused.

"I am unworthy to approach you too closely, my Queen."

Salmissra bent her head to examine the parchment the trembling eunuch held out for her to read. "There appears to be some discrepancy," she hissed. "This document is the same as the one you showed me, Polgara, but it is *not* the document to which I ordered my seal affixed. How is this possible?"

"May I speak, my Queen?" the eunuch who held the parchment asked in a quavering voice.

"Of course, Adiss," she replied almost pleasantly, "so long as you realize that if your words displease me, the kiss I will give you in payment will bring you death." Her forked tongue flickered out toward him.

The eunuch's face went a ghastly gray color, and his trembling became so violent that he very nearly collapsed.

"Speak, Adiss," she whispered. "It is my command that you disclose your mind to me. We will determine then whether you live or die. Speak. Now."

"My Queen," he quavered, "the Chief Eunuch is the only person in the palace permitted to touch your Majesty's royal seal. If the document in question is false, must we not look to him for an explanation?"

The serpent considered that, her head swaying rhythmically back and forth and her forked tongue flickering. At last she stopped her reptilian dance and leaned slowly forward until her tongue brushed the cringing eunuch's cheek. "Live, Adiss," she murmured. "Your words have not displeased me, and so my kiss grants the gift of life." Then she reared her mottled form again and regarded Sariss with her dead eyes. "Do you have an explanation, Sariss? As our most excellent servant Adiss has pointed out, you are my Chief Eunuch. You affixed my seal. How did this discrepancy come to pass?"

"My Queen—" His mouth gaped open, and his dead-white face froze in an expression of stark terror.

The still-shaken Adiss half rose, his eyes filled with a sudden wild hope. He held up the parchment in his hand and turned to his crimson-robed companions kneeling to one side of the dais. "Behold," he cried in a triumphant voice. "Behold the proof of the Chief Eunuch's misconduct!"

The other eunuchs looked first at Adiss and then at the groveling and terrified Chief Eunuch. Their eyes also furtively tried to read the enigmatic expression on Salmissra's face. "Ah," they said in unison at last.

"I'm still waiting, Sariss," the Serpent Queen whispered.

Sariss, however, quite suddenly scrambled to his feet and bolted toward the throne room door, squealing in mindless, animal panic. As fast as his sudden flight was, though, Issus was even faster. The shabby, one-eyed assassin bounded after the fleeing fat man, his horrid dagger leaping into his hand. With the other he caught the back of the Chief Eunuch's crimson robe and jerked him up short. He raised his knife and looked inquiringly at Salmissra.

"Not yet, Issus," she decided. "Bring him to me."

Issus grunted and dragged his struggling captive toward the throne. Sariss, squealing and gibbering in terror, scrambled his feet ineffectually on the polished floor.

"I will have an answer from you, Sariss," Salmissra whispered.

"Talk," Issus said in a flat voice, setting his dagger point against the eunuch's lower eyelid. He pushed slightly, and a sudden trickle of bright-red blood ran down the fat man's cheek.

Sariss squealed and began to blubber. "Forgive me, your Majesty," he begged. "The Mallorean Nadaras compelled it of me."

"How did you do it, Sariss?" the serpent demanded implacably.

"I-I put your seal at the very bottom of the page, Divine Salmissra," he blurted. "Then when I was alone, I added the other orders."

"And were there other orders as well?" Aunt Pol asked him. "Will we encounter hindrances and traps on the trail of Zandramas?"

"No. Nothing. I gave no orders other than that Zandramas be escorted to the Murgo border and provided the maps she required. I pray you, your Majesty. Forgive me."

"That is quite impossible, Sariss," she hissed. "It had been my intention to hold myself aloof in the dispute between Polgara and Zandramas, but now I am involved because you have abused my trust in you."

"Shall I kill him?" Issus asked calmly.

"No, Issus," she replied. "Sariss and I will share a kiss, as is the custom in this place." She looked oddly at him. "You are an interesting man, assassin," she said. "Would you like to enter my service? I am certain that a position can be found for one of your talents."

Adiss the eunuch gasped, his face suddenly going pale. "But your Majesty," he protested, leaping to his feet, "your servants have always been eunuchs, and this man is—" He faltered, suddenly realizing the temerity of his rash outburst.

Salmissra's dead eyes locked on his, and he sank white-faced to the floor again.

"You disappoint me, Adiss," she said in that dusty whisper. She turned back to the one-eyed assassin. "Well, Issus?" she said. "A man of your talents could rise to great eminence, and the procedure, I'm told, is a minor one. You would soon recover and enter the service of your queen."

"Ah—I'm honored, your Majesty," he replied carefully, "but I'd really prefer to remain more or less intact. There's a certain edge my profession requires, and I'd rather not endanger that by tampering with things."

"I see." She swung her head briefly to look at the cowering Adiss and then back to the assassin. "You have made an enemy today, however, I think—and one that may some day grow quite powerful."

Issus shrugged. "I've had many enemies," he replied. "A few of them are even still alive." He gave the cowering eunuch a flinty look. "If Adiss wants to pursue the matter, he and I can discuss it privately some day—or perhaps late some night when our discussions won't disturb anyone."

"We must leave now," Polgara said. "You have been most helpful, Salmissra. Thank you."

"I am indifferent to your gratitude," Salmissra replied. "I do not think that I will see you again, Polgara. I think that Zandramas is more powerful than you and that she will destroy you."

"Only time can reveal that."

"Indeed. Farewell, Polgara."

"Good-bye, Salmissra." Polgara deliberately turned her back on the dais. "Come along, Garion—Issus," she said.

"Sariss," Salmissra said in a peculiar, almost singing tone, "come to me." Garion glanced back over his shoulder and saw that she had reared her mottled body until it rose high above the dais and her velvet-covered throne. She swayed rhythmically back and forth. Her dead eyes had come alight with a kind of dreadful hunger and they burned irresistibly beneath her scaly brows.

Sariss, his mouth agape and with his piglike eyes frozen and devoid of all thought, lurched toward the dais with jerky, stiff-legged steps.

"Come, Sariss," Salmissra crooned. "I long to embrace you and give you my kiss."

Aunt Pol, Garion, and Issus reached the ornately carved door and went quietly into the corridor outside. They had gone no more than a few yards when there came from the throne room a sudden shrill scream of horror, dying hideously into a gurgling, strangled squeal.

"I think that the position of Chief Eunuch just became vacant," Issus observed drily. Then, as they continued on down the dimly lighted hallway he turned to Polgara. "Now, my Lady," he said, ticking the items off on his fingers, "first of all there was the fee for getting you and the young man into the palace. Then there was the business of persuading Sariss to take us to the throne room, and then . . ."

PART TWO

RAK URGA

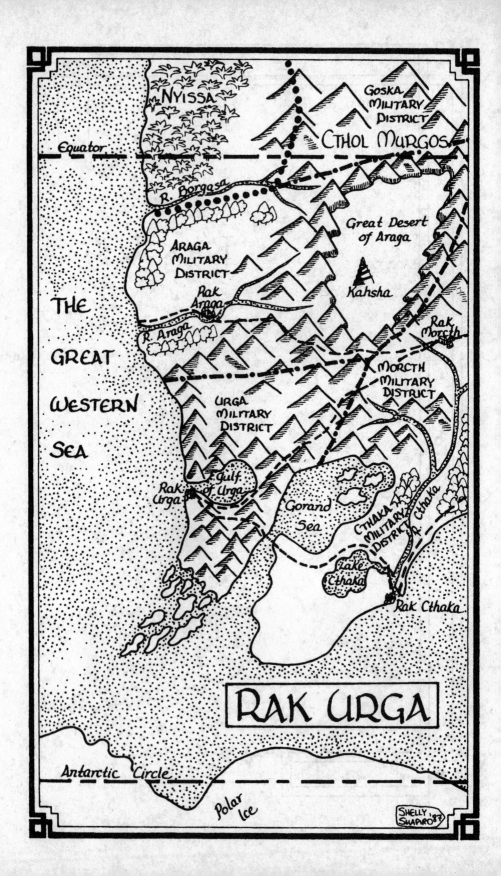

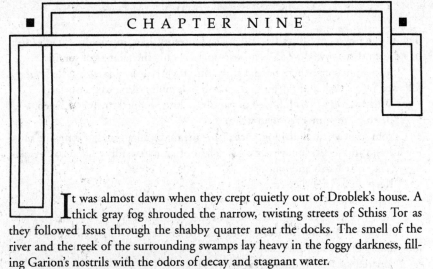

It was almost dawn when they crept quietly out of Droblek's house. A thick gray fog shrouded the narrow, twisting streets of Sthiss Tor as they followed Issus through the shabby quarter near the docks. The smell of the river and the reek of the surrounding swamps lay heavy in the foggy darkness, filling Garion's nostrils with the odors of decay and stagnant water.

They emerged from a narrow alleyway, and Issus motioned them to a halt as he peered into the mist. Then he nodded. "Let's go," he whispered. "Try not to make any noise." They hurried across a glistening cobblestone street, ill-lit by torches, each surrounded by a nimbus of hazy red light, and entered the deeper shadows of another garbage-strewn alley. At the far end of that alley, Garion could see the slow-moving surface of the river sliding ponderously by, pale in the fog.

The one-eyed assassin led them along another cobblestone street to the foot of a rickety wharf jutting out into the fog. He stopped in the shadows beside a dilapidated shack that stood partially out over the water and fumbled briefly at the door. He opened it slowly, muffling the protesting creak of a rusty hinge with a tattered piece of rag. "In here," he muttered, and they followed him into the dank-smelling shack. "There's a boat tied at the end of this wharf," he told them in a half whisper. "Wait here while I go get it." He went to the front of the shack, and Garion heard the creak of hinges as a trapdoor opened.

They waited, listening nervously to the skittering and squeaking of the rats that infested this part of town. The moments seemed to creep by as Garion stood watch beside the door, peering out through a crack between two rotting boards at the foggy street running along the edge of the river.

"All right," he heard Issus say from below after what seemed like hours. "Be careful on the ladder. The rungs are slippery."

One by one, they climbed down the ladder into the boat the one-eyed man had pulled into place under the wharf. "We have to be quiet," he cautioned them after they had seated themselves. "There's another boat out there on the river somewhere."

"A boat?" Sadi asked in alarm. "What are they doing?"

Issus shrugged. "Probably something illegal." Then he pushed his craft out into the shadows at the side of the wharf, settled himself on the center seat, and began to row, dipping his oars carefully into the oily surface of the river so that they made almost no sound.

The fog rose from the dark water in little tendrils, and the few lighted windows high in the towers of Sthiss Tor had a hazy unreality, like tiny golden candles seen in a dream. Issus rowed steadily, his oars making only the faintest of sounds.

Then from somewhere not far upstream, there was a sudden muffled outcry, followed by a splash and the gurgling sound of bubbles rising to the surface.

"What was that?" Sadi hissed nervously as Issus stopped rowing to listen.

"Be still," the one-eyed man whispered.

From somewhere in the fog, there came the thumping sound of someone moving around in a boat, followed by the splash of an awkwardly pulled oar. A man swore, his voice harsh and loud.

"Keep quiet," another voice said.

"What for?"

"Let's not tell everybody in Sthiss Tor that we're out here."

"You worry too much. That rock I tied to his ankles will keep him down for a long time." The creaking oarlocks faded off into the fog.

"Amateurs," Issus muttered derisively.

"An assassination, perhaps?" Silk asked with a certain professional curiosity. "Or a private killing?"

"What difference does it make?" Issus started to row again, his oars dipping slowly into the water. Behind them Sthiss Tor had disappeared in the fog. Without the reference point of its dim lights, it seemed to Garion that they were not moving at all, but sat motionless on the surface of the dark river. Then, at last, a shadowy shore appeared ahead in the clinging fog; after a few more minutes, he was able to make out the hazy shape of individual treetops outlined by the pale mist.

A low whistle came to them from the bank, and Issus angled their boat slightly, making for that signal. "Garion, is that you?" Durnik's whispered voice came out of the shadows.

"Yes."

Issus pulled their boat under the overhanging branches, and Durnik caught the bow. "The others are waiting on the far side of the road," he said quietly as he helped Polgara from the boat.

"You've been most helpful, Issus," Sadi said to his hireling.

The one-eyed man shrugged. "Isn't that what you paid me for?"

Silk looked at him. "If you decide to consider my offer, talk to Droblek."

"I'll think about it," Issus replied. He paused, then looked at Polgara. "Good luck on your journey, Lady," he said quietly. "I get the feeling that you're going to need it."

"Thank you, Issus."

Then he pushed his boat back out into the fog and disappeared.

"What was that all about?" Sadi asked Silk.

"Oh, nothing much. Drasnian Intelligence is always looking for a few good men, is all."

Durnik was looking curiously at the shaven-headed eunuch.

"We'll explain when we get back to the others, dear," Polgara assured him.

"Yes, Pol," he agreed. "We go this way." He led them up the brushy bank to the broken stones of the road and then pushed his way into the tangled undergrowth on the far side, with the rest of them close behind him.

Ce'Nedra, Eriond, Toth, and Velvet sat in a little hollow behind the moss-covered trunk of a fallen tree. A single, well-shielded lantern gave forth a dim glow, illuminating the hollow with faint light. "Garion," Ce'Nedra exclaimed with relief, coming quickly to her feet. "What took you so long?"

"We had to make a side trip," he replied, taking her into his arms. As he nestled his face into her hair, he found that it still had that warm, sweet fragrance that had always touched his heart.

"All right," Belgarath said, looking out into the tag end of the foggy night, "I want to get moving, so I'll keep this short." He sat down on the spongy moss beside the lantern. "This is Sadi." He pointed at the shaven-headed eunuch. "Most of you know him already. He'll be going with us."

"Is that altogether wise, Belgarath?" Durnik asked dubiously.

"Probably not," the old man replied, "but it wasn't my idea. He seems to feel that Zandramas has gone down into southern Cthol Murgos and plans to cross the continent to the Isle of Verkat off the southeast coast."

"That's a very dangerous part of the world just now, Ancient One," Velvet murmured.

"We'll have no trouble, dear lady," Sadi assured her in his contralto voice. "If we pose as slavers, no one will interfere with us."

"So you say," Belgarath said somewhat skeptically. "That might have been true before the war started down there, but we still don't know for sure how the Malloreans view the slave trade."

"There's one other thing you should all know," Polgara added quietly. "Garion and I went to the palace to find out if Salmissra was involved in this in any way. She told us that Zandramas is a woman."

"A woman?" Ce'Nedra exclaimed.

"That's what she said, and she had no reason to lie to us."

Durnik scratched at his head. "That's a bit of a surprise, isn't it? Are you sure Salmissra knew what she was talking about?"

She nodded. "She was very certain—and quite smug about the fact that she knew something that I didn't."

"It *does* sort of fit," Velvet said thoughtfully. "Most of the things Zandramas has done were done the way a woman would do them."

"I can't quite follow that," Durnik admitted.

"A man does things one way, Goodman. A woman does them differently. The fact that Zandramas is a woman explains a great deal."

"She's also going to great lengths to conceal the fact," Silk added. "She's made sure that just about everybody who's seen her isn't alive to tell anybody about it."

"We can talk about all this some more later," Belgarath said, standing up and looking around at the gradually lightening fog. "I want to get away from this place before the people on the other side of the river start moving around. Let's saddle the horses."

It took a bit of readjustment of their equipment to free one of the pack horses for Sadi's use, but a short time later they rode out from their sheltered place of concealment and on along the weedy track that followed the winding course of the River of the Serpent. They moved at first at a cautious walk, but once they had passed the outskirts of Sthiss Tor, lying hidden in the fog across the river, they picked up their pace to a canter, clattering along the abandoned road that stretched through the rank jungle and reeking swamps of the land of the snake-people.

As the sun rose, it gave the fog surrounding them a kind of mystical glow, and the droplets hanging along the edges of individual leaves drooping from the under-growth at the side of the road took on a jewel-like sparkle. Garion, sandy-eyed and tired from a night without sleep, looked bemused at the jeweled green leaves, mar-veling that such beauty could exist in this stinking swamp.

"The whole world is beautiful, Belgarion," Eriond assured him in response to that unspoken thought. "You just have to know how to look at it."

Once the fog had burned off, they were able to move at a much more rapid pace. They encountered no other travelers that day. By the time the sun began to sink into the heavy banks of purple cloud that seemed to hover perpetually over the western horizon, they were well upriver.

"How far is it to the Murgo border?" Garion asked Sadi as the two of them gathered firewood while Durnik and Toth set up the tents for their night's encamp-ment.

"Several more days," the eunuch replied. "The highway fords the river up near the headwaters and then angles down toward Araga. There's a village on the other side of the ford. I'll need to stop there for a few things—suitable garments and the like."

Velvet and Ce'Nedra were unpacking Polgara's cooking utensils not far away, and the blond Drasnian girl looked over at Sadi. "Excuse me," she said, "but I think I've discovered a flaw in your plan."

"Oh?"

"How can we pose as slavers when some of us are obviously women?"

"But there are always women in any party of slave traders, my dear lady," he an-swered, dropping an armload of firewood beside the stone-lined cooking pit. "I'm sure that if you think about it, you'll understand why."

"I certainly don't," Ce'Nedra declared.

Sadi coughed rather delicately. "We trade in female slaves as well as males, your Majesty," he explained, "and a female who's been guarded by women brings a higher price."

A slow flush crept up her face. "That's revolting."

Sadi shrugged. "I didn't make the world, your Majesty," he replied. "I only try to live in it."

After they had eaten, Sadi took an earthenware bowl, filled it with hot water, and began to lather his stubbled scalp.

"There's something I've been meaning to ask you, Sadi," Silk said from the other side of the fire. "Exactly what was it that you did to make Salmissra so discon-tented with you?"

Sadi gave him a wry look. "Those of us in the queen's service are an extraordi-narily corrupt lot, Kheldar," he replied. "We're all knaves and scoundrels and worse. A number of years ago Salmissra laid down certain guidelines to keep our plotting and deceit within reasonable limits—just to keep the government from falling apart. I overstepped a few of those limits—most of them, actually. Sariss found out about it and ran to the Queen to tattle." He sighed. "I do so wish that I'd been able to see his reaction when she kissed him." He picked up his razor.

"Why do all Nyissan men shave their heads?" Ce'Nedra asked him curiously.

"There are all manner of nasty little insects in Nyissa, your Majesty, and hair provides them with a perfect nesting place."

She gave him a startled look, her hand going unconsciously to her coppery curls.

"I shouldn't worry too much," he smiled. "*Most* of the time, they're dormant in winter."

About noon several days later, the road they were following began to climb up out of the jungles into the foothills. The damp chill that had lain over the normally steaming swamps of Nyissa moderated as they climbed, and it was pleasantly warm as they moved up into the hardwood forest lying along the eastern frontier. The river began to tumble over stones beside the road, and its murky waters grew clear as they rode deeper into the hills.

"The ford is just up ahead," Sadi told them as he led them around a broad curve in the road. A stone bridge had once crossed the river there, but time and the turbulent water had eaten away its foundations and tumbled it into the riverbed. The green water rushed over the fallen stones, swift and foaming. Upstream from the fallen bridge, there was a wide stretch of gravel-bottomed shallows that rippled, sparkling in the sun. A well-traveled trail led down to the ford.

"What about the leeches?" Silk asked, eyeing the water with suspicion.

"The water's a little too fast for them, Prince Kheldar," Sadi replied. "Their bodies are too soft to take much bouncing around on rocks." He rode confidently down into the rippling stream and led them on across.

"That village I mentioned is just up ahead," he told them as they emerged from the stream. "It should only take me an hour or so to pick up what we'll need."

"The rest of us can wait here, then," Belgarath said, swinging down from his saddle. "You go with him, Silk."

"I can manage," Sadi protested.

"I'm sure you can. Let's just call it a precaution."

"How am I going to explain to the shopkeeper what a Drasnian is doing with me?"

"Lie to him. I'm sure you'll be very convincing."

Garion dismounted and walked up the slope of the river bank. These were the people he loved most in the world, but sometimes their idle banter set his teeth on edge. Even though he knew that they really meant nothing by it, it seemed somehow to reflect an indifferent frivolity, a callous lack of concern for his personal tragedy—and more importantly, for Ce'Nedra's. He stood atop the river bank, looking with unseeing eyes down the descending gorge of the River of the Serpent and out over the dense green canopy of the jungles of the snake-people. He would be glad to get out of Nyissa. It was not so much the clinging mud, the stink of the swamps, nor even the clouds of insects that hovered perpetually in the air. The real problem with Nyissa was the fact that one could seldom see for more than a few feet in any direction. For some reason, Garion felt an overpowering need to see for long distances, and the obscuring trees and undergrowth that had blocked his vision since they had been in Nyissa had increasingly irritated him. A number of times he had caught himself just on the verge of clenching his will and blasting out long, clear avenues through the jungle.

When Silk and Sadi returned, the little Drasnian's face was angry.

"They're only for show, Prince Kheldar," Sadi protested mildly. "We're not actually going to have any slaves with us anyway, so there won't really be anyone to wear them, will there?"

"It's the idea of them that offends me."

"What's this?" Belgarath asked.

Sadi shrugged. "I purchased a few shackles and slave bells. Kheldar doesn't approve."

"I didn't like the whips either," Silk added.

"I explained that to you, Kheldar."

"I know. It's still disgusting."

"Of course it is. Nyissans are a disgusting people. I thought you knew that."

"We can sort out comparative moralities later on," Belgarath said. "Let's move along."

The road they followed rose steeply up from the river, taking them deeper and deeper into the foothills. The hardwoods gave way to gnarled evergreens and low-lying heather. Great, rounded white boulders lay in scattered profusion among the dark green trees, and the sky overhead was an intense blue. They camped that night in a grove of low, twisted junipers, building their fire against a boulder so that its white surface could reflect back both light and heat. Above them rose a steep ridge that stood jaggedly outlined against the starry eastern sky.

"Once we cross that ridge, we'll be in Cthol Murgos," Sadi told them as they sat around the fire after supper. "The Murgos watch their borders very carefully, so it's probably time to start wearing our disguises." He opened the large bundle he had brought from the village near the ford and took out a number of dark green silk robes. He looked speculatively at Ce'Nedra and the gigantic Toth. "There may be a slight problem here," he murmured. "The shopkeeper didn't have a wide variety of sizes."

"I'll fix it, Sadi," Polgara said, taking the rolled-up robes from him and opening one of the packs in search of her sewing kit.

Belgarath had been staring thoughtfully at a large map. "There's something that's been bothering me," he said. He turned to Sadi. "Is there any way Zandramas might have taken a ship from one of these ports on the west coast and sailed around the southern end of the continent to Verkat?"

Sadi shook his head, his shaven scalp gleaming in the orange firelight. "Impossible, Ancient One. A Mallorean fleet slipped up behind the Murgos a few years back, and King Urgit still has nightmares about it. He's closed all the west coast ports and has ships patrolling the sea lanes all the way around the tip of the Urga peninsula. No one sails along that coast without his specific permission."

"How far is it to Verkat?" Durnik asked.

Sadi squinted up at the stars. "Three or four months at this time of the year, Goodman."

Polgara had been humming quietly to herself as her needle flashed in the firelight. "Come here, Ce'Nedra," she said.

The little queen rose and went over to where she sat. Polgara held up the green silk robe, measuring it against her tiny frame, then nodded in satisfaction.

Ce'Nedra wrinkled her nose. "Do they have to smell so bad?" she asked Sadi.

"I don't suppose they have to, but they always do, for some reason. Slaves have a certain odor about them, and it seems to rub off."

Aunt Pol was looking at Toth as she held another of the slaver's robes in her hands. "This could be a bit more challenging," she murmured.

The giant gave her a brief, almost shy smile and rose to put more wood on the fire. As he poked the coals with a stick, a column of winking red sparks rose to greet the stars hanging low in the night sky. From somewhere down the ridge, as if in response to those sparks, there came a deep, coughing roar.

"What's that?" Ce'Nedra cried.

"Lion." Sadi shrugged. "Sometimes they hunt along the slave route—the old and crippled ones at any rate."

"Why would they do that?"

"Sometimes slaves get too sick to walk any farther and they have to be left behind. An old lion can't chase anything that's very nimble, and . . ." He left it hanging in the air.

She stared at him in horror.

"You did ask, after all, your Majesty," he reminded her. "As a matter of fact, I don't like the idea very much myself. That's one of the reasons I left the slave trade to go into politics." He stood up and brushed off the back of his robe. "Now, if you dear people will excuse me, I have to go feed Zith. Please be careful when you go to your beds tonight. Sometimes she sneaks away after she's been fed. I think it amuses her to hide from me, and one never knows where she might turn up." He walked out of the circle of golden firelight toward the place where he had spread his blankets.

Silk stared after him, then turned back to the fire. "I don't know about the rest of you," he declared, "but I'm sleeping right here tonight."

The next morning after breakfast, they donned the evil-smelling robes of Nyissan slavers. At Belgarath's instruction, Garion once again covered the hilt of Iron-grip's sword. "I think we'd better keep the Orb well wrapped as long as we're in Cthol Murgos," the old man said. "It tends to get excited when there are Angaraks about."

They mounted their horses and followed the ancient highway up a ravine toward the jagged ridge top. As they rounded a bend, Polgara suddenly reined in her horse with a sharp hiss.

"What's the matter, Pol?" Durnik asked her.

She did not reply immediately, but her face grew pale. Her eyes flashed, and the white lock at her brow suddenly flamed. "Monstrous!" she said.

"What is it, Aunt Pol?" Garion asked.

"Look over there," she answered, pointing with a trembling hand. There were white bones scattered about on the rocky ground several yards from the road; lying among them was a vacant-eyed human skull.

"One of the slaves Sadi mentioned last night?" Silk suggested.

Polgara shook her head. "A part of the arrangement between Sariss and Naradas involved several men to escort Zandramas to the Murgo border," she reminded him. "When she got this far, she didn't need them any more."

Silk's face grew grim. "That seems to be in character. Every time she finishes with somebody, she kills him."

"She didn't just kill them," Polgara said with a look of revulsion. "She broke their legs and left them for the lions. They waited all day for nightfall, and then the lions came."

Ce'Nedra's face blanched. "How horrible!"

"Are you sure, Pol?" Durnik asked, his face slightly sick.

"Some things are so dreadful that they leave their traces in the very rocks."

Belgarath had been staring bleakly at the gnawed bones. "This isn't the first time she's done this. She's not satisfied with just killing people to cover her tracks. She has to commit atrocities."

"She's a monster," Ce'Nedra declared. "She feeds on horror."

"It's a bit more than that," Belgarath replied. "I think she's trying to leave messages for us." He jerked his head toward the scattered bones. "That wasn't really necessary. I think she's trying to scare us off."

"It won't work," Garion said very quietly. "All she's doing is adding to the final reckoning. When the time finally comes for her to pay it, I think she's going to find that all of this is more than she can afford."

At the top of the ridge, the ancient road they had been following ended abruptly, sharply marking the invisible line where Nyissa ended and Cthol Murgos began. From the ridge top they looked out over an endless, unbroken expanse of shattered black rock and miles-wide beds of dark brown gravel, shimmering under a broiling sun.

"Which way did Zandramas go from here?" Durnik asked Garion.

"She turned south," Garion replied, feeling the Orb pulling in a new direction.

"We could gain time if we cut straight across that out there, couldn't we?"

"Absolutely out of the question, Goodman Durnik," Sadi declared. "That's the Great Desert of Araga. It's as big as Algaria. The only water there is in the wells of the Dagashi, and you wouldn't want to get caught dipping into a Dagashi well."

"The Dagashi live out there?" Durnik asked, shading his eyes with one hand to look out at the fiery wasteland.

"They're the only ones who can," Sadi replied. "Perhaps that explains why they're so fearsome. We're going to have to follow this ridge line south for a hundred leagues or so to get around that waste. Then we'll strike out due southeast across Morcth and on down into the Great Southern Forest in Gorut."

Belgarath nodded. "Let's get started then."

They rode south, skirting the western edge of the Desert of Araga and staying well up in the hills, which sloped steeply down to the desert floor. As they rode, Garion noticed that the trees on this side of the ridge were stunted and sparsely distributed. There was no grass growing in the rock-strewn ground, and the heather had given way to scrubby thorn bushes. The sharp ridge line appeared to be an abrupt demarcation between two entirely different climates. What had been only pleasantly warm on the west side became oppressively hot here on the east. There were almost no streams, and the few springs they found were tiny and seeped their water grudgingly into tepid little puddles hidden among the rust-colored boulders.

On the morning of the third day after they had entered Cthol Murgos, Toth belted his blanket across one shoulder, took up his staff, and walked down to the mouth of the ravine where they had spent the night, to look out over the rocky desert lying below. The sun had not yet risen, and the light from the dawn sky was steely and shadowless, etching each rock and crag of the sun-blasted wasteland in sharp detail. After a moment, the giant returned and touched Durnik's shoulder.

"What is it, Toth?" the smith asked.

The mute pointed to the mouth of the ravine.

"All right," Durnik said, rising from the spot where he had been kindling their morning fire. The two of them went on down the ravine in the pale light and stood looking out. After a few moments, Durnik called back over his shoulder. "Belgarath, I think you'd better come here and look at this."

The old sorcerer finished pulling on his scuffed and mismatched boots and went down to join them, with his green silk robe flapping about his ankles. He stared out for a while, then muttered a curse. "We've got a problem," he announced without turning.

The problem became apparent as soon as the rest of them reached the entrance to the ravine. Some distance out on the desert, a large cloud of dust was rising to hang motionless in the still morning air.

"How many men do you think it would take to raise that much dust?" Garion asked quietly.

"At least several hundred," Silk told him.

"Murgos?"

"Not unless the Murgos have changed their habits," Velvet murmured. "Those men are dressed in red."

Silk peered intently out at the dust cloud. "You've got good eyes," he said finally to the blond girl.

"One of the advantages of youth," she replied sweetly.

He gave her a quick, irritable look.

"I thought this was Murgo territory," Durnik objected. "It is," Sadi said, "but the Malloreans send patrols out every so often. 'Zakath's been trying to find a way to come at Urgit from behind for a number of years now."

"How did they find water out there?"

"I'm sure they brought it with them."

Toth turned toward the south side of the ravine and scrambled up the steep, rocky bank, sending long streams of dusty brown gravel slithering down behind him.

"Do you think we can outrun them?" Silk asked Belgarath.

"That probably wouldn't be a very good idea. I think we'd better stay here until they're out of the area."

Toth gave a low whistle from the top of the bank he had just climbed.

"Go see what he wants, Durnik," Belgarath said.

The smith nodded and started up the steep slope.

"Do you think they'll find us up here?" Ce'Nedra asked tensely.

"It's not too likely, your Majesty," Sadi replied. "I doubt that they're going to take the time to search every ravine and gully in these mountains."

Belgarath squinted out at the dust cloud. "They're moving toward the southwest," he noted. "If we sit tight for a day or so, they'll move on out of our vicinity."

"I hate to lose the time," Garion fretted.

"So do I, but I don't think we've got much choice."

Durnik came sliding back down the bank of the ravine. "There's another group of men up ahead," he reported tersely. "Murgos, I think."

Belgarath uttered a fairly rancid curse. "I really don't want to get caught in the middle of a skirmish," he said. "Go up there and keep an eye on things," he told Silk. "Let's not have any more surprises."

Silk started up the steep bank of the ravine. On an impulse, Garion followed him. When they reached the top, they took cover behind a scrubby thorn bush.

The fiery ball of the sun slid up out of the desert lying to the east, and the obscuring cloud of dust raised by the advancing Mallorean column turned it to an ominous red. The figures of the men below, both the mounted Malloreans and the concealed Murgos, were tiny in the distance, like toy figures on a miniature landscape.

"As closely as I can tell, they're about evenly matched," Silk noted, looking down at the two parties of troops.

Garion considered it. "The Murgos are going to have the advantage, though. They're on higher ground and they'll have the element of surprise."

Silk grinned. "You're turning into quite a tactician."

Garion let that pass.

"Sadi was right," Silk said. "The Malloreans brought water with them." He pointed at two dozen or so cumbersome-looking wagons loaded with large casks, trailing along at the rear of the column advancing across the desert.

The Malloreans reached the first of the shallow ravines stretching up into the foothills, then halted, while their scouts fanned out to search the rocky terrain. It was only a short time before alarmed shouts announced that at least some of the Murgos had been seen.

"That doesn't make any sense," Garion said. "They didn't even try to keep from being found."

"Murgos aren't notorious for intelligence," Silk replied. As the red-clad Malloreans massed up for a charge, the concealed Murgos rose from their hiding places and began to shower their foes with arrows, but after only a few volleys, they began to pull back.

"Why are they retreating?" Garion demanded in disgust. "What's the point of setting up an ambush and then turning around and running away from it?"

"Nobody's *that* stupid," Silk muttered his agreement. "They're up to something else."

The retreating Murgos kept up a steady rain of arrows, littering the ravines stretching up into the hills with windrows of red-garbed dead as the Malloreans doggedly charged up into the foothills. Once again, the toylike quality of all those men so far below became apparent. At closer range, the carnage at the edge of that vast desert would have sickened Garion, but from up here he could watch with little more than curiosity.

And then, when the great majority of the charging Malloreans were far up the ravines and gullies, a force of axe-wielding Murgo cavalry came pounding around the tip of a long, rocky ridge that protruded out into the wasteland.

"That's what they were up to," Garion said. "They lured the Malloreans into a charge so that they could attack from the rear."

"I don't think so," Silk disagreed. "I think they're after the supply wagons."

The galloping Murgo cavalry swept across the intervening space and then thundered along the sides of the poorly guarded Mallorean supply column, their axes rising and falling as they chopped open the water casks. With each stroke, sparkling water gushed out to soak into the arid floor of the desert. The sun, obscured by the dust of the charge, glowed red through the choking clouds to dye the gushing streams of water. From their vantage point high above the battle, it looked almost to Garion that the fluid spurting from the ruptured barrels was not water, but blood.

With a great outcry of chagrin, the Mallorean charge faltered. Then the red-clad figures far below turned and desperately ran back toward the desert to protect their precious water supply. But it was too late. With brutal efficiency, the Murgo cavalry had already axed open every barrel and cask and was riding back the way they had come with triumphant jeers.

The Murgos, whose feigned retreat had drawn the Mallorean troops into their fatal charge, ran back down the ridges to resume their former positions. From their vantage points above the now-demoralized Malloreans, they sent great sheets of arrows arching up into the morning sky to rain down upon their enemies. In the midst of that deadly rain, the Malloreans desperately tried to salvage what little water was left in the bottoms of their shattered barrels, but their losses from the arrow storm soon grew unacceptable. The men in red tunics broke and ran out into the waiting desert, leaving their wagons behind.

"That's a brutal way to make war," Silk said.

"The battle's pretty much over then, isn't it?" Garion said as the black-robed Murgos moved down into the ravines to butcher the wounded.

"Oh, yes," Silk replied, sounding almost sick. "The fighting's all done. The dying isn't, though."

"Maybe the ones who are left can make it back across the desert."

"Not a chance."

"All right, then," a lean man in a black robe said, stepping out from behind a nearby rocky outcrop with a half-drawn bow in his hands. "Now that you've seen it all, why don't we go back down to your camp and join the others?"

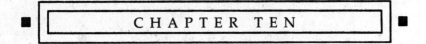

CHAPTER TEN

Silk rose to his feet slowly, keeping both hands in plain sight. "You're very quiet on your feet, friend," he observed.

"I'm trained to be so," the man with the bow replied. "Move. Your friends are waiting."

Silk gave Garion a quick warning look.—*Let's go along until we can size up the situation.*—His fingers cautioned.—*I'm sure this one isn't alone.*—

They turned and slid down the bank to the floor of the ravine, with the stranger following watchfully behind them, his bow at the ready. At the upper end of the gully where they had pitched their tents the previous night, a score of black-robed men armed with bows guarded the others. They all had the scarred cheeks and angular eyes of Murgos, but there were certain subtle differences. The Murgos Garion had seen before had always been heavy-shouldered, and their stance had been marked by a stiff arrogance. These men were leaner, and their bearing was at once wary and peculiarly relaxed.

"You see, noble Tajak," Sadi said obsequiously to the lean-faced man who seemed to be in charge, "it is exactly as I told you. I have only these two other servants."

"We know your numbers, slaver," the lean-faced man replied in a harshly accented voice. "We've been watching you since you entered Cthol Murgos."

"We made no effort to hide," Sadi protested mildly. "The only reason we remained concealed here was to avoid becoming involved in that unpleasantness down at the edge of the desert." He paused. "One is curious, however, to know why the noble Dagashi would choose to concern themselves with the activities of a party of Nyissan slavers. Surely we are not the first to come this way."

Tajak ignored that, looking carefully at Garion and his friends with his slate-hard black eyes. "What's your name, slaver?" he asked Sadi finally.

"I am Ussa of Sthiss Tor, good master, a duly registered slave trader. I have all the proper documents, if you'd care to examine them."

"How is it that none of your servants are Nyissan?"

Sadi spread his hands innocently. "The war here in the south makes most of my countrymen a bit reluctant to venture into Cthol Murgos just now," he explained, "so I was forced to hire foreign adventurers instead."

"Perhaps," the Dagashi said in a flat, unemotional voice. He gave Sadi a penetrating look. "Are you interested in money, Ussa of Sthiss Tor?" he asked suddenly.

Sadi's dead eyes brightened, and he rubbed his hands together eagerly. "Well, now," he said, "why don't we talk about that? Just exactly how may I serve you? And how much would you be willing to pay me?"

"You will need to discuss that with my master," Tajak replied. "My orders were to find a party of slavers and tell them that I could put them in touch with someone who could see that they were well-paid for a fairly minor service. Are you interested in such a proposition?"

Sadi hesitated, glancing surreptitiously at Belgarath for some kind of instruction.

"Well?" Tajak said impatiently. "Are you interested?"

"Of course," Sadi answered carefully. "Who is your master, Tajak? Just who is this benefactor who wants to make me rich?"

"He will tell you his name and what you must do for him when you meet him—at Kahsha."

"Kahsha?" Sadi exclaimed. "You didn't say that I'd have to go there."

"There are many things I didn't say. Well? Do you agree to go with us to Kahsha?"

"Do I have any choice?"

"No."

Sadi spread his arms helplessly.

—*What's Kahsha?*—Garion's fingers asked Silk.

—*The headquarters of the Dagashi. It's got an unsavory reputation.*—

"All right," Tajak said decisively, "let's break down these tents and get ready to leave. It's many hours to Kahsha, and midafternoon is not a good time to be out in the desert."

The sun was well up when they rode out of the mouth of the ravine with Tajak's Dagashi formed up watchfully around them. Out in the wasteland, the defeated Malloreans had begun their hopeless trek.

"Will they not attempt to use your wells, noble Tajak?" Sadi asked.

"Probably—but they won't be able to find them. We cover our wells with piles of rock, and all piles of rock in the desert look the same."

There were Murgo troops at the base of the foothills, watching the dispirited retreat of the Malloreans. As Tajak approached them, he made a quick, imperious gesture to them, and they grudgingly stood aside.

As they rode through a narrow defile that opened out into the desert, Garion took the opportunity to pull his horse in beside Belgarath's. "Grandfather," he whispered urgently, "what should we do?"

"We wait and see what this is all about," the old man replied. "Let's not do anything to give away our disguise—not yet, anyway."

As they rode out into the furnace heat of the desert, Sadi looked back at the Murgo soldiers lining the tops of the last low line of hills. "Your countrymen are most accommodating," he said to Tajak. "I'm surprised, though, that they didn't stop us to ask one or two questions."

"They know who we are," Tajak said shortly, "and they know better than to interfere with us." He looked at the already-sweating eunuch. "It would be wise of you to keep your mouth closed now, Ussa. The sun draws the moisture out of a man's body very quickly in this desert, and an open mouth is the first thing it attacks. It's quite possible to talk yourself to death out here."

Sadi gave him a startled look and then clamped his lips tightly together.

The heat was unbelievable. The desert floor was for the most part a vast, flat bed of reddish-brown gravel, broken only by occasional heaps of dark boulders and widely scattered stretches of gleaming white sand. The world seemed to shimmer and undulate as heat waves rose from the blistering gravel. The sun was like a club beating down on Garion's head and neck; though he was sweating profusely, the moisture evaporated from his body so quickly that his clothing remained totally dry.

They rode into that furnace for an hour, and then Tajak signaled for a halt. With a quick gesture, he sent five of his men off across a low rock ridge lying to the northeast. A short while later they returned, carrying lukewarm water in bags made of whole goatskins.

"Water the horses first," Tajak said tersely. Then he strode to the base of the ridge, bent, and scooped up a handful of what appeared to be white sand. He came back. "Hold out your right hands," he said, then spilled perhaps a spoonful into each outstretched palm. "Eat it," he ordered.

Sadi cautiously licked at the white stuff in his palm and then immediately spat. "Issa!" he swore. "Salt!"

"Eat it all," Tajak told him. "If you don't, you'll die."

Sadi stared at him.

"The sun is baking the salt out of your body. Without salt in your blood, you die."

They all reluctantly ate the salt. When they had finished, the Dagashi allowed each of them to drink sparingly; then they remounted and rode on into the inferno.

Ce'Nedra began to droop in her saddle like a wilted flower. The heat seemed to crush her. Garion pulled his horse in beside hers. "Are you all right?" he asked through parched lips.

"No talking!" a Dagashi snapped.

The little queen lifted her face and gave Garion a wan smile and then rode on.

Time lost all meaning in that dreadful place, and even thought became impossible. Garion rode dumbly, his head bent beneath the hammerlike blows of the sun. Hours—or years—later, he raised his head, squinting against the brilliant light around him. He stared stupidly ahead, and only slowly did the realization come to him that what he was seeing was utterly impossible. There, looming in the air before them, floated a vast black island. It hovered above the shimmering, sun-blasted gravel, defying all reason. What manner of sorcery could perform such a feat? How could anyone have that much power?

But it was not sorcery. As they rode nearer, the undulating heat waves began to thin, dispelling the mirage and revealing the fact that what they approached was not an island in the air, but instead a single rock peak rising precipitously from the desert floor. Encircling it was a narrow trail, hacked out of the solid rock and spiraling upward around the mountain.

"Kahsha," Tajak said shortly. "Dismount and lead your horses."

The trail was very steep. After the second spiral around the mountain the shimmering gravel floor of the desert lay far below. Up and up they went, round and round the blisteringly hot peak. And then the trail went directly into the mountain through a large, square opening.

"More caves?" Silk whispered bitterly. "Why is it always caves?"

Garion, however, moved eagerly. He would gladly have entered a tomb to get away from the intolerable sun.

"Take the horses," Tajak instructed some of his men, "and see to them at once. The rest of you, come with me." He led them into a long corridor chopped out of the rock itself. Garion groped along blindly until his eyes became adjusted to the dimness. Though by no means cold, the air in the corridor was infinitely cooler than it had been outside. He breathed deeply, straightened, and looked around. The brutal amount of physical labor it had taken to hack this long corridor out of solid rock was clearly evident.

Sadi, noticing that as well, looked at the grim-faced man striding beside him. "I didn't know that Dagashi were such expert stonecutters," he observed.

"We aren't. The corridor was cut by slaves."

"I didn't know that the Dagashi kept slaves."

"We don't. Once our fortress was finished, we turned them loose."

"Out there?" Sadi's voice was aghast.

"Most of them preferred to jump off the mountain instead."

The corridor ended abruptly in a cavern quite nearly as vast as some Garion had seen in the land of the Ulgos. Here, however, narrow windows high in the wall admitted light. As he looked up, he saw that this was not a natural cave, but rather was a large hollow that had been roofed over with stone slabs supported by vaults and buttresses. On the floor of the cave stood a city of low stone houses, and rising in the center of that city stood a bleak, square fortress.

"The house of Jaharb," their guide said shortly. "He waits. We must hurry."

Silk drew in his breath with a sharp hiss.

"What's the matter?" Garion whispered.

"We're going to have to be very careful here," Silk murmured. "Jaharb is the chief elder of the Dagashi and he has a very nasty reputation."

The houses in the city of the Dagashi all had flat roofs and narrow windows. Garion noticed that there was none of the bustle in the streets which one might see in a western city. The black-robed, unsmiling Dagashi went about their business in silence, and each man he saw moving through that strange, half-lit town seemed to carry a kind of vacant space about him, a circle into which none of his fellow townsmen would intrude.

The fortress of Jaharb was solidly built of huge basalt blocks, and the guards at the heavy front door were formidably armed. Tajak spoke briefly to them, and the door swung open.

The room to which Tajak took them was large and was illuminated by costly oil lamps, swinging on chains from the ceiling. The only furnishings were heaps of yellow cushions scattered on the floor and a row of stout, iron-bound chests standing along the rear wall. Seated in the midst of one of the heaps of cushions was an ancient man with white hair and a dark face that was incredibly wrinkled. He wore a yellow robe and he was eating grapes as they entered, carefully selecting them one by one and then languidly raising them to his lips.

"The Nyissan slavers, Revered Elder," Tajak announced in tones of profoundest respect.

Jaharb set aside his bowl of grapes and leaned forward, resting his elbows on his knees and looking at them intently with his smoky, penetrating eyes. There was something infinitely chilling about that steady gaze. "How are you called?" he asked Sadi finally. His voice was as cold as his eyes, very quiet and with a kind of dusty dryness to it.

"I am Ussa, Revered One," Sadi replied with a sinuous bow.

"So? And what is your business in the lands of the Murgos?" The ancient man spoke slowly, drawing out his words almost as if he were singing them.

"The slave trade, Great Elder," Sadi answered quickly.

"Buying or selling?"

"A bit of each. The present turmoil offers certain opportunities."

"I'm sure it does. You are here for gain, then?"

"A reasonable profit is all, Revered Jaharb."

The Elder's expression did not change, but his eyes bored into the face of the suddenly sweating eunuch. "You seem uncomfortable, Ussa," the dusty voice crooned softly. "Why is that?"

"The heat, Revered Jaharb," Sadi said nervously. "Your desert is very hot."

"Perhaps." The smoky eyes continued their unrelenting gaze. "Is it your purpose to enter the lands controlled by the Malloreans?"

"Why, yes," Sadi replied, "as a matter of fact it is. I am told that many slaves took advantage of the chaos that accompanied the Mallorean invasions to hide themselves in the Forest of Gorut. They are free for the taking, and the fields and vineyards of Hagga and Cthan lie untended for lack of slaves to work them. There is profit in such a situation."

"You will have little time for pursuing runaway slaves, Ussa. You must be in Rak Hagga before two months have passed."

"But—"

Jaharb held up one hand. "You will proceed from this place to Rak Urga, where you are expected. A new servant will join you there. His name is Kabach, and you will find him in the Temple of Torak under the protection of Agachak, the Grolim Hierarch of that place. Agachak and King Urgit will place you and your servants on board a ship which will take you around the southern end of the Urga peninsula to Rak Cthaka. From there you will go directly overland to Rak Hagga. Do you understand all that I have said?"

"Most certainly, Revered Jaharb—and what is it that you want me to do in Rak Hagga?"

"When you reach Rak Hagga, Kabach will leave you, and your task will be complete. Your entire service to me consists of concealing him within your party as you journey to Rak Hagga—a small thing, but your reward will be great."

"The ship will certainly save me months of difficult travel on horseback, Revered Elder, but will I not have difficulty explaining my presence to the Malloreans if I have no slaves to sell in the mart at Rak Hagga?"

"You will buy slaves in Cthaka or Gorut. The Malloreans will have no reason to question you."

"Forgive me, Revered Elder," Sadi said with a slightly embarrassed cough, "but my purse is slender. That's why my plan was to capture runaway slaves. They cost no more than the effort of running them down."

Jaharb did not reply, and his probing eyes remained flat and emotionless. He turned his gaze to Tajak. "Open that chest at the end," he said.

Tajak moved quickly to obey. When he lifted the lid of the chest, Garion heard Ce'Nedra gasp involuntarily. The chest was filled to its very brim with bright red gold coins.

"Take what you need, Ussa," Jaharb said indifferently. Then a faintly amused look flickered in his smoldering eyes. "*But* no more than you can hold in both your hands."

Sadi gaped at the gold-filled chest, his eyes filled with greed and his face and shaven scalp sweating profusely. He looked at the red gold, then down at his own two rather delicately shaped hands. A sudden look of undisguised cunning came over his face. "Gold is heavy, most Revered Jaharb, and my hands are quite weak as a result of a recent illness. Might I have one of my servants gather up your most generous payment?"

"That's not an unreasonable request, Ussa," Jaharb replied, his eyes openly amused now. "But mind, no more than he can hold in his two hands."

"Naturally," Sadi said. "I certainly wouldn't want you to overpay me." He turned. "You there," he said to Toth, "go to that chest and remove a double handful of coins—and be certain that you take no more."

Impassively Toth went to the chest and scooped out perhaps a half pailful of the gleaming red coins in his huge hands.

Jaharb regarded the nervously sweating eunuch for a long moment, his wrinkled face expressionless. Then quite suddenly he threw back his head and laughed a dusty laugh. "Excellent, Ussa," he crooned softly. "Your mind is agile. I like that quality in those who serve me. It may be that you will even live long enough to spend some of the gold you have just so cleverly obtained."

"It was merely a demonstration of my intelligence, Revered Jaharb," Sadi answered quickly, "to prove to you that you made no mistake in selecting me. I'll have him put the coins back if you wish—some of them, anyway."

"No, Ussa. Keep them all. You will earn every one of them by the time you reach Rak Hagga, I think."

"I am much honored to be of service to the Dagashi. Even if it were not for your open-handed generosity, I would be no poorer for having befriended you." He hesitated, glancing quickly at Belgarath. "I have been told, Revered Elder, that the Dagashi know many things."

"Few secrets are hidden from us in this part of the world."

"Might I be so bold as to ask a question? A small thing, but one of some interest to me?"

"You may ask, Ussa. I will decide whether or not to answer after I hear the question."

"I have an extremely wealthy customer in Tol Honeth, Revered Jaharb," Sadi said. "He has an absolute passion for rare books and he would pay me a fortune for a copy of the Grolim Prophecies of Rak Cthol. Do you possibly know where I might find such a book?"

Jaharb frowned slightly, rubbing at his wrinkled cheek. "The Dagashi have little interest in books," he said. "The volume you seek would certainly have been in the library of Ctuchik at Rak Cthol, but I'm sure it was lost when Belgarath the Sorcerer destroyed the city." He thought a moment longer. "You might ask Agachak when you get to Rak Urga, however. The Temple library there is most extensive; since the prophecies deal with religion, Agachak is certain to have a copy—if one still exists."

"I am profoundly grateful for the information, Revered Elder," Sadi said, bowing again.

Jaharb straightened. "And now you and your servants will need to rest. You depart for Rak Urga at first light tomorrow morning. A room has been prepared for you." He turned back to his bowl of grapes.

The room to which they were taken was quite large. The stone walls had been whitewashed to enhance the dim light which lay over the city of the assassins, but the furnishings were rudimentary at best, consisting only of a low stone table and heaps of cushions.

As soon as the black-robed Tajak left them alone, Garion pulled off his green slaver's robe. "Grandfather," he said, "what are we going to do? We can't go to Rak Urga. If we're ever going to catch Zandramas, we're going to have to get to Verkat as soon as we can."

The old man sprawled in a pile of cushions. "Actually, Garion, things couldn't have worked out better for us. Once we have the ship that Agachak and Urgit have waiting for us, we can sail directly on to Verkat. That's going to save us months of difficult travel."

"But won't the Dagashi—this Kabach who's waiting at Rak Urga—object if we don't land where Jaharb said we were going to?"

Sadi unlatched his leather case. "Set your mind at ease, Belgarion." He took out a small vial containing a thick blue liquid and held it up. "Two drops of this in his food and he'll be so happy that he won't care *where* we're going."

"You're a very versatile fellow, Sadi," Belgarath said. "How did you know that I was looking for the Prophecies of the Western Grolims?"

Sadi shrugged. "It wasn't hard to deduce, Ancient One. A part of the arrangement between Sariss and Naradas involved the burning of the only copy of that book in the palace library at Sthiss Tor. If Zandramas wanted it destroyed, it was fairly obvious that she didn't want you to get your hands on it."

"I'm starting to revise my opinion of you, Sadi. I still don't entirely trust you, but you certainly can be useful when you set your mind to it."

"Why, thank you, Ancient Belgarath." The eunuch took out the small earthenware bottle.

"Are you going to feed that snake?" Silk asked.

"She *does* get hungry, Kheldar."

"I'll wait outside, then."

"Tell me, Prince Kheldar," Velvet said curiously, "what is the source of this peculiar aversion of yours toward reptiles?"

"Most normal people don't like snakes."

"Oh, they aren't that bad."

"Are you trying to be funny?"

She opened her brown eyes very wide in an expression of exaggerated innocence. "Would I do that?"

He went out into the hallway muttering to himself.

Velvet laughed and then went over to join Ce'Nedra on the pile of cushions near the window. Garion had noticed that the two of them had grown quite close during the weeks since they had left Tol Honeth. Because Polgara had always seemed so totally self-sufficient, he had not fully realized the deep-seated need that most women had for the companionship of other women. As Sadi fed his little green snake, the two of them sat side by side on the cushions and brushed the dust of their journey out of their hair.

"Why do you tease him so much, Liselle?" Ce'Nedra asked, pulling her brush through her flaming locks.

"I'm getting even with him," Velvet replied with an impish smile. "When I was a little girl, he used to tease me outrageously. Now it's my turn."

"You always seem to know just exactly what to say to offend him the most."

"I know him very well, Ce'Nedra. I've been watching him for years now. I know every single one of his weaknesses and I know exactly where he's the most sensitive." The blond girl's eyes grew soft. "He's a legend in Drasnia, you know. At the Academy, whole seminars are devoted to his exploits. We all try to emulate him, but none of us has his outrageous flair."

Ce'Nedra stopped brushing and gave her friend a long, speculative look.

"Yes?" Velvet said, returning the look.

"Oh, nothing," Ce'Nedra said and went back to brushing her hair.

The desert night was surprisingly chill. The air was so totally devoid of moisture that each day's heat evaporated almost as soon as the sun went down. As they set out from Kahsha in the steely dawn light, Garion found that he was actually shivering. By midmorning, however, the burning sun had once again turned the barren waste of Araga into an inferno. It was nearly noon by the time they reached the foothills along the western rim of the desert and began the climb that took them up out of that hideous furnace.

"How long until we get to Rak Urga, good Master?" Sadi asked Tajak, who once again escorted them.

"A week or so."

"Distances are very great in this part of Cthol Murgos, aren't they?"

"It's a very large country."

"And very empty."

"Only if you don't look around you."

Sadi looked at him inquiringly.

"Along that ridge, for example." Taak pointed toward the ragged stretch of rock outlined against the western sky where a single black-robed Murgo sat astride his horse, watching them.

"How long has he been there?" Sadi asked.

"For the past hour. Don't you ever look up?"

"In Nyissa, we always watch the ground. Snakes, you know."

"That explains it, I suppose."

"What's he doing up there?"

"Watching us. King Urgit likes to keep track of strangers."

"Is he likely to cause trouble?"

"We are Dagashi, Nyissan. Other Murgos do not cause us trouble."

"It's a great comfort to have so formidable an escort, good Tajak."

The country through which they rode for the next week was rocky and only sparsely vegetated. Garion had some difficulty adjusting to the notion that it was late summer here in the southern latitudes. The turn of the seasons had always been so immutable that emotionally and perhaps in his very blood, he found that he could not actually accept the idea that they were reversed here at the bottom of the world.

At a certain point in their journey southward, he felt the well-covered Orb on the pommel of the sword that rode across his back tug strongly off toward the left. He nudged his horse up beside Belgarath's. "Zandramas turned east here," he reported quietly.

The old man nodded.

"I hate to lose the trail," Garion said. "If Sadi's wrong about where she's going, it could take months to find it again."

"We wasted a lot of time on the Bear-cult, Garion," the old man replied. "We have to make that up, and that means taking a few gambles."

"I suppose you're right, Grandfather, but I still don't like it."

"I don't much either, but I don't think we have any choice, do we?"

A series of squalls blew in off the Great Western Sea as they proceeded down the rocky spine of the Urga peninsula, an indication that autumn was rapidly approaching. Although the squalls were blustery, they carried only fitful spates of rain, and the journey continued without interruption. They more frequently saw mounted Murgo patrols now, ranging along the ridge tops and outlined against the dirty gray sky. The Murgos, however, prudently gave the Dagashi a wide berth.

And then, about noon on a windy day when heavy clouds rolled in off the vast ocean, they topped a hill and looked down at a large body of water embraced by steep rock cliffs.

"The Gulf of Urga," Tajak said tersely, pointing at that leaden sea.

A peninsula jutted out from the far shore, sheltering the entrance to the gulf with a rocky headland. Embraced by the curve of that headland was a harbor dotted with black-hulled ships, and rising from that harbor was a fair-sized town.

"Is that it?" Sadi asked.

Tajak nodded. "Rak Urga," he said.

A ferry awaited them on the narrow beach, bobbing in the sullen waves rolling in from the open sea. It was a large, wide-beamed barge manned by two score wretched-looking slaves under the watchful eye of a Murgo boatman armed with a long whip. Tajak and his men led the way down to the gravel strand, then turned without a word and rode back up the trail.

The channel running from the Great Western Sea into the Gulf of Urga was not wide, and Garion could clearly make out the low stone buildings of Rak Urga squatting under a murky sky on the far side. Sadi spoke briefly with the Murgo, a few coins changed hands, and then they led their horses aboard. The Murgo barked a short command to his slaves, cracking his whip over their heads by way of emphasis. Desperately, the slaves pushed the barge off the gravel beach with their oars, casting fearful glances at their cruel-faced master and his whip. Once they were clear of the beach, they quickly took their places and began to row, pulling hard for the city across the narrow channel. The Murgo paced up and down the length of the barge, his face alert, and his eyes intently on his slaves, watching for any hint of flagging effort. Once, when they were about halfway across, he partially raised his whip, apparently for no other reason than out of a desire to use it.

"Excuse me, noble ferryman," Silk said, stepping in front of him, "but did you know that your boat is leaking?"

"Leaking?" the Murgo replied sharply, lowering his whip. "Where?"

"I can't really be sure, but there's quite a bit of water down in the bottom."

The Murgo called to his steersman in the stern and then quickly raised a wooden grating so that the two of them could peer down into the shallow bottom of his boat. "That's bilgewater," he said in disgust, motioning his steersman back to his post. "Don't you know anything about boats?"

"Not much," Silk admitted. "I saw the water and thought you ought to know about it. Sorry to have bothered you." He walked forward to rejoin the others.

"What was that all about?" Belgarath asked.

"Durnik's face was getting a bit bleak." Silk shrugged. "I didn't want his passion for justice to get the better of him."

Belgarath looked at the smith.

"I'm not going to stand around idly, if he starts flogging those poor men," Durnik declared, his face stiff. "The minute he raises that whip, he's going to find himself swimming."

"You see what I mean?" Silk said.

Belgarath looked as if he were about to say something, but Polgara stepped in front of him. "Leave him alone, father," she said. "It's the way he is, and I wouldn't change him for the world."

The harbor of Rak Urga was even more congested with ships than it had appeared to be from the other side. The steersman of the barge picked his way carefully through all those anchored vessels toward the stone quays jutting out into the lead-gray chop of the channel. A dozen or more of the wide-beamed Murgo ships were moored to the quays, bumping against woven rope fenders as gangs of slaves unloaded them.

The barge drew in close to the sheltered side of one of the quays, and the horses were carefully led up a slanting stone ramp, made slippery by clinging seaweed. Ce'Nedra looked down at the garbage-strewn water sloshing below and sniffed disdainfully. "Why do seaports always look—and smell—the same?" she murmured.

"Probably because the people who live in them find all that water irresistible," Velvet replied.

Ce'Nedra looked puzzled.

"It's just too convenient," the Drasnian girl explained. "They always seem to forget that the garbage they throw into the harbor this morning will come back to haunt them with the afternoon tide."

When they reached the top of the ramp, a self-important Murgo stood waiting for them, his heavy black robe flapping in the stiff breeze. "You there," he said arrogantly. "State your business."

Sadi stepped forward and gave the Murgo an oily bow. "I am Ussa," he replied, "registered slave trader from Sthiss Tor. I have all the necessary documents."

"There's no slave market in Rak Urga," the Murgo declared suspiciously. "Hand over your documents."

"Of course." Sadi dipped his hand inside his green robe and brought out a packet of folded parchment.

"If you're not dealing in slaves, what are you doing here?" the Murgo demanded, taking the packet from him.

"I'm merely doing a favor for my good friend Jaharb, Chief Elder of the Dagashi," Sadi told him.

The Murgo paused in the very act of opening the packet. "Jaharb?" he said a bit apprehensively.

Sadi nodded. "Since I was passing this way anyhow, he asked me to stop by and deliver a message to Agachak, the Hierarch of Rak Urga."

The Murgo swallowed hard and thrust the documents back into Sadi's hands as if they had suddenly grown hot. "On your way, then," he said shortly.

"My thanks, noble sir," Sadi said with another bow. "Excuse me, but could you direct me to the Temple of Torak? This is my first visit to Rak Urga."

"It lies at the head of the street running up from this quay," the Murgo answered.

"Again my thanks. If you'll give me your name, I'll tell Agachak how helpful you were."

The Murgo's face took on a pasty hue. "That won't be necessary," he said quickly, then turned and walked away.

"The names Jaharb and Agachak appear to have a certain impact here," Silk suggested.

Sadi smiled. "I imagine that, if you were to mention them in the same breath, every door in town would open for you," he agreed.

Rak Urga was not an attractive city. The streets were narrow, and the buildings were built of roughly squared-off stones and topped by gray slate roofs that over-hung the streets, putting the thoroughfares into a perpetually gloomy twilight. It was not merely that gray bleakness, however, that made the city so dreary. There was about it an air of cold unconcern for normal human feelings, coupled with a sense of lingering fear. Grim-faced Murgos in their black robes moved through the streets, neither speaking nor even acknowledging the presence of their fellow townsmen.

"Why are these people all so unfriendly toward each other?" Eriond asked Polgara.

"It's a cultural trait," she told him. "Murgos were the aristocracy at Cthol Mishrak before Torak ordered them to migrate to this continent. They are absolutely convinced that Murgos are the supreme creation of the universe—and every one of them is convinced that he's superior to all the rest. It doesn't leave them very much to talk about."

There was a pall of greasy black smoke hanging over the city, bringing with it a sickening stench.

"What is that dreadful smell?" Velvet asked, wrinkling her nose.

"I don't think you really want to know," Silk told her with a bleak look on his face.

"Surely they aren't still—" Garion left it hanging.

"It seems so," the little man replied.

"But Torak's dead. What's the sense of it?"

"Grolims have never really been all that much concerned about the fact that what they do doesn't make sense, Garion," Belgarath said. "The source of their power has always been terror. If they want to keep the power, they have to continue the terror."

They rounded a corner and saw a huge black building ahead of them. A column of dense smoke rose from a large chimney jutting up from the slate roof, blowing first this way and then that in the gusty wind coming up from the harbor.

"Is that the Temple?" Durnik asked.

"Yes," Polgara replied. She pointed at the two massive, nail-studded doors forming the only break in the blank, featureless wall. Directly above those doors there hung the polished steel replica of the face of Torak. Garion felt the familiar chill in his blood as he looked at the brooding face of his enemy. Even now, after all that had happened in the City of Endless Night, the face of Torak filled him with dread, and he was not particularly surprised to find that he was actually trembling as he approached the entrance to the Temple of the maimed God of Angarak.

■ ┌──────────────────────────────┐ ■

CHAPTER ELEVEN

└──────────────────────────────┘

Sadi slid down from his saddle, went up to the nail-studded doors, and clanged the rusty iron knocker, sending hollow echoes reverberating back into the Temple.

"Who comes to the House of Torak?" a muffled voice demanded from inside.

"I bear a message from Jaharb, Chief Elder at Mount Kahsha, for the ears of Agachak, Hierarch of Rak Urga."

There was a momentary pause inside, and then one of the doors creaked open and a pock-marked Grolim looked cautiously out at them. "You are not of the Dagashi," he said accusingly to Sadi.

"No, as a matter of fact, I'm not. There's an arrangement between Jaharb and Agachak, and I'm part of it."

"I have not heard of such an arrangement."

Sadi looked pointedly at the unadorned hood of the Grolim's robe, an obvious indication that the priest was of low rank. "Forgive me, servant of Torak," he said coolly, "but is your Hierarch in the habit of confiding in his doorman?"

The Grolim's face darkened as he glared at the eunuch. "Cover your head, Nyissan," he said after a long moment. "This is a holy place."

"Of course." Sadi pulled the hood of his green robe up over his shaven scalp. "Will you have someone see to our horses?"

"They will be taken care of. Are these your servants?" The Grolim looked past Sadi's shoulder at the others, who still sat their horses in the cobbled street.

"They are, noble priest."

"Tell them to come with us. I will take you all to Chabat."

"Excuse me, priest of the Dragon God. My message is for Agachak."

"No one sees Agachak without first seeing Chabat. Bring your servants and follow me."

The rest of them dismounted and passed through the grim doors into the torchlit corridor beyond. The sickening odor of burning flesh which had pervaded the city was even stronger here in the Temple. A sense of dread came over Garion as he followed the Grolim and Sadi along the smoky hallway into the Temple. The place reeked of an ancient evil, and the hollow-faced priests they passed in the corridor all looked at them with heavy suspicion and undisguised malice.

And then there came from somewhere in the building an agonized shriek, followed by a great iron clang. Garion shuddered, fully aware of the meaning of those sounds.

"Is the ancient rite of sacrifice still performed?" Sadi asked the Grolim in some surprise. "I would have thought that the practice might have fallen into disuse—all things considered."

"Nothing has happened to make us discontinue the performance of our holiest duty, Nyissan," the Grolim replied coldly. "Each hour we offer up a human heart to the God Torak."

"But Torak is no more."

The Grolim stopped, his face angry. "*Never* speak those words again!" he snapped. "It is not the place of a foreigner to utter such blasphemy within the walls of the Temple. The spirit of Torak lives on, and one day he will be reborn to rule the world. He himself will wield the knife when his enemy, Belgarion of Riva, lies screaming on the altar."

"Now there's a cheery thought," Silk murmured to Belgarath. "We get to do it all over again."

"Just shut up, Silk," Belgarath muttered.

The chamber to which the Grolim underpriest led them was large and dimly lighted by several oil lamps. The walls were lined with black drapes, and the air was thick with incense. A slim, hooded figure sat behind a large table with a guttering black candle at its elbow and a heavy, black-bound book before it. A kind of warning tingle prickled Garion's scalp as he sensed the power emanating from that figure. He glanced quickly at Polgara, and she nodded gravely.

"Forgive me, Holy Chabat," the pock-marked Grolim said in a slightly trembling voice as he genuflected before the table, "but I bring a messenger from Jaharb the assassin."

The figure at the table looked up, and Garion suppressed a start of surprise. It was a woman. There was about her face a kind of luminous beauty, but it was not that which struck his eye. Cruelly inscribed into each of her pale cheeks were deep red scars that ran down from her temples to her chin in an ornate design, a design which appeared to represent flames. Her eyes were dark and smoldering, and her full-lipped mouth was drawn into a contemptuous sneer. A deep purple piping marked the edge of her black hood. "So?" she said in a harshly rasping voice. "And how is it that the Dagashi now entrust their messages to foreigners?"

"I—I thought not to ask, Holy Chabat," the Grolim faltered. "This one claims to be a friend of Jaharb."

"And you chose not to question him further?" Her harsh voice sank into a menacing whisper, and her eyes bored into the suddenly trembling underpriest. Then her gaze slowly shifted to Sadi. "Say your name," she commanded.

"I am Ussa of Sthiss Tor, Holy Priestess," he replied. "Jaharb instructed me to present myself to your Hierarch and to give him a message."

"And what is that message?"

"Ah—forgive me, Holy Priestess, but I was told that it was for Agachak's ears alone."

"I *am* Agachak's ears," she told him, her voice dreadfully quiet. "Nothing reaches his ears that I have not heard first." It was the tone of her voice that made Garion suddenly understand. Although this cruelly scarred woman had somehow risen to a position of power here in the temple, she was still uncertain about that power. She bore her uncertainty like an open wound, and the slightest questioning of her authority roused in her an abiding hatred for whomever doubted her. Fervently he hoped that Sadi realized how extremely dangerous she was.

"Ah," Sadi said with polished aplomb. "I was not fully aware of the situation here. I was told that Jaharb, Agachak, and King Urgit have reason to want one Kabach transported safely to Rak Hagga. I am the one who is to provide that transportation."

Her eyes narrowed suspiciously. "That is certainly not the entire message," she accused.

"I'm afraid it is, Noble Priestess. I presume that Agachak will understand its meaning."

"Jaharb said nothing else to you?"

"Only that this Kabach is here in the Temple under Agachak's protection."

"Impossible," she snapped. "I would have known about it if he were. Agachak conceals nothing from me."

Sadi spread his hands in a mollifying gesture. "I can only repeat what Jaharb told me, Holy Priestess."

She gnawed at one knuckle, her eyes suddenly filled with doubt. "If you're lying to me, Ussa—or trying to conceal something—I will have your heart ripped out," she threatened.

"That is the entire message, Holy Priestess. May I now deliver it to your Hierarch?"

"The Hierarch is at the Drojim Palace, consulting with the High King. He is not likely to return until midnight."

"Is there someplace where my servants and I could await his return, then?"

"I have not yet finished with you, Ussa of Sthiss Tor. What is it that this Kabach is to do in Rak Hagga?"

"Jaharb did not think I needed to know that."

"I think you're lying to me, Ussa," she said, her fingernails rapping a nervous staccato on the table top.

"I have no reason to lie to you, Holy Chabat," he protested.

"Agachak would have told me of this matter. He conceals nothing from me—nothing."

"Perhaps he overlooked it. It may not be anything of much importance."

She looked at each of the others in turn then, her eyes hooded beneath her dark brows. She turned a cold gaze on the still-trembling Grolim. "Tell me," she said in a voice scarcely more than a whisper, "how is it that the one over there was permitted to come into my presence bearing a sword?" She pointed at Garion.

The Priest's face grew stricken. "Forgive me, Chabat," he stammered, "I—I failed to notice the sword."

"Failed? How can one fail to see so large a weapon? Can you possibly explain that to me?"

The Grolim began to tremble even more violently.

"Is the sword perhaps invisible? Or is it, perhaps, that my safety is of no concern to you?" Her scarred face grew even more cruel. "Or might it be that you bear me some malice and hoped that this foreigner might decide to slay me?"

The Grolim's face grew ashen.

"I think perhaps that I should bring this matter to the attention of Agachak upon his return. He will doubtless wish to speak with you about this invisible sword—at some length."

The door to the chamber opened and an emaciated Grolim, black-robed, but with his green-lined hood pushed back, entered the chamber. His black hair was greasy and hung in lank tangles about his shoulders. He had the bulging eyes of a fanatic and there was the acrid odor of a long-unwashed body about him. "It's nearly time, Chabat," he announced in a strident voice.

Chabat's smoldering eyes softened as she looked at him. "Thank you, Sorchak," she replied, lowering her eyelashes in an oddly coquettish fashion. She rose, opened a drawer in the table, and took out a black leather case. She opened the case and lovingly lifted out a long, gleaming knife. Then she looked coldly at the Grolim priest she had just chastised. "I go now to the Sanctum to perform the rite of sacrifice," she told him, absently testing the edge of her heavy-bladed knife. "If one single word of anything that has happened here escapes your lips, you yourself will die at the next sounding of the bell. Now take these slavers to suitable quarters where they can await the return of the Hierarch." She turned back to the greasy-haired Sorchak, her eyes alight with a sudden, dreadful eagerness. "Will you escort me to the Sanctum so that you can witness my performance of the rite?"

"I would be honored, Chabat," he replied with a jerky bow; but as the priestess turned from him, his lip curled into a sneer of contempt.

"I will leave you in the care of this bungler," she told Sadi as she passed him. "You and I have not yet finished our discussion, but I must go prepare myself for the sacrifice." With Sorchak at her side, she left the room.

When the door closed, the pock-marked underpriest spat on the floor where she had just stood.

"I had not known that a priestess could rise to the Purple in one of the Temples of Torak," Sadi said to him.

"She is the favorite of Agachak," the Grolim muttered darkly. "Her ability at sorcery is very limited, so her elevation came at his insistence. The Hierarch has a peculiar preference for ugly things. It is only his power that keeps her from getting her throat cut."

"Politics." Sadi sighed. "It's the same the world over. She seems most zealous about the performance of her religious duties, however."

"Her eagerness to perform the rite of sacrifice has little to do with religion. She delights in blood. I myself have seen her drink it as it gushes from the chest of the sacrifice and bathe her face and arms in it." The priest glanced around quickly as if afraid of being overheard. "One day, however, Agachak will discover that she practices witchcraft in the House of Torak and that she and Sorchak celebrate their black sabbaths with obscene rites when all the others in the Temple have gone to their beds. When our Hierarch discovers their corruption, she herself will go screaming under the knife, and every Grolim in the Temple will volunteer to slit her open as she lies on the altar." He straightened. "Come with me," he ordered them.

The rooms to which he led them were little more than a series of narrow, dim cells. In each cell stood a low cot, and, hanging on a peg protruding from the wall in each, was a black Grolim robe. The priest nodded briefly, then silently left. Silk looked around the somewhat larger central room with its single lamp and the rough table and benches in its center. "Hardly what I'd call luxurious," he sniffed.

"We can lodge a complaint, if you'd like," Velvet suggested.

"What happened to her face?" Ce'Nedra asked in a horrified voice. "She's hideous."

"It was a custom in certain Grolim temples in parts of Hagga," Polgara replied. "Priestesses with some ability at sorcery carved their faces in that fashion to seal themselves to Torak forever. The practice has largely been abandoned."

"But she could have been so beautiful. Why did she disfigure herself that way?"

"People sometimes do strange things in the grip of religious hysteria."

"How did that Grolim miss seeing Garion's sword?" Silk asked Belgarath.

"The Orb is taking steps to make itself inconspicuous."

"Did you tell it to do that?"

"No. Sometimes it gets certain ideas on its own."

"Well, things seem to be going rather well, don't you think?" Sadi said, rubbing his hands together in a self-congratulatory manner. "I told you I could be very useful down here."

"Very useful, Sadi," Silk replied sardonically. "So far you've led us into the middle of a battle, directly into the headquarters of the Dagashi, and now to the very center of Grolim power in Cthol Murgos. What did you have planned for us next—assuming that the lady with the interesting face doesn't gut you before morning?"

"We *are* going to get the ship, Kheldar," Sadi assured him. "Not even Chabat would dare to counter the wishes of Agachak—no matter how injured her pride may be. And the ship will save us months."

"There's something else Garion and I need to attend to," Belgarath said. "Durnik, take a look out in that hallway and see if they posted any guards to watch us."

"Where are you going?" Silk asked him.

"I need to find the library. I want to see if Jaharb was right about that book being here."

"Wouldn't it be better to wait until tonight—after everybody's gone to bed?"

The old man shook his head. "It might take us a while to find what we need. Agachak's going to be at the palace until midnight, so this is probably the best time to paw through his library." He gave the little Drasnian a brief smile. "Besides," he added, "although it might upset your notion of order, sometimes you can move around in the daytime more easily than you can by sneaking around corners after midnight."

"That's a terribly unnatural thing to suggest, Belgarath."

"The hallway looks clear," Durnik reported from the doorway.

"Good." Belgarath stepped back into the cells and emerged with a couple of the Grolim robes. "Here," he said, extending one of them to Garion, "put this on." As the two of them pulled off their green robes and replaced them with the black ones, Durnik kept watch at the door. "It's still clear, Belgarath," he said, "but you'd better hurry. I can hear people moving around down at the far end."

The old man nodded, puffing up the hood of his robe. "Let's go," he said to Garion.

The corridors were dim, lighted only by smoky torches set in iron rings protruding from the stone walls. They encountered but few of the black-robed Grolim priests in the hallways. The Grolims walked with an odd, swaying gait, their arms folded in their sleeves, their heads down, and the cowls of their robes covering their faces. Garion guessed that there was some obscure significance to that stiff-legged walk and tried to emulate it as he followed his grandfather along the half-lit halls.

Belgarath moved with feigned confidence, as if he knew precisely where they were going. They reached a broader corridor, and the old man glanced once toward its far end where a pair of heavy doors stood open. Beyond those doors lay a room filled with the flickering light of seething flames. "Not that way," he whispered to Garion.

"What is it?"

"The Sanctum. That's where the altar is." He quickly led the way across the corridor and entered an intersecting hallway.

"This could take hours, Grandfather," Garion said in a low voice.

Belgarath shook his head. "Grolim architecture is fairly predictable," he disagreed. "We're in the right part of the Temple. You check the doors on that side, and I'll take these over here."

They moved along the hall, cautiously opening each door as they came to it.

"Garion," the old man whispered, "it's over here."

The room they entered was quite large and smelled of old parchment and moldy leather bindings. It was filled with row upon row of tall, cluttered bookshelves. Solitary tables, each with a pair of wooden benches and with a single dimly glowing oil lamp hanging over it on a long chain, stood in little alcoves along the walls.

"Take a book—any book," Belgarath said. "Sit at that table over there and try to look as if you're studying. Keep your hood up and your eye on the door. I'm going to have a look around. Cough if anybody comes in."

Garion nodded, took a heavy volume from one of the shelves, and seated himself at the table. The minutes dragged by as he looked unseeing at the pages of his book with his ears straining for the slightest sound. Then, shockingly, there came the now-familiar shriek, a long drawn-out cry of despairing agony, followed by the sullen iron clang of the huge gong in the Sanctum where the Grolims conducted their unspeakable rites. Unbidden, an image rose in his mind—the image of the scar-faced Chabat gleefully butchering a victim. He clenched his teeth together, forcing himself not to leap to his feet to stop that abomination.

Then Belgarath whistled softly to him from a narrow aisle leading back between two of the high-standing bookshelves. "I've got it," he said. "Keep watch on the door. I'll be back here."

Garion sat nervously at the table, his eyes and ears alert. He was not good at this sort of thing. His nerves seemed to wind tighter and tighter as he waited, listening and watching for someone to open that door. What would he do if some black-robed priest entered? Should he speak or just remain silent with his head down over his book? What was customary here? He formulated a half-dozen different strategies, but when the latch of the door clicked loudly, he followed one that he had not even considered—he bolted. He swung his legs over the bench upon which he sat and noiselessly dodged back among the high, dark shelves looking for Belgarath.

"Is it safe to talk in here?" he heard someone say.

Another man grunted. "Nobody comes in here any more. What was it you wanted to talk about?"

"Have you endured enough of her yet? Are you ready to do something about her?"

"Keep your voice down, you fool. If someone hears you and carries your words back to her, your heart will fry in the coals at the next sounding of the bell."

"I loathe that scar-faced wench," the first Grolim spat.

"We all do, but our lives depend on not letting her know that. As long as she's Agachak's favorite, her power is absolute."

"She won't be his favorite if he finds out that she's practicing magic here in the Temple."

"How will he find out? Will you denounce her? She would deny it, and then Agachak would let her have you to do with as she chose."

There was a long, fearful silence.

"Besides," the second Grolim continued, "I don't think Agachak would even care about her petty amusements. The only thing that concerns him at the moment is his search for Cthrag Sardius. He and the other Hierarchs are bending all their thought to locating it. If she wants to dally with Sorchak and try to raise demons in the middle of the night, that's her affair and no business of ours."

"It's an abomination!" The first priest's voice was choked with outrage. "She defiles our Temple."

"I won't listen to such talk. I want to keep my heart inside my chest."

"Very well." The first Grolim's tone grew sly. "It may be as you say. You and I are both of the Green, however, and our elevation to the Purple will be more genuine than hers was. If we came upon her when no one else was around, you could use your power to lock her muscles, and I could sink my knife into her heart. Then she could stand before Torak and listen to *his* judgment upon her for violating his commandment forbidding magic."

"I refuse to listen to this any more." There was the sound of rapid footsteps, and the door slammed.

"Coward," the first priest muttered; then he too went out and closed the door behind him.

"Grandfather," Garion whispered hoarsely, "where are you?"

"Back here. Did they leave?"

"They're gone."

"Interesting conversation, wasn't it?"

Garion joined the old man at the back of the library. "Do you think Chabat could really be trying to raise demons—the way the Morindim do?"

"A fair number of Grolims here seem to think so. If she is, she's walking on very dangerous ground. Torak absolutely forbade the practice of magic. Favorite or no, Agachak would have to condemn her if he found out about it."

"Did you find anything?" Garion looked at the book the old man had on the table in front of him.

"I think this might help. Listen: 'The path that has been lost will be found again on the Southern Isle.' "

"Verkat?"

"It almost has to be. Verkat is the only island of any size in southern Cthol Murgos. It confirms what Sadi told us, and I always like to get confirmation whenever I can."

"But it still means that we're only trailing after Zandramas. Did you find anything that tells us how to get ahead of her?"

"Not yet," Belgarath admitted. He turned a page. "What's this?" he said in a startled voice.

"What is it?"

"Listen." The old man lifted the book so that the lamp light fell upon the page. " 'Behold:' " he read, " 'In the days which shall follow the ascension of the Dark God into the heavens shall the King of the East and the King of the South do war upon each other, and this shall be a sign unto ye that the day of the meeting is at hand. Hasten therefore unto the Place which is No More when battles do rage upon the plains of the south. Take with thee the chosen sacrifice and a King of Angarak to bear witness to what shall come to pass. For lo, whichever of ye cometh into the presence of Cthrag Sardius with the sacrifice and an Angarak King shall be exalted above all the rest and shall have dominion over them. And know further that in the moment of the sacrifice shall the Dark God be reborn, and he shall triumph over the Child of Light in the instant of his rebirth.' "

Garion stared at him, feeling the blood drain from his face. "Sacrifice?" he exclaimed. "Is that what Zandramas plans to do with my son?"

"So it would seem," Belgarath grunted. He thought about it for a moment. "This explains a few things, but I still don't quite follow this business about needing an Angarak King present at the meeting. Cyradis didn't say anything about that, and neither did the Prophecy."

"That's a Grolim book you've got there, Grandfather," Garion pointed out. "Maybe it's wrong."

"That's possible, too, but it does help to explain why Zandramas is moving around so stealthily. If Urvon knows about this the way Agachak obviously does, they'll both be doing everything in their power to get your son away from her. Whichever one of them gets to the Sardion with Geran and one of the Kings of Angarak is going to gain absolute control of the Grolim Church."

"Why my son?" Garion demanded. "Why would he be the one chosen for sacrifice?"

"I'm not sure, Garion. We haven't found an explanation for that yet."

"I don't think we'd better tell Ce'Nedra about this," Garion said. "She has problems enough as it is."

The door opened again, and Garion spun, his hand going over his shoulder to the hilt of his sword.

"Belgarath? Are you in here?" It was Silk's voice.

"Back here," Belgarath answered. "Keep your voice down."

"We've got trouble," the little man said, coming to the back of the library to join them. "Eriond is missing."

"What?" Garion exclaimed.

"He slipped out when none of us was watching."

Belgarath slammed his fist down on the table and swore. "What's the matter with that boy?" he burst out.

Silk pushed back the hood of the Grolim robe he wore. "Polgara was going to go looking for him, but Durnik and I talked her out of it. I said I'd come and find you instead."

"We'd better find him," the old man said, rising to his feet. "Pol will only wait for so long before she starts acting on her own. We'd better split up. We can cover more ground that way." He led them to the door of the library, glanced out quickly, and then went out into the hall. "Don't do anything unusual," he cautioned Garion in a whisper. "There are Grolims in this place with enough talent to hear you if you start making any noise."

Garion nodded.

"And check back with the others from time to time. We won't accomplish much if one of us finds Eriond and then has to go looking for the other two. Let's go." He moved quickly off down the dimly lighted hallway.

"How did he manage to slip past Aunt Pol?" Garion whispered to Silk as the two of them went side by side back the way they had come.

"Ce'Nedra had a bout of hysterics," Silk replied. "The sacrifices upset her. Polgara had her in one of the cells trying to calm her down. That's when Eriond slipped out."

"Is she all right?" Garion demanded, the sinking fear that had been with him since Prolgu returning with sudden force.

"I think so. Polgara gave her something, and she's sleeping." Silk carefully looked around a corner. "I'll go this way," he whispered. "Be careful." He moved off on silent feet.

Garion stood waiting for his friend to get well out of sight, then cautiously stepped out into the next corridor, folding his hands on his chest and lowering his cowled head in an imitation of Grolim piety. What could Eriond possibly be thinking of? The sheer irresponsibility of the boy's act made Garion want to pound his fist against the wall. He moved down the corridor, trying his best not to do anything that might look suspicious and carefully cracking open each door he came to.

"What is it?" a harshly accented voice demanded from inside a dark room when he opened the door.

"Sorry, brother," Garion muttered, trying to imitate the thickly accented Angarak speech, "wrong door." He quickly closed it again and went on down the corridor, moving as fast as he dared.

The door behind him was suddenly yanked open, and a half-dressed Grolim stepped out, his face angry. "You there," he shouted after Garion, "stop!"

Garion threw a quick look over his shoulder and was around the corner into the broad central corridor of the Temple in two steps.

"Come back here!" the Grolim shouted, and Garion heard his bare feet slapping on the flagstone floor as he ran in pursuit. Garion swore and then took a gamble. He yanked open the first door that presented itself and darted inside. A quick glance told him that the room was empty, and he closed the door and set his ear against its panel to listen.

"What's the trouble?" he heard someone demand from the corridor outside.

"Someone just tried to come into my cell." Garion recognized the outraged voice of the Grolim upon whom he had just intruded.

There was a sly chuckle. "Perhaps you should have waited to see what she wanted."

"It was a man."

There was a pause. "Well," the first voice said. "Well, well, well."

"What's that supposed to mean?"

"Nothing. Nothing at all. You'd better go put on some clothes. If Chabat catches you in the hall in your undergarments, she might get some peculiar ideas."

"I'm going to look for this intruder. There's something very strange going on here. Will you help me?"

"Why not? I haven't got anything better to do."

From far up the corridor Garion heard a slow, groaning chant and the sound of many shuffling feet.

"Quick," one of the voices outside the door warned, "back down this side passage. If they see us, they'll insist that we join them."

Garion heard their scurrying feet as they dodged back out of sight. Carefully, he opened the door a crack and peered out. The slow shuffling march and the deep-toned chanting came nearer. A line of Grolims, the cowls of their hoods raised and with their hands clasped in front of them, came into view, moving at a ceremonial pace along the torchlit corridor toward the very heart of the Temple. He waited in the dark room for them to pass, and then, on a sudden impulse so strong that he moved without even thinking, he boldly opened the door, stepped out into the corridor, and fell in at the end of the column.

The slow, rhythmic march continued on down the broad hallway, and the reek of burning flesh grew stronger in Garion's nostrils as the file which he had joined approached the Sanctum. Then, chanting even louder, they passed through the arched doorway into the vaulted Sanctum itself.

The ceiling was very high, lost in smoky shadows. On the wall facing the door hung that polished steel mask—the calm, beautiful replica of the unblemished face of the God Torak. Under that uncaring mask stood the black altar with bright rivulets of fresh blood streaking its sides. There stood the glowing brazier, awaiting the next quivering heart to be offered up to the long-dead God; and there the fire pit yawned for the body of the next butchered victim.

Shaking himself, Garion dodged quickly out of sight behind a column standing to one side of the doorway and stood sweating and trembling for several moments, struggling to control his emotions. Better perhaps than any man alive, he knew the full meaning of this awful place. Torak was dead. He himself had felt the faltering beat of the stricken God's heart thrilling down the blazing length of Iron-grip's sword, sunk deep in his enemy's chest. The slaughter that had drenched this foul place with blood in the years since that awful night was senseless, empty—homage paid to a maimed and demented God who had died weeping fire and crying piteously to the indifferent stars. A slow burning rage began to build up in his chest, filling his mouth with a fiery taste as bitter as gall. Unbidden, his will began to clench itself as he envisioned the shattering of the mask and the altar and the sudden destruction of this filthy place.

"That's not why you're here, Belgarion!" the voice in his mind cracked.

Slowly, as if, were he to release it all at once, it might destroy the entire city, Garion relaxed his will. Time enough to crush this horror later. Right now, he had to find Eriond. Cautiously, he poked his head around the column which concealed him. A priest with the purple-lined hood of his robe pushed back had just entered from the far side of the Sanctum. In his hands he carried a dark red cushion, and gleaming on that cushion lay a long, cruel knife. He faced the image of his dead God and reverently lifted the cushion and the knife in supplication. "Behold the instrument of thy will, Dragon God of Angarak," he intoned, "and behold him whose heart is to be offered unto thee."

Four Grolims dragged a naked, screaming slave into the Sanctum, ignoring his helpless struggles and panic-stricken pleas for mercy. Without thinking, Garion reached over his shoulder for his sword.

"Stop that!" the voice commanded.

"No! I'm not going to let it happen!"

"It won't happen. Now get your hand off your sword!"

"No chance!" Garion said aloud, drawing his blade and lunging around the pillar. And then as if he had suddenly been turned to stone, he found that he could not move so much as an eyelash. *"Let go of me!"* he grated.

"No! You're here to watch this time, not to act. Now stand there and keep your eyes open."

Garion stared in sudden disbelief as Eriond, his pale blond curls gleaming in the cruel light of the Temple, entered by way of the same door through which the slave had just been dragged. The young man's face bore an expression of almost regretful determination as he entered and walked directly toward the astonished priest. "I'm sorry," he said quite firmly, "but you can't do this any more."

"Seize this desecrator," the priest at the altar shouted. "It shall be *his* heart which shall sizzle in the coals!"

A dozen Grolims leaped to their feet, but suddenly froze, caught in that same stasis which locked Garion's muscles.

"This can't continue," Eriond said in that same determined voice. "I know how much it means to all of you, but it just can't go on. Someday—very soon, I think—you'll all understand."

There was no sound, no rushing surge such as Garion had come to expect, but the yawning fire pit before the altar suddenly roared to a furnace note, sending leaping flames and glowing sparks shooting upward to lick at the very vaults of the ceiling. The suffocatingly hot Sanctum suddenly cooled as if a cleansing breeze had just swept through it. Then the seething fire guttered briefly like a dying candle—and went out. The glowing brazier at the side of the altar also flared into blinding incandescence, and its steel body grew suddenly soft, drooping and sagging as it began to collapse under its own weight. With a flicker, it also went out.

The priest dropped his knife in horror and leaped to the still-glowing brazier. Irrationally, he put forth his hands as if he would force the softened metal back into its original shape, but he howled in pain as the red-hot steel seared deeply into his flesh.

Eriond regarded the dead fires with a look of satisfaction, then turned to the stunned Grolims still holding the naked slave. "Let that man go," he told them.

They stared at him.

"You might as well," Eriond said almost conversationally. "You can't sacrifice him without the fires, and the fires won't burn any more. No matter what you do, you won't ever be able to start them again."

"Done!" the voice in Garion's mind said in a tone of such exultation that it buckled his knees.

The burned priest, still moaning and cradling his charred hands at his chest, raised his ashen face. "Seize him!" he shrieked, pointing at Eriond with a blackened hand. "Seize him and take him to Chabat!"

CHAPTER TWELVE

There was no longer any need for stealth. Alarm bells rang in every quarter of the Temple, and frightened Grolims scurried this way and that, shouting contradictory orders to each other. Garion ran among them, desperately looking for Belgarath and Silk.

As he rounded a corner, a wild-faced Grolim caught him by the arm. "Were you there in the Sanctum when it happened?" he demanded.

"No," Garion lied, trying to free his arm.

"They say that he was ten feet tall, and that he blasted a dozen priests into nothingness before he extinguished the fires."

"Oh?" Garion said, still trying to free himself from the Grolim's grasp.

"Some people say that it was Belgarath the Sorcerer himself."

"I find that hard to believe."

"Who else would have that much power?" The Grolim stopped suddenly, his eyes going very wide. "You know what this means, don't you?" he asked in a trembling voice.

"What?"

"The Sanctum will have to be rededicated, and that requires Grolim blood. Dozens of us will have to die before the Sanctum is purified."

"I really have to go," Garion told him, tugging at the arm the man held fast in both hands.

"Chabat will wade to the hips in our blood," the priest moaned hysterically, ignoring Garion's words.

There was really no choice. Things were much too urgent for diplomacy. Garion feigned a frightened expression as he looked past the babbling Grolim's shoulder. "Is that her coming?" he whispered hoarsely.

The Grolim turned his head to look in fright back over his shoulder. Garion carefully measured him and then smashed his fist into the unprotected side of the terrified man's face. The Grolim slammed back against the wall, his eyes glazed and vacant. Then he collapsed in a heap on the floor.

"Neat," Silk said from a dark doorway a few yards up the hall, "but the reason for it escapes me."

"I couldn't get loose from him," Garion explained, bending to take hold of the unconscious man. He dragged him into a shadowy alcove and propped him up in a sitting position. "Have you got any idea where Grandfather is?"

"He's in here," Silk replied, jerking his thumb over his shoulder at the door behind him. "What happened?"

"I'll tell you in a minute. Let's get in out of sight."

They went through the doorway to find Belgarath seated on the edge of a table. "What's going on out there?" he demanded.

"I found Eriond."

"Good."

"No, not really. He went into the Sanctum just as the Grolims were about to sacrifice a slave and put out the fires."

"He did *what*?"

"I think it was him. I was there and I know that it wasn't me. He just walked in and told them that they couldn't sacrifice people any more, and then the fires went out. Grandfather, he didn't make a sound when he did it—no surge, no noise, nothing."

"Are you sure it was him? I mean—it wasn't something natural?"

Garion shook his head. "No. The fires flared up and then went out like blown-out candles. There were other things going on, too. The voice talked to me and I couldn't even move a muscle. The Grolims who were dragging the slave to the altar just let him go when Eriond told them to. Then he told them all that they won't ever be able to relight the fires."

"Where's the boy now?"

"They're taking him to Chabat."

"Couldn't you stop them?"

"I was told not to." Garion tapped his forehead.

"I should have expected that," Belgarath said irritably. "We'd better go warn Pol and the others. We may have to free Eriond and then fight our way out of here." He opened the door, looked out into the hallway, and motioned Garion and Silk to follow him.

Polgara's face was deathly pale when the three of them re-entered the room where she and the others were waiting. "You didn't find him," she said. It was not exactly a question.

"Garion did," Belgarath replied.

She turned to Garion. "Why isn't he with you, then?" she demanded.

"I'm afraid the Grolims have him, Aunt Pol."

"We've got a problem here, Pol," Belgarath said gravely. "From what Garion says, Eriond went into the Sanctum and put out the fires."

"What?" she exclaimed.

Garion spread his hands helplessly. "He just walked in and made the fires go out. The Grolims seized him and they're taking him to Chabat."

"This is very serious, Belgarath," Sadi said. "Those fires are supposed to burn perpetually. If the Grolims believe that the boy was responsible, he's in very great danger."

"I know," the old man agreed.

"All right, then," Durnik said quietly. "We'll just have to go take him away from them." He stood up, and Toth silently joined him.

"But our ship is almost ready," Sadi protested. "We could be out of here with no one the wiser."

"There's nothing we can do about that now." Belgarath's face was grimly determined.

"Let me see if I can salvage something out of this mess before any of you do anything irreversible," Sadi pleaded. "There'll always be time for more direct action if I can't talk our way out of this."

Garion looked around. "Where's Ce'Nedra?" he asked.

"She's asleep," Polgara replied. "Liselle's with her."

"Is she all right? Silk said that she was upset. She isn't sick again, is she?"

"No, Garion. It was the sounds coming from the Sanctum. She couldn't tolerate them."

A heavy fist suddenly pounded on the bolted door. Garion jumped and instinctively reached for his sword. "Open up in there!" a harsh voice commanded from outside.

"Quickly," Sadi hissed, "all of you get back into your cells and try to look as if you've been sleeping when you come out."

They hurried back into the cells and waited breathlessly while the thin eunuch went to the door and unbolted it. "What's the matter, reverend sirs?" he asked mildly as the Grolims burst into the room with drawn weapons.

"You have been summoned to an audience with the Hierarch, slaver," one of them snarled. "You and all your servants."

"We're honored," Sadi murmured.

"You're not being honored. You're to be interrogated. I'd advise you to speak the truth, because Agachak has the power to pull you very slowly out of your skin if you lie to him."

"What an unpleasant notion. Has the Hierarch returned from the Drojim Palace then?"

"Word has been sent to him of the monstrous crime one of your servants has committed."

"Crime? What crime?"

The Grolim ignored him. "On Chabat's orders, you are all to be confined until Agachak returns to the Temple."

Garion and the others were roughly shaken out of their feigned sleep and marched through the smoky corridors and down a narrow flight of stone steps into the basement. Unlike the rooms above, these cells were secured with barred iron doors, and the narrow halls had about them that peculiar sour odor that permeates prisons and dungeons the world over. One of the Grolims opened a barred door and gestured for them to enter.

"Is this really necessary, good Priest?" Sadi protested.

The Grolim put his hand threateningly on his sword hilt.

"Calm yourself, sir," Sadi said. "I was merely asking."

"Inside! Now!"

They all filed into the cell, and the black-robed priest slammed it behind them. The sound of the key grating in the lock seemed very loud for some reason.

"Garion," Ce'Nedra said in a frightened little voice, "What's happening? Why are they doing this?"

He put his arm comfortingly about her shoulders. "Eriond got into trouble," he explained. "Sadi's going to try to talk us all out of this."

"What if he can't?"

"Then we'll do it the other way."

Silk looked around at the dimly lit cell with a disdainful sniff. "Dungeons always show such a lack of imagination," he remarked, scuffing at the moldy straw littering the floor with one foot.

"Have you had such a wide experience with dungeons, Kheldar?" Velvet asked him.

"I've been in a few from time to time." He shrugged. "I've never found it convenient to stay for more than a few hours." He raised up on his tiptoes to peer out through the small barred window in the door. "Good," he said, "no guards." He looked at Belgarath. "Do you want me to open this?" he asked, tapping on the door with one knuckle. "I don't think we can accomplish very much from in here."

"Please be patient, Prince Kheldar," Sadi said. "If we break out of this cell, I'll never be able to smooth this over."

"I've got to find out what they've done with Eriond," Polgara told the eunuch firmly. "Go ahead and open it, Silk."

"Polgara?" a light, familiar voice came from the next cell. "Is that you?"

"Eriond!" she said with relief. "Are you all right?"

"I'm fine, Polgara. They put chains on me, but they aren't too uncomfortable."

"Why did you do that—what you did in the Sanctum?"

"I didn't like those fires."

"I didn't either, but—"

"I *really* didn't like them, Polgara. That sort of thing has to be stopped, and we have to start somewhere."

"How did you put them out?" Belgarath asked through the barred window in the door. "Garion was there when you did it and he says that he didn't hear or feel anything."

"I'm not sure, Belgarath. I don't think I actually did anything special to make them go out. I just decided that I didn't want them to burn any more, so I sort of let them know how I felt, and they just went out."

"That's all?"

"As closely as I can remember, yes."

Belgarath turned from the door, his face baffled. "When we get out of here, that boy and I are going to have a very long talk about this. I've meant to do that about a half-dozen times, and every time I make up my mind, I get smoothly diverted." He looked at Garion. "The next time you talk to your friend, tell him to stop that. It irritates me."

"He already knows that, Grandfather. I think that's why he does it."

Somewhere down the corridor outside, a heavy iron door clanged open, and there came the sound of marching feet.

"Grolims," Silk said quietly from the barred window.

"Who else?" Belgarath asked sourly.

The approaching group stopped outside, and a key grated in the lock of Eriond's cell. The door creaked open. "You, boy," a harsh voice barked. "Come with us."

"Father," Polgara whispered urgently.

The old man held up one hand. "Wait," he muttered.

Then someone rattled a key in the lock of their cell door, and it also clanged open. "Agachak has returned," the Grolim in the open doorway announced curtly. "You will come out of there now."

"Splendid," Sadi said with relief. "Whatever this is all about, I'm sure it can be cleared up in just a few minutes."

"No talking!" The Grolim turned abruptly and started down the corridor while a dozen of his fellows fell in behind the prisoners with drawn weapons.

Agachak, the Hierarch of Rak Urga, was a cadaverous-looking man with a long beard. He sat upon a thronelike chair in a large room lighted by glaring torches and hung with dark maroon drapes. The Hierarch's hooded robe was blood-red, and his sunken eyes burned beneath their shaggy gray brows. Eriond, still in chains, sat calmly on a rough wooden stool before him, and the slim priestess, Chabat, her purple-lined hood pushed back and the red scars on her cheeks seeming to reflect the torchlight, stood at her master's elbow with a look of cruel triumph on her face.

"Which one of you is Ussa of Sthiss Tor?" the Hierarch demanded in a hollow-sounding voice.

Sadi stepped forward with an oily bow. "I am Ussa, Holy One," he said.

"You're in a great deal of trouble, Ussa," Chabat told him, her throaty voice almost purring. Her lips twisted into an ugly smirk.

"But I have done nothing."

"Here in Cthol Murgos, the master is responsible for the misdeeds of the servant."

Agachak's eyes bored into Sadi, though his bony white face remained expressionless. "Let us proceed," he commanded. "Who is to present the evidence in this matter?"

Chabat turned and gestured to a hooded Grolim standing near the wall. "Sorchak will serve as the priest-inquisitor, Master," she replied in the tone of one who feels fully in charge of a situation. "I'm sure you're aware of his zeal."

"Ah, yes," Agachak said in a noncommittal tone. "I might have guessed that it would be Sorchak." The faintest hint of sardonic amusement touched his lips. "Very well, priest-inquisitor, you may present the charges."

The black-robed Grolim stepped forward, pushing his green-lined hood back from his tangled hair. "The matter itself is simple, my Lord," he declared in his strident voice. "There were dozens of witnesses present, so there can be no question of this young villain's guilt. The implications of that guilt, however, must be pursued."

"Pronounce your sentence, Great Hierarch," Chabat urged the dead-looking man on the throne. "I will wring the whole truth from this greasy Nyissan and from his servants."

"I have heard talk of guilt, Chabat," he replied, "but I have still not heard the charges or the evidence."

Chabat looked slightly taken aback by his words. "I but thought to spare you the tedium of a formal inquiry, Master. I am convinced of the truth of Sorchak's words. You have always accepted my judgment in such matters before."

"Perhaps," Agachak said, "but I think that this time I might like to judge for myself." He looked at the greasy-haired priest standing before him. "The charges, Sorchak," he said. "Exactly what is it that the young man is accused of doing?" There was a faint note of dislike in the Hierarch's voice.

Sorchak's bulging eyes grew slightly less certain as he sensed Agachak's unspoken animosity. Then he drew himself up. "Early this evening," he began, "just as the holiest rite of our faith was about to be performed on the altar in the Sanctum, this young man entered and extinguished the altar fires. That is what he did, and it is that of which I accuse him. I swear that he is guilty."

"Absurd," Sadi protested. "Are the fires at the altar not perpetually attended? How could this boy have gotten close enough to them to put them out?"

"How *dare* you question the sworn word of a priest of Torak?" Chabat said angrily, her scarred cheeks writhing. "Sorchak has sworn to his guilt, and therefore he is guilty. To question the word of a priest is death."

Agachak's sunken eyes were veiled as he looked at her. "I think that I might like to hear the evidence that has so persuaded you and the priest-inquisitor for myself, Chabat," he said in a flat voice. "Accusation and guilt are not always the same thing, and the question raised by Ussa is quite relevant."

A faint hope surged through Garion at the Hierarch's words. Agachak *knew*. He was completely aware of Chabat's involvement with Sorchak, and the very eagerness with which she defended the rancid-smelling Grolim's every word affronted her master.

"Well, priest-inquisitor," Agachak continued, "how *did* this boy manage to put out the altar fires? Has there been some laxity in guarding them?"

Sorchak's eyes grew wary as he realized that he was on dangerous ground. "I have many witnesses, my Lord," he declared. "There is universal agreement by all who were present that the Sanctum was desecrated by means of sorcery."

"Ah, sorcery, is it? That would explain everything, of course." Agachak paused, his dreadful eyes fixed on the now-sweating Sorchak. "I have noticed, however, that the cry 'witch' or 'sorcerer' is frequently raised when there is a lack of solid evidence. Is there no other explanation for what happened in the Sanctum? Is the priest-inquisitor's case so weak that he must fall back on so tired and worn-out an accusation?"

Chabat's expression was incredulous, and Sorchak began to tremble.

"Fortunately, the matter is easily resolved," Agachak added. "The gift of sorcery has a slight drawback. Others with the same gift can clearly sense the use of the power." He paused. "You didn't know that, did you, Sorchak? A priest of the Green hoping for elevation to the Purple would have been more diligent in his studies and would have known that—but you have been otherwise occupied, haven't you?" He turned to the priestess at his side. "I am surprised, however, that you did not instruct your protege here more completely before you let him make this kind of charge, Chabat. You might have prevented his making a fool of himself—and of you."

Her eyes blazed, and the flamelike scars on her face went livid; then suddenly they began to glow as if an inner fire were running beneath her skin.

"Well, Chabat," he said in a calm, deadly voice, "has the moment come then? Will you finally try your will against mine?"

The awful question hung in the air, and Garion found that he was holding his breath. Chabat, however, averted her eyes and turned her face away from the Hierarch, the fires in her cheeks fading.

"A wise decision, Chabat." Agachak turned to Sadi. "Well, Ussa of Sthiss Tor, how say you to the charge that your servant here is a sorcerer?"

"The priest of Torak is in error, my Lord," Sadi replied diplomatically. "Believe me, this young dunce is no sorcerer. He spends ten minutes every morning trying to decide which of his shoes goes on which foot. Look at him. There's not the faintest glimmer of intelligence in those eyes. He doesn't even have sense enough to be afraid."

Chabat's eyes grew angry again, though there was in them now a faint hint that she was no longer so sure of herself. "What would a Nyissan slaver know of sorcery, Master?" she sneered. "You know of the habits of the snake-people. Doubtless this Ussa's mind is so fuddled with drugs that one of his servants could be Belgarath himself, and he wouldn't know it."

"A very interesting point," Agachak murmured. "Now, let us examine this matter. We know that the altar fires went out. That much is certain. Sorchak declares that this young man extinguished them by means of sorcery—though he has no proof to substantiate that charge. Ussa of Sthiss Tor, who may be drugged to the point of insensibility, maintains that the young man is a simpleton and thus totally incapable of so extraordinary an act. Now, how may we resolve this dilemma?"

"Put them to the torment, Holy One," Chabat suggested eagerly. "I myself will wring the truth from them—one by one."

Garion tensed himself and looked carefully at Belgarath. The old man stood quite calmly with his short, silvery beard gleaming in the ruddy torchlight. He gave no sign that he might be preparing for any kind of direct action.

"Your fondness for the torture chamber is well known, Chabat," Agachak was saying coldly. "Your skill is such that your victims usually say exactly what you want them to say—which is not always the absolute truth."

"I do but serve my God, Master," she declared proudly.

"We *all* serve here, my Holy Priestess," he rebuked her, "and you would be wise not to assert your own excessive piety in order to elevate yourself—or your underling for that matter." He looked at Sorchak with undisguised contempt. "I am still Hierarch here, and *I* will make the final decision in this matter."

The scar-faced priestess shrank back, her eyes suddenly fearful. "Forgive me, Agachak," she stammered. "This monstrous crime has filled me with righteous outrage, but as you say, the final decision is wholly yours."

"I find your acceptance of my authority gratifying, Chabat. I thought you might have forgotten."

Just then there was a stir at the back of the torchlit room. Two burly Murgos with long, polished halberds in their hands rudely pushed aside the Grolims clustered near the door. With their dark faces impassive, they banged the butts of their weapons on the floor in unison. "Make way!" one of them boomed. "Make way for Urgit, High King of Cthol Murgos!"

The man who sauntered into the room surrounded by guards looked like no Murgo Garion had ever seen before. He was short and had a slender but wiry build. His black hair was lank and his features narrow. His robe was carelessly open at the front, revealing the fact that, instead of the customary mail shirt, he wore a western-style doublet and hose of rich purple. His iron crown was perched somewhat rakishly on one side of his head. His expression was sardonic, but his eyes were wary. "Agachak," he greeted the Hierarch perfunctorily, "I gave some thought to the news which was brought to you at the Drojim, and I finally concluded that I might be of some use to you in sorting out the cause of this regrettable incident."

"The Temple is honored by the presence of the High King," Agachak intoned formally.

"And the High King is honored to be so kindly received by the Hierarch of Rak Urga," Urgit replied. He looked around. "Do you have a chair handy?" he asked. "I've had a long, tiring day."

"See to it," Agachak said flatly to the priestess standing beside his throne.

Chabat blinked, then a slow flush mounted her cheeks. "A chair for his Majesty," she commanded harshly, "and be quick about it."

One of the Grolims near the door scurried out and returned a moment later with a heavy chair.

"Thanks awfully," the King said, sinking into the chair. He looked at Agachak. "I have a small confession to make, Holy One," he said with an apologetic cough. "As I was about to enter your presence in this room, I lingered for a time in the hallway outside, hoping to acquaint myself with the details of this affair." He laughed shortly. "Listening at doors is an old habit of mine, I'm afraid. It comes from my anxious childhood. Anyway, I managed to hear the charges presented by the priest-inquisitor. To be perfectly candid, Agachak, he's got a very shaky case." He gave the Hierarch a quick, ingratiating look. "But of course you've already pointed that out, haven't you?"

Agachak nodded briefly, his face unreadable.

"Now," Urgit went on quickly, "I most certainly wouldn't want to interfere in what is clearly a Church matter, but wouldn't you say that there are dozens of possible natural explanations for this incident?" He looked hopefully at Agachak; then reassured by the look of agreement on the Hierarch's face, he continued. "I mean, we've all seen fires go out before, haven't we? Do we really need to go so far afield to come up with a reason for this really unremarkable occurrence? Isn't it more likely that the keepers of the Temple fires grew careless and that the fires just went out on their own—as fires starved for fuel are likely to do?"

"Absolute nonsense!" the greasy-haired Sorchak snapped.

Urgit flinched visibly, his eyes going in appeal to Agachak.

"You forget yourself, priest-inquisitor," the Hierarch said. "Our guest is the High King of Cthol Murgos; if you offend him, I may decide to give him your head by way of apology."

Sorchak swallowed hard. "Please forgive me, your Majesty," he choked. "I spoke before I thought."

"Quite all right, old boy." Urgit forgave him with a magnanimous wave of his hand. "Sometimes we all speak too quickly when we're excited." He turned back to the Hierarch. "I regret this catastrophe as much as anyone, Agachak," he said, "but this Nyissan slaver was sent here by Jaharb, and both you and I know how desperately urgent his mission is to the Church and to the State. Don't you think that as a matter of policy we could let this incident pass?"

"Surely you're not just going to let these charges drop?" Chabat's voice was shrill as she faced the Hierarch. "Who is to be punished for the desecration of the Sanctum?"

Urgit's face grew unhappy, and he once again appealed to Agachak for support with pleading eyes. Garion clearly saw that this was not a strong king. Even the slightest resistance to his diffidently offered proposals made him instinctively retreat or seek support from someone he perceived to be stronger.

Agachak turned slowly to look the scarred priestess full in the face. "All this shouting is beginning to weary me, Chabat," he told her bluntly. "If you can't modulate your voice, you can leave."

She stared at him in stunned disbelief.

"There is far more at stake here than the fact that some fires went out," he said to her. "As was foretold ages ago, the time for the final meeting between the Child of Light and the Child of Dark is at hand. If *I* am not the one who is present at that meeting, you will find yourself bowing to either Urvon or Zandramas. I doubt that either one of them would find your antics amusing enough to make them decide to let you go on living. As for the charge of sorcery, there's an easy way to settle that once and for all." He rose from his throne, walked across to Eriond, and placed one hand on each side of his head.

Aunt Pol drew in her breath sharply, and Garion carefully began to gather in his will.

Eriond looked up into the face of the dead-looking Hierarch with a gentle smile on his face.

"Faugh!" Agachak said in disgust, pulling his hands quickly back. "This beardless boy is an innocent. There's no evidence in his mind that he has ever tasted power." He turned to look at Sorchak. "I find your charges groundless, priest-inquisitor, and I dismiss them."

Sorchak's face went white, and his eyes bulged.

"Have a care, Sorchak," the Hierarch said ominously. "If you protest my decision too strenuously, I might just decide that this whole incident was *your* fault. Chabat is sick with disappointment that she has no one to torture to death." His look grew sly as he glanced at the priestess. "Would you like to have Sorchak, my dear?" he asked her. "I have always delighted in giving you these little gifts. I'll even watch with some pleasure while you slowly pull out his entrails with red-hot hooks."

Chabat's flame-marked face was filled with chagrin. Garion saw that she had been convinced that the Hierarch, as he apparently had so many times in the past, would meekly accede to her peremptory demands, and she had staked all of her prestige on the punishment of Sadi, for whom she had developed an instantaneous dislike. Agachak's unexpected and almost contemptuous rejection of the accusations she and Sorchak had leveled struck at the very foundations of her puffed-up self-esteem, but more importantly at her position of power here in the Temple. Unless she could somehow salvage something—anything—out of this, her many enemies would inevitably pull her down. Garion fervently hoped that Sadi realized that she was even more dangerous now than she had been when she had thought she held the upper hand.

Her narrowed eyes grew cautious as she assessed the Hierarch's mood, then she drew herself up and addressed King Urgit. "There is also a civil crime here, your Majesty," she told him. "I had believed that the desecration of the Sanctum was more serious, but since our revered Hierarch has discovered in his wisdom that those charges were unfounded, it is now my duty to advise you of a crime against the State."

Urgit exchanged a quick look with Agachak, then slouched lower in his chair, his eyes unhappy. "The Crown is always ready to listen to the words of the priesthood," he replied without much enthusiasm.

Chabat gave Sadi another look of smug triumph and open hatred. "Since the founding of our nation, the vile drugs and poisons of the snake-people have been forbidden in Cthol Murgos by royal decree," she pointed out. "After this Ussa and his servants were confined in the dungeon, I had their belongings searched." She turned. "Bring in that case," she ordered.

A side door opened, and an obsequious underpriest entered, carrying Sadi's red leather case. The fanatic Sorchak took it from him, his face also gleefully triumphant. "Behold the evidence that Ussa of Sthiss Tor has violated our law and that his life is forfeit," he said in his strident voice. He undid the latch, opened the case, and displayed Sadi's many vials and the earthenware bottle where Zith resided.

Urgit's face grew even more unhappy. He looked uncertainly at Sadi. "Is there some explanation for this, Ussa?" he asked hopefully.

Sadi's face took on an exaggerated expression of innocence. "Surely your Majesty could not believe that I ever intended to try to distribute those items here in Cthol Murgos," he protested.

"Well," Urgit said lamely, "you have got them with you."

"Of course, but they're for trade with the Malloreans. There's quite a market for this sort of thing among those people."

"I wouldn't be in the least surprised," Urgit said, straightening in his chair. "Then you had no intention of peddling your drugs to my subjects?"

"Most certainly not, your Majesty," Sadi replied indignantly.

Urgit's expression grew relieved. "Well," he said to the glowering Chabat, "there you have it, then. Certainly none of us could object to the fact that our Nyissan friend here is bent on corrupting the Malloreans—the more the better, I'd say."

"What about this?" Sorchak said, putting Sadi's case on the floor and lifting out the earthenware bottle. "What secret is hidden in here, Ussa of Sthiss Tor?" He shook the bottle.

"Be careful, man!" Sadi exclaimed, leaping forward with his hand outstretched.

"Ah-ha!" Chabat exclaimed triumphantly. "It appears that there is something in that bottle that the slaver considers important. Let us examine the contents. It may yet be that some undiscovered crime lurks here. Open the bottle, Sorchak."

"I beg of you," Sadi pleaded. "If you value your life, do not tamper with that bottle."

"Open it, Sorchak," Chabat ordered relentlessly.

The smirking Grolim shook the bottle again and then began to work out the stopper.

"Please, noble Priest!" Sadi's voice was anguished.

"We'll just have a look." Sorchak grinned. "I'm sure that one look won't hurt anything." He drew out the cork and raised the bottle to his eye to peer in.

Zith, of course, took immediate action.

With a strangled shriek, Sorchak arched backward, flinging both arms into the air. The earthenware bottle sailed upward, and Sadi caught it just before it struck the floor. The stricken priest clapped both hands over his eye. There was a look of horror on his face, and blood spurted out from between his fingers. He began to squeal like a pig, all of his limbs convulsing. He suddenly pitched forward, threshing wildly and clawing tatters of skin from his face. He began to bang his head on the floor. His convulsions grew more violent and he began to froth at the mouth. With a shrill shriek, he suddenly leaped high into the air. When he came down, he was dead.

There was a moment of stunned silence, then Chabat suddenly shrieked, "Sorchak!" Her voice was filled with anguish and insupportable loss. She flew to the side of the dead man and fell across his body, sobbing uncontrollably.

Urgit stared in open-mouthed revulsion at Sorchak's corpse. "Torak's teeth!" he swore in a strangled whisper, "what have you got in that bottle, Ussa?"

"Uh—it's a pet, your Majesty," Sadi replied nervously. "I did try to warn him."

"Indeed you did, Ussa," Agachak crooned. "We all heard you. Do you suppose I might see this pet of yours?" A cruel smile crossed his face as he looked gloatingly at the hysterically sobbing Chabat.

"Certainly, Holy One," Sadi answered quickly. He carefully laid the bottle on the floor. "Just a precaution," he apologized. "She's a little excited, and I wouldn't want her to make any mistakes." He leaned over the bottle. "It's all right now, dear," he said soothingly to the vengeful little reptile lurking inside. "The bad man has gone away, and everything is fine now."

Zith sulked in her bottle, still greatly offended.

"Really, dear," Sadi assured her, "it's all right. Don't you trust me?"

There was a snippy little hiss from inside the bottle.

"That's a very naughty thing to say, Zith," Sadi gently reproved her. "I did everything I could to keep him from disturbing you." He looked apologetically at Agachak. "I really don't know where she picks up such language, Holy One," he declared. He turned his attention back to the bottle. "Please, dear, don't be nasty."

Another spiteful little hiss came from the bottle.

"Now that's going entirely too far, Zith. You come out of there at once."

Cautiously the little green snake poked her head out of the bottle, raised herself, and looked at the corpse on the floor. Sorchak's face was a ghastly blue color, and the foam was drying on his lips. Chabat, still weeping hysterically, clung to his stiffening body. Zith slithered the rest of the way out of her little house, dismissed the dead man with a contemptuous flick of her tail, and crawled to Sadi, purring with a smug little sound of self-satisfaction. Sadi reached down his hand to her, and she nuzzled affectionately at his fingers. "Isn't she adorable?" he said fondly. "She's always so kittenish after she bites someone."

A slight movement caught Garion's eye. Velvet was leaning forward, looking at the contentedly purring little reptile with an expression of wholly absorbed fascination.

"You've got her under control, haven't you, Ussa?" Urgit asked in a faintly apprehensive voice.

"Oh, yes, your Majesty," Sadi assured him. "She's perfectly content now. In a little bit, I'll give her a light snack and a nice little bath, and she'll sleep like a baby."

Urgit turned back to the Hierarch. "Well, Agachak?" he said, "what's your decision? Personally, I see no reason to continue this investigation. The slaver and his servants appear to be quite blameless."

The Hierarch considered it, his eyes hooded. "I believe you're right, your Majesty." He turned to one of his Grolims. "Free this idiot boy," he said, pointing at Eriond.

Chabat, her scarred face ravaged by grief, slowly raised herself from Sorchak's body. She looked first at Urgit and then at Agachak. "And what of this?" she demanded in a voice vibrant with her emotion. "What of this?" She indicated the stiffening Sorchak at her feet. "Who is to be punished for this? Upon whom shall I wreak my vengeance?"

"The man died through his own act, Chabat," Agachak dismissed her demand. "There was no crime involved."

"No crime?" Her voice was choked. "No crime?" It rose in a crescendo. "Are Grolim lives so cheap that you will now throw them away?" She spun and fixed Sadi with her burning eyes. "You will pay for this, Ussa of Sthiss Tor," she declared. "I swear it upon the body of Sorchak and upon that of Torak. You will never escape me. I will have revenge upon you and all your servants for the death of Sorchak."

"Why are you so upset, Chabat?" Agachak asked with malicious amusement in his hollow voice. "There are scores of Grolims in the Temple. Sorchak was one like all the rest—greedy, ambitious, and deceitful. His death was the result of his own folly—and of yours." A cruel smile touched his thin lips. "Could it be that your interest in this dead Grolim was personal? You have long been my favorite, Chabat. I trusted you entirely. Is it possible that you have been unfaithful to me, seeking entertainment in the arms of another?"

Her face blanched, and she lifted one trembling hand to her lips as she realized that she had gone too far and revealed too much.

Agachak laughed, a chilling sound. "Did you actually believe that I was so engrossed in my search for the Sardion that I was not aware of your private amusements?" He paused. "Tell me, Chabat," he said in an offhand way, "did you and Sorchak ever succeed in raising a demon?"

She drew back, her eyes wide with sudden terror as she faced her master.

"I thought not," he murmured. "What a shame. All that effort wasted. Perhaps you need a new partner in your midnight rites, Chabat. Sorchak's heart was never really in your attempts anyway. He was nothing more than a cheap opportunist, so your loss is not as great as you might think. Do you know what he called you in private?" he asked her, his eyes alight.

She shook her head numbly.

"I have it on the very best authority that he customarily referred to you as 'that scar-faced hag.' Does that in any way mollify your grief?"

Chabat recoiled from him, her face suffused with mortification as she realized that she had just been cruelly humiliated in public. She whirled in rage and kicked the dead man in his unfeeling side. "Scar-faced hag?" she shrieked, kicking the body again. "Scar-faced hag? Rot, Sorchak! And may the worms enjoy your stinking carcass!" Then she spun and fled, sobbing, from the room.

"She seems a trifle distraught," Urgit observed mildly.

Agachak shrugged. "The shattering of illusions is always painful."

Urgit pulled absently at his pointed nose. "Her distraction, however, raises certain risks here, Agachak," he said thoughtfully. "The mission of this slaver is vital to both of us, and an hysterical woman—particularly one with the kind of power Chabat possesses—can be very dangerous. She obviously bears Ussa here a certain enmity, and since he was involved in both her humiliation and the death of Sorchak, I'd say that right now the Temple might not be the safest place in the world for him."

Agachak nodded gravely. "Your Majesty's point is well taken."

Urgit's face brightened as if an idea had just occurred to him. "Agachak," he said, "what would you say to the notion of my keeping Ussa and his servants at the Drojim until we can see him safely on his way? That would put him beyond Chabat's reach in the event that her distraction impels her into any kind of rashness." He paused nervously. "It's entirely up to you, Holy Agachak," he added quickly.

"There is much to what you say, Urgit," Agachak replied. "A small slip here could put you at the mercy of Kal Zakath and me on my knees before either Urvon or Zandramas. Let us by all means avoid those disasters." He turned to Sadi. "You and your servants will accompany his Majesty to the Drojim Palace, Ussa. I'll have your belongings sent along later. You'll be safe there, and your ship will be ready in a few days." He smiled ironically. "I hope you appreciate our tender concern for your well-being."

Sadi bowed. "I am overwhelmed with gratitude, Holy One," he said.

"I'll keep the Dagashi Kabach here in the Temple, however," Agachak said to the King. "That way each of us will have in his hands a vital element in the mission to Rak Hagga. It should encourage us to cooperate."

"Of course," Urgit agreed hastily, "I quite understand." He rose to his feet. "The hour grows late," he noted. "I'll return to the Drojim now and leave you to your many religious duties, Dread Hierarch."

"Give my regards to the Lady Tamazin, your noble mother," Agachak responded.

"I will, Agachak. I know that she'll be smothered with joy to know that you remembered her. Come along then, Ussa." He turned and started toward the door.

"May the spirit of Torak go with you, your Majesty," Agachak called after him.

"I certainly *hope* not," Urgit muttered to Sadi as they passed through the doorway.

"Your Majesty's arrival came at a critical moment," Sadi said quietly as the two of them led the way down the hall. "Things were getting a bit tense."

"Don't flatter yourself," Urgit said sourly. "If it weren't for the absolute necessity of getting Kabach to Rak Hagga, I'd never have risked a confrontation with the Grolims. I'm sure you're a nice enough fellow, but I have my own skin to consider."

When they were outside the nail-studded doors of the Temple, the Murgo King straightened and drew in a deep breath of the cool night air. "I'm always glad to get out of that stinking place," he declared. He motioned to one of his guards. "Go get the horses," he commanded.

"At once, your Majesty."

Then Urgit turned back to the shaven-headed Nyissan. "All right, you sly fox," he said in an amused tone, "now perhaps you'd like to tell me what you're doing down here in Cthol Murgos—and why you've assumed this pose. I almost fainted dead away when I discovered that the mysterious Ussa of Sthiss Tor was none other than my old friend Sadi, Chief Eunuch in the palace of Queen Salmissra."

CHAPTER THIRTEEN

They clattered through the deserted midnight streets of Rak Urga with the king's torch-bearing guards drawn up closely around them. "It's all a sham, of course," Urgit was saying to Sadi. "I bow and scrape to Agachak, mouth pious platitudes to make him happy, and keep my real opinions to myself. I need his support, so I have to stay on the good side of him. He knows that, so he takes every possible advantage of the situation."

"The bond between Church and State here in Cthol Murgos is well known," Sadi noted as they entered a broad square where flaring torches painted the sides of nearby buildings a smoky orange.

Urgit made an indelicate sound. "Bond!" he snorted, "More like a chain, Sadi—and it's around *my* neck." He looked up at the murky sky, his sharp-featured face ruddy in the torchlight. "Agachak and I agree on one thing, though. It's absolutely essential to get the Dagashi Kabach to Rak Hagga before winter sets in. Jaharb's had his people combing all of western Cthol Murgos for months looking for a slaver to slip Kabach through Mallorean lines." He suddenly grinned at Sadi. "As luck had it, the one he found just happened to be an old friend of mine. I don't know that we need to let Agachak know that we're acquainted, though. I like to keep a few secrets from him."

Sadi made a sour face. "It's not too hard to guess why you're sending an assassin to the city where Kal Zakath's headquarters are located."

"I wouldn't advise lingering for any sight-seeing after you get him there," Urgit agreed. "But then, Rak Hagga's not a very attractive town anyway."

Sadi nodded glumly. "That's more or less what I thought." He considered it, running one long-fingered hand over his shaven scalp. "The death of 'Zakath won't really solve your problem, though, will it? I can't really see the Mallorean generals packing up and going home just because their emperor's been killed."

Urgit sighed. "One thing at a time, Sadi. I can probably bribe the generals, or pay them tribute or something. The first step is to get rid of 'Zakath. You can't reason with that man." He looked around at the bleak stone buildings, harshly illuminated by flickering torchlight. "I hate this place," he said suddenly. "I absolutely hate it."

"Rak Urga?"

"Cthol Murgos, Sadi. I hate the whole stinking country. Why couldn't I have been born in Tolnedra—or maybe Sendaria? Why did I have to get stuck in Cthol Murgos?"

"But you're the king."

"That wasn't by choice. One of our charming customs is that when a new king is crowned, all other possible contenders for the throne are put to death. For me, it was either the throne or the grave. I had a number of brothers when I became king, but now I'm an only child." He shuddered. "This is a gloomy subject, don't you think? Why don't we talk about something else? Just what are you doing in Cthol Murgos, Sadi? I thought you were Salmissra's right hand."

Sadi coughed. "Her Majesty and I had a slight misunderstanding, so I thought it might be better for me to leave Nyissa for a while."

"Why Cthol Murgos? Why didn't you go to Tol Honeth instead? It's much more civilized and much, much more comfortable." He sighed again. "I'd give anything to be able to live in Tol Honeth."

"I've made some powerful enemies in Tolnedra, your Majesty," Sadi replied. "I know my way around Cthol Murgos, so I hired these Alorn mercenaries to protect me and came here posing as a slaver."

"And then Jaharb picked you up," Urgit guessed. "Poor old Sadi, no matter where you go, you always seem to get mixed up in politics—even when you don't want to."

"It's a curse," Sadi told him mournfully. "It's been following me for all my life."

They rounded a corner and approached a vast, sprawling building surrounded by a high wall. Its domes and towers rose in barbaric, torchlit profusion, and, unlike the rest of Rak Urga, it was garishly painted in a half-dozen conflicting colors.

"Behold the Drojim Palace," King Urgit said extravagantly to Sadi, "the hereditary home of the House of Urga."

"A most unusual structure, your Majesty," Sadi murmured.

"That's a diplomatic way to put it." Urgit looked critically at his palace. "It's gaudy, ugly, and in terribly bad taste. It does, however, suit my personality almost perfectly." He turned to one of his guards. "Be a good fellow and ride on ahead," he instructed. "Tell the gatekeepers that the High King approaches and that if I have to wait while they open the gate for me, I'll have their ears cut off."

"At once, your Majesty."

Urgit grinned at Sadi. "One of my few amusements," he explained. "The only people I'm allowed to bully are servants and common soldiers, and all Murgos have a deep-seated need to bully somebody."

They rode on through the hastily opened gate and dismounted in a ruddily torchlit courtyard. Urgit looked around at the garishly painted walls of the house. "Ghastly, isn't it?" He shuddered. "Let's go inside."

There was a large door at the top of a flight of stone stairs, and Urgit led them inside and down a long, vaulted corridor. He stopped before a pair of polished double doors guarded by two scar-faced soldiers. "Well?" he said to them.

"Yes, your Majesty?" one replied.

"Do you suppose that I could prevail upon you to open the door?" Urgit asked him. "Or would you prefer an immediate transfer to the war zone?"

"At once, your Majesty," the soldier replied, quickly yanking the door open.

"Excellently done, my dear fellow. Just try not to jerk it off its hinges next time." The king strolled through the door and into the room beyond. "My throne room," he said grandiosely. "The product of whole generations of diseased imaginations."

The room was larger than the Hall of the Rivan King in Garion's Citadel. The ceiling was a maze of intersecting vaults, all covered with sheets of the beaten red gold from the mines of Cthol Murgos. The walls and columns were ablaze with inset jewels, and the chairs lined up at the sides of the room were inlaid with more Angarak gold. At the far end of the room stood a bejeweled throne, backed by blood-red drapes. Seated in a simple chair beside that throne was a silver-haired lady, calmly embroidering.

"Hideous, isn't it?" Urgit said. "The Urgas have been pillaging the treasury at Rak Goska for centuries to decorate the Drojim Palace, but would you believe that the roof still leaks?" He sauntered to the far end of the room and stopped before the black-gowned lady, who was still busy at her needlework. "Mother," he greeted her with a slightly mocking bow, "you're up late, aren't you?"

"I don't need as much sleep as I did when I was younger, Urgit." She set her sewing aside. "Besides," she added, "we usually talk over the day's events before you retire for the night."

"It's the high point of my day, mother," he replied with a faint smile tugging at his lips.

She returned his smile with good-humored affection. She was, Garion saw as that smile lighted her face, a remarkably attractive woman. Despite the silvery hair and the few lines at the corners of her eyes, her face still bore the signs of what had once been an extraordinary beauty. A faint movement caught his eye, and he saw Silk shrinking behind Toth's broad back and drawing up the hood of his green robe to conceal his face.

"Who are your friends, Urgit?" the silver-haired lady asked her son.

"Ah, forgive me, mother. My manners must be slipping. Allow me to present Sadi, Chief Eunuch to Queen Salmissra of the land of the snake-people."

"*Formerly* Chief Eunuch, I'm afraid," Sadi corrected. He bowed deeply. "I'm honored to meet the Queen Mother of the Kingdom of the Murgos."

"Oh," Urgit said, mounting the dais and sprawling on the throne with one leg cocked up over one of its jeweled arms, "I keep forgetting the amenities. Sadi, this is my royal mother, the Lady Tamazin, jewel of the House of Hagga and grieving widow of my royal father, Taur Urgas the Deranged—may blessings rain down on the hand that sent him to the bosom of Torak."

"Can't you ever be serious about anything, Urgit?" his mother chided him.

"But you *do* grieve, don't you mother? I know that in your heart you miss all those wonderful moments you spent with my father—watching him gnaw on the furniture, listening to his insane gibbering, and enjoying all those playful blows to the stomach and kicks to the head with which he demonstrated his affection for his wives."

"That will do, Urgit," she said firmly.

"Yes, mother."

"Welcome to the Drojim, Sadi," Lady Tamazin greeted the eunuch formally. She looked inquiringly at the others.

"My servants, Lady Tamazin," Sadi said quickly. "Alorns for the most part."

"A most unusual turn of circumstances," she murmured. "The age-old war between Murgo and Alorn has denied me the opportunity to meet very many of that race." She looked directly then at Aunt Pol. "Surely this lady is no servant," she said skeptically.

"A temporary arrangement, my Lady Tamazin," Polgara replied with a profoundly graceful curtsy. "I needed some time in another place to avoid some unpleasantness at home."

The Queen Mother smiled. "I do understand," she said. "Men play at politics, and women must pay the price for their folly." She turned back to her son. "And how did your interview with the Hierarch go?" she asked him.

"Not bad." He shrugged. "I groveled enough to keep him happy."

"That's enough, Urgit." Her voice was sharp. "Agachak's in a position to do you a great service, so show him the proper respect."

Urgit flinched slightly at her tone. "Yes, mother," he replied meekly. "Oh, I almost forgot," he went on. "The priestess Chabat had a bit of a setback."

The Queen Mother's expression became one of disgust. "Her behavior is a public scandal," she declared. "I can't understand why Agachak tolerates her."

"I think he finds her amusing, mother. Grolims have a peculiar sense of humor. Anyway, she had this friend—a very *close* friend—who had a bit of an accident. She'll need to find another playmate before she can scandalize the good people of Rak Urga any more."

"Why do you persist in being so frivolous, Urgit?"

"Why don't we just call it a symptom of my incipient madness?"

"You're not going to go mad," she said firmly.

"Of course I'm going to go mad, mother. I'm rather looking forward to it."

"You're impossible to talk with when you're like this," she chided him. "Are you going to stay up much longer?"

"I don't think so. Sadi and I have a few things to discuss, but they can wait until tomorrow."

The Queen Mother turned back to Polgara. "My quarters are most spacious, Lady," she said. "Would you and your attendants care to share them with me during your stay here in the Drojim?"

"We would be honored, my Lady," Polgara said.

"Very well, then," Urgit's mother said. "Prala," she called.

The girl who stepped from the shadows behind the throne was slender and perhaps sixteen years old. She wore a black gown and had long, lustrous black hair. The dark, angular eyes that made most Murgo men look so alien were in her case very large and delicately almond-shaped, giving her features an exotic beauty. Her expression, however, was filled with a resolve uncommon in one so young. She stepped to Lady Tamazin's chair and helped her to her feet.

Urgit's face darkened, and his eyes grew flinty as he watched his mother limp down from the dais, leaning heavily on the girl's shoulder. "A little gift from the inestimable Taur Urgas," he said to Sadi. "One evening when he was feeling playful, he knocked my mother down a flight of stairs and broke her hip. She's had that limp ever since."

"I don't even notice it any more, Urgit."

"It's amazing how all of our minor aches and pains got better right after King Cho-Hag's saber slid through my father's guts." Urgit paused. "I wonder if it's too late to send Cho-Hag some small token of appreciation," he added.

"Oh," the Queen Mother said to Polgara, "this is Lady Prala, a princess of the House of Cthan."

"Princess," Polgara greeted the slender girl supporting Lady Tamazin.

"My Lady," Prala responded in a clear voice.

Lady Tamazin, leaning on Prala's shoulder, slowly limped from the room with Polgara, Ce'Nedra, and Velvet close behind her.

"That girl makes me very nervous for some reason," Urgit muttered to Sadi. "My mother dotes on her, but she has something else on her mind. She never takes her eyes off me." He shook his head as if to dismiss an unwelcome thought. "You and your people have had a very busy day, Sadi. We can talk further tomorrow after we've both had a good night's sleep." He reached out and tugged at a silken bellpull, and there was the heavy note of a large gong somewhere outside the throne room. Urgit rolled his eyes toward the ceiling. "Why does it always have to be those great bongs and clangs?" he complained. "Someday, I'd like to tug on a bellpull and hear a tiny little tinkle."

The door at the far end of the throne room opened, and a heavy-shouldered Murgo of late middle age entered. His hair was gray, and his scarred face was heavily lined. There was no hint that a smile had ever touched that grim face. "Your Majesty rang?" he said in a rasping voice.

"Yes, Oskatat," Urgit replied in an oddly respectful tone. "Do you suppose that you could escort my good friend Sadi and his servants to suitable quarters?" He turned back to Sadi. "Oskatat is Lord High Seneschal here," he said. "He served my father in the same capacity at Rak Goska." There was no hint of his usual mockery as he spoke. "My mother and I were not popular in my father's house, and Oskatat was the closest thing to a friend either of us had there."

"My Lord," Sadi said to the big, gray-haired man with a deep bow.

The seneschal nodded a curt response, then returned his bleak gaze to the king. "Has my Lady Tamazin retired for the night?" he asked.

"Yes, Oskatat."

"Then you should also seek your bed. The hour is late."

"I was just on my way," Urgit answered, getting quickly to his feet. Then he stopped. "Oskatat," he said plaintively, "I'm not a sickly little boy any more. I don't really need to spend twelve hours in bed every night the way I used to."

"The burdens of the crown are many," the seneschal said shortly. "You need your rest." He turned back to Sadi. "Follow me," he said, starting toward the door.

"Until tomorrow then, Sadi," Urgit said. "Sleep well."

"My thanks, your Majesty."

The rooms to which the bleak-faced Oskatat took them were as garish as the rest of the Drojim Palace. The walls were painted an unwholesome mustard-yellow and hung with splotchy tapestries. The furnishings were carved from rare, priceless woods, and the blue Mallorean carpet was as deep as the wool on the back of a sheep. Once he had opened the door for them, Oskatat jerked his head in the briefest of nods, then turned and left them alone.

"Charming fellow there," Sadi murmured.

Garion had been looking curiously at Silk, who still had his face covered by his hood. "Why are you trying so hard to hide?" he asked.

The little man pulled back his hood with a rueful expression. "One of the disadvantages of being a world traveler is that one keeps running into old friends."

"I'm not sure I follow you."

"Do you remember that time when we were on our way to Rak Cthol and Taur Urgas caught me and stuck me in that pit?"

"Yes."

"And do you remember why he did that—and why he planned to peel off my skin inch by inch the next day?"

"You said that you'd been in Rak Goska once and accidentally killed his eldest son."

"Right. You have an excellent memory, Garion. Well, as it happened, I'd been engaged in some negotiations with Taur Urgas himself before that unfortunate incident. I visited the palace in Rak Goska frequently and met the Lady Tamazin several times. She's almost certain to remember me—particularly in view of the fact that she said that she knew my father."

"That could cause some problems," Belgarath said.

"Not if I avoid her." Silk shrugged. "Murgo women seldom socialize with men—particularly with strangers—so I don't imagine we'll be bumping into each other very often in the next few days. Oskatat could be a different matter, though. I also met him while I was there."

"I think that, if it's at all possible, you ought to stay here in our rooms," the old man suggested. "It might even keep you out of trouble for a change."

"Why, Belgarath," Silk said mildly, "what a thing to say."

"Has King Urgit always been like this?" Durnik asked Sadi. "He seems awfully—well—humorous, I guess the word is. I didn't think that Murgos even knew how to smile."

"He's a very complex fellow," Sadi replied.

"Have you known him long?"

"He frequently visited Sthiss Tor when he was younger—usually on missions for his father. I think he jumped at any excuse to get out of Rak Goska. He and Salmissra got on rather well together. Of course, that was before Lady Polgara changed her into a snake." The eunuch rubbed his hand absently over his scalp. "He's not a very strong king," he noted. "His childhood in the palace of Taur Urgas made him timid, and he backs away from any sort of confrontation. He's a survivor, though. He's spent his entire life just trying to stay alive, and that tends to make a man very alert."

"You'll be talking with him again tomorrow," Belgarath said. "See if you can get him to give you some definite information about this ship they plan to give us. I want to get to the Isle of Verkat before the onset of winter, and various people in our party have been doing things that might attract attention, if we have to stay here too long." He gave Eriond a reproving look.

"It wasn't really my fault, Belgarath," the young man protested mildly. "I didn't like the fires in the Sanctum, that's all."

"Try to keep a grip on your prejudices, Eriond," the old man said in a faintly sarcastic voice. "Let's not get sidetracked on these moral crusades just now."

"I'll try, Belgarath."

"I'd appreciate it."

The next morning, the seneschal, Oskatat, summoned them all to another audience with the Murgo King in a brightly candlelit chamber that was smaller and less garish than the vast throne room. Garion noticed that Silk remained carefully hooded until the gray-haired functionary had left the room. Urgit and Sadi spoke quietly together while the rest of them sat unobtrusively in the chairs lining the wall.

"It was probably the first hint that anyone really had that my father's brains were starting to come off their hinges," the Murgo King was saying. He was dressed again in his purple doublet and hose and was sprawled in a chair with his feet thrust out in front of him. "He was suddenly seized with the wild ambition to make himself Overking of Angarak. Personally, I think that Ctuchik planted the notion in his head as a means of irritating Urvon. Anyway," he continued, twisting the heavy gold ring on one of his fingers, "it took the combined efforts of all his generals to convince my manic father that 'Zakath's army was about five times the size of ours and that 'Zakath could squash him like a bug any time he chose. Once that notion had finally seeped into his head, he went absolutely wild."

"Oh?" Sadi said.

Urgit grinned. "Threw himself on the floor and started chewing on the carpet. After he calmed down, he decided to try subversion instead. He inundated Mallorea with Murgo agents—and Murgos are probably the clumsiest spies in the world. To keep it short—'Zakath was about nineteen at the time and desperately in love with a Melcene girl. Her family was deeply in debt, so my father's agents bought up all their obligations and started putting pressure on them. The brilliant plan that emerged from my father's diseased wits was that the girl should encourage the love-struck young 'Zakath, marry him, and then slip a knife between the imperial ribs at her earliest opportunity. One of the Melcenes these highly intelligent Murgo spies had bought to help them in their scheme ran to 'Zakath with the whole sordid story, and the girl and her entire family were immediately put to death."

"What a tragic story," Sadi murmured.

"You haven't heard the best part yet. Several of the Murgo spies were persuaded to reveal the whole story—Malloreans tend to be very good persuaders—and 'Zakath discovered to his horror that the girl had known absolutely nothing about my father's plan. He locked himself in his room in the palace at Mal Zeth for an entire month. When he went in, he was a pleasant, open young man who showed much promise of becoming one of Mallorea's greatest emperors. When he came out, he was the cold-blooded monster we all know and love. He rounded up every Murgo in Mallorea—including a fair number of my father's relatives—and he used to amuse himself by sending bits and pieces of them in ornate containers to Rak Goska, accompanied by highly insulting notes."

"But didn't the two of them join forces at the battle of Thull Mardu?"

Urgit laughed. "That may be the popular perception, Sadi, but in point of fact, the Imperial Princess Ce'Nedra's army was just unlucky enough to get between two opposing Angarak monarchs. They didn't care a thing about her or about that dungheap people call Mishrak ac Thull. All they were trying to do was kill each other. Then my addled father made the mistake of challenging King Cho-Hag of Algaria to single combat, and Cho-Hag gave him a *very* pointed lesson in swords-manship." He looked thoughtfully into the fire. "I still think I ought to send Cho-Hag some token of appreciation," he mused.

"Excuse me, your Majesty." Sadi frowned. "But I don't altogether understand. Kal Zakath's quarrel was with your father, and Taur Urgas is dead."

"Oh yes, quite dead," Urgit agreed. "I cut his throat before I buried him—just to make sure. I think that 'Zakath's problem stems from the fact that he didn't get the chance to kill my father personally. Failing that, I guess he's willing to settle for me." He rose and began to pace moodily up and down. "I've sent him a dozen peace over-tures, but all he does is send me back the heads of my emissaries. I think he's as crazy as my father was." He stopped his restless pacing. "You know, maybe I was a bit hasty on my way to the throne. I had a dozen brothers—all of the blood of Taur Urgas. If I'd kept a few of them alive, I might have been able to give them to 'Zakath. Perhaps, if he had drunk enough Urga blood, it might have made him lose his taste for it."

The door opened and a bulky Murgo with an ornate gold chain about his neck entered the room. "I need your signature on this," he said rudely to Urgit, thrust-ing a sheet of parchment at him.

"What is it, General Kradak?" Urgit asked meekly.

The officer's face darkened.

"All right," Urgit said in a mollifying tone, "don't get yourself excited." He took the parchment to a nearby table where a quill pen lay beside a silver ink-pot. He dipped the pen, scribbled his name on the bottom of the sheet, and handed it back.

"Thank you, your Majesty," General Kradak said in a flat voice. Then he turned on his heel and left the room.

"One of my father's generals," Urgit told Sadi sourly. "They all treat me like that." He began to pace up and down again, scuffing his feet at the carpet. "How much do you know about King Belgarion, Sadi?" he asked suddenly.

The eunuch shrugged. "Well, I've met him once or twice."

"Didn't you say that most of your servants are Alorns?"

"Alorn mercenaries, yes. They're dependable and very good to have around if a fight breaks out."

The Murgo King turned to Belgarath, who sat dozing in a chair. "You—old man," he said abruptly. "Have you ever met Belgarion of Riva?"

"Several times," Belgarath admitted calmly.

"What kind of man is he?"

"Sincere," Belgarath replied. "He tries very hard to be a good king."

"Just how powerful is he?"

"Well, he has the whole Alorn Alliance to back him up, and technically he's the Overlord of the West—although the Tolnedrans are likely to go their own way, and the Arends would rather fight each other."

"That's not what I meant. How good a sorcerer is he?"

"Why ask me, your Majesty? Do I look like the kind of man who'd know very much about that sort of thing? He managed to kill Torak, though, and I'd imagine that took a bit of doing."

"How about Belgarath? Is there really such a person, or is he just a myth?"

"No, Belgarath is a real person."

"And he's seven thousand years old?"

"Seven thousand or so." Belgarath shrugged. "Give or take a few centuries."

"And his daughter Polgara?"

"She's also a real person."

"And she's thousands of years old?"

"Something like that. I could probably figure it out if I needed to, but a gentleman doesn't ask questions about a lady's age."

Urgit laughed—a short, ugly, barking sound. "The words 'gentleman' and 'Murgo' are mutually exclusive, my friend," he said. "Do you think Belgarion would receive my emissaries, if I sent them to Riva?"

"He's out of the country just now," Belgarath told him blandly.

"I hadn't heard that."

"He does it from time to time. Every so often he gets bored with all the ceremonies and goes away."

"How does he manage that? How can he just pick up and leave?"

"Who's going to argue with him?"

Urgit began to gnaw worriedly on one fingernail. "Even if the Dagashi Kabach succeeds in killing 'Zakath, I'm still going to have a Mallorean army on my doorstep. I'm going to need an ally if I'm ever going to get rid of them." He began to pace up and down again. "Besides," he added, "if I can reach an agreement with

Belgarion, maybe I'll be able to get Agachak's fist off my throat. Do you think he'd listen to a proposal from me?"

"You could ask him and find out, I suppose."

The door opened again and the Queen Mother, assisted by the girl Prala, entered.

"Good morning, mother," Urgit greeted her. "Why are you out roaming the halls of this madhouse?"

"Urgit," she said firmly, "you'd be much more admirable if you stopped trying to make a joke out of everything."

"It keeps me from brooding about my circumstances," he told her flippantly. "I'm losing a war, half of my subjects want to depose me and send my head to 'Zakath on a plate, I'll be going mad soon, and I think I'm developing a boil on my neck. There are only a few things left for me to laugh about, mother, so please let me enjoy a joke or two while I still can."

"Why do you keep insisting that you're going to go mad?"

"Every male in the Urga family for the past five hundred years has gone mad before he reached fifty," he reminded her. "It's one of the reasons we make such good kings. Nobody in his right mind would want the throne of Cthol Murgos. Was there anything special you wanted, mother? Or did you just want to enjoy my fascinating companionship?"

She looked around the room. "Which of you gentlemen is married to that little red-haired girl?" she asked.

Garion looked up quickly. "Is she all right, my Lady?"

"Pol, the lady with the white lock at her brow, said that you should come at once. The young woman seems to be in some distress."

Garion stood up to follow as the Queen Mother started slowly back toward the door. Just before she reached it, she stopped and glanced at Silk, who had pulled up his hood as soon as she had entered. "Why don't you accompany your friend?" she suggested, "Just for the sake of appearances?"

They went out of the room and on down one of the garish halls of the Drojim to a dark-paneled door guarded by a pair of mail-shirted men-at-arms. One of them opened the door with a respectful bow to Lady Tamazin, and she led them inside. Her quarters were decorated much more tastefully than the rest of the Drojim. The walls were white, and the decor much more subdued. Aunt Pol sat on a low divan, holding the weeping Ce'Nedra in her arms with Velvet standing nearby.

—*Is she all right?*—Garion's fingers asked quickly.

—*I don't think it's too serious.*—Polgara's hands replied.

—*A bout of nerves most likely, but I don't want any of these fits of depression to go on for too long. She still hasn't fully recovered from her melancholia. See if you can comfort her.*—

Garion went to the divan and enclosed Ce'Nedra gently in his arms. She clung to him, still weeping.

"Is the young lady subject to these crying-spells, Pol?" the Queen Mother asked as the two of them took chairs on opposite sides of the cheery fire that danced on the grate.

"Not all that frequently, Tamazin," Polgara answered. "There's been a recent tragedy in her family, though, and sometimes her nerves get the best of her."

"Ah," Urgit's mother said. "Could I offer you a cup of tea, Pol? I always find tea in the morning so comforting."

"Why, thank you, Tamazin. I think that would be very nice."

Gradually, Ce'Nedra's weeping subsided, though she still clung tightly to Garion. At last she raised her head and wiped at her eyes with her fingertips. "I'm so very sorry," she apologized. "I don't know what came over me."

"It's all right, dear," Garion murmured, his arms still about her shoulders.

She dabbed at her eyes again, using a wispy little handkerchief. "I must look absolutely terrible," she said with a teary little laugh.

"Moderately terrible, yes," he agreed, smiling.

"I told you once, dear, that you should never cry in public," Polgara said to her. "You just don't have the right coloring for it."

Ce'Nedra smiled tremulously and stood up. "Perhaps I should go wash my face," she said. "And then I think I'd like to lie down for a bit." She turned to Garion. "Thank you for coming," she said simply.

"Any time you need me," he replied.

"Why don't you go with the lady, Prala?" Lady Tamazin suggested.

"Of course," the slender Murgo Princess agreed, coming quickly to her feet.

Silk had been standing nervously near the door with the hood of his green robe pulled up and his head down to keep his face concealed.

"Oh, *do* stop that, Prince Kheldar," the Queen Mother told him after Ce'Nedra and Prala had left the room. "I recognized you last night, so it's no good your trying to hide your face."

He sighed and pushed his hood back. "I was afraid you might have," he said.

"That hood doesn't hide your most salient feature anyway," she told him.

"And which feature was that, my Lady?"

"Your nose, Kheldar, that long, sharp, pointed nose that precedes you wherever you go."

"But it's such a noble nose, my Lady," Velvet said with a dimpled smile. "He wouldn't be nearly the man he is without it."

"Do you mind?" Silk asked her.

"You do get around, don't you, Prince Kheldar?" Lady Tamazin said to him. "How long has it been since you left Rak Goska with half of the Murgo army hot on your heels?"

"Fifteen or twenty years, my Lady," he replied, coming closer to the fire.

"I was sorry to hear that you'd left," she said. "You're not a very prepossessing-looking fellow, but your conversation was most entertaining, and there was very little in the way of entertainment in the house of Taur Urgas."

"You don't plan to make a general announcement about my identity then, I take it?" he said carefully.

"It's not my concern, Kheldar." She shrugged. "Murgo women do not involve themselves in the affairs of men. Over the centuries, we've found that it's safer that way."

"You're not upset, then, my Lady?" Garion asked her. "What I mean is, I'd heard that Prince Kheldar here accidentally killed the eldest son of Taur Urgas. Didn't that offend you just a little?"

"It had nothing to do with me," she replied. "The one Kheldar killed was the child of Taur Urgas' first wife—an insufferable, toothless hag of the House of Gorut who used to gloat over the fact that she had given birth to the heir apparent and that, as soon as he ascended the throne, she was going to have the rest of us strangled."

"I'm relieved to hear that you had no particular fondness for the young man," Silk told her.

"Fondness? He was a monster—just like his father. When he was just a little boy, he used to amuse himself by dropping live puppies into boiling water. The world's a better place without him."

Silk assumed a lofty expression. "I always like to perform these little public services," he declared. "I feel that it's a gentleman's civic duty."

"I thought you said that his death was accidental," Garion said.

"Well, sort of. Actually, I was trying to stab him in the belly—painful perhaps, but seldom fatal—but he bumped my arm as I made the thrust, and somehow my knife went straight into his heart."

"What a shame," Tamazin murmured. "I'd be sort of careful here in the Drojim though, Kheldar. I have no intention of revealing your identity, but the seneschal, Oskatat, also knows you by sight and he would probably feel obliged to denounce you."

"I'd already guessed as much, my Lady. I'll try to avoid him."

"Now tell me, Prince Kheldar, how is your father?"

Silk sighed. "He died, I'm afraid," he replied sadly, "quite a few years ago. It was rather sudden."

As chance had it, Garion was looking directly at the Queen Mother's face as Silk spoke and he saw the momentary flicker of anguish touch her beautiful features. She recovered quickly, though her eyes still brimmed with sorrow. "Ah," she said very quietly. "I'm sorry, Kheldar—more sorry than you could possibly know. I liked your father very much. The memories of the months he was in Rak Goska are among the happiest of my life."

To avoid being caught staring, Garion turned his head, and his eyes fell on Velvet, whose expression was faintly speculative. She returned his look, and her eyes conveyed a world of meaning and several unanswered questions.

CHAPTER FOURTEEN

The following morning dawned clear and cold. Garion stood at the window of his room, looking out over the slate rooftops of Rak Urga. The low, squat houses seemed to huddle together fearfully under the twin presence of the garish Drojim Palace at one end of town and the black Temple of Torak at the other. The smoke from hundreds of chimneys rose in straight blue columns toward the windless sky.

"Depressing sort of place, isn't it?" Silk said as he came into the room with his green robe carelessly slung over one shoulder.

Garion nodded. "It looks almost as if they deliberately went out of their way to make it ugly."

"It's a reflection of the Murgo mind. Oh, Urgit wants to see us again." The little man caught Garion's inquiring look. "I don't think it's anything particularly important," he added. "He's probably just starved for conversation. I imagine that talking with Murgos can get tedious after a while."

They all trooped through the garish halls on the heels of the mail-shirted guard who had brought the king's summons, returning to the room where they had met with Urgit the previous day. They found him lounging in a chair by the fire with one leg cocked up over the arm and a half-eaten chicken leg in his hand. "Good morning, gentlemen," he greeted them. "Please sit down." He waved his breakfast at the chairs lined against one wall. "I'm not much of a one for formality." He looked at Sadi. "Did you sleep well?" he asked.

"It got a bit cold on toward morning, your Majesty."

"It's the slipshod construction of this place. There are cracks in the walls big enough to push a horse through. In the wintertime we have snow storms in the corridors." He sighed. "Do you realize that it's spring in Tol Honeth right now?" He sighed again, then glanced at Belgarath, who stood smiling peculiarly at him. "Was there something amusing, old boy?"

"Not really. Just remembering something I heard once." The old man went to the fire and held out his hands to the crackling flames. "How are your people coming on that ship?"

"I expect that it's going to be tomorrow at the earliest before it's ready," Urgit replied. "Winter's coming on, and the seas around the southern tip of the Urga peninsula are never what you'd call placid, even in the best of seasons, so I ordered the shipwrights to take special pains." He leaned forward and negligently tossed his chicken leg into the fireplace. "It was burned," he said absently. "Every meal I get in this place is either burned or raw." He looked peculiarly at Belgarath. "You intrigue me, old man. You don't seem like the type to wind up his career hiring himself out to a Nyissan slaver."

"Appearances can be deceiving." Belgarath shrugged. "You don't look much like a king, either, but you *do* have the crown, after all."

Urgit reached up and pulled off his iron circlet. He looked at it distastefully and then held it out to Belgarath. "You want this thing?" he asked. "I'm sure you'd look more regal than I do, and I'd be very happy to get rid of it—particularly in view of the fact that Kal Zakath so keenly wants to take my head out from under it." He dropped it on the floor beside his chair with a dull clink. "Let's go back to something we were discussing yesterday. You told me that you know Belgarion."

Belgarath nodded.

"How well?"

"How well can any man know another?"

"You're evading my question."

"It seems that way, doesn't it?"

Urgit let that pass. He looked intently at the old man. "How do you think Belgarion would really react if I proposed that he ally himself with me to drive the Malloreans off the continent? I'm sure their presence here worries him almost as much as it does me."

"The chances aren't very good," Belgarath told him. "You might be able to persuade Belgarion that it's a good idea, but the rest of the Alorn monarchs would probably object."

"They reached an accommodation with Drosta, didn't they?"

"That was between Rhodar and Drosta. There's always been a certain wary friendship between the Drasnians and the Nadraks. The one you'd need to get to accept your idea would be Cho-Hag, and Cho-Hag's never been exactly cordial to Murgos."

"I need allies, old man, not platitudes." Urgit paused. "What if I got word to Belgarath?"

"What would you say to him?"

"I'd try to persuade him that 'Zakath's a much greater danger to the Kingdoms of the West than I am. Maybe he could make the Alorns listen to reason."

"I don't think you'd have much luck there, either." The old man looked into the dancing flames with the firelight gleaming on his short, silvery beard. "You have to understand that Belgarath doesn't live in the same world with ordinary men. He lives in the world of first causes and primal forces. I'd imagine that he looks upon Kal Zakath as little more than a minor irritation."

"Torak's teeth!" Urgit swore. "Where am I going to get the troops I need?"

"Hire mercenaries," Silk suggested without turning from the window where he stood.

"What?"

"Dip into the royal vaults and bring out some of the fabled red gold of Angarak. Send word into the Kingdoms of the West that you need good men and that you're willing to pay them good gold. You'll be swamped with volunteers."

"I prefer men who fight for patriotism—or religion," Urgit declared stiffly.

Silk turned with an amused expression. "I've noticed that preference in many kings," he observed. "It doesn't put such a strain on royal treasuries. But believe me, your Majesty, loyalty to an ideal can vary in its intensity, but loyalty to money never changes. That's why mercenaries are better fighters."

"You're a cynic," Urgit accused.

Silk shook his head. "No, your Majesty. I'm a realist." He stepped over to Sadi and murmured something. The eunuch nodded, and the rat-faced little Drasnian quietly left the room.

Urgit raised one eyebrow inquiringly.

"He's going to go start packing, your Majesty," Sadi explained. "If we're going to sail tomorrow, we need to start getting ready."

Urgit and Sadi talked quietly for about a quarter of an hour, and then the door at the far end of the room opened again. Polgara and the other ladies entered with the Lady Tamazin.

"Good morning, mother," Urgit greeted her. "You slept well, I trust?"

"Quite well, thank you." She looked critically at him. "Urgit, where's your crown?"

"I took it off. It gives me a headache."

"Put it back on at once."

"What for?"

"Urgit, you don't look very much like a king. You're short and thin and you've got a face like a weasel. Murgos are not bright. If you don't wear your crown all the time, it's altogether possible that they'll forget who you are. Now put it back on."

"Yes, mother." He picked up his crown and clapped it on his head. "How's that?"

"It's lopsided, dear," she said in a calm tone so familiar that Garion gave Polgara a quick, startled look. "Now you look like a drunken sailor."

Urgit laughed and straightened his crown.

Garion looked closely at Ce'Nedra to see if there were any traces left of the storm of weeping that had swept over her the previous day, but he saw no evidence that it might immediately return. She was engaged in a murmured conversation with the Cthan Princess, Prala, and the Murgo girl's face clearly showed that she had already fallen under the queen's spell.

"And you, Urgit," Lady Tamazin said, "did you sleep well?"

"I never really sleep, mother. You know that. I decided years ago that sleeping nervously is infinitely preferable to sleeping permanently."

Garion found himself making a difficult readjustment in his thinking. He had never liked Murgos. He had always distrusted and even feared them. King Urgit's personality, however, was as un-Murgoish as his appearance. He was quick and volatile, and his moods swung from sardonic amusement to gloom so rapidly that Garion was quite uncertain what to expect next. He was obviously not a strong king, and Garion had been a king long enough himself to see where Urgit was making his mistakes. In spite of himself, though, Garion found that he actually liked him and felt a peculiar sympathy for him as he struggled with a job for which he was hopelessly unsuited. That, of course, created a problem. Garion did not *want* to like this man, and this unwanted sympathy seemed wildly out of place. He rose from his chair and withdrew to the far end of the room, making some pretense of looking out the window so that he might put himself beyond the range of the Murgo King's urbane wit. With a kind of unbearable urgency, he wanted to be on board ship and away from this ugly Murgo city, huddled on its barren coast, and from the weak, fearful man who was not really such a bad fellow, but whom Garion knew he should regard as an enemy.

"What's the trouble, Garion?" Polgara asked quietly, coming up behind him.

"Impatience, I guess, Aunt Pol. I want to get moving."

"We all do, dear," she told him, "but we have to endure this for one more day."

"Why can't he just leave us alone?"

"Who's that?"

"Urgit. I'm not interested in his problems, so why does he have to sit around telling us about them all the time?"

"Because he's lonely, Garion."

"All kings are lonely. It comes with the crown. Most of us learn how to endure it, though. We don't sit around and snivel about it."

"That's unkind, Garion," she told him firmly, "and it's unworthy of you."

"Why are we all so concerned about a weak king with a clever mouth?"

"Perhaps it's because he's the first Murgo we've met in eons who shows some human qualities. Because he's the way he is, he raises the possibility that Alorns and Murgos might someday find ways to settle their differences without resorting to bloodshed."

He continued to stare out the window, although a slow flush began to creep up his neck. "I'm being childish, aren't I?" he admitted.

"Yes, dear, I'm afraid you are. Your prejudices are running away with you. Ordinary people can afford that. Kings cannot. Go back to where he's sitting, Garion, and watch him very closely. Don't pass up this opportunity to get to know him. The time may come when that knowledge will help you."

"All right, Aunt Pol." Garion sighed, squaring his shoulders resolutely.

It was almost noon when Oskatat entered the room. "Your Majesty," he announced in his rasping voice, "Agachak, Hierarch of Rak Urga, craves audience with you."

"Show him in, Oskatat," Urgit replied wearily. He turned to his mother. "I think I'm going to have to find another place to hide," he muttered. "Too many people know where to find me."

"I have a splendid closet, Urgit," she replied, "warm and dry and dark. You could hide in there and cover yourself with a blanket. We'll slip food in to you from time to time."

"Are you making fun of me, mother?"

"No, dear," she said. "But like it or not, you're the king. You can either *be* king or you can be a spoiled child. The choice is entirely up to you."

Garion glanced guiltily at Polgara.

"Yes?" she murmured.

But he decided not to answer.

The cadaverous-looking Agachak entered and bowed perfunctorily to his king. "Your Majesty," he said in his hollow voice.

"Dread Hierarch," Urgit responded, his voice betraying no hint of his true feeling.

"Time is passing, your Majesty."

"It has a way of doing that, I've noticed."

"My point is that the weather is about to turn stormy. Is the ship nearly ready?"

"I expect it to sail tomorrow," Urgit replied.

"Excellent. I shall instruct Kabach to make ready."

"Has the Priestess Chabat regained her composure?" Urgit asked.

"Not really, your Majesty. She still keenly feels the loss of her paramour."

"Even after she found out what his true feelings were about her? Who can ever hope to understand the workings of the female mind?"

"Chabat is not that difficult to fathom, your Majesty." Agachak shrugged. "A disfigured woman has little chance to attract lovers, and the loss of even an insincere one is most painful. Her loss in this particular case goes a bit deeper, however. Sorchak assisted her in the performance of certain rites of magic. Without him, she will not be able to continue her efforts to summon up demons."

Urgit shuddered. "I thought that she was a sorceress. Isn't that enough for her? Why would she want to dabble in magic, too?"

"Chabat is not really that powerful a sorceress," Agachak replied. "She thinks that she will have a greater advantage when she finally confronts me if she has demons to aid her."

"Confront you? Is that what she's planning?"

"Of course. Her occasional dallying is merely an amusement. Her central goal has always been power. In time, she will have to try to wrest mine from me."

"If that's the case, why did you allow her to gain so much authority in the Temple?"

"It amused me," Agachak said with a chill smile. "I am not as repelled by ugliness as others are, and Chabat, despite her ambition—or perhaps because of it—is very efficient."

"You knew about her affair with Sorchak. Didn't that offend you?"

"Not really," the dead-looking Hierarch answered. "That's just a part of the entertainment I'm preparing for myself. Eventually, Chabat will succeed in raising a demon, and then she will challenge me. At the very instant that her triumph seems complete, I shall also raise a demon, and mine will destroy hers. Then I shall have her stripped and dragged to the Sanctum. There she will be bent backward across the altar and I myself will slowly cut out her heart. I look forward to that moment with a great deal of anticipation, and it will be all the sweeter because it will come just when she thinks she has beaten me." His dead face had come alive with a dreadful pleasure. His eyes burned, and there were flecks of spittle in the corners of his mouth.

Urgit, however, looked faintly sick. "Grolims appear to have more exotic amusements than ordinary men."

"Not really, Urgit. The only reason for power is to be able to use it to destroy your enemies, and it's particularly enjoyable to be able to drag them down from a height before you destroy them. Wouldn't you like to be present when the mighty Kal Zakath dies with a Dagashi knife in his heart?"

"Not really. I just want him out of the way. I don't particularly want to watch the procedure."

"You have not yet learned the true meaning of power, then. The understanding may come when you and I stand in the presence of Cthrag Sardius and witness the rebirth of the Dark God and the final triumph of the Child of Dark."

Urgit's expression grew pained.

"Do not flinch from your destiny, Urgit," Agachak said in his hollow voice. "It is foretold that a King of Angarak will be present at the final meeting. You will be that king—just as I will be the one to make the sacrifice and thus become the first disciple of the reborn God. We are bound together by a chain forged of fate. Your destiny is to become Overking of Angarak, and mine is to rule the Church."

Urgit sighed in resignation. "Whatever you say, Agachak," he said disconsolately. "We still have a few problems to overcome, however."

"They are of little concern to me," the Hierarch declared.

"Well, they do concern me," Urgit said with surprising heat. "First we have to deal with 'Zakath, and then we'll need to get rid of Gethel and Drosta—just to be on the safe side. I've been involved in a race for a throne before and I think I'd feel more confident if I were the only one running. Your problems, however, are a bit more weighty. Urvon and Zandramas are very serious opponents."

"Urvon is a doddering old fool, and Zandramas is only a woman."

"Agachak," Urgit said pointedly, "Polgara is also only a woman. Would you care to face *her*? No, Dread Hierarch, I think that Urvon doesn't dodder as much as you think, and Zandramas is probably more dangerous than you'd like to believe. She's managed to spirit away Belgarion's son, and that was no mean trick. She's also slipped past you and all the other Hierarchs as if you weren't even here. Let's neither of us take any of this too lightly."

"I know where Zandramas is," Agachak said with a chill smile, "and I will wrest Belgarion's son from her at the proper time. It is foretold that you and I and the babe who is to be sacrificed will come into the presence of the Sardion at the appointed time. There I will perform the sacrifice, and you will witness the rite, and we shall both be exalted. It is so written."

"Depending on how you read it," Urgit added morosely.

Garion moved to Ce'Nedra's side, trying to look casual. As the meaning of what the Grolim Hierarch had just said came to her, the blood slowly drained from her face. "It's not going to happen," he told her in a firm, quiet voice. "Nobody's going to do that to our baby."

"You knew," she accused him in a choked whisper.

"Grandfather and I found it in the Grolim Prophecies in the Temple library."

"Oh, Garion," she said, biting her lip to keep back the tears.

"Don't worry about it," he said. "The same Prophecy said that Torak was going to win at Cthol Mishrak. That didn't happen, and this isn't going to happen, either."

"But what if—"

"There aren't any ifs," he said firmly. "It's *not* going to happen."

After the Hierarch had left, King Urgit's mood changed. He sat in his chair, brooding sourly.

"Perhaps your Majesty might prefer to be left alone," Sadi ventured.

"No, Sadi." Urgit sighed. "No amount of worrying at it is going to change what we've already set in motion." He shook his head and then shrugged as if dismissing the whole matter. "Why don't you tell me the details of the little misdemeanor that made Salmissra so vexed with you? I adore stories of deceit and dishonesty. They always seem to hint that the world's not really such a bad place after all."

It was not long after, as Sadi was elaborating at some length on the involuted scheme that had caused his downfall, when the seneschal entered the room again. "A dispatch has arrived from the military governor at Cthaka, your Majesty," he rasped.

"What does he want now?" Urgit muttered plaintively.

"He reports that the Malloreans are mounting a major campaign in the south. Rak Gorut is under siege and must inevitably fall within a week."

"In the autumn?" Urgit exclaimed, coming up out of his chair in dismay. "They're mounting a campaign when the summer's already over?"

"So it appears," Oskatat replied. "I think that Kal Zakath's hoping to take you by surprise. Once Rak Gorut falls, there won't be anything between his forces and Rak Cthaka."

"And the garrison there is virtually nonexistent, isn't it?"

"I'm afraid so, Urgit. Rak Cthaka will also fall, and then 'Zakath will have all winter to consolidate his hold on the south."

Urgit began to swear and moved quickly to a map tacked up on the wall. "How many troops do we have up here in Morcth?" he demanded, tapping the map with one finger.

"A few score thousand. But by the time they had received the order to march south, the Malloreans would already be halfway to Rak Cthaka."

Urgit stared in consternation at the map. Then he suddenly smashed his fist against it. "He's outsmarted me again!" he raged. He returned to his chair and collapsed in it.

"I think I'd better go get Kradak," Oskatat said. "The General Staff will need to know about this."

"Whatever you think best, Oskatat," Urgit replied in a defeated tone.

As the seneschal strode from the room, Garion crossed to look at the map. After only the briefest of glances, he saw a solution to Urgit's problem, but he was reluctant to speak. He did not want to become involved in this. There were a dozen good reasons why he should keep his mouth shut—the most important being the fact that should he offer his solution to the Murgo King, he would in a sense be committed, and he firmly desired to avoid any commitment to the man, no matter how slight. An unresolved problem, however, nagged at his sense of responsibility; to turn his back on one—even one that was not his own—violated something deep within him. He muttered a curse under his breath, then turned to the stricken Urgit. "Excuse me, your Majesty," he said, approaching the matter obliquely, "but how well fortified is Rak Cthaka?"

"It's like every Murgo city," Urgit replied abstactedly. "The walls are seventy feet high and thirty feet thick. What difference does it make?"

"The city could withstand a seige, then—if you had enough men there?"

"That's the whole problem—I don't."

"Then you need to get reinforcements there before the Malloreans can reach the city."

"What a brilliant observation. But if I can't get relief columns there in time, how could I possibly get reinforcements there before the streets are filled with Malloreans?"

Garion shrugged. "Send them by sea."

"By sea?" Urgit suddenly looked stunned.

"Your harbor is full of ships, and your city's bulging with troops. Load enough men on the ships to reinforce the garrison at Rak Cthaka and sail them around to the city. Even if Rak Gorut fell tomorrow, it's still going to take the Malloreans ten days to march overland. Your ships could be there in less than a week. Your reinforced garrison will be able to hold until the relief columns arrive."

Urgit shook his head. "Murgo armies do not move by ship," he said. "My generals wouldn't hear of it."

"You're the king, aren't you? *Make* them hear of it."

Urgit's face grew apprehensive. "They never listen to me."

Garion had a sudden urge to shake him. With some effort he got his irritation under control. "There's nothing holy about walking," he said, "particularly if marching your men to Rak Cthaka is going to cost you the city. Tell your generals to load the men on those ships and also tell them that the matter isn't open to discussion."

"They'll refuse."

"Then dismiss them from their posts and promote a few colonels."

Urgit stared at him, aghast. "I couldn't do that."

"You're the king. You can do anything you want to."

Urgit wrestled with it indecisively.

"Do as he says, Urgit," Lady Tamazin commanded abruptly. "It's the only way to save Rak Cthaka."

He looked at her, a lost expression on his face. "Do you really think I should, mother?" he asked in a small voice.

"Just do it. As the young man said, you're the king—and I think it's about time that you started acting like one."

"There's something else we need to consider, your Majesty," Sadi said, his face grave. "If the Malloreans lay seige to Rak Cthaka, I won't be able to land there. I'm going to have to get past that vicinity before any fighting breaks out. Slavers can move around with very little interference, unless there's an actual battle going on, but once the fighting starts, the Malloreans are sure to detain us. If we don't move very quickly, your Dagashi won't reach Rak Hagga until sometime next summer."

Urgit's face grew even more disconsolate. "I hadn't considered that," he admitted. "I think you and your people had better get ready to leave here immediately. I'll send word to the Temple and tell Agachak that the plans have changed."

The door opened. Oskatat entered, and at his side was the Murgo officer who had so rudely demanded Urgit's signature the previous day.

"Ah, General Kradak," Urgit greeted the officer with an obviously feigned joviality, "so good of you to join us. You've heard about what's going on in the south?"

The general nodded shortly. "The situation is grave," he said. "Rak Gorut and Rak Cthaka are in great peril."

"What do you advise, General?" Urgit asked.

"There's nothing to advise," Kradak said. "We'll have to accept the fact that Gorut and Cthaka are lost and concentrate our efforts on holding Urga, Morcth, and Araga."

"General, that only leaves three of the nine military districts of Cthol Murgos under my control. 'Zakath is eating my kingdom one bite at a time."

The general shrugged. "We cannot reach Rak Cthaka before the Malloreans do. The city will fall. There's nothing we can do about it."

"What if we were to reinforce the garrison there? Would that change things at all?"

"Certainly, but it's impossible."

"Maybe not," Urgit said with a quick look at Garion. "What do you think of moving reinforcements there by ship?"

"By ship?" The general blinked, and then his face hardened. "That's absurd."

"Why absurd?"

"It's never been done in Cthol Murgos before."

"I imagine that there are a lot of things that have never been done in Cthol Murgos before. Is there any specific reason why it won't work?"

"Ships sink, your Majesty," Kradak pointed out acidly, as if speaking to a child. "The troops know that and they'll refuse to go on board."

Oskatat stepped forward. "Not if you crucify the first ten or so who refuse right there on the dock," he said firmly. "That sort of example should lessen the reluctance of the rest."

Kradak gave the gray-haired man a look of undisguised hatred. "What would a house servant know about command?" he demanded. He looked back at Urgit with a barely concealed sneer. "Just stay on your throne, Urgit," he said harshly. "Play with your crown and your scepter and pretend that you're a real king. But keep your nose out of the business of running the war."

Urgit's face blanched, and he shrank back in his chair.

"Shall I send for the headsman, your Majesty?" Oskatat inquired in an icy voice. "It appears that General Kradak has outlived his usefulness."

Kradak stared at him incredulously. "You wouldn't dare!" he gasped.

"Your life hangs on his Majesty's pleasure just now, Kradak. One word from him, and your head will roll in the dust."

"I am a general officer in the armies of Cthol Murgos." Kradak clutched at the gold chain about his neck as if for reassurance. "My appointment comes from Taur Urgas himself. You have no authority over me, Oskatat."

Urgit straightened in his chair, an angry flush moving up into his face. "Oh, really?" he said in a dangerously quiet voice. "Maybe it's time that we got a few things clarified." He took off his crown and held it up. "Do you recognize this, Kradak?"

The general glared at him with a stony face.

"Answer me!"

"It's the crown of Cthol Murgos," Kradak replied sullenly.

"And the man who wears it has absolute authority, right?"

"Taur Urgas did."

"Taur Urgas is dead. I sit upon the throne now, and you will obey me in the same way you obeyed him. Do you understand me?"

"You are not Taur Urgas."

"That's painfully obvious, General Kradak," Urgit replied coldly. "I am your king, however, and I'm also an Urga. When I grow agitated, I feel the madness of the Urgas creeping up on me—and it's creeping very fast just now. If you don't do exactly as I tell you to do, you're going to be a head shorter before the sun sets. Now go give the order to load the troops on those ships."

"And if I refuse?"

Urgit's expression grew hesitant. For some reason he looked appealingly at Garion.

"Kill him," Garion said in the flat unemotional voice he had discovered immediately got people's attention.

Urgit straightened again and firmly yanked his bellpull. The great gong outside in the hallway clanged. Two burly guards responded immediately. "Yes, your Majesty?" one of them asked.

"Well, Kradak?" Urgit asked. "What's it to be? The ships or the block? Speak up, man. I haven't got all day."

Kradak's face went ashen. "The ships, your Majesty," he replied in a shaky voice.

"Splendid. I'm so happy that we were able to settle our little differences with-out unpleasantness." Urgit turned to his guards. "General Kradak is going directly to the barracks of the Third Cohort now," he told them, "and you will accompany him. He's going to order those men to board the ships in the harbor and to sail to the relief of the garrison at Rak Cthaka." He gave Kradak a narrow, distrustful look. "If he gives them any other order, you will cut off his head immediately and bring it to me—in a bucket."

"As your Majesty commands," the Murgos replied in unison, each banging his fist against his mail shirt.

Kradak turned, trembling and suddenly broken, and went out with the grim Murgo guards flanking him closely.

Urgit retained his imperious expression until the door closed, and then he threw both arms in the air and began beating his feet on the floor, whooping with delight. "Oh, Gods!" he said ecstatically. "I loved that! I've been wanting to do that all my life!"

The Lady Tamazin rose gravely from her chair, limped to where her son sat, and wordlessly embraced him.

"Affection, mother?" he asked lightly, a broad grin still creasing his sharp-featured face. "How terribly un-Murgoish." And then he laughed and caught her in a rough bear hug.

"There may be hope after all," she observed calmly to Oskatat.

A slow smile crept across the big Murgo's lips. "It looks a bit more promising, my Lady," he agreed.

"Thank you for your support, Oskatat," Urgit said to his friend. "I might not have gotten through that without your help." He paused. "I must say, though, that I'm a little surprised that you approved of my scheme."

"I don't. I think it's an absurd idea almost certainly doomed from the start."

Urgit blinked.

"There was another issue at stake, however—one that is much more important." There was a peculiar pride on the big man's face. "Do you realize that this is the very first time you've ever faced down one of your generals? They've been running roughshod over you since the day you took the throne. The loss of a few ships and a few thou-sand men is a small price to pay for a real king on the throne of Cthol Murgos."

"Thank you for your candor, Oskatat," Urgit said gravely. "It may just be, though, that things may not turn out so disastrously as you think."

"Perhaps, but Taur Urgas would not have done this."

"It might just be that someday we'll all rejoice in the fact that Taur Urgas is no longer with us, Oskatat." A faint ironic smile crossed the king's lips. "As a matter of fact, I seem to feel a small surge of rejoicing coming over me already. I'm losing this war, my old friend, and a man who's losing can't afford to be conservative. I've got to take a few gambles if I want to keep Kal Zakath from parading through the streets of Rak Urga with my head on a pole."

"As your Majesty commands," the seneschal said with a bow. "I'm also going to have to give certain orders. Have I your permission to withdraw?"

"Of course."

Oskatat turned and started toward the door. Before he reached it, however, it opened and Silk came into the room. The seneschal stopped, staring hard at the Drasnian. Silk's hand moved swiftly toward the hood of his robe, but then he let it drop with a rueful grimace.

Garion groaned inwardly. He moved carefully into position not far behind Oskatat, aware that Durnik and the gigantic Toth were also coming up on either side of him, ready to move quickly to prevent any outcry.

"You!" Oskatat exclaimed to Silk. "What are you doing here?"

Silk's expression grew resigned. "Just passing through, Oskatat," he replied casually. "You've been well, I trust?"

Urgit looked up. "What's this?"

"The seneschal and I are old friends, your Majesty," Silk replied. "We met in Rak Goska some years ago."

"Is your Majesty aware of this man's true identity?" Oskatat demanded.

Urgit shrugged. "He's one of Sadi's servants," he said. "Or so I was told."

"Hardly that, Urgit. This is Prince Kheldar of Drasnia, the most notorious spy in the entire world."

"The seneschal is perhaps a bit lavish in his praise," Silk noted modestly.

"Do you deny that you murdered the soldiers Taur Urgas sent to detain you when your scheme in Rak Goska was exposed?" Oskatat said accusingly.

"I don't know that I'd use the word 'murdered,' exactly, my Lord." Silk winced. "Oh, I'll admit that there was a bit of unpleasantness, but that's such an awkward way to sum up."

"Your Majesty," the grim old Murgo said. "This man was responsible for the death of Dorak Urgas, your eldest brother. There is a long-standing warrant for his immediate execution, so I will send for the headsman at once."

CHAPTER FIFTEEN

U rgit's face had grown cold. His eyes were narrowed, and he chewed nervously on a fingernail. "All right, Sadi," he said, "what's this all about?"

"Your Majesty—I—" The eunuch spread his hand.

"Don't try to play the innocent with me," Urgit snapped. "Did you know about this man?" He pointed at Silk.

"Well, yes, but—"

"And you chose not to tell me? What's your game, Sadi?"

The eunuch hesitated, and Garion saw beads of sweat breaking out on his forehead. Durnik and Toth, moving casually as if merely removing themselves from the vicinity of the confrontation, went past Oskatat and leaned idly against the wall, one on each side of the door.

"Well, Sadi?" Urgit pressed. "I've heard about this Prince Kheldar. He's not merely a spy; he's an assassin as well." His eyes suddenly grew wide. "So that's it!" he gasped, staring at Silk. "Belgarion sent you here to kill me, didn't he—you and these other Alorns."

"Don't be absurd, Urgit," Lady Tamazin said from her chair. "You've been alone with these people for hours at a time since they arrived here. If they were here to kill you, you'd already be dead."

He thought about that. "All right, you—Prince Kheldar—speak up. I want to know exactly what you're doing here. Now talk."

Silk shrugged. "It's as I told my Lord Oskatat, your Majesty. I'm merely passing through. My business is in another part of the world."

"Which part?"

"Here and there," Silk said evasively.

"I'm going to get some straight answers here," Urgit declared.

"Shall I send for the headsman, your Majesty?" Oskatat asked ominously.

"Perhaps that might not be a bad idea," Urgit agreed.

The seneschal turned, but found Durnik and the impassive Toth barring his way from the room. Urgit, perceiving the situation at once, reached quickly for the bellpull which would fill the room with armed Murgos.

"Urgit!" Lady Tamazin snapped. "No!"

He hesitated.

"Do as I say!"

"What's this?" he asked.

"Look around you," she told him. "If you even touch that cord, one of these people will have a knife against your throat before you can tug it even once."

His expression grew suddenly frightened, and he slowly lowered his hand.

Sadi cleared his throat. "Ah—your Majesty," he said. "I believe that the Queen Mother has seen directly to the heart of the matter here. We are both in positions to greatly inconvenience each other. Wouldn't it be wiser for us to discuss things rationally before we resort to any unpleasantness?"

"What is it that you want, Sadi?" Urgit asked him in a slightly quavering voice.

"Only what you had intended all along, your Majesty. As Kheldar said, our business is in another part of the world, and it does not directly concern you. Give us the ship that you were going to give us anyway, and in return we'll deliver your Dagashi to Rak Hagga as we promised. After that, we'll proceed with our own affairs. What could be fairer than that?"

"Listen to him, Urgit," Lady Tamazin urged. "He makes a great deal of sense."

Urgit's expression was filled with doubt. "Do you really think so, mother?"

"What harm can they do you, once they've crossed the Mallorean lines?" she asked. "If you're nervous about them, then get them out of Rak Urga as quickly as possible."

"All except this one." Oskatat pointed at Silk.

"We really need him, my Lord," Sadi said politely.

"He killed Dorak Urgas," the seneschal said stubbornly.

"We can give him a medal for that later, Oskatat," Urgit said.

Oskatat stared at him.

"Oh, come now, my friend. You despised Dorak as much as I did."

"He was a Murgo prince, your Majesty. His murder cannot go unpunished."

"You seem to forget that *I* murdered a dozen of my other brothers—also

Murgo princes—on my way to the throne. Were you planning to punish me as well?" Urgit looked back at Sadi. "I think, however, that it might not hurt for me to keep Kheldar here in the Drojim. Sort of as a performance bond. As soon as you deliver Kabach to Rak Hagga, I'll release him. He can catch up with you later."

Sadi's expression grew pained.

"You're overlooking something important here, Urgit," Lady Tamazin said, leaning forward intently.

"Oh? What's that, mother?"

"Prince Kheldar of Drasnia is reputed to be one of King Belgarion's closest friends. You have there the perfect envoy to convey a message to the Rivan King."

He looked sharply at Silk. "Is that true?" he asked. "Do you really know Belgarion?"

"Quite well, actually," Silk replied. "I've known him since he was a little boy."

"That old man over there said that Belgarion isn't at Riva just now. Do you have any idea where you might be able to find him?"

"Your Majesty," Silk answered with a perfectly straight face, "I can honestly tell you that I know exactly where Belgarion is at this very moment."

Urgit scratched at one cheek, his eyes suspicious. "I don't think I like this," he said. "Let's say that I give you a message to deliver to Belgarion. What's to prevent you from just throwing it away and then circling around to rejoin your friends?"

"Ethics." Silk shrugged. "I always do the things I'm paid to do. You *were* planning to pay me, weren't you?"

Urgit stared at Silk for a moment and then he threw back his head and laughed. "You're absolutely outrageous, Kheldar," he said. "Here you are, about two steps from the headsman's block, and you have the nerve to try to extort money from me."

Silk sighed and looked around tragically. "Why is it that the word 'pay' always brings that same look of consternation into the eyes of kings the world over?" he asked. "Surely your Majesty would not expect me to perform this truly unique service for you without some small recompense, would you?"

"Wouldn't you say that getting to keep your head is more than adequate payment?"

"Oh, I'm fairly safe, I think. Since I'm the only one in the world who can guarantee delivery of your message, I'm far too valuable to kill, wouldn't you say?"

Lady Tamazin suddenly laughed, a whimsical expression on her face as she looked at the two of them.

"Something amusing, mother?" Urgit asked her.

"Nothing, Urgit. Nothing at all."

The king's eyes were still indecisive. He looked hopefully at his seneschal. "What do you think, Oskatat?" he asked. "Can I trust this little knave?"

"It's your Majesty's decision," the big Murgo replied stiffly.

"I'm not asking you as your king," Urgit told him. "I'm asking as a friend."

Oskatat winced. "That's cruel, Urgit," he said. "You're forcing me to decide between duty and friendship."

"All right, then. Let's put it on that basis. What should I do?"

"As king, you should obey the law—even if it means flying in the face of your own best interests. As a man, however, you should seize every opportunity that presents itself to avert disaster."

"Well? What should I do? Should I be a king or a man? Which do you advise?"

It hung there in the air between them. The seneschal refused to meet Urgit's eyes. Instead, he cast one quick, appealing look at Lady Tamazin. "Torak forgive me," he muttered finally. He straightened and looked his king full in the face. "Save yourself, Urgit," he said. "If this Drasnian can arrange an alliance with Belgarion, then pay him whatever he demands and send him on his way. Belgarion may deceive you at some later date, but Kal Zakath seeks your head now. You need that alliance, no matter what the cost."

"Thank you, Oskatat," the king said with genuine gratitude. He turned back to Silk. "How quickly do you think you could reach Belgarion with my message?" he asked.

"Your Majesty," Silk replied, "I can have your message in Belgarion's hands more quickly than you could possibly imagine. Now, shall we talk about money?" His long, pointed nose began to twitch in a manner Garion recognized at once.

"How much do you want?" Urgit asked warily.

"Oh," Silk pretended to think about it, "I suppose a hundred Tolnedran gold-marks ought to cover it."

Urgit gaped at him. "A hundred marks? You're insane!"

Silk casually examined the fingernails of one hand. "The figure's open to negotiation, your Majesty," he admitted. "I just wanted to establish a general price range sort of to get things off to a smooth start."

Urgit's eyes took on a strange light. He leaned forward, tugging absently at his nose. "I might be able to see my way clear to pay you ten—or so," he countered. "I don't really have all that much Tolnedran coin in my vaults."

"Oh, that's all right, your Majesty," Silk said magnanimously. "I'd be willing to accept Angarak coins—at a slight discount, of course."

"Discount?"

"Angarak gold is obviously adulterated, King Urgit. That's why it's red instead of yellow."

Urgit eyed him narrowly. "Why don't you draw up a chair, old boy?" he suggested. "This might take a while." Strangely enough, his nose had also begun to twitch.

What followed was a display of astonishing virtuosity on the part of both negotiators. Garion had seen Silk in this sort of situation many times before and had always believed that his sharp-nosed friend was without peer when it came to getting the best of every bargain he struck. Urgit, however, quickly demonstrated that he too was an expert at the game. When Silk pointed out in suitably exaggerated terms the dangers he would have to face on his way to deliver the message, Urgit countered by offering an escort of Murgo soldiers rather than increased compensation. Silk dropped that line of attack and concentrated for a time on the unusual expenses he would incur—fresh horses, food and lodging, bribes, and the like. In each case the Murgo King proposed assistance rather than money—horses, food and lodging at Murgo embassies or trade missions, and the good offices of Murgo officials to step around the necessity for bribes. Silk made some pretense at considering that, his watchful eyes never leaving his adversary's face. Then he fell back to his previously prepared position, re-emphasizing his friendship with the Rivan King and the fact that he, perhaps better than any man in the world, could present the proposed alliance to Belgarion in the most favorable light. "After all," he concluded, "what it finally comes down to is how much the alliance is worth to you, doesn't it?"

"It's worth a very great deal," Urgit admitted with deceptive candor, "but, although I'd be the first to admit that you're probably the perfect messenger, there's no guarantee that Belgarion will agree to an alliance, now is there?" He paused, his expression announcing that a notion had just struck him. "I'll tell you what," he said then with an artfully feigned enthusiasm, "why don't we set a relatively modest figure for the actual delivery of the message—oh, let's say the ten marks I suggested previously."

Silk's face grew flinty, but Urgit lifted one hand. "Hear me out, your Highness," he said. "As I just suggested, we agree on that figure as payment for carrying the message. Then, if Belgarion agrees to an alliance, I'd be more than happy to pay you the rest of the money you asked for."

"That's hardly fair, your Majesty," Silk protested. "You're putting the entire question into the hands of a third party. I can guarantee delivery, but not acceptance. Belgarion is a sovereign king. I can't tell him what to do, and I have no way of knowing how he would react to your proposal."

"Didn't you say that you were his oldest friend? Surely you know him well enough to have at least some idea of how he would view the matter."

"You're shifting the entire basis of the negotiations, your Majesty," Silk accused him.

"Yes, I know." Urgit smirked.

"The payment for actually cementing an alliance between you and Belgarion would have to be much, much higher," Silk countered. "What you propose is extremely hazardous, after all."

"Hazardous? I don't follow you, old boy."

"Belgarion is not entirely a free agent. Even though he's the Overlord of the West, he's still answerable to the other kings—particularly the Alorns; and let's be honest about it, Alorns despise Murgos. If I persuade him to accept an alliance with you, those other Alorn Kings might very well believe that I'm a traitor. I could find myself dodging their assassins for the rest of my life."

"I find that very hard to believe, Kheldar."

"You don't know them. The Alorns are a fearfully unforgiving race. Even my aunt would give orders to have me hunted down if she thought that I'd betrayed a basic Alorn concept of the world. What you propose is absolutely out of the question—unless we start talking about really significant amounts of money, of course."

"Just how significant?" Urgit asked warily.

"Well now, let's see—" Silk pretended to consider the matter. "Naturally I'd have to abandon all my enterprises in the Kingdoms of the West. If the Alorn Kings declare me an outlaw, all my assets would be expropriated anyway. My commercial ventures are far-flung, and it's going to take some time to establish their fair value. Then, of course, I'll have the expense of setting up operations in a part of the world where the Alorns can't track me down."

"That's simplicity in itself, Kheldar. Come to Cthol Murgos. I'll protect you."

"No offense, your Majesty, but Cthol Murgos doesn't suit me. I was thinking perhaps of Mal Zeth or maybe Melcene. I could probably do quite well in Melcene."

"Silk," Belgarath said abruptly, "what's the point of all this?"

"I was just—"

"I know what you were doing. You can amuse yourself some other time. Right now we've got a ship to catch."

"But, Belg—" Silk caught himself abruptly with a quick sidelong glance at Urgit.

"You're not in a position to be giving orders, old man," the Murgo King said. Then he looked around suspiciously. "There's something going on here that I don't like. I don't think anybody's going anyplace today. I'm not going to turn any of you loose until I get to the bottom of all this."

"Don't be absurd, Urgit," his mother interrupted him. "These people must leave at once."

"Don't interfere, mother."

"Then stop acting like a child. Sadi must get past Rak Cthaka before the fighting starts there, and Kheldar must be on his way to Belgarion within the hour. Don't throw away this opportunity out of sheer pique."

Their eyes locked. Urgit's face was suddenly angry, and his mother's unrelenting. After a long moment, his eyes dropped. "This isn't like you, mother," he mumbled. "Why are you deliberately trying to humiliate me in public?"

"I'm not, Urgit. I'm just trying to bring you to your senses. A king must always bow to reality—even if it injures his pride."

He gave her a long, penetrating look. "The time isn't really all that pressing, mother," he said. "Sadi has time to spare, and Kheldar really doesn't have to leave for a day or so. If I didn't know better, I'd say that you have some personal reason for not wanting me to talk to them any more."

"Nonsense!" But her face had grown quite pale.

"You're upset, mother," he pressed. "Why is that?"

"She can't tell you," Eriond said suddenly. The young man was seated on a bench in front of a nearby window with the autumn sun streaming golden on his pale hair.

"What?"

"Your mother can't tell you," Eriond repeated. "There's a secret she's had locked in her heart since before you were born."

"No!" Lady Tamazin gasped involuntarily. "You musn't!"

"What is this secret?" Urgit demanded, his eyes flickering suspiciously from face to face.

A slow flush crept up Eriond's cheeks. "I'd really rather not say," he replied in a slightly embarrassed tone.

Velvet had been watching the exchange with wholly absorbed fascination; even as a startling suspicion dawned in Garion's mind, she suddenly began to laugh.

"What's so funny, young lady?" Urgit asked irritably.

"A peculiar thought just occurred to me, your Majesty," she replied. She turned to Lady Tamazin. "Didn't you say that you knew Prince Kheldar's father, my Lady?"

Tamazin's chin lifted suddenly. Her face was still deadly pale, and she did not answer.

"How long ago would you say that was?" Velvet asked.

Tamazin's lips remained tightly closed.

Velvet sighed, then looked at Silk. "Kheldar," she said, "quite a long time back your father visited Rak Goska, didn't he? I think it had something to do with some trade negotiations on behalf of King Rhodar. Do you happen to recall just how many years ago that was?"

He looked puzzled. "I don't know," he replied. "It must have been—" He thought about it. "I remember that my mother and I stayed at the palace in Boktor while he was gone. I think I was eight or so at the time. That would make it about forty years, I guess. What's this all about, Liselle?"

"Interesting," she murmured, ignoring his question. "My Lady Tamazin," she said, "you keep telling your son that he isn't going to go mad—but doesn't every male in the Urga line fall prey to that hereditary affliction? What is it that makes you so positive that he's somehow going to escape the family curse?"

Tamazin's face grew even paler, and her lips were resolutely sealed.

"My Lord High Seneschal," Velvet said to Oskatat, "just out of curiosity, how old is his Majesty?"

Oskatat's face had also gone deadly pale. He looked at Lady Tamazin with a stricken expression, and then his lips also clamped shut.

"I'm thirty-nine," Urgit snapped. "What difference does it—" Then he suddenly stopped, his eyes going very wide. He turned with a look of stunned incredulity.

"Mother!" he gasped.

Sadi began to laugh.

"I just adore happy endings, don't you?" Velvet said brightly to Ce'Nedra. She looked impishly at Silk. "Well, don't just sit there, Kheldar. Go embrace your brother."

The Lady Tamazin rose slowly from her chair, her face proud. "Summon the executioner, Oskatat," she said. "I am ready."

"No, my Lady," he replied. "I won't do that."

"It's the law, Oskatat," she insisted. "A Murgo woman who dishonors her husband is to be put to death immediately."

"Oh, sit down, mother," Urgit said, abstractedly gnawing at one of his knuckles. "This is no time for histrionics."

Silk's eyes were a bit wild. "You're very quick, Liselle," he said in a strained voice.

"Not really," she admitted. "I should have guessed quite some time ago. You and his Majesty could almost use each other for shaving mirrors, and he negotiates almost as shrewdly as you do." She looked at the stunned Murgo King, her cheeks dimpling. "If your Majesty ever grows weary of the throne, I'm certain that my uncle could find work for you."

"This alters things quite a bit, Urgit," Belgarath said. "The prejudices of your subjects are well known. If they find out that you're not a real Murgo, it might agitate them just a bit, wouldn't you say?"

Urgit had been staring at Silk. "Oh, just shut up, old man," he said absently. "Let me think my way through this."

"I'm sure that your Majesty realizes that you can rely totally on our discretion," Sadi said smoothly.

"Of course," Urgit replied drily. "Just as long as I do exactly what you tell me to do."

"Well, there's that, naturally."

Urgit looked at his seneschal. "Well, Oskatat," he said, "will you now dash to the highest window of the Drojim to proclaim this to the entire city?"

"Why should I?" Oskatat shrugged. "I've known since you were a little boy that you were not the son of Taur Urgas."

Lady Tamazin gasped, her hand going suddenly to her lips. "You've known, Oskatat? And you've kept my shame a secret?"

"My Lady," he said with a stiff bow, "I would not have betrayed you even on the rack."

She gave him a peculiar look. "And why is that, Oskatat?" she asked gently.

"You are of the House of Hagga," he replied, "as am I. Loyalty to blood is very strong in Cthol Murgos."

"And is that all, Oskatat? Is that the only reason you befriended me and protected my son?"

He looked her full in the face. "No, my Lady," he said almost proudly, "it is not."

She lowered her eyelashes.

"There were other reasons for my keeping your secret, however," he continued, "less personal, perhaps, but just as compelling. The Urga Dynasty has brought Cthol Murgos to the brink of disaster. I saw in young Urgit the best hope for the kingdom. I might have wished him to be stronger, but his agility of mind showed much promise. In the long run a clever king is often preferable to a strong one without any brains."

Belgarath rose from his chair. "I hate to break up these festivities," he said, "but it's time for us to leave. Too many secrets are starting to come out into the open." He looked at Urgit. "Did you send that messenger to the Temple? If Agachak's Dagashi wants to go along with us, he's going to have to get down to the harbor at once."

Urgit started to rise from his chair, his face angry. Then he stopped, his eyes narrowing. "Just who are you, old man?" he demanded. "You look like a vagabond, but you've been throwing commands around here like an emperor."

Lady Tamazin, however, had been looking at Belgarath with eyes suddenly gone wide. Then she turned to stare in awe at Aunt Pol. "Urgit!" she said in a half-strangled whisper.

"What is it, mother?"

"Look at him. Look very closely—and then look at his daughter here."

"His daughter? I didn't know they were related."

"Neither did I—until just now." The Queen Mother looked directly at Polgara. "He is your father, isn't he, Lady Polgara?"

Polgara straightened, and the white lock at her brow caught the candlelight. "I think this has gone far enough, father," she said to the old man with a wry expression. "There's not much point in trying to hide things any more, is there?"

"Old friend," Silk said lightly, "you really ought to do something about your appearance, you know. Your description's been noised about the world for all these centuries, so people are bound to recognize you every so often. Have you ever considered shaving off your beard?"

Urgit was staring at the old man with an expression of near-terror.

"Oh, don't do that," Belgarath said in disgust.

Urgit flinched.

"And don't do that either. No matter what you've been told, I don't make a practice of biting off the heads of Murgo babies just for amusement." He tugged thoughtfully at one ear, looking first at Urgit, then at Lady Tamazin, and finally at Oskatat and Prala. "I think there's going to have to be a small change of plans," he said. "I believe that you people are all going to develop an irresistible craving for sea travel—just as a precaution. You have some secrets you want kept, and so do we. This way we can sort of keep an eye on each other."

"You're not serious!" Urgit burst out.

"Yes, as a matter of fact, I am. I don't like leaving loose ends behind me."

The door opened, and Garion spun quickly, but stopped his hand halfway to his sword hilt. The Murgo officer who had just entered looked curiously at the people in the room, sensing the tension. "Uh—excuse me, your Majesty," he said a bit warily.

Urgit looked at him, a swift flash of hope fleeting across his face. Then he cast a quick, fearful glance at Belgarath. "Yes, Colonel," he replied in a carefully neutral voice.

"A message has just arrived from the Hierarch, your Majesty. I am directed to advise you that the Dagashi Kabach will be at the harbor within the hour."

Durnik and Toth, moving in unison, had carefully sidled up until one of them stood on each side of Oskatat, and Polgara had crossed to Lady Tamazin's chair.

Urgit's face was faintly sick with fright. "Very good, Colonel," he replied. "Thank you for your trouble."

The officer bowed and then turned toward the door.

"Colonel," Prala's clear voice stopped him.

He turned back, his face respectful. "Yes, Princess?"

Velvet was moving toward the Murgo girl with a deceptive casualness. Garion inwardly flinched at the potential for sudden, awful violence that hung heavily in the air—even as he measured the distance to the unsuspecting colonel.

"Have you had any reports about the weather conditions along the coast to the south?" Prala asked calmly.

"There's some wind, your Highness," the colonel replied, "and there are almost always rain squalls around the tip of the peninsula."

"Thank you, Colonel."

He bowed and quietly left the room.

Garion let out his breath explosively.

"Lord Belgarath." Prala's voice was crisp. "You cannot expose the Lady Tamazin to that kind of weather. I will not permit it."

Belgarath blinked. "Will not permit?" he asked incredulously.

"Absolutely not. If you persist, I'll scream the roof down." She turned coolly to Velvet. "Don't come one step closer, Liselle," she warned. "I can scream at least twice before you can kill me, and that will bring every guard in the Drojim to this room on the run."

"She's right, you know, father," Polgara said very calmly. "Tamazin could not possibly endure the rigors of the voyage."

"Couldn't we—"

"No, father," she said firmly, "it's absolutely out of the question."

He muttered a sour curse and jerked his head at Sadi. The two of them moved down to the far end of the room for a brief, murmured conversation.

"You've got a knife under your doublet, haven't you, Kheldar?" Urgit asked.

"Two, actually," Silk replied in a matter-of-fact tone, "and one in my boot and another on a string at the back of my neck. I like to be prepared for little emergencies when they arise—but why dwell on an unpleasantness that never happened?"

"You're a dreadful man, Kheldar."

"I know."

Belgarath came back from his low-voiced conference with Sadi. "Lady Tamazin," he said.

The Queen Mother's chin lifted. "Yes?" she replied.

"Under the circumstances, I believe we can rely on your discretion," he said. "You've already proved that you know how to keep a secret. You *do* realize that your life—and your son's—depends on your not revealing what you've learned here, don't you?"

"Yes, I suppose I do."

"We're going to need to leave someone ostensibly in charge here anyway, so things will work out, I suppose."

"What you propose is quite impossible, Lord Belgarath."

"I do wish people would stop using that word. What's the problem now?"

"Murgos will not take orders from a woman."

Belgarath grunted sourly. "Oh, yes. I'd forgotten about that peculiar Murgo prejudice."

"My Lord Oskatat," Sadi said.

The seneschal's face was stony as he glanced briefly at Durnik and Toth standing one on each side of him.

"Wouldn't you be the logical one to attend to the affairs of state during his Majesty's absence?"

"It's possible."

"Just how far does your loyalty to your kinswoman, the Lady Tamazin, go?"

Oskatat scowled at him.

"Eriond," Ce'Nedra said then.

"Yes?"

"Can the seneschal be trusted not to send a fleet after us as soon as we leave?"

Garion looked up sharply. He had forgotten his young friend's peculiar ability to see directly into the minds and hearts of others.

"He won't say anything," Eriond replied confidently.

"Are you sure?" Ce'Nedra asked.

"Absolutely. He'd rather die than betray Tamazin."

A dull flush crept up into the big Murgo's scarred cheeks, and he turned his face so that he could avoid the Queen Mother's eyes.

"All right then." Belgarath's tone was decisive. "Urgit will go with us." He looked at the seneschal. "We'll drop him off not far from Rak Cthaka. You have my word on that. You stay here with Tamazin. It's up to you, but I'd recommend that you follow through on the plan to send reinforcements to the city by sea. Otherwise, your king may have to hold off the Malloreans all by himself."

"What about Prala?" Ce'Nedra asked.

Belgarath scratched his ear. "There's no real point in taking her along," he said. "I'm sure that if she stays here, Tamazin and Oskatat can keep her from blurting out any secrets."

"No, my Lord Belgarath," the slender Cthan Princess said firmly. "I will not stay behind. If his Majesty is going to Rak Cthaka, then so am I. I will not give you my word to remain silent. You have no choice but to take me along—or to kill me."

"What's this?" Urgit asked, puzzled.

Silk, however, had already guessed. "If you want to start running right now, Urgit, I'll try to hold her until you get a good head start."

"What are you talking about, Kheldar?"

"If you're very, very lucky, my brother, Kal Zakath won't get you, but I'm afraid that your chances of escaping this young lady are far more slender. Take my advice and start running right now."

CHAPTER SIXTEEN

A heavy bank of gray cloud had moved in off the Great Western Sea, and a stiff offshore breeze tugged at their garments as they mounted their horses in the courtyard of the Drojim.

"You know what to do, Oskatat?" Urgit asked his seneschal.

The big Murgo nodded. "The ships carrying the reinforcements will depart within two days, your Majesty. You have my word on that."

"Good. I'd rather not fight this battle all by myself. Try not to use any more of those warrants than you absolutely have to."

"Trust me." Oskatat's face creased into a bleak smile.

Urgit's quick answering grin was wolfish. "And look after my mother," he added.

"I've done that for many years—without her even being aware of it."

Gravely the Murgo King leaned down from his saddle and shook hands with his friend. Then he straightened resolutely. "All right," he said to the officer in charge of the guard detachment, "let's go."

They clattered out of the courtyard, and Silk drew in beside his brother. "What was that business about warrants?" he asked curiously.

Urgit laughed. "The generals might want to refuse to obey Oskatat's orders," he explained, "so I signed warrants for the execution of every one of them and left them with him to use as he sees fit."

"Clever."

"I should have thought of it years ago." Urgit looked up at the racing clouds overhead, with his robe flapping in the rising wind. "I'm not a very good sailor, Kheldar," he admitted with a shudder. "I tend to throw up a lot in rough weather."

Silk laughed. "Then just remember always to stand at the leeward rail."

The murky sky seemed somehow to Garion to be suited to the bleakness of Rak Urga. A city so devoid of any kind of beauty seemed unnatural when the sky was clear and the sun was shining. Now, however, it squatted under the roiling clouds like some torpid stone toad. The black-robed Murgos in the narrow streets stood aside for their king. Some of them bowed; others stood stony-faced and unbending as the party passed.

They rode through a square and then on down the stone-paved street that led to the Temple. "Captain," Urgit called to the officer in the lead, "have one of your men stop by and tell the Hierarch that we're leaving. He has someone in the Temple that he wants to send along with us."

"As your Majesty commands," the officer replied.

The cobbled street they were following rounded a corner, and they were able to see the harbor. It lay in a sheltered bay behind the headland standing at the narrow mouth of the Gulf of Urga and was dotted with black-painted Murgo ships. The familiar smell of the meeting of sea and land, a mixture of brine, seaweed, and dead fish, rose to meet Garion's nostrils, and his blood began to race at the prospect of once again going to sea.

The black ship moored at the side of the stone quay onto which they rode was larger than most of the other vessels in the harbor. It was a squat, broad-beamed scow with slanting masts and tarred planking. Silk eyed it distrustfully. "Do you really call that thing a ship?" he asked his brother.

"I warned you about Murgo boats."

There was a brief disagreement about the horses when they reached the ship. "Totally out of the question, your Majesty," the ship captain, a huge, evil-looking man, declared adamantly. "I don't carry livestock on board my ship." He stood towering over his king with a self-important expression slightly tinged with contempt on his face.

Urgit's expression became one of distress.

"I'd say that it's time for another exercise of the royal assertiveness," Silk murmured to him.

Urgit gave him a quick look and then squared his shoulders. He turned back to the hulking ship's master. "Load these horses on your ship, Captain," he repeated his command in a firmer tone.

"I just told you that I don't—"

"Did I say it too fast for you? Listen carefully this time. Put-the-horses-on-the-boat. If you don't do exactly what I tell you to do, I'll have you nailed to the prow of your ship in place of a figurehead. Do we understand each other?"

The captain stepped back, his look of arrogance becoming one of doubt and apprehension. "Your Majesty—"

"Do it, Captain!" Urgit barked, "Now!"

The captain drew himself up sharply, saluted, and then turned to his crew. "You heard the king," he said harshly. "Load the horses." He stalked away, muttering to himself.

"You see," Silk said. "It gets easier every time you do it, doesn't it? All you have to remember is that your commands are not subjects for debate."

"You know," Urgit said with a tight grin, "I could actually get to like that."

The sailors began to push the skittish horses up the narrow gangplank and then down a steeply slanting ramp into the hold of the vessel. They had loaded perhaps half of the animals when Garion heard the sound of a sullen drum coming from the narrow, cobbled street leading down to the quay. A double file of black-robed Grolims in polished steel masks marched down the hill toward the water, moving with that peculiar, swaying gait Garion had seen in the Temple. Belgarath took Urgit by the sleeve and drew him out of earshot of his guards and the busy sailors. "We don't need any surprises, here, Urgit," he said firmly, "so let's get through the formalities with Agachak as quickly as possible. Tell him that you're going to Rak Cthaka to take personal command of the defense of the city. Let's get your Dagashi on board ship and get out of here."

"I don't really have any choice about this, do I?" Urgit asked unhappily.

"No," Belgarath replied. "Not very much at all."

The cadaverous Agachak rode in a litter carried by a dozen Grolims. At his side, her head erect, came the scarred priestess Chabat. Her eyes were ravaged from weeping, and her face was dreadfully pale. The look she directed at Sadi, however, was filled with implacable hatred.

Behind Agachak's litter there came a hooded figure that did not walk with the stiff-legged, swaying gait of the Grolims in the Hierarch's entourage, and Garion surmised that this man was the mysterious Kabach. He looked at the man curiously, but could not see the face concealed beneath the hood.

As the litter reached the gangway, Agachak signaled his bearers to a halt. "Your Majesty," he greeted Urgit hollowly as his litter was lowered to the stones.

"Dread Hierarch."

"I received your message. Is the situation in the south as grave as I was led to believe?"

"I'm afraid so, Agachak. I'm going to take advantage of this ship to go to Rak Cthaka and take personal command."

"You, your Majesty?" Agachak looked startled. "Is that altogether wise?"

"Perhaps not, but I'm sure I can't do much worse than my generals have done. I've left orders that reinforcements are to be sent to the city by ship."

"By ship? A daring innovation, your Majesty. I'm surprised that your generals agreed to it."

"I didn't ask them to agree. I finally realized that their duty to advise me doesn't give them the authority to order me around."

Agachak looked at him, his eyes thoughtful. "This is a new side of you, your Majesty," he noted, stepping out of his litter to stand on the stones of the quay.

"I thought it was time for a change."

It was at that point that Garion felt a warning tingle and an oppressive kind of weight that seemed centered just above his ears. He glanced quickly at Polgara, and she nodded. It did not appear to be emanating from the Hierarch, who seemed wholly engrossed in his conversation with Urgit. Chabat stood to one side with her burning eyes fixed balefully on Sadi, but there was no hint of any mounting of her will. The quiet probing was coming from somewhere else.

"We should be able to reach Rak Cthaka in five or six days," Urgit was saying to the red-robed Hierarch. "As soon as we arrive, I'll get Ussa and his people started toward Rak Hagga with our Dagashi. They might have to swing south a bit to avoid the Mallorean advance, but they won't lose too much time."

"You must be very careful at Rak Cthaka, your Majesty," Agachak cautioned. "It's not only the fate of Cthol Murgos you carry on your shoulders; it's the fate of the entire world."

"I don't concern myself too much with fate, Agachak. A man whose main concern has always been staying alive for the next hour or so doesn't have much time to worry about next year. Where's Kabach?"

The man in the hooded robe stepped out from behind the litter. "I'm here, your Majesty," he said in a deep, resonant voice. There was something familiar about that voice, and a warning prickle ran up between Garion's shoulder blades.

"Good," Urgit said. "Have you any final instructions for him, Agachak?"

"I have said to him all that needs to be said," the Hierarch responded.

"That covers everything, then." Urgit looked around. "All right," he said, "let's all get on board that ship."

"Perhaps not just yet, your Majesty," the black-robed Dagashi said to him, stepping forward and pushing back his hood. Garion suppressed a start of surprise. Although his black beard had been shaved off, there was no question about the man's identity. It was Harakan.

"There is one last thing your Majesty should know before we board," Harakan declared in a voice clearly intended to be heard by everyone on the quay. "Were you aware of the fact that the man with the sword over there is Belgarion of Riva?"

Urgit's eyes went very wide as a ripple of amazement went through the priests and the soldiers standing on the slippery stones of the quay. The Murgo King, however, was quick to recover. "That's a very interesting thing to suggest, Kabach," he said carefully. "I'd be interested to know what makes you so sure."

"It's absolute nonsense," Sadi spluttered.

Agachak's sunken eyes were boring into Garion's face. "I have seen Belgarion myself," he intoned hollowly. "He was much younger then, but there *is* a resemblance."

"A resemblance certainly, Dread Hierarch," Sadi agreed quickly, "but that's all. The young man has been in my service since he was a boy. Oh, I'll admit that there are some superficial similarities of features, but I can assure you that this most definitely is *not* Belgarion."

Silk was standing just behind Urgit, and his lips were moving very fast as he whispered to his new-found brother. The Murgo King was a skilled enough politician to control his expression, but his eyes darted nervously this way and that as he began to realize that he stood at the very center of an incipient explosion. Finally, he cleared his throat. "You still haven't told us what makes you believe that this is Belgarion, Kabach," he said.

"I was in Tol Honeth some years ago." Harakan shrugged. "Belgarion was there at the same time—for a funeral, I think. Someone pointed him out to me."

"I think the noble Dagashi is mistaken," Sadi said. "His identification is based entirely on a fleeting glance from a distance. That hardly qualifies as definitive proof. I tell you that this is not Belgarion."

"He lies," Harakan said flatly. "I am of the Dagashi. We are trained observers."

"That raises an interesting point, Agachak," Urgit said, his eyes narrowing as he looked at Harakan. "In spite of everything, the Dagashi are still Murgos, and every Murgo alive slashes his face as a blood offering to Torak." He turned and pointed at two faint, thin white lines on his cheek. The king's scarcely visible scars gave mute evidence that his self-mutilation had been none too fervent. "Look at our Dagashi there," he continued. "I don't see a single mark on his face, do you?"

"I was instructed by my elder not to make the customary blood offering," Harakan said quickly. "He wanted me unmarked so that I could move around freely in the Kingdoms of the West."

"I'm sorry, Kabach," Urgit said with heavy skepticism, "but that story doesn't hold water at all. The blood offering to Torak is a part of the rite of passage into manhood. Were you so precocious as a child that your elder decided to make you a spy before you were ten years old? And even if he had, you would still have been required to go through the rite before you could marry or even enter the Temple. The scars may not be on your face, but if you're a Murgo, you've got scars on you someplace. Show us your scars, noble Dagashi. Let us see the proof of your fidelity to Torak and your uncontaminated Murgo blood."

"Dread Hierarch," Sadi said with a thoughtful expression on his face, "this is not the first accusation leveled at one of my servants." He looked meaningfully at Chabat. "Is it possible that there is a faction among your Grolims that does not want this mission to succeed—some group hiding behind false beards?"

"Beard!" Silk exclaimed, snapping his fingers. "That's why I couldn't place him! He's shaved off his beard!"

Urgit turned to look inquiringly at him. "What are you talking about, fellow?"

"Excuse me, your Majesty," Silk said with exaggerated humility. "I just realized something, and it surprised me. I think I can clarify things here."

"I certainly hope someone can. All right, go ahead."

"Thank you, your Majesty." Silk looked around with a beautifully feigned expression of nervousness. "I'm an Alorn, your Majesty," he said, then held up one hand quickly. "Please hear me out," he begged, half of the king and half of the surrounding Murgos. "I'm an Alorn, but I'm not a fanatic about it. The way I look at it, there's plenty of room in the world for Alorns and Murgos. Live and let live, I always say. Anyway, last year I hired myself out as a soldier in King Belgarion's army— the one that he raised to lay seige to the Bear-cult at Rheon in northeastern Drasnia. Well, to make it short, I was present when Belgarion and his friend from Sendaria—

Durnik, I think his name is—captured the cult leader, Ulfgar. He had a beard then, but I swear to you that this Kabach is the selfsame man. I ought to know. I helped to carry him into a house after Durnik knocked him senseless."

"What would a Dagashi be doing in Drasnia?" Urgit asked with an artfully puzzled expression on his face.

"Oh, he's not a Dagashi, your Majesty," Silk explained. "When King Belgarion and his friends questioned him, it came out that he's a Mallorean Grolim. Harakan, I think his name is."

"Harakan?" Agachak said, turning quickly to fix the counterfeit Dagashi with his suddenly smoldering eyes.

"Ridiculous," Harakan scoffed. "This little weasel is one of Belgarion's servants. He's lying to protect his master."

"Is the name Harakan in any way significant, Agachak?" Urgit asked.

The Hierarch straightened, his eyes intent. "Harakan is Urvon's underling," he replied, "and I've heard that he's been seen here in the west."

"I think we've got a problem on our hands here, Agachak," Urgit said. "These charges—both of them—are too serious to be ignored. We've got to get to the truth here."

The priestess Chabat's eyes were narrowed, and her expression cunning. "Finding that truth is a simple matter, your Majesty," she declared. "My master Agachak is the most powerful sorcerer in all of Cthol Murgos. He will have no difficulty in probing the minds of all who are here to find out who is speaking truth and who is lying."

"Can you really do that, Agachak?" Urgit asked.

Agachak shrugged. "It's a simple matter."

"Then by all means, do it. I'm not going on board that scow over there until I find out exactly who my shipmates are going to be."

Agachak took a deep breath and began to draw in his will.

"Master!" a Grolim with a purple satin lining on the hood of his robe exclaimed, leaping forward with one hand outstretched. "Beware!"

"How dare you?" Chabat shrieked at him, her eyes blazing.

The Grolim ignored her. "Master," he said to Agachak, "there is great danger in what the priestess proposes. Should either of these men be telling the truth, you will be probing the mind of a powerful sorcerer, and your own mind will be totally vulnerable. A single thought could erase your entire consciousness."

Agachak slowly relaxed his will. "Ah, yes," he murmured. "I had not considered that danger." He turned to Chabat, catching the brief flicker of disappointment that crossed her face. "How curious that my Holy Priestess did not think of that before she suggested the probing—or did you, Chabat? Have you given up the notion of raising a demon to destroy me, then? Will you now fall back on so commonplace a thing as simple deceit? I'm terribly disappointed in you, my beloved."

She shrank back, her scar-laced face frightened.

"This matter has to be settled, Agachak," Urgit said. "I'm not going to go near that ship until I find out the truth here. I haven't succeeded in staying alive for all these years by being foolhardy."

"The question is largely academic now anyway," Agachak replied. "None of these people will be leaving."

"Agachak, I have to get to Rak Cthaka immediately."

"Then go. I will find another party of slavers and hire another Dagashi."

"That could take months," Urgit protested. "Personally, I'm inclined to believe these slavers. Ussa has been very honest with me, and the young man over there has none of the bearing of a king. This one who calls himself Kabach, however, is highly suspect. If you were to look along the trail between here and Mount Kahsha, I think you might find the real Kabach in a shallow grave someplace. This man—whoever he is—has come very close to forestalling the mission to Rak Hagga with his accusation. Wouldn't that be exactly what Urvon would want?"

"There's a logic to what you say, your Majesty, but I don't think I want any of them going on board that ship until I find out the truth."

"Why not let *them* settle it for us, then?"

"I don't follow you."

"One of them—or possibly both—is a sorcerer. Let them fight each other, and we'll see which one tries to destroy the other by sorcery."

"Trial by combat?"

"Why not? It's a bit antique, but the circumstances here seem to be appropriate."

"There is merit in your plan, your Majesty."

Urgit suddenly grinned. "Why don't we clear a space?" he suggested. "We wouldn't want to get singed when these two start hurling thunderbolts at each other." He came over and took Garion's arm. "Just stay calm," he whispered, "and don't do anything conspicuous. Try to force him to use sorcery." Then he pushed Garion forward into the circle that had quickly been formed on the stone quay. "Here is the supposed King of Riva," he said to Agachak. "Now, if the ostensible Mallorean Grolim will be so good as to step forth, we'll find out who's been telling the truth."

"I have no sword," Harakan said sullenly.

"Simplicity in itself. Somebody give him a sword."

Several were offered at once.

"I think you're in deep trouble, Harakan," Urgit smirked. "If you so much as twitch one finger, you'll reveal yourself as a Mallorean Grolim, and my soldiers will shoot you full of arrows. On the other hand, if this is really Belgarion and you don't use sorcery to defend yourself, he'll burn you right down into a little pile of cinders. All in all, I think you're in for a very bad afternoon."

Garion ground his teeth together and began talking fervently to the Orb, telling the stone over and over again not to do anything out of the ordinary. Then he steeled himself and reached back over his shoulder. The great blade made a steely hiss as it came out of the scabbard.

Harakan handled his borrowed sword nervously, but the way he held it and his stance clearly indicated that he was a competent swordsman. A sudden anger filled Garion. This was the man who had been responsible for the attempt on Ce'Nedra's life and for the murder of Brand. He dropped into a half crouch with Iron-grip's sword extended in front of him. Harakan desperately tried to slap that great blade away with his own sword, and there was a steely ring as the two swords came together. Implacably, Garion stalked his enemy. His anger was so great that he had even forgotten the reason for this duel. He was no longer interested in unmasking Harakan. All he wanted to do was to kill him.

There was a rapid exchange of thrusts and parries, and the entire harbor rang with the steel song of the swords. Step by step Harakan retreated, and his eyes began to fill with fear. But finally Garion lost all patience with fencing. With his eyes ablaze he seized the hilt of his huge sword in both hands and swung it back over his shoulder. Had he delivered that blow, nothing could have stopped it.

Harakan's cheeks blanched as he looked directly into the face of death. "Curse you!" he shouted at Garion, then flickered and vanished, to reappear briefly at the far end of the quay. He shimmered and swooped away in the form of a swift sea hawk.

"That sort of answers the question, doesn't it, Agachak?" Urgit said quite calmly.

Agachak, however, his eyes ablaze with hate, also flashed into the form of a hawk. With two powerful strokes of his pinions, he drove himself into the air, shrieking for blood as he raced after the fleeing Harakan.

Garion's hands were shaking. He turned and stalked toward Urgit with a scorching fury rising in his throat. With a great effort he restrained his sudden desire to take hold of the front of the smaller man's doublet and hurl him far out into the harbor.

"Now—now don't be hasty," Urgit said, backing fearfully away.

Garion spoke from between clenched teeth in a dreadfully quiet voice. "Don't *ever* do that again."

"Naturally not," Urgit agreed hastily. He stopped, a curious expression suddenly crossing his ratlike face. "Are you *really* Belgarion?" he asked in a hoarse whisper.

"Would you like some proof?"

"No, no—that's quite all right." Urgit's words came tumbling out. He stepped quickly around the still infuriated Garion and crossed the quay to where Chabat stood. "Let us pray that your Hierarch succeeds in capturing that imposter," he said. "Give him my regards upon his return. I'd wait, but I must board ship and depart at once."

"Of course, your Majesty," she replied in a voice that was nearly a purr. "I will take charge of these slavers until the Hierarch's return."

He stared at her.

"Since the entire purpose of this mission was to convey the Dagashi assassin to Rak Hagga, there's no point in their going now, is there? They will have to remain here while we send to Kahsha for another Dagashi." She looked at Sadi with an unconcealed smirk. "I will place them under my personal protection."

Urgit looked at her narrowly. "Holy Priestess," he said to her, "to be quite candid about it, I don't think you can be trusted. Your personal enmity toward this Nyissan is painfully obvious, and he's far too important to risk. I don't think that you would be able to restrain yourself, once both Agachak and I are gone from Rak Urga. I think I'll just take Ussa and his people with me—just to be on the safe side. When the Dagashi arrives from Mount Kahsha, send him along."

Chabat's eyes hardened, and her face grew angry. "The purpose of the mission to Rak Hagga is to fulfill a prophecy," she declared, "and the fulfillment of prophecy is clearly in the domain of the Church."

Urgit drew in a deep breath. Then he straightened from his usual slouching posture. "The mission is also a State matter, Holy Priestess. Agachak and I have been cooperating in this affair, and in his absence I assert the authority of the crown. Ussa and his people will go with me, and you will take your Grolims back to the Temple to await the return of your Hierarch."

Chabat seemed taken aback by his sudden show of strength. She had obviously expected to brush aside any feeble objections he might raise, but this seemed to be a new Urgit. Her face hardened, and the flamelike scars writhed on her pale cheeks. "So," she said, "it appears that our king is finally maturing. I think, however, that you will come to regret your passage into manhood at this particular time. Watch closely, High King of Cthol Murgos." She bent, holding something in her hand, and began to mark symbols on the stones of the quay—symbols that glowed with an unholy light.

"Garion!" Silk cried in alarm, "Stop her!"

But Garion had also seen the glowing circle Chabat had drawn on the wet stones and the burning five-pointed star she was inscribing in its center and he recognized the meaning of those symbols immediately. He took a half step toward Chabat, even as she stepped into the protection of the circle and began muttering words in some unknown language.

As fast as he was, however, Polgara was even faster. "Chabat!" she said sharply, "Stop! This is forbidden!"

"Nothing is forbidden to one who has the power," the priestess replied, her scarred and beautiful face filled with an overwhelming pride, "and who here can prevent me?"

Polgara's face grew grim. "I can," she said calmly. She raised her hand in a curious lifting gesture, and Garion felt the surge of her will. The sullen swells washing against the stones of the quay slowly rose until they broke across the top to swirl about the ankles of those who stood there. The burning symbols Chabat had marked on the stones vanished as the water washed over them.

The Grolim priestess drew in her breath sharply and stared at Aunt Pol, realization slowly dawning in her eyes. "Who are you?"

"One who would save your life, Chabat," Polgara answered. "The punishment for raising demons has always been the same. You might succeed once or twice—or even a few more times—but in the end, the demon will turn on you and tear you to pieces. Not even Torak in all his twisted madness would have dared to step across this line."

"But I *do* dare! Torak is dead, and Agachak is not here to prevent me. No one can stop me."

"I can, Chabat," Polgara said quietly. "I will not permit you to do this."

"And how will you stop me? I have the power."

"But mine is greater." Polgara let her cloak fall to the stones at her feet, bent, and removed her shoes. "You may have been able to control your demon the first time you raised him," she said, "but your control is only temporary. You are no more than the doorway through which he enters this world. As soon as he feels his full strength, he will destroy you and be loosed upon this world to raven as he chooses. I beg of you, my sister, do not do this. Your life—and your very soul—are in deadly peril."

"I have no fear," Chabat rasped. "Not of my demon and not of you."

"Then you're a fool—on both counts."

"You challenge me?"

"If I must. Will you meet me on my own ground, Chabat?" Polgara's blue eyes were suddenly like ice, and the white lock at her brow flamed incandescently as she gathered in her will. Once again she raised her hand and the lead-gray swells again raised obediently to the edge of the quay. With that same dreadful calm, she stepped out onto the surface of the water and stood there, as if what lay under her feet was firm earth. A sudden moan rose from the Grolims as she turned to look at the awe-stricken priestess. "Well, Chabat," she said, "will you join me here? *Can* you join me?"

Chabat's scarred face grew ashen, but her eyes clearly showed that she could not refuse Aunt Pol's challenge. "I will," she rasped through clenched teeth. Then she, too, stepped off the quay, but floundered awkwardly as she sank to the knees in the dirty waters of the harbor.

"Is it so very difficult for you, then?" Polgara asked her. "If this little thing takes all of your will, how do you imagine that you will have enough power to control a demon? Abandon this desperate plan, Chabat. There is still time to save your own life."

"Never!" Chabat shrieked with flecks of froth coming to her lips. With an enormous effort, she lifted herself until she stood on the surface and laboriously strode out several yards. Then, with her face once again twisted into that over-whelming triumph, she drew the symbols on the face of the water, inscribing them with sooty orange flame. Her voice rose again in the evil incantation of the summoning, rising and falling in its hideous cadences. The red scars on her cheeks seemed to grow pale, then suddenly glowed with a burning white light as she continued to recite the spell.

"Kheldar, what's happening?" Urgit's voice was shrill as he stared at the impossibility that was occurring before his eyes.

"Something very unpleasant," Silk told him.

Chabat's voice had risen to a shriek, and the surface of the harbor suddenly erupted before her in a seething cauldron of steam and fire. Out of the midst of those flames there arose something so hideous that it was beyond comprehension. It was vast and clawed and fanged, but the worst of all were its red, glowing eyes.

"Kill her!" Chabat cried, pointing at Polgara with a trembling hand. "I command thee to kill this witch!"

The demon looked at the priestess standing safely within the flaming circle of her protective symbols and then, with the still-boiling water surging around his vast trunk, he turned and started toward Polgara. But, with her face still calm, she raised one hand. "Stop!" she commanded, and Garion felt the enormous jolting force of her will.

The demon suddenly howled, his fanged muzzle lifted toward the gray clouds in a sudden agony of frustration.

"I said kill her!" Chabat shrieked again.

The monster slowly sank into the water, extending his two huge arms just beneath the surface. He began to turn, rotating slowly in the seething water. Faster and faster he spun, with the water sizzling around him. A vortex began to appear around him as he whirled, a sudden maelstrom very nearly as dreadful as the Cherek Bore.

Chabat howled her triumph, dancing on the surface of the water in an obscene caper, unaware that the flames with which she had drawn her symbols had been suddenly whirled away by the surging vortex.

As the spinning waters reached the spot where Polgara stood, she began to be drawn toward the deadly whirlpool and the slavering demon still whirling in its center.

"Pol!" Durnik shouted. "Look out!"

But it was too late. Caught in that inexorable maelstrom, she was carried round and round, slowly at first but then faster and faster as she was pulled in long spirals toward the center. As she neared it, however, she once again raised her hand and very suddenly she disappeared beneath the surging surface.

"Pol!" Durnik shouted again, his face suddenly gone deathly white. Struggling to pull off his tunic, he ran toward the edge of the quay. Belgarath, however, his face grimly set, caught the smith's arm. "Stay out of it, Durnik!" he snapped, his voice cracking like a whip.

Durnik struggled with him, trying to pull himself free. "Let me go!" he yelled.

"I said not to interfere!"

Beyond the edge of the demon-created vortex, a single rose bobbed to the surface. It was a curiously familiar flower, its petals white on the outside and a deep, blushing crimson in the center. Garion stared at it, a sudden wild hope springing up in him.

At the center of the swirling vortex, the monstrous demon suddenly stopped, his burning eyes filled with bafflement. Without any warning he rose, arched forward, and plunged headfirst into the seething water.

"Find her!" the flame-marked Chabat screamed after her enslaved fiend. "Find her and kill her!"

The leaden waters of the harbor boiled and steamed as the huge demon surged this way and that beneath the surface. Quite suddenly, the movement stopped, and the air and the water grew deadly calm.

Chabat, still standing on the water and with the glowing light still illuminating the cruel scars on her cheeks, lifted both arms above her head in a gesture of exaltation. "Die, witch!" she shouted. "Feel the fangs of my servant rend your flesh!"

Suddenly a monstrous, scaly claw came up out of the water directly in front of her. "No!" she shrieked, "you cannot!" Then she looked in horror at the water upon which she stood, realizing at last that her protective symbols had been swept away. She took a faltering step backward, but the huge hand closed on her, its needle-sharp claws biting deeply into her body. Her blood spurted, and she screamed in agony, writhing in that awful grasp.

Then, with a huge bellow, the demon rose from the depths with his great, fanged muzzle agape. He lifted the struggling priestess aloft with a howl of hellish triumph. The Grolims and the Murgo soldiers on the quay broke and fled in terror as the monster started toward them.

The single rose that had floated to the surface of the harbor, however, had begun to glow with a strange blue light. It seemed to grow larger as the glow intensified. Then, her face calm, Polgara appeared in the very center of that coruscating incandescence. A few feet to her left there also appeared a nimbus of flickering light. Before the stunned eyes of those on the quay, the nimbus suddenly coalesced, and there, standing beside Polgara, Garion saw the glowing form of the God Aldur.

"Must it be so, Master?" Polgara asked in a voice that clearly revealed her reluctance.

"It must, my daughter," Aldur replied sadly.

Polgara sighed. "Then so be it, Master." She extended her left hand, and the God enclosed it in his. The gathering-in of her will roared in Garion's mind like a tornado, and the force of it pushed against him with an awful power. Enclosed in blue light and linked by their touching hands, Polgara and Aldur stood side by side on the surface of the water, facing the hideous demon who still held the weakly struggling Chabat high in the air.

"I abjure thee, creature of darkness," Polgara said in a great voice. "Return to the hell that spawned thee and never more corrupt this world by thy foul presence. Begone and take with thee the one who summoned thee." She raised her hand, and the force of her will, combined with the will of the God Aldur, blazed forth from her palm. There was a vast thunderclap as the demon suddenly exploded into a huge ball of fire with the waters of the harbor geysering up around it. Then he was gone, and with him disappeared the priestess Chabat.

When Garion looked back, Aldur no longer stood at Polgara's side. She turned and slowly walked back across the waves toward the quay. As she approached, Garion clearly saw that her eyes were filled with anguish.

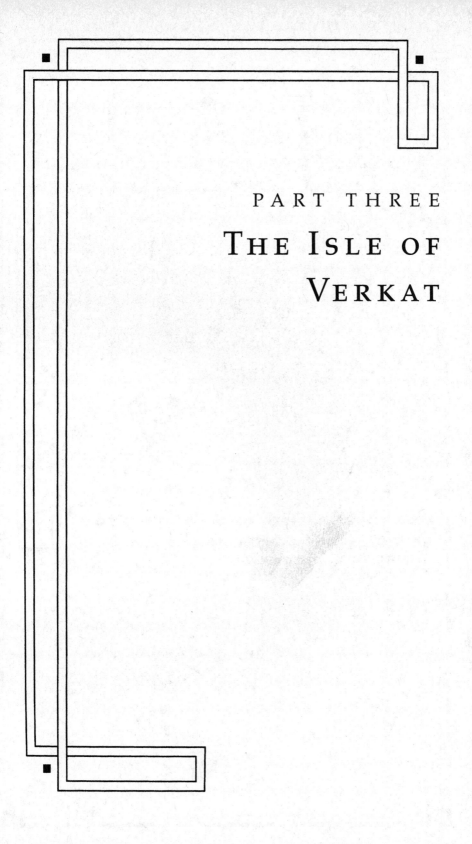

PART THREE

THE ISLE OF VERKAT

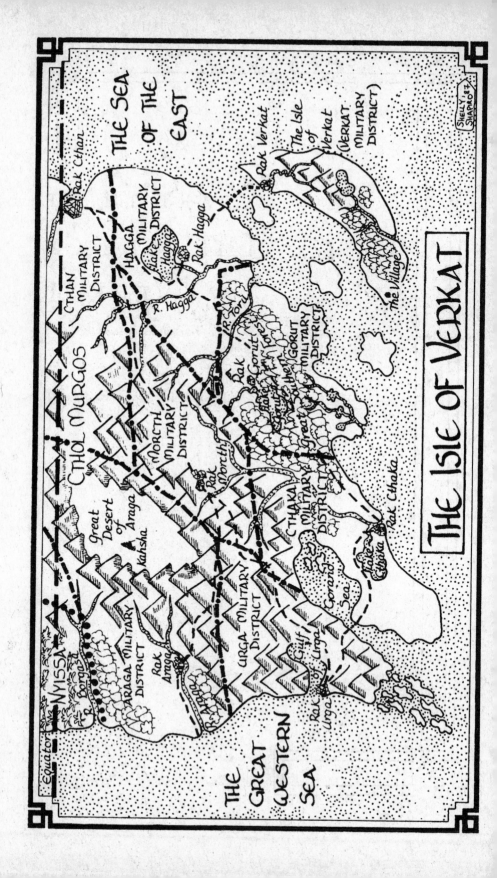

The Isle of Verkat

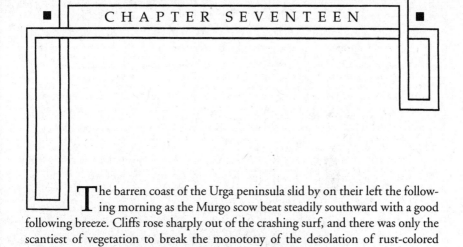

The barren coast of the Urga peninsula slid by on their left the following morning as the Murgo scow beat steadily southward with a good
following breeze. Cliffs rose sharply out of the crashing surf, and there was only the
scantiest of vegetation to break the monotony of the desolation of rust-colored
rock. The autumn sky was a deep, chill blue, but the sun stood far to the north, for
winter came early to these extreme southern latitudes.

Garion, as he always did when he was at sea, had risen at first light of day and
gone up on deck. He stood at the rail amidships, half-bemused by the sparkle of
the morning sun on the waves and by the steady creak and roll of the vessel under
his feet.

The slanting door that opened onto the short flight of steps leading down to
the aft companionway creaked, and Durnik came out on deck, bracing himself
against the awkward roll of the ship and squinting in the bright sunlight. The smith
wore his usual plain brown tunic, and his face was somber.

Garion crossed the deck to his friend's side. "Is she all right?" he asked.

"She's very tired," Durnik replied wearily. His own nearly exhausted face
clearly showed that he had slept very little himself. "She tossed and fretted for a long
time before she finally went to sleep last night. That was a terrible thing she had
to do."

"Did she talk to you about it at all?"

"Some. The demon had to be sent back to where he came from. Otherwise he'd
have spread horror and death across the whole world. Since Chabat summoned
him, he could have used her as a doorway to come into this world any time he
wanted to. That's why Chabat had to go with him—to close that doorway."

"Exactly where do they come from—demons, I mean?"

"She didn't say very much about that, but I got the feeling that I wouldn't
really want to know about it."

"Is she sleeping now?"

Durnik nodded. "I'm going to go talk with the ship's cook. I want to have
something hot for her to eat when she wakes up."

"You'd better get some sleep yourself."

"Perhaps. Would you excuse me, Garion? I don't want to stay away too long—
just in case she wakes up and needs me." He went on forward toward the ship's
galley.

Garion straightened and looked around. The Murgo sailors worked with fearful looks on their faces. What had taken place the previous afternoon had washed

away all traces of the stiff arrogance that usually marked a Murgo's expression, and they all cast frightened, sidelong glances at every one of their passengers, as if expecting them to turn into ogres or sea monsters without any warning.

Silk and Urgit had emerged from the companionway door while Garion and Durnik had been talking and stood at the rail near the stern, idly watching the bubbly wake tracing its path across the dark green swells and the white-winged gulls screeching and hovering in a greedy cloud behind them. Garion moved a bit closer, but did not actually join them.

"Uninviting sort of place," Silk observed, looking at the stark cliffs rising from the sea. The little man had discarded the shabby clothing he had worn when they had begun this journey and he now wore a plain, unadorned gray doublet.

Urgit grunted morosely. Idly, he tossed chunks of stale bread into their wake, watching without much interest as the squawking gulls trailing the ship swooped down to fight over them. "Kheldar," he said, "does she do that all the time?"

"Who's that?"

"Polgara." Urgit shuddered. "Does she obliterate everybody who displeases her?"

"No," Silk replied. "Polgara doesn't do that—none of them do. It's not allowed."

"I'm sorry, Kheldar. Allowed or not, I know what I saw yesterday."

"I talked to Belgarath about it," Silk told him, "and he explained it. Chabat and the demon weren't actually destroyed. They were just sent back to the place where the demon came from. The demon absolutely had to be sent back; unfortunately, Chabat had to go with him."

"Unfortunately? I didn't feel all that much sympathy for her."

"I don't think you quite understand, Urgit. Killing somebody is one thing, but destroying someone's soul is quite something else. That's what made Polgara miserable. She was forced to condemn Chabat to eternal pain and horror. That's the most terrible thing anybody can be forced to do."

"Who was that who came up out of the water with her?"

"Aldur."

"You're not serious!"

"Oh, yes. I've seen him once or twice. It was Aldur, all right."

"A God? Here? What was he doing?"

"He had to be here." Silk shrugged. "No human, however powerful, can face a demon unaided. When the magicians of the Morindim raise a demon, they always are very careful to set rigid limits on him. Chabat just unleashed hers without any limits at all. Only a God can deal with a demon with that kind of freedom; and since the Gods work through us, Polgara had to be involved as well. It was a very tricky business."

Urgit shuddered. "I don't think I'm going to be able to deal with this."

They stood side by side, leaning on the rail and looking out at the long waves rolling in off the Great Western Sea to crash against the barren cliffs. As Garion looked at the two of them, he wondered how it had been possible for anyone to miss the relationship. Although they were not exactly identical, their features were so much alike that there could be no doubt they were brothers.

"Kheldar," Urgit said finally, "what was our father really like?"

"He was taller than either of us," Silk replied, "and very distinguished-looking. His hair was sort of iron-gray, and this nose we've all got made him look more like an eagle than a rat."

"We do look a bit like rodents, don't we?" Urgit agreed with a brief smile. "That's not what I meant, though. What was he really like?"

"Polished. He had exquisite manners, and he was very civilized and urbane. I never heard him use a harsh word to anyone." Silk's face was melancholy.

"But he was deceitful, wasn't he?"

"What makes you say that?"

"He did cheat, after all. I'm not the product of any sort of lasting fidelity."

"You don't exactly understand," Silk disagreed. He looked thoughtfully out at the green swells topped by an occasional whitecap. "For all his polish, our father was very much an adventurer. He'd accept any challenge—just for the fun involved—and he had an insatiable wanderlust. He was always looking for something new. I think that when you put the two of those traits together, you might begin to understand exactly why he was attracted to your mother. I visited the palace in Rak Goska when Taur Urgas was still alive. His wives were all either closely guarded or kept under lock and key. It was the sort of thing our father would have viewed as a challenge."

Urgit made a sour face. "You aren't bolstering my ego very much, Kheldar. I'm here because a Drasnian gentleman liked to pick locks."

"Not entirely. I didn't have much chance to talk with your mother about it, but I gather that she and our father were genuinely fond of each other. Taur Urgas was never fond of anyone. At least our father and your mother were having fun."

"Maybe that explains my sunny disposition."

Silk sighed. "He didn't have too much fun after my mother's illness, though. That put an end to all the wandering and adventures."

"What kind of illness was it?"

"A pestilence that breaks out in Drasnia from time to time. It disfigures its victims horribly. My mother was blinded by its effects, fortunately."

"Fortunately?"

"She couldn't look into a mirror. Our father stayed by her side for the rest of his life and never once gave any hint about what he saw whenever he looked at her." Silk's face was bleak, and his jaws were tightly clenched together. "It was the bravest thing I've ever seen any man do—and it was all the worse because it went on and on and on until the day he died." He looked away quickly. "Do you suppose we could talk about something else?"

"I'm sorry, Kheldar," Urgit said sympathetically. "I didn't mean to open old wounds."

"What was it like growing up in Rak Goska?" Silk asked after a moment.

"Grim," Urgit replied. "Taur Urgas had begun to show signs of his madness much earlier than was usual in the Urga family, and there were all kinds of rituals we had to observe."

"I've seen some of them."

"Not just the ones in the Temple, Kheldar—although there were plenty of those as well. I'm talking about his personal peculiarities. No one was ever supposed to stand to his right, and it was worth a man's life to let his shadow fall on the royal person. My brothers and I were taken from our mothers at the age of seven and set to training—military exercises for the most part—involving a great deal of grunting and sweating. Lapses of any kind were punished with flogging—usually at the supper table."

"That might tend to cool one's appetite."

"It does indeed. I don't even eat supper any more—too many unpleasant memories. My brothers and I all started plotting against each other very early. Taur Urgas had many wives and whole platoons of children. Since the crown falls to the eldest surviving son, we all schemed against our older brothers and tried to protect ourselves against the plots of the younger ones. One charming little fellow ran a knife into one of the others when he was nine."

"Precocious," Silk murmured.

"Oh, he was indeed. Taur Urgas was delighted, of course. For a time, the little back stabber was his favorite. That made me and my older brothers quite nervous, since it was entirely possible that our insane sire might have seen fit to have us all strangled to make room for the little monster, so we took steps."

"Oh?"

"We caught him alone in the upper floors of the palace one day and threw him out a window." Urgit looked somberly out over the long swells sweeping in off the Great Western Sea. "From the day we were taken from our mothers, we lived a life of constant fear and senseless brutality. We were supposed to be perfect Murgos—strong, brave, insanely loyal, and absolutely dedicated to Torak. Each of us had a Grolim for a tutor, and we had to listen to hours of gibberish about the God of Angarak every day. It wasn't what you might call a pleasant childhood."

"Taur Urgas never showed any kind of affection?"

"Not to me, he didn't. I was always the smallest, and he had a great deal of contempt for me. Murgos are supposed to be big and muscular. Even after I'd managed to work my way up to the point where I was heir apparent, he never had a civil word for me and he encouraged my younger brothers to try to murder me."

"How did you manage to survive?"

"By my wits—and by using a key I managed to steal."

"A key?"

"To the palace strong room. You'd be amazed at how much help a man with unlimited funds at his command can get—even in Cthol Murgos."

Silk shivered. "It's getting definitely chilly out here on deck," he said. "Why don't we go inside and share a flagon of spiced wine?"

"I don't drink, Kheldar."

"You don't?" Silk sounded amazed.

"I need to keep my wits about me. A man with his head stuck in a wine barrel can't see someone creeping up behind him with a knife, can he?"

"You're quite safe with me, brother."

"I'm not safe with anyone, Kheldar—particularly not with a brother. Nothing personal, you understand—just the result of a very nervous childhood."

"All right," Silk said amiably. "Let's go inside, and you can watch *me* drink. I'm very good at it."

"I can imagine. You're an Alorn, after all."

"So are you, dear brother." Silk laughed. "So are you. Come along, and I'll introduce you to all the fun that goes with your heritage."

Garion was on the verge of turning to follow them, but at that moment Belgarath came out on deck, stretching and yawning. "Is Pol up yet?" he asked Garion.

Garion shook his head. "I talked with Durnik a little while ago. He said that she's very tired after what she did yesterday."

Belgarath frowned slightly. "It really shouldn't have tired her all that much," he said. "It was spectacular, I'll admit, but hardly exhausting."

"I don't think it's that kind of exhaustion, Grandfather. Durnik said she was troubled for about half the night."

The old man scratched at his beard. "Oh," he said, "sometimes I lose sight of the fact that Pol's a woman. She can't seem to put things behind her, and sometimes her compassion gets the better of her."

"That's not necessarily a bad trait, Grandfather."

"Not for a woman, perhaps."

"I seem to remember something that happened in the fens once," Garion told him. "Didn't you sort of go out of your way to do something for Vordai—more or less out of compassion?"

Belgarath looked around guiltily. "I thought we agreed that you weren't going to mention that."

"You know something, Grandfather?" Garion said with a faint smile. "You're a fraud. You pretend to be as cold as ice and as hard as a rock, but underneath you've got the same emotions as all the rest of us."

"Please, Garion, don't bandy that about too much."

"Does it bother you being human?"

"Well, not really, but after all, I do sort of have a reputation to maintain."

By late afternoon the coastline they had been following had grown even more jagged, and the surf boiled and thundered against the rocks. Silk and Urgit came up out of the aft companionway, and Garion noted that both were a trifle unsteady as they walked.

"Hello there, Belgarion," Urgit said expansively. "How would you like to join us? Kheldar and I have decided that we'd like to sing for a bit."

"Uh—thanks all the same," Garion replied carefully, "but I don't sing very well."

"That doesn't matter, old boy. It doesn't matter in the slightest. I might not be very good at it myself. I can't say for sure, because I've never sung a note in my whole life." He giggled suddenly. "There are a lot of things I've never done before, and I think it might be time I tried a few."

Ce'Nedra and the Murgo girl, Prala, came up on deck. Instead of her customary black, Prala was dressed in a stunning gown of pale rose, and her jet-black hair was caught in an intricate coil at the nape of her neck.

"My ladies," Urgit greeted them with a formal bow, marred only slightly by an unsteady lurch.

"Careful, old boy," Silk said, catching him by the elbow. "I don't want to have to fish you out of the sea."

"You know something, Kheldar?" Urgit said, blinking owlishly. "I don't think I've ever felt quite this good." He looked at Ce'Nedra and the dark-haired Prala. "You know something else? Those are a couple of awfully pretty girls there. Do you think they might like to sing with us?"

"We could ask them."

"Why don't we?"

The pair of them descended on Ce'Nedra and her Murgo companion, imploring them outrageously to join them in song. Prala laughed as the Murgo King lurched forward and back with the roll of the ship. "I think you two are drunk," she declared.

"Are we drunk?" Urgit asked Silk, still swaying on his feet.

"I certainly hope so," Silk replied. "If we aren't, we've wasted a great deal of very good wine."

"I guess we're drunk then. Now that's been settled, what shall we sing?"

"Alorns!" Ce'Nedra sighed, rolling her eyes skyward.

It was raining the following morning when they awoke, a chill drizzle that hissed into the sea and collected to run in heavy droplets down the tarred ropes of the rigging. Polgara joined them for breakfast in the larger cabin at the extreme aft end of the companionway, though she seemed silent and withdrawn.

Velvet looked brightly around the cabin, where stoutly constructed windows instead of portholes stretched across the stern and heavy beams held up a ceiling which was actually the deck above. She looked pointedly at the two conspicuously empty chairs at the breakfast table. "What's become of Prince Kheldar and his wayward royal brother?" she asked.

"I think they lingered a bit too long over their wine cups yesterday," Ce'Nedra replied with a slightly malicious smirk. "I'd imagine that they're feeling just a bit delicate this morning."

"Would you believe that they were singing?" Prala said.

"Oh?" Velvet said. "Were they doing it well?"

Prala laughed. "They frightened away the seagulls. I've never heard such dreadful noise."

Polgara and Durnik had been talking quietly at the far end of the table. "I'm perfectly fine, Durnik," she assured him. "You go right ahead."

"I don't want to leave you alone, Pol," he told her.

"I won't be alone, dear. Ce'Nedra, Prala, and Liselle will all be with me. If you don't find out for yourself, you'll wonder about it for the rest of your life and always regret the fact that you passed the opportunity by."

"Well—if you're sure, Pol."

"I'm certain, dear," she said, laying her hand fondly on his and kissing his cheek.

After breakfast, Garion pulled on a cloak and went out on deck. He stood squinting up into the drizzle for a few minutes, then turned as he heard the companionway door open behind him. Durnik and Toth emerged with fishing poles in their hands. "It only stands to reason, Toth," Durnik was saying. "With that much water, there almost have to be fish."

Toth nodded, then made a peculiar gesture, extending both his arms out as if measuring something.

"I don't quite follow you."

Toth made the gesture again.

"Oh, I'm sure they wouldn't be all that big," the smith disagreed. "Fish don't get that big, do they?"

Toth nodded vigorously.

"I don't mean to doubt you," Durnik said seriously, "but I'd have to see that."

Toth shrugged.

"Quite a beautiful morning, isn't it, Garion?" Durnik said, smiling up at the dripping sky. Then he went up the three steps to the aft deck, nodded pleasantly to the steersman at the tiller, and then made a long, smooth cast out into the frothy wake. He looked critically at his trailing lure. "I think we're going to need some weight on the lines to hold them down, don't you?" he said to Toth.

The giant smiled slightly, then nodded his agreement.

"Have Silk and Urgit managed to get up yet?" Garion called to them.

"Hmm?" Durnik replied, his eyes fixed intently on his brightly colored lure bobbing far back in their wake.

"I said, are Silk and his brother up yet?"

"Oh—yes, I think I heard them stirring around in their cabin. Toth, we're definitely going to need something to weight down the lines."

Belgarath came up on deck just then, with his shabby old cloak pulled tightly around his shoulders. He looked sourly out through the drizzle at the half-concealed coast sliding by to port and went forward to stand amidships.

Garion joined him there. "How long do you think it's going to take us to get to Verkat, Grandfather?" he asked.

"A couple of weeks," the old man replied, "if this weather doesn't get any worse. We're a long way south and we're coming up on the stormy season."

"There's a faster way, though, isn't there?" Garion suggested.

"I don't quite follow you."

"You remember how we got from Jarviksholm to Riva? Couldn't you and I do it that way? The others could catch up later."

"I don't think we're supposed to. I think the others are supposed to be with us when we catch up with Zandramas."

Garion suddenly banged his fist on the rail in frustration. "Supposed to!" he burst out. "I don't care about what we're *supposed* to do. I want my son back. I'm tired of creeping around trying to satisfy all the clever little twists and turns of the Prophecy. What's wrong with just ignoring it and going right straight to the point?"

Belgarath's face was calm as he looked out at the rust-colored cliffs half-hidden in the gray drizzle. "I've tried that a few times myself," he admitted, "but it never worked—and usually it put me even further behind. I know you're impatient, Garion, and sometimes it's hard to accept the idea that following the Prophecy is really the fastest way to get where you want to go, but that's the way it always seems to work out." He put his hand on Garion's shoulder. "It's sort of like digging a well. The water's at the bottom, but you have to start at the top. I don't think anybody's ever had much luck digging a well from the bottom up."

"What's that got to do with it, Grandfather? I don't see any connection at all."

"Maybe you will if you think about it for a while."

Durnik came running forward. His eyes were wide in stunned amazement, and his hands were shaking.

"What's wrong?" Belgarath asked him.

"That was the biggest fish I've ever seen in my life!" the smith exclaimed. "He was as big as a horse!"

"He got away, I take it."

"Snapped my line on the second jump." Durnik's voice had a peculiar pride in it, and his eyes grew very bright. "He was beautiful, Belgarath. He came up out of the water as if he'd just been shot out of a catapult and he actually walked across the waves on his tail. What a tremendous fish!"

"What are you going to do?"

"I'm going to catch him, of course—but I'm going to need a stouter line— maybe even a rope. What a fish! Excuse me." He hurried toward the bow to talk to the Murgo ship captain about some rope.

Belgarath smiled. "I love that man, Garion," he said. "I really love him."

The door to the aft companionway opened again, and Silk and his brother emerged. Although Garion was usually the first one on deck, he had noticed that, sooner or later during the course of any day, everyone came out to take a turn or two in the bracing salt air.

The two weasel-faced men came forward along the rain-slick deck. Neither of them looked particularly well. "Are we making any headway?" Silk asked. His face was pale, and his hands were trembling noticeably.

"Some," Belgarath grunted. "You two slept late this morning."

"I think we should have slept longer," Urgit replied with a mournful look. "I seem to have this small headache—in my left eye." He was sweating profusely, and there was a faint greenish cast to his skin. "I feel absolutely dreadful," he declared. "Why didn't you warn me about this, Kheldar?"

"I wanted to surprise you."

"Is it always like this the next morning?"

"Usually," Silk admitted. "Sometimes it's worse."

"Worse? How could it possibly get any worse? Excuse me." Urgit hurried to the rail and leaned over it, retching noisily.

"He's not handling this too well, is he?" Belgarath noted clinically.

"Inexperience," Silk explained.

"I honestly believe I'm going to die," Urgit said weakly, wiping at his mouth with a shaking hand. "Why did you let me drink so much?"

"That's a decision a man has to make for himself," Silk told him.

"You seemed to be having a good time," Garion added.

"I really wouldn't know. I've lost track of several hours. What did I do?"

"You were singing."

"Singing? Me?" Urgit sank onto a bench and dropped his face into his trembling hands. "Oh dear," he moaned. "Oh dear, oh dear, oh dear."

Prala came out of the aft door wearing a black coat and a smug little smile. She carried a pair of tankards forward through the drizzle to the two suffering men. "Good morning, my Lords," she said brightly with a little curtsey. "Lady Polgara says that you're to drink this."

"What's in it?" Urgit asked suspiciously.

"I'm not sure, your Majesty. She and the Nyissan mixed it up."

"Maybe it's poison," he said hopefully. "I would sort of like to die quickly and get it over with." He seized a tankard and gulped it down noisily. Then he shuddered, and his face went deathly pale. His expression was one of sheer horror, and he began to shake violently. "That's terrible!" he gasped.

Silk watched him closely for a moment, then took the other tankard and carefully dumped it out over the side.

"Aren't you going to drink yours?" Urgit asked accusingly.

"I don't think so. Polgara has a peculiar sense of humor sometimes. I'd rather not take any chances—until I see how many fish come floating to the top."

"How are you feeling this morning, your Majesty?" Prala asked the suffering Urgit with a feigned look of sympathy on her face.

"I'm sick."

"It's your own fault, you know."

"Please don't."

She smiled sweetly at him.

"You're enjoying this, aren't you?" he accused.

"Why, yes, your Majesty," she replied with a little toss of her head, "As a matter of fact, I am." Then she took the two tankards and went back along the rail toward the stern.

"Are they all like that?" Urgit asked miserably. "So cruel?"

"Women?" Belgarath shrugged. "Of course. It's in their blood."

Somewhat later that gloomy morning, after Silk and Belgarath had returned aft to seek refuge from the weather in one of the cabins and also, Garion suspected, for a touch of something to ward off the chill, Urgit sat miserably on a rain-wet bench with his head in his hands while Garion moodily paced the deck not far away. "Belgarion," the Murgo King said plaintively, "do you have to stamp your feet so hard?"

Garion gave him a quick, amused smile. "Silk really should have warned you about this," he said.

"Why do people call him Silk?"

"It's a nickname he picked up from his colleagues in Drasnian Intelligence."

"Why would a member of the Drasnian royal family want to be a spy?"

"It's their national industry."

"Is he really any good at it?"

"He's just about the best there is."

Urgit's face had definitely grown green. "This is dreadful," he groaned. "I can't be sure if it's the drink or seasickness. I wonder if I'd feel better if I stuck my head in a bucket of water."

"Only if you held it down long enough."

"That's a thought." Urgit laid his head back on the rail to let the rain drizzle into his face. "Belgarion," he said finally, "what am I doing wrong?"

"You drank a little too much."

"That's not what I'm talking about. Where am I making my mistakes—as a king, I mean?"

Garion looked at him. The little man was obviously sincere, and the sympathy for him which had welled up back in Rak Urga rose again. Garion finally admitted to himself that he liked this man. He drew in a deep breath and sat down beside the suffering Urgit. "You know part of it already," he said. "You let people bully you."

"It's because I'm afraid, Belgarion. When I was a boy, I let them bully me because it kept them from killing me. I guess it just got to be a habit."

"Everybody's afraid."

"You aren't. You faced Torak at Cthol Mishrak, didn't you?"

"It wasn't altogether my idea—and believe me, you can't even begin to guess how frightened I was when I was on my way there for that meeting."

"You?"

"Oh, yes. You're beginning to get some control over that problem, though. You handled that general—Kradak, wasn't it?—fairly well back at the Drojim. Just keep remembering that you're the king, and that you're the one who gives the orders."

"I can try, I guess. What else am I doing wrong?"

Garion thought about it. "You're trying to do it all yourself," he replied finally. "Nobody can do that. There are just too many details for one man to keep up with. You need help—good, honest help."

"Where am I going to find good help in Cthol Murgos? Whom can I trust?"

"You trust Oskatat, don't you?"

"Well, yes, I suppose so."

"That's a start, then. You see, Urgit, what's happening is that you've got people in Rak Urga who are making decisions that you should be making. They're taking it upon themselves to do that because you've been too afraid or too busy with other things to assert your authority."

"You're being inconsistent, Belgarion. First you say that I should get some people to help me, then you turn around and tell me that I shouldn't let other people make my decisions."

"You weren't listening. The people who are making your decisions for you aren't the people you might have chosen. They've just stepped in on their own. In a lot of cases, you probably don't even know who they are. That simply won't work. You have to choose your people rather carefully. Their first qualification has to be ability. Right behind that comes personal loyalty to you—and to your mother."

"Nobody's loyal to me, Belgarion. My subjects despise me."

"You might be surprised. I don't think there's any question about Oskatat's loyalty—or his ability. That's probably a good place to start. Let him pick your administrators. They'll start out by being loyal to him, but in time they'll come to respect you as well."

"I hadn't even considered that. Do you think it might work?"

"It won't hurt to try. To be perfectly honest with you, my friend, you've made a mess of things. It's going to take you a while to straighten them out, but you've got to start somewhere."

"You've given me quite a bit to think about, Belgarion." Urgit shivered and looked around. "It's really miserable out here," he said. "Where did Kheldar go?"

"Back inside. I think he's trying to get well."

"You mean that there's actually something that will cure this?"

"Some Alorns recommend some more of what made you sick in the first place."

Urgit's face went pale. "More?" he said in a horrified voice. "How can they?"

"Alorns are notoriously brave people."

Urgit's eyes grew suspicious. "Wait a minute," he said. "Wouldn't that just make me feel exactly the same way tomorrow morning?"

"Probably, yes. That could explain why Alorns are usually so foul-tempered when they first get up."

"That's stupid, Belgarion."

"I know. Murgos don't have an absolute monopoly on stupidity." Garion looked at the shivering man. "I think you'd better go inside, Urgit," he advised. "You don't want a chill on top of all your other problems."

The rain let up by late afternoon. The Murgo captain looked up at the still-threatening sky and then at the cliffs and the jagged reefs jutting out of the turbulent water and prudently ordered his crew to lower the sails and drop the anchor.

Durnik and Toth rather regretfully rolled up their stout fishing lines and stood looking proudly at the dozen or so gleaming silver fish lying on the deck at their feet.

Garion drifted back to where they stood and looked admiringly at their catch. "Not bad," he said.

Durnik carefully measured the biggest fish with his hands. "About three feet," he said, "but they're minnows compared to the big one that got away."

"It always seems to work out that way," Garion said. "Oh," he added, "one thing, Durnik. I'd clean them before I showed them to Aunt Pol. You know how she feels about that."

Durnik sighed. "You're probably right," he agreed.

That evening, after they had all dined on some of the catch, they sat around the table in the aft cabin conversing idly.

"Do you think Agachak's caught up with Harakan yet?" Durnik asked Belgarath.

"I sort of doubt it," the old man replied. "Harakan's tricky. If Beldin couldn't catch him, I don't think Agachak's going to have much luck either."

"Lady Polgara," Sadi suddenly protested in a tone of outrage, "make her stop that."

"What's that, Sadi?"

"The Margravine Liselle. She's subverting my snake."

Velvet, with a mysterious little smile on her face, was delicately feeding Zith fish eggs taken from one of the large fish Durnik and Toth had caught. The little green snake was purring contentedly and was half-raised in anticipation of the next morsel.

CHAPTER EIGHTEEN

The wind came up during the night, a raw, gusty wind, smelling strongly of dusty old ice, and the drizzle which had fallen for most of the previous day turned to sleet that rattled in the rigging and clattered on the deck like hand-fuls of pebbles. As usual, Garion rose early and tiptoed on unshod feet from the tiny cabin he shared with his sleeping wife. He made his way down the dark companion-way past the doors to the cabins where the others slept and entered the aft cabin. He stood for a time at the windows running across the stern of the ship, looking out at the wind-tossed waves and listening to the slow creak of the tiller post running down through the center of the cabin to the rudder that probed the dark water be-neath the stern.

As he sat down to put on his boots, the door opened and Durnik came in, brushing the ice pellets of the sleet squall chattering on the decks from the folds of his cloak. "It's going to be slow going for a while, I'm afraid," he said to Garion. "The wind's swung around and it's coming directly up out of the south. We're run-ning right straight into it. The sailors are breaking out the oars."

"Could you get any idea of how far it is to the tip of the peninsula?" Garion asked, standing up and stamping his feet to settle his boots into place.

"I talked with the captain a bit. From what he said, it's only a few leagues. There's a cluster of islands that runs off the south end of it, though, and he wants to let this blow over before he tries to thread his way through the passage. He's not much of a sailor, and this isn't much of a boat, so I guess he's a little timid."

Garion leaned forward, put his hands on the sill of one of the stern windows and looked out again at the stormy sea. "This could blow for a week," he observed. He turned to look at his friend. "Has our captain recovered his composure at all?" he asked. "He was a little wild-eyed when we sailed out of Rak Urga."

Durnik smiled. "I think he's been talking to himself very hard. He's trying to convince himself that he didn't really see what happened back there. He still tends to cringe a lot when Pol goes out on deck, though."

"Good. Is she awake?"

Durnik nodded. "I fixed her morning tea for her before I went out on deck."

"How do you think she'd react if I asked her to bully the captain for me—just a little bit?"

"I don't know that I'd use the word 'bully,' Garion," Durnik advised seriously. "Try 'talk to' or 'persuade' instead. Pol doesn't really think of what she does as bul-lying."

"It is, though."

"Of course, but she doesn't think of it that way."

"Let's go see her."

The cabin Polgara shared with Durnik was as tiny and cramped as all the rest aboard this ungainly vessel. Two-thirds of the space inside was given over to the high-railed bed, built of planks and seeming to grow out of the bulkheads themselves. Polgara sat in the center of the bed in her favorite blue dressing gown, holding a cup of tea and gazing out the porthole at the sleet-spattered waves.

"Good morning, Aunt Pol," Garion greeted her.

"Good morning, dear. How nice of you to visit."

"Are you all right, now?" he asked. "What I mean is, I understand that you were quite upset about what happened back at the harbor."

She sighed. "I think the worst part was that I had no choice in the matter. Once Chabat raised the demon, she was doomed—but I was the one who had to destroy her soul." Her expression was somber with a peculiar overtone of a deep and abiding regret. "Could we talk about something else?" she asked.

"All right. Would you like to speak to someone for me?"

"Who's that?"

"The ship's captain. He wants to drop his anchor until this weather clears, and I'd rather not wait."

"Why don't you talk with him yourself, Garion?"

"Because people tend to listen to you more attentively than they do me. Could you do it, Aunt Pol—talk to him, I mean?"

"You want me to bully him."

"I wouldn't exactly say 'bully,' Aunt Pol," he protested.

"But that's what you mean, Garion. Always say what you mean."

"Will you?"

"All right, if you want me to. Now, will you do something for me?"

"Anything, Aunt Pol."

She held out her cup. "Do you suppose you could fix me another cup of tea?"

After breakfast, Polgara put on her blue cloak and went out on deck. The Murgo captain changed his plans almost as soon as she began to speak to him. Then he climbed the mainmast and spent the rest of the morning with the lookout in the wildly swaying crow's nest high aloft.

At the southern tip of the Urga peninsula, the steersman swung his tiller over, and the ship heeled sharply to port. It was not hard to understand why the captain had originally wanted to avoid the passage through the islands in anything remotely resembling rough weather. The currents and tides swirled through the narrow channels, the wind tore the tops of the dark-rolling waves to tatters, and the surf boomed and crashed on the knife-edged rocks rearing up out of the sea. The Murgo sailors rowed fearfully, casting wild-eyed looks at the looming cliffs on all sides of them. After the first league or so, the captain clambered down the mast to stand tensely beside the steersman as the ship cautiously crawled through the gale-lashed islands.

It was midafternoon when they finally passed the last of the rocky islets, and the sailors began to row away from the land toward open water where the wind-driven sleet sizzled into the whitecaps.

Belgarath and Garion, with their cloaks pulled tightly about them, stood on the deck watching the oarsmen for a few minutes; then the old man went to the companionway door. "Urgit!" he shouted down the narrow hall, "come out here!"

The Murgo King stumbled up the stairs out onto the deck, his eyes fearful.

"Don't your people know how to set their rigging so that they can quarter into the wind?" Belgarath demanded.

Urgit looked at him blankly. "I have absolutely no idea what you're talking about," he said.

"Durnik!" Belgarath shouted.

The smith, standing with Toth at the stern of the ship, was intently watching his trailing lure and did not answer.

"Durnik!"

"Hmmm?"

"We have to reset the rigging. Come and show the captain how it's done."

"In a minute."

"Now, Durnik!"

The smith sighed and began to coil up his line. The fish struck without warning, and Durnik's excited whoop was whipped away by the rising wind. He seized the line and jerked hard to set his hook. The great, silver-sided fish came boiling up out of the water, shaking his head angrily and threshing his way across the wind-driven chop. Durnik's shoulders bowed as he pulled hard on his line, struggling manfully to haul the huge fish in hand over hand.

Belgarath started to swear.

"I'll show the captain how to set his rigging, Grandfather," Garion said.

"How much do you know about it?"

"I've been on at least as many ships as Durnik has. I know how it's done." He went toward the bow to talk to the Murgo captain who now stood staring ahead at the tossing sea. "You want to slack off your lines on this side over here," Garion explained to him, "and draw them in on the other. The idea is to angle your sails so that they catch the wind. Then you put your rudder over to compensate."

"Nobody's ever done it that way before," the captain declared stubbornly.

"The Alorns do, and they're the best sailors in the world."

"The Alorns control the wind by sorcery. You can't use your sails unless the wind is behind you."

"Just try it, Captain," Garion said patiently. He looked at the heavy-shouldered sailor and saw that he was wasting his time. "If you'd rather not do it because I ask you to," he added, "I could probably persuade Lady Polgara to ask you—as a personal favor."

The captain stared at him. Then he swallowed hard. "How was it you said you wanted the rigging reset, my Lord?" he asked in a much milder tone.

It took perhaps a quarter of an hour to set the lines to Garion's satisfaction. Then, with the dubious captain in tow, he went aft and took the tiller from the steersman. "All right," he said, "raise the sails."

"It's not going to work," the captain predicted under his breath. Then he lifted his voice to a bellow. "Hoist the sails!"

The pulleys began to creak, and the sails, flapping in the wind, crawled up the masts. Then they boomed and bellied out, angled sharply to catch the wind. Garion pulled the tiller over as the ship heeled sharply to leeward. The prow knifed sharply through the heaving waves.

The Murgo captain gaped up at his sails. "I don't believe it!" he exclaimed. "Nobody's ever done that before."

"You see how it works now, don't you?" Garion asked him.

"Of course. It's so simple that I can't understand why I didn't think of it myself."

Garion had an answer, but he decided to keep it to himself. The captain had already had a bad enough day. He turned to the steersman. "You have to keep your tiller over like this to compensate for the force of the wind coming in on your starboard beam," he explained.

"I understand, my Lord."

Garion relinquished the tiller and stepped back to watch Durnik and Toth. They were still hauling at their line, and the great fish, no longer dancing on the sleet-swept surface, swept back and forth in long arcs across the boiling wake; the stout rope connecting his jaw to the two fishermen sizzled through the water as if it were hot.

"Nice fish," Garion called to the struggling pair.

Durnik's quick answering grin was like the sun coming up.

They quartered into an increasingly stiff wind for the remainder of the day. As the light began to fade, they were far from land. Garion was by now certain that the captain and the steersman could manage and he went forward to join the little group standing amidships around Durnik's huge fish.

"Now that you've got him, where are you going to find a pan big enough to cook him in?" Silk was asking the smith.

A brief frown crossed Durnik's face, but then he smiled again. "Pol will know how to take care of it," he said and went back to admiring the monster lying on the deck. "Pol knows how to take care of everything."

The sleet had abated, and the dark-rolling waves stretched sullenly to the faintly luminous line of the horizon that divided the black waves from an even blacker sky. The Murgo captain came forward in the windy twilight with a worried look on his face. Respectfully, he touched Urgit's sleeve.

"Yes, Captain?"

"I'm afraid there's trouble, your Majesty."

"What kind of trouble?"

The captain pointed toward the line of the southern horizon. A half-dozen ships were running before the wind, coming directly toward them.

Urgit's face grew slightly sick. "Malloreans?"

The captain nodded.

"Do you think they've seen us?"

"Almost certainly, your Majesty."

"We'd better go talk to Belgarath," Silk said. "I don't think any of us counted on this."

The conference in the aft cabin was tense. "They're making much better time than we are, Grandfather," Garion said. "We're quartering the wind, and they're running with it dead astern. I think we're going to have to turn north—at least until we can get out of their sight."

The old man was staring at a tattered map the captain had brought with him. He shook his head. "I don't like it," he said. "This gulf we're in right now funnels into the mouth of the Gorand Sea, and I don't want to get trapped in there." He turned to Silk. "You've been to Mallorea a few times. How good are their ships?"

Silk shrugged. "About the same as this one. I'm not trying to be offensive, Captain, but Angaraks aren't the same kind of sailors—or shipbuilders—that Chereks are." He considered it. "There might be a way to escape them," he said. "Malloreans are timid sailors, so they won't spread all sail at night. If we turned north and put up every ounce of canvas we can, we could be a long way ahead of them—no more than a blinking light on the horizon once it gets dark. Then we drop the sails, reset the rigging, and put out every light on board ship."

"But we can't do that," the captain objected. "It's against the law."

"I'll write you an excuse, Captain," Urgit said drily.

"It's too dangerous, your Majesty. If we run without lights, we could collide with another ship out there in the dark. We could be sunk."

"Captain," Urgit said in a patient tone, "there are six Mallorean ships chasing us. What do you imagine they're going to do if they catch up with us?"

"They'll sink us, of course."

"What difference does it make, then? At least if we put out the lights, we'll have a chance. Go ahead, Kheldar."

Silk shrugged. "There isn't much more. After we blow out the running lights, we hoist sail and run east again. The Malloreans won't be able to see us, and they'll charge right on across our wake. By tomorrow morning, they won't have any idea about where we are."

"It might just work," Belgarath conceded.

"It's dangerous," the captain said disapprovingly.

"Sometimes even breathing is dangerous, Captain," Urgit told him. "Let's try it and see what happens. What I can't understand, though, is what Mallorean ships are doing this far west."

"It's possible that they're marauders sent to harry the coastlines," Sadi suggested.

"Perhaps," Urgit said dubiously.

They ran due north before the rising wind that swept up from the south polar icecap. The deck lanterns swung and bobbed in the wind, peopling the storm-whipped rigging with wildly dancing shadows. The six Mallorean vessels, running cautiously under half sail, dropped behind until their running lights looked no larger than tiny twinkling stars on the horizon far astern. Then, about midnight, the captain gave the order to drop the sails. The sailors quickly reset the rigging and the ship's master came aft to where Garion stood beside the steersman. "Everything's ready, my Lord," he reported.

"All right then. Let's blow out all the lights and see if we can sneak out of here."

The Murgo's stiff face creased uncertainly into a rueful grin. "When we get out of this—if we get out of it—I think I'll take to my bed for a month," he said. He raised his voice to a shout. "Extinguish all the deck lights!" he commanded.

The resulting blackness was so intense as to be very nearly palpable.

"Hoist the sails!" the captain shouted.

Garion could hear the creaking pulleys and the flapping of canvas. Then there was the heavy boom of the sails catching the wind and the ship heeled over as she swung to starboard.

"There's no way to be sure of our direction, my Lord," the captain warned. "We haven't got a fixed point of any kind to refer to."

"Use those," Garion suggested, pointing at the winking deck lights on the Mallorean vessels trailing far behind. "We might as well get some use out of them."

Their darkened scow moved eastward with her sharply angled sails cracking in the wind. The deck lights of the Mallorean ships that had been pursuing them continued their cautious northward course, crossed far behind, and winked out of sight.

"May Torak guide them to a reef," the captain muttered fervently.

"It worked!" Urgit said delightedly, clapping the seaman on the shoulder. "By the Gods, it actually worked!"

"I just hope that nobody catches me running at night without any lights," the captain brooded.

Dawn came smudged and bleary to the murky eastern horizon, rising slowly up out of a low-lying shadow some ten leagues or so ahead. "That's the coast of Cthaka," the captain said, pointing.

"Is there any sign of those Mallorean ships?" Urgit asked, peering around at the heaving sea.

The captain shook his head. "They passed astern of us during the dogwatch, your Majesty. They're halfway up the Gorand Sea by now." The seaman looked at Garion. "You wanted to get closer in to shore and then swing around to starboard again, my Lord?"

"To starboard, of course."

The captain squinted up at the sails. "We'll have to reset the rigging again, I suppose."

"I'm afraid not," Garion told him regretfully. "When we turn south, we'll be sailing directly into the wind. You'll have to furl your sails and break out the oars." He noted the disappointed expression on the seaman's face. "I'm sorry, Captain, but there are limits. Your sails are the wrong shape, and when you get right down to it, rowing in this case will actually be faster. How far north were we swept last night?"

"A goodly way, my Lord," the captain replied, peering at the indistinct coastline lying ahead. "You can put a lot of water behind you moving under full sail before a wind like that. I wouldn't be surprised to see the mouth of the Gorand Sea somewhere ahead."

"We don't want to go in there. Let's not start playing tag with those Mallorean ships again—particularly in tight quarters. I'm going below for a bite of breakfast and some dry clothes. Send someone down if anything happens."

"I will, my Lord."

They had fish for breakfast that morning. At Polgara's suggestion, Durnik's huge catch had been cut into steaks and then delicately broiled over a low flame.

"Delicious, isn't he?" Durnik asked proudly.

"Yes, dear," Polgara agreed. "He's a very nice fish."

"Did I tell you how I caught him, Pol?"

"Yes, dear—but that's all right. You can tell me again, if you'd like."

As they were just finishing their meal, the Murgo captain entered, wearing a tarred cape and an anxious expression. "There's more of them, my Lord," he blurted to Garion.

"More of what?"

"Malloreans. There's another squadron coming up the Cthaka coast."

Urgit's face blanched, and his hands started to tremble.

"Are you sure they aren't the same ones who were chasing us last night?" Garion asked, getting quickly to his feet.

"There's no way they could be, my Lord. It's a different group of ships."

Silk was looking narrowly at the ship's master. "Captain," he said, "have you ever been in business for yourself?"

The captain threw a brief, guilty glance at Urgit. "I don't know what you're talking about," he mumbled.

"This is no time for false modesty, Captain," Silk said. "We're charging head-long into the midst of a Mallorean squadron. Are there any coves or inlets around here where we could get out of sight?"

"Not along this coast, your Highness; but right after you go through the channel into the Gorand Sea, there's a small bay to starboard. It's well hidden by some reefs. If we were to unstep the masts and tie bushes along the sides, I think we could escape notice."

"Let's do it then, Captain," Belgarath said shortly. "What's the weather look like?"

"Not very pleasant. There's a heavy cloud bank coming up from the south. I think we can expect a gale before noon."

"Good."

"Good?"

"We're not alone in these waters," Belgarath reminded him. "A nice gale ought to give the Malloreans something to do besides line the rails of their ships looking for us. Go give the orders, Captain. Let's turn around and make a run for it."

"How were you so sure that the captain knew about a secluded cove or bay somewhere?" Urgit asked Silk after the seaman had left.

Silk shrugged. "You levy taxes on merchandise that gets moved from one place to another, don't you?"

"Of course. I need the revenue."

"A resourceful man with his own boat can sort of forget to stop by the customs dock at the end of a voyage—or he can locate some quiet place to store things until he finds customers for them."

"That's smuggling!"

"Why, yes, I believe some people do call it that. Anyway, I'd guess that every sea captain in the world has dabbled in the business at one time or another."

"Not Murgos," Urgit insisted.

"Then how is it that your captain knew of a perfect hiding place not five leagues from our present location—and probably knows of hundreds more?"

"You're a corrupt and disgusting man, Kheldar."

"I know. Smuggling is a very profitable business, though. You ought to give some thought to going into it."

"Kheldar, I'm the king. I'd be stealing from myself."

"Trust me," Silk said. "It's a bit complicated, but I can show you how to set things up so that you can make a very handsome profit."

The ship rolled then, and they all looked out through the windows along the stern to watch the waves sweep by as the steersman pulled his tiller over hard and the ship came about. Far astern they could see a half-dozen red sails looking tiny in the distance.

"Are there any Grolims on board those ships, Pol?" Belgarath asked his daughter.

Her lavender eyes became distant for a moment, then she passed one hand over her brow. "No, father," she replied, "just ordinary Malloreans."

"Good. We shouldn't have too much trouble hiding from them, then."

"That storm the captain mentioned is coming up behind them," Durnik said.

"Won't it just hurry them along?" Urgit asked nervously.

"Probably not," the smith answered. "Most likely they'll come about to head into the wind. That's the only safe way to ride out a storm."

"Won't we have to do the same thing?"

"We're outnumbered six to one, my brother," Silk pointed out. "We're going to have to take a few chances, I think."

The advancing wave of darkness that marked the leading edge of the oncoming storm engulfed the red sails far astern and came racing up the coast. The waves grew higher, and the Murgo ship bucked and plunged as the wind picked up. The timbers shrieked and groaned in protest as the heavy seas wrenched at their vessel, and high overhead there was the heavy booming of the sails. Garion actually listened to that booming sound for several minutes before the significance of it began to dawn on him. It was an ominous grinding noise from amidships that finally alerted him. "That idiot!" he exclaimed, leaping to his feet and snatching up his cloak.

"What's the matter?" Sadi asked in alarm.

"He's carrying full sail! If his mainmast doesn't break, we'll be driven under!" Garion whirled, dashed out of the cabin, and staggered along the lurching companionway to the three steps leading up to the deck. "Captain!" he shouted as he dashed out onto the rain-swept deck. He caught one of the hastily strung lifelines as a wave broke over the stern and came rushing knee-deep down the deck, sweeping his feet out from under him. "Captain!" he shouted again, hauling himself hand over hand up the rope toward the aft deck.

"My Lord?" the captain shouted back with a startled look.

"Shorten your sail! Your mainmast is starting to tear free!"

The captain stared aloft, his face filled with sudden chagrin. "Impossible, my Lord," he protested as Garion reached him. "The men can't furl sail in this storm."

Garion rubbed the rain out of his eyes and looked back up over his shoulder at the tautly bellied mainsail. "They'll have to cut it away, then."

"Cut it? But, my Lord, that's a new sail."

"Right now it's the sail or the ship. If the wind uproots your mainmast, it's going to tear your ship apart—and if it doesn't, we'll be driven under. Now get that sail off the mast—or I will."

The captain stared at him.

"Believe me," Garion told him, "if I have to do it, I'll sweep your deck clean—masts, rigging, sails, and all."

The captain immediately began giving orders.

Once the mainsail had been cut free and allowed to kite off into the storm, the dreadful shuddering and grinding eased, and the vessel ran before the wind more smoothly, propelled only by a small foresail.

"How far is it to the mouth of the Gorand Sea?" Garion asked.

"Not far, my Lord," the captain replied, mopping his face. He looked around at the storm-lashed morning and the low, nearly invisible coast sliding by on their right. "There it is," he said, pointing at a scarcely visible hillock jutting up a mile or so ahead. "You see that headland—the one with the white bluff facing us? The channel's just on the other side of it." He turned to the sailors clinging to the aft rail. "Drop the sea anchor," he commanded.

"What's that for?" Garion asked him.

"We've got too much headway, my Lord," the seaman explained. "The channel's a little difficult, and we have to turn sharply to get through it. We have to slow down. The sea anchor drags behind and keeps us from going quite so fast."

Garion thought about it, frowning. Something seemed wrong, but he couldn't quite put his finger on it. He watched as the sailors rolled what appeared to be a long canvas sack on a heavy rope over the stern rail. The sack streamed out behind them; the rope went taut, and the ship shuddered and slowed perceptibly.

"That's better," the captain said with some satisfaction.

Garion shielded his eyes from the icy rain being driven into his face and peered back behind them. The Malloreans were nowhere in sight. "Just how tricky is this channel you mentioned?" he asked.

"There are some reefs in the center, my Lord. You have to hug the coast on one side or the other to avoid them. We'll stay close to the south shore, since that bay I mentioned is on that side."

Garion nodded. "I'll go warn the others that we're about to make a turn to the right. A sudden change of direction might toss them around a bit down there."

"Starboard," the captain said disapprovingly.

"What? Oh, no. To most of them, it's to the right." Garion started forward, peering out through the rain at the low coast sliding past. The bluff and the rounded headland looming above it was almost dead amidships now. He could see the channel just ahead cluttered with jagged, up-thrusting rocks. He swung down into the narrow, dark companionway and shook as much water out of his cloak as possible as he stumbled aft. He opened the main cabin door and poked his head inside. "We're at the mouth of the Gorand Sea," he announced. "We'll be turning to starboard here." Then he cursed at forgetting.

"Which way is starboard?" Ce'Nedra asked.

"Right."

"Why didn't you say right, then?"

He let that pass. "When we come about, we could bounce around a bit, so you'd all better hang on to something. There's a reef in the center of the channel, so we're going to have to swing in tight to the south shore to avoid—" Then it came to him, even as the ship heeled over and plunged into the channel. "Belar!" he swore. He spun, reaching over his shoulder for Iron-grip's sword, and then plunged back down the companionway. He banged out through the slanting companionway doors and jumped up to the rain-swept aft deck with the great blade aloft. "Cut it!" he screamed. "Cut the rope to the sea anchor!"

The captain gaped at him, uncomprehending.

"Cut the cursed rope!" Garion bellowed. Then he was on them, and they stumbled clumsily over each other, trying to get out of his way. The ship had already swept in a tight curve close in to the headland, avoiding the reefs and up-thrusting boulders in mid-channel. The submerged sea anchor, however, pulled by the force of the waves running before the wind, continued on across the mouth of the channel. The rope that had slackened until it was lost in the whitecaps suddenly snapped taut, jerking the Murgo scow askew. The force of that sudden sideways jerk threw Garion off his feet, and he crashed into the tangle of arms and legs at the rail. "Cut it!" he shouted, struggling to free himself. "Cut the rope!"

But it was too late. The heavy sea anchor, pulled by the irresistible force of the storm-driven waves, had not only jerked the Murgo vessel to a halt but was now pulling her inexorably backward—not toward the safe channel through which she had just passed, but instead directly toward the jagged reefs.

Garion staggered to his feet, kicking the floundering sailors out from around his ankles. Desperately he swung a massive blow at the tautly thrumming rope, shearing away not merely the rope itself but the stout windlass to which it was attached.

"My Lord!" the captain protested.

"Get that tiller!" Garion shouted. "Turn starboard! Turn! Turn! Turn!" He pointed at the deadly reefs foaming directly in their path.

The captain gaped at the huge knife-edged rocks standing in his vessel's course. Then he whirled and tore the tiller from the hands of his frozen steersman. Instinctively, he swung the tiller hard over for a turn to port.

"Starboard!" Garion shouted. "Turn to starboard!"

"No, my Lord," the captain disagreed. "We have to turn to port—to the left."

"We're going backward, you jackass! Turn right!"

"Starboard," the captain corrected absently, still wrestling with an idea he was not yet fully prepared to grasp—all the while still firmly holding the tiller locked into the fatal course he had originally set.

Garion began to clamber over the still-floundering sailors, desperately trying to reach the bemused captain, but there came a sudden tearing sound from below the waterline and a lurching jolt as their ship crashed stern-first into the reef. Timbers shrieked and snapped as the sharp rocks knifed into the vessel's bottom. Then they hung there, impaled on the rocks, while the waves began the deadly pounding that would soon break the ship to pieces.

CHAPTER NINETEEN

Garion struggled to his feet, shaking his head to clear it of the ringing sound and to chase the dancing sparks from before his eyes. The sudden jolt of the ship's striking the reef had tumbled him headlong into the aft rail, and there was a great, stinging welt across the top of his scalp. The air around him was filled with sounds. There were shouts from the deck and cries for help coming from the water. The ship groaned and shook as she hung on the reef, and the surging waves pounded her splintered bottom on the unseen rocks beneath her keel. Wincing, Garion shook his head again and began to slip and slide his way across the heaving aft deck toward the companionway door. As he reached it, however, Belgarath and Durnik came crashing out. "What's happened?" the old man demanded.

"We hit a reef," Garion said. "Is anybody down there hurt?"

"They're all right—a little tumbled about is all."

Garion touched the welt on top of his head, wincing at the sharp sting. Then he looked at his fingers, noting that there didn't seem to be any blood.

"What's the matter?" Belgarath asked.

"I hit my head."

"I thought we all decided that you weren't going to do that any more."

A deadly, jarring boom came from under their feet and with it the sound of splintering timbers.

"Belgarath," Durnik said with alarm, "we're caught on the reef. This surf is going to pound the ship to pieces."

Belgarath looked around quickly. "Where's the captain?" he demanded.

Garion turned to look aft. "He was right there at the tiller, Grandfather," he said. He clambered up the short incline to the aft deck and caught hold of the steersman, who was stumbling forward. "Where's the captain?" he shouted.

"Lost. He was thrown over the aft rail when we hit the reef." The steersman's eyes were filled with shock and fright. "We're all doomed!" he cried, clinging to Garion.

"Oh, stop that!" Garion snapped. "The captain's gone, Grandfather," he shouted over the noise of the storm and the confusion on deck. "He fell over the side."

Belgarath and Durnik came quickly up the three steps to the aft deck. "We'll have to take care of it ourselves, then," the old man said. "How much time do you think we've got, Durnik?"

"Not much. There are a lot of timbers breaking down in the hold, and you can hear water pouring in."

"We have to get her off this reef, then—before the rocks break any more holes in her bottom."

"The reef's the only thing that's keeping us up right now, Belgarath," the smith objected. "If we lift her off, she'll sink in minutes."

"Then we'll have to beach her. Come along, both of you." He led them aft and took hold of the tiller bar. He jiggled it back and forth a couple of times and then swore. "The rudder's gone." He drew in a deep breath to calm himself and then turned to Garion and Durnik. "We'll do this all at one time and all together," he told them. "If we start heaving and hauling and bouncing her around, we'll just tear her up all the more." He wiped the rain and spray out of his face and peered toward the shore, perhaps a mile distant. He pointed at the up-thrusting headland with the white bluff on one side dropping straight down into the thundering surf. "There's a beach just to the left of that bluff," he said. "We'll try for that. It's not too well sheltered, and there are a lot of rocks sticking up out of the sand, but it's the closest."

Durnik leaned far out over the aft rail and peered down. "She's been badly broached, Belgarath," he reported gravely. He squinted across the intervening water toward the beach. "Our only hope is speed. Once she's clear of the reef, she'll start to go down. We're going to have to push her toward the beach as fast as we can—and without a rudder, it's going to be very hard to control our direction."

"Do we have any other options?" Belgarath asked him.

"Not that I can think of, no."

"Let's do it then." The old man looked at them. "Are we ready?"

Garion and Durnik both nodded, then straightened, concentrating hard as each of them drew in and focused his will. Garion began to tingle all over and clenched himself tightly, holding in the pent-up force.

"Now!" Belgarath barked.

"Lift!" the three of them said in unison.

The battered stern of the ship came sluggishly up out of the churning waves with her shattered timbers shrieking as the hull pulled free of the jagged reef.

"There!" Belgarath snapped, pointing at the half-obscured beach.

Garion thrust, bracing his will astern at the boiling reef. The ship settled sickeningly as she came free, going down rapidly by the stern; then, slowly at first, but quickly gaining speed, she surged forward. Even over the sound of the howling wind, he could hear the rushing wash of water along her sides as she raced toward the safety of the beach.

When they hit the currents in the main channel, however, the rudderless ship began to veer and yaw, threatening to swing broadside. "Keep her straight!" Belgarath shouted. The veins were standing out in his forehead, and his jaws were tightly clenched.

Garion labored at it. As long as their broken ship moved fast enough, they could keep the water from pouring in through the shattered stern, but if she went broadside to the waves, the loss of momentum would be fatal. The sea would inexorably drag her under. Garion gripped the bow with the force of his will, holding the ship rigidly on course, even as he continued to drive toward the beach with all his strength.

Three hundred more yards. Sweating and straining, Garion could see the foaming surf seething on the sandy, boulder-strewn beach.

Two hundred yards. He could hear the thunder of the waves.

One hundred yards. He could feel the ponderous, upward-heaving swell of the great wave that rose beneath them and rushed them toward the safety only scant yards away.

And then, even as the prow touched the froth-covered sand, the great swell that had driven them up onto the beach subsided, and there was a dreadful, shocking crash from amidships as they came down onto a submerged boulder lurking beneath the surf. Again Garion was thrown facedown on the deck and half stunned by the impact.

The surf still boomed about them, and the snapping and splintering of timbers amidships was deafening, but they were safe. The prow of the stricken vessel was firmly embedded in the wet sand of the beach. As Garion painfully hauled himself to his feet, he felt drained and weak from his efforts. Then the deck beneath his feet gave a peculiar, sickening lurch, and there were more cracking and splintering noises coming from amidships.

"I think we broke the keel when we hit that rock," Durnik said shakily. His face was gray with exhaustion, and he was shaking visibly. "We'd better get everybody off the ship and onto the beach."

Belgarath rose from the scuppers. There was a ruddy contusion on his cheek, rain and spray streaming down his face, and a vast anger in his eyes. He was swearing sulfurously. Then his rage suddenly vanished. "The horses!" he exclaimed. "They're down in the hold! Durnik!"

But the smith was already running forward toward the sprung hatchway amidships. "Get Toth to come and help me!" he shouted back over his shoulder. "We have to get those horses out!"

"Garion!" Belgarath barked. "Let's get everybody out of the cabins and onto dry land. I don't think we've got a lot of time before this wreck starts to break apart."

They started forward, moving carefully on the slanting deck of the broken ship, with the wind-whipped spray and driving rain stinging their faces. They ducked into the slanting aft door and down the companionway. The narrow hall echoed and rang with the noise of cracking timbers coming from amidships.

The aft cabin was a total shambles. The shock of striking the reef and the even worse one that had broken the ship's back had torn most of the bolted-down furniture loose. Sprung timbers flopped and clattered, and the windows across the stern had all been broken and wrenched from their casings. Spray and rain were splashing in through those gaping holes.

Ce'Nedra and Prala looked frightened as they clung to each other, Urgit held tightly to the keel-post as if expecting yet another crashing impact, and Sadi half-lay in a corner with his arms protectively wrapped around his red leather case. Polgara, however, looked dreadfully angry. She was also wet. The water pouring in through the shattered stern had drenched her clothes and her hair, and her expression was that of one who has been enormously offended. "Exactly what did you do, old man?" she demanded of Belgarath as he and Garion entered through the broken door.

"We hit a reef, Pol," he replied. "We were taking water, so we had to beach the ship."

She considered that for a moment, obviously trying to find something wrong with it.

"We can talk about it later," he said. He looked around. "Is everyone all right? We've got to get off this wreck immediately."

"We're as well as can be expected, father," she said. "What's the problem? I thought you said we were on the beach."

"We hit a submerged rock and broke the keel. This part of the ship's still in the water, and about the only thing that's holding this tub in one piece right now is the pitch in her seams. We've got to get forward and off the ship at once."

She nodded. "I understand, father." She turned to the others. "Gather up whatever you can carry," she instructed. "We have to get ashore."

"I'll go help Durnik with the horses," Garion said to Belgarath. "Toth, Eriond, come with me." He turned toward the door, but paused a moment to look at Ce'Nedra. "Are you all right?" he asked her.

"I think so," she replied, sounding frightened and rubbing at an ugly bruise on her knee.

"Stay with Aunt Pol," he instructed curtly and then went out.

The scene in the ship's hold was even worse than he had expected. Knee-deep water swirled and sloshed in the half-light coming in through the splintered hull. Boxes, bags, and bales floated everywhere, and the top of the sloshing, bilge-smelling water was littered with splinters from the broken timbers. Durnik had herded the wild-eyed horses forward, and they were bunched together in the ship's bow where the water was the shallowest. "We lost three of them," he reported, "two with broken necks and one that drowned."

"Horse?" Eriond asked quickly.

"He's all right, Eriond," Durnik assured him. He turned back to Garion. "I've been trying to gather up our packs. Everything's pretty wet, I'm afraid. The food packs were all back in the stern, though. There's no way to get to them."

"We can deal with that later," Garion said. "The main thing now is to get the horses out."

Durnik squinted at the jagged edges of the two-foot square keel grinding together as the aft end of the ship swung sluggishly in the surging waves. "Too dangerous," he said shortly. "We'll have to go out through the bow. I'll get my axe."

Garion shook his head. "If the aft end breaks loose, the bow-section's likely to roll. We could lose another four or five horses if that happens and we might not have too much time left."

Durnik drew in a deep breath and squared his broad shoulders. His face was not happy.

"I know," Garion said, putting his hand on his friend's arm. "I'm tired, too. Let's do it up forward. There's no point in breaking out of the hull someplace where we'll have to jump into deep water."

It was not quite as difficult as they had expected. The assistance of Toth made a noticeable difference. They selected a space in the ship's side between a pair of stout ribs and went to work. As Durnik and Garion began carefully to break out the ship's timbers between those ribs with the force of concentrated will, Toth attacked the same area with a large iron pry bar. The combination of sorcery and the mute's enormous physical strength quickly opened a low, narrow opening in the ship's bow.

Silk stood on the beach out of range of the splinters their efforts had sent flying. His cloak was whipping wildly in the wind, and the surf was swirling about his ankles. "Are you all right?" he shouted over the noise of the storm.

"Good enough," Garion shouted back. "Give us a hand with the horses."

It eventually took blindfolds. Despite the best efforts of Durnik and Eriond to calm them, the terrified horses could be moved only if they could not see the dangers in the sloshing water surging around their knees. One by one they had to be led and coaxed through the litter lying half-awash in the shattered hold and out into the foaming surf. When the last of their animals was clear and stood flinching on the sand with the driving rain lashing at his flanks, Garion turned back to the sluggishly heaving wreck. "Let's get the packs out," he shouted at the others. "Save what you can, but don't take any chances."

The Murgo sailors, after leaping from the bow of the ship to the sand, had retreated up the beach and taken dubious shelter on the leeward side of a large, upthrusting rock. They stood clustered together, sullenly watching the unloading. Garion and the others heaped up the packs above the frothy line that marked the highest point reached by the waves.

"We lost three horses and all the food packs," Garion reported to Belgarath and Polgara. "I think we got everything else—except what we had to leave behind in the cabins."

Belgarath squinted upward into the rain. "We can redistribute the packs," he said, "but we're going to need food."

"Is the tide going in or out?" Silk asked as he deposited the last pack on their heap of belongings.

Durnik squinted at the storm-tossed channel leading into the Gorand Sea. "I think it's just turning."

"We don't really have too much of a problem, then," the little man said. "Let's find someplace out of the wind and wait for the tide to go out. Then we can come back and ransack the wreck at our leisure. She ought to be completely out of the water at low tide."

"There's just one thing wrong with your plan, Prince Kheldar," Sadi told him, squinting toward the upper end of the beach. "You're forgetting those Murgo sailors. They're stranded on a deserted coast with at least a dozen Mallorean ships cruising up and down the shore line looking for them. Malloreans enjoy killing Murgos almost as much as Alorns do, so those sailors are going to want to get far away from here. It might be wise to get these horses quite some distance away—if we want to keep them."

"Let's load the pack horses and get mounted," Belgarath decided. "I think Sadi's right. We can come back and pick over what's left of the ship later."

They broke down the packs and redistributed the weight to make up for the three lost animals, then began to saddle their mounts.

The sailors, led by a tall, heavy-shouldered Murgo with an evil-looking scar under his left eye, came back down the beach. "Where do you think you're taking those horses?" he demanded.

"I can't really see where that's any of your business," Sadi replied coolly.

"We're going to make it our business, aren't we, mates?" There was a rumble of agreement from the rain-soaked sailors.

"The horses belong to us," Sadi told him.

"We don't care about that. There are enough of us so that we can take anything we want."

"Why waste time with talk?" one of the sailors behind the scar-faced man shouted.

"Right," the big Murgo agreed. He drew a short, rusty sword from the sheath at his hip, looked back over his shoulder as he raised it aloft, and shouted, "Follow me!" Then he fell writhing and bellowing in pain to the wet sand, clutching at his broken right arm. Toth, without any change of expression and with an almost negligent side-arm flip, had sent the iron pry bar he still held in one hand spin-ning through the air with a whirring flutter that ended with a sharp crack as the sword-wielding Murgo's arm snapped.

The sailors drew back, alarmed by their leader's sudden collapse. Then a stubble-cheeked fellow in the front rank lifted a heavy boat hook. "Rush them!" he bel-lowed. "We want those horses and we outnumber them."

"I think you might want to count again," Polgara said in a cool voice. Even as Garion stepped forward, drawing his sword out of its sheath, he felt a peculiar shad-owy presence to his left. He blinked unbelievingly. As real as if he were actually there, the huge, red-bearded shape of Barak stood at his side.

A clinking sound came from the right, and there, his armor gleaming wet in the rain, stood Mandorallen, and somewhat beyond him, the hawk-faced Hettar. "What thinkest thou, my Lords?" the figure that appeared to be the invincible Baron of Vo Mandor said gaily. "Should we afford these knaves the opportunity to flee, ere we fall upon them and spill out their lifeblood?"

"It seems like the decent thing to do," the apparition of Barak rumbled its agreement. "What do you think, Hettar?"

"They're Murgos," the shade of Hettar said in his quiet, chilling voice as he drew his saber. "Kill them all right here and now. That way we won't have to waste time chasing them down one by one later."

"Somehow I knew you were going to look at it that way." Barak laughed. "All right, my Lords, let's go to work." He drew his heavy sword.

The three images, larger actually than they were in life, advanced grimly on the shrinking sailors. In their midst, painfully aware that he was in fact quite alone, Garion moved forward, his huge sword held low. Then, on the far side of the ap-parition of Barak, he saw Toth advancing with his huge staff. Beyond him, Sadi held a small poisoned dagger. At the opposite end of the line, Durnik and Silk moved into place.

The image of Barak glanced over at Garion. "Now, Garion!" Polgara's whis-pered voice came from those bearded lips.

Instantly he understood. He relaxed the restraints he usually kept on the Orb. The great sword he held leaped into flame, spurting blue fire from its tip almost into the faces of the now-terrified Murgos.

"Will all of you who would like to die immediately and save yourselves the in-convenience and discomfort of being chased down and slowly hacked to pieces please step forward?" the red-bearded shadow at Garion's side roared in tones more grandiose than Barak himself could ever have managed. "We can have you in the arms of your one-eyed God in the blinking of an eye."

It hung there for a moment; then the sailors fled.

"Oh, Gods!" Garion heard Polgara's ringing voice coming from behind him. "I've wanted to do that for a thousand years!" He turned and saw her, standing with the raging sea and racing black clouds behind her and the wind tearing at her blue cloak. The rain had plastered her hair to her face and neck, but her glorious eyes were triumphant.

"My Pol!" Belgarath exulted, catching her in a rough embrace. "Gods, what a son you'd have made!"

"I'm your daughter, Belgarath," she replied simply, "but could any son have done better?"

"No, Pol." He laughed suddenly, crushing her to him and soundly planting a kiss on her rain-wet cheek. "Not one bit."

They stopped, startled and even a little embarrassed that the enormous love they had each tried to conceal for millennia had finally come out into the open on this storm-swept beach here at the bottom of the world. Almost shyly they looked at each other and then, unable to hold it in, they began to laugh.

Garion turned away, his eyes suddenly brimming.

Urgit was bending over the sailor with the broken arm. "If you wouldn't mind taking some advice from your king, my man," he said urbanely, "might I remind you that the sea out there is crawling with Malloreans, and Malloreans take a child-like delight in crucifying every Murgo they come across. Don't you think it might be prudent for you and your shipmates to remove yourselves from the vicinity of all that scrap lumber?" He looked meaningfully at the wreck.

The sailor cast a sudden, frightened glance at the storm-tossed channel and scrambled to his feet. Cradling his broken arm, he scurried back up the beach to re-join his frightened mates.

"He shows a remarkable grasp of the situation, doesn't he?" Urgit said to Silk.

"He does seem uncharacteristically alert," Silk agreed. He looked at the rest of them. "Why don't we mount up and get off this beach?" he suggested. "That wreck stands out like a beacon, and our injured friend and his companions might decide to give horse rustling another try." He looked appraisingly at the hulking images Polgara had conjured up. "Just out of curiosity, Polgara, could those apparitions of yours actually have done any good if it had gotten down to a fight?"

Polgara was still laughing, her lavender eyes alight. "To be perfectly honest with you, my dear Silk," she replied gaily, "I haven't got the faintest idea."

For some reason her answer sent them all off into helpless gales of laughter.

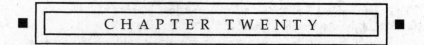

CHAPTER TWENTY

The slope leading to the top of the headland was covered with rank grass, drooping under the rain that swept in from the south. As they started up from the beach, Garion looked back. The Murgo sailors had swarmed over the wreck to salvage whatever they could, stopping often to look fearfully out at the storm-racked channel.

At the top of the headland, the full force of the gale struck them, tearing at their clothes and raking them with sheets of rain. Belgarath pulled to a halt, held one hand above his eyes to shield them, and surveyed the treeless expanse of grass-land lying sodden and wind-whipped ahead.

"This is totally impossible, father," Polgara declared, drawing her wet cloak more tightly about her. "We're going to have to find shelter and wait this out."

"That might be difficult, Pol." He gazed out over a grassland that showed no signs of any sort of human habitation. The broad valley lying below them was laced with deep gullies where turbulent creeks had cut down through the turf and exposed the rounded boulders and beds of gravel lying beneath the thin topsoil and its tenacious cover of grass. The wind sheeted across that grass, tossing it like waves, and the rain, mingled with icy sleet, raked at it. "Urgit," the old man said, "are there any villages or settlements hereabouts?"

Urgit wiped his face and looked around. "I don't think so," he replied. "The maps don't show anything in this part of Cthaka except the high road leading inland. We might stumble across some isolated farmstead, but I doubt it. The soil here is too thin for crops, and the winters are too severe for cattle."

The old man nodded gloomily. "That's more or less what I thought."

"We might be able to pitch the tents," Durnik said, "but we'll be right out in the open, and there's no firewood anywhere out there."

Eriond had been patiently sitting astride his stallion, staring out at the featureless landscape with a peculiar look of recognition. "Couldn't we take shelter in the watchtower?" he asked.

"What watchtower?" Belgarath asked him, looking around again, "I don't see anything."

"You can't see it from here. It's mostly all tumbled down. The cellar's still all right, though."

"I don't know of any watchtowers on this coast," Urgit said.

"It hasn't been used for a long time."

"Where, Eriond?" Polgara asked. "Can you show us where it is?"

"Of course. It's not too far." The young man turned his stallion and angled up toward the very top of the headland. As they climbed the hill, Garion looked down and saw a fair number of stone blocks protruding up out of the grass. It was difficult to say for sure, but at least some of those blocks bore what looked vaguely like chisel marks.

When they reached the top, the gale shrieked around them, and the tossing grass whipped at their horses' legs.

"Are you sure, Eriond?" Polgara shouted over the wind.

"We can get in from the other side," he replied confidently. "It might be better to lead the horses, though. The entrance is fairly close to the edge of the bluff." He slid out of his saddle and led the way across the grassy, rounded top of the hill. The rest of them followed him. "Be careful here," he warned, moving around a slight depression. "Part of the roof is sagging a bit."

Just past that grass-covered depression was a bank that angled steeply downward to a narrow ledge. Beyond that, the bluff broke away sharply. Eriond picked his way down the bank and led his horse along the ledge. Garion followed him; when he reached the ledge, he glanced over the edge of the bluff. Far below, he saw the wreck lying on the beach. A broad line of footprints stretched away from it at the water's edge to disappear in the rain.

"Here it is," Eriond said. Then he disappeared, leading his horse, it seemed, directly into the grass-covered bank.

The rest of them followed curiously and found a narrow, arched opening that had quite obviously been built by human hands. The long grass above and on each side of the arch had grown over it until it was barely visible. Gratefully, Garion pushed his way through that grass-obscured opening into a calm, musty-smelling darkness.

"Did anyone think to bring any torches?" Sadi asked.

"They were with the food packs, I'm afraid," Durnik apologized. "Here, let's see what I can do." Garion felt a light surge and heard a faint rushing sound. A dimly glowing spot of light appeared, balanced on the palm of Durnik's hand. Gradually that dim light grew until they could see the interior of the ancient ruin. Like so many structures that had been built in antiquity, this low-ceilinged cellar was vaulted. Stone arches supported the ceiling, and the walls were solidly buttressed. Garion had seen precisely the same construction in King Anheg's eons-old palace in Val Alorn, in the ruins of Vo Wacune, in the lower floors of his own Citadel at Riva, and even in the echoing tomb of the one-eyed God in Cthol Mishrak.

Silk was looking speculatively at Eriond. "I'm sure you have an explanation," he said. "How did you know that this place was here?"

"I lived here for a while with Zedar. It was while he was waiting until I'd grow old enough to steal the Orb."

Silk looked slightly disappointed. "How prosaic," he said.

"I'm sorry," Eriond said as he led the horses over to one side of the vaulted room. "Would you like to have me make up some kind of story for you instead?"

"Never mind, Eriond," the little man told him.

Urgit had been examining one of the buttresses. "No Murgo ever built this," he declared. "The stones fit too closely."

"It was built before the Murgos came to this part of the world," Eriond said.

"By the slave race?" Urgit asked incredulously. "All they know how to make are mud huts."

"That's what they wanted you to think. They were building towers—and cities—when Murgos were still living in goatskin tents."

"Could somebody please make a fire?" Ce'Nedra asked through chattering teeth. "I'm freezing." Garion looked at her closely and saw that her lips had a bluish tinge to them.

"The firewood's over here," Eriond said. He went behind one of the buttresses and emerged with an armload of white-bleached sticks. "Zedar and I used to carry driftwood up from the beach. There's still quite a bit left." He went to the fireplace in the back wall, dropped the wood, and bent over to peer up the chimney. "It seems to be clear," he said.

Durnik went to work immediately with his flint, steel, and tinder. In a few moments, a small curl of orange flame was licking up through the little peaked roof of splinters he had built on the bed of ash in the fireplace. They all crowded around that tiny flame, thrusting twigs and sticks at it in their eagerness to force it to grow more quickly.

"That won't do," Durnik said with uncharacteristic sternness. "You'll only knock it apart and put it out."

They reluctantly backed away from the fireplace.

Durnik carefully laid twigs and splinters on the growing flame, then small sticks, and finally larger ones. The flames grew higher and began to spread quickly through the bone-dry wood. The light from the fireplace began to fill the musty cellar, and Garion could feel a faint warmth on his face.

"All right, then," Polgara said in a crisp, businesslike way, "what are we going to do about food?"

"The sailors have left the wreck," Garion said, "and the tide's gone out enough so that all but the very aft end of the ship is out of the water. I'll take some pack horses and go back down there to see what I can find."

Durnik's fire had begun to crackle. He stood up and looked at Eriond. "Can you manage here?" he asked.

Eriond nodded and went behind the buttress for more wood.

The smith bent and picked up his cloak. "Toth and I can go with you, Garion," he said, "just in case those sailors decide to come back. But we're going to have to hurry. It's going to start getting dark before too long."

The gale still howled across the weather-rounded top of the headland, driving rain and sleet before it. Garion and his two friends picked their way carefully down the slope again toward the forlorn-looking ship, lying twisted and broken-backed on the boulder that had claimed her life.

"How long do you think this storm is going to last?" Garion shouted to Durnik.

"It's hard to say," Durnik shouted back. "It could blow over tonight or it could keep it up for several days."

"I was afraid you might say that."

They reached the wreck, dismounted, and entered the hold through the opening they had previously made in the bow. "I don't think we'll find too much down here," Durnik said. "Our own food is all spoiled, and I don't think the sailors stored anything perishable in the hold."

Garion nodded. "Can we get Aunt Pol's cooking things?" he asked. "She'll want those, I think."

Durnik peered aft at the bilge-soaked bags and bales lying in a tumbled heap in the shattered stern, with surf sloshing over them through the holes rent in the hull in that end of the ship. "I think so," he said. "I'll take a look."

"As long as we're here, we might as well pick up the rest of the things we had in those aft cabins," Garion said. "I'll go gather them up while you and Toth see what the sailors left behind in the galley." He climbed carefully over the splintered timbers at the point where the keel had broken and went up a ladder to the hatch above. Then he slipped and slid down the deck to the aft companionway.

It took him perhaps a quarter of an hour to gather up the belongings they had left behind when they had fled the wreck. He wrapped them all in a sheet of sail-cloth and went back up on deck. He carried his bundle forward and dropped it over the side onto the wet sand of the beach.

Durnik poked his head out of the forward companionway. "There isn't much, Garion," he said. "The sailors picked it over pretty thoroughly."

"We'll have to make do with whatever we can find, I guess." Garion squinted up through the rain. The sky was growing noticeably darker. "We'd better hurry," he added.

They reached the top of the headland in a gale-torn twilight and carefully led their horses along the edge of the bluff to the entrance of the cellar as the last tatters of daylight faded from the sky. The inside of the vaulted chamber was warm now and filled with the light of the fire dancing on the hearth. The others had strung lines from the arches during their absence, and their blankets and clothing hung dripping and steaming along the walls.

"Any luck?" Silk asked as Garion led his horse inside.

"Not much," Garion admitted. "The sailors cleaned out the galley pretty thoroughly."

Durnik and Toth led in the other horses and lifted down a number of makeshift packs. "We found a bag of beans," the smith reported, "and a crock full of honey. There was a sack of meal back in a corner and a couple of sides of bacon. The sailors left the bacon behind because it was moldy, but we ought to be able to cut most of the mold away."

"That's all?" Polgara asked.

"I'm afraid so, Pol," Durnik replied. "We picked up a brazier and a couple of bags of charcoal—since there doesn't seem to be any firewood in this part of the world."

She frowned slightly, running over the inventory he had just given her.

"It's not very much, Pol," he apologized, "but it was the best we could do."

"I can manage with it, dear," she said, smiling at him.

"I picked up the clothes we left in those aft cabins, too," Garion said as he unsaddled his horse. "A few of them are even dry."

"Good," Polgara said. "Let's all change into whatever dry clothing will fit, and I'll see what I can do about something to eat."

Silk had been looking suspiciously at the sack of meal. "Gruel?" he asked, looking unhappy.

"Beans would take much too long to cook," she replied. "Porridge and honey—and a bit of bacon—will get us through the night."

He sighed.

The following morning, the rain and sleet had let up, although the wind still tore at the long grass atop the headland. Garion, wrapped in his cloak, stood on the ledge outside the entrance to the cellar, looking out over the froth-tipped waves in the gulf and the surf pounding on the beach far below. Off to the southeast, the clouds seemed to be growing thinner, and patches of blue raced along through the dirty-looking murk covering the rest of the sky. Sometime during the night, the tide had once again washed over the wreck of their ship, and the aft end had broken away and been carried off. A number of huddled lumps bobbed limply at the edge of the surf, and Garion resolutely kept his eyes away from those mute remains of the Murgo sailors who had been washed overboard and drowned when the ship had crashed into the reef.

Then, far up the coast, he saw a number of red-sailed ships beating their way along the south shore of the Gorand Sea toward the broken remains of the ship lying on the beach below.

Belgarath and Eriond pushed their way past the sailcloth door Durnik had hung across the arched entrance to the cellar the night before to join Garion on the ledge. "It's quit raining at least," Garion reported, "and the wind seems to be dropping. There's that problem though." He pointed at the Mallorean ships coming up the coast.

Belgarath grunted. "They're certain to come ashore when they see the wreck," he agreed. "I think it's time for us to leave here."

Eriond was looking around with a strange expression on his face. "It hasn't changed much," he noted. He pointed toward a small, grassy bench at the far end of the ledge. "I used to play there," he said, "when Zedar let me come outside, anyway."

"Did he talk to you very much while you were staying here?" Belgarath asked him.

"Not very often." Eriond shrugged. "He kept pretty much to himself. He had some books with him and he used to spend most of his time with them."

"It must have been a lonely way to grow up," Garion said.

"It wasn't so bad. I used to spend a lot of my time watching the clouds—or the birds. In the springtime the birds nest in holes in the face of this bluff. If you lean out over the edge, you can see them coming and going, and I always used to like watching the fledglings when they first tried out their wings."

"Do you have any idea of how far it is to the high road that leads inland?" Belgarath asked him.

"It used to take us about a day to get there. Of course I was small then, and I couldn't walk very fast."

Belgarath nodded. He shaded his eyes with one hand and looked at the Mallorean ships laboring up the coast. "I think we'd better tell the others," he said. "We won't accomplish too much by trying to hold this place against several shiploads of the Mallorean sailors."

It took perhaps an hour to gather up their still-wet clothing and their meager food supply and load the pack horses. Then they pushed their way out past the sailcloth door and led their horses to the far side of the headland. Garion noticed that Eriond looked back once with a faintly regretful expression, then resolutely turned his back on his childhood home to face the grassland lying ahead. "I sort of know the way," he said. "Those creeks out there are running bank-full, though, so we'll have to be careful." He swung lightly up into his saddle. "I'll go on ahead and pick the best route." He leaned forward and stroked his stallion's neck. Then he smiled. "Horse wants to run a bit anyway." He moved off down the hill at a rolling gallop.

"That's a very strange boy," Urgit said as he mounted. "Did he really know Zedar?"

"Oh, yes," Silk replied, "and also Ctuchik." He gave Polgara a sly look. "He's been consorting with strange people all his life, so his peculiarities aren't really all that hard to understand."

The small patches of blue that had touched the southeastern sky when Garion had first awakened had spread now, and columns of bright morning sunlight streamed down through the misty air to stalk ponderously across the stream-laced grassland below. The wind had abated to little more than a gusty breeze, and they rode on down through the still-wet grass at a brisk canter, following the trail of Eriond and his exuberant horse.

Ce'Nedra, dressed now in one of Eriond's tunics and a pair of woolen leggings, pulled in beside Garion.

"I like your outfit, my Queen." He grinned.

"All my dresses were still wet," she said. She paused, her face growing somber. "It's not working out very well, is it, Garion? We were counting so much on that ship."

"Oh, I don't know," he replied. "We saved a bit of time and we managed to get around most of the war zone. Once we get past Rak Cthaka, maybe we'll be able to find another ship. I don't think we actually lost any time."

"But we didn't gain any either, did we?"

"It's hard to say exactly."

She sighed and rode on beside him in silence.

They reached the high road about noon and turned eastward, making good time for the rest of the day. There was no sign that any other travelers had recently used the road, but Silk ranged out in front of them as a precautionary scout. A clump of willows at the side of the road afforded some shelter that night and also provided the poles necessary for erecting their tents. Supper that evening consisted of beans and bacon, a meal which Urgit in particular found less than satisfying. "I'd give anything for a chunk of beef right now," he complained, "even one as badly prepared as the cooks at the Drojim used to offer me."

"Would you prefer a bowl of boiled grass, your Majesty?" Prala asked him pertly, "or perhaps a nice plate of fried willow bark?"

He gave her a sour look, then turned to Garion. "Tell me," he said, "do you and your friends plan to remain long in Cthol Murgos?"

"Not too long, why?"

"Western ladies seem to have a broad streak of independence in their nature— and a regrettable tendency to speak their minds. I find their influence on certain impressionable Murgo ladies to be unwholesome." Then, as if suddenly realizing that he might have gone too far, he threw an apprehensive glance in Polgara's direction. "No offense intended, my Lady," he apologized quickly. "Just an old Murgo prejudice."

"I see," she replied.

Belgarath set aside his plate and looked over at Silk. "You were out in front all day," he noted. "Did you happen to see any game moving around?"

"There were herds of what looked like some sort of large deer moving north," the little man answered, "but they stayed a long way out of bow shot."

"What have you got in mind, old man?" Polgara asked.

"We need fresh meat, Pol," he replied, rising to his feet. "Moldy bacon and boiled beans aren't going to get us very far." He stepped out of the small circle of light and squinted up at the moon-speckled clouds drifting across the stars. "It might be a good night for hunting," he observed. "What do you think?"

A curious smile touched her lips, and she also rose. "Do you think you can still keep up, old wolf?" she asked him.

"Well enough, I suppose," he said blandly. "Come along, Garion. Let's get a little way away from the horses."

"Where are they going?" Urgit asked Silk.

"You don't want to know, my brother. You really don't want to know."

The moon touched the grass waving in the night breeze with silvery light. The scents of the grassland around them came sharply to Garion's nostrils as his ten-fold heightened sense of smell tasted the odors of the night. He loped easily at the side of the great silvery wolf while the snowy owl ghosted through the moonlight above them. It was good again to run tirelessly with the wind ruffling his fur and his toe-nails digging into the damp turf as he and his grandfather wolf ranged out across the moon-silvered grass in the ancient rite of the hunt.

They started a herd of deerlike creatures from their matted grass beds some leagues east of their camp and pursued them hard for miles across the rolling hills. Then, as the terrified animals plunged across a rain-swollen creek, an old buck, pushed to exhaustion, missed his footing, tumbled end over end, throwing up a great spray of water, and came to rest against the far bank, his antlers dug into the shore and his grotesquely twisted head proclaiming that his fall had snapped his neck.

Without thinking, Garion leaped from the bank into the swollen creek, drove himself rapidly across, and caught the dead buck by the foreleg with his powerful jaws. Straining, he dragged the still-warm carcass up onto the bank before the rushing creek could sweep it away.

Belgarath and Polgara, who had once again resumed their natural forms, came sauntering up the gravel bank as calmly as if they were on an evening stroll. "He's very good, isn't he?" Polgara observed.

"Not bad," Belgarath admitted. Then he drew his knife from his belt and tested its edge with his thumb. "We'll dress the deer out," he said to her. "Why don't you go back and get Durnik and a pack horse?"

"All right, father," she agreed, shimmered in the moonlight, and swooped away on silent wings.

"You're going to need your hands, Garion," the old man said pointedly.

"Oh," Garion said in the manner of wolves and rose from his haunches. "Sorry, Grandfather. I forgot." He changed back into his own form a little regretfully.

There were some queer looks the following morning when Polgara served up steaks instead of porridge, but no one chose to say anything about the sudden change of diet.

They rode on for the next two days, with the last wrack and tatter of the dying storm flowing overhead. About noon, they crested a long hill and saw before them the broad blue expanse of a great body of water.

"Lake Cthaka," Urgit said. "Once we circle that, we're only two days from Rak Cthaka itself."

"Sadi," Belgarath said, "have you got your map?"

"Right here, Ancient One," the eunuch replied, reaching inside his robe.

"Let's have a look." The old sorcerer swung down from his horse, took the parchment map from Sadi, and opened it. The wind coming off the lake rattled and fluttered it, threatening to tear it from his grasp. "Oh, stop that," he snapped irritably. Then he stared at the map for several long moments. "I think we're going to have to get off the road," he said finally. "The storm and the wreck delayed us, and we can't be absolutely certain how far the Malloreans have marched since we left Rak Urga. I don't want an army catching us with the lake at our backs. The Malloreans don't have any reason to be on the south side of the lake, so we'll go that way instead." He pointed at a large area on the map covered with a representation of trees. "We'll find out what the situation is in Rak Cthaka," he said, "and if we need to, we'll be able to get into the Great Southern Forest."

"Belgarath," Durnik said urgently, pointing toward the north, "what's that?"

A low smudge of black smoke was streaming low to the horizon in the stiff breeze.

"Grass fire perhaps?" Sadi suggested.

Belgarath began to swear. "No," he said shortly, "it's not the right color." He pulled the map open again. "There are some villages up there," he said. "I think it's one of them."

"Malloreans!" Urgit gasped.

"How could they have gotten this far west?" Silk asked.

"Wait a minute," Garion said as a sudden thought came to him. He looked at Urgit. "Who wins when you fight the Malloreans in the mountains?" he asked.

"We do, of course. We know how to use the mountains to our advantage."

"But when you fight them on the plains, who wins?"

"They do. They've got more people."

"Then your armies are safe only as long as they stay in the mountains?"

"I already said that, Belgarion."

"If I were the one who was fighting you then, I'd try to figure out a way to lure you down onto the plains. If I moved around, making threatening noises at Rak Cthaka, you'd almost have to respond, wouldn't you? You'd send all your troops out of Urga and Morcth to defend the city. But if, instead of attacking the city, I moved my forces north and west, I could intercept and ambush you out in the open on flat ground. I could pick my battlefields and destroy both your armies in a single day."

Urgit's face had grown very pale. "*That's* what those Mallorean ships were doing in the Gorand Sea!" he exclaimed. "They were there to spy out the movements of my troops coming from Rak Urga. 'Zakath's setting traps for me." He spun, his eyes wild. "Belgarath, you've got to let me go warn my troops. They're completely unprepared for an attack. The Malloreans will wipe my army out, and they're the only force between here and Rak Urga."

Belgarath tugged at one earlobe, squinting at him.

"Please, Belgarath!"

"Do you think you can move fast enough to get ahead of the Malloreans?"

"I have to. If I don't, Cthol Murgos will fall. Blast it, old man, I've got a responsibility."

"I think you're finally beginning to learn, Urgit," Belgarath told him. "We might make a king out of you, after all. Durnik, give him whatever food we can spare." He turned back to Silk's anxious brother. "Don't take chances," he cautioned. "Stay off the hilltops where you'll be outlined against the sky. Make the best time you can, but don't kill your horse in the process." He stopped, then gruffly grasped the weasel-faced man by the shoulders. "Good luck," he said shortly.

Urgit nodded, then turned toward his horse.

Prala was right behind him.

"What do you think you're doing?" he demanded.

"I'm going with you."

"You most certainly are not!"

"We're wasting time."

"There's probably going to be a battle, girl. Use your head."

"I'm a Murgo, too," she declared defiantly, "I'm descended from the Cthan Dynasty. I'm not afraid of battles!" She caught the reins of her horse and lifted the long black leather case down from her saddle. She untied the fastenings and snapped the case open. Inside lay a sword, its hilt encrusted with rubies. She lifted it from the case and held it aloft. "This is the sword of the last king of the Cthan Dynasty," she announced dramatically. "He took the field with it at Vo Mimbre. Do not dishonor it." She reversed the blade and offered him the hilt across her forearm.

He stared first at her and then at the sword.

"It was to have been my gift to you on our wedding day," she said to him, "but you need it now. Take the sword, King of the Murgos, and get on your horse. We have a battle to win."

He took the sword and held it up. The rubies caught the sun like drops of blood on the hilt. Then he suddenly turned, as if on an impulse. "Cross swords with me, Belgarion," he said, "for luck."

Garion nodded and drew his great sword. The fire that ran up its blade was a bright blue; when he touched Urgit's extended weapon with it, the smaller man winced as if the hilt of his sword had suddenly burned his hand. Then he stared at it incredulously. The stones on the hilt of his sword were no longer rubies, but bright blue sapphires. "Did you do that?" he gasped.

"No," Garion replied. "The Orb did. It seems to like you for some reason. Good luck, your Majesty."

"Thanks, your Majesty," Urgit answered. "And good luck to you, too—all of you." He started toward his horse again, then turned back and wordlessly caught Silk in a rough embrace. "All right, girl," he said to Prala, "let's go."

"Good-bye, Ce'Nedra," Prala called as she mounted her horse. "Thank you— for everything." The two of them wheeled their horses and raced off toward the north.

Silk sighed. "I'm afraid I'm going to lose him," he said mournfully.

"To the Malloreans, you mean?" Durnik asked.

"No—to that girl. She had a marrying sort of expression on her face when they left."

"I think it's sweet," Ce'Nedra sniffed.

"Sweet? I think it's revolting." He looked around. "If we're going around the south end of the lake, we'd better get started."

They galloped south along the lake shore through the long, golden-slanting beams of afternoon sunlight until they were a couple of leagues from the place where Urgit and Prala had so abruptly left them. Then Silk, ranging once again ahead of them, crested a hill and motioned them to come ahead, but cautiously.

"What is it?" Belgarath asked when they joined him.

"There's something else burning up ahead," the little man reported. "I didn't get too close, but it looks like an isolated farmstead."

"Let's go look," Durnik said to Toth, and the two of them rode off in the direction of the smudge of smoke lying low on the horizon to the east.

"I'd certainly like to know if Urgit's doing all right," Silk said with a worried frown.

"You really like him, don't you?" Velvet asked him.

"Urgit? Yes, I think I do. We're very much alike in many ways." He looked at her. "I suppose that you're going to mention all of this in your report to Javelin?"

"Naturally."

"I really wish you wouldn't, you know."

"Why on earth not?"

"I'm not entirely sure. It's just that for some reason I don't think I want Drasnian Intelligence using my relationship to the King of Cthol Murgos for its own advantage. I think I want to keep it private."

A silver twilight was settling over the lake when Durnik and Toth returned with grim faces. "It was a Murgo farmstead," Durnik reported. "Some Malloreans had been there. I don't think they were regular troops—probably deserters of some kind. They looted and burned, and regular troops don't usually do that, if they've got officers around to control them. The house is gone, but the barn is still partially intact."

"Is there enough of it left to shelter us for the night?" Garion wanted to know.

Durnik looked dubious, then shrugged. "The roof's still mostly there."

"Is something wrong?" Belgarath asked him.

Durnik made a small gesture and then walked away until he was out of earshot of the rest. Garion and Belgarath followed him.

"What's the matter, Durnik?" Belgarath asked.

"The barn's good enough to give us shelter," the smith said quietly, "but I think you ought to know that those Mallorean deserters impaled everybody on the farmstead. I don't think you want the ladies to see that. It isn't very pleasant."

"Is there someplace where you can get the bodies under cover?" the old man asked.

"I'll see what we can do," Durnik sighed. "Why do people do that sort of thing?"

"Ignorance, usually. An ignorant man falls back on brutality out of a lack of imagination. Go with them, Garion. They might need some help. Wave a torch to let us know when you get finished."

The fact that it was nearly dark helped a little. Garion was unable to see the faces of the people on the stakes. There was a sod-roofed cellar at the back of the still-smoldering house, and they put the bodies there. Then Garion took up a torch and walked some distance from the house to signal to Belgarath. The barn was dry, and the fire Durnik built in a carefully cleared area on the stone floor soon warmed it.

"This is actually pleasant," Ce'Nedra declared with a smile as she looked around at the dancing shadows on the walls and rafters. She sat on a pile of fragrant hay and bounced tentatively a few times. "And this will make wonderful beds. I hope we can find a place like this every night."

Garion walked over to the door and looked out, not trusting himself to answer. He had grown up on a farm not really all that much different from this one, and the thought of a band of marauding soldiers swooping down on Faldor's farm, burning and killing, filled him with a vast outrage. A sudden image rose in his mind. The shadowy faces of the dead Murgos hanging on those stakes might very well have been the faces of his childhood friends, and that thought shook him to the very core of his being. The dead here had been Murgos, but they had also been farmers, and he felt a sudden kinship with them. The savagery that had befallen them began to take on the aspect of a personal affront, and dark thoughts began to fill his mind.

CHAPTER TWENTY-ONE

By morning it was raining again, a drizzly sort of rain that made the surrounding countryside hazy and indistinct. They rode out from the ruins of the farmstead, dressed again in their slaver's robes, and turned northward along the eastern shore of the lake.

Garion rode in silence, his thoughts as somber as the leaden waters of the lake lying to his left. The rage he had felt the previous evening had settled into an icy resolve. Justice, he had been told, was an abstraction, but he was determined that, should the Mallorean deserters responsible for the atrocity at the farm ever cross his path, he would turn the abstract into an immediate reality. He knew that Belgarath and Polgara did not approve of the sort of thing he had in mind, so he kept his peace and contemplated the idea of vengeance, if not justice.

When they reached the muddy road coming in off the northern end of the lake and stretching out toward the southeast and the city of Rak Cthaka, they found it clogged with a horde of terrified civilians, dressed for the most part in ragged clothing and carrying bundles of what few possessions they had been able to salvage.

"I think we'll stay off the road," Belgarath decided. "We could never make any time through that mob."

"Are we going on to Rak Cthaka?" Sadi asked him.

Belgarath looked at the crowd streaming along the road. "I don't think you could find a raft in Rak Cthaka right now, much less a ship. Let's go on into the forest and work our way south through the trees. I don't much like staying out in the open in hostile territory, and fishing villages are better places to hire boats than the piers of a major city."

"Why don't you and the others ride on," Silk suggested. "I'd like to ask a few questions."

Belgarath grunted. "That might not be a bad idea. Just don't be too long at it. I'd like to reach the Great Southern Forest sometime before the end of winter, if I can possibly manage it."

"I'll go with him, Grandfather," Garion offered. "I need to get my mind off some things I've seen lately, anyway."

The two of them rode through the knee-high grass toward the broad stream of frightened refugees fleeing southward. "Garion," Silk said, reining in his horse, "isn't that a Sendar—the one pushing the wheelbarrow?"

Garion shielded his eyes from the rain and peered at the sturdy fellow Silk had pointed out. "He sort of looks like a Sendar," he agreed. "What would a Sendar be doing down here in Cthol Murgos?"

"Why don't we go ask him? Sendars love to gossip, so he can probably give us some idea of what's happening." The little man walked his horse over until he was riding beside the stout man with the wheelbarrow. "Morning, friend," he said pleasantly. "You're a long way from home, aren't you?"

The stout man set down his barrow and eyed Silk's green Nyissan robe apprehensively. "I'm not a slave," he declared, "so don't get any ideas."

"This?" Silk laughed, plucking at the front of the robe. "Don't worry, friend, we're not Nyissans. We just found these on some bodies back there a ways. We thought they might be a help if we happened to run into somebody official. What in the world are you doing in Cthol Murgos?"

"Running," the Sendar said ruefully, "just like all the rest of this rabble. Didn't you hear about what's been happening?"

"No. We've been out of touch."

The stout man lifted the handles of his barrow again and trudged along the grassy shoulder of the road. "There's a whole Mallorean army marching west out of Gorut," he said. "They burned the town I lived in and killed half the people. They didn't even bother with Rak Cthaka, so that's where we're all going. I'm going to see if I can find a sea captain who's going in the general direction of Sendaria. For some reason, I'm suddenly homesick."

"You've been living in a Murgo town?" Silk asked with some surprise.

The fellow made a face. "It wasn't altogether by choice," he replied. "I had some trouble with the law in Tolnedra when I was there on business ten years ago and I took passage on board a merchantman to get out of the country. The captain was a scoundrel; when my money ran out, he sailed off and left me on the wharf at Rak Cthaka. I drifted on up to a town on the north side of the lake. They let me stay because I was willing to do things that are beneath Murgo dignity, but were too important to trust a slave to do. It was sort of degrading, but it was a living. Anyway, a couple of days ago the Malloreans marched through. When they left, there wasn't a single building standing."

"How did you escape?" Silk asked him.

"I hid under a haystack until dark. That's when I joined this mob." He glanced over at the crowd of refugees slogging through the ankle-deep mud of the road. "Isn't that pathetic? They don't even have sense enough to spread out and walk on the grass. You certainly wouldn't see soldiers doing that, let me tell you."

"You've had some military experience, then?"

"I most certainly have," the stout man replied proudly. "I was a sergeant in Princess Ce'Nedra's army. I was at Thull Mardu with her."

"I missed that one," Silk told him with aplomb. "I was busy someplace else. Are there any Malloreans between here and the Great Southern Forest?"

"Who knows? I don't go looking for Malloreans. You don't really want to go into the forest, though. All this killing has stirred up the Raveners."

"Raveners? What's that?"

"Ghouls. They feed on dead bodies most of the time, but I've heard some very ugly stories lately. I'd make a special point of staying out of the forest, my friend."

"We might have to keep that in mind. Thanks for the information. Good luck when you get to Rak Cthaka, and I hope you make it back to Camaar."

"Right now, I'd settle for Tol Honeth. Tolnedran jails aren't really all that bad."

Silk grinned at him quickly, turned his horse, and led Garion away from the road at a gallop to rejoin the others.

That afternoon they forded the River Cthaka some leagues upstream from the coast. The drizzle slackened as evening approached, though the sky remained cloudy. Once they had reached the far side of the river, they could see the irregular, dark shape of the edge of the Great Southern Forest, looming up beyond perhaps a league of open grassland.

"Shall we try for it?" Silk asked.

"Let's wait," Belgarath decided. "I'm just a little concerned about what that fellow you talked with said. I'm not sure I want any surprises—particularly in the dark."

"There's a willow thicket downstream a ways," Durnik said, pointing at a fair-sized grove of spindly trees bordering the river a half mile or so to the south. "Toth and I can pitch the tents there."

"All right," Belgarath agreed.

"How far is it to Verkat now, Grandfather?" Garion asked as they rode down along the rain-swollen river toward the willows.

"According to the map, it's about fifty leagues to the southeast before we reach the coast opposite the island. Then we'll have to find a boat to get us across."

Garion sighed.

"Don't get discouraged," Belgarath told him. "We're making better time than I'd originally expected, and Zandramas can't run forever. There's only so much land in the world. Sooner or later we'll chase her down."

As Durnik and Toth pitched the tents, Garion and Eriond ranged out through the sodden willow thicket in search of firewood. It was difficult to find anything sufficiently dry to burn, and the effort of an hour yielded only enough twigs and small branches from under fallen trees to make a meager cook fire for Polgara. As she began to prepare their evening meal of beans and venison, Garion noted that Sadi was walking about their campsite, combing the ground with his eyes. "This isn't funny, dear," he said quite firmly. "Now you come out this very minute."

"What's the matter?" Durnik asked him.

"Zith isn't in her bottle," Sadi replied, still searching.

Durnik rose from where he was sitting quite rapidly. "Are you sure?"

"She thinks it's amusing to hide from me sometimes. Now, you come out immediately, you naughty snake."

"You probably shouldn't tell Silk," Belgarath advised. "He'll go directly into hysterics if he finds out that she's loose." The old man looked around. "Where is he, by the way?"

"He and Liselle went for a walk," Eriond told him.

"In all this wet? Sometimes I wonder about him."

Ce'Nedra came over and sat on the log beside Garion. He put his arm about her shoulders and drew her close to him. She snuggled down and sighed. "I wonder what Geran is doing tonight," she said wistfully.

"Sleeping, probably."

"He always looked so adorable when he was asleep." She sighed again and then closed her eyes.

There was a crashing back in the willows, and Silk suddenly ran into the circle of firelight, his eyes very wide and his face deathly pale.

"What's the matter?" Durnik exclaimed.

"She had that snake in her bodice!" Silk blurted.

"Who did?"

"Liselle!"

Polgara, holding a ladle in one hand, turned to regard the violently trembling little man with one raised eyebrow. "Tell me, Prince Kheldar," she said in a cool voice, "exactly what were you doing in the Margravine Liselle's bodice?"

Silk endured that steady gaze for a moment; then he actually began to blush furiously.

"Oh," she said, "I see." She turned back to her cooking.

It was past midnight, and Garion was not sure what it was that had awakened him. He moved slowly to avoid waking Ce'Nedra and carefully parted the tent flap to look out. A dense, clinging fog had arisen from the river, and all that he could see was a curtain of solid, dirty white. He lay quietly, straining his ears to catch any sound.

From somewhere off in the fog, he heard a faint clinking sound; it took him a moment to identify it. Finally he realized that what he was hearing was the sound of a mounted man wearing a mail shirt. He reached over in the darkness and took up his sword.

"I still think you ought to tell us what you found in that house before you set it on fire," he heard someone say in a gruff, Mallorean-accented voice. The speaker was not close, but sounds at night traveled far, so Garion could clearly understand what was being said.

"Oh, it wasn't much, Corporal," another Mallorean voice replied evasively. "A bit of this; a bit of that."

"I think you ought to share those things with the rest of us. We're all in this together, after all."

"Isn't it odd that you didn't think of that until after I managed to pick up a few things? If you want to share in the loot, then you should pay attention to the houses and not spend all your time impaling the prisoners."

"We're at war," the corporal declared piously. "It's our duty to kill the enemy."

"Duty," the second Mallorean snorted derisively. "We're deserters, Corporal. Our only duty is to ourselves. If you want to spend your time butchering Murgo farmers, that's up to you, but I'm saving up for my retirement."

Garion carefully rolled out from under the tent flap. He felt a peculiar calm, almost as if his emotions had somehow been set aside. He rose and moved silently to where the packs were piled and burrowed his hand into them one by one until his fingers touched steel. Then, carefully, so that it made no sound, he drew out his heavy mail shirt. He pulled it on and shrugged his shoulders a couple of times to settle it into place.

Toth was standing guard near the horses, his huge bulk looming in the fog.

"There's something I have to take care of," Garion whispered softly to the mute giant.

Toth looked at him gravely, then nodded. He turned, untied a horse from the picket line, and handed him the reins. Then he put one huge hand on Garion's shoulder, squeezed once in silent approval, and stepped back.

Garion did not want to give the Mallorean deserters time to lose themselves in the fog, so he pulled himself up onto the unsaddled horse and moved out of the willow thicket at a silent walk.

The fading voices that had come out of the fog had seemed to be moving in the direction of the forest, and Garion rode quietly after them, probing the foggy darkness ahead with his ears and with his mind.

After he had ridden for perhaps a mile, he heard a raucous laugh coming from somewhere ahead and slightly to the left. "Did you hear the way they squealed when we impaled them?" a coarse voice came out of the clinging mist.

"That does it," Garion grated from between clenched teeth as he drew his sword. He directed his horse toward the sound, then nudged his heels at the animal's flanks. The horse moved faster, his hooves making no sound on the damp earth.

"Let's have some light," one of the deserters said.

"Do you think it's safe? There are patrols out looking for deserters."

"It's after midnight. The patrols are all in bed. Go ahead and light the torch."

After a moment, there was a fatally ruddy beacon glowing in the dark and reaching out to Garion.

His charge caught the deserters totally by surprise. Several of them were dead before they even knew that he was upon them. There were screams and shouts from both sides as he crashed through them, chopping them out of their saddles with huge strokes to the right and the left. His great blade sheared effortlessly through mail, bone, and flesh. He sent five of them tumbling to the ground as he thundered through their ranks. Then he whirled on the three who still remained. After one startled look, one of them fled; another dragged his sword from its sheath, and the third, who held the torch, sat frozen in astonished terror.

The Mallorean with the sword feebly raised his weapon to protect his head from the dreadful blow Garion had already launched. The great overhand sweep, however, shattered the doomed man's sword blade and sheared down through his helmet halfway to his waist. Roughly, Garion kicked the twitching body off his sword and turned on the torch bearer.

"Please!" the terrified man cried, trying to back his horse away. "Have mercy!"

For some reason, that plaintive cry infuriated Garion all the more. He clenched his teeth together. With a single broad swipe, he sent the murderer's head spinning off into the foggy darkness.

He pulled his horse up sharply, cocked his head for a moment to pick up the sound of the last Mallorean's galloping flight, and set out in pursuit.

It took him only a few minutes to catch up with the fleeing deserter. At first he had only the sound to follow, but then he was able to make out the dim, shadowy form racing ahead of him in the fog. He veered slightly to the right, plunged on past the desperate man, then pulled his horse directly into the shadowy deserter's path.

"Who are you?" the unshaven Mallorean squealed as he hauled his mount to a sudden, rearing stop. "Why are you doing this?"

"I am justice," Garion grated at him and quite deliberately ran the man through.

The deserter stared in horrified amazement at the huge sword protruding from his chest. With a gurgling sigh, he toppled to one side, sliding limply off the blade.

Still without any real sense of emotion, Garion dismounted and wiped the blade of his sword on the dead man's tunic. Almost as an afterthought, he caught the reins of the fellow's horse, remounted, and turned back toward the place where he had killed the others. Carefully, one by one, he checked each fallen body for signs of life, then rounded up three more horses and rode back to the camp concealed in the willows.

Silk stood beside the huge Toth near the picket line. "Where have you been?" he demanded in a hoarse whisper as Garion dismounted.

"We needed some more horses," Garion replied tersely, handing the reins of the captured mounts to Toth.

"Mallorean ones, judging from the saddles," Silk noted. "How did you find them?"

"Their riders were talking as they went by. They seemed to be quite amused by a visit they paid to a Murgo farmstead a few days ago."

"And you didn't even invite me to go along?" Silk accused.

"Sorry," Garion said, "but I had to hurry. I didn't want to lose them in the fog."

"Four of them?" Silk asked, counting horses.

"I couldn't find the other four mounts." Garion shrugged. "These ought to be enough to make up for the ones we lost during the shipwreck, though."

"Eight?" Silk looked a bit startled at that.

"I came on them by surprise. It wasn't much of a fight. Why don't we get some sleep?"

"Uh—Garion," Silk suggested, "it might not be a bad idea for you to wash up before you go back to bed. Ce'Nedra's nerves are a little delicate, and she might be upset, if she wakes up and sees you covered with blood the way you are."

The fog was even thicker the following morning. It was a heavy fog, chill and clinging, lying densely along the river bank and bedewing the tangled limbs of the willow thicket at their backs with strings of pearl-like droplets.

"It hides us, at least," Garion observed, still feeling that peculiar remoteness.

"It also hides anybody else who might be out there," Sadi told him, "or any *thing*. That forest up ahead has a bad reputation."

"Just how big is it?"

"It's probably the largest forest in the world," Sadi replied, lifting a pack up onto a horse's back. "It goes on for hundreds of leagues." He looked curiously down the picket line. "Is it my imagination, or do we have more horses this morning?"

"I happened across a few last night," Garion replied.

After breakfast, they packed up Polgara's cooking utensils, mounted, and started out across the intervening grassland toward the forest lying hidden in the fog.

As Garion rode, he heard Silk and Durnik talking right behind him. "Just what were you doing last night?" Durnik asked directly. "When you found Zith in Liselle's bodice, I mean?"

"She's going to make a report to Javelin when this is all over," Silk replied. "There are some things I'd rather he didn't know. If I can get on friendly terms with her, maybe I can persuade her to overlook those things in her report."

"That's really rather contemptible, you know. She's just a girl."

"Believe me, Durnik, Liselle can take care of herself. The two of us are playing a game. I'll admit that I hadn't counted on Zith, though."

"Do Drasnians always have to play games?"

"Of course. It helps to pass the time. Winters are very long and tedious in Drasnia. The games we play sharpen our wits and make us better at what we do when we aren't playing." The little man raised his voice slightly. "Garion?" he said.

"Yes?"

"Are we avoiding the place where you found those horses last night? We wouldn't want to upset the ladies so soon after breakfast."

"It was over that way." Garion gestured off to the left.

"What's this?" Durnik asked.

"The extra animals came from a group of Mallorean deserters who used to creep up on isolated Murgo farmlands," Silk replied lightly. "Garion saw to it that they won't be needing horses any more."

"Oh," Durnik said. He thought about it for a moment. "Good," he said finally.

The dark trees loomed out of the fog as the company approached the edge of the forest. The leaves had turned brown and clung sparsely to the branches, for winter was not far off. As they rode in under the twisted branches, Garion looked about, trying to identify the trees, but they were of kinds that he did not recognize. They were gnarled into fantastic shapes, and their limbs seemed almost to writhe up and out from their massy trunks, reaching toward the sunless sky. Their gnarled stems were dotted with dark knots, deeply indented in the coarse bark, and those knots seemed somehow to give each tree a grotesque semblance of a distorted human face with wide, staring eyes and a gaping mouth twisted into an expression of unspeakable horror. The forest floor was deep with fallen leaves, blackened and sodden, and the fog hung gray beneath the branches spreading above.

Ce'Nedra drew her cloak more tightly about her and shuddered. "Do we have to go through this forest?" she asked plaintively.

"I thought you liked trees," Garion said.

"Not these." She looked about fearfully. "There's something very cruel about them. They hate each other."

"Hate? Trees?"

"They struggle and push each other, trying to reach the sunlight. I don't like this place, Garion."

"Try not to think about it," he advised.

They pushed deeper and deeper into the gloomy wood, riding in silence for the most part, their spirits sunk low by the pervasive gloom and by the cold antagonism seeping from the strange, twisted trees.

They took a brief, cold lunch, then rode on toward a somber twilight which seemed hardly more than a deepening of the foggy half-dark spread beneath the hateful trees.

"I guess we've gone far enough," Belgarath said finally. "Let's get a fire going and put up the tents."

It might have been only Garion's imagination or perhaps the cry of some hunting bird of prey, but as the first few flickering tongues of flame curled up around the sticks in the fire pit, it seemed that he heard a shriek coming from the trees themselves—a shriek of fear mingled with a dreadful rage. And as he looked around, the distorted semblances of human faces deeply indented in the surrounding tree trunks seemed to move in the flickering light, silently howling at the hated fire.

After they had eaten, Garion walked away from the fire. He still felt strangely numb inside, as if his emotions had been enclosed in some kind of protective blanket. He found that he could no longer even remember the details of last night's encounter, but only brief, vivid flashes of blood spurting in ruddy torchlight, of riders tumbling limply out of their saddles, and of the torch bearer's head flying off into the fog.

"Do you want to talk about it?" Belgarath asked quietly from just behind him.

"Not really, Grandfather. I don't think you'll approve of what I did, so why don't we just let it go at that? There's no way that I could make you understand."

"Oh, I understand, Garion. I just don't think that you accomplished anything, that's all. You killed—how many was it?"

"Eight."

"That many? All right—eight Malloreans. What did you prove by it?"

"I wasn't really out to prove anything, Grandfather. I just wanted to make sure that they never did it again. I can't even be absolutely certain that they were the men who killed those Murgo farmers. They did kill some people someplace, though, and people who do that sort of thing need to be stopped."

"You did that, all right. Does it make you feel any better?"

"No. I suppose not. I wasn't even angry when I killed them. It was just something that had to be done, so I did it. Now it's over, and I'd just as soon forget about it."

Belgarath gave him a long, steady look. "All right," he said finally. "As long as you keep that firmly in mind, I guess you haven't done yourself any permanent injury. Let's go back to the fire. It's chilly out here in the woods."

Garion slept badly that night, and Ce'Nedra, huddled almost fearfully in his arms, stirred restlessly and often whimpered in her sleep.

The next morning, Belgarath rose and looked about with a dark scowl. "This is absurd," he burst out quite suddenly. "Where *is* the sun?"

"Behind the clouds and fog, father," Polgara replied as she calmly brushed her long, dark hair.

"I know that, Pol," he retorted testily, "but I need to see it—even if only briefly—to get our direction. We could wind up wandering around in circles."

Toth, who had been building up the fire, looked over at the old man, his face impassive as always. He raised one hand and pointed in a direction somewhat at an oblique from that which they had been following the previous evening.

Belgarath frowned. "Are you absolutely sure?" he asked the giant.

Toth nodded.

"Have you been through these woods before?"

Again the mute nodded, then firmly pointed once more in the same direction.

"And if we go that way, we're going to come out on the south coast in the vicinity of the Isle of Verkat?"

Toth nodded again and went back to tending the fire.

"Cyradis said that he was coming along to aid us in the search, Grandfather," Garion reminded him.

"All right. Since he knows the way, we'll let him lead us through this forest. I'm tired of guessing."

They had gone perhaps two leagues that cloudy morning, with Toth confidently leading them along a scarcely perceptible track, when Polgara quite suddenly reined in her horse with a warning cry. "Look out!"

An arrow sizzled through the foggy air directly at Toth, but the huge man swept it aside with his staff. Then a gang of rough-looking men, some Murgos and some of indeterminate race, came rushing out of the woods, brandishing a variety of weapons.

Without a moment's hesitation, Silk rolled out of his saddle, his hands diving under his slaver's robe for his daggers. As the bawling ruffians charged forward, he leaped to meet them, his heavy daggers extended in front of him like a pair of spears.

Even as Garion jumped to the ground, he saw Toth already advancing, his huge staff whirling as he bore down on the attackers, and Durnik, holding his axe in both hands, circling to the other side.

Garion swept Iron-grip's sword from its scabbard and ran forward, swinging the flaming blade in great arcs. One of the ruffians launched himself into the air, twisting as he did so in a clumsy imitation of a maneuver Garion had seen Silk perform so many times in the past. This time, however, the technique failed. Instead of driving his heels into Garion's face or chest, the agile fellow encountered the point of the burning sword, and his momentum quite smoothly skewered him on the blade.

Silk ripped open an attacker with one of his daggers, spun, and drove his other knife directly into the forehead of another.

Toth and Durnik, moving in from opposite sides, drove several of the assailants into a tight knot, and methodically began to brain them one after another as they struggled to disentangle themselves from each other.

"Garion!" Ce'Nedra cried, and he whirled to see a burly, unshaven man pull the struggling little queen from her saddle with one hand, even as he raised the knife he held in the other. Then he dropped the knife, and both his hands flew up to grasp the slim, silken cord that had suddenly been looped about his neck from the rear. Calmly, the golden-haired Velvet, her knee pushed firmly against the wildly thrashing man's back, pulled her cord tighter and tighter. Ce'Nedra watched in horror as her would-be killer was efficiently strangled before her eyes.

Garion grimly turned and began to chop his way through the now-disconcerted attackers. The air around him was suddenly filled with shrieks, groans, and chunks of clothing and flesh. The ragged-looking men he faced flinched back as his huge sword laid a broad windrow of quivering dead in his wake. Then they broke and ran.

"Cowards!" a black-robed man screamed after the fleeing villains. He held a bow in his hand and he raised it, pointing his arrow directly at Garion. Then he suddenly doubled over sharply, driving his arrow into the ground before him as one of Silk's daggers flickered end over end to sink solidly into his stomach.

"Is anybody hurt?" Garion demanded, spinning around quickly, his dripping sword still in his hand.

"They are." Silk laughed gaily, looking around with some satisfaction at the carnage in the forest clearing.

"Please stop!" Ce'Nedra cried to Velvet in an anguished voice.

"What?" the blond girl asked absently, still leaning back against the silken cord drawn tightly about the neck of the now-limp man she had just strangled. "Oh, I'm sorry, Ce'Nedra," she apologized. "My attention wandered a bit, I guess." She released the cord, and the black-faced dead man toppled to the ground at her feet.

"Nice job," Silk congratulated her.

"Fairly routine." She shrugged, carefully coiling up her garrote.

"You seem to be taking it quite calmly."

"There's no particular reason to get excited, Kheldar. It's part of what we were trained to do, after all."

He looked as if he were about to reply, but her matter-of-fact tone obviously baffled him.

"Yes?" she asked.

"Nothing."

■ | CHAPTER TWENTY-TWO | ■

"Stop that!" Durnik said in disgust to Sadi, who was moving about the clearing casually sticking his small, poisoned dagger into each of the bodies littering the ground.

"Just making sure, Goodman," Sadi replied coolly. "It's not prudent to leave an enemy behind you who might be feigning death." He moved over to the black-robed man whom Silk had felled. "What's this?" he said with some surprise. "This one's still alive." He reached down to push the dying man's hood aside to look at his face, then pulled back his hand with a sharp intake of his breath. "You'd better have a look at this one, Belgarath," he said.

Belgarath crossed the clearing to the eunuch's side.

"Doesn't that purple lining on the inside of his hood mean that he's a Grolim?" Sadi asked.

Belgarath nodded bleakly. He bent and lightly touched the hilt of Silk's dagger that still protruded from the robed man's stomach. "He doesn't have much time left," he said. "Can you get him conscious enough to answer a few questions?"

"I can try," Sadi told him. He went to his horse and took a vial of yellow liquid from his red case. "Could you get me a cup of water, Goodman?" he asked Durnik.

The smith's face was disapproving, but he fetched a tin cup from one of the packs and filled it from one of their water bags.

Sadi carefully measured a few drops of the yellow liquid into the cup, then swirled it around a few times. He knelt beside the dying man and almost tenderly lifted his head. "Here," he said gently, "drink this. It might make you feel better." He supported the Grolim's head on his arm and held the cup to his lips. Weakly, the stricken man drank, then lay back. After a moment, a serene smile came to his ashen face.

"There, isn't that better?"

"Much better," the dying man croaked.

"That was quite a skirmish, wasn't it?"

"We thought to surprise you," the Grolim admitted, "but we were the ones who got the surprise."

"Your Master—what was his name again? I'm terrible at names."

"Morgat," the Grolim supplied with a bemused look on his face, "Hierarch of Rak Cthan."

"Oh, yes, now I remember. Anyway, Morgat should have given you more men to help you."

"I hired the men myself—at Rak Cthaka. They told me that they were profes-sionals, but—" He began to cough weakly.

"Don't tire yourself," Sadi said. He paused. "What's Morgat's interest in us?" he asked.

"He's acting on the instructions of Agachak," the Grolim replied, his voice lit-tle more than a whisper. "Agachak is not one to take chances, and some very serious accusations were made back at Rak Urga, I understand. Agachak has ordered that every Grolim priest of the purple seek you out."

Sadi sighed. "It's more or less what I'd expected," he said mournfully. "People always seem to distrust me. Tell me, how did you ever manage to find us?"

"It was Cthrag Yaska," the Grolim replied, his breathing growing even more la-bored. "Its accursed song rings across Cthol Murgos like a beacon, drawing every Grolim of the purple directly to you." The dying man drew in a deep breath, and his unfocused eyes suddenly became alert. "What was in that cup?" he demanded sharply. He pushed Sadi's arm away and tried to rise to a sitting position. A great gush of blood spurted from his mouth, and his eyes went blank. He shuddered once with a long, gurgling groan. Then he fell limply back.

"Dead," Sadi noted clinically. "That's the problem with oret. It's a little hard on the heart, and this fellow wasn't in very good shape to begin with. I'm sorry, Belgarath, but it was the best I could do."

"It was enough, Sadi," the old man replied bleakly. "Come with me, Garion," he said. "Let's go someplace quiet. You and I are going to have to have a long talk with the Orb."

"Do you suppose that you could hold off on that, Belgarath?" Sadi asked, looking around nervously. "I think we want to get as far away from here as we can—almost immediately."

"I hardly expect those fellows to come back, Sadi," Silk drawled.

"That's not what concerns me, Kheldar. It's not prudent to remain in the vicinity of so many dead bodies in this forest, and we've lingered much too long already."

"Would you like to explain that?" Garion asked.

"Do you remember the warning the Sendar on the road gave to you and Kheldar?"

"About something he called the Raveners, you mean?"

"Yes. How much did he tell you?"

"He said that they're ghouls—creatures that feed on the dead. But that's just a ghost story, isn't it?"

"I'm afraid not. I've heard the story from people who've actually seen them. We definitely want to get away from here. Most of the people who live in this forest—or near it—don't bury their dead. They burn them instead."

"I've never cared much for that idea," Durnik said.

"It has nothing to do with respect, Goodman—or the lack of it. It's done to protect the living."

"All right," Silk said. "What are these ghouls supposed to look like? There are a lot of animals around that try to dig up dead bodies."

"The Raveners aren't animals, Kheldar. They're men—or at least that's what they look like. Normally, they're quite torpid and only come out at night, but during a war or a pestilence, when there are a large number of bodies unburied, they go into a kind of frenzy. The smell of death attracts them and makes them wild. They'll attack anything when they're like that."

"Father," Polgara said, "is this true?"

"It's possible," he admitted. "I've heard some unpleasant things about these woods myself. I don't usually pursue ghost stories, so I didn't bother to investigate."

"Every country has its stories of ogres and monsters," Silk said skeptically. "Only children are frightened by them."

"I'll strike a bargain with you, Kheldar," Sadi said. "If we make it through these woods without seeing any Raveners, you can laugh at my timidity if you like, but for the sake of the ladies, let's get away from here."

Belgarath was frowning. "I don't altogether accept the notion of ghouls," he said, "but then, I didn't believe there was such a thing as an Eldrak either—until I saw one. We want to move along anyway, and Garion and I can talk with the Orb later."

With Toth once more in the lead, they rode away at a gallop, still following the scarcely visible track that angled off toward the southeast. Their horses' hooves tossed up clots of the leaves lying thick-spread on the forest floor as they plunged through the misty wood. The misshapen trees seemed to gape at them as they pounded past, and, though Garion knew it was only his imagination, those grotesque, almost human features seemed somehow to have taken on expressions of malicious glee.

"Wait!" Silk barked suddenly. "Stop!"

They all reined in.

"I thought I heard something—off that way," Silk said. They all sat straining their ears, trying to listen over the heavy panting of their horses.

Faintly, from somewhere to the east, a scream came out of the fog.

"There it is again," Silk said. He pulled his horse around.

"What are you doing?" Belgarath asked him.

"I'm going to have a look."

But Toth had moved his horse around until it was blocking the Drasnian's path. Gravely the giant shook his head.

"Toth, we have to know what's happening," Silk said.

Toth shook his head again.

"Toth," Garion said, "is what Sadi told us really true? Is there really such a thing as a Ravener?"

Toth's face grew bleak, and he nodded.

Another scream came out of the dim woods, seeming much closer this time. The scream was filled with horror and agony.

"Who is it?" Ce'Nedra demanded, her voice shrill with fright. "Who's screaming?"

"The men who attacked us," Eriond replied in a sick voice. "The ones who survived the fight. Something's running them down one by one."

"Raveners?" Garion asked him.

"I think so. Whatever it is, it's horrible."

"They're coming this way," Sadi said. "Let's get away from here." He drove his heels into his horse's flanks.

They plunged off into the gloomy wood, no longer even trying to follow the track. Their blind flight took them perhaps a half mile farther into the forest when Polgara suddenly pulled her horse to a halt. "Stop!" she commanded.

"What is it, Pol?" Durnik asked her.

But she pushed forward carefully to peer at a thicket half-obscured in the mist. "There's someone ahead," she whispered.

"A Ravener?" Garion asked in a low voice.

She concentrated for a moment. "No. It's one of the attackers. He's trying to hide."

"How far away is he?"

"Not far." She continued to peer into the shrouding mist. "There," she said. "He's behind that tree at the edge of the thicket—the one with the broken limb hanging down."

Garion vaguely saw a dark patch half-concealed behind a gnarled tree root rising out of the sodden leaves. Then a movement caught his eye, and he glimpsed a shambling figure coming out of the trees. It seemed gray, almost invisible in the hazy fog, and it was so gaunt that it resembled a skeleton. It was dressed in rags, stained with earth and blood. Its pale skull was covered with scanty hair, and it was half-crouched, snuffling audibly as it walked with its arms hanging loosely. Its eyes were vacant and its mouth agape.

Then another emerged from the woods, and yet another. As the creatures advanced, they made a low moaning sound that expressed nothing remotely intelligible, but rather seemed to convey only a dreadful hunger.

"He's going to run!" Polgara said.

With a despairing cry, the hidden assassin leaped to his feet and desperately began to run. The Raveners took up the chase, their moaning coming faster. Their shambling gait quickened, and their emaciated legs carried them through the wood at a surprising rate of speed.

Twisting and dodging, the panic-stricken ruffian fled among the trees, with his hideous pursuers gaining on him at every step. When he finally disappeared far back into the fog and gloom, they were no more than a few yards behind him.

His shriek was a shocking, horrible sound. Again he screamed—and again.

"Are they killing him?" Ce'Nedra's voice was shrill.

Polgara's face had gone absolutely white, and her eyes were filled with horror. "No," she replied in a shaking voice.

"What are they doing?" Silk demanded.

"They're eating him."

"But—" Silk broke off as more shrieks came out of the fog. "He's still—" He stared at her, his eyes gone very wide and the blood draining from his cheeks.

Ce'Nedra gasped. "Alive?" she said in a choked whisper. "They're eating him while he's still alive?"

"That's what I was trying to warn you about, your Majesty," Sadi said grimly. "When they go into their frenzy, they don't make any distinction between the living and the dead. They feed on anything."

"Toth," Belgarath said sharply. "Can they be frightened off?"

The mute shook his head, then turned to Durnik, gesturing rapidly, touching his head and then his stomach.

"He says that they aren't able to think enough to be afraid," the smith told him. "All they know is hunger."

"What are we going to do, father?" Polgara demanded.

"We're going to try to outrun them," he replied, "and if any of them get in our way, we'll have to kill them." He looked back at Toth. "How far can they run?" he asked.

Toth raised one hand and traced an arc over his head, then another, and then another.

"For days," Durnik interpreted.

Belgarath's face became very grim. "Let's go," he said, "and stay together."

Their pace through the dreadful wood was more measured now, and the men all rode with their weapons in their hands.

The first attack came after they had gone no more than a mile. A dozen gray-faced Raveners shambled out from among the trees, moaning their hideous hunger and spreading out to block the path.

Garion spurred forward, swinging his sword in great arcs. Savagely, he chopped a path through the ranks of the slavering Raveners, who reached out mindlessly to pull him from his saddle. A terrible, rotting stink rose from them as he rode them down. He killed fully half of them as he crashed through, then whirled his horse to smash into them again, but pulled up sharply, his gorge rising. The Raveners who had escaped his sword were tearing at the bodies of those who had gone down, ripping out dripping gobbets of flesh and feeding them into their gaping mouths with their clawlike hands, even as they continued their awful moan.

Cautiously Belgarath and the others circled around that dreadful feeding, averting their eyes as they passed.

"It won't work, father," Polgara declared. "Sooner or later one of us is going to make a mistake. We're going to have to shield."

He thought about it for a moment. "You might be right, Pol," he admitted finally. He looked at Garion. "You and Durnik pay attention to how this is done," he instructed. "I want you to be able to take over when we get tired."

They started out at a walk as Belgarath and Polgara adjusted the barrier they were creating with the force of their combined will. They had gone no more than a little way when a gray-faced Ravener came loping out from among the twisted trees, slobbering and moaning. When it was perhaps ten yards from Durnik's horse, it suddenly stumbled back as if it had just run headlong into something solid. Moaning dreadfully, it came forward again and began to claw at the empty air with its filthy, long-nailed hands.

"Durnik," Polgara said quite calmly, "would you deal with it, please?"

"All right, Pol." The smith's face creased into an expression of extreme concentration, and he muttered a single word. The Ravener flickered and popped momentarily out of sight. When it reappeared, it was twenty yards away, beside a large tree. It struggled to lurch forward at them again, but seemed for some reason unable to move.

"That should hold it," Durnik said.

"What did you do?" Silk asked, peering at the struggling creature.

"I stuck its arm into that tree," Durnik replied. "If it wants to attack again, it's either going to have to bring the tree along or leave the arm behind. I didn't really hurt it, but it's going to take it a day or so to get its arm loose."

"Have you got a good hold on our shield, Pol?" Belgarath asked over his shoulder.

"Yes, father."

"Let's pick up the pace a trifle then. A bit of momentum won't hurt."

They moved, first at a trot and then at a loping canter. The shield Belgarath was projecting to the front ran ahead of them like a battering ram, hurling the rag-clothed Raveners from their path.

"Where do they get those clothes?" Silk asked as he rode.

Toth made a kind of digging motion with one hand.

"He says that they take them off the bodies of the dead that they dig up," Durnik translated.

Silk shuddered. "That would explain the smell, then."

The next few days began to blur in Garion's mind. It was necessary to relieve Polgara and Belgarath every four hours or so, and the weight of the shield he and Durnik erected seemed to grow with each passing mile. The fog continued, making it impossible to see more than a hundred yards in any direction, and the twisted trees, with their semblance of human faces, emerged with a shocking suddenness out of that obscuring mist. Shapes, gray and emaciated, moved through that fog, and the mindless moaning came from all around them as they plunged through the ghoul-haunted wood.

Night was a time of dreadful terror as the Raveners gathered around the shield, clawing at it and moaning their hideous longing. Exhausted by his efforts of the day, Garion was forced to use every ounce of his will—not merely to hold the shield in place when his turn came to maintain it, but also to ward off sleep. Even more than the Raveners, sleep was the enemy. He forced himself to walk up and down. He pinched himself. He even went so far as to put a large pebble in his left boot in hopes that the discomfort would help to keep him awake. Once all his devices failed, his head began to sag slowly forward as sleep finally overcame him.

It was the putrid smell that jerked him awake. There, directly before him as his head came up, stood a Ravener. Its eyes were empty of all thought, its gaping mouth revealed broken, rotting teeth, and its black-nailed hands groped out—reaching for him. With a startled cry, he unleashed a heavy blow with his will, hurling the creature backward. Trembling violently, he re-established the barrier that had begun to falter.

Then, at last, they reached the southernmost fringe of the dreadful forest and rode out from under the twisted trees onto a fog-shrouded heath.

"Will they keep up the chase?" Durnik asked his giant friend. The smith's voice dropped from his lips with a great weariness.

Toth made a number of obscure gestures.

"What did he say?" Garion asked.

Durnik's face was bleak. "He says that for as long as the fog lasts, they probably won't give up. They don't like the sun, but the fog's hiding it, so—" He shrugged.

"We have to keep the shield up then, don't we?"

"I'm afraid so."

The heath across which they rode was a blasted, ugly place, covered with low thorn bushes and dotted with shallow tarns filled with rusty-looking water. The fog eddied and billowed, and always at the farthest edge of vision lurked the shadowy forms of the Raveners.

They rode on. Polgara and Belgarath took the burden of the shield, and Garion slumped in his saddle, trembling with exhaustion.

Then, very faintly, he caught the smell of salt brine.

"The sea!" Durnik exulted. "We've reached the sea."

"Now all we need is a boat," Silk reminded him.

Toth, however, pointed ahead confidently and made a curious gesture.

"He says that there's a ship waiting for us," Durnik told them.

"There is?" Silk seemed astonished. "How did he manage that?"

"I really don't know," Durnik replied. "He didn't say."

"Durnik," Silk said, "exactly how do you know what he's saying? Those gestures of his don't make much sense to me at all."

Durnik frowned. "I really don't know," he admitted. "I hadn't even thought about it. I just seem to know what he wants to say."

"Are you using sorcery?"

"No. Maybe it's because we've worked with each other a few times. That always seems to bring men closer together."

"I'll take your word for it."

They crested a moundlike hill to look down at a gravel beach where long rollers came in off the foggy sea to crash against the rounded pebbles and then slide back with a mournful hissing sound as the foam-flecked water slithered down the strand, only to pause and then crash back up again.

"I don't see your ship, Toth," Silk said almost accusingly. "Where is it?"

Toth pointed out into the fog.

"Really?" Silk's voice was skeptical.

The mute nodded.

The Raveners trailing behind grew more agitated as the company started down toward the beach. Their moans became more urgent, and they began to run back and forth along the crest of the hill, reaching out their clawed hands with a kind of desperate longing. They did not, however, pursue any farther.

"Is it my imagination, or does it seem that they're afraid of something?" Velvet suggested.

"They aren't coming down the hill," Durnik agreed. He turned to Toth. "Are they afraid?" he asked.

Toth nodded.

"I wonder what it is," Velvet said.

The giant made a motion with both hands.

"He says that it has to do with something being even more hungry than they are," Durnik said. "They're afraid of it."

"Sharks, maybe?" Silk suggested.

"No. It's the sea itself."

When they reached the gravel strand, they dismounted and stood in a weary little group at the water's edge. "Are you all right, father?" Polgara asked the old man, who was leaning against his saddle, staring out into the fog that lay thick and pale on the dark water.

"What? Oh, yes. I'm fine, Pol—just a little puzzled, that's all. If there *is* a ship out there, I'd sort of like to know who arranged for it and how they knew that we were going to arrive at this particular spot."

"More important than that," Silk added, "I'd like to know how we're going to tell them that we've arrived. That fog's like a blanket out there."

"Toth says they already know we're here," Durnik told him. "They'll probably show up in the next half hour or so."

"Oh?" Belgarath said curiously. "And who sent this ship in the first place?"

"He said it was Cyradis."

"I'm going to have to have a long talk with that young lady one of these days," Belgarath said. "She's starting to make me just a little uneasy about certain things."

"They went back," Eriond told them as he stood stroking the bowed neck of his stallion.

"Who did?" Garion asked.

"The Raveners," the boy replied, pointing back up the hill. "They gave up and started back toward the woods."

"And without even saying good-bye," Silk added with a tight grin. "I don't know what's happened to people's manners these days."

The ship that came ghosting out of the fog was curiously built with a high prow and stern and broad sails on her twin masts.

"What's making it go?" Ce'Nedra asked, staring curiously at the shadowy shape.

"I don't quite follow you," Garion said.

"They aren't rowing," she pointed out, "and there isn't even a hint of a breeze."

He looked sharply back at the ship and saw immediately that she was right. There were no oars protruding from the ghostly ship's sides; but in spite of the dead-calm, foggy air, the sails were bellied outward, and the vessel moved smoothly through the oily-looking water.

"Is it sorcery?" she asked him.

He pushed his mind out, searching for some hint. "It doesn't seem to be," he replied. "At least not any kind that I know about."

Belgarath stood not far away, his expression profoundly disapproving.

"How are they moving the ship, Grandfather?" Garion asked him.

"It's a form of witchcraft," the old man told him, still scowling, "unpredictable and usually not very reliable." He turned to Toth. "You want us to go on board that?" he asked.

Toth nodded.

"Will it take us to Verkat?"

Toth nodded again.

"You mean that it will, if the sprite that's pushing it doesn't get bored with the idea—or decide that it might be funny to take us in the opposite direction."

Toth held out both hands.

"He says to trust him," Durnik supplied.

"I wish people would quit saying that to me."

The ship slowed, and her keel ground gently on the gravel bottom. A broad ramp came sliding out over the side, and its weighted end sank in about three feet of water. Toth, leading his reluctant horse, waded out to the ramp. Then he turned and looked inquiringly back at the rest of them. He motioned with his arm.

"He says we're supposed to board now," Durnik said.

"I heard him," Belgarath growled. "All right, I suppose we might as well." Sourly, he took his horse's reins and waded out into the water.

CHAPTER TWENTY-THREE

The crew of the strange ship all wore rough, cowled tunics made of heavy cloth. The bones of their faces were prominent, giving their features a peculiarly hewn-out look and, like Toth, they were all mutes. They went about their work in absolute silence. Garion, accustomed to the bawling and cursing which accompanied the labors of Cherek sailors, found this stillness peculiar, even slightly unnerving. The ship itself made none of the usual sounds. There was no rasp of oars in their locks, no creak of rigging, no groaning of timbers—only the faint wash and run of water along the sides as they were propelled out across the fog-muffled sea by some force or spirit Garion could not even comprehend.

Once the shore behind had sunk into the fog, there was no reference point, no hint of direction. The silent ship moved on.

Garion stood with his arm about Ce'Nedra's shoulders. The peculiar combination of his near-exhaustion from the ordeal in the wood of the Raveners and the pervading gloom of dark, unbroken water and thick-hanging fog made his mood melancholy and his thoughts abstracted. It was enough merely to stand at the side of his weary wife, holding her in the protecting curve of his arm and to look blankly, uncomprehendingly into the fog.

"What in the world is that?" Velvet exclaimed from somewhere behind him. He turned and looked toward the stern. From out of the pearly fog, there came a ghostly white bird with impossible wings—pinions that appeared longer than a tall man might stretch his arms. The wings did not move, and yet the silent bird came on, gliding through the misty air like a disembodied spirit.

"Albatross," Polgara identified the magnificent creature.

"Aren't they supposed to be bad luck?" Silk asked.

"Are you superstitious, Prince Kheldar?"

"Not exactly, but—" He left it hanging.

"It's a sea bird, nothing more," she told him.

"Why does it have such enormous wings?" Velvet asked curiously.

"It flies great distances over open water," Polgara said. "The wings hold it aloft without any effort. It's very practical."

The great-winged bird tilted in the air, giving forth a strange, lonely cry, a sound that carried in it all the emptiness of a vast, rolling sea.

Polgara inclined her head in response to that strange greeting.

"What did he say, Pol?" Durnik asked her in an oddly subdued voice.

"It was quite formal," she replied. "Sea birds have a great deal of dignity—perhaps because they spend so much time alone. It gives them leisure to formulate their thoughts, I suppose. Land birds babble a great deal, but sea birds try to be profound."

"They're strange creatures, aren't they—birds I mean?"

"Not once you get used to them." She looked out at the alabaster bird coasting in the silent air beside the ship with an indecipherable expression on her face.

The albatross moved his great wings and pulled ahead of the ship to station himself just in front of the prow, hanging apparently motionless in the mist.

Belgarath had been staring up at the sails, which bellied out improbably in the dead-calm air. Finally he grunted and turned to Toth. "How long does the trip to Verkat take?" he asked.

Toth measured out a short space with his hands.

"That's not very specific, my friend."

Toth pointed upward and spread his fingers wide.

"He says about five hours, Belgarath," Durnik translated.

"We're moving faster than it appears then," the old man observed. "I wonder how they managed to persuade the sprite to concentrate on one thing for that long, though. I've never run into one before that could keep hold of an idea for more than a minute."

"Do you want me to ask him?" Durnik offered.

Belgarath squinted back up at the sails. "No," he said. "I guess not. I might not like the answer."

The northwest coast of the Isle of Verkat rose dark and indistinct out of the fog as evening approached. They sailed closer, with the gleaming albatross hovering just ahead, and Garion saw that the low hills behind the gravel strand were thickly covered with dark evergreens wreathed in fog. Some distance back up from the beach, a few scattered lights gleamed golden in the windows of a village, and a line of torches wound down from that village toward the shore. Faintly, Garion could hear the sound of singing. The words were indistinct, but the overall tone of the song conveyed a great sadness and an endless longing.

Their ship moved silently across a shallow bay, then coasted gently up beside a rude stone quay that looked more like a natural rock formation than any man-made structure.

A tall man in a white linen robe stood on the quay. Although his face was unlined and his eyebrows were black as ravens' wings, his flowing hair was as silver as Belgarath's. "Welcome," he greeted them. His voice was deep and peculiarly gentle. "I am Vard. We have long awaited your coming, which the Book of the Heavens revealed to us ages past."

"Now you see why I don't like these people," Belgarath muttered. "I hate it when someone pretends to know everything."

"Forgive us, Holy Belgarath," the man on the quay said with a slight smile. "If it will make you more comfortable, we will conceal what we have read in the stars."

"You've got sharp ears, Vard," the old man noted.

"If you wish to believe so." Vard shrugged. "A place has been made ready for you—and food prepared. Your journey has been long and difficult, and I'm sure you are all very tired. If you will come with me, I will show you the way. My people will bring your mounts and your belongings."

"You are very kind, Vard," Polgara said across the rail of the ship as the mute sailors ran their ramp out to the stones of the quay.

Vard bowed. "We are honored by your presence, Lady Polgara," he replied. "We have stood in awe of you since the beginning of the Third Age."

The path leading up from the bay was narrow and it wound about with no seeming purpose. "I fear that you will find our village rude by comparison with the mighty cities of the west," the white-robed man apologized. "We have ever been indifferent to our surroundings."

"One place is much the same as another," Belgarath agreed, peering ahead toward the cluster of lighted windows glowing in the mist.

The village consisted of a score or so buildings constructed of rough field stone and thatched with straw. They seemed scattered at random with nothing resembling an organized street anywhere in sight. The place was tidy, however, with none of the clutter that inevitably seemed to spring up in such places, and the doorstep of each house showed signs of frequent scrubbing.

Vard led them to a fair-sized house in the center of the village and opened the door for them. "This will be yours for as long as you remain," he said. "The table is prepared, and some of my people will attend you. Should you require anything else, please send for me." Then he bowed, turned, and walked away into the foggy twilight.

The inside of the house was by no means palatial, but it belied the crude-appearing exterior. Each room contained a low, cheery fireplace, exuding warmth and light. The doorways were arched and the walls all whitewashed. The furniture was plain, but stoutly made, and the beds were covered with thick, down-filled comforters.

A table and benches stood in the central room, and a number of covered earthenware pots stood on that table. The smells coming from those pots reminded Garion that he had not eaten a hot meal in several days.

"They're a strange sort of people," Velvet observed, removing her cloak, "but you certainly can't fault their hospitality."

Silk had been eyeing the table. "We wouldn't want to offend them by letting supper get cold, would we? I don't know about the rest of you, but I'm famished."

The supper that had been laid for them was delicious. None of the dishes were anything out of the ordinary, but each was delicately seasoned. The main course was a well-browned haunch of some animal Garion did not recognize, but he found it rich and full-flavored.

"What *is* this delicious roast?" Ce'Nedra asked, helping herself to another piece.

"Goat, I think," Polgara replied.

"Goat?"

"It seems to be."

"But I *hate* goat."

"That's your third slice, dear," Polgara pointed out.

After they had eaten, they sat around the fireplace. Garion felt a vast weariness and knew that he should go to bed, but he was simply too comfortable to move.

"Did you get any hints that Zandramas came through here?" Silk asked him.

"What? Oh—no. Nothing."

"She seems to want to avoid inhabited places," Belgarath noted. "I don't think she'd have come to the village here. Probably tomorrow you're going to have to ride out and see if you can cross her trail."

"Wouldn't she have gone straight to Rak Verkat?" Silk suggested. "That's where all the ships are, and she wants to go to Mallorea, doesn't she?"

"She might have made other arrangements," the old man told him. "She *does* have a price on her head, and the Malloreans at Rak Verkat are probably as interested in collecting it as the ones at Rak Hagga. She's made careful preparations in advance for every step of this journey. I don't think she'd have left anything to chance, once she got this far."

Sadi came back into the room, holding the small earthenware bottle. "Margravine Liselle," he said acidly, "do you suppose I could have my snake back?"

"Oh, I'm ever so sorry, Sadi," she apologized. "I completely forgot I had her." She dipped into the front of her dress and gently removed the little green reptile.

Silk drew back with a sharp intake of his breath.

"I wasn't really trying to steal her," Velvet assured Sadi. "It was just that the poor dear was cold."

"Of course." He took his snake from her.

"I was only trying to keep her warm, Sadi. You certainly wouldn't want her to get sick, would you?"

"Your concern touches my heart." He turned and went back toward the sleeping rooms with Zith lazily coiled about his wrist.

The following morning, Garion went into the shed attached to the back of the house, saddled his horse, and rode back down to the gravel strand, where the waves rolled endlessly in off the foggy sea to crash against the shore. He stopped, looking first up the beach, then down. He shrugged and turned his horse toward the northeast.

The upper edge of the rock-strewn beach was thick with windrows of white-bleached driftwood. As he rode, he idly ran his eyes along those tangled heaps of branches and broken logs. Occasionally, he noted a squared-off timber lying among the other bits and pieces, mute evidence that some ship had come to grief. The possibility occurred to him that the shipwreck that had set those timbers adrift might have taken place as long as a century ago and that the debris might well have floated half around the world to wash up on this strand of salt-crusted pebbles.

"That's all very interesting," the dry voice in his mind told him, *"but you're going the wrong way."*

"Where have you been?" Garion asked, reining in.

"Why do we always have to start these conversations with that same question? The answer wouldn't mean anything to you, so why pursue it? Turn around and go back. The trail is on the other side of the village, and you don't have time to ride all the way around the island."

"Is Zandramas still here with my son?" Garion asked quickly, wanting to get that question out in the open before the elusive voice went off again.

"No," the voice replied. *"She left about a week ago."*

"We're gaining on her then," Garion said aloud, a sudden hope springing up in him.

"That would be a logical assumption."

"Where did she go?"

"Mallorea—but you knew that already, didn't you?"

"Could you get a little more specific? Mallorea's a big place."

"Don't do that, Garion," the voice told him. *"UL told you that finding your son was your task. I'm not permitted to do it for you any more than he was. Oh, incidentally, keep an eye on Ce'Nedra."*

"Ce'Nedra? What for?"

But the voice had already gone. Garion swore and rode back the way he had come.

A league or so to the south of the village, where a cove sheltered by two jutting headlands ran back into the shore line, the sword strapped across his back tugged at him. He reined in sharply and drew the blade. It turned in his hand to point unerringly due inland.

He trotted his horse up the hill, with the blade of Iron-grip's sword resting on the pommel of his saddle. The trail did not veer. Ahead of him lay a long, grassy slope and then the misty edge of the evergreen forest. He considered the situation for a moment and decided that it might be better to go back and tell the others, rather than pursue Zandramas alone. As he turned his horse toward the village, he glanced down at the shallow waters of the cove. There, lying on its side beneath the water, lay the sunken wreck of a small ship. His face grew bleak. Once again, Zandramas had rewarded those who had aided her by killing them. He kicked his mount into a loping canter and rode back across the foggy meadows lying between the sea and the dark forest toward the village.

It was nearly noon when he reached the house Vard had provided for them, and he swung down out of his saddle, controlling his excitement as best he could.

"Well?" Belgarath, who sat before the fire with a mug in his hand, asked as Garion entered the room.

"The trail's about a league to the south."

Polgara, seated at the table, looked up quickly from the piece of parchment she had been examining. "Are you sure?" she asked.

"The Orb is." Garion unfastened his cloak. "Oh—I had another visit from our friend." He tapped his forehead. "He told me that Zandramas left the island about a week ago and that she's going to Mallorea. That's about all I could get out of him. Where's Ce'Nedra? I want to tell her that we're getting closer."

"She's asleep," Polgara said, carefully folding the parchment.

"Is that part of one of those books Grandfather's been looking for?" he asked.

"No, dear. It's the recipe for that soup we had at supper last night." She turned to Belgarath. "Well, father? Do we take up the trail again?"

He thought about it, staring absently into the fire dancing on the hearth. "I'm not sure, Pol," he answered finally. "We were deliberately brought here to this island for something, and I don't think that locating the trail was the only reason. I think we ought to stay here for another day or so."

"We've gained a great deal of time on Zandramas, father," she reminded him. "Why waste it by just sitting in one place?"

"Call it a hunch, Pol. I've got a very strong feeling that we're supposed to wait here for something—something fairly important."

"I think it's a mistake, father."

"That's your privilege, Pol. I've never told you what to think."

"Only what to do," she added tartly.

"That's *my* privilege. It's a father's duty to guide his children. I'm sure you understand."

The door opened, and Silk and Velvet came in out of the sunless noon. "Did you find the trail?" Silk asked, removing his cloak.

Garion nodded. "She came ashore a league or so down the beach. Then she sank the boat that brought her. It's lying on the bottom with the full crew aboard, about fifty yards from shore."

"She's running true to form, then," Silk noted.

"What have you been up to this morning?" Garion asked him.

"Snooping."

"The term is 'intelligence gathering,' Kheldar," Velvet said primly, also removing her cloak and smoothing the front of her dress.

"It amounts to the same thing, doesn't it?"

"Of course, but 'snooping' has such a nasty ring to it."

"Did you find out anything?" Garion asked.

"Not much," Silk admitted, coming to the fire to warm himself. "All these people are terribly polite, but they're very good at evading direct questions. I can tell you one thing, though. This place isn't a real village—at least not in the sense that we understand it. It's all very carefully set up to look crude and rustic, and the people here go through the motions of tending crops and herds, but it's all for show. Their tools show almost no signs of use, and their animals are just a bit too well groomed."

"What are they doing, then?" Garion asked.

"I think they spend their time in study," Velvet replied. "I was visiting with one of the women, and there was a sort of a chart on the table in her house. I got a look at it before she put it away. It looked like a map of some constellations—a sort of a picture of the night sky."

Belgarath grunted. "Astrologers. I've never had much faith in astrology. The stars seem to say something different every quarter hour or so." He thought about it for a moment. "Back at Prolgu, the Gorim said that these people are Dals—the same as the ones who live in southern Mallorea—and no one has ever been able to figure out what the Dals are up to. They seem to be docile and placid, but I suspect that's only a mask. There are several centers of learning in Dalasia, and I wouldn't be surprised to find out that this place is very similar. Did either of you see anyone wearing a blindfold—the way Cyradis does?"

"A seer?" Silk said. "I didn't." He looked at Velvet.

She shook her head.

"Toth might be able to give us some answers, father," Polgara said. "He seems to be able to communicate with these people in ways that we can't."

"How do you propose to get answers out of a mute, Polgara?" Silk asked her.

"Durnik seems to be able to talk with him," she replied. "Where are they, by the way?"

"They found a pond on the upper edge of the village," Velvet answered. "They're checking to see if it's occupied. Eriond is with them."

"Inevitably." Polgara smiled.

"Doesn't it get a little tedious?" Velvet asked. "Having him spend all his time fishing, I mean?"

"It's a healthy activity," Polgara said. She looked meaningfully at the mug in Belgarath's hand. "And probably much better for him than the amusements of some others I could name."

"What next, old friend?" Silk asked Belgarath.

"Let's sit tight for a while and keep our eyes and ears open. I've got a nagging sort of feeling that something important's going to happen here."

That afternoon a faint breeze began to stir the fog that had plagued them for the past week or so. When evening approached, the sky had blown clear except for a heavy cloud bank off toward the west, dyed a deep scarlet by the setting sun.

Sadi had spent the day with Vard; when he returned, his expression was frustrated.

"Were you able to get anything out of him?" Silk asked.

"Nothing that I could make any sense out of," the eunuch replied. "I think the grip these people have on reality is rather tenuous. The only thing that seems to interest them is some obscure thing they call the task. Vard wouldn't tell me exactly what this task is, but they seem to have been gathering information about it since the beginning of time."

As twilight began to settle over the Isle, Durnik, with Eriond at his side, returned with his fishing pole across his shoulder and a frustrated look on his face.

"Where's Toth?" Garion asked him.

"He said that he had something to attend to," Durnik replied, carefully examining his tackle. "I think that maybe I need a smaller hook," he mused.

As Polgara and Velvet began preparing supper, Silk looked over at Garion. "Why don't we go stretch our legs?" he suggested.

"You mean right now?"

"I'm a little restless." The weasel-faced man rose from his chair. "Come along," he said. "If you sit in that chair much longer, you're going to put down roots."

Puzzled, Garion followed his friend outside. "What was that all about?" he asked.

"I want to find out what Toth's up to and I don't want Liselle tagging along."

"I thought you liked her."

"I do, but I'm getting a little tired of having her looking over my shoulder every place I go." He stopped. "Where are *they* going?" he said, pointing at a line of torches strung out across the meadow lying between the village and the edge of the forest.

"We could follow them and find out," Garion suggested.

"Right. Let's go."

Vard led the line of torch-bearing villagers toward the dark forest at the upper end of the meadow, and Toth, towering above all the rest, strode beside him. Garion and Silk, bent low to the tall grass, paralleled their course, but remained some distance away.

As the torchlit file of villagers approached the edge of the woods, several dim figures emerged from the shadows under the trees and stood waiting. "Can you make them out at all?" Garion whispered.

Silk shook his head. "Too far," he murmured, "and there's not enough light. We're going to have to get closer." He dropped down onto his stomach and began to worm his way through the grass.

The meadow was still wet from the days of dense fog; by the time Garion and Silk reached the protecting shadows at the edge of the trees, they were both soaking wet.

"I'm not enjoying this much, Silk," Garion whispered somewhat crossly.

"I don't think you'll melt," Silk whispered back. Then he raised his head and peered out through the trees. "Are those people blindfolded?" he asked.

"It sort of looks that way," Garion replied.

"That would mean that they're seers then, wouldn't it? We didn't see any of them in the village, so maybe they live somewhere in these woods. Let's see if we can get a little closer. All of this is definitely stirring up my curiosity."

The villagers, still carrying their torches, moved into the damp forest for several hundred yards and finally stopped in a large clearing. Around the edge of that clearing stood a series of roughly squared-off blocks of stone, each of them about twice the height of a tall man. The villagers spaced themselves among those stone blocks, forming a torchlit circle, and the blindfolded seers, perhaps a dozen or so of them, gathered in the center and joined hands to form another circle. Standing immediately behind each of the seers was a large, muscular man—their guides and protectors, Garion surmised. In the very center, enclosed within that inner ring of seers, stood the silver-haired Vard and the giant Toth.

Garion and Silk crept closer.

The only sound in the clearing was the guttering of torches; then, very quietly at first, but with growing strength, the people in the circle began to sing. In many ways, their song was similar to the discordant hymn of the Ulgos, yet there were subtle differences. Though he was not schooled in musicology or harmony, Garion perceived that this hymn was older and perhaps more pure than the one which had rung through the caves of Ulgo for five millennia. In a sudden flash of insight, he also understood how endless centuries of confusing echos had gradually corrupted the Ulgos' song. This hymn, moreover, was not raised to UL, but to a God unknown, and it was a plea to that unnamed God to manifest himself and to come forth to guide and protect the Dals, even as UL guided and protected the Ulgos.

Then he heard or felt another sound joining with that unbelievably ancient hymn. A peculiar sighing within his mind signaled that these people, gathered in their strange circles, were bringing their combined wills to bear in a mystic accompaniment to the song their voices raised to the starry sky.

There was a shimmering in the air in the very center of the clearing, and the glowing form of Cyradis appeared, robed and cowled in white linen and with her eyes covered by a strip of cloth.

"Where did she come from?" Silk breathed.

"She's not really there," Garion whispered. "It's a projection. Listen."

"Welcome, Holy Seeress," Vard greeted the glowing image. "We are grateful that thou hast responded to our summons."

"Thy gratitude is unnecessary, Vard," the clear voice of the blindfolded girl replied. "I respond out of the duty imposed upon me by my task. Have the seekers arrived, then?"

"They have, Holy Cyradis," Vard answered, "and the one called Belgarion hath found that which he sought here."

"The quest of the Child of Light hath but only begun," the image stated. "The Child of Dark hath reached the coast of far-off Mallorea and even now doth journey toward the House of Torak at Ashaba. The time hath come for the Eternal man to open the *Book of Ages*."

Vard's face grew troubled. "Is that wise, Cyradis?" he asked. "Can even Ancient Belgarath be trusted with what he may find in that volume? His entire life hath been devoted to but *one* of the two spirits which control all things."

"It must be so, Vard, else the meeting of the Child of Light and the Child of Dark will not come to pass at the appointed time, and *our* task will remain uncompleted." She sighed. "The time draws nigh," she told them. "That for which we have waited since the beginning of the First Age fast approaches, and all must be accomplished ere the moment in which I must perform that task which hath lain upon us throughout the weary centuries. Give the *Book of Ages* to Eternal Belgarath that he may lead the Child of Light to the place which is no more—where all will be decided forever." Then she turned to the towering mute standing impassively beside the white-robed Vard. "My heart is empty without thee," she told him in a voice very near to tears. "My steps falter, and I am alone. I pray thee, my dear companion, make haste in the completion of thy task, for I am made desolate by thine absence."

Quite clearly in the flickering torchlight Garion could see the tears in Toth's eyes and the anguish on his face. The giant reached out toward the glowing image, then let his hand fall helplessly.

Cyradis also raised her hand, it seemed almost involuntarily.

Then she vanished.

CHAPTER TWENTY-FOUR

"Are you sure she said Ashaba?" Belgarath asked intently.

"I heard her, too, Grandfather," Garion confirmed what Silk had just reported. "She said that the Child of Dark had reached Mallorea and was journeying to the House of Torak at Ashaba."

"But there's nothing there," Belgarath objected. "Beldin and I ransacked that place right after Vo Mimbre." He began to pace up and down, scowling darkly. "What could Zandramas possibly want there? It's just an empty house."

"Maybe you can find some answers in the *Book of Ages*," Silk suggested.

Belgarath stopped and stared at him.

"Oh, I guess we hadn't got to that part yet," the little man said. "Cyradis told Vard that he was supposed to give you the book. He didn't like it very much, but she insisted."

Belgarath's hands began to tremble, and he controlled himself with an obvious effort.

"Is it important?" Silk asked curiously.

"So that's what this has all been about!" the old man burst out. "I knew there was a reason for bringing us here."

"What's the *Book of Ages,* Belgarath?" Ce'Nedra asked him.

"It's a part of *The Mallorean Gospels*—the holy book of the Seers at Kell. It looks as if we were led here specifically for the purpose of putting that book into my hands."

"This is all just a little obscure for me, old friend," Silk said, shivering. "Let's go get cleaned up, Garion. I'm soaked all the way through."

"How did you two get so wet?" Velvet asked.

"We were crawling around in the grass."

"That would account for it, I suppose."

"Do you really *have* to do that, Liselle?"

"Do what?"

"Never mind. Come on, Garion."

"What is it about her that irritates you so much?" Garion asked as the two of them went down the hall toward the back of the house.

"I'm not really sure," Silk replied. "I get the feeling that she's laughing at me all the time—and that she's got something on her mind that she isn't telling me. For some reason, she makes me very nervous."

After they had dried themselves and changed into clean clothing, they returned to the warm, firelit main room of the house to find that Toth had returned. He sat impassively on a bench near the door, with his huge hands folded on his knees. All traces of the anguish Garion had seen on his face in the clearing were gone now, and his expression was as enigmatic as ever.

Belgarath sat beside the fire holding a large leather-bound book tilted to catch the light, his eyes poring over it intently.

"Is that the book?" Silk asked.

"Yes," Polgara replied. "Toth brought it."

"I hope that it says something to make this trip worth all the trouble."

As Garion, Silk, and Toth ate, Belgarath continued to read, turning the crackling pages of the *Book of Ages* impatiently. "Listen to this," he said. He cleared his throat and began to read aloud: " 'Know ye, oh my people, that all adown the endless avenues of time hath division marred all that is—for there is division at the very heart of creation. But the stars and the spirits and the voices within the rocks speak of the day when the division will end and all will be made one again, for creation itself knows that the day will come. And two spirits contend with each other at the very center of time, and these spirits are the two sides of that which hath divided creation. Now the day must come when we must choose between them, and the choice we must make is the choice between absolute good and absolute evil, and that which *we* choose—good or evil—will prevail until the end of days. But how may we know which is good and which is evil?

" 'Behold also this truth; the rocks of the world and of all other worlds murmur continually of the two stones which lie at the center of the division. Once these stones were one, and they stood at the very center of all of creation, but, like all else, they were divided, and in the instant of division were they rent apart with a force that destroyed whole suns. And where these stones are found together, there surely will be the last confrontation between the two spirits. Now the day will come when all division will end and all will be made as one again—*except* that the division between the two stones is so great that they can never be rejoined. And in the day when the division ends shall one of the stones cease forever to exist, and in that day also shall one of the spirits forever vanish.' "

"Are they trying to say that the Orb is only *half* of this original stone?" Garion asked incredulously.

"And the other half would be the Sardion," Belgarath agreed. "That would explain a great deal."

"I didn't know there was any connection between the two."

"Neither did I, but it does sort of fit together, doesn't it? Everything about this whole business has come in pairs from the very beginning—two Prophecies, two fates, a Child of Light and a Child of Dark—it only stands to reason that there'd have to be two stones, doesn't it?"

"And the Sardion would have the same power as the Orb," Polgara added gravely.

Belgarath nodded. "In the hands of the Child of Dark, it could do just about anything that Garion can do with the Orb—and we haven't even tested the limits of that yet."

"It gives us just a little more incentive to keep Zandramas from reaching the Sardion, doesn't it?" Silk said.

"I already have all the incentive in the world," Ce'Nedra said sadly.

Garion rose early the next morning. When he came out of the room he shared with Ce'Nedra, he found Belgarath seated at the table in the main room with the *Book of Ages* lying before him in the light of a guttering candle.

"Didn't you go to bed, Grandfather?"

"What? Oh—no. I wanted to read this all the way through without any interruptions."

"Did you find anything helpful?"

"A great deal, Garion. A very great deal. Now I know what Cyradis is doing."

"Is she really involved in this?"

"She believes that she is." He closed the book and leaned back, staring thoughtfully at the far wall. "You see, these people, and the ones at Kell in Dalasia, believe that it's their task to choose between the two Prophecies—the two forces that have divided the universe—and they believe that it's their choice that's going to settle the matter once and for all."

"A choice? That's all? You mean that all they have to do is pick one or the other, and that's the end of it?"

"Roughly, yes. They believe that the choice has to be made during one of the meetings of the Child of Light and the Child of Dark—and both stones, the Orb and the Sardion, have to be present. Down through history, the task of making the choice has always been laid on just one of the seers. At every meeting between the Child of Light and the Child of Dark, that particular seer has been present. I expect that there was one lurking about somewhere at Cthol Mishrak when you met Torak. At any rate, the task has finally fallen to Cyradis. She knows where the Sardion is and she knows when this meeting is going to take place. She'll be there. If all the conditions have been met, she'll choose."

Garion sat down in a chair by the dying fire. "You don't actually believe all that, do you?"

"I don't know, Garion. We've spent our entire lives living out the pronouncements of the Prophecy, and it's gone to a great deal of trouble to get me here and put this book into my hands. I may not entirely believe all this mysticism, but I'm certainly not going to ignore it."

"Did it say anything at all about Geran? What's his part in all this?"

"I'm not sure. It could be as a sacrifice—the way Agachak believes. Or, it's possible that Zandramas abducted him just to force you to come after her and bring the Orb with you. Nothing is ever going to be settled until the Orb and the Sardion are brought together in the same place."

"The place which is no more," Garion added sourly.

Belgarath grunted. "There's something about that phrase that keeps nagging at me," he said. "Sometimes I can almost put my finger on it, but it keeps slipping away from me. I've seen it or heard it before, but I can't seem to remember where."

Polgara came into the room. "You're both up early," she said.

"Garion is," Belgarath replied. "I'm up late."

"Did you stay up all night, father?"

"It seems that way. I think that this was what I was waiting for." He laid his hand on the book in front of him. "As soon as the others get up, let's pack and get ready to leave. It's time for us to move on."

There was a light tap on the outer door. Garion rose, crossed the room, and opened it.

Vard stood outside in the pale gray light of the dawning day. "There's something I need to tell you," he said.

"Come in." Garion held the door open for him.

"Good morning, Vard," Belgarath greeted the white-robed man. "I didn't get the chance to thank you for this book."

"You must thank Cyradis for that. We gave it to you at her instruction. I think you and your friends should leave. There are soldiers coming."

"Malloreans?"

Vard nodded. "There's a column moving out from Rak Verkat. They'll probably reach our village before noon."

"Can you give us a ship of any kind?" Belgarath asked him. "We need to get to Mallorea."

"That wouldn't be wise just now. There are also Mallorean ships patrolling the coast."

"Do you think they're searching for us?" Polgara asked.

"It's possible, Lady Polgara," Vard admitted, "but the commander at Rak Verkat has ordered these sweeps through the countryside before—usually to round up any Murgos who still might be hidden on the Isle. They stir around for a few days and then return to their garrison in Rak Verkat. If this present excursion is merely one of those periodic searches, the troops won't be very thorough and they won't be in this vicinity for long. As soon as they're gone, you can come back here, and we'll provide you with a ship."

"Just how extensive is that forest out there?" Belgarath asked him.

"It's quite large, Ancient One."

"Good. Malloreans aren't comfortable in forests. Once we get back into the trees, it shouldn't be much of a problem to slip around them."

"You will need to avoid the hermit who dwells in the forest, however."

"The hermit?"

"A poor deranged fellow. He's not really an evil person, but he's mischievous and he likes to play tricks on travelers."

"We'll keep that in mind," Belgarath said. "Garion, go wake the others. Let's get ready to leave."

By the time everything was ready for their departure, the sun had risen over the low range of hills to the east. Sadi looked out the door at the bright sunlight streaming over the village and sparkling on the waves in the harbor. "Where's the fog when you need it?" he asked of no one in particular.

Belgarath looked around. "We've got about four hours until the Malloreans get here," he told them. "Let's use that time to put some distance between us and this place." He turned to Vard. "Thank you," he said simply, "for everything."

"May all of the Gods be with you," the silvery-haired man replied. "Now go—quickly."

They rode out of the village and up across the meadow to the edge of the dark forest.

"Any particular direction, old friend?" Silk asked Belgarath.

"I don't think it matters all that much," the old man replied. "Probably about all we're going to need is a thicket to hide in. Malloreans get nervous when they can't see for a mile or so in every direction, so they aren't very likely to search these woods too extensively."

"I'll see what I can find," the little man offered. He turned his horse toward the northeast, but suddenly reined in sharply as two figures stepped out from among the trees. One was robed and cowled, and the other was a large, watchful man.

"I greet thee, Ancient Belgarath," the hooded figure said in the clear voice of a woman. She lifted her face, and Garion saw that her eyes were bound with a dark strip of cloth. "I am Onatel," she continued, "and I am here to point out a safe path to thee."

"We're grateful for your aid, Onatel."

"Thy path lies southward, Belgarath. Some small way into this wood thou wilt discover an ancient track, much overgrown. It will lead thee to a place of concealment."

"And have you seen what is to come, Onatel?" Polgara asked. "Will the soldiers search this wood?"

"Thou and thy companions are the ones they seek, Polgara, and they will search in all parts of the island, but they will not find thee and thy friends—unless it come to pass that someone doth point thee out to them. Beware of the hermit who doth dwell in this wood, however. He will seek to test thee." She turned then with one hand outstretched. The large man standing in the shadows took that groping hand and gently led her back into the forest.

"How convenient," Velvet murmured. "Perhaps a little *too* convenient."

"She wouldn't lie, Liselle," Polgara said.

"But she's not obliged to tell the whole truth, is she?"

"You've got a very suspicious nature," Silk told her.

"Let's just say that I'm cautious. When a perfect stranger goes out of her way to help me, it always makes me a little nervous."

"Let's go ahead and find this path of hers," Belgarath said. "If we decide later on to change direction, we can do it some place private."

They pushed into the shadows beneath the spreading evergreens. The forest floor was damp and thickly covered with fallen needles from the limbs overhead. The sun streamed down in long, slanting shafts of golden light, and the shadows had that faint bluish tinge of morning. The thick loam muffled the sound of their passage, and they rode in a kind of hushed silence.

The track to which the seeress had directed them lay perhaps a mile back in the wood. It was deeply indented in the forest floor, as if at some time in the long-distant past it had been much traveled. Now, however, it lay unused, and weeds and grass had reclaimed it.

As the sun mounted in the sky, the blue cast to the shadows beneath the trees faded, and a myriad of tiny insects swirled and darted in the shafts of sunlight. Then, quite suddenly, Belgarath reined in his horse. "Listen!" he said sharply.

From far behind them, Garion heard a series of sharp yelps.

"Dogs?" Sadi asked, looking nervously back over his shoulder. "Did they bring dogs to sniff out our trail?"

"Those aren't dogs," Belgarath told him. "They're wolves."

"Wolves?" Sadi exclaimed. "We must flee!"

"Don't get excited, Sadi," the old man told him. "Wolves don't hunt people."

"I'd rather not chance that, Belgarath," the eunuch said. "I've heard some very alarming stories."

"That's all they were—stories. Believe me, I know wolves. No self-respecting wolf would even consider eating a human. Stay here, all of you. I'll go see what they want." He slid down out of his saddle.

"Not too close to the horses, father," Polgara warned. "You know how horses feel about wolves."

He grunted and went off into the forest.

"What's he doing?" Sadi asked nervously.

"You wouldn't believe it," Silk replied.

They waited in the cool dampness of the forest, listening to the faint yelping sounds and an occasional bell-like howl echoing among the trees.

When Belgarath returned some time later, he was swearing angrily.

"Whatever is the matter, father?" Polgara asked him.

"Somebody's playing games," he retorted angrily. "There aren't any wolves back there."

"Belgarath," Sadi said, "I can *hear* them. They've been yapping and howling on our trail for the past half hour."

"And that's all there is back there—just the noise. There isn't a wolf within miles of here."

"What's making all the noise, then?"

"I told you. Somebody's playing games. Let's move on—and keep your eyes open."

They rode warily now, with the phantom baying filling the woods behind them. Then there came a sudden, high-pitched bellow from somewhere in front of them.

"What's that?" Durnik exclaimed, reaching for his axe.

"It's an absurdity," Belgarath snapped. "Ignore it. It's no more real than the wolves were."

But there was something swaying in the shadows beneath the spreading trees ahead—something gray and ponderously vast.

"There! What *is* that thing?" Ce'Nedra's voice was shrill.

"It's an elephant, dear," Polgara told her calmly. "They live in the jungles of Gandahar on the east coast of Mallorea."

"How did it get here, then?"

"It didn't. It's an apparition. Father was right. Someone in these woods has a very twisted sense of humor."

"And I'm going to show this comedian exactly what I think of his little jokes," Belgarath growled.

"No, father," Polgara disagreed. "I think that perhaps you should leave it to me. You're irritated, and that sometimes makes you go a little far with things. I'll take care of it."

"Polgara—" he started angrily.

"Yes, father?" Her look was cool and direct.

He controlled himself with some effort. "All right, Pol," he said. "Don't take any chances, though. This funny fellow might have some other tricks in his bag."

"I'm always careful, father," she replied. Then she moved her horse at a walk until she was several yards in advance of the rest of the party. "It's a very nice elephant," she called into the woods as she eyed the huge gray shape swaying menacingly in the shadows ahead of her. "Have you anything else you might like to show us?"

There was a long pause.

"You don't seem very impressed," a rusty-sounding voice growled from somewhere nearby.

"Well, you *did* make a few mistakes. The ears aren't big enough, for one thing, and the tail is much too long."

"The feet and tusks are about right, though," the voice in the woods snapped, "as you're about to find out."

The gray shape raised its huge snout and bellowed. Then it lumbered forward directly toward Polgara.

"How tiresome," she said, making a negligent-appearing gesture with one hand.

The elephant vanished in mid-stride.

"Well?" she asked.

A figure stepped out from behind a tree. It was a tall, gaunt man with wild hair and a very long beard, with twigs and straw clinging to it. He was dressed in a filthy smock, and his bare legs were as white as fish bellies, with knobby knees and broken veins. In one hand he carried a slender stick.

"I see that you have power, woman," he said to her, his voice filled with an unspoken threat.

"Some," she admitted calmly. "You must be the hermit I've heard about."

A look of cunning came into his eyes. "Perhaps," he replied. "And who are you?"

"Let's just say that I'm a visitor."

"I don't want any visitors. These woods are mine, and I prefer to be left alone."

"That's hardly civil. You must learn to control yourself." His face suddenly twisted into an insane grimace. "Don't tell me what to do!" he screamed at her. "I am a God!"

"Hardly that," she disagreed.

"Feel the weight of my displeasure!" he roared. He raised the stick in his hand, and a glowing spark appeared at its tip. Suddenly, out of the insubstantial air, a monster leaped directly at her. It had scaly hide, a gaping muzzle filled with pointed fangs, and great paws tipped with needle-sharp claws.

Polgara lifted one hand, palm outward, and the thing suddenly stopped and hung motionless in midair. "A trifle better," she said critically. "This one even seems to have a bit of substance to it."

"Release it!" the hermit howled at her, jumping up and down in fury.

"Are you really sure you want me to?"

"Release it! Release it! Release it!" His voice rose to a shriek as he danced about wildly.

"If you insist," she replied. Slowly the slavering monster turned about in midair and then dropped to the ground. With a roar, it charged the startled hermit.

The gaunt man recoiled, thrusting his wand out in front of him. The creature vanished.

"You always have to be careful with monsters," she advised. "You never know when one of them might turn on you."

His mad eyes narrowed, and he leveled his stick at her. A series of incandescent fireballs burst from its tip, sizzling through the air directly at her.

She held up her hand again, and the smoldering chunks of fire bounced off into the woods. Garion glanced at one and saw that it was actually burning, setting the damp needles on the forest floor to smoking. He put his heels to his horse's flanks, even as Durnik also spurred forward, brandishing his cudgel.

"Stay out of it, you two!" Belgarath barked. "Pol can take care of herself."

"But, Grandfather," Garion protested, "that was real fire."

"Just do as I say, Garion. You'll throw her off balance if you go blundering in there now."

"Why are you being so difficult?" Polgara asked the madman who stood glaring at her. "All we're doing is traveling through these woods."

"The woods are mine!" he shrieked. "Mine! Mine! Mine!" Again he danced his insane caper of fury and shook both his fists at her.

"Now you're being ridiculous," she told him.

The hermit leaped backward with a startled exclamation as the ground directly in front of his feet erupted with a seething green fire and a boiling cloud of bright purple smoke.

"Did you like the colors?" she inquired. "I like a little variety now and then, don't you?"

"Pol," Belgarath said in exasperation, "will you stop playing?"

"This isn't play, father," she replied firmly. "It's education."

A tree some yards behind the hermit suddenly bent forward, enfolding him in its stout limbs and then straightening back up again, lifting him struggling into the air.

"Have you had enough of this yet?" she asked, looking up at the startled man, who was trying desperately to free himself from the branches wrapped about his waist. "Decide quickly, my friend. You're a long way from the ground, and I'm losing interest in keeping you up there."

With a curse, the hermit wrenched himself free and tumbled heavily to the loam beneath the tree.

"Did you hurt yourself?" she inquired solicitously.

Snarling, he cast a wave of absolute blackness at her.

Still sitting her horse with unruffled calm, she began to glow with an intensely blue light that pushed the blackness away.

Again the look of mad cunning came into his eyes. Garion felt a disjointed surge. Jerkily, one portion of his body at a time, the deranged hermit began to expand, growing larger and larger. His face was wholly insane now, and he lashed out with one huge fist, shattering a nearby tree. He bent, picked up a long branch, and broke it in two. He discarded the shorter end and advanced upon Polgara, swinging his great club.

"Pol!" Belgarath shouted in sudden alarm. "Be careful of him!"

"I can manage, father," she replied. Then she faced the ten-foot-tall madman. "I think this has gone quite far enough," she told him. "I hope you know how to run." She made a peculiar gesture.

The wolf that appeared between them was impossibly large—half again as big as a horse—and its snarl was thunderous.

"I do not fear your apparitions, woman," the towering hermit roared. "I am God, and I fear nothing."

The wolf bit him, its teeth sinking into his shoulder. He screamed and jerked back, dropping his cloth. "Get away!" he shouted at the snarling wolf.

The beast crouched, its fangs bared.

"Get away!" the hermit screamed again. He flopped his hands in the air, and Garion again felt that disorganized surge as the insane man tried with all his might to make the wolf vanish.

"I recommend immediate flight," Polgara suggested. "That wolf hasn't been fed for a thousand years and it's dreadfully hungry."

The hermit's nerve broke at that point. He spun and ran desperately back into the woods, his pale, skinny legs flashing and his hair and beard streaming behind him. The wolf gave chase at a leisurely lope, snapping at his heels and growling horribly.

"Have a pleasant day," Polgara called after him.

CHAPTER TWENTY-FIVE

Polgara's expression was unreadable as she looked after the fleeing hermit. At last she sighed. "Poor fellow," she murmured.

"Will the wolf catch him?" Ce'Nedra asked in a small voice.

"The wolf? Oh no, dear. The wolf was only an illusion."

"But it bit him. I saw the blood."

"Just a small refinement, Ce'Nedra."

"Then why did you say 'poor fellow'?"

"Because he's completely mad. His mind is filled with all kinds of shadows."

"That happens sometimes, Polgara," Belgarath told her. "Let's move along. I want to get deeper into these woods before the sun goes down."

Garion pulled his horse in beside Belgarath's as they rode on into the forest. "Do you think he might have been a Grolim at one time?" he asked.

"What makes you say that?"

"Well—I sort of thought—" Garion struggled to put it into words. "What I mean is, there are two groups of sorcerers in the world—the Grolims and us. He wasn't one of us, was he?"

"What a peculiar notion," Belgarath said. "The talent is latent in everybody. It can show up any place—and does. It takes different directions in different cultures, but it's all related—magic, witchcraft, sorcery, wizardry, and even the peculiar gift of the seers. It all comes from the same place, and it's all basically the same thing. It just shows up in different ways, that's all."

"I didn't know that."

"Then you've learned something today. No day in which you learn something is a complete loss."

The autumn sun was very bright, though it was low on the northern horizon. Winter was almost upon them. Once again Garion was reminded that they were in a strange part of the world where the seasons were reversed. Back at Faldor's farm it was nearly summer now. The fields had been plowed and the crops planted, and the days were long and warm. Here at the bottom of the world, however, it was quite the opposite. With a start, he realized that, except for that brief time in the desert of Araga, he had entirely missed summer this year. For some reason, he found that thought profoundly depressing.

They had been climbing steadily for the past hour or more as they moved up into the low range of hills that formed the spine of the island. The land became more broken, with wooded gullies and ravines wrinkling the floor of the forest.

"I hate mountain country," Sadi complained, looking at a cliff that suddenly reared up out of the trees. "Broken terrain is always so inconvenient."

"It's going to be just as troublesome for the Malloreans," Silk pointed out.

"That's true, I suppose," Sadi admitted, "but I'm afraid I still don't like hills and valleys. They seem so unnatural for some reason. Give me a nice flat swamp any time."

"Let me check that ravine just ahead," Durnik said. "It's getting on toward sunset, and we're going to need a safe place to spend the night." He cantered his horse to a narrow notch, splashed across the turbulent brook that issued from its mouth, and disappeared upstream.

"How far do you think we've come today?" Velvet asked.

"Six or eight leagues," Belgarath replied. "We should be deep enough into the forest to avoid being noticed—unless the Malloreans intend to take this search of theirs seriously."

"Or unless that seeress we met accidentally happens to mention the fact that we're here," she added.

"Why are you so suspicious about those people?" Ce'Nedra asked her.

"I'm not entirely sure," the blond girl replied, "but I get an uneasy feeling every time one of them sends us off in some direction or other. If they're supposed to be so neutral, why are they going out of their way to help us?"

"It's her Academy training, Ce'Nedra," Silk said. "Skepticism is one of the major branches of study there."

"Do *you* trust her, Kheldar?" Velvet asked pointedly.

"Of course not—but then I graduated from the Academy, too."

Durnik came back out of the ravine with a satisfied look on his face. "It's a good place," he announced. "It's secure, sheltered, and well out of sight."

"Let's have a look," Belgarath said.

They followed the smith up the ravine, with the brook gurgling and splashing beside them. After a few hundred yards, the ravine angled sharply to the left; farther along, it twisted back to the right again and opened out into a wooded basin. The brook they had been following upstream spilled out over the edge of a steep limestone cliff above the basin to fall as a misty spray into a pond at the upper end of the little canyon.

"Very nice, Durnik," Polgara congratulated her husband. "And that pond really didn't have anything at all to do with your choice, did it?"

"Well—" he said.

She laughed a rich, warm laugh, leaned across, and kissed him lightly. "It's all right, Durnik," she said, "but first we'll need shelter. *Then* you can see if the pond is occupied."

"Oh, it is, Pol," he assured her. "I saw one jumping." He hesitated. "I mean— well, I just happened to notice it in passing, is all."

"Of course, dear."

He lowered his head slightly, much like an abashed schoolboy, but Garion could see the faint flicker of a smile playing about the smith's lips. It was almost with a shock that he realized that his plain, honest friend was far more devious than he sometimes appeared. Since Polgara enjoyed catching him in these little subterfuges so much, Durnik often arranged things so that she *could* catch him—just for the sake of the pleasure it gave her.

They set the tents back under the trees, not too far from the edge of the pond. As usual, the chore of gathering firewood fell to Garion and Eriond while Durnik and Toth put up the tents. Also, as usual, Silk and Belgarath disappeared until all the work was completed. Sadi sat chatting with Velvet and Ce'Nedra, and his contralto voice seemed somehow as feminine as theirs.

As Polgara began to busy herself with supper, Durnik looked critically around at the campsite. "I guess that's about it," he said.

"Yes, dear," Polgara agreed.

"Do you need anything else?"

"No, dear."

"Well, I suppose—" He glanced toward the pond.

"Go ahead, Durnik," she told him. "Just be sure to come back when supper's ready."

"Are you coming, Toth?" Durnik asked his friend.

As evening darkened their concealed basin, and the stars came out in the velvety sky overhead, they gathered about the fire and ate a supper consisting of lightly grilled lamb, steamed vegetables, and dark bread, all drawn from the supplies Vard had pressed upon them before they had left the village near the beach.

"A meal fit for a king, Lady Polgara," Sadi said expansively, leaning back.

"Yes," Garion murmured.

Sadi laughed. "I keep forgetting," he said. "You're such an unassuming fellow, Belgarion. If you asserted yourself a bit, people might take more note of your royalty."

"I couldn't agree more, Sadi," Ce'Nedra said.

"I'm not sure that's such a good idea at the moment," Garion told them. "Just now, I don't really *want* that kind of recognition."

Silk rose from the place where he had been sitting.

"Where are you going, Kheldar?" Velvet asked him.

"I'm going to have a look around," he replied. "I'll give you a full report when I come back, so that you can make note of it in the document you're preparing for Javelin."

"You're not taking this situation well at all, Prince Kheldar."

"I just don't like being spied on."

"Try to look at it as a friendly concern for your welfare. It's not really spying, if you consider it in that light, is it?"

"It amounts to the same thing, Liselle."

"Of course, but it doesn't *seem* quite so unpleasant that way, now does it?"

"Very clever."

"I thought so myself. Try not to get lost out there."

He went off into the darkness muttering to himself.

"How long do you think the soldiers will keep searching, Grandfather?" Garion asked.

The old man scratched absently at his bearded chin. "It's hard to say," he replied. "Malloreans don't have the same kind of brainless tenacity that Murgos do; but if the orders came from someone with enough authority, they probably won't give up until they've at least gone through the motions of making a thorough search."

"Several days, then?"

"At least."

"And all the time Zandramas is getting farther and farther ahead of us with my son."

"I'm afraid that can't be helped."

"Don't you think the slavers' robes would deceive them, Belgarath?" Sadi asked.

"I don't believe I want to take the chance. Murgos have seen Nyissan slavers moving around down here for so many years that they don't give them a second glance. Malloreans are probably more alert—besides, we don't know exactly what they're looking for. For all we know, they could be specifically looking for a group of slavers."

Silk quietly came back to the fire. "We've got company," he said. "I saw several campfires out there." He gestured off to the northeast.

"How close?" Garion asked quickly.

"Probably several leagues or so. I was up on top of that ridge, and you can see for quite a distance. The fires are pretty well spread out."

"Malloreans?" Durnik asked him.

"Probably. I'd say that they're making a sweep through the woods."

"Well, father?" Polgara asked.

"I don't think we can make any decisions until daylight," the old man replied. "If they're just making a cursory pass, we can probably sit tight. If they're serious about it, we might have to think of something else. We'd all better get some sleep. Tomorrow might be hectic."

Silk was up the next morning before daylight. As the rest of them rose to gather about the fire in the growing light of the dawn, he came back down the ridge. "They're coming," he announced, "and they're combing the woods inch by inch. I think we can be fairly sure that some of them will come up this ravine."

Belgarath stood up. "One of you put that fire out," he said. "We don't want the smoke to lead them right to us."

As Durnik quickly shoveled dirt over their cook fire, Toth stood up and peered off across the basin. Then he tapped Belgarath on the shoulder and pointed.

"What did he say, Durnik?" the old man asked.

The smith and his huge friend exchanged a series of somewhat obscure gestures.

"He says that there's a bramble thicket on the other side of the pond," Durnik interpreted. "He thinks that if we go around to the back side where the cliff comes down behind it, we might be able to find a good place to hide."

"Go look," Belgarath said shortly, "while the rest of us brush out any traces to show we've been here."

It took about a quarter of an hour to break down their tents and to obliterate any footprints that might alert the soldiers to the fact that someone had spent the night in this secluded place. As Silk was giving the campsite a critical last scrutiny, Durnik and Toth returned. "It's adequate," the smith reported. "There's an open place in the center of the thicket. We won't leave any tracks, if we're careful getting in there with the horses."

"What about from up there?" Garion asked him, pointing at the top of the cliff.

"We can cover the open place over with brambles," Durnik replied. "It shouldn't take too long." He looked at Silk. "How much time do you think we have? How close are the soldiers?"

"Probably about an hour away."

"That's more than enough time."

"All right," Belgarath said, "let's do it. I'd rather hide than run, anyway."

It was necessary to push the brambles aside to lead the horses into the center of the thicket. As Garion and Silk carefully rearranged them to conceal the game trail that had given them access to the hiding place, Durnik and Toth cut enough of the long, thorny tendrils to roof over the opening in the center. In the very midst of the task, Toth stopped suddenly, and his eyes grew distant, as if he were listening to something. His expression became oddly reluctant, and then he sighed.

"What's the matter, Toth?" Durnik asked him.

The giant shrugged and went back to his work.

"Grandfather," Garion said, "if there are Grolims with the soldiers, won't they look for us with their minds?"

"It's not very likely that any Grolims would be along, Garion," Silk told him. "This is a fairly small expedition, and the church and the army don't get along very well in Mallorea."

"They're coming, father," Polgara told him.

"How far are they?"

"A mile or so."

"Let's work our way out to the edge of the thicket," Silk suggested to Garion. "I'd sort of like to keep an eye on things." He dropped to the ground and began to worm his way among the roots of the prickly brambles.

After a few yards, Garion began to mutter a few choice curses. No matter which way he twisted, the sharp thorns managed to find any number of sensitive spots.

"I don't want to interrupt your devotions," Silk whispered, "but it might be a good time for a fair amount of silence."

"Can you see anything?" Garion whispered back.

"Not yet, but you can hear them crashing around at the mouth of the ravine. Stealth is not a Mallorean's strong point."

Faintly from far down the ravine, Garion could hear several men talking. The sound, distorted by echoes bouncing off the twisting-rock walls, came in odd bursts. Then there was a clatter of hooves on the rocks beside the tumbling brook as the Malloreans began their search of the narrow course.

There were a dozen or so soldiers in the party. They wore the usual red tunics and they rode their horses stiffly, like men who were not at all comfortable in the saddle.

"Did anybody ever say why we're looking for these people?" one of them asked, sounding a bit surly about it.

"You've been in the army long enough to know better than that, Brek," one of his companions replied. "They never tell you why. When an officer tells you to jump, you don't ask why. You just say, 'How far?' "

"Officers." Brek spat. "They get all the best of everything and they never do any work. Someday the ordinary soldiers like you and me are going to get sick of it, and then all those fine generals and captains had better look out."

"You're talking mutiny, Brek," his companion said, looking around nervously. "If the captain hears you, he'll have you crucified on the spot."

Brek scowled darkly. "Well, they'd better look out, that's all," he muttered. "A man can take being pushed around for just so long."

The red-clad soldiers rode directly through the campsite Garion and his friends had carefully obliterated and rode along the edge of the pond.

"Sergeant," Brek said in his complaining voice to the heavy man in the lead, "isn't it about time to stop and rest?"

"Brek," the sergeant replied, "sometime not too far off, I'd like to get through a day without hearing you whine about everything that happens."

"You don't have any reason to talk to me like that," Brek objected. "I follow my orders, don't I?"

"But you complain, Brek. I'm so sick of hearing you snivel about everything that happens that, about the next time you open your mouth, I'm going to bash in your teeth."

"I'm going to tell the captain what you just said," Brek threatened. "You heard what he told you about hitting us."

"How do you plan to make him understand you, Brek?" the sergeant asked ominously. "A man mumbles when he doesn't have any teeth, you know. Now, water your horse and keep your mouth shut."

Then a stern-faced man with iron-gray hair astride a raw-boned horse came cantering up the ravine and into the basin. "Any signs?" he demanded curtly.

The sergeant saluted. "Nothing at all, Captain," he reported.

The officer glanced around. "Did you look into that thicket?" he asked, pointing toward the place where Garion and the others were concealed.

"We were just about to, sir," the sergeant replied. "There aren't any tracks, though."

"Tracks can be brushed out. Have your men go look."

"Right away, Captain."

As the soldiers rode up to the thicket, the officer dismounted and led his horse to the pond to drink.

"Did the general say anything about why he wants these people captured, sir?" the sergeant asked, also dismounting.

"Nothing that concerns you, Sergeant."

The soldiers were riding around the thicket, making some show of peering through the brambles.

"Tell them to get off their horses, Sergeant," the captain said disgustedly. "I want that thicket thoroughly searched. That white-haired man back at the village said that the ones we're looking for would be in this part of the forest."

Garion muffled a sudden gasp. "Vard!" he whispered to Silk. "He told them exactly where to find us."

"So it would seem," Silk breathed back grimly. "Let's get back a little farther into the thicket. Those soldiers are likely to get a bit more serious about this now."

"The thicket's all thorn bushes, Captain," Brek shouted back his report. "We can't get in there at all."

"Use your spears," the captain ordered. "Poke around and see if you can flush anybody out."

The Mallorean troopers untied their spears from their saddles and began to stab them into the thicket.

"Keep down," Silk whispered.

Garion pressed himself closer to the ground, wincing as he found a fair number of thorns with his thighs.

"It's solid brambles, Captain," Brek shouted after several moments of probing. "Nobody could possibly be in there—not with horses."

"All right," the officer told him. "Mount up and come on back down here. We'll try the next ravine."

Garion carefully let out the breath he had been holding. "That was close," he breathed to Silk.

"Too close," Silk replied. "I think I'll have a talk with Vard about this."

"Why would he betray us like that?"

"That's one of the things we're going to talk about when I see him."

As the soldiers reached the pond, the captain swung back up into his saddle. "All right, Sergeant," he said, "form up your men, and let's move on."

Then, directly in front of him, there was a peculiar shimmering in the air, and Cyradis, robed and cowled, appeared.

The officer's startled horse reared, and the man kept his saddle only with difficulty. "Torak's teeth!" he swore. "Where did you come from?"

"That is of no moment," she replied. "I have come to aid thee in thy search."

"Look out, Captain!" Brek called warningly. "That's one of those Dalasian witches. She'll put a curse on you if you're not careful."

"Shut up, Brek," the sergeant snapped.

"Explain yourself, woman," the captain said imperiously. "Just what did you mean by that last remark?"

Cyradis turned until she was facing the bramble thicket. She raised her hand and pointed. "The ones you seek are concealed there," she said.

From somewhere behind him Garion heard Ce'Nedra gasp.

"We just searched there," Brek objected. "There's nobody in that thicket."

"Thy sight is faulty then," she told him.

The captain's face had grown cold. "You're wasting my time," he told her. "I watched my men make the search with my own eyes." He gave her a narrow glance. "What is a Seeress from Kell doing here in Cthol Murgos?" he demanded. "You people are neither wanted nor welcome here. Go home and fill your mind with the shadows of brain-sickly imagining. I have no time for the babblings of adolescent witches."

"Then I must prove to thee that my words are true," she replied. She lifted her face and stood quite still.

From somewhere behind where Garion and Silk lay concealed there came a crashing sound, and a moment later the huge Toth, responding to the silent summons of his mistress, burst out of the bramble thicket, carrying the struggling Ce'Nedra in his arms.

The captain stared at him.

"That's one of them, Captain!" Brek exclaimed. "That's the big one you told us to look for—and the red-haired wench!"

"It is as I told thee," Cyradis said. "Seek the others in the same place." Then she vanished.

"Take those two!" the sergeant commanded, and several of his men jumped down from their saddles and surrounded Toth and the still-struggling Ce'Nedra with drawn weapons.

"What are we going to do?" Garion whispered to Silk. "They've got Ce'Nedra."

"I can see that."

"Let's go, then." Garion reached for his sword.

"Use your head," the little man snapped. "You'll only put her in more danger if you go running down there."

"Garion—Silk," Belgarath's whispered voice came to them, "what's happening?"

Garion twisted around to look back over his shoulder and saw his grandfather peering through the brambles. "They've got Toth and Ce'Nedra," he reported softly. "It was Cyradis, Grandfather. She told them exactly where we are."

Belgarath's face went stony, and Garion could see his lips shaping a number of curses.

The Mallorean captain rode up to the thicket with the sergeant and the rest of his men closely behind him. "I think that the rest of you had better come out of there," he ordered crisply. "I have your two friends already and I know that you're in there."

No one answered.

"Oh, come now," he said, "be reasonable. If you don't come out, I'll just send for more soldiers and have them cut down the thicket with their swords. No one's been hurt yet, and I give you my word that none of you will be harmed in any way, if you come out now. I'll even let you keep your weapons—as a gesture of good faith."

Garion heard a brief whispered consultation back in the center of the thicket.

"All right, Captain," Belgarath called in a disgusted tone of voice. "Keep your men under control. We're coming out. Garion, you and Silk, too."

"Why did he do that?" Garion asked. "We could have stayed hidden and then worked out a way to get them all free again."

"The Malloreans know how many of us there are," Silk replied. "That captain's got the upper hand for the moment. Let's go." He started to worm his way out of the thicket.

Garion swore and then followed him.

The others emerged from the back of the thicket and began to walk toward the Mallorean officer. Durnik, however, pushed past them, his face livid with anger. He strode quickly down the slope to confront Toth. "Is this your idea of friendship?" he demanded. "Is this the way you repay all our kindness?"

Toth's face grew melancholy, but he made no gesture of reply or explanation.

"I was wrong about you, Toth," the smith continued in a dreadfully quiet voice. "You were never a friend. Your mistress just put you in a position where the two of you could betray us. Well, you won't get the chance again." He started to raise his hand, and Garion could feel the surge as he gathered in his will.

"Durnik!" Polgara cried. "No!"

"He betrayed us, Pol. I'm not going to let him get away with that."

The two of them stared at each other for a long moment, their eyes locked. In that moment, something passed between them, and Durnik finally lowered his gaze. He turned back to the mute. "You and I are through, Toth. I'll never trust you again. I don't even want to see your face any more. Give me the princess. I don't want you touching her."

Wordlessly Toth held out Ce'Nedra's tiny form. Durnik took her and then deliberately turned his back on the huge mute.

"All right, Captain," Belgarath said, "what now?"

"My orders are to escort you all safely to Rak Verkat, Ancient Belgarath. The military governor there awaits your arrival. It will, of course, be necessary for me to separate certain of your companions from you—just as a precaution. Your power, and that of Lady Polgara, is well known. The well-being of your friends will depend upon your restraint. I'm sure you understand."

"Of course," Belgarath replied drily.

"And do the plans of your military governor involve dungeons and the like?" Silk asked him.

"You do his Excellency an injustice, Prince Kheldar," the captain told him. "He has been instructed to treat you all with the utmost respect."

"You seem remarkably well informed as to our identities, Captain," Polgara observed.

"The one who ordered you detained was most specific, my Lady," he answered with a curt, military bow.

"And just who might that have been?"

"Can there be any doubt in your mind, Lady Polgara? The orders come directly from his Imperial Majesty, Kal Zakath. He has been aware of the presence of your party in Cthol Murgos for some time now." He turned to his men. "Form up around the prisoners," he ordered sharply. Then he turned back to Polgara. "Forgive me, my Lady," he apologized. "I meant guests, of course. The military vocabulary is sometimes blunt. A ship awaits you at Rak Verkat. Immediately upon your arrival there, you will set sail. His Imperial Majesty awaits your arrival at Rak Hagga with the keenest anticipation."

Demon Lord
of Karanda

For Patrick Janson-Smith,
a very special friend,
from writer, wife, and Fatso.

At this time I would again like to express my indebtedness to my wife, Leigh Eddings, for her support, her contributions, and her wholehearted collaboration in this ongoing story. Without her help, none of this would have been possible.

I would also like to take this opportunity to thank my editor, Lester del Rey, for his patience and forbearance, as well as for contributions too numerous to mention.

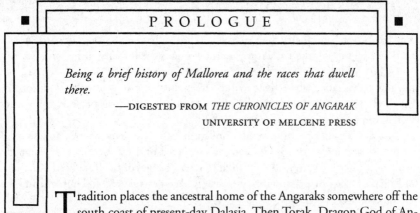

Being a brief history of Mallorea and the races that dwell there.

—DIGESTED FROM *THE CHRONICLES OF ANGARAK*
UNIVERSITY OF MELCENE PRESS

Tradition places the ancestral home of the Angaraks somewhere off the south coast of present-day Dalasia. Then Torak, Dragon God of Angarak, used the power of the Stone, Cthrag Yaska, in what has come to be called "the cracking of the world." The crust of the earth split, releasing liquid magma from below and letting the waters of the southern ocean in to form the Sea of the East. This cataclysmic process continued for decades before the world gradually assumed its present form.

As a result of this upheaval, the Alorns and their allies were forced to retreat into the unexplored reaches of the western continent, while the Angaraks fled into the wilderness of Mallorea.

Torak had been maimed and disfigured by the Stone, which rebelled at the use to which the God put it, and the Grolim priests were demoralized. Thus leadership fell by default to the military; by the time the Grolims recovered, the military had established *de facto* rule of all Angarak. Lacking their former preeminence, the priests set up an opposing center of power at Mal Yaska, near the tip of the Karandese mountain range.

At this point, Torak roused himself to prevent the imminent civil war between priesthood and military rule. But he made no move against the military headquarters at Mal Zeth; instead, he marched to the extreme northwest of Malorea Antiqua with a quarter of the Angarak people to build the Holy City of Cthol Mishrak. There he remained, so absorbed by efforts to gain control of Cthrag Yaska that he was oblivious to the fact that the people had largely turned from their previous preoccupation with theological matters. Those with him in Cthol Mishrak were mostly a hysterical fringe of fanatics under the rigid control of Torak's three disciples, Zedar, Ctuchik, and Urvon. These three maintained the old forms in the society of Cthol Mishrak while the rest of Angarak changed.

When the continuing friction between the Church and military finally came to Torak's attention, he summoned the military High Command and the Grolim Hierarchy to Cthol Mishrak and delivered his commands in terms that brooked no demur. Exempting only Mal Yaska and Mal Zeth, all towns and districts were to be ruled jointly by the military and priesthood. The subdued Hierarchy and High Command immediately settled their differences and returned to their separate enclaves. This enforced truce freed the generals to turn their attention to the other peoples living in Mallorea.

The origins of these people are lost in myth, but three races had predated the

Angaraks on the continent: the Dalasians of the southwest; the Karands of the north; and the Melcenes of the East. It was to the Karands the military turned its efforts.

The Karands were a warlike race with little patience for cultural niceties. They lived in crude cities where hogs roamed freely in the muddy streets. Traditionally, they were related to the Morindim of the far north of Gar og Nadrak. Both races were given to the practice of demon worship.

At the beginning of the second millennium, roving bands of Karandese brigands had become a serious problem along the eastern frontier, and the Angarak army now moved out of Mal Zeth to the western fringes of the Karandese Kingdom of Pallia. The city of Rakand in southwestern Pallia was sacked and burned, and the inhabitants were taken captives.

At this point, one of the greatest decisions of Angarak history was made. While the Grolims prepared for an orgy of human sacrifice, the generals paused. They had no desire to occupy Pallia, and the difficulties of long-distance communication made the notion unattractive. To the generals, it seemed far better to keep Pallia as a subject kingdom and exact tribute, rather than to occupy a depopulated territory. The Grolims were outraged, but the generals were adamant. Ultimately, both sides agreed to take the matter before Torak for his decision.

Not surprisingly, Torak agreed with the High Command; if the Karands could be converted, he would nearly double the congregation of his Church as well as the size of his army for any future confrontation with the Kings of the West. "Any man who liveth in boundless Mallorea shall bow down and worship me," he told his reluctant missionaries. And to insure their zeal, he sent Urvon to Mal Yaska to oversee the conversion of the Karands. There Urvon established himself as temporal head of the Mallorean Church in pomp and luxury hitherto unknown to the ascetic Grolims.

The army moved against Katakor, Jenno, and Delchin, as well as Pallia. But the missionaries fared poorly as the Karandese magicians conjured up hordes of demons to defend their society. Urvon finally journeyed to Cthol Mishrak to consult with Torak. It is not clear what Torak did, but the Karandese magicians soon discovered that the spells previously used to control the demons were no longer effective. Any magician could now reach into the realms of darkness only at the peril of life and soul.

The conquest of the Karands absorbed the attention of both military and priesthood for the next several centuries, but ultimately the resistance collapsed and Karanda became a subject nation, its peoples generally looked upon as inferiors.

When the army advanced down the Great River Magan against the Melcene Empire, however, it met a sophisticated and technologically superior people. In several disastrous battles, in which Melcene war chariots and elephant cavalry destroyed whole battalions, the Angaraks abandoned their efforts. The Angarak generals made overtures of peace. To their astonishment, the Melcenes quickly agreed to normalize relations and offered to trade horses, which the Angaraks previously lacked. They refused, however, even to discuss the sale of elephants.

The army then turned to Dalasia, which proved to be an easy conquest. The Dalasians were simple farmers and herdsmen with little skill for war. The Angaraks moved into Dalasia and established military protectorates during the next ten years. The priesthood seemed at first equally successful. The Dalasians meekly accepted the forms of Angarak worship. But they were a mystical people, and the Grolims soon discovered that the power of the witches, seers, and prophets remained unbroken. Moreover, copies of the infamous *Mallorean Gospels* still circulated in secret among the Dalasians.

In time, the Grolims might have succeeded in stamping out the secret Dalasian religion. But then a disaster occurred that was to change forever the complexion of Angarak life. Somehow, the legendary sorcerer Belgarath, accompanied by three Alorns, succeeded in evading all the security measures and came unobserved at night to steal Cthrag Yaska from the iron tower of Torak in the center of Cthol Mishrak. Although pursued, they managed to escape with the stolen Stone to the West.

In furious rage, Torak destroyed his city. Then he ordered that the Murgos, Thulls, and Nadraks be sent to the western borders of the Sea of the East. More than a million lives were lost in the crossing of the northern land bridge, and the society and culture of the Angaraks took long to recover.

Following the dispersal and the destruction of Cthol Mishrak, Torak became almost inaccessible, concentrating totally on various schemes to thwart the growing power of the Kingdoms of the West. The God's neglect gave the military time to exploit fully its now virtually total control of Mallorea and the subject kingdoms.

For many centuries, the uneasy peace between Angaraks and Melcenes continued, broken occasionally only by little wars in which both sides avoided committing their full forces. The two nations eventually established the practice of each sending children of the leaders to be raised by leaders of the other side. This led to a fuller understanding by both, as well as to the growth of a body of cosmopolitan youths that eventually became the norm for the ruling class of the Mallorean Empire.

One such youth was Kallath, the son of a high-ranking Angarak general. Brought up in Melcene, he returned to Mal Zeth to become the youngest man ever to be elevated to the General Staff. Returning to Melcene, he married the daughter of the Melcene Emperor and managed to have himself declared Emperor following the old man's death in 3830. Then, using the Melcene army as a threat, he managed to get himself declared hereditary Commander in Chief of the Angaraks.

The integration of Melcene and Angarak was turbulent. But in time, the Melcene patience won out over Angarak brutality. Unlike other peoples, the Melcenes were ruled by a bureaucracy. And in the end, that bureaucracy proved far more efficient than the Angarak military administration. By 4400, the ascendancy of the bureaucracy was complete. By that time, also, the title of Commander in Chief had been forgotten and the ruler of both peoples was simply the Emperor of Mallorea.

To the sophisticated Melcenes, the worship of Torak remained largely superficial. They accepted the forms out of expediency, but the Grolims were never able to command the abject submission to the Dragon God that had characterized the Angaraks.

Then in 4850, Torak suddenly emerged from his eons of seclusion to appear before the gates of Mal Zeth. Wearing a steel mask to conceal his maimed face, he set aside the Emperor and declared himself Kal Torak, King and God. He immediately began mustering an enormous force to crush the Kingdoms of the West and bring all the world under his domination.

The mobilization that followed virtually stripped Mallorea of able-bodied males. The Angaraks and Karands were marched north to the land bridge, crossing to northernmost Gar og Nadrak, and the Dalasians and Melcenes moved to where fleets had been constructed to ferry them across the Sea of the East to southern Cthol Murgos. The northern Malloreans joined with the Nadraks, Thulls, and northern Murgos to strike toward the Kingdoms of Drasnia and Algaria. The second group of Malloreans joined with the southern Murgos and were to march northwesterly. Torak meant to crush the West between the two huge armies.

The southern forces, however, were caught in a freak storm that swept off the Western Sea in the spring of 4875 and that buried them alive in the worst blizzard of recorded history. When it finally abated, the column was mired in fourteen-foot snowdrifts that persisted until early summer. No theory has yet been able to explain this storm, which was clearly not of natural origin. Whatever the cause, the southern army perished. The few survivors who struggled back to the East told tales of horror that were truly unthinkable.

The northern force was also beset by various disasters, but eventually laid siege to Vo Mimbre, where they were completely routed by the combined armies of the West. And there Torak was struck down by the power of Cthrag Yaska (there called the Orb of Aldur) and lay in a coma that was to last centuries, though his body was rescued and taken to a secret hiding place by his disciple Zedar.

In the years following these catastrophes, Mallorean society began to fracture back into its original components of Melcene, Karanda, Dalasia, and the lands of the Angaraks. The Empire was saved only by the emergence of Korzeth as Emperor.

Korzeth was only fourteen when he seized the throne from his aged father. Deceived by his youth, the separatist regions began to declare independence of the imperial throne. Korzeth moved decisively to stem the revolution. He spent the rest of his life on horseback in one of the greatest bloodbaths of history, but when he was done, he delivered a strong and united Mallorea to his successors. Henceforth, the descendants of Korzeth ruled in total and unquestioned power from Mal Zeth.

This continued until the present Emperor, 'Zakath, ascended the throne. For a time, he gave promise of being an enlightened ruler of Mallorea and the western kingdoms of the Angaraks. But soon there were signs of trouble.

The Murgos were ruled by Taur Urgas, and it was evident that he was both mad and unscrupulously ambitious. He instigated some plot against the young Emperor. It has never been established clearly what form his scheming took. But 'Zakath discovered that Taur Urgas was behind it and vowed vengeance. This took the form of a bitter war in which 'Zakath began a campaign to destroy the mad ruler utterly.

It was in the middle of this struggle that the West struck. While the Kings of the West sent an army against the East, Belgarion, the young Overlord of the West and descendant of Belgarath the Sorcerer, advanced on foot across the north and across the land bridge into Mallorea. He was accompanied by Belgarath and a Drasnian and he bore the ancient Sword of Riva, on the pommel of which was Cthrag Yaska, the Orb of Aldur. His purpose was to slay Torak, apparently in response to some prophecy known in the West.

Torak had been emerging from his long coma in the ruins of his ancient city of Cthol Mishrak. Now he roused himself to meet the challenger. But in the confrontation, Belgarion overcame the God and slew him with the Sword, leaving the priesthood of Mallorea in chaos and confusion.

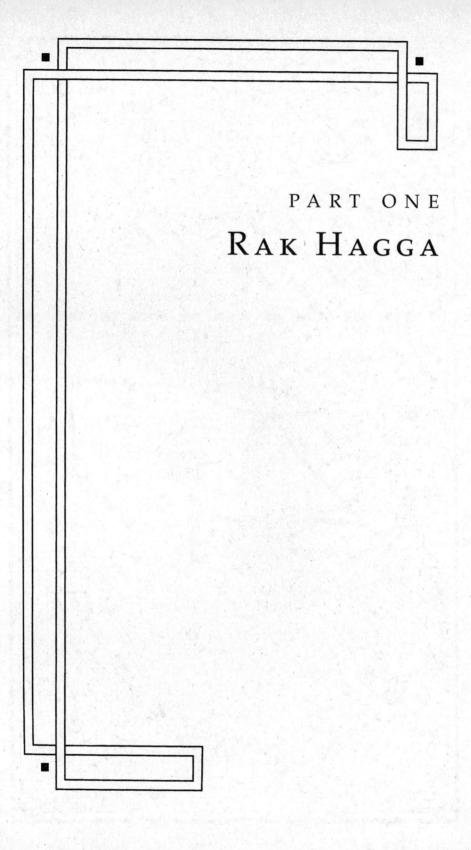

PART ONE

Rak Hagga

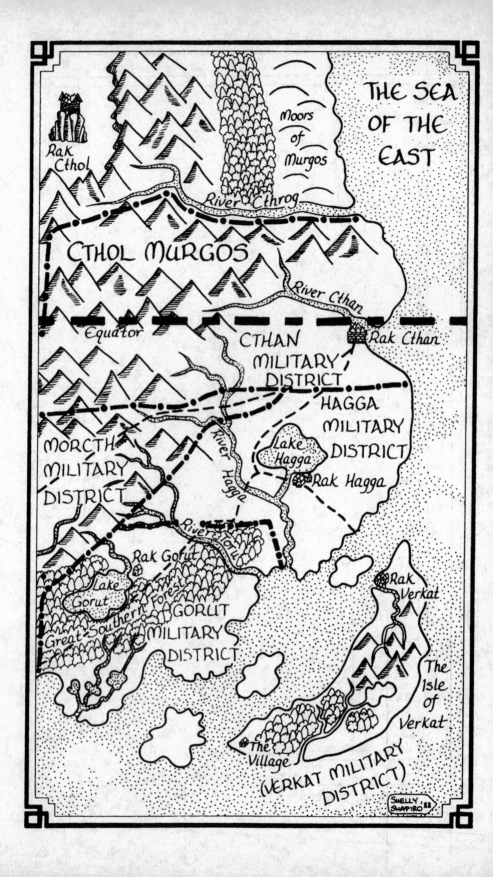

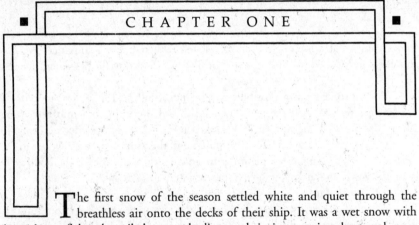

The first snow of the season settled white and quiet through the breathless air onto the decks of their ship. It was a wet snow with large, heavy flakes that piled up on the lines and rigging, turning the tarred ropes into thick, white cables. The sea was black, and the swells rose and fell without sound. From the stern came the slow, measured beat of a muffled drum that set the stroke for the Mallorean oarsmen. The sifting flakes settled on the shoulders of the sailors and in the folds of their scarlet cloaks as they pulled steadily through the snowy morning. Their breath steamed in the chill dampness as they bent and straightened in unison to the beat of the drum.

Garion and Silk stood at the rail with their cloaks pulled tightly around them, staring somberly out through the filmy snowfall.

"Miserable morning," the rat-faced little Drasnian noted, distastefully brushing snow from his shoulders.

Garion grunted sourly.

"You're in a cheerful humor today."

"I don't really have all that much to smile about, Silk." Garion went back to glowering out at the gloomy black-and-white morning.

Belgarath the Sorcerer came out of the aft cabin, squinted up into the thickly settling snow, and raised the hood of his stout old cloak. Then he came forward along the slippery deck to join them at the rail.

Silk glanced at the red-cloaked Mallorean soldier who had unobstrusively come up on deck behind the old man and who now stood leaning with some show of idleness on the rail several yards aft. "I see that General Atesca is still concerned about your well-being," he said, pointing at the man who had dogged Belgarath's steps since they had sailed out of the harbor at Rak Verkat. "Stupidity,"

Belgarath threw a quick disgusted glance in the soldier's direction. "Stupidity," he said shortly. "Where does he think I'm going?"

A sudden thought came to Garion. He leaned forward and spoke very quietly. "You know," he said, "we *could* go someplace, at that. We've got a ship here, and a ship goes wherever you point it—Mallorea just as easily as the coast of Hagga."

"It's an interesting notion, Belgarath," Silk agreed.

"There are four of us, Grandfather," Garion pointed out. "You, me, Aunt Pol, and Durnik. I'm sure we wouldn't have much difficulty in taking over this ship. Then we could change course and be halfway to Mallorea before Kal Zakath realized that we weren't coming to Rak Hagga after all." The more he thought about it, the more the idea excited him. "Then we could sail north along the Mallorean coast and anchor in a cove or inlet someplace on the shore of Camat. We'd only be a week or so from Ashaba. We might even be able to get there before Zandramas does." A bleak smile touched his lips. "I'd sort of like to be waiting for her when she gets there."

"It's got some definite possibilities, Belgarath," Silk said. "Could you do it?"

Belgarath scratched thoughtfully at his beard, squinting out into the sifting snow. "It's possible," he admitted. He looked at Garion. "But what do you think we ought to do with all these Mallorean soldiers and the ship's crew, once we get to the coast of Camat? You weren't planning to sink the ship and drown them all, were you, the way Zandramas does when she's finished using people?"

"Of course not!"

"I'm glad to hear that—but then how did you plan to keep them from running to the nearest garrison just as soon as we leave them behind? I don't know about you, but the idea of having a regiment or so of Mallorean troops hot on our heels doesn't excite me all that much."

Garion frowned. "I guess I hadn't thought about that," he admitted.

"I didn't think you had. It's usually best to work your way completely through an idea before you put it into action. It avoids a great deal of spur-of-the-moment patching later on."

"All right," Garion said, feeling slightly embarrassed.

"I know you're impatient, Garion, but impatience is a poor substitute for a well-considered plan."

"Do you mind, Grandfather?" Garion said acidly.

"Besides, it might just be that we're *supposed* to go to Rak Hagga and meet with Kal Zakath. Why would Cyradis turn us over to the Malloreans, after she went to all the trouble of putting the *Book of Ages* into my hands? There's something else going on here, and I'm not sure we want to disrupt things until we find out a little more about them."

The cabin door opened, and General Atesca, the commander of the Mallorean forces occupying the Isle of Verkat, emerged. From the moment they had been turned over to him, Atesca had been polite and strictly correct in all his dealings with them. He had also been very firm about his intention to deliver them personally to Kal Zakath in Rak Hagga. He was a tall, lean man, and his uniform was bright scarlet, adorned with numerous medals and decorations. He carried himself with erect dignity, though the fact that his nose had been broken at some time in the past made him look more like a street brawler than a general in an imperial army. He came up the slush-covered deck, heedless of his highly polished boots. "Good morning, gentlemen," he greeted them with a stiff, military bow. "I trust you slept well?"

"Tolerably," Silk replied.

"It seems to be snowing," the general said, looking about and speaking in the tone of one making small talk for the sake of courtesy.

"I noticed that," Silk said. "How long is it likely to take us to reach Rak Hagga?"

"A few more hours to reach the coast, your Highness, and then a two-day ride to the city."

Silk nodded. "Have you any idea why your Emperor wants to see us?" he asked.

"He didn't say," Atesca answered shortly, "and I didn't think it appropriate to ask. He merely told me to apprehend you and to bring you to him at Rak Hagga. You are all to be treated with utmost courtesy as long as you don't try to escape. If you do that, his Imperial Majesty instructed me to be more firm." His tone as he spoke was neutral, and his face remained expressionless. "I hope you gentlemen will excuse me now," he said. "I have some matters that need my attention." He bowed curtly, turned, and left them.

"He's a gold mine of information, isn't he?" Silk noted dryly. "Most Melcenes love to gossip, but you've got to pry every word out of this one."

"Melcene?" Garion said. "I didn't know that."

Silk nodded. "Atesca's a Melcene name. Kal Zakath has some peculiar ideas about the aristocracy of talent. Angarak officers don't like the idea, but there's not too much they can do about it—if they want to keep their heads."

Garion was not really that curious about the intricacies of Mallorean politics, so he let the matter drop, to return to the subject they had been discussing previously. "I'm not quite clear about what you were saying, Grandfather," he said, "about our going to Rak Hagga, I mean."

"Cyradis believes that she has a choice to make," the old man replied, "and there are certain conditions that have to be met before she can make it. I've got a suspicion that your meeting with 'Zakath might be one of those conditions."

"You don't actually believe her, do you?"

"I've seen stranger things happen and I always walk very softly around the Seers of Kell."

"I haven't seen anything about a meeting of that kind in the Mrin Codex."

"Neither have I, but there are more things in the world than the Mrin Codex. You've got to keep in mind the fact that Cyradis is drawing on the prophecies of *both* sides, and if the prophecies are equal, they have equal truth. Not only that, Cyradis is probably drawing on some prophecies that only the Seers know about. Wherever this list of preconditions came from, though, I'm fairly certain that she won't let us get to this 'place which is no more' until every item's been crossed off her list."

"Won't *let* us?" Silk said.

"Don't underestimate Cyradis, Silk," Belgarath cautioned. "She's the receptacle of all the power the Dals possess. That means that she can probably do things that the rest of us couldn't even begin to dream of. Let's look at things from a practical point of view, though. When we started out, we were a half a year behind Zandramas and we were planning a very tedious and time-consuming trek across Cthol Murgos—but we kept getting interrupted."

"Tell me about it," Silk said sardonically.

"Isn't it curious that after all these interruptions, we've reached the eastern side of the continent ahead of schedule and cut Zandramas' lead down to a few weeks?"

Silk blinked, and then his eyes narrowed.

"Gives you something to think about, doesn't it?" The old man pulled his cloak more tightly about him and looked around at the settling snow. "Let's go inside," he suggested. "It's really unpleasant out here."

The coast of Hagga was backed by low hills, filmy-looking and white in the thick snowfall. There were extensive salt marshes at the water's edge, and the brown reeds bent under their burden of wet, clinging snow. A black-looking wooden pier extended out across the marshes to deeper water, and they disembarked from the Mallorean ship without incident. At the landward end of the pier a wagon track ran up into the hills, its twin ruts buried in snow.

Sadi the eunuch looked upward with a slightly bemused expression as they rode off the pier and onto the road. He lightly brushed one long-fingered hand across his shaved scalp. "They feel like fairy wings," he smiled.

"What's that?" Silk asked him.

"The snowflakes. I've almost never seen snow before—only when I was visiting a northern kingdom—and I actually believe that this is the first time I've ever been out of doors when it was snowing. It's not too bad, is it?"

Silk gave him a sour look. "The first chance I get, I'll buy you a sled," he said.

Sadi looked puzzled. "Excuse me, Kheldar, but what's a sled?" he asked.

Silk sighed. "Never mind, Sadi. I was only trying to be funny."

At the top of the first hill a dozen or so crosses leaned at various angles beside the road. Hanging from each cross was a skeleton with a few tattered rags clinging to its bleached bones and a clump of snow crowning its vacant-eyed skull.

"One is curious to know the reason for that, General Atesca," Sadi said mildly, pointing at the grim display at the roadside.

"Policy, your Excellency," Atesca replied curtly. "His Imperial Majesty seeks to alienate the Murgos from their king. He hopes to make them realize that Urgit is the cause of their misfortunes."

Sadi shook his head dubiously. "I'd question the reasoning behind that particular policy," he disagreed. "Atrocities seldom endear one to the victims. I've always preferred bribery myself."

"Murgos are accustomed to being treated atrociously." Atesca shrugged. "It's all they understand."

"Why haven't you taken them down and buried them?" Durnik demanded, his face pale and his voice thick with outrage.

Atesca gave him a long, steady look. "Economy, Goodman," he replied. "An empty cross really doesn't prove very much. If we took them down, we'd just have to replace them with fresh Murgos. That gets to be tedious after a while, and sooner or later one starts to run out of people to crucify. Leaving the skeletons there proves our point—and it saves time."

Garion did his best to keep his body between Ce'Nedra and the gruesome object lesson at the side of the road, trying to shield her from that hideous sight. She rode on obliviously, however, her face strangely numb and her eyes blank and unseeing. He threw a quick, questioning glance at Polgara and saw a slight frown on her face. He dropped back and pulled his horse in beside hers. "What's wrong with her?" he asked in a tense whisper.

"I'm not entirely sure, Garion," she whispered back.

"Is it the melancholia again?" There was a sick, sinking feeling in the pit of his stomach.

"I don't think so." Her eyes were narrowed in thought, and she absently pulled the hood of her blue robe forward to cover the white lock in the midnight of her hair. "I'll keep an eye on her."

"What can I do?"

"Stay with her. Try to get her to talk. She might say something to give us some clues."

Ce'Nedra, however, made few responses to Garion's efforts to engage her in conversation, and her answers for the remainder of that snowy day quite frequently had little relevance to either his questions or his observations.

As evening began to settle over the war-ravaged countryside of Hagga, General Atesca called a halt, and his soldiers began to erect several scarlet pavilions in the lee of a fire-blackened stone wall, all that remained of a burned-out village. "We should reach Rak Hagga by late tomorrow afternoon," he advised them. "That large pavilion in the center of the encampment will be yours for the night. My men will bring you your evening meal in a little while. Now, if you'll all excuse me—" He inclined his head briefly, then turned his horse around to supervise his men.

When the soldiers had completed the erection of the pavilions, Garion and his friends dismounted in front of the one Atesca had indicated. Silk looked around at the guard detachment moving into position around the large red tent. "I wish he'd make up his mind," he said irritably.

"I don't quite follow you, Prince Kheldar," Velvet said to him. "Just who should make up his mind?"

"Atesca. He's the very soul of courtesy, but he surrounds us with armed guards."

"The troops might just be there to protect us, Kheldar," she pointed out. "This *is* a war zone, after all."

"Of course," he said dryly, "and cows might fly, too—if they had wings."

"What a fascinating observation," she marveled.

"I wish you wouldn't do that all the time."

"Do what?" Her brown eyes were wide and innocent.

"Forget it."

The supper Atesca's cooks prepared for them was plain, consisting of soldiers' rations and served on tin plates, but it was hot and filling. The interior of the pavilion was heated by charcoal braziers and filled with the golden glow of hanging oil lamps. The furnishings were of a military nature, the kinds of tables and beds and chairs that could be assembled and disassembled rapidly, and the floors and walls were covered with Mallorean carpets dyed a solid red color.

Eriond looked around curiously after he had pushed his plate back. "They seem awfully partial to red, don't they?" he noted.

"I think it reminds them of blood," Durnik declared bleakly. "They like blood." He turned to look coldly at the mute Toth. "If you've finished eating, I think we'd prefer it if you left the table," he said in a flat tone.

"That's hardly polite, Durnik," Polgara said reprovingly.

"I wasn't trying to be polite, Pol. I don't see why he has to be with us in the first place. He's a traitor. Why doesn't he go stay with his friends?"

The giant mute rose from the table, his face melancholy. He lifted one hand as if he were about to make one of those obscure gestures with which he and the smith communicated, but Durnik deliberately turned his back on him. Toth sighed and went over to sit unobstrusively in one corner.

"Garion," Ce'Nedra said suddenly, looking around with a worried little frown, "where's my baby?"

He stared at her.

"Where's Geran?" she demanded, her voice shrill.

"Ce'Nedra—" he started.

"I hear him crying. What have you done with him?" She suddenly sprang to her feet and began to dash about the tent, flinging back the curtains that partitioned off the sleeping quarters and yanking back the blankets on each bed. "Help me!" she cried to them. "Help me find my baby!"

Garion crossed the tent quickly to take her by the arm. "Ce'Nedra—"

"No!" she shouted at him. "You've hidden him somewhere! Let me go!" She wrenched herself free of his grasp and began overturning the furniture in her desperate search, sobbing and moaning unintelligibly.

Again Garion tried to restrain her, but she suddenly hissed at him and extended her fingers like talons to claw at his eyes.

"Ce'Nedra! Stop that!"

But she darted around him and bolted out of the pavilion into the snowy night.

As Garion burst through the tent flap in pursuit, he found his way barred by a red-cloaked Mallorean soldier. "You! Get back inside!" the man barked, blocking Garion with the shaft of his spear. Over the guard's shoulder, Garion saw Ce'Nedra struggling with another soldier; without even thinking, he smashed his fist into the face in front of him. The guard reeled backward and fell. Garion leaped over him, but found himself suddenly seized from behind by a half-dozen more men. "Leave her alone!" he shouted at the guard who was cruelly holding one of the little Queen's arms behind her.

"Get back inside the tent!" a rough voice barked, and Garion found himself being dragged backward step by step toward the tent flap. The soldier holding Ce'Nedra was half lifting, half pushing her back toward the same place. With a tremendous effort, Garion got control of himself and coldly began to draw in his will.

"That will be enough!" Polgara's voice cracked from the doorway to the tent.

The soldiers stopped, looking uncertainly at each other and somewhat fearfully at the commanding presence in the doorway.

"Durnik!" she said then. "Help Garion bring Ce'Nedra back inside."

Garion shook himself free of the restraining hands and he and Durnik took the violently struggling little Queen from the soldier and pulled her back toward the pavilion.

"Sadi," Polgara said as Durnik and Garion entered the tent with Ce'Nedra between them, "do you have any oret in that case of yours?"

"Certainly, Lady Polgara," the eunuch replied, "but are you sure that oret is appropriate here? I'd be more inclined toward naladium, personally."

"I think we've got more than a case of simple hysteria on our hands, Sadi. I want something strong enough to insure that she doesn't wake up the minute my back's turned."

"Whatever you think best, Lady Polgara." He crossed the carpeted floor, opened his red leather case, and took out a vial of dark blue liquid. Then he went to the table and picked up a cup of water. He looked at her inquiringly.

She frowned. "Make it three drops," she decided.

He gave her a slightly startled look, then gravely measured out the dosage.

It took several moments of combined effort to get Ce'Nedra to drink the contents of the cup. She continued to sob and struggle for several moments, but then her struggles grew gradually weaker, and her sobbing lessened. Finally she closed her eyes with a deep sigh, and her breathing became regular.

"Let's get her to bed," Polgara said, leading the way to one of the curtained-off sleeping chambers.

Garion picked up the tiny form of his sleeping wife and followed. "What's wrong with her, Aunt Pol?" he demanded as he laid her gently on the bed.

"I'm not positive," Polgara replied, covering Ce'Nedra with a rough soldier's blanket. "I'll need more time to pin it down."

"What can we do?"

"Not very much while we're on the road," she admitted candidly. "We'll keep her asleep until we get to Rak Hagga. Once I get her into a more stable situation, I'll be able to work on it. Stay with her. I want to talk with Sadi for a few moments."

Garion sat worriedly by the bed, gently holding his wife's limp little hand while Polgara went back out to consult with the eunuch concerning the various drugs in his case. Then she returned, drawing the drape shut behind her. "He has most of what I need," she reported quietly. "I'll be able to improvise the rest." She touched Garion's shoulder and bent forward. "General Atesca just came in," she whispered to him. "He wants to see you. I wouldn't be too specific about the cause of Ce'Nedra's attack. We can't be sure just how much 'Zakath knows about our reasons for being here, and Atesca's certain to report everything that happens, so watch what you say."

He started to protest.

"You can't do anything here, Garion, and they need you out there. I'll watch her."

"Is she subject to these seizures often?" Atesca was asking as Garion came through the draped doorway.

"She's very high-strung," Silk replied. "Sometimes circumstances get the best of her. Polgara knows what to do."

Atesca turned to face Garion. "Your Majesty," he said in a chilly tone, "I don't appreciate your attacking my soldiers."

"He got in my way, General," Garion replied. "I don't think I hurt him all that much."

"There's a principle involved, your Majesty."

"Yes," Garion agreed, "there is. Give the man my apologies, but advise him not to interfere with me again—particularly when it concerns my wife. I don't really like hurting people, but I can make exceptions when I have to."

Atesca's look grew steely, and the gaze Garion returned was just as bleak. They stared at each other for a long moment. "With all due respect, your Majesty," Atesca said finally, "don't abuse my hospitality again."

"Only if the situation requires it, General."

"I'll instruct my men to prepare a litter for your wife," Atesca said then, "and let's plan to get an early start tomorrow. If the Queen is ill, we want to get her to Rak Hagga as soon as possible."

"Thank you, General," Garion replied.

Atesca bowed coldly, then turned and left.

"Wouldn't you say that was a trifle blunt, Belgarion?" Sadi murmured. "We *are* in Atesca's power at the moment."

Garion grunted. "I didn't like his attitude." He looked at Belgarath, whose expression was faintly disapproving. "Well?" he asked.

"I didn't say anything."

"You didn't have to. I could hear you thinking all the way over here."

"Then I don't have to say it, do I?"

The next day dawned cold and raw, but the snow had stopped. Garion rode at the side of Ce'Nedra's horse-borne litter with his face mirroring his concern. The road they followed ran northwesterly past more burned-out villages and shattered towns. The ruins were covered with a thick coating of the clinging wet snow that had fallen the previous day, and each of them was encircled by a ring of those grim, occupied crosses and stakes.

It was about midafternoon when they crested a hill and saw the lead-gray expanse of Lake Hagga stretching far to the north and east; on the near shore was a large, walled city.

"Rak Hagga," Atesca said with a certain relief.

They rode on down the hill toward the city. A brisk wind was blowing in off the lake, whipping their cloaks about them and tossing the manes of their horses.

"All right, gentlemen," Atesca said over his shoulder to his troops, "let's form up and try to look like soldiers." The red-cloaked Malloreans pulled their horses into a double file and straightened in their saddles.

The walls of Rak Hagga had been breached in several places, and the tops of the battlements were chipped and pitted from the storms of steel-tipped arrows that had swept over them. The heavy gates had been burst asunder during the final assault on the city and hung in splinters from their rusty iron hinges.

The guards at the gate drew themselves up and saluted smartly as Atesca led the way into the city. The battered condition of the stone houses within the walls attested to the savagery of the fighting which had ensued when Rak Hagga had fallen. Many of them stood unroofed to the sky, their gaping, soot-blackened windows staring out at the rubble-choked streets. A work gang of sullen Murgos, dragging clanking chains behind them, labored to clear the fallen building stones out of the slushy streets under the watchful eyes of a detachment of Mallorean soldiers.

"You know," Silk said, "that's the first time I've ever seen a Murgo actually work. I didn't think they even knew how."

The headquarters of the Mallorean army in Cthol Murgos was in a large, imposing yellow-brick house near the center of the city. It faced a broad, snowy square, and a marble staircase led up to the main door with a file of red-cloaked Mallorean soldiers lining each side.

"The former residence of the Murgo Military Governor of Hagga," Sadi noted as they drew near the house.

"You've been here before, then?" Silk asked.

"In my youth," Sadi replied. "Rak Hagga has always been the center of the slave trade."

Atesca dismounted and turned to one of his officers. "Captain," he said, "have your men bring the Queen's litter. Tell them to be very careful."

As the rest of them swung down from their mounts, the captain's men unfastened the litter from the saddles of the two horses that had carried it and started up the marble stairs in General Atesca's wake.

Just inside the broad doors stood a polished table, and seated behind it was an arrogant-looking man with angular eyes and an expensive-looking scarlet uniform. Against the far wall stood a row of chairs occupied by bored-looking officials.

"State your business," the officer behind the table said brusquely.

Atesca's face did not change expression as he silently stared at the officer.

"I said to state your business."

"Have the rules changed, Colonel?" Atesca asked in a deceptively mild voice. "Do we no longer rise in the presence of a superior?"

"I'm too busy to jump to my feet for every petty Melcene official from the outlying districts," the colonel declared.

"Captain," Atesca said flatly to his officer, "if the colonel is not on his feet in the space of two heartbeats, would you be so good as to cut his head off for me?"

"Yes, sir," the captain replied, drawing his sword even as the startled colonel jumped to his feet.

"Much better," Atesca told him. "Now, let's begin over again. Do you by chance remember how to salute?"

The colonel saluted smartly, though his face was pale.

"Splendid. We'll make a soldier of you yet. Now, one of the people I was escorting—a lady of high station—fell ill during our journey. I want a warm, comfortable room prepared for her immediately."

"Sir," the colonel protested, "I'm not authorized to do that."

"Don't put your sword away just yet, Captain."

"But, General, the members of his Majesty's household staff make all those decisions. They'll be infuriated if I overstep my bounds."

"I'll explain it to his Majesty, Colonel," Atesca told him. "The circumstances are a trifle unusual, but I'm sure he'll approve."

The colonel faltered, his eyes filled with indecison.

"Do it, Colonel! Now!"

"I'll see to it at once, General," the colonel replied, snapping to attention. "You men," he said to the soldiers holding Ce'Nedra's litter, "follow me."

Garion automatically started to follow the litter, but Polgara took his arm firmly. "No, Garion. I'll go with her. There's nothing you can do right now, and I think 'Zakath's going to want to talk to you. Just be careful of what you say." And she went off down the hallway behind the litter.

"I see that Mallorean society still has its little frictions," Silk said blandly to General Atesca.

"Angaraks," Atesca grunted. "Sometimes they have a little difficulty coping with the modern world. Excuse me, Prince Kheldar. I want to let his Majesty know that we're here." He went to a polished door at the other end of the room and spoke briefly with one of the guards. Then he came back. "The Emperor is being advised of our arrival," he said to them. "I expect that he'll see us in a few moments."

A rather chubby, bald-headed man in a plain, though obviously costly, brown robe and with a heavy gold chain about his neck approached them. "Atesca, my dear fellow," he greeted the general, "they told me that you were stationed at Rak Verkat."

"I have some business with the Emperor, Brador. What are you doing in Cthol Murgos?"

"Cooling my heels," the chubby man replied. "I've been waiting for two days to see Kal Zakath."

"Who's minding the shop at home?"

"I've arranged it so that it more or less runs itself," Brador replied. "The report I have for his Majesty is so vital that I decided to carry it myself."

"What could be so earthshaking that it would drag the Chief of the Bureau of Internal Affairs away from the comforts of Mal Zeth?"

"I believe that it's time for his Imperial Exaltedness to tear himself away from his amusements here in Cthol Murgos and come back to the capital."

"Careful, Brador," Atesca said with a brief smile. "Your fine-tuned Melcene prejudices are showing."

"Things are getting grim at home, Atesca," Brador said seriously. "I've *got* to talk with the Emperor. Can you help me to get in to see him?"

"I'll see what I can do."

"Thank you, my friend," Brador said, clasping the general's arm. "The whole fate of the empire may depend on my persuading Kal Zakath to come back to Mal Zeth."

"General Atesca," one of the spear-armed guards at the polished door said in a loud voice, "his Imperial Majesty will see you and your prisoners now."

"Very good," Atesca replied, ignoring the ominous word "prisoners." He looked at Garion. "The Emperor must be very eager to see you, your Majesty," he noted. "It often takes weeks to gain an audience with him. Shall we go inside?"

CHAPTER TWO

Kal Zakath, the Emperor of boundless Mallorea, lounged in a red-cushioned chair at the far end of a large plain room. The Emperor wore a simple white linen robe, severe and unadorned. Though Garion knew that he was at least in his forties, his hair was untouched by gray and his face was unlined. His eyes, however, betrayed a kind of dead weariness, devoid of any joy or even any interest in life. Curled in his lap lay a common mackerel-striped alley cat, her eyes closed and her forepaws alternately kneading his thigh. Although the Emperor himself wore the simplest of clothes, the guards lining the walls all wore steel breastplates deeply inlaid with gold.

"My Emperor," General Atesca said with a deep bow, "I have the honor to present his Royal Majesty, King Belgarion of Riva."

Garion nodded briefly, and 'Zakath inclined his head in response. "Our meeting is long overdue, Belgarion," he said in a voice as dead as his eyes. "Your exploits have shaken the world."

"Yours have also made a certain impression, 'Zakath." Garion had decided even before he had left Rak Verkat that he would not perpetuate the absurdity of the Mallorean's self-bestowed "Kal."

A faint smile touched 'Zakath's lips. "Ah," he said in a tone which indicated that he saw through Garion's attempt to be subtle. He nodded briefly to the others, and his attention finally fixed itself upon the rumpled untidy form of Garion's grandfather. "And of course you, sir, would be Belgarath," he noted. "I'm a bit surprised to find you so ordinary-looking. The Grolims of Mallorea all agree that you're a hundred feet tall—possible two hundred—and that you have horns and a forked tail."

"I'm in disguise," Belgarath replied with aplomb.

'Zakath chuckled, though there was little amusement in that almost mechanical sound. Then he looked around with a faint frown. "I seem to note some absences," he said.

"Queen Ce'Nedra fell ill during our journey, your Majesty," Atesca advised him. "Lady Polgara is attending her."

"Ill? Is it serious?"

"It's difficult to say at this point, your Imperial Majesty," Sadi replied unctuously, "but we have given her certain medications, and I have every confidence in Lady Polgara's skill."

'Zakath looked at Garion. "You should have sent word on ahead, Belgarion. I have a healer on my personal staff—a Dalasian woman with remarkable gifts. I'll send her to the Queen's chambers at once. Our first concern must be your wife's health."

"Thank you," Garion replied with genuine gratitude.

'Zakath touched a bellpull and spoke briefly with the servant who responded immediately to his summons.

"Please," the Emperor said then, "seat yourselves. I have no particular interest in ceremony."

As the guards hastily brought chairs for them, the cat sleeping in 'Zakath's lap half opened her golden eyes and looked around at them. She rose to her paws, arched her back, and yawned. Then she jumped heavily to the floor with an audible grunt and waddled over to sniff at Eriond's fingers. With a faintly amused look, 'Zakath watched his obviously pregnant cat make her matronly way across the carpet. "You'll note that my cat has been unfaithful to me—again." He sighed in mock resignation. "It happens fairly frequently, I'm afraid, and she never seems to feel the slightest guilt about it."

The cat jumped up into Eriond's lap, nestled down, and began to purr contentedly.

"You've grown, boy," 'Zakath said to the young man. "Have they taught you how to talk as yet?"

"I've picked up a few words, 'Zakath," Eriond said in his clear voice.

"I know the rest of you—by reputation at least," 'Zakath said then. "Goodman Durnik and I met on the plains of Mishrak ac Thull, and of course I've heard of the Margravine Liselle of Drasnian Intelligence and of Prince Kheldar, who strives to become the richest man in the world."

Velvet's graceful curtsy of acknowledgement was not quite so florid as Silk's grandiose bow.

"And here, of course," the Emperor continued, "is Sadi, Chief Eunuch in the palace of Queen Salmissra."

Sadi bowed with fluid grace. "I must say that your Majesty is remarkably well informed," he said in his contralto voice. "You have read us all like an open book."

"My chief of intelligence tries to keep me informed, Sadi. He may not be as gifted as the inestimable Javelin of Boktor, but he knows about *most* of what's going on in this part of the world. He's mentioned that huge fellow over in the corner, but so far he hasn't been able to discover his name."

"He's called Toth," Eriond supplied. "He's a mute, so we have to do his talking for him."

"And a Dalasian besides," 'Zakath noted. "A very curious circumstance."

Garion had been closely watching this man. Beneath the polished, urbane exterior, he sensed a kind of subtle probing. The idle greetings, which seemed to be no more than a polite means of putting them at their ease, had a deeper motive behind them. In some obscure way he sensed that 'Zakath was somehow testing each of them.

The Emperor straightened then. "You have an oddly assorted company with you, Belgarion," he said, "and you're a long way from home. I'm curious about your reasons for being here in Cthol Murgos."

"I'm afraid that's a private matter, 'Zakath."

One of the Emperor's eyebrows rose slightly. "Under the circumstances, that's hardly a satisfactory answer, Belgarion. I can't really take the chance that you're allied with Urgit."

"Would you accept my word that I'm not?"

"Not until I know a bit more about your visit to Rak Urga. Urgit left there quite suddenly—apparently in your company—and reappeared just as suddenly on the plains of Morcth, where he and a young woman led his troops out of an ambush I'd gone to a great deal of trouble to arrange. You'll have to admit that's a peculiar set of circumstances."

"Not when you look at it from a practical standpoint," Belgarath said. "The decision to take Urgit with us was mine. He'd found out who we are, and I didn't want an army of Murgos on our heels. Murgos aren't too bright, but they can be an inconvenience at times."

'Zakath looked surprised. "He was your prisoner?"

Belgarath shrugged. "In a manner of speaking."

The Emperor laughed rather wryly. "You could have wrung almost any concession from me if you had just delivered him into my hands, you know. Why did you let him go?"

"We didn't need him anymore," Garion replied. "We'd reached the shores of Lake Cthaka, so he really wasn't any kind of threat to us."

'Zakath's expression narrowed slightly. "A few other things happened as well, I think," he observed. "Urgit has always been a notorious coward, wholly under the domination of the Grolim Agachak and of his father's generals. But he didn't seem very timid while he was extricating his troops from the trap I'd laid for them, and all the reports filtering out of Rak Urga seem to suggest that he's actually behaving like a king. Did you by any chance have anything to do with that?"

"It's possible, I suppose," Garion answered. "Urgit and I talked a few times, and I told him what he was doing wrong."

'Zakath tapped one forefinger against his chin, and his eyes were shrewd. "You may not have made a lion of him, Belgarion," he said, "but at least he's no longer a rabbit." A chill smile touched the Mallorean's lips. "In a way, I'm rather glad about that. I've never taken much satisfaction in hunting rabbits." He shaded his eyes with one hand, although the light in the room was not particularly bright. "But what I can't understand is how you managed to spirit him out of the Drojim Palace and away from the city. He has whole regiments of bodyguards."

"You're overlooking something, 'Zakath," Belgarath said to him. "We have certain advantages that aren't available to others."

"Sorcery, you mean? Is it really all that reliable?"

"I've had some luck with it from time to time."

'Zakath's eyes had become suddenly intent. "They tell me that you're five thousand years old, Belgarath. Is that true?"

"Seven, actually—or a little more. Why do you ask?"

"In all those years, hasn't it ever occurred to you simply to seize power? You could have made yourself king of the world, you know."

Belgarath looked amused. "Why would I want to?" he asked.

"All men want power. It's human nature."

"Has all your power really made you happy?"

"It has certain satisfactions."

"Enough to make up for all the petty distractions that go with it?"

"I can endure those. At least I'm in a position where no one tells me what to do."

"No one tells me what to do either, and I'm not saddled with all those tedious responsibilities." Belgarath straightened. "All right, 'Zakath, shall we get to the point? What are your intentions concerning us?"

"I haven't really decided that yet." The Emperor looked around at them. "I presume that we can all be civilized about the present situation?"

"How do you mean, civilized?" Garion asked him.

"I'll accept your word that none of you will try to escape or do anything rash. I'm aware that you and a number of your friends have certain specialized talents. I don't want to be forced to take steps to counteract them."

"We have some rather pressing business," Garion replied carefully, "so we can only delay for just so long. For the time being, however, I think we can agree to be reasonable about things."

"Good. We'll have to talk later, you and I, and come to know one another. I've had comfortable quarters prepared for you and your friends, and I know that you're anxious about your wife. Now, I hope you'll excuse me, but I have some of those tedious responsibilities Belgarath mentioned to attend to."

Although the house was very large, it was not, strictly speaking, a palace. It appeared that the Murgo governors-general of Hagga who had ordered it built had not shared the grandiose delusions which afflicted the rulers of Urga, and so the building was more functional than ornate.

"I hope you'll excuse me," General Atesca said to them when they had emerged from the audience chamber. "I'm obliged to deliver a full report to his Majesty—about various matters—and then I must return immediately to Rak Verkat." He looked at Garion. "The circumstances under which we met were not the happiest, your Majesty," he said, "but I hope you won't think too unkindly of me." He bowed rather stiffly and then left them in the care of a member of the Emperor's staff.

The man who led them down a long, dark-paneled hallway toward the center of the house was obviously not an Angarak. He had not the angular eyes nor the stiff, bleak-faced arrogance that marked the men of that race. His cheerful, round face seemed to hint at a Melcene heritage, and Garion remembered that the bureaucracy which controlled most aspects of Mallorean life was made up almost excusively of Melcenes. "His Majesty asked me to assure you that your quarters are not intended to be a prison," the official told them as they approached a heavily barred iron door blocking off one portion of the hallway. "This was a Murgo house before we took the city, and it has certain structural peculiarities. Your rooms are in what once were the women's quarters, and Murgos are fanatically protective of their women. It has to do with their concept of racial purity, I think."

At the moment, Garion had little interest in sleeping arrangements. All his concern was for Ce'Nedra. "Do you happen to know where I might find my wife?" he asked the moon-faced bureaucrat.

"There at the end of this corridor, your Majesty," the Melcene replied, pointing toward a blue-painted door at the far end of the hall.

"Thank you." Garion glanced at the others. "I'll be back in a little while," he told them and strode on ahead.

The room he entered was warm and the lighting subdued. Deep, ornately woven Mallorean carpets covered the floor and soft green velvet drapes covered the tall, narrow windows. Ce'Nedra lay in a high-posted bed against the wall opposite the door, and Polgara was seated at the bedside, her expression grave.

"Has there been any change?" Garion asked her, softly closing the door behind him.

"Nothing as yet," she replied.

Ce'Nedra's face was pale as she slept with her crimson curls tumbled on her pillow.

"She *is* going to be all right, isn't she?" Garion asked.

"I'm sure of it, Garion."

Another woman sat near the bed. She wore a light green, cowled robe; despite the fact that she was indoors, she had the hood pulled up, partially concealing her face. Ce'Nedra muttered something in a strangely harsh tone and tossed her head restlessly on her pillow. The cowled woman frowned. "Is this her customary voice, Lady Polgara?" she asked.

Polgara looked at her sharply. "No," she replied. "As a matter of fact, it's not."

"Would the drug you gave her in some way affect the sound of her speech?"

"No, it wouldn't. Actually, she shouldn't be making any sounds at all."

"Ah," the woman said. "I think perhaps I understand now." She leaned forward and very gently laid the fingertips of one hand on Ce'Nedra's lips. She nodded then and withdrew her hand. "As I suspected," she murmured.

Polgara also reached out to touch Ce'Nedra's face. Garion heard the faint whisper of her will, and the candle at the bedside flared up slightly, then sank back until its flame was scarcely more than a pinpoint. "I should have guessed," Polgara accused herself.

"What is it?" Garion asked in alarm.

"Another mind is seeking to dominate your wife and to subdue her will, your Majesty," the cowled woman told him. "It's an art sometimes practiced by the Grolims. They discovered it quite by accident during the third age."

"This is Andel, Garion," Polgara told him. " 'Zakath sent her here to help care for Ce'Nedra."

Garion nodded briefly to the hooded woman. "Exactly what do we mean by the word 'dominate'?" he asked.

"You should be more familiar with that than most people, Garion," Polgara said. "I'm sure you remember Asharak the Murgo."

Garion felt a sudden chill, remembering the force of the mind that had from his earliest childhood sought that same control over his awareness. "Drive it out," he pleaded. "Get whomever it is out of her mind."

"Perhaps not quite yet, Garion," Polgara said coldly. "We have an opportunity here. Let's not waste it."

"I don't understand."

"You will, dear," she told him. Then she rose, sat on the edge of the bed and lightly laid one hand on each of Ce'Nedra's temples. The faint whisper came again, stronger this time, and once again the candles all flared and then sank back as if suffocating. "I know you're in there," she said then. "You might as well speak."

Ce'Nedra's expression grew contorted, and she tossed her head back and forth as if trying to escape the hands touching her temples. Polgara's face grew stern, and she implacably kept her hands in place. The pale lock in her hair began to glow, and a strange chill came into the room, seeming to emanate from the bed itself.

Ce'Nedra suddenly screamed.

"Speak!" Polgara commanded. "You cannot flee until I release you, and I will not release you until you speak."

Ce'Nedra's eyes suddenly opened. They were filled with hate. "I do not fear thee, Polgara," she said in a harsh, rasping voice delivered in a peculiar accent.

"And I fear you even less. Now, who are you?"

"Thou knowest me, Polgara."

"Perhaps, but I will have your name from you." There was a long pause, and the surge of Polgara's will grew stronger.

Ce'Nedra screamed again—a scream filled with an agony that made Garion flinch. "Stop!" the harsh voice cried. "I will speak!"

"Say your name," Polgara insisted implacably.

"I am Zandramas."

"So. What do you hope to gain by this?"

An evil chuckle escaped Ce'Nedra's pale lips. "I have already stolen her heart, Polgara—her child. Now I will steal her mind as well. I could easily kill her if I chose, but a dead Queen may be buried and her grave left behind. A mad one, on the other hand, will give thee much to distract thee from thy search for the Sardion."

"I can banish you with a snap of my fingers, Zandramas."

"And I can return just as quickly."

A frosty smile touched Polgara's lips. "You're not nearly as clever as I thought," she said. "Did you actually believe that I twisted your name out of you for my own amusement? Were you ignorant of the power over you that you gave me when you spoke your own name? The power of the name is the most elementary of all. I can keep you out of Ce'Nedra's mind now. There's much more, though. For example, I know now that you're at Ashaba, haunting the bat-infested ruins of the House of Torak like a poor ragged ghost."

A startled gasp echoed through the room.

"I could tell you more, Zandramas, but this is all beginning to bore me." She straightened, her hands still locked to the sides of Ce'Nedra's head. The white lock at her brow flared into incandescence, and the faint whisper became a deafening roar. "Now, begone!" she commanded.

Ce'Nedra moaned, and her face suddenly contorted into an expression of agony. An icy, stinking wind seemed to howl through the room, and the candles and glowing braziers sank even lower until the room was scarcely lit.

"Begone!" Polgara repeated.

An agonized wail escaped Ce'Nedra's lips, and then that wail became disembodied, coming it seemed from the empty air above the bed. The candles went out, and all light ceased to glow out of the braziers. The wailing voice began to fade, moving swiftly until it came to them as no more than a murmur echoing from an unimaginable distance.

"Is Zandramas gone?" Garion asked in a shaking voice.

"Yes," Polgara replied calmly out of the sudden darkness.

"What are we going to say to Ce'Nedra? When she wakes up, I mean."

"She won't remember any of this. Just tell her something vague. Make some light, dear."

Garion fumbled for one of the candles, brushed his sleeve against it, and then deftly caught it before it hit the floor. He was sort of proud of that.

"Don't play with it, Garion. Just light it."

Her tone was so familiar and so commonplace that he began to laugh, and the little surge of his will that he directed at the candle was a stuttering sort of thing. The flame that appeared bobbled and hiccuped at the end of the wick in a soundless golden chortle.

Polgara looked steadily at the giggling candle, then closed her eyes. "Oh, Garion," she sighed in resignation.

He moved about the room relighting the other candles and fanning the braziers back into life. The flames were all quite sedate—except for the original one, which continued to dance and laugh in blithe glee.

Polgara turned to the hooded Dalasian healer. "You're most perceptive, Andel," she said. "That sort of thing is difficult to recognize unless you know precisely what you're looking for."

"The perception was not mine, Lady Polgara," Andel replied. "I was advised by another of the cause of her Majesty's illness."

"Cyradis?"

Andel nodded. "The minds of all our race are joined with hers, for we are but the instruments of the task which lies upon her. Her concern for the Queen's well-being prompted her to intervene." The hooded woman hesitated. "The Holy Seeress also asked me to beg you to intercede with your husband in the matter of Toth. The Goodman's anger is causing that gentle guide extreme anguish, and his pain is also hers. What happened at Verkat had to happen—otherwise the meeting between the Child of Light and the Child of Dark could not come to pass for ages hence."

Polgara nodded gravely. "I thought it might have been something like that. Tell her that I'll speak with Durnik in Toth's behalf."

Andel inclined her head gratefully.

"Garion," Ce'Nedra murmured drowsily, "where are we?"

He turned to her quickly. "Are you all right?" he asked, taking her hand in his.

"Mmmm," she said. "I'm just so very sleepy. What happened—and where are we?"

"We're at Rak Hagga." He threw a quick glance at Polgara, then turned back to the bed. "You just had a little fainting spell is all," he said with a slightly exaggerated casualness. "How are you feeling?"

"I'm fine, dear, but I think I'd like to sleep now." And her eyes went closed. Then she opened them again with a sleepy little frown. "Garion," she murmured, "why is that candle acting like that?"

He kissed her lightly on the cheek. "Don't worry about it, dear," he told her, but she had already fallen fast asleep.

It was well past midnight when Garion was awakened by a light tapping on the door of the room in which he slept. "Who is it?" he asked, half rising in his bed.

"A messenger from the Emperor, your Majesty," a voice replied from the other side of the door. "He instructed me to ask if you would be so good as to join him in his private study."

"Now? In the middle of the night?"

"Such was the Emperor's instruction, your Majesty."

"All right," Garion said, throwing off his blankets and swinging around to put his feet on the cold floor. "Give me a minute or so to get dressed."

"Of course, your Majesty."

Muttering to himself, Garion began to pull on his clothes by the faint light coming from the brazier in the corner. When he was dressed, he splashed cold water on his face and raked his fingers through his sandy hair, trying to push it into some semblance of order. Almost as an afterthought he ducked his head and arm through the strap attached to the sheath of Iron-grip's sword and shrugged it into place across his back. Then he opened the door. "All right," he said to the messenger, "let's go."

Kal Zakath's study was a book-lined room with several leather-upholstered chairs, a large polished table and a crackling fire on the hearth. The Emperor, still clad in plain white linen, sat in a chair at the table, shuffling through a stack of parchment sheets by the light of a single oil lamp.

"You wanted to see me, 'Zakath?" Garion asked as he entered the room.

"Ah, yes, Belgarion," 'Zakath said, pushing aside the parchments. "So good of you to come. I understand that your wife is recovering."

Garion nodded. "Thank you again for sending Andel. Her aid was very helpful."

"My pleasure, Belgarion." 'Zakath reached out and lowered the wick in the lamp until the corners of the room filled with shadows. "I thought we might talk a little," he said.

"Isn't it sort of late?"

"I don't sleep very much, Belgarion. A man can lose a third of his life in sleep. The day is filled with bright lights and distractions; the night is dim and quiet and allows much greater concentration. Please, sit down."

Garion unbuckled his sword and leaned it against a bookcase.

"I'm not really all *that* dangerous, you know," the Emperor said, looking pointedly at the great weapon.

Garion smiled slightly, settling into a chair by the fire. "I didn't bring it because of you, 'Zakath. It's just a habit. It's not the kind of sword you want to leave lying around."

"I don't think anyone would steal it, Belgarion."

"It *can't* be stolen. I just don't want anybody getting hurt by accidentally touching it."

"Do you mean to say that it's *that* sword?"

Garion nodded. "I'm sort of obliged to take care of it. It's a nuisance most of the time, but there've been a few occasions when I was glad I had it with me."

"What *really* happened at Cthol Mishrak?" 'Zakath asked suddenly. "I've heard all sorts of stories."

Garion nodded wryly. "So have I. Most of them get the names right, but not very much else. Neither Torak nor I had very much control over what happened. We fought, and I stuck that sword into his chest."

"And he died?" 'Zakath's face was intent.

"Eventually, yes."

"Eventually?"

"He vomited fire first and wept flames. Then he cried out."

"What did he say?"

" 'Mother,' " Garion replied shortly. He didn't really want to talk about it.

"What an extraordinary thing for him to do. Whatever happened to his body? I had the entire ruin of Cthol Mishrak searched for him."

"The other Gods came and took it. Do you suppose we could talk about something else? Those particular memories are painful."

"He *was* your enemy."

Garion sighed. "He was also a God, 'Zakath—and killing a God is a terrible thing to have to do."

"You're a strangely gentle man, Belgarion. I think I respect you more for that than I do for your invincible courage."

"I'd hardly say invincible. I was terrified the whole time—and so was Torak, I think. Was there something you really wanted to talk about?"

'Zakath leaned back in his chair, tapping thoughtfully at his pursed lips. "You know that eventually you and I will have to confront each other, don't you?"

"No," Garion disagreed. "That's not absolutely certain."

"There can only be one King of the World."

Garion's look grew pained. "I've got enough trouble trying to rule one small island. I've never wanted to be King of the World."

"But I have—and do."

Garion sighed. "Then we probably will fight at that—sooner or later. I don't think the world was intended to be ruled by one man. If you try to do that, I'll have to stop you."

"I am unstoppable, Belgarion."

"So was Torak—or at least he thought so."

"That's blunt enough."

"It helps to avoid a lot of misunderstandings later on. I'd say that you've got enough trouble at home without trying to invade my kingdom—or those of my friends. That's not to mention the stalemate here in Cthol Murgos."

"You're well informed."

"Queen Porenn is a close personal friend. She keeps me advised, and Silk picks up a great deal of information during the course of his business dealings."

"Silk?"

"Excuse me. Prince Kheldar, I mean. Silk's a nickname of sorts."

'Zakath looked at him steadily. "In some ways we're very much alike, Belgarion, and in other ways very different, but we still do what necessity compels us to do. Frequently, we're at the mercy of events over which we have no control."

"I suppose you're talking about the two Prophecies?"

'Zakath laughed shortly. "I don't believe in prophecy. I only believe in power. It's curious, though, that we've both been faced with similar problems of late. You recently had to put down an uprising in Aloria—a group of religious fanatics, I believe. I have something of much the same nature going on in Darshiva. Religion is a constant thorn in the side of any ruler, wouldn't you say?"

"I've been able to work around it—most of the time."

"You've been very lucky then. Torak was neither a good nor kindly God, and his Grolim priesthood is vile. If I weren't busy here in Cthol Murgos, I think I might endear myself to the next thousand or so generations by obliterating every Grolim on the face of the earth."

Garion grinned at him. "What would you say to an alliance with that in mind?" he suggested.

'Zakath laughed briefly, and then his face grew somber again. "Does the name Zandramas mean anything to you?" he asked.

Garion edged around that cautiously, not knowing how much information 'Zakath had about their real reason for being in Cthol Murgos. "I've heard some rumors," he said.

"How about Cthrag Sardius?"

"I've heard of it."

"You're being evasive, Belgarion." 'Zakath gave him a steady look, then passed his hand wearily across his eyes.

"I think you need some sleep," Garion told him.

"Time for that soon enough—when my work is done."

"That's up to you, I guess."

"How much do you know about Mallorea, Belgarion?"

"I get reports—a little disjointed sometimes, but fairly current."

"No. I mean our past."

"Not too much, I'm afraid. Western historians tried very hard to ignore the fact that Mallorea was even there."

'Zakath smiled wryly. "The University of Melcena has the same shortsightedness regarding the West," he noted. "Anyway, over the past several centuries—since the disaster at Vo Mimbre—Mallorean society has become almost completely secular. Torak was bound in sleep, Ctuchik was practicing his perversions here in Cthol Murgos, and Zedar was wandering around the world like a rootless vagabond—what ever happened to him, by the way? I thought he was at Cthol Mishrak."

"He was."

"We didn't find his body."

"He isn't dead."

"He's not?" 'Zakath looked stunned. "Where is he, then?"

"Beneath the city. Belgarath opened the earth and sealed him up in solid rock under the ruin."

"Alive?" 'Zakath's exclamation came out in a choked gasp.

"There was a certain amount of justification for it. Go on with your story."

'Zakath shuddered and then recovered. "With the rest of them out of the way, the only religious figure left in Mallorea was Urvon, and he devoted himself almost exclusively to trying to make his palace at Mal Yaska more opulent than the imperial one at Mal Zeth. Every so often he'd preach a sermon filled with mumbo jumbo and nonsense, but most of the time he seemed to have forgotten Torak entirely. With the Dragon God and his disciples no longer around, the real power of the Grolim Church was gone—oh, the priests babbled about the return of Torak and they all paid lip service to the notion that one day the sleeping God would awaken, but the memory of him grew dimmer and dimmer. The power of the Church grew less and less, while that of the army—which is to say the imperial throne—grew more and more."

"Mallorean politics seem to be very murky," Garion observed.

'Zakath nodded. "It's part of our nature, I suppose. At any rate, our society was functioning and moving out of the dark ages—slowly, perhaps, but moving. Then you suddenly appeared out of nowhere and awakened Torak—and just as suddenly put him permanently back to sleep again. That's when all our problems started."

"Shouldn't it have ended them? That's sort of what I had in mind."

"I don't think you grasp the nature of the religious mind, Belgarion. So long as Torak was there—even though he slept—the Grolims and the other hysterics in the empire were fairly placid, secure and comfortable in the belief that one day he would awaken, punish all their enemies, and reassert the absolute authority of the unwashed and stinking priesthood. But when you killed Torak, you destroyed their comfortable sense of security. They were forced to face the fact that without Torak they were nothing. Some of them were so chagrined that they went mad. Others fell into absolute despair. A few, however, began to hammer together a new mythology—something to replace what you had destroyed with a single stroke of that sword over there."

"It wasn't entirely my idea," Garion told him.

"It's results that matter, Belgarion, not intentions. Anyway, Urvon was forced to tear himself away from his quest for opulence and his wallowing in the adoration of the sycophants who surrounded him and get back to business. For a time he was in an absolute frenzy of activity. He resurrected all the moth-eaten old prophecies and twisted and wrenched at them until they seemed to say what he wanted them to say."

"And what was that?"

"He's trying to convince people that a new God will come to rule over Angarak—either a resurrection of Torak himself or some new deity infused with Torak's spirit. He's even got a candidate in mind for this new God of Angarak."

"Oh? Who's that?"

'Zakath's expression became amused. "He sees his new God every time he looks in a mirror."

"You're not serious!"

"Oh, yes. Urvon's been trying to convince himself that he's at least a demigod for several centuries now. He'd probably have himself paraded all over Mallorea in a golden chariot—except that he's afraid to leave Mal Yaska. As I understand it, there's a very nasty hunchback who's been hungering to kill him for eons—one of Aldur's disciples, I believe."

Garion nodded. "Beldin," he said. "I've met him."

"Is he really as bad as the stories make him out to be?"

"Probably even worse. I don't think you'd want to be around to watch what he does, if he ever catches up with Urvon."

"I wish him good hunting, but Urvon's not my only problem, I'm afraid. Not long after the death of Torak, certain rumors started coming out of Darshiva. A Grolim priestess—Zandramas by name—also began to predict the coming of a new God."

"I didn't know that she was a Grolim," Garion said with some surprise.

'Zakath nodded gravely. "She formerly had a very unsavory reputation in Darshiva. Then the so-called ecstacy of prophecy fell on her, and she was suddenly transformed by it. Now when she speaks, no one can resist her words. She preaches to multitudes and fires them with invincible zeal. Her message of the coming of a new God ran through Darshiva like wildfire and spread into Regel, Voresebo, and Zamad as well. Virtually the entire northeast coast of Mallorea is hers."

"What's the Sardion got to do with all this?" Garion asked.

"I think it's the key to the whole business," 'Zakath replied. "Both Zandramas and Urvon seem to believe that whoever finds and possesses it is going to win out."

"Agachak—the Hierarch of Rak Urga—believes the same thing," Garion told him.

'Zakath nodded moodily. "I suppose I should have realized that. A Grolim is a Grolim—whether he comes from Mallorea or Cthol Murgos."

"It seems to me that maybe you should go back to Mallorea and put things in order."

"No, Belgarion, I won't abandon my campaign here in Cthol Murgos."

"Is personal revenge worth it?"

'Zakath looked startled.

"I know why you hated Taur Urgas, but he's dead, and Urgit's not at all like him. I can't really believe that you'd sacrifice your whole empire just for the sake of revenging yourself on a man who can't feel it."

"You know?" 'Zakath's face looked stricken. "Who told you?"

"Urgit did. He told me the whole story."

"With pride, I expect." 'Zakath's teeth were clenched, and his face pale.

"No, not really. It was with regret—and with contempt for Taur Urgas. He hated him even more than you do."

"That's hardly possible, Belgarion. To answer your question, yes, I *will* sacrifice my empire—the whole world if need be—to spill out the last drop of the blood of Taur Urgas. I will neither sleep nor rest nor be turned aside from my vengeance, and I will crush whomever stands in my path."

"*Tell him,*" the dry voice in Garion's mind said suddenly.

"*What?*"

"*Tell him the truth about Urgit.*"

"*But—*"

"*Do it, Garion. He needs to know. There are things he has to do, and he won't do them until he puts this obsession behind him.*"

'Zakath was looking at him curiously.

"Sorry, just receiving instructions," Garion explained lamely.

"Instructions? From whom?"

"You wouldn't believe it. I was told to give you some information." He drew in a deep breath. "Urgit isn't a Murgo," he said flatly.

"What are you talking about?"

"I said that Urgit isn't a Murgo—at least not entirely. His mother was, of course, but his father was not Taur Urgas."

"You're lying!"

"No, I'm not. We found out about it while we were at the Drojim Palace in Rak Urga. Urgit didn't know about it either."

"I don't believe you, Belgarion!" 'Zakath's face was livid, and he was nearly shouting.

"Taur Urgas is dead," Garion said wearily. "Urgit made sure of that by cutting his throat and burying him head down in his grave. He also claims that he had every one of his brothers—the *real* sons of Taur Urgas—killed to make himself secure on the throne. I don't think there's one drop of Urga blood left in the world."

'Zakath's eyes narrowed. "It's a trick. You've allied yourself with Urgit and brought me this absurd lie to save his life."

"Use the Orb, Garion," the voice instructed.

"How?"

"Take it off the pommel of the sword and hold it in your right hand. It'll show 'Zakath the truths that he needs to know."

Garion rose to his feet. "If I can show you the truth, will you look?" he asked the agitated Mallorean Emperor.

"Look? Look at what?"

Garion walked over to his sword and peeled off the soft leather sleeve covering the hilt. He put his hand on the Orb, and it came free with an audible click. Then he turned back to the man at the table. "I'm not exactly sure how this works," he said. "I'm told that Aldur was able to do it, but I've never tried it for myself. I think you're supposed to look into this." He extended his right arm until the Orb was in front of 'Zakath's face.

"What is that?"

"You people call it Cthrag Yaska," Garion replied.

'Zakath recoiled, his face blanching.

"It won't hurt you—as long as you don't touch it."

The Orb, which for the past months had rather sullenly obeyed Garion's continued instruction to restrain itself, slowly began to pulsate and glow in his hand, bathing 'Zakath's face in its blue radiance. The Emperor half lifted his hand as if to push the glowing stone aside.

"Don't touch it," Garion warned again. "Just look."

But 'Zakath's eyes were already locked on the stone as its blue light grew stronger and stronger. His hands gripped the edge of the table in front of him so tightly that his knuckles grew white. For a long moment he stared into that blue incandescence. Then, slowly, his fingers lost their grip on the table edge and fell back onto the arms of his chair. An expression of agony crossed his face. "They have escaped me," he groaned with tears welling out of his closed eyes, "and I have slaughtered tens of thousands for nothing." The tears began to stream down his contorted face.

"I'm sorry, 'Zakath," Garion said quietly, lowering his hand. "I can't change what's already happened, but you had to know the truth."

"I cannot thank you for this truth," 'Zakath said, his shoulders shaking in the storm of his weeping. "Leave me, Belgarion. Take that accursed stone from my sight."

Garion nodded with a great feeling of compassion and shared sorrow. Then he replaced the Orb on the pommel of his sword, re-covered the hilt, and picked up the great weapon. "I'm very sorry, 'Zakath," he said again, and then he quietly went out of the room, leaving the Emperor of boundless Mallorea alone with his grief.

■ | CHAPTER THREE | ■

"Really, Garion, I'm perfectly fine," Ce'Nedra objected again. "I'm glad to hear that."

"Then you'll let me get out of bed?"

"No."

"That's not fair," she pouted.

"Would you like a little more tea?" he asked, going to the fireplace, taking up a poker, and swinging out the iron arm from which a kettle was suspended.

"No, I don't," she replied in a sulky little voice. "It smells, and it tastes awful."

"Aunt Pol says that it's very good for you. Maybe if you drink some more of it, she'll let you get out of bed and sit in a chair for a while." He spooned some of the dried, aromatic leaves from an earthenware pot into a cup, tipped the kettle carefully with the poker, and filled the cup with steaming water.

Ce'Nedra's eyes had momentarily come alight, but narrowed again almost immediately. "Oh, *very* clever, Garion," she said in a voice heavy with sarcasm. "Don't patronize me."

"Of course not," he agreed blandly, setting the cup on the stand beside the bed. "You probably ought to let that steep for a while," he suggested.

"It can steep all year if it wants to. I'm not going to drink it."

He sighed with resignation. "I'm sorry, Ce'Nedra," he said with genuine regret, "but you're wrong. Aunt Pol says that you're supposed to drink a cup of this every other hour. Until she tells me otherwise, that's exactly what you're going to do."

"What if I refuse?" Her tone was belligerent.

"I'm bigger than you are," he reminded her.

Her eyes went wide with shock. "You wouldn't actually *force* me to drink it, would you?"

His expression grew mournful. "I'd really hate to do something like that," he told her.

"But you'd do it, wouldn't you?" she accused.

He thought about it a moment, then nodded. "Probably," he admitted, "if Aunt Pol told me to."

She glared at him. "All right," she said finally. "Give me the stinking tea."

"It doesn't smell all *that* bad, Ce'Nedra."

"Why don't *you* drink it, then?"

"I'm not the one who's been sick."

She proceeded then to tell him—at some length—exactly what she thought of the tea and him and her bed and the room and of the whole world in general. Many of the terms she used were very colorful—even lurid—and some of them were in languages that he didn't recognize.

"What on earth is all the shouting about?" Polgara asked, coming into the room.

"I absolutely *hate* this stuff!" Ce'Nedra declared at the top of her lungs, waving the cup about and spilling most of the contents.

"I wouldn't drink it then," Aunt Pol advised calmly.

"Garion says that if I don't drink it, he'll pour it down my throat."

"Oh. Those were *yesterday's* instructions." Polgara looked at Garion. "Didn't I tell you that they change today?"

"No," he replied. "As a matter of fact, you didn't." He said it in a very level tone. He was fairly proud of that.

"I'm sorry, dear. I must have forgotten."

"When can I get out of bed?" Ce'Nedra demanded.

Polgara gave her a surprised look. "Any time you want, dear," she said. "As a matter of fact, I just came by to ask if you planned to join us for breakfast."

Ce'Nedra sat up in bed, her eyes like hard little stones. She slowly turned an icy gaze upon Garion and then quite deliberately stuck her tongue out at him.

Garion turned to Polgara. "Thanks awfully," he said to her.

"Don't be snide, dear," she murmured. She looked at the fuming little Queen. "Ce'Nedra, weren't you told as a child that sticking out one's tongue is the worst possible form of bad manners?"

Ce'Nedra smiled sweetly. "Why, yes, Lady Polgara, as a matter of fact I was. That's why I only do it on special occasions."

"I think I'll take a walk," Garion said to no one in particular. He went to the door, opened it, and left.

Some days later he lounged in one of the sitting rooms that had been built in the former women's quarters where he and the others were lodged. The room was peculiarly feminine. The furniture was softly cushioned in mauve, and the broad windows had filmy curtains of pale lavender. Beyond the windows lay a snowy garden, totally embraced by the tall wings of this bleak Murgo house. A cheery fire crackled in the half-moon arch of a broad fireplace, and at the far corner of the room an artfully contrived grotto, thick with green fern and moss, flourished about a trickling fountain. Garion sat brooding out at a sunless noon—at an ash-colored sky spitting white pellets that were neither snow nor hail, but something in between—and realized all of a sudden that he was homesick for Riva. It was a peculiar thing to come to grips with here on the opposite end of the world. Always before, the word "homesick" had been associated with Faldor's farm—the kitchen, the broad central courtyard, Durnik's smithy, and all the other dear, treasured memories. Now, suddenly, he missed that storm-lashed coast, the security of that grim fortress hovering above the bleak city lying below, and the mountains, heavy with snow, rising stark white against a black and stormy sky.

There was a faint knock at the door.

"Yes?" Garion said absently, not looking around.

The door opened almost timidly. "Your Majesty?" a vaguely familiar voice said.

Garion turned, looking back over his shoulder. The man was chubby and bald and he wore brown, a plain serviceable color, though his robe was obviously costly, and the heavy gold chain about his neck loudly proclaimed that this was no minor official. Garion frowned slightly. "Haven't we met before?" he asked. "Aren't you General Atesca's friend—uh—"

"Brador, your Majesty," the brown-robed man supplied. "Chief of the Bureau of Internal Affairs."

"Oh, yes. Now I remember. Come in, your Excellency, come in."

"Thank you, your Majesty." Brador came into the room and moved toward the fireplace, extending his hands to its warmth. "Miserable climate." He shuddered.

"You should try a winter in Riva," Garion said, "although it's summer there right now."

Brador looked out the window at the snowy garden. "Strange place, Cthol Murgos," he said. "One's tempted to believe that all of Murgodom is deliberately ugly, and then one comes across a room like this."

"I suspect that the ugliness was to satisfy Ctuchik—and Taur Urgas," Garion replied. "Underneath, Murgos probably aren't much different from the rest of us."

Brador laughed. "That sort of thinking is considered heresy in Mal Zeth," he said.

"The people in Val Alorn feel much the same way." Garion looked at the bureaucrat. "I expect that this isn't just a social call, Brador," he said. "What's on your mind?"

"Your Majesty," Brador said soberly, "I absolutely *have* to speak with the Emperor. Atesca tried to arrange it before he went back to Rak Verkat, but—" He spread his hands helplessly. "Could you possibly speak to him about it? The matter is of the utmost urgency."

"I really don't think there's very much I can do for you, Brador," Garion told him. "Right now I'm probably the last person he'd want to talk to."

"Oh?"

"I told him something that he didn't want to hear."

Brador's shoulders slumped in defeat. "You were my last hope, your Majesty," he said.

"What's the problem?"

Brador hesitated, looking around nervously as if to assure himself that they were alone. "Belgarion," he said then in a very quiet voice, "have you ever seen a demon?"

"A couple of times, yes. It's not the sort of experience I'd care to repeat."

"How much do you know about the Karands?"

"Not a great deal. I've heard that they're related to the Morindim in northern Gar og Nadrak."

"You know more about them than most people, then. Do you know very much about the religious practices of the Morindim?"

Garion nodded. "They're demon worshippers. It's not a particularly safe form of religion, I've noticed."

Brador's face was bleak. "The Karands share the beliefs and practices of their cousins on the arctic plains of the West," he said. "After they were converted to the worship of Torak, the Grolims tried to stamp out those practices, but they persisted in the mountains and forests." He stopped and looked fearfully around again. "Belgarion," he said, almost in a whisper, "does the name Mengha mean anything to you?"

"No. I don't think so. Who's Mengha?"

"We don't know—at least not for certain. He seems to have come out of the forest to the north of Lake Karanda about six months ago."

"And?"

"He marched—alone—to the gates of Calida in Jenno and called for the surrender of the city. They laughed at him, of course, but then he marked some symbols on the ground. They didn't laugh any more after that." The Melcene bureaucrat's face was gray. "Belgarion, he unloosed a horror on Calida such as man has never seen before. Those symbols he drew on the ground summoned up a host of demons—not one, or a dozen, but a whole army of them. I've talked with survivors of that attack. They're mostly mad—mercifully so, I think—and what happened at Calida was utterly unspeakable."

"An *army* of them?" Garion exclaimed.

Brador nodded. "That's what makes Mengha so dreadfully dangerous. As I'm sure you know, usually when someone summons a demon, sooner or later it gets away from him and kills him, but Mengha appears to have absolute control of all the fiends he raises and he can call them up by the hundreds. Urvon is terrified and he's even begun to experiment with magic himself, hoping to defend Mal Yaska against Mengha. We don't know where Zandramas is, but her apostate Grolim cohorts are desperately striving also to summon up these fiends. Great Gods, Belgarion, help me! This unholy infection will spread out of Mallorea and sweep the world. We'll all be engulfed by howling fiends, and no place, no matter how remote, will provide a haven for the pitiful remnants of mankind. Help me to persuade Kal Zakath that his petty little war here in Cthol Murgos has no real meaning in the face of the horror that's emerging in Mallorea."

Garion gave him a long, steady look, then rose to his feet. "You'd better come with me, Brador," he said quietly. "I think we need to talk with Belgarath."

They found the old sorcerer in the book-lined library of the house, poring over an ancient volume bound in green leather. He set his book aside and listened as Brador repeated what he had told Garion. "Urvon and Zandramas are also engaging in this insanity?" he asked when the Melcene had finished.

Brador nodded. "According to our best information, Ancient One," he replied.

Belgarath slammed his fist down and began to swear. "What are they thinking of?" he burst out, pacing up and down. "Don't they know that UL himself had forbidden this?"

"They're afraid of Mengha," Brador said helplessly. "They feel that they must have some way to protect themselves from his horde of fiends."

"You don't protect yourself from demons by raising more demons," the old man fumed. "If even one of them breaks free, they'll all get loose. Urvon or Zandramas might be able to handle them, but sooner or later some underling is going to make a mistake. Let's go see 'Zakath."

"I don't think we can get in to see him just now, Grandfather," Garion said dubiously. "He didn't like what I told him about Urgit."

"That's too bad. This is something that won't wait for him to regain his composure. Let's go."

The three of them went quickly through the corridors of the house to the large antechamber they had entered with General Atesca upon their arrival from Rak Verkat.

"Absolutely impossible," the colonel at the desk beside the main door declared when Belgarath demanded to see the Emperor immediately.

"As you grow older, Colonel," the old man said ominously, "you'll discover just how meaningless the word 'impossible' really is." He raised one hand, gestured somewhat theatrically, and Garion heard and felt the surge of his will.

A number of battle flags mounted on stout poles projected out from the opposite wall perhaps fifteen feet from the floor. The officious colonel vanished from his chair and reappeared precariously astride one of those poles with his eyes bulging and his hands desperately clinging to his slippery perch.

"Where would you like to go next, Colonel?" Belgarath asked him. "As I recall, there's a very tall flagpole out front. I could set you on top of it if you wish."

The colonel stared at him in horror.

"Now, as soon as I bring you down from there, you're going to persuade your Emperor to see us at once. You're going to be very convincing, Colonel—that's unless you want to be a permanent flagpole ornament, of course."

The colonel's face was still pasty white when he emerged from the guarded door leading to the audience chamber, and he flinched violently every time Belgarath moved his hand. "His Majesty consents to see you," he stammered.

Belgarath grunted. "I was almost sure that he would."

Kal Zakath had undergone a noticeable transformation since Garion had last seen him. His white linen robe was wrinkled and stained, and there were dark circles under his eyes. His face was deathly pale, his hair was unkempt, and he was unshaven. Spasmlike tremors ran through his body, and he looked almost too weak to stand. "What do you want?" he demanded in a barely audible voice.

"Are you sick?" Belgarath asked him.

"A touch of fever, I think." 'Zakath shrugged. "What's so important that you felt you had to force your way in here to tell me about it?"

"Your empire's collapsing, 'Zakath," Belgarath told him flatly. "It's time you went home to mend your fences."

'Zakath smiled faintly. "Wouldn't that be so very convenient for you?" he said.

"What's going on in Mallorea isn't convenient for anybody. Tell him, Brador."

Nervously, the Melcene bureaucrat delivered his report.

"Demons?" 'Zakath retorted sceptically. "Oh, come now, Belgarath. Surely you don't expect me to believe that, do you? Do you honestly think that I'll run back to Mallorea to chase shadows and leave you behind to raise an army here in the West to confront me when I return?" The palsylike shaking Garion had noted when they had entered the room seemed to be growing more severe. 'Zakath's head bobbed and jerked on his neck, and a stream of spittle ran unnoticed from one corner of his mouth.

"You won't be leaving us behind, 'Zakath," Belgarath replied. "We're going with you. If even a tenth of what Brador says is true, I'm going to have to go to Karanda and stop this Mengha. If he's raising demons, we're *all* going to have to put everything else aside to stop him."

"Absurd!" 'Zakath declared agitatedly. His eyes were unfocused now, and his weaving and trembling had become so severe that he was unable to control his limbs. "I'm not going to be tricked by a clever old man into—" He suddenly started up from his chair with an animal-like cry, clutching at the sides of his head. Then he toppled forward to the floor, twitching and jerking.

Belgarath jumped forward and took hold of the convulsing man's arms. "Quick!" he snapped. "Get something between his teeth before he bites off his tongue!"

Brador grabbed up a sheaf of reports from a nearby table, wadded them up, and jammed them into the frothing Emperor's mouth.

"Garion!" Belgarath barked. "Get Pol—fast!"

Garion started toward the door at a run.

"Wait!" Belgarath said, sniffing suspiciously at the air above the face of the man he was holding down. "Bring Sadi, too. There's a peculiar smell here. Hurry!"

Garion bolted. He ran through the hallways past startled officials and servants and finally burst into the room where Polgara was quietly talking with Ce'Nedra and Velvet. "Aunt Pol!" he shouted, "Come quickly! 'Zakath just collapsed!" Then he spun, ran a few more steps down the hall, and shouldered open the door to Sadi's room. "We need you," he barked at the startled eunuch. "Come with me."

It took only a few moments for the three of them to return to the polished door in the anteroom.

"What's going on?" the Angarak colonel demanded in a frightened voice, barring their way.

"Your Emperor is sick," Garion told him. "Get out of the way." Roughly he pushed the protesting officer to one side and yanked the door open.

'Zakath's convulsions had at least partially subsided, but Belgarath still held him down.

"What is it, father?" Polgara asked, kneeling beside the stricken man.

"He threw a fit."

"The falling sickness?"

"I don't think so. It wasn't quite the same. Sadi, come over here and smell his breath. I'm getting a peculiar odor from him."

Sadi approached cautiously, leaned forward, and sniffed several times. Then he straightened, his face pale. "Thalot," he announced.

"A poison?" Polgara asked him.

Sadi nodded. "It's quite rare."

"Do you have an antidote?"

"No, my lady," he replied. "There isn't an antidote for thalot. It's always been universally fatal. It's seldom used because it acts very slowly, but no one ever recovers from it."

"Then he's dying?" Garion asked with a sick feeling.

"In a manner of speaking, yes. The convulsions will subside, but they'll recur with increasing frequency. Finally . . ." Sadi shrugged.

"There's no hope at all?" Polgara asked.

"None whatsoever, my lady. About all we can do is make his last few days more comfortable."

Belgarath started to swear. "Quiet him down, Pol," he said. "We need to get him into bed and we can't move him while he's jerking around that way."

She nodded and put one hand on 'Zakath's forehead. Garion felt the faint surge, and the struggling Emperor grew quiet.

Brador, his face very pale, looked at them. "I don't think we should announce this just yet," he cautioned. "Let's just call it a slight illness for the moment until we can decide what to do. I'll send for a litter."

The room to which the unconscious 'Zakath was taken was plain to the point of severity. The Emperor's bed was a narrow cot. The only other furniture was a single plain chair and a low chest. The walls were white and unadorned, and a charcoal brazier glowed in one corner. Sadi went back to their chambers and returned with his red case and the canvas sack in which Polgara kept her collection of herbs and remedies. The two of them consulted in low tones while Garion and Brador pushed the litter bearers and curious soldiers from the room. Then they mixed a steaming cup of a pungent-smelling liquid. Sadi raised 'Zakath's head and held it while Polgara spooned the medicine into his slack-lipped mouth.

The door opened quietly, and the green-robed Dalasian healer, Andel, entered. "I came as soon as I heard," she said. "Is the Emperor's illness serious?"

Polgara looked at her gravely. "Close the door, Andel," she said quietly.

The healer gave her a strange look, then pushed the door shut. "Is it that grave, my lady?"

Polgara nodded. "He's been poisoned," she said. "We don't want word of it to get out just yet."

Andel gasped. "What can I do to help?" she asked, coming quickly to the bed.

"Not very much, I'm afraid," Sadi told her.

"Have you given him the antidote yet?"

"There is no antidote."

"There must be. Lady Polgara—"

Polgara sadly shook her head.

"I have failed, then," the hooded woman said in a voice filled with tears. She turned from the bed, her head bowed, and Garion heard a faint murmur that somehow seemed to come from the air above her—a murmur that curiously was not that of a single voice. There was a long silence, and then a shimmering appeared at the foot of the bed. When it cleared, the blindfolded form of Cyradis stood there, one hand slightly extended. "This must not be," she said in her clear, ringing voice. "Use thine art, Lady Polgara. Restore him. Should he die, all our tasks will fail. Bring thy power to bear."

"It won't work, Cyradis," Polgara replied, setting the cup down. "If a poison affects only the blood, I can usually manage to purge it, and Sadi has a whole case full of antidotes. This poison, however, sinks into every particle of the body. It's killing his bones and organs as well as his blood, and there's no way to leech it out."

The shimmering form at the foot of the bed wrung its hands in anguish. "It cannot be so," Cyradis wailed. "Hast thou even applied the sovereign specific?"

Polgara looked up quickly. "Sovereign specific? A universal remedy? I know of no such agent."

"But it doth exist, Lady Polgara. I know not its origins nor its composition, but I have felt its gentle power abroad in the world for some years now."

Polgara looked at Andel, but the healer shook her head helplessly. "I do not know of such a potion, my lady."

"Think, Cyradis," Polgara said urgently. "Anything you can tell us might give us a clue."

The blindfolded Seeress touched the fingertips of one hand lightly to her temple. "Its origins are recent," she said, half to herself. "It came into being less than a score of years ago—some obscure flower, or so it seemeth to me."

"It's hopeless, then," Sadi said. "There are millions of kinds of flowers." He rose and crossed the room to Belgarath. "I think we might want to leave here—almost immediately," he murmured. "At the first suggestion of the word 'poison,' people start looking for the nearest Nyissan—and those associated with him. I think we're in a great deal of danger right now."

"Can you think of *anything* else, Cyradis?" Polgara pressed. "No matter how remote?"

The Seeress struggled with it, her face strained as she reached deeper into her strange vision. Her shoulders finally sagged in defeat. "Nothing," she said. "Only a woman's face."

"Describe it."

"She is tall," the Seeress replied. "Her hair is very dark, but her skin is like marble. Her husband is much involved with horses."

"Adara!" Garion exclaimed, the beautiful face of his cousin suddenly coming before his eyes.

Polgara snapped her fingers. "And Adara's rose!" Then she frowned. "I examined that flower very closely some years back, Cyradis," she said. "Are you absolutely sure? There are some unusual substances in it, but I didn't find any particular medicinal qualities in any of them—either in any distillation or powder."

Cyradis concentrated. "Can healing be accomplished by means of a fragrance, Lady Polgara?"

Polgara's eyes narrowed in thought. "There are some minor remedies that are inhaled," she said doubtfully, "but—"

"There are poisons that can be administered in that fashion, Lady Polgara," Sadi supplied. "The fumes are drawn into the lungs and from there into the heart. Then the blood carries them to every part of the body. It could very well be the only way to neutralize the effects of thalot."

Belgarath's expression had grown intent. "Well, Pol?" he asked.

"It's worth a try, father," she replied. "I've got a few of the flowers. They're dried, but they *might* work."

"Any seeds?"

"A few, yes."

"Seeds?" Andel exclaimed. "Kal Zakath would be months in his grave before any bush could grow and bloom."

The old man chuckled slyly. "Not quite," he said, winking at Polgara. "I have quite a way with plants sometimes. I'm going to need some dirt—and some boxes or tubs to put it in."

Sadi went to the door and spoke briefly with the guards outside. They looked baffled, but a short command from Andel sent them scurrying.

"What is the origin of this strange flower, Lady Polgara?" Cyradis asked curiously, "How is it that thou art so well acquainted with it?"

"Garion made it." Polgara shrugged, looking thoughtfully at 'Zakath's narrow cot. "I think we'll want the bed out from the wall, father," she said. "I want it surrounded by flowers."

"Made?" the Seeress exclaimed.

Polgara nodded. "Created, actually," she said absently. "Do you think it's warm enough in here, father? We're going to want big, healthy blooms, and even at best the flower's a bit puny."

"I did my best," Garion protested.

"Created?" Cyradis' voice was awed. Then she bowed to Garion with profound respect.

When the tubs of half-frozen dirt had been placed about the stricken Emperor's bed, smoothed, and dampened with water, Polgara took a small leather pouch from her green canvas sack, removed a pinch of miniscule seeds, and carefully sowed them in the soil.

"All right," Belgarath said, rolling up his sleeves in a workmanlike fashion, "stand back." He bent and touched the dirt in one of the tubs. "You were right, Pol," he muttered. "Just a little too cold." He frowned slightly, and Garion saw his lips move. The surge was not a large one, and the sound of it was little more than a whisper. The damp earth in the tubs began to steam. "That's better," he said. Then he extended his hands out over the narrow cot and the steaming tubs. Again Garion felt the surge and the whisper.

At first nothing seemed to happen, but then tiny specks of green appeared on the top of the dampened dirt. Even as Garion watched those little leaves grow and expand, he remembered where he had seen Belgarath perform this same feat before. As clearly as if he were there, he saw the courtyard before King Korodullin's palace at Vo Mimbre and he saw the apple twig the old man had thrust down between two flagstones expand and reach up toward the old sorcerer's hand as proof to the skeptical Sir Andorig that he was indeed who he said he was.

The pale green leaves had grown darker, and the spindly twigs and tendrils that had at first appeared had already expanded into low bushes.

"Make them vine up across the bed, father," Polgara said critically. "Vines produce more blossoms, and I want a lot of blossoms."

He let out his breath explosively and gave her a look that spoke volumes. "All right," he said finally. "You want vines? Vines it is."

"Is it too much for you, father?" she asked solicitously.

He set his jaw, but did not answer. He did, however, start to sweat. Longer tendrils began to writhe upward like green snakes winding up around the legs of the Emperor's cot and reaching upward to catch the bedframe. Once they had gained that foothold, they seemed to pause while Belgarath caught his breath. "This is harder than it looks," he puffed. Then he concentrated again, and the vines quickly overspread the cot and Kal Zakath's inert body until only his ashen face remained uncovered by them.

"All right," Belgarath said to the plants, "that's far enough. You can bloom now." There was another surge and a peculiar ringing sound.

The tips of all the myriad twiglets swelled, and then those buds began to split, revealing their pale lavender interiors. Almost shyly the lopsided little flowers opened, filling the room with a gentle-seeming fragrance. Garion straightened as he breathed in that delicate odor. For some reason, he suddenly felt very good, and the cares and worries which had beset him for the past several months seemed to fall away.

The slack-faced 'Zakath stirred slightly, took a breath, and sighed deeply. Polgara laid her fingertips to the side of his neck. "I think it's working, father," she said. "His heart's not laboring so hard now, and his breathing's easier."

"Good," Belgarath replied. "I hate to go through something like that for nothing."

Then the Emperor opened his eyes. The shimmering form of Cyradis hovered anxiously at the foot of his bed. Strangely, he smiled when he saw her, and her shy, answering smile lighted her pale face. Then 'Zakath sighed once more and closed his eyes again. Garion leaned forward to make sure that the sick man was still breathing. When he looked back toward the foot of the bed, the Seeress of Kell was gone.

CHAPTER FOUR

A warm wind came in off the lake that night, and the wet snow that had blanketed Rak Hagga and the surrounding countryside turned to a dreary slush that sagged and fell from the limbs of the trees in the little garden at the center of the house and slid in sodden clumps from the gray slate roof. Garion and Silk sat near the fire in the mauve-cushioned room, looking out at the garden and talking quietly.

"We'd know a great deal more, if I could get in touch with Yarblek," Silk was saying. The little man was dressed again in the pearl-gray doublet and black hose which he had favored during those years before they had begun this search, although he wore only a few of the costly rings and ornaments which had made him appear so ostentatiously wealthy at that time.

"Isn't he in Gar og Nadrak?" Garion asked. Garion had also discarded his serviceable travel clothing and reverted to his customary silver-trimmed blue.

"It's hard to say exactly where Yarblek is at any given time, Garion. He moves around a great deal; but no matter where he goes, the reports from our people in Mal Zeth, Melcene, and Maga Renn are all forwarded to him. Whatever this

Mengha is up to is almost certain to have disrupted trade. I'm sure that our agents have gathered everything they could find out about him and sent it along to Yarblek. Right now my scruffy-looking partner probably knows more about Mengha than Brador's secret police do."

"I don't want to get sidetracked, Silk. Our business is with Zandramas, not Mengha."

"Demons are everybody's business," Silk replied soberly, "but no matter what we decide to do, we have to get to Mallorea first—and that means persuading 'Zakath that this is serious. Was he listening at all when you told him about Mengha?"

Garion shook his head. "I'm not sure if he even understood what we were telling him. He wasn't altogether rational."

Silk grunted. "When he wakes up, we'll have to try again." A sly grin crossed the little man's face. "I've had a certain amount of luck negotiating with sick people," he said.

"Isn't that sort of contemptible?"

"Of course it is—but it gets results."

Later that morning, Garion and his rat-faced friend stopped by the Emperor's room, ostensibly to inquire about his health. Polgara and Sadi were seated on either side of the bed, and Andel sat quietly in the corner. The vines that had enveloped the narrow cot had been pulled aside, but the air in the room was still heavy with the fragrance of the small, lavender flowers. The sick man was propped into a half-sitting position by pillows, but his eyes were closed as Silk and Garion entered. His cat lay contentedly purring at the foot of the bed.

"How is he?" Garion asked quietly.

"He's been awake a few times," Sadi replied. "There are still some traces of thalot in his extremities, but they seem to be dissipating." The eunuch was picking curiously at one of the small flowers. "I wonder if these would work if they were distilled down to an essence," he mused, "or perhaps an attar. It might be very interesting to wear a perfume that would ward off any poison." He frowned slightly. "And I wonder if they'd be effective against snake venom."

"Have Zith bite someone," Silk suggested. "Then you can test it."

"Would you like to volunteer, Prince Kheldar?"

"Ah, no, Sadi," Silk declined. "Thanks all the same." He looked at the red case lying open on the floor in the corner. "Is she confined, by the way?" he asked nervously.

"She's sleeping," Sadi replied. "She always takes a little nap after breakfast."

Garion looked at the dozing Emperor. "Is he coherent at all—when he's awake, I mean?"

"His mind seems to be clearing," Polgara told him.

"Hysteria and delirium are some of the symptoms brought on by thalot," Sadi said. "Growing rationality is an almost certain sign of recovery."

"Is that you, Belgarion?" 'Zakath asked almost in a whisper and without opening his eyes.

"Yes," Garion replied. "How are you feeling?"

"Weak. Light-headed—and every muscle in my body screams like an abscessed tooth. Aside from that, I'm fine." He opened his eyes with a wry smile. "What happened? I seem to have lost track of things."

Garion glanced briefly at Polgara, and she nodded. "You were poisoned," he told the sick man.

'Zakath looked a bit surprised. "It must not have been a very good one then," he said.

"Actually, it's one of the very best, your Imperial Majesty," Sadi disagreed mildly. "It's always been universally lethal."

"I'm dying then?" 'Zakath said it with a peculiar kind of satisfaction, almost as if he welcomed the idea. "Ah, well," he sighed. "That should solve many problems."

"I'm very sorry, your Majesty," Silk said with mock regret, "but I think you'll live. Belgarath tampers with the normal course of events from time to time. It's a bad habit he picked up in his youth, but a man needs *some* vices, I suppose."

'Zakath smiled weakly. "You're a droll little fellow, Prince Kheldar."

"If you're really keen on dying, though," Silk added outrageously, "we could always wake Zith. One nip from her almost guarantees perpetual slumber."

"Zith?"

"Sadi's pet—a little green snake. She could even curl up at your ear after she bites you and purr you into eternity."

'Zakath sighed, and his eyes drooped shut again.

"I think we should let him sleep," Polgara said quietly.

"Not just yet, Lady Polgara," the Emperor said. "I've shunned sleep and the dreams which infest it for so long that it comes unnaturally now."

"You *must* sleep, Kal Zakath," Andel told him. "There are ways to banish evil dreams, and sleep is the greatest healer."

'Zakath sighed and shook his head. "I'm afraid you won't be able to banish *these* dreams, Andel." Then he frowned slightly. "Sadi, is hallucination one of the symptoms of the poison I was given?"

"It's possible," the eunuch admitted. "What horrors have you seen?"

"Not a horror," 'Zakath replied. "I seem to see the face of a young woman. Her eyes are bound with a strip of cloth. A peculiar peace comes over me when I see her face."

"Then it was not an hallucination, Kal Zakath," Andel told him.

"Who is this strange blind child, then?"

"My mistress," Andel said proudly. "The face which came to you in your direst hour was the face of Cyradis, the Seeress of Kell, upon whose decision rests the fate of all the world—and of all other worlds as well."

"So great a responsibility to lie upon such slender shoulders," 'Zakath said.

"It is her task," Andel said simply.

The sick man seemed to fall again into a doze, his lips lightly touched with a peculiar smile. Then his eyes opened again, seemingly more alert now. "Am I healed, Sadi?" he asked the shaved-headed eunuch. "Has your excellent Nyissan poison quite run its course?"

"Oh," Sadi replied speculatively, "I wouldn't say that you're entirely well yet, your Majesty, but I'd guess that you're out of any immediate danger."

"Good," 'Zakath said crisply, trying to shoulder his way up into a sitting position. Garion reached out to help him. "And has the knave who poisoned me been apprehended yet?"

Sadi shook his head. "Not as far as I know," he answered.

"I think that might be the first order of business, then. I'm starting to feel a little hungry and I'd rather not go through this again. Is the poison common in Cthol Murgos?"

Sadi frowned. "Murgo law forbids poisons and drugs, your Majesty," he replied. "They're a backward sort of people. The Dagashi assassins probably have access to thalot, though."

"You think my poisoner might have been a Dagashi, then?"

Sadi shrugged. "Most assassinations in Cthol Murgos are carried out by the Dagashi. They're efficient and discreet."

'Zakath's eyes narrowed in thought. "That would seem to point a finger directly at Urgit, then. The Dagashi are expensive, and Urgit has access to the royal treasury."

Silk grimaced. "No," he declared. "Urgit wouldn't do that. A knife between your shoulder blades maybe, but not poison."

"How can you be so sure, Kheldar?"

"I know him," Silk replied a bit lamely. "He's weak and a little timid, but he wouldn't be a party to a poisoning. It's a contemptible way to resolve political differences."

"Prince Kheldar!" Sadi protested.

"Except in Nyissa, of course," Silk conceded. "One always needs to take quaint local customs into account." He pulled at his long, pointed nose. "I'll admit that Urgit wouldn't grieve too much if you woke up dead some morning," he said to the Mallorean Emperor, "but it's all just a little too pat. If your generals believed that it was Urgit who arranged to have you killed, they'd stay here for the next ten generations trying to obliterate all of Murgodom, wouldn't they?"

"I'd assume so," 'Zakath said.

"Who would benefit the most by disposing of you and rather effectively making sure that the bulk of your army doesn't return to Mallorea in the foreseeable future? Not Urgit, certainly. More likely it would be somebody in Mallorea who wants a free hand there." Silk squared his shoulders. "Why don't you let Liselle and me do a little snooping around before you lock your mind in stone on this? Obvious things always make me suspicious."

"That's all very well, Kheldar," 'Zakath said rather testily, "but how can I be sure that my next meal won't have another dose of exotic spices in it?"

"You have at your bedside the finest cook in the world," the rat-faced man said, pointing grandly at Polgara, "and I can absolutely guarantee that she won't poison you. She might turn you into a radish if you offend her, but she'd never poison you."

"All right, Silk, that will do," Polgara told him.

"I'm only paying tribute to your extraordinary gifts, Polgara."

Her eyes grew hard.

"I think that perhaps it might be time for me to be on my way," Silk said to Garion.

"Wise decision," Garion murmured.

The little man turned and quickly left the room.

"Is he really as good as he pretends to be?" 'Zakath asked curiously.

Polgara nodded. "Between them, Kheldar and Liselle can probably ferret out any secret in the world. Silk doesn't always like it, but they're almost a perfect team. And now, your Majesty, what would you like for breakfast?"

A curious exchange was taking place in the corner. Throughout the previous conversation, Garion had heard a faint, drowsy purr coming from Zith's earthenware bottle. Either the little snake was expressing a general sense of contentment, or it may have been one of the peculiarities of her species to purr while sleeping. 'Zakath's pregnant, mackerel-striped cat, attracted by that sound, jumped down from the bed and curiously waddled toward Zith's little home. Absently, probably without even thinking about it, she responded to the purr coming from the bottle with one of her own. She sniffed at the bottle, then tentatively touched it with one soft paw. The peculiar duet of purring continued.

Then, perhaps because Sadi had not stoppered the bottle tightly enough or because she had long since devised this simple means of opening her front door, the little snake nudged the cork out of the bottle with her blunt nose. Both creatures continued to purr, although the cat was now obviously afire with curiosity. For a time Zith did not reveal herself, but lurked shyly in her bottle, still purring. Then, cautiously, she poked out her head, her forked tongue flickering as she tested the air.

The cat jumped straight up to a height of about three feet, giving vent to a startled yowl. Zith retreated immediately back into the safety of her house, though she continued to purr.

Warily, but still burning with curiosity, the cat approached the bottle again, moving one foot at a time.

"Sadi," 'Zakath said, his voice filled with concern.

"There's no immediate danger, your Majesty," the eunuch assured him. "Zith never bites while she's purring."

Again the little green snake slid her head out of the bottle. This time the cat recoiled only slightly. Then, curiosity overcoming her natural aversion to reptiles, she continued her slow advance, her nose reaching out toward this remarkable creature. Zith, still purring, also extended her blunt nose. Their noses touched, and both flinched back slightly. Then they cautiously sniffed at each other, the cat with her nose, the snake with her tongue. Both were purring loudly now.

"Astonishing," Sadi murmured. "I think they actually like each other."

"Sadi, please," 'Zakath said plaintively. "I don't know how you feel about your snake, but I'm rather fond of my cat, and she *is* about to become a mother."

"I'll speak with them, your Majesty," Sadi assured him. "I'm not sure that they'll listen, but I'll definitely speak with them."

Belgarath had once again retired to the library, and Garion found him later that day poring over a large map of northern Mallorea. "Ah," he said, looking up as Garion entered, "there you are. I was just about to send for you. Come over here and look at this."

Garion went to the table.

"The appearance of this Mengha fellow might just work to our advantage, you know."

"I don't quite follow that, Grandfather."

"Zandramas is here at Ashaba, right?" Belgarath stabbed his finger at a spot in the representation of the Karandese mountains.

"Yes," Garion said.

"And Mengha's moving west and south out of Calida, over here." The old man poked at the map again.

"That's what Brador says."

"He's got her blocked off from most of the continent, Garion. She's been very careful here in Cthol Murgos to avoid populated areas. There's no reason to believe that she's going to change once she gets to Mallorea. Urvon's going to be to the south of her at Mal Yaska, and the wastes to the north are virtually impassable—even though it's nearly summer."

"Summer?"

"In the northern half of the world it is."

"Oh. I keep forgetting." Garion peered at the map. "Grandfather, we don't have any idea of where 'the place which is no more' might be. When Zandramas leaves Ashaba, she could go in any direction."

Belgarath squinted at the map. "I don't think so, Garion. In the light of all that's happened in Mallorea—coupled with the fact that by now she knows that we're on her trail—I think she almost *has* to be trying to get back to her power base in Darshiva. Everybody in the world is after her, and she needs help."

"*We* certainly aren't threatening her all that much," Garion said moodily. "We can't even get out of Cthol Murgos."

"That's what I wanted to talk to you about. You've got to persuade 'Zakath that it's vital for us to leave here and get to Mallorea as quickly as possible."

"Persuade?"

"Just do whatever you have to, Garion. There's a great deal at stake."

"Why me?" Garion said it without thinking.

Belgarath gave him a long, steady look.

"Sorry," Garion muttered. "Forget that I said it."

"All right. I'll do that."

Late that evening, 'Zakath's cat gave birth to seven healthy kittens while Zith hovered in anxious attendance, warning off all other observers with ominous hisses. Peculiarly, the only person the protective little reptile would allow near the newborn kittens was Velvet.

Garion had little success during the next couple of days in his efforts to steer his conversations with the convalescing 'Zakath around to the subject of the necessity for returning to Mallorea. The Emperor usually pleaded a lingering weakness as a result of his poisoning, though Garion privately suspected subterfuge on that score, since the man appeared to have more than enough energy for his usual activities and only protested exhaustion when Garion wanted to talk about a voyage.

On the evening of the fourth day, however, he decided to try negotiation one last time before turning to more direct alternatives. He found 'Zakath seated in the chair near his bed with a book in his hands. The dark circles beneath his eyes had vanished, the trembling had disappeared entirely, and he seemed totally alert. "Ah, Belgarion," he said almost cheerfully, "so good of you to stop by."

"I thought I'd come in and put you to sleep again," Garion replied with slightly exaggerated sarcasm.

"Have I been that obvious?" 'Zakath asked.

"Yes, as a matter of fact you have. Every time I mention the words 'ship' and 'Mallorea' in the same sentence, your eyes snap shut. 'Zakath, we've got to talk about this, and time is starting to run out."

'Zakath passed one hand across his eyes with some show of weariness.

"Let me put it this way," Garion pressed on. "Belgarath's starting to get impatient. I'm trying to keep our discussions civil, but if he steps in, I can almost guarantee that they're going to turn unpleasant—very quickly."

'Zakath lowered his hand, and his eyes narrowed. "That sounds vaguely like a threat, Belgarion."

"No," Garion disagreed. "As a matter of fact, it's in the nature of friendly advice. If you want to stay here in Cthol Murgos, that's up to you, but *we* have to get to Mallorea—and soon."

"And if I choose not to permit you to go?"

"Permit?" Garion laughed. " 'Zakath, did you grow up in the same world with the rest of us? Have you got even the remotest idea of what you're talking about?"

"I think that concludes this interview, Belgarion," the Emperor said coldly. He rose stiffly to his feet and turned to his bed. As usual, his cat had deposited her mewling little brood in the center of his coverlet and then gone off to nap alone in her wool-lined box in the corner. The irritated Emperor looked with some exasperation at the furry little puddle on his bed. "You have my permission to withdraw, Belgarion," he said over his shoulder. Then he reached down with both hands to scoop up the cluster of kittens.

Zith reared up out of the very center of the furry heap, fixed him with a cold eye, and hissed warningly.

"Torak's teeth!" 'Zakath swore, jerking his hands away. "This is going too far! Go tell Sadi that I want his accursed snake out of my room immediately!"

"He's taken her out four times already, 'Zakath," Garion said mildly. "She just keeps crawling back." He suppressed a grin. "Maybe she likes you."

"Are you trying to be funny?"

"Me?"

"Get the snake out of here."

Garion put his hands behind his back. "Not me, 'Zakath. I'll go get Sadi."

In the hallway outside, however, he encountered Velvet, who was coming toward the Emperor's room with a mysterious smile on her face.

"Do you think you could move Zith?" Garion asked her. "She's in the middle of 'Zakath's bed with those kittens."

"*You* can move her, Belgarion," the blond girl said, smiling the dimples into her cheeks. "She trusts you."

"I think I'd rather not try that."

The two of them went back into the Emperor's bedchamber.

"Margravine," 'Zakath greeted her courteously, inclining his head.

She curtsied. "Your Majesty."

"Can you deal with this?" he asked, pointing at the furry pile on his bed with the snake still half-reared out of the center, her eyes alert.

"Of course, your Majesty." She approached the bed, and the snake flickered her tongue nervously. "Oh, *do* stop that, Zith," the blond girl chided. Then she lifted the front of her skirt to form a kind of pouch and began picking up kittens and depositing them in her improvised basket. Last of all she lifted Zith and laid her in the middle. She crossed the room and casually put them all into the box with the mother cat, who opened one golden eye, made room for her kittens and their bright green nursemaid, and promptly went back to sleep.

"Isn't that sweet?" Velvet murmured softly. Then she turned back to 'Zakath. "Oh, by the way, your Majesty, Kheldar and I managed to find out who it was who poisoned you."

"What?"

She nodded, frowning slightly. "It came as something of a surprise, actually."

The Emperor's eyes had become intent. "You're sure?"

"As sure as one can be in these cases. You seldom find an eyewitness to a poisoning; but he was in the kitchen at the right time, he left right after you fell ill, and we know him by reputation." She smiled at Garion. "Have you noticed how people always tend to remember a man with white eyes?"

"*Naradas?*" Garion exclaimed.

"Surprising, isn't it?"

"Who's Naradas?" 'Zakath demanded.

"He works for Zandramas," Garion replied. He frowned. "That doesn't make any sense, Velvet. Why would Zandramas want to kill him? Wouldn't she want to keep him alive?"

She spread her hands. "I don't know, Belgarion—not yet, anyway."

"Velvet?" 'Zakath asked in puzzlement.

She smiled the dimples into her cheeks again. "Isn't it silly?" She laughed. "I suppose these little nicknames are a form of affection, though. Belgarion's question is to the point, however. Can you think of any reason why Zandramas might want to kill you?"

"Not immediately, but we can wring that answer out of her when I catch her— and I'll make a point of doing that, even if I have to take Cthol Murgos apart stone by stone."

"She isn't here," Garion said absently, still struggling with the whole idea. "She's at Ashaba—in the House of Torak."

'Zakath's eyes narrowed suspiciously. "Isn't this convenient, Belgarion?" he said. "I *happen* to get poisoned right after your arrival. Belgarath *happens* to cure me. Kheldar and Liselle *happen* to discover the identity of the poisoner, who *happens* to work for Zandramas, who *happens* to be at Ashaba, which *happens* to be in Mallorea—a place which just *happens* to be where you so desperately want to go. The coincidence staggers the imagination, wouldn't you say?"

" 'Zakath, you're starting to make me tired," Garion said irritably. "If I decide that I need a boat to get to Mallorea, I'll *take* one. All that's kept me from doing that so far are the manners Lady Polgara drilled into me when I was a boy."

"And how do you propose to leave this house?" 'Zakath snapped, his temper also starting to rise.

That did it. The rage that came over Garion was totally irrational. It was the result of a hundred delays and stumbling blocks and petty interruptions that had dogged him for almost a year now. He reached over his shoulder, ripped Iron-grip's sword from its sheath, and peeled the concealing leather sleeve from its hilt. He held the great blade before him and literally threw his will at the Orb. The sword exploded into blue flame. "How do I propose to leave this house?" he half shouted at the stunned Emperor. "I'll use *this* for a key. It works sort of like this." He straightened his arm, leveling the blazing sword at the door. "Burst!" he commanded.

Garion's anger was not only irrational, it was also somewhat excessive. He had intended no more than the door—and possibly a part of the doorframe—simply to illustrate to 'Zakath the intensity of his feeling about the matter. The Orb, however, startled into wakefulness by the sudden jolt of his angry will, had overreacted. The door, certainly, disappeared, dissolving into splinters that blasted out into the hall-way. The doorframe also vanished. What Garion had *not* intended, however, was what happened to the wall.

White-faced and shaking, 'Zakath stumbled back, staring at the hallway out-side that had suddenly been revealed and at the rubble that filled it—rubble that had a moment before been the solid, two-foot-thick stone wall of his bedroom.

"My goodness," Velvet murmured mildly.

Knowing that it was silly and melodramatic, but still caught up in that tower-ing, irrational anger, Garion caught the stunned 'Zakath by the arm with his left hand and gestured with the sword he held in his right. "Now, we're going to go talk with Belgarath," he announced. "We'll go through the hallways *if* you'll give me your word not to call soldiers every time we go around a corner. Otherwise, we'll just cut straight through the house. The library's sort of in that direction, isn't it?" he pointed at one of the still-standing walls with his sword.

"Belgarion," Velvet chided him gently, "now really, that's no way to behave. Kal Zakath has been a very courteous host. I'm sure that now that he understands the situation, he'll be more than happy to cooperate, won't you, your Imperial Majesty?" She smiled winsomely at the Emperor. "We wouldn't want the Rivan King to get *really* angry, now would we? There are so many breakable things about—windows, walls, houses, the city of Rak Hagga—that sort of thing."

They found Belgarath in the library again. He was reading a small scroll, and there was a large tankard at his elbow.

"Something's come up," Garion said shortly as he entered.

"Oh?"

"Velvet tells us that she and Silk found out that it was Naradas who poisoned 'Zakath."

"Naradas?" the old man blinked. "That's a surprise, isn't it?"

"What's she up to, Grandfather? Zandramas, I mean."

"I'm not sure." Belgarath looked at 'Zakath. "Who's likely to succeed you if somebody manages to put you to sleep?"

'Zakath shrugged. "There are a few distant cousins scattered about—mostly in the Melcene Islands and Celanta. The line of the succession is a little murky."

"Perhaps that's what she has in mind, Belgarath," Velvet said seriously. "If there's any truth in that Grolim Prophecy you found in Rak Hagga, she's got to have an Angarak king with her at the time of the final meeting. A tame king would suit her purposes much better than someone like his Majesty here—some third or fourth cousin she could crown and anoint and proclaim king. Then she could have her Grolims keep an eye on him and deliver him to her at the proper time."

"It's possible, I suppose," he agreed. "I think there may be a bit more to it than that, though. Zandramas has never been that straightforward about anything before."

"I hope you all realize that I haven't the faintest notion of what you're talking about," 'Zakath said irritably.

"Just how much does he know?" Belgarath asked Garion.

"Not very much, Grandfather."

"All right. Maybe if he does know what's going on, he won't be quite so difficult." He turned to the Mallorean Emperor. "Have you ever heard of the Mrin Codex?" he asked.

"I've heard that it was written by a madman—like most of the other so-called prophecies."

"How about the Child of Light and the Child of Dark?"

"That's part of the standard gibberish used by religious hysterics."

" 'Zakath, you're going to have to believe in *something*. This is going to be very difficult for you to grasp if you don't."

"Would you settle for a temporary suspension of skepticism?" the Emperor countered.

"Fair enough, I suppose. All right, now, this gets complicated, so you're going to have to pay attention, listen carefully, and stop me if there's anything you don't understand."

The old man then proceeded to sketch in the ancient story of the "accident" that had occurred before the world had begun and the divergence of the two possible courses of the future and of the two consciousnesses which had somehow infused those courses.

"All right," 'Zakath said. "That's fairly standard theology so far. I've had Grolims preaching to the same nonsense since I was a boy."

Belgarath nodded. "I just wanted to start us off from common ground." He went on then, telling 'Zakath of the events spanning the eons between the cracking of the world and the Battle of Vo Mimbre.

"Our point of view is somewhat different," 'Zakath murmured.

"It would be," Belgarath agreed. "All right, there were five hundred years between Vo Mimbre and the theft of the Orb by Zedar the Apostate."

"Recovery," 'Zakath corrected. "The Orb was stolen from Cthol Mishrak by Iron-grip the thief and by—" He stopped, and his eyes suddenly widened as he stared at the seedy-looking old man.

"Yes," Belgarath said, "I really *was* there, 'Zakath—and I was there two thousand years before, when Torak originally stole the Orb from my master."

"I've been sick, Belgarath," the Emperor said weakly, sinking into a chair. "My nerves aren't really up for too many of these shocks."

Belgarath looked at him, puzzled.

"Their Majesties were having a little discussion," Velvet explained brightly. "King Belgarion gave the Emperor a little demonstration of some of the more flamboyant capabilities of the Sword of the Rivan King. The Emperor was quite impressed. So was most everybody else who happened to be in that part of the house."

Belgarath gave Garion a chill look. "Playing again?" he asked.

Garion tried to reply, but there was nothing he could really say.

"All right, let's get on with this," Belgarath continued briskly. "What happened after the emergence of Garion here is all recent history, so I'm sure you're familiar with it."

"Garion?" 'Zakath asked.

"A more common—and familiar—form. 'Belgarion' is a bit ostentatious, wouldn't you say?"

"No more so than 'Belgarath.' "

"I've worn 'Belgarath' for almost seven thousand years, 'Zakath, and I've sort of rubbed off the rough edges and corners. Garion's only been wearing his 'Bel' for a dozen years, and it still squeaks when he turns around too quickly."

Garion felt slightly offended by that.

"Anyway," the old man continued, "after Torak was dead, Garion and Ce'Nedra got married. About a year or so ago, she gave birth to a son. Garion's attention at that time was on the Bear-cult. Someone had tried to kill Ce'Nedra and had succeeded in killing the Rivan Warder."

"I'd heard about that," 'Zakath said.

"Anyway, he was in the process of stamping out the cult—he stamps quite well once he puts his mind to it—when someone crept into the Citadel at Riva and abducted his infant son—my great-grandson."

"No!" 'Zakath exclaimed.

"Oh, yes," Belgarath continued grimly. "We thought that it was the cult and marched to Rheon in Drasnia, their headquarters, but it was all a clever ruse. Zandramas had abducted Prince Geran and misdirected us to Rheon. The leader of the cult turned out to be Harakan, one of the henchmen of Urvon—is this coming too fast for you?"

'Zakath's face was startled, and his eyes had gone wide again. "No," he said, swallowing hard. "I think I can keep up."

"There isn't too much more. After we discovered our mistakes, we took up the abductor's trail. We know that she's going to Mallorea—to a 'place which is no more.' That's where the Sardion is. We have to stop her, or at least arrive there at the same time. Cyradis believes that when we all arrive at this 'place which is no more,' there's going to be one of those confrontations between the Child of Light and the Child of Dark which have been happening since before the beginning of time—except that this is going to be the last one. She'll choose between them, and that's supposed to be the end of it."

"I'm afraid that it's at that point that my skepticism reasserts itself, Belgarath," 'Zakath said. "You don't acutally expect me to believe that these two shadowy figures that predate the world are going to arrive at this mysterious place to grapple once more, do you?"

"What makes you think they're shadowy? The spirits that are at the core of the two possible destinies infuse real people to act as their instruments during these meetings. Right now, for example, Zandramas is the Child of Dark. It used to be Torak—until Garion killed him."

"And who's the Child of Light?"

"I thought that would be obvious."

'Zakath turned to stare incredulously into Garion's blue eyes. "You?" he gasped.

"That's what they tell me," Garion replied.

CHAPTER FIVE

Kal Zakath, dread Emperor of boundless Mallorea, looked first at Belgarath, then again at Garion, and finally at Velvet. "Why do I feel that I'm losing control of things here?" he asked. "When you people came here, you were more or less my prisoners. Now somehow I'm yours."

"We told you some things you didn't know before, that's all," Belgarath told him.

"Or some things that you've cleverly made up."

"Why would we do that?"

"I can think of any number of reasons. For the sake of argument I'll accept your story about the abduction of Belgarion's son, but don't you see how that makes all your motives completely obvious? You need my aid in your search. All this mystical nonsense, *and* your wild story about Urgit's parentage, could have been designed to divert me from my campaign here in Cthol Murgos and to trick me into returning with you to Mallorea. Everything you've done or said since you've come here could have been directed toward that end."

"Do you really think we'd do that?" Garion asked him.

"Belgarion, if *I* had a son and someone had abducted him, I'd do *anything* to get him back. I sympathize with your situation, but I have my own concerns, and they're here, not in Mallorea. I'm sorry, but the more I think about this, the less of it I believe. I could not have misjudged the world so much. Demons? Prophecies? Magic? Immortal old men? It's all been very entertaining, but I don't believe one word of it."

"Not even what the Orb showed you about Urgit?" Garion asked.

"Please, Belgarion, don't treat me like a child." 'Zakath's lips were twisted into an ironic smile. "Isn't it altogether possible that the poison had already crept into my mind? And isn't it also possible that you, like any other of the charlatans who infest village fairs, used a show of mysterious lights and suggestions to make me see what you wanted me to see?"

"What *do* you believe, Kal Zakath?" Velvet asked him.

"What I can see and touch—and precious little else."

"So great a skepticism," she murmured. "Then you do not accept one single out-of-the-ordinary thing?"

"Not that I can think of, no."

"Not even the peculiar gift of the Seers at Kell? It's been fairly well documented, you know."

He frowned slightly. "Yes," he admitted, "as a matter of fact, it has."

"How can you document a vision?" Garion asked curiously.

"The Grolims were seeking to discredit the Seers," 'Zakath replied. "They felt that the easiest way to do that was to have these pronouncements about the future written down and then wait to see what happened. The bureaucracy was instructed to keep records. So far, not one of the predictions of the Seers has proven false."

"Then you *do* believe that the Seers have the ability to know things about the past and the present and the future in ways that the rest of us might not completely understand?" Velvet pressed.

'Zakath pursed his lips. "All right, Margravine," he said reluctantly, "I'll concede that the Seers have certain abilities that haven't been explained as yet."

"Do you believe that a Seer could lie to you?"

"Good girl," Belgarath murmured approvingly.

"No," 'Zakath replied after a moment's thought. "A Seer is incapable of lying. Their truthfulness is proverbial."

"Well, then," she said with a dimpled smile, "all you need to do to find out if what we've told you is the truth is to send for a Seer, isn't it?"

"Liselle," Garion protested, "that could take weeks. We don't have that much time."

"Oh," she said, "I don't think it would take all that long. If I remember correctly, Lady Polgara said that Andel summoned Cyradis when his Majesty here lay dying. I'm fairly sure we could persuade her to do it for us again."

"Well, 'Zakath," Belgarath said. "Will you agree to accept what Cyradis tells you as the truth?"

The Emperor squinted at him suspiciously, searching for some kind of subterfuge. "You've manipulated me into a corner," he accused. He thought about it. "All right, Belgarath," he said finally. "I'll accept whatever Cyradis says as the truth—if you'll agree to do the same."

"Done then," Belgarath said. "Let's send for Andel and get on with this."

As Velvet stepped out into the hall to speak with one of the guards who trailed along behind the Emperor wherever he went, 'Zakath leaned back in his chair. "I can't believe that I'm even considering all the wild impossibilities you've been telling me," he said.

Garion exchanged a quick look with his grandfather, and then they both laughed.

"Something funny, gentlemen?"

"Just a family joke, 'Zakath," Belgarath told him. "Garion and I have been discussing the possible and the impossible since he was about nine years old. He was even more stubborn about it than you are."

"It gets easier to accept after the first shock wears off," Garion added. "It's sort of like swimming in very cold water. Once you get numb, it doesn't hurt quite so much."

It was not long until Velvet reentered the room with the hooded Andel at her side.

"I believe you said that the Seeress of Kell is your mistress, Andel," 'Zakath said to her.

"Yes, she is, your Majesty."

"Can you summon her?"

"Her semblance, your Majesty, if there is need and if she will consent to come."

"I believe there's a need, Andel. Belgarath has told me certain things that I have to have confirmed. I know that Cyradis speaks only the truth. Belgarath, on the other hand, has a more dubious reputation." He threw a rather sly, sidelong glance at the old man.

Belgarath grinned at him and winked.

"I will speak with my mistress, your Majesty," Andel said, "and entreat her to send her semblance here. Should she consent, I beg of you to ask your questions quickly. The effort of reaching half around the world exhausts her, and she is not robust." Then the Dalasian woman knelt reverently and lowered her head, and Garion once again heard that peculiar murmur as of many voices, followed by a long moment of silence. Again there was that same shimmer in the air; when it had cleared, the hooded and blindfolded form of Cyradis stood there.

"We thank you for coming, Holy Seeress," 'Zakath said to her in an oddly respectful tone of voice. "My guests here have told me certain things that I am loath to believe, but I have agreed to accept whatever you can confirm."

"I will tell thee what I can, 'Zakath," she replied. "Some things are hidden from me, and some others may not yet be revealed."

"I understand the limitations, Cyradis. Belgarion tells me that Urgit, the King of the Murgos, is not of the blood of Taur Urgas. Is this true?"

"It is," she replied simply. "King Urgit's father was an Alorn."

"Are any of the sons of Taur Urgas still alive?"

"Nay, 'Zakath. The line of Taur Urgas became extinct some twelve years ago when his last son was strangled in a cellar in Rak Goska upon the command of Oskatat, King Urgit's Seneschal."

'Zakath sighed and shook his head sadly. "And so it has ended," he said. "My enemy's line passed unnoticed from this world in a dark cellar—passed so quietly that I could not even rejoice that they were gone, nor curse the ones who stole them from my grasp."

"Revenge is a hollow thing, 'Zakath."

"It's the only thing I've had for almost thirty years now." He sighed again, then straightened his shoulders. "Did Zandramas really steal Belgarion's son?"

"She did, and now she carries him to the Place Which Is No More."

"And where's that?"

Her face grew very still. "I may not reveal that," she replied finally, "but the Sardion is there."

"Can you tell me what the Sardion is?"

"It is one half of the stone which was divided."

"Is it really all *that* important?"

"In all of Angarak there is no thing of greater worth. The Grolims all know this. Urvon would give all his wealth for it. Zandramas would abandon the adoration of multitudes for it. Mengha would give his soul for it—indeed, he hath done so already in his enlistment of demons to aid him. Even Agachak, Hierarch of Rak Urga, would abandon his ascendancy in Cthol Murgos to possess it."

"How is it that a thing of such value has escaped my notice?"

"Thine eyes are on worldly matters, 'Zakath. The Sardion is not of this world—no more than the other half of the divided stone is of this world."

"The other half?"

"That which the Angaraks call Cthrag Yaska and the men of the West call the Orb of Aldur. Cthrag Sardius and Cthrag Yaska were sundered in the moment which saw the birth of the opposing necessities."

'Zakath's face had grown quite pale, and he clasped his hands tightly in front of him to control their trembling. "It's all true, then?" he asked in a hoarse voice.

"All, Kal Zakath. All."

"Even that Belgarion and Zandramas are the Child of Light and the Child of Dark?"

"Yes, they are." He started to ask her another question, but she raised her hand. "My time is short, 'Zakath, and I must now reveal something of greater import unto thee. Know that thy life doth approach a momentous crossroads. Put aside thy lust for power and thy hunger for revenge, as they are but childish toys. Return thou even to Mal Zeth to prepare thyself for *thy* part in the meeting which is to come."

"*My* part?" He sounded startled.

"Thy name and thy task are written in the stars."

"And what is this task?"

"I will instruct thee when thou art ready to understand what it is that thou must do. First thou must cleanse thy heart of that grief and remorse which hath haunted thee."

His face grew still, and he sighed. "I'm afraid not, Cyradis," he said. "What you ask is quite impossible."

"Then thou wilt surely die before the seasons turn again. Consider what I have told thee, and consider it well, Emperor of Mallorea. I will speak with thee anon." And then she shimmered and vanished.

'Zakath stared at the empty spot where she had stood. His face was pale, and his jaws were set.

"Well, 'Zakath?" Belgarath said. "Are you convinced?"

The Emperor rose from his chair and began to pace up and down. "This is an absolute absurdity!" he burst out suddenly in an agitated voice.

"I know," Belgarath replied calmly, "but a willingness to believe the absurd is an indication of faith. It might just be that faith is the first step in the preparation Cyradis mentioned."

"It's not that I don't *want* to believe, Belgarath," 'Zakath said, in a strangely humble tone. "It's just—"

"Nobody said that it was going to be easy," the old man told him. "But you've done things before that weren't easy, haven't you?"

'Zakath dropped into his chair again, his eyes lost in thought. "Why me?" he said plaintively. "Why do *I* have to get involved in this?"

Garion suddenly laughed.

'Zakath gave him a cold stare.

"Sorry," Garion apologized, "but *I've* been saying 'why me?' since I was about fourteen. Nobody's ever given me a satisfactory answer, but you get used to the injustice of it after a while."

"It's not that I'm trying to avoid any kind of responsibility, Belgarion. It's just that I can't see what possible help I could be. You people are going to track down Zandramas, retrieve your son, and destroy the Sardion. Isn't that about it?"

"It's a little more complicated than that," Belgarath told him. "Destroying the Sardion is going to involve something rather cataclysmic."

"I don't quite follow that. Can't you just wave your hand and make it cease to exist? You *are* a sorcerer, after all—or so they say."

"That's forbidden," Garion said automatically. "You can't unmake things. That's what Ctuchik tried to do, and he destroyed himself."

'Zakath frowned and looked at Belgarath. "I thought *you* killed him."

"Most people do." The old man shrugged. "It adds to my reputation, so I don't argue with them." He tugged at one earlobe. "No," he said, "I think we're going to have to see this all the way through to the end. I'm fairly sure that the only way the Sardion can be destroyed is as a result of the final confrontation between the Child of Light and the Child of Dark." He paused, then sat up suddenly, his face intent. "I think Cyradis slipped and gave us something she hadn't intended, though. She said that the Grolim priesthood all desperately wanted the Sardion, and she included Mengha in her list. Wouldn't that seem to indicate that Mengha's also a Grolim?" He looked at Andel. "Is your young mistress subject to these little lapses?"

"Cyradis cannot misspeak herself, Holy Belgarath," the healer replied. "A Seeress does not speak in her own voice, but in the voice of her vision."

"Then she *wanted* us to know that Mengha is—or was—a Grolim, and that the reason he's raising demons is to help him in his search for the Sardion." He thought about it. "There's another rather bleak possibility, too," he added. "It might just be that his demons are using him to get the Sardion for themselves. Maybe that's why they're so docile where he's concerned. Demons by themselves are bad enough, but if the Sardion has the same power as the Orb, we *definitely* don't want it to fall into their hands." He turned to 'Zakath. "Well?" he said.

"Well what?"

"Are you with us or against us?"

"Isn't that a little blunt?"

"Yes, it is—but it saves time, and time's starting to be a factor."

'Zakath sank lower in his chair, his expression unreadable. "I find very little benefit for *me* in this proposed arrangement," he said.

"You get to keep living," Garion reminded him. "Cyradis said that you'll die before spring if you don't take up the task she's going to lay in front of you."

'Zakath's faint smile was melancholy, and the dead indifference returned to his eyes. "My life hasn't really been so enjoyable that I'd consider going out of my way to prolong it, Belgarion," he replied.

"Don't you think you're being just a little childish, 'Zakath?" Garion snapped, his temper starting to heat up again. "You're not accomplishing a single thing here in Cthol Murgos. There's not one solitary drop of Urga blood left for you to spill, and you've got a situation at home that verges on disaster. Are you a King—or an Emperor, or whatever you want to call it—or are you a spoiled child? You refuse to go back to Mal Zeth just because somebody told you that you ought to. You even dig in your heels when someone assures you that you'll die if you don't go back. That's not only childish, it's irrational, and I don't have the time to try to reason with somebody whose wits have deserted him. Well, you can huddle here in Rak Hagga and nurse all your tired old griefs and disappointments until Cyradis' predictions catch up with you, for all I care, but Geran is my son, and I'm going to Mallorea. I've got work to do, and I don't have time to coddle you." He had saved something up for last. "Besides," he added in an insulting, offhand tone, "I don't need you anyway."

'Zakath came to his feet, his eyes ablaze. "You go too far!" he roared, slamming his fist down on the table.

"Amazing," Garion said sarcastically. "You *are* alive after all. I thought I might have to step on your foot to get any kind of response out of you. All right, now that you're awake, let's fight."

"What do you mean, fight?" 'Zakath demanded, his face still flushed with anger. "Fight about what?"

"About whether or not you're going with us to Mallorea."

"Don't be stupid. Of course I'm going with you. What we *are* going to fight about is your incredible lack of common courtesy."

Garion stared at him for a moment and then suddenly doubled over in a gale of helpless laughter.

'Zakath's face was still red, and his fists were clenching and unclenching. Then a slightly sheepish expression came over his face, and he, too, began to laugh.

Belgarath let out an explosive breath. "Garion," he said irritably, "let me know when you're going to do something like that. My veins aren't what they used to be."

'Zakath wiped at his eyes, though he was still laughing. "How long do you think it might take for you and your friends to get packed?" he asked them.

"Not too long," Garion replied. "Why?"

"I'm suddenly homesick for Mal Zeth. It's spring there now, and the cherry trees are in bloom. You and Ce'Nedra will love Mal Zeth, Garion."

Garion was not entirely sure if the omission of the "Bel" was inadvertent or an overture of friendship. He *was*, however, quite sure that the Emperor of Mallorea was a man of even greater complexity than he had imagined.

"I hope you'll all excuse me now," 'Zakath said, "but I want to talk with Brador and get a few more details about what's been going on in Karanda. This Mengha he told me about seems to be mounting an open insurrection against the crown, and I've always had a violent prejudice against that sort of thing."

"I can relate to that," Garion agreed blandly.

For the next few days the road between Rak Hagga and the port city of Rak

Cthan was thick with imperial messengers. Finally, on a frosty morning when the sun was bright and the sky dark blue and when misty steam rose from the dark waters of Lake Hagga, they set out, riding across a winter-browned plain toward the coast. Garion, his gray Rivan cloak drawn about him, rode at the head of the column with 'Zakath, who seemed for some reason to be in better spirits than he had been at any time since the two had met. The column which followed them stretched back for miles.

"Vulgar, isn't it?" the Mallorean said wryly, looking back over his shoulder. "I'm absolutely surrounded by parasites and toadies, and they proliferate like maggots in rotten meat."

"If they bother you so much, then why not dismiss them?" Garion suggested.

"I can't. They all have powerful relatives. I have to balance them very carefully—one from this tribe to match the one from that clan. As long as no one family has too many high offices, they spend all their time plotting against each other. That way they don't have the time to plot against me."

"I suppose that's one way to keep things under control."

As the sun moved up through the bright blue winter sky at this nether end of the world, the frost gently dissolved from the long stems of dead grass or fell lightly from the fern and bracken to leave ghostly white imprints of those drooping brown fronds on the short green moss spread beneath.

They paused for a noon meal that was every bit as sumptuous as one that might have been prepared back in Rak Hagga and was served on snowy damask beneath a wide-spread canvas roof. "Adequate, I suppose," 'Zakath said critically after they had eaten.

"You're overpampered, my lord," Polgara told him. "A hard ride in wet weather and a day or so on short rations would probably do wonders for your appetite."

'Zakath gave Garion an amused look. "I thought it was just you," he said, "but this blunt outspokenness seems to be a characteristic of your whole family."

Garion shrugged. "It saves time."

"Forgive my saying this, Belgarion," Sadi interjected, "but what possible interest can an immortal have in time?" He sighed rather mournfully. "Immortality must give one a great deal of satisfaction—watching all one's enemies grow old and die."

"It's much overrated," Belgarath said, leaning back in his chair with a brimming silver tankard. "Sometimes whole centuries go by when one doesn't *have* any enemies and there's nothing to do but watch the years roll by."

'Zakath suddenly smiled broadly. "Do you know something?" he said to them all. "I feel better right now than I've felt in over twenty-five years. It's as if a great weight has been lifted from me."

"Probably an aftereffect of the poison," Velvet suggested archly. "Get plenty of rest, and it should pass in a month or so."

"Is the Margravine always like this?" 'Zakath asked.

"Sometimes she's even worse," Silk replied morosely.

As they emerged from beneath the wide-spread canvas, Garion looked around for his horse, a serviceable roan with a long, hooked nose, but he could not seem to see the animal. Then he suddenly noticed that his saddle and packs were on a dif-

ferent horse, a very large dark gray stallion. Puzzled, he looked at 'Zakath, who was
watching him intently. "What's this?" he asked.

"Just a little token of my unbounded respect, Garion," 'Zakath said, his eyes
alight. "Your roan was an adequate mount, I suppose, but he was hardly a regal animal. A King needs a kingly horse, and I think you'll find that Chretienne can lend
himself to any occasion that requires ceremony."

"Chretienne?"

"That's his name. He's been the pride of my stable here in Cthol Murgos. Don't
you have a stable at Riva?"

Garion laughed. "My kingdom's an island, 'Zakath. We're more interested in
boats than in horses." He looked at the proud gray standing with his neck arched
and with one hoof lightly pawing the earth and was suddenly overcome with gratitude. He clasped the Mallorean Emperor's hand warmly. "This is a magnificent gift,
'Zakath," he said.

"Of course it is. I'm a magnificent fellow—or hadn't you noticed? Ride him,
Garion. Feel the wind in your face and let the thunder of his hooves fill your blood."

"Well," Garion said, trying to control his eagerness, "maybe he and I really
ought to get to know each other."

'Zakath laughed with delight. "Of course," he said.

Garion approached the big gray horse, who watched him quite calmly.

"I guess we'll be sharing a saddle for a while," he said to the animal. Chretienne
nickered and nudged at Garion with his nose.

"He wants to run," Eriond said. "I'll ride with you, if you don't mind. Horse
wants to run, too."

"All right," Garion agreed. "Let's go then." He gathered the reins, set his foot
in the stirrup, and swung up into the saddle. The gray was running almost before
Garion was in place.

It was a new experience. Garion had spent many hours riding—sometimes for
weeks on end. He had always taken care of his mounts, as any good Sendar would,
but there had never really been any personal attachment before. For him, a horse
had simply been a means of conveyance, a way to get from one place to another, and
riding had never been a particular source of pleasure. With this great stallion, Chretienne, however, it was altogether different. There was a kind of electric thrill to the
feel of the big horse's muscles bunching and flowing beneath him as they ran out
across the winter-brown grass toward a rounded hill a mile or so distant, with
Eriond and his chestnut stallion racing alongside.

When they reached the hilltop, Garion was breathless and laughing with sheer
delight. He reined in, and Chretienne reared, pawing at the air with his hooves,
wanting to be off again.

"Now you know, don't you?" Eriond asked with a broad smile.

"Yes," Garion admitted, still laughing, "I guess I do. I wonder how I missed it
all these years."

"You have to have the right horse," Eriond told him wisely. He gave Garion a
sidelong glance. "You know that you'll never be the same again, don't you?"

"That's all right," Garion replied. "I was getting tired of the old way anyhow."

He pointed at a low string of hills outlined against the crisp blue sky a league or so on ahead. "Why don't we go over there and see what's on the other side?" he suggested.

"Why not?" Eriond laughed.

And so they did.

The Emperor's household staff was well organized, and a goodly number of them rode on ahead to prepare their night's encampment at a spot almost precisely halfway to the coast. The column started early the following morning, riding again along a frosty track beneath a deep blue sky. It was late afternoon when they crested a hill to look out over the expanse of the Sea of the East, rolling a dark blue under the winter sun and with smoky-looking cloud banks the color of rust blurring the far horizon. Two dozen ships with their red sails furled stood at anchor in the indented curve of a shallow bay far below, and Garion looked with some puzzlement at 'Zakath.

"Another symptom of the vulgar ostentation I mentioned." The Emperor shrugged. "I ordered this fleet down here from the port at Cthan. A dozen or so of those ships are here to transport all my hangers-on and toadies—as well as the humbler people who actually do the work. The other dozen are here to escort our royal personages with suitable pomp. You have to have pomp, Garion. Otherwise people might mistake a King or an Emperor for an honest man."

"You're in a whimsical humor this afternoon."

"Maybe it's another of those lingering symptoms Liselle mentioned. We'll sleep on board ship tonight and sail at first light tomorrow."

Garion nodded, touching Chretienne's bowed neck with an odd kind of regret as he handed his reins to a waiting groom.

The vessel to which they were ferried from the sandy beach was opulent. Unlike the cramped cabins on most of the other ships Garion had sailed aboard, the chambers on this one were nearly as large as the rooms in a fair-sized house. It took him a little while to pin down the reason for the difference. The other ships had devoted so little room to cabins because the bulk of the space on board had been devoted to cargo. The only cargo *this* ship customarily carried, however, was the Emperor of Mallorea.

They dined that evening on lobster, served in the low-beamed dining room aboard 'Zakath's floating palace. So much of Garion's attention for the past week or more had been fixed on the unpredictable Emperor that he had not had much opportunity to talk with his friends. Thus, when they took their places at the table, he rather deliberately sat at the opposite end from the Mallorean. It was with a great deal of relief that he took his seat between Polgara and Durnik, while Ce'Nedra and Velvet diverted the Emperor with sparkling feminine chatter.

"You look tired, Garion," Polgara noted.

"I've been under a certain strain," he replied. "I wish that man wouldn't keep changing every other minute. Every time I think I've got him figured out, he turns into somebody else."

"It's not a good idea to categorize people, dear," she advised placidly, touching his arm. "That's the first sign of fuzzy thinking."

"Are we actually supposed to eat these things?" Durnik asked in a disgusted sort of voice, pointing his knife at the bright red lobster staring up at him from his plate with its claws seemingly at the ready.

"That's what the pliers are for, Durnik," Polgara explained in a peculiarly mild tone. "You have to crack it out of its shell."

He pushed his plate away. "I'm not going to eat something that looks like a big red bug," he declared with uncharacteristic heat. "I draw the line at some things."

"Lobster is a delicacy, Durnik," she said.

He grunted. "Some people eat snails, too."

Her eyes flashed, but then she gained control of her anger and continued to speak to him in that same mild tone. "I'm sure we can have them take it away and bring you something else," she said.

He glared at her.

Garion looked back and forth between the two of them. Then he decided that they had all known each other for far too long to step delicately around any problems. "What's the matter, Durnik?" he asked bluntly. "You're as cross as a badger with a sore nose."

"Nothing," Durnik almost snapped at him.

Garion began to put a few things together. He remembered the plea Andel had made to Aunt Pol concerning Toth. He looked down the table to where the big mute, his eyes lowered to his plate, seemed almost to be trying to make himself invisible. Then he looked back at Durnik, who kept his face stiffly turned away from his former friend. "Oh," he said, "now I think I understand. Aunt Pol told you something you didn't want to hear. Someone you liked very much did something that made you angry. You said some things to him that you wish now you hadn't said. Then you found out that he didn't really have any choice in the matter and that what he did was really right after all. Now you'd like to make friends with him again, but you don't know how. Is that sort of why you're behaving this way—and being so impolite to Aunt Pol?"

Durnik's look was at first stricken. Then his face grew red—then pale. "I don't have to listen to this," he burst out, coming to his feet.

"Oh, sit down, Durnik," Garion told him. "We all love each other too much to behave this way. Instead of being embarrassed and bad-tempered about it, why don't we see what we can do to fix it?"

Durnik tried to meet Garion's eyes, but finally lowered his head, his face flaming. "I treated him badly, Garion," he mumbled, sinking back into his chair again.

"Yes," Garion agreed, "you did. But it was because you didn't understand what he was doing—and why. I didn't understand myself until the day before yesterday— when 'Zakath finally changed his mind and decided to take us all to Mal Zeth. Cyradis knew that he was going to do that, and that's why she made Toth turn us over to Atesca's men. She *wants* us to get to the Sardion and meet Zandramas, and so she's going to arrange it. Toth will be the one who does what she thinks has to be done to accomplish that. Under the present circumstances, we couldn't find a better friend."

"How can I possibly—I mean, after the way I treated him?"

"Be honest. Admit that you were wrong and apologize."

Durnik's face grew stiff.

"It doesn't have to be in words, Durnik," Garion told his friend patiently. "You and Toth have been talking together without words for months." He looked speculatively up at the low-beamed ceiling. "This is a ship," he noted, "and we're going out onto an ocean. Do you imagine that there might be a few fish out there in all that water?"

Durnik's smile was immediate.

Polgara's sigh, however, was pensive.

The smith looked almost shyly across the table. "How did you say that I'm supposed to get this bug out of its shell, Pol?" he asked, pointing at the angry-looking lobster on his plate.

They sailed northeasterly from the coast of Hagga and soon left winter behind. At some point during the voyage they crossed that imaginary line equidistant from the poles and once again entered the northern half of the world. Durnik and Toth, shyly at first, but then with growing confidence, resumed their friendship and spent their days at the ship's stern, probing the sea with lines, bright-colored lures, and various baits gleaned from the galley.

'Zakath's humor continued to remain uncharacteristically sunny, though his discussions with Belgarath and Polgara centered on the nature of demons, a subject about which there was very little to smile. Finally, one day when they had been at sea for about a week, a servant came up to Garion, who stood at the portside rail watching the dance of the wind atop the sparkling waves, and advised him that the Emperor would like to see him. Garion nodded and made his way aft to the cabin where 'Zakath customarily held audience. Like most of the cabins aboard the floating palace, this one was quite large and ostentatiously decorated. Owing to the broad windows stretching across the ship's stern, the room was bright and airy. The drapes at the sides of the windows were of crimson velvet, and the fine Mallorean carpet was a deep blue. 'Zakath, dressed as always in plain white linen, sat on a low, leather-upholstered divan at the far end of the cabin, looking out at the whitecaps and the flock of snowy gulls trailing the ship. His cat lay purring in his lap as he absently stroked her ears.

"You wanted to see me, 'Zakath?" Garion asked as he entered.

"Yes. Come in, Garion," the Mallorean replied. "I haven't seen much of you for the past few days. Are you cross with me?"

"No," Garion said. "You've been busy learning about demons. I don't know that much about them, so I couldn't have added all that much to the discussions." He crossed the cabin, pausing at one point to stoop and unwrap a ferociously playful kitten from around his left ankle.

"They love to pounce." 'Zakath smiled.

A thought came to Garion, and he looked around warily. "Zith isn't in here, is she?"

'Zakath laughed. "No. Sadi's devised a means of keeping her at home." He looked whimsically at Garion. "Is she really as deadly as he says?"

Garion nodded. "She bit a Grolim at Rak Urga," he said. "He was dead in about a half a minute."

'Zakath shuddered. "You don't have to tell Sadi about this," he said, "but snakes make my flesh creep."

"Talk to Silk. He could give you a whole dissertation about how much he dislikes them."

"He's a complicated little fellow, isn't he?"

Garion smiled. "Oh, yes. His life is filled with danger and excitement, and so his nerves are as tightly wound as lute strings. He's erratic sometimes, but you get used to that after a while." He looked at the other man critically. "You're looking particularly fit," he noted, sitting down on the other end of the leather couch. "Sea air must agree with you."

"I don't think it's really the air, Garion. I think it has to do with the fact that I've been sleeping eight to ten hours a night."

"Sleep? You?"

"Astonishing, isn't it?" 'Zakath's face went suddenly quite somber. "I'd rather that this didn't go any further, Garion," he said.

"Of course."

"Urgit told you what happened when I was young?"

Garion nodded. "Yes."

"My habit of not sleeping very much dates from then. A face that had been particularly dear to me haunted my dreams, and sleep became an agony to me."

"That didn't diminish? Not even after some thirty years?"

"Not one bit. I lived in continual grief and guilt and remorse. I lived only to revenge myself on Taur Urgas. Cho-Hag's saber robbed me of that. I had planned a dozen different deaths for the madman—each more horrible than the one before—but he cheated me by dying cleanly in battle."

"No," Garion disagreed. "His death was worse than anything you could possibly have devised. I've talked with Cho-Hag about it. Taur Urgas went totally mad before Cho-Hag killed him, but he lived long enough to realize that he had finally been beaten. He died biting and clawing at the earth in frustration. Being beaten was more than he could bear."

'Zakath thought about it. "Yes," he said finally. "That would have been quite dreadful for him, wouldn't it? I think that maybe I'm less disappointed now."

"And was it your discovery that the Urga line is now extinct that finally laid the ghost that's haunted your sleep all these years?"

"No, Garion. I don't think that had anything to do with it. It's just that instead of the face that had always been there before, now I see a different face."

"Oh?"

"A blindfolded face."

"Cyradis? I don't know that I'd recommend thinking about her in that fashion."

"You misunderstand, Garion. She's hardly more than a child, but somehow she's touched my life with more peace and comfort than I've ever known. I sleep like a baby and I walk around all day with this silly euphoria bubbling up in me." He shook his head. "Frankly, I can't stand myself like this, but I can't help it for some reason."

Garion stared out the window, not even seeing the play of sunlight on the waves nor the hovering gulls. Then it came to him so clearly that he knew that it was undeniably true. "It's because you've come to that crossroads in your life that

Cyradis mentioned," he said. "You're being rewarded because you've chosen the right fork."

"Rewarded? By whom?"

Garion looked at him and suddenly laughed. "I don't think you're quite ready to accept that information yet," he said. "Could you bring yourself to believe that it's Cyradis who's making you feel good right now?"

"In some vague way, yes."

"It goes a little deeper, but that's a start." Garion looked at the slightly perplexed man before him. "You and I are caught up together in something over which we have absolutely no control," he said seriously. "I've been through it before, so I'll try to cushion the shocks that are in store for you as much as I can. Just try to keep an open mind about a peculiar way of looking at the world." He thought about it some more. "I think that we're going to be working together—at least up to a point—so we might as well be friends." He held out his right hand.

'Zakath laughed. "Why not?" he said, taking Garion's hand in a firm grip. "I think we're both as crazy as Taur Urgas, but why not? We're the two most powerful men in the world. We should be deadly enemies, and you propose friendship. Well, why not?" He laughed again delightedly.

"We have much more deadly enemies, 'Zakath," Garion said gravely, "and all of your armies—and all of mine—won't mean a thing when we get to where we're going."

"And where's that, my young friend?"

"I think it's called 'the place which is no more.' "

"I've been meaning to ask you about that. The whole phrase is a contradiction in terms. How can you go someplace which doesn't exist any more?"

"I don't really know," Garion told him. "I'll tell you when we get there."

Two days later, they arrived at Mal Gemila, a port in southern Mallorea Antiqua, and took to horse. They rode eastward at a canter on a well-maintained highway that crossed a pleasant plain, green with spring. A regiment of red-tunicked cavalrymen cleared the road ahead of them, and their pace left the entourage which usually accompanied the Emperor far behind. There were way stations along the highway—not unlike the Tolnedran hostels dotting the roads in the west—and the imperial guard rather brusquely ejected other guests at these roadside stops to make way for the Emperor and his party.

As they pressed onward, day after day, Garion began slowly to comprehend the true significance of the word "boundless" as it was applied to Mallorea. The plains of Algaria, which had always before seemed incredibly vast, shrank into insignificance. The snowy peaks of the Dalasian mountains, lying to the south of the road they traveled, raked their white talons at the sky. Garion drew in on himself, feeling smaller and smaller the deeper they rode into this vast domain.

Peculiarly, Ce'Nedra seemed to be suffering a similar shrinkage, and she quite obviously did not like it very much. Her comments became increasingly waspish; her observations more acid. She found the loose-fitting garments of the peasantry uncouth. She found fault with the construction of the gangplows that opened whole acres at a time behind patiently plodding herds of oxen. She didn't like the food. Even the water—as clear as crystal, and as cold and sweet as might have sprung from any crevice in the Tolnedran mountains—offended her taste.

Silk, his eyes alight with mischief, rode at her side on the sunny midmorning of the last day of their journey from Mal Gemila. "Beware, your Majesty," he warned her slyly as they neared the crest of a hillside sheathed in pale spring grass so verdant that it almost looked like a filmy green mist. "The first sight of Mal Zeth has sometimes struck the unwary traveler blind. To be safe, why don't you cover one eye with your hand? That way you can preserve at least partial sight."

Her face grew frosty, and she drew herself to her full height in her saddle—a move that might have come off better had she been only slightly taller—and said to him in her most imperious tone, "*We* are not amused, Prince Kheldar, and *we* do not expect to find a barbarian city at the far end of the world a rival to the splendors of Tol Honeth, the only truly imperial city in the—"

And then she stopped—as they all did.

The valley beyond the crest stretched not for miles, but for leagues, and it was filled to overflowing with the city of Mal Zeth. The streets were as straight as tautly stretched strings, and the buildings gleamed—not with marble, for there was not marble enough in all the world to sheath the buildings of this enormous city—but rather with an intensly gleaming, thick white mortar that seemed somehow to shoot light at the eye. It was stupendous.

"It's not much," 'Zakath said in an exaggeratedly deprecating tone. "Just a friendly little place we like to call home." He looked at Ce'Nedra's stiff, pale little face with an artful expression. "We really should press on, your Majesty," he told her. "It's a half-day's ride to the imperial palace from here."

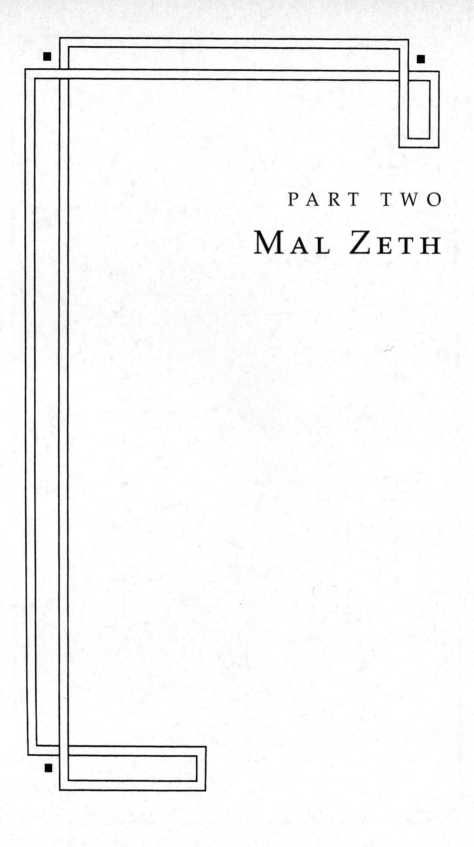

PART TWO

MAL ZETH

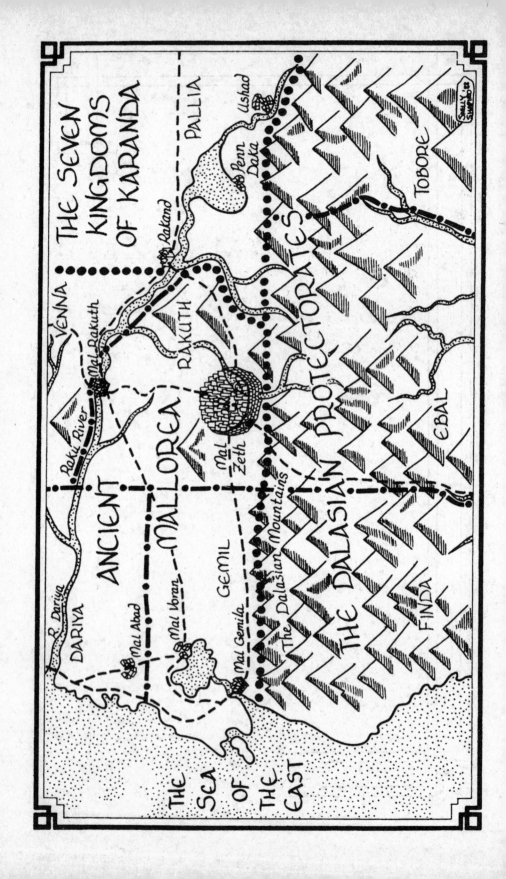

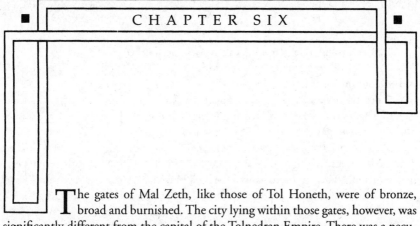

CHAPTER SIX

The gates of Mal Zeth, like those of Tol Honeth, were of bronze, broad and burnished. The city lying within those gates, however, was significantly different from the capital of the Tolnedran Empire. There was a peculiar sameness about the structures, and they were built so tightly against each other that the broad avenues of the city were lined on either side by solid, mortar-covered walls, pierced only by deeply inset, arched doorways with narrow white stairways leading up to the flat rooftops. Here and there, the mortar had crumbled away, revealing the fact that the buildings beneath that coating were constructed of squared-off timbers. Durnik, who believed that all buildings should be made of stone, noted that fact with a look of disapproval.

As they moved deeper into the city, Garion noticed the almost total lack of windows. "I don't want to seem critical," he said to 'Zakath, "but isn't your city just a little monotonous?"

'Zakath looked at him curiously.

"All the houses are the same, and there aren't very many windows."

"Oh," 'Zakath smiled, "that's one of the drawbacks of leaving architecture up to the military. They're great believers in uniformity, and windows have no place in military fortifications. Each house has its own little garden, though, and the windows face that. In the summertime, the people spend most of their time in the gardens—or on the rooftops."

"Is the whole city like this?" Durnik asked, looking at the cramped little houses all packed together.

"No, Goodman," the Emperor replied. "This quarter of the city was built for corporals. The streets reserved for officers are a bit more ornate, and those where the privates and workmen live are much shabbier. Military people tend to be very conscious of rank and the appearances that go with it."

A few doors down a side street branching off from the one they followed, a stout, red-faced woman was shrilly berating a scrawny-looking fellow with a hang-dog expression as a group of soldiers removed furniture from a house and piled it in a rickety cart. "You had to go and do it, didn't you, Actas?" she demanded. "You had to get drunk and insult your captain. Now what's to become of us? I spent all those years living in those pigsty privates' quarters waiting for you to get promoted, and just when I think things are taking a turn for the better, you have to destroy it all by getting drunk and being reduced to private again."

He mumbled something.

"What was that?"

"Nothing, dear."

"I'm not going to let you forget this, Actas, let me tell you."

"Life does have its little ups and downs, doesn't it?" Sadi murmured as they rode on out of earshot.

"I don't think it's anything to laugh about," Ce'Nedra said with surprising heat. "They're being thrown out of their home over a moment's foolishness. Can't someone do something?"

'Zakath gave her an appraising look, then beckoned to one of the red-cloaked officers riding respectfully along behind them. "Find out which unit that man's in," he instructed. "Then go to his captain and tell him that I'd take it as a personal favor if Actas were reinstated in his former rank—on the condition that he stays sober."

"At once, your Majesty." The officer saluted and rode off.

"Why, thank you, 'Zakath," Ce'Nedra said, sounding a little startled.

"My pleasure, Ce'Nedra." He bowed to her from his saddle. Then he laughed shortly. "I suspect that Actas' wife will see to it that he suffers sufficiently for his misdeeds anyway."

"Aren't you afraid that such acts of compassion might damage your reputation, your Majesty?" Sadi asked him.

"No," 'Zakath replied. "A ruler must always strive to be unpredictable, Sadi. It keeps the underlings off balance. Besides, an occasional act of charity toward the lower ranks helps to strengthen their loyalty."

"Don't you ever do anything that isn't motivated by politics?" Garion asked him. For some reason, 'Zakath's flippant explanation of his act irritated him.

"Not that I can think of," 'Zakath said. "Politics is the greatest game in the world, Garion, but you have to play it all the time to keep your edge."

Silk laughed. "I've said the exact same thing about commerce," he said. "About the only difference I can see is that in commerce you have money as a way of keeping score. How do you keep score in politics?"

'Zakath's expression was peculiarly mixed—half amused and half deadly serious. "It's very simple, Kheldar," he said. "If you're still on the throne at the end of the day, you've won. If you're dead, you've lost—and each day is a complete new game."

Silk gave him a long, speculative look, then looked over at Garion, his fingers moving slightly.—*I need to talk to you—at once*—

Garion nodded briefly, then leaned over in his saddle. He reined in.

"Something wrong?" 'Zakath asked him.

"I think my cinch is loose," Garion replied, dismounting. "Go on ahead. I'll catch up."

"Here, I'll help you, Garion," Silk offered, also swinging down from his saddle.

"What's this all about?" Garion asked when the Emperor, chatting with Ce'Nedra and Velvet, had ridden out of earshot.

"Be very careful with him, Garion," the little man replied quietly, pretending to check the straps on Garion's saddle. "He let something slip there. He's all smiles and courtesy on the surface, but underneath it all he hasn't really changed all that much."

"Wasn't he just joking?"

"Not even a little. He was deadly serious. He's brought us all to Mal Zeth for reasons that have nothing to do with Mengha or our search for Zandramas. Be on your guard with him. That friendly smile of his can fall off his face without any warning at all." He spoke a little more loudly then. "There," he said, tugging at a strap, "that ought to hold it. Let's catch up with the others."

They rode into a broad square surrounded on all sides by canvas booths dyed in various hues of red, green, blue, and yellow. The square teemed with merchants and citizens, all dressed in varicolored, loose-fitting robes that hung to their heels.

"Where do the common citizens live if the whole city's divided up into sections based on military rank?" Durnik asked.

Brador, the bald, chubby Chief of the Bureau of Internal Affairs, who happened to be riding beside the smith, looked around with a smile. "They all have their ranks, Goodman," he replied, "each according to his individual accomplishments. It's all very rigidly controlled by the Bureau of Promotions. Housing, places of business, suitable marriages—they're all determined by rank."

"Isn't that sort of overregimented?" Durnik asked pointedly.

"Malloreans love to be regimented, Goodman Durnik." Brador laughed. "Angaraks bow automatically to authority; Melcenes have a deep inner need to compartmentalize things; Karands are too stupid to take control of their own destinies; and the Dals—well, nobody knows what the Dals want."

"We aren't really all that different from the people in the West, Durnik," 'Zakath said back over his shoulder. "In Tolnedra and Sendaria, such matters are determined by economics. People gravitate to the houses and shops and marriages they can afford. We've just formalized it, that's all."

"Tell me, your Majesty," Sadi said, "how is it that your people are so undemonstrative?"

"I don't quite follow you."

"Shouldn't they at least salute as you ride by? You *are* the Emperor, after all."

"They don't recognize me." 'Zakath shrugged. "The Emperor is a man in crimson robes who rides in a golden carriage, wears a terribly heavy jeweled crown, and is accompanied by at least a regiment of imperial guards all blowing trumpets. I'm just a man in white linen riding through town with a few friends."

Garion thought about that, still mindful of Silk's half-whispered warning. The almost total lack of any kind of self-aggrandizement implicit in 'Zakath's statement revealed yet another facet of the man's complex personality. He was quite sure that not even King Fulrach of Sendaria, the most modest of all the monarchs of the West, could be quite so self-effacing.

The streets beyond the square were lined with somewhat larger houses than those they had passed near the city gates, and there had been some attempt at ornamentation here. It appeared, however, that Mallorean sculptors had limited talent, and the mortar-cast filigree surmounting the front of each house was heavy and graceless.

"The sergeants' district," 'Zakath said laconically.

The city seemed to go on forever. At regular intervals there were squares and marketplaces and bazaars, all filled with people wearing the bright, loose-fitting robes that appeared to be the standard Mallorean garb. When they passed the last of the rigidly similar houses of the sergeants and of those civilians of equal rank, they entered a broad belt of trees and lawns where fountains splashed and sparkled in the sunlight and where broad promenades were lined with carefully sculptured green hedges interspersed with cherry trees laden with pink blossoms shimmering in the light breeze.

"How lovely," Ce'Nedra exclaimed.

"We do have some beauty here in Mal Zeth," 'Zakath told her. "No one—not even an army architect—could make a city this big uniformly ugly."

"The officers' districts aren't quite so severe," Silk told the little Queen.

"You're familiar with Mal Zeth, then, your Highness?" Brador asked.

Silk nodded. "My partner and I have a facility here," he replied. "It's more in the nature of a centralized collection point than an actual business. It's cumbersome doing business in Mal Zeth—too many regulations."

"Might one inquire as to the rank you were assigned?" the moon-faced bureaucrat asked delicately.

"We're generals," Silk said in a rather grandly offhand manner. "Yarblek wanted to be a field marshal, but I didn't think the expense of buying that much rank was really justified."

"Is rank for sale?" Sadi asked.

"In Mal Zeth, everything's for sale," Silk replied. "In most respects it's almost exactly like Tol Honeth."

"Not entirely, Silk," Ce'Nedra said primly.

"Only in the broadest terms, your Imperial Highness," he agreed quickly. "Mal Zeth has never been graced by the presence of a divinely beautiful Imperial Princess, glowing like a precious jewel and shooting beams of her fire back at the sun."

She gave him a hard look, then turned her back on him.

"What did I say?" the little man asked Garion in an injured tone.

"People always suspect you, Silk," Garion told him. "They can never quite be sure that you're not making fun of them. I thought you knew that."

Silk sighed tragically. "Nobody understands me," he complained.

"Oh, I think they do."

The plazas and boulevards beyond the belt of parks and gardens were more grand, and the houses larger and set apart from each other. There was still, however, a stiff similarity about them, a kind of stern sameness that insured that men of equal rank would be assigned to rigidly equal quarters.

Another broad strip of lawns and trees lay beyond the mansions of the generals and their mercantile equivalents, and within that encircling green there arose a fair-sized marble city with its own walls and burnished gates.

"The imperial palace," 'Zakath said indifferently. He frowned. "What have you done over there?" he asked Brador, pointing at a long row of tall buildings rising near the south wall of the enclosed compound.

Brador coughed delicately. "Those are the bureaucratic offices, your Majesty," he replied in a neutral tone. "You'll recall that you authorized their construction just before the battle of Thull Mardu."

'Zakath pursed his lips. "I hadn't expected something on quite such a grand scale," he said.

"There are quite a lot of us, your Majesty," Brador explained, "and we felt that things might be more harmonious if each bureau had its own building." He looked a bit apologetic. "We really *did* need the space," he explained defensively to Sadi. "We were all jumbled together with the military, and very often men from different bureaus had to share the same office. It's really much more efficient this way, wouldn't you say?"

"I think I'd prefer it if you didn't involve me in this discussion, your Excellency," Sadi answered.

"I was merely attempting to draw upon your Excellency's expertise in managing affairs of state."

"Salmissra's palace is somewhat unique," Sadi told him. "We *like* being jumbled together. It gives us greater opportunities for spying and murder and intrigue and the other normal functions of government."

As they approached the gates to the imperial complex, Garion noticed with some surprise that the thick bronze gates had been overlaid with beaten gold, and his thrifty Sendarian heritage recoiled from the thought of such wanton lavishness. Ce'Nedra, however, looked at the priceless gates with undisguised acquisitiveness.

"You wouldn't be able to move them," Silk advised her.

"What?" she said inattentively.

"The gates. They're much too heavy to steal."

"Shut up, Silk," she said absently, her eyes still appraising the gates.

He began to laugh uproariously, and she looked at him, her green eyes narrowing dangerously.

"I think I'll ride back to see what's keeping Belgarath," the little man said.

"Do," she said. Then she looked at Garion, who was trying to conceal a broad grin. "Something funny?" she asked him.

"No, dear," he replied quickly. "Just enjoying the scenery is all."

The detachment of guards at the gates was neither as burnished nor plumed as the ceremonial guards at the gates of Tol Honeth. They wore polished shirts of chain mail over the customary red tunic, baggy breeches tucked into the tops of knee-high boots, red cloaks, and pointed conical helmets. They nonetheless looked very much like soldiers. They greeted Kal Zakath with crisp military salutes, and, as the Emperor passed through the gilded gates, trumpeters announced his entrance into the imperial compound with a brazen fanfare.

"I've always hated that," the Mallorean ruler said confidentially to Garion. "The sound grates on my ears."

"What irritated me were the people who used to follow me around hoping that I might need something," Garion told him.

"That's convenient sometimes."

Garion nodded. "Sometimes," he agreed, "but it stopped being convenient when one of them threw a knife at my back."

"Really? I thought your people universally adored you."

"It was a misunderstanding. The young man and I had a talk about it, and he promised not to do it any more."

"That's all?" 'Zakath exclaimed in astonishment. "You didn't have him executed?"

"Of course not. Once he and I understood each other, he turned out to be extraordinarily loyal." Garion sighed sadly. "He was killed at Thull Mardu."

"I'm sorry, Garion," 'Zakath said. "We all lost friends at Thull Mardu."

The marble-clad buildings inside the imperial complex were a jumble of conflicting architectural styles, ranging from the severely utilitarian to the elaborately ornate. For some reason Garion was reminded of the vast rabbit warren of King Anheg's palace at Val Alorn. Although 'Zakath's palace did not consist of one single building, the structures were all linked to each other by column-lined promenades and galleries which passed through parklike grounds studded with statues and marble pavilions.

'Zakath led them through the confusing maze toward the middle of the complex, where a single palace stood in splendid isolation, announcing by its expanse and height that it was the center of all power in boundless Mallorea. "The residence of Kallath the Unifier," the Emperor announced with grand irony, "my revered ancestor."

"Isn't it just a bit overdone?" Ce'Nedra asked tartly, still obviously unwilling to concede the fact that Mal Zeth far outstripped her girlhood home.

"Of course it is," the Mallorean replied, "but the ostentation was necessary. Kallath had to demonstrate to the other generals that he outranked them, and in Mal Zeth one's rank is reflected by the size of one's residence. Kallath was an undisguised knave, a usurper and a man of little personal charm, so he had to assert himself in other ways."

"Don't you just love politics?" Velvet said to Ce'Nedra. "It's the only field where the ego is allowed unrestricted play—as long as the treasury holds out."

'Zakath laughed. "I should offer you a position in the government, Margravine Liselle," he said. "I think we need an imperial deflator—someone to puncture all our puffed-up self-importance."

"Why, thank you, your Majesty," she said with a dimpled smile. "If it weren't for my commitments to the family business, I might even consider accepting such a post. It sounds like so much fun."

He sighed with mock regret. "Where were you when I needed a wife?"

"Probably in my cradle, your Majesty," she replied innocently.

He winced. "That was unkind," he accused.

"Yes," she agreed. "True, though," she added clinically.

He laughed again and looked at Polgara. "I'm going to steal her from you, my lady," he declared.

"To be your court jester, Kal Zakath?" Liselle asked, her face no longer lightly amused. "To entertain you with clever insults and banter? Ah, no. I don't think so. There's another side to me that I don't think you'd like very much. They call me 'Velvet' and think of me as a soft-winged butterfly, but this particular butterfly has a poisoned sting—as several people have discovered after it was too late."

"Behave, dear," Polgara murmured to her. "And don't give away trade secrets in a moment of pique."

Velvet lowered her eyes. "Yes, Lady Polgara," she replied meekly.

'Zakath looked at her, but did not say anything. He swung down from his saddle, and three grooms dashed to his side to take the reins from his hand. "Come along, then," he said to Garion and the others. "I'd like to show you around." He threw a sly glance at Velvet. "I hope that the Margravine will forgive me if I share every home owner's simple pride in his domicile—no matter how modest."

She laughed a golden little laugh.

Garion dismounted and laid an affectionate hand on Chretienne's proud neck. It was with a pang of almost tangible regret that he handed the reins to a waiting groom.

They entered the palace through broad, gilded doors and found themselves in a vaulted rotunda, quite similar in design to the one in the Emperor's palace in Tol Honeth, though this one lacked the marble busts that made Varana's entryway appear vaguely like a mausoleum. A crowd of officials, military and civilian, awaited their Emperor, each with a sheaf of important-looking documents in his hand.

'Zakath sighed as he looked at them. "I'm afraid we'll have to postpone the grand tour," he said. "I'm certain that you'll all want to bathe and change anyway—and perhaps rest a bit before we start the customary formalities. Brador, would you be good enough to show our guests to their rooms and arrange to have a light lunch prepared for them?"

"Of course, your Majesty."

"I think the east wing might be pleasant. It's away from all the scurrying through the halls in this part of the palace."

"My very thought, your Majesty."

'Zakath smiled at them all. "We'll dine together this evening," he promised. Then he smiled ironically. "An intimate little supper with no more than two or three hundred guests." He looked at the nervous officials clustered nearby and made a wry face. "Until this evening, then."

Brador led them through the echoing marble corridors teeming with servants and minor functionaries.

"Big place," Belgarath observed after they had been walking for perhaps ten minutes. The old man had said very little since they had entered the city, but had ridden in his customary half doze, although Garion was quite sure that very little escaped his grandfather's half-closed eyes.

"Yes," Brador agreed with him. "The first Emperor, Kallath, had grandiose notions at times."

Belgarath grunted. "It's a common affliction among rulers. I think it has something to do with insecurity."

"Tell me, Brador," Silk said, "didn't I hear somewhere that the state secret police are under the jurisdiction of your bureau?"

Brador nodded with a deprecating little smile. "It's one of my many responsibilities, Prince Kheldar," he replied. "I need to know what's going on in the empire in order to stay on top of things, so I had to organize a modest little intelligence service—nothing on nearly the scale of Queen Porenn's, however."

"It will grow with time," Velvet assured him. "Those things always do, for some reason."

The east wing of the palace was set somewhat apart from the rest of the buildings in the complex and it embraced a kind of enclosed courtyard or atrium that was green with exotic flowering plants growing about a mirrorlike pool at its center.

Jewel-like hummingbirds darted from blossom to blossom, adding splashes of vi-brant, moving color.

Polgara's eyes came alight when Brador opened the door to the suite of rooms she was to share with Durnik. Just beyond an arched doorway leading from the main sitting room was a large marble tub sunk into the floor with little tendrils of steam rising from it. "Oh, my," she sighed. "Civilization—at last."

"Just try not to get waterlogged, Pol," Belgarath said.

"Of course not, father," she agreed absently, still eyeing the steaming tub with undisguised longing.

"Is it really all that important, Pol?" he asked her.

"Yes, father," she replied. "It really is."

"It's an irrational prejudice against dirt." He grinned at the rest of them. "I've always been sort of fond of dirt myself."

"Quite obviously," she said. Then she stopped. "Incidentally, Old Wolf," she said critically as they all began to file out, "if your room happens to be similarly equipped, you should make use of the facilities yourself."

"Me?"

"You smell, father."

"No, Pol," he corrected. "I stink. *You* smell."

"Whatever. Go wash, father." She was already absently removing her shoes.

"I've gone as much as ten years at a time without a bath," he declared.

"Yes, father," she said. "I know—only the Gods know how well I know. Now," she said in a very businesslike tone, "if you'll all excuse me . . ." She very deliberately began to unbotton the front of her dress.

The suite of rooms to which Garion and Ce'Nedra were led was, if anything, even more opulent than that shared by Durnik and Polgara. As Garion moved about the several large chambers, examining the furnishings, Ce'Nedra went directly toward the bath, her eyes dreamy and her clothes falling to the floor behind her as she went. His wife's tendency toward casual nudity had occasionally shocked Garion in the past. He did not *personally* object to Ce'Nedra's skin. What disturbed him had been that she had seemed oblivious to the fact that sometimes her unclad state was highly inappropriate. He recalled with a shudder the time when he and the Sendar-ian ambassador had entered the royal apartment at Riva just as Ce'Nedra was in the process of trying on several new undergarments she had received from her dress-maker that very morning. Quite calmly, she had asked the ambassador's opinion of various of the frilly little things, modeling each in turn for him. The ambassador, a staid and proper Sendarian gentleman in his seventies, received more shocks in that ten minutes than he had encountered in the previous half century, and his next dis-patch to King Fulrach had plaintively requested that he be relieved of his post.

"Ce'Nedra, aren't you at least going to close the door?" Garion asked her as she tested the water's temperature with a tentative toe.

"That makes it very hard for us to talk, Garion," she replied reasonably as she stepped down into the tub. "I hate to have to shout."

"Oh?" he said. "I hadn't noticed that."

"Be nice," she told him, sinking into the water with a contented sigh. Curi-ously she began to unstopper and sniff the crystal decanters lined along one side of the tub which contained, Garion assumed, the assorted condiments with which ladies seasoned their bath water. Some of these she restoppered disapprovingly. Others she liberally sprinkled into her bath. One or two of them she rubbed on herself in various places.

"What if somebody comes in?" Garion asked her pointedly. "Some official or messenger or servant or something?"

"Well, what if they do?"

He stared at her.

"Garion, darling," she said in that same infuriatingly reasonable tone, "if they hadn't intended for the bath to be used, they wouldn't have prepared it, would they?"

Try as he might, he could not find an answer to that question.

She laid her head back in the water, letting her hair fan out around her face. Then she sat up. "Would you like to wash my back for me?" she asked him.

An hour or so later, after an excellent lunch served by efficient servants, Silk stopped by. The little thief had also bathed and changed clothes once again. His pearl-gray doublet was formally elegant, and he once again dripped jewels. His short, scraggly beard had been neatly trimmed, and there was a faint air of exotic perfume lingering about him. "Appearances," he responded to Garion's quizzical look. "One always wants to put one's best foot forward in a new situation."

"Of course," Garion said dryly.

"Belgarath asked me to stop by," the little man continued. "There's a large room upstairs. We're gathering there for a council of war."

"War?"

"Metaphorically speaking, of course."

"Oh. Of course."

The room at the top of a flight of marble stairs to which Silk led Garion and Ce'Nedra was quite large, and there was a thronelike chair on a dais against the back wall. Garion looked about at the lush furnishings and heavy crimson drapes. "This isn't the throne room, is it?" he asked.

"No," Silk replied. "At least not Kal Zakath's official one. It's here to make visiting royalty feel at home. Some kings get nervous when they don't have official-looking surroundings to play in."

"Oh."

Belgarath sat with his mismatched boots up on a polished table. His hair and beard were slightly damp, evidence that, despite his pretended indifference to bathing, he had in fact followed Polgara's instructions. Polgara and Durnik were talking quietly at one side, and Eriond and Toth were nearby. Velvet and Sadi stood looking out the window at the formal garden lying to the east of 'Zakath's sprawling palace.

"All right," the old sorcerer said, "I guess we're all here now. I think we need to talk."

—*I wouldn't say anything too specific*— Silk's fingers said in the gestures of the Drasnian secret language.—*It's almost certain that there are a few spies about*—

Belgarath looked at the far wall, his eyes narrowed as he searched it inch by inch for hidden peepholes. He grunted and looked at Polgara.

"I'll look into it, father," she murmured. Her eyes grew distant, and Garion felt the familiar surge. After a moment she nodded and held up three fingers. She concentrated for a moment, and the quality of the surge changed, seeming somehow languorous. Then she straightened and relaxed her will. "It's all right now," she told them calmly. "They fell asleep."

"That was very smooth, Pol," Durnik said admiringly.

"Why, thank you, dear," she smiled, laying her hand on his.

Belgarath put his feet on the floor and leaned forward. "That's one more thing for us all to keep in mind," he said seriously. "We're likely to be watched all the time that we're here in Mal Zeth, so be careful. 'Zakath's a skeptic, so we can't really be sure just how much of what we've told him he believes. It's altogether possible that he has other things in mind for us. Right now he needs our help in dealing with Mengha, but he still hasn't entirely abandoned his campaign in Cthol Murgos, and he might want to use us to bring the Alorns and the others into that war on his side. He's also got problems with Urvon and Zandramas. We don't have the time to get caught up in internal Mallorean politics. At the moment, though, we're more or less in his power, so let's be careful."

"We can leave any time we need to, Belgarath," Durnik said confidently.

"I'd rather not do it that way unless we have absolutely no other choice," the old man replied. " 'Zakath's the kind of man who's very likely to grow testy if he's thwarted, and I don't want to have to creep around dodging his soldiers. It takes too much time and it's dangerous. I'll be a lot happier if we can leave Mal Zeth with his blessing—or at least with his consent."

"I want to get to Ashaba before Zandramas has time to escape again," Garion insisted.

"So do I, Garion," his grandfather said, "but we don't know what she's doing there, so we don't know how long she's likely to stay."

"She's been looking for something, father," Polgara told the old man. "I saw that in her mind when I trapped her back in Rak Hagga."

He looked at her thoughtfully. "Could you get any idea of what it was, Pol?"

She shook her head. "Not specifically," she replied. "I think it's information of some kind. She can't go any further until she finds it. I was able to pick that much out of her thoughts."

"Whatever it is has to be well hidden," he said. "Beldin and I took Ashaba apart after the Battle of Vo Mimbre and we didn't find anything out of the ordinary—if you can accept the idea that Torak's house was in any way ordinary."

"Can we be sure that she's still there with my baby?" Ce'Nedra asked intently.

"No, dear," Polgara told her. "She's taken steps to hide her mind from me. She's rather good, actually."

"Even if she's left Ashaba, the Orb can pick up her trail again," Belgarath said. "The chances are pretty good that she hasn't found what she's looking for, and that effectively nails her down at Ashaba. If she has found it, she won't be hard to follow."

"We're going on to Ashaba, then?" Sadi asked. "What I'm getting at is that our concern about Mengha was just a ruse to get us to Mallorea, wasn't it?"

"I think I'm going to need more information before I make any decisions about that. The situation in northern Karanda is serious, certainly, but let's not lose sight of the fact that our primary goal is Zandramas, and she's at Ashaba. Before I can decide anything, though, I need to know more about what's going on here in Mallorea."

"My department," Silk volunteered.

"And mine," Velvet added.

"I might be able to help a bit as well," Sadi noted with a faint smile. He frowned then. "Seriously though, Belgarath," he continued, "you and your family here represent power. I don't think we're going to have much luck at persuading Kal Zakath to let you go willingly—no matter how cordial he may appear on the surface."

The old man nodded glumly. "It might turn out that way after all," he agreed. Then he looked at Silk, Velvet, and Sadi. "Be careful," he cautioned them. "Don't let your instincts run away with you. I need information, but don't stir up any hornets' nests getting it for me." He looked pointedly at Silk. "I hope I've made myself clear about this," he said. "Don't complicate things just for the fun of it."

"Trust me, Belgarath," Silk replied with a bland smile.

"Of course he trusts you, Kheldar," Velvet assured the little man.

Belgarath looked at his impromptu spy network and shook his head. "Why do I get the feeling that I'm going to regret this?" he muttered.

"I'll keep an eye on them, Belgarath," Sadi promised.

"Of course, but who's going to keep an eye on you?"

CHAPTER SEVEN

That evening they were escorted with some ceremony through the echoing halls of 'Zakath's palace to a banquet hall that appeared to be only slightly smaller than a parade ground. The hall was approached by way of a broad, curved stairway lined on either side with branched candelabra and liveried trumpeters. The stairway was obviously designed to facilitate grand entrances. Each new arrival was announced by a stirring fanfare and the booming voice of a gray-haired herald so thin that it almost appeared that a lifetime of shouting had worn him down to a shadow.

Garion and his friends waited in a small antechamber while the last of the local dignitaries were announced. The fussy chief of protocol, a small Melcene with an elaborately trimmed brown beard, wanted them to line up in ascending order of rank, but the difficulties involved in assigning precise rank to the members of this strange group baffled him. He struggled with it, manfully trying to decide if Sorcerer outranked King or Imperial Princess until Garion solved his problem for him by leading Ce'Nedra out onto the landing at the top of the stairs.

"Their Royal Majesties, King Belgarion and Queen Ce'Nedra of Riva," the herald declaimed grandly, and the trumpets blared.

Garion, dressed all in blue and with his ivory-gowned Queen on his arm, paused on the marble landing at the top of the stairs to allow the brightly clad throng below the time to gawk at him. The somewhat dramatic pause was not entirely his idea. Ce'Nedra had dug her fingernails into his arm with a grip of steel and hissed, "Stand still!"

It appeared that 'Zakath also had some leaning toward the theatrical, since the stunned silence which followed the herald's announcement clearly indicated that the Emperor had given orders that the identity of his guests remain strictly confidential until this very moment. Garion was honest enough with himself to admit that the startled buzz which ran through the crowd below was moderately gratifying.

He began down the stairway, but found himself reined in like a restive horse. "Don't run!" Ce'Nedra commanded under her breath.

"Run?" he objected. "I'm barely moving."

"Do it slower, Garion."

He discovered then that his wife had a truly amazing talent. She could speak without moving her lips! Her smile was gracious, though somewhat lofty, but a steady stream of low-voiced commands issued from that smile.

The buzzing murmur that had filled the banquet hall when they had been announced died into a respectful silence when they reached the foot of the stair, and a vast wave of bows and curtsies rippled through the crowd as they moved along the carpeted promenade leading to the slightly elevated platform upon which sat the table reserved for the Emperor and his special guests, domestic and foreign.

'Zakath himself, still in his customary white, but wearing a gold circlet artfully hammered into the form of a wreath woven of leaves as a concession to the formality of the occasion, rose from his seat and came to meet them, thereby avoiding that awkward moment when two men of equal rank meet in public. "So good of you to come, my dear," he said, taking Ce'Nedra's hand and kissing it. He sounded for all the world like a country squire or minor nobleman greeting friends from the neighborhood.

"So good of you to invite us," she replied with a whimsical smile.

"You're looking well, Garion," the Mallorean said, extending his hand and still speaking in that offhand and informal manner.

"Tolerable, 'Zakath," Garion responded, taking his cue from his host. If 'Zakath wanted to play, Garion felt that he should show him that he could play, too.

"Would you care to join me at the table?" 'Zakath asked. "We can chat while we wait for the others to arrive."

"Of course," Garion agreed in a deliberately commonplace tone of voice.

When they reached their chairs, however, his curiosity finally got the better of him. "Why are we playing 'just plain folks'?" he asked 'Zakath as he held Ce'Nedra's chair for her. "This affair's a trifle formal for talking about the weather and asking after each other's health, wouldn't you say?"

"It's baffling the nobility," 'Zakath replied with aplomb. "Never do the expected, Garion. The hint that we're old, old friends will set them afire with curiosity and make people who thought that they knew everything just a little less sure of themselves." He smiled at Ce'Nedra. "You're positively ravishing tonight, my dear," he told her.

Ce'Nedra glowed then looked archly at Garion. "Why don't you take a few notes, dear?" she suggested. "You could learn a great deal from his Majesty here." She turned back to 'Zakath. "You're so very kind to say it," she told him, "but my hair is an absolute disaster." Her expression was faintly tragic as she lightly touched her curls with her fingertips. Actually, her hair was stupendous, with a coronet of braids interwoven with strings of pearls and with a cascade of coppery ringlets spilling down across the front of her left shoulder.

During this polite exchange, the others in their party were being introduced. Silk and Velvet caused quite a stir, he in his jewel-encrusted doublet and she in a gown of lavender brocade.

Ce'Nedra sighed enviously. "I wish I could wear that color," she murmured.

"You can wear any color you want to, Ce'Nedra," Garion told her.

"Are you color-blind, Garion?" she retorted. "A girl with red hair can *not* wear lavender."

"If that's all that's bothering you, I can change the color of your hair any time you want."

"Don't you dare!" she gasped, her hands going protectively to the cascade of auburn curls at her shoulder.

"Just a suggestion, dear."

The herald at the top of the stairs announced Sadi, Eriond, and Toth as a group, obviously having some difficulty with the fact that the boy and the giant had no rank that he could discern. The next presentation, however, filled his voice with awe and his bony limbs with trembling. "Her Grace, the Duchess of Erat," he declaimed, "Lady Polgara the Sorceress." The silence following that announcement was stunned. "And Goodman Durnik of Sendaria," the herald added, "the man with two lives."

Polgara and the smith descended the stairs to the accompaniment of a profound silence.

The bows and curtsies which acknowledged the legendary couple were so deep as to resemble genuflections before an altar. Polgara, dressed in her customary silver-trimmed blue, swept through the hall with all the regal bearing of an Empress. She wore a mysterious smile, and the fabled white lock at her brow glowed in the candlelight as she and Durnik approached the platform.

Meanwhile, at the top of the stairs, the herald had shrunk back from the next guest, his eyes wide and his face gone quite pale.

"Just say it," Garion heard his grandfather tell the frightened man. "I'm fairly sure that they'll all recognize the name."

The herald stepped to the marble railing at the front of the landing. "Your Majesty," he said falteringly, "My lords and ladies, I have the unexpected honor to present Belgarath the Sorcerer."

A gasp ran through the hall as the old man, dressed in a cowled robe of soft gray wool, stumped down the stairs with no attempt at grace or dignity. The assembled Mallorean notables pulled back from him as he walked toward the table where the others had already joined 'Zakath.

About halfway to the imperial platform, however, a blond Melcene girl in a low-cut gown caught his eye. She stood stricken with awe, unable to curtsy or even to move as the most famous man in all the world approached her. Belgarath stopped and looked her up and down quite slowly and deliberately, noting with appreciation just how revealing her gown was. A slow, insinuating smile crept across his face, and his blue eyes twinkled outrageously.

"Nice dress," he told her.

She blushed furiously.

He laughed, reached out, and patted her cheek. "There's a good girl," he said.

"Father," Polgara said firmly.

"Coming, Pol." He chuckled and moved along the carpet toward the table. The pretty Melcene girl looked after him, her eyes wide and her hand pressed to the cheek he had touched.

"Isn't he disgusting?" Ce'Nedra muttered.

"It's just the way he is, dear," Garion disagreed. "He doesn't pretend to be anything else. He doesn't have to."

The banquet featured a number of exotic dishes that Garion could not put a name to and several which he did not even know how to eat. A deceptively innocent-looking rice dish was laced with such fiery seasonings that it brought tears to his eyes and sent his hand clutching for his water goblet.

"Belar, Mara, and Nedra!" Durnik choked as he also groped about in search of water. So far as he could remember, it was the first time Garion had ever heard Durnik swear. He did it surprisingly well.

"Piquant," Sadi commented as he calmly continued to eat the dreadful concoction.

"How can you eat that?" Garion demanded in amazement.

Sadi smiled. "You forget that I'm used to being poisoned, Belgarion. Poison tends to toughen the tongue and fireproof the throat."

'Zakath had watched their reactions with some amusement. "I should have warned you," he apologized. "The dish comes from Gandahar, and the natives of that region entertain themselves during the rainy season by trying to build bonfires in each other's stomachs. They're elephant trappers, for the most part, and they pride themselves on their courage."

After the extended banquet, the brown-robed Brador approached Garion. "If your Majesty wouldn't mind," he said, leaning forward so that Garion could hear him over the sounds of laughter and sprightly conversation from nearby tables, "there are a number of people who are most eager to meet you."

Garion nodded politely even though he inwardly winced. He had been through this sort of thing before and knew how tedious it usually became. The Chief of the Bureau of Internal Affairs led him down from the platform into the swirl of brightly clad celebrants, pausing occasionally to exchange greetings with various fellow officials and to introduce Garion. Garion braced himself for an hour or two of total boredom. The plump, bald-headed Brador, however, proved to be an entertaining escort. Though he seemed to be engaging Garion in light conversation, he was in fact providing a succinct and often pointed briefing even as they went.

"We'll be talking with the kinglet of Pallia," he murmured as they approached a group of men in tall, conical felt caps who wore leather which had been dyed an unhealthy-looking green color. "He's a fawning bootlicker, a liar, a coward, and absolutely not to be trusted."

"Ah, there you are, Brador," one of the felt-capped men greeted the Melcene with a forced heartiness.

"Your Highness," Brador replied with a florid bow. "I have the honor to present his Royal Majesty, Belgarion of Riva." He turned to Garion. "Your Majesty, this is his Highness, King Warasin of Pallia."

"Your Majesty," Warasin gushed, bowing awkwardly. He was a man with a narrow, pockmarked face, close-set eyes, and a slack-lipped mouth. His hands, Garion noticed, were not particularly clean.

"Your Highness," Garion replied with a slightly distant note.

"I was just telling the members of my court here that I'd have sooner believed that the sun would rise in the north tomorrow than that the Overlord of the West would appear at Mal Zeth."

"The world is full of surprises."

"By the beard of Torak, you're right, Belgarion—you don't mind if I call you Belgarion, do you, your Majesty?"

"Torak didn't have a beard," Garion corrected shortly.

"What?"

"Torak—he didn't have a beard. At least he didn't when I met him."

"When you—" Warasin's eyes suddenly widened. "Are you telling me that all those stories about what happened at Cthol Mishrak are actually *true?*" he gasped.

"I'm not sure, your Highness," Garion told him. "I haven't heard all the stories yet. It's been an absolute delight meeting you, old boy," he said, clapping the stunned-looking kinglet on the shoulder with exaggerated camaraderie. "It's a shame that we don't have more time to talk. Coming, Brador?" He nodded to the petty king of Pallia, turned, and led the Melcene away.

"You're very skilled, Belgarion," Brador murmured. "Much more so than I would have imagined, considering—" He hesitated.

"Considering the fact that I look like an unlettered country oaf?" Garion supplied.

"I don't know that I'd put it exactly that way."

"Why not?" Garion shrugged. "It's the truth, isn't it? What was pigeyes back there trying to maneuver the conversation around to? It was pretty obvious that he was leading up to something."

"It's fairly simple," Brador replied. "He recognizes your current proximity to Kal Zakath. All power in Mallorea derives from the throne, and the man who has the Emperor's ear is in a unique position. Warasin is currently having a border dispute with the Prince Regent of Delchin and he probably wants you to put in a good word for him." Brador gave him an amused look. "You're in a position right now to make millions, you know."

Garion laughed. "I couldn't carry it, Brador," he said. "I visited the royal treasury at Riva once, and I know how much a million weighs. Who's next?"

"The Chief of the Bureau of Commerce—an unmitigated, unprincipled ass. Like most Bureau Chiefs."

Garion smiled. "And what does *he* want?"

Brador tugged thoughtfully at one earlobe. "I'm not entirely certain. I've been out of the country. Vasca's a devious one, though, so I'd be careful of him."

"I'm always careful, Brador."

The Baron Vasca, Chief of the Bureau of Commerce, was wrinkled and bald. He wore the brown robe that seemed to be almost the uniform of the bureaucracy, and the gold chain of his office seemed almost too heavy for his thin neck. Though at first glance he appeared to be old and frail, his eyes were as alert and shrewd as those of a vulture. "Ah, your Majesty," he said after they had been introduced, "I'm so pleased to meet you at last."

"My pleasure, Baron Vasca," Garion said politely.

They chatted together for some time, and Garion could not detect anything in the baron's conversation that seemed in the least bit out of the ordinary.

"I note that Prince Kheldar of Drasnia is a member of your party," the baron said finally.

"We're old friends. You're acquainted with Kheldar then, Baron?"

"We've had a few dealings together—the customary permits and gratuities, you understand. For the most part, though, he tends to avoid contact with the authorities."

"I've noticed that from time to time," Garion said.

"I was certain that you would have. I won't keep your Majesty. Many others here are eager to meet you, and I wouldn't want to be accused of monopolizing your time. We must talk again soon." The baron turned to the Chief of the Bureau of Internal Affairs. "So good of you to introduce us, my dear Brador," he said.

"It's nothing, my dear Baron," Brador replied. He took Garion by the arm, and they moved away from Vasca.

"What was that all about?" Garion asked.

"I'm not altogether sure," Brador replied, "but whatever he wanted, he seems to have gotten."

"We didn't really say anything."

"I know. That's what worries me. I think I'll have my old friend Vasca watched. He's managed to arouse my curiosity."

During the next couple of hours Garion met two more gaudily dressed petty kings, a fair number of more soberly garbed bureaucrats, and a sprinkling of semi-important nobles and their ladies. Many of them, of course, wanted nothing more than to be seen talking to him so that later they could say in a casual, offhand fashion, "I was talking with Belgarion the other day, and he said—" Others made some point of suggesting that a private conversation might be desirable at some later date. A few even tried to set up specific appointments.

It was rather late when Velvet finally came to his rescue. She approached the place where Garion was trapped by the royal family of Peldane, a stodgy little kinglet in a mustard-yellow turban, his simpering, scrawny wife in a pink gown that clashed horribly with her orange hair, and three spoiled royal brats who spent their time whining and hitting each other. "Your Majesty," the blond girl said with a curtsy, "Your wife asks your permission to retire."

"Asks?"

"She's feeling slightly unwell."

Garion gave her a grateful look. "I must go to her at once, then," he said quickly. He turned to the Peldane royalty. "I hope you'll all excuse me," he said to them.

"Of course, Belgarion," the kinglet replied graciously.

"And please convey our regards to your lovely wife," the queenlet added.

The royal brood continued to howl and kick each other.

"You looked a bit harried," Velvet murmured as she led Garion away.

"I could kiss you."

"Now that's an interesting suggestion."

Garion glanced sourly back over his shoulder. "They should drown those three little monsters and raise a litter of puppies instead," he muttered.

"Piglets," she corrected.

He looked at her.

"At least they could sell the bacon," she explained. "That way the effort wouldn't be a total loss."

"Is Ce'Nedra really ill?"

"Of course not. She's made as many conquests as she wants to this evening, that's all. She wants to save a few for future occasions. Now it's time for the grand withdrawal, leaving a horde of disappointed admirers, who were all panting to meet her, crushed with despair."

"That's a peculiar way to look at it."

She laughed affectionately, linking her arm in his. "Not if you're a woman, it's not."

The following morning shortly after breakfast, Garion and Belgarath were summoned to meet with 'Zakath and Brador in the Emperor's private study. The room was large and comfortable, lined with books and maps and with deeply up-holstered chairs clustered about low tables. It was a warm day outside, and the windows stood open, allowing a blossom-scented spring breeze to ruffle the curtains.

"Good morning, gentlemen," 'Zakath greeted them as they were escorted into the room. "I hope you slept well."

"Once I managed to get Ce'Nedra out of the tub." Garion laughed. "It's just a bit too convenient, I think. Would you believe that she bathed three times yester-day?"

"Mal Zeth is very hot and dusty in the summertime," 'Zakath said. "The baths make it bearable."

"How does the hot water get to them?" Garion asked curiously. "I haven't seen anyone carrying pails up and down the halls."

"It's piped in under the floors," the Emperor replied. "The artisan who devised the system was rewarded with a baronetcy."

"I hope you don't mind if we steal the idea. Durnik's already making sketches."

"I think it's unhealthy myself," Belgarath said. "Bathing should be done out of doors—in cold water. All this pampering softens people." He looked at 'Zakath. "I'm sure you didn't ask us here to discuss the philosophical ramifications of bathing, though."

"Not unless you really want to, Belgarath," 'Zakath replied. He straightened in his chair. "Now that we've all had a chance to rest from our journey, I thought that maybe it was time for us to get to work. Brador's people have made their reports to him, and he's ready to give us his assessment of the current situation in Karanda. Go ahead, Brador."

"Yes, your Majesty." The plump, bald Melcene rose from his chair and crossed to a very large map of the Mallorean continent hanging on the wall. The map was exquisitely colored with blue lakes and rivers, green prairies, darker green forests and brown, white-topped mountains. Instead of simply being dots on the map, the cities were represented by pictures of buildings and fortifications. The Mallorean highway system, Garion noted, was very nearly as extensive as the Tolnedran network in the west.

Brador cleared his throat, fought for a moment with one of 'Zakath's ferocious kittens for the long pointer he wanted to use, and began. "As I reported to you in Rak Hagga," he said, "a man named Mengha came out of this immense forest to the north of Lake Karanda some six months ago." He tapped the representation of a large belt of trees stretching from the Karandese Range to the Mountains of Zamad. "We know very, very little about his background."

"That's not entirely true, Brador," Belgarath disagreed. "Cyradis told us that he's a Grolim priest—or he used to be. That puts us in a position to deduce quite a bit."

"I'd be interested to hear whatever you can come up with," 'Zakath said.

Belgarath squinted around the room, and his eyes fixed on several full crystal decanters and some polished glasses sitting on a sideboard across the room. "Do you mind?" he asked, pointing at the decanters. "I think better with a glass in my hand."

"Help yourself," 'Zakath replied.

The old man rose, crossed to the sideboard, and poured himself a glass of ruby-red wine. "Garion?" he asked, holding out the decanter.

"No, thanks all the same, Grandfather."

Belgarath replaced the crystal stopper with a clink and began to pace up and down on the blue carpet. "All right," he said. "We know that demon worship persists in the back country of Karanda, even though the Grolim priests tried to stamp out the practice when the Karands were converted to the worship of Torak in the second millennium. We also know that Mengha was a priest himself. Now, if the Grolims here in Mallorea reacted in the same way that the ones in Cthol Murgos did when they heard about the death of Torak, then we know that they were thoroughly demoralized. The fact that Urvon spent several years scrambling around trying to find prophecies that would hint at the possibility of a justification for keeping the Church intact is fairly good evidence that he was faced with almost universal despair in the ranks of the Grolims." He paused to sip at his wine. "Not bad," he said to 'Zakath approvingly. "Not bad at all."

"Thank you."

"Now," the old man continued, "there are many possible reactions to religious despair. Some men go mad, some men try to lose themselves in various forms of dissipation, some men refuse to admit the truth and try to keep the old forms alive. A few men, however, go in search of some new kind of religion—usually something the exact opposite of what they believed before. Since the Grolim Church in Karanda had concentrated for eons on eradicating demon worship, it's only logical that a few of the despairing priests would seek out demon-masters in the hope of learning their secrets. Remember, if you can actually control a demon, it gives you a great deal of power, and the hunger for power has always been at the core of the Grolim mentality."

"It does fit together, Ancient One," Brador admitted.

"I thought so myself. All right, Torak is dead, and Mengha suddenly finds that his theological ground has been cut out from under him. He probably goes through a period of doing all the things that he wasn't allowed to do as a priest—drinking, wenching, that sort of thing. But if you do things to excess, eventually they become empty and unsatisfying. Even debauchery can get boring after a while."

"Aunt Pol will be amazed to hear that you said that," Garion said.

"You just keep it to yourself," Belgarath told him. "Our arguments about my bad habits are the cornerstone of our relationship." He took another sip of his wine. "This is really excellent," he said, holding up the glass to admire the color of the wine in the sunlight. "Now then, here we have Mengha waking up some morning with a screaming headache, a mouth that tastes like a chicken coop, and a fire in his stomach that no amount of water will put out. He has no real reason to go on living. He might even take out his sacrificial gutting knife and set the point against his chest."

"Isn't your speculation going a bit far afield?" 'Zakath asked.

Belgarath laughed. "I used to be a professional storyteller," he apologized. "I can't stand to let a good story slip by without a few artistic touches. All right, maybe he did or maybe he didn't think about killing himself. The point is that he had reached the absolute rock bottom. That's when the idea of demons came to him. Raising demons is almost as dangerous as being the first man up the scaling ladder during an assault on a fortified city, but Mengha has nothing to lose. So, he journeys into the forest up there, finds a Karandese magician, and somehow persuades him to teach him the art—if that's what you want to call it. It takes him about a dozen years to learn all the secrets."

"How did you arrive at that number?" Brador asked.

Belgarath shrugged. "It's been fourteen years since the death of Torak—or thereabouts. No normal man can seriously mistreat himself for more than a couple of years before he starts to fall apart, so it was probably about twelve years ago that Mengha went in search of a magician to give him instruction. Then, once he's learned all the secrets, he kills his teacher, and—"

"Wait a minute," 'Zakath objected. "Why would he do that?"

"His teacher knew too much about him, and *he* could also raise demons to send after our defrocked Grolim. Then there's the fact that the arrangement between teacher and pupil in these affairs involves lifetime servitude enforced with a curse. Mengha could not leave his master until the old man was dead."

"How do you know so much about this, Belgarath?" 'Zakath asked.

"I went through it all among the Morindim a few thousand years ago. I wasn't doing anything very important and I was curious about magic."

"Did you kill your master?"

"No—well, not exactly. When I left him, he sent his familiar demon after me. I took control of it and sent it back to him."

"And it killed him?"

"I assume so. They usually do. Anyway, getting back to Mengha. He arrives at the gates of Calida about six months ago and raises a whole army of demons. Nobody in his right mind raises more than one at a time because they're too difficult to control." He frowned, pacing up and down staring at the floor. "The only thing I can think of is that somehow he's managed to raise a Demon Lord and get it under control."

"Demon Lord?" Garion asked.

"They have rank, too—just as humans do. If Mengha has a grip on a Demon Lord, then it's that creature that's calling up the army of lesser demons." He refilled his glass, looking faintly satisfied with himself. "That's probably fairly close to Mengha's life story," he said, sitting down again.

"A virtuoso performance, Belgarath," 'Zakath congratulated him.

"Thank you," the old man replied. "I thought so myself." He looked at Brador. "Now that we know him, why don't you tell us what he's been up to?"

Brador once again took his place beside the map, fending off the same kitten with his pointer. "After Mengha took Calida, word of his exploits ran all through Karanda," he began. "It appears that the worship of Torak was never really very firmly ingrained in the Karands to begin with, and about the only thing that kept them in line was their fear of the sacrificial knives of the Grolims."

"Like the Thulls?" Garion suggested.

"Very much so, your Majesty. Once Torak was dead, however, and his Church in disarray, the Karands began to revert. The old shrines began to reappear, and the old rituals came back into practice." Brador shuddered. "Hideous rites," he said. "Obscene."

"Even worse than the Grolim rite of sacrifice?" Garion asked mildly.

"There was some justification for that, Garion," 'Zakath objected. "It was an honor to be chosen, and the victims went under the knife willingly."

"Not any of them that I ever saw," Garion disagreed.

"We can discuss comparative theology some other time," Belgarath told them. "Go on, Brador."

"Once the Karands heard about Mengha," the Melcene official continued, "they began to flock to Calida to support him and to enlist themselves on the side of the demons. There's always been a subterranean independence movement in the seven kingdoms of Karanda, and many hotheads there believe that the demons offer the best hope of throwing off the yoke of Angarak oppression." He looked at the Emperor. "No offense intended, your Majesty," he murmured.

"None taken, Brador," 'Zakath assured him.

"Naturally, the little kinglets in Karanda tried to keep their people from joining Mengha. The loss of subjects is always painful to a ruler. The army—our army—was also alarmed by the hordes of Karands flocking to Mengha's banner, and they tried to block off borders and the like. But, since a large portion of the army was in Cthol Murgos with his Majesty here, the troops in Karanda just didn't have the numbers. The Karands either slipped around them or simply overwhelmed them. Mengha's army numbers almost a million by now—ill-equipped and poorly trained, perhaps, but a million is a significant number, even if they're armed with sticks. Not only Jenno but also Ganesia are totally under Mengha's domination, and he's on the verge of overwhelming Katakor. Once he succeeds there, he'll inevitably move on Pallia and Delchin. If he isn't stopped, he'll be knocking on the gates of Mal Zeth by Erastide."

"Is he unleashing his demons in these campaigns?" Belgarath asked intently.

"Not really," Brador replied. "After what happened at Calida, there's no real need for that. The sight of them alone is usually enough to spring open the gates of any city he's taken so far. He's succeeded with remarkably little actual fighting."

The old man nodded. "I sort of thought that might have been the case. A demon is very hard to get back under control once it's tasted blood."

"It's not really the demons that are causing the problems," Brador continued. "Mengha's flooded all the rest of Karanda with his agents, and the stories that they're circulating are whipping previously uncommitted people into a frenzy." He looked at the Emperor. "Would you believe that we actually caught one of his missionaries in the Karandese barracks right here in Mal Zeth?" he said.

'Zakath looked up sharply. "How did he get in?" he demanded.

"He disguised himself as a corporal returning from convalescent leave at home," Brador replied. "He'd even gone so far as to give himself a wound to make his story look authentic. It was very believable the way he cursed Murgos."

"What did you do to him?"

"Unfortunately, he didn't survive the questioning," Brador said, frowning. He bent to remove the kitten from around his ankle.

"Unfortunately?"

"I had some interesting plans for him. I take it rather personally when someone manages to circumvent my secret police. It's a matter of professional pride."

"What do you advise, then?" 'Zakath asked.

Brador began to pace. "I'm afraid that you're going to have to bring the army back from Cthol Murgos, your Majesty," he said. "You can't fight a war on two fronts."

"Absolutely out of the question." 'Zakath's tone was adamant.

"I don't think we have much choice," Brador told him. "Almost half of the forces left here in Mallorea are of Karandese origin, and it's my considered opinion that to rely upon them in any kind of confrontation with Mengha would be sheer folly."

'Zakath's face grew bleak.

"Put it this way, your Majesty," Brador said smoothly. "If you weaken your forces in Cthol Murgos, it's quite possible that you'll lose Rak Cthaka and maybe Rak Gorut, but if you don't bring the army home, you're going to lose Mal Zeth."

'Zakath glared at him.

"There's still time to consider the matter, Sire," Brador added in a reasonable tone of voice. "This is only *my* assessment of the situation. I'm sure you'll want confirmation of what I've said from military intelligence, and you'll need to consult with the High Command."

"No," 'Zakath said bluntly. "The decision is mine." He scowled at the floor.

"All right, Brador, we'll bring the army home. Go tell the High Command that I want to see them all at once."

"Yes, your Majesty."

Garion had risen to his feet. "How long will it take to ship your troops back from Cthol Murgos?" he asked with a sinking feeling.

"About three months," 'Zakath replied.

"I can't wait that long, 'Zakath."

"I'm very sorry, Garion, but none of us has any choice. Neither you nor I will leave Mal Zeth until the army gets here."

CHAPTER EIGHT

The following morning, Silk came early to the rooms Garion shared with Ce'Nedra. The little man once again wore his doublet and hose, though he had removed most of his jewelry. Over his arm he carried a pair of Mallorean robes, the lightweight, varicolored garments worn by most of the citizens of Mal Zeth. "Would you like to go into the city?" he asked Garion.

"I don't think they'll let us out of the palace."

"I've already taken care of that. Brador gave his permission—provided that we don't try to get away from the people who are going to be following us."

"That's a depressing thought. I hate being followed."

"You get used to it."

"Have you got anything specific in mind, or is this just a sight-seeing tour?"

"I want to stop by our offices here and have a talk with our factor."

Garion gave him a puzzled look.

"The agent who handles things for us here in Mal Zeth."

"Oh. I hadn't heard the word before."

"That's because you aren't in business. Our man here is named Dolmar. He's a Melcene—very efficient, and he doesn't steal too much."

"I'm not sure that I'd enjoy listening to you talk business," Garion said.

Silk looked around furtively. "You might learn all kinds of things, Garion," he said, but his fingers were already moving rapidly. —*Dolmar can give us a report on what's really happening in Karanda*— he gestured. —*I think you'd better come along*—

"Well," Garion said with slightly exaggerated acquiescence, "maybe you're right. Besides, the walls here are beginning to close in on me."

"Here," Silk said, holding out one of the robes, "wear this."

"It's not really cold, Silk."

"The robe isn't to keep you warm. People in western clothing attract a lot of attention on the streets of Mal Zeth, and I don't like being stared at." Silk grinned quickly. "It's very hard to pick pockets when everybody in the street is watching you. Shall we go?"

The robe Garion put on was open at the front and hung straight from his shoulders to his heels. It was a serviceable outer garment with deep pockets at the sides. The material of which it was made was quite thin, and it flowed out behind him as he moved around. He went to the door of the adjoining room. Ce'Nedra was combing her hair, still damp from her morning bath.

"I'm going into the city with Silk," he told her. "Do you need anything?"

She thought about that. "See if you can find me a comb," she said, holding up the one she had been using. "Mine's starting to look a little toothless."

"All right." He turned to leave.

"As long as you're going anyway," she added, "why don't you pick me up a bolt of silk cloth—teal green, if you can find it. I'm told that there's a dressmaker here in the palace with a great deal of skill."

"I'll see what I can do." He turned again.

"And perhaps a few yards of lace—not too ornate, mind. Tasteful."

"Anything else?"

She smiled at him. "Buy me a surprise of some kind. I love surprises."

"A comb, a bolt of teal green silk, a few yards of tasteful lace, and a surprise." He ticked them off on his fingers.

"Get me one of those robes like you're wearing, too."

He waited.

She pursed her lips thoughtfully. "That's all I can think of, Garion, but you and Silk might ask Liselle and Lady Polgara if they need anything."

He sighed.

"It's only polite, Garion."

"Yes, dear. Maybe I'd better make out a list."

Silk's face was blandly expressionless as Garion came back out.

"Well?" Garion asked him.

"I didn't say anything."

"Good."

They started out the door.

"Garion," Ce'Nedra called after him.

"Yes, dear?"

"See if you can find some sweetmeats, too."

Garion went out into the hall behind Silk and firmly closed the door behind him.

"You handle that sort of thing very well," Silk said.

"Practice."

Velvet added several items to Garion's growing list, and Polgara several more. Silk looked at the list as they walked down the long, echoing hallway toward the main part of the palace. "I wonder if Brador would lend us a pack mule," he murmured.

"Quit trying to be funny."

"Would I do that?"

"Why were we talking with our fingers back there?"

"Spies."

"In our private quarters?" Garion was shocked, remembering Ce'Nedra's sometimes aggressive indifference to the way she was dressed—or not dressed—when they were alone.

"Private places are where the most interesting secrets are to be found. No spy ever passes up the opportunity to peek into a bedroom."

"That's disgusting!" Garion exclaimed, his cheeks burning.

"Of course it is. Fairly common practice, though."

They passed through the vaulted rotunda just inside the gold-plated main door of the palace and walked out into a bright spring morning touched with a fragrant breeze.

"You know," Silk said, "I like Mal Zeth. It always smells so good. Our office here is upstairs over a bakery, and some mornings the smells from downstairs almost make me swoon."

There was only the briefest of pauses at the gates of the imperial complex. A curt gesture from one of the pair of unobtrusive men who were following them advised the gate guards that Silk and Garion were to be allowed to pass into the city.

"Policemen do have their uses sometimes," Silk said as they started down a broad boulevard leading away from the palace.

The streets of Mal Zeth teemed with people from all over the empire and not a few from the West as well. Garion was a bit surprised to see a sprinkling of Tolnedran mantles among the varicolored robes of the local populace, and here and there were Sendars, Drasnians, and a fair number of Nadraks. There were, however, no Murgos. "Busy place," he noted to Silk.

"Oh, yes. Mal Zeth makes Tol Honeth look like a country fair and Camaar like a village market."

"It's the biggest commercial center in the world, then?"

"No. That's Melcene—of course Melcene concentrates on money instead of goods. You can't even buy a tin pot in Melcene. All you can buy there is money."

"Silk, how can you make any kind of profit buying money with money?"

"It's a little complicated." Silk's eyes narrowed. "Do you know something?" he said. "If you could put your hands on the royal treasury of Riva, I could show you how to double it in six months on Basa Street in Melcene—with a nice commission for the both of us thrown in for good measure."

"You want me to speculate with the royal treasury? I'd have an open insurrection on my hands if anybody ever found out about it."

"That's the secret, Garion. You don't let anybody find out."

"Have you ever had an honest thought in your entire life?"

The little man thought about it. "Not that I recall, no," he replied candidly. "But then, I've got a well-trained mind."

The offices of the commercial empire of Silk and Yarblek here in Mal Zeth were, as the little man had indicated, rather modest and were situated above a busy bakeshop. Access to that second floor was by way of an outside stairway rising out of a narrow side street. As Silk started up those stairs, a certain tension that Garion had not even been aware of seemed to flow out of his friend. "I *hate* not being able to talk freely," he said. "There are so many spies in Mal Zeth that every word you say here is delivered to Brador in triplicate before you get your mouth shut."

"There are bound to be spies around your office, too."

"Of course, but they can't hear anything. Yarblek and I had a solid foot of cork built into the floors, ceilings, and walls."

"Cork?"

"It muffles all sounds."

"Didn't that cost a great deal?"

Silk nodded. "But we made it all back during the first week we were here by managing to keep certain negotiations secret." He reached into an inside pocket and took out a large brass key. "Let's see if I can catch Dolmar with his hands in the cash box," he half whispered.

"Why? You already know that he's stealing from you."

"Certainly I do, but if I can catch him, I can reduce his year-end bonus."

"Why not just pick his pocket?"

Silk tapped the brass key against his cheek as he thought about it. "No," he decided finally. "That's not really good business. A relationship like this is founded on trust."

Garion began to laugh.

"You have to draw the line *somewhere*, Garion." Silk quietly slipped his brass key into the lock and slowly turned it. Then he abruptly shoved the door open and jumped into the room.

"Good morning, Prince Kheldar," the man seated behind a plain table said quite calmly. "I've been expecting you."

Silk looked a bit crestfallen.

The man sitting at the table was a thin Melcene with crafty, close-set eyes, thin lips, and scraggly, mud-brown hair. He had the kind of face that one instantly distrusts.

Silk straightened. "Good morning, Dolmar," he said. "This is Belgarion of Riva."

"Your Majesty." Dolmar rose and bowed.

"Dolmar."

Silk closed the door and pulled a pair of chairs out from the brown, cork-sheathed wall. Although the floor was of ordinary boards, the way that all sounds of walking or moving pieces of furniture were muted testified to the thickness of the cork lying beneath.

"How's business?" Silk asked, seating himself and pushing the other chair to Garion with his foot.

"We're paying the rent," Dolmar replied cautiously.

"I'm sure that the baker downstairs is overjoyed. Specifics, Dolmar. I've been away from Mal Zeth for quite a while. Stun me with how well my investments here are doing."

"We're up fifteen percent from last year."

"That's all?" Silk sounded disappointed.

"We've just made quite a large investment in inventory. If you take the current value of that into account, the number would be much closer to forty percent."

"That's more like it. Why are we accumulating inventory?"

"Yarblek's instructions. He's at Mal Camat right now arranging for ships to take the goods to the west. I expect that he'll be here in a week or so—he and that foulmouthed wench of his." Dolmar stood up, carefully gathered the documents from the table, and crossed to an iron stove sitting in the corner. He bent, opened the stove door, and calmly laid the parchment sheets on the small fire inside.

To Garion's amazement, Silk made no objection to his factor's blatant incendiarism. "We've been looking into the wool market," the Melcene reported as he returned to his now-empty table. "With the growing mobilization, the Bureau of Military Procurement is certain to need wool for uniforms, cloaks, and blankets. If we can buy up options from all the major sheep producers, we'll control the market and perhaps break the stranglehold that the Melcene consortium has on military purchases. If we can just get our foot in the door of the Bureau, I'm sure that we can get a chance to bid on all sorts of contracts."

Silk was pulling at his long, pointed nose, his eyes narrowed in thought. "Beans," he said shortly.

"I beg your pardon?"

"Look into the possibility of tying up this year's bean crop. A soldier can live in a worn-out uniform, but he has to eat. If we control the bean crop—and maybe coarse flour as well—the Bureau of Military Procurement won't have any choice. They'll *have* to come to us."

"Very shrewd, Prince Kheldar."

"I've been around for a while," Silk replied.

"The consortium is meeting this week in Melcene," the factor reported. "They'll be setting the prices of common items. We really want to get our hands on that price list if we can."

"I'm in the palace," Silk said. "Maybe I can pry it out of somebody."

"There's something else you should know, Prince Kheldar. Word has leaked out that the consortium is also going to propose certain regulations to Baron Vasca of the Bureau of Commerce. They'll present them under the guise of protecting the economy, but the fact of the matter is that they're aimed at you and Yarblek. They want to restrict western merchants who gross more than ten million a year to two or three enclaves on the west coast. That wouldn't inconvenience smaller merchants, but it would probably put us out of business."

"Can we bribe someone to put a stop to it?"

"We're already paying Vasca a fortune to leave us alone, but the consortium is throwing money around like water. It's possible that the baron won't stay bribed."

"Let me nose around inside the palace a bit," Silk said, "before you double Vasca's bribe or anything."

"Bribery's the standard procedure, Prince Kheldar."

"I know, but sometimes blackmail works even better." Silk looked over at Garion, then back at his factor. "What do you know about what's happening in Karanda?" he asked.

"Enough to know that it's disastrous for business. All sorts of perfectly respectable and otherwise sensible merchants are closing up their shops and flocking off to Calida to enlist in Mengha's army. Then they march around in circles singing 'Death to the Angaraks' while they wave rusty swords in the air."

"Any chance of selling them weapons?" Silk asked quickly.

"Probably not. There's not enough real money in northern Karanda to make it worthwhile to try to deal with them, and the political unrest has closed down all the mines. The market in gem stones has just about dried up."

Silk nodded glumly. "What's really going on up there, Dolmar?" he asked. "The reports Brador passed on to us were sort of sketchy."

"Mengha arrived at the gates of Calida with demons." The factor shrugged. "The Karands went into hysterics and then fell down in the throes of religious ecstasy."

"Brador told us about certain atrocities," Garion said.

"I expect that the reports he received were a trifle exaggerated, your Majesty," Dolmar replied. "Even the most well trained observer is likely to multiply mutilated corpses lying in the streets by ten. In point of fact, the vast majority of the casualties were either Melcene or Angarak. Mengha's demons rather scrupulously avoided killing Karands—except by accident. The same has held true in every city that he's taken so far." He scratched at his head, his close-set eyes narrowing. "It's really very shrewd, you know. The Karands see Mengha as a liberator and his demons as an invincible spearhead of their army. I can't swear to his *real* motives, but those barbarians up there believe that he's a savior come to sweep Karanda clean of Angaraks and the Melcene bureaucracy. Give him another six months or so, and he'll accomplish what no one has ever been able to do before."

"What's that?" Silk asked.

"Unify all of Karanda."

"Does he use his demons in the assault on every city he takes?" Garion asked, wanting to confirm what Brador had told them.

Dolmar shook his head. "Not anymore, your Majesty. After what happened at Calida and several other towns he took early in his campaign, he doesn't really have to. All he's been doing lately is marching up to the city. The demons are with him, of course, but they don't have to do anything but stand there looking awful. The Karands butcher all the Angaraks and Melcenes in town, throw open their gates, and welcome him with open arms. Then his demons vanish." He thought a moment. "He always has one particular one of them with him, though—a shadowy sort of creature that doesn't seem to be gigantic the way they're supposed to be. He stands directly behind Mengha's left shoulder at any public appearance."

A sudden thought occurred to Garion. "Are they desecrating Grolim temples?" he asked.

Dolmar blinked. "No," he replied with some surprise, "as a matter of fact, they're not—and there don't seem to be any Grolims among the dead, either. Of course it's possible that Urvon pulled all his Grolims out of Karanda when the trouble started."

"That's unlikely," Garion disagreed. "Mengha's arrival at Calida came without any kind of warning. The Grolims wouldn't have had time to escape." He stared up at the ceiling, thinking hard.

"What is it, Garion?" Silk asked.

"I just had a chilling sort of notion. We know that Mengha's a Grolim, right?"

"I didn't know that," Dolmar said with some surprise.

"We got a bit of inside information," Silk told him. "Go ahead, Garion."

"Urvon spends all of his time in Mal Yaska, doesn't he?"

Silk nodded. "So I've heard. He doesn't want Beldin to catch him out in the open."

"Wouldn't that make him a fairly ineffective leader? All right, then. Let's suppose that Mengha went through his period of despair after the death of Torak and then found a magician to teach him how to raise demons. When he comes back, he offers his former Grolim brethren an alternative to Urvon—along with access to a kind of power they'd never experienced before. A demon in the hands of an illiterate and fairly stupid Karandese magician is one thing, but a demon controlled by a Grolim sorcerer would be much worse, I think. If Mengha is gathering disaffected Grolims around him and training them in the use of magic, we have a *big* problem. I don't think I'd care to face a legion of Chabats, would you?"

Silk shuddered. "Not hardly," he replied fervently.

"He has to be uprooted then," Dolmar said, "and soon."

Garion made a sour face. " 'Zakath won't move until he gets his army back from Cthol Murgos—about three months from now."

"In three months, Mengha's going to be invincible," the factor told him.

"Then we'll have to move now," Garion said, "with 'Zakath or without him."

"How do you plan to get out of the city?" Silk asked.

"We'll let Belgarath work that out." Garion looked at Silk's agent. "Can you tell us anything else?" he asked.

Dolmar tugged at his nose in a curious imitation of Silk's habitual gesture. "It's only a rumor," he said.

"Go ahead."

"I've been getting some hints out of Karanda that Mengha's familiar demon is named Nahaz."

"Is that significant?"

"I can't be altogether sure, your Majesty. When the Grolims went into Karanda in the second millennium, they destroyed all traces of Karandese mythology, and no one has ever tried to record what few bits and pieces remained. All that's left is a hazy oral tradition, but the rumors I've heard say that Nahaz was the tribal demon of the original Karands who migrated into the region before the Angaraks came to Mallorea. The Karands follow Mengha not only because he's a political leader, but also because he's resurrected the closest thing they've ever had to a God of their own."

"A Demon Lord?" Garion asked him.

"That's a very good way to describe him, your Majesty. If the rumors are true, the demon Nahaz has almost unlimited power."

"I was afraid you were going to say that."

Later, when they were back out in the street, Garion looked curiously at Silk. "Why didn't you object when he burned those documents?" he asked.

"It's standard practice." The rat-faced man shrugged. "We never keep anything in writing. Dolmar has everything committed to memory."

"Doesn't that make it fairly easy for him to steal from you?"

"Of course, but he keeps his thievery within reasonable limits. If the Bureau of Taxation got its hands on written records, though, it could be a disaster. Do you want to go back to the palace now?"

Garion took out his list. "No," he said. "We've got to take care of this first." He looked glumly at the sheet. "I wonder how we're going to carry it all."

Silk glanced back over his shoulder at the two unobtrusive spies trailing along behind them. "Help is only a few paces away." He laughed. "As I said before, there are many uses for policemen."

During the next several days, Garion discovered that the imperial palace at Mal Zeth was unlike any court in the West. Since all power rested in 'Zakath's hands, the bureaucrats and palace functionaries contested with each other for the Emperor's favor and strove with oftentimes wildly complicated plots to discredit their enemies. The introduction of Silk, Velvet, and Sadi into this murky environment added whole new dimensions to palace intrigue. The trio rather casually pointed out the friendship between Garion and 'Zakath and let it be generally known that they had the Rivan King's complete trust. Then they sat back to await developments.

The officials and courtiers in the imperial palace were quick to grasp the significance and the opportunities implicit in this new route to the Emperor's ear. Perhaps even without formally discussing it, the trio of westerners neatly divided up the possible spheres of activity. Silk concentrated his attention on commercial matters, Velvet dabbled in politics, and Sadi delicately dipped his long-fingered hands into the world of high-level crime. Though all of them subtly let it be known that they were susceptible to bribery, they also expressed a willingness to pass along various requests in exchange for information. Thus, almost by accident, Garion found that he had a very efficient espionage apparatus at his disposal. Silk and Velvet manipulated the fears, ambitions, and open greed of those who contacted them with a musicianlike skill, delicately playing the increasingly nervous officials like well-tuned instruments. Sadi's methods, derived from his extensive experience in Salmissra's court, were in some instances even more subtle, but in others, painfully direct. The contents of his red leather case brought premium prices, and several high-ranking criminals, men who literally owned whole platoons of bureaucrats and even generals, quite suddenly died under suspicious circumstances—one of them even toppling over with a blackened face and bulging eyes in the presence of the Emperor himself.

'Zakath, who had watched the activities of the three with a certain veiled amusement, drew the line at that point. He spoke quite firmly with Garion about the matter during their customary evening meeting on the following day.

"I don't really mind what they're doing, Garion," he said, idly stroking the head of an orange kitten who lay purring in his lap. "They're confusing all the insects who scurry around in the dark corners of the palace, and a confused bug can't consolidate his position. I like to keep all these petty bootlickers frightened and off balance, since it makes it easier to control them. I really must object to poison, however. It's far too easy for an unskilled poisoner to make mistakes."

"Sadi could poison one specific person at a banquet with a hundred guests," Garion assured him.

"I have every confidence in his ability," 'Zakath agreed, "but the trouble is that he's not doing the actual poisoning himself. He's selling his concoctions to rank amateurs. There are *some* people here in the palace that I need. Their identities are general knowledge, and that keeps the daggers out of their entrails. A mistake with some poison, however, could wipe out whole branches of my government. Could you ask him not to sell any more of it here in the palace? I'd speak to him personally, but I don't want it to seem like an official reprimand."

"I'll have a talk with him," Garion promised.

"I'd appreciate it, Garion." The Emperor's eyes grew sly. "Just the poisons, though. I find the effects of some of his other compounds rather amusing. Just yesterday, I saw an eighty-five-year-old general in hot pursuit of a young chambermaid. The old fool hasn't had that kind of thought for a quarter of a century. And the day before that, the Chief of the Bureau of Public Works—a pompous ass who makes me sick just to look at him—tried for a solid half hour in front of dozens of witnesses to walk up the side of a building. I haven't laughed so hard in years."

"Nyissan elixirs do strange things to people." Garion smiled. "I'll ask Sadi to confine his dealings to recreational drugs."

"Recreational drugs," 'Zakath laughed. "I like that description."

"I've always had a way with words," Garion replied modestly.

The orange kitten rose, yawned, and jumped down from the Emperor's lap. The mackerel-tabby mother cat promptly caught a black and white kitten by the scruff of the neck and deposited it exactly where the orange one had been lying. Then she looked at 'Zakath's face and meowed questioningly.

"Thank you," 'Zakath murmured to her.

Satisfied, the cat jumped down, caught the orange kitten, and began to bathe it, holding it down with one paw.

"Does she do that all the time?" Garion asked.

'Zakath nodded. "She's busy being a mother, but she doesn't want me to get lonely."

"That's considerate of her."

'Zakath looked at the black and white kitten in his lap, who had all four paws wrapped around his hand and was gnawing on one of his knuckles in mock ferocity. "I think I could learn to survive without it," he said, wincing.

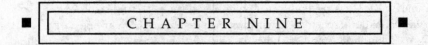

CHAPTER NINE

The simplest way to avoid the omnipresent spies infesting the imperial palace was to conduct any significant conversations out in the open, and so Garion frequently found himself strolling around the palace grounds with one or more of his companions. On a beautiful spring morning a few days later he walked with Belgarath and Polgara through the dappled shade of a cherry orchard, listening to Velvet's latest report on the political intrigues which seethed through the corridors of 'Zakath's palace.

"The surprising thing is that Brador is probably aware of most of what's going

on," the blond girl told them. "He doesn't *look* all that efficient, but his secret police are everywhere." Velvet was holding a spray of cherry blossoms in front of her
face, rather ostentatiously inhaling their fragrance.

"At least they can't hear us out here," Garion said.

"No, but they can *see* us. If I were you, Belgarion, I still wouldn't talk too
openly—even out of doors. I happened to come across one industrious fellow yesterday who was busily writing down every word of a conversation being conducted
in whispers some fifty yards away."

"That's a neat trick," Belgarath said. "How did he manage it?"

"He's stone-deaf," she replied. "Over the years, he's learned to understand what
people are saying by reading the shape of the words from their lips."

"Clever," the old man murmured. "Is that why you're so busily sniffing cherry
blossoms?"

She nodded with a dimpled smile. "That and the fact that they have such a
lovely fragrance."

He scratched at his beard, his hand covering his mouth. "All right," he said.
"What I need is some sort of disruption—something to draw Brador's police off so
that we can slip out of Mal Zeth without being followed. 'Zakath is rock hard on
the point of not doing anything until his army gets back from Cthol Murgos, so it's
obvious that we're going to have to move without him. Is there anything afoot that
might distract all the spies around here?"

"Not really, Ancient One. The petty kinglet of Pallia and the Prince Regent of
Delchin are scheming against each other, but that's been going on for years. The old
King of Voresebo is trying to get imperial aid in wresting his throne back from his
son, who deposed him a year or so ago. Baron Vasca, the Chief of the Bureau of
Commerce, is trying to assimilate the Bureau of Military Procurement, but the generals have him stalemated. Those are the major things in the air right now. There
are a number of minor plots going on as well, but nothing earthshaking enough to
divert the spies who are watching us."

"Can you stir anything up?" Polgara asked, her lips scarcely moving.

"I can try, Lady Polgara," Velvet replied, "but Brador is right on top of everything that's happening here in the palace. I'll talk with Kheldar and Sadi. It's remotely possible that the three of us can engineer something unexpected enough to
give us a chance to slip out of the city."

"It's getting fairly urgent, Liselle," Polgara said. "If Zandramas finds what she's
looking for at Ashaba, she'll be off again, and we'll wind up trailing along behind
her in the same way that we were back in Cthol Murgos."

"I'll see what we can come up with, my lady," Velvet promised.

"Are you going back inside?" Belgarath asked her.

She nodded.

"I'll go with you." He looked around distastefully. "All this fresh air and exercise is a little too wholesome for my taste."

"Walk a bit farther with me, Garion," Polgara said.

"All right."

As Velvet and Belgarath turned back toward the east wing of the palace,

Garion and his aunt strolled on along the neatly trimmed green lawn lying beneath the blossom-covered trees. A wren, standing on the topmost twig of a gnarled, ancient tree, sang as if his heart would burst.

"What's he singing about?" Garion asked, suddenly remembering his aunt's unusual affinity for birds.

"He's trying to attract the attention of a female," she replied, smiling gently. "It's that time of year again. He's being very eloquent and making all sorts of promises—most of which he'll break before the summer's over."

He smiled and affectionately put his arm about her shoulders.

She sighed happily. "This is pleasant," she said. "For some reason when we're apart, I still think of you as a little boy. It always sort of surprises me to find that you've grown so tall."

There wasn't too much that he could say to that. "How's Durnik?" he asked. "I almost never see him these days."

"He and Toth and Eriond managed to find a well-stocked trout pond on the southern end of the imperial grounds," she replied with a slightly comical upward roll of her eyes. "They're catching large numbers of fish, but the kitchen staff is beginning to get a bit surly about the whole thing."

"Trust Durnik to find water." Garion laughed. "Is Eriond actually fishing too? That seems a little out of character for him."

"I don't think he's very serious about it. He goes along mostly for Durnik's company, I think—and because he likes to be outside." She paused and then looked directly at him. As so many times in the past, he was suddenly struck to the heart by her luminous beauty. "How has Ce'Nedra been lately?" she asked him.

"She's managed to locate a number of young ladies to keep her company," he replied. "No matter where we go, she's always able to surround herself with companions."

"Ladies like to have other ladies about them, dear," she said. "Men are nice enough, I suppose, but a woman needs other women to talk to. There are so many important things that men just don't understand." Her face grew serious. "There hasn't been any recurrence of what happened in Cthol Murgos, then?" she asked.

"Not so far as I can tell. She seems fairly normal to me. About the only unusual thing I've noticed is that she never talks about Geran anymore."

"That could just be her way of protecting herself, Garion. She might not be able to put it into words exactly, but she's aware of the melancholia that came over her at Prolgu, and I'm sure that she realizes that if she gives in to it, she'll be incapacitated. She still thinks about Geran, I'm sure—probably most of the time—but she just won't talk about him." She paused again. "What about the physical side of your marriage?" she asked him directly.

Garion blushed furiously and coughed. "Uh—there really hasn't been much opportunity for that sort of thing, Aunt Pol—and I think she has too many other things on her mind."

She pursed her lips thoughtfully. "It's not a good idea just to ignore that, Garion," she told him. "After a while, people grow apart if they don't periodically renew their intimacy."

He coughed again, still blushing. "She doesn't really seem very interested, Aunt Pol."

"That's your fault, dear. All it takes is a little bit of planning and attention to detail."

"You make it sound awfully calculated and cold-blooded."

"Spontaneity is very nice, dear, but there's a great deal of charm to a well-planned seduction, too."

"Aunt Pol!" he gasped, shocked to the core.

"You're an adult, Garion dear," she reminded him, "and that's one of an adult man's responsibilities. Think about it. You can be quite resourceful at times. I'm sure you'll come up with something." She looked out over the sun-washed lawns. "Shall we go back inside now?" she suggested. "I think it's almost lunch time."

That afternoon, Garion once again found himself strolling about the palace grounds, this time accompanied by Silk and Sadi the eunuch. "Belgarath needs a diversion," he told them seriously. "I think he has a plan to get us out of the city, but we've got to shake off all the spies who are watching us long enough for him to put it into motion." He was busily scratching at his nose as he spoke, his hand covering his mouth.

"Hay fever?" Silk asked him.

"No. Velvet told us that some of Brador's spies are deaf, but that they can tell what you're saying by watching your lips."

"What an extraordinary gift," Sadi murmured. "I wonder if an undeaf man could learn it."

"I can think of some times myself when it might have been useful," Silk agreed, covering his mouth as he feigned a cough. He looked at Sadi. "Can I get an honest answer out of you?" he asked.

"That depends on the question, Kheldar."

"You're aware of the secret language?"

"Of course."

"Do you understand it?"

"I'm afraid not. I've never met a Drasnian who trusted me enough to teach me."

"I wonder why."

Sadi flashed him a quick grin.

"I think we can manage if we cover our mouths when we speak," Garion said.

"Won't that become a little obvious after a while?" Sadi objected.

"What are they going to do? Tell us to stop?"

"Probably not, but we might want to pass on some disinformation sometimes, and if they know that we know about this way of listening, we won't be able to do that." The eunuch sighed about the lost opportunity, then shrugged. "Oh, well," he said.

Garion looked at Silk. "Do you know of anything that's going on that we could use to pull the police off our trail?"

"No, not really," the little man replied. "At the moment the Melcene consortium seems to be concentrating on keeping this year's price list a secret and trying to persuade Baron Vasca that Yarblek and I should be restrained to those enclaves on the west coast. We've got Vasca pretty much in our pockets, though—as long as he stays bribed. There's a great deal of secret maneuvering going on, but I don't think anything is close to coming to a head right now. Even if it did, it probably wouldn't cause a big enough stink to make the secret police abandon their assignment to watch us."

"Why not go right to the top?" Sadi suggested. "I could talk to Brador and see if he's susceptible to bribery."

"I don't think so," Garion said. "He's having us watched on specific orders from 'Zakath. I doubt that any amount of money would make him consider risking his head."

"There are other ways to bribe people, Belgarion." Sadi smiled slyly. "I have some things in my case that make people feel *very* good. The only trouble with them is that after you've used them a few times, you have to keep on using them. The pain of stopping is really quite unbearable. I could *own* Brador within the space of a week and make him do anything I told him to do."

Garion felt a sudden surge of profound distaste for the entire notion. "I'd really rather not do that," he said, "or only as a last resort."

"You Alorns have a peculiar notion of morality," the eunuch said, rubbing at his shaved scalp. "You chop people in two without turning a hair, but you get queasy at the idea of poisons or drugs."

"It's a cultural thing, Sadi," Silk told him.

"Have you found anything else that might work to our advantage?" Garion asked.

Sadi considered it. "Not by itself, no," he replied. "A bureaucracy lends itself to endemic corruption, though. There are a number of people in Mallorea who take advantage of that. Caravans have a habit of getting waylaid in the Dalasian Mountains or on the road from Maga Renn. A caravan needs a permit from the Bureau of Commerce, and Vasca has been known on occasion to sell information about departure times and routes to certain robber chiefs. Or, if the price is right, he sells his silence to the merchant barons in Melcene." The eunuch chuckled. "Once he sold information about one single caravan to three separate robber bands. There was a pitched battle on the plains of Delchin, or so I'm told."

Garion's eyes narrowed in thought. "I'm beginning to get the feeling that we might want to concentrate our attention on this Baron Vasca," he said. "Velvet told us that he's *also* trying to take the Bureau of Military Procurement away from the army."

"I didn't know that," Silk said with some surprise. "Little Liselle is developing quite rapidly, isn't she?"

"It's the dimples, Prince Kheldar," Sadi said. "I'm almost totally immune to any kind of feminine blandishment, but I have to admit that when she smiles at me, my knees turn to butter. She's absolutely adorable—and totally unscrupulous, of course."

Silk nodded. "Yes," he said. "We're moderately proud of her."

"Why don't you two go look her up?" Garion suggested. "Pool your information about this highly corruptible Baron Vasca. Maybe we can stir something up—

something noisy. Open fighting in the halls of the palace might just be the sort of thing we need to cover our escape."

"You have a genuine flair for politics, Belgarion," Sadi said admiringly.

"I'm a quick learner," Garion admitted, "and, of course, I keep company with some very disreputable men."

"Thank you, your Majesty," the eunuch replied with mock appreciation.

Shortly after supper, Garion walked through the halls of the palace for his customary evening conversation with 'Zakath. As always, a soft-footed secret policeman trailed along some distance behind.

'Zakath's mood that evening was pensive—almost approaching the bleak, icy melancholy that had marked him back in Rak Hagga.

"Bad day?" Garion asked him, removing a sleeping kitten from the carpet-covered footstool in front of his chair. Then he leaned back and set his feet on the stool.

'Zakath made a sour face. "I've been whittling away at all the work that piled up while I was in Cthol Murgos," he said. "The problem is that now that I'm back, the pile just keeps getting higher."

"I know the feeling," Garion agreed. "When I get back to Riva, it's probably going to take me a year to clear my desk. Are you open to a suggestion?"

"Suggest away, Garion. Right now, I'll listen to anything." He looked reprovingly at the black and white kitten who was biting his knuckles again. "Not so hard," he murmured, tapping the ferocious little beast on the nose with his forefinger.

The kitten laid back its ears and growled a squeaky little growl at him.

"I'm not trying to be offensive or anything," Garion began cautiously, "but I think you're making the same mistake that Urgit made."

"That's an interesting observation. Go on."

"It seems to me that you need to reorganize your government."

'Zakath blinked. "Now, that *is* a major proposal," he said. "I don't get the connection, though. Urgit was a hopeless incompetent—at least he was before you came along and taught him the fundamentals of ruling. What is this mistake that he and I have in common?"

"Urgit's a coward," Garion said, "and probably always will be. You're not a coward—sometimes a bit crazy, maybe, but never a coward. The problem is that you're both making the same mistake. You're trying to make all the decisions yourselves—even the little ones. Even if you stop sleeping altogether, you won't find enough hours in the day to do that."

"So I've noticed. What's the solution?"

"Delegate responsibility. Your Bureau Chiefs and generals are competent—corrupt, I'll grant you, but they know their jobs. Tell them to take care of things and only bring you the major decisions. And tell them that if anything goes wrong, you'll replace them."

"That's not the Angarak way, Garion. The ruler—or Emperor, in this case—has always made all decisions. It's been that way since before the cracking of the world. Torak made every decision in antiquity, and the Emperors of Mallorea have followed that example—no matter what we may have felt about him personally."

"Urgit made the exact same mistake," Garion told him. "What you're both forgetting is that Torak was a God, and his mind and will were unlimited. Human beings can't possibly hope to imitate that sort of thing."

"None of my Bureau Chiefs or generals could be trusted with that kind of authority," 'Zakath said, shaking his head. "They're almost out of control as it is."

"They'll learn the limits," Garion assured him. "After a few of them have been demoted or dismissed, the rest will get the idea."

'Zakath smiled bleakly. "That is also not the Angarak way, Garion. When I make an example of someone, it usually involves the headsman's block."

"That's an internal matter, of course," Garion admitted. "You know your people better than I do, but if a man has talent, you can't really call on him again if you've removed his head, can you? Don't waste talent, 'Zakath. It's too hard to come by."

"You know something?" 'Zakath said with a slightly amused look. "They call me the man of ice, but in spite of your mild-seeming behavior, you're even more cold-blooded than I am. You're the most practical man I've ever met."

"I was raised in Sendaria, 'Zakath," Garion reminded him. "Practicality is a religion there. I learned to run a kingdom from a man named Faldor. A kingdom is very much like a farm, really. Seriously, though, the major goal of any ruler is to keep things from flying apart, and gifted subordinates are too valuable a resource to waste. I've had to reprimand a few people, but that's as far as it ever went. That way they were still around in case I needed them. You might want to think about that a little bit."

"I'll consider it." 'Zakath straightened. "By the way," he said, "speaking of corruption in government—"

"Oh? Were we speaking about that?"

"We're about to. My Bureau Chiefs are all more or less dishonest, but your three friends are adding levels of sophistication to the petty scheming and deceit here in the palace that we're not really prepared to cope with."

"Oh?"

"The lovely Margravine Liselle has actually managed to persuade the King of Pallia *and* the Prince Regent of Delchin that she's going to intercede with you in their behalf. Each of them is absolutely convinced that their long-term squabble is about to come out into the open. I don't want them to declare war on each other. I've got trouble in Karanda already."

"I'll have a word with her," Garion promised.

"And Prince Kheldar virtually owns whole floors of the Bureau of Commerce. He's getting more information out of there than I am. The merchants in Melcene gather every year to set prices for just about everything that's sold in Mallorea. It's the most closely guarded secret in the empire, and Kheldar just bought it. He's deliberately undercutting those prices, and he's disrupting our whole economy."

Garion frowned. "He didn't mention that."

"I don't mind his making a reasonable profit—as long as he pays his taxes—but I can't really have him gaining absolute control over all commerce in Mallorea, can I? He *is* an Alorn, after all, and his political loyalties are a little obscure."

"I'll suggest that he moderate his practices a bit. You have to understand Silk, though. I don't believe he even cares about the money. All he's interested in is the game."

"It's still Sadi who concerns me the most, though."

"Oh?"

"He's become rather intensely involved in agriculture."

"Sadi?"

"There's a certain plant that grows wild in the marshes of Camat. Sadi's paying a great deal for it, and one of our prominent bandit chiefs has put all of his men to work harvesting it—and protecting the crop, of course. There have already been some pitched battles up there, I understand."

"A bandit who's harvesting crops is too busy to be robbing travelers on the highways, though," Garion pointed out.

"That's not exactly the point, Garion. I didn't mind so much when Sadi was making a few officials feel good and act foolish, but he's importing this plant into the city by the wagon load and spreading it around through the work force—and the army. I don't care for the idea at all."

"I'll see what I can do to get him to suspend operations," Garion agreed. Then he looked at the Mallorean Emperor through narrowed eyes. "You do realize, though, that if I rein the three of them in, they'll just switch over to something new—and probably just as disruptive. Wouldn't it be better if I just took them out of Mal Zeth entirely?"

'Zakath smiled. "Nice try, Garion," he said, "but I don't think so. I think we'll just wait until my army gets back from Cthol Murgos. Then we can all ride out of Mal Zeth together."

"You are the most stubborn man I've ever met," Garion said with some heat. "Can't you get it through your head that time is slipping away from us? This delay could be disastrous—not only for you and me, but for the whole world."

"The fabled meeting between the Child of Light and the Child of Dark again? I'm sorry, Garion, but Zandramas is just going to have to wait for you. I don't want you and Belgarath roaming at will through my empire. I *like* you, Garion, but I don't altogether trust you."

Garion's temper began to heat up. He thrust his jaw out pugnaciously as he rose to his feet. "My patience is starting to wear a little thin, 'Zakath. I've tried to keep things between us more or less civil, but there *is* a limit, and we're getting rather close to it. I am *not* going to lie around your palace for three months."

"That's where you're wrong," 'Zakath snapped, also rising to his feet and unceremoniously dumping the surprised kitten to the floor.

Garion ground his teeth together, trying to get his temper under control. "Up to now, I've been polite, but I'd like to remind you about what happened back at Rak Hagga. We can leave here any time we want to, you know."

"And the minute you do, you're going to have three of my regiments right on your heels." 'Zakath was shouting now.

"Not for very long," Garion replied ominously.

"What are you going to do?" 'Zakath demanded scornfully. "Turn all my troops into toads or something? No, Garion, I know you well enough to know that you wouldn't do that."

Garion straightened. "You're right," he said, "I wouldn't, but I was thinking of something a bit more elemental. Torak used the Orb to crack the world, remember? I know how it was done and I could do it myself if I had to. Your troops are going to have a great deal of trouble following us if they suddenly run into a trench—ten miles deep and fifty miles wide—stretching all the way across the middle of Mallorea."

"You wouldn't!" 'Zakath gasped.

"Try me." With a tremendous effort, Garion brought his anger under control. "I think perhaps it's time for us to break this off," he said. "We're starting to shout threats at each other like a pair of schoolboys. Why don't we continue this conversation some other time, after we've both had a chance to cool off a bit?"

He could see a hot retort hovering on 'Zakath's lips, but then the Emperor also drew himself up and regained his composure, though his face was still pale with anger. "I think perhaps you're right," he said.

Garion nodded curtly and started toward the door.

"Garion," 'Zakath said then.

"Yes?"

"Sleep well."

"You too." Garion left the room.

Her Imperial Highness, the Princess Ce'Nedra, Queen of Riva and beloved of Belgarion, Overlord of the West, was feeling pecky. "Pecky" was not a word that her Imperial Highness would normally have used to describe her mood. "Disconsolate" or "out of sorts" might have had a more aristocratic ring, but Ce'Nedra was honest enough with herself privately to admit that "pecky" probably came closer to the mark. She moved irritably from room to room in the luxurious apartment 'Zakath had provided for her and Garion with the hem of her favorite teal-green dressing gown trailing along behind her bare feet. She suddenly wished that breaking a few dishes wouldn't appear quite so unlady-like.

A chair got in her way. She almost kicked it, but remembered at the last instant that she was not wearing shoes. Instead she deliberately took the cushion from the chair and set it on the floor. She plumped it a few times, then straightened. She lifted the hem of her dressing gown to her knees, squinted, swung her leg a few times for practice, and then kicked the cushion completely across the room. "There!" she said. "Take that!" For some reason it made her feel a little better.

Garion was away from their rooms at the moment, engaged in his customary evening conversation with Emperor 'Zakath. Ce'Nedra wished that he were here so that she could pick a fight with him. A nice little fight right now might modify her mood.

She went through a door and looked at the steaming tub sunk in the floor. Perhaps a bath might help. She even went so far as to dip an exploratory toe in the water, then decided against it. She sighed and moved on. She paused for a few moments at the window of the unlighted sitting room that overlooked the verdant atrium at the center of the east wing of the palace. The full moon had risen early that day and stood high in the sky, filling the atrium with its pale, colorless light, and the pool at the center of the private little court reflected back the perfect white circle of the queen of the night. Ce'Nedra stood for quite some time, looking out the window, lost in thought.

She heard the door open and then slam shut. "Ce'Nedra, where are you?" Garion's voice sounded a trifle testy.

"I'm in here, dear."

"Why are you standing around in the dark?" he asked, coming into the room.

"I was just looking at the moon. Do you realize that it's the same moon that shines down on Tol Honeth—and Riva, too, for that matter?"

"I hadn't really thought about it," he replied shortly.

"Why are you being so grumpy with me?"

"It's not you, Ce'Nedra," he answered apologetically. "I had another fight with 'Zakath, is all."

"That's getting to be a habit."

"Why is he so unreasonably stubborn?" Garion demanded.

"That's part of the nature of Kings and Emperors, dear."

"What's that supposed to mean?"

"Nothing."

"Do you want something to drink? I think we've still got some of that wine left."

"I don't think so. Not right now."

"Well I do. After my little chat with his pigheaded imperialness, I need something to calm my nerves." He went back out, and she heard the clink of a decanter against the rim of a goblet.

Out in the moon-bright atrium something moved out from the shadows of the tall, broad-leafed trees. It was Silk. He was wearing only his shirt and hose, he had a bath sheet over his shoulder, and he was whistling. He bent at the edge of the pool and dipped his fingers into the water. Then he stood up and began to unbutton his shirt.

Ce'Nedra smiled, drew back behind the drape, and watched as the little man disrobed. Then he stepped down into the pool, shattering the reflected moon into a thousand sparkling fragments. Ce'Nedra continued to watch as he lazily swam back and forth in the moon-dappled water.

Then there was another shadow under the trees, and Liselle came out into the moonlight. She wore a loose-fitting robe, and there was a flower in her hair. The flower was undoubtedly red, but the wan light of the full spring moon leeched away the color, making it appear black against the blond girl's pale hair. "How's the water?" she asked quite calmly. Her voice seemed very close, almost as if she were in the same room with the watching Ce'Nedra.

Silk gave a startled exclamation, then coughed as his mouth and nose filled with water. He spluttered, then recovered his composure. "Not bad," he replied in an unruffled tone.

"Good," Liselle said. She moved to the edge of the pool. "Kheldar, I think it's time that we had a talk."

"Oh? About what?"

"About this." Quite calmly she unbelted her robe and let it fall to the ground about her feet.

She wasn't wearing anything under the robe.

"You seem to have a little difficulty grasping the idea that things change with the passage of time," she continued, dipping one foot into the water. Quite deliberately, she pointed at herself. "This is one of those things."

"I noticed that," he said admiringly.

"I'm so glad. I was beginning to be afraid that your eyes might be failing." She stepped down into the pool and stood waist-deep in the water. "Well?" she said then.

"Well what?"

"What do you plan to do about it?" She reached up and took the flower from her hair and carefully laid it on the surface of the pool.

Ce'Nedra darted to the door on silent, bare feet. "Garion!" she called in an urgent whisper. "Come here!"

"Why?"

"Keep your voice down and come here."

He grumbled slightly and came into the darkened room. "What is it?"

She pointed at the window with a muffled giggle. "Look!" she commanded in a delighted little whisper.

Garion went to the window and looked out. After a single glance, he quickly averted his eyes. "Oh, my," he said in a strangled whisper.

Ce'Nedra giggled again, came to his side, and burrowed her way under his arm. "Isn't that sweet?" she said softly.

"I'm sure it is," he whispered back, "but I don't think we ought to watch."

"Why not?"

The flower Liselle had laid on the water had floated across the intervening space, and Silk, his expression bemused, picked it up and smelled it. "Yours, I believe," he said, holding it out to the pale-skinned girl sharing the pool with him.

"Why, yes, I believe it is," she replied. "But you haven't answered my question."

"Which question?"

"What are you going to do about this?"

"I'll think of something."

"Good. I'll help you."

Garion firmly reached out and pulled the drape shut.

"Spoilsport," Ce'Nedra pouted.

"Never mind," he told her. "Now come away from the window." He drew her out of the room. "I can't understand what she's up to," he said.

"I thought that was fairly obvious."

"Ce'Nedra!"

"She's seducing him, Garion. She's been in love with him since she was a little girl and she's finally decided to take steps. I'm so happy for her that I could just burst."

He shook his head. "I will *never* understand women," he said. "Just when I think I've got everything worked out, you all get together and change the rules. You wouldn't believe what Aunt Pol said to me just this morning."

"Oh? What was that?"

"She said that I ought to—" He stopped abruptly, his face suddenly going beet red. "Ah—never mind," he added lamely.

"What was it?"

"I'll tell you some other time." He gave her a peculiar look then. It was a look she thought she recognized. "Have you taken your evening bath yet?" he asked with exaggerated casualness.

"Not yet. Why?"

"I thought I might join you—if you don't mind."

Ce'Nedra artfully lowered her lashes. "If you really want to," she said in a girlish voice.

"I'll light some candles in there," he said. "The lamp's a bit bright, don't you think?"

"Whatever you prefer, dear."

"And I think I'll bring in the wine, too. It might help us to relax."

Ce'Nedra felt an exultant little surge of triumph. For some reason her irritability had entirely disappeared. "I think that would be just lovely, dear."

"Well," he said, extending a slightly trembling hand to her, "shall we go in, then?"

"Why don't we?"

CHAPTER TEN

The following morning when they gathered for breakfast, Silk's expression was faintly abstracted as if he had just realized that someone had somehow outbargained him. The little man steadfastly refused to look at Velvet, who kept her eyes demurely on the bowl of strawberries and cream she was eating.

"You seem a trifle out of sorts this morning, Prince Kheldar," Ce'Nedra said to him in an offhand manner, though her eyes sparkled with suppressed mirth. "Whatever is the matter?"

He threw her a quick, suspicious look.

"There, there," she said, fondly patting his hand. "I'm sure that you'll feel much better after breakfast."

"I'm not very hungry," he replied. His voice was just a little sullen. He stood up abruptly. "I think I'll go for a walk," he said.

"But my dear fellow," she protested, "you haven't eaten your strawberries. They're absolutely delicious, aren't they, Liselle?"

"Marvelous," the blond girl agreed with only the faintest hint of her dimples showing.

Silk's scowl deepened, and he marched resolutely toward the door.

"May I have yours, Kheldar?" Velvet called after him. "If you're not going to eat them, that is?"

He slammed the door as he went out, and Ce'Nedra and Velvet exploded into gales of silvery laughter.

"What's this?" Polgara asked them.

"Oh, nothing," Ce'Nedra said, still laughing. "Nothing at all, Lady Polgara. Our Prince Kheldar had a little adventure last night that didn't turn out exactly the way he expected it to."

Velvet gave Ce'Nedra a quick look and flushed slightly. Then she laughed again.

Polgara looked at the giggling pair, and then one of her eyebrows went up. "Oh. I see," she said.

The flush on Velvet's cheeks grew rosier, although she continued to laugh.

"Oh, dear." Polgara sighed.

"Is something wrong, Pol?" Durnik asked her.

She looked at the good, honest man, assessing his strict Sedarian principles. "Just a small complication, Durnik," she replied, "Nothing that can't be managed."

"That's good." He pushed back his bowl. "Do you need me for anything this morning?"

"No, dear," she replied, kissing him.

He returned her kiss and then stood up, looking across the table at Toth and Eriond, who sat waiting expectantly. "Shall we go then?" he asked them.

The three of them trooped out, their faces alight with anticipation.

"I wonder how long it's going to take them to empty all the fish out of that pond," Polgara mused.

"Forever, I'm afraid, Lady Polgara," Sadi told her, popping a strawberry into his mouth. "The grounds keepers restock it every night."

She sighed. "I was afraid of that," she said.

About midmorning, Garion was pacing up and down one of the long, echoing halls. He felt irritable, and a sort of frustrated impatience seemed to weigh him down. The urgent need to get to Ashaba before Zandramas escaped him again was so constantly on his mind now that he could think of almost nothing else. Although they had come up with several possible schemes, Silk, Velvet, and Sadi were still searching for a suitable diversion—something startling enough to draw off Brador's secret policemen so that they could all make good their escape. There was obviously little chance of changing 'Zakath's mind, and it began to look increasingly as if Garion and his friends were going to have to "do it the other way," as Belgarath sometimes put it. Despite his occasional threats to 'Zakath, Garion didn't really want to do that. He was quite sure that to do so would permanently end his growing friendship with the strange man who ruled Mallorea. He was honest enough to admit that it was not only the friendship he would regret losing but the political possibilities implicit in the situation as well.

He was about to return to his rooms when a scarlet-liveried servant came up to him. "Your Majesty," the servant said with a deep bow, "Prince Kheldar asked me to find you for him. He'd like to have a word with you."

"Where is he?" Garion asked.

"In the formal garden near the north wall of the complex, your Majesty. There's a half-drunk Nadrak with him—and a woman with a remarkably foul mouth. You wouldn't believe some of the things she said to me."

"I think I know her," Garion replied with a faint smile. "I'd believe it." He turned then and walked briskly through the hallways and out into the palace grounds.

Yarblek had not changed. Though it was pleasantly warm in the neatly manicured formal garden, he nonetheless still wore his shabby felt overcoat and his shaggy fur hat. He was sprawled on a marble bench under a leafy arbor with a broached ale keg conveniently at hand. Vella, as lush as ever, wandered idly among the flower beds, dressed in her tight-fitting Nadrak vest and leather trousers. Her silver-hilted daggers protruded from the tops of her boots and from her belt, and her walk was still that same challenging, sensual strut, a mannerism she had practiced for so long that it was by now automatic and probably even unconscious. Silk sat on the grass near Yarblek's bench, and he, too, held an ale cup.

"I was just about to come looking for you," he said as Garion approached.

The rangy Yarblek squinted at Garion. "Well, well," he said, blinking owlishly, "if it isn't the boy-King of Riva. I see that you're still wearing that big sword of yours."

"It's a habit," Garion shrugged. "You're looking well, Yarblek—aside from being a little drunk, that is."

"I've been cutting down," Yarblek said rather piously. "My stomach isn't what it used to be."

"Did you happen to see Belgarath on your way here?" Silk asked Garion.

"No. Should I have?"

"I sent for him, too. Yarblek's got some information for us, and I want the old man to get it firsthand."

Garion looked at Silk's coarse-faced partner. "How long have you been in Mal Zeth?" he asked.

"We got in last night," Yarblek replied, dipping his cup into the ale keg again. "Dolmar told me that you were all here in the palace, so I came by this morning to look you up."

"How long are you going to stay in town?" Silk asked him.

Yarblek tugged at his scraggly beard and squinted up at the arbor. "That's kind of hard to say," he said. "Dolmar picked up *most* of what I need, but I want to nose around the markets a bit. There's a Tolnedran in Boktor who said that he's interested in uncut gem stones. I could pick up a quick fortune on that transaction— particularly if I could sneak the stones past Drasnian customs."

"Don't Queen Porenn's customs agents search your packs pretty thoroughly?" Garion asked him.

"From top to bottom," Yarblek laughed, "And they pat me down as well. They *don't*, however, lay one finger on Vella. They've all learned how quick she is with her daggers. I've made back what I paid for her a dozen times over by hiding little packages here and there in her clothes." He laughed coarsely. "And of course the hiding is sort of fun, too." He belched thunderously. "Par'me," he said.

Belgarath came across the lawn. The old man had resisted all of 'Zakath's tactful offers of less disreputable raiment, and still wore, defiantly, Garion thought, his stained tunic, patched hose, and mismatched boots. "Well, I see that you finally got here," he said to Yarblek without any preamble.

"I got tied up in Mal Camat," the Nadrak replied. "Kal Zakath is commandeering ships all up and down the west coast to bring his army back from stinking Cthol Murgos. I had to hire boats and hide them in the marshes north of the ruins of Cthol Mishrak." He pointed at the ale keg. "You want some of this?" he asked.

"Naturally. Have you got another cup?"

Yarblek patted here and there at his voluminous coat, reached into an inside pocket, and drew out a squat, dented tankard.

"I like a man who comes prepared."

"A proper host is always ready. Help yourself. Just try not to spill too much." The Nadrak looked at Garion. "How about you?" he asked. "I think I could find another cup."

"No. Thanks anyway, Yarblek. It's a little early for me."

Then a short, gaudily dressed man came around the arbor. His clothes were a riot of frequently conflicting colors. One sleeve was green, the other red. One leg of his hose was striped in pink and yellow and the other covered with large blue polka dots. He wore a tall, pointed cap with a bell attached to the peak. It was not his outrageous clothing that was so surprising, however. What caught Garion's eye first was the fact that the man was quite casually walking on his hands with both feet extended into the air. "Did I hear somebody offer somebody a little drap of somethin' to drink" he asked in a strange, lilting brogue that Garion did not quite recognize.

Yarblek gave the colorful little fellow a sour look and reached inside his coat again.

The acrobat flexed his shoulders, thrusting himself into the air, flipped over in midair, and landed on his feet. He briskly brushed off his hands and came toward Yarblek with an ingratiating smile. His face was nondescript, the kind of face that would be forgotten almost as soon as it was seen, but for some reason, it seemed to Garion to be naggingly familiar.

"Ah, good Master Yarblek," the man said to Silk's partner, "I'm sure that yer the kindest man alive. I was near to perishin' of thirst, don't y' know?" He took the cup, dipped into the ale keg, and drank noisily. Then he let out his breath with a gusty sound of appreciation. " 'Tis a good brew ye have there, Master Yarblek," he said, dipping again into the keg.

Belgarath had a peculiar expression on his face, partly puzzled but at the same time partially amused.

"He came tagging along when we left Mal Camat," Yarblek told them. "Vella finds him amusing, so I haven't chased him off yet. She turns a little shrill when she doesn't get her own way."

"The name is Feldegast, fine gentlemen," the gaudy little fellow introduced himself with an exaggerated bow. "Feldegast the juggler. I be also an acrobat—as ye've seen fer yerselves—a comedian of no mean ability, and an accomplished magician. I can baffle yer eyes with me unearthly skill at prestidigitation, don't y' know. I kin also play rousin' tunes on a little wooden whistle—or, if yer mood be melancholy, I kin play ye sad songs on the lute to bring a lump to yer throat and fill yer eyes with sweet, gentle tears. Would ye be wantin' to witness some of me unspeakable talent?"

"Maybe a little later," Belgarath told him, his eyes still a little bemused. "Right now we have some business to discuss."

"Take another cup of ale and go entertain Vella, comedian," Yarblek said to him. "Tell her some more off-color stories."

" 'Twill be me eternal delight, good Master Yarblek," the outrageous fellow said grandly. "She's a good strappin' wench with a lusty sense of humor and a fine appreciation fer bawdy stories." He dipped out more ale and then capered across the lawn toward the dark-haired Nadrak girl.

"Disgusting," Yarblek growled, looking after him. "Some of the stories he tells her make *my* ears burn, but the nastier they are, the harder she laughs." He shook his head moodily.

"Let's get down to business," Belgarath said. "We need to know what's going on in Karanda right now."

"That's simple," Yarblek told him. "Mengha, that's what's going on. Mengha and his cursed demons."

"Dolmar filled us in," Silk said. "We know about what happened at Calida and about the way that Karands are flocking in to join his army from all over the seven kingdoms. Is he making any moves toward the south yet?"

"Not that I've heard," Yarblek replied. "He seems to be consolidating things through the north right now. He's whipping all of the Karands into hysteria, though. If 'Zakath doesn't do something quickly, he's going to have a full-scale revolution on his hands. I can tell you, though, that it's not safe to travel in northern Karanda right now. Mengha's shrieking Karands control everything to the coast of Zamad."

"We have to go to Ashaba," Garion told him.

"I wouldn't advise it," Yarblek said bluntly. "The Karands are picking up some very unsavory habits."

"Oh?" Silk said.

"I'm an Angarak," Yarblek said, "and I've been watching Grolims cut out human hearts to offer to Torak since I was a boy, but what's happening in Karanda turns even *my* stomach. The Karands stake captives out on the ground and then call up their demons. The demons are all getting fat."

"Would you care to be a little more specific?"

"Not really. Use your imagination, Silk. You've been in Morindland. You know what demons eat."

"You're not serious!"

"Oh, yes—and the Karands eat the scraps. As I said—some very unsavory habits. There are also some rumors about the demons breeding with human females."

"That's abominable!" Garion gasped.

"It is indeed," Yarblek agreed with him. "The women usually don't survive their pregnancies, but I've heard of a few live births."

"We have to put a stop to that," Belgarath said bleakly.

"Good luck," Yarblek said. "Me, I'm going back to Gar og Nadrak just as soon as I can get my caravan put together. I'm not going anywhere near Mengha—or the tame demon he keeps on a leash."

"Nahaz?" Garion asked.

"You've heard the name then?"

"Dolmar told us."

"We should probably start with him," Belgarath said. "If we can drive Nahaz back to where he came from, it's likely that the rest of the demons will follow their lord."

"Neat trick," Yarblek grunted.

"I have certain resources," the old man told him. "Once the demons are gone, Mengha won't have anything left but a ragtag army of Karandese fanatics. We'll be able to go on about our business and leave the mopping up to 'Zakath." He smiled briefly. "That might occupy his mind enough to keep him from breathing down our necks."

Vella was laughing raucously as she and Feldegast the juggler approached the arbor. The little comedian was walking on his hands again—erratically and with his feet waving ludicrously in the air.

"He tells a good story," the lush-bodied Nadrak girl said, still laughing, "but he can't hold his liquor."

"I didn't think he drank all that much," Silk said.

"It wasn't the ale that fuddled him so bad," she replied. She drew a silver flask from under her belt. "I gave him a pull or two at this." Her eyes suddenly sparkled with mischief. "Care to try some, Silk?" she offered, holding out the flask.

"What's in it?" he asked suspiciously.

"Just a little drink we brew in Gar og Nadrak," she said innocently. "It's as mild as mothers' milk." She demonstrated by taking a long drink from the flask.

"Othlass?"

She nodded.

"No thanks." He shuddered. "The last time I drank that, I lost track of a whole week."

"Don't be so chicken-livered, Silk," she told him scornfully. She took another drink. "See? It doesn't hurt a bit." She looked at Garion. "My lord," she said to him. "How's your pretty little wife?"

"She's well, Vella."

"I'm glad to hear that. Have you got her pregnant again yet?"

Garion flushed. "No," he replied.

"You're wasting time, my lord. Why don't you run back to the palace and chase her around the bedroom a time or two?" Then she turned to Belgarath. "Well?" she said to him.

"Well what?"

She smoothly drew one of her knives from her belt. "Would you like to try again?" she asked, turning deliberately so that her well-rounded posterior was available to him.

"Ah, thanks all the same, Vella," he said with a kind of massive dignity, "but it's a bit early."

"That's all right, old man," she said. "I'm ready for you this time. Any time you're in a patting frame of mind, feel free. I sharpened all my knives before we came—especially for you."

"You're too kind."

The drunken Feldegast lurched, tried to regain his balance, and toppled over in an unceremonious heap. When he stumbled to his feet, his plain face was splotched and distorted, and he stood hunched over with his back bowed to the point where he almost looked deformed.

"I think the girl got the best of you, my friend," Belgarath said jovially as he moved quickly to help the inebriated juggler to right himself. "You really ought to straighten up, though. If you stand around bent over like that, you'll tie your insides in knots." Garion saw his grandfather's lips moving slightly as he whispered something to the tipsy entertainer. Then, so faint that it was barely discernible, he felt the surge of the old man's will.

Feldegast straightened, his face buried in his hands. "Oh dear, oh dear, oh dear," he said. "Have y' poisoned me, me girl?" he demanded of Vella. "I can't remember ever bein' taken by the drink so fast." He took his hands away. The splotches and distortion were gone from his face, and he looked as he had before.

"Don't ever try to drink with a Nadrak woman," Belgarath advised him, "particularly when she's the one who brewed the liquor."

"It seems that I heard a snatch of conversation whilst I was entertainin' the wench here. Is it Karanda ye be talkin' about—and the woeful things happenin' there?"

"We were," Belgarath admitted.

"I display me talents betimes in wayside inns and taverns—for pennies and a drink or two, don't y' know—and a great deal of information comes into places like that. Sometimes if ye make a man laugh and be merry, ye kin draw more out of him than ye can with silver or strong drink. As it happened, I was in such a place not long ago—dazzlin' the onlookers with the brilliance of me performance—and happens that whilst I was there, a wayfarer came in from the east. A great brute of a man he was, and he told us the distressful news from Karanda. And after he had eaten and finished more pots of good strong ale than was good for him, I sought him out and questioned him further. A man in me profession can't never know too much about the places where he might be called upon to display his art, don't y' know. This great brute of a man, who should not have feared anythin' that walks, was shakin' and tremblin' like a frightened babe, and he tells me that I should stay out of Karanda as I valued me life. And then he tells me a very strange thing, which I have not yet put the meanin' to. He tells me that the road between Calida and Mal Yaska is thick with messengers goin' to and fro, hither and yon. Isn't that an amazin' thing? How could a man account fer it? But there be strange things goin' on in the world, good masters, and wonders to behold that no man at all could ever begin to imagine."

The juggler's lilting brogue was almost hypnotic in its charm and liquidity, and Garion found himself somehow caught up in the really quite commonplace narrative. He felt a peculiar disappointment as the gaudy little man broke off his story.

"I hope that me tale has brought ye some small entertainment an' enlightenment, good masters," Feldegast said ingratiatingly, his grass-stained hand held out suggestively. "I make me way in the world with me wits and me talents, givin' of them as free as the birds, but I'm always grateful fer little tokens of appreciation, don't y' know."

"Pay him," Belgarath said shortly to Garion.

"What?"

"Give him some money."

Garion sighed and reached for the leather purse at his belt.

"May the Gods all smile down on ye, young master," Feldegast thanked Garion effusively for the few small coins which changed hands. Then he looked slyly at Vella. "Tell me, me girl," he said, "have ye ever heard the story of the milkmaid and the peddler? I must give ye fair warnin' that it's a naughty little story, and I'd be covered with shame to bring a blush to yer fair cheeks."

"I haven't blushed since I was fourteen," Vella said to him.

"Well then, why don't we go apart a ways, an' I'll see if I can't remedy that? I'm told that blushin' is good fer the complexion."

Vella laughed and followed him back out onto the lawn.

"Silk," Belgarath said brusquely, "I need that diversion—now."

"We don't really have anything put together yet," Silk objected.

"Make something up, then." The old man turned to Yarblek. "And I don't want you to leave Mal Zeth until I give you the word. I might need you here."

"What's the matter, Grandfather?" Garion asked.

"We have to leave here as quickly as possible."

Out on the lawn, Vella stood wide-eyed and with the palms of her hands pressed to her flaming cheeks.

"Ye'll have to admit that I warned ye, me girl," Feldegast chortled triumphantly. "Which is more than I can say about the deceitful way ye slipped yer dreadful brew into me craw." He looked at her admiringly. "I must say, though, that ye bloom like a red, red rose when ye blush like that, and yer a joy to behold in yer maidenlike confusion. Tell me, have ye by chance heard the one about the shepherdess and the knight-errant?"

Vella fled.

That afternoon, Silk, who normally avoided anything remotely resembling physical exertion, spent several hours in the leafy atrium in the center of the east wing, busily piling stones across the mouth of the tiny rivulent of fresh, sparkling water which fed the pool at the center of the little garden. Garion watched curiously from the window of his sitting room until he could stand it no longer. He went out into the atrium to confront the sweating little Drasnian. "Are you taking up landscaping as a hobby?" he asked.

"No," Silk replied, mopping his forehead, "just taking a little precaution, is all."

"Precaution against what?"

Silk held up one finger. "Wait," he said, gauging the level of the water rising behind his improvised dam. After a moment, the water began to spill over into the pool with a loud gurgling and splashing. "Noisy, isn't it?" he said proudly.

"Won't that make sleep in these surrounding rooms a little hard?" Garion asked.

"It's also going to make listening almost impossible," the little man said smugly. "As soon as it gets dark, why don't you and I and Sadi and Liselle gather here. We need to talk, and my cheerful little waterfall should cover what we say to each other."

"Why after dark?"

Silk slyly laid one finger alongside his long, pointed nose. "So that the night will hide our lips from those police who don't use their ears to listen with."

"That's clever," Garion said.

"Why, yes. I thought so myself." Then Silk made a sour face. "Actually, it was Liselle's idea," he confessed.

Garion smiled. "But she let you do the work."

Silk grunted. "She claimed that she didn't want to break any of her fingernails. I was going to refuse, but she threw her dimples at me, and I gave in."

"She uses those very well, doesn't she? They're more dangerous than your knives."

"Are you trying to be funny, Garion?"

"Would I do that, old friend?"

As the soft spring evening descended over Mal Zeth, Garion joined his three friends in the dim atrium beside Silk's splashing waterfall.

"Very nice work, Kheldar," Velvet complimented the little man.

"Oh, shut up."

"Why, Kheldar!"

"All right," Garion said, by way of calling the meeting to order, "what have we got that we can work with? Belgarath wants us out of Mal Zeth almost immediately."

"I've been following your advice, Belgarion," Sadi murmured, "and I've been concentrating my attention on Baron Vasca. He's a man of eminent corruption and he has his fingers in so many pies that he sometimes loses track of just who's bribing him at any given moment."

"Exactly what's he up to right now?" Garion asked.

"He's still trying to take over the Bureau of Military Procurement," Velvet reported. "That bureau is controlled by the General Staff, however. It's mostly composed of colonels, but there's a General Bregar serving as Bureau Chief. The colonels aren't *too* greedy, but Bregar has a large payroll. He has to spread quite a bit of money around among his fellow generals to keep Vasca in check."

Garion thought about that. "Aren't you bribing Vasca as well?" he asked Silk.

Silk nodded glumly. "The price is going up, though. The consortium of Melcene merchant barons is laying a lot of money in his path, trying to get him to restrict Yarblek and me to the west coast."

"Can he raise any sort of force? Fighting men, I mean?"

"He has contacts with a fair number of robber chiefs," Sadi replied, "and they have some pretty rough-and-ready fellows working for them."

"Is there any band operating out of Mal Zeth right now?"

Sadi coughed rather delicately. "I just brought a string of wagons down from Camat," he admitted. "Agricultural products for the most part."

Garion gave him a hard look. "I thought I asked you not to do that anymore."

"The crop had already been harvested, Belgarion," the eunuch protested. "It doesn't make sense to just let it rot in the fields, does it?"

"That's sound business thinking, Garion," Silk interceded.

"Anyway," Sadi hurried on, "the band that's handling the harvesting and transport for me is one of the largest in this part of Mallorea—two or three hundred anyway, and I have a goodly number of stout fellows involved in local distribution."

"You did all this in just a few weeks?" Garion was incredulous.

"One makes very little profit by allowing the grass to grow under one's feet," Sadi stated piously.

"Well put," Silk approved.

"Thank you, Prince Kheldar."

Garion shook his head in defeat. "Is there any way you can get your bandits into the palace grounds?"

"Bandits?" Sadi sounded injured.

"Isn't that what they are?"

"I prefer to think of them as entrepreneurs."

"Whatever. Can you get them in?"

"I sort of doubt it, Belgarion. What did you have in mind?"

"I thought we might offer their services to Baron Vasca to help in his forthcoming confrontation with the General Staff."

"Is there going to be a confrontation?" Sadi looked surprised. "I hadn't heard about that."

"That's because we haven't arranged it yet. Vasca's going to find out—probably tomorrow—that his activities have irritated the General Staff, and that they're going to send troops into his offices to arrest him and to dig through his records to find enough incriminating evidence to take to the Emperor."

"That's brilliant," Silk said.

"I liked it—but it won't work unless Vasca's got enough men to hold off a fair number of troops."

"It can still work," Sadi said. "At about the same time that Vasca finds out about his impending arrest, I'll offer him the use of my men. He can bring them into the palace complex under the guise of workmen. All the Bureau Chiefs are continually renovating their offices. It has to do with status, I think."

"What's the plan here, Garion?" Silk asked.

"I want open fighting right here in the halls of the palace. *That* should attract the attention of Brador's policemen."

"He was born to be a King, wasn't he?" Velvet approved. "Only royalty has the ability to devise a deception of that scale."

"Thanks," Garion said dryly. "It's not going to work, though, if Vasca just takes up defensive positions in his bureau offices. We also have to persuade him to strike first. The soldiers won't really be coming after him, so we're going to have to make him start the fight himself. What kind of man is Vasca?"

"Deceitful, greedy, and not really all that bright," Silk replied.

"Can he be pressured into any kind of rashness?"

"Probably not. Bureaucrats tend to be cowardly. I don't think he'd make a move until he sees the soldiers coming."

"I believe I can make him bolder," Sadi said. "I have something very nice in a green vial that would make a mouse attack a lion."

Garion made a face. "I don't much care for that way," he said.

"It's the results that count, Belgarion," Sadi pointed out. "If things are that urgent right now, delicate feelings might be a luxury we can't afford."

"All right," Garion decided. "Do whatever you have to."

"Once things are in motion, I might be able to throw in just a bit of additional confusion," Velvet said. "The King of Pallia and the Prince Regent of Delchin both have sizeable retinues, and they're on the verge of open war anyway. There's also the King of Veresebo, who's so senile that he distrusts everybody. I could probably persuade each of them that any turmoil in the halls is directed at *them* personally. They'd put their men-at-arms into the corridors at the first sound of fighting."

"Now that's got some interesting possibilities," Silk said, rubbing his hands together gleefully. "A five-way brawl in the palace ought to give us all the opportunity we need to leave town."

"And it wouldn't necessarily have to be confined to the palace," Sadi added thoughtfully. "A bit of judicious misdirection could probably spread it out into the city itself. A general riot in the streets would attract quite a bit of attention, wouldn't you say?"

"How long would it take to set it up?" Garion asked.

Silk looked at his partners in crime. "Three days?" he asked them, "Maybe four?"

They both considered it, then nodded.

"That's it then, Garion," Silk said. "Three or four days."

"All right. Do it."

They all turned and started back toward the entrance to the atrium. "Margravine Liselle," Sadi said firmly.

"Yes, Sadi?"

"I'll take my snake back now, if you don't mind."

"Oh, of course, Sadi." She reached into her bodice for Zith.

Silk's face blanched, and he stepped back quickly.

"Something wrong, Kheldar?" she asked innocently.

"Never mind." The little man turned on his heel and went on through the green-smelling evening gesticulating and talking to himself.

CHAPTER ELEVEN

His name was Balsca. He was a rheumy-eyed seafaring man with bad habits and mediocre skills who hailed from Kaduz, a fish-reeking town on one of the northern Melcene Islands. He had signed on as a common deck hand for the past six years aboard a leaky merchantman grandiosely named *The Star of Jarot*, commanded by an irascible peg-leg captain from Celanta who called himself

"Woodfoot," a colorful name which Balsca privately suspected was designed to conceal the captain's true identity from the maritime authorities.

Balsca did not like Captain Woodfoot. Balsca had not liked any ships' officers since he had been summarily flogged ten years back for pilfering grog from ship's stores aboard a ship of the line in the Mallorean navy. Balsca had nursed his grievance from that incident until he had found an opportunity to jump ship, and then he had gone in search of kindlier masters and more understanding officers in the merchant marine.

He had not found them aboard *The Star of Jarot*.

His most recent disillusionment had come about as the result of a difference of views with the ship's bosun, a heavy-fisted rascal from Pannor in Rengel. That altercation had left Balsca without his front teeth, and his vigorous protest to the captain had evoked jeering laughter followed by his being unceremoniously kicked off the quarterdeck by a nail-studded leg constructed of solid oak. The humiliation and the bruises were bad enough, but the splinters which festered for weeks in Balsca's behind made it almost impossible for him to sit down, and sitting down was Balsca's favorite position.

He brooded about it, leaning on the starboard rail well out of Captain Woodfoot's view and staring out at the lead-gray swells surging through the straits of Perivor as *The Star of Jarot* beat her way northwesterly past the swampy coast of the southwestern Dalasian Protectorates and on around the savage breakers engulfing the Turim Reef. By the time they had cleared the reef and turned due north along the desolate coast of Finda, Balsca had concluded that life was going out of its way to treat him unfairly, and that he might be far better off seeking his fortune ashore.

He spent several nights prowling through the cargo hold with a well-shielded lantern until he found the concealed compartment where Woodfoot had hidden a number of small, valuable items that he didn't want to trouble the customs people with. Balsca's patched canvas sea bag picked up a fair amount of weight rather quickly that night.

When *The Star of Jarot* dropped anchor in the harbor of Mal Gemila, Balsca feigned illness and refused his shipmates' suggestion that he go ashore with them for the customary end-of-voyage carouse. He lay instead in his hammock, moaning theatrically. Late during the dogwatch, he pulled on his tarred canvas sea coat, the only thing of any value that he owned, picked up his sea bag and went on silent feet up on deck. The solitary watch, as Balsca had anticipated, lay snoring in the scuppers, snuggled up to an earthenware jug; there were no lights in the aft cabins, where Woodfoot and his officers lived in idle luxury; and the moon had already set. A small ship's boat swung on a painter on the starboard side, and Balsca deftly dropped his sea bag into it, swung over the rail, and silently left *The Star of Jarot* forever. He felt no particular regret about that. He did not even pause to mutter a curse at the vessel which had been his home for the past six years. Balsca was a philosophical sort of fellow. Once he had escaped from an unpleasant situation, he no longer held any grudges.

When he reached the docks, he sold the small ship's boat to a beady-eyed man with a missing right hand. Balsca feigned drunkenness during the transaction, and the maimed man—who had undoubtedly had his hand chopped off as punishment for theft—paid him quite a bit more for the boat than would have been the case had the sale taken place in broad daylight. Balsca immediately knew what that meant. He shouldered his sea bag, staggered up the wharf, and began to climb the steep cobblestone street from the harbor. At the first corner, he made a sudden turn to the left and ran like a deer, leaving the surprised press gang the beady-eyed man had sent after him floundering far behind. Balsca was stupid, certainly, but he was no fool.

He ran until he was out of breath and quite some distance from the harbor with all its dangers. He passed a number of alehouses along the way, regretfully perhaps, but there was still business to attend to, and he needed his wits about him.

In a dim little establishment, well hidden up a dank, smelly alleyway, he sold Captain Woodfoot's smuggled treasures, bargaining down to the last copper with the grossly fat woman who ran the place. He even traded his sea coat for a landsman's tunic, and emerged from the alley with all trace of the sea removed from him, except for the rolling gait of a man whose feet have not touched dry land for several months.

He avoided the harbor with its press gangs and cheap grog shops and chose instead a quiet street that meandered past boarded-up warehouses. He followed that until he found a sedate workman's alehouse where a buxom barmaid rather sullenly served him. Her mood, he surmised, was the result of the fact that he was her only customer, and that she had quite obviously intended to close the doors and seek her bed—or someone else's, for all he knew. He jollied her into some semblance of good humor for an hour or so, left a few pennies on the table, and squeezed her ample bottom by way of farewell. Then he lurched into the empty street in search of further adventure.

He found true love under a smoky torch on the corner. Her name, she said, was Elowanda. Balsca suspected that she was not being entirely honest about that, but it was not her name he was interested in. She was quite young and quite obviously sick. She had a racking cough, a hoarse, croaking voice, and her reddened nose ran constantly. She was not particularly clean and she exuded the rank smell of a week or more of dried sweat. Balsca, however, had a sailor's strong stomach and an appetite whetted by six months' enforced abstinence at sea. Elowanda was not very pretty, but she was cheap. After a brief haggle, she led him to a rickety crib in an alley that reeked of moldy sewage. Although he was quite drunk, Balsca grappled with her on a lumpy pallet until dawn was staining the eastern sky.

It was noon when he awoke with a throbbing head. He might have slept longer, but the cry of a baby coming from a wooden box in the corner drove into his ears like a sharp knife. He nudged the pale woman lying beside him, hoping that she would rise and quiet her squalling brat. She moved limply under his hand, her limbs flaccid.

He nudged her again, harder this time. Then he rose up and looked at her. Her stiff face was locked in a dreadful rictus—a hideous grin that made his blood run cold. He suddenly realized that her skin was like clammy ice. He jerked his hand away, swearing under his breath. He reached out gingerly and peeled back one of her eyelids. He swore again.

The woman who had called herself Elowanda was as dead as last week's mackerel.

Balsca rose and quickly pulled on his clothes. He searched the room thoroughly, but found nothing worth stealing except for the few coins he had given the dead woman the previous night. He took those, then glared at the naked corpse lying on the pallet. "Rotten whore!" he said and kicked her once in the side. She rolled limply off the pallet and lay facedown on the floor.

Balsca slammed out into the stinking alley, ignoring the wailing baby he had left behind him.

He had a few moments' concern about the possibility of certain social diseases. *Something* had killed Elowanda, and he had not really been all that rough with her. As a precaution, he muttered an old sailors' incantation which was said to be particularly efficacious in warding off the pox; reassured, he went looking for something to drink.

By midafternoon, he was pleasantly drunk and he lurched out of a congenial little wine shop and stopped, swaying slightly, to consider his options. By now Woodfoot would certainly have discovered that his hidden cabinet was empty and that Balsca had jumped ship. Since Woodfoot was a man of limited imagination, he and his officers would certainly be concentrating their search along the waterfront. It would take them some time to realize that their quarry had moved somewhat beyond the sight, if not the smell, of salt water. Balsca prudently decided that if he were to maintain his lead on his vengeful former captain, it was probably time for him to head inland. It occurred to him, moreover, that someone might have seen him with Elowanda, and that her body probably had been found by now. Balsca felt no particular responsibility for her death, but he was by nature slightly shy about talking with policemen. All in all, he decided, it might just be time to leave Mal Gemila.

He started out confidently, striding toward the east gate of the city; but after several blocks, his feet began to hurt. He loitered outside a warehouse where several workmen were loading a large wagon. He carefully stayed out of sight until the work was nearly done, then heartily offered to lend a hand. He put two boxes on the wagon, then sought out the teamster, a shaggy-bearded man smelling strongly of mules.

"Where be ye bound, friend?" Balsca asked him as if out of idle curiosity.

"Mal Zeth," the teamster replied shortly.

"What an amazing coincidence," Balsca exclaimed. "I have business there myself." In point of fact, Balsca had cared very little where the teamster and his wagon had been bound. All he wanted to do was to go inland to avoid Woodfoot or the police. "What say I ride along with you—for company?"

"I don't get all that lonesome," the teamster said churlishly.

Balsca sighed. It was going to be one of *those* days. "I'd be willing to pay," he offered sadly.

"How much?"

"I don't really have very much."

"Ten coppers," the teamster said flatly.

"Ten? I haven't got that much."

"You'd better start walking then. It's that way."

Balsca sighed and gave in. "All right," he said. "Ten."

"In advance."

"Half now and half when we get to Mal Zeth."

"In advance."

"That's hard."

"So's walking."

Balsca stepped around a corner, reached into an inside pocket, and carefully counted out the ten copper coins. The hoard he had accumulated as a result of his pilferage aboard *The Star of Jarot* had dwindled alarmingly. A number of possibilities occurred to him. He shifted his sheath knife around until it was at his back. If the teamster slept soundly enough and if they stopped for the night in some secluded place, Balsca was quite certain that he could ride into Mal Zeth the proud owner of a wagon and a team of mules—not to mention whatever was in the boxes. Balsca had killed a few men in his time—when it had been safe to do so—and he was not particularly squeamish about cutting throats, if it was worth his while.

The wagon clattered and creaked as it rumbled along the cobbled street in the slanting afternoon sunlight.

"Let's get a few things clear before we start," the teamster said. "I don't like to talk and I don't like having people jabber at me."

"All right."

The teamster reached back and picked up a wicked-looking hatchet out of the wagon bed. "Now," he said, "give me your knife."

"I don't have a knife."

The teamster reined in his mules. "Get out," he said curtly.

"But I paid you?"

"Not enough for me to take any chances with you. Come up with a knife or get out of my wagon."

Balsca glared at him, then at the hatchet. Slowly he drew out his dagger and handed it over.

"Good. I'll give it back to you when we get to Mal Zeth. Oh, by the way, I sleep with one eye open and with this in my fist." He held the hatchet in front of Balsca's face. "If you even come near me while we're on the road, I'll brain you."

Balsca shrank back.

"I'm glad that we understand each other." The teamster shook his reins, and they rumbled out of Mal Gemila.

Balsca was not feeling too well when they reached Mal Zeth. He assumed at first that it was a result of the peculiar swaying motion of the wagon. Though he had never been seasick in all his years as a sailor, he was frequently land-sick. This time, however, was somewhat different. His stomach, to be sure, churned and heaved, but, unlike his previous bouts of malaise, this time he also found that he was sweating profusely, and his throat was so sore that he could barely swallow. He had alternating bouts of chills and fever, and a foul taste in his mouth.

The surly teamster dropped him off at the main gates of Mal Zeth, idly tossed his dagger at his feet and then squinted at his former passenger. "You don't look so good," he observed. "You ought to go see a physician or something."

Balsca made an indelicate sound. "People die in the hands of physicians," he said, "or if they do manage to get well, they go away with empty purses."

"Suit yourself." The teamster shrugged and drove his wagon into the city without looking back.

Balsca directed a number of muttered curses after him, bent, picked up his knife, and walked into Mal Zeth. He wandered about for a time, trying to get his bearings, then finally accosted a man in a sea coat.

"Excuse me, mate," he said, his voice raspy as a result of his sore throat, "but where's a place where a man can get a good cup of grog at a reasonable price?"

"Try the Red Dog Tavern," the sailor replied. "It's two streets over on the corner."

"Thanks, mate," Balsca said.

"You don't look like you're feeling too good."

"A little touch of a cold, I think." Balsca flashed him a toothless grin. "Nothing that a few cups of grog won't fix."

"That's the honest truth." The sailor laughed his agreement. "It's the finest medicine in the world."

The Red Dog Tavern was a dark grogshop that faintly resembled the forecastle of a ship. It had a low, beamed ceiling of dark wood and portholes instead of windows. The proprietor was a bluff, red-faced man with tattoos on both arms and an exaggerated touch of salt water in his speech. His "Ahoys" and "Mateys" began to get on Balsca's nerves after a while, but after three cups of grog, he didn't mind so much. His sore throat eased, his stomach settled down, and the trembling in his hands ceased. He still, however, had a splitting headache. He had two more cups of grog and then fell asleep with his head cradled on his crossed arms.

"Ahoy, mate. Closing time," the Red Dog's proprietor said some time later, shaking his shoulder.

Balsca sat up, blinking. "Must have dropped off for a few minutes," he mumbled hoarsely.

"More like a few hours, matey." The man frowned, then laid his hand on Balsca's forehead. "You're burning up, matey," he said. "You'd better get you to bed."

"Where's a good place to get a cheap room?" Balsca asked, rising unsteadily. His throat hurt worse now than it had before, and his stomach was in knots again.

"Try the third door up the street. Tell them that I sent you."

Balsca nodded, bought a bottle to take with him and surreptitiously filched a rope-scarred marlinespike from the rack beside the door on his way out. "Good tavern," he croaked to the proprietor as he left. "I like the way you've got it fixed up."

The tattooed man nodded proudly. "My own idea," he said. "I thought to myself that a seafaring man might like a homelike sort of place to do his drinking in— even when he's this far from deep water. Come back again."

"I'll do that," Balsca promised.

It took him about a half an hour to find a solitary passerby hurrying home with his head down and his hands jammed into his tunic pockets. Balsca stalked him for a block or so, his rope-soled shoes making no sound on the cobblestones. Then, as the passerby went by the dark mouth of an alleyway, Balsca stepped up behind him and rapped him smartly across the base of the skull with his marlinespike. The man dropped like a poleaxed ox. Balsca had been in enough shipboard fights and tavern brawls to know exactly where and how hard to hit his man. He rolled the fellow over, hit him alongside the head once again just to be on the safe side, and then methodically began to go through the unconscious man's pockets. He found several coins and a stout knife. He put the coins in his pocket, tucked the knife under his broad leather belt, and pulled his victim into the alley out of the light. Then he went on down the street, whistling an old sea song.

He felt much worse the following day. His head throbbed, and his throat was so swollen that he could barely talk. His fever, he was sure, was higher, and his nose ran constantly. It took three pulls on his bottle to quiet his stomach. He knew that he should go out and get something to eat, but the thought of food sickened him. He took another long drink from his bottle, lay back on the dirty bed in the room he had rented, and fell back into a fitful doze.

When he awoke again, it was dark outside, and he was shivering violently. He finished his bottle without gaining any particular relief, then shakily pulled on his clothing, which he absently noted exuded a rank odor, and stumbled down to the street and three doors up to the inviting entrance to the Red Dog.

"By the Gods, matey," the tattooed man said, "ye look positively awful."

"Grog," Balsca croaked. "Grog."

It took nine cups of grog to stem the terrible shaking which had seized him.

Balsca was not counting.

When his money ran out, he staggered into the street and beat a man to death with his marlinespike for six pennies. He lurched on, encountered a fat merchant, and knifed him for his purse. The purse even had some gold in it. He reeled back to the Red Dog and drank until closing time.

"Have a care, matey," the proprietor cautioned him as he thrust him out the door. "There be murdering footpads about, or so I've been told—and the police are as thick as fleas on a mangy dog in the streets and alleys in the neighborhood."

Balsca took the jug of grog he had bought back to his shabby room and drank himself into unconsciousness.

He was delirious the following morning and he raved for hours, alternating between drinking from his jug of grog and vomiting on his bed.

It took him until sunset to die. His last words were, "Mother, help me."

When they found him, some days later, he was arched rigidly backward, and his face was fixed in a hideous grin.

Three days later, a pair of wayfarers found the body of a bearded teamster lying in a ditch beside his wagon on the road to Mal Gemila. His body was arched stiffly backward, and his face was locked in a grotesque semblance of a grin. The wayfarers concluded that he had no further need of his team and wagon, and so they stole it. As an afterthought, they also stole his clothes and covered the body with dead leaves. Then they turned the wagon around and rode on back to Mal Zeth.

Perhaps a week after Balsca's largely unnoticed death, a man in a tarred sea coat came staggering into a run-down street in broad daylight. He was raving and clutching at his throat. He lurched along the cobblestone street for perhaps a hundred feet before he collapsed and died. The dreadful grin fixed on his foam-flecked lips gave several onlookers nightmares that night.

The tatooed proprietor of the Red Dog Tavern was found dead in his establishment the following morning. He lay amidst the wreckage of the several tables and chairs he had smashed during his final delirium. His face was twisted into a stiff, hideous grin.

During the course of that day, a dozen more men in that part of the city, all regular patrons of the Red Dog Tavern, also died.

The next day, three dozen more succumbed. The authorities began to take note of the matter.

But by then it was too late. The curious intermingling of classes characteristic of a great city made the confining of the infection to any one district impossible. Servants who lived in that shabby part of town carried the disease into the houses of the rich and powerful. Workmen carried it to construction sites, and their fellow workmen carried it home to other parts of the city. Customers gave it to merchants, who in turn gave it to other customers. The most casual contact was usually sufficient to cause infection.

The dead had at first been numbered in the dozens, but by the end of the week hundreds had fallen ill. The houses of the sick were boarded up despite the weak cries of the inhabitants from within. Grim carts rumbled through the streets, and workmen with camphor-soaked cloths about their lower faces picked up the dead with long hooks. The bodies were stacked in the carts like logs of wood, conveyed to cemeteries, and buried without rites in vast common graves. The streets of Mal Zeth became deserted as the frightened citizens barricaded themselves inside their houses.

There was some concern inside the palace, naturally, but the palace, walled as it was, was remote from the rest of the city. As a further precaution, however, the Emperor ordered that no one be allowed in or out of the compound. Among those locked inside were several hundred workmen who had been hired by Baron Vasca, the Chief of the Bureau of Commerce, to begin the renovations of the bureau offices.

It was about noon on the day after the locking of the palace gates that Garion, Polgara, and Belgarath were summoned to an audience with 'Zakath. They entered his study to find him gaunt and hollow-eyed, poring over a map of the imperial city. "Come in. Come in," he said when they arrived. They entered and sat down in the chairs he indicated with an absent wave of his hand.

"You look tired," Polgara noted.

"I haven't slept for the past four days," 'Zakath admitted. He looked wearily at Belgarath. "You say that you're seven thousand years old?"

"Approximately, yes."

"You've lived through pestilence before?"

"Several times."

"How long does it usually last?"

"It depends on which disease it is. Some of them run their course in a few months. Others persist until everybody in the region is dead. Pol would know more about that than I would. She's the one with all the medical experience."

"Lady Polgara?" the Emperor appealed to her.

"I'll need to know the symptoms before I can identify the disease," she replied.

'Zakath burrowed through the litter of documents on the table in front of him. "Here it is." He picked up a scrap of parchment and read from it. "High fever, nausea, vomiting. Chills, profuse sweating, sore throat, and headache. Finally delirium, followed shortly by death."

She looked at him gravely. "That doesn't sound too good," she said. "Is there anything peculiar about the bodies after they've died?"

"They all have an awful grin on their faces," he told her, consulting his parchment.

She shook her head. "I was afraid of that."

"What is it?"

"A form of plague."

"Plague?" His face had gone suddenly pale. "I thought there were swellings on the body with that. This doesn't mention that." He held up the scrap of parchment.

"There are several different varieties of the disease, 'Zakath. The most common involves the swellings you mentioned. Another attacks the lungs. The one you have here is quite rare, and dreadfully virulent."

"Can it be cured?"

"Not cured, no. Some people manage to survive it, but that's probably the result of mild cases or their body's natural resistance to disease. Some people seem to be immune. They don't catch it no matter how many times they've been exposed."

"What can I do?"

She gave him a steady look. "You won't like this," she told him.

"I like the plague even less."

"Seal up Mal Zeth. Seal the city in the same way that you've sealed the palace."

"You can't be serious!"

"Deadly serious. You have to keep the infection confined to Mal Zeth, and the only way to do that is to prevent people from carrying the disease out of the city to other places." Her face was bleak. "And when I say to seal the city, 'Zakath, I mean totally. *Nobody* leaves."

"I've got an empire to run, Polgara. I can't seal myself up here and just let it run itself. I have to get messengers in and send orders out."

"Then, inevitably, you will rule an empire of the dead. The symptoms of the disease don't begin to show up until a week or two after the initial infection, but during the last several days of that period, the carrier is already dreadfully contagious. You can catch it from somebody who looks and feels perfectly healthy. If you send out messengers, sooner or later one of them will be infected, and the disease will spread throughout all of Mallorea."

His shoulders slumped in defeat as the full horror of what she was describing struck him. "How many?" he asked quietly.

"I don't quite understand the question."

"How many will die here in Mal Zeth, Polgara?"

She considered it. "Half," she replied, "if you're lucky."

"*Half?*" he gasped. "Polgara, this is the largest city in the world. You're talking about the greatest disaster in the history of mankind."

"I know—and that's only if you're lucky. The death rate could go as high as four-fifths of the population."

He sank his face into his trembling hands. "Is there anything at all that can be done?" he asked in a muffled voice.

"You must burn the dead," she told him. "The best way is just to burn their houses without removing them. That reduces the spread of the disease."

"You'd better have the streets patrolled, too," Belgarath added grimly. "There's bound to be looting, and the looters are going to catch the disease. Send out archers with orders to shoot looters on sight. Then their bodies should be pushed back into the infected houses with long poles and burned along with the bodies already in the houses."

"You're talking about the destruction of Mal Zeth!" 'Zakath protested violently, starting to his feet.

"No," Polgara disagreed. "We're talking about saving as many of your citizens as possible. You have to steel your heart about this, 'Zakath. You may eventually have to drive all the healthy citizens out into the fields, surround them with guards to keep them from getting away, and then burn Mal Zeth to the ground."

"That's unthinkable!"

"Perhaps you ought to start thinking about it," she told him. "The alternative could be much, much worse."

CHAPTER TWELVE

"Silk," Garion said urgently, "you've got to stop it."

"I'm sorry, Garion," the little man replied, looking cautiously around the moonlit atrium for hidden spies, "but it's already in motion. Sadi's bandits are inside the palace grounds and they're taking their orders from Vasca. Vasca's so brave now that he's almost ready to confront 'Zakath himself. General Bregar of the Bureau of Military Procurement knows that something's afoot, so he's surrounded himself with troops. The King of Pallia, the Prince Regent of Delchin, and the old King of Voresebo have armed every one of their retainers. The palace is sealed, and nobody can bring in any outside help—not even 'Zakath himself. The way things stand right now, one word could set it off."

Garion started to swear, walking around the shadowy atrium and kicking at the short-cropped turf.

"You *did* tell us to go ahead," Silk reminded him.

"Silk, we can't even get out of the palace right now—much less the city. We've stirred up a fight, and now we're going to be caught right in the middle of it."

Silk nodded glumly. "I know," he said.

"I'll have to go to 'Zakath," Garion said. "Tell him the whole story. He can have his imperial guards disarm everybody."

"If you thought it was hard to come up with a way to get out of the palace, start thinking about how we're going to get out of the imperial dungeon. 'Zakath's been polite so far, but I don't think his patience—or his hospitality—would extend to this."

Garion grunted.

"I'm afraid that we've outsmarted ourselves," Silk said. He scratched at his head. "I do that sometimes," he added.

"Can you think of *any* way to head it off?"

"I'm afraid not. The whole situation is just too inflammable. Maybe we'd better tell Belgarath."

Garion winced. "He won't be happy."

"He'll be a lot less happy if we don't tell him."

Garion sighed. "I suppose you're right. All right, let's go get it over with."

It took quite some time to locate Belgarath. They finally found him standing at a window in a room high up in the east wing. The window looked out over the palace wall. Beyond that wall fires ranged unchecked in the stricken city. Sheets of sooty flame belched from whole blocks of houses, and a pall of thick smoke blotted out the starry sky. "It's getting out of hand," the old man said. "They should be pulling down houses to make firebreaks, but I think the soldiers are afraid to leave their barracks." He swore. "I hate fires," he said.

"Something's sort of come up," Silk said cautiously, looking around to see if he could locate the spy holes in the walls of the room.

"What is it?"

"Oh, nothing all that much," Silk replied with exaggerated casualness. "We just thought that we'd bring it to your attention, is all." His fingers, however, were twitching and flickering. Even as he spoke quite calmly, improvising some minor problem with the horses for the edification of the spies they all knew were watching and listening, his dancing fingers laid out the entire situation for the old man.

"You *what*?" Belgarath exclaimed, then covered the outburst with a cough.

—*You told us to devise a diversion, Grandfather*—Garion's hands said as Silk continued to ramble on about the horses.

—*A diversion, yes*— Belgarath's fingers replied, —*but not pitched battles inside the palace. What were you thinking of?*—

—*It was the best we could come up with*— Garion replied lamely.

"Let me think about this for a minute," the old man said aloud. He paced back and forth for a while, his hands clasped behind his back and his face furrowed with concentration. "Let's go talk with Durnik," he said finally. "He's more or less in charge of the horses, so we'll need his advice." Just before he turned to lead them from the room, however, his fingers flickered one last time. —*Try not to walk too softly on the way downstairs*— he told them. —*I need to give you some instructions, and wiggling our fingers takes too long*—

As they left the room, Garion and Silk scuffed their feet and brought the heels of their boots down hard on the marble floor to cover Belgarath's whispering voice.

"All right," the old man breathed, scarcely moving his lips as they moved along the corridor toward the stairs leading down. "The situation isn't really irretrievable. Since we can't stop this little brawl you've arranged anyway, let it go ahead and happen. We *will* need the horses, though, so, Garion, I want you to go to 'Zakath and tell him that we'd like to isolate our mounts from the rest of the stables. Tell him that it's to avoid having them catch the plague."

"Can horses catch the plague?" Garion whispered in some surprise.

"How should I know? But if *I* don't, you can be sure that 'Zakath won't either. Silk, you sort of ease around and let everybody know—quietly—that we're just about to leave and to get ready without being too obvious about it."

"Leave?" Garion's whisper was startled. "Grandfather, do you know a way to get out of the palace—and the city?"

"No, but I know someone who does. Get to 'Zakath with your request about the horses as quickly as you can. He's got his mind on so many other things right now that he probably won't give you any argument about it." He looked at Silk. "Can you give me any kind of idea as to when your little explosion is going to take place?"

"Not really," Silk whispered back, still scuffing his feet on the stairs as they went down. "It could happen at any minute, I suppose."

Belgarath shook his head in disgust. "I think you need to go back to school," he breathed irritably. "*How* to do something is important, yes, but *when* is sometimes even more important."

"I'll try to remember that."

"Do. We'd all better hurry, then. We want to be ready when this unscheduled little eruption takes place."

There were a dozen high-ranking officers with 'Zakath when Garion was admitted to the large, red-draped room where the Emperor was conferring with his men. "I'll be with you in a bit, Garion," the haggard-looking man said. Then he turned back to his generals. "We *have* to get orders to the troops," he told them. "I need a volunteer to go out into the city."

The generals looked at each other, scuffing their feet on the thick blue carpet.

"Am I going to have to order someone to go?" 'Zakath demanded in exasperation.

"Uh—excuse me," Garion interjected mildly, "but why does anybody have to go at all?"

"Because the troops are all sitting on their hands in their barracks while Mal Zeth burns," 'Zakath snapped. "They have to start tearing down houses to make firebreaks, or we'll lose the whole city. Someone has to order them out."

"Have you got troops posted outside the palace walls?" Garion asked.

"Yes. They have orders to keep the populace away."

"Why not just shout at them from the top of the wall?" Garion suggested. "Tell one of them to go get a colonel or somebody, then yell your orders down to him. Tell him to put the troops to work. Nobody can catch the plague from a hundred yards away—I don't think."

'Zakath stared at him and then suddenly began to laugh ruefully. "Why didn't I think of that?" he asked.

"Probably because you weren't raised on a farm," Garion replied. "If you're plowing a different field from the man you want to talk to, you shout back and forth. Otherwise, you do an awful lot of unnecessary walking."

"All right," 'Zakath said briskly, looking at his generals, "which one of you has the biggest mouth?"

A red-faced officer with a big paunch and snowy white hair grinned suddenly. "In my youth, I could be heard all the way across a parade ground, your Majesty," he said.

"Good. Go see if you can still do it. Get hold of some colonel with a glimmer of intelligence. Tell him to abandon any district that's already burning and to tear down enough houses around the perimeter to keep the fire from spreading. Tell him that there's a generalcy in it for him if he saves at least half of Mal Zeth."

"Provided that he doesn't get the plague and die," one of the other generals muttered.

"That's what soldiers get paid for, gentlemen—taking risks. When the trumpet blows, you're supposed to attack, and I'm blowing the trumpet—right now."

"Yes, your Majesty," they all replied in unison, turned smartly, and marched out.

"That was a clever idea, Garion," 'Zakath said gratefully. "Thank you." He sprawled wearily in a chair.

"Just common sense." Garion shrugged, also sitting down.

"Kings and Emperors aren't supposed to have common sense. It's too common."

"You're going to have to get some sleep, 'Zakath," Garion told him seriously. "You look like a man on his last legs."

"Gods," 'Zakath replied, "I'd give half of Karanda right now for a few hours' sleep—of course, I don't *have* half of Karanda anymore."

"Go to bed, then."

"I can't. There's too much to do."

"How much can you do if you collapse from exhaustion? Your generals can take care of things until you wake up. That's what generals are for, isn't it?"

"Maybe." 'Zakath slumped lower in his chair. He looked across at Garion. "Was there something on your mind?" he asked. "I'm sure this isn't just a social visit."

"Well," Garion said, trying to make it sound only incidental, "Durnik's worried about our horses," he said. "We've talked with Aunt Pol—Lady Polgara—and she's not really sure whether horses can catch plague or not. Durnik wanted me to ask you if it would be all right if we took our animals out of the main stables and picketed them someplace near the east wing where he can keep an eye on them."

"Horses?" 'Zakath said incredulously. "He's worried about horses at a time like this?"

"You sort of have to understand Durnik," Garion replied. "He's a man who takes his responsibilities very seriously. He looks on it as a duty, and I think we can both appreciate that."

'Zakath laughed a tried laugh. "The legendary Sendarian virtues," he said, "duty, rectitude, and practicality." He shrugged. "Why not?" he said. "If it makes Goodman Durnik happy, he can stable your horses in the corridors of the east wing if he wants."

"Oh, I don't think he'd want to do that," Garion replied after a moment's thought. "One of the Sendarian virtues you neglected to mention was propriety.

Horses don't belong inside the house. Besides," he added, "the marble floors might bruise their hooves."

'Zakath smiled weakly. "You're a delight, Garion," he said. "Sometimes you're so serious about the littlest things."

"Big things are made up of little things, 'Zakath," Garion replied sententiously. He looked at the exhausted man across the table, feeling a peculiar regret at being forced to deceive somebody he genuinely liked. "Are you going to be all right?" he asked.

"I'll survive, I expect," 'Zakath said. "You see, Garion, one of the big secrets about this world is that the people who desperately cling to life are usually the ones who die. Since I don't really care one way or the other, I'll probably live to be a hundred."

"I wouldn't base any plans on that kind of superstition," Garion told him. Then a thought came to him. "Would it upset you if we locked the doors of the east wing from the inside until this all blows over?" he asked. "I'm not particularly timid about getting sick myself, but I'm sort of concerned about Ce'Nedra and Liselle and Eriond. None of them are really terribly robust, and Aunt Pol said that stamina was one of the things that help people survive the plague."

'Zakath nodded. "That's a reasonable request," he agreed, "and really a very good idea. Let's protect the ladies and the boy, if at all possible."

Garion stood up. "You've got to get some sleep," he said.

"I don't think I *can* sleep. There are so many things on my mind just now."

"I'll have someone send Andel to you," Garion suggested. "If she's half as good as Aunt Pol thinks she is, she should be able to give you something that would put a regiment to sleep." He looked at the exhausted man he cautiously considered to be his friend. "I won't be seeing you for a while," he said. "Good luck, and try to take care of yourself, all right?"

"I'll try, Garion. I'll try."

Gravely they shook hands, and Garion turned and quietly left the room.

They were busy for the next several hours. Despite Garion's subterfuges, Brador's secret police dogged their every step. Durnik and Toth and Eriond went to the stables and came back with the horses, trailed closely by the ubiquitous policemen.

"What's holding things up?" Belgarath demanded when they had all gathered once again in the large room at the top of the stairs with its dais and the thronelike chair at one end.

"I'm not sure," Silk replied carefully, looking around. "It's just a matter of time, though."

Then, out on the palace grounds beyond the bolted doors of the east wing, there was the sound of shouting and the thud of running feet, followed by the ring of steel on steel.

"Something seems to be happening," Velvet said clinically.

"It's about time," Belgarath grunted.

"Be nice, Ancient One."

Within their locked-off building there also came the rapid staccato sound of running. The doors leading out into the rest of the palace and to the grounds began to bang open and then slam shut.

"Are they all leaving, Pol?" Belgarath asked.

Her eyes grew distant for a moment. "Yes, father," she said.

The running and slamming continued for several minutes.

"My," Sadi said mildly, "weren't there a lot of them?"

"Will you three stop congratulating yourselves and go bolt those doors again?" Belgarath said.

Silk grinned and slipped out the door. He came back a few minutes later, frowning. "We've got a bit of a problem," he said. "The guards at the main door seem to have a strong sense of duty. They haven't left their posts."

"Great diversion, Silk," Belgarath said sarcastically.

"Toth and I can deal with them," Durnik said confidently. He went to the box beside the fireplace and picked up a stout chunk of oak firewood.

"That might be just a bit direct, dear," Polgara murmured. "I'm sure you don't want to kill them, and sooner or later they'll wake up and run straight to 'Zakath. I think we'll need to come up with something a little more sneaky."

"I don't care much for that word, Pol," he said stiffly.

"Would 'diplomatic' put a better light on it?"

He thought about it. "No," he said, "not really. It means the same thing, doesn't it?"

"Well," she conceded, "yes, probably. But it sounds nicer, doesn't it?"

"Polgara," the smith said firmly. It was the first time Garion had ever heard him use her full name. "I'm not trying to be unreasonable, but how can we face the world if we lie and cheat and sneak every time we go around a corner? I mean—really, Pol."

She looked at him. "Oh, my Durnik," she said, "I love you." She threw her arms about her husband's neck with a sort of girlish exuberance. "You're too good for this world, do you know that?"

"Well," he said, slightly abashed by a show of affection that he obviously believed should be kept very private, "it's a matter of decency, isn't it?"

"Of course, Durnik," she agreed in an oddly submissive tone. "Whatever you say."

"What are we going to do about the guards?" Garion asked.

"I can manage them, dear." Polgara smiled. "I can arrange it so that they won't see or hear a thing. We'll be able to leave with no one the wiser—assuming that father knows what he's talking about."

Belgarath looked at her, then suddenly winked. "Trust me," he said. "Durnik, bring the horses inside."

"Inside?" the smith looked startled.

Belgarath nodded. "We have to take them down into the cellar."

"I didn't know that this wing had a cellar," Silk said.

"Neither does 'Zakath," Belgarath smirked. "Or Brador."

"Garion," Ce'Nedra said sharply.

Garion turned to see a shimmering in the center of the room. Then the blind-folded form of Cyradis appeared.

"Make haste," she urged them. "Ye must reach Ashaba 'ere the week is out."

"Ashaba?" Silk exclaimed. "We have to go to Calida. A man named Mengha is raising demons there."

"That is of no moment, Prince Kheldar. The demons are thy least concern. Know, however, that the one called Mengha also journeys toward Ashaba. He will be caught up in one of the tasks which must be completed 'ere the meeting of the Child of Light and the Child of Dark can come to pass in the Place Which Is No More." She turned her blindfolded face toward Garion. "The time to complete this task is at hand, Belgarion of Riva, and shouldst those of thy companions upon whom the task hath been laid fail in its accomplishment, the world is lost. I pray thee, therefore, go to Ashaba." And then she vanished.

There was a long silence as they all stared at the spot where she had stood.

"That's it, then," Belgarath said flatly. "We go to Ashaba."

"*If* we can get out of the palace," Sadi murmured.

"We'll get out. Leave that to me."

"Of course, Ancient One."

The old man led them out into the hallway, down the stairs, and along the main corridor toward the stout door leading to the rest of the palace.

"Just a moment, father," Polgara said. She concentrated for a moment, the white lock at her brow glowing. Then Garion felt the surge of her will. "All right," she said. "The guards are asleep now."

The old man continued on down the corridor. "Here we are," he said, stopping before a large tapestry hanging on the marble wall. He reached behind the tapestry, took hold of an age-blackened iron ring, and pulled. There was a squeal of protesting metal and then a solid-sounding clank. "Push on that side," he said, gesturing toward the far end of the tapestry.

Garion went on down a few steps and set his shoulder to the tapestry. There was a metallic shriek as the covered marble slab turned slowly on rusty iron pivots set top and bottom in its precise center.

"Clever," Silk said, peering into the dark, cobweb-choked opening beyond the slab. "Who put it here?"

"A long time ago one of the Emperors of Mallorea was a bit nervous about his position," the old man replied. "He wanted to have a quick way out of the palace in case things started to go wrong. The passageway's been forgotten, so nobody's likely to follow us. Let's go bring out our packs and other belongings. We won't be coming back."

It took about five minutes for them to pile their things in front of the tapestry-covered panel, and by then Durnik, Toth, and Eriond were leading the horses along the marble corridor with a great clatter of hooves.

Garion stepped to the corner and peered around it at the main door. The two guards were standing rigidly, their faces blank and their eyes glassy and staring. Then he walked back to join the others. "Someday you'll have to show me how to do that," he said to Polgara, jerking his thumb back over his shoulder toward the two comatose soldiers.

"It's very simple, Garion," she told him.

"For you, maybe," he said. Then a thought suddenly came to him. "Grandfather," he said with a worried frown, "if this passage of yours comes out in the city, won't we be worse off than we were here in the palace? There's plague out there, you know, and all the gates are locked."

"It doesn't come out inside Mal Zeth," the old man replied. "Or so I've been told."

Out on the palace grounds the sounds of fighting intensified.

"They seem very enthusiastic, don't they?" Sadi murmured in a self-congratulatory way.

"Well, now," a familiar lilting voice came up out of the cellar beyond the panel. "Will ye stand there for hours pattin' yerselves on the backs an' allowin' the night to fly by with nothin' more accomplished at all? We've miles and miles to go, don't y' know? An' we won't get out of Mal Zeth this month unless we make a start, now will we?"

"Let's go," Belgarath said shortly.

The horses were reluctant to enter the dark, musty place behind the marble panel, but Eriond and Horse confidently went through with Garion's big gray, Chretienne, close behind; and the other animals somewhat skittishly followed.

It was not really a cellar, Garion realized. A flight of shallow stairs led down to what could be more properly described as a rough stone passageway. The horses had some difficulty negotiating the stairs, but eventually, following Eriond, Horse, and Chretienne, they reached the bottom.

At the top of the stairs the giant Toth pushed the hidden panel shut again, and the latch made an ominously heavy clank as it closed.

"One moment, father," Polgara said. In the close and musty-smelling darkness, Garion felt the faint surge of her will. "There," she said. "The soldiers are awake again, and they don't even know that we've been here."

At the bottom of the stairs the comic juggler, Feldegast, stood holding a well-shielded lantern. " 'Tis a fine night fer a little stroll," he observed. "Shall we be off, then?"

"I hope you know what you're doing," Belgarath said to him.

"How could ye possibly doubt me, old man?" the comedian said with an exaggerated expression of injury. "I'm the very soul of circumspection, don't y' know." He made a faint grimace. "There's only one teensy-weensy little problem. It seems that a certain portion of this passageway collapsed in on itself a while back, so we'll be forced to go through the steets up above for a triflin' bit of a way."

"Just *how* triflin'—trifling?" Belgarath demanded. He glared at the impudent comedian. "I wish you'd stop that," he said irritably. "What possessed you to resurrect a dialect that died out two thousand years ago?"

" 'Tis a part of me charm, Ancient Belgarath. Any man at all kin throw balls in the air an' catch 'em again, but it's the way a performer talks that sets the tone of his act."

"You two have met before, I take it?" Polgara said with one raised eyebrow.

"Yer honored father an' me are old, old friends, me dear Lady Polgara," Feldegast said with a sweeping bow. "I know ye all by his description. I must admit, however, that I'm overcome altogether by yer unearthly beauty."

"This is a rare rogue you've found, father," she said with a peculiar smile on her face. "I think I could grow to like him."

"I don't really advise it, Pol. He's a liar and a sneak and he has uncleanly habits.

You're evading the question, Feldegast—if that's what you want to call yourself. How far do we have to go through the streets?"

"Not far at all, me decrepit old friend—a half a mile perhaps until the roof of the passage is stout enough again to keep the pavin' stones where they belong instead of on the top of our heads. Let's press on, then. 'Tis a long, long way to the north wall of Mal Zeth, an' the night is wearin' on."

"Decrepit?" Belgarath objected mildly.

"Merely me way of puttin' things, Ancient One," Feldegast apologized. "Be sure that I meant no offense." He turned to Polgara. "Will ye walk with me, me girl? Ye've got an absolutely ravishin' fragrance about ye that quite takes me breath away. I'll walk along beside ye, inhalin' and perishin' with sheer delight."

Polgara laughed helplessly and linked her arm with that of the outrageous little man.

"I *like* him," Ce'Nedra murmured to Garion as they followed along through the cobwebby passageway.

"Yer supposed to, me girl," Garion said in a not altogether perfect imitation of the juggler's brogue. " 'Tis a part of his charm, don't y' know?"

"Oh, Garion," she laughed, "I love you."

"Yes," he said. "I know."

She gave him an exasperated look and then punched him in the shoulder with her little fist.

"Ouch."

"Did I hurt you?" she asked, taking his arm in sudden concern.

"I think I can stand it, dear," he replied. "We noble heroes can bear all sorts of things."

They followed Feldegast's lantern for a mile or more with the horses clattering along behind them through the cobweb-draped passageway. Occasionally they heard the rumble of the dead-carts bearing their mournful freight through the streets above. Here in the musty darkness, however, there was only the sound of the furtive skittering of an occasional errant mouse and the whisperlike tread of watchful spiders moving cautiously across the vaulted ceiling.

"I hate this," Silk said to no one in particular. "I absolutely hate it."

"That's all right, Kheldar," Velvet replied, taking the little man's hand. "I won't let anything hurt you."

"Thanks awfully," he said, though he did not remove his hand from hers.

"Who's there?" The voice came from somewhere ahead.

" 'Tis only me, good Master Yarblek," Feldegast replied. "Me an' a few lost, strayed souls tryin' to find their way on this dark, dark night."

"Do you really enjoy him all that much?" Yarblek said sourly to someone else.

"He's the delight of my life," Vella's voice came through the darkness. "At least with him I don't have to look to my daggers every minute to defend my virtue."

Yarblek sighed gustily. "I had a feeling that you were going to say something like that," he said.

"My lady," Vella said, making an infinitely graceful curtsy to Polgara as the sorceress and the juggler, arm in arm, moved up to the place where a moss-grown rockfall blocked the passageway.

"Vella," Polgara responded in an oddly Nadrak accent. "May your knives always be bright and keen." There was a strange formality in her greeting, and Garion knew that he was hearing an ancient ritual form of address.

"And may you always have the means at hand to defend your person from unwanted attentions," the Nadrak dancing girl responded automatically, completing the ritual.

"What's happening up above?" Belgarath asked the felt-coated Yarblek.

"They're dying," Yarblek answered shortly, "whole streets at a time."

"Have you been avoiding the city?" Silk asked his partner.

Yarblek nodded. "We're camped outside the gates," he said. "We got out just before they chained them shut. Dolmar died, though. When he realized that he had the plague, he got out an old sword and fell on it."

Silk sighed. "He was a good man—a little dishonest, maybe, but a good man all the same."

Yarblek nodded sadly. "At least he died clean," he said. Then he shook his head. "The stairs up to the street are over here," he said, pointing off into the darkness. "It's late enough so that there's nobody much abroad—except for the dead-carts and the few delirious ones stumbling about and looking for a warm gutter to die in." He squared his shoulders. "Let's go," he said. "The quicker we can get through those streets up there, the quicker we can get back underground where it's safe."

"Does the passage go all the way to the city wall?" Garion asked him.

Yarblek nodded. "And a mile or so beyond," he said. "It comes out in an old stone quarry." He looked at Feldegast. "You never did tell me how you found out about it," he said.

" 'Tis one of me secrets, good Master Yarblek," the juggler replied. "No matter how honest a man might be, it's always good to know a quick way out of town, don't y' know."

"Makes sense," Silk said.

"You ought to know," Yarblek replied. "Let's get out of here."

They led the horses to a flight of stone stairs reaching up into the darkness beyond the circle of light from Feldegast's lantern and then laboriously hauled the reluctant animals up the stairway, one step at a time. The stairway emerged in a rickety shed with a straw-littered floor. After the last horse had been hauled up, Feldegast carefully lowered the long trap door again and scuffed enough straw over it to conceal it. " 'Tis a useful sort of thing," he said, pointing downward toward the hidden passage, "but a secret's no good at all if just anybody kin stumble over it."

Yarblek stood at the door peering out into the narrow alleyway outside.

"Anybody out there?" Silk asked him.

"A few bodies," the Nadrak replied laconically. "For some reason they always seem to want to die in alleys." He drew in a deep breath. "All right, let's go, then."

They moved out into the alley, and Garion kept his eyes averted from the contorted bodies of the plague victims huddled in corners or sprawled in the gutters.

The night air was filled with smoke from the burning city, the reek of burning flesh, and the dreadful smell of decay.

Yarblek also sniffed, then grimaced. "From the odor, I'd say that the dead-carts have missed a few," he said. He led the way to the mouth of the alley and peered out into the street. "It's clear enough," he grunted. "Just a few looters picking over the dead. Come on."

They went out of the alley and moved along a street illuminated by a burning house. Garion saw a furtive movement beside the wall of another house and then made out the shape of a raggedly dressed man crouched over a sprawled body. The man was roughly rifling through the plague victim's clothes. "Won't he catch it?" he asked Yarblek, pointing at the looter.

"Probably." Yarblek shrugged. "I don't think the world's going to miss him very much if he does, though."

They rounded a corner and entered a street where fully half the houses were on fire. A dead-cart had stopped before one of the burning houses, and two rough-looking men were tossing bodies into the fire with casual brutality.

"Stay back!" one of the men shouted to them. "There's plague here!"

"There's plague everywhere in this mournful city, don't y' know," Feldegast replied. "But we thank ye fer yer warnin' anyway. We'll just go on by on the other side of the street, if ye don't mind." He looked curiously at the pair. "How is it that yer not afraid of the contagion yerselves?" he asked.

"We've already had it," one replied with a short laugh. "I've never been so sick in my life, but at least I didn't die from it—and they say you can only catch it once."

" 'Tis a fortunate man y' are, then," Feldegast congratulated him.

They moved on past the rough pair and on down to the next corner.

"We go this way," Feldegast told them.

"How much farther is it?" Belgarath asked him.

"Not far, an' then we'll be back underground where it's safe."

"*You* might feel safe underground," Silk said sourly, "but *I* certainly don't."

Halfway along the street Garion saw a sudden movement in one of the deeply inset doorways, and then he heard a feeble wail. He peered at the doorway. Then, one street over, a burning house fell in on itself, shooting flame and sparks high into the air. By that fitful light he was able to see what was in the shadows. The crumpled figure of a woman lay huddled in the doorway, and seated beside the body was a crying child, not much more than a year old. His stomach twisted as he started at the horror before his eyes.

Then, with a low cry, Ce'Nedra darted toward the child with her arms extended.

"Ce'Nedra!" he shouted, trying to shake his hand free of Chretienne's reins. "No!"

But before he could move in pursuit, Vella was already there. She caught Ce'Nedra by the shoulder and spun her around roughly. "Ce'Nedra!" she snapped. "Stay away!"

"Let me go!" Ce'Nedra almost screamed. "Can't you see that it's a baby?" She struggled to free herself.

Very coolly, Vella measured the little Queen, then slapped her sharply across the face. So far as Garion knew, it was the first time anyone had ever hit Ce'Nedra. "The baby's dead, Ce'Nedra," Vella told her with brutal directness, "and if you go near it, you'll die, too." She began to drag her captive back toward the others.

Ce'Nedra stared back over her shoulder at the sickly wailing child, her hand out-stretched toward it.

Then Velvet moved to her side, put an arm about her shoulders, and gently turned her so that she could no longer see the child. "Ce'Nedra," she said, "you must think first of your own baby. Would you want to carry this dreadful disease to him?"

Ce'Nedra stared at her.

"Or do you want to die before you ever see him again?"

With a sudden wail, Ce'Nedra fell into Velvet's arms, sobbing bitterly.

"I hope she won't hold any grudges," Vella murmured.

"You're very quick, Vella," Polgara said, "and you think very fast when you have to."

Vella shrugged. "I've found that a smart slap across the mouth is the best cure for hysterics."

Polgara nodded. "It usually works," she agreed approvingly.

They went on down the street until Feldegast led them into another smelly alley. He fumbled with the latch to the wide door of a boarded-up warehouse, then swung it open. "Here we are, then," he said, and they all followed him inside. A long ramp led down into a cavernous cellar, where Yarblek and the little juggler moved aside a stack of crates to reveal the opening of another passageway.

They led their horses into the dark opening, and Feldegast remained outside to hide the passage again. When he was satisfied that the opening was no longer visible, he wormed his way through the loosely stacked crates to rejoin them. "An' there we are," he said, brushing his hands together in a self-congratulatory way. "No man at all kin possibly know that we've come this way, don't y' know, so let's be off."

Garion's thoughts were dark as he trudged along the passageway, following Feldegast's winking lantern. He had slipped away from a man for whom he had begun to develop a careful friendship and had left him behind in a plague-stricken and burning city. There was probably very little that he could have done to aid 'Zakath, but his desertion of the man did not make him feel very proud. He knew, however, that he had no real choice. Cyradis had been too adamant in her instructions. Compelled by necessity, he turned his back on Mal Zeth and resolutely set his face toward Ashaba.

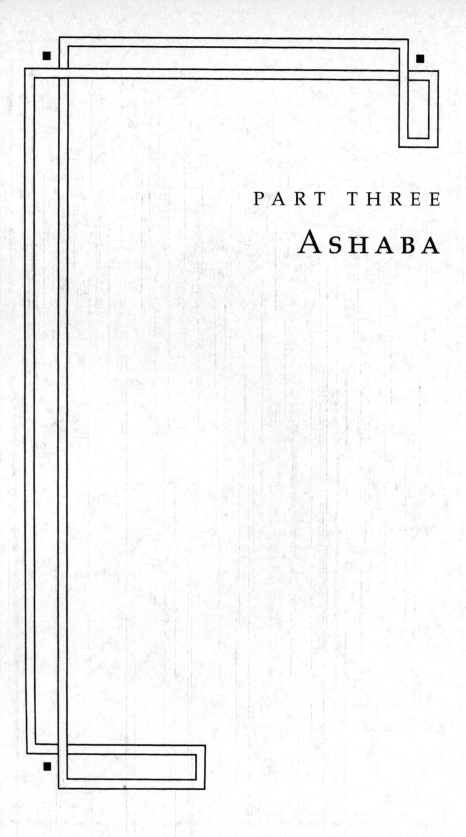

PART THREE
ASHABA

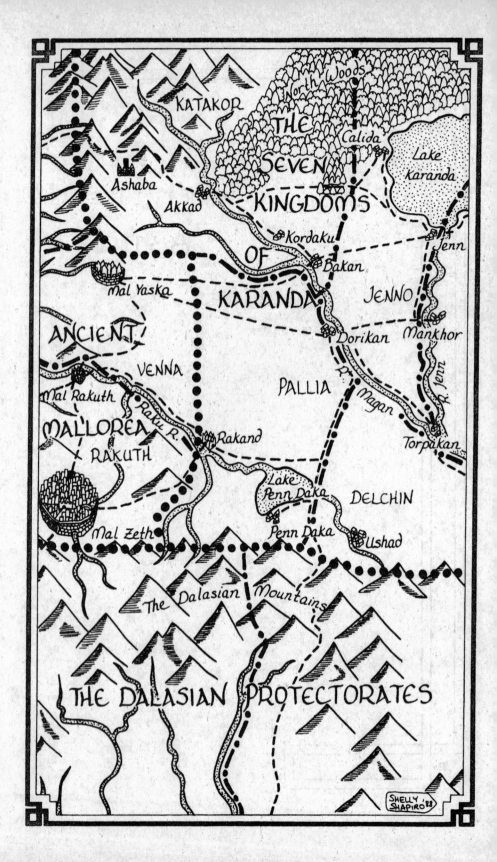

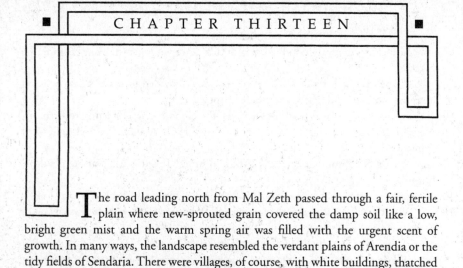

The road leading north from Mal Zeth passed through a fair, fertile plain where new-sprouted grain covered the damp soil like a low, bright green mist and the warm spring air was filled with the urgent scent of growth. In many ways, the landscape resembled the verdant plains of Arendia or the tidy fields of Sendaria. There were villages, of course, with white buildings, thatched roofs, and dogs that came out to stand at the roadside and bark. The spring sky was an intense blue dotted with puffy white clouds grazing like sheep in their azure pastures.

The road was a dusty brown ribbon laid straight where the surrounding green fields were flat, and folded and curved where the land rose in gentle, rounded hills.

They rode out that morning in glistening sunshine with the sound of the bells fastened about the necks of Yarblek's mules providing a tinkling accompaniment to the morning song of flights of birds caroling to greet the sun. Behind them there rose a great column of dense black smoke, marking the huge valley where Mal Zeth lay burning.

Garion could not bring himself to look back as they rode away.

There were others on the road as well, for Garion and his friends were not the only ones fleeing the plague-stricken city. Singly or in small groups, wary travelers moved north, fearfully avoiding any contact with each other, leaving the road and angling far out into the fields whenever they overtook other refugees, and returning to the brown, dusty ribbon only when they were safely past. Each solitary traveler or each group thus rode in cautious isolation, putting as much empty air about itself as possible.

The lanes branching off from the road and leading across the bright green fields were all blocked with barricades of fresh-cut brush, and bleak-faced peasants stood guard at those barricades, awkwardly handling staffs and heavy, graceless crossbows and shouting warnings at any and all who passed to stay away.

"Peasants," Yarblek said sourly as the caravan plodded past one such barricade. "They're the same the world over. They're glad to see you when you've got something they want, but they spend all the rest of their time trying to chase you away. Do you think they actually believe that anybody would really *want* to go into their stinking little villages?" Irritably he crammed his fur cap down lower over his ears.

"They're afraid," Polgara told him. "They know that their village isn't very luxurious, but it's all they have, and they want to keep if safe."

"Do those barricades and threats really do any good?" he asked. "To keep out the plague, I mean?"

"Some," she said, "if they put them up early enough."

Yarblek grunted, then looked over at Silk. "Are you open to a suggestion?" he asked.

"Depends," Silk replied. The little man had returned to his customary travel clothing—dark, unadorned, and nondescript.

"Between the plague and the demons, the climate here is starting to turn unpleasant. What say we liquidate all our holdings here in Mallorea and sit tight until things settle down?"

"You're not thinking, Yarblek," Silk told him. "Turmoil and war are good for business."

Yarblek scowled at him. "Somehow I thought you might look at it that way."

About a half mile ahead, there was another barricade, this one across the main road itself.

"What's this?" Yarblek demanded angrily, reining in.

"I'll go find out," Silk said, thumping his heels against his horse's flanks. On an impulse, Garion followed his friend.

When they were about fifty yards from the barricade, a dozen mud-spattered peasants dressed in smocks made of brown sackcloth rose from behind it with leveled crossbows. "Stop right there!" one of them commanded threateningly. He was a burly fellow with a coarse beard and eyes that looked off in different directions.

"We're just passing through, friend," Silk told him.

"Not without paying toll, you're not."

"Toll?" Silk exclaimed. "This is an imperial highway. There's no toll."

"There is now. You city people have cheated and swindled us for generations and now you want to bring your diseases to us. Well, from now on, you're going to pay. How much gold have you got?"

"Keep him talking," Garion muttered, looking around.

"Well," Silk said to the walleyed peasant in the tone of voice he usually saved for serious negotiations, "why don't we talk about that?"

The village stood about a quarter of a mile away, rising dirty and cluttered-looking atop a grassy knoll. Garion concentrated, drawing in his will, then he made a slight gesture in the direction of the village. "Smoke," he muttered, half under his breath.

Silk was still haggling with the armed peasants, taking up as much time as he could.

"Uh—excuse me," Garion interrupted mildly, "but is that something burning over there?" He pointed.

The peasants turned to stare in horror at the column of dense smoke rising from their village. With startled cries, most of them threw down their crossbows and ran out across the fields in the direction of the apparent catastrophe. The walleyed man ran after them, shouting at them to return to their posts. Then he ran back, waving his crossbow threateningly. A look of anguish crossed his face as he hopped about in an agony of indecision, torn between his desire for money that could be extorted from these travelers and the horrid vision of a fire raging unchecked through his house and outbuildings. Finally, no longer able to stand it, he also threw down his weapon and ran after his neighbors.

"Did you really set their village on fire?" Silk sounded a little shocked.

"Of course not," Garion said.

"Where's the smoke coming from then?"

"Lots of places." Garion winked. "Out of the thatch on their roofs, up from between the stones in the streets, boiling up out of their cellars and granaries—lots of places. But it's only smoke." He swung down from Chretienne's back and gathered up the discarded crossbows. He lined them up, nose down, in a neat row along the brushy barricade. "How long does it take to restring a crossbow?" he asked.

"Hours." Silk suddenly grinned. "Two men to bend the limbs with a windlass and another two to hook the cable in place."

"That's what I thought," Garion agreed. He drew his old belt knife and went down the line of weapons, cutting each twisted rope cable. Each bow responded with a heavy twang. "Shall we go, then?" he asked.

"What about this?" Silk pointed at the brushy barricade.

Garion shrugged. "I think we can ride around it."

"What were they trying to do?" Durnik asked when they returned.

"An enterprising group of local peasants decided that the highway needed a tollgate about there." Silk shrugged. "They didn't really have the temperament for business affairs, though. At the first little distraction, they ran off and left the shop untended."

They rode on past the now-deserted barricade with Yarblek's laden mules plodding along behind them, their bells clanging mournfully.

"I think we're going to have to leave you soon," Belgarath said to the furcapped Nadrak. "We have to get to Ashaba within the week, and your mules are holding us back."

Yarblek nodded. "Nobody ever accused a pack mule of being fast on his feet," he agreed. "I'll be turning toward the west before long anyway. You can go into Karanda if you want to, but I want to get to the coast as quickly as possible."

"Garion," Polgara said. She looked meaningfully at the column of smoke rising from the village behind them.

"Oh," he replied. "I guess I forgot." He raised his hand, trying to make it look impressive. "Enough," he said, releasing his will. The smoke thinned at its base, and the column continued to rise as a cloud, cut off from its source.

"Don't overdramatize, dear," Polgara advised. "It's ostentatious."

"You do it all the time," he accused.

"Yes, dear, but I know how."

It was perhaps noon when they rode up a long hill, crested it in the bright sunshine, and found themselves suddenly surrounded by mailed, red-tunicked Mallorean soldiers, who rose up out of ditches and shallow gullies with evil-looking javelins in their hands.

"You! Halt!" the officer in charge of the detachment of soldiers commanded brusquely. He was a short man, shorter even than Silk, though he strutted about as if he were ten feet tall.

"Of course, Captain," Yarblek replied, reining in his horse.

"What do we do?" Garion hissed to Silk.

"Let Yarblek handle it," Silk murmured. "He knows what he's doing."

"Where are you bound?" the officer asked when the rangy Nadrak had dismounted.

"Mal Dariya," Yarblek answered, "or Mal Camat—wherever I can hire ships to get my goods to Yar Marak."

The captain grunted as if trying to find something wrong with that. "What's more to the point is where you've come from." His eyes were narrowed.

"Maga Renn." Yarblek shrugged.

"Not Mal Zeth?" The little captain's eyes grew even harder and more suspicious.

"I don't do business in Mal Zeth very often, Captain. It costs too much—all those bribes and fees and permits, you know."

"I assume that you can prove what you say?" The captain's tone was belligerent.

"I suppose I could—if there's a need for it."

"There's a need, Nadrak, because, unless you can prove that you haven't come from Mal Zeth, I'm going to turn you back." He sounded smug about that.

"Turn back? That's impossible. I have to be in Boktor by midsummer."

"That's *your* problem, merchant." The little soldier seemed rather pleased at having upset the larger man. "There's plague in Mal Zeth, and *I'm* here to make sure that it doesn't spread." He tapped himself importantly on the chest.

"Plague!" Yarblek's eyes went wide, and his face actually paled. "Torak's teeth! And I almost stopped there!" He suddenly snapped his fingers. "So *that's* why all the villages hereabouts are barricaded."

"Can you prove that you came from Maga Renn?" the captain insisted.

"Well—" Yarblek unbuckled a well-worn saddlebag hanging under his right stirrup and began to rummage around in it. "I've got a permit here issued by the Bureau of Commerce," he said rather dubiously. "It authorizes me to move my goods from Maga Renn to Mal Dariya. If I can't find ships there, I'll have to get another permit to go on to Mal Camat, I guess. Would that satisfy you?"

"Let's see it." The captain held out his hand, snapping his fingers impatiently. Yarblek handed it over.

"It's a little smeared," the captain accused suspiciously.

"I spilled some beer on it in a tavern in Penn Daka." Yarblek shrugged. "Weak, watery stuff it was. Take my advice, Captain. Don't ever plan to do any serious drinking in Penn Daka. It's a waste of time and money."

"Is drinking all you Nadraks ever think about?"

"It's the climate. There's nothing else to do in Gar og Nadrak in the wintertime."

"Have you got anything else?"

Yarblek pawed through his saddlebag some more. "Here's a bill of sale from a carpet merchant on Yorba Street in Maga Renn—pockmarked fellow with bad teeth. Do you by any chance know him?"

"Why would I know a carpet merchant in Maga Renn? I'm an officer in the imperial army. I don't associate with riffraff. Is the date on this accurate?"

"How should I know? We use a different calendar in Gar og Nadrak. It was about two weeks ago, if that's any help."

The captain thought it over, obviously trying very hard to find some excuse to exert his authority. Finally his expression became faintly disappointed. "All right," he said grudgingly, handing back the documents. "Be on your way. But don't make any side trips, and make sure that none of your people leave your caravan."

"They'd better not leave—not if they want to get paid. Thank you, Captain." Yarblek swung back up into his saddle.

The officer grunted and waved them on.

"Little people should never be given any kind of authority," the Nadrak said sourly when they were out of earshot. "It lies too heavily on their brains."

"*Yarblek!*" Silk objected.

"Present company excepted, of course."

"Oh. That's different, then."

"Ye lie like ye were born to it, good Master Yarblek," Feldegast the juggler said admiringly.

"I've been associating with a certain Drasnian for too long."

"How did you come by the permit and the bill of sale?" Silk asked him.

Yarblek winked and tapped his forehead slyly. "Official types are always over-whelmed by official-looking documents—and the more petty the official, the more he's impressed. I could have proved to that obnoxious little captain back there that we came from any place at all—Melcene, Aduma in the Mountains of Zamad, even Crol Tibu on the coast of Gandahar—except that all you can buy in Crol Tibu are elephants, and I don't have any of those with me, so that might have made even him a little suspicious."

Silk looked around with a broad grin. "Now you see why I went into partner-ship with him," he said to them all.

"You seem well suited to each other," Velvet agreed.

Belgarath was tugging at one ear. "I think we'll leave you after dark tonight," he said to Yarblek. "I don't want some other officious soldier to stop us and count noses—or decide that we need a military escort."

Yarblek nodded. "Are you going to need anything?"

"Just some food is all." Belgarath glanced back at their laden packhorses plod-ding along beside the mules. "We've been on the road for quite some time now and we've managed to gather up what we really need and discard what we don't."

"I'll see to it that you've got enough food," Vella promised from where she was riding between Ce'Nedra and Velvet. "Yarblek sometimes forgets that full ale kegs are not the *only* things you need on a journey."

"An' will ye be ridin' north, then?" Feldegast asked Belgarath. The little comic had changed out of his bright-colored clothes and was now dressed in plain brown.

"Unless they've moved it, that's where Ashaba is," Belgarath replied.

"If it be all the same to ye, I'll ride along with ye fer a bit of a ways."

"Oh?"

"There was a little difficulty with the authorities the last time I was in Mal Dariya, an' I'd like to give 'em time t' regain their composure before I go back fer me triumphant return engagement. Authorities tend t' be a stodgy an' unfergivin' lot, don't y' know—always dredgin' up old pranks an' bits of mischief perpetrated in the spirit of fun an' throwin' 'em in yer face."

Belgarath gave him a long, steady look, then shrugged. "Why not?" he said.

Garion looked sharply at the old man. His sudden acquiescence seemed wildly out of character, given his angry protests at the additions of Velvet and Sadi to their party. Garion then looked over at Polgara, but she showed no signs of concern either. A peculiar suspicion began to creep over him.

As evening settled over the plains of Mallorea, they drew off the road to set up their night's encampment in a parklike grove of beech trees. Yarblek's muleteers sat about one campfire, passing an earthenware jug around and becoming increasingly rowdy. At the upper end of the grove, Garion and his friends sat around another fire, eating supper and talking quietly with Yarblek and Vella.

"Be careful when you cross into Venna," Yarblek cautioned his rat-faced partner. "Some of the stories coming out of there are more ominous than the ones coming out of Karanda."

"Oh?"

"It's as if a kind of madness has seized them all. Of course, Grolims were never very sane to begin with."

"Grolims?" Sadi looked up sharply.

"Venna's a Church-controlled state," Silk explained. "All authority there derives from Urvon and his court at Mal Yaska."

"It *used* to," Yarblek corrected. "Nobody seems to know *who's* got the authority now. The Grolims gather in groups to talk. The talk keeps getting louder until they're sceaming at each other, and then they all reach for their knives. I haven't been able to get the straight of it. Even the Temple Guardsmen are taking sides."

"The idea of Grolims cutting each other to pieces is one I can live with," Silk said.

"Truly," Yarblek agreed. "Just try not to get caught in the middle."

Feldegast had been softly strumming his lute and he struck a note so sour that even Garion noticed it.

"That string's out of tune," Durnik advised him.

"I know," the juggler replied. "The peg keeps slippin'."

"Let me see it," Durnik offered. "Maybe I can fix it."

" 'Tis too worn, I fear, friend Durnik. 'Tis a grand instrument, but it's old."

"Those are the ones that are worth saving." Durnik took the lute and twisted the loose peg, tentatively testing the pitch of the string with his thumb. Then he took his knife and cut several small slivers of wood. He carefully inserted them around the peg, tapping them into place with the hilt of his knife. Then he twisted the peg, retuning the string. "That should do it," he said. He took up the lute and strummed it a few times. Then, to a slow measure, he picked out an ancient air, the single notes quivering resonantly. He played the air through once, his fingers seeming to grow more confident as he went along. Then he returned to the beginning again, but this time, to Garion's amazement, he accompanied the simple melody with a rippling counterpoint so complex that it seemed impossible that it could come from a single instrument. "It has a nice tone," he observed to Feldegast.

" 'Tis a marvel that ye are, master smith. First ye repair me lute, an' then ye turn around an' put me t' shame by playin' it far better than I could ever hope to."

Polgara's eyes were very wide and luminous. "Why haven't you told me about this, Durnik?" she asked.

"Actually, it's been so long that I almost forgot about it." He smiled, his fingers still dancing on the strings and bringing forth that rich-toned cascade of sound. "When I was young, I worked for a time with a lute maker. He was old, and his fingers were stiff, but he needed to hear the tone of the instruments he made, so he taught me how to play them for him."

He looked across the fire at his giant friend, and something seemed to pass between them. Toth nodded, reached inside the rough blanket he wore across one shoulder, and produced a curious-looking set of pipes, a series of hollow reeds, each longer than the one preceding it, all bound tightly together. Quietly, the mute lifted the pipes to his lips as Durnik returned again to the beginning of the air. The sound he produced from his simple pipes had an aching poignancy about it that pierced Garion to the heart, soaring through the intricate complexity of the lute song.

"I'm beginnin' t' feel altogether unnecessary," Feldegast said in wonder. "Me own playin' of lute or pipe be good enough fer taverns an' the like, but I be no virtuoso like these two." He looked at the huge Toth. "How is it possible fer a man so big t' produce so delicate a sound?"

"He's very good," Eriond told him. "He plays for Durnik and me sometimes—when the fish aren't biting."

"Ah, 'tis a grand sound," Feldegast said, "an' far too good t' be wasted." He looked across the fire at Vella. "Would ye be willin' t' give us a bit of a dance, me girl, t' sort of round out the evenin'?"

"Why not?" She laughed with a toss of her head. She rose to her feet and moved to the opposite side of the fire. "Follow this beat," she instructed, raising her rounded arms above her head and snapping her fingers to set the tempo. Feldegast picked up the beat, clapping his hands rhythmically.

Garion had seen Vella dance before—long ago in a forest tavern in Gar og Nadrak—so he knew more or less what to expect. He was sure, however, that Eriond certainly—and Ce'Nedra probably—should not watch a performance of such blatant sensuality. Vella's dance began innocuously enough, though, and he began to think that perhaps he had been unduly sensitive the last time he had watched her.

When the sharp staccato of her snapping fingers and Feldegast's clapping increased the tempo, however, and she began to dance with greater abandon, he realized that his first assessment had been correct. Eriond should really not be watching this dance, and Ce'Nedra should be sent away almost immediately. For the life of him, however, he could not think of any way to do it.

When the tempo slowed again and Durnik and Toth returned to a simple restatement of the original air, the Nadrak girl concluded her dance with that proud, aggressive strut that challenged every man about the fire.

To Garion's absolute astonishment, Eriond warmly applauded with no trace of embarrassment showing on his young face. He knew that his own neck was burning and that his breath was coming faster.

Ce'Nedra's reaction was about what he had expected. Her cheeks were flaming and her eyes were wide. Then she suddenly laughed with delight. "Wonderful!" she exclaimed, and her eyes were full of mischief as she cast a sidelong glance at Garion. He coughed nervously.

Feldegast wiped a tear from his eye and blew his nose gustily. Then he rose to his feet. "Ah, me fine, lusty wench," he said fulsomely to Vella, hanging a regretful embrace about her neck and—endangering life and limb just a little in view of her ever-ready daggers—bussing her noisily on the lips, "it's destroyed altogether I am that we must part. I'll miss ye, me girl, an' make no mistake about that. But I make ye me promise that we'll meet again, an' I'll delight ye with a few of me naughty little stories, an' ye'll fuddle me brains with yer wicked brew, an' we'll laugh an' sing together an' enjoy spring after spring in the sheer delight of each others' company." Then he slapped her rather familiarly on the bottom and moved quickly out of range before she could find the hilt of one of her daggers.

"Does she dance for you often, Yarblek?" Silk asked his partner, his eyes very bright.

"*Too* often," Yarblek replied mournfully, "and every time she does, I find myself starting to think that her daggers aren't really all *that* sharp and that a little cut or two wouldn't really hurt too much."

"Feel free to try at any time, Yarblek," Vella offered, her hand suggestively on the hilt of one of her daggers. Then she looked at Ce'Nedra with a broad wink.

"Why do you dance like that?" Ce'Nedra asked, still blushing slightly. "You *know* what it does to every man who watches."

"That's part of the fun, Ce'Nedra. First you drive them crazy, and then you hold them off with your daggers. It makes them absolutely wild. Next time we meet, I'll show you how it's done." She looked at Garion and laughed a wicked laugh.

Belgarath returned to the fire. He had left at some time during Vella's dance, though Garion's eyes had been too busy to notice. "It's dark enough," he told them all. "I think we can leave now without attracting any notice."

They all rose from where they had been sitting.

"You know what to do?" Silk asked his partner.

Yarblek nodded.

"All right. Do whatever you have to keep me out of the soup."

"Why do you persist in playing around in politics, Silk?"

"Because it gives me access to greater opportunities to steal."

"Oh," Yarblek said. "That's all right then." He extended his hand. "Take care, Silk," he said.

"You, too, Yarblek. Try to keep us solvent if you can, and I'll see you in a year or so."

"If you live."

"There's that, too."

"I enjoyed your dance, Vella," Polgara said, embracing the Nadrak girl.

"I'm honored, Lady," Vella replied a bit shyly. "And we'll meet again, I'm sure."

"I'm certain that we will."

"Are ye sure that ye won't reconsider yer outrageous askin' price, Master Yarblek?" Feldegast asked.

"Talk to *her* about it," Yarblek replied, jerking his head in Vella's direction. "She's the one who set it."

" 'Tis a hardhearted woman ye are, me girl," the juggler accused her.

She shrugged. "If you buy something cheap, you don't value it."

"Now that's the truth, surely. I'll see what I kin do t' put me hands on some money, fer make no mistake, me fine wench, I mean t' own ye."

"We'll see," she replied with a slight smile.

They went out of the circle of firelight to their picketed horses—and the juggler's mule—and mounted quietly. The moon had set, and the stars lay like bright jewels across the warm, velvet throat of night as they rode out of Yarblek's camp and moved at a cautious walk toward the north. When the sun rose several hours later, they were miles away, moving northward along a well-maintained highway toward Mal Rukuth, the Angarak city lying on the south bank of the Raku River, the stream that marked the southern border of Venna. The morning was warm, the sky was clear, and they made good time.

Once again there were refugees on the road, but unlike yesterday, significant numbers of them were fleeing toward the south.

"Is it possible that the plague has broken out in the north as well?" Sadi asked.

Polgara frowned. "It's possible, I suppose," she told him.

"I think it's more likely that those people are fleeing from Mengha," Belgarath disagreed.

"It's going to get a bit chaotic hereabouts," Silk noted. "If you've got people fleeing in one direction from the plague and people fleeing in the other from the demons, about all they'll be able to do is mill around out here on these plains."

"That could work to our advantage, Kheldar," Velvet pointed out. "Sooner or later, 'Zakath is going to discover that we left Mal Zeth without saying good-bye and he's likely to send troops out looking for us. A bit of chaos in this region should help to confuse their search, wouldn't you say?"

"You've got a point there," he admitted.

Garion rode on in a half doze, a trick he had learned from Belgarath. Though he had occasionally missed a night's sleep in the past, he had never really gotten used to it. He rode along with his head down, only faintly aware of what was happening around him.

He heard a persistent sound that seemed to nag at the edge of his consciousness. He frowned, his eyes still closed, trying to identify the sound. And then he remembered. It was a faint, despairing wail, and the full horror of the sight of the dying child in the shabby street in Mal Zeth struck him. Try though he might, he could not wrench himself back into wakefulness, and the continuing cry tore at his heart.

Then he felt a large hand on his shoulder, shaking him gently. Struggling, he raised his head to look full into the sad face of the giant Toth.

"Did you hear it, too?" he asked.

Toth nodded, his face filled with sympathy.

"It was only a dream, wasn't it?"

Toth spread his hands, and his look was uncertain.

Garion squared his shoulders and sat up in his saddle, determined not to drift off again.

They rode some distance away from the road and took a cold lunch of bread, cheese, and smoked sausage in the shade of a large elm tree standing quite alone in the middle of a field of oats. There was a small spring surrounded by a mossy rock wall not far away, where they were able to water the horses and fill their water bags.

Belgarath stood looking out over the fields toward a distant village and the barricaded lane which approached it. "How much food do we have with us, Pol?" he asked. "If every village we come to is closed up the way the ones we've passed so far have been, it's going to be difficult to replenish our stores."

"I think we'll be all right, father," she replied. "Vella was very generous."

"I like her." Ce'Nedra smiled. "Even though she does swear all the time."

Polgara returned the smile. "It's the Nadrak way, dear," she said. "When I was in Gar og Nadrak, I had to draw on my memories of the more colorful parts of my father's vocabulary to get by."

"Halloo!" someone hailed them.

"He's over there." Silk pointed toward the road.

A man who was wearing one of the brown robes that identified him as a Melcene bureaucrat sat looking at them longingly from the back of a bay horse.

"What do you want?" Durnik called to him.

"Can you spare a bit of food?" the Melcene shouted. "I can't get near any of these villages and I haven't eaten in three days. I can pay."

Durnik looked questioningly at Polgara.

She nodded. "We have enough," she said.

"Which way was he coming?" Belgarath asked.

"South, I think," Silk replied.

"Tell him that it's all right, Durnik," the old man said. "He can probably give us some recent news from the north."

"Come on in," Durnik shouted to the hungry man.

The bureaucrat rode up until he was about twenty yards away. Then he stopped warily. "Are you from Mal Zeth?" he demanded.

"We left before the plague broke out," Silk lied.

The official hesitated. "I'll put the money on this rock here," he offered, pointing at a white boulder. "Then I'll move back a ways. You can take the money and leave some food. That way neither one of us will endanger the other."

"Makes sense," Silk replied pleasantly.

Polgara took a loaf of brown bread and a generous slab of cheese from her stores and gave them to the sharp-faced Drasnian.

The Melcene dismounted, laid a few coins on the rock, and then led his horse back some distance.

"Where have you come from, friend?" Silk asked as he approached the rock.

"I was in Akkad in Katakor," the hungry man answered, eyeing the loaf and the cheese. "I was senior administrator there for the Bureau of Public Works—you know, walls, aqueducts, streets, that sort of thing. The bribes weren't spectacular, but I managed to get by. Anyway, I got out just a few hours before Mengha and his demons got there."

Silk laid the food on the rock and picked up the money. Then he backed away. "We heard that Akkad fell quite some time ago."

The Melcene almost ran to the rock and snatched up and bread and cheese. He took a large bite of cheese and tore a chunk off the loaf. "I hid out in the mountains," he replied around the mouthful.

"Isn't that where Ashaba is?" Silk asked, sounding very casual.

The Melcene swallowed hard and nodded. "That's why I finally left," he said, stuffing bread in his mouth. "The area's infested with huge wild dogs—ugly brutes as big as horses—and there are roving bands of Karands killing everyone they come across. I could have avoided all that, but there's something terrible going on at Ashaba. There are dreadful sounds coming from the castle and strange lights in the sky over it at night. I don't hold with the supernatural, my friend, so I bolted." He sighed happily, tearing off another chunk of bread. "A month ago I'd have turned my nose up at brown bread and cheese. Now it tastes like a banquet."

"Hunger's the best sauce," Silk quoted the old adage.

"That's the honest truth."

"Why didn't you stay up in Venna? Didn't you know that there's plague in Mal Zeth?"

The Melcene shuddered. "What's going on in Venna's even worse than what's going on in Katakor or Mal Zeth," he replied. "My nerves are absolutely destroyed by all this. I'm an engineer. What do I know about demons and new Gods and magic? Give me paving stones and timbers and mortar and a few modest bribes and don't even mention any of that other nonsense to me."

"New Gods?" Silk asked. "Who's been talking about new Gods?"

"The Chandim. You've heard of them?"

"Don't they belong to Urvon the Disciple?"

"I don't think they belong to anybody right now. They've gone on a rampage in Venna. Nobody's seen Urvon for more than a month now—not even the people in Mal Yaska. The Chandim are completely out of control. They're erecting altars out in the fields and holding double sacrifices—the first heart to Torak and the second to this new God of Angarak—and anybody up there that doesn't bow to *both* altars gets his heart cut out right on the spot."

"That seems like a very good reason to stay out of Venna," Silk said wryly. "Have they put a name to this new God of theirs?"

"Not that I ever heard. They just call him 'The new God of Angarak, come to replace Torak and to take dreadful vengeance on the Godslayer.' "

"That's you," Velvet murmured to Garion.

"Do you mind?"

"I just thought you ought to know, that's all."

"There's an open war going on in Venna, my friend," the Melcene continued, "and I'd advise you to give the place a wide berth."

"War?"

"Within the Church itself. The Chandim are slaughtering all the old Grolims— the ones who are still faithful to Torak. The Temple Guardsmen are taking sides and they're having pitched battles on the plains up there—that's when they're not marauding through the countryside, burning farmsteads, and massacring whole villages. You'd think that the whole of Venna's gone crazy. It's as much as a man's life is worth to go through there just now. They stop you and ask you which God you worship, and a wrong answer is fatal." He paused, still eating. "Have you heard about any place that's quiet—and safe?" he asked plaintively.

"Try the coast," Silk suggested. "Mal Abad, maybe—or Mal Camat."

"Which way are you going?"

"We're going north to the river and see if we can find a boat to take us down to Lake Penn Daka."

"It won't be safe there for very long, friend. If the plague doesn't get there first, Mengha's demons will—or the crazed Grolims and their Guardsmen out of Venna."

"We don't plan to stop," Silk told him. "We're going to cut on across Delchin to Maga Renn and then on down the Magan."

"That's a long journey."

"Friend, I'll go to Gandahar if necessary to get away from demons and plague and mad Grolims. If worse comes to worst, we'll hide out among the elephant herders. Elephants aren't all that bad."

The Melcene smiled briefly. "Thanks for the food," he said, tucking his loaf and his cheese inside his robe and looking around for his grazing horse. "Good luck when you get to Gandahar."

"The same to you on the coast," Silk replied.

They watched the Melcene ride off.

"Why did you take his money, Kheldar?" Eriond asked curiously. "I thought we were just going to give him the food."

"Unexpected and unexplained acts of charity linger in people's minds, Eriond, and curiosity overcomes gratitude. I took his money to make sure that by tomorrow he won't be able to describe us to any curious soldiers."

"Oh," the boy said a bit sadly. "It's too bad that things are like that, isn't it?"

"As Sadi says, I didn't make the world; I only try to live in it."

"Well, what do you think?" Belgarath said to the juggler.

Feldegast squinted off toward the horizon. "Yer dead set on goin' right straight up through the middle of Venna—past Mal Yaska an' all?"

"We don't have any choice. We've got just so much time to get to Ashaba."

"Somehow I thought y' might feel that way about it."

"Do you know a way to get us through?"

Feldegast scratched his head. " 'Twill be dangerous, Ancient One," he said dubiously, "what with Grolims and Chandim and Temple Guardsmen an' all."

"It won't be nearly as dangerous as missing our appointment at Ashaba would be."

"Well, if yer dead set on it, I suppose I kin get ye through."

"All right," Belgarath said. "Let's get started then."

The peculiar suspicion which had come over Garion the day before grew stronger. Why would his grandfather ask these questions of a man they scarcely knew? The more he thought about it, the more he became convinced that there was a great deal more going on here than met the eye.

CHAPTER FOURTEEN

It was late afternoon when they reached Mal Rakuth, a grim fortress city crouched on the banks of a muddy river. The walls were high, and black towers rose within those walls. A large crowd of people was gathered outside, imploring the citizens to let them enter, but the city gates were locked, and archers with half-drawn bows lined the battlements, threatening the refugees below.

"That sort of answers that question, doesn't it?" Garion said as he and his companions reined in on a hilltop some distance from the frightened city.

Belgarath grunted. "It's more or less what I expected," he said. "There's nothing we really need in Mal Rakuth anyway, so there's not much point in pressing the issue."

"How are we going to get across the river, though?"

"If I remember correctly, there be a ferry crossin' but a few miles upstream," Feldegast told him.

"Won't the ferryman be just as frightened of the plague as the people in that city are?" Durnik asked him.

" 'Tis an ox-drawn ferry, Goodman—with teams on each side an' cables an' pulleys an' all. The ferryman kin take our money an' put us on the far bank an' never come within fifty yards of us. I fear the crossin' will be dreadful expensive, though."

The ferry proved to be a leaky old barge attached to a heavy cable stretched across the yellow-brown river.

"Stay back!" the mud-covered man holding the rope hitched about the neck of the lead ox on the near side commanded as they approached. "I don't want any of your filthy diseases."

"How much to go across?" Silk called to him.

The muddy fellow squinted greedily at them, assessing their clothing and horses. "One gold piece," he said flatly.

"That's outrageous!"

"Try swimming."

"Pay him," Belgarath said.

"Not likely," Silk replied. "I refuse to be cheated—even here. Let me think a minute." His narrow face became intent as he stared hard at the rapacious ferryman. "Durnik," he said thoughtfully, "do you have your axe handy?"

The smith nodded, patting the axe which hung from a loop at the back of his saddle.

"Do you suppose you could reconsider just a bit, friend?" the little Drasnian called plaintively to the ferryman.

"One gold piece," the ferryman repeated stubbornly.

Silk sighed. "Do you mind if we look at your boat first? It doesn't look all that safe to me."

"Help yourself—but I won't move it until I get paid."

Silk looked at Durnik. "Bring the axe," he said.

Durnik dismounted and lifted his broad-bladed axe from its loop. Then the two of them climbed down the slippery bank to the barge. They went up the sloping ramp and onto the deck. Silk stamped his feet tentatively on the planking. "Nice boat," he said to the ferryman, who stood cautiously some distance away. "Are you sure you won't reconsider the price?"

"One gold piece. Take it or leave it."

Silk sighed. "I was afraid you might take that position." He scuffed one foot at the muddy deck. "You know more about boats than I do, friend," he observed. "How long do you think it would take this tub to sink if my friend here chopped a hole in the bottom?"

The ferryman gaped at him.

"Pull up the decking in the bow, Durnik," Silk suggested pleasantly. "Give yourself plenty of room for a good swing."

The desperate ferryman grabbed up a club and ran down the bank.

"Careful, friend," Silk said to him. "We left Mal Zeth only yesterday, and I'm already starting to feel a little feverish—something I ate, no doubt."

The ferryman froze in his tracks.

Durnik was grinning as he began to pry up the decking at the front of the barge.

"My friend here is an expert woodsman," Silk continued in a conversational tone, "and his axe is terribly sharp. I'll wager that he can have this scow lying on the bottom inside of ten minutes."

"I can see into the hold now," Durnik reported, suggestively testing the edge of his axe with his thumb. "Just how big a hole would you like?"

"Oh," Silk replied, "I don't know, Durnik—a yard or so square, maybe. Would that sink it?"

"I'm not sure. Why don't we try it and find out?" Durnik pushed up the sleeves of his short jacket and hefted his axe a couple of times.

The ferryman was making strangled noises and hopping up and down.

"What's your feeling about negotiation at this point, friend?" Silk asked him. "I'm almost positive that we can reach an accommodation—now that you fully understand the situation."

When they were partway across the river and the barge was wallowing heavily in the current, Durnik walked forward to the bow and stood looking into the opening he had made by prying up the deck. "I wonder how big a hole it *would* take to sink this thing," he mused.

"What was that, dear?" Polgara asked him.

"Just thinking out loud, Pol," he said. "But do you know something? I just realized that I've never sunk a boat before."

She rolled her eyes heavenward. "Men," she sighed.

"I suppose I'd better put the planks back so that we can lead the horses off on the other side," Durnik said almost regretfully.

They erected their tents in the shelter of a grove of cedar trees near the river that evening. The sky, which had been serene and blue since they had arrived in

Mallorea, had turned threatening as the sun sank, and there were rumbles of thunder and brief flickers of lightning among the clouds off to the west.

After supper, Durnik and Toth went out of the grove for a look around and returned with sober faces. "I'm afraid that we're in for a spell of bad weather," the smith reported. "You can smell it coming."

"I hate riding in the rain," Silk complained.

"Most people do, Prince Kheldar," Feldegast told him. "But bad weather usually keeps others in as well, don't y' know; an' if what that hungry traveler told us this afternoon be true, we'll not be wantin' t' meet the sort of folk that be abroad in Venna when the weather's fine."

"He mentioned the Chandim," Sadi said, frowning. "Just exactly who are they?"

"The Chandim are an order within the Grolim Church," Belgarath told him. "When Torak built Cthol Mishrak, he converted certain Grolims into Hounds to patrol the region. After Vo Mimbre, when Torak was bound in sleep, Urvon converted about half of them back. The ones who reassumed human form are all sorcerers of greater or lesser talent, and they can communicate with the ones who are still Hounds. They're very close-knit—like a pack of wild dogs—and they're all fanatically loyal to Urvon."

"An' that be much of the source of Urvon's power," Feldegast added. "Ordinary Grolims be always schemin' against each other an' against their superiors, but Urvon's Chandim have kept the Mallorean Grolims in line fer five hundred years now."

"And the Temple Guardsmen?" Sadi added. "Are they Chandim, or Grolims, too?"

"Not usually," Belgarath replied. "There are Grolims among them, of course, but most of them are Mallorean Angaraks. They were recruited before Vo Mimbre to serve as Torak's personal bodyguard."

"Why would a God need a bodyguard?"

"I never entirely understood that myself," the old man admitted. "Anyway, after Vo Mimbre, there are still a few of them left—new recruits, veterans who'd been wounded in earlier battles and sent home, that sort of thing. Urvon persuaded them that *he* spoke for Torak, and now their allegiance is to him. After that, they recruited more young Angaraks to fill up the holes in their ranks. They do more than just guard the Temple now, though. When Urvon started having difficulties with the Emperors at Mal Zeth, he decided that he needed a fighting force, so he expanded them into an army."

" 'Tis a practical arrangement," Feldegast pointed out. "The Chandim provide Urvon with the sorcery he needs t' keep the other Grolims toein' the mark, an' the Temple Guardsmen provide the muscle t' keep the ordinary folk from protestin' their lot."

"These Guardsmen, they're just ordinary soldiers, then?" Durnik asked.

"Not really. They're closer to being knights," Belgarath replied.

"Like Mandorallen, you mean—all dressed in steel plate and with shields and lances and war horses and all that?"

"No, Goodman," Feldegast answered. "They're not nearly so grand. Lances an' helmets and shields they have, certainly, but fer the rest, they rely on chain mail. They be most nearly as stupid as Arends, however. Somethin' about wearin' all that steel empties the mind of every knight the world around."

Belgarath was looking speculatively at Garion. "How muscular are you feeling?" he asked.

"Not very—why?"

"We've got a bit of a problem here. We're far more likely to encounter Guardsmen than we are Chandim, but if we start unhorsing all these tin men with our minds, the noise is going to attract the Chandim like a beacon."

Garion stared at him. "You're not serious! I'm not Mandorallen, Grandfather."

"No. You've got better sense than he has."

"I will *not* stand by and hear my knight insulted!" Ce'Nedra declared hotly.

"Ce'Nedra," Belgarath said almost absently, "hush."

"Hush?"

"You heard me." He scowled at her so blackly that she faltered and drew back behind Polgara for protection. "The point, Garion," the old man continued, "is that you've received a certain amount of training from Mandorallen in this sort of thing and you've had a bit of experience. None of the rest of us have."

"I don't have any armor."

"You've got a mail shirt."

"I don't have a helmet—or a shield."

"I could probably manage those, Garion," Durnik offered.

Garion looked at his old friend. "I'm terribly disappointed in you, Durnik," he said.

"You aren't afraid, are you, Garion?" Ce'Nedra asked in a small voice.

"Well, no. Not really. It's just that it's so stupid—and it *looks* so ridiculous."

"Have you got an old pot I could borrow, Pol?" Durnik asked.

"How big a pot?"

"Big enough to fit Garion's head."

"Now that's going too far!" Garion exclaimed. "I'm not going to wear a kitchen pot on my head for a helmet. I haven't done that since I was a boy."

"I'll modify it a bit," Durnik assured him. "And then I'll take the lid and make you a shield."

Garion walked away swearing to himself.

Velvet's eyes had narrowed. She looked at Feldegast with no hint of her dimples showing. "Tell me, master juggler," she said, "how is it that an itinerant entertainer, who plays for pennies in wayside taverns, knows so very much about the inner working of Grolim society here in Mallorea?"

"I be not nearly so foolish as I look, me lady," he replied, "an' I do have eyes an' ears, an' know how t' use 'em."

"You avoided that question rather well," Belgarath complimented him.

The juggler smirked. "I thought so meself. Now," he continued seriously, "as me ancient friend here says, 'tis not too likely that we'll be encounterin' the Chandim if it rains, fer a dog has usually the good sense t' take t' his kennel when the weather be foul—unless there be pressin' need fer him t' be out an' about. 'Tis far more probable fer us t' meet Temple Guardsmen, fer a knight, be he Arendish or Mallorean, seems deaf t' the gentle patter of rain on his armor. I shouldn't wonder that our young warrior King over there be of sufficient might t' be a match fer any Guardsman we might meet alone, but there always be the possibility of comin' across 'em in groups. Should there be such encounters, keep yer wits about ye an' remember that once a knight has started his charge, 'tis very hard fer him t' swerve or change direction very much at all. A sidestep an' a smart rap across the back of the head be usually enough t' roll 'em out of the saddle, an' a man in armor—once he's off his horse—be like a turtle on his back, don't y' know."

"You've done it a few times yourself, I take it?" Sadi murmured.

"I've had me share of misunderstandin's with Temple Guardsmen," Feldegast admitted, "an' ye'll note that I still be here t' talk about 'em."

Durnik took the cast iron pot Polgara had given him and set it in the center of their fire. After a time, he pulled it glowing out of the coals with a stout stick, placed the blade of a broken knife on a rounded rock, and then set the pot over it. He took up his axe, reversed it, and held the blunt end over the pot.

"You'll break it," Silk predicted. "Cast iron's too brittle to take any pounding."

"Trust me, Silk," the smith said with a wink. He took a deep breath and began to tap lightly on the pot. The sound of his hammering was not the dull clack of cast iron, but the clear ring of steel, a sound that Garion remembered from his earliest boyhood. Deftly the smith reshaped the pot into a flat-topped helmet with a fierce nose guard and heavy cheek pieces. Garion knew that his old friend was cheating just a bit by the faint whisper and surge he was directing at the emerging helmet.

Then Durnik dropped the helmet into a pail of water, and it hissed savagely, sending off a cloud of steam. The pot lid that the smith intended to convert into a shield, however, challenged even *his* ingenuity. It became quite obvious that, should he hammer it out to give it sufficient size to offer protection, it would be so thin that it would not even fend off a dagger stroke, much less a blow from a lance or sword. He considered that, even as he pounded on the ringing lid. He shifted his axe and made an obscure gesture at Toth. The giant nodded, went to the river bank, returned with a pail full of clay, and dumped the bucket out in the center of the glowing shield. It gave off an evil hiss, and Durnik continued to pound.

"Uh—Durnik," Garion said, trying not to be impolite, "a ceramic shield was not exactly what I had in mind, you know."

Durnik gave him a grin filled with suppressed mirth. "Look at it, Garion," he suggested, not changing the tempo of his hammering.

Garion stared at the shield, his eyes suddenly wide. The glowing circle upon which Durnik was pounding was solid, cherry-red steel. "How did you do that?"

"Transmutation!" Polgara gasped. "Changing one thing into something else! Durnik, where on earth did you ever learn to do that?"

"It's just something I picked up, Pol." He laughed. "As long as you've got a bit of steel to begin with—like that old knife blade—you can make as much more as you want, out of anything that's handy: cast iron, clay, just about anything."

Ce'Nedra's eyes had suddenly gone very wide. "Durnik," she said in an almost reverent whisper, "could you have made it out of gold?"

Durnik thought about it, still hammering. "I suppose I could have," he admitted, "but gold's too heavy and soft to make a good shield, wouldn't you say?"

"Could you make another one?" she wheedled. "For me? It wouldn't have to be so big—at least not quite. Please, Durnik."

Durnik finished the rim of the shield with a shower of crimson sparks and the musical ring of steel on steel. "I don't think that would be a good idea, Ce'Nedra," he told her. "Gold is valuable because it's so scarce. If I started making it out of clay, it wouldn't be long before it wasn't worth anything at all. I'm sure you can see that."

"But—"

"No, Ce'Nedra," he said firmly.

"Garion—" she appealed, her voice anguished.

"He's right, dear."

"But—"

"Never mind, Ce'Nedra."

The fire had burned down to a bed of glowing coals. Garion awoke with a start, sitting up suddenly. He was covered with sweat and trembling violently. Once again he had heard the wailing cry that he had heard the previous day, and the sound of it wrenched at his heart. He sat for a long time staring at the fire. In time, the sweat dried and his trembling subsided.

Ce'Nedra's breathing was regular as she lay beside him, and there was no other sound in their well-shielded encampment. He rolled carefully out of his blankets and walked to the edge of the grove of cedars to stare bleakly out across the fields lying dark and empty under an inky sky. Then, because there was nothing he could do about it, he returned to his bed and slept fitfully until dawn.

It was drizzling rain when he awoke. He got up quietly and went out of the tent to join Durnik, who was building up the fire. "Can I borrow your axe?" he asked his friend.

Durnik looked up at him.

"I guess I'm going to need a lance to go with all that." He looked rather distastefully at the helmet and shield lying atop his mail shirt near the packs and saddles.

"Oh," the smith said. "I almost forgot about that. Is one going to be enough? They break sometimes, you know—at least Mandorallen's always did."

"I'm certainly not going to carry more than one." Garion jabbed his thumb back over his shoulder at the hilt of his sword. "Anyway, I've always got this big knife to fall back on."

The chill drizzle that had begun shortly before dawn was the kind of rain that made the nearby fields hazy and indistinct. After breakfast, they took heavy cloaks out of their packs and prepared to face a fairly unpleasant day. Garion had already put on his mail shirt, and he padded the inside of his helmet with an old tunic and jammed it down on his head. He felt very foolish as he clinked over to saddle Chretienne. The mail already smelled bad and it seemed, for some reason, to attract the chill of the soggy morning. He looked at his new-cut lance and his round shield. "This is going to be awkward," he said.

"Hang the shield from the saddle bow, Garion," Durnik suggested, "and set the butt of your lance in the stirrup beside your foot. That's the way Mandorallen does it."

"I'll try it," Garion said. He hauled himself up into his saddle, already sweating under the weight of his mail. Durnik handed him the shield, and he hooked the strap of it over the saddle bow. Then he took his lance and jammed its butt into his stirrup, pinching his toes in the process.

"You'll have to hold it," the smith told him. "It won't stay upright by itself."

Garion grunted and took the shaft of his lance in his right hand.

"You look very impressive, dear," Ce'Nedra assured him.

"Wonderful," he replied dryly.

They rode out of the cedar grove into the wet, miserable morning with Garion in the lead, feeling more than a little absurd in his warlike garb.

The lance, he discovered almost immediately, had a stubborn tendency to dip its point toward the ground. He shifted his grip on it, sliding his hand up until he found its center of balance. The rain collected on the shaft of the lance, ran down across his clammy hand, and trickled into his sleeve. After a short while, a steady stream of water dribbled from his elbow. "I feel like a downspout," he grumbled.

"Let's pick up the pace," Belgarath said to him. "It's a long way to Ashaba, and we don't have too much time."

Garion nudged Chretienne with his heels, and the big gray moved out, at first at a trot and then in a rolling canter. For some reason that made Garion feel a bit less foolish.

The road which Feldegast had pointed out to them the previous evening was little traveled and this morning it was deserted. It ran past abandoned farmsteads, sad, bramble-choked shells with the moldy remains of their thatched roofs all tumbled in. A few of the farmsteads had been burned, some only recently.

The road began to turn muddy as the earth soaked up the steady rain. The cantering hooves of their horses splashed the mud up to coat their legs and bellies and to spatter the boots and cloaks of the riders.

Silk rode beside Garion, his sharp face alert, and just before they reached the crest of each hill, he galloped on ahead to have a quick look at the shallow valley lying beyond.

By midmorning, Garion was soaked through, and he rode on bleakly, enduring the discomfort and the smell of new rust, wishing fervently that the rain would stop.

Silk came back down the next hill after scouting on ahead. His face was tight with a sudden excitement, and he motioned them all to stop.

"There are some Grolims up ahead," he reported tersely.

"How many?" Belgarath asked.

"About two dozen. They're holding some kind of religious ceremony."

The old man grunted. "Let's take a look." He looked at Garion. "Leave your lance with Durnik," he said. "It sticks up too high into the air, and I'd rather not attract attention."

Garion nodded and passed his lance over to the smith, then followed Silk, Belgarath, and Feldegast up the hill. They dismounted just before they reached the crest and moved carefully to the top, where a brushy thicket offered some conceal-ment.

The black-robed Grolims were kneeling on the wet grass before a pair of grim altars some distance down the hill. A limp, unmoving form lay sprawled across each of them, and there was a great deal of blood. Sputtering braziers stood at the end of each altar, sending twin columns of black smoke up into the drizzle. The Grolims were chanting in the rumbling groan Garion had heard too many times before. He could not make out what they were saying.

"Chandim?" Belgarath softly asked the juggler.

" 'Tis hard t' say fer certain, Ancient One," Feldegast replied. "The twin altars would suggest it, but the practice might have spread. Grolims be very quick t' pick up changes in Church policy. But Chandim or not, 'twould be wise of us t' avoid 'em. There be not much point in engagin' ourselves in casual skirmishes with Grolims."

"There are trees over on the east side of the valley," Silk said, pointing. "If we stay in among them, we'll be out of sight."

Belgarath nodded.

"How much longer are they likely to be praying?" Garion asked.

"Another half hour at least," Feldegast replied.

Garion looked at the pair of altars, feeling an icy rage building up in him. "I'd like to cap their ceremony with a little personal visit," he said.

"Forget it," Belgarath told him. "You're not here to ride around the countryside righting wrongs. Let's go back and get the others. I'd like to get around those Grolims before they finish with their prayers."

They picked their way carefully through the belt of dripping trees that wound along the eastern rim of the shallow valley where the Grolims were conducting their grim rites and returned to the muddy road about a mile beyond. Again they set out at the same distance-eating canter, with Garion once more in the lead.

Some miles past the valley where the Grolims had sacrificed the two unfortu-nates, they passed a burning village that was spewing out a cloud of black smoke. There seemed to be no one about, though there were some signs of fighting near the burning houses.

They rode on without stopping.

The rain let up by midafternoon, though the sky remained overcast. Then, as they crested yet another hilltop in the rolling countryside, they saw another rider on the far side of the valley. The distance was too great to make out details, but Garion *could* see that the rider was armed with a lance.

"What do we do?" he called back over his shoulder at the rest of them.

"That's why you're wearing armor and carrying a lance, Garion," Belgarath replied.

"Shouldn't I at least give him the chance to stand aside?"

"To what purpose?" Feldegast asked. "He'll not do it. Yer very presence here with yer lance an' yer shield be a challenge, an' he'll not be refusin' it. Ride him down, young Master. The day wears on, don't y' know."

"All right," Garion said unhappily. He buckled his shield to his left arm, settled his helmet more firmly in place, and lifted the butt of his lance out of his stirrup. Chretienne was already pawing at the earth and snorting defiantly.

"Enthusiast," Garion muttered to him. "All right, let's go, then."

The big gray's charge was thunderous. It was not a gallop, exactly, nor a dead run, but rather was a deliberately implacable gait that could only be called a charge.

The armored man across the valley seemed a bit startled by the unprovoked attack, there having been none of the customary challenges, threats, or insults. After a bit of fumbling with his equipment, he managed to get his shield in place and his lance properly advanced. He seemed to be quite bulky, though that might have been his armor. He wore a sort of chain-mail coat reaching to his knees. His helmet was round and fitted with a visor, and he had a large sword sheathed at his waist. He clanged down his visor, then sank his spurs into his horse's flanks and also charged.

The wet fields at the side of the road seemed to blur as Garion crouched behind his shield with his lance lowered and aimed directly at his opponent. He had seen Mandorallen do this often enough to understand the basics. The distance between him and the stranger was narrowing rapidly, and Garion could clearly see the mud spraying out from beneath the hooves of his opponent's horse. At the last moment, just before they came together, Garion raised up in his stirrups as Mandorallen had instructed him, leaned forward so that his entire body was braced for the shock, and took careful aim with his lance at the exact center of the other man's shield.

There was a dreadful crashing impact, and he was suddenly surrounded by flying splinters as his opponent's lance shattered. His own lance, however, though it was as stout as that of the Guardsman, was a freshly cut cedar pole and it was quite springy. It bent into a tight arch like a drawn bow, then snapped straight again. The startled stranger was suddenly lifted out of his saddle. His body described a high, graceful arc through the air, which ended abruptly as he came down on his head in the middle of the road.

Garion thundered on past and finally managed to rein in his big gray horse. He wheeled and stopped. The other man lay on his back in the mud of the road. He was not moving. Carefully, his lance at the ready, Garion walked Chretienne back to the splinter-littered place where the impact had occurred.

"Are you all right?" he asked the Temple Guardsman lying in the mud.

There was no answer.

Cautiously, Garion dismounted, dropped his lance, and drew Iron-grip's sword. "I say, man, are you all right?" he asked again. He reached out with his foot and nudged the fellow.

The Guardsman's visor was closed, and Garion put the tip of his sword under the bottom of it and lifted. The man's eyes were rolled back in his head until only the whites showed, and there was blood gushing freely from his nose.

The others came galloping up, and Ce'Nedra flung herself out of the saddle almost before her horse and stopped and hurled herself into her husband's arms. "You were magnificent, Garion! Absolutely magnificent!"

"It did go rather well, didn't it?" he replied modestly, trying to juggle sword, shield, and wife all at the same time. He looked at Polgara, who was also dismounting. "Do you think he's going to be all right, Aunt Pol?" he asked. "I hope I didn't hurt him too much."

She checked the limp man lying in the road. "He'll be fine, dear," she assured him. "He's just been knocked senseless, is all."

"Nice job," Silk said.

Garion suddenly grinned broadly. "You know something," he said. "I think I'm starting to understand why Mandorallen enjoys this so much. It *is* sort of exhilarating."

"I think it has t' do with the weight of the armor," Feldegast observed sadly to Belgarath. "It bears down on 'em so much that it pulls all the juice out of their brains, or some such."

"Let's move on," Belgarath suggested.

By midmorning the following day, they had moved into the broad valley which was the location of Mal Yaska, the ecclesiastical capital of Mallorea and the site of the Disciple Urvon's palace. Though the sky remained overcast, the rain had blown on through, and a stiff breeze had begun to dry the grass and the mud which had clogged the roads. There were encampments dotting the valley, little clusters of people who had fled from the demons to the north and the plague to the south. Each group was fearfully isolated from its neighbors, and all of them kept their weapons close at hand.

Unlike those of Mal Rakuth, the gates of Mal Yaska stood open, though they were patrolled by detachments of mail-armored Temple Guardsmen.

"Why don't they go into the city?" Durnik asked, looking at the clusters of refugees.

"Mal Yaska's not the sort of place ye visit willin'ly, Goodman," Feldegast replied. "When the Grolims be lookin' fer people t' sacrifice on their altars, 'tis unwise t' make yerself too handy." He looked at Belgarath. "Would ye be willin' t' accept a suggestion, me ancient friend?" he asked.

"Suggest away."

"We'll be needin' information about what's happenin' up there." He pointed at the snow-capped mountains looming across the northern horizon. "Since I know me way about Mal Yaska an' know how t' avoid the Grolims, wouldn't ye say that it might be worth the investment of an hour or so t' have me nose about the central marketplace an' see what news I kin pick up?"

"He's got a point, Belgarath," Silk agreed seriously. "I don't like riding into a situation blind."

Belgarath considered it. "All right," he said to the juggler, "but be careful—and stay out of the alehouses."

Feldegast sighed. "There be no such havens in Mal Yaska, Belgarath. The Grolims there be fearful strict in their disapproval of simple pleasures." He shook the reins of his mule and rode on across the plain toward the black walls of Urvon's capital.

"Isn't he contradicting himself?" Sadi asked. "First he says it's too dangerous to go into the city and then he rides on in anyway."

"He knows what he's doing," Belgarath said. "He's in no danger."

"We might as well have some lunch while we're waiting, father," Polgara suggested.

He nodded, and they rode some distance into an open field and dismounted.

Garion laid aside his lance, pulled his helmet from his sweaty head, and stood looking across the intervening open space at the center of Church power in Mallorea. The city was large, certainly, though not nearly so large as Mal Zeth. The walls were high and thick, surmounted by heavy battlements, and the towers rising inside were square and blocky. There was a kind of unrelieved ugliness about it, and it seemed to exude a brooding menace as if the eons of cruelty and blood lust had sunk into its very stones. From somewhere near the center of the city, the telltale black column of smoke rose into the air, and faintly, echoing across the plain with its huddled encampments of frightened refugees, he thought he could hear the sullen iron clang of the gong coming from the Temple of Torak. Finally, he sighed and turned his head away.

"It will not last forever," Eriond, who had come up beside him, said firmly. "We're almost to the end of it now. All the altars will be torn down, and the Grolims will put their knives away to rust."

"Are you sure, Eriond?"

"Yes, Belgarion. I'm very sure."

They ate a cold lunch, and, not long after, Feldegast returned, his face somber. " 'Tis perhaps a bit more serious than we had expected, Ancient One," he reported, swinging down from his mule. "The Chandim be in total control of the city, an' the Temple Guardsmen be takin' their orders directly from them. The Grolims who hold t' the old ways have all gone into hidin', but packs of Torak's Hounds be sniffin' out the places where they've hidden an' they be tearin' 'em t' pieces wherever they find 'em."

"I find it very hard to sympathize with Grolims," Sadi murmured.

"I kin bear their discomfort meself," Feldegast agreed, "but 'tis rumored about the marketplace that the Chandim an' their dogs an' their Guardsmen *also* be movin' about across the border in Katakor."

"In spite of the Karands and Mengha's demons?" Silk asked with some surprise.

"Now that's somethin' I could not get the straight of," the juggler replied. "No one could tell me why or how, but the Chandim an' the Guardsmen seem not t' be concerned about Mengha nor his army nor his demons."

"That begins to smell of some kind of accommodation," Silk said.

"There were hints of that previously," Feldegast reminded him.

"An alliance?" Belgarath frowned.

" 'Tis hard t' say fer sure, Ancient One, but Urvon be a schemer, an' he's always had this dispute with the imperial throne at Mal Zeth. If he's managed t' put Mengha in his pocket, Kal Zakath had better look t' his defenses."

"Is Urvon in the city?" Belgarath asked.

"No. No one knows where he's gone fer sure, but he's not in his palace there."

"That's very strange," Belgarath said.

"Indeed," the juggler replied, "but whatever he's doin' or plannin' t' do, I think we'd better be walkin' softly once we cross the border into Katakor. When ye add the Hounds an' the Temple Guardsmen t' the demons an' Karands already there, 'tis goin' t' be fearful perilous t' approach the House of Torak at Ashaba."

"That's a chance we'll have to take," the old man said grimly. "We're going to Ashaba, and if anything—Hound, human, or demon—gets in our way, we'll just have to deal with it as it comes."

■ CHAPTER FIFTEEN ■

The sky continued to lower as they rode past the brooding city of the Grolim Church under the suspicious gaze of the armored Guardsmen at the gate and the hooded Grolims on the walls.

"Is it likely that they'll follow us?" Durnik asked.

"It's not very probable, Goodman," Sadi replied. "Look around you. There are thousands encamped here, and I doubt that either Guardsmen or Grolims would take the trouble to follow them all when they leave."

"I suppose you're right," the smith agreed.

By late afternoon they were well past Mal Yaska, and the snow-topped peaks in Katakor loomed higher ahead of them, starkly outlined against the dirty gray clouds scudding in from the west.

"Will ye be wantin' t' stop fer the night before we cross the border?" Feldegast asked Belgarath.

"How far is it to there from here?"

"Not far at all, Ancient One."

"Is it guarded?"

"Usually, yes."

"Silk," the old man said, "ride on ahead and have a look."

The little man nodded and nudged his horse into a gallop.

"All right," Belgarath said, signaling for a halt so that they could all hear him. "Everybody we've seen this afternoon was going south. Nobody's fleeing *toward* Katakor. Now, a man who's running away from someplace doesn't stop when the border's in sight. He keeps on going. That means that there's a fair chance that there's not going to be anybody within miles of the border on the Katakor side. If the border's not guarded, we can just go on across and take shelter for the night on the other side."

"And if the border *is* guarded?" Sadi asked.

Belgarath's eyes grew flat. "We're still going to go through," he replied.

"That's likely to involve fighting."

"That's right. Let's move along, shall we?"

About fifteen minutes later, Silk returned. "There are about ten Guardsmen at the crossing," he reported.

"Any chance of taking them by surprise?" Belgarath asked him.

"A little, but the road leading to the border is straight and flat for a half mile on either side of the guard post."

The old man muttered a curse under his breath. "All right then," he said.

"They'll at least have time to get to their horses. We don't want to give them the leisure to get themselves set. Remember what Feldegast said about keeping your wits. Don't take any chances, but I want all of those Guardsmen on their backs after our first charge. Pol, you stay back with the ladies—and Eriond."

"But—" Velvet began to protest.

"Don't argue with me, Liselle—just this once."

"Couldn't Lady Polgara just put them to sleep?" Sadi asked. "The way she did with the spies back in Mal Zeth?"

Belgarath shook his head. "There are a few Grolims among the Guardsmen, and that particular technique doesn't work on Grolims. This time we're going to have to do it by main strength—just to be on the safe side."

Sadi nodded glumly, dismounted, and picked up a stout tree limb from the side of the road. He thumped it experimentally on the turf. "I want you all to know that this is not my preferred way of doing things," he said.

The rest of them also dismounted and armed themselves with cudgels and staffs. Then they moved on.

The border was marked by a stone shed painted white and by a gate consisting of a single white pole resting on posts on either side of the road. A dozen horses were tethered just outside the shed, and lances leaned against the wall. A single, mail-coated Guardsman paced back and forth across the road on the near side of the gate, his sword leaning back over his shoulder.

"All right," Belgarath said. "Let's move as fast as we can. Wait here, Pol."

Garion sighed. "I guess I'd better go first."

"We were hoping that you'd volunteer." Silk's grin was tight.

Garion ignored that. He buckled on his shield, settled his helmet in place, and once again lifted the butt of his lance out of his stirrup. "Is everybody ready?" he asked, looking around. Then he advanced his lance and spurred his horse into a charge with the others close on his heels.

The Guardsman at the gate took one startled look at the warlike party bearing down on him, ran to the door of the shed, and shouted at his comrades inside. Then he struggled into the saddle of his tethered horse, leaned over to pick up his lance, and moved out into the road. Other Guardsmen came boiling out of the shed, struggling with their equipment and stumbling over each other.

Garion had covered half the distance to the gate before more than two or three of the armored men were in their saddles, and so it was that the man who had been standing watch was forced to meet his charge alone.

The results were relatively predictable.

As Garion thundered past his unhorsed opponent, another Guardsman came out into the road at a half gallop, but Garion gave him no time to set himself or to turn his horse. The crashing impact against the unprepared man's shield hurled his horse from its feet. The Guardsman came down before the horse did, and the animal rolled over him, squealing and kicking in fright.

Garion tried to rein in, but Chretienne had the bit in his teeth. He cleared the pole gate in a long, graceful leap and charged on. Garion swore and gave up on the reins. He leaned forward and seized the big gray by one ear and hauled back. Startled, Chretienne stopped so quickly that his rump skidded on the road.

"The fight's back that way," Garion told his horse, "or did you forget already?"

Chretienne gave him a reproachful look, turned, and charged back toward the gate again.

Because of the speed of their attack, Garion's friends were on top of the Guardsmen before the armored men could bring their lances into play, and the fight had quickly turned ugly. Using the blunt side of his axe, Durnik smashed in one Guardsman's visor, denting it so severely that the man could no longer see. He rode in circles helplessly, both hands clutching at his helmet until he rode under a low-hanging limb, which smoothly knocked him off his horse.

Silk ducked under a wide, backhand sword stroke, reached down with his dagger, and neatly cut his attacker's girth strap. The fellow's horse leaped forward, jumping out from under his rider. Saddle and all, the Guardsman tumbled into the road. He struggled to his feet, sword in hand, but Feldegast came up behind him and methodically clubbed him to earth again with an ugly lead mace.

It was Toth, however, who was the hardest pressed. Three Guardsmen closed in on the giant. Even as Chretienne leaped the gate again, Garion saw the huge man awkwardly flailing with his staff for all the world like someone who had never held one in his hands before. When the three men came within range however, Toth's skill miraculously reemerged. His heavy staff whirled in a blurring circle. One Guardsman fell wheezing to earth, clutching at his broken ribs. Another doubled over sharply as Toth deftly poked him in the pit of the stomach with the butt of his staff. The third desperately raised his sword, but the giant casually swiped it out of his hand, then reached out and took the surprised man by the front of his mail coat. Garion clearly heard the crunch of crushed steel as Toth's fist closed. Then the giant looked about and almost casually threw the armored man against a roadside tree so hard that it shook the spring leaves from the highest twig.

The three remaining Guardsmen began to fall back, trying to give themselves room to use their lances, but they seemed unaware that Garion was returning to the fray—from behind them.

As Chretienne thundered toward the unsuspecting trio, a sudden idea came to Garion. Quickly he turned his lance sideways so that its center rested just in front of his saddlebow and crashed into the backs of the Guardsmen. The springy cedar pole swept all three of them out of their saddles and over the heads of their horses. Before they could stumble to their feet, Sadi, Feldegast, and Durnik were on them, and the fight ended as quickly as it had begun.

"I don't think I've ever seen anybody use a lance that way before," Silk said gaily to Garion.

"I just made it up," Garion replied with an excited grin.

"I'm sure that there are at least a half-dozen rules against it."

"We probably shouldn't mention it, then."

"I won't tell anybody if you don't."

Durnik was looking around critically. The ground was littered with Guardsmen who were either unconscious or groaning over assorted broken bones. Only the man Toth had poked in the stomach was still in his saddle, though he was doubled over, gasping for breath. Durnik rode up to him. "Excuse me," he said politely, removed the poor fellow's helmet, and then rapped him smartly on top of the head with the butt of his axe. The Guardsman's eyes glazed, and he toppled limply out of the saddle.

Belgarath suddenly doubled over, howling with laughter. *"Excuse me?"* he demanded of the smith.

"There's no need to be uncivil to people, Belgarath," Durnik replied stiffly.

Polgara came riding sedately down the hill, followed by Ce'Nedra, Velvet, and Eriond. "Very nice, gentlemen," she complimented them all, looking around at the fallen Guardsmen. Then she rode up to the pole gate. "Garion, dear," she said pleasantly, reining in her mount, "would you mind?"

He laughed, rode Chretienne over to the gate, and kicked it out of her way.

"Why on earth were you jumping fences in the very middle of the fight?" she asked him curiously.

"It wasn't altogether my idea," he replied.

"Oh," she said, looking critically at the big horse. "I think I understand."

Chretienne managed somehow to look slightly ashamed of himself.

They rode on past the border as evening began imperceptibly to darken an already gloomy sky. Feldegast pulled in beside Belgarath. "Would yer morals be at all offended if I was t' suggest shelterin' fer the night in a snug little smugglers' cave I know of a few miles or so farther on?" he asked.

Belgarath grinned and shook his head. "Not in the slightest," he replied. "When I need a cave, I never concern myself about the previous occupants." Then he laughed. "I shared quarters for a week once with a sleeping bear—nice enough bear, actually, once I got used to his snoring."

" 'Tis a fascinatin' story, I'm sure, an' I'd be delighted t' hear it—but the night's comin' on, an' ye kin tell me about it over supper. Shall we be off, then?" The juggler thumped his heels into his mule's flanks and led them on up the rutted road in the rapidly descending twilight at a jolting gallop.

As they moved into the first of the foothills, they found the poorly maintained road lined on either side by mournful-looking evergreens. The road, however, was empty, though it showed signs of recent heavy traffic—all headed south.

"How much farther to this cave of yours?" Belgarath called to the juggler.

" 'Tis not far, Ancient One," Feldegast assured him. "There be a dry ravine that crosses the road up ahead, an' we go up that a bit of a ways, an' there we are."

"I hope you know what you're doing."

"Trust me."

Somewhat surprisingly, Belgarath let that pass.

They pounded on up the road as a sullen dusk settled into the surrounding foothills and deep shadows began to gather about the trunks of the evergreens.

"Ah, an' there it is," Feldegast said, pointing at the rocky bed of a dried-up stream. "The footin' be treacherous here, so we'd best lead the mounts." He swung down from his mule and cautiously began to lead the way up the ravine. It grew steadily darker, the light fading quickly from the overcast sky. As the ravine narrowed and rounded a sharp bend, the juggler rummaged through the canvas pack strapped to the back of his mule. He lifted out the stub of a candle and looked at Durnik. "Kin ye be makin' me a bit of a flame, Goodman?" he asked. "I'd do it meself, but I seem t' have misplaced me tinder."

Durnik opened his pouch, took out his flint and steel and his wad of tinder, and, after several tries, blew a lighted spark into a tiny finger of fire. He held it out, shielded between his hands, and Feldegast lit his bit of candle.

"An' here we are now," the juggler said grandly, holding up his candle to illuminate the steep banks of the ravine.

"Where?" Silk asked, looking about in puzzlement.

"Well now, Prince Kheldar, it wouldn't be much of a hidden cave if the openin' was out in plain sight fer just anybody t' stumble across, now would it?" Feldegast went over to the steep side of the ravine to where a huge slab of water-scoured granite leaned against the bank. He lowered his candle, shielding it with his hand, ducked slightly, and disappeared behind it with his mule trailing along behind him.

The interior of the cave was floored with clean white sand, and the walls had been worn smooth by centuries of swirling water. Feldegast stood in the center of the cave holding his candle aloft. There were crude log bunks along the walls, a table and some benches in the center of the cave, and a rough fireplace near the far wall with a fire already laid. Feldegast crossed to the fireplace, bent, and lit the kindling lying under the split logs resting on a rough stone grate with his candle. "Well now, that's better," he said, holding his hands out to the crackling flames. "Isn't this a cozy little haven?"

Just beyond the fireplace was an archway, in part natural and in part the work of human hands. The front of the archway was closed off with several horizontal poles. Feldegast pointed at it. "There be the stable fer the horses, an' also a small spring at the back of it. 'Tis altogether the finest smugglers' cave in this part of Mallorea."

"A cunning sort of place," Belgarath agreed, looking around.

"What do they smuggle through here?" Silk asked with a certain professional curiosity.

"Gem stones fer the most part. There be rich deposits in the cliffs of Katakor, an' quite often whole gravel bars of the shiny little darlin's lyin' in the streams t' be had fer the trouble it takes t' pick 'em up. The local taxes be notorious cruel, though, so the bold lads in this part of these mountains have come up with various ways t' take their goods across the border without disturbin' the sleep of the hard-workin' tax collectors."

Polgara was inspecting the fireplace. There were several iron pothooks protruding from its inside walls and a large iron grill sitting on stout legs to one side. "Very nice," she murmured approvingly. "Is there adequate firewood?"

"More than enough, me dear lady," the juggler replied. " 'Tis stacked in the stable, along with fodder fer the horses."

"Well, then," she said, removing her blue cloak and laying it across one of the bunks, "I think I might be able to expand the menu I'd planned for this evening's meal. As long as we have such complete facilities here, it seems a shame to waste them. I'll need more firewood stacked here—and water, of course." She went to the packhorse that carried her cooking utensils and her stores, humming softly to herself.

Durnik, Toth, and Eriond led the horses into the stable and began to unsaddle them. Garion, who had left his lance outside, went to one of the bunks, removed his helmet and laid it, along with his shield, under the bunk, and then he began to struggle out of his mail shirt. Ce'Nedra came over to assist him.

"You were magnificent today, dear," she told him warmly.

He grunted noncommittally, leaning forward and extending his arms over his head so that she could pull the shirt off.

She tugged hard, and the mail shirt came free all at once. Thrown off balance by the weight, she sat down heavily on the sandy floor with the shirt in her lap.

Garion laughed and quickly went to her. "Oh, Ce'Nedra," he said, still laughing, "I do love you." He kissed her and then helped her to her feet.

"This is terribly heavy, isn't it?" she said, straining to lift the steel-link shirt.

"You noticed," he said, rubbing at one aching shoulder. "And here you thought I was just having fun."

"Be nice, dear. Do you want me to hang it up for you?"

He shrugged. "Just kick it under the bunk."

Her look was disapproving.

"I don't think it's going to wrinkle, Ce'Nedra."

"But it's untidy to do it that way, dear." She made some effort to fold the thing, then gave up, rolled it in a ball, and pushed it far back under the bunk with her foot.

Supper that evening consisted of thick steaks cut from a ham Vella had provided them, a rich soup so thick that it hovered on the very edge of stew, large slabs of bread that had been warmed before the fire, and baked apples with honey and cinnamon.

After they had eaten, Polgara rose and looked around the cave again. "The ladies and I are going to need a bit of privacy now," she said, "and several basins of hot water."

Belgarath sighed. "Again, Pol?" he said.

"Yes, father. It's time to clean up and change clothes—for all of us." She pointedly sniffed at the air in the small cave. "It's definitely time," she added.

They curtained off a portion of the cave to give Polgara, Ce'Nedra, and Velvet the privacy they required and began heating water over the fire.

Though at first reluctant even to move, Garion had to admit that after he had washed up and changed into clean, dry clothes, he did feel much better. He sat back on one of the bunks beside Ce'Nedra, not even particularly objecting to the damp smell of her hair. He had that comfortable sense of being clean, well fed, and warm after a day spent out of doors in bad weather. He was, in fact, right on the edge of dozing off when there echoed up the narrow ravine outside a vast bellow that seemed to be part animal and part human, a cry so dreadful that it chilled his blood and made the hair rise on the back of his neck.

"What's that?" Ce'Nedra exclaimed in fright.

"Hush now, girl," Feldegast warned softly. He jumped to his feet and quickly secured a piece of canvas across the opening of the fireplace, plunging the cave into near-darkness.

Another soulless bellow echoed up the ravine. The sound seemed filled with a dreadful malevolence.

"Can we put a name to whatever it is?" Sadi asked in a quiet voice.

"It's nothing I've ever heard before," Durnik assured him.

"I think I have," Belgarath said bleakly. "When I was in Morindland, there was a magician up there who thought it was amusing to turn his demon out at night to hunt. It made a sound like that."

"What an unsavory practice," the eunuch murmured. "What do demons eat?"

"You really wouldn't want to know," Silk replied. He turned to Belgarath. "Would you care to hazard a guess at just how big that thing might be?"

"It varies. From the amount of noise it's making, though, I'd say that it's fairly large."

"Then it wouldn't be able to get into this cave, would it?"

"That's a gamble I think I'd rather not take."

"It can sniff out our tracks, I assume?"

The old man nodded.

"Things are definitely going to pieces here, Belgarath. Can you do anything at all to drive it off?" The little man turned to Polgara. "Or perhaps you, Polgara. You dealt with the demon Chabat raised back in the harbor at Rak Urga."

"I had help, Silk," she reminded him. "Aldur came to my aid."

Belgarath began to pace up and down, scowling at the floor.

"Well?" Silk pressed.

"Don't rush me," the old man growled. "I *might* be able to do something," he said grudgingly, "but if I *do,* it's going to make so much noise that every Grolim in Katakor is going to hear it—and probably Zandramas as well. We'll have the Chandim or her Grolims hot on our heels all the way to Ashaba."

"Why not use the Orb?" Eriond suggested, looking up from the bridle he was repairing.

"Because the Orb makes even more noise than I do. If Garion uses the Orb to chase off a demon, they're going to hear it in Gandahar all the way on the other side of the continent."

"But it *would* work, wouldn't it?"

Belgarath looked at Polgara.

"I think he's right, father," she said. "A demon *would* flee from the Orb—even if it were fettered by its master. An unfettered demon would flee even faster."

"Can you think of anything else?" he asked her.

"A God," she shrugged. "All demons—no matter how powerful—flee from the Gods. Do you happen to know any Gods?"

"A few," he replied, "but they're busy right now."

Another shattering bellow resounded through the mountains. It seemed to come from right outside the cave.

"It's time for some kind of decision, old man," Silk said urgently.

"It's the noise the Orb makes that bothers you?" Eriond asked.

"That and the light. That blue beacon that lights up every time Garion draws the sword attracts a lot of attention, you know."

"You aren't all suggesting that I fight a demon, are you?" Garion demanded indignantly.

"Of course not," Belgarath snorted. "Nobody fights a demon—nobody *can.* All we're discussing is the possibility of driving it off." He began to pace up and down again, scuffing his feet in the sand. "I hate to announce our presence here," he muttered.

Outside, the demon bellowed again, and the huge granite slab partially covering the cave mouth began to grate back and forth as if some huge force were rocking it to try to move it aside.

"Our options are running out, Belgarath," Silk told him. "And so is our time. If you don't do something quickly, that thing's going to be in here with us."

"Try not to pinpoint our location to the Grolims," Belgarath said to Garion.

"You really want me to go out there and do it?"

"Of course I do. Silk was right. Time's run out on us."

Garion went to his bunk and fished his mail shirt out from under it.

"You won't need that. It wouldn't do any good anyway."

Garion reached over his shoulder and drew his great sword. He set its point in the sand and peeled the soft leather sheath from its hilt. "I think this is a mistake," he declared. Then he reached out and put his hand on the Orb.

"Let me, Garion," Eriond said. He rose, came over, and covered Garion's hand with his own.

Garion gave him a startled look.

"It knows me, remember?" the young man explained, "and I've got a sort of an idea."

A peculiar tingling sensation ran through Garion's hand and arm, and he became aware that Eriond was communing with the Orb in a manner even more direct than he himself was capable of. It was is if during the months that the boy had been the bearer of the Orb, the stone had in some peculiar way taught him its own language.

There was a dreadful scratching coming from the mouth of the cave, as if huge talons were clawing at the stone slab.

"Be careful out there," Belgarath cautioned. "Don't take any chances. Just hold up the sword so that it can see it. The Orb should do the rest."

Garion sighed. "All right," he said, moving toward the cave mouth with Eriond directly behind him.

"Where are you going?" Polgara asked the blond young man.

"With Belgarion," Eriond replied. "We both need to talk with the Orb to get this right. I'll explain it later, Polgara."

The slab at the cave mouth was rocking back and forth again. Garion ducked quickly out from behind it and ran several yards up the ravine with Eriond on his heels. Then he turned and held up the sword.

"Not yet," Eriond warned. "It hasn't seen us."

There was an overpoweringly foul odor in the ravine, and then, as Garion's eyes slowly adjusted to the darkness, he saw the demon outlined against the clouds rolling overhead. It was enormous, its shoulders blotting out half the sky. It had long, pointed ears like those of a vast cat, and its dreadful eyes burned with a green fire that cast a fitful glow across the floor of the ravine.

It bellowed and reached toward Garion and Eriond with a great, scaly claw.

"Now, Belgarion," Eriond said quite calmly.

Garion lifted his arms, holding his sword directly in front of him with its point aimed at the sky, and then he released the curbs he had placed on the Orb.

He was not in the least prepared for what happened. A huge noise shook the earth and echoed off nearby mountains, causing giant trees miles away to tremble. Not only did the great blade take fire, but the entire sky suddenly shimmered an intense sapphire blue as if it had been ignited. Blue flame shot from horizon to horizon, and the vast sound continued to shake the earth.

The demon froze, its vast, tooth-studded muzzle turned upward to the blazing blue sky in terror. Grimly, Garion advanced on the thing, still holding his burning sword before him. The beast flinched back from him, trying to shield its face from the intense blue light. It screamed as if suddenly gripped by an intolerable agony. It stumbled back, falling and scrambling to its feet again. Then it took one more look at the blazing sky, turned, and fled howling back down the ravine with a peculiar loping motion as all four of its claws tore at the earth.

"*That* is your idea of quiet?" Belgarath thundered from the cave mouth. "And what's all that?" He pointed a trembling finger at the still-illuminated sky.

"It's really all right, Belgarath," Eriond told the infuriated old man. "You didn't want the sound to lead the Grolims to us, so we just made it general through the whole region. Nobody could have pinpointed its source."

Belgarath blinked. Then he frowned for a moment. "What about all the light?" he asked in a more mollified tone of voice.

"It's more or less the same with that," Eriond explained calmly. "If you've got a single blue fire in the mountains on a dark night, everybody can see it. If the whole sky catches on fire, though, nobody can really tell where it's coming from."

"It does sort of make sense, Grandfather," Garion said.

"Are they all right, father?" Polgara asked from behind the old man.

"What could possibly have hurt them? Garion can level mountains with that sword of his. He very nearly did, as a matter of fact. The whole Karandese range rang like a bell." He looked up at the still-flickering sky. "Can you turn that off?" he asked.

"Oh," Garion said. He reversed his sword and resheathed it in the scabbard strapped across his back. The fire in the sky died.

"We really had to do it that way, Belgarath," Eriond continued. "We needed the light and the sound to frighten off the demon and we had to do it in such a way that the Grolims couldn't follow it, so—" He spread both hands and shrugged.

"Did you know about this?" Belgarath asked Garion.

"Of course, Grandfather," Garion lied.

Belgarath grunted. "All right. Come back inside," he said.

Garion bent slightly toward Eriond's ear. "Why didn't you tell me what we were going to do?" he whispered.

"There wasn't really time, Belgarion."

"The next time we do something like that, *take* time. I almost dropped the sword when the ground started shaking under me."

"That wouldn't have been a good idea at all."

"I know."

A fair number of rocks had been shaken from the ceiling of the cave and lay on the sandy floor. Dust hung thickly in the air.

"What happened out there?" Silk demanded in a shaky voice.

"Oh, not much," Garion replied in a deliberately casual voice. "We just chased it away, that's all."

"There wasn't really any help for it, I guess," Belgarath said, "but just about everybody in Katakor knows that *something's* moving around in these mountains, so we're going to have to start being very careful."

"How much farther is it to Ashaba?" Sadi asked him.

"About a day's ride."

"Will we make it in time?"

"Only just. Let's all get some sleep."

Garion had the same dream again that night. He was not really sure that it was a dream, since dreaming usually involved sight as well as sound, but all there was to this one was that persistent, despairing wail and the sense of horror with which it filled him. He sat up on his bunk, trembling and sweat-covered. After a time, he drew his blanket about his shoulders, clasped his arms about his knees, and stared at the ruddy coals in the fireplace until he dozed off again.

It was still cloudy the following morning, and they rode cautiously back down the ravine to the rutted track leading up into the foothills of the mountains. Silk and Feldegast ranged out in front of them as scouts to give them warning should any dangers arise.

After they had ridden a league or so, the pair came back down the narrow road. Their faces were sober, and they motioned for silence.

"There's a group of Karands camped around the road up ahead," Silk reported in a voice scarcely louder than a whisper.

"An ambush?" Sadi asked him.

"No," Feldegast replied in a low voice. "They're asleep fer the most part. From the look of things, I'd say that they spent the night in some sort of religious observance, an' so they're probably exhausted—or still drunk."

"Can we get around them?" Belgarath asked.

"It shouldn't be too much trouble," Silk replied. "We can just go off into the trees and circle around until we're past the spot where they're sleeping."

The old man nodded. "Lead the way," he said.

They left the road and angled off into the timber, moving at a cautious walk.

"What sort of ceremony were they holding?" Durnik asked quietly.

Silk shrugged. "It looked pretty obscure," Silk told him. "They've got an altar set up with skulls on posts along the back of it. There seems to have been quite a bit of drinking going on—as well as some other things."

"What sort of things?"

Silk's face grew slightly pained. "They have women with them," he answered disgustedly. "There's some evidence that things got a bit indiscriminate."

Durnik's cheeks suddenly turned bright red.

"Aren't you exaggerating a bit, Kheldar?" Velvet asked him.

"No, not really. Some of them were still celebrating."

"A bit more important than quaint local religious customs, though," Feldegast added, still speaking quietly, "be the peculiar pets the Karands was keepin'."

"Pets?" Belgarath asked.

"Perhaps 'tis not the right word, Ancient One, but sittin' round the edges of the camp was a fair number of the Hounds—an' they was makin' no move t' devour the celebrants."

Belgarath looked at him sharply. "Are you sure?"

"I've seen enough of the Hounds of Torak t' recognize 'em when I see 'em."

"So there *is* some kind of an alliance between Mengha and Urvon," the old man said.

"Yer wisdom is altogether a marvel, old man. It must be a delight beyond human imagination t' have the benefit of ten thousand years experience t' guide ye in comin' t' such conclusions."

"*Seven* thousand," Belgarath corrected.

"Seven—ten—what matter?"

"*Seven* thousand," Belgarath repeated with a slightly offended expression.

■ CHAPTER SIXTEEN ■

They rode that afternoon into a dead wasteland, a region foul and reeking, where white snags poked the skeleton-like fingers of their limbs imploringly at a dark, roiling sky and where dank ponds of oily, stagnant water exuded the reek of decay. Clots of fungus lay in gross profusion about the trunks of long-dead trees and matted-down weeds struggled up through ashy soil toward a sunless sky.

"It looks almost like Cthol Mishrak, doesn't it?" Silk asked, looking about distastefully.

"We're getting very close to Ashaba," Belgarath told him. "Something about Torak did this to the ground."

"Didn't he know?" Velvet said sadly.

"Know what?" Ce'Nedra asked her.

"That his very presence befouled the earth?"

"No," Ce'Nedra replied, "I don't think he did. His mind was so twisted that he couldn't even see it. The sun hid from him, and he saw that only as a mark of his power and not as a sign of its repugnance for him."

It was a peculiarly astute observation, which to some degree surprised Garion. His wife oftentimes seemed to have a wide streak of giddiness in her nature which made it far too easy to think of her as a child, a misconception reinforced by her diminutive size. But he had frequently found it necessary to reassess this tiny, often willful little woman who shared his life. Ce'Nedra might sometimes behave foolishly, but she was never stupid. She looked out at the world with a clear, unwavering vision that saw much more than gowns and jewels and costly perfumes. Quite suddenly he was so proud of her that he thought his heart would burst.

"How much farther is it to Ashaba?" Sadi asked in a subdued tone. "I hate to admit it, but this particular swamp depresses me."

"You?" Durnik said. "I thought you liked swamps."

"A swamp should be green and rich with life, Goodman," the eunuch replied. "There's nothing here but death." He looked at Velvet. "Have you got Zith, Margravine?" he asked rather plaintively. "I'm feeling a bit lonesome just now."

"She's sleeping at the moment, Sadi," she told him, her hand going to the front of her bodice in an oddly protective fashion. "She's safe and warm and very content. She's even purring."

"Resting in her perfumed little bower." He sighed. "There are times when I envy her."

"Why, Sadi," she said, blushing slightly, lowering her eyes, and then flashing her dimples at him.

"Merely a clinical observation, my dear Liselle," he said to her rather sadly. "There are times when I wish it could be otherwise, but . . ." He sighed again.

"Do you really have to carry that snake there?" Silk asked the blond girl.

"Yes, Kheldar," she replied, "as a matter of fact, I do."

"You didn't answer my question, Ancient One," Sadi said to Belgarath. "How much farther is it to Ashaba?"

"It's up there," the old sorcerer replied shortly, pointing toward a ravine angling sharply up from the reeking wasteland. "We should make it by dark."

"A particularly unpleasant time to visit a haunted house," Feldegast added.

As they started up the ravine, there came a sudden hideous growling from the dense undergrowth to one side of the weedy track, and a huge black Hound burst out of the bushes, its eyes aflame and with foam dripping from its cruel fangs. "Now you are mine!" it snarled, its jaws biting off the words.

Ce'Nedra screamed, and Garion's hand flashed back over his shoulder; but quick as he was, Sadi was even quicker. The eunuch spurred his terrified horse directly at the hulking dog. The beast rose, its jaws agape, but Sadi hurled a strangely colored powder of about the consistency of coarse flour directly into its face.

The Hound shook its head, still growling horribly. Then it suddenly screamed, a shockingly human sound. Its eyes grew wide in terror. Then it began desperately to snap at the empty air around it, whimpering and trying to cringe back. As suddenly as it had attacked, it turned and fled howling back into the undergrowth.

"What did you do?" Silk demanded.

A faint smile touched Sadi's slender features. "When ancient Belgarath told me about Torak's Hounds, I took certain precautions," he replied, his head slightly cocked as he listened to the terrified yelps of the huge dog receding off into the distance.

"Poison?"

"No. It's really rather contemptible to poison a dog if you don't have to. The Hound simply inhaled some of that powder I threw in its face. Then it began to see some very distracting things—*very* distracting." He smiled again. "Once I saw a cow accidentally sniff the flower that's the main ingredient of the powder. The last time I saw her, she was trying to climb a tree." He looked over at Belgarath. "I hope you didn't mind my taking action without consulting you, Ancient One, but as you've pointed out, your sorcery might alert others in the region, and I had to move quickly to deal with the situation before you felt compelled to unleash it anyway."

"That's quite all right, Sadi," Belgarath replied. "I may have said it before, but you're a very versatile fellow."

"Merely a student of pharmacology, Belgarath. I've found that there are chemicals suitable for almost every situation."

"Won't the Hound report back to its pack that we're here?" Durnik asked, looking around worriedly.

"Not for several days." Sadi chuckled, brushing off his hands, holding them as far away from his face as possible.

They rode slowly up the weed-grown track along the bottom of the ravine where mournful, blackened trees spread their branches, filling the deep cut with a pervading gloom. Off in the distance they could hear the baying of Torak's Hounds as they coursed through the forest. Above them, sooty ravens flapped from limb to limb, croaking hungrily.

"Disquieting sort of place," Velvet murmured.

"And *that* adds the perfect touch," Silk noted, pointing at a large vulture perched on the limb of a dead snag at the head of the ravine.

"Are we close enough to Ashaba yet for you to be able to tell if Zandramas is still there?" Garion asked Polgara.

"Possibly," she replied. "But even that faint a sound could be heard."

"We're close enough now that we can wait," Belgarath said. "I'll tell you one thing, though," he added. "If my great-grandson *is* at Ashaba, I'll take the place apart stone by stone until I find him and I don't care *how* much noise it makes."

Impulsively, Ce'Nedra pulled her horse in beside his, leaned over, and locked her arms about his waist. "Oh, Belgarath," she said, "I love you." And she burrowed her face into his shoulder.

"What's this?" His voice was slightly surprised.

She pulled back, her eyes misty. She wiped at them with the back of her hand, then gave him an arch look. "You're the dearest man in all the world," she told him. "I might even consider throwing Garion over for you," she added, "if it weren't for the fact that you're twelve thousand years old, that is."

"Seven," he corrected automatically.

She gave him a sadly whimsical smile, a melancholy sign of her final victory in an ongoing contest that no longer had any meaning for her. "Whatever," she sighed.

And then in a peculiarly uncharacteristic gesture, he enfolded her in his arms and gently kissed her. "My dear child," he said with brimming eyes. Then he looked back over his shoulder at Polgara. "How did we ever get along without her?" he asked.

Polgara's eyes were a mystery. "I don't know, father," she replied. "I really don't."

At the head of the ravine, Sadi dismounted and dusted the leaves of a low bush growing in the middle of the track they were following with some more of his powder. "Just to be on the safe side," he explained, pulling himself back into his saddle.

The region they entered under a lowering sky was a wooded plateau, and they rode on along the scarcely visible track in a generally northerly direction with the rising wind whipping at their cloaks. The baying of Torak's Hounds still sounded from some distance off, but seemed to be coming no closer.

As before, Silk and Feldegast raged out ahead, scouting for possible dangers. Garion again rode at the head of their column, his helmet in place and the butt of his lance riding in his stirrup. As he rounded a sharp bend in the track, he saw Silk and the juggler ahead. They had dismounted and were crouched behind some bushes. Silk turned quickly and motioned Garion back. Garion quickly passed on that signal and, step by step, backed his gray stallion around the bend again. He dismounted, leaned his lance against a tree, and took off his helmet.

"What is it?" Belgarath asked, also swinging down from his horse.

"I don't know," Garion replied. "Silk motioned us to stay out of sight."

"Let's go have a look," the old man said.

"Right."

The two of them crouched over and moved forward on silent feet to join the rat-faced man and the juggler. Silk put his finger to his lips as they approached. When Garion reached the brush, he carefully parted the leaves and looked out.

There was a road there, a road that intersected the track they had been following. Riding along that road were half-a-hundred men dressed mostly in furs, with rusty helmets on their heads and bent and dented swords in their hands. The men at the head of the column, however, wore mail coats. Their helmets were polished, and they carried lances and shields.

Tensely, without speaking, Garion and his friends watched the loosely organized mob ride past.

When the strangers were out of sight, Feldegast turned to Belgarath. "It sort of confirms yer suspicion, old friend," he said.

"Who were they?" Garion asked in a low voice.

"The ones in fur be Karands," Feldegast replied, "an' the ones in steel be Temple Guardsmen. 'Tis more evidence of an alliance between Urvon and Mengha, y' see."

"Can we be sure that the Karands were Mengha's men?"

"He's overcome Katakor altogether, an' the only armed Karands in the area be his. Urvon an' his Chandim control the Guardsmen—*an'* the Hounds. When ye see Karands an' Hounds together the way we did yesterday, it's fair proof of an alliance, but when ye see Karandese fanatics escorted by armed Guardsmen, it doesn't leave hardly any doubt at all."

"What *is* that fool up to?" Belgarath muttered.

"Who?" Silk asked.

"Urvon. He's done some fairly filthy things in his life, but he's never consorted with demons before."

"Perhaps 'twas because Torak had forbid it," Feldegast suggested. "Now that Torak's dead, though, maybe he's throwin' off all restraints. The demons would be a powerful factor if the final confrontation between the Church an' the imperial throne that's been brewin' all these years should finally come."

"Well," Belgarath grunted, "we don't have time to sort it out now. Let's get the others and move on."

They quickly crossed the road that the Karands and the Guardsmen had been following and continued along the narrow track. After a few more miles, they crested a low knoll that at some time in the past had been denuded by fire. At the far end of the plateau, just before a series of stark cliffs rose sharply up into the mountains, there stood a huge black building, rearing up almost like a mountain it-self. It was surmounted by bleak towers and surrounded by a battlement-topped wall, half-smothered in vegetation.

"Ashaba," Belgarath said shortly, his eyes flinty.

"I thought it was a ruin," Silk said with some surprise.

"Parts of it are, I've been told," the old man replied. "The upper floors aren't habitable anymore, but the ground floor's still more or less intact—at least it's sup-posed to be. It takes a very long time for wind and weather to tear down a house that big." The old man nudged his horse and led them down off the knoll and back into the wind-tossed forest.

It was nearly dark by the time they reached the edge of the clearing surround-ing the House of Torak. Garion noted that the vegetation half covering the walls of the black castle consisted of brambles and thick-stemmed ivy. The glazing in the windows had long since succumbed to wind and weather, and the vacant casements seemed to stare out at the clearing like the eye sockets of a dark skull.

"Well, father?" Polgara said.

He scratched at his beard, listening to the baying of the Hounds back in the forest.

"If yer open t' a bit of advice, me ancient friend," Feldegast said, "wouldn't it be wiser t' wait until dark before we go in? Should there be watchers in the house, the night will conceal us from their eyes. An' then, too, once it grows dark, there'll undoubtedly be lights inside if the house be occupied. 'Twill give us some idea of what t' expect."

"It makes sense, Belgarath," Silk agreed. "Walking openly up to an unfriendly house in broad daylight disturbs my sense of propriety."

"That's because you've got the soul of a burglar. But it's probably the best plan anyhow. Let's pull back into the woods a ways and wait for dark."

Though the weather had been warm and springlike on the plains of Rakuth and Venna, here in the foothills of the Karandese mountains there was still a per-vading chill, for winter only reluctantly released its grip on these highlands. The wind was raw, and there were some places back under the trees where dirty windrows of last winter's snow lay deep and unyielding.

"Is that wall around the house going to cause us any problems?" Garion asked.

"Not unless someone's repaired the gates," Belgarath replied. "When Beldin and I came in here after Vo Mimbre, they were all locked, so we had to break them down to get in."

"Walkin' openly up to them gates might not be the best idea in the world, Bel-garath," Feldegast said, "fer if the house do be occupied by Chandim or Karands or

Guardsmen, 'tis certain that the gates are goin' t' be watched, an' there be a certain amount of light even on the darkest night. There be a sally port on the east side of the house though, an' it gives entry into an inner court that's sure t' be filled with deep shadows as soon as the night comes on."

"Won't it be barred off?" Silk asked him.

"T' be sure, Prince Kheldar, it was indeed. The lock, however, was not difficult fer a man with fingers as nimble as mine."

"You've been inside, then?"

"I like t' poke around in abandoned houses from time t' time. One never knows what the former inhabitants might have left behind, an' findin' is oftentimes as good as earnin' or stealin'."

"I can accept that," Silk agreed.

Durnik came back from the edge of the woods where he had been watching the house. He had a slightly worried look on his face. "I'm not entirely positive," he said, "but it looks as if there are clouds of smoke coming out of the towers of that place."

"I'll just go along with ye an' have a bit of a look," the juggler said, and he and the smith went back through the deepening shadows beneath the trees. After a few minutes they came back. Durnik's expression was faintly disgusted.

"Smoke?" Belgarath asked.

Feldegast shook his head. "Bats," he replied. "Thousands of the little beasties. They be comin' out of the towers in great black clouds."

"Bats?" Ce'Nedra exclaimed, her hands going instinctively to her hair.

"It's not uncommon," Polgara told her. "Bats need protected places to nest in, and a ruin or an abandoned place is almost ideal for them."

"But they're so *ugly*!" Ce'Nedra declared with a shudder.

" 'Tis only a flyin' mouse, me little darlin'," Feldegast told her.

"I'm not fond of mice, either."

" 'Tis a very unforgivin' woman ye've married, young Master," Feldegast said to Garion, "brim-full of prejudices an' unreasonable dislikes."

"More important, did you see any lights coming from inside?" Belgarath asked.

"Not so much as a glimmer, Ancient One, but the house be large, an' there be chambers inside which have no windows. Torak was unfond of the sun, as ye'll recall."

"Let's move around through the woods until we're closer to this sally port of yours," the old man suggested, "before the light goes entirely."

They stayed back from the edge of the trees as they circled around the clearing with the great black house in its center. The last light was beginning to fade from the cloud-covered sky as they cautiously peered out from the edge of the woods.

"I can't quite make out the sally port," Silk murmured, peering toward the house.

" 'Tis partially concealed," Feldegast told him. "If ye give ivy the least bit of a toehold, it can engulf a whole buildin' in a few hundred years. Quiet yer fears, Prince Kheldar. I know me way, an' I kin find the entrance t' the House of Torak on the blackest of nights."

"The Hounds are likely to be patrolling the area around here after dark, aren't they?" Garion said. He looked at Sadi. "I hope you didn't use up all of your powder back there."

"There's more than enough left, Belgarion." The eunuch smiled, patting his pouch. "A light dusting at the entrance to Master Feldegast's sally port should insure that we won't be disturbed once we're inside."

"What do you think?" Durnik asked, squinting up at the dark sky.

"It's close enough," Belgarath grunted. "I want to get inside."

They led their horses across the weed-choked clearing until they reached the looming wall.

" 'Tis this way just a bit," Feldegast said in a low voice as he began to feel his way along the rough black stones of the wall.

They followed him for several minutes, guided more by the faint rustling sound of his feet among the weeds than by sight.

"An' here we are, now," Feldegast said with some satisfaction. It was a low, arched entrance in the wall, almost totally smothered in ivy and brambles. Durnik and the giant Toth, moving slowly to avoid making too much noise, pulled the obstructing vines aside to allow the rest of them and the horses to enter. Then they followed, pulling the vines back in place once again to conceal the entrance.

Once they were inside, it was totally dark, and there was the musty smell of mildew and fungus. "May I borrow yer flint an' steel an' tinder again, Goodman Durnik?" Feldegast whispered. Then there was a small clinking sound, followed by a rapid clicking accompanied by showers of glowing sparks as Feldegast, kneeling so that his body concealed even those faint glimmers, worked with Durnik's flint and steel. After a moment, he blew on the tinder, stirring a tiny flame to life. There was another clink as he opened the front of a square lantern he had taken from a small niche in the wall.

"Is that altogether wise?" Durnik asked doubtfully as the juggler lighted the candle stub inside the lantern and returned the flint and steel.

" 'Tis a well-shielded little bit of a light, Goodman," Feldegast told him, "an' it be darker than the inside of yer boots in this place. Trust me in this, fer I kin keep it so well concealed that not the tiniest bit of a glow will escape me control."

"Isn't that what they call a burglar's lantern?" Silk asked curiously.

"Well, now." Feldegast's whisper sounded slightly injured. "I don't know that I'd call it that, exactly. 'Tis a word that has an unsavory ring t' it."

"Belgarath," Silk chuckled softly. "I think your friend here has a more checkered past than we've been led to believe. I wondered why I liked him so much."

Feldegast had closed down the tin sides of his little lantern, allowing only a single, small spot of light feebly to illuminate the floor directly in front of his feet. "Come along, then," he told them. "The sally port goes back a way under the wall here, an' then we come t' the grate that used t' close it off. Then it makes a turn t' the right an' a little farther on, another t' the left, an' then it comes out in the courtyard of the house."

"Why so many twists and turns?" Garion asked him.

"Torak was a crooked sort, don't y' know. I think he hated straight lines almost as much as he hated the sun."

They followed the faint spot of light the lantern cast. Leaves had blown in through the entrance over the centuries to lie in a thick, damp mat on the floor, effectively muffling the sounds of their horses' hooves.

The grate that barred the passageway was a massively constructed crisscross of rusty iron. Feldegast fumbled for a moment with the huge latch, then swung it clear. "An' now, me large friend," he said to Toth, "we'll be havin' need of yer great strength here. The gate is cruel heavy, let me warn ye, an' the hinges be so choked with rust that they'll not likely yield easily." He paused a moment. "An' that reminds me—ah, where have me brains gone? We'll be needin' somethin' t' mask the dreadful squeakin' when ye swing the grate open." He looked back at the others. "Take a firm grip on the reins of yer horses," he warned them, "fer this is likely t' give 'em a bit of a turn."

Toth place his huge hands on the heavy grate, then looked at the juggler.

"Go!" Feldegast said sharply, then he lifted his face and bayed, his voice almost perfectly imitating the sound of one of the great Hounds prowling outside, even as the giant slowly swung the grate open on shrieking hinges.

Chretienne snorted and shied back from the dreadful howl, but Garion held his reins tightly.

"Oh, that was clever," Silk said in quiet admiration.

"I have me moments from time to time," Feldegast admitted. "With all the dogs outside raisin' their awful caterwaulin', 'tis certain that one more little yelp won't attract no notice, but the squealin' of them hinges could have been an altogether different matter."

He led them on through the now-open grate and on along the dank passageway to a sharp right-hand turn. Somewhat farther along, the passage bent again to the left. Before he rounded that corner, the juggler closed down his lantern entirely, plunging them into total darkness. "We be approachin' the main court now," he whispered to them. " 'Tis the time for silence an' caution, fer if there be others in the house, they'll be payin' a certain amount of attention t' be sure that no one creeps up on 'em. There be a handrail along the wall there, an' I think it might be wise t' tie the horses here. Their hooves would make a fearful clatter on the stones of the court, an' we'll not be wantin' t' ride them up an' down the corridors of this accursed place."

Silently they tied the reins of their mounts to the rusty iron railing and then crept on quiet feet to the turn in the passageway. There was a lessening of the darkness beyond the turn—not light, certainly, but a perceptible moderation of the oppressive gloom. And then they reached the inside entrance to the sally port and looked out across the broad courtyard toward the looming black house beyond. There was no discernible grace to the construction of that house. It rose in blocky ugliness almost as if the builders had possessed no understanding of the meaning of the word beauty, but had striven instead for a massive kind of arrogance to reflect the towering pride of its owner.

"Well," Belgarath whispered grimly, "that's Ashaba."

Garion looked at the dark house before him, half in apprehension and half with a kind of dreadful eagerness.

Something caught his eye then, and he thrust his head out to look along the front of the house across the court. At the far end, in a window on a lower floor, a dim light glowed, looking for all the world like a watchful eye.

CHAPTER SEVENTEEN

"Now what?" Silk breathed, looking at the dimly lighted window. "We've got to cross that courtyard to get to the house, but we can't be sure if there's somebody watching from that window or not."

"You've been out of the academy for too long, Kheldar," Velvet murmured. "You've forgotten your lessons. If stealth is impossible, then you try boldness."

"You're suggesting that we just walk up to the door and knock?"

"Well, I hadn't planned to knock, exactly."

"What have you got in mind, Liselle?" Polgara asked quietly.

"If there are people in the house, they're probably Grolims, right?"

"It's more than likely," Belgarath said. "Most other people avoid this place."

"Grolims pay little attention to other Grolims, I've noticed," she continued.

"You're forgetting that we don't have any Grolim robes with us," Silk pointed out.

"It's very dark in that courtyard, Kheldar, and in shadows that deep, any dark color would appear black, wouldn't it?"

"I suppose so," he admitted.

"And we still have those green silk slavers' robes in our packs, don't we?"

He squinted at her in the darkness, then looked at Belgarath. "It goes against all my instincts," he said, "but it might just work, at that."

"One way or another, we've got to get into the house. We have to find out who's in there—and why—before we can decide anything."

"Would Zandramas have Grolims with her?" Ce'Nedra asked. "If she's alone in that house and she sees a line of Grolims walking across the courtyard, wouldn't that frighten her into running away with my baby?"

Belgarath shook his head. "Even if she does run, we're close enough to catch her—particularly since the Orb can follow her no matter how much she twists and dodges. Besides, if she's here, she's probably got some of her own Grolims with her. It's not really so far from here to Darshiva that she couldn't have summoned them."

"What about him?" Durnik whispered the question and pointed at Feldegast. "He hasn't got a slavers' robe."

"We'll improvise something," Velvet murmured. She smiled at the juggler. "I've got a nice dark blue dressing gown that should set off his eyes marvelously. We can add a kerchief to resemble a hood and we can slip him by—if he stays in the middle of the group."

" 'Twould be beneath me dignity," he objected.

"Would you prefer to stay behind and watch the horses?" she asked pleasantly.

" 'Tis a hard woman y' are, me lady," he complained.

"Sometimes, yes."

"Let's do it," Belgarath decided. "I've got to get inside that house."

It took only a few moments to retrace their steps to the place where the horses were tied and to pull the neatly folded slavers' robes from their packs by the dim light of Feldegast's lantern.

"Isn't this ridiculous, now?" the juggler grumbled indignantly, pointing down at the blue satin gown Velvet had draped about him.

"I think it looks just darling," Ce'Nedra said.

"If there are people in there, aren't they likely to be patrolling the corridors?" Durnik asked.

"Only on the main floor, Goodman," Feldegast replied. "The upper stories of the house be almost totally uninhabitable—on account of all the broken windows an' the weather blowin' around in the corridors fer all the world like they was part of the great outdoors. There be a grand staircase just opposite the main door, an' with just a bit of luck we kin nip up the stairs an' be out of sight with no one the wiser. Once we're up there, we're not likely t' encounter a livin' soul—unless ye be countin' the bats an' mice an' an occasional adventuresome rat."

"You absolutely had to say that, didn't you?" Ce'Nedra said caustically.

"Ah, me poor little darlin'." He grinned at her. "But quiet yer fears. I'll be beside ye an' I've yet t' meet the bat or mouse or rat I couldn't best in a fair fight."

"It makes sense, Belgarath," Silk said. "If we all go trooping through the lower halls, sooner or later someone's bound to notice us. Once we're upstairs and out of sight, though, I'll be able to reconnoiter and find out exactly what we're up against."

"All right," the old man agreed, "but the first thing is to get inside."

"Let's be off, then," Feldegast said, swirling his dressing gown about him with a flourish.

"Hide that light," Belgarath told him.

They filed out through the entrance to the sally port and marched into the shadowy courtyard, moving in the measured, swaying pace Grolim priests assumed on ceremonial occasions. The lighted window at the end of the house seemed somehow like a burning eye that followed their every move.

The courtyard was really not all that large, but it seemed to Garion that crossing it took hours. Eventually, however, they reached the main door. It was large, black, and nail-studded, like the door of every Grolim temple Garion had ever seen. The steel mask mounted over it, however, was no longer polished. In the faint light coming from the window at the other end of the house, Garion could see that over the centuries it had rusted, making the coldly beautiful face look scabrous and diseased. What made it look perhaps even more hideous were the twin gobbets of lumpy, semiliquid rust running from the eye sockets down the cheeks. Garion remembered with a shudder the fiery tears that had run down the stricken God's face before he had fallen.

They mounted the three steps to that bleak door, and Toth slowly pushed it open.

The corridor inside was dimly illuminated by a single flickering torch at the far end. Opposite the door, as Feldegast had told them, was a broad staircase reaching up into the darkness. The treads were littered with fallen stones, and cobwebs hung in long festoons from a ceiling lost in shadows. Still moving at that stately Grolim pace, Belgarath led them across the corridor and started up the stairs. Garion followed close behind him with measured tread, though every nerve screamed at him to run. They had gone perhaps halfway up the staircase when they heard a clinking sound behind them, and there was a sudden light at the foot of the stairs. "What are you doing?" a rough voice demanded. "Who are you?"

Garion's heart sank, and he turned. The man at the foot of the stairs wore a long, coatlike shirt of mail. He was helmeted and had a shield strapped to his left arm. With his right he held aloft a sputtering torch.

"Come back down here," the mailed man commanded them.

The giant Toth turned obediently, his hood pulled far over his face with his arms crossed so that his hands were inside his sleeves. With an air of meekness he started down the stairs again.

"I mean all of you," the Temple Guardsman insisted. "I order you in the name of the God of Angarak."

As Toth reached the foot of the stairs, the Guardsman's eyes widened as he realized that the robe the huge man wore was not Grolim black. "What's this?" he exclaimed. "You're not Chandim! You're—" He broke off suddenly as one of Toth's huge hands seized him by the throat and lifted him off the floor. He dropped his torch, kicking and struggling. Then, almost casually, Toth removed his helmet with his other hand and banged his head several times against the stone wall of the corridor. With a shudder, the mail-coated man went limp. Toth draped the unconscious form across his shoulder and started back up the stairs.

Silk bounded back down to the corridor, picked up the steel helmet and extinguished torch, and came back up again. "Always clean up the evidence," he murmured to Toth. "No crime is complete until you've tidied up."

Toth grinned at him.

As they neared the top of the stairs, they found the treads covered with leaves that had blown in from the outside, and the cobwebs hung in tatters like rotted curtains, swaying in the wind that came moaning in from the outside through the shattered windows.

The hall at the top of the stairs was littered. Dry leaves lay in ankle-deep windrows on the floor, skittering before the wind. A large, empty casement at the end of the corridor behind them was half covered with thick ivy that shook and rustled in the chill night wind blowing down off the slopes of the mountains. Doors had partially rotted away and hung in chunks from their hinges. The rooms beyond those doors were choked with leaves and dust, and the furniture and bedding had long since surrendered every scrap of cloth or padding to thousands of generations of industrious mice in search of nesting materials. Toth carried his unconscious captive into one of those rooms, bound him hand and foot, and then gagged him to muffle any outcry, should he awaken before dawn.

"That light was at the other end of the house, wasn't it?" Garion asked. "What's at that end?"

" 'Twas the livin' quarters of Torak himself," Feldegast replied, adjusting his little lantern so that it emitted a faint beam of light. "His throne room be there, an' his private chapel. I could even show ye t' his personal bedroom, an' ye could bounce up an' down on his great bed—or what's left of it—just fer fun, if yer of a mind."

"I think I could live without doing that."

Belgarath had been tugging at one earlobe. "Have you been here lately?" he asked the juggler.

"Perhaps six months ago."

"Was anybody here?" Ce'Nedra demanded.

"I'm afraid not, me darlin'. 'Twas as empty as a tomb."

"That was before Zandramas got here, Ce'Nedra," Polgara reminded her gently.

"Why do ye ask, Belgarath?" Feldegast said.

"I haven't been here since just after Vo Mimbre," Belgarath said as they continued down the littered hall. "The house was fairly sound then, but Angaraks aren't really notorious for the permanence of their construction. How's the mortar holding out?"

"'Tis as crumbly as year-old bread."

Belgarath nodded. "I thought it might be," he said. "Now, what we're after here is information, not open warfare in the corridors."

"Unless the one who's here happens to be Zandramas," Garion corrected. "If she's still here with my son, I'll start a war that's going to make Vo Mimbre look like a country fair."

"And I'll clean up anything he misses," Ce'Nedra added fiercely.

"Can't you control them?" Belgarath asked his daughter.

"Not under the circumstances, no," she replied. "I might even decide to join in myself."

"I thought that we'd more or less erased the Alorn side of your nature, Pol," he said to her.

"That's not the side that was just talking, father."

"My point," Belgarath said, "at least the point I was trying to make before everybody started flexing his—or her—muscles, is that it's altogether possible that we'll be able to hear and maybe even see what's going on in the main part of the house from up here. If the mortar's as rotten as Feldegast says it is, it shouldn't be too hard to find—or make—some little crevices in the floor of one of these rooms and find out what we need to know. If Zandramas is here, that's one thing, and we'll deal with her in whatever way seems appropriate. But if the only people down there are some of Urvon's Chandim and Guardsmen or a roving band of Mengha's Karandese fanatics, we'll pick up Zandramas' trail and go on about our business without announcing our presence."

"That sounds reasonable," Durnik agreed. "It doesn't make much sense to get involved in unnecessary fights."

"I'm glad that *someone* in this belligerent little group has some common sense," the old man said.

"Of course, if it *is* Zandramas down there," the smith added, "I'll have to take steps myself."

"You, too?" Belgarath groaned.

"Naturally. After all, Belgarath, right is right."

They moved on along the leaf-strewn corridor where the cobwebs hung from the ceiling in tatters and where there were skittering sounds in the corners.

As they passed a large double door so thick that it was still intact, Belgarath seemed to remember something. "I want to look in here," he muttered. As he opened those doors, the sword strapped across Garion's back gave a violent tug that very nearly jerked him off his feet. "Grandfather!" he gasped. He reached back, instructing the Orb to restrain itself, and drew the great blade. The point dipped to the floor, and then he was very nearly dragged into the room. "She's been here," he exulted.

"What?" Durnik asked.

"Zandramas. She's been in this room with Geran."

Feldegast opened the front of his lantern wider to throw more light into the room. It was a library, large and vaulted, with shelves reaching from the floor to the ceiling and filled with dusty, moldering books and scrolls.

"So *that* was what she was looking for," Belgarath said.

"For what?" Silk asked.

"A book. A prophecy, most likely." His face grew grim. "She's following the same trail that I am, and this would probably be just about the only place where she could find an uncorrupted copy of the Ashabine Oracles."

"Oh!" Ce'Nedra's little cry was stricken. She pointed a trembling hand at the dust-covered floor. There were footprints there. Some of them had obviously been made by a woman's shoes, but there were others as well—quite tiny. "My baby's been here," Ce'Nedra said in a voice near tears, and then she gave a little wail and began to weep. "H-he's walking," she sobbed, "and I'll never be able to see his first steps."

Polgara moved to her and took her into a comforting embrace.

Garion's eyes also filled with tears, and his grip on the hilt of his sword grew so tight that his knuckles turned white. He felt an almost overpowering need to smash things.

Belgarath was swearing under his breath.

"What's the matter?" Silk asked him.

"That was the main reason I had to come here," the old man grated. "I need a clean copy of the Ashabine Oracles, and Zandramas has beaten me to it."

"Maybe there's another."

"Not a chance. She's been running ahead of me burning books at every turn. If there was more than one copy here, she'd have made sure that I couldn't get my hands on it. That's why she stayed here so long—ransacking this place to make sure that she had the only copy." He started to swear again.

"Is this in any way significant?" Eriond said, going to a table that, unlike the others in the room, had been dusted and even polished. In the precise center of that table lay a book bound in black leather and flanked on each side by a candlestick. Eriond picked it up, and as he did so, a neatly folded sheet of parchment fell out from between its leaves. The young man bent, picked it up, and glanced at it.

"What's that?" Belgarath demanded.

"It's a note," Eriond replied. "It's for you." He handed the parchment and the book to the old man.

Belgarath read the note. His face went suddenly pale and then beet red. He ground his teeth together with the veins swelling in his face and neck. Garion felt the sudden building up of the old sorcerer's will.

"Father!" Polgara snapped, "No! Remember that we aren't alone here!"

He controlled himself with a tremendous effort, then crumpled the parchment into a ball and hurled it at the floor so hard that it bounced high into the air and rolled across the room. He swung back the hand holding the book as if he were about to send it after the ball of parchment, but then seemed to think better of it. He opened the book at random, turned a few pages, and then began to swear sulfurously. He shoved the book at Garion. "Here," he said, "hold on to this." Then he began to pace up and down, his face as black as a thundercloud, muttering curses and waving his hands in the air.

Garion opened the book, tilting it to catch the light. He saw at once the reason for Belgarath's anger. Whole passages had been neatly excised—not merely blotted out, but cut entirely from the page with a razor or a very sharp knife. Garion also started to swear.

Silk curiously went over, picked up the parchment, and looked at it. He swallowed hard and looked apprehensively at the swearing Belgarath. "Oh, my," he said.

"What is it?" Garion asked.

"I think we'd all better stay out of your grandfather's way for a while," the rat-faced man replied. "It might take him a little bit to get hold of himself."

"Just read it, Silk," Polgara said. "Don't editorialize."

Silk looked again at Belgarath, who was now at the far end of the room pounding on the stone wall with his fist. " 'Belgarath,' " he read. " 'I have beaten thee, old man. Now I go to the Place Which Is No More for the final meeting. Follow me if thou canst. Perhaps this book will help thee.' "

"Is it signed?" Velvet asked him.

"Zandramas," he replied. "Who else?"

"That is a truly offensive letter," Sadi murmured. He looked at Belgarath, who continued to pound his fist on the wall in impotent fury. "I'm surprised that he's taking it so well—all things considered."

"It answers a lot of questions, though," Velvet said thoughtfully.

"Such as what?" Silk asked.

"We were wondering if Zandramas was still here. Quite obviously, she's not. Not even an idiot would leave that kind of message for Belgarath and then stay around where he could get his hands on her."

"That's true," he agreed. "There's no real point in our staying here, then, is there? The Orb has picked up the trail again, so why don't we just slip out of the house again and go after Zandramas?"

"Without findin' out who's here?" Feldegast objected. "Me curiosity has been aroused, an' I'd hate t' go off with it unsatisfied." He glanced across the room at the fuming Belgarath. "Besides, it's goin' t' be a little while before our ancient friend there regains his composure. I think I'll go along t' the far end of the hall an' see if I kin find a place where I kin look down into the lower part of the house—just t' answer some burnin' questions which have been naggin' at me." He went to the table and lighted one of the candles from his little lantern. "Would ye be wantin' t' come along with me, Prince Kheldar?" he invited.

Silk shrugged. "Why not?"

"I'll go, too," Garion said. He handed the book to Polgara and then pointedly looked at the raging Belgarath. "Is he going to get over that eventually?"

"I'll talk with him, dear. Don't be too long."

He nodded, and then he, Silk, and the juggler quietly left the library.

There was a room at the far end of the hall. It was not particularly large, and there were shelves along the walls. Garion surmised that it had at one time been a storeroom or a linen closet. Feldegast squinted appraisingly at the leaf-strewn floor, then closed his lantern.

The leaves had piled deep in the corners and along the walls, but in the sudden darkness a faint glow shone up through them, and there came the murmur of voices from below.

"Me vile-tempered old friend seems t' have been right," Feldegast whispered. " 'Twould appear that the mortar has quite crumbled away along that wall. 'Twill be but a simple matter t' brush the leaves out of the way an' give ourselves some convenient spy holes. Let's be havin' a look an' find out who's taken up residence in the House of Torak."

Garion suddenly had that strange sense of reexperiencing something that had happened a long time ago. It had been in King Anheg's palace at Val Alorn, and he had followed the man in the green cloak through the deserted upper halls until they had come to a place where crumbling mortar had permitted the sound of voices to come up from below. Then he remembered something else. When they had been at Tol Honeth, hadn't Belgarath said that most of the things that had happened while they were pursuing Zedar and the Orb were likely to happen again, since everything was leading up to another meeting between the Child of Light and the Child of Dark? He tried to shake off the feeling, but without much success.

They removed the leaves from the crack running along the far wall of the storeroom carefully, trying to avoid sifting any of them down into the room below. Then each of them selected a vantage point from which to watch and listen.

The room into which they peered was very large. Ragged drapes hung at the windows, and the corners were thick with cobwebs. Smoky torches hung in iron rings along the walls, and the floor was thick with dust and the litter of ages. The room was filled with black-robed Grolims, a sprinkling of roughly clad Karands, and a large number of gleaming Temple Guardsmen. Near the front, drawn up like a platoon of soldiers, a group of the huge black Hounds of Torak sat on their haunches expectantly. In front of the Hounds stood a black altar, showing signs of recent use, flanked on either side by a glowing brazier. Against the wall on a high dais was a golden throne, backed by thick, tattered black drapes and by a huge replica of the face of Torak.

" 'Twas Burnt-face's throne room, don't y' know," Feldegast whispered.

"Those are Chandim, aren't they?" Garion whispered back.

"The very same—both human an' beast—along with their mail-shirted bully boys. I'm a bit surprised that Urvon has chosen t' occupy the place with his dogs— though the best use fer Ashaba has probably always been as a kennel."

It was obvious that the men in the throne room were expecting something by the nervous way they kept looking at the throne.

Then a great gong sounded from below, shimmering in the smoky air.

"On your knees!" a huge voice commanded the throng in the large room. "Pay obeisance and homage to the new God of Angarak!"

"What?" Silk exclaimed in a choked whisper.

"Watch an' be still!" Feldegast snapped.

From below there came a great roll of drums, followed by a brazen fanfare. The rotten drapes near the golden throne parted, and a double file of robed Grolims entered, chanting fervently, even as the assembled Chandim and Guardsmen fell to their knees and the Hounds and the Karands groveled and whined.

The booming of the drums continued, and then a figure garbed in cloth of gold and wearing a crown strode imperiously out from between the drapes. A glowing nimbus surrounded the figure, though Garion could clearly sense that the will that maintained the glow emanated from the gold-clad man himself. Then the figure lifted its head in a move of overweening arrogance. The man's face was splotched—some patches showing the color of healthy skin and others a hideous dead white. What chilled Garion's blood the most, however, was the fact that the man's eyes were totally mad.

"Urvon!" Feldegast said with a sudden intake of his breath. "You piebald son of a mangy dog!" All trace of his lilting accent had disappeared.

Directly behind the patch-faced madman came a shadowy figure, cowled so deeply that its face was completely obscured. The black that covered it was not that of a simple Grolim robe, but seemed to grow out of the figure itself, and Garion felt a cold dread as a kind of absolute evil permeated the air about that black shape.

Urvon mounted the dais and seated himself on the throne, his insane eyes bulging and his face frozen in that expression of imperious pride. The shadow-covered figure took its place behind his left shoulder and bent forward toward his ear, whispering, whispering.

The Chandim, Guardsmen, and Karands in the throne room continued to grovel, fawning and whining, even as did the Hounds, while the last disciple of Torak preened himself in the glow of their adulation. A dozen or so of the black-robed Chandim crept forward on their knees, bearing gilded chests and reverently placing them on the altar before the dais. When they opened the chests, Garion saw that they were all filled to the brim with red Angarak gold and with jewels.

"These offerings are pleasing to mine eyes," the enthroned Disciple declared in a shrill voice. "Let others come forth to make also their offerings unto the new God of Angarak."

There was a certain amount of consternation among the Chandim and a few hasty consultations.

The next group of offerings were in plain wooden boxes; when they were opened, they revealed only pebbles and twigs. Each of the Chandim who bore those boxes to the altar surreptitiously removed one of the gilded chests after depositing his burden on the black stone.

Urvon gloated over the chests and boxes, apparently unable to distinguish between gold and gravel, as the line continued to move toward the altar, each priest laying one offering on the altar and removing another before returning to the end of the line.

"I am well pleased with ye, my priests," Urvon said in his shrill voice when the charade had been played out. "Truly, ye have brought before me the wealth of nations."

As the Chandim, Karands, and Guardsmen rose to their feet, the shadowy figure at Urvon's shoulder continued to whisper.

"And now will I receive Lord Mengha" the madman announced, "most favored of all who serve me, for he has delivered unto me this familiar spirit who revealed my high divinity unto me." He indicated the shadow behind him.

"Summon the Lord Mengha that he may pay homage to the God Urvon and be graciously received by the new God of Angarak." The voice that boomed that command was as hollow as a voice issuing from a tomb.

From the door at the back of the hall came another fanfare of trumpets, and another hollow voice responded. "All hail Urvon, new God of Angarak," it intoned. "Lord Mengha approacheth to make his obeisance and to seek counsel with the living God."

Again there came the booming of drums, and a man robed in Grolim black paced down the broad aisle toward the altar and the dais. As he reached the altar, he genuflected to the madman seated on Torak's throne.

"Look now upon the awesome face of Lord Mengha, most favored servant of the God Urvon and soon to become First Disciple," the hollow voice boomed.

The figure before the altar turned and pushed back his hood to reveal his face to the throng.

Garion stared, supressing a gasp of surprise. The man standing before the altar was Harakan.

CHAPTER EIGHTEEN

"Belar!" Silk swore under his breath.

"All bow down to the First Disciple of your God!" Urvon declaimed in his shrill voice. "It is my command that ye honor him."

There was a murmur of amazement among the assembled Chandim, and Garion, peering down from above, thought that he could detect a certain reluctance on the faces of some of them.

"Bow to him!" Urvon shrieked, starting to his feet. "He is my Disciple!"

The Chandim looked first at the frothing madman on the dais and then at the cruel face of Harakan. Fearfully they sank to their knees.

"I am pleased to see such willing obedience to the commands of our God," Harakan observed sardonically. "I shall remember it always." There was a scarcely veiled threat in his voice.

"Know ye all that my Disciple speaks with my voice," Urvon announced, resuming his seat upon the throne. "His words are my words, and ye will obey him even as ye obey me."

"Hear the words of our God," Harakan intoned in that same sardonic voice, "for mighty is the God of Angarak, and swift to anger should any fail to heed him. Know further that I, Mengha, am now the sword of Urvon as well as his voice, and that the chastisement of the disobedient is in *my* hands." The threat was no longer veiled, and Harakan swept his eyes slowly across the faces of the assembled priests as if challenging each of them to protest his elevation.

"Hail Mengha, Disciple of the living God!" one of the mailed Guardsmen shouted.

"Hail Mengha!" the other Guardsmen responded, smashing their fists against their shields in salute.

"Hail Mengha!" the Karands shrieked.

"Hail Mengha!" the kneeling Chandim said at last, cowed finally into submission. And then the great Hounds crept forward on their bellies to fawn about Harakan's feet and to lick his hands.

"It is well," the enthroned madman declared in his shrill voice. "Know that the God of Angarak is pleased with ye."

And then another figure appeared in the throne room below, coming through the same rotted drapes which had admitted Urvon. The figure was slender and dressed in a robe of clinging black satin. Its head was partially covered by a black hood, and it was carrying something concealed beneath its robe. When it reached the altar, it tipped back its head in a derisive laugh, revealing a face with at once an unearthly beauty and an unearthly cruelty all cast in marble white. "You poor fools," the figure rasped in a harsh voice. "Think you to raise a new God over Angarak without my permission?"

"I have not summoned thee, Zandramas!" Urvon shouted at her.

"I feel no constraint to heed thy summons, Urvon," she replied in a voice filled with contempt, "nor its lack. I am not thy creature, as are these dogs. I serve the God of Angarak, in whose coming shalt thou be cast down."

"*I* am the God of Angarak!" he shrieked.

Harakan had begun to come around the altar toward her.

"And wilt thou pit thy puny will against the Will of the Child of Dark, Harakan?" she asked coolly. "Thou mayest change thy name, but thy power is no greater." Her voice was like ice.

Harakan stopped in his tracks, his eyes suddenly wary.

She turned back to Urvon. "I am dismayed that I was not notified of thy deification, Urvon," she continued, "for should I have known, I would have come before thee to pay thee homage and seek thy blessing." Then her lip curled in a sneer that distorted her face. "*Thou?*" she said. "*Thou*, a God? Thou mayest sit upon the throne of Torak for all eternity whilst this shabby ruin crumbles about thee, and thou wilt never become a God. Thou mayest fondle dross and call it gold, and thou wilt never become a God. Thou mayest bask in the canine adulation of thy cringing dogs, who even now befoul thy throne room with their droppings, and thou wilt never become a God. Thou mayest hearken greedily to the words of thy tame demon, Nahaz, who even now whispers the counsels of madness in thine ear, and thou wilt never become a God."

"I *am* a God!" Urvon shrieked, starting to his feet again.

"So? It may be even as thou sayest, Urvon," she almost purred. "But if thou *art* a God, I must tell thee to enjoy thy Godhood whilst thou may, then, for even as maimed Torak, thou art doomed."

"Who hath the might to slay a God?" he foamed at her.

Her laugh was dreadful. "Who hath the might? Even he who reft Torak of *his* life. Prepare thyself to receive the mortal thrust of the burning sword of Iron-grip, which spilled out the life of thy master, for *thus* I summon the Godslayer!"

And then she reached forward and placed the cloth-wrapped bundle which she had been concealing beneath her robe on the black altar. She raised her face and looked directly at the crack through which Garion was staring in frozen disbelief. "Behold thy son, Belgarion," she called up to him, "and hear his crying!" She turned back the cloth to reveal the infant Geran. The baby's face was contorted with fear, and he began to wail, a hopeless, lost sound.

All thought vanished from Garion's mind. The wailing was the sound he had been hearing over and over again since he had left Mal Zeth. It was *not* the wail of that doomed child in those plague-stricken streets that had haunted his dreams. It was the voice of his own son! Powerless to resist that wailing call, he leaped to his feet. It was as if there were suddenly sheets of flame before his eyes, flames that erased everything from his mind but the desperate need to go to the child wailing on the altar below.

He realized dimly that he was running through the shadowy, leaf-strewn halls, roaring insanely even as he ripped Iron-grip's sword from its sheath.

The moldering doors of long-empty rooms flashed by as he ran full tilt along the deserted corridor. Dimly behind him, he heard Silk's startled cry. "Garion! No!" Heedless, his brain afire, he ran on with the great Sword of Riva blazing in his hand before him as he went.

Even years later, he did not remember the stairs. Vaguely, he remembered emerging in the lower hall, raging.

There were Temple Guardsmen and Karands there, flinching before him and trying feebly to face him, but he seized the hilt of his sword in both hands and moved through them like a man reaping grain. They fell in showers of blood as he sheared his way through their ranks.

The great door to the dead God's throne room was closed and bolted, but Garion did not even resort to sorcery. He simply destroyed the door—and those who were trying desperately to hold it closed—with his burning sword.

The fire of madness filled his eyes as he burst into the throne room, and he roared at the terrified men there, who gaped at the dreadful form of the Godslayer, advancing on them, enclosed in a nimbus of blue light. His lips were peeled back from his teeth in a snarl, and his terrible sword, all ablaze, flickered back and forth before him like the shears of fate.

A Grolim jumped in front of him with one arm upraised as Garion gathered his will with an inrushing sound he scarcely heard. Garion did not stop, and the other Grolims in the throne room recoiled in horror as the point of his flaming sword came sliding out from between the rash priest's shoulder blades. The mortally wounded Grolim stared at the sizzling blade sunk into his chest. He tried with shaking hands to clutch at the blade, but Garion kicked him off the sword and continued his grim advance.

A Karand with a skull-surmounted staff stood in his path, desperately muttering an incantation. His words cut off abruptly, however, as Garion's sword passed through his throat.

"Behold the Godslayer, Urvon!" Zandramas exulted. "Thy life is at an end, God of Angarak, for Belgarion hath come to spill it out, even as he spilled out the life of Torak!" Then she turned her back on the cringing madman. "All hail the Child of Light!" she announced in ringing tones. She smiled her cruel smile at him. "Hail, Belgarion," she taunted him. "Slay once again the God of Angarak, for that hath ever been thy task. I shall await thy coming in the Place Which Is No More." And then she took up the wailing babe in her arms, covered it with her cloak again, shimmered, and vanished.

Garion was suddenly filled with chagrin as he realized that he had been cruelly duped. Zandramas had not actually been here with his son, and all his overpowering rage had been directed at an empty projection. Worse than that, he had been manipulated by the haunting nightmare of the wailing child which he now realized *she* had put into his mind to force him to respond to her taunting commands. He faltered then, his blade lowering and its fire waning.

"Kill him!" Harakan shouted. "Kill the one who slew Torak!"

"Kill him!" Urvon echoed in his insane shriek. "Kill him and offer his heart up to me in sacrifice!"

A half-dozen Temple Guardsmen began a cautious, clearly reluctant, advance. Garion raised his sword again; its light flared anew, and the Guardsmen jumped back.

Harakan sneered as he looked at the armored men. "Behold the reward for cowardice," he snapped. He extended one hand, muttered a single word, and one of the Guardsmen shrieked and fell writhing to the floor as his mail coat and helmet turned instantly white-hot, roasting him alive.

"Now obey me!" Harakan roared. "Kill him!"

The terrified Guardsmen attacked more fervently then, forcing Garion back step by step. Then he heard the sound of running feet in the corridor outside. He glanced quickly over his shoulder and saw the others come bursting into the throne room.

"Have you lost your mind?" Belgarath demanded angrily.

"I'll explain later," Garion told him, still half-sick with frustration and disappointment. He returned his attention to the armored men before him and began swinging his great sword in wide sweeps, driving them back again.

Belgarath faced the Chandim on one side of the central aisle, concentrated for an instant, then gestured shortly. Suddenly a raging fire erupted from the stones of the floor all along the aisle.

Something seemed to pass between the old man and Polgara. She nodded, and quite suddenly the other side of the aisle was also walled off by flame.

Two of the Guardsmen had fallen beneath Garion's sword, but others, accompanied by wild-eyed Karands, were rushing to the aid of their comrades, though they flinched visibly from the flames on either side of the aisle up which they were forced to attack.

"Combine your wills!" Harakan was shouting to the Chandim. "Smother the flames!"

Even as he closed with the Guardsmen and the Karands, beating down their upraised swords and hacking at them with Iron-grip's blade, Garion felt the rush and surge of combined will. Despite the efforts of Belgarath and Polgara, the fires on either side of the aisle flickered and grew low.

One of the huge Hounds came loping through the ranks of the Guardsmen facing Garion. Its eyes were ablaze, and its tooth-studded muzzle agape. It leaped directly at his face, snapping and growling horribly, but fell twitching and biting at the floor as he split its head with his sword.

And then Harakan thrust his way through the Guardsmen and Karands to confront Garion. "And so we meet again, Belgarion," he snarled in an almost dog-like voice. "Drop your sword, or I will slay your friends—and your wife. I have a hundred Chandim with me, and not even you are a match for so many." And he began to draw in his will.

Then, to Garion's amazement, Velvet ran forward past him, her arms stretched toward the dread Grolim. "Please!" she wailed. "Please don't kill me!" And she threw herself at Harakan's feet, clutching at his black robe imploringly as she cringed and groveled before him.

Thrown off balance by this sudden and unexpected display of submissiveness, Harakan let his will dissipate and he backed away, trying to shake her hand from his robe and kicking at her to free himself. But she clung to him, weeping and begging for her life.

"Get her off me!" he snapped at his men, turning his head slightly. And that briefest instant of inattention proved fatal. Velvet's hand moved so quickly that it seemed to blur in the air. She dipped swiftly into her bodice; when her hand emerged, she held a small, bright-green snake.

"A present for you, Harakan!" she shouted triumphantly. "A present for the leader of the Bear-cult from Hunter!" And she threw Zith full into his face.

He screamed once the first time Zith bit him, and his hands came up to claw her away from his face, but the scream ended with a horrid gurgle, and his hands convulsed helplessly in the air in front of him. Squealing and jerking, he reeled backward as the irritated little reptile struck again and again. He stiffened and arched back across the altar, his feet scuffing and scrabbling on the floor and his arms flopping uselessly. He banged his head on the black stone, his eyes bulging and his swollen tongue protruding from his mouth. Then a dark froth came from his lips, he jerked several more times, and his body slid limply off the altar.

"And *that* was for Bethra," Velvet said to the crumpled form of the dead man lying on the floor before the altar.

The Chandim and their cohorts again drew back in fear as they stared at the body of their fallen pack leader.

"They are few!" Urvon shrieked at them. "We are many! Destroy them all! Your God commands it!"

The Chandim gaped first at Harakan's contorted body, then at the crowned madman on the throne, then at the terrible little snake who had coiled herself atop the altar with her head raised threateningly as she gave vent to a series of angry hisses.

"That's about enough of this," Belgarath snapped. He let the last of the flames die and began to refocus his will. Garion also straightened, pulling in his own will even as he felt the frightened Chandim start to focus their power for a final, dreadful confrontation.

"What is all this now?" Feldegast laughed, suddenly coming forward until he stood between Garion and his foes. "Surely, good masters, we can put aside all this hatred and strife. I'll tell ye what I'll do. Let me give ye a demonstration of me skill, an' we'll laugh together an' make peace between us once an' fer all. No man at all kin keep so great a hatred in his heart while he's bubblin' with laughter, don't y' know."

Then he began to juggle, seeming to pull brightly colored balls out of the air. The Grolims gaped at him, stunned by this unexpected interruption, and Garion stared incredulously at the performer, who seemed deliberately bent on self-destruction. Still juggling, Feldegast flipped his body onto the back of a heavy bench, holding himself upside down over it with one hand while he continued to juggle with his free hand and his feet. Faster and faster the balls whirled, more and more of them coming, it seemed out of thin air. The more the balls whirled, the brighter they became until at last they were incandescent, and the inverted little man was juggling balls of pure fire.

Then he flexed the arm that was holding him in place, tossing himself high over the bench. When his feet touched the floor, however, it was no longer Feldegast the juggler who stood there. In place of the roguish entertainer stood the gnarled, hunchbacked shape of the sorcerer Beldin. With a sudden evil laugh, he began to hurl his fireballs at the startled Grolims and their warriors.

His aim was unerring, and the deadly fireballs pierced Grolim robes, Guardsmen's mail coats, and Karandese fur vests with equal facility. Smoking holes appeared in the chests of his victims, and he felled them by the dozen. The throne room filled with smoke and the reek of burning flesh as the grinning, ugly little sorcerer continued his deadly barrage.

"*You!*" Urvon shrieked in terror, the sudden appearance of the man he had feared for so many thousands of years shocking him into some semblance of sanity, even as the terrified Chandim and their cohorts broke and fled, howling in fright.

"So good to see you again, Urvon," the hunchback said to him pleasantly. "Our conversation was interrupted the last time we were talking, but as I recall, I'd just promised to sink a white-hot hook into your belly and yank out all your guts." He held out his gnarled right hand, snapped his fingers, and there was a sudden flash. A cruel hook, smoking and glowing, appeared in his fist. "Why don't we continue with that line of thought?" he suggested, advancing on the splotchy-faced man cowering on the throne.

Then the shadow which had lurked behind the madman's shoulder came out from behind the throne. "Stop," it said in a voice that was no more than a crackling whisper. No human throat could have produced that sound. "I need this thing," it said, pointing a shadowy hand in the direction of the gibbering Disciple of Torak. "It serves my purposes, and I will not let you kill it."

"You would be Nahaz, then," Beldin said in an ominous voice.

"I am," the figure whispered. "Nahaz, Lord of Demons and Master of Darkness."

"Go find yourself another plaything, Demon Lord," the hunchback grated. "This one is mine."

"Will you pit your will against mine, sorcerer?"

"If need be."

"Look upon my face, then, and prepare for death." The demon pushed back its hood of darkness, and Garion recoiled with a sharp intake of his breath. The face of Nahaz was hideous, but it was not the misshapen features alone which were so terrifying. There emanated from its burning eyes a malevolent evil so gross that it froze the blood. Brighter and brighter those eyes burned with evil green fire until their beams shot forth toward Beldin. The gnarled sorcerer clenched himself and raised one hand. The hand suddenly glowed an intense blue, a light that seemed to cascade down over his body to form a shield against the demon's power.

"Your will is strong," Nahaz hissed. "But mine is stronger."

Then Polgara came down the littered aisle, the white lock at her brow gleaming. On one side of her strode Belgarath and on the other Durnik. As they reached him, Garion joined them. They advanced slowly to take up positions flanking Beldin, and Garion became aware that Eriond had also joined them, standing slightly off to one side.

"Well, Demon," Polgara said in a deadly voice, "will you face us all?"

Garion raised his sword and unleashed its fire. "And *this* as well?" he added, releasing all restraints on the Orb.

The Demon flinched momentarily, then drew itself erect again, its horrid face bathed in that awful green fire. From beneath its robe of shadow, it took what appeared to be a scepter or a wand of some kind that blazed an intense green. As it raised that wand, however, it seemed to see something that had previously escaped its notice. An expression of sudden fear crossed its hideous face, and the fire of the wand died, even as the intense green light bathing its face flickered and grew wan and weak. Then it raised its face toward the vaulted ceiling and howled—a dreadful, shocking sound. It spun quickly, moving toward the terrified Urvon. It reached out with shadowy hands, seized the gold-robed madman, and lifted him easily from the throne. Then it fled, its fire pushing out before it like a great battering ram, blasting out the walls of the House of Torak as it went.

The crown which had surmounted Urvon's brow fell from his head as Nahaz carried him from the crumbling house, and it clanked when it hit the floor with the tinny sound of brass.

PART FOUR

THE MOUNTAINS
OF ZAMAD

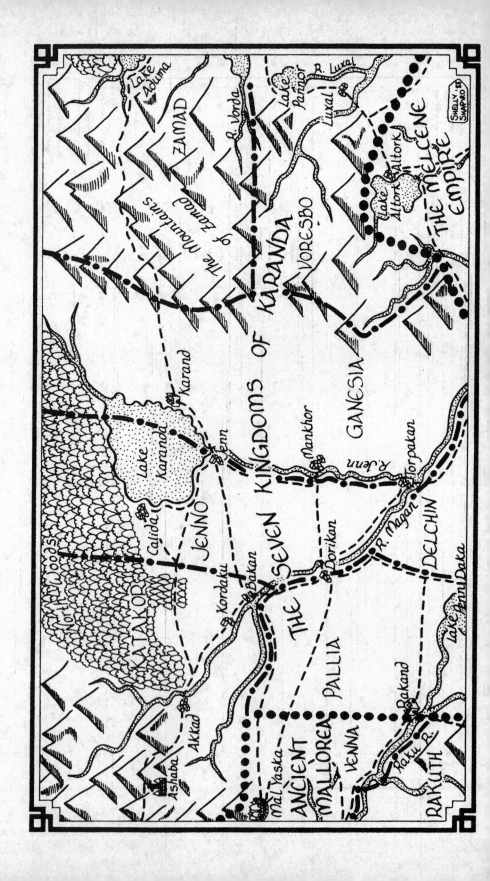

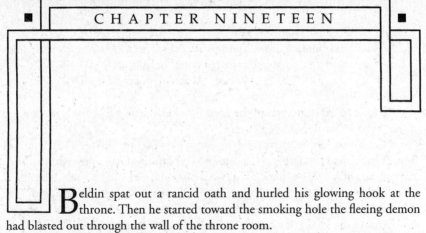

Beldin spat out a rancid oath and hurled his glowing hook at the throne. Then he started toward the smoking hole the fleeing demon had blasted out through the wall of the throne room.

Belgarath, however, managed to place himself in front of the angry hunchback. "No, Beldin," he said firmly.

"Get out of my way, Belgarath."

"I'm not going to let you chase after a demon who could turn on you at any minute."

"I can take care of myself. Now stand aside."

"You're not thinking, Beldin. There'll be time enough to deal with Urvon later. Right now we need to make some decisions."

"What's to decide? You go after Zandramas and I go after Urvon. It's all pretty much cut and dried, isn't it?"

"Not entirely. In any event, I'm not going to let you chase after Nahaz in the dark. You know as well as I do that the darkness multiplies his power—and I haven't got so many brothers left that I can afford to lose one just because he's irritated."

Their eyes locked, and the ugly hunchback finally turned away. He stumped back toward the dais, pausing long enough to kick a chair to pieces on his way, muttering curses all the while.

"Is everyone all right?" Silk asked, looking around as he resheathed his knife.

"So it would seem," Polgara replied, pushing back the hood of her blue cloak.

"It was a bit tight there for a while, wasn't it?" The little man's eyes were very bright.

"Also unnecessary," she said, giving Garion a hard look. "You'd better take a quick look through the rest of the house, Kheldar. Let's make sure that it's really empty. Durnik, you and Toth go with him."

Silk nodded and started back up the blood-splashed aisle, stepping over bodies as he went, with Durnik and Toth close behind him.

"I don't understand," Ce'Nedra said, staring in bafflement at the gnarled Beldin, who was once again dressed in rags and had the usual twigs and bits of straw clinging to him. "How did you change places with Feldegast—and where is he?"

A roguish smile crossed Beldin's face. "Ah, me little darlin'," he said to her in the juggler's lilting brogue, "I'm right here, don't y' know. An' if yer of a mind, I kin still charm ye with me wit an' me unearthly skill."

"But I *liked* Feldegast," she almost wailed.

"All ye have t' do is transfer yer affection t' me, darlin'."

"It's not the same," she objected.

Belgarath was looking steadily at the twisted sorcerer. "Have you got any idea of how much that particular dialect irritates me?" he said.

"Why, yes, brother." Beldin grinned. "As a matter of fact I do. That's one of the reasons I selected it."

"I don't entirely understand the need for so elaborate a disguise," Sadi said as he put away his small poisoned dagger.

"Too many people know me by sight in this part of Mallorea," Beldin told him. "Urvon's had my description posted on every tree and fence post within a hundred leagues of Mal Yaska for the last two thousand years, and let's be honest about it, it wouldn't be too hard to recognize me from even the roughest description."

"You are a unique sort of person, uncle," Polgara said to him, smiling fondly.

"Ah, yer too kind t' say it, me girl," he replied with an extravagant bow.

"*Will* you stop that?" Belgarath said. Then he turned to Garion. "As I remember, you said that you were going to explain something later. All right—it's later."

"I was tricked," Garion admitted glumly.

"By whom?"

"Zandramas."

"She's still here?" Ce'Nedra exclaimed.

Garion shook his head. "No. She sent a projection here—a projection of herself and of Geran."

"Couldn't you tell the difference between a projection and the real thing?" Belgarath demanded.

"I wasn't in any condition to tell the difference when it happened."

"I suppose you can explain that."

Garion took a deep breath and sat down on one of the benches. He noticed that his bloodstained hands were shaking. "She's very clever," he said. "Ever since we left Mal Zeth, I've been having the same dream over and over again."

"Dream?" Polgara asked sharply. "What kind of dream?"

"Maybe dream isn't the right word," he replied, "but over and over again, I kept hearing the cry of a baby. At first I thought that I was remembering the cry of that sick child we saw in the streets back in Mal Zeth, but that wasn't it at all. When Silk and Beldin and I were in that room just above this one, we could see down into the throne room here and we saw Urvon come in with Nahaz right behind him. He's completely insane now. He think's he's a God. Anyway, he summoned Mengha—only Mengha turned out to be Harakan, and then—"

"Wait a minute," Belgarath interrupted him. "*Harakan* is Mengha?"

Garion glanced over at the limp form sprawled in front of the altar. Zith was still coiled atop the black stone, muttering and hissing to herself. "Well, he *was*," he said.

"Urvon made the announcement before all this broke out," Beldin added. "We didn't have the time to fill you in."

"That explains a great many things, doesn't it?" Belgarath mused. He looked at Velvet. "Did you know about this?" he asked her.

"No, Ancient One," she replied, "as a matter of fact, I didn't. I just seized the opportunity when it arose."

Silk, Durnik, and Toth came back into the body-strewn throne room. "The house is empty," the little man reported. "We've got it all to ourselves."

"Good," Belgarath said. "Garion was just telling us why he saw fit to start his own private war."

"Zandramas told him to." Silk shrugged. "I'm not sure why he started taking orders from her, but that's what happened."

"I was just getting to that," Garion said. "Urvon was down here telling all the Chandim that Harakan—Mengha—was going to be his first disciple. That's when Zandramas came in—or at least she seemed to. She had a bundle under her cloak. I didn't know it at first, but it was Geran. She and Urvon shouted at each other for a while, and Urvon finally insisted that he was a God. She said something like, 'All right. Then I will summon the Godslayer to deal with you.' That's when she put the bundle on the altar. She opened it, and it was Geran. He started to cry, and I realized all at once that it was *his* cry I'd been hearing all along. I just totally stopped thinking at that point."

"Obviously," Belgarath said.

"Well, anyway, you know all the rest." Garion looked around at the corpse-littered throne room and shuddered. "I hadn't altogether realized just how far things went," he said. "I guess I was sort of crazy."

"The word is berserk, Garion," Belgarath told him. "It's fairly common among Alorns. I'd sort of thought you might be immune, but I guess I was wrong."

"There was some justification for it, father," Polgara said.

"There's never a justification for losing your wits, Pol," he growled.

"He was provoked." She pursed her lips thoughtfully, then came over and lightly placed her hands on Garion's temples. "It's gone now," she said.

"What is?" Ce'Nedra sounded concerned.

"The possession."

"Possession?"

Polgara nodded. "Yes. That's how Zandramas tricked him. She filled his mind with the sound of a crying child. Then, when she laid the bundle that *seemed* to be Geran on the altar and Garion heard that same crying, he had no choice but to do what she wanted him to do." She looked at Belgarath. "This is very serious, father. She's already tampered with Ce'Nedra, and now it's Garion. She may try the same thing with others as well."

"What would be the point?" he asked. "You can catch her at it, can't you?"

"Usually, yes—*if* I know what's going on. But Zandramas is very skilled at this and she's very subtle. In many ways she's even better at it than Asharak the Murgo was." She looked around at them. "Now listen carefully, all of you," she told them. "If anything unusual begins to happen to you—dreams, notions, peculiar ideas, strange feelings—anything at all, I want you to tell me about it at once. Zandramas knows that we're after her and she's using this to delay us. She tried it with Ce'Nedra while we were on our way to Rak Hagga, and now—"

"Me?" Ce'Nedra said in amazement. "I didn't know that."

"Remember your illness on the road from Rak Verkat?" Polgara said. "It wasn't exactly an illness. It was Zandramas putting her hand on your mind."

"But nobody told me."

"Once Andel and I drove Zandramas away, there was no need to worry you about it. Anyway, Zandramas tried it first with Ce'Nedra and now with Garion. She could try it on any one of the rest of us as well, so let me know if you start feeling in the least bit peculiar."

"Brass," Durnik said.

"What was that, dear?" Polgara asked him.

He held up Urvon's crown. "This thing is brass," he said. "So's that throne. I didn't really think there'd be any gold left here. The house has been abandoned and wide open for looters for too many centuries."

"That's usually the way it is with the gifts of demons," Beldin told him. "They're very good at creating illusions." He looked around. "Urvon probably saw all this as unearthly splendor. He couldn't see the rotten drapes, or cobwebs, or all the trash on the floor. All he could see was the glory that Nahaz wanted him to see." The dirty, twisted man chuckled. "I sort of enjoy the idea of Urvon spending his last days as a raving lunatic," he added, "right up until the moment when I sink a hook into his guts."

Silk had been looking narrowly at Velvet. "Do you suppose you could explain something for me?" he asked.

"I'll try," she said.

"You said something rather strange when you threw Zith into Harakan's face."

"Did I say something?"

"You said, 'A present for the leader of the Bear-cult from Hunter.' "

"Oh, that." She smiled her dimples into life. "I just wanted him to know who was killing him, that's all."

He stared at her.

"You *are* getting rusty, my dear Kheldar," she chided him. "I was certain that you'd have guessed by now. I've done everything but hit you over the head with it."

"Hunter?" he said incredulously. "*You?*"

"I've been Hunter for quite some time now. That's why I hurried to catch up with you at Tol Honeth." She smoothed the front of her plain gray traveling gown.

"At Tol Honeth you told us that *Bethra* was Hunter."

"She *had* been, Kheldar, but her job was finished. She was supposed to make sure that we'd get a reasonable man as a successor to Ran Borune. First she had to eliminate a few members of the Honeth family before they could consolidate their positions, and then she made a few suggestions about Varana to Ran Borune while the two of them were—" She hesitated, glancing at Ce'Nedra, and then she coughed. "—ah—shall we say, entertaining each other?" she concluded.

Ce'Nedra blushed furiously.

"Oh, dear," the blond girl said, putting one hand to her cheek. "That didn't come out at all well, did it? Anyway," she hurried on, "Javelin decided that Bethra's task was complete and that it was time for there to be a new Hunter with a new mission. Queen Porenn was *very* cross about what Harakan did in the west—the attempt on Ce'Nedra's life, the murder of Brand, and everything that went on at Rheon—so she instructed Javelin to administer some chastisement. He selected me to deliver it. I was fairly sure that Harakan would come back to Mallorea. I knew that you were all coming here, too—eventually—so that's why I joined you." She looked over at the sprawled form of Harakan. "I was absolutely amazed when I saw him standing in front of the altar," she admitted, "but I couldn't allow an opportunity like that to slip by." She smiled. "Actually, it worked out rather well. I was just on the verge of leaving you and going back to Mal Yaska to look for him. The fact that he turned out to be Mengha, too, was just sort of a bonus."

"I thought you were tagging along to keep an eye on *me.*"

"I'm very sorry, Prince Kheldar. I just made that up. I needed some reason to join you, and sometimes Belgarath can be very stubborn." She smiled winsomely at the old sorcerer, then turned back to the baffled-looking Silk. "Actually," she continued, "my uncle isn't really upset with you at all."

"But you said—" He stared at her. "You *lied*!" he accused.

" 'Lie' is such an ugly word, Kheldar," she replied, patting his cheek fondly. "Couldn't we just say that I exaggerated a trifle? I wanted to keep an eye on you, certainly, but it was for reasons of my own—which had nothing whatsoever to do with Drasnian state policy."

A slow flush crept up his cheeks.

"Why, Kheldar," she exclaimed delightedly, "you're actually blushing—almost like a simple village girl who's just been seduced."

Garion had been struggling with something. "What was the point of it, Aunt Pol?" he asked. "What Zandramas did to me, I mean?"

"Delay," she replied, "but more importantly, there was the possibility of defeating us before we ever get to the final meeting."

"I don't follow that."

She sighed. "We know that one of us is going to die," she said. "Cyradis told us that at Rheon. But there's always a chance that in one of these random skirmishes, someone *else* could be killed—entirely by accident. If the Child of Light—you—meets with the Child of Dark and he's lost someone whose task hasn't been completed, he won't have any chance of winning. Zandramas could win by default. The whole point of that cruel game she played was to lure you into a fight with the Chandim and Nahaz. The rest of us, quite obviously, would come to your aid. In that kind of fight, it's always possible for accidents to happen."

"Accident? How can there be accidents when we're all under the control of a prophecy?"

"You're forgetting something, Belgarion," Beldin said. "This whole business started with an accident. That's what divided the Prophecies in the first place. You can read prophecies until your hair turns gray, but there's always room for random chance to step in and disrupt things."

"You'll note that my brother is a philosopher," Belgarath said, "always ready to look on the dark side of things."

"Are you two really brothers?" Ce'Nedra asked curiously.

"Yes," Beldin told her, "but in a way that you could never begin to understand. It was something that our master impressed upon us."

"And Zedar was *also* one of your brothers?" She suddenly stared in horror at Belgarath.

The old man set his jaw. "Yes," he admitted.

"But you—"

"Go ahead and say it, Ce'Nedra," he said. "There's nothing you can possibly say to me that I haven't already said to myself."

"Someday," she said in a very small voice, "someday when this is all over, will you let him out?"

Belgarath's eyes were stony. "I don't think so, no."

"And if he *does* let him out, I'll go find him and stuff him right back in again," Beldin added.

"There's not much point in chewing over ancient history," Belgarath said. He thought a moment, then said, "I think it's time for us to have another talk with the young lady from Kell." He turned to Toth. "Will you summon your mistress?" he asked.

The giant's face was not happy. When he finally nodded, it was obviously with some reluctance.

"I'm sorry, my friend," Belgarath said to him, "but it's really necessary."

Toth sighed and then he sank to one knee and closed his eyes in an oddly prayerful fashion. Once again, as it had happened back on the Isle of Verkat and again at Rak Hagga, Garion heard a murmur as of many voices. Then there came that peculiar, multicolored shimmering in the air not far from Urvon's shoddy throne. The air cleared, and the unwavering form of the Seeress of Kell appeared on the dais. For the first time, Garion looked closely at her. She was slender and somehow looked very vulnerable, a helplessness accentuated by her white robe and her blindfolded eyes. There was, however, a serenity in her face—the serenity of someone who has looked full in the face of Destiny and has accepted it without question or reservation. For some reason, he felt almost overcome with awe in her radiant presence.

"Thank you for coming, Cyradis," Belgarath said simply. "I'm sorry to have troubled you. I know how difficult it is for you to do this, but there are some answers I need before we can go any further."

"I will tell thee as much as I am permitted to say, Ancient One," she replied. Her voice was light and musical, but there was, nonetheless, a firmness in it that spoke of an unearthly resolve. "I must say unto thee, however, that thou must make haste. The time for the final meeting draws nigh."

"That's one of the things I wanted to talk about. Can you be any more specific about this appointed time?"

She seemed to consider it as if consulting with some power so immense that Garion's imagination shuddered back from the very thought of it. "I know not time in thy terms, Holy Belgarath," she said simply, "but only for so long as a babe lieth beneath his mother's heart remains ere the Child of Light and the Child of Dark must face each other in the Place Which Is No More, and my task must be completed."

"All right," he said. "That's clear enough, I guess. Now, when you came to us at Mal Zeth, you said that there was a task here at Ashaba that needed to be accomplished before we could move on. A great deal has happened here, so I can't pinpoint exactly what that task was. Can you be a bit more specific?"

"The task is completed, Eternal One, for the Book of the Heavens sayeth that the Huntress must find her prey and bring him low in the House of Darkness in the sixteenth moon. And lo, even as the stars have proclaimed, it hath come to pass."

The old man's face took on a slightly puzzled expression.

"Ask further, Disciple of Aldur," she told him. "My time with you grows short."

"I'm supposed to follow the trail of the Mysteries," he said, "but Zandramas cut certain key passages out of the copy of the Ashabine Oracles she left here for me to find."

"Nay, Ancient One. It was not the hand of Zandramas which mutilated thy book, but rather the hand of its author."

"*Torak?*" he sounded startled.

"Even so. For know thou that the words of prophecy come unbidden, and ofttimes their import is not pleasing unto the prophet. So it was with the master of this house."

"But Zandramas managed to put her hands on a copy that hadn't been mutilated?" he asked.

The seeress nodded.

"Are there any other copies that Burnt-face didn't tamper with?" Beldin asked intently.

"Only two," she replied. "One is in the house of Urvon the Disciple, but that one lieth under the hand of Nahaz, the accursed. Seek not to wrest it from him, lest ye die."

"And the other?" the hunchback demanded.

"Seek out the clubfooted one, for he will aid thee in thy search."

"That's not too helpful, you know."

"I speak to thee in the words that stand in the Book of the Heavens and were written ere the world began. These words have no language but speak instead directly to the soul."

"Naturally," he said. "All right. You spoke of Nahaz. Is he going to line our path with demons all the way across Karanda?"

"Nay, gentle Beldin. Nahaz hath no further interest in Karanda, and his legions of darkness abide no longer there and respond to no summons, however powerful. They infest instead the plains of Darshiva where they do war upon the minions of Zandramas."

"Where is Zandramas now?" Belgarath asked her.

"She doth journey unto the place where the Sardion lay hidden for unnumbered centuries. Though it is no longer there, she hopes to find traces of it sunk into the very rocks and to follow those traces to the Place Which Is No More."

"Is that possible?"

Her face grew very still. "That I may not tell thee," she replied. Then she straightened. "I may say no more unto thee in this place, Belgarath. Seek instead the mystery which will guide thee. Make haste, however, for Time will not stay nor falter in its measured pace." And then she turned toward the black altar standing before the dais where Zith was coiled, still muttering and hissing in irritation. "Be tranquil, little sister," she said, "for the purpose of all thy days is now accomplished, and that which was delayed may now come to pass." She then seemed, even though blindfolded, to turn her serene face toward each of them, pausing briefly only to bow her head to Polgara in a gesture of profound respect. At last she turned to Toth. Her face was filled with anguish, but she said nothing. And then she sighed and vanished.

Beldin was scowling. "That was fairly standard," he said. "I *hate* riddles. They're the entertainment of the preliterate."

"Stop trying to show off your education and let's see if we can sort this out," Belgarath told him. "We know that this is all going to be decided one way or the other in nine more months. That was the number I needed."

Sadi was frowning in perplexity. "How did we arrive at that number?" he asked. "To be perfectly frank, I didn't understand very much of what she said."

"She said that we have only as much time as a baby lies in its mother's womb," Polgara explained. "That's nine months."

"Oh," he said. Then he smiled a bit sadly. "That's the sort of thing I don't pay too much attention to, I guess."

"What was that business about the sixteenth moon?" Silk asked. "I didn't follow that at all."

"This whole thing began with the birth of Belgarion's son," Beldin told him. "We found a reference to that in the Mrin Codex. Your friend with the snake had to be here at Ashaba sixteen moons later."

Silk frowned, counting on his fingers. "It hasn't been sixteen months yet," he objected.

"Moons, Kheldar," the hunchback said. "Moons, not months. There's a difference, you know."

"Oh. That explains it, I guess."

"Who's this clubfoot who's supposed to have the third uncorrupted copy of the Oracles?" Belgarath said.

"It rings a bell somehow," Beldin replied. "Let me think about it."

"What's Nahaz doing in Darshiva?" Garion asked.

"Apparently attacking the Grolims there," Belgarath replied. "We know that Darshiva is where Zandramas originally came from and that the church in that region belongs to her. If Nahaz wants to put the Sardion in Urvon's hands, he's going to have to stop her. Otherwise, she'll get to it first."

Ce'Nedra seemed to suddenly remember something. She looked at Garion, her eyes hungry. "You said that you saw Geran—when Zandramas tricked you."

"A projection of him, yes."

"How did he look?"

"The same. He hadn't changed a bit since the last time I saw him."

"Garion, dear," Polgara said gently. "That's not really reasonable, you know. Geran's almost a year older now. He wouldn't look the same at all. Babies grow and change a great deal during their first few years."

He nodded glumly. "I realize that now," he replied. "At the time, I wasn't really in any condition to think my way through it." Then he stopped. "Why didn't she project an image of him the way he looks now?"

"Because she wanted to show you something she was sure you'd recognize."

"Now you stop that!" Sadi exclaimed. He was standing near the altar and he had just jerked his hand back out of Zith's range. The little green snake was growling ominously at him. The eunuch turned toward Velvet. "Do you see what you've done?" he accused. "You've made her terribly angry."

"Me?" she asked innocently.

"How would *you* like to be pulled out of a warm bed and thrown into somebody's face?"

"I suppose I hadn't thought about that. I'll apologize to her, Sadi—just as soon as she regains her composure a bit. Will she crawl into her bottle by herself?"

"Usually, yes."

"That might be the safest course, then. Lay the bottle on the altar and let her crawl inside and sulk a bit."

"You're probably right," he agreed.

"Are any of the other rooms in the house habitable?" Polgara asked Silk.

He nodded. "More or less. The Chandim and the Guardsmen were staying in them."

She looked around at the corpse-littered throne room. "Why don't we move out of here, then?" she suggested to Belgarath. "This place looks like a battlefield, and the smell of blood isn't that pleasant."

"Why bother?" Ce'Nedra said. "We're leaving to follow Zandramas, aren't we?"

"Not until morning, dear," Polgara replied. "It's dark and cold outside, and we're all tired and hungry."

"But—"

"The Chandim and the Guardsmen ran away, Ce'Nedra—but we can't be at all sure how far they went. And, of course, there are the Hounds as well. Let's not make the mistake of blundering out into a forest at night when we can't see what might be hiding behind the first tree we come to."

"It makes sense, Ce'Nedra," Velvet told her. "Let's try to get some sleep and start out early in the morning."

The little Queen sighed. "I suppose you're right," she admitted. "It's just that—"

"Zandramas can't get away from me, Ce'Nedra," Garion assured her. "The Orb knows which way she went."

They followed Silk out of the throne room and along the blood-spattered corridor outside. Garion tried as best he could to shield Ce'Nedra from the sight of the crumpled forms of the Guardsmen and Karands he had killed in his raging dash to the throne room of Torak. About halfway down the corridor Silk pushed open a door and held up the guttering torch he had taken from one of the iron rings sticking out of the wall. "This is about the best I can do," he told Polgara. "At least someone made an effort to clean it up."

She looked around. The room had the look of a barracks. Bunks protruded from the walls and there was a long table with benches in the center. There was a fireplace at the far end with the last embers of a fire glowing inside. "Adequate," she said.

"I'd better go look after the horses," Durnik said. "Is there a stable anywhere on the grounds?"

"It's down at the far end of the courtyard," Beldin told him, "and the Guardsmen who were here probably put in a supply of fodder and water for their own mounts."

"Good," Durnik said.

"Would you bring in the packs with my utensils and the stores, dear?" Polgara asked him.

"Of course." Then he went out, followed by Toth and Eriond.

"Suddenly I'm so tired that I can barely stand," Garion said, sinking onto a bench.

"I wouldn't be at all surprised." Beldin grunted. "You've had a busy evening."

"Are you coming along with us?" Belgarath asked him.

"No, I don't think so," Beldin replied, sprawling on the bench. "I want to find out where Nahaz took Urvon."

"Will you be able to follow him?"

"Oh, yes." Beldin tapped his nose. "I can smell a demon six days after he passes. I'll trail Nahaz just like a bloodhound. I won't be gone too long. You go ahead and follow Zandramas, and I'll catch up with you somewhere along the way." The hunchback rubbed at his jaw thoughtfully. "I think we can be fairly sure that Nahaz isn't going to let Urvon out of his sight. Urvon is—or was—a Disciple of Torak, after all. Even as much as I detest him, I still have to admit that he's got a very strong mind. Nahaz is going to have to talk to him almost constantly to keep his sanity from returning, so if our Demon Lord went to Darshiva to oversee his creatures there, he's almost certain to have taken Urvon along."

"You *will* be careful, won't you?"

"Don't get sentimental on me, Belgarath. Just leave me some kind of trail I can follow. I don't want to have to look all over Mallorea for you."

Sadi came from the throne room with his red leather case in one hand and Zith's little bottle in the other. "She's still very irritated," he said to Velvet. "She doesn't appreciate being used as a weapon."

"I told you that I'd apologize to her, Sadi," she replied. "I'll explain things to her. I'm sure she'll understand."

Silk was looking at the blond girl with an odd expression. "Tell me," he said. "Didn't it bother you at all the first time you put her down the front of your dress?"

She laughed. "To be perfectly honest with you, Prince Kheldar, the first time it was all I could do to keep from screaming."

CHAPTER TWENTY

At first light the following morning, a light that was little more than a lessening of the darkness of a sky where dense clouds scudded before the chill wind blowing down off the mountains, Silk returned to the room in which they had spent the night. "The house is being watched," he told them.

"How many are there?" Belgarath asked.

"I saw one. I'm sure there are others."

"Where is he? The one that you saw?"

Silk's quick grin was vicious. "He's watching the sky. At least he looks like he's watching. His eyes are open and he's lying on his back." He slid his hand down into his boot, pulled out one of his daggers, and looked sorrowfully at its once-keen edge. "Do you have any idea of how hard it is to push a knife through a chain-mail shirt?"

"I think that's why people wear them, Kheldar," Velvet said to him. "You should use one of these." From somewhere amongst her soft, feminine clothing she drew out a long-bladed poniard with a needlelike point.

"I thought you were partial to snakes."

"Always use the appropriate weapon, Kheldar. I certainly wouldn't want Zith to break her teeth on a steel shirt."

"Could you two talk business some other time?" Belgarath said to them. "Can you put a name to this fellow who's suddenly so interested in the sky?"

"We didn't really have time to introduce ourselves," Silk replied, sliding his jagged-edged knife back into his boot.

"I meant what—not who."

"Oh. He was a Temple Guardsman."

"Not one of the Chandim?"

"All I had to go by was his clothing."

The old man grunted.

"It's going to be slow going if we have to look behind every tree and bush as we ride along," Sadi said.

"I realize that," Begarath answered, tugging at one earlobe. "Let me think my way through this."

"And while you're deciding, I'll fix us some breakfast," Polgara said, laying aside her hairbrush. "What would you all like?"

"Porridge?" Eriond asked hopefully.

Silk sighed. "The word is gruel, Eriond. Gruel." Then he looked quickly at Polgara, whose eyes had suddenly turned frosty. "Sorry, Polgara," he apologized, "but it's our duty to educate the young, don't you think?"

"What I think is that I need more firewood," she replied.

"I'll see to it at once."

"You're too kind."

Silk rather quickly left the room.

"Any ideas?" the hunchbacked Beldin asked Belgarath.

"Several. But they all have certain flaws in them."

"Why not let me handle it for you?" the gnarled sorcerer asked, sprawling on a bench near the fire and scratching absently at his belly. "You've had a hard night, and a ten-thousand-year-old man needs to conserve his strength."

"You really find that amusing, don't you? Why not say twenty—or fifty? Push absurdity to its ultimate edge."

"My," Beldin said, "aren't we testy this morning? Pol, have you got any beer handy?"

"Before breakfast, uncle?" she said from beside the fireplace where she was stirring a large pot.

"Just as a buffer for the gruel," he said.

She gave him a very steady look.

He grinned at her, then turned back toward Belgarath. "Seriously, though," he went on, "why not let me deal with all the lurkers in the bushes around the house? Kheldar could dull every knife he's carrying, and Liselle could wear that poor little snake's fangs down to the gums, and you still wouldn't be sure if you'd cleaned out the woods hereabouts. I'm going off in a different direction anyway, so why not let me do something flamboyant to frighten off the Guardsmen and the Karands and then leave a nice, wide trail for the Chandim and the Hounds? They'll follow me, and that should leave you an empty forest to ride through."

Belgarath gave him a speculative look. "Exactly what have you got in mind?" he asked.

"I'm still working on it." The dwarf leaned back reflectively. "Let's face it, Belgarath, the Chandim and Zandramas already know that we're here, so there's not much point in tiptoeing around anymore. A little noise isn't going to hurt anything."

"That's true, I suppose," Belgarath agreed. He looked at Garion. "Are you getting any hints from the Orb about the direction Zandramas took when she left here?"

"A sort of a steady pull toward the east is all."

Beldin grunted. "Makes sense. Since Urvon's people were wandering all over Katakor, she probably wanted to get to the nearest unguarded border as quickly as possible. That would be Jenno."

"Is the border between Jenno and Katakor unguarded?" Velvet asked.

"They don't even know for sure where the border is." He snorted. "At least not up in the forest. There's nothing up there but trees anyway, so they don't bother with it." He turned back to Belgarath. "Don't get your mind set in stone on some of these things," he advised. "We did a lot of speculating back at Mal Zeth, and the theories we came up with were related to the truth only by implication. There's a great deal of intrigue going on here in Mallorea, so it's a good idea to expect things to turn out not quite the way you thought they would."

"Garion," Polgara said from the fireplace, "would you see if you can find Silk? Breakfast is almost ready."

"Yes, Aunt Pol," he replied automatically.

After they had eaten, they repacked their belongings and carried the packs out to the stable.

"Go out through the sally port," Beldin said as they crossed the courtyard again. "Give me about an hour before you start."

"You're leaving now?" Belgarath asked him.

"I might as well. We're not accomplishing very much by sitting around talking. Don't forget to leave me a trail to follow."

"I'll take care of it. I wish you'd tell me what you're going to do here."

"Trust me." The gnarled sorcerer winked. "Take cover someplace and don't come out again until all the noise subsides." He grinned wickedly and rubbed his dirty hands together in anticipation. Then he shimmered and swooped away as a blue-banded hawk.

"I think we'd better go back inside the house," Belgarath suggested. "Whatever he's going to do out here is likely to involve a great deal of flying debris."

They reentered the house and went back to the room where they had spent the night. "Durnik," Belgarath said, "can you get those shutters closed? I don't think we want broken glass sheeting across the room."

"But then we won't be able to see," Silk objected.

"I'm sure you can live without seeing it. As a matter of fact, you probably *wouldn't* want to watch, anyway."

Durnik went to the window, opened it slightly, and pulled the shutters closed.

Then, from high overhead where the blue-banded hawk had been circling, there came a huge roar almost like a continuous peal of swirling thunder, accompanied by a rushing surge. The House of Torak shook as if a great wind were tearing at it, and the faint light coming from between the slats of the shutters Durnik had closed vanished, to be replaced by inky darkness. Then there came a vast bellow from high in the air above the house.

"A demon?" Ce'Nedra gasped. "Is it a demon?"

"A *semblance* of a demon," Polgara corrected.

"How can anybody see it when it's so dark outside?" Sadi asked.

"It's dark around the house because the house is *inside* the image. The people hiding in the forest should be able to see it very well—too well, in fact."

"It's *that* big?" Sadi looked stunned. "But this house is enormous."

Belgarath grinned. "Beldin was never satisfied with halfway measures," he said.

There came another of those huge bellows from high above, followed by faint shrieks and cries of agony.

"Now what's he doing?" Ce'Nedra asked.

"Some kind of visual display, I'd imagine." Belgarath shrugged. "Probably fairly graphic. My guess is that everyone in the vicinity is being entertained by the spectacle of an illusory demon eating imaginary people alive."

"Will it frighten them off?" Silk asked.

"Wouldn't it frighten you?"

From high overhead, a dreadful booming voice roared. "Hungry!" it said. "Hungry! Want food! More food!" There came a ponderous, earthshaking crash, the sound of a titanic foot crushing an acre of forest. Then there was another and yet another as Beldin's enormous image stalked away. The light returned, and Silk hurried toward the window.

"I wouldn't," Belgarath warned him.

"But—"

"You don't want to see it, Silk. Take my word for it. You don't want to see it."

The gigantic footsteps continued to crash through the nearby woods.

"How much longer?" Sadi asked in a shaken voice.

"He said about an hour," Belgarath replied. "He'll probably make use of all of it. He wants to make a lasting impression on everybody in the area,"

There were screams of terror coming from the woods now, and the crashing continued. Then there was another sound—a great roaring that receded off into the distance toward the southwest, accompanied by the fading surge of Beldin's will.

"He's leading the Chandim off now," Belgarath said. "That means he's already chased off the Guardsmen and the Karands. Let's get ready to leave."

It took them a while to calm the wild-eyed horses, but they were finally able to mount and ride into the courtyard. Garion had once again donned his mail shirt and helmet, and his heavy shield hung from the bow of Chretienne's saddle. "Do I still need to carry the lance?" he asked.

"Probably not," Belgarath replied. "We're not likely to meet anybody out there now."

They went through the sally port and into the brushy woods. They circled the black house until they reached the east side, then Garion drew Iron-grip's sword. He held it lightly and swept it back and forth until he felt it pull at his hand. "The trail's over there," he said, pointing toward a scarcely visible path leading off into the woods.

"Good," Belgarath said. "At least we won't have to beat our way through the brush."

They crossed the weed-grown clearing that surrounded the House of Torak and entered the forest. The path they followed showed little sign of recent use, and it was at times difficult to see.

"It looks as if some people left here in a hurry." Silk grinned, pointing at various bits and pieces of equipment lying scattered along the path.

They came up over the top of a hill and saw a wide strip of devastation stretching through the forest toward the southwest.

"A tornado?" Sadi asked.

"No," Belgarath replied. "Beldin. The Chandim won't have much trouble finding his trail."

The sword in Garion's hand was still pointed unerringly toward the path they were following. He led the way confidently, and they increased their pace to a trot and pushed on through the forest. After a league or so, the path began to run downhill, moving out of the foothills toward the heavily forested plains lying to the east of the Karandese range.

"Are there any towns out there?" Sadi asked, looking out over the forest.

"Akkad is the only one of any size between here and the border," Silk told him.

"I don't think I've ever heard of it. What's it like?"

"It's a pigpen of a place," Silk replied. "Most Karandese towns are. They seem to have a great affinity for mud."

"Wasn't Akkad the place where the Melcene bureaucrat was from?" Velvet asked.

"That's what he said," Silk answered.

"And didn't he say that there are demons there?"

"There *were*," Belgarath corrected. "Cyradis told us that Nahaz has pulled all of his demons out of Karanda and sent them off to Darshiva to fight the Grolims there." He scratched at his beard. "I think we'll avoid Akkad anyway. The demons may have left, but there are still going to be Karandese fanatics there, and I don't think that the news of Mengha's death has reached them yet. In any event, there's going to be a fair amount of chaos here in Karanda until 'Zakath's army gets back from Cthol Murgos and he moves in to restore order."

They rode on, pausing only briefly for lunch.

By midafternoon, the clouds that had obscured the skies over Ashaba had dissipated, and the sun came back out again. The path they had been following grew wider and more well traveled, and it finally expanded into a road. They picked up the pace and made better time.

As evening drew on, they rode some distance back from the road and made their night's encampment in a small hollow where the light from their fire would be well concealed. They ate, and, immediately after supper, Garion sought his bed. For some reason he felt bone weary.

After half an hour, Ce'Nedra joined him in their tent. She settled down into the blankets and nestled her head against his back. Then she sighed disconsolately. "It was all a waste of time, wasn't it?" she said. "Going to Ashaba, I mean."

"No, Ce'Nedra, not really," he replied, still on the verge of sleep. "We had to go there so that Velvet could kill Harakan. That was one of the tasks that have to be completed before we get to the Place Which Is No More."

"Does all that really have any meaning, Garion?" she asked. "Half the time you act as if you believe it, and the other half you don't. If Zandramas had been there with our son, you wouldn't have just let her walk away because all the conditions hadn't been met, would you?"

"Not by so much as one step," he said grimly.

"Then you *don't* really believe it, do you?"

"I'm not an absolute fatalist, if that's what you mean, but I've seen things come out exactly the way the Prophecy said they were going to far too many times for me to ignore it altogether."

"Sometimes I think that I'll never see my baby again," she said in a weary little voice.

"You mustn't ever think that," he told her. "We *will* catch up with Zandramas, and we *will* take Geran home with us again."

"Home," she sighed. "We've been gone for so long that I can barely remember what it looks like."

He took her into his arms, buried his face in her hair, and held her close. After a time she sighed and fell asleep. In spite of his own deep weariness, however, it was quite late before he himself drifted off.

The next day dawned clear and warm. They made their way back to the road again and continued eastward with Iron-grip's sword pointing the way.

About midmorning, Polgara called ahead to Belgarath. "Father, there's someone hiding off to the side of the road just ahead."

He slowed his horse to a walk. "Chandim?" he asked tersely.

"No. It's a Mallorean Angarak. He's very much afraid—and not altogether rational."

"Is he planning any mischief?"

"He's not actually planning anything, father. His thoughts aren't coherent enough for that."

"Why don't you go flush him out, Silk?" the old man suggested. "I don't like having people lurking behind me—sane or not."

"About where is he?" the little man asked Polgara.

"Some distance back in the woods from that dead tree," she replied.

He nodded. "I'll go talk with him," he said. He loped his horse on ahead and reined in beside the dead tree. "We know you're back there, friend," he called pleasantly. "We don't mean you any harm, but why don't you come out in the open where we can see you?"

There was a long pause.

"Come along now," Silk called. "Don't be shy."

"Have you got any demons with you?" The voice sounded fearful.

"Do I look like the sort of fellow who'd be consorting with demons?"

"You won't kill me, will you?"

"Of course not. We only want to talk with you, that's all."

There was another long, fearful pause. "Have you got anything to eat?" The voice was filled with a desperate need.

"I think we can spare a bit."

The hidden man thought about that. "All right," he said finally. "I'm coming out. Remember that you promised not to kill me." Then there was a crashing in the bushes, and a Mallorean soldier came stumbling out into the road. His red tunic was in shreds, he had lost his helmet, and the remains of his boots were tied to his legs with leather thongs. He had quite obviously neither shaved nor bathed for at least a month. His eyes were wild and his head twitched on his neck uncontrollably. He stared at Silk with a terrified expression.

"You don't look to be in very good shape, friend," Silk said to him. "Where's your unit?"

"Dead, all dead, and eaten by the demons." The soldier's eyes were haunted. "Were you at Akkad?" he asked in a terrified voice. "Were you there when the demons came?"

"No, friend. We just came up from Venna."

"You said that you had something for me to eat."

"Durnik," Silk called, "could you bring some food for this poor fellow?"

Durnik rode to the packhorse carrying their stores and took out some bread and dried meat. Then he rode on ahead to join Silk and the fear-crazed soldier.

"Were *you* at Akkad when the demons came?" the fellow asked him.

Durnik shook his head. "No," he replied, "I'm with him." He pointed at Silk. Then he handed the fellow the bread and meat.

The soldier snatched them and began to wolf them down in huge bites.

"What happened at Akkad?" Silk asked.

"The demons came," the soldier replied, still cramming food into his mouth. Then he stopped, his eyes fixed on Durnik with an expression of fright. "Are you going to kill me?" he demanded.

Durnik stared at him. "No, man," he replied in a sick voice.

"Thank you." The soldier sat down at the roadside and continued to eat.

Garion and the others slowly drew closer, not wanting to frighten the skittish fellow off.

"What *did* happen at Akkad?" Silk pressed. "We're going in that direction, and we'd sort of like to know what to expect."

"Don't go there," the soldier said, shuddering. "It's horrible—horrible. The demons came through the gates with howling Karands all around them. The Karands started hacking people to pieces and then they fed the pieces to the demons. They cut off both of my captain's arms and then his legs as well, and then a demon picked up what was left of him and ate his head. He was screaming the whole time." He lowered his chunk of bread and fearfully stared at Ce'Nedra. "Lady, are you going to kill me?" he demanded.

"Certainly not!" she replied in a shocked voice.

"If you are, please don't let me see it when you do. And pleasy bury me someplace where the demons won't dig me up and eat me."

"She's not going to kill you," Polgara told him firmly.

The man's wild eyes filled with a kind of desperate longing. "Would *you* do it then, Lady?" he pleaded. "I can't stand the horror any more. Please kill me gently— the way my mother would—and then hide me so that the demons won't get me." He put his face into his shaking hands and began to cry.

"Give him some more food, Durnik," Belgarath said, his eyes suddenly filled with compassion. "He's completely mad, and there's nothing else we can do for him."

"I think I might be able to do something, Ancient One," Sadi said. He opened his case and took out a vial of amber liquid. "Sprinkle a few drops of this on the bread you give him, Goodman," he said to Durnik. "It will calm him and give him a few hours of peace."

"Compassion seems out of character for you, Sadi," Silk said.

"Perhaps," the eunuch murmured, "but then, perhaps you don't fully understand me, Prince Kheldar."

Durnik took some more bread and meat from the pack for the hysterical Mallorean soldier, sprinkling them liberally with Sadi's potion. Then he gave them to the poor man, and they all rode slowly past and on down the road. After they had gone a ways, Garion heard him calling after them. "Come back! Come back! Somebody—anybody—please come back and kill me. Mother, please kill me!"

Garion's stomach wrenched with an almost overpowering sense of pity. He set his teeth and rode on, trying not to listen to the desperate pleas coming from behind.

They circled to the north of Akkad that afternoon, bypassing the city and returning to the road some two leagues beyond. The pull of the sword Garion held on the pommel of his saddle confirmed the fact that Zandramas had indeed passed this way and had continued on along this road toward the northeast and the relative safety of the border between Katakor and Jenno.

They camped in the forest a few miles north of the road that night and started out once more early the following morning. The road for a time stretched across open fields. It was deeply rutted and still quite soft at the shoulders.

"Karands don't take road maintenance very seriously," Silk observed, squinting into the morning sun.

"I noticed that," Durnik replied.

"I thought you might have."

Some leagues farther on, the road they were following reentered the forest, and they rode along through a cool, damp shade beneath towering evergreens.

Then, from somewhere ahead they heard a hollow, booming sound.

"I think we might want to go rather carefully until we're past that," Silk said quietly.

"What is that sound?" Sadi asked.

"Drums. There's a temple ahead."

"Out here in the forest?" The eunuch sounded surprised. "I thought that the Grolims were largely confined to the cities."

"This isn't a Grolim Temple, Sadi. It was nothing to do with the worship of Torak. As a matter of fact, the Grolims used to burn these places whenever they came across them. They were a part of the old religion of the area."

"Demon worship, you mean?"

Silk nodded. "Most of them have been long abandoned, but every so often you come across one that's still in use. The drums are a fair indication that the one just ahead is still open for business."

"Will we be able to go around them?" Durnik asked.

"It shouldn't be much trouble," the little man replied. "The Karands burn a certain fungus in their ceremonial fires. The fumes have a peculiar effect on one's senses."

"Oh?" Sadi said with a certain interest.

"Never mind," Belgarath told him. "That red case of yours has quite enough in it already."

"Just scientific curiosity, Belgarath."

"Of course."

"What are they worshipping?" Velvet asked. "I thought that the demons had all left Karanda."

Silk was frowning. "The beat isn't right," he said.

"Have you suddenly become a music critic, Kheldar?" she asked him.

He shook his head. "I've come across these places before, and the drumming's usually pretty frenzied when they're holding their rites. That beat up ahead is too measured. It's almost as if they're waiting for something."

Sadi shrugged. "Let them wait," he said. "It's no concern of ours, is it?"

"We don't know that for sure, Sadi," Polgara told him. She looked at Belgarath. "Wait here, father," she suggested. "I'll go on ahead and take a look."

"It's too dangerous, Pol," Durnik objected.

She smiled. "They won't even pay any attention to me, Durnik." She dismounted and walked a short way up the path. Then, momentarily, she was surrounded with a kind of glowing nimbus, a hazy patch of light that had not been there before. When the light cleared, a great snowy owl hovered among the trees and then ghosted away on soft, silent wings.

"For some reason that always makes my blood run cold," Sadi murmured.

They waited while the measured drumming continued. Garion dismounted and checked his cinch strap. Then he walked about a bit, stretching his legs.

It was perhaps ten minutes later when Polgara returned, drifting on white wings under the low-hanging branches. When she resumed her normal shape, her face was pale and her eyes were filled with loathing. "Hideous!" she said. "Hideous!"

"What is it, Pol?" Durnik's voice was concerned.

"There's a woman in labor in that temple."

"I don't know that a temple is the right sort of place for that, but if she needed shelter—" The smith shrugged.

"The temple was chosen quite deliberately," she replied. "The infant that's about to be born isn't human."

"But—"

"It's a demon."

Ce'Nedra gasped.

Polgara looked at Belgarath. "We have to intervene, father," she told him. "This *must* be stopped."

"How can it be stopped?" Velvet asked in perplexity. "I mean, if the woman's already in labor . . ." She spread her hands.

"We may have to kill her," Polgara said bleakly. "Even that may not prevent this monstrous birth. We may have to deliver the demon child and then smother it."

"No!" Ce'Nedra cried. "It's just a baby! You can't kill it."

"It's not that kind of baby, Ce'Nedra. It's half human and half demon. It's a creature of *this* world and a spawn of the other. If it's allowed to live, it won't be possible to banish it. It will be a perpetual horror."

"Garion!" Ce'Nedra cried. "You can't let her."

"Polgara's right, Ce'Nedra," Belgarath told her. "The creature can't be allowed to live."

"How many Karands are gathered up there?" Silk asked.

"There are a half dozen outside the temple," Polgara replied. "There may be more inside."

"However many they are, we're going to have to dispose of them," he said. "They're waiting for the birth of what they believe is a God, and they'll defend the newborn demon to the death."

"All right, then," Garion said bleakly, "let's go oblige them."

"You're not condoning this?" Ce'Nedra exclaimed.

"I don't like it," he admitted, "but I don't see that we've got much choice." He looked at Polgara. "There's absolutely no way it could be sent back to the place where demons originate?" he asked her.

"None whatsoever," she said flatly. "*This* world will be it's home. It wasn't summoned and it has no master. Within two years, it will be a horror such as this world has never seen. It *must* be destroyed."

"Can you do it, Pol?" Belgarath asked her.

"I don't have any choice, father," she replied. "I *have* to do it."

"All right, then," the old man said to the rest of them. "We have to get Pol inside that temple—and that means dealing with the Karands."

Silk reached inside his boot and pulled out his dagger. "I should have sharpened this," he muttered, looking ruefully at his jagged blade.

"Would you like to borrow one of mine?" Velvet asked him.

"No, that's all right, Liselle," he replied. "I've got a couple of spares." He returned the knife to his boot and drew another from its place of concealment at the small of his back and yet a third from its sheath down the back of his neck.

Durnik lifted his axe from its loop at the back of his saddle. His face was unhappy. "Do we really have to do this, Pol?" he asked.

"Yes, Durnik. I'm afraid we do."

He sighed. "All right, then," he said. "Let's go get it over with."

They started forward, riding at a slow walk to avoid alerting the fanatics ahead.

The Karands were sitting around a large, hollowed-out section of log, pounding on it with clubs in rhythmic unison. It gave forth a dull booming sound. They were dressed in roughly tanned fur vests and cross-tied leggings of dirty sackcloth. They were raggedly bearded, and their hair was matted and greasy. Their faces were hideously painted, but their eyes seemed glazed and their expressions slack-lipped.

"I'll go first," Garion muttered to the others.

"Shouting a challenge, I suppose," Silk whispered.

"I'm not an assassin, Silk," Garion replied quietly. "One or two of them might be rational enough to run, and that means a few less we'll have to kill."

"Suit yourself, but expecting rationality from Karands is irrational all by itself."

Garion quickly surveyed the clearing. The wooden temple was constructed of half-rotten logs, sagging badly at one end and surmounted along its ridgepole by a line of mossy skulls staring out vacantly. The ground before the building was hard-packed dirt, and there was a smoky firepit not far from the drummers.

"Try not to get into that smoke," Silk cautioned in a whisper. "You might start to see all sorts of peculiar things if you inhale too much of it."

Garion nodded and looked around. "Are we all ready?" he asked in a low voice.

They nodded.

"All right then." He spurred Chretienne into the clearing. "Throw down your weapons!" he shouted at the startled Karands.

Instead of obeying, they dropped their clubs and seized up a variety of axes, spears, and swords, shrieking their defiance.

"You see?" Silk said.

Garion clenched his teeth and charged, brandishing his sword. Even as he thundered toward the fur-clad men, he saw four others come bursting out of the temple.

Even with these reinforcements, however, the men on foot were no match for Garion and his mounted companions. Two of the howling Karands fell beneath Iron-grip's sword on Garion's first charge, and the one who tried to thrust at his back with a broad-bladed spear fell in a heap as Durnik brained him with his axe. Sadi caught a sword thrust with a flick of his cloak and then, with an almost delicate motion, dipped his poisoned dagger into the swordsman's throat. Using his heavy staff like a club, Toth battered two men to the ground, the sound of his blows punctuated by the snapping of bones. Their howls of frenzy turned to groans of pain as they fell. Silk launched himself from his saddle, rolled with the skill of an acrobat, and neatly ripped open one fanatic with one of his daggers while simultaneously plunging the other into the chest of a fat man who was clumsily trying to wield an axe. Chretienne whirled so quickly that Garion was almost thrown from his saddle as the big stallion trampled a Karand into the earth with his steel-shod hooves.

The lone remaining fanatic stood in the doorway of the crude temple. He was much older than his companions, and his face had been tattooed into a grotesque mask. His only weapon was a skull-surmounted staff, and he was brandishing it at them even as he shrieked an incantation. His words broke off suddenly, however, as Velvet hurled one of her knives at him with a smooth underhand cast. The wizard gaped down in amazement at the hilt of her knife protruding from his chest. Then he slowly toppled over backward.

There was a brief silence, punctuated only by the groans of the two men Toth had crippled. And then a harsh scream came from the temple—a woman's scream.

Garion jumped from his saddle, stepped over the body in the doorway, and looked into the large, smoky room.

A half-naked woman lay on the crude altar against the far wall. She had been bound to it in a spread-eagle position and she was partially covered by a filthy blanket. Her features were distorted, and her belly grossly, impossibly distended. She screamed again and then spoke in gasps.

"Nahaz! Magrash Klat Grichak! Nahaz!"

"I'll deal with this, Garion," Polgara said firmly from behind him. "Wait outside with the others."

"Were there any others in there?" Silk asked him as he came out.

"Just the woman. Aunt Pol's with her." Garion suddenly realized that he was shaking violently.

"What was that language she was speaking?" Sadi asked, carefully cleaning his poisoned dagger.

"The language of the demons," Belgarath replied. "She was calling out to the father of her baby."

"Nahaz?" Garion asked, his voice startled.

"She *thinks* it was Nahaz," the old man said. "She could be wrong—or maybe not."

From inside the temple the woman screamed again.

"Is anybody hurt?" Durnik asked.

"They are," Silk replied, pointing at the fallen Karands. Then he squatted and repeatedly plunged his daggers into the dirt to cleanse the blood off them.

"Kheldar," Velvet said in a strangely weak voice, "would you get my knife for me?" Garion looked at her and saw that her face was pale and that her hands were trembling slightly. He realized then that this self-possessed young woman was perhaps not quite so ruthless as he had thought.

"Of course, Liselle," Silk replied in a neutral tone. The little man quite obviously also understood the cause of her distress. He rose, went to the doorway, and pulled the knife out of the wizard's chest. He wiped it carefully and returned it to her. "Why don't you go back and stay with Ce'Nedra?" he suggested. "We can clean up here."

"Thank you, Kheldar," she said, turned her horse, and rode out of the clearing.

"She's only a girl," Silk said to Garion in a defensive tone. "She *is* good, though," he added with a certain pride.

"Yes," Garion agreed. "Very good." He looked around at the twisted shapes lying in heaps in the clearing. "Why don't we drag all these bodies over behind the temple?" he suggested. "This place is bad enough without all of this."

There was another scream from the temple.

Noon came and went unnoticed as Garion and the others endured the cries of the laboring woman. By midafternoon, the screams had grown much weaker, and as the sun was just going down, there came one dreadful last shriek that seemed to dwindle off into silence. No other sound came from inside, and after several minutes, Polgara came out. Her face was pale, and her hands and clothing were drenched with blood.

"Well, Pol?" Belgarath asked her.

"She died."

"And the demon?"

"Stillborn. Neither one of them survived the birth." She looked down at her clothing. "Durnik, please bring me a blanket and water to wash in."

"Of course, Pol."

With her husband shielding her by holding up the blanket, Polgara deliberately removed all of her clothing, throwing each article through the temple doorway. Then she drew the blanket about her. "Now burn it," she said to them. "Burn it to the ground."

■ CHAPTER TWENTY-ONE ■

They crossed the border into Jenno about noon the following day, still following the trail of Zandramas. The experiences of the previous afternoon and evening had left them all subdued, and they rode on in silence. A league or so past the rather indeterminate border, they pulled off to the side of the road to eat. The spring sunlight was very bright and the day pleasantly warm. Garion walked a little ways away from the others and reflectively watched a cloud of yellow-striped bees industriously working at a patch of wild flowers.

"Garion," Ce'Nedra said in a small voice, coming up behind him.

"Yes, Ce'Nedra?" He put his arm around her.

"What really happened back there?"

"You saw about as much of it as I did."

"That's not what I mean. What happened inside the temple? Did that poor woman and her baby *really* just die—or did Polgara kill them?"

"Ce'Nedra!"

"I have to know, Garion. She was so grim about it before she went inside that place. She was going to kill the baby. Then she came out and told us that the mother and baby had both died in the birth. Wasn't that very convenient?"

He drew in a deep breath. "Ce'Nedra, think back. You've known Aunt Pol for a long time now. Has she ever told you a lie—ever?"

"Well—sometimes she hasn't told me the whole truth. She's told me part of it and kept the rest a secret."

"That's not the same as lying, Ce'Nedra, and you know it."

"Well—"

"You're angry because she said we might have to kill that thing."

"Baby," she corrected firmly.

He took her by the shoulders and looked directly into her face. "No, Ce'Nedra. It was a thing—half human, half demon, and all monster."

"But it was so little—so helpless."

"How do you know that?"

"All babies are little when they're born."

"I don't think that one was. I saw the woman for just a minute before Aunt Pol told me to leave the temple. Do you remember how big you were just before Geran was born? Well, that woman's stomach was at least five times as big as yours was— and she wasn't a great deal taller than you are."

"You aren't serious!"

"Oh, yes, I am. There was no way that the demon could have been born without killing its mother. For all I know, it might just simply have clawed its way out."

"It's own mother?" she gasped.

"Did you think it would love its mother? Demons don't know how to love, Ce'Nedra. That's why they're demons. Fortunately the demon died. It's too bad that the woman had to die, too, but it was much too late to do anything for her by the time we got there."

"You're a cold, hard person, Garion."

"Oh, Ce'Nedra, you know better than that. What happened back there was unpleasant, certainly, but none of us had any choice but to do exactly what we did."

She turned her back on him and started to stalk away.

"Ce'Nedra," he said, hurrying to catch her.

"What?" She tried to free her arm from his grasp.

"We didn't have any choice," he repeated. "Would you want Geran to grow up in a world filled with demons?"

She stared at him. "No," she firmly admitted. "It's just that . . ." She left it hanging.

"I know." He put his arms about her.

"Oh, Garion." She suddenly clung to him, and everything was all right again.

After they had eaten, they rode on through the forest, passing occasional villages huddled deep among the trees. The villages were rude, most of them consisting of a dozen or so rough log houses and surrounded by crude log palisades. There were usually a rather surprising number of hogs rooting among the stumps that surrounded each village.

"There don't seem to be very many dogs," Durnik observed.

"These people prefer pigs as house pets," Silk told him. "As a race, Karands have a strong affinity for dirt, and pigs satisfy certain deep inner needs among them."

"Do you know something, Silk," the smith said then. "You'd be a much more pleasant companion if you didn't try to turn everything into a joke."

"It's a failing I have. I've looked at the world for quite a few years now and I've found that if I don't laugh, I'll probably end up crying."

"You're really serious, aren't you?"

"Would I do that to an old friend?"

About midafternoon, the road they were following curved slightly, and they soon reached the edge of the forest and a fork in the rutted track.

"All right. Which way?" Belgarath asked.

Garion lifted his sword from the pommel of his saddle and swept it slowly back and forth until he felt the familiar tug. "The right fork," he replied.

"I'm *so* glad you said that," Silk told him. "The left fork leads to Calida. I'd expect that news of Harakan's death has reached there by now. Even without the demons, a town full of hysterics doesn't strike me as a very nice place to visit. The followers of Lord Mengha might be just a bit upset when they hear that he's gone off and left them."

"Where does the right fork go?" Belgarath asked him.

"Down to the lake," Silk replied. "Lake Karanda. It's the biggest lake in the world. When you stand on the shore, it's like looking at an ocean."

Garion frowned. "Grandfather," he said, starting to worry, "Do you think that Zandramas knows that the Orb can follow her?"

"It's possible, yes."

"And would she know that it can't follow her over water?"

"I couldn't say for sure."

"But if she *does,* isn't it possible that she went to the lake in order to hide her trail from us? She could have sailed out a ways, doubled back, and come ashore just about anyplace. Then she could have struck out in a new direction, and we'd never pick up her trail again."

Belgarath scratched at his beard, squinting in the sunlight. "Pol," he said. "Are there any Grolims about?"

She concentrated a bit. "Not in the immediate vicinity, father," she replied.

"Good. When Zandramas was trying to tamper with Ce'Nedra back at Rak Hagga, weren't you able to lock your thought with hers for a while?"

"Yes, briefly."

"She was at Ashaba then, right?"

She nodded.

"Did you get any kind of notion about which direction she was planning to go when she left?"

She frowned. "Nothing very specific, father—just a vague hint about wanting to go home.

"Darshiva," Silk said, snapping his fingers. "We know that Zandramas is a Darshivan name, and 'Zakath told Garion that it was in Darshiva that she started stirring up trouble."

Belgarath grunted. "It's a little thin," he said. "I'd feel a great deal more comfortable with some confirmation." He looked at Polgara. "Do you think you could reestablish contact with her—even for just a moment? All I need is a direction."

"I don't think so, father. I'll try, but . . ." she shrugged. Then her face grew very calm, and Garion could feel her mind reaching out with a subtle probing. After a few minutes, she relaxed her will. "She's shielding, father," she told the old man. "I can't pick up anything at all."

He muttered a curse under his breath. "We'll just have to go on down to the lake and ask a few questions. Maybe somebody saw her."

"I'm sure they did," Silk said, "but Zandramas likes to drown sailors, remember? Anyone who saw where she landed is probably sleeping under thirty feet of water."

"Can you think of an alternative plan?"

"Not offhand, no."

"Then we go on to the lake."

As the sun began to sink slowly behind them, they passed a fair-sized town set perhaps a quarter of a mile back from the road. The inhabitants were gathered outside the palisade surrounding it. They had a huge bonfire going, and just in front of the fire stood a crude, skull-surmounted altar of logs. A skinny man wearing several feathers in his hair and with lurid designs painted on his face and body was before the altar, intoning an incantation at the top of his lungs. His arms were stretched imploringly at the sky, and there was a note of desperation in his voice.

"What's he doing?" Ce'Nedra asked.

"He's trying to raise a demon so that the townspeople can worship it," Eriond told her calmly.

"Garion!" she said in alarm. "Shouldn't we run?"

"He won't succeed," Eriond assured her. "The demon won't come to him anymore. Nahaz has told them all not to."

The wizard broke off his incantation. Even from this distance, Garion could see that there was a look of panic on his face.

An angry mutter came from the townspeople.

"That crowd is starting to turn ugly," Silk observed. "The wizard had better raise his demon on the next try, or he might be in trouble."

The gaudily painted man with feathers in his hair began the incantation again, virtually shrieking and ranting at the sky. He completed it and stood waiting expectantly.

Nothing happened.

After a moment, the crowd gave an angry roar and surged forward. They seized the cringing wizard and tore his log altar apart. Then, laughing raucously, they nailed his hands and feet to one of the logs with long spikes and, with a great shout, they hurled the log up onto the bonfire.

"Let's get out of here," Belgarath said. "Mobs tend to go wild once they've tasted blood." He led them away at a gallop.

They made camp that night in a willow thicket on the banks of a small stream, concealing their fire as best they could.

It was foggy the following morning, and they rode warily with their hands close to their weapons.

"How much farther to the lake?" Belgarath asked as the sun began to burn off the fog.

Silk looked around into the thinning mist. "It's kind of hard to say. I'd guess a couple more leagues at least."

"Let's pick up the pace, then. We're going to have to find a boat when we get there, and that might take a while."

They urged their horses into a canter and continued on. The road had taken on a noticeable downhill grade.

"It's a bit closer than I thought," Silk called to them. "I remember this stretch of road. We should reach the lake in an hour or so."

They passed occasional Karands, clad in brown fur for the most part and heavily armed. The eyes of these local people were suspicious, even hostile, but Garion's mail shirt, helmet, and sword were sufficient to gain the party passage without incident.

By midmorning the gray fog had completely burned off. As they crested a knoll, Garion reined in. Before him there lay an enormous body of water, blue and sparkling in the midmorning sun. It looked for all the world like a vast inland sea, with no hint of a far shore, but it did not have that salt tang of the sea.

"Big, isn't it?" Silk said, pulling his horse in beside Chretienne. He pointed toward a thatch-and-log village standing a mile or so up the lake shore. A number of fair-sized boats were moored to a floating dock jutting out into the water. "That's where I've usually hired boats when I wanted to cross the lake."

"You've done business around here, then?"

"Oh, yes. There are gold mines in the mountains of Zamad, and deposits of gem stones up in the forest."

"How big are those boats?"

"Big enough. We'll be a little crowded, but the weather's calm enough for a safe crossing, even if the boat might be a bit overloaded." Then he frowned. "What are *they* doing?"

Garion looked at the slope leading down to the village and saw a crowd of people moving slowly down toward the lakeshore. There seemed to be a great deal of fur involved in their clothing in varying shades of red and brown, though many of them wore cloaks all dyed in hues of rust and faded blue. More and more of them came over the hilltop, and other people came out of the village to meet them.

"Belgarath," the little Drasnian called. "I think we've got a problem."

Belgarath came jolting up to the crest of the knoll at a trot. He looked at the large crowd gathering in front of the village.

"We need to get into that village to hire a boat," Silk told him. "We're well enough armed to intimidate a few dozen villagers, but there are two or three hundred people down there now. That could require some fairly serious intimidation."

"A country fair, perhaps?" the old man asked.

Silk shook his head. "I wouldn't think so. It's the wrong time of year for it, and those people don't have any carts with them." He swung down from his saddle and went back to the packhorses. A moment or so later, he came back with a poorly tanned red fur vest and a baggy fur hat. He pulled them on, bent over, and wrapped a pair of sackcloth leggings about his calves, tying them in place with lengths of cord. "How do I look?" he asked.

"Shabby," Garion told him.

"That's the idea. Shab's in fashion here in Karanda." He remounted.

"Where did you get the clothes?" Belgarath asked curiously.

"I pillaged one of the bodies back at the temple." The little man shrugged. "I like to keep a few disguises handy. I'll go find out what's happening down there."

He dug his heels into his horse's flanks and galloped down toward the throng gathering near the lakeside village.

"Let's pull back out of sight," Belgarath suggested. "I'd rather not attract too much attention."

They walked their horses down the back side of the knoll and then some distance away from the road to a shallow gully that offered concealment and dismounted there. Garion climbed back up out of the gully on foot and lay down in the tall grass to keep watch.

About a half hour later, Silk came loping back over the top of the knoll. Garion rose from the grass and signaled to him.

When the little man reached the gully and dismounted, his expression was disgusted. "Religion," he snorted. "I wonder what the world would be like without it. That gathering down there is for the purpose of witnessing the performance of a powerful wizard, who absolutely guarantees that he can raise a demon—despite the notable lack of success of others lately. He's even hinting that he might be able to persuade the Demon Lord Nahaz himself to put in an appearance. That crowd's likely to be there all day."

"Now what?" Sadi asked.

Belgarath walked down the gully a ways, looking thoughtfully up at the sky. When he came back, his look was determined. "We're going to need a couple more of those," he said, pointing at Silk's disguise.

"Nothing simpler," Silk replied. "There are still enough latecomers going down that hill for me to be able to waylay a few. What's the plan?"

"You, Garion, and I are going down there."

"Interesting notion, but I don't get the point."

"The wizard, whoever he is, is promising to raise Nahaz, but Nahaz is with Urvon and isn't very likely to show up. After what we saw happen at that village yesterday, it's fairly obvious that failing to produce a demon is a serious mistake for a wizard to make. If our friend down there is so confident, it probably means that he's going to create an illusion—since nobody's been able to produce the real thing lately. I'm good at illusions myself, so I'll just go down and challenge him."

"Won't they just fall down and worship *your* illusion?" Velvet asked him.

His smile was chilling. "I don't really think so, Liselle," he replied. "You see, there are demons, and then there are *demons*. If I do it right, there won't be a Karand within five leagues of this place by sunset—depending on how fast they can run, of course." He looked at Silk. "Haven't you left yet?" he asked pointedly.

While Silk went off in search of more disguises, the old sorcerer made a few other preparations. He found a long, slightly crooked branch to use as a staff and a couple of feathers to stick in his hair. Then he sat down and laid his head back against one of their packs. "All right, Pol," he instructed his daughter, "make me hideous."

She smiled faintly and started to raise one hand.

"Not *that* way. Just take some ink and draw some designs on my face. They don't have to be too authentic-looking. The Karands have corrupted their religion so badly that they wouldn't recognize authenticity if they stepped in it."

She laughed and went to one of the packs, returning a moment later with an inkpot and a quill pen.

"Why on earth are you carrying ink, Lady Polgara?" Ce'Nedra asked.

"I like to be prepared for eventualities as they arise. I went on a long journey once and had to leave a note for someone along the way. I didn't have ink with me, so I ended up opening a vein to get something to write with. I seldom make the same mistake twice. Close your eyes, father. I always like to start with the eyelids and work my way out."

Belgarath closed his eyes. "Durnik," he said as Polgara started drawing designs on his face with her quill, "you and the others will stay back here. See if you can find someplace a little better hidden than this gully."

"All right, Belgarath," the smith agreed. "How will we know when it's safe to come down to the lakeshore?"

"When the screaming dies out."

"Don't move your lips, father," Polgara told him, frowning in concentration as she continued her drawing. "Did you want me to blacken your beard, too?"

"Leave it the way it is. Superstitious people are always impressed by venerability, and I look older than just about anybody."

She nodded her agreement. "Actually, father, you look older than dirt."

"Very funny, Pol," he said acidly. "Are you just about done?"

"Did you want the death symbol on your forehead?" she asked.

"Might as well," he grunted. "Those cretins down there won't recognize it, but it looks impressive."

By the time Polgara had finished with her artwork, Silk returned with assorted garments.

"Any problems?" Durnik asked him.

"Simplicity itself." Silk shrugged. "A man whose eyes are fixed on heaven is fairly easy to approach from behind, and a quick rap across the back of the head will usually put him to sleep."

"Leave your mail shirt and helmet, Garion," Belgarath said. "Karands don't wear them. Bring your sword, though."

"I'd planned to." Garion began to struggle out of his mail shirt. After a moment, Ce'Nedra came over to help him.

"You're getting rusty," she told him after they had hauled off the heavy thing. She pointed at a number of reddish-brown stains on the padded linen tunic he wore under the shirt.

"It's one of the drawbacks to wearing armor," he replied.

"That and the smell," she added, wrinkling her nose. "You *definitely* need a bath, Garion."

"I'll see if I can get around to it one of these days," he said. He pulled on one of the fur vests Silk had stolen. Then he tied on the crude leggings and crammed on a rancid-smelling fur cap. "How do I look?" he asked her.

"Like a barbarian," she replied.

"That was sort of the whole idea."

"I didn't steal you a hat," Silk was saying to Belgarath. "I thought you might prefer to wear feathers."

Belgarath nodded. "All of us mighty wizards wear feathers," he agreed. "It's a passing fad, I'm sure, but I always like to dress fashionably." He looked over at the horses. "I think we'll walk," he decided. "When the noise starts, the horses might get a bit skittish." He looked at Polgara and the others who were staying behind. "This shouldn't take us too long," he told them confidently and strode off down the gully with Garion and Silk close behind him.

They emerged from the mouth of the gully at the south end of the knoll and walked down the hill toward the crowd gathering on the lakeshore.

"I don't see any sign of their wizard yet," Garion said, peering ahead.

"They always like to keep their audiences waiting for a bit," Belgarath said. "It's supposed to heighten the anticipation or something."

The day was quite warm as they walked down the hill, and the rancid smell coming from their clothing grew stronger. Although they did not really look that much like Karands, the people in the crowd they quietly joined paid them scant attention. Every eye seemed to be fixed on a platform and one of those log altars backed by a line of skulls on stakes.

"Where do they get all the skulls?" Garion whispered to Silk.

"They used to be headhunters," Silk replied. "The Angaraks discouraged that practice, so now they creep around at night robbing graves. I doubt if you could find a whole skeleton in any graveyard in all of Karanda."

"Let's get closer to the altar," Belgarath muttered. "I don't want to have to shove my way through this mob when things start happening." They pushed through the crowd. A few of the greasy-haired fanatics started to object to being thrust aside, but one look at Belgarath's face with the hideous designs Polgara had drawn on it convinced them that here was a wizard of awesome power and that it perhaps might be wiser not to interfere with him.

Just as they reached the front near the altar, a man in a black Grolim robe strode out through the gate of the lakeside village, coming directly toward the altar.

"I think that's our wizard," Belgarath said quietly.

"A Grolim?" Silk sounded slightly surprised.

"Let's see what he's up to."

The black-robed man reached the platform and stepped up to stand in front of the altar. He raised both hands and spoke harshly in a language Garion did not understand. His words could have been either a benediction or a curse. The crowd fell immediately silent. Slowly the Grolim pushed back his hood and let his robe fall to the platform. He wore only a loincloth, and his head had been shaved. His body was covered from crown to toe with elaborate tattoos.

Silk winced. "That must have *really* hurt," he muttered.

"Prepare ye all to look upon the face of your God," the Grolim announced in a large voice, then bent to inscribe the designs on the platform before the altar.

"That's what I thought," Belgarath whispered. "That circle he drew isn't complete. If he were *really* going to raise a demon, he wouldn't have made that mistake."

The Grolim straightened and began declaiming the words of the incantation in a rolling, oratorical style.

"He's being very cautious," Belgarath told them. "He's leaving out certain key phrases. He doesn't want to raise a *real* demon accidentally. Wait." The old man smiled bleakly. "Here he goes."

Garion also felt the surge as the Grolim's will focused and then he heard the familiar rushing sound.

"Behold the Demon Lord Nahaz," the tattooed Grolim shouted, and a shadow-encased form appeared before the altar with a flash of fire, a peal of thunder, and a cloud of sulfur-stinking smoke. Although the figure was no larger than an ordinary man, it looked very substantial for some reason.

"Not too bad, really," Belgarath admitted grudgingly.

"It looks awfully solid to me, Belgarath," Silk said nervously.

"It's only an illusion, Silk," the old man quietly reassured him. "A good one, but still only an illusion."

The shadowy form on the platform before the altar rose to its full height and then pulled back its hood of darkness to reveal the hideous face Garion had seen in Torak's throne room at Ashaba.

As the crowd fell to its knees with a great moan, Belgarath drew in his breath sharply. "When this crowd starts to disperse, don't let the Grolim escape," he instructed. "He's actually seen the real Nahaz, and that means that he was one of Harakan's cohorts. I want some answers out of him." Then the old man drew himself up. "Well, I guess I might as well get started with this," he said. He stepped up in front of the platform. "Fraud!" he shouted in a great voice. "Fraud and fakery!"

The Grolim stared at him, his eyes narrowing as he saw the designs drawn on his face. "On your knees before the Demon Lord," he blustered.

"Fraud!" Belgarath denounced him again. He stepped up onto the platform and faced the stunned crowd. "This is no wizard, but only a Grolim trickster," he declared.

"The Demon Lord will tear all your flesh from your bones," the Grolim shrieked.

"All right," Belgarath replied with calm contempt. "Let's see him do it. Here. I'll even help him." He pulled back his sleeve, approached the shadowy illusion hovering threateningly before the altar and quite deliberately ran his bare arm into the shadow's gaping maw. A moment later, his hand emerged, coming, or so it appeared, out of the back of the Demon Lord's head. He pushed his arm further until his entire wrist and forearm were sticking out of the back of the illusion. Then, quite deliberately, he wiggled his fingers at the people gathered before the altar.

A nervous titter ran through the crowd.

"I think you missed a shred or two of flesh, Nahaz," the old man said to the shadowy form standing before him. "There still seems to be quite a bit of meat clinging to my fingers and arm." He pulled his arm back out of the shadow and then passed both hands back and forth through the Grolim's illusion. "It appears to lack a bit of substance, friend," he said to the tattooed man. "Why don't we send it back where you found it? Then I'll show you and your parishoners here a *real* demon."

He put his hands derisively on his hips, leaned forward slightly from the waist, and blew at the shadow. The illusion vanished, and the tattooed Grolim stepped back fearfully.

"He's getting ready to run," Silk whispered to Garion. "You get on that side of the platform, and I'll get on this. Thump his head for him if he comes your way."

Garion nodded and edged around toward the far side of the platform.

Belgarath raised his voice again to the crowd. "You fall upon your knees before the reflection of the Demon Lord," he roared at them. "What will you do when I bring before you the King of Hell?" He bent and quickly traced the circle and pentagram about his feet. The tattooed priest edged further away from him.

"Stay, Grolim," Belgarath said with a cruel laugh. "The King of Hell is always hungry, and I think he might like to devour you when he arrives." He made a hooking gesture with one hand, and the Grolim began to struggle as if he had been seized by a powerful, invisible hand.

Then Belgarath began to intone an incantation quite different from the one the Grolim had spoken, and his words reverberated from the vault of heaven as he subtly amplified them into enormity. Seething sheets of varicolored flame shot through the air from horizon to horizon.

"Behold the Gates of Hell!" he roared, pointing.

Far out on the lake, two vast columns seemed to appear; between them were great billowing clouds of smoke and flame. From behind that burning gate came the sound of a multitude of hideous voices shrieking some awful hymn of praise.

"And now I call upon the King of Hell to reveal himself!" the old man shouted, raising his crooked staff. The surging force of his will was vast, and the great sheets of flame flickering in the sky actually seemed to blot out the sun and to replace its light with a dreadful light of its own.

From beyond the gate of fire came a huge whistling sound that descended into a roar. The flames parted, and the shape of a mighty tornado swept between the two pillars. Faster and faster the tornado whirled, turning from inky black to pale, frozen white. Ponderously, that towering white cloud advanced across the lake, congealing as it came. At first it appeared to be some vast snow wraith with hollow eyes and gaping mouth. It was quite literally hundreds of feet tall, and its breath swept across the now-terrified crowd before the altar like a blizzard.

"Ye have tasted ice," Belgarath told them. "Now taste fire! Your worship of the false Demon Lord hath offended the King of Hell, and now will ye roast in perpetual flames!" He made another sweeping gesture with his staff, and a deep red glow appeared in the center of the seething white shape that even now approached the shore of the lake. The sooty red glow grew more and more rapidly, expanding until it filled the encasing white entirely. Then the wraithlike figure of flame and swirling ice raised its hundred-foot-long arms and roared with a deafening sound. The ice seemed to shatter, and the wraith stood as a creature of fire. Flames shot from its mouth and nostrils, and steam rose from the surface of the lake as it moved across the last few yards of water before reaching the shore.

It reached down one enormous hand, placing it atop the altar, palm turned up. Belgarath calmly stepped up onto that burning hand, and the illusion raised him high into the air.

"Infidels!" he roared at them in an enormous voice. "Prepare ye all to suffer the wrath of the King of Hell for your foul apostasy!"

There was a dreadful moan from the Karands, followed by terrified screams as the fire-wraith reached out toward the crowd with its other huge, burning hand. Then, as one man, they turned and fled, shrieking in terror.

Somehow, perhaps because Belgarath was concentrating so much of his attention on the vast form he had created and was struggling to maintain, the Grolim broke free and jumped down off the platform.

Garion, however, was waiting for him. He reached out and stopped the fleeing man with one hand placed flat against his chest, even as he swept the other back and then around in a wide swing that ended with a jolting impact against the side of the tattooed man's head.

The Grolim collapsed in a heap. For some reason, Garion found that very satisfying.

CHAPTER TWENTY-TWO

"Which boat did you want to steal?" Silk asked as Garion dropped the unconscious Grolim on the floating dock that stuck out into the lake.

"Why ask me?" Garion replied, feeling just a bit uncomfortable with Silk's choice of words.

"Because you and Durnik are the ones who are going to have to sail it. I don't know the first thing about getting a boat to move through the water without tipping over."

"Capsizing," Garion corrected absently, looking at the various craft moored to the dock.

"What?"

"The word is 'capsize,' Silk. You tip over a wagon. You capsize a boat."

"It means the same thing, doesn't it?"

"Approximately, yes."

"Why make an issue of it, then? How about this one?" The little man pointed at a broad-beamed vessel with a pair of eyes painted on the bow.

"Not enough freeboard," Garion told him. "The horses are heavy, so any boat we take is going to settle quite a bit."

Silk shrugged. "You're the expert. You're starting to sound as professional as Barak or Greldik." He grinned suddenly. "You know, Garion, I've never stolen anything as big as a boat before. It's really very challenging."

"I wish you'd stop using the word 'steal.' Couldn't we just say that we're borrowing a boat?"

"Did you plan to sail it back and return it when we're finished with it?"

"No. Not really."

"Then the proper word is 'steal.' You're the expert on ships and sailing; I'm the expert on theft."

They walked farther out on the dock.

"Let's go on board this one and have a look around," Garion said, pointing at an ungainly-looking scow painted an unwholesome green color.

"It looks like a washtub."

"I'm not planning to win any races with it." Garion leaped aboard the scow. "It's big enough for the horses and the sides are high enough to keep the weight from swamping it." He inspected the spars and rigging. "A little crude," he noted, "but Durnik and I should be able to manage."

"Check the bottom for leaks," Silk suggested. "Nobody would paint a boat that color if it didn't leak."

Garion went below and checked the hold and the bilges. When he came back up on deck, he had already made up his mind. "I think we'll borrow this one," he said, jumping back to the pier.

"The term is still 'steal,' Garion."

Garion sighed. "All right, steal—if it makes you happy."

"Just trying to be precise, that's all."

"Let's go get that Grolim and drag him up here," Garion suggested. "We'll throw him in the boat and tie him up. I don't *think* he'll wake up for a while, but there's no point in taking chances."

"How hard did you hit him?"

"Quite hard, actually. For some reason he irritated me." They started back to where the Grolim lay.

"You're getting to be more like Belgarath every day," Silk told him. "You do more damage out of simple irritation than most men can do in a towering rage."

Garion shrugged and rolled the tattooed Grolim over with his foot. He took hold of one of the unconscious man's ankles. "Get his other leg," he said.

The two of them walked back toward the scow with the Grolim dragging limply along behind them, his shaved head bouncing up and down on the logs of the dock. When they reached the scow, Garion took the man's arms while Silk took his ankles. They swung him back and forth a few times, then lobbed him across the rail like a sack of grain. Garion jumped across again and bound him hand and foot.

"Here comes Belgarath with the others," Silk said from the dock.

"Good. Here—catch the other end of this gangplank." Garion swung the ungainly thing around and pushed it out toward the waiting little Drasnian. Silk caught hold of it, pulled it out farther, and set the end down on the dock.

"Did you find anything?" he asked the others as they approached.

"We did quite well, actually," Durnik replied. "One of those buildings is a storehouse. It was crammed to the rafters with food."

"Good. I wasn't looking forward to making the rest of this trip on short rations."

Belgarath was looking at the scow. "It isn't much of a boat, Garion," he objected. "If you were going to steal one, why didn't you steal something a little fancier?"

"You see?" Silk said to Garion. "I told you that it was the right word."

"I'm not stealing it for its looks, Grandfather," Garion said. "I don't plan to keep it. It's big enough to hold the horses, and the sails are simple enough so that Durnik and I can manage them. If you don't like it, go steal one of your own."

"Grumpy today, aren't we?" the old man said mildly. "What did you do with my Grolim?"

"He's lying up here in the scuppers."

"Is he awake yet?"

"Not for some time, I don't think. I hit him fairly hard. Are you coming on board, or would you rather go steal a different boat?"

"Be polite, dear," Polgara chided.

"No, Garion," Belgarath said. "If you've got your heart set on this one, then we'll take this one."

It took a while to get the horses aboard, and then they all fell to the task of raising the boat's square-rigged sails. When they were raised and set to Garion's satisfaction, he took hold of the tiller. "All right," he said. "Cast off the lines."

"You sound like a real sailor, dear," Ce'Nedra said in admiration.

"I'm glad you approve." He raised his voice slightly. "Toth, would you take that boat hook and push us out from the pier, please? I don't want to have to crash through all these other boats to get to open water."

The giant nodded, picked up the long boat hook, and shoved against the dock with it. The bow swung slowly out from the dock with the sails flapping in the fitful breeze.

"Isn't the word 'ship,' Garion?" Ce'Nedra asked.

"What?"

"You called them boats. Aren't they called ships?"

He gave her a long, steady look.

"I was only asking," she said defensively.

"Don't. Please."

"What did you hit this man with, Garion?" Belgarath asked peevishly. He was kneeling beside the Grolim.

"My fist," Garion replied.

"Next time, use an axe or a club. You almost killed him."

"Would anyone else like to register any complaints?" Garion asked in a loud voice. "Let's pile them all up in a heap right now."

They all stared at him, looking a bit shocked.

He gave up. "Just forget that I said it." He squinted up at the sails, trying to swing the bow to the exact angle which would allow the sails to catch the offshore breeze. Then, quite suddenly, they bellied out and boomed, and the scow began to pick up speed, plowing out past the end of the pier and into open water.

"Pol," Belgarath said. "Why don't you come over here and see what you can do with this man? I can't get a twitch out of him, and I want to question him."

"All right, father." She went to the Grolim, knelt beside him, and put her hands on his temples. She concentrated for a moment, and Garion felt the surge of her will.

The Grolim groaned.

"Sadi," she said thoughtfully, "Do you have any nephara in that case of yours?"

The eunuch nodded. "I was just going to suggest it myself, Lady Polgara." He knelt and opened his red case.

Belgarath looked at his daughter quizzically.

"It's a drug, father," she explained. "It induces truthfulness."

"Why not do it the regular way?" he asked.

"The man's a Grolim. His mind is likely to be very strong. I could probably overcome him, but it would take time—and it would be very tiring. Nephara works just as well and it doesn't take any effort."

He shrugged. "Suit yourself, Pol."

Sadi had taken a vial of a thick green liquid from his case. He unstoppered it and then took hold of the Grolim's nose, holding it until the half-conscious man was forced to open his mouth in order to breathe. Then the eunuch delicately tilted three drops of the green syrup onto the man's tongue. "I'd suggest giving him a few moments before you wake him, Lady Polgara," he said, squinting clinically at the Grolim's face. "Give the drug time to take effect first." He restoppered the vial and put it back in his case.

"Will the drug hurt him in any way?" Durnik asked.

Sadi shook his head. "It simply relaxes the will," he replied. "He'll be rational and coherent, but very tractable."

"He *also* won't be able to focus his mind sufficiently to use any talent he may have," Polgara added. "We won't have to worry about his translocating himself away from us the moment he wakes up." She critically watched the Grolim's face, occasionally lifting one of his eyelids to note the drug's progress. "I think it's taken hold now," she said finally. She untied the prisoner's hands and feet. Then she put her hands on the man's temples and gently brought him back to consciousness. "How are you feeling?" she asked him.

"My head hurts," the Grolim said plaintively.

"That will pass," she assured him. She rose and looked at Belgarath. "Speak to him calmly, father," she said, "and start out with simple questions. With nephara it's best to lead them rather gently up to the important things."

Belgarath nodded. He picked up a wooden pail, inverted it, put it on the deck beside the Grolim, and sat on it. "Good morning, friend," he said pleasantly, "or is it afternoon?" He squinted up at the sky.

"You're not really a Karand, are you?" the Grolim asked. His voice sounded dreamy. "I thought you were one of their wizards, but now that I look at you more closely, I can see that you're not."

"You're very astute, friend," Belgarath congratulated him. "What's your name?"

"Arshag," the Grolim replied.

"And where are you from?"

"I am of the Temple at Calida."

"I thought you might be. Do you happen to know a Chandim named Harakan, by any chance?"

"He now prefers to be known as Lord Mengha."

"Ah, yes, I'd heard about that. That illusion of Nahaz you raised this morning was very accurate. You must have seen him several times in order to get everything right."

"I have frequently been in close contact with Nahaz," the Grolim admitted. "It was I who delivered him to Lord Mengha."

"Why don't you tell me about that? I'm sure it's a fascinating story and I'd really like to hear it. Take your time, Arshag. Tell me the whole story, and don't leave out any of the details."

The Grolim smiled almost happily. "I've been wanting to tell someone the story for a long time now," he said. "Do you really want to hear it?"

"I'm absolutely dying to hear it," Belgarath assured him.

The Grolim smiled again. "Well," he began, "it all started quite a number of years ago—not too long after the death of Torak. I was serving in the Temple at Calida. Though we were all in deepest despair, we tried to keep the faith alive. Then one day Harakan came to our temple and sought me out privately. I had journeyed at times to Mal Yaska on Church business and I knew Harakan to be of high rank among the Chandim and very close to the Holy Disciple Urvon. When we were alone, he told me that Urvon had consulted the Oracles and Prophecies concerning the direction the Church must take in her blackest hour. The Disciple had discovered that a new God was destined to rise over Angarak, and that he will hold Cthrag Sardius in his right hand and Cthrag Yaska in his left. And he will be the almighty Child of Dark, and the Lord of Demons shall do his bidding."

"That's a direct quotation, I take it?"

Arshag nodded. "From the eighth antistrophe of the Ashabine Oracles," he confirmed.

"It's a little obscure, but prophecies usually are. Go on."

Arshag shifted his position and continued. "The Disciple Urvon interpreted the passage to mean that our new God would have the aid of the demons in quelling his enemies."

"Did Harakan identify these enemies for you?"

Arshag nodded again. "He mentioned Zandramas—of whom I have heard—and one named Agachak, whose name is strange to me. He also warned me that the Child of Light would probably attempt to interfere."

"That's a reasonable assumption," Silk murmured to Garion.

"Harakan, who is the Disciple's closest advisor, had selected *me* to perform a great task," Arshag continued proudly. "He charged me to seek out the wizards of Karanda and to study their arts so that I might summon up the Demon Lord Nahaz and beseech him to aid the Disciple Urvon in his struggles with his enemies."

"Did he tell you how dangerous that task would be?" Belgarath asked him.

"I understood the perils," Arshag said, "but I accepted them willingly, for my rewards were to be great."

"I'm sure," Belgarath murmured. "Why didn't Harakan do it himself?"

"The Disciple Urvon had placed another task upon Harakan—somewhere in the West, I understand—having to do with a child."

Belgarath nodded blandly. "I think I've heard about it."

"Anyway," Arshag went on, "I journeyed into the forest of the north, seeking out the wizards who still practiced their rites in places hidden from the eyes of the Church. In time, I found such a one." His lip curled in a sneer. "He was an ignorant savage of small skill, at best only able to raise an imp or two, but he agreed to accept me as his pupil—and slave. It was he who saw fit to put these marks upon my body." He glanced with distaste at his tattoos. "He kept me in a kennel and made me serve him and listen to his ravings. I learned what little he could teach me and then I strangled him and went in search of a more powerful teacher."

"Note how deep the gratitude of Grolims goes," Silk observed quietly to Garion, who was concentrating half on the story and half on the business of steering the scow.

"The years that followed were difficult," Arshag continued. "I went from teacher to teacher, suffering enslavement and abuse." A bleak smile crossed his face. "Occasionally, they used to sell me to other wizards—as one might sell a cow or a pig. After I learned the arts, I retraced my steps and repaid each one for his impertinences. At length, in a place near the barrens of the north, I was able to apprentice myself to an ancient man reputed to be the most powerful wizard in Karanda. He was very old, and his eyes were failing, so he took me for a young Karand seeking wisdom. He accepted me as his appentice, and my training began in earnest. The raising of minor demons is no great chore, but summoning a Demon Lord is much more difficult and much more perilous. The wizard claimed to have done it twice in his life, but he may have been lying. He did, however, show me how to raise the *image* of the Demon Lord Nahaz and also how to communicate with him. No spell or incantation is powerful enough to *compel* a Demon Lord to come when he is called. He will come only if he *consents* to come—and usually for reasons of his own.

"Once I had learned all that the old wizard could teach me, I killed him and journeyed south toward Calida again." He sighed a bit regretfully. "The old man was a kindly master, and I was sorry that I had to kill him." Then he shrugged. "But he was old," he added, "and I sent him off with a single knife stroke to the heart."

"Steady, Durnik," Silk said, putting his hand on the angry smith's arm.

"At Calida, I found the Temple in total disarray," Arshag went on. "My brothers had finally succumbed to absolute despair, and the Temple had become a vile sink of corruption and degeneracy. I suppressed my outrage, however, and kept to myself. I dispatched word to Mal Yaska, advising Harakan that I had been successful in my mission and that I awaited his commands in the Temple at Calida. In time, I received a reply from one of the Chandim, who told me that Harakan had not yet returned from the West." He paused. "Do you suppose that I could have a drink of water?" he asked. "I have a very foul taste in my mouth for some reason."

Sadi went to the water cask in the stern and dipped out a tin cup of water. "No drug is *completely* perfect," he murmured defensively to Garion in passing.

Arshag gratefully took the cup from Sadi and drank.

"Go on with your story," Belgarath told him when he had finished.

Arshag nodded. "It was a bit less than a year ago that Harakan returned from the West," he said. "He came up to Calida, and he and I met in secret. I told him what I had accomplished and advised him of the limitations involved in any attempts to raise a Demon Lord. Then we went to a secluded place, and I instructed him in the incantations and spells which would raise an image of Nahaz and permit us to speak through the gate that lies between the worlds and communicate directly with Nahaz. Once I had established contact with the Demon Lord, Harakan began to speak with him. He mentioned Cthrag Sardius, but Nahaz already knew of it.

And then Harakan told Nahaz that during the long years that Torak slept, the Disciple Urvon had become more and more obsessed with wealth and power and had at last convinced himself that he was in fact a demigod, and but one step removed from divinity. Harakan proposed an alliance between himself and Nahaz. He suggested that the Demon Lord nudge Urvon over the edge into madness and then aid him in defeating all the others who were seeking the hiding place of Cthrag Sardius. Unopposed, Urvon would easily gain the stone."

"I gather that you chose to go along with them—instead of warning Urvon what was afoot? What did *you* get out of the arrangement?"

"They let me live." Arshag shrugged. "I think Harakan wanted to kill me—just to be safe—but Nahaz told him that I could still be useful. He promised me kingdoms of my own to rule—and demon children to do my bidding. Harakan was won over by the Demon Lord and he treated me courteously."

"I don't exactly see that there's much advantage to Nahaz in giving the Sardion to Urvon," Belgarath confessed.

"Nahaz wants Cthrag Sardius for himself," Arshag told him. "If Urvon has been driven mad, Nahaz will simply take Cthrag Sardius from him and replace it with a piece of worthless rock. Then the Demon Lord and Harakan will put Urvon in a house somewhere—Ashaba perhaps, or some other isolated castle—and they'll surround him with imps and lesser demons to blind him with illusions. There he will play at being God in blissful insanity while Nahaz and Harakan rule the world between them."

"Until the *real* new God of Angarak arises," Polgara added.

"There will *be* no new God of Angarak," Arshag disagreed. "Once Nahaz puts his hand on Cthrag Sardius—the Sardion—*both* Prophecies will cease to exist. The Child of Light and the Child of Dark will vanish forever. The Elder Gods will be banished, and Nahaz will be Lord of the Universe and Master of the destinies of all mankind."

"And what does Harakan get out of this?" Belgarath asked.

"Dominion of the Church—and the secular throne of all the world."

"I hope he got that in writing," Belgarath said dryly. "Demons are notorious for not keeping their promises. Then what happened?"

"A messenger arrived at Calida with instructions for Harakan from Urvon. The Disciple told him that there must be a disruption in Karanda so violent that Kal Zakath would have no choice but to return from Cthol Murgos. Once the Emperor was back in Mallorea, it would be a simple matter to have him killed, and once he is dead, Urvon believes that he can manipulate the succession to place a tractable man on the throne—one he can take with him when he goes to the place where the Sardion lies hidden. Apparently, this is one of the conditions which must be met before the new God arises."

Belgarath nodded. "A great many things are starting to fall into place," he said. "What happened then?"

"Harakan and I journeyed again in secret to that secluded place, and I once again opened the gate and brought forth the image of Nahaz. Harakan and the Demon Lord spoke together for a time, and suddenly the image was made flesh, and Nahaz himself stood before us.

"Harakan instructed me that I should henceforth call him by the name Mengha, since the name Harakan is widely known in Mallorea, and then we went again to Calida, and Nahaz went with us. The Demon Lord summoned his hordes, and Calida fell. Nahaz demanded a certain repayment for his aid, and Lord Mengha instructed me to provide it. It was then that I discovered why Nahaz had let me live. We spoke together, and he told me what he wanted. I did not care for the notion, but the people involved were only Karands, so—" He shrugged. "The Karands regard Nahaz as their God, and so it was not difficult for me to persuade young Karandese women that receiving the attentions of the Demon Lord would be a supreme honor. They went to him willingly, each one of them hoping in her heart to bear his offspring—not knowing, of course, that such a birth would rip them apart like fresh-gutted pigs." He smirked contemptuously. "The rest I think you know."

"Oh, yes, we do indeed." Belgarath's voice was like a nail scraping across a flat stone. "When did they leave? Harakan and Nahaz, I mean? We know that they're no longer in this part of Karanda."

"It was about a month ago. We were preparing to lay siege to Torpakan on the border of Delchin, and I awoke one morning to discover that Lord Mengha and the Demon Nahaz were gone and that none of their familiar demons were any longer with the army. Everyone looked to me, but none of my spells or incantations could raise even the least of demons. The army grew enraged, and I barely escaped with my life. I journeyed north again toward Calida, but found things there in total chaos. Without the demons to hold them in line, the Karands had quickly become unmanageable. I found that I *could*, however, still call up the *image* of Nahaz. It seemed likely to me that with Mengha and Nahaz gone, I could sway Karandese loyalty to me, if I used the image cleverly enough, and thus come to rule all of Karanda myself. I was attempting a beginning of that plan this morning when you interrupted."

"I see," Belgarath said bleakly.

"How long have you been in this vicinity?" Polgara asked the captive suddenly.

"Several weeks," the Grolim replied.

"Good," she said. "Some few weeks ago, a woman came from the west carrying a child."

"I pay little attention to women."

"This one might have been a bit different. We know that she came to that village back on the lakeshore and that she would have hired a boat. Did any word of that reach you?"

"There are few travelers in Karanda right now," he told her. "There's too much turmoil and upheaval. There's only one boat that left that village in the past month. I'll tell you this, though. If the woman you seek was a friend of yours, and if she *was* on board that boat, prepare to mourn her."

"Oh?"

"The boat sank in a sudden storm just off the city of Karand on the east side of the lake in Ganesia."

"The nice thing about Zandramas is her predictability," Silk murmured to Garion. "I don't think we're going to have much trouble picking up her trail again, do you?"

Arshag's eyelids were drooping now, and he seemed barely able to hold his head erect.

"If you have any more questions for him, Ancient One, you should ask them quickly," Sadi advised. "The drug is starting to wear off, and he's very close to sleep again."

"I think I have all the answers I need," the old man replied.

"And I have what I need as well," Polgara added grimly.

Because of the size of the lake, there was no possibility of reaching the eastern shore before nightfall, and so they lowered the sails and set a sea anchor to minimize the nighttime drift of their scow. They set sail again at first light and shortly after noon saw a low, dark smudge along the eastern horizon.

"That would be the east coast of the lake," Silk said to Garion. "I'll go up to the bow and see if I can pick out some landmarks. I don't think we'll want to run right up to the wharves of Karand, do you?"

"No. Not really."

"I'll see if I can find us a quiet cove someplace, and then we can have a look around without attracting attention."

They beached the scow in a quiet bay surrounded by high sand dunes and scrubby brush about midafternoon.

"What do you think, Grandfather?" Garion asked after they had unloaded the horses.

"About what?"

"The boat. What should we do with it?"

"Set it adrift. Let's not announce that we came ashore here."

"I suppose you're right." Garion sighed a bit regretfully. "It wasn't a bad boat, though, was it?"

"It didn't tip over."

"Capsize," Garion corrected.

Polgara came over to where they were standing. "Do you have any further need for Arshag?" she asked the old man.

"No, and I've been trying to decide what to do with him."

"I'll take care of it, father," she said. She turned and went back to where Arshag still lay, once more bound and half asleep on the beach. She stood over him for a moment, then raised one hand. The Grolim flinched wildly even as Garion felt the sudden powerful surge of her will.

"Listen carefully, Arshag," she said. "You provided the Demon Lord with women so that he could unloose an abomination upon the world. That act must not go unrewarded. This, then, is your reward. You are now invincible. No one can kill you—no man, no demon—not even you yourself. *But,* no one will ever again believe a single word that you say. You will be faced with constant ridicule and derision all the days of your life and you will be driven out wherever you go, to wander the world as a rootless vagabond. Thus are you repaid for aiding Mengha and helping him to unleash Nahaz and for sacrificing foolish women to the Demon Lord's unspeakable lust." She turned to Durnik. "Untie him," she commanded.

When his arms and legs were free, Arshag stumbled to his feet, his tattooed face ashen. "Who are you, woman?" he demanded in a shaking voice, "and what power do you have to pronounce so terrible a curse?"

"I am Polgara," she replied. "You may have heard of me. Now go!" She pointed up the beach with an imperious finger.

As if suddenly seized by an irresistible compulsion, Arshag turned, his face filled with horror. He stumbled up one of the sandy dunes and disappeared on the far side.

"Do you think it was wise to reveal your identity, my lady?" Sadi asked dubiously.

"There's no danger, Sadi." She smiled. "He can shout my name from every rooftop, but no one will believe him."

"How long will he live?" Ce'Nedra's voice was very small.

"Indefinitely, I'd imagine. Long enough, certainly, to give him time to appreciate fully the enormity of what it was that he did."

Ce'Nedra stared at her. "Lady Polgara!" she said in a sick voice. "How could you do it? It's horrible."

"Yes," Polgara replied, "it is—but so was what happened back at that temple we burned."

CHAPTER TWENTY-THREE

The street, if it could be called that, was narrow and crooked. An attempt had been made at some time in the past to surface it with logs, but they had long since rotted and been trodden into the mud. Decaying garbage lay in heaps against the walls of crudely constructed log houses, and herds of scrawny pigs rooted dispiritedly through those heaps in search of food.

As Silk and Garion, once again wearing their Karandese vests and caps and their cross-tied sackcloth leggings, approached the docks jutting out into the lake, they were nearly overcome by the overpowering odor of long-dead fish.

"Fragrant sort of place, isn't it?" Silk noted, holding a handkerchief to his face.

"How can they stand it?" Garion asked, trying to keep from gagging.

"Their sense of smell has probably atrophied over the centuries," Silk replied. "The city of Karand is the ancestral home of all the Karands in all the seven kingdoms. It's been here for eons, so the debris—and the smell—has had a long time to build up."

A huge sow, trailed by a litter of squealing piglets, waddled out into the very center of the street and flopped over on her side with a loud grunt. The piglets immediately attacked, pushing and scrambling to nurse.

"Any hints at all?" Silk asked.

Garion shook his head. The sword strapped across his back had neither twitched nor tugged since the two of them had entered the city early that morning on foot by way of the north gate. "Zandramas might not have even entered the city at all," he said. "She's avoided populated places before, you know."

"That's true, I suppose," Silk admitted, "but I don't think we should go any farther until we locate the place where she landed. She could have gone in any direction once she got to this side of the lake—Darshiva, Zamad, Voresebo—even down into Delchin and then on down the Magan into Rengel or Peldane."

"I know," Garion said, "but all this delay is very frustrating. We're getting closer to her. I can feel it, and every minute we waste gives her that much more time to escape again with Geran."

"It can't be helped." Silk shrugged. "About all we can do here is follow the inside of the wall and walk along the waterfront. If she came through the city at all, we're certain to cross her path."

They turned a corner and looked down another muddy street toward the lakeshore where fishnets hung over long poles. They slogged through the mud until they reached the street that ran along the shore line where floating docks reached out into the lake and then followed it along the waterfront.

There was a certain amount of activity here. A number of sailors dressed in faded blue tunics were hauling a large boat half-full of water up onto the shore with a great deal of shouting and contradictory orders. Here and there on the docks, groups of fishermen in rusty brown sat mending nets, and farther on along the street several loiterers in fur vests and leggings sat on the log stoop in front of a sour-smelling tavern, drinking from cheap tin cups. A blowzy young woman with frizzy orange hair and a pockmarked face leaned out of a second-story window, calling to passersby in a voice she tried to make seductive, but which Garion found to be merely coarse.

"Busy place," Silk murmured.

Garion grunted, and they moved on along the littered street.

Coming from the other direction, they saw a group of armed men. Though they all wore helmets of one kind or another, the rest of their clothing was of mismatched colors and could by no stretch of the imagination be called uniforms. Their self-important swagger, however, clearly indicated that they were either soldiers or some kind of police.

"You two! Halt!" one of them barked as they came abreast of Garion and Silk.

"Is there some problem, sir?" Silk asked ingratiatingly.

"I haven't seen you here before," the man said, his hand on his sword hilt. He was a tall fellow with lank red hair poking out from under his helmet. "Identify yourselves."

"My name is Saldas," Silk lied. "This is Kvasta." He pointed at Garion. "We're strangers here in Karand."

"What's your business here—and where do you come from?"

"We're from Dorikan in Jenno," Silk told him, "and we're here looking for my older brother. He sailed out from the village of Dashun on the other side of the lake a while back and hasn't returned."

The redheaded man looked suspicious.

"We talked with a fellow near the north gate," Silk continued, "and he told us that there was a boat that sank in a storm just off the docks here." His face took on a melancholy expression. "The time would have been just about right, I think, and the description he gave us of the boat matched the one my brother was sailing. Have you by any chance heard about it, sir?" The little man sounded very sincere.

Some of the suspicion faded from the red-haired man's face. "It seems to me that I heard some mention of it," he conceded.

"The fellow we talked with said that he thought there might have been some survivors," Silk added, "one that he knew of, anyway. He said that a woman in a dark cloak and carrying a baby managed to get away in a small boat. Do *you* by chance happen to know anything about that?"

The Karand's face hardened. "Oh, yes," he said. "We know about *her*, all right."

"Could you by any chance tell me where she went?" Silk asked him. "I'd really like to talk with her and find out if she knows anything about my brother." He leaned toward the other man confidentially. "To be perfectly honest with you, good sir, I can't stand my brother. We've hated each other since we were children, but I promised my old father that I'd find out what happened to him." Then he winked outrageously. "There's an inheritance involved, you understand. If I can take definite word back to father that my brother's dead, I stand to come into a nice piece of property."

The red-haired man grinned. "I can understand your situation, Saldas." he said. "I had a dispute with my *own* brothers about our patrimony." His eyes narrowed. "You say you're from Dorikan?" he asked.

"Yes. On the banks of the northern River Magan. Do you know our city?"

"Does Dorikan follow the teachings of Lord Mengha?"

"The Liberator? Of course. Doesn't all of Karanda?"

"Have you seen any of the Dark Lords in the last month or so?"

"The minions of the Lord Nahaz? No, I can't say that I have—but then Kvasta and I haven't attended any worship services for some time. I'm sure that the wizards are still raising them, though."

"I wouldn't be all that sure, Saldas. We haven't seen one here in Karand for over five weeks. Our wizards have tried to summon them, but they refuse to come. Even the Grolims who now worship Lord Nahaz haven't been successful and they're all powerful magicians, you know."

"Truly," Silk agreed.

"Have you heard anything at all about Lord Mengha's whereabouts?"

Silk shrugged. "The last I heard, he was in Katakor someplace. In Dorikan we're just waiting for his return so that we can sweep the Angaraks out of all Karanda."

The answer seemed to satisfy the tall fellow. "All right, Saldas," he said. "I'd say that you've got a legitimate reason to be in Karand after all. I don't think you're going to have much luck in finding the woman you want to talk to, though. From what I've heard, she *was* on your brother's boat and she *did* get away before the storm hit. She had a small boat, and she landed to the south of the city. She came to the south gate with her brat in her arms and went straight to the Temple. She talked with the Grolims inside for about an hour. When she left, they were all following her."

"Which way did they go?" Silk asked him.

"Out the east gate."

"How long ago was it?"

"Late last week. I'll tell you something, Saldas. Lord Mengha had better stop whatever he's doing in Katakor and come back to central Karanda where he belongs. The whole movement is starting to falter. The Dark Lords have deserted us, and the Grolims are trailing after this woman with the baby. All we have left are the wizards, and they're mostly mad, anyway."

"They always have been, haven't they?" Silk grinned. "Tampering with the supernatural tends to unsettle a man's brains, I've noticed."

"You seem like a sensible man, Saldas," the redhead said, clapping him on the shoulder. "I'd like to stay and talk with you further, but my men and I have to finish our patrol. I hope you find your brother." He winked slyly. "Or *don't* find him, I should say."

Silk grinned back. "I thank you for your wishes about my brother's growing ill health," he replied.

The soldiers moved off along the street.

"You tell better stories than Belgarath does," Garion said to his little friend.

"It's a gift. That was a very profitable encounter, wasn't it? Now I understand why the Orb hasn't picked up the trail yet. We came into the city by way of the north gate, and Zandramas came up from the south. If we go straight to the Temple, the Orb's likely to jerk you off your feet."

Garion nodded. "The important thing is that we're only a few days behind her." He paused, frowning. "Why is she gathering Grolims, though?"

"Who knows? Reinforcements maybe. She knows that we're right behind her. Or, maybe she thinks she's going to need Grolims who have training in Karandese magic when she gets home to Darshiva. If Nahaz has sent his demons down there, she's going to need all the help she can get. We'll let Belgarath sort it out. Let's go to the Temple and see if we can pick up the trail."

As they approached the Temple in the center of the city, the Orb began to pull at Garion again, and he felt a surge of exultation. "I've got it," he said to Silk.

"Good." The little man looked up at the Temple. "I see that they've made some modifications," he observed.

The polished steel mask of the face of Torak which normally occupied the place directly over the nail-studded door had been removed, Garion saw, and in its place was a red-painted skull with a pair of horns screwed down into its brow.

"I don't know that the skull is all that big an improvement," Silk said, "but then, it's no great change for the worse either. I was getting a little tired of that mask staring at me every time I turned around."

"Let's follow the trail," Garion suggested, "and make certain that Zandramas left the city before we go get the others."

"Right," Silk agreed.

The trail led from the door of the Temple through the littered streets to the east gate of the city. Garion and Silk followed it out of Karand and perhaps a half mile along the highway leading eastward across the plains of Ganesia.

"Is she veering at all?" Silk asked.

"Not yet. She's following the road."

"Good. Let's go get the others—and our horses. We won't make very good time on foot."

They moved away from the road, walking through knee-high grass.

"Looks like good, fertile soil here," Garion noted. "Have you and Yarblek ever considered buying farmland? It might be a good investment."

"No, Garion." Silk laughed. "There's a major drawback to owning land. If you have to leave a place in a hurry, there's no way that you can pick it up and carry it along with you."

"That's true, I guess."

The others waited in a grove of large old willows a mile or so north of the city, and their faces were expectant as Garion and Silk ducked in under the branches.

"Did you find it?" Belgarath asked.

Garion nodded. "She went east," he replied.

"And apparently she took all the Grolims from the Temple along with her," Silk added.

Belgarath looked puzzled. "Why would she do that?"

"I haven't got a clue. I suppose we could ask her when we catch up with her."

"Could you get any idea of how far ahead of us she is?" Ce'Nedra asked.

"Just a few days," Garion said. "With any luck we'll catch her before she gets across the Mountains of Zamad."

"Not if we don't get started," Belgarath said.

They rode on back across the wide, open field to the highway leading across the plains toward the upthrusting peaks lying to the east. The Orb picked up the trail again, and they followed it at a canter.

"What kind of a city was it?" Velvet asked Silk as they rode along.

"Nice place to visit," he replied, "but you wouldn't want to live there. The pigs are clean enough, but the people are awfully dirty."

"Cleverly put, Kheldar."

"I've always had a way with words," he conceded modestly.

"Father," Polgara called to the old man, "a large number of Grolims have passed this way."

He looked around and nodded. "Silk was right, then," he said. "For some reason she's subverting Mengha's people. Let's be alert for any possible ambushes."

They rode on for the rest of the day and camped that night some distance away from the road, starting out again at first light in the morning. About midday they saw a roadside village some distance ahead. Coming from that direction was a solitary man in a rickety cart being pulled by a bony white horse.

"Do you by any change have a flagon of ale, Lady Polgara?" Sadi asked as they slowed to a walk.

"Are you thirsty?"

"Oh, it's not for me. I detest ale personally. It's for that carter just ahead. I thought we might want some information." He looked over at Silk. "Are you feeling at all sociable today, Kheldar?"

"No more than usual. Why?"

"Take a drink or two of this," the eunuch said, offering the little man the flagon

Polgara had taken from one of the packs. "Not too much, mind. I only want you to *smell* drunk."

"Why not?" Silk shrugged, taking a long drink.

"That should do it," Sadi approved. "Now give it back."

"I thought you didn't want any."

"I don't. I'm just going to add a bit of flavoring." He opened his red case. "Don't drink any more from this flagon," he warned Silk as he tapped four drops of a gleaming red liquid into the mouth of the flagon. "If you do, we'll all have to listen to you talk for days on end." He handed the flagon back to the little man. "Why don't you go offer that poor fellow up there a drink," he suggested. "He looks like he could use one."

"You didn't poison it, did you?"

"Of course not. It's very hard to get information out of somebody who's squirming on the ground clutching at his belly. One or two good drinks from that flagon, though, and the carter will be seized by an uncontrollable urge to talk— about anything at all and to anybody who asks him a question in a friendly fashion. Go be friendly to the poor man, Kheldar. He looks dreadfully lonesome."

Silk grinned, then turned and trotted his horse toward the oncoming cart, swaying in his saddle and singing loudly and very much off-key.

"He's very good," Velvet murmured to Ce'Nedra, "but he always overacts his part. When we get back to Boktor, I think I'll send him to a good drama coach."

Ce'Nedra laughed.

By the time they reached the cart, the seedy-looking man in a rust-red smock had pulled his vehicle off to the side of the road, and he and Silk had joined in song—a rather bawdy one.

"Ah, there you are," Silk said, squinting owlishly at Sadi. "I wondered how long it was going to take you to catch up. Here—" He thrust the flagon at the eunuch. "Have a drink."

Sadi feigned taking a long drink from the flagon. Then he sighed lustily, wiped his mouth on his sleeve, and handed the flagon back.

Silk passed it to the carter. "Your turn, friend."

The carter took a drink and then grinned foolishly. "I haven't felt this good in weeks," he said.

"We're riding toward the east," Sadi told him.

"I saw that right off," the carter said. "That's unless you've taught your horses to run backward." He laughed uproariously at that, slapping his knee in glee.

"How droll," the eunuch murmured. "Do you come from that village just up ahead?"

"Lived there all my life," the carter replied, "and my father before me—and his father before him—and his father's father before that and—"

"Have you seen a dark-cloaked woman with a babe in her arms go past here within the last week?" Sadi interrupted him. "She probably would have been in the company of a fairly large party of Grolims."

The carter made the sign to ward off the evil eye at the mention of the word "Grolim." "Oh, yes. She came by all right," he said, "and she went into the local Temple here—if you can really call it a Temple. It's no bigger than my own house and it's only got three Grolims in it—two young ones and an old one. Anyway, this woman with the babe in her arms, she goes into the Temple, and we can hear her talking, and pretty soon she comes out with our three Grolims—only the old one was trying to talk the two young ones into staying, and then she says something to the young ones and they pull out their knives and start stabbing the old one, and he yells and falls down on the ground dead as mutton, and the woman takes our two young Grolims back out to the road, and they join in with the others and they all go off, leaving us only that old dead one lying on his face in the mud and—"

"How many Grolims would you say she had with her?" Sadi asked.

"Counting our two, I'd say maybe thirty or forty—or it could be as many as fifty. I've never been very good at quick guesses like that. I can tell the difference between three and four, but after that I get confused, and—"

"Could you give us any idea of exactly how long ago all that was?"

"Let's see." The carter squinted at the sky, counting on his fingers. "It couldn't have been yesterday, because yesterday I took that load of barrels over to Toad-face's farm. Do you know Toad-face? Ugliest man I ever saw, but his daughter's a real beauty. I could tell you stories about *her*, let me tell you."

"So it wasn't yesterday?"

"No. It definitely wasn't yesterday. I spent most of yesterday under a haystack with Toad-face's daughter. And I know it wasn't the day before, because I got drunk that day and I don't remember a thing that happened after midmorning." He took another drink from the flagon.

"How about the day before that?"

"It could have been," the carter said, "or the day before that."

"Or even before?"

The carter shook his head. "No, that was the day our pig farrowed, and I know that the woman came by after that. It had to have been the day before the day before yesterday or the day before that."

"Three or four days ago, then?"

"If that's the way it works out," the carter shrugged, drinking again.

"Thanks for the information, friend," Sadi said. He looked at Silk. "We should be moving on, I suppose," he said.

"Did you want your jar back?" the carter asked.

"Go ahead and keep it, friend," Silk said. "I think I've had enough anyway."

"Thanks for the ale—and the talk," the carter called after them as they rode away. Garion glanced back and saw that the fellow had climbed down from his cart and was engaging in an animated conversation with his horse.

"Three days!" Ce'Nedra exlaimed happily.

"Or, at the most, four," Sadi said.

"We're gaining on her!" Ce'Nedra said, suddenly leaning over and throwing her arms about the eunuch's neck.

"So it appears, your Majesty," Sadi agreed, looking slightly embarrassed.

They camped off the road again that night and started out again early the following morning. The sun was just coming up when the large, blue-banded hawk came spiraling in, flared, and shimmered into the form of Beldin at the instant its talons touched the road. "You've got company waiting for you just ahead," he told them, pointing at the first line of foothills of the Mountains of Zamad lying perhaps a mile in front of them.

"Oh?" Belgarath said, reining in his horse.

"About a dozen Grolims," Beldin said. They're hiding in the bushes on either side of the road."

Belgarath swore.

"Have you been doing things to annoy the Grolims?" the hunchback asked.

Belgarath shook his head. "Zandramas has been gathering them as she goes along. She's got quite a few of them with her now. She probably left that group behind to head off pursuit. She knows that we're right behind her."

"What are we going to do, Belgarath?" Ce'Nedra asked. "We're so *close*. We can't stop now."

The old man looked at his brother sorcerer. "Well?" he said.

Beldin scowled at him. "All right," he said. "I'll do it, but don't forget that you owe me, Belgarath."

"Write it down with all the other things. We'll settle up when this is all over."

"Don't think I won't."

"Did you find out where Nahaz took Urvon?"

"Would you believe they went back to Mal Yaska?" Beldin sounded disgusted.

"They'll come out eventually," Belgarath assured him. "Are you going to need any help with the Grolims? I could send Pol along if you like."

"Are you trying to be funny?"

"No. I was just asking. Don't make too much noise."

Beldin made a vulgar sound, changed again, and swooped away.

"Where's he going?" Silk asked.

"He's going to draw off the Grolims."

"Oh? How?"

"I didn't ask him," Belgarath shrugged. "We'll give him a little while and then we should be able to ride straight on through."

"He's very good, isn't he?"

"Beldin? Oh, yes, very, very good. There he goes now."

Silk looked around. "Where?"

"I didn't see him—I heard him. He's flying low a mile or so to the north of where the Grolims are hiding, and he's kicking up just enough noise to make it sound as if the whole group of us are trying to slip around them without being seen." He glanced at his daughter. "Pol, would you take a look and see if it's working?"

"All right, father." She concentrated, and Garion could feel her mind reaching out, probing. "They've taken the bait," she reported. "They all ran off after Beldin."

"That was accommodating of them, wasn't it? Let's move on."

They pushed their horses into a gallop and covered the distance to the first foothills of the Mountains of Zamad in a short period of time. They followed the road up a steep slope and through a shallow notch. Beyond that the terrain grew more rugged, and the dark green forest rose steeply up the flanks of the peaks.

Garion began to sense conflicting signals from the Orb as he rode. At first he had only felt its eagerness to follow the trail of Zandramas and Geran, but now he began to feel a sullen undertone, a sound of ageless, implacable hatred, and at his back where the sword was sheathed, he began to feel an increasing heat.

"Why is it burning red?" Ce'Nedra asked from behind him.

"What's burning red?"

"The Orb, I think. I can see it glowing right through the leather covering you have over it."

"Let's stop a while," Belgarath told them, reining in his horse.

"What is it, Grandfather?"

"I'm not sure. Take the sword out and slip off the sleeve. Let's see what's happening."

Garion drew the sword from its sheath. It seemed heavier than usual for some reason, and when he peeled off the soft leather covering, they were all able to see that instead of its usual azure blue, the Orb of Aldur was glowing a dark, sooty red.

"What is it, father?" Polgara asked.

"It feels the Sardion," Eriond said in a calm voice.

"Are we that close?" Garion demanded. "Is this the Place Which Is No More?"

"I don't think so, Belgarion," the young man replied. "It's something else."

"What is it, then?"

"I'm not sure, but the Orb is responding to the other stone in some way. They talk to each other in a fashion I can't understand."

They rode on, and some time later the blue-banded hawk came swirling in, blurred into Beldin's shape, and stood in front of them. The gnarled dwarf had a slightly self-satisfied look on his face.

"You look like a cat that just got into the cream," Belgarath said.

"Naturally. I just sent a dozen or so Grolims off in the general direction of the polar icecap. They'll have a wonderful time when the pan ice starts to break up and they get to float around up there for the rest of the summer."

"Are you going to scout on ahead?" Belgarath asked him.

"I suppose so," Beldin replied. He held out his arms, blurred into feathers, and drove himself into the air.

They rode more cautiously now, climbing deeper and deeper into the Mountains of Zamad. The surrounding country grew more broken. The reddish-hued peaks were jagged, and their lower flanks were covered with dark firs and pines. Rushing streams boiled over rocks and dropped in frothy waterfalls over steep cliffs. The road, which had been straight and flat on the plains of Ganesia, began to twist and turn as it crawled up the steep slopes.

It was nearly noon when Beldin returned again. "The main party of Grolims turned south," he reported. "There are about forty of them."

"Was Zandramas with them?" Garion asked quickly.

"No. I don't think so—at least I didn't pick up the sense of anyone unusual in the group."

"We haven't lost her, have we?" Ce'Nedra asked in alarm.

"No," Garion replied. "The Orb still has her trail." He glanced over his shoulder. The stone on the hilt of his sword was still burning a sullen red.

"About all we can do is follow her," Belgarath said. "It's Zandramas we're interested in, not a party of stray Grolims. Can you pinpoint exactly where we are?" he asked Beldin.

"Mallorea."

"Very funny."

"We've crossed into Zamad. This road goes on down into Voresebo, though. Where's my mule?"

"Back with the packhorses," Durnik told him.

As they moved on, Garion could feel Polgara probing on ahead with her mind.

"Are you getting anything, Pol?" Belgarath asked her.

"Nothing specific, father," she replied. "I can sense the fact that Zandramas is close, but she's shielding, so I can't pinpoint her."

They rode on, moving at a cautious walk now. Then, as the road passed through a narrow gap and descended on the far side, they saw a figure in a gleaming white robe standing in the road ahead. As they drew closer, Garion saw that it was Cyradis.

"Move with great care in this place," she cautioned, and there was a note of anger in her voice. "The Child of Dark seeks to circumvent the ordered course of events and hath laid a trap for ye."

"There's nothing new or surprising about that," Beldin growled. "What does she hope to accomplish?"

"It is her thought to slay one of the companions of the Child of Light and thereby prevent the completion of one of the tasks which must be accomplished ere the final meeting. Should she succeed, all that hath gone before shall come to naught. Follow me, and I will guide you safely to the next task."

Toth stepped down from his horse and quickly led it to the side of his slender mistress. She smiled at him, her face radiant, and laid a slim hand on his huge arm. With no apparent effort, the huge man lifted her into the saddle of his horse and then took the reins in his hand.

"Aunt Pol," Garion whispered, "is it my imagination, or is she really there this time?"

Polgara looked intently at the blindfolded Seeress. "It's not a projection," she said. "It's much more substantial. I couldn't begin to guess how she got here, but I think you're right, Garion. She's really here."

They followed the Seeress and her mute guide down the steeply descending road into a grassy basin surrounded on all sides by towering firs. In the center of the basin was a small mountain lake sparkling in the sunlight.

Polgara suddenly drew in her breath sharply. "We're being watched," she said.

"Who is it, Pol?" Belgarath asked.

"The mind is hidden, father. All I can get is the sense of watching—and anger." A smile touched her lips. "I'm sure it's Zandramas. She's shielding, so I can't reach her mind, but she can't shield out my sense of being watched, and she can't control her anger enough to keep me from picking up the edges of it."

"Who's she so angry with?"

"Cyradis, I think. She went to a great deal of trouble to lay a trap for us, and

Cyradis came along and spoiled it. She still might try something, so I think we'd all better be on our guard."

He nodded bleakly. "Right," he agreed.

Toth led the horse his mistress was riding out into the basin and stopped at the edge of the lake. When the rest of them reached her, she pointed down through the crystal water. "The task lies there," she said. "Below lies a submerged grot. One of ye must enter that grot and then return. Much shall be revealed there."

Belgarath looked hopefully at Beldin.

"Not this time, old man," the dwarf said, shaking his head. "I'm a hawk, not a fish, and I don't like cold water any more than you do."

"Pol?" Belgarath said rather plaintively.

"I don't think so, father," she replied. "I think it's your turn this time. Besides, I need to concentrate on Zandramas."

He bent over and dipped his hand into the sparkling water. Then he shuddered. "This is cruel," he said.

Silk was grinning at him.

"Don't say it, Prince Kheldar." Belgarath scowled, starting to remove his clothing. "Just keep your mouth shut."

They were perhaps all a bit surprised at how sleekly muscular the old man was. Despite his fondness for rich food and good brown ale, his stomach was as flat as a board; although he was as lean as a rail, his shoulders and chest rippled when he moved.

"My, my," Velvet murmured appreciatively, eyeing the loincloth-clad old man.

He suddenly grinned at her impishly. "Would you care for another frolic in a pool, Liselle?" he invited with a wicked look in his bright blue eyes.

She suddenly blushed a rosy red, glancing guiltily at Silk.

Belgarath laughed, arched himself forward, and split the water of the lake as cleanly as the blade of a knife. Several yards out, he breached, leaping high into the air with the sun gleaming on his silvery scales and his broad, forked tail flapping and shaking droplets like jewels across the sparkling surface of the lake. Then his dark, heavy body drove down and down into the depths of the crystal lake.

"Oh, my," Durnik breathed, his hands twitching.

"Never mind, dear." Polgara laughed. "He wouldn't like it at all if you stuck a fishhook in his jaw."

The great, silver-sided salmon swirled down and disappeared into an irregularly shaped opening near the bottom of the lake.

They waited, and Garion found himself unconsciously holding his breath.

After what seemed an eternity, the great fish shot from the mouth of the submerged cave, drove himself far out into the lake, and then returned, skipping across the surface of the water on his tail, shaking his head and almost seeming to balance himself with his fins. Then he plunged forward into the water near the shore, and Belgarath emerged dripping and shivering. "Invigorating," he observed, climbing back up onto the bank. "Have you got a blanket handy, Pol?" he asked, stripping the water from his arms and legs with his hands.

"Show-off," Beldin grunted.

"What was down there?" Garion asked.

"It looks like an old temple of some kind," the old man answered, vigorously drying himself with the blanket Polgara had handed him. "Somebody took a natural cave and walled up the sides to give it some kind of shape. There was an altar there with a special kind of niche in it—empty, naturally—but the place was filled with an overpowering presence, and all the rocks glowed red."

"The Sardion?" Beldin demanded intently.

"Not any more," Belgarath replied, drying his hair. "It *was* there, though, for a long, long time—and it had built a barrier of some kind to keep anybody from finding it. It's gone now, but I'll recognize the signs of it the next time I get close."

"Garion!" Ce'Nedra cried. "Look!" With a trembling hand she was pointing at a nearby crag. High atop that rocky promontory stood a figure wrapped in shiny black satin. Even before the figure tossed back its hood with a gesture of supreme arrogance, he knew who it was. Without thinking, he reached for Iron-grip's sword, his mind suddenly aflame.

But then Cyradis spoke in a clear, firm voice. "I am wroth with thee, Zandramas," she declared. "Seek not to interfere with that which must come to pass, lest I make my choice here and now."

"And if thou dost, sightless, creeping worm, then all will turn to chaos, and thy task will be incomplete, and blind chance will supplant prophecy. Behold, I am the Child of Dark, and I fear not the hand of chance, for chance is *my* servant even more than it is the servant of the Child of Light."

Then Garion heard a low snarl, a dreadful sound—more dreadful yet because it came from his wife's throat. Moving faster than he thought was possible, Ce'Nedra dashed to Durnik's horse and ripped the smith's axe from the rope sling which held it. With a scream of rage, she ran around the edge of the tiny mountain lake brandishing the axe.

"Ce'Nedra!" he shouted, lunging after her. "No!"

Zandramas laughed with cruel glee. "Choose, Cyradis!" she shouted. "Make thine empty choice, for in the death of the Rivan Queen, I triumph!" and she raised both hands over her head.

Though he was running as fast as he could, Garion saw that he had no hope of catching Ce'Nedra before she moved fatally close to the satin-robed sorceress atop the crag. Even now, his wife had begun scrambling up the rocks, screeching curses and hacking at the boulders that got in her way with Durnik's axe.

Then the form of a glowing blue wolf suddenly appeared between Ce'Nedra and the object of her fury. Ce'Nedra stopped as if frozen, and Zandramas recoiled from the snarling wolf. The light around the wolf flickered briefly, and there, still standing between Ce'Nedra and Zandramas stood the form of Garion's ultimate grandmother, Belgarath's wife and Polgara's mother. Her tawny hair was aflame with blue light, and her golden eyes blazed with unearthly fire.

"You!" Zandramas gasped, shrinking back even further.

Poledra reached back, took Ce'Nedra to her side, and protectively put one arm about her tiny shoulders. With her other hand she gently removed the axe from the little Queen's suddenly nerveless fingers. Ce'Nedra's eyes were wide and unseeing, and she stood immobilized as if in a trance.

"She is under my protection, Zandramas," Poledra said, "and you may not harm her."

The sorceress atop the crag howled in sudden, frustrated rage. Her eyes ablaze, she once again drew herself erect.

"Will it be now, Zandramas?" Poledra asked in a deadly voice. "Is this the time you have chosen for our meeting? You know even as I that should we meet at the wrong time and in the wrong place, we will *both* be destroyed."

"I do not fear thee, Poledra!" the sorceress shrieked.

"Nor I you. Come then, Zandramas, let us destroy each other here and now— for should the Child of Light go on to the Place Which Is No More unopposed and find no Child of Dark awaiting him there, then *I* triumph! If this be the time and place of your choosing, bring forth your power and let it happen—for I grow weary of you."

The face of Zandramas was twisted with rage, and Garion could feel the force of her will building up. He tried to reach over his shoulder for his sword, thinking to unleash its fire and blast the hated sorceress from atop her crag, but even as Ce'Nedra's apparently were, he found that his muscles were all locked in stasis. From behind him he could feel the others also struggling to shake free of the force which seemed to hold them in place as well.

"No," Poledra's voice sounded firmly in the vaults of his mind. "This is between Zandramas and me. Don't interfere."

"Well, Zandramas," she said aloud then, "what is your decision? Will you cling to life a while longer, or will you die now?"

The sorceress struggled to regain her composure, even as the glowing nimbus about Poledra grew more intense. Then Zandramas howled with enraged disappointment and disappeared in a flash of orange fire.

"I thought she might see it my way," Poledra said calmly. She turned to face Garion and the others. There was a twinkle in her golden eyes. "What took you all so long?" she asked. "I've been waiting for you here for months." She looked rather critically at the half-naked Belgarath, who was staring at her with a look of undisguised adoration. "You're as thin as a bone, Old Wolf," she told him. "You really ought to eat more, you know." She smiled fondly at him. "Would you like to have me go catch you a nice fat rabbit?" she asked. Then she laughed, shimmered back into the form of the blue wolf, and loped away, her paws seeming scarcely to touch the earth.

ABOUT THE AUTHOR

DAVID EDDINGS published his first novel, *High Hunt,* in 1973, before turning to the field of fantasy with The Belgariad, soon followed by The Malloreon. Born in Spokane, Washington, in 1931, and raised in the Puget Sound area north of Seattle, he received his bachelor of arts degree from Reed College in Portland, Oregon, in 1954, and a master of arts degree from the University of Washington in 1961. He has served in the United States Army, has worked as a buyer for the Boeing Company, and has been a grocery clerk and a college English teacher. He now lives with Leigh, his wife and collaborator, in Nevada.